海外优秀数学类教材系列丛书 Pearson

影印版

Thomas' CALCULUS

(Eleventh Edition)

托马斯微积分(第11版)(下册)

Based on the original work by
George B.Thomas,Jr.
Massachusetts Institute of Technology

as revised by
Maurice D. Weir
Naval Postgraduate School

Joel Hass
University of California, Davis

Frank R. Giordano
Naval Postgraduate School

高等教育出版社·北京

图字：01-2016-1854 号

图书在版编目（CIP）数据

托马斯微积分：第 11 版 = Thomas' Calculus (Eleventh Edition). 下册：英文 /（美）韦尔，（美）哈斯，（美）吉尔当诺著. --影印本. -- 北京：高等教育出版社，2016.6（2022.4 重印）
（海外优秀数学类教材系列丛书）
ISBN 978-7-04-045254-9

Ⅰ. ①托… Ⅱ. ①韦… ②哈… ③吉… Ⅲ. ①微积分-高等学校-教材-英文 Ⅳ. ①O172

中国版本图书馆 CIP 数据核字(2016)第 102087 号

策划编辑 于丽娜　　责任编辑 徐 可　　封面设计 李小璐　　版式设计 马 云
责任印制 高 峰

出版发行	高等教育出版社	网　　址	http://www.hep.edu.cn
社　　址	北京市西城区德外大街 4 号		http://www.hep.com.cn
邮政编码	100120	网上订购	http://www.hepmall.com.cn
印　　刷	北京市密东印刷有限公司		http://www.hepmall.com
开　　本	889mm×1194mm 1/16		http://www.hepmall.cn
印　　张	43.25		
字　　数	960千字	版　　次	2016 年 6 月第 1 版
购书热线	010-58581118	印　　次	2022 年 4 月第 6 次印刷
咨询电话	400-810-0598	定　　价	79.80 元

本书如有缺页、倒页、脱页等质量问题，请到所购图书销售部门联系调换

物 料 号 45254-00

出版说明

本书是“海外优秀数学类教材系列丛书”之一。

该系列教材经国内高校一线教师、专家、学者推荐和评介，遴选 Pearson Education，John Wiley & Sons，McGraw-Hill，Cengage Learning 等国外出版公司近几年出版的优秀教材，由高等教育出版社影印出版，原汁原味呈献给读者。

遴选出来的原版教材具有以下特点：

1. 在国际上被广泛使用，在同类教材中具有一定的权威性；
2. 历经多年教学实践检验，取材广泛，内容翔实准确；
3. 教学资源配套完善，方便教师教学、学生学习；
4. 插图精美、丰富，图文并茂，可读性强；
5. 语言简练、流畅，注重可接受性，适合非英语国家的学生阅读。

希望该系列教材的出版能为国内教师吸收、借鉴国外优秀教学理念和教学成果，为高等教育提高教学质量、提升人才培养水平做出贡献。

高等教育出版社

2014 年 2 月

Contents

Preface ix

1 Preliminaries 1

1.1 Real Numbers and the Real Line 1
1.2 Lines, Circles, and Parabolas 9
1.3 Functions and Their Graphs 19
1.4 Identifying Functions; Mathematical Models 28
1.5 Combining Functions; Shifting and Scaling Graphs 38
1.6 Trigonometric Functions 48
1.7 Graphing with Calculators and Computers 59
Questions to Guide Your Review 68
Practice Exercises 69
Additional and Advanced Exercises 71

2 Limits and Continuity 73

2.1 Rates of Change and Limits 73
2.2 Calculating Limits Using the Limit Laws 84
2.3 The Precise Definition of a Limit 91
2.4 One-Sided Limits and Limits at Infinity 102
2.5 Infinite Limits and Vertical Asymptotes 115
2.6 Continuity 124
2.7 Tangents and Derivatives 134
Questions to Guide your Review 141
Practice Exercises 142
Additional and Advanced Exercises 144

3 Differentiation 147

3.1 The Derivative as a Function 147
3.2 Differentiation Rules 159

3.3 The Derivative as a Rate of Change 171
3.4 Derivatives of Trigonometric Functions 183
3.5 The Chain Rule and Parametric Equations 190
3.6 Implicit Differentiation 205
3.7 Related Rates 213
3.8 Linearization and Differentials 221
Questions to Guide Your Review 235
Practice Exercises 235
Additional and Advanced Exercises 240

4 Applications of Derivatives 244

4.1 Extreme Values of Functions 244
4.2 The Mean Value Theorem 255
4.3 Monotonic Functions and the First Derivative Test 262
4.4 Concavity and Curve Sketching 267
4.5 Applied Optimization Problems 278
4.6 Indeterminate Forms and L'Hôpital's Rule 292
4.7 Newton's Method 299
4.8 Antiderivatives 307
Questions to Guide Your Review 318
Practice Exercises 318
Additional and Advanced Exercises 322

5 Integration 325

5.1 Estimating with Finite Sums 325
5.2 Sigma Notation and Limits of Finite Sums 335
5.3 The Definite Integral 343
5.4 The Fundamental Theorem of Calculus 356
5.5 Indefinite Integrals and the Substitution Rule 368
5.6 Substitution and Area Between Curves 376
Questions to Guide Your Review 387
Practice Exercises 388
Additional and Advanced Exercises 391

6 Applications of Definite Integrals 396

6.1 Volumes by Slicing and Rotation About an Axis 396
6.2 Volumes by Cylindrical Shells 409
6.3 Lengths of Plane Curves 416
6.4 Moments and Centers of Mass 424
6.5 Areas of Surfaces of Revolution and the Theorems of Pappus 436
6.6 Work 447
6.7 Fluid Pressures and Forces 456

QUESTIONS TO GUIDE YOUR REVIEW 461
PRACTICE EXERCISES 461
ADDITIONAL AND ADVANCED EXERCISES 464

7 Transcendental Functions 466

7.1 Inverse Functions and Their Derivatives 466
7.2 Natural Logarithms 476
7.3 The Exponential Function 486
7.4 a^x and $\log_a x$ 495
7.5 Exponential Growth and Decay 502
7.6 Relative Rates of Growth 511
7.7 Inverse Trigonometric Functions 517
7.8 Hyperbolic Functions 535
QUESTIONS TO GUIDE YOUR REVIEW 546
PRACTICE EXERCISES 547
ADDITIONAL AND ADVANCED EXERCISES 550

8 Techniques of Integration 553

8.1 Basic Integration Formulas 553
8.2 Integration by Parts 561
8.3 Integration of Rational Functions by Partial Fractions 570
8.4 Trigonometric Integrals 581
8.5 Trigonometric Substitutions 586
8.6 Integral Tables and Computer Algebra Systems 593
8.7 Numerical Integration 603
8.8 Improper Integrals 619
QUESTIONS TO GUIDE YOUR REVIEW 633
PRACTICE EXERCISES 634
ADDITIONAL AND ADVANCED EXERCISES 638

9 Further Applications of Integration 642

9.1 Slope Fields and Separable Differential Equations 642
9.2 First-Order Linear Differential Equations 650
9.3 Euler's Method 659
9.4 Graphical Solutions of Autonomous Differential Equations 665
9.5 Applications of First-Order Differential Equations 673
QUESTIONS TO GUIDE YOUR REVIEW 682
PRACTICE EXERCISES 682
ADDITIONAL AND ADVANCED EXERCISES 683

10 Conic Sections and Polar Coordinates 685

10.1 Conic Sections and Quadratic Equations 685
10.2 Classifying Conic Sections by Eccentricity 697
10.3 Quadratic Equations and Rotations 702
10.4 Conics and Parametric Equations; The Cycloid 709
10.5 Polar Coordinates 714
10.6 Graphing in Polar Coordinates 719
10.7 Areas and Lengths in Polar Coordinates 725
10.8 Conic Sections in Polar Coordinates 732
Questions to Guide Your Review 739
Practice Exercises 739
Additional and Advanced Exercises 742

11 Infinite Sequences and Series 746

11.1 Sequences 747
11.2 Infinite Series 761
11.3 The Integral Test 772
11.4 Comparison Tests 777
11.5 The Ratio and Root Tests 781
11.6 Alternating Series, Absolute and Conditional Convergence 787
11.7 Power Series 794
11.8 Taylor and Maclaurin Series 805
11.9 Convergence of Taylor Series; Error Estimates 811
11.10 Applications of Power Series 822
11.11 Fourier Series 833
Questions to Guide Your Review 839
Practice Exercises 840
Additional and Advanced Exercises 843

12 Vectors and the Geometry of Space 848

12.1 Three-Dimensional Coordinate Systems 848
12.2 Vectors 853
12.3 The Dot Product 862
12.4 The Cross Product 873
12.5 Lines and Planes in Space 880
12.6 Cylinders and Quadric Surfaces 889
Questions to Guide Your Review 899
Practice Exercises 900
Additional and Advanced Exercises 902

13 Vector-Valued Functions and Motion in Space 906

13.1 Vector Functions 906
13.2 Modeling Projectile Motion 920
13.3 Arc Length and the Unit Tangent Vector **T** 931
13.4 Curvature and the Unit Normal Vector **N** 936
13.5 Torsion and the Unit Binormal Vector **B** 943
13.6 Planetary Motion and Satellites 950
Questions to Guide Your Review 959
Practice Exercises 960
Additional and Advanced Exercises 962

14 Partial Derivatives 965

14.1 Functions of Several Variables 965
14.2 Limits and Continuity in Higher Dimensions 976
14.3 Partial Derivatives 984
14.4 The Chain Rule 996
14.5 Directional Derivatives and Gradient Vectors 1005
14.6 Tangent Planes and Differentials 1015
14.7 Extreme Values and Saddle Points 1027
14.8 Lagrange Multipliers 1038
14.9 Partial Derivatives with Constrained Variables 1049
14.10 Taylor's Formula for Two Variables 1054
Questions to Guide Your Review 1059
Practice Exercises 1060
Additional and Advanced Exercises 1063

15 Multiple Integrals 1067

15.1 Double Integrals 1067
15.2 Areas, Moments, and Centers of Mass 1081
15.3 Double Integrals in Polar Form 1092
15.4 Triple Integrals in Rectangular Coordinates 1098
15.5 Masses and Moments in Three Dimensions 1109
15.6 Triple Integrals in Cylindrical and Spherical Coordinates 1114
15.7 Substitutions in Multiple Integrals 1128
Questions to Guide Your Review 1137
Practice Exercises 1138
Additional and Advanced Exercises 1140

16 Integration in Vector Fields 1143

16.1 Line Integrals 1143
16.2 Vector Fields, Work, Circulation, and Flux 1149
16.3 Path Independence, Potential Functions, and Conservative Fields 1160
16.4 Green's Theorem in the Plane 1169
16.5 Surface Area and Surface Integrals 1182
16.6 Parametrized Surfaces 1192
16.7 Stokes' Theorem 1201
16.8 The Divergence Theorem and a Unified Theory 1211
Questions to Guide Your Review 1222
Practice Exercises 1223
Additional and Advanced Exercises 1226

Appendices AP-1

A.1 Mathematical Induction AP-1
A.2 Proofs of Limit Theorems AP-4
A.3 Commonly Occurring Limits AP-7
A.4 Theory of the Real Numbers AP-9
A.5 Complex Numbers AP-12
A.6 The Distributive Law for Vector Cross Products AP-22
A.7 The Mixed Derivative Theorem and the Increment Theorem AP-23
A.8 The Area of a Parallelogram's Projection on a Plane AP-28
A.9 Basic Algebra, Geometry, and Trigonometry Formulas AP-29

Answers A-1

Index I-1

A Brief Table of Integrals T-1

Credits C-1

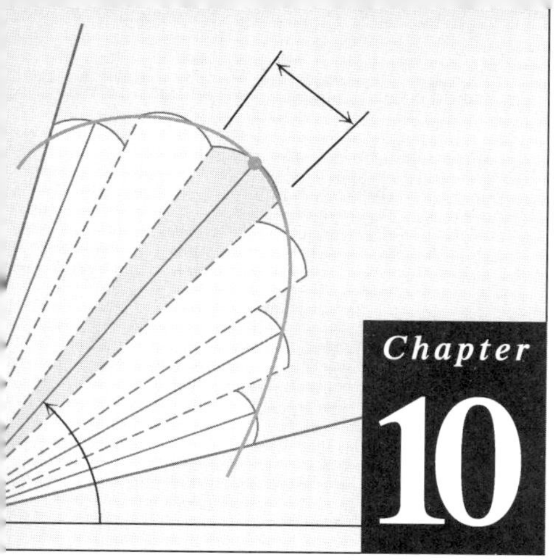

Chapter

10

CONIC SECTIONS AND POLAR COORDINATES

OVERVIEW In this chapter we give geometric definitions of parabolas, ellipses, and hyperbolas and derive their standard equations. These curves are called *conic sections*, or *conics*, and model the paths traveled by planets, satellites, and other bodies whose motions are driven by inverse square forces. In Chapter 13 we will see that once the path of a moving body is known to be a conic, we immediately have information about the body's velocity and the force that drives it. Planetary motion is best described with the help of polar coordinates, so we also investigate curves, derivatives, and integrals in this new coordinate system.

10.1 Conic Sections and Quadratic Equations

In Chapter 1 we defined a **circle** as the set of points in a plane whose distance from some fixed center point is a constant radius value. If the center is (h, k) and the radius is a, the standard equation for the circle is $(x - h)^2 + (y - k)^2 = a^2$. It is an example of a conic section, which are the curves formed by cutting a double cone with a plane (Figure 10.1); hence the name *conic section.*

We now describe parabolas, ellipses, and hyperbolas as the graphs of quadratic equations in the coordinate plane.

Parabolas

> **DEFINITIONS** **Parabola, Focus, Directrix**
> A set that consists of all the points in a plane equidistant from a given fixed point and a given fixed line in the plane is a **parabola**. The fixed point is the **focus** of the parabola. The fixed line is the **directrix**.

If the focus F lies on the directrix L, the parabola is the line through F perpendicular to L. We consider this to be a degenerate case and assume henceforth that F does not lie on L.

A parabola has its simplest equation when its focus and directrix straddle one of the coordinate axes. For example, suppose that the focus lies at the point $F(0, p)$ on the positive y-axis and that the directrix is the line $y = -p$ (Figure 10.2). In the notation of the figure,

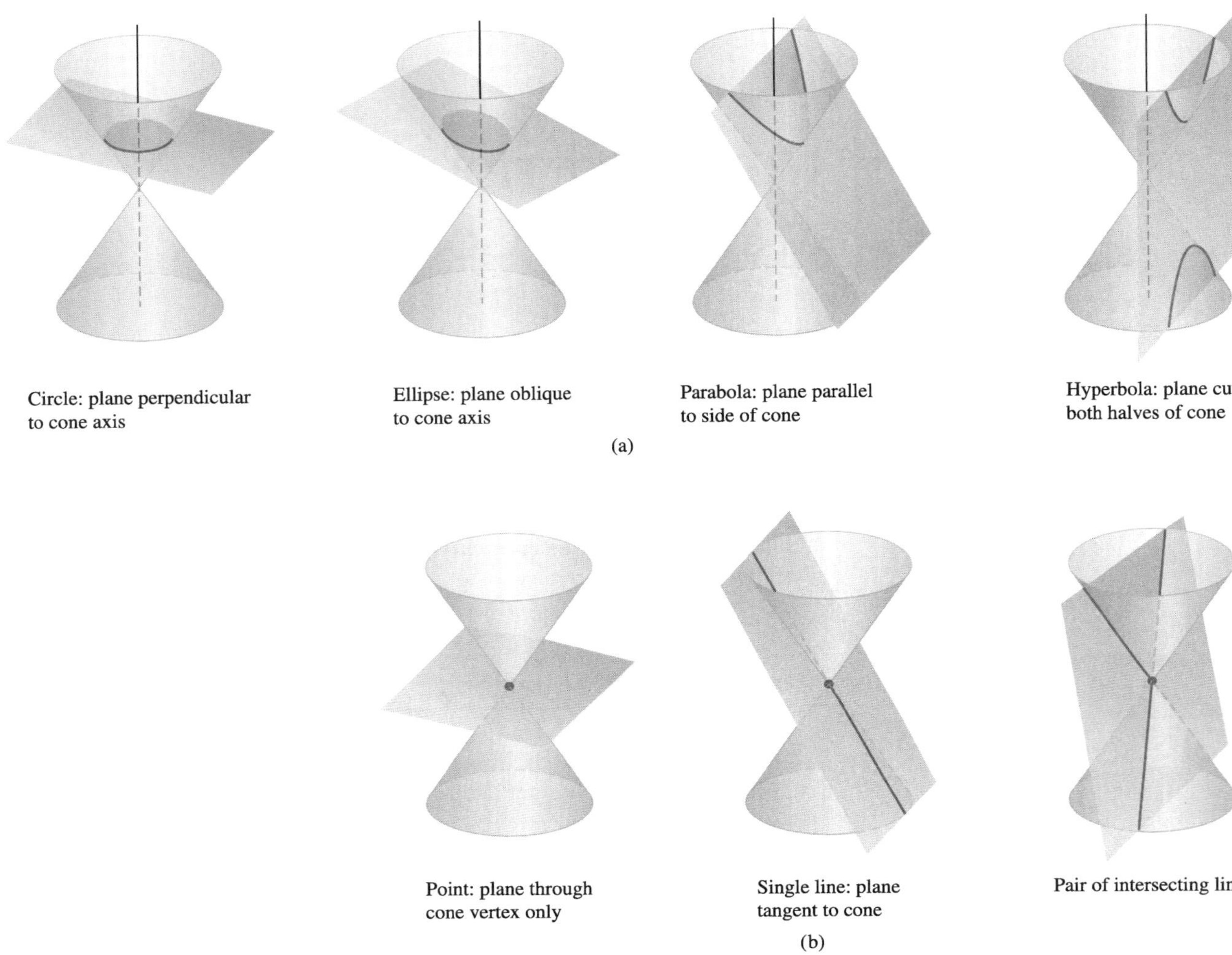

FIGURE 10.1 The standard conic sections (a) are the curves in which a plane cuts a double cone. Hyperbolas come in two parts, called *branches*. The point and lines obtained by passing the plane through the cone's vertex (b) are *degenerate* conic sections.

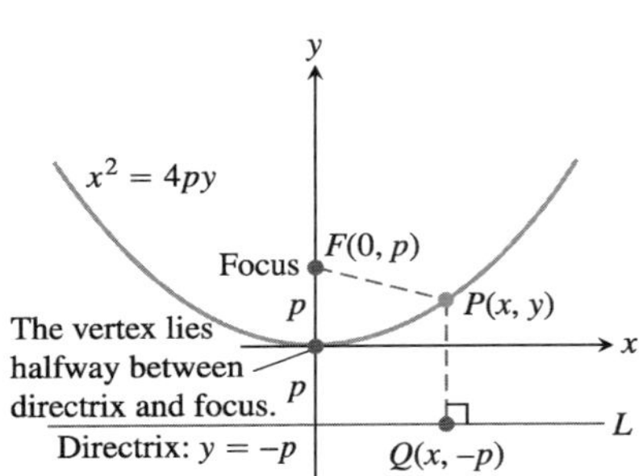

FIGURE 10.2 The standard form of the parabola $x^2 = 4py, p > 0$.

a point $P(x, y)$ lies on the parabola if and only if $PF = PQ$. From the distance formula,

$$PF = \sqrt{(x-0)^2 + (y-p)^2} = \sqrt{x^2 + (y-p)^2}$$

$$PQ = \sqrt{(x-x)^2 + (y-(-p))^2} = \sqrt{(y+p)^2}.$$

When we equate these expressions, square, and simplify, we get

$$y = \frac{x^2}{4p} \quad \text{or} \quad x^2 = 4py. \qquad \text{Standard form} \tag{1}$$

These equations reveal the parabola's symmetry about the y-axis. We call the y-axis the **axis** of the parabola (short for "axis of symmetry").

The point where a parabola crosses its axis is the **vertex**. The vertex of the parabola $x^2 = 4py$ lies at the origin (Figure 10.2). The positive number p is the parabola's **focal length**.

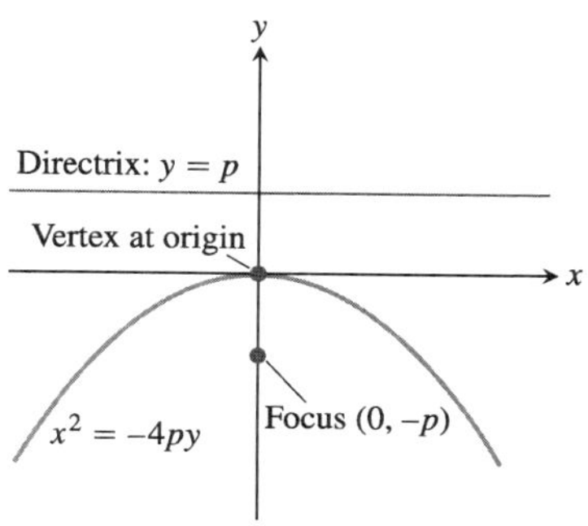

FIGURE 10.3 The parabola $x^2 = -4py, p > 0$.

If the parabola opens downward, with its focus at $(0, -p)$ and its directrix the line $y = p$, then Equations (1) become

$$y = -\frac{x^2}{4p} \quad \text{and} \quad x^2 = -4py$$

(Figure 10.3). We obtain similar equations for parabolas opening to the right or to the left (Figure 10.4 and Table 10.1).

TABLE 10.1 Standard-form equations for parabolas with vertices at the origin $(p > 0)$

Equation	Focus	Directrix	Axis	Opens
$x^2 = 4py$	$(0, p)$	$y = -p$	y-axis	Up
$x^2 = -4py$	$(0, -p)$	$y = p$	y-axis	Down
$y^2 = 4px$	$(p, 0)$	$x = -p$	x-axis	To the right
$y^2 = -4px$	$(-p, 0)$	$x = p$	x-axis	To the left

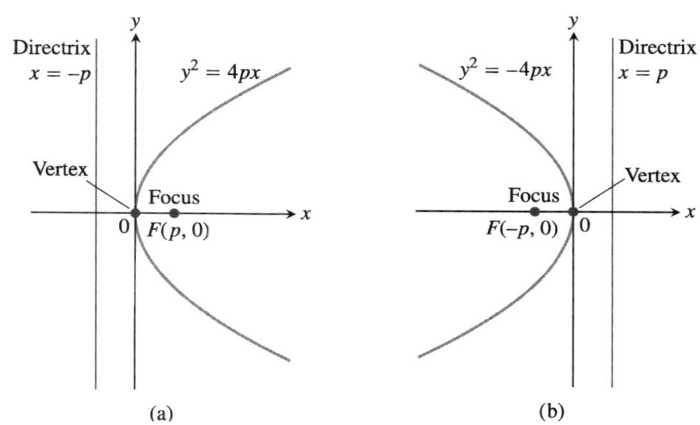

FIGURE 10.4 (a) The parabola $y^2 = 4px$. (b) The parabola $y^2 = -4px$.

EXAMPLE 1 Find the focus and directrix of the parabola $y^2 = 10x$.

Solution We find the value of p in the standard equation $y^2 = 4px$:

$$4p = 10, \quad \text{so} \quad p = \frac{10}{4} = \frac{5}{2}.$$

Then we find the focus and directrix for this value of p:

$$\text{Focus:} \quad (p, 0) = \left(\frac{5}{2}, 0\right)$$

$$\text{Directrix:} \quad x = -p \quad \text{or} \quad x = -\frac{5}{2}.$$

■

The horizontal and vertical shift formulas in Section 1.5, can be applied to the equations in Table 10.1 to give equations for a variety of parabolas in other locations (see Exercises 39, 40, and 45–48).

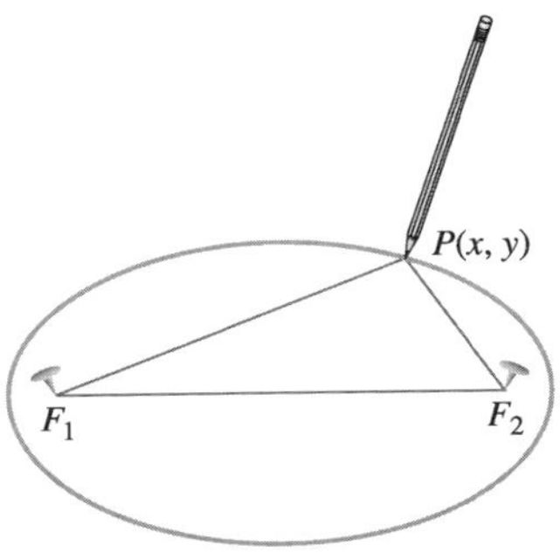

FIGURE 10.5 One way to draw an ellipse uses two tacks and a loop of string to guide the pencil.

Ellipses

> **DEFINITIONS Ellipse, Foci**
> An **ellipse** is the set of points in a plane whose distances from two fixed points in the plane have a constant sum. The two fixed points are the **foci** of the ellipse.

The quickest way to construct an ellipse uses the definition. Put a loop of string around two tacks F_1 and F_2, pull the string taut with a pencil point P, and move the pencil around to trace a closed curve (Figure 10.5). The curve is an ellipse because the sum $PF_1 + PF_2$, being the length of the loop minus the distance between the tacks, remains constant. The ellipse's foci lie at F_1 and F_2.

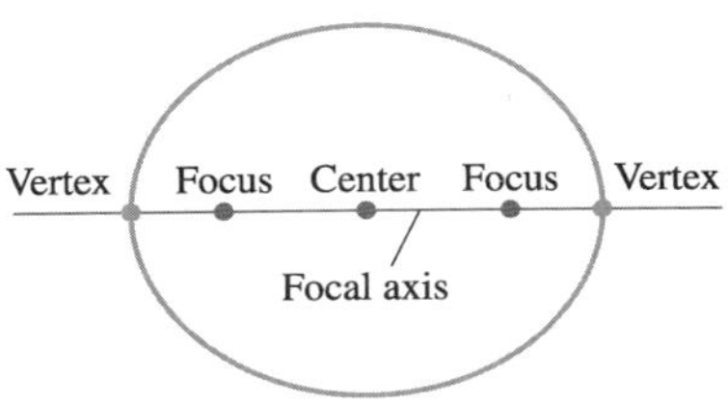

FIGURE 10.6 Points on the focal axis of an ellipse.

> **DEFINITIONS Focal Axis, Center, Vertices**
> The line through the foci of an ellipse is the ellipse's **focal axis**. The point on the axis halfway between the foci is the **center**. The points where the focal axis and ellipse cross are the ellipse's **vertices** (Figure 10.6).

If the foci are $F_1(-c, 0)$ and $F_2(c, 0)$ (Figure 10.7), and $PF_1 + PF_2$ is denoted by $2a$, then the coordinates of a point P on the ellipse satisfy the equation

$$\sqrt{(x + c)^2 + y^2} + \sqrt{(x - c)^2 + y^2} = 2a.$$

To simplify this equation, we move the second radical to the right-hand side, square, isolate the remaining radical, and square again, obtaining

$$\frac{x^2}{a^2} + \frac{y^2}{a^2 - c^2} = 1. \tag{2}$$

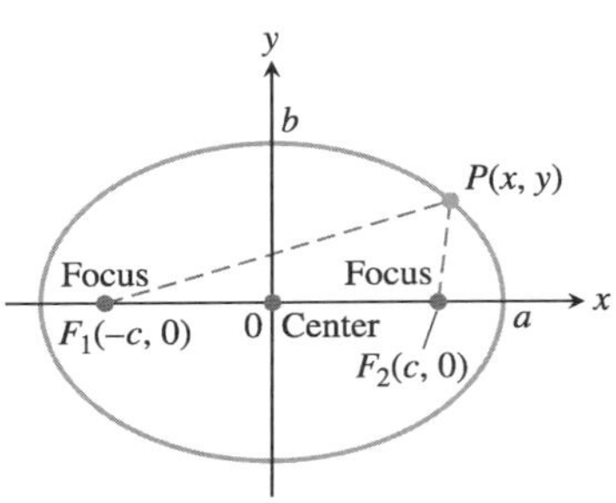

FIGURE 10.7 The ellipse defined by the equation $PF_1 + PF_2 = 2a$ is the graph of the equation $(x^2/a^2) + (y^2/b^2) = 1$, where $b^2 = a^2 - c^2$.

Since $PF_1 + PF_2$ is greater than the length F_1F_2 (triangle inequality for triangle PF_1F_2), the number $2a$ is greater than $2c$. Accordingly, $a > c$ and the number $a^2 - c^2$ in Equation (2) is positive.

The algebraic steps leading to Equation (2) can be reversed to show that every point P whose coordinates satisfy an equation of this form with $0 < c < a$ also satisfies the equation $PF_1 + PF_2 = 2a$. A point therefore lies on the ellipse if and only if its coordinates satisfy Equation (2).

If

$$b = \sqrt{a^2 - c^2}, \tag{3}$$

then $a^2 - c^2 = b^2$ and Equation (2) takes the form

$$\frac{x^2}{a^2} + \frac{y^2}{b^2} = 1. \tag{4}$$

Equation (4) reveals that this ellipse is symmetric with respect to the origin and both coordinate axes. It lies inside the rectangle bounded by the lines $x = \pm a$ and $y = \pm b$. It crosses the axes at the points $(\pm a, 0)$ and $(0, \pm b)$. The tangents at these points are perpendicular to the axes because

$$\frac{dy}{dx} = -\frac{b^2 x}{a^2 y} \quad \text{Obtained from Equation (4) by implicit differentiation}$$

is zero if $x = 0$ and infinite if $y = 0$.

The **major axis** of the ellipse in Equation (4) is the line segment of length $2a$ joining the points $(\pm a, 0)$. The **minor axis** is the line segment of length $2b$ joining the points $(0, \pm b)$. The number a itself is the **semimajor axis**, the number b the **semiminor axis**. The number c, found from Equation (3) as

$$c = \sqrt{a^2 - b^2},$$

is the **center-to-focus distance** of the ellipse.

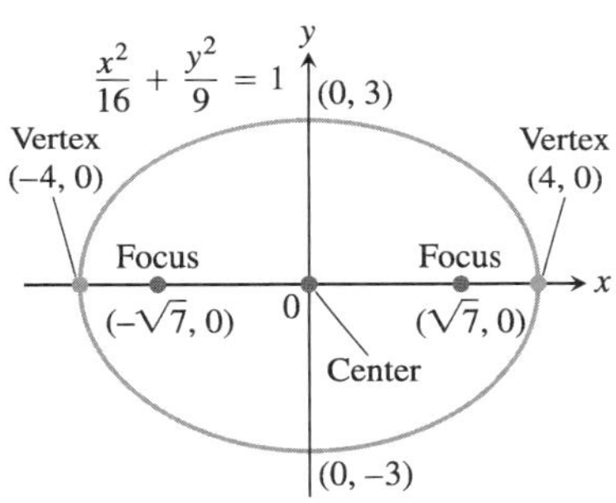

FIGURE 10.8 An ellipse with its major axis horizontal (Example 2).

EXAMPLE 2 Major Axis Horizontal

The ellipse

$$\frac{x^2}{16} + \frac{y^2}{9} = 1 \tag{5}$$

(Figure 10.8) has

Semimajor axis: $a = \sqrt{16} = 4$, Semiminor axis: $b = \sqrt{9} = 3$

Center-to-focus distance: $c = \sqrt{16 - 9} = \sqrt{7}$

Foci: $(\pm c, 0) = \left(\pm\sqrt{7}, 0\right)$

Vertices: $(\pm a, 0) = (\pm 4, 0)$

Center: $(0, 0)$. ■

EXAMPLE 3 Major Axis Vertical

The ellipse

$$\frac{x^2}{9} + \frac{y^2}{16} = 1, \tag{6}$$

obtained by interchanging x and y in Equation (5), has its major axis vertical instead of horizontal (Figure 10.9). With a^2 still equal to 16 and b^2 equal to 9, we have

Semimajor axis: $a = \sqrt{16} = 4$, Semiminor axis: $b = \sqrt{9} = 3$

Center-to-focus distance: $c = \sqrt{16 - 9} = \sqrt{7}$

Foci: $(0, \pm c) = \left(0, \pm\sqrt{7}\right)$

Vertices: $(0, \pm a) = (0, \pm 4)$

Center: $(0, 0)$. ■

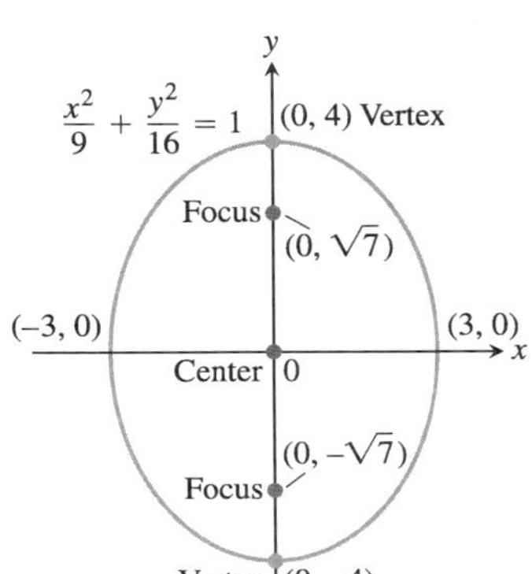

FIGURE 10.9 An ellipse with its major axis vertical (Example 3).

There is never any cause for confusion in analyzing Equations (5) and (6). We simply find the intercepts on the coordinate axes; then we know which way the major axis runs because it is the longer of the two axes. The center always lies at the origin and the foci and vertices lie on the major axis.

Standard-Form Equations for Ellipses Centered at the Origin

Foci on the x-axis: $\dfrac{x^2}{a^2} + \dfrac{y^2}{b^2} = 1 \quad (a > b)$

Center-to-focus distance: $c = \sqrt{a^2 - b^2}$

Foci: $(\pm c, 0)$

Vertices: $(\pm a, 0)$

Foci on the y-axis: $\dfrac{x^2}{b^2} + \dfrac{y^2}{a^2} = 1 \quad (a > b)$

Center-to-focus distance: $c = \sqrt{a^2 - b^2}$

Foci: $(0, \pm c)$

Vertices: $(0, \pm a)$

In each case, a is the semimajor axis and b is the semiminor axis.

Hyperbolas

DEFINITIONS Hyperbola, Foci

A **hyperbola** is the set of points in a plane whose distances from two fixed points in the plane have a constant difference. The two fixed points are the **foci** of the hyperbola.

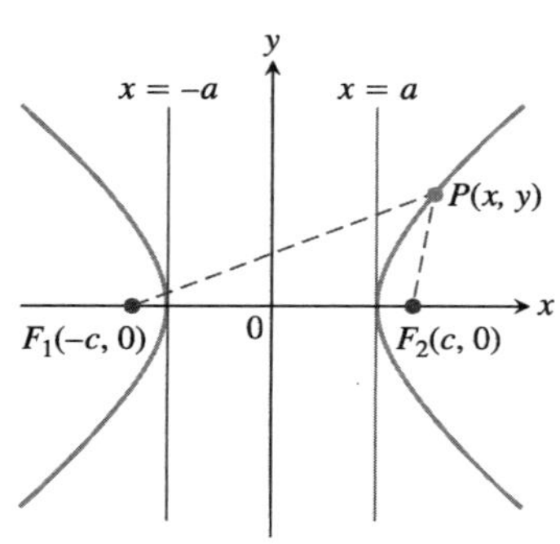

FIGURE 10.10 Hyperbolas have two branches. For points on the right-hand branch of the hyperbola shown here, $PF_1 - PF_2 = 2a$. For points on the left-hand branch, $PF_2 - PF_1 = 2a$. We then let $b = \sqrt{c^2 - a^2}$.

If the foci are $F_1(-c, 0)$ and $F_2(c, 0)$ (Figure 10.10) and the constant difference is $2a$, then a point (x, y) lies on the hyperbola if and only if

$$\sqrt{(x + c)^2 + y^2} - \sqrt{(x - c)^2 + y^2} = \pm 2a. \tag{7}$$

To simplify this equation, we move the second radical to the right-hand side, square, isolate the remaining radical, and square again, obtaining

$$\frac{x^2}{a^2} + \frac{y^2}{a^2 - c^2} = 1. \tag{8}$$

So far, this looks just like the equation for an ellipse. But now $a^2 - c^2$ is negative because $2a$, being the difference of two sides of triangle PF_1F_2, is less than $2c$, the third side.

The algebraic steps leading to Equation (8) can be reversed to show that every point P whose coordinates satisfy an equation of this form with $0 < a < c$ also satisfies Equation (7). A point therefore lies on the hyperbola if and only if its coordinates satisfy Equation (8).

If we let b denote the positive square root of $c^2 - a^2$,

$$b = \sqrt{c^2 - a^2}, \tag{9}$$

then $a^2 - c^2 = -b^2$ and Equation (8) takes the more compact form

$$\frac{x^2}{a^2} - \frac{y^2}{b^2} = 1. \tag{10}$$

The differences between Equation (10) and the equation for an ellipse (Equation 4) are the minus sign and the new relation

$$c^2 = a^2 + b^2. \qquad \text{From Equation (9)}$$

Like the ellipse, the hyperbola is symmetric with respect to the origin and coordinate axes. It crosses the x-axis at the points $(\pm a, 0)$. The tangents at these points are vertical because

$$\frac{dy}{dx} = \frac{b^2x}{a^2y} \qquad \text{Obtained from Equation (10) by implicit differentiation}$$

is infinite when $y = 0$. The hyperbola has no y-intercepts; in fact, no part of the curve lies between the lines $x = -a$ and $x = a$.

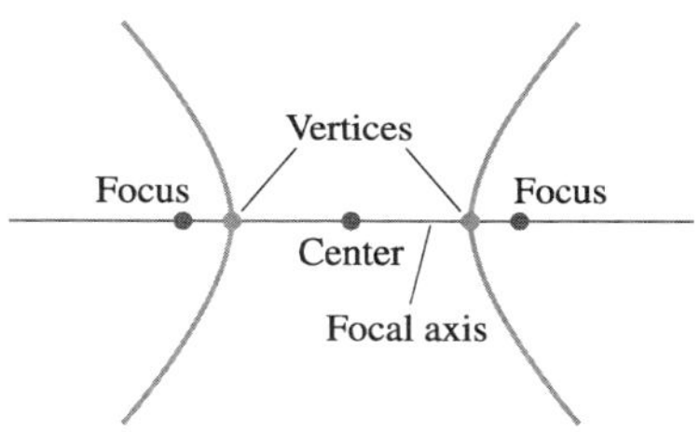

FIGURE 10.11 Points on the focal axis of a hyperbola.

DEFINITIONS Focal Axis, Center, Vertices
The line through the foci of a hyperbola is the **focal axis**. The point on the axis halfway between the foci is the hyperbola's **center**. The points where the focal axis and hyperbola cross are the **vertices** (Figure 10.11).

Asymptotes of Hyperbolas and Graphing

If we solve Equation (10) for y we obtain

$$\begin{aligned} y^2 &= b^2\left(\frac{x^2}{a^2} - 1\right) \\ &= \frac{b^2}{a^2}x^2\left(1 - \frac{a^2}{x^2}\right) \end{aligned}$$

or, taking square roots,

$$y = \pm\frac{b}{a}x\sqrt{1 - \frac{a^2}{x^2}}.$$

As $x \to \pm\infty$, the factor $\sqrt{1 - a^2/x^2}$ approaches 1, and the factor $\pm(b/a)x$ is dominant. Thus the lines

$$y = \pm\frac{b}{a}x$$

are the two **asymptotes** of the hyperbola defined by Equation (10). The asymptotes give the guidance we need to graph hyperbolas quickly. The fastest way to find the equations of the asymptotes is to replace the 1 in Equation (10) by 0 and solve the new equation for y:

$$\underbrace{\frac{x^2}{a^2} - \frac{y^2}{b^2} = 1}_{\text{hyperbola}} \to \underbrace{\frac{x^2}{a^2} - \frac{y^2}{b^2} = 0}_{\text{0 for 1}} \to \underbrace{y = \pm\frac{b}{a}x.}_{\text{asymptotes}}$$

Standard-Form Equations for Hyperbolas Centered at the Origin

Foci on the x-axis: $\dfrac{x^2}{a^2} - \dfrac{y^2}{b^2} = 1$	*Foci on the y-axis:* $\dfrac{y^2}{a^2} - \dfrac{x^2}{b^2} = 1$
Center-to-focus distance: $c = \sqrt{a^2 + b^2}$	Center-to-focus distance: $c = \sqrt{a^2 + b^2}$
Foci: $(\pm c, 0)$	Foci: $(0, \pm c)$
Vertices: $(\pm a, 0)$	Vertices: $(0, \pm a)$
Asymptotes: $\dfrac{x^2}{a^2} - \dfrac{y^2}{b^2} = 0$ or $y = \pm\dfrac{b}{a}x$	Asymptotes: $\dfrac{y^2}{a^2} - \dfrac{x^2}{b^2} = 0$ or $y = \pm\dfrac{a}{b}x$

Notice the difference in the asymptote equations (b/a in the first, a/b in the second).

EXAMPLE 4 Foci on the x-axis

The equation

$$\frac{x^2}{4} - \frac{y^2}{5} = 1 \tag{11}$$

is Equation (10) with $a^2 = 4$ and $b^2 = 5$ (Figure 10.12). We have

Center-to-focus distance: $c = \sqrt{a^2 + b^2} = \sqrt{4 + 5} = 3$

Foci: $(\pm c, 0) = (\pm 3, 0)$, Vertices: $(\pm a, 0) = (\pm 2, 0)$

Center: $(0, 0)$

Asymptotes: $\dfrac{x^2}{4} - \dfrac{y^2}{5} = 0$ or $y = \pm\dfrac{\sqrt{5}}{2}x$. ■

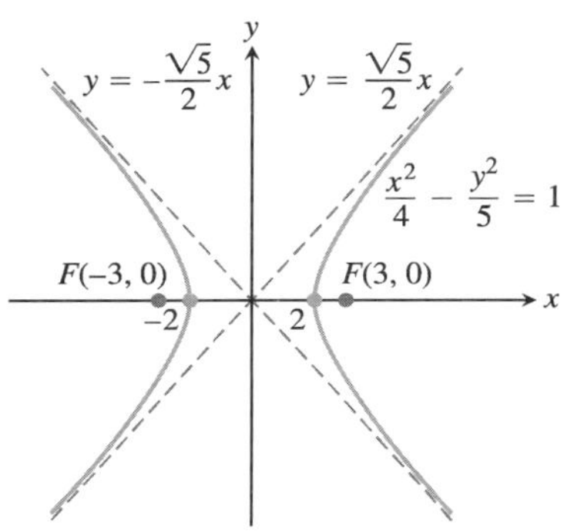

FIGURE 10.12 The hyperbola and its asymptotes in Example 4.

EXAMPLE 5 Foci on the y-axis

The hyperbola

$$\frac{y^2}{4} - \frac{x^2}{5} = 1,$$

obtained by interchanging x and y in Equation (11), has its vertices on the y-axis instead of the x-axis (Figure 10.13). With a^2 still equal to 4 and b^2 equal to 5, we have

Center-to-focus distance: $c = \sqrt{a^2 + b^2} = \sqrt{4 + 5} = 3$

Foci: $(0, \pm c) = (0, \pm 3)$, Vertices: $(0, \pm a) = (0, \pm 2)$

Center: $(0, 0)$

Asymptotes: $\dfrac{y^2}{4} - \dfrac{x^2}{5} = 0$ or $y = \pm\dfrac{2}{\sqrt{5}}x$. ■

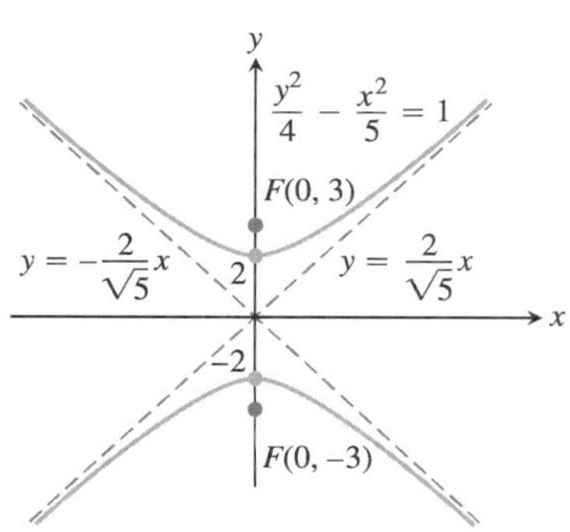

FIGURE 10.13 The hyperbola and its asymptotes in Example 5.

Reflective Properties

The chief applications of parabolas involve their use as reflectors of light and radio waves. Rays originating at a parabola's focus are reflected out of the parabola parallel to the parabola's axis (Figure 10.14 and Exercise 90). Moreover, the time any ray takes from the focus to a line parallel to the parabola's directrix (thus perpendicular to its axis) is the same for each of the rays. These properties are used by flashlight, headlight, and spotlight reflectors and by microwave broadcast antennas.

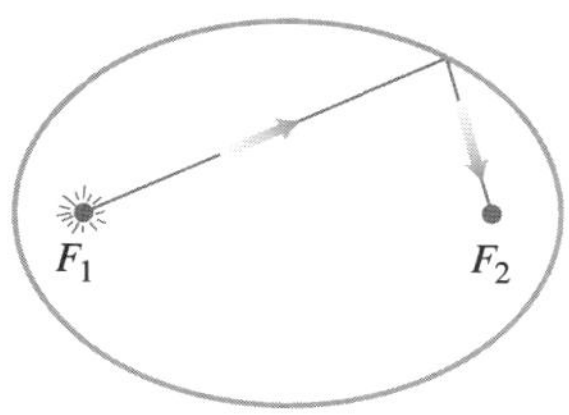

FIGURE 10.15 An elliptical mirror (shown here in profile) reflects light from one focus to the other.

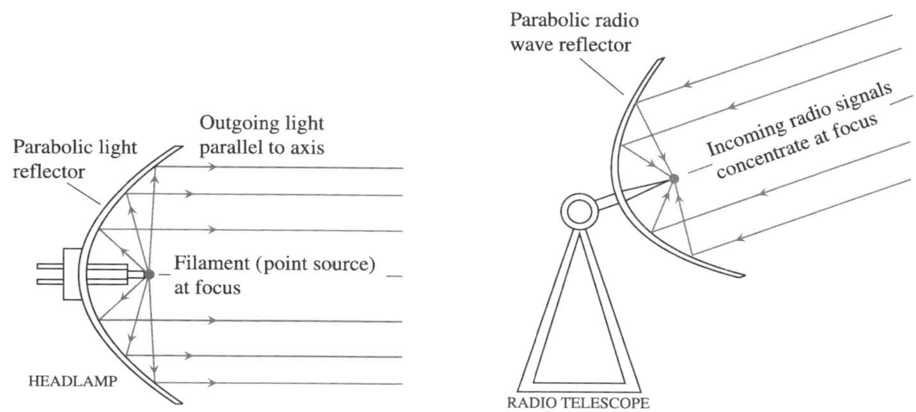

FIGURE 10.14 Parabolic reflectors can generate a beam of light parallel to the parabola's axis from a source at the focus; or they can receive rays parallel to the axis and concentrate them at the focus.

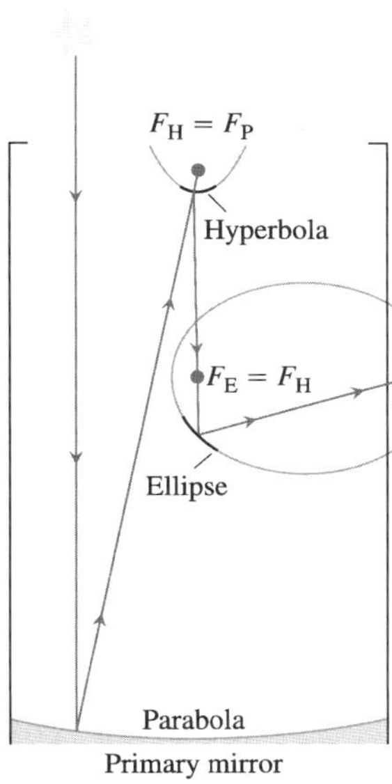

FIGURE 10.16 Schematic drawing of a reflecting telescope.

If an ellipse is revolved about its major axis to generate a surface (the surface is called an *ellipsoid*) and the interior is silvered to produce a mirror, light from one focus will be reflected to the other focus (Figure 10.15). Ellipsoids reflect sound the same way, and this property is used to construct *whispering galleries*, rooms in which a person standing at one focus can hear a whisper from the other focus. (Statuary Hall in the U.S. Capitol building is a whispering gallery.)

Light directed toward one focus of a hyperbolic mirror is reflected toward the other focus. This property of hyperbolas is combined with the reflective properties of parabolas and ellipses in designing some modern telescopes. In Figure 10.16 starlight reflects off a primary parabolic mirror toward the mirror's focus F_P. It is then reflected by a small hyperbolic mirror, whose focus is $F_H = F_P$, toward the second focus of the hyperbola, $F_E = F_H$. Since this focus is shared by an ellipse, the light is reflected by the elliptical mirror to the ellipse's second focus to be seen by an observer.

EXERCISES 10.1

Identifying Graphs

Match the parabolas in Exercises 1–4 with the following equations:

$$x^2 = 2y, \quad x^2 = -6y, \quad y^2 = 8x, \quad y^2 = -4x.$$

Then find the parabola's focus and directrix.

1.

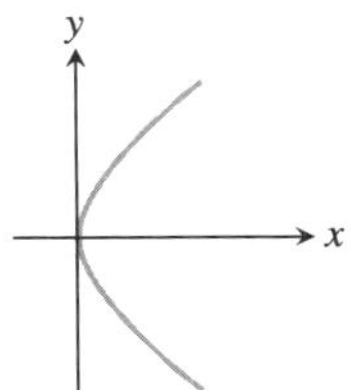

2.

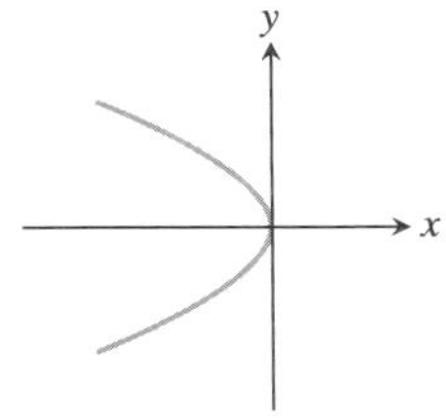

3.

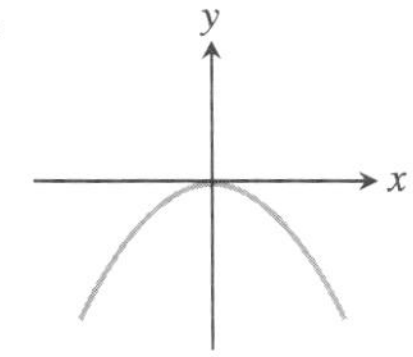

4.

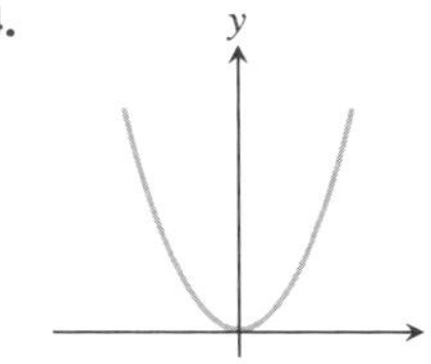

Match each conic section in Exercises 5–8 with one of these equations:

$$\frac{x^2}{4} + \frac{y^2}{9} = 1, \quad \frac{x^2}{2} + y^2 = 1,$$

$$\frac{y^2}{4} - x^2 = 1, \quad \frac{x^2}{4} - \frac{y^2}{9} = 1.$$

Then find the conic section's foci and vertices. If the conic section is a hyperbola, find its asymptotes as well.

5.

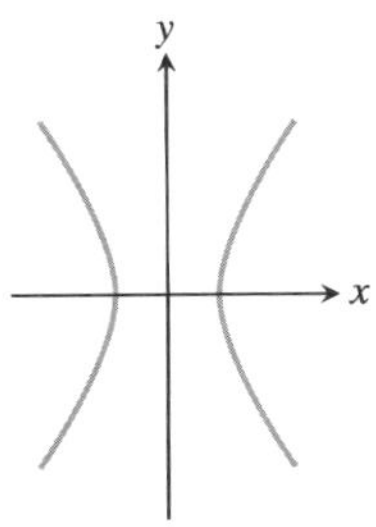

6.

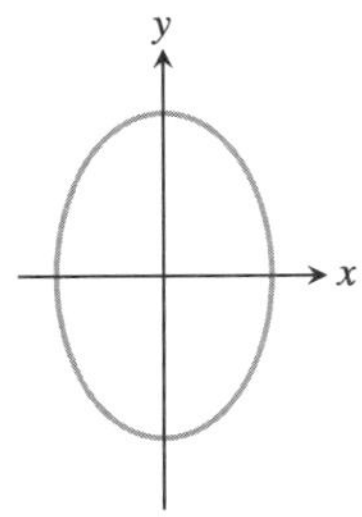

7.

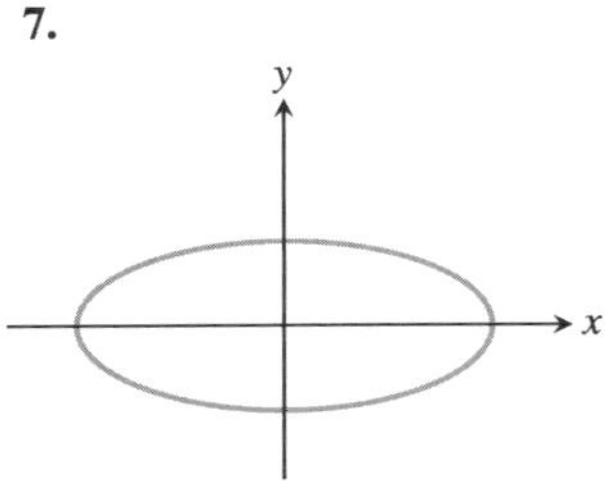

8.

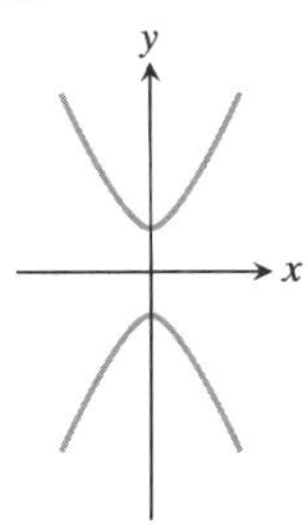

Parabolas

Exercises 9–16 give equations of parabolas. Find each parabola's focus and directrix. Then sketch the parabola. Include the focus and directrix in your sketch.

9. $y^2 = 12x$ **10.** $x^2 = 6y$ **11.** $x^2 = -8y$

12. $y^2 = -2x$ **13.** $y = 4x^2$ **14.** $y = -8x^2$

15. $x = -3y^2$ **16.** $x = 2y^2$

Ellipses

Exercises 17–24 give equations for ellipses. Put each equation in standard form. Then sketch the ellipse. Include the foci in your sketch.

17. $16x^2 + 25y^2 = 400$ **18.** $7x^2 + 16y^2 = 112$

19. $2x^2 + y^2 = 2$ **20.** $2x^2 + y^2 = 4$

21. $3x^2 + 2y^2 = 6$ **22.** $9x^2 + 10y^2 = 90$

23. $6x^2 + 9y^2 = 54$ **24.** $169x^2 + 25y^2 = 4225$

Exercises 25 and 26 give information about the foci and vertices of ellipses centered at the origin of the *xy*-plane. In each case, find the ellipse's standard-form equation from the given information.

25. Foci: $\left(\pm\sqrt{2}, 0\right)$ Vertices: $(\pm 2, 0)$

26. Foci: $(0, \pm 4)$ Vertices: $(0, \pm 5)$

Hyperbolas

Exercises 27–34 give equations for hyperbolas. Put each equation in standard form and find the hyperbola's asymptotes. Then sketch the hyperbola. Include the asymptotes and foci in your sketch.

27. $x^2 - y^2 = 1$ **28.** $9x^2 - 16y^2 = 144$

29. $y^2 - x^2 = 8$ **30.** $y^2 - x^2 = 4$

31. $8x^2 - 2y^2 = 16$ **32.** $y^2 - 3x^2 = 3$

33. $8y^2 - 2x^2 = 16$ **34.** $64x^2 - 36y^2 = 2304$

Exercises 35–38 give information about the foci, vertices, and asymptotes of hyperbolas centered at the origin of the *xy*-plane. In each case, find the hyperbola's standard-form equation from the information given.

35. Foci: $\left(0, \pm\sqrt{2}\right)$ Asymptotes: $y = \pm x$

36. Foci: $(\pm 2, 0)$ Asymptotes: $y = \pm \frac{1}{\sqrt{3}}x$

37. Vertices: $(\pm 3, 0)$ Asymptotes: $y = \pm \frac{4}{3}x$

38. Vertices: $(0, \pm 2)$ Asymptotes: $y = \pm \frac{1}{2}x$

Shifting Conic Sections

39. The parabola $y^2 = 8x$ is shifted down 2 units and right 1 unit to generate the parabola $(y + 2)^2 = 8(x - 1)$.

a. Find the new parabola's vertex, focus, and directrix.

b. Plot the new vertex, focus, and directrix, and sketch in the parabola.

40. The parabola $x^2 = -4y$ is shifted left 1 unit and up 3 units to generate the parabola $(x + 1)^2 = -4(y - 3)$.

a. Find the new parabola's vertex, focus, and directrix.

b. Plot the new vertex, focus, and directrix, and sketch in the parabola.

41. The ellipse $(x^2/16) + (y^2/9) = 1$ is shifted 4 units to the right and 3 units up to generate the ellipse

$$\frac{(x-4)^2}{16} + \frac{(y-3)^2}{9} = 1.$$

a. Find the foci, vertices, and center of the new ellipse.

b. Plot the new foci, vertices, and center, and sketch in the new ellipse.

42. The ellipse $(x^2/9) + (y^2/25) = 1$ is shifted 3 units to the left and 2 units down to generate the ellipse

$$\frac{(x+3)^2}{9} + \frac{(y+2)^2}{25} = 1.$$

a. Find the foci, vertices, and center of the new ellipse.

b. Plot the new foci, vertices, and center, and sketch in the new ellipse.

43. The hyperbola $(x^2/16) - (y^2/9) = 1$ is shifted 2 units to the right to generate the hyperbola

$$\frac{(x-2)^2}{16} - \frac{y^2}{9} = 1.$$

a. Find the center, foci, vertices, and asymptotes of the new hyperbola.

b. Plot the new center, foci, vertices, and asymptotes, and sketch in the hyperbola.

44. The hyperbola $(y^2/4) - (x^2/5) = 1$ is shifted 2 units down to generate the hyperbola

$$\frac{(y+2)^2}{4} - \frac{x^2}{5} = 1.$$

a. Find the center, foci, vertices, and asymptotes of the new hyperbola.

b. Plot the new center, foci, vertices, and asymptotes, and sketch in the hyperbola.

Exercises 45–48 give equations for parabolas and tell how many units up or down and to the right or left each parabola is to be shifted. Find an equation for the new parabola, and find the new vertex, focus, and directrix.

45. $y^2 = 4x$, left 2, down 3 **46.** $y^2 = -12x$, right 4, up 3

47. $x^2 = 8y$, right 1, down 7 **48.** $x^2 = 6y$, left 3, down 2

Exercises 49–52 give equations for ellipses and tell how many units up or down and to the right or left each ellipse is to be shifted. Find an equation for the new ellipse, and find the new foci, vertices, and center.

49. $\frac{x^2}{6} + \frac{y^2}{9} = 1$, left 2, down 1

50. $\frac{x^2}{2} + y^2 = 1$, right 3, up 4

51. $\frac{x^2}{3} + \frac{y^2}{2} = 1$, right 2, up 3

52. $\frac{x^2}{16} + \frac{y^2}{25} = 1$, left 4, down 5

Exercises 53–56 give equations for hyperbolas and tell how many units up or down and to the right or left each hyperbola is to be shifted. Find an equation for the new hyperbola, and find the new center, foci, vertices, and asymptotes.

53. $\frac{x^2}{4} - \frac{y^2}{5} = 1$, right 2, up 2

54. $\frac{x^2}{16} - \frac{y^2}{9} = 1$, left 2, down 1

55. $y^2 - x^2 = 1$, left 1, down 1

56. $\frac{y^2}{3} - x^2 = 1$, right 1, up 3

Find the center, foci, vertices, asymptotes, and radius, as appropriate, of the conic sections in Exercises 57–68.

57. $x^2 + 4x + y^2 = 12$

58. $2x^2 + 2y^2 - 28x + 12y + 114 = 0$

59. $x^2 + 2x + 4y - 3 = 0$ **60.** $y^2 - 4y - 8x - 12 = 0$

61. $x^2 + 5y^2 + 4x = 1$ **62.** $9x^2 + 6y^2 + 36y = 0$

63. $x^2 + 2y^2 - 2x - 4y = -1$

64. $4x^2 + y^2 + 8x - 2y = -1$

65. $x^2 - y^2 - 2x + 4y = 4$ **66.** $x^2 - y^2 + 4x - 6y = 6$

67. $2x^2 - y^2 + 6y = 3$ **68.** $y^2 - 4x^2 + 16x = 24$

Inequalities

Sketch the regions in the xy-plane whose coordinates satisfy the inequalities or pairs of inequalities in Exercises 69–74.

69. $9x^2 + 16y^2 \le 144$

70. $x^2 + y^2 \ge 1$ and $4x^2 + y^2 \le 4$

71. $x^2 + 4y^2 \ge 4$ and $4x^2 + 9y^2 \le 36$

72. $(x^2 + y^2 - 4)(x^2 + 9y^2 - 9) \le 0$

73. $4y^2 - x^2 \ge 4$ **74.** $|x^2 - y^2| \le 1$

Theory and Examples

75. Archimedes' formula for the volume of a parabolic solid The region enclosed by the parabola $y = (4h/b^2)x^2$ and the line $y = h$ is revolved about the y-axis to generate the solid shown here. Show that the volume of the solid is $3/2$ the volume of the corresponding cone.

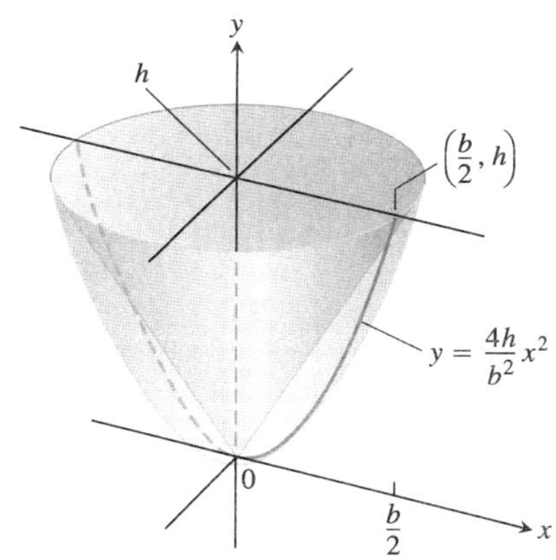

76. Suspension bridge cables hang in parabolas The suspension bridge cable shown here supports a uniform load of w pounds per horizontal foot. It can be shown that if H is the horizontal tension of the cable at the origin, then the curve of the cable satisfies the equation

$$\frac{dy}{dx} = \frac{w}{H}x.$$

Show that the cable hangs in a parabola by solving this differential equation subject to the initial condition that $y = 0$ when $x = 0$.

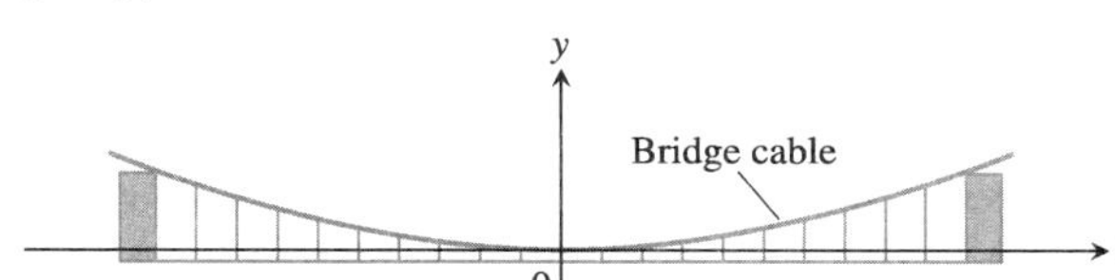

77. Find an equation for the circle through the points (1, 0), (0, 1), and (2, 2).

78. Find an equation for the circle through the points (2, 3), (3, 2), and $(-4, 3)$.

79. Find an equation for the circle centered at $(-2, 1)$ that passes through the point (1, 3). Is the point (1.1, 2.8) inside, outside, or on the circle?

80. Find equations for the tangents to the circle $(x - 2)^2 + (y - 1)^2 = 5$ at the points where the circle crosses the coordinate axes. (*Hint:* Use implicit differentiation.)

81. If lines are drawn parallel to the coordinate axes through a point P on the parabola $y^2 = kx$, $k > 0$, the parabola partitions the rectangular region bounded by these lines and the coordinate axes into two smaller regions, A and B.

a. If the two smaller regions are revolved about the y-axis, show that they generate solids whose volumes have the ratio 4:1.

b. What is the ratio of the volumes generated by revolving the regions about the x-axis?

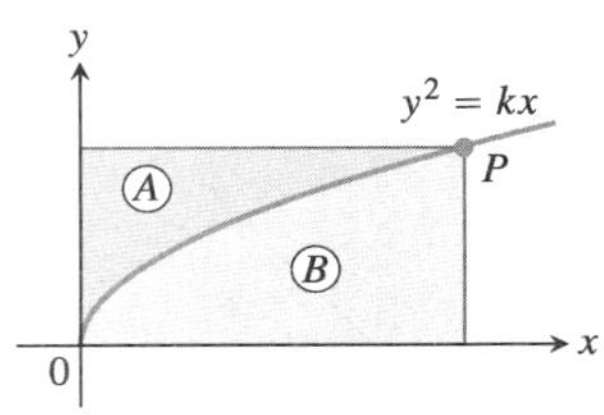

82. Show that the tangents to the curve $y^2 = 4px$ from any point on the line $x = -p$ are perpendicular.

83. Find the dimensions of the rectangle of largest area that can be inscribed in the ellipse $x^2 + 4y^2 = 4$ with its sides parallel to the coordinate axes. What is the area of the rectangle?

84. Find the volume of the solid generated by revolving the region enclosed by the ellipse $9x^2 + 4y^2 = 36$ about the **(a)** x-axis, **(b)** y-axis.

85. The "triangular" region in the first quadrant bounded by the x-axis, the line $x = 4$, and the hyperbola $9x^2 - 4y^2 = 36$ is revolved about the x-axis to generate a solid. Find the volume of the solid.

86. The region bounded on the left by the y-axis, on the right by the hyperbola $x^2 - y^2 = 1$, and above and below by the lines $y = \pm 3$ is revolved about the y-axis to generate a solid. Find the volume of the solid.

87. Find the centroid of the region that is bounded below by the x-axis and above by the ellipse $(x^2/9) + (y^2/16) = 1$.

88. The curve $y = \sqrt{x^2 + 1}, 0 \le x \le \sqrt{2}$, which is part of the upper branch of the hyperbola $y^2 - x^2 = 1$, is revolved about the x-axis to generate a surface. Find the area of the surface.

89. The circular waves in the photograph here were made by touching the surface of a ripple tank, first at A and then at B. As the waves expanded, their point of intersection appeared to trace a hyperbola. Did it really do that? To find out, we can model the waves with circles centered at A and B.

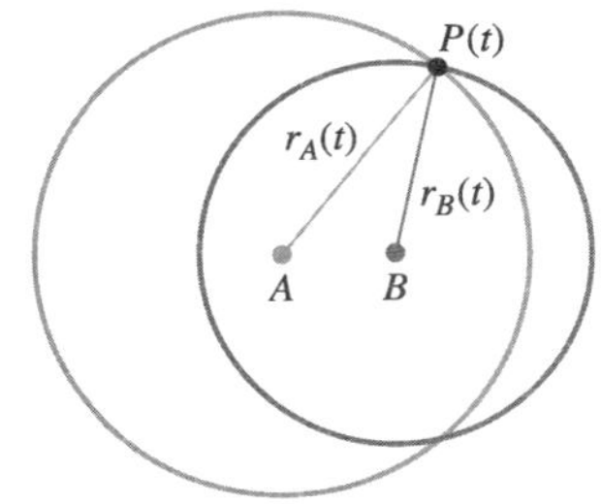

At time t, the point P is $r_A(t)$ units from A and $r_B(t)$ units from B. Since the radii of the circles increase at a constant rate, the rate at which the waves are traveling is

$$\frac{dr_A}{dt} = \frac{dr_B}{dt}.$$

Conclude from this equation that $r_A - r_B$ has a constant value, so that P must lie on a hyperbola with foci at A and B.

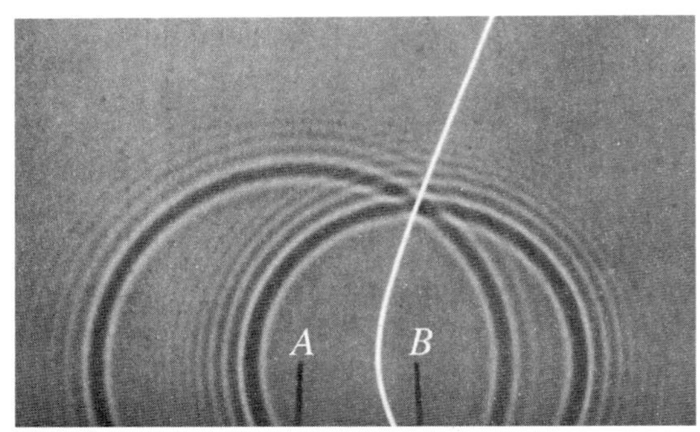

90. The reflective property of parabolas The figure here shows a typical point $P(x_0, y_0)$ on the parabola $y^2 = 4px$. The line L is tangent to the parabola at P. The parabola's focus lies at $F(p, 0)$. The ray L' extending from P to the right is parallel to the x-axis. We show that light from F to P will be reflected out along L' by showing that β equals α. Establish this equality by taking the following steps.

a. Show that $\tan \beta = 2p/y_0$.

b. Show that $\tan \phi = y_0/(x_0 - p)$.

c. Use the identity

$$\tan \alpha = \frac{\tan \phi - \tan \beta}{1 + \tan \phi \tan \beta}$$

to show that $\tan \alpha = 2p/y_0$.

Since α and β are both acute, $\tan\beta = \tan\alpha$ implies $\beta = \alpha$.

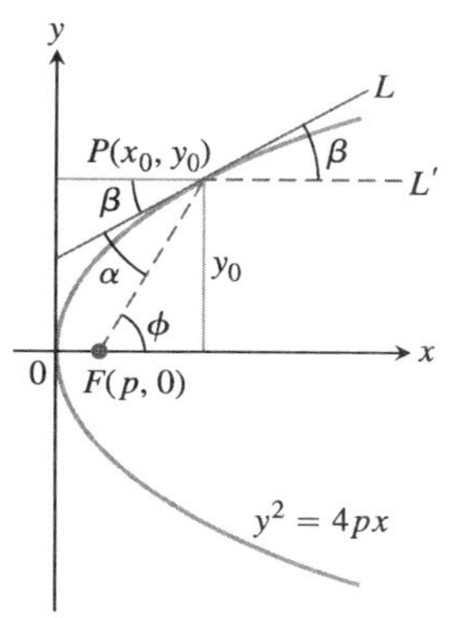

91. How the astronomer Kepler used string to draw parabolas Kepler's method for drawing a parabola (with more modern tools) requires a string the length of a T square and a table whose edge can serve as the parabola's directrix. Pin one end of the string to the point where you want the focus to be and the other end to the upper end of the T square. Then, holding the string taut against the T square with a pencil, slide the T square along the table's edge. As the T square moves, the pencil will trace a parabola. Why?

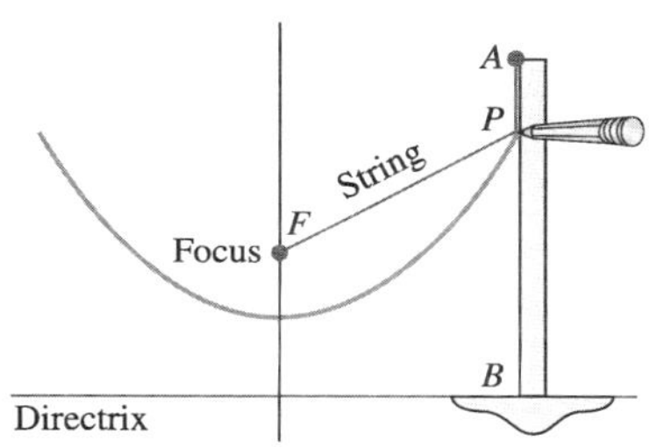

92. Construction of a hyperbola The following diagrams appeared (unlabeled) in Ernest J. Eckert, "Constructions Without Words," *Mathematics Magazine*, Vol. 66, No. 2, Apr. 1993, p. 113. Explain the constructions by finding the coordinates of the point P.

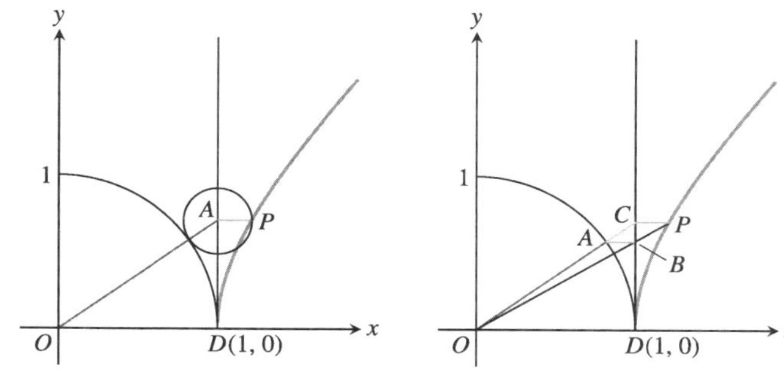

(a) (b)

93. The width of a parabola at the focus Show that the number $4p$ is the *width* of the parabola $x^2 = 4py$ $(p > 0)$ at the focus by showing that the line $y = p$ cuts the parabola at points that are $4p$ units apart.

94. The asymptotes of $(x^2/a^2) - (y^2/b^2) = 1$ Show that the vertical distance between the line $y = (b/a)x$ and the upper half of the right-hand branch $y = (b/a)\sqrt{x^2 - a^2}$ of the hyperbola $(x^2/a^2) - (y^2/b^2) = 1$ approaches 0 by showing that

$$\lim_{x\to\infty}\left(\frac{b}{a}x - \frac{b}{a}\sqrt{x^2 - a^2}\right) = \frac{b}{a}\lim_{x\to\infty}\left(x - \sqrt{x^2 - a^2}\right) = 0.$$

Similar results hold for the remaining portions of the hyperbola and the lines $y = \pm(b/a)x$.

10.2 Classifying Conic Sections by Eccentricity

We now show how to associate with each conic section a number called the conic section's *eccentricity*. The eccentricity reveals the conic section's type (circle, ellipse, parabola, or hyperbola) and, in the case of ellipses and hyperbolas, describes the conic section's general proportions.

Eccentricity

Although the center-to-focus distance c does not appear in the equation

$$\frac{x^2}{a^2} + \frac{y^2}{b^2} = 1, \qquad (a > b)$$

for an ellipse, we can still determine c from the equation $c = \sqrt{a^2 - b^2}$. If we fix a and vary c over the interval $0 \le c \le a$, the resulting ellipses will vary in shape (Figure 10.17). They are circles if $c = 0$ (so that $a = b$) and flatten as c increases. If $c = a$, the foci and vertices overlap and the ellipse degenerates into a line segment.

We use the ratio of c to a to describe the various shapes the ellipse can take. We call this ratio the ellipse's eccentricity.

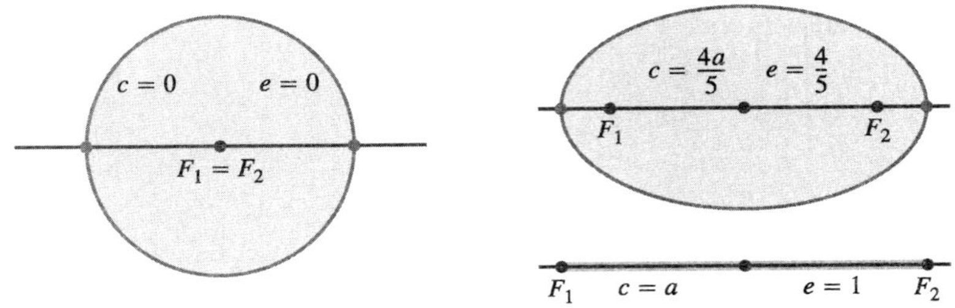

FIGURE 10.17 The ellipse changes from a circle to a line segment as c increases from 0 to a.

DEFINITION Eccentricity of an Ellipse

The **eccentricity** of the ellipse $(x^2/a^2) + (y^2/b^2) = 1$ $(a > b)$ is

$$e = \frac{c}{a} = \frac{\sqrt{a^2 - b^2}}{a}.$$

TABLE 10.2 Eccentricities of planetary orbits

Mercury	0.21	Saturn	0.06
Venus	0.01	Uranus	0.05
Earth	0.02	Neptune	0.01
Mars	0.09	Pluto	0.25
Jupiter	0.05		

The planets in the solar system revolve around the sun in (approximate) elliptical orbits with the sun at one focus. Most of the orbits are nearly circular, as can be seen from the eccentricities in Table 10.2. Pluto has a fairly eccentric orbit, with $e = 0.25$, as does Mercury, with $e = 0.21$. Other members of the solar system have orbits that are even more eccentric. Icarus, an asteroid about 1 mile wide that revolves around the sun every 409 Earth days, has an orbital eccentricity of 0.83 (Figure 10.18).

HISTORICAL BIOGRAPHY

Edmund Halley
(1656–1742)

EXAMPLE 1 Halley's Comet

The orbit of Halley's comet is an ellipse 36.18 astronomical units long by 9.12 astronomical units wide. (One *astronomical unit* [AU] is 149,597,870 km, the semimajor axis of Earth's orbit.) Its eccentricity is

$$e = \frac{\sqrt{a^2 - b^2}}{a} = \frac{\sqrt{(36.18/2)^2 - (9.12/2)^2}}{(1/2)(36.18)} = \frac{\sqrt{(18.09)^2 - (4.56)^2}}{18.09} \approx 0.97. \quad ■$$

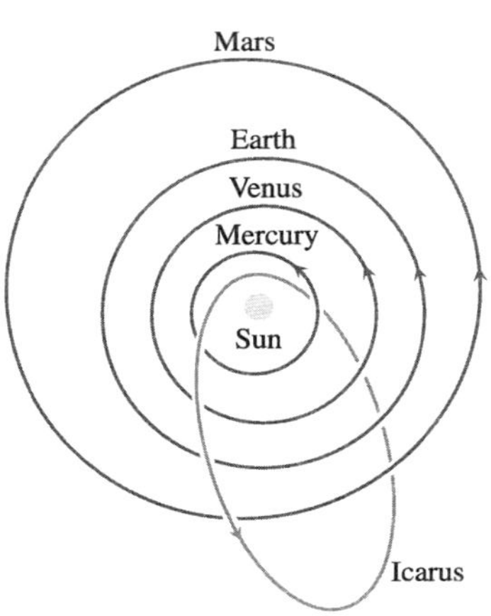

FIGURE 10.18 The orbit of the asteroid Icarus is highly eccentric. Earth's orbit is so nearly circular that its foci lie inside the sun.

Whereas a parabola has one focus and one directrix, each **ellipse** has two foci and two **directrices**. These are the lines perpendicular to the major axis at distances $\pm a/e$ from the center. The parabola has the property that

$$PF = 1 \cdot PD \tag{1}$$

for any point P on it, where F is the focus and D is the point nearest P on the directrix. For an ellipse, it can be shown that the equations that replace Equation (1) are

$$PF_1 = e \cdot PD_1, \qquad PF_2 = e \cdot PD_2. \tag{2}$$

Here, e is the eccentricity, P is any point on the ellipse, F_1 and F_2 are the foci, and D_1 and D_2 are the points on the directrices nearest P (Figure 10.19).

In both Equations (2) the directrix and focus must correspond; that is, if we use the distance from P to F_1, we must also use the distance from P to the directrix at the same end of the ellipse. The directrix $x = -a/e$ corresponds to $F_1(-c, 0)$, and the directrix $x = a/e$ corresponds to $F_2(c, 0)$.

The eccentricity of a hyperbola is also $e = c/a$, only in this case c equals $\sqrt{a^2 + b^2}$ instead of $\sqrt{a^2 - b^2}$. In contrast to the eccentricity of an ellipse, the eccentricity of a hyperbola is always greater than 1.

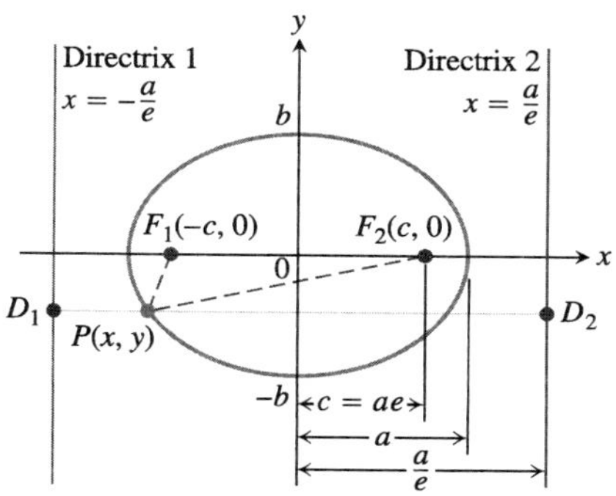

FIGURE 10.19 The foci and directrices of the ellipse $(x^2/a^2) + (y^2/b^2) = 1$. Directrix 1 corresponds to focus F_1, and directrix 2 to focus F_2.

DEFINITION Eccentricity of a Hyperbola

The **eccentricity** of the hyperbola $(x^2/a^2) - (y^2/b^2) = 1$ is

$$e = \frac{c}{a} = \frac{\sqrt{a^2 + b^2}}{a}.$$

In both ellipse and hyperbola, the eccentricity is the ratio of the distance between the foci to the distance between the vertices (because $c/a = 2c/2a$).

$$\text{Eccentricity} = \frac{\text{distance between foci}}{\text{distance between vertices}}$$

In an ellipse, the foci are closer together than the vertices and the ratio is less than 1. In a hyperbola, the foci are farther apart than the vertices and the ratio is greater than 1.

EXAMPLE 2 Finding the Vertices of an Ellipse

Locate the vertices of an ellipse of eccentricity 0.8 whose foci lie at the points $(0, \pm 7)$.

Solution Since $e = c/a$, the vertices are the points $(0, \pm a)$ where

$$a = \frac{c}{e} = \frac{7}{0.8} = 8.75,$$

or $(0, \pm 8.75)$. ■

EXAMPLE 3 Eccentricity of a Hyperbola

Find the eccentricity of the hyperbola $9x^2 - 16y^2 = 144$.

Solution We divide both sides of the hyperbola's equation by 144 to put it in standard form, obtaining

$$\frac{9x^2}{144} - \frac{16y^2}{144} = 1 \quad \text{and} \quad \frac{x^2}{16} - \frac{y^2}{9} = 1.$$

With $a^2 = 16$ and $b^2 = 9$, we find that $c = \sqrt{a^2 + b^2} = \sqrt{16 + 9} = 5$, so

$$e = \frac{c}{a} = \frac{5}{4}.$$ ■

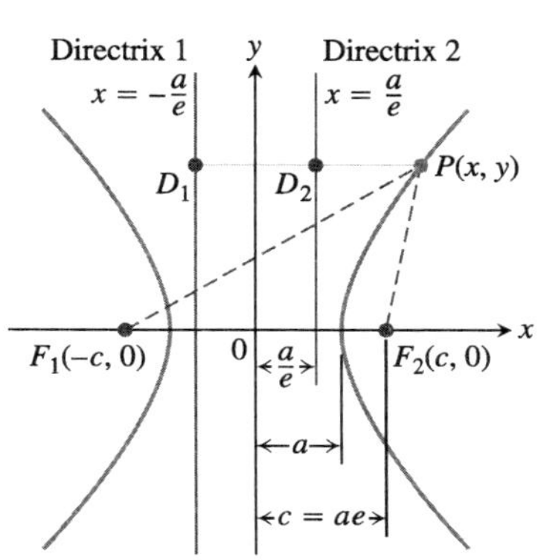

FIGURE 10.20 The foci and directrices of the hyperbola $(x^2/a^2) - (y^2/b^2) = 1$. No matter where P lies on the hyperbola, $PF_1 = e \cdot PD_1$ and $PF_2 = e \cdot PD_2$.

As with the ellipse, it can be shown that the lines $x = \pm a/e$ act as **directrices** for the **hyperbola** and that

$$PF_1 = e \cdot PD_1 \quad \text{and} \quad PF_2 = e \cdot PD_2. \tag{3}$$

Here P is any point on the hyperbola, F_1 and F_2 are the foci, and D_1 and D_2 are the points nearest P on the directrices (Figure 10.20).

To complete the picture, we define the eccentricity of a parabola to be $e = 1$. Equations (1) to (3) then have the common form $PF = e \cdot PD$.

DEFINITION Eccentricity of a Parabola

The **eccentricity** of a parabola is $e = 1$.

The "focus–directrix" equation $PF = e \cdot PD$ unites the parabola, ellipse, and hyperbola in the following way. Suppose that the distance PF of a point P from a fixed point F (the focus) is a constant multiple of its distance from a fixed line (the directrix). That is, suppose

$$PF = e \cdot PD, \tag{4}$$

where e is the constant of proportionality. Then the path traced by P is

(a) a *parabola* if $e = 1$,

(b) an *ellipse* of eccentricity e if $e < 1$, and

(c) a *hyperbola* of eccentricity e if $e > 1$.

There are no coordinates in Equation (4) and when we try to translate it into coordinate form it translates in different ways, depending on the size of e. At least, that is what happens in Cartesian coordinates. However, in polar coordinates, as we will see in Section 10.8, the equation $PF = e \cdot PD$ translates into a single equation regardless of the value of e, an equation so simple that it has been the equation of choice of astronomers and space scientists for nearly 300 years.

Given the focus and corresponding directrix of a hyperbola centered at the origin and with foci on the x-axis, we can use the dimensions shown in Figure 10.20 to find e. Knowing e, we can derive a Cartesian equation for the hyperbola from the equation $PF = e \cdot PD$, as in the next example. We can find equations for ellipses centered at the origin and with foci on the x-axis in a similar way, using the dimensions shown in Figure 10.19.

EXAMPLE 4 Cartesian Equation for a Hyperbola

Find a Cartesian equation for the hyperbola centered at the origin that has a focus at (3, 0) and the line $x = 1$ as the corresponding directrix.

Solution We first use the dimensions shown in Figure 10.20 to find the hyperbola's eccentricity. The focus is

$$(c, 0) = (3, 0) \qquad \text{so} \qquad c = 3.$$

The directrix is the line

$$x = \frac{a}{e} = 1, \qquad \text{so} \qquad a = e.$$

When combined with the equation $e = c/a$ that defines eccentricity, these results give

$$e = \frac{c}{a} = \frac{3}{e}, \qquad \text{so} \qquad e^2 = 3 \quad \text{and} \quad e = \sqrt{3}.$$

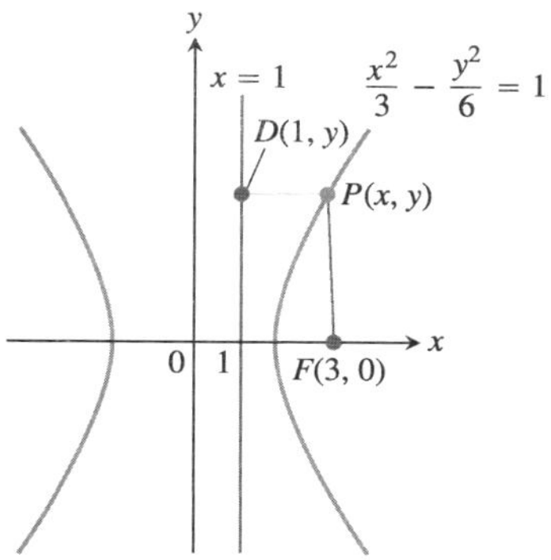

FIGURE 10.21 The hyperbola and directrix in Example 4.

Knowing e, we can now derive the equation we want from the equation $PF = e \cdot PD$. In the notation of Figure 10.21, we have

$$PF = e \cdot PD \qquad \text{Equation (4)}$$

$$\sqrt{(x-3)^2 + (y-0)^2} = \sqrt{3}\,|x-1| \qquad e = \sqrt{3}$$

$$x^2 - 6x + 9 + y^2 = 3(x^2 - 2x + 1)$$

$$2x^2 - y^2 = 6$$

$$\frac{x^2}{3} - \frac{y^2}{6} = 1.$$

■

EXERCISES 10.2

Ellipses

In Exercises 1–8, find the eccentricity of the ellipse. Then find and graph the ellipse's foci and directrices.

1. $16x^2 + 25y^2 = 400$
2. $7x^2 + 16y^2 = 112$
3. $2x^2 + y^2 = 2$
4. $2x^2 + y^2 = 4$
5. $3x^2 + 2y^2 = 6$
6. $9x^2 + 10y^2 = 90$
7. $6x^2 + 9y^2 = 54$
8. $169x^2 + 25y^2 = 4225$

Exercises 9–12 give the foci or vertices and the eccentricities of ellipses centered at the origin of the xy-plane. In each case, find the ellipse's standard-form equation.

9. Foci: $(0, \pm 3)$
Eccentricity: 0.5

10. Foci: $(\pm 8, 0)$
Eccentricity: 0.2

11. Vertices: $(0, \pm 70)$
Eccentricity: 0.1

12. Vertices: $(\pm 10, 0)$
Eccentricity: 0.24

Exercises 13–16 give foci and corresponding directrices of ellipses centered at the origin of the xy-plane. In each case, use the dimensions in Figure 10.19 to find the eccentricity of the ellipse. Then find the ellipse's standard-form equation.

13. Focus: $(\sqrt{5}, 0)$
Directrix: $x = \frac{9}{\sqrt{5}}$

14. Focus: $(4, 0)$
Directrix: $x = \frac{16}{3}$

15. Focus: $(-4, 0)$
Directrix: $x = -16$

16. Focus: $(-\sqrt{2}, 0)$
Directrix: $x = -2\sqrt{2}$

17. Draw an ellipse of eccentricity $4/5$. Explain your procedure.

18. Draw the orbit of Pluto (eccentricity 0.25) to scale. Explain your procedure.

19. The endpoints of the major and minor axes of an ellipse are (1, 1), (3, 4), (1, 7), and (−1, 4). Sketch the ellipse, give its equation in standard form, and find its foci, eccentricity, and directrices.

20. Find an equation for the ellipse of eccentricity $2/3$ that has the line $x = 9$ as a directrix and the point (4, 0) as the corresponding focus.

21. What values of the constants a, b, and c make the ellipse

$$4x^2 + y^2 + ax + by + c = 0$$

lie tangent to the x-axis at the origin and pass through the point $(-1, 2)$? What is the eccentricity of the ellipse?

22. The reflective property of ellipses An ellipse is revolved about its major axis to generate an ellipsoid. The inner surface of the ellipsoid is silvered to make a mirror. Show that a ray of light emanating from one focus will be reflected to the other focus. Sound waves also follow such paths, and this property is used in constructing "whispering galleries." (*Hint:* Place the ellipse in standard position in the xy-plane and show that the lines from a point P on the ellipse to the two foci make congruent angles with the tangent to the ellipse at P.)

Hyperbolas

In Exercises 23–30, find the eccentricity of the hyperbola. Then find and graph the hyperbola's foci and directrices.

23. $x^2 - y^2 = 1$
24. $9x^2 - 16y^2 = 144$
25. $y^2 - x^2 = 8$
26. $y^2 - x^2 = 4$
27. $8x^2 - 2y^2 = 16$
28. $y^2 - 3x^2 = 3$
29. $8y^2 - 2x^2 = 16$
30. $64x^2 - 36y^2 = 2304$

Exercises 31–34 give the eccentricities and the vertices or foci of hyperbolas centered at the origin of the xy-plane. In each case, find the hyperbola's standard-form equation.

31. Eccentricity: 3
Vertices: $(0, \pm 1)$

32. Eccentricity: 2
Vertices: $(\pm 2, 0)$

33. Eccentricity: 3
Foci: $(\pm 3, 0)$

34. Eccentricity: 1.25
Foci: $(0, \pm 5)$

Exercises 35–38 give foci and corresponding directrices of hyperbolas centered at the origin of the xy-plane. In each case, find the hyperbola's eccentricity. Then find the hyperbola's standard-form equation.

35. Focus: $(4, 0)$
Directrix: $x = 2$

36. Focus: $(\sqrt{10}, 0)$
Directrix: $x = \sqrt{2}$

37. Focus: $(-2, 0)$
Directrix: $x = -\dfrac{1}{2}$

38. Focus: $(-6, 0)$
Directrix: $x = -2$

39. A hyperbola of eccentricity $3/2$ has one focus at $(1, -3)$. The corresponding directrix is the line $y = 2$. Find an equation for the hyperbola.

T **40. The effect of eccentricity on a hyperbola's shape** What happens to the graph of a hyperbola as its eccentricity increases? To find out, rewrite the equation $(x^2/a^2) - (y^2/b^2) = 1$ in terms of a and e instead of a and b. Graph the hyperbola for various values of e and describe what you find.

41. The reflective property of hyperbolas Show that a ray of light directed toward one focus of a hyperbolic mirror, as in the accompanying figure, is reflected toward the other focus. (*Hint:* Show that the tangent to the hyperbola at P bisects the angle made by segments PF_1 and PF_2.)

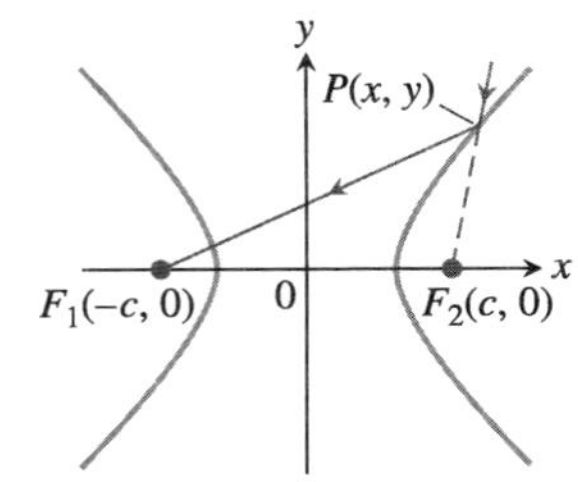

42. A confocal ellipse and hyperbola Show that an ellipse and a hyperbola that have the same foci A and B, as in the accompanying figure, cross at right angles at their point of intersection. (*Hint:* A ray of light from focus A that met the hyperbola at P would be reflected from the hyperbola as if it came directly from B (Exercise 41). The same ray would be reflected off the ellipse to pass through B (Exercise 22).)

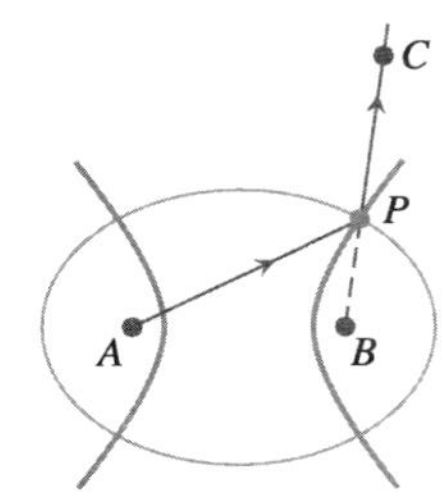

10.3 Quadratic Equations and Rotations

In this section, we examine the Cartesian graph of any equation

$$Ax^2 + Bxy + Cy^2 + Dx + Ey + F = 0, \tag{1}$$

in which A, B, and C are not all zero, and show that it is nearly always a conic section. The exceptions are the cases in which there is no graph at all or the graph consists of two parallel lines. It is conventional to call all graphs of Equation (1), curved or not, **quadratic curves**.

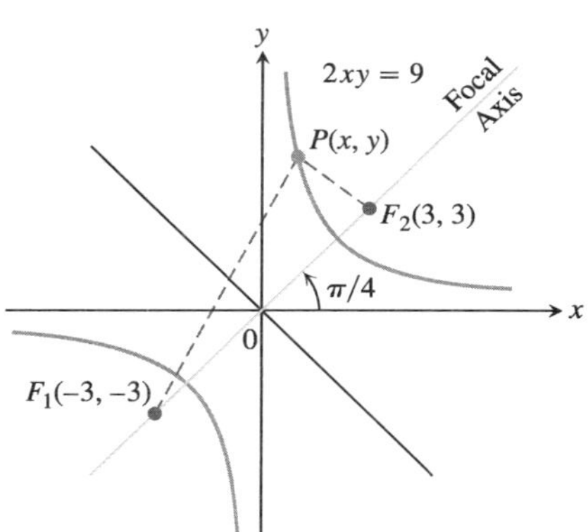

FIGURE 10.22 The focal axis of the hyperbola $2xy = 9$ makes an angle of $\pi/4$ radians with the positive x-axis.

The Cross Product Term

You may have noticed that the term Bxy did not appear in the equations for the conic sections in Section 10.1. This happened because the axes of the conic sections ran parallel to (in fact, coincided with) the coordinate axes.

To see what happens when the parallelism is absent, let us write an equation for a hyperbola with $a = 3$ and foci at $F_1(-3, -3)$ and $F_2(3, 3)$ (Figure 10.22). The equation $|PF_1 - PF_2| = 2a$ becomes $|PF_1 - PF_2| = 2(3) = 6$ and

$$\sqrt{(x + 3)^2 + (y + 3)^2} - \sqrt{(x - 3)^2 + (y - 3)^2} = \pm 6.$$

When we transpose one radical, square, solve for the radical that still appears, and square again, the equation reduces to

$$2xy = 9, \tag{2}$$

a case of Equation (1) in which the cross product term is present. The asymptotes of the hyperbola in Equation (2) are the x- and y-axes, and the focal axis makes an angle of $\pi/4$

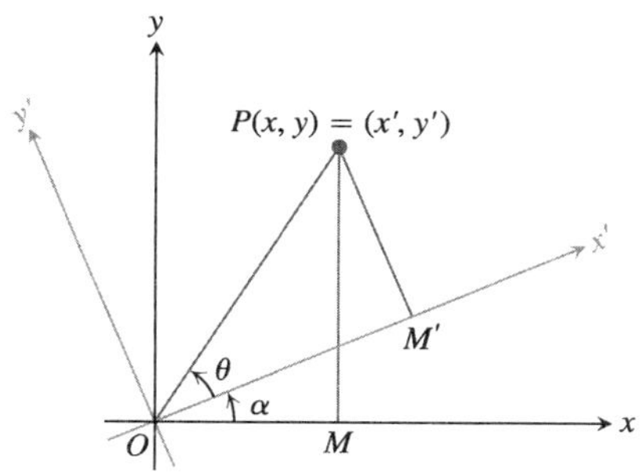

FIGURE 10.23 A counterclockwise rotation through angle α about the origin.

radians with the positive x-axis. As in this example, the cross product term is present in Equation (1) only when the axes of the conic are tilted.

To eliminate the xy-term from the equation of a conic, we rotate the coordinate axes to eliminate the "tilt" in the axes of the conic. The equations for the rotations we use are derived in the following way. In the notation of Figure 10.23, which shows a counterclockwise rotation about the origin through an angle α,

$$\begin{aligned} x &= OM = OP\cos(\theta+\alpha) = OP\cos\theta\cos\alpha - OP\sin\theta\sin\alpha \\ y &= MP = OP\sin(\theta+\alpha) = OP\cos\theta\sin\alpha + OP\sin\theta\cos\alpha. \end{aligned} \tag{3}$$

Since

$$OP\cos\theta = OM' = x'$$

and

$$OP\sin\theta = M'P = y',$$

Equations (3) reduce to the following.

Equations for Rotating Coordinate Axes

$$\begin{aligned} x &= x'\cos\alpha - y'\sin\alpha \\ y &= x'\sin\alpha + y'\cos\alpha \end{aligned} \tag{4}$$

EXAMPLE 1 Finding an Equation for a Hyperbola

The x- and y-axes are rotated through an angle of $\pi/4$ radians about the origin. Find an equation for the hyperbola $2xy = 9$ in the new coordinates.

Solution Since $\cos\pi/4 = \sin\pi/4 = 1/\sqrt{2}$, we substitute

$$x = \frac{x'-y'}{\sqrt{2}}, \qquad y = \frac{x'+y'}{\sqrt{2}}$$

from Equations (4) into the equation $2xy = 9$ and obtain

$$\begin{aligned} 2\left(\frac{x'-y'}{\sqrt{2}}\right)\left(\frac{x'+y'}{\sqrt{2}}\right) &= 9 \\ x'^2 - y'^2 &= 9 \\ \frac{x'^2}{9} - \frac{y'^2}{9} &= 1. \end{aligned}$$

See Figure 10.24. ■

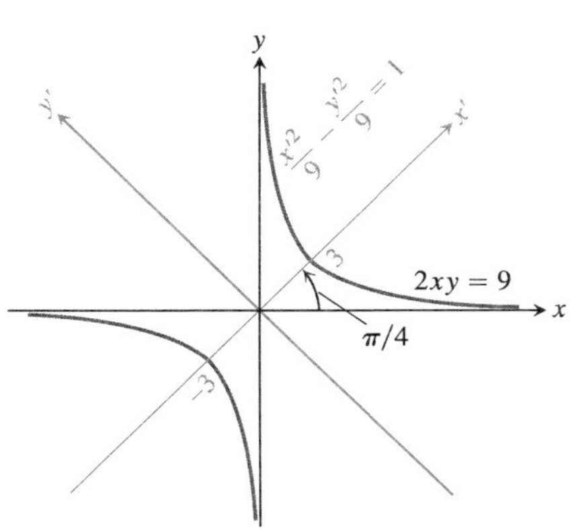

FIGURE 10.24 The hyperbola in Example 1 (x' and y' are the coordinates).

If we apply Equations (4) to the quadratic equation (1), we obtain a new quadratic equation

$$A'x'^2 + B'x'y' + C'y'^2 + D'x' + E'y' + F' = 0. \tag{5}$$

The new and old coefficients are related by the equations

$$\begin{aligned} A' &= A\cos^2\alpha + B\cos\alpha\sin\alpha + C\sin^2\alpha \\ B' &= B\cos 2\alpha + (C - A)\sin 2\alpha \\ C' &= A\sin^2\alpha - B\sin\alpha\cos\alpha + C\cos^2\alpha \\ D' &= D\cos\alpha + E\sin\alpha \\ E' &= -D\sin\alpha + E\cos\alpha \\ F' &= F. \end{aligned} \tag{6}$$

These equations show, among other things, that if we start with an equation for a curve in which the cross product term is present ($B \neq 0$), we can find a rotation angle α that produces an equation in which no cross product term appears ($B' = 0$). To find α, we set $B' = 0$ in the second equation in (6) and solve the resulting equation,

$$B\cos 2\alpha + (C - A)\sin 2\alpha = 0,$$

for α. In practice, this means determining α from one of the two equations

Angle of Rotation

$$\cot 2\alpha = \frac{A - C}{B} \quad \text{or} \quad \tan 2\alpha = \frac{B}{A - C}. \tag{7}$$

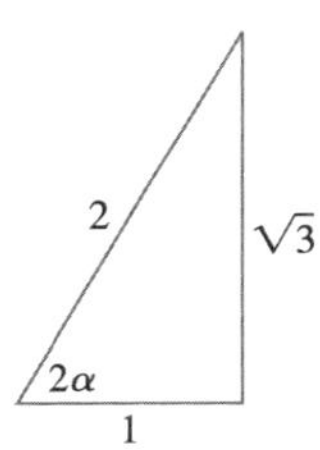

FIGURE 10.25 This triangle identifies $2\alpha = \cot^{-1}(1/\sqrt{3})$ as $\pi/3$ (Example 2).

EXAMPLE 2 Finding the Angle of Rotation

The coordinate axes are to be rotated through an angle α to produce an equation for the curve

$$2x^2 + \sqrt{3}\,xy + y^2 - 10 = 0$$

that has no cross product term. Find α and the new equation. Identify the curve.

Solution The equation $2x^2 + \sqrt{3}\,xy + y^2 - 10 = 0$ has $A = 2, B = \sqrt{3}$, and $C = 1$. We substitute these values into Equation (7) to find α:

$$\cot 2\alpha = \frac{A - C}{B} = \frac{2 - 1}{\sqrt{3}} = \frac{1}{\sqrt{3}}.$$

From the right triangle in Figure 10.25, we see that one appropriate choice of angle is $2\alpha = \pi/3$, so we take $\alpha = \pi/6$. Substituting $\alpha = \pi/6$, $A = 2$, $B = \sqrt{3}$, $C = 1$, $D = E = 0$, and $F = -10$ into Equations (6) gives

$$A' = \frac{5}{2}, \quad B' = 0, \quad C' = \frac{1}{2}, \quad D' = E' = 0, \quad F' = -10.$$

Equation (5) then gives

$$\frac{5}{2}x'^2 + \frac{1}{2}y'^2 - 10 = 0, \quad \text{or} \quad \frac{x'^2}{4} + \frac{y'^2}{20} = 1.$$

The curve is an ellipse with foci on the new y'-axis (Figure 10.26). ■

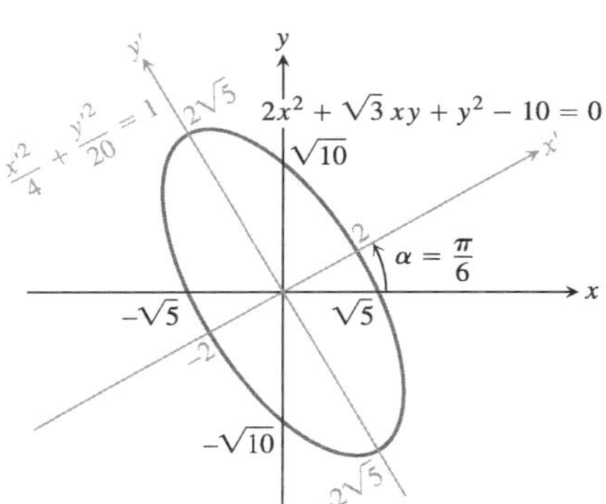

FIGURE 10.26 The conic section in Example 2.

Possible Graphs of Quadratic Equations

We now return to the graph of the general quadratic equation.

Since axes can always be rotated to eliminate the cross product term, there is no loss of generality in assuming that this has been done and that our equation has the form

$$Ax^2 + Cy^2 + Dx + Ey + F = 0. \tag{8}$$

Equation (8) represents

(a) a *circle* if $A = C \neq 0$ (special cases: the graph is a point or there is no graph at all);

(b) a *parabola* if Equation (8) is quadratic in one variable and linear in the other;

(c) an *ellipse* if A and C are both positive or both negative (special cases: circles, a single point, or no graph at all);

(d) a *hyperbola* if A and C have opposite signs (special case: a pair of intersecting lines);

(e) a *straight line* if A and C are zero and at least one of D and E is different from zero;

(f) *one or two straight lines* if the left-hand side of Equation (8) can be factored into the product of two linear factors.

See Table 10.3 for examples.

TABLE 10.3 Examples of quadratic curves $Ax^2 + Bxy + Cy^2 + Dx + Ey + F = 0$

	A	B	C	D	E	F	Equation	Remarks
Circle	1		1			−4	$x^2 + y^2 = 4$	$A = C; F < 0$
Parabola			1	−9			$y^2 = 9x$	Quadratic in y, linear in x
Ellipse	4		9			−36	$4x^2 + 9y^2 = 36$	A, C have same sign, $A \neq C; F < 0$
Hyperbola	1		−1			−1	$x^2 - y^2 = 1$	A, C have opposite signs
One line (still a conic section)	1						$x^2 = 0$	y-axis
Intersecting lines (still a conic section)		1		1	−1	−1	$xy + x - y - 1 = 0$	Factors to $(x - 1)(y + 1) = 0$, so $x = 1, y = -1$
Parallel lines (not a conic section)	1			−3		2	$x^2 - 3x + 2 = 0$	Factors to $(x - 1)(x - 2) = 0$, so $x = 1, x = 2$
Point	1		1				$x^2 + y^2 = 0$	The origin
No graph	1					1	$x^2 = -1$	No graph

The Discriminant Test

We do not need to eliminate the xy-term from the equation

$$Ax^2 + Bxy + Cy^2 + Dx + Ey + F = 0 \tag{9}$$

to tell what kind of conic section the equation represents. If this is the only information we want, we can apply the following test instead.

As we have seen, if $B \neq 0$, then rotating the coordinate axes through an angle α that satisfies the equation

$$\cot 2\alpha = \frac{A - C}{B} \tag{10}$$

will change Equation (9) into an equivalent form

$$A'x'^2 + C'y'^2 + D'x' + E'y' + F' = 0 \tag{11}$$

without a cross product term.

Now, the graph of Equation (11) is a (real or degenerate)

(a) *parabola* if A' or $C' = 0$; that is, if $A'C' = 0$;

(b) *ellipse* if A' and C' have the same sign; that is, if $A'C' > 0$;

(c) *hyperbola* if A' and C' have opposite signs; that is, if $A'C' < 0$.

It can also be verified from Equations (6) that for any rotation of axes,

$$B^2 - 4AC = B'^2 - 4A'C'. \tag{12}$$

This means that the quantity $B^2 - 4AC$ is not changed by a rotation. But when we rotate through the angle α given by Equation (10), B' becomes zero, so

$$B^2 - 4AC = -4A'C'.$$

Since the curve is a parabola if $A'C' = 0$, an ellipse if $A'C' > 0$, and a hyperbola if $A'C' < 0$, the curve must be a parabola if $B^2 - 4AC = 0$, an ellipse if $B^2 - 4AC < 0$, and a hyperbola if $B^2 - 4AC > 0$. The number $B^2 - 4AC$ is called the **discriminant** of Equation (9).

The Discriminant Test

With the understanding that occasional degenerate cases may arise, the quadratic curve $Ax^2 + Bxy + Cy^2 + Dx + Ey + F = 0$ is

(a) a **parabola** if $B^2 - 4AC = 0$,
(b) an **ellipse** if $B^2 - 4AC < 0$,
(c) a **hyperbola** if $B^2 - 4AC > 0$.

EXAMPLE 3 Applying the Discriminant Test

(a) $3x^2 - 6xy + 3y^2 + 2x - 7 = 0$ represents a parabola because

$$B^2 - 4AC = (-6)^2 - 4 \cdot 3 \cdot 3 = 36 - 36 = 0.$$

(b) $x^2 + xy + y^2 - 1 = 0$ represents an ellipse because

$$B^2 - 4AC = (1)^2 - 4 \cdot 1 \cdot 1 = -3 < 0.$$

(c) $xy - y^2 - 5y + 1 = 0$ represents a hyperbola because

$$B^2 - 4AC = (1)^2 - 4(0)(-1) = 1 > 0.$$

■

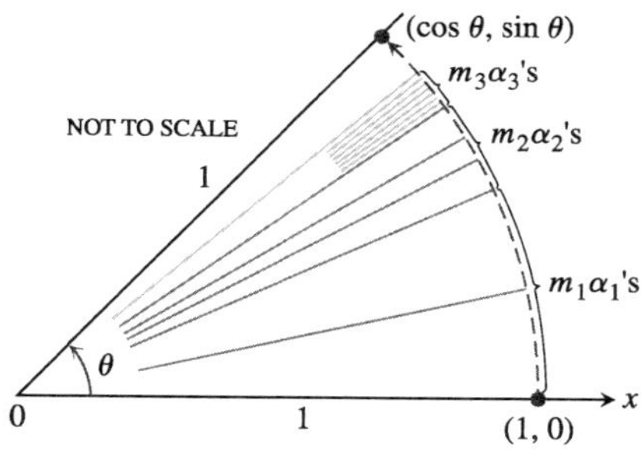

FIGURE 10.27 To calculate the sine and cosine of an angle θ between 0 and 2π, the calculator rotates the point (1, 0) to an appropriate location on the unit circle and displays the resulting coordinates.

USING TECHNOLOGY **How Calculators Use Rotations to Evaluate Sines and Cosines**

Some calculators use rotations to calculate sines and cosines of arbitrary angles. The procedure goes something like this: The calculator has, stored,

1. ten angles or so, say

$$\alpha_1 = \sin^{-1}(10^{-1}), \qquad \alpha_2 = \sin^{-1}(10^{-2}), \qquad \ldots, \qquad \alpha_{10} = \sin^{-1}(10^{-10}),$$

and

2. twenty numbers, the sines and cosines of the angles $\alpha_1, \alpha_2, \ldots, \alpha_{10}$.

To calculate the sine and cosine of an arbitrary angle θ, we enter θ (in radians) into the calculator. The calculator subtracts or adds multiples of 2π to θ to replace θ by the angle between 0 and 2π that has the same sine and cosine as θ (we continue to call the angle θ). The calculator then "writes" θ as a sum of multiples of α_1 (as many as possible without overshooting) plus multiples of α_2 (again, as many as possible), and so on, working its way to α_{10}. This gives

$$\theta \approx m_1\alpha_1 + m_2\alpha_2 + \cdots + m_{10}\alpha_{10}.$$

The calculator then rotates the point (1, 0) through m_1 copies of α_1 (through α_1, m_1 times in succession), plus m_2 copies of α_2, and so on, finishing off with m_{10} copies of α_{10} (Figure 10.27). The coordinates of the final position of (1, 0) on the unit circle are the values the calculator gives for $(\cos\theta, \sin\theta)$.

EXERCISES 10.3

Using the Discriminant

Use the discriminant $B^2 - 4AC$ to decide whether the equations in Exercises 1–16 represent parabolas, ellipses, or hyperbolas.

1. $x^2 - 3xy + y^2 - x = 0$
2. $3x^2 - 18xy + 27y^2 - 5x + 7y = -4$
3. $3x^2 - 7xy + \sqrt{17}y^2 = 1$
4. $2x^2 - \sqrt{15}xy + 2y^2 + x + y = 0$
5. $x^2 + 2xy + y^2 + 2x - y + 2 = 0$
6. $2x^2 - y^2 + 4xy - 2x + 3y = 6$
7. $x^2 + 4xy + 4y^2 - 3x = 6$
8. $x^2 + y^2 + 3x - 2y = 10$
9. $xy + y^2 - 3x = 5$
10. $3x^2 + 6xy + 3y^2 - 4x + 5y = 12$
11. $3x^2 - 5xy + 2y^2 - 7x - 14y = -1$
12. $2x^2 - 4.9xy + 3y^2 - 4x = 7$
13. $x^2 - 3xy + 3y^2 + 6y = 7$
14. $25x^2 + 21xy + 4y^2 - 350x = 0$
15. $6x^2 + 3xy + 2y^2 + 17y + 2 = 0$
16. $3x^2 + 12xy + 12y^2 + 435x - 9y + 72 = 0$

Rotating Coordinate Axes

In Exercises 17–26, rotate the coordinate axes to change the given equation into an equation that has no cross product (xy) term. Then identify the graph of the equation. (The new equations will vary with the size and direction of the rotation you use.)

17. $xy = 2$
18. $x^2 + xy + y^2 = 1$
19. $3x^2 + 2\sqrt{3}xy + y^2 - 8x + 8\sqrt{3}y = 0$
20. $x^2 - \sqrt{3}xy + 2y^2 = 1$
21. $x^2 - 2xy + y^2 = 2$
22. $3x^2 - 2\sqrt{3}xy + y^2 = 1$
23. $\sqrt{2}x^2 + 2\sqrt{2}xy + \sqrt{2}y^2 - 8x + 8y = 0$
24. $xy - y - x + 1 = 0$
25. $3x^2 + 2xy + 3y^2 = 19$
26. $3x^2 + 4\sqrt{3}xy - y^2 = 7$
27. Find the sine and cosine of an angle in Quadrant I through which the coordinate axes can be rotated to eliminate the cross product term from the equation

$$14x^2 + 16xy + 2y^2 - 10x + 26{,}370y - 17 = 0.$$

Do not carry out the rotation.

28. Find the sine and cosine of an angle in Quadrant II through which the coordinate axes can be rotated to eliminate the cross product term from the equation

$$4x^2 - 4xy + y^2 - 8\sqrt{5}x - 16\sqrt{5}y = 0.$$

Do not carry out the rotation.

T The conic sections in Exercises 17–26 were chosen to have rotation angles that were "nice" in the sense that once we knew $\cot 2\alpha$ or $\tan 2\alpha$ we could identify 2α and find $\sin\alpha$ and $\cos\alpha$ from familiar triangles.

In Exercises 29–34, use a calculator to find an angle α through which the coordinate axes can be rotated to change the given equation into a quadratic equation that has no cross product term. Then find $\sin\alpha$ and $\cos\alpha$ to two decimal places and use Equations (6) to find the coefficients of the new equation to the nearest decimal place. In each case, say whether the conic section is an ellipse, a hyperbola, or a parabola.

29. $x^2 - xy + 3y^2 + x - y - 3 = 0$

30. $2x^2 + xy - 3y^2 + 3x - 7 = 0$

31. $x^2 - 4xy + 4y^2 - 5 = 0$

32. $2x^2 - 12xy + 18y^2 - 49 = 0$

33. $3x^2 + 5xy + 2y^2 - 8y - 1 = 0$

34. $2x^2 + 7xy + 9y^2 + 20x - 86 = 0$

Theory and Examples

35. What effect does a 90° rotation about the origin have on the equations of the following conic sections? Give the new equation in each case.

a. The ellipse $(x^2/a^2) + (y^2/b^2) = 1 \quad (a > b)$

b. The hyperbola $(x^2/a^2) = (y^2/b^2) = 1$

c. The circle $x^2 + y^2 = a^2$

d. The line $y = mx$ **e.** The line $y = mx + b$

36. What effect does a 180° rotation about the origin have on the equations of the following conic sections? Give the new equation in each case.

a. The ellipse $(x^2/a^2) + (y^2/b^2) = 1 \quad (a > b)$

b. The hyperbola $(x^2/a^2) = (y^2/b^2) = 1$

c. The circle $x^2 + y^2 = a^2$

d. The line $y = mx$ **e.** The line $y = mx + b$

37. The Hyperbola $xy = a$ The hyperbola $xy = 1$ is one of many hyperbolas of the form $xy = a$ that appear in science and mathematics.

a. Rotate the coordinate axes through an angle of 45° to change the equation $xy = 1$ into an equation with no xy-term. What is the new equation?

b. Do the same for the equation $xy = a$.

38. Find the eccentricity of the hyperbola $xy = 2$.

39. Can anything be said about the graph of the equation $Ax^2 + Bxy + Cy^2 + Dx + Ey + F = 0$ if $AC < 0$? Give reasons for your answer.

40. Degenerate conics Does any nondegenerate conic section $Ax^2 + Bxy + Cy^2 + Dx + Ey + F = 0$ have all of the following properties?

a. It is symmetric with respect to the origin.

b. It passes through the point (1, 0).

c. It is tangent to the line $y = 1$ at the point $(-2, 1)$.

Give reasons for your answer.

41. Show that the equation $x^2 + y^2 = a^2$ becomes $x'^2 + y'^2 = a^2$ for every choice of the angle α in the rotation equations (4).

42. Show that rotating the axes through an angle of $\pi/4$ radians will eliminate the xy-term from Equation (1) whenever $A = C$.

43. a. Decide whether the equation

$$x^2 + 4xy + 4y^2 + 6x + 12y + 9 = 0$$

represents an ellipse, a parabola, or a hyperbola.

b. Show that the graph of the equation in part (a) is the line $2y = -x - 3$.

44. a. Decide whether the conic section with equation

$$9x^2 + 6xy + y^2 - 12x - 4y + 4 = 0$$

represents a parabola, an ellipse, or a hyperbola.

b. Show that the graph of the equation in part (a) is the line $y = -3x + 2$.

45. a. What kind of conic section is the curve $xy + 2x - y = 0$?

b. Solve the equation $xy + 2x - y = 0$ for y and sketch the curve as the graph of a rational function of x.

c. Find equations for the lines parallel to the line $y = -2x$ that are normal to the curve. Add the lines to your sketch.

46. Prove or find counterexamples to the following statements about the graph of $Ax^2 + Bxy + Cy^2 + Dx + Ey + F = 0$.

a. If $AC > 0$, the graph is an ellipse.

b. If $AC > 0$, the graph is a hyperbola.

c. If $AC < 0$, the graph is a hyperbola.

47. A nice area formula for ellipses When $B^2 - 4AC$ is negative, the equation

$$Ax^2 + Bxy + Cy^2 = 1$$

represents an ellipse. If the ellipse's semi-axes are a and b, its area is πab (a standard formula). Show that the area is also given by the formula $2\pi/\sqrt{4AC - B^2}$. (*Hint:* Rotate the coordinate axes to eliminate the xy-term and apply Equation (12) to the new equation.)

48. Other invariants We describe the fact that $B'^2 - 4A'C'$ equals $B^2 - 4AC$ after a rotation about the origin by saying that the discriminant of a quadratic equation is an *invariant* of the equation.

Use Equations (6) to show that the numbers **(a)** $A + C$ and **(b)** $D^2 + E^2$ are also invariants, in the sense that

$$A' + C' = A + C \quad \text{and} \quad D'^2 + E'^2 = D^2 + E^2.$$

We can use these equalities to check against numerical errors when we rotate axes.

49. A proof that $B'^2 - 4A'C' = B^2 - 4AC$ Use Equations (6) to show that $B'^2 - 4A'C' = B^2 - 4AC$ for any rotation of axes about the origin.

10.4 Conics and Parametric Equations; The Cycloid

Curves in the Cartesian plane defined by parametric equations, and the calculation of their derivatives, were introduced in Section 3.5. There we studied parametrizations of lines, circles, and ellipses. In this section we discuss parametrization of parabolas, hyperbolas, cycloids, brachistocrones, and tautocrones.

Parabolas and Hyperbolas

In Section 3.5 we used the parametrization

$$x = \sqrt{t}, \qquad y = t, \qquad t > 0$$

to describe the motion of a particle moving along the right branch of the parabola $y = x^2$. In the following example we obtain a parametrization of the entire parabola, not just its right branch.

EXAMPLE 1 An Entire Parabola

The position $P(x, y)$ of a particle moving in the xy-plane is given by the equations and parameter interval

$$x = t, \qquad y = t^2, \qquad -\infty < t < \infty.$$

Identify the particle's path and describe the motion.

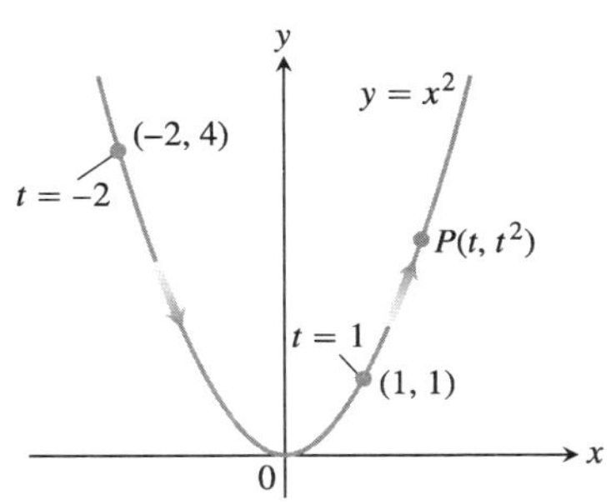

FIGURE 10.28 The path defined by $x = t, y = t^2, -\infty < t < \infty$ is the entire parabola $y = x^2$ (Example 1).

Solution We identify the path by eliminating t between the equations $x = t$ and $y = t^2$, obtaining

$$y = (t)^2 = x^2.$$

The particle's position coordinates satisfy the equation $y = x^2$, so the particle moves along this curve.

In contrast to Example 10 in Section 3.5, the particle now traverses the entire parabola. As t increases from $-\infty$ to ∞, the particle comes down the left-hand side, passes through the origin, and moves up the right-hand side (Figure 10.28). ■

As Example 1 illustrates, any curve $y = f(x)$ has the parametrization $x = t$, $y = f(t)$. This is so simple we usually do not use it, but the point of view is occasionally helpful.

EXAMPLE 2 A Parametrization of the Right-hand Branch of the Hyperbola $x^2 - y^2 = 1$

Describe the motion of the particle whose position $P(x, y)$ at time t is given by

$$x = \sec t, \qquad y = \tan t, \qquad -\frac{\pi}{2} < t < \frac{\pi}{2}.$$

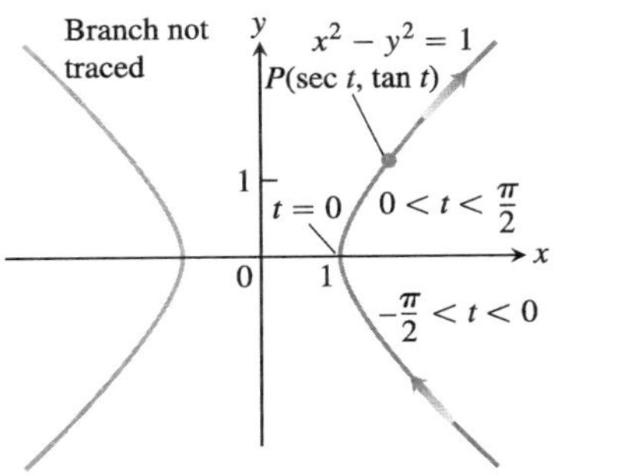

FIGURE 10.29 The equations $x = \sec t$, $y = \tan t$ and interval $-\pi/2 < t < \pi/2$ describe the right-hand branch of the hyperbola $x^2 - y^2 = 1$ (Example 2).

Solution We find a Cartesian equation for the coordinates of P by eliminating t between the equations

$$\sec t = x, \qquad \tan t = y.$$

We accomplish this with the identity $\sec^2 t - \tan^2 t = 1$, which yields

$$x^2 - y^2 = 1.$$

Since the particle's coordinates (x, y) satisfy the equation $x^2 - y^2 = 1$, the motion takes place somewhere on this hyperbola. As t runs between $-\pi/2$ and $\pi/2$, $x = \sec t$ remains positive and $y = \tan t$ runs between $-\infty$ and ∞, so P traverses the hyperbola's right-hand branch. It comes in along the branch's lower half as $t \rightarrow 0^-$, reaches $(1, 0)$ at $t = 0$, and moves out into the first quadrant as t increases toward $\pi/2$ (Figure 10.29). ■

Cycloids

The problem with a pendulum clock whose bob swings in a circular arc is that the frequency of the swing depends on the amplitude of the swing. The wider the swing, the longer it takes the bob to return to center (its lowest position).

This does not happen if the bob can be made to swing in a *cycloid*. In 1673, Christiaan Huygens designed a pendulum clock whose bob would swing in a cycloid, a curve we define in Example 3. He hung the bob from a fine wire constrained by guards that caused it to draw up as it swung away from center (Figure 10.30).

HISTORICAL BIOGRAPHY

Christiaan Huygens (1629–1695)

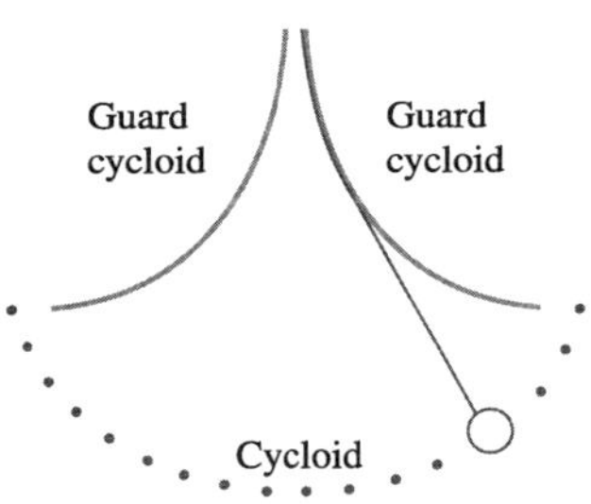

FIGURE 10.30 In Huygens' pendulum clock, the bob swings in a cycloid, so the frequency is independent of the amplitude.

EXAMPLE 3 Parametrizing a Cycloid

A wheel of radius a rolls along a horizontal straight line. Find parametric equations for the path traced by a point P on the wheel's circumference. The path is called a **cycloid**.

Solution We take the line to be the x-axis, mark a point P on the wheel, start the wheel with P at the origin, and roll the wheel to the right. As parameter, we use the angle t through which the wheel turns, measured in radians. Figure 10.31 shows the wheel a short while later, when its base lies at units from the origin. The wheel's center C lies at (at, a) and the coordinates of P are

$$x = at + a\cos\theta, \qquad y = a + a\sin\theta.$$

To express θ in terms of t, we observe that $t + \theta = 3\pi/2$ in the figure, so that

$$\theta = \frac{3\pi}{2} - t.$$

This makes

$$\cos\theta = \cos\left(\frac{3\pi}{2} - t\right) = -\sin t, \qquad \sin\theta = \sin\left(\frac{3\pi}{2} - t\right) = -\cos t.$$

The equations we seek are

$$x = at - a\sin t, \qquad y = a - a\cos t.$$

These are usually written with the a factored out:

$$x = a(t - \sin t), \qquad y = a(1 - \cos t). \tag{1}$$

Figure 10.32 shows the first arch of the cycloid and part of the next. ■

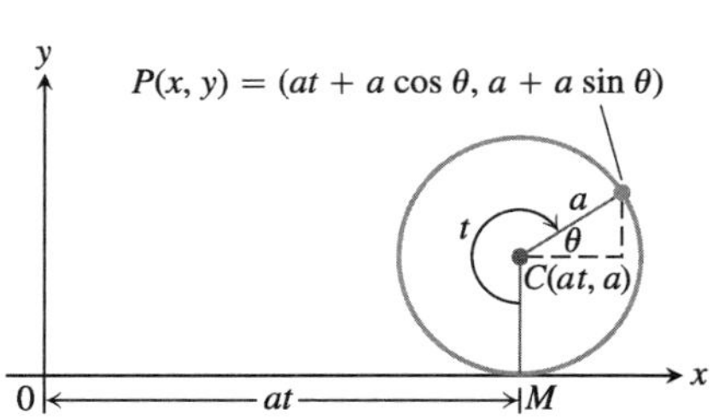

FIGURE 10.31 The position of $P(x, y)$ on the rolling wheel at angle t (Example 3).

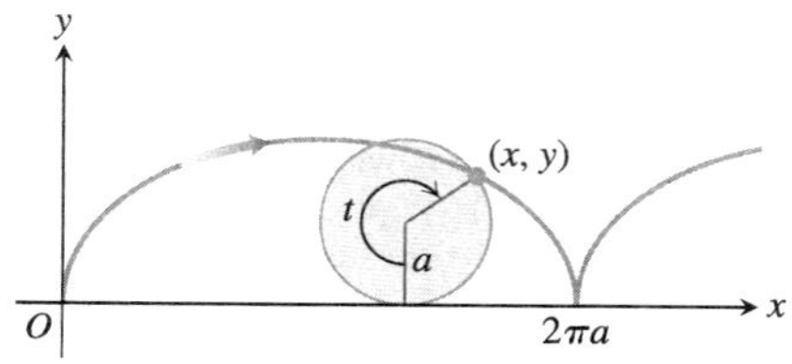

FIGURE 10.32 The cycloid $x = a(t - \sin t), y = a(1 - \cos t)$, for $t \geq 0$.

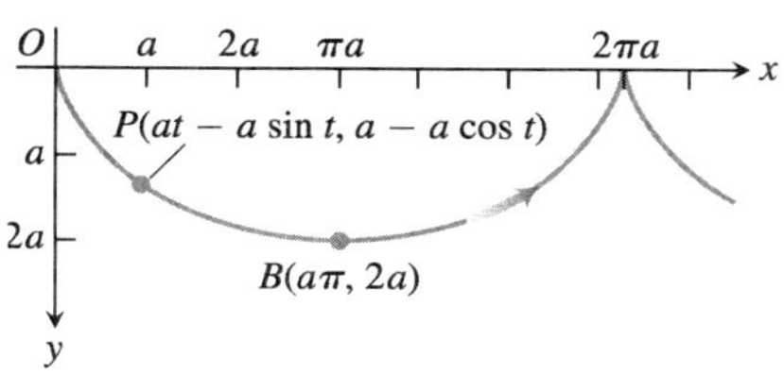

FIGURE 10.33 To study motion along an upside-down cycloid under the influence of gravity, we turn Figure 10.32 upside down. This points the y-axis in the direction of the gravitational force and makes the downward y-coordinates positive. The equations and parameter interval for the cycloid are still

$$x = a(t - \sin t),$$
$$y = a(1 - \cos t), \quad t \geq 0.$$

The arrow shows the direction of increasing t.

Brachistochrones and Tautochrones

If we turn Figure 10.32 upside down, Equations (1) still apply and the resulting curve (Figure 10.33) has two interesting physical properties. The first relates to the origin O and the point B at the bottom of the first arch. Among all smooth curves joining these points, the cycloid is the curve along which a frictionless bead, subject only to the force of gravity, will slide from O to B the fastest. This makes the cycloid a **brachistochrone** ("brah-*kiss*-toe-krone"), or shortest time curve for these points. The second property is that even if you start the bead partway down the curve toward B, it will still take the bead the same amount of time to reach B. This makes the cycloid a **tautochrone** ("*taw*-toe-krone"), or same-time curve for O and B.

Are there any other brachistochrones joining O and B, or is the cycloid the only one? We can formulate this as a mathematical question in the following way. At the start, the kinetic energy of the bead is zero, since its velocity is zero. The work done by gravity in moving the bead from (0, 0) to any other point (x, y) in the plane is mgy, and this must equal the change in kinetic energy. That is,

$$mgy = \frac{1}{2}mv^2 - \frac{1}{2}m(0)^2.$$

Thus, the velocity of the bead when it reaches (x, y) has to be

$$v = \sqrt{2gy}.$$

That is,

$$\frac{ds}{dt} = \sqrt{2gy} \qquad \text{ds is the arc length differential along the bead's path.}$$

or

$$dt = \frac{ds}{\sqrt{2gy}} = \frac{\sqrt{1 + (dy/dx)^2}\,dx}{\sqrt{2gy}}.$$

The time T_f it takes the bead to slide along a particular path $y = f(x)$ from O to $B(a\pi, 2a)$ is

$$T_f = \int_{x=0}^{x=a\pi} \sqrt{\frac{1 + (dy/dx)^2}{2gy}}\,dx. \tag{2}$$

What curves $y = f(x)$, if any, minimize the value of this integral?

At first sight, we might guess that the straight line joining O and B would give the shortest time, but perhaps not. There might be some advantage in having the bead fall vertically at first to build up its velocity faster. With a higher velocity, the bead could travel a longer path and still reach B first. Indeed, this is the right idea. The solution, from a branch of mathematics known as the *calculus of variations,* is that the original cycloid from O to B is the one and only brachistochrone for O and B.

While the solution of the brachistrochrone problem is beyond our present reach, we can still show why the cycloid is a tautochrone. For the cycloid, Equation (2) takes the form

$$\begin{aligned} T_{\text{cycloid}} &= \int_{x=0}^{x=a\pi} \sqrt{\frac{dx^2 + dy^2}{2gy}} \\ &= \int_{t=0}^{t=\pi} \sqrt{\frac{a^2(2 - 2\cos t)}{2ga(1 - \cos t)}}\,dt \\ &= \int_0^{\pi} \sqrt{\frac{a}{g}}\,dt = \pi\sqrt{\frac{a}{g}}. \end{aligned}$$

From Equations (1), $dx = a(1 - \cos t)\,dt$, $dy = a \sin t\,dt$, and $y = a(1 - \cos t)$

Thus, the amount of time it takes the frictionless bead to slide down the cycloid to B after it is released from rest at O is $\pi\sqrt{a/g}$.

Suppose that instead of starting the bead at O we start it at some lower point on the cycloid, a point (x_0, y_0) corresponding to the parameter value $t_0 > 0$. The bead's velocity at any later point (x, y) on the cycloid is

$$v = \sqrt{2g(y - y_0)} = \sqrt{2ga(\cos t_0 - \cos t)}. \qquad y = a(1 - \cos t)$$

Accordingly, the time required for the bead to slide from (x_0, y_0) down to B is

$$\begin{aligned}
T &= \int_{t_0}^{\pi}\sqrt{\frac{a^2(2 - 2\cos t)}{2ga(\cos t_0 - \cos t)}}\,dt = \sqrt{\frac{a}{g}}\int_{t_0}^{\pi}\sqrt{\frac{1 - \cos t}{\cos t_0 - \cos t}}\,dt \\
&= \sqrt{\frac{a}{g}}\int_{t_0}^{\pi}\sqrt{\frac{2\sin^2(t/2)}{(2\cos^2(t_0/2) - 1) - (2\cos^2(t/2) - 1)}}\,dt \\
&= \sqrt{\frac{a}{g}}\int_{t_0}^{\pi}\frac{\sin(t/2)\,dt}{\sqrt{\cos^2(t_0/2) - \cos^2(t/2)}} \\
&= \sqrt{\frac{a}{g}}\int_{t=t_0}^{t=\pi}\frac{-2\,du}{\sqrt{a^2 - u^2}} \qquad \begin{aligned} u &= \cos(t/2) \\ -2\,du &= \sin(t/2)\,dt \\ c &= \cos(t_0/2) \end{aligned} \\
&= 2\sqrt{\frac{a}{g}}\left[-\sin^{-1}\frac{u}{c}\right]_{t=t_0}^{t=\pi} \\
&= 2\sqrt{\frac{a}{g}}\left[-\sin^{-1}\frac{\cos(t/2)}{\cos(t_0/2)}\right]_{t_0}^{\pi} \\
&= 2\sqrt{\frac{a}{g}}(-\sin^{-1}0 + \sin^{-1}1) = \pi\sqrt{\frac{a}{g}}.
\end{aligned}$$

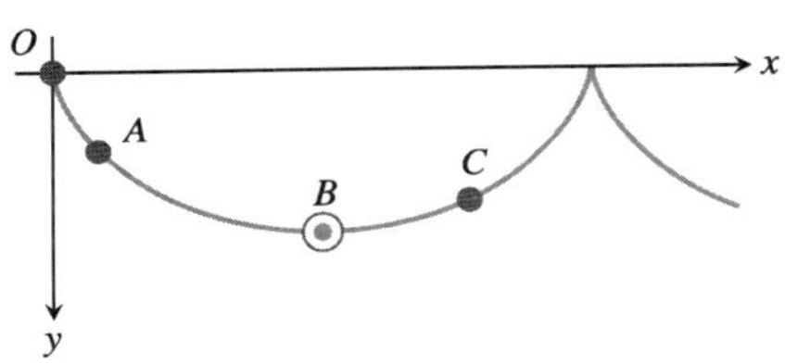

FIGURE 10.34 Beads released simultaneously on the cycloid at O, A, and C will reach B at the same time.

This is precisely the time it takes the bead to slide to B from O. It takes the bead the same amount of time to reach B no matter where it starts. Beads starting simultaneously from O, A, and C in Figure 10.34, for instance, will all reach B at the same time. This is the reason that Huygens' pendulum clock is independent of the amplitude of the swing.

EXERCISES 10.4

Parametric Equations for Conics

Exercises 1–12 give parametric equations and parameter intervals for the motion of a particle in the xy-plane. Identify the particle's path by finding a Cartesian equation for it. Graph the Cartesian equation. (The graphs will vary with the equation used.) Indicate the portion of the graph traced by the particle and the direction of motion.

1. $x = \cos t, \quad y = \sin t, \quad 0 \le t \le \pi$
2. $x = \sin(2\pi(1 - t)), \quad y = \cos(2\pi(1 - t)); \quad 0 \le t \le 1$
3. $x = 4\cos t, \quad y = 5\sin t; \quad 0 \le t \le \pi$
4. $x = 4\sin t, \quad y = 5\cos t; \quad 0 \le t \le 2\pi$
5. $x = t, \quad y = \sqrt{t}; \quad t \ge 0$
6. $x = \sec^2 t - 1, \quad y = \tan t; \quad -\pi/2 < t < \pi/2$
7. $x = -\sec t, \quad y = \tan t; \quad -\pi/2 < t < \pi/2$
8. $x = \csc t, \quad y = \cot t; \quad 0 < t < \pi$
9. $x = t, \quad y = \sqrt{4 - t^2}; \quad 0 \le t \le 2$
10. $x = t^2, \quad y = \sqrt{t^4 + 1}; \quad t \ge 0$
11. $x = -\cosh t, \quad y = \sinh t; \quad -\infty < t < \infty$
12. $x = 2\sinh t, \quad y = 2\cosh t; \quad -\infty < t < \infty$
13. **Hypocycloids** When a circle rolls on the inside of a fixed circle, any point P on the circumference of the rolling circle describes a *hypocycloid*. Let the fixed circle be $x^2 + y^2 = a^2$, let the radius of the rolling circle be b, and let the initial position of the tracing point P be $A(a, 0)$. Find parametric equations for the hypocycloid, using as the parameter the angle θ from the positive x-axis to the line joining the circles' centers. In particular, if

$b = a/4$, as in the accompanying figure, show that the hypocycloid is the astroid

$$x = a\cos^3\theta, \quad y = a\sin^3\theta.$$

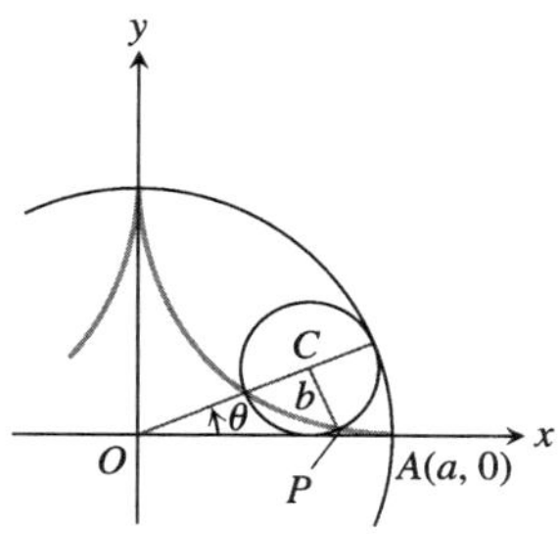

14. **More about hypocycloids** The accompanying figure shows a circle of radius a tangent to the inside of a circle of radius $2a$. The point P, shown as the point of tangency in the figure, is attached to the smaller circle. What path does P trace as the smaller circle rolls around the inside of the larger circle?

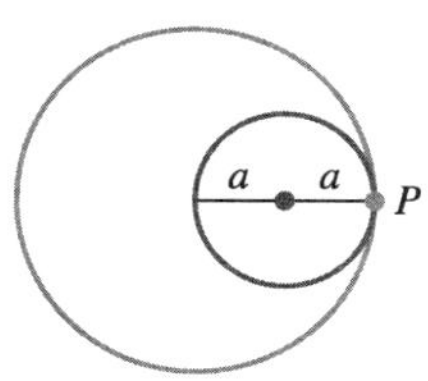

15. As the point N moves along the line $y = a$ in the accompanying figure, P moves in such a way that $OP = MN$. Find parametric equations for the coordinates of P as functions of the angle t that the line ON makes with the positive y-axis.

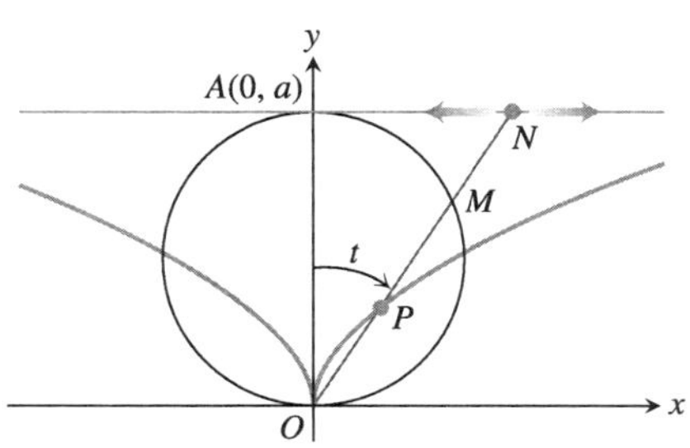

16. **Trochoids** A wheel of radius a rolls along a horizontal straight line without slipping. Find parametric equations for the curve traced out by a point P on a spoke of the wheel b units from its center. As parameter, use the angle θ through which the wheel turns. The curve is called a *trochoid*, which is a cycloid when $b = a$.

Distance Using Parametric Equations

17. Find the point on the parabola $x = t, y = t^2, -\infty < t < \infty$, closest to the point $(2, 1/2)$. (*Hint:* Minimize the square of the distance as a function of t.)

18. Find the point on the ellipse $x = 2\cos t, y = \sin t, 0 \le t \le 2\pi$ closest to the point $(3/4, 0)$. (*Hint:* Minimize the square of the distance as a function of t.)

T GRAPHER EXPLORATIONS

If you have a parametric equation grapher, graph the following equations over the given intervals.

19. **Ellipse** $x = 4\cos t, \quad y = 2\sin t,$ over
 a. $0 \le t \le 2\pi$ **b.** $0 \le t \le \pi$
 c. $-\pi/2 \le t \le \pi/2$.

20. **Hyperbola branch** $x = \sec t$ (enter as $1/\cos(t)$), $y = \tan t$ (enter as $\sin(t)/\cos(t)$), over
 a. $-1.5 \le t \le 1.5$ **b.** $-0.5 \le t \le 0.5$
 c. $-0.1 \le t \le 0.1$.

21. **Parabola** $x = 2t + 3, \quad y = t^2 - 1, \quad -2 \le t \le 2$

22. **Cycloid** $x = t - \sin t, \quad y = 1 - \cos t,$ over
 a. $0 \le t \le 2\pi$ **b.** $0 \le t \le 4\pi$
 c. $\pi \le t \le 3\pi$.

23. **A nice curve (a deltoid)**

$$x = 2\cos t + \cos 2t, \quad y = 2\sin t - \sin 2t; \quad 0 \le t \le 2\pi$$

What happens if you replace 2 with -2 in the equations for x and y? Graph the new equations and find out.

24. **An even nicer curve**

$$x = 3\cos t + \cos 3t, \quad y = 3\sin t - \sin 3t; \quad 0 \le t \le 2\pi$$

What happens if you replace 3 with -3 in the equations for x and y? Graph the new equations and find out.

25. **Three beautiful curves**
 a. *Epicycloid:*

$$x = 9\cos t - \cos 9t, \quad y = 9\sin t - \sin 9t; \quad 0 \le t \le 2\pi$$

 b. *Hypocycloid:*

$$x = 8\cos t + 2\cos 4t, \quad y = 8\sin t - 2\sin 4t; \quad 0 \le t \le 2\pi$$

 c. *Hypotrochoid:*

$$x = \cos t + 5\cos 3t, \quad y = 6\cos t - 5\sin 3t; \quad 0 \le t \le 2\pi$$

26. **More beautiful curves**
 a. $x = 6\cos t + 5\cos 3t, \quad y = 6\sin t - 5\sin 3t;$ $0 \le t \le 2\pi$
 b. $x = 6\cos 2t + 5\cos 6t, \quad y = 6\sin 2t - 5\sin 6t;$ $0 \le t \le \pi$
 c. $x = 6\cos t + 5\cos 3t, \quad y = 6\sin 2t - 5\sin 3t;$ $0 \le t \le 2\pi$
 d. $x = 6\cos 2t + 5\cos 6t, \quad y = 6\sin 4t - 5\sin 6t;$ $0 \le t \le \pi$

10.5 Polar Coordinates

In this section, we study polar coordinates and their relation to Cartesian coordinates. While a point in the plane has just one pair of Cartesian coordinates, it has infinitely many pairs of polar coordinates. This has interesting consequences for graphing, as we will see in the next section.

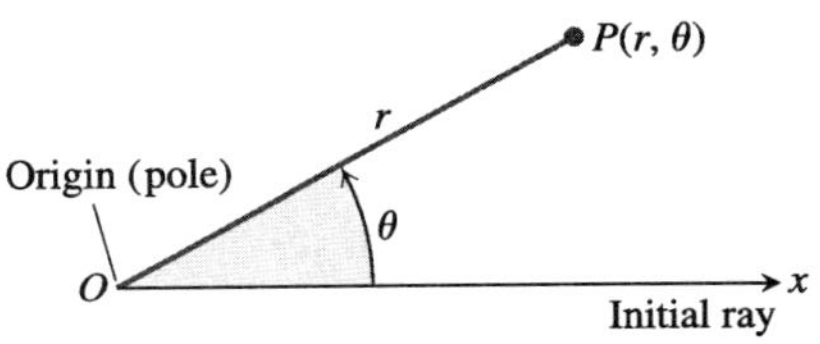

FIGURE 10.35 To define polar coordinates for the plane, we start with an origin, called the pole, and an initial ray.

Definition of Polar Coordinates

To define polar coordinates, we first fix an **origin** O (called the **pole**) and an **initial ray** from O (Figure 10.35). Then each point P can be located by assigning to it a **polar coordinate pair** (r, θ) in which r gives the directed distance from O to P and θ gives the directed angle from the initial ray to ray OP.

Polar Coordinates

$P(r, \theta)$

Directed distance from O to P — Directed angle from initial ray to OP

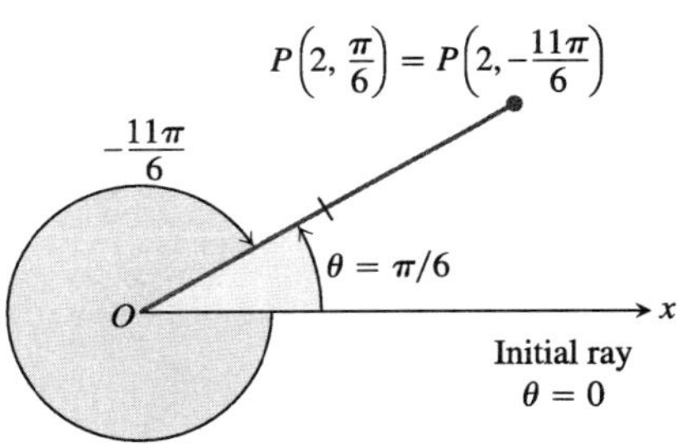

FIGURE 10.36 Polar coordinates are not unique.

As in trigonometry, θ is positive when measured counterclockwise and negative when measured clockwise. The angle associated with a given point is not unique. For instance, the point 2 units from the origin along the ray $\theta = \pi/6$ has polar coordinates $r = 2$, $\theta = \pi/6$. It also has coordinates $r = 2$, $\theta = -11\pi/6$ (Figure 10.36). There are occasions when we wish to allow r to be negative. That is why we use directed distance in defining $P(r, \theta)$. The point $P(2, 7\pi/6)$ can be reached by turning $7\pi/6$ radians counterclockwise from the initial ray and going forward 2 units (Figure 10.37). It can also be reached by turning $\pi/6$ radians counterclockwise from the initial ray and going *backward* 2 units. So the point also has polar coordinates $r = -2$, $\theta = \pi/6$.

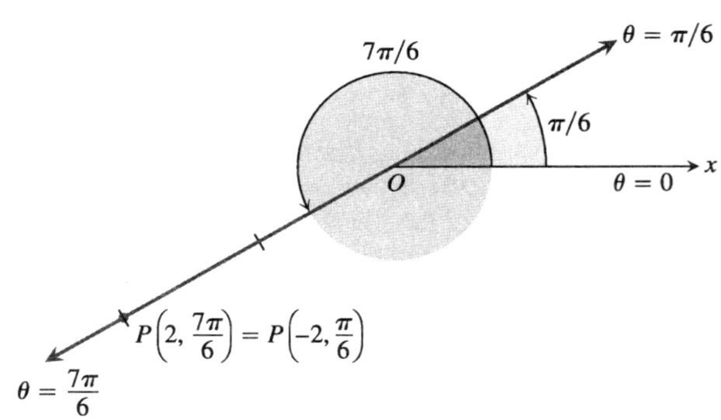

FIGURE 10.37 Polar coordinates can have negative r-values.

EXAMPLE 1 Finding Polar Coordinates

Find all the polar coordinates of the point $P(2, \pi/6)$.

Solution We sketch the initial ray of the coordinate system, draw the ray from the origin that makes an angle of $\pi/6$ radians with the initial ray, and mark the point $(2, \pi/6)$ (Figure 10.38). We then find the angles for the other coordinate pairs of P in which $r = 2$ and $r = -2$.

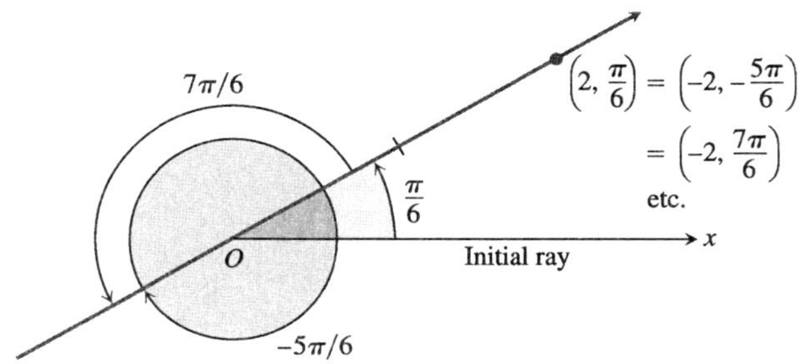

FIGURE 10.38 The point $P(2, \pi/6)$ has infinitely many polar coordinate pairs (Example 1).

For $r = 2$, the complete list of angles is

$$\frac{\pi}{6}, \quad \frac{\pi}{6} \pm 2\pi, \quad \frac{\pi}{6} \pm 4\pi, \quad \frac{\pi}{6} \pm 6\pi, \quad \ldots.$$

For $r = -2$, the angles are

$$-\frac{5\pi}{6}, \quad -\frac{5\pi}{6} \pm 2\pi, \quad -\frac{5\pi}{6} \pm 4\pi, \quad -\frac{5\pi}{6} \pm 6\pi, \quad \ldots.$$

The corresponding coordinate pairs of P are

$$\left(2, \frac{\pi}{6} + 2n\pi\right), \qquad n = 0, \pm 1, \pm 2, \ldots$$

and

$$\left(-2, -\frac{5\pi}{6} + 2n\pi\right), \qquad n = 0, \pm 1, \pm 2, \ldots.$$

When $n = 0$, the formulas give $(2, \pi/6)$ and $(-2, -5\pi/6)$. When $n = 1$, they give $(2, 13\pi/6)$ and $(-2, 7\pi/6)$, and so on. ■

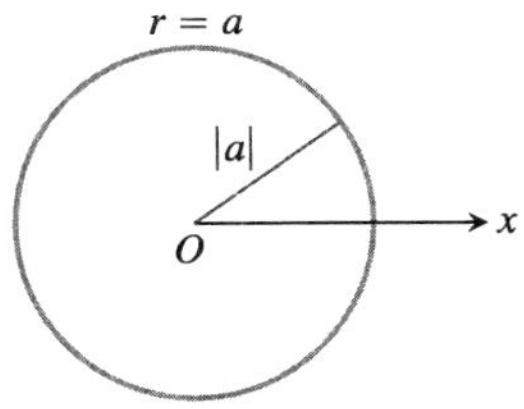

FIGURE 10.39 The polar equation for a circle is $r = a$.

Polar Equations and Graphs

If we hold r fixed at a constant value $r = a \neq 0$, the point $P(r, \theta)$ will lie $|a|$ units from the origin O. As θ varies over any interval of length 2π, P then traces a circle of radius $|a|$ centered at O (Figure 10.39).

If we hold θ fixed at a constant value $\theta = \theta_0$ and let r vary between $-\infty$ and ∞, the point $P(r, \theta)$ traces the line through O that makes an angle of measure θ_0 with the initial ray.

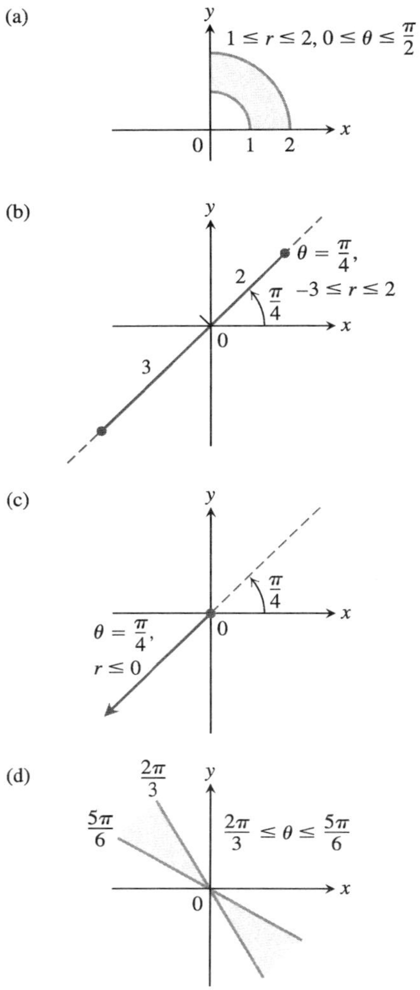

FIGURE 10.40 The graphs of typical inequalities in r and θ (Example 3).

Equation	**Graph**
$r = a$	Circle radius $\lvert a \rvert$ centered at O
$\theta = \theta_0$	Line through O making an angle θ_0 with the initial ray

EXAMPLE 2 Finding Polar Equations for Graphs

(a) $r = 1$ and $r = -1$ are equations for the circle of radius 1 centered at O.

(b) $\theta = \pi/6$, $\theta = 7\pi/6$, and $\theta = -5\pi/6$ are equations for the line in Figure 10.38. ■

Equations of the form $r = a$ and $\theta = \theta_0$ can be combined to define regions, segments, and rays.

EXAMPLE 3 Identifying Graphs

Graph the sets of points whose polar coordinates satisfy the following conditions.

(a) $1 \le r \le 2$ and $0 \le \theta \le \frac{\pi}{2}$

(b) $-3 \le r \le 2$ and $\theta = \frac{\pi}{4}$

(c) $r \le 0$ and $\theta = \frac{\pi}{4}$

(d) $\frac{2\pi}{3} \le \theta \le \frac{5\pi}{6}$ (no restriction on r)

Solution The graphs are shown in Figure 10.40. ■

Relating Polar and Cartesian Coordinates

When we use both polar and Cartesian coordinates in a plane, we place the two origins together and take the initial polar ray as the positive x-axis. The ray $\theta = \pi/2, r > 0$, becomes the positive y-axis (Figure 10.41). The two coordinate systems are then related by the following equations.

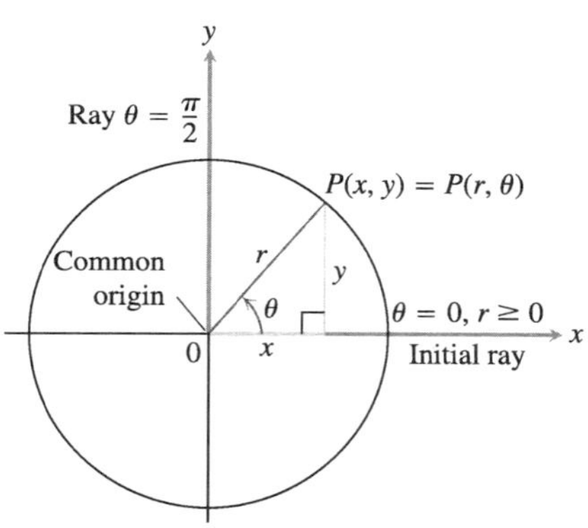

FIGURE 10.41 The usual way to relate polar and Cartesian coordinates.

Equations Relating Polar and Cartesian Coordinates

$$x = r\cos\theta, \qquad y = r\sin\theta, \qquad x^2 + y^2 = r^2$$

The first two of these equations uniquely determine the Cartesian coordinates x and y given the polar coordinates r and θ. On the other hand, if x and y are given, the third equation gives two possible choices for r (a positive and a negative value). For each selection, there is a unique $\theta \in [0, 2\pi)$ satisfying the first two equations, each then giving a polar coordinate representation of the Cartesian point (x, y). The other polar coordinate representations for the point can be determined from these two, as in Example 1.

EXAMPLE 4 Equivalent Equations

Polar equation	Cartesian equivalent
$r\cos\theta = 2$	$x = 2$
$r^2\cos\theta\sin\theta = 4$	$xy = 4$
$r^2\cos^2\theta - r^2\sin^2\theta = 1$	$x^2 - y^2 = 1$
$r = 1 + 2r\cos\theta$	$y^2 - 3x^2 - 4x - 1 = 0$
$r = 1 - \cos\theta$	$x^4 + y^4 + 2x^2y^2 + 2x^3 + 2xy^2 - y^2 = 0$

With some curves, we are better off with polar coordinates; with others, we aren't. ■

EXAMPLE 5 Converting Cartesian to Polar

Find a polar equation for the circle $x^2 + (y - 3)^2 = 9$ (Figure 10.42).

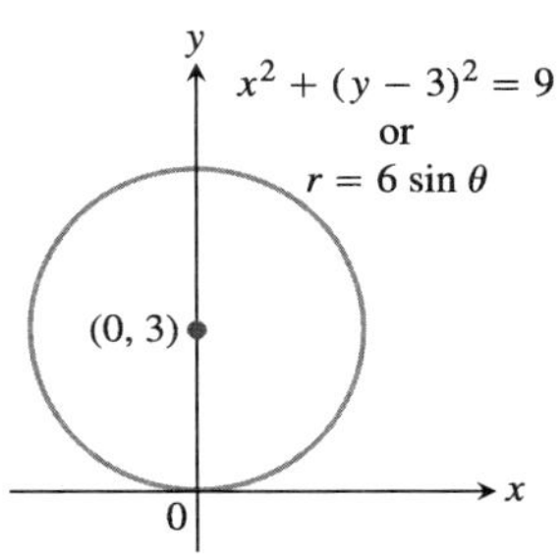

FIGURE 10.42 The circle in Example 5.

Solution

$$
\begin{aligned}
x^2 + y^2 - 6y + 9 &= 9 && \text{Expand } (y-3)^2. \\
x^2 + y^2 - 6y &= 0 && \text{The 9's cancel.} \\
r^2 - 6r\sin\theta &= 0 && x^2 + y^2 = r^2 \\
r = 0 \quad \text{or} \quad r - 6\sin\theta &= 0 \\
r &= 6\sin\theta && \text{Includes both possibilities}
\end{aligned}
$$

We will say more about polar equations of conic sections in Section 10.8. ■

EXAMPLE 6 Converting Polar to Cartesian

Replace the following polar equations by equivalent Cartesian equations, and identify their graphs.

(a) $r\cos\theta = -4$

(b) $r^2 = 4r\cos\theta$

(c) $r = \dfrac{4}{2\cos\theta - \sin\theta}$

Solution We use the substitutions $r\cos\theta = x$, $r\sin\theta = y$, $r^2 = x^2 + y^2$.

(a) $r\cos\theta = -4$

The Cartesian equation:
$$
\begin{aligned}
r\cos\theta &= -4 \\
x &= -4
\end{aligned}
$$

The graph: Vertical line through $x = -4$ on the x-axis

(b) $r^2 = 4r\cos\theta$

The Cartesian equation:
$$
\begin{aligned}
r^2 &= 4r\cos\theta \\
x^2 + y^2 &= 4x \\
x^2 - 4x + y^2 &= 0 \\
x^2 - 4x + 4 + y^2 &= 4 && \text{Completing the square} \\
(x - 2)^2 + y^2 &= 4
\end{aligned}
$$

The graph: Circle, radius 2, center $(h, k) = (2, 0)$

(c) $r = \dfrac{4}{2\cos\theta - \sin\theta}$

The Cartesian equation:

$$\begin{aligned} r(2\cos\theta - \sin\theta) &= 4 \\ 2r\cos\theta - r\sin\theta &= 4 \\ 2x - y &= 4 \\ y &= 2x - 4 \end{aligned}$$

The graph: Line, slope $m = 2$, y-intercept $b = -4$ ■

EXERCISES 10.5

Polar Coordinate Pairs

1. Which polar coordinate pairs label the same point?
   a. $(3, 0)$ b. $(-3, 0)$ c. $(2, 2\pi/3)$
   d. $(2, 7\pi/3)$ e. $(-3, \pi)$ f. $(2, \pi/3)$
   g. $(-3, 2\pi)$ h. $(-2, -\pi/3)$
2. Which polar coordinate pairs label the same point?
   a. $(-2, \pi/3)$ b. $(2, -\pi/3)$ c. (r, θ)
   d. $(r, \theta + \pi)$ e. $(-r, \theta)$ f. $(2, -2\pi/3)$
   g. $(-r, \theta + \pi)$ h. $(-2, 2\pi/3)$
3. Plot the following points (given in polar coordinates). Then find all the polar coordinates of each point.
   a. $(2, \pi/2)$ b. $(2, 0)$
   c. $(-2, \pi/2)$ d. $(-2, 0)$
4. Plot the following points (given in polar coordinates). Then find all the polar coordinates of each point.
   a. $(3, \pi/4)$ b. $(-3, \pi/4)$
   c. $(3, -\pi/4)$ d. $(-3, -\pi/4)$

Polar to Cartesian Coordinates

5. Find the Cartesian coordinates of the points in Exercise 1.
6. Find the Cartesian coordinates of the following points (given in polar coordinates).
   a. $(\sqrt{2}, \pi/4)$ b. $(1, 0)$
   c. $(0, \pi/2)$ d. $(-\sqrt{2}, \pi/4)$
   e. $(-3, 5\pi/6)$ f. $(5, \tan^{-1}(4/3))$
   g. $(-1, 7\pi)$ h. $(2\sqrt{3}, 2\pi/3)$

Graphing Polar Equations and Inequalities

Graph the sets of points whose polar coordinates satisfy the equations and inequalities in Exercises 7–22.

7. $r = 2$
8. $0 \le r \le 2$
9. $r \ge 1$
10. $1 \le r \le 2$
11. $0 \le \theta \le \pi/6, \quad r \ge 0$
12. $\theta = 2\pi/3, \quad r \le -2$
13. $\theta = \pi/3, \quad -1 \le r \le 3$
14. $\theta = 11\pi/4, \quad r \ge -1$
15. $\theta = \pi/2, \quad r \ge 0$
16. $\theta = \pi/2, \quad r \le 0$
17. $0 \le \theta \le \pi, \quad r = 1$
18. $0 \le \theta \le \pi, \quad r = -1$
19. $\pi/4 \le \theta \le 3\pi/4, \quad 0 \le r \le 1$
20. $-\pi/4 \le \theta \le \pi/4, \quad -1 \le r \le 1$
21. $-\pi/2 \le \theta \le \pi/2, \quad 1 \le r \le 2$
22. $0 \le \theta \le \pi/2, \quad 1 \le |r| \le 2$

Polar to Cartesian Equations

Replace the polar equations in Exercises 23–48 by equivalent Cartesian equations. Then describe or identify the graph.

23. $r\cos\theta = 2$
24. $r\sin\theta = -1$
25. $r\sin\theta = 0$
26. $r\cos\theta = 0$
27. $r = 4\csc\theta$
28. $r = -3\sec\theta$
29. $r\cos\theta + r\sin\theta = 1$
30. $r\sin\theta = r\cos\theta$
31. $r^2 = 1$
32. $r^2 = 4r\sin\theta$
33. $r = \dfrac{5}{\sin\theta - 2\cos\theta}$
34. $r^2\sin 2\theta = 2$
35. $r = \cot\theta\csc\theta$
36. $r = 4\tan\theta\sec\theta$
37. $r = \csc\theta\, e^{r\cos\theta}$
38. $r\sin\theta = \ln r + \ln\cos\theta$
39. $r^2 + 2r^2\cos\theta\sin\theta = 1$
40. $\cos^2\theta = \sin^2\theta$
41. $r^2 = -4r\cos\theta$
42. $r^2 = -6r\sin\theta$
43. $r = 8\sin\theta$
44. $r = 3\cos\theta$
45. $r = 2\cos\theta + 2\sin\theta$
46. $r = 2\cos\theta - \sin\theta$
47. $r\sin\left(\theta + \dfrac{\pi}{6}\right) = 2$
48. $r\sin\left(\dfrac{2\pi}{3} - \theta\right) = 5$

Cartesian to Polar Equations

Replace the Cartesian equations in Exercises 49–62 by equivalent polar equations.

49. $x = 7$
50. $y = 1$
51. $x = y$
52. $x - y = 3$
53. $x^2 + y^2 = 4$
54. $x^2 - y^2 = 1$
55. $\dfrac{x^2}{9} + \dfrac{y^2}{4} = 1$
56. $xy = 2$

57. $y^2 = 4x$

58. $x^2 + xy + y^2 = 1$

59. $x^2 + (y - 2)^2 = 4$

60. $(x - 5)^2 + y^2 = 25$

61. $(x - 3)^2 + (y + 1)^2 = 4$

62. $(x + 2)^2 + (y - 5)^2 = 16$

Theory and Examples

63. Find all polar coordinates of the origin.

64. **Vertical and horizontal lines**

   a. Show that every vertical line in the xy-plane has a polar equation of the form $r = a \sec \theta$.

   b. Find the analogous polar equation for horizontal lines in the xy-plane.

10.6 Graphing in Polar Coordinates

This section describes techniques for graphing equations in polar coordinates.

Symmetry

Figure 10.43 illustrates the standard polar coordinate tests for symmetry.

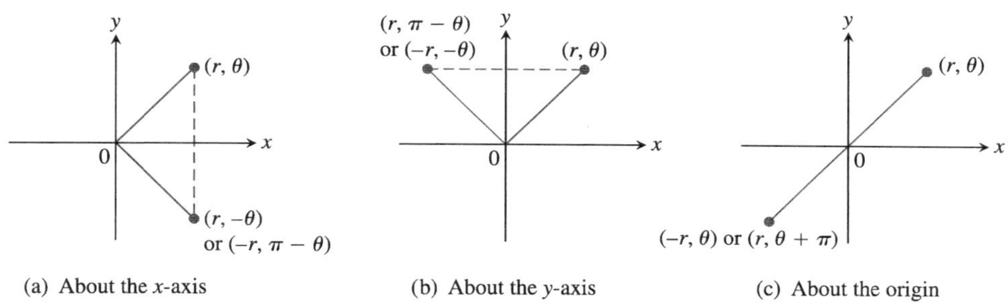

FIGURE 10.43 Three tests for symmetry in polar coordinates.

> **Symmetry Tests for Polar Graphs**
>
> 1. *Symmetry about the x-axis:* If the point (r, θ) lies on the graph, the point $(r, -\theta)$ or $(-r, \pi - \theta)$ lies on the graph (Figure 10.43a).
> 2. *Symmetry about the y-axis:* If the point (r, θ) lies on the graph, the point $(r, \pi - \theta)$ or $(-r, -\theta)$ lies on the graph (Figure 10.43b).
> 3. *Symmetry about the origin:* If the point (r, θ) lies on the graph, the point $(-r, \theta)$ or $(r, \theta + \pi)$ lies on the graph (Figure 10.43c).

Slope

The slope of a polar curve $r = f(\theta)$ is given by dy/dx, not by $r' = df/d\theta$. To see why, think of the graph of f as the graph of the parametric equations

$$x = r\cos\theta = f(\theta)\cos\theta, \qquad y = r\sin\theta = f(\theta)\sin\theta.$$

If f is a differentiable function of θ, then so are x and y and, when $dx/d\theta \neq 0$, we can calculate dy/dx from the parametric formula

$$\frac{dy}{dx} = \frac{dy/d\theta}{dx/d\theta} \qquad \text{Section 3.5, Equation (2) with } t = \theta$$

$$= \frac{\dfrac{d}{d\theta}(f(\theta) \cdot \sin\theta)}{\dfrac{d}{d\theta}(f(\theta) \cdot \cos\theta)}$$

$$= \frac{\dfrac{df}{d\theta}\sin\theta + f(\theta)\cos\theta}{\dfrac{df}{d\theta}\cos\theta - f(\theta)\sin\theta} \qquad \text{Product Rule for derivatives}$$

Slope of the Curve $r = f(\theta)$

$$\left.\frac{dy}{dx}\right|_{(r,\,\theta)} = \frac{f'(\theta)\sin\theta + f(\theta)\cos\theta}{f'(\theta)\cos\theta - f(\theta)\sin\theta},$$

provided $dx/d\theta \neq 0$ at (r, θ).

If the curve $r = f(\theta)$ passes through the origin at $\theta = \theta_0$, then $f(\theta_0) = 0$, and the slope equation gives

$$\left.\frac{dy}{dx}\right|_{(0,\,\theta_0)} = \frac{f'(\theta_0)\sin\theta_0}{f'(\theta_0)\cos\theta_0} = \tan\theta_0.$$

If the graph of $r = f(\theta)$ passes through the origin at the value $\theta = \theta_0$, the slope of the curve there is $\tan\theta_0$. The reason we say "slope at $(0, \theta_0)$" and not just "slope at the origin" is that a polar curve may pass through the origin (or any point) more than once, with different slopes at different θ-values. This is not the case in our first example, however.

EXAMPLE 1 A Cardioid

Graph the curve $r = 1 - \cos\theta$.

Solution The curve is symmetric about the x-axis because

$$(r, \theta) \text{ on the graph} \Rightarrow r = 1 - \cos\theta$$
$$\Rightarrow r = 1 - \cos(-\theta) \qquad \cos\theta = \cos(-\theta)$$
$$\Rightarrow (r, -\theta) \text{ on the graph}.$$

As θ increases from 0 to π, $\cos\theta$ decreases from 1 to -1, and $r = 1 - \cos\theta$ increases from a minimum value of 0 to a maximum value of 2. As θ continues on from π to 2π, $\cos\theta$ increases from -1 back to 1 and r decreases from 2 back to 0. The curve starts to repeat when $\theta = 2\pi$ because the cosine has period 2π.

The curve leaves the origin with slope $\tan(0) = 0$ and returns to the origin with slope $\tan(2\pi) = 0$.

We make a table of values from $\theta = 0$ to $\theta = \pi$, plot the points, draw a smooth curve through them with a horizontal tangent at the origin, and reflect the curve across the x-axis to complete the graph (Figure 10.44). The curve is called a *cardioid* because of its heart shape. Cardioid shapes appear in the cams that direct the even layering of thread on bobbins and reels, and in the signal-strength pattern of certain radio antennas. ■

θ	$r = 1 - \cos\theta$
0	0
$\frac{\pi}{3}$	$\frac{1}{2}$
$\frac{\pi}{2}$	1
$\frac{2\pi}{3}$	$\frac{3}{2}$
π	2

(a)

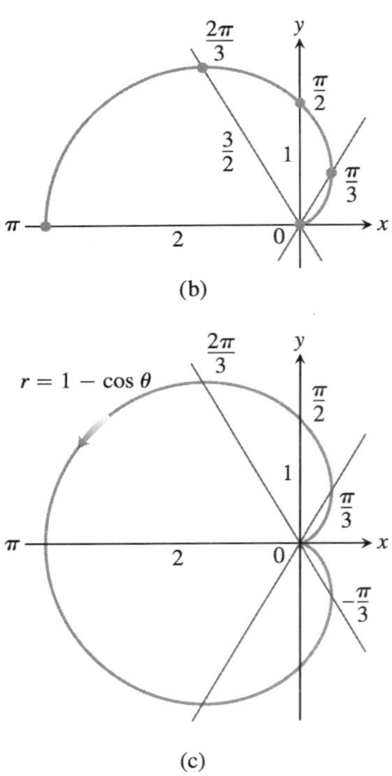

FIGURE 10.44 The steps in graphing the cardioid $r = 1 - \cos\theta$ (Example 1). The arrow shows the direction of increasing θ.

EXAMPLE 2 Graph the Curve $r^2 = 4\cos\theta$.

Solution The equation $r^2 = 4\cos\theta$ requires $\cos\theta \geq 0$, so we get the entire graph by running θ from $-\pi/2$ to $\pi/2$. The curve is symmetric about the x-axis because

$$\begin{aligned}(r, \theta) \text{ on the graph} &\Rightarrow r^2 = 4\cos\theta \\ &\Rightarrow r^2 = 4\cos(-\theta) \qquad \cos\theta = \cos(-\theta) \\ &\Rightarrow (r, -\theta) \text{ on the graph.}\end{aligned}$$

The curve is also symmetric about the origin because

$$\begin{aligned}(r, \theta) \text{ on the graph} &\Rightarrow r^2 = 4\cos\theta \\ &\Rightarrow (-r)^2 = 4\cos\theta \\ &\Rightarrow (-r, \theta) \text{ on the graph.}\end{aligned}$$

Together, these two symmetries imply symmetry about the y-axis.

The curve passes through the origin when $\theta = -\pi/2$ and $\theta = \pi/2$. It has a vertical tangent both times because $\tan\theta$ is infinite.

For each value of θ in the interval between $-\pi/2$ and $\pi/2$, the formula $r^2 = 4\cos\theta$ gives two values of r:

$$r = \pm 2\sqrt{\cos\theta}.$$

We make a short table of values, plot the corresponding points, and use information about symmetry and tangents to guide us in connecting the points with a smooth curve (Figure 10.45). ■

θ	$\cos\theta$	$r = \pm 2\sqrt{\cos\theta}$
0	1	± 2
$\pm\frac{\pi}{6}$	$\frac{\sqrt{3}}{2}$	$\approx \pm 1.9$
$\pm\frac{\pi}{4}$	$\frac{1}{\sqrt{2}}$	$\approx \pm 1.7$
$\pm\frac{\pi}{3}$	$\frac{1}{2}$	$\approx \pm 1.4$
$\pm\frac{\pi}{2}$	0	0

(a)

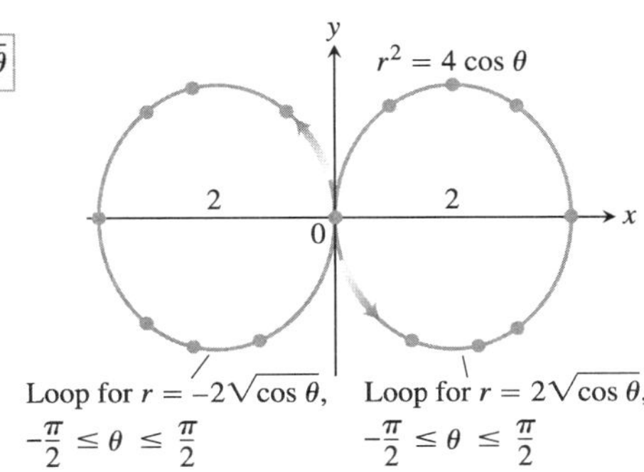

(b)

FIGURE 10.45 The graph of $r^2 = 4\cos\theta$. The arrows show the direction of increasing θ. The values of r in the table are rounded (Example 2).

A Technique for Graphing

One way to graph a polar equation $r = f(\theta)$ is to make a table of (r, θ)-values, plot the corresponding points, and connect them in order of increasing θ. This can work well if enough points have been plotted to reveal all the loops and dimples in the graph. Another method of graphing that is usually quicker and more reliable is to

1. first graph $r = f(\theta)$ in the *Cartesian* $r\theta$-plane,
2. then use the Cartesian graph as a "table" and guide to sketch the *polar* coordinate graph.

This method is better than simple point plotting because the first Cartesian graph, even when hastily drawn, shows at a glance where r is positive, negative, and nonexistent, as well as where r is increasing and decreasing. Here's an example.

EXAMPLE 3 A Lemniscate

Graph the curve

$$r^2 = \sin 2\theta.$$

Solution Here we begin by plotting r^2 (not r) as a function of θ in the Cartesian $r^2\theta$-plane. See Figure 10.46a. We pass from there to the graph of $r = \pm\sqrt{\sin 2\theta}$ in the $r\theta$-plane (Figure 10.46b), and then draw the polar graph (Figure 10.46c). The graph in Figure 10.46b "covers" the final polar graph in Figure 10.46c twice. We could have managed with either loop alone, with the two upper halves, or with the two lower halves. The double covering does no harm, however, and we actually learn a little more about the behavior of the function this way. ■

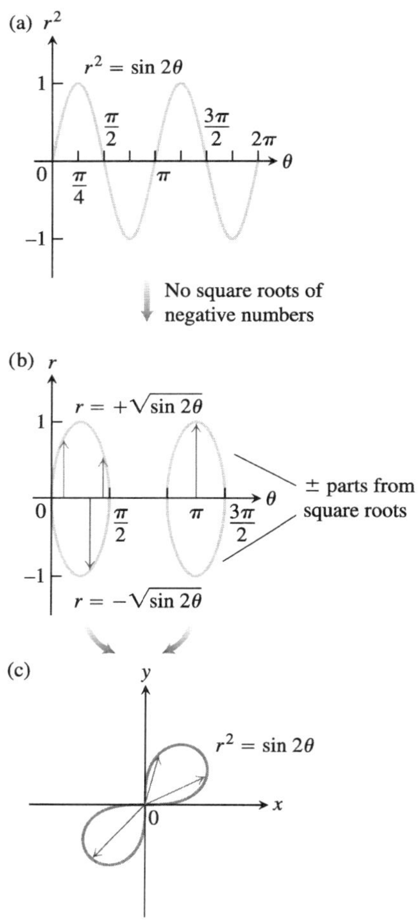

FIGURE 10.46 To plot $r = f(\theta)$ in the Cartesian $r\theta$-plane in (b), we first plot $r^2 = \sin 2\theta$ in the $r^2\theta$-plane in (a) and then ignore the values of θ for which $\sin 2\theta$ is negative. The radii from the sketch in (b) cover the polar graph of the lemniscate in (c) twice (Example 3).

Finding Points Where Polar Graphs Intersect

The fact that we can represent a point in different ways in polar coordinates makes extra care necessary in deciding when a point lies on the graph of a polar equation and in determining the points in which polar graphs intersect. The problem is that a point of intersection may satisfy the equation of one curve with polar coordinates that are different from the ones with which it satisfies the equation of another curve. Thus, solving the equations of two curves simultaneously may not identify all their points of intersection. One sure way to identify all the points of intersection is to graph the equations.

EXAMPLE 4 Deceptive Polar Coordinates

Show that the point $(2, \pi/2)$ lies on the curve $r = 2\cos 2\theta$.

Solution It may seem at first that the point $(2, \pi/2)$ does not lie on the curve because substituting the given coordinates into the equation gives

$$2 = 2\cos 2\left(\frac{\pi}{2}\right) = 2\cos\pi = -2,$$

which is not a true equality. The magnitude is right, but the sign is wrong. This suggests looking for a pair of coordinates for the same given point in which r is negative, for example, $(-2, -(\pi/2))$. If we try these in the equation $r = 2\cos 2\theta$, we find

$$-2 = 2\cos 2\left(-\frac{\pi}{2}\right) = 2(-1) = -2,$$

and the equation is satisfied. The point $(2, \pi/2)$ does lie on the curve. ■

EXAMPLE 5 Elusive Intersection Points

Find the points of intersection of the curves

$$r^2 = 4\cos\theta \quad \text{and} \quad r = 1 - \cos\theta.$$

HISTORICAL BIOGRAPHY

Johannes Kepler
(1571–1630)

Solution In Cartesian coordinates, we can always find the points where two curves cross by solving their equations simultaneously. In polar coordinates, the story is different. Simultaneous solution may reveal some intersection points without revealing others. In this example, simultaneous solution reveals only two of the four intersection points. The others are found by graphing. (Also, see Exercise 49.)

If we substitute $\cos\theta = r^2/4$ in the equation $r = 1 - \cos\theta$, we get

$$r = 1 - \cos\theta = 1 - \frac{r^2}{4}$$

$$4r = 4 - r^2$$

$$r^2 + 4r - 4 = 0$$

$$r = -2 \pm 2\sqrt{2}. \qquad \text{Quadratic formula}$$

The value $r = -2 - 2\sqrt{2}$ has too large an absolute value to belong to either curve. The values of θ corresponding to $r = -2 + 2\sqrt{2}$ are

$$\begin{aligned}\theta &= \cos^{-1}(1 - r) && \text{From } r = 1 - \cos\theta\\ &= \cos^{-1}\left(1 - \left(2\sqrt{2} - 2\right)\right) && \text{Set } r = 2\sqrt{2} - 2.\\ &= \cos^{-1}\left(3 - 2\sqrt{2}\right)\\ &= \pm 80^\circ. && \text{Rounded to the nearest degree}\end{aligned}$$

We have thus identified two intersection points: $(r, \theta) = (2\sqrt{2} - 2, \pm 80^\circ)$.

If we graph the equations $r^2 = 4\cos\theta$ and $r = 1 - \cos\theta$ together (Figure 10.47), as we can now do by combining the graphs in Figures 10.44 and 10.45, we see that the curves also intersect at the point $(2, \pi)$ and the origin. Why weren't the r-values of these points revealed by the simultaneous solution? The answer is that the points $(0, 0)$ and $(2, \pi)$ are not on the curves "simultaneously." They are not reached at the same value of θ. On the curve $r = 1 - \cos\theta$, the point $(2, \pi)$ is reached when $\theta = \pi$. On the curve $r^2 = 4\cos\theta$, it is reached when $\theta = 0$, where it is identified not by the coordinates $(2, \pi)$, which do not satisfy the equation, but by the coordinates $(-2, 0)$, which do. Similarly, the cardioid reaches the origin when $\theta = 0$, but the curve $r^2 = 4\cos\theta$ reaches the origin when $\theta = \pi/2$. ■

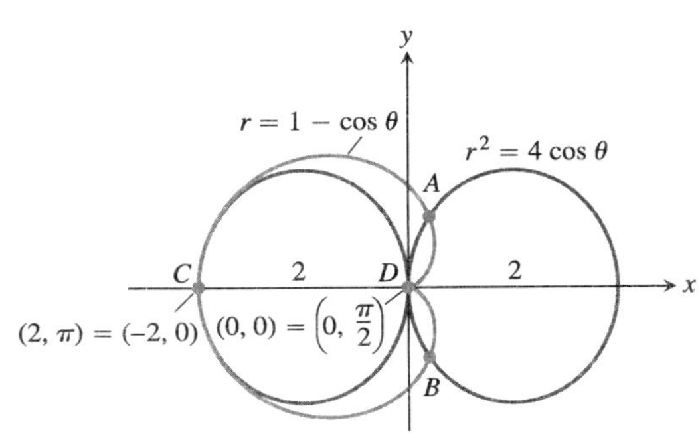

FIGURE 10.47 The four points of intersection of the curves $r = 1 - \cos\theta$ and $r^2 = 4\cos\theta$ (Example 5). Only A and B were found by simultaneous solution. The other two were disclosed by graphing.

USING TECHNOLOGY Graphing Polar Curves Parametrically

For complicated polar curves we may need to use a graphing calculator or computer to graph the curve. If the device does not plot polar graphs directly, we can convert $r = f(\theta)$ into parametric form using the equations

$$x = r\cos\theta = f(\theta)\cos\theta, \qquad y = r\sin\theta = f(\theta)\sin\theta.$$

Then we use the device to draw a parametrized curve in the Cartesian xy-plane. It may be required to use the parameter t rather than θ for the graphing device.

EXERCISES 10.6

Symmetries and Polar Graphs

Identify the symmetries of the curves in Exercises 1–12. Then sketch the curves.

1. $r = 1 + \cos\theta$
2. $r = 2 - 2\cos\theta$
3. $r = 1 - \sin\theta$
4. $r = 1 + \sin\theta$
5. $r = 2 + \sin\theta$
6. $r = 1 + 2\sin\theta$
7. $r = \sin(\theta/2)$
8. $r = \cos(\theta/2)$
9. $r^2 = \cos\theta$
10. $r^2 = \sin\theta$
11. $r^2 = -\sin\theta$
12. $r^2 = -\cos\theta$

Graph the lemniscates in Exercises 13–16. What symmetries do these curves have?

13. $r^2 = 4\cos 2\theta$
14. $r^2 = 4\sin 2\theta$
15. $r^2 = -\sin 2\theta$
16. $r^2 = -\cos 2\theta$

Slopes of Polar Curves

Find the slopes of the curves in Exercises 17–20 at the given points. Sketch the curves along with their tangents at these points.

17. **Cardioid** $r = -1 + \cos\theta;\quad \theta = \pm\pi/2$
18. **Cardioid** $r = -1 + \sin\theta;\quad \theta = 0, \pi$
19. **Four-leaved rose** $r = \sin 2\theta;\quad \theta = \pm\pi/4, \pm 3\pi/4$
20. **Four-leaved rose** $r = \cos 2\theta;\quad \theta = 0, \pm\pi/2, \pi$

Limaçons

Graph the limaçons in Exercises 21–24. Limaçon ("*lee*-ma-sahn") is Old French for "snail." You will understand the name when you graph the limaçons in Exercise 21. Equations for limaçons have the form $r = a \pm b\cos\theta$ or $r = a \pm b\sin\theta$. There are four basic shapes.

21. **Limaçons with an inner loop**

    a. $r = \frac{1}{2} + \cos\theta$ b. $r = \frac{1}{2} + \sin\theta$

22. **Cardioids**

    a. $r = 1 - \cos\theta$ b. $r = -1 + \sin\theta$

23. **Dimpled limaçons**

    a. $r = \frac{3}{2} + \cos\theta$ b. $r = \frac{3}{2} - \sin\theta$

24. **Oval limaçons**

    a. $r = 2 + \cos\theta$ b. $r = -2 + \sin\theta$

Graphing Polar Inequalities

25. Sketch the region defined by the inequalities $-1 \le r \le 2$ and $-\pi/2 \le \theta \le \pi/2$.
26. Sketch the region defined by the inequalities $0 \le r \le 2\sec\theta$ and $-\pi/4 \le \theta \le \pi/4$.

In Exercises 27 and 28, sketch the region defined by the inequality.

27. $0 \le r \le 2 - 2\cos\theta$
28. $0 \le r^2 \le \cos\theta$

Intersections

29. Show that the point $(2, 3\pi/4)$ lies on the curve $r = 2\sin 2\theta$.
30. Show that $(1/2, 3\pi/2)$ lies on the curve $r = -\sin(\theta/3)$.

Find the points of intersection of the pairs of curves in Exercises 31–38.

31. $r = 1 + \cos\theta,\quad r = 1 - \cos\theta$
32. $r = 1 + \sin\theta,\quad r = 1 - \sin\theta$
33. $r = 2\sin\theta,\quad r = 2\sin 2\theta$
34. $r = \cos\theta,\quad r = 1 - \cos\theta$
35. $r = \sqrt{2},\quad r^2 = 4\sin\theta$
36. $r^2 = \sqrt{2}\sin\theta,\quad r^2 = \sqrt{2}\cos\theta$
37. $r = 1,\quad r^2 = 2\sin 2\theta$
38. $r^2 = \sqrt{2}\cos 2\theta,\quad r^2 = \sqrt{2}\sin 2\theta$

T Find the points of intersection of the pairs of curves in Exercises 39–42.

39. $r^2 = \sin 2\theta,\quad r^2 = \cos 2\theta$
40. $r = 1 + \cos\frac{\theta}{2},\quad r = 1 - \sin\frac{\theta}{2}$
41. $r = 1,\quad r = 2\sin 2\theta$
42. $r = 1,\quad r^2 = 2\sin 2\theta$

Grapher Explorations

43. Which of the following has the same graph as $r = 1 - \cos\theta$?

a. $r = -1 - \cos\theta$ **b.** $r = 1 + \cos\theta$

Confirm your answer with algebra.

44. Which of the following has the same graph as $r = \cos 2\theta$?

a. $r = -\sin(2\theta + \pi/2)$ **b.** $r = -\cos(\theta/2)$

Confirm your answer with algebra.

45. A rose within a rose Graph the equation $r = 1 - 2\sin 3\theta$.

46. The nephroid of Freeth Graph the nephroid of Freeth:

$$r = 1 + 2\sin\frac{\theta}{2}.$$

47. Roses Graph the roses $r = \cos m\theta$ for $m = 1/3, 2, 3$, and 7.

48. Spirals Polar coordinates are just the thing for defining spirals. Graph the following spirals.

a. $r = \theta$ **b.** $r = -\theta$

c. *A logarithmic spiral:* $r = e^{\theta/10}$

d. *A hyperbolic spiral:* $r = 8/\theta$

e. *An equilateral hyperbola:* $r = \pm 10/\sqrt{\theta}$

(Use different colors for the two branches.)

Theory and Examples

49. (*Continuation of Example 5.*) The simultaneous solution of the equations

$$r^2 = 4\cos\theta \qquad (1)$$

$$r = 1 - \cos\theta \qquad (2)$$

in the text did not reveal the points (0, 0) and $(2, \pi)$ in which their graphs intersected.

a. We could have found the point $(2, \pi)$, however, by replacing the (r, θ) in Equation (1) by the equivalent $(-r, \theta + \pi)$ to obtain

$$\begin{aligned} r^2 &= 4\cos\theta \\ (-r)^2 &= 4\cos(\theta + \pi) \qquad (3) \\ r^2 &= -4\cos\theta. \end{aligned}$$

Solve Equations (2) and (3) simultaneously to show that $(2, \pi)$ is a common solution. (This will still not reveal that the graphs intersect at (0, 0).)

b. The origin is still a special case. (It often is.) Here is one way to handle it: Set $r = 0$ in Equations (1) and (2) and solve each equation for a corresponding value of θ. Since $(0, \theta)$ is the origin for *any* θ, this will show that both curves pass through the origin even if they do so for different θ-values.

50. If a curve has any two of the symmetries listed at the beginning of the section, can anything be said about its having or not having the third symmetry? Give reasons for your answer.

***51.** Find the maximum width of the petal of the four-leaved rose $r = \cos 2\theta$, which lies along the x-axis.

***52.** Find the maximum height above the x-axis of the cardioid $r = 2(1 + \cos\theta)$.

10.7 Areas and Lengths in Polar Coordinates

This section shows how to calculate areas of plane regions, lengths of curves, and areas of surfaces of revolution in polar coordinates.

Area in the Plane

The region *OTS* in Figure 10.48 is bounded by the rays $\theta = \alpha$ and $\theta = \beta$ and the curve $r = f(\theta)$. We approximate the region with n nonoverlapping fan-shaped circular sectors based on a partition P of angle *TOS*. The typical sector has radius $r_k = f(\theta_k)$ and central angle of radian measure $\Delta\theta_k$. Its area is $\Delta\theta_k/2\pi$ times the area of a circle of radius r_k, or

$$A_k = \frac{1}{2} r_k^2\, \Delta\theta_k = \frac{1}{2}\left(f(\theta_k)\right)^2 \Delta\theta_k.$$

The area of region *OTS* is approximately

$$\sum_{k=1}^{n} A_k = \sum_{k=1}^{n} \frac{1}{2}\left(f(\theta_k)\right)^2 \Delta\theta_k.$$

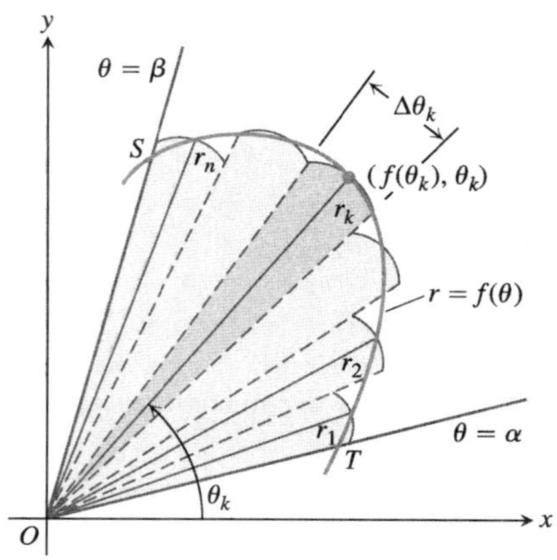

FIGURE 10.48 To derive a formula for the area of region *OTS*, we approximate the region with fan-shaped circular sectors.

If f is continuous, we expect the approximations to improve as the norm of the partition $\|P\| \to 0$, and we are led to the following formula for the region's area:

$$\begin{aligned} A &= \lim_{\|P\|\to 0} \sum_{k=1}^{n} \frac{1}{2}\left(f(\theta_k)\right)^2 \Delta\theta_k \\ &= \int_{\alpha}^{\beta} \frac{1}{2}\left(f(\theta)\right)^2 d\theta. \end{aligned}$$

Area of the Fan-Shaped Region Between the Origin and the Curve $r = f(\theta), \alpha \le \theta \le \beta$

$$A = \int_{\alpha}^{\beta} \frac{1}{2} r^2 \, d\theta.$$

This is the integral of the **area differential** (Figure 10.49)

$$dA = \frac{1}{2} r^2 \, d\theta = \frac{1}{2} (f(\theta))^2 \, d\theta.$$

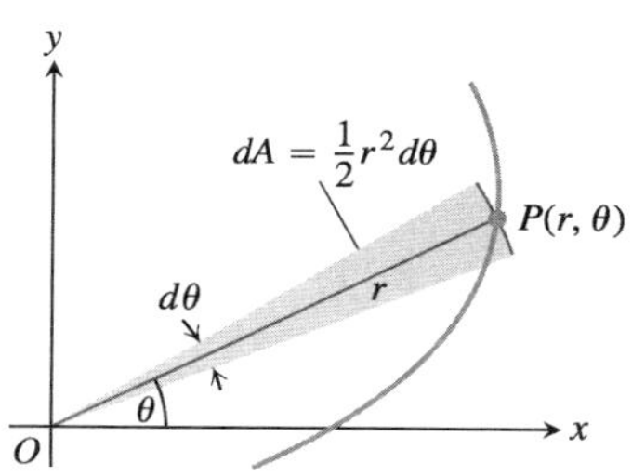

FIGURE 10.49 The area differential dA for the curve $n = f(\theta)$.

EXAMPLE 1 Finding Area

Find the area of the region in the plane enclosed by the cardioid $r = 2(1 + \cos\theta)$.

Solution We graph the cardioid (Figure 10.50) and determine that the radius OP sweeps out the region exactly once as θ runs from 0 to 2π. The area is therefore

$$\begin{aligned} \int_{\theta=0}^{\theta=2\pi} \frac{1}{2} r^2 \, d\theta &= \int_0^{2\pi} \frac{1}{2} \cdot 4(1 + \cos\theta)^2 \, d\theta \\ &= \int_0^{2\pi} 2(1 + 2\cos\theta + \cos^2\theta)\, d\theta \\ &= \int_0^{2\pi} \left(2 + 4\cos\theta + 2\frac{1 + \cos 2\theta}{2}\right) d\theta \\ &= \int_0^{2\pi} (3 + 4\cos\theta + \cos 2\theta)\, d\theta \\ &= \left[3\theta + 4\sin\theta + \frac{\sin 2\theta}{2}\right]_0^{2\pi} = 6\pi - 0 = 6\pi. \end{aligned}$$

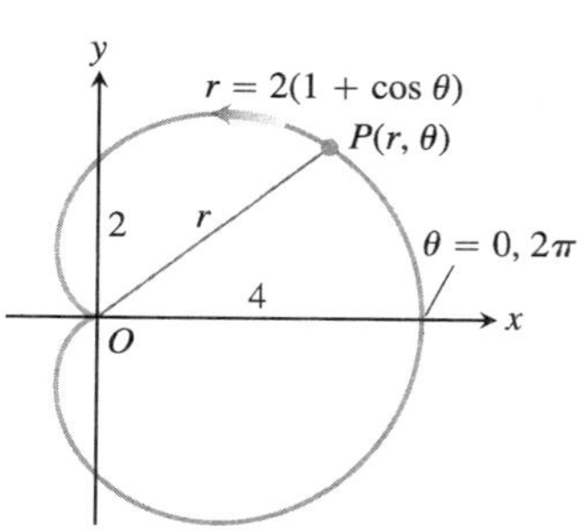

FIGURE 10.50 The cardioid in Example 1.

EXAMPLE 2 Finding Area

Find the area inside the smaller loop of the limaçon

$$r = 2\cos\theta + 1.$$

Solution After sketching the curve (Figure 10.51), we see that the smaller loop is traced out by the point (r, θ) as θ increases from $\theta = 2\pi/3$ to $\theta = 4\pi/3$. Since the curve is symmetric about the x-axis (the equation is unaltered when we replace θ by $-\theta$), we may calculate the area of the shaded half of the inner loop by integrating from $\theta = 2\pi/3$ to $\theta = \pi$. The area we seek will be twice the resulting integral:

$$A = 2\int_{2\pi/3}^{\pi} \frac{1}{2} r^2 \, d\theta = \int_{2\pi/3}^{\pi} r^2 \, d\theta.$$

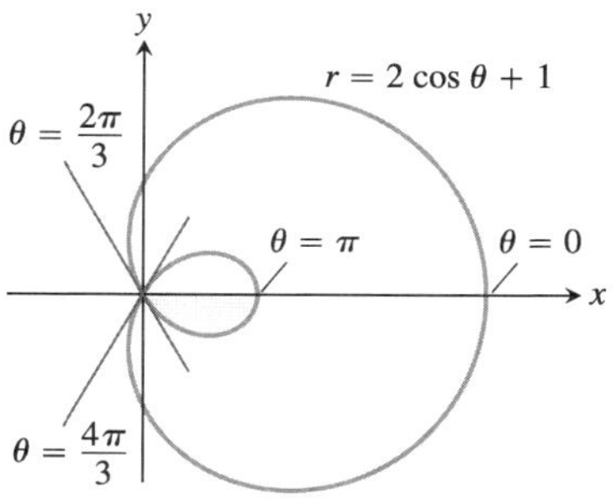

FIGURE 10.51 The limaçon in Example 2. Limaçon (pronounced LEE-ma-sahn) is an old French word for *snail*.

Since

$$\begin{aligned} r^2 &= (2\cos\theta + 1)^2 = 4\cos^2\theta + 4\cos\theta + 1 \\ &= 4\cdot\frac{1+\cos 2\theta}{2} + 4\cos\theta + 1 \\ &= 2 + 2\cos 2\theta + 4\cos\theta + 1 \\ &= 3 + 2\cos 2\theta + 4\cos\theta, \end{aligned}$$

we have

$$\begin{aligned} A &= \int_{2\pi/3}^{\pi} (3 + 2\cos 2\theta + 4\cos\theta)\, d\theta \\ &= \Big[3\theta + \sin 2\theta + 4\sin\theta\Big]_{2\pi/3}^{\pi} \\ &= (3\pi) - \left(2\pi - \frac{\sqrt{3}}{2} + 4\cdot\frac{\sqrt{3}}{2}\right) \\ &= \pi - \frac{3\sqrt{3}}{2}. \end{aligned}$$ ■

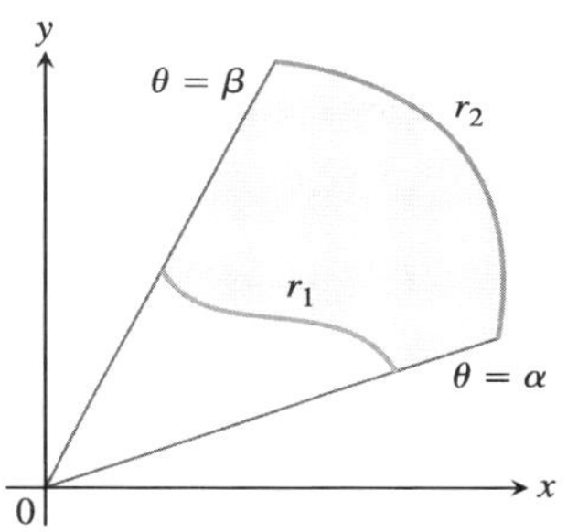

FIGURE 10.52 The area of the shaded region is calculated by subtracting the area of the region between r_1 and the origin from the area of the region between r_2 and the origin.

To find the area of a region like the one in Figure 10.52, which lies between two polar curves $r_1 = r_1(\theta)$ and $r_2 = r_2(\theta)$ from $\theta = \alpha$ to $\theta = \beta$, we subtract the integral of $(1/2){r_1}^2\, d\theta$ from the integral of $(1/2){r_2}^2\, d\theta$. This leads to the following formula.

Area of the Region $0 \le r_1(\theta) \le r \le r_2(\theta), \qquad \alpha \le \theta \le \beta$

$$A = \int_{\alpha}^{\beta} \frac{1}{2}{r_2}^2\, d\theta - \int_{\alpha}^{\beta} \frac{1}{2}{r_1}^2\, d\theta = \int_{\alpha}^{\beta} \frac{1}{2}\left({r_2}^2 - {r_1}^2\right) d\theta \qquad (1)$$

EXAMPLE 3 Finding Area Between Polar Curves

Find the area of the region that lies inside the circle $r = 1$ and outside the cardioid $r = 1 - \cos\theta$.

Solution We sketch the region to determine its boundaries and find the limits of integration (Figure 10.53). The outer curve is $r_2 = 1$, the inner curve is $r_1 = 1 - \cos\theta$, and θ runs from $-\pi/2$ to $\pi/2$. The area, from Equation (1), is

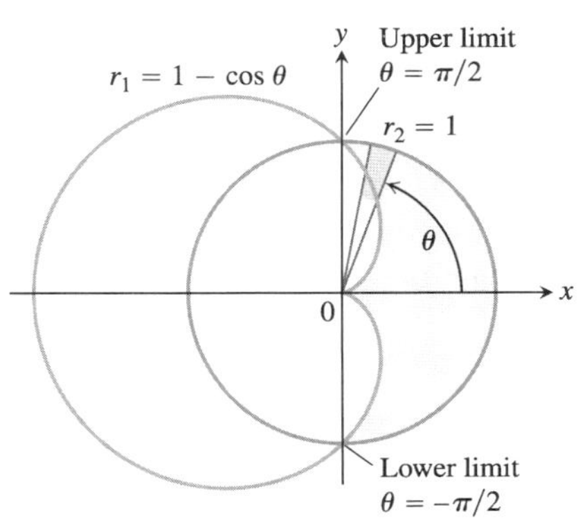

FIGURE 10.53 The region and limits of integration in Example 3.

$$\begin{aligned} A &= \int_{-\pi/2}^{\pi/2} \frac{1}{2}\left({r_2}^2 - {r_1}^2\right) d\theta \\ &= 2\int_{0}^{\pi/2} \frac{1}{2}\left({r_2}^2 - {r_1}^2\right) d\theta \qquad \text{Symmetry} \\ &= \int_{0}^{\pi/2} (1 - (1 - 2\cos\theta + \cos^2\theta))\, d\theta \\ &= \int_{0}^{\pi/2} (2\cos\theta - \cos^2\theta)\, d\theta = \int_{0}^{\pi/2} \left(2\cos\theta - \frac{1+\cos 2\theta}{2}\right) d\theta \\ &= \left[2\sin\theta - \frac{\theta}{2} - \frac{\sin 2\theta}{4}\right]_0^{\pi/2} = 2 - \frac{\pi}{4}. \end{aligned}$$ ■

Length of a Polar Curve

We can obtain a polar coordinate formula for the length of a curve $r = f(\theta)$, $\alpha \le \theta \le \beta$, by parametrizing the curve as

$$x = r\cos\theta = f(\theta)\cos\theta, \qquad y = r\sin\theta = f(\theta)\sin\theta, \qquad \alpha \le \theta \le \beta. \tag{2}$$

The parametric length formula, Equation (1) from Section 6.3, then gives the length as

$$L = \int_\alpha^\beta \sqrt{\left(\frac{dx}{d\theta}\right)^2 + \left(\frac{dy}{d\theta}\right)^2}\, d\theta.$$

This equation becomes

$$L = \int_\alpha^\beta \sqrt{r^2 + \left(\frac{dr}{d\theta}\right)^2}\, d\theta$$

when Equations (2) are substituted for x and y (Exercise 33).

Length of a Polar Curve
If $r = f(\theta)$ has a continuous first derivative for $\alpha \le \theta \le \beta$ and if the point $P(r, \theta)$ traces the curve $r = f(\theta)$ exactly once as θ runs from α to β, then the length of the curve is

$$L = \int_\alpha^\beta \sqrt{r^2 + \left(\frac{dr}{d\theta}\right)^2}\, d\theta. \tag{3}$$

EXAMPLE 4 Finding the Length of a Cardioid

Find the length of the cardioid $r = 1 - \cos\theta$.

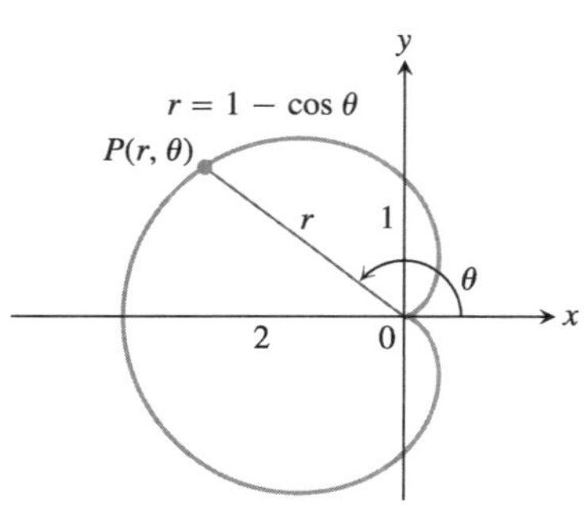

FIGURE 10.54 Calculating the length of a cardioid (Example 4).

Solution We sketch the cardioid to determine the limits of integration (Figure 10.54). The point $P(r, \theta)$ traces the curve once, counterclockwise as θ runs from 0 to 2π, so these are the values we take for α and β.

With

$$r = 1 - \cos\theta, \qquad \frac{dr}{d\theta} = \sin\theta,$$

we have

$$\begin{aligned} r^2 + \left(\frac{dr}{d\theta}\right)^2 &= (1 - \cos\theta)^2 + (\sin\theta)^2 \\ &= 1 - 2\cos\theta + \underbrace{\cos^2\theta + \sin^2\theta}_{1} = 2 - 2\cos\theta \end{aligned}$$

and

$$\begin{aligned} L &= \int_\alpha^\beta \sqrt{r^2 + \left(\frac{dr}{d\theta}\right)^2}\, d\theta = \int_0^{2\pi} \sqrt{2 - 2\cos\theta}\, d\theta \\ &= \int_0^{2\pi} \sqrt{4\sin^2\frac{\theta}{2}}\, d\theta \qquad 1 - \cos\theta = 2\sin^2\frac{\theta}{2} \end{aligned}$$

$$= \int_0^{2\pi} 2\left|\sin\frac{\theta}{2}\right| d\theta$$

$$= \int_0^{2\pi} 2\sin\frac{\theta}{2}\, d\theta \qquad \sin\frac{\theta}{2} \geq 0 \quad \text{for} \quad 0 \leq \theta \leq 2\pi$$

$$= \left[-4\cos\frac{\theta}{2}\right]_0^{2\pi} = 4 + 4 = 8.$$

■

Area of a Surface of Revolution

To derive polar coordinate formulas for the area of a surface of revolution, we parametrize the curve $r = f(\theta)$, $\alpha \leq \theta \leq \beta$, with Equations (2) and apply the surface area equations for parametrized curves in Section 6.5.

Area of a Surface of Revolution of a Polar Curve

If $r = f(\theta)$ has a continuous first derivative for $\alpha \leq \theta \leq \beta$ and if the point $P(r, \theta)$ traces the curve $r = f(\theta)$ exactly once as θ runs from α to β, then the areas of the surfaces generated by revolving the curve about the x- and y-axes are given by the following formulas:

1. Revolution about the x-axis ($y \geq 0$):

$$S = \int_\alpha^\beta 2\pi r \sin\theta \sqrt{r^2 + \left(\frac{dr}{d\theta}\right)^2}\, d\theta \tag{4}$$

2. Revolution about the y-axis ($x \geq 0$):

$$S = \int_\alpha^\beta 2\pi r \cos\theta \sqrt{r^2 + \left(\frac{dr}{d\theta}\right)^2}\, d\theta \tag{5}$$

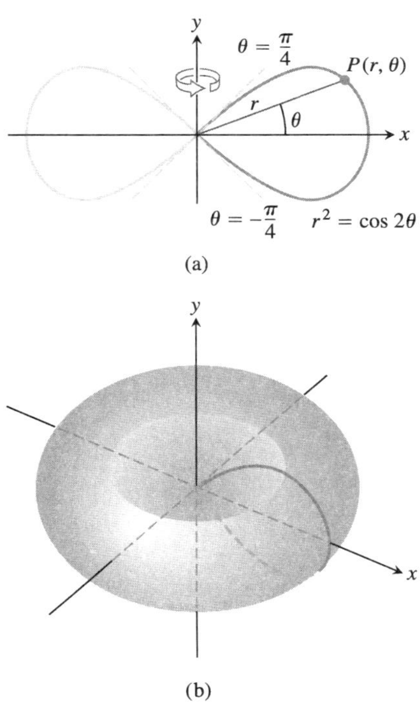

FIGURE 10.55 The right-hand half of a lemniscate (a) is revolved about the y-axis to generate a surface (b), whose area is calculated in Example 5.

EXAMPLE 5 Finding Surface Area

Find the area of the surface generated by revolving the right-hand loop of the lemniscate $r^2 = \cos 2\theta$ about the y-axis.

Solution We sketch the loop to determine the limits of integration (Figure 10.55a). The point $P(r, \theta)$ traces the curve once, counterclockwise as θ runs from $-\pi/4$ to $\pi/4$, so these are the values we take for α and β.

We evaluate the area integrand in Equation (5) in stages. First,

$$2\pi r\cos\theta\sqrt{r^2 + \left(\frac{dr}{d\theta}\right)^2} = 2\pi\cos\theta\sqrt{r^4 + \left(r\frac{dr}{d\theta}\right)^2}. \tag{6}$$

Next, $r^2 = \cos 2\theta$, so

$$2r\frac{dr}{d\theta} = -2\sin 2\theta$$

$$r\frac{dr}{d\theta} = -\sin 2\theta$$

$$\left(r\frac{dr}{d\theta}\right)^2 = \sin^2 2\theta.$$

Finally, $r^4 = (r^2)^2 = \cos^2 2\theta$, so the square root on the right-hand side of Equation (6) simplifies to

$$\sqrt{r^4 + \left(r\frac{dr}{d\theta}\right)^2} = \sqrt{\cos^2 2\theta + \sin^2 2\theta} = 1.$$

All together, we have

$$\begin{aligned} S &= \int_\alpha^\beta 2\pi r\cos\theta\sqrt{r^2 + \left(\frac{dr}{d\theta}\right)^2}\,d\theta \qquad \text{Equation (5)} \\ &= \int_{-\pi/4}^{\pi/4} 2\pi\cos\theta\cdot(1)\,d\theta \\ &= 2\pi\Big[\sin\theta\Big]_{-\pi/4}^{\pi/4} \\ &= 2\pi\left[\frac{\sqrt{2}}{2} + \frac{\sqrt{2}}{2}\right] = 2\pi\sqrt{2}. \end{aligned}$$

■

EXERCISES 10.7

Areas Inside Polar Curves

Find the areas of the regions in Exercises 1–6.

1. Inside the oval limaçon $r = 4 + 2\cos\theta$
2. Inside the cardioid $r = a(1 + \cos\theta)$, $a > 0$
3. Inside one leaf of the four-leaved rose $r = \cos 2\theta$
4. Inside the lemniscate $r^2 = 2a^2\cos 2\theta$, $a > 0$
5. Inside one loop of the lemniscate $r^2 = 4\sin 2\theta$
6. Inside the six-leaved rose $r^2 = 2\sin 3\theta$

Areas Shared by Polar Regions

Find the areas of the regions in Exercises 7–16.

7. Shared by the circles $r = 2\cos\theta$ and $r = 2\sin\theta$
8. Shared by the circles $r = 1$ and $r = 2\sin\theta$
9. Shared by the circle $r = 2$ and the cardioid $r = 2(1 - \cos\theta)$
10. Shared by the cardioids $r = 2(1 + \cos\theta)$ and $r = 2(1 - \cos\theta)$
11. Inside the lemniscate $r^2 = 6\cos 2\theta$ and outside the circle $r = \sqrt{3}$
12. Inside the circle $r = 3a\cos\theta$ and outside the cardioid $r = a(1 + \cos\theta)$, $a > 0$
13. Inside the circle $r = -2\cos\theta$ and outside the circle $r = 1$
14. **a.** Inside the outer loop of the limaçon $r = 2\cos\theta + 1$ (See Figure 10.51.)

    b. Inside the outer loop and outside the inner loop of the limaçon $r = 2\cos\theta + 1$
15. Inside the circle $r = 6$ above the line $r = 3\csc\theta$
16. Inside the lemniscate $r^2 = 6\cos 2\theta$ to the right of the line $r = (3/2)\sec\theta$
17. **a.** Find the area of the shaded region in the accompanying figure.

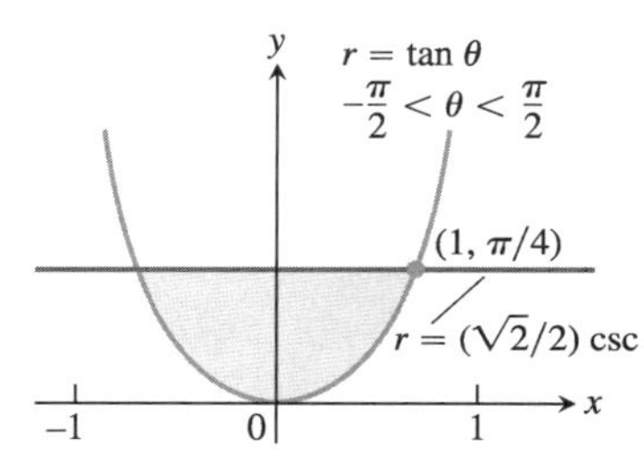

    b. It looks as if the graph of $r = \tan\theta$, $-\pi/2 < \theta < \pi/2$, could be asymptotic to the lines $x = 1$ and $x = -1$. Is it? Give reasons for your answer.
18. The area of the region that lies inside the cardioid curve $r = \cos\theta + 1$ and outside the circle $r = \cos\theta$ is not

$$\frac{1}{2}\int_0^{2\pi}[(\cos\theta + 1)^2 - \cos^2\theta]\,d\theta = \pi.$$

Why not? What *is* the area? Give reasons for your answers.

Lengths of Polar Curves

Find the lengths of the curves in Exercises 19–27.

19. The spiral $r = \theta^2, \quad 0 \le \theta \le \sqrt{5}$

20. The spiral $r = e^{\theta}/\sqrt{2}, \quad 0 \le \theta \le \pi$

21. The cardioid $r = 1 + \cos\theta$

22. The curve $r = a\sin^2(\theta/2), \quad 0 \le \theta \le \pi, \quad a > 0$

23. The parabolic segment $r = 6/(1 + \cos\theta), \quad 0 \le \theta \le \pi/2$

24. The parabolic segment $r = 2/(1 - \cos\theta), \quad \pi/2 \le \theta \le \pi$

25. The curve $r = \cos^3(\theta/3), \quad 0 \le \theta \le \pi/4$

26. The curve $r = \sqrt{1 + \sin 2\theta}, \quad 0 \le \theta \le \pi\sqrt{2}$

27. The curve $r = \sqrt{1 + \cos 2\theta}, \quad 0 \le \theta \le \pi\sqrt{2}$

28. Circumferences of circles As usual, when faced with a new formula, it is a good idea to try it on familiar objects to be sure it gives results consistent with past experience. Use the length formula in Equation (3) to calculate the circumferences of the following circles ($a > 0$):

a. $r = a$ **b.** $r = a\cos\theta$ **c.** $r = a\sin\theta$

Surface Area

Find the areas of the surfaces generated by revolving the curves in Exercises 29–32 about the indicated axes.

29. $r = \sqrt{\cos 2\theta}, \quad 0 \le \theta \le \pi/4, \quad y\text{-axis}$

30. $r = \sqrt{2}e^{\theta/2}, \quad 0 \le \theta \le \pi/2, \quad x\text{-axis}$

31. $r^2 = \cos 2\theta, \quad x\text{-axis}$

32. $r = 2a\cos\theta, \quad a > 0, \quad y\text{-axis}$

Theory and Examples

33. The length of the curve $r = f(\theta), \alpha \le \theta \le \beta$ Assuming that the necessary derivatives are continuous, show how the substitutions

$$x = f(\theta)\cos\theta, \quad y = f(\theta)\sin\theta$$

(Equations 2 in the text) transform

$$L = \int_{\alpha}^{\beta}\sqrt{\left(\frac{dx}{d\theta}\right)^2 + \left(\frac{dy}{d\theta}\right)^2}\,d\theta$$

into

$$L = \int_{\alpha}^{\beta}\sqrt{r^2 + \left(\frac{dr}{d\theta}\right)^2}\,d\theta.$$

34. Average value If f is continuous, the average value of the polar coordinate r over the curve $r = f(\theta), \alpha \le \theta \le \beta$, with respect to θ is given by the formula

$$r_{\text{av}} = \frac{1}{\beta - \alpha}\int_{\alpha}^{\beta} f(\theta)\,d\theta.$$

Use this formula to find the average value of r with respect to θ over the following curves ($a > 0$).

a. The cardioid $r = a(1 - \cos\theta)$

b. The circle $r = a$

c. The circle $r = a\cos\theta, \quad -\pi/2 \le \theta \le \pi/2$

35. $r = f(\theta)$ vs. $r = 2f(\theta)$ Can anything be said about the relative lengths of the curves $r = f(\theta), \alpha \le \theta \le \beta$, and $r = 2f(\theta)$, $\alpha \le \theta \le \beta$? Give reasons for your answer.

36. $r = f(\theta)$ vs. $r = 2f(\theta)$ The curves $r = f(\theta), \alpha \le \theta \le \beta$, and $r = 2f(\theta), \alpha \le \theta \le \beta$, are revolved about the x-axis to generate surfaces. Can anything be said about the relative areas of these surfaces? Give reasons for your answer.

Centroids of Fan-Shaped Regions

Since the centroid of a triangle is located on each median, two-thirds of the way from the vertex to the opposite base, the lever arm for the moment about the x-axis of the thin triangular region in the accompanying figure is about $(2/3)r\sin\theta$. Similarly, the lever arm for the moment of the triangular region about the y-axis is about $(2/3)r\cos\theta$. These approximations improve as $\Delta\theta \to 0$ and lead to the following formulas for the coordinates of the centroid of region AOB:

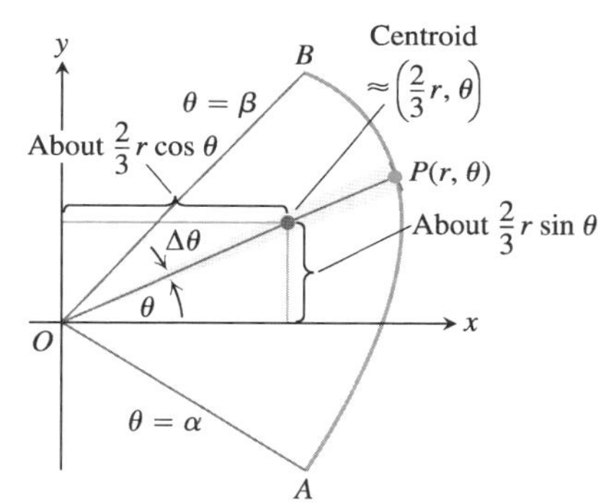

$$\bar{x} = \frac{\int \frac{2}{3}r\cos\theta\cdot\frac{1}{2}r^2\,d\theta}{\int \frac{1}{2}r^2\,d\theta} = \frac{\frac{2}{3}\int r^3\cos\theta\,d\theta}{\int r^2\,d\theta},$$

$$\bar{y} = \frac{\int \frac{2}{3}r\sin\theta\cdot\frac{1}{2}r^2\,d\theta}{\int \frac{1}{2}r^2\,d\theta} = \frac{\frac{2}{3}\int r^3\sin\theta\,d\theta}{\int r^2\,d\theta},$$

with limits $\theta = \alpha$ to $\theta = \beta$ on all integrals.

37. Find the centroid of the region enclosed by the cardioid $r = a(1 + \cos\theta)$.

38. Find the centroid of the semicircular region $0 \le r \le a$, $0 \le \theta \le \pi$.

10.8 Conic Sections in Polar Coordinates

Polar coordinates are important in astronomy and astronautical engineering because the ellipses, parabolas, and hyperbolas along which satellites, moons, planets, and comets approximately move can all be described with a single relatively simple coordinate equation. We develop that equation here.

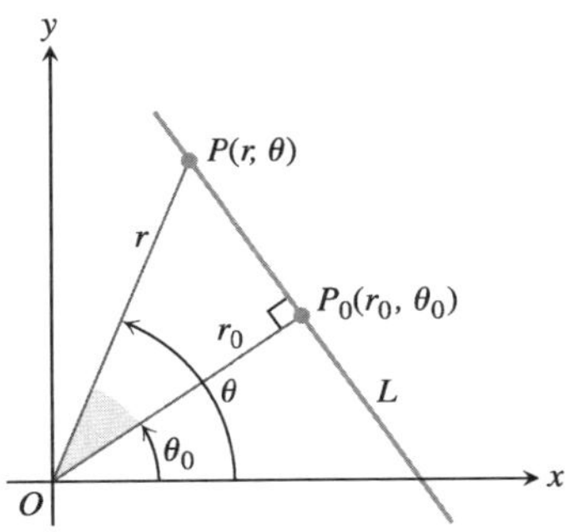

FIGURE 10.56 We can obtain a polar equation for line L by reading the relation $r_0 = r\cos(\theta - \theta_0)$ from the right triangle OP_0P.

Lines

Suppose the perpendicular from the origin to line L meets L at the point $P_0(r_0, \theta_0)$, with $r_0 \geq 0$ (Figure 10.56). Then, if $P(r, \theta)$ is any other point on L, the points P, P_0, and O are the vertices of a right triangle, from which we can read the relation

$$r_0 = r\cos(\theta - \theta_0).$$

The Standard Polar Equation for Lines

If the point $P_0(r_0, \theta_0)$ is the foot of the perpendicular from the origin to the line L, and $r_0 \geq 0$, then an equation for L is

$$r\cos(\theta - \theta_0) = r_0. \tag{1}$$

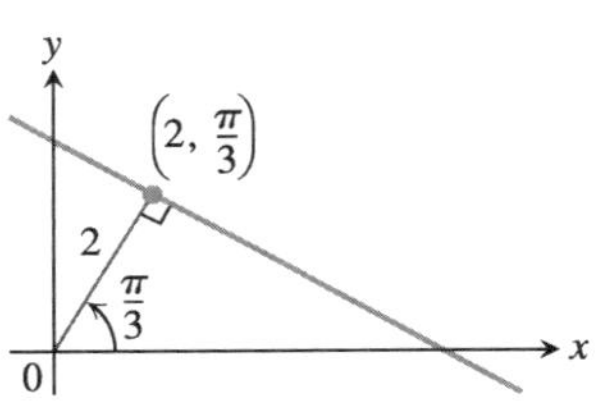

FIGURE 10.57 The standard polar equation of this line converts to the Cartesian equation $x + \sqrt{3}y = 4$ (Example 1).

EXAMPLE 1 Converting a Line's Polar Equation to Cartesian Form

Use the identity $\cos(A - B) = \cos A\cos B + \sin A\sin B$ to find a Cartesian equation for the line in Figure 10.57.

Solution

$$r\cos\left(\theta - \frac{\pi}{3}\right) = 2$$

$$r\left(\cos\theta\cos\frac{\pi}{3} + \sin\theta\sin\frac{\pi}{3}\right) = 2$$

$$\frac{1}{2}r\cos\theta + \frac{\sqrt{3}}{2}r\sin\theta = 2$$

$$\frac{1}{2}x + \frac{\sqrt{3}}{2}y = 2$$

$$x + \sqrt{3}y = 4$$

■

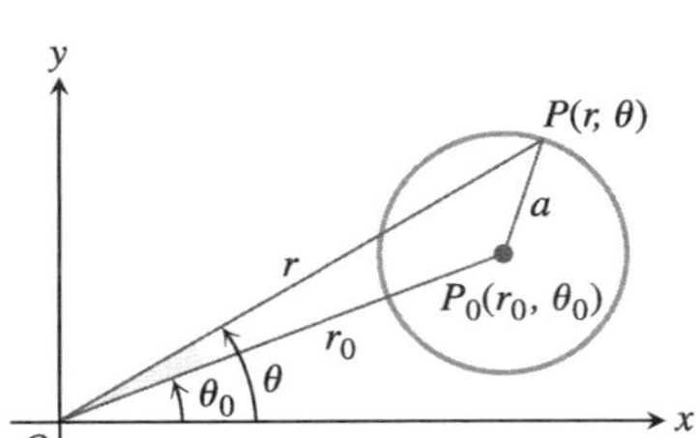

FIGURE 10.58 We can get a polar equation for this circle by applying the Law of Cosines to triangle OP_0P.

Circles

To find a polar equation for the circle of radius a centered at $P_0(r_0, \theta_0)$, we let $P(r, \theta)$ be a point on the circle and apply the Law of Cosines to triangle OP_0P (Figure 10.58). This gives

$$a^2 = r_0^2 + r^2 - 2r_0 r\cos(\theta - \theta_0).$$

If the circle passes through the origin, then $r_0 = a$ and this equation simplifies to

$$a^2 = a^2 + r^2 - 2ar\cos(\theta - \theta_0)$$
$$r^2 = 2ar\cos(\theta - \theta_0)$$
$$r = 2a\cos(\theta - \theta_0).$$

If the circle's center lies on the positive x-axis, $\theta_0 = 0$ and we get the further simplification

$$r = 2a\cos\theta$$

(see Figure 10.59a).

If the center lies on the positive y-axis, $\theta = \pi/2$, $\cos(\theta - \pi/2) = \sin\theta$, and the equation $r = 2a\cos(\theta - \theta_0)$ becomes

$$r = 2a\sin\theta$$

(see Figure 10.59b).

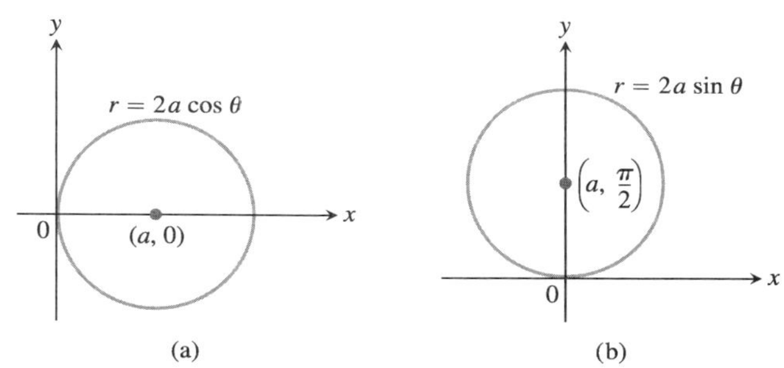

FIGURE 10.59 Polar equation of a circle of radius a through the origin with center on (a) the positive x-axis, and (b) the positive y-axis.

Equations for circles through the origin centered on the negative x- and y-axes can be obtained by replacing r with $-r$ in the above equations (Figure 10.60).

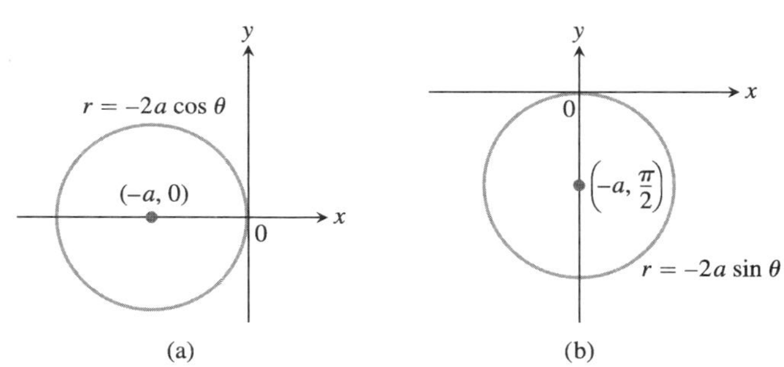

FIGURE 10.60 Polar equation of a circle of radius a through the origin with center on (a) the negative x-axis, and (b) the negative y-axis.

EXAMPLE 2 Circles Through the Origin

Radius	Center (polar coordinates)	Polar equation
3	$(3, 0)$	$r = 6\cos\theta$
2	$(2, \pi/2)$	$r = 4\sin\theta$
1/2	$(-1/2, 0)$	$r = -\cos\theta$
1	$(-1, \pi/2)$	$r = -2\sin\theta$

■

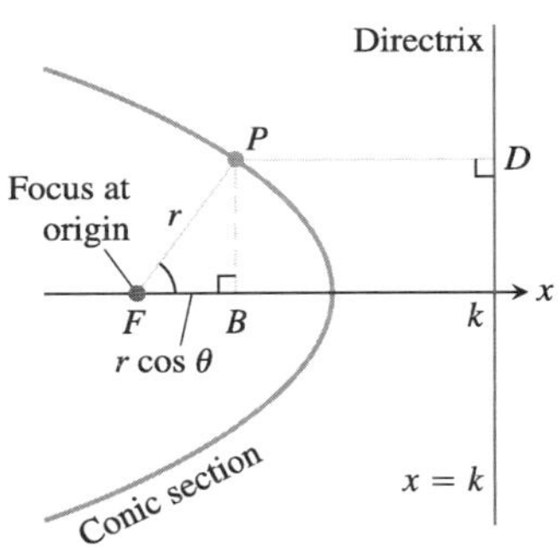

FIGURE 10.61 If a conic section is put in the position with its focus placed at the origin and a directrix perpendicular to the initial ray and right of the origin, we can find its polar equation from the conic's focus–directrix equation.

Ellipses, Parabolas, and Hyperbolas

To find polar equations for ellipses, parabolas, and hyperbolas, we place one focus at the origin and the corresponding directrix to the right of the origin along the vertical line $x = k$ (Figure 10.61). This makes

$$PF = r$$

and

$$PD = k - FB = k - r\cos\theta.$$

The conic's focus–directrix equation $PF = e \cdot PD$ then becomes

$$r = e(k - r\cos\theta),$$

which can be solved for r to obtain

Polar Equation for a Conic with Eccentricity e

$$r = \frac{ke}{1 + e\cos\theta}, \tag{2}$$

where $x = k > 0$ is the vertical directrix.

This equation represents an ellipse if $0 < e < 1$, a parabola if $e = 1$, and a hyperbola if $e > 1$. That is, ellipses, parabolas, and hyperbolas all have the same basic equation expressed in terms of eccentricity and location of the directrix.

EXAMPLE 3 Polar Equations of Some Conics

$e = \frac{1}{2}$: ellipse $r = \dfrac{k}{2 + \cos\theta}$

$e = 1$: parabola $r = \dfrac{k}{1 + \cos\theta}$

$e = 2$: hyperbola $r = \dfrac{2k}{1 + 2\cos\theta}$

■

You may see variations of Equation (2) from time to time, depending on the location of the directrix. If the directrix is the line $x = -k$ to the left of the origin (the origin is still a focus), we replace Equation (2) by

$$r = \frac{ke}{1 - e\cos\theta}.$$

The denominator now has a $(-)$ instead of a $(+)$. If the directrix is either of the lines $y = k$ or $y = -k$, the equations have sines in them instead of cosines, as shown in Figure 10.62.

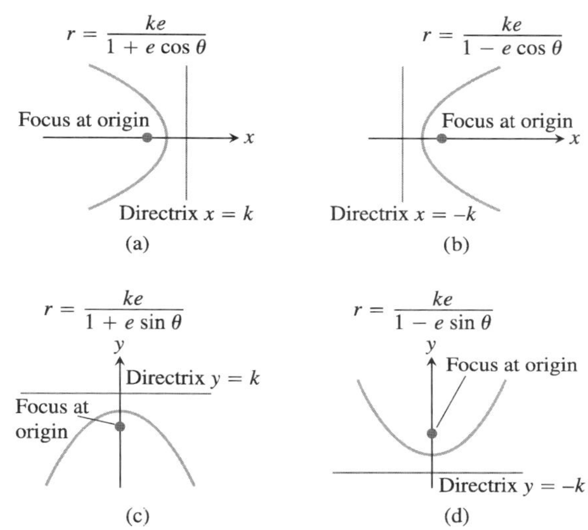

FIGURE 10.62 Equations for conic sections with eccentricity $e > 0$, but different locations of the directrix. The graphs here show a parabola, so $e = 1$.

EXAMPLE 4 Polar Equation of a Hyperbola

Find an equation for the hyperbola with eccentricity $3/2$ and directrix $x = 2$.

Solution We use Equation (2) with $k = 2$ and $e = 3/2$:

$$r = \frac{2(3/2)}{1 + (3/2)\cos\theta} \quad \text{or} \quad r = \frac{6}{2 + 3\cos\theta}.$$ ■

EXAMPLE 5 Finding a Directrix

Find the directrix of the parabola

$$r = \frac{25}{10 + 10\cos\theta}.$$

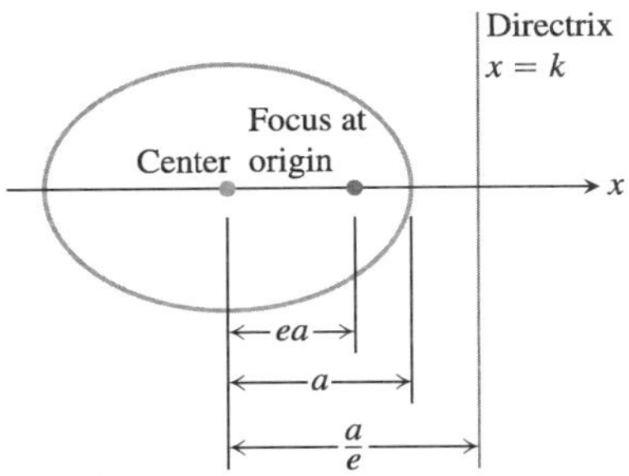

FIGURE 10.63 In an ellipse with semimajor axis a, the focus–directrix distance is $k = (a/e) - ea$, so $ke = a(1 - e^2)$.

Solution We divide the numerator and denominator by 10 to put the equation in standard form:

$$r = \frac{5/2}{1 + \cos\theta}.$$

This is the equation

$$r = \frac{ke}{1 + e\cos\theta}$$

with $k = 5/2$ and $e = 1$. The equation of the directrix is $x = 5/2$. ■

From the ellipse diagram in Figure 10.63, we see that k is related to the eccentricity e and the semimajor axis a by the equation

$$k = \frac{a}{e} - ea.$$

From this, we find that $ke = a(1 - e^2)$. Replacing ke in Equation (2) by $a(1 - e^2)$ gives the standard polar equation for an ellipse.

Polar Equation for the Ellipse with Eccentricity e and Semimajor Axis a

$$r = \frac{a(1 - e^2)}{1 + e\cos\theta} \tag{3}$$

Notice that when $e = 0$, Equation (3) becomes $r = a$, which represents a circle.

Equation (3) is the starting point for calculating planetary orbits.

EXAMPLE 6 The Planet Pluto's Orbit

Find a polar equation for an ellipse with semimajor axis 39.44 AU (astronomical units) and eccentricity 0.25. This is the approximate size of Pluto's orbit around the sun.

Solution We use Equation (3) with $a = 39.44$ and $e = 0.25$ to find

$$r = \frac{39.44(1 - (0.25)^2)}{1 + 0.25\cos\theta} = \frac{147.9}{4 + \cos\theta}.$$

At its point of closest approach (perihelion) where $\theta = 0$, Pluto is

$$r = \frac{147.9}{4 + 1} = 29.58 \text{ AU}$$

from the sun. At its most distant point (aphelion) where $\theta = \pi$, Pluto is

$$r = \frac{147.9}{4 - 1} = 49.3 \text{ AU}$$

from the sun (Figure 10.64). ■

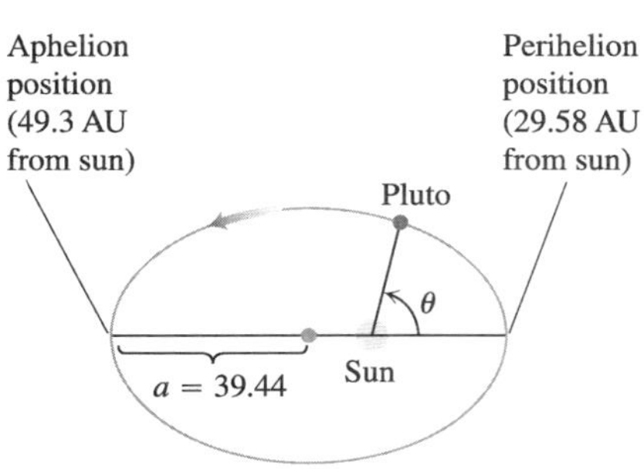

FIGURE 10.64 The orbit of Pluto (Example 6).

EXERCISES 10.8

Lines

Find polar and Cartesian equations for the lines in Exercises 1–4.

1.

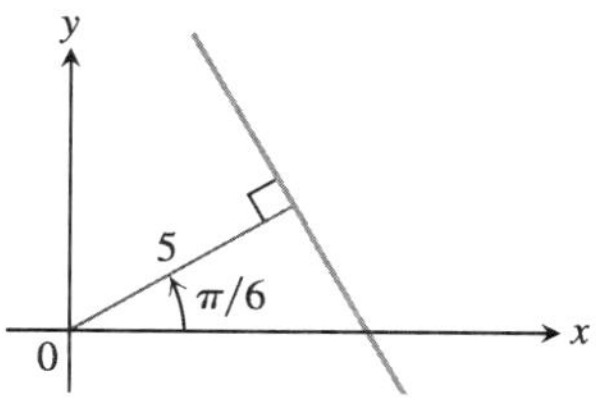

2.

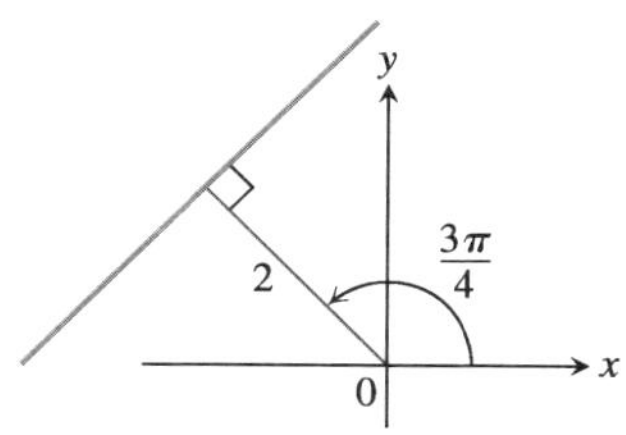

3.

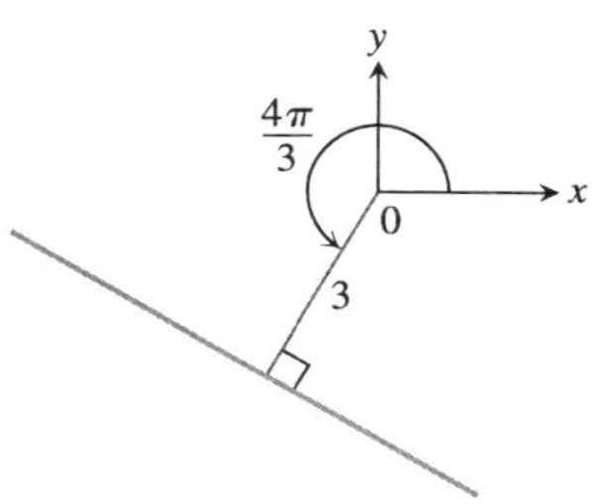

4.

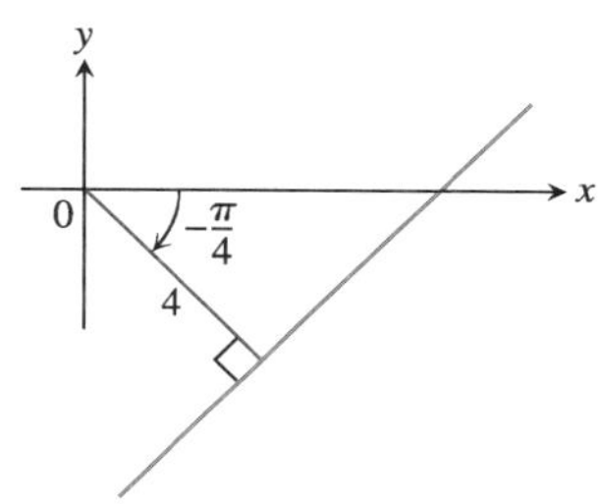

Sketch the lines in Exercises 5–8 and find Cartesian equations for them.

5. $r\cos\left(\theta-\frac{\pi}{4}\right)=\sqrt{2}$ **6.** $r\cos\left(\theta+\frac{3\pi}{4}\right)=1$

7. $r\cos\left(\theta-\frac{2\pi}{3}\right)=3$ **8.** $r\cos\left(\theta+\frac{\pi}{3}\right)=2$

Find a polar equation in the form $r\cos(\theta-\theta_0)=r_0$ for each of the lines in Exercises 9–12.

9. $\sqrt{2}x+\sqrt{2}y=6$ **10.** $\sqrt{3}x-y=1$

11. $y=-5$ **12.** $x=-4$

Circles

Find polar equations for the circles in Exercises 13–16.

13.

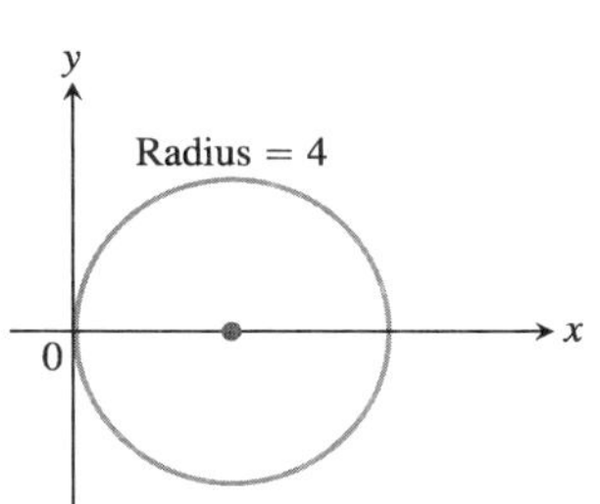

14.

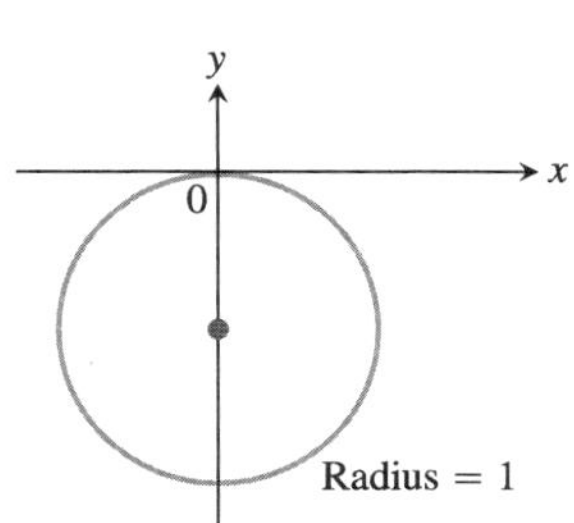

15.

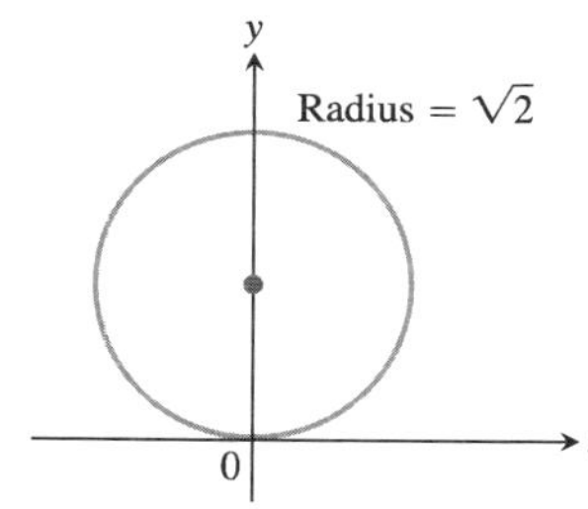

16.

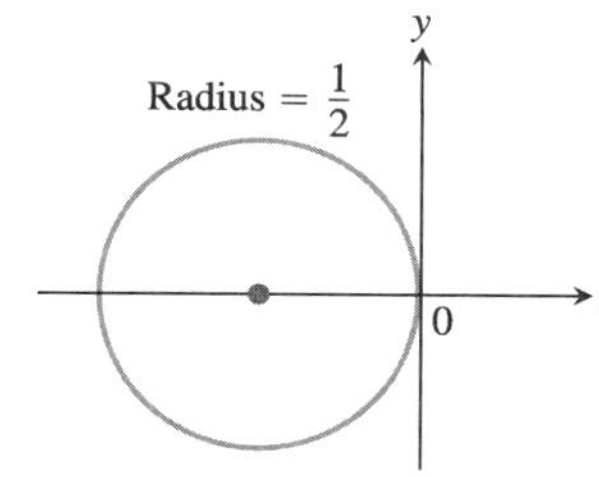

Sketch the circles in Exercises 17–20. Give polar coordinates for their centers and identify their radii.

17. $r=4\cos\theta$ **18.** $r=6\sin\theta$

19. $r=-2\cos\theta$ **20.** $r=-8\sin\theta$

Find polar equations for the circles in Exercises 21–28. Sketch each circle in the coordinate plane and label it with both its Cartesian and polar equations.

21. $(x-6)^2+y^2=36$ **22.** $(x+2)^2+y^2=4$

23. $x^2+(y-5)^2=25$ **24.** $x^2+(y+7)^2=49$

25. $x^2+2x+y^2=0$ **26.** $x^2-16x+y^2=0$

27. $x^2+y^2+y=0$ **28.** $x^2+y^2-\frac{4}{3}y=0$

Conic Sections from Eccentricities and Directrices

Exercises 29–36 give the eccentricities of conic sections with one focus at the origin, along with the directrix corresponding to that focus. Find a polar equation for each conic section.

29. $e=1,\quad x=2$ **30.** $e=1,\quad y=2$

31. $e=5,\quad y=-6$ **32.** $e=2,\quad x=4$

33. $e=1/2,\quad x=1$ **34.** $e=1/4,\quad x=-2$

35. $e=1/5,\quad y=-10$ **36.** $e=1/3,\quad y=6$

Parabolas and Ellipses

Sketch the parabolas and ellipses in Exercises 37–44. Include the directrix that corresponds to the focus at the origin. Label the vertices with appropriate polar coordinates. Label the centers of the ellipses as well.

37. $r=\dfrac{1}{1+\cos\theta}$ **38.** $r=\dfrac{6}{2+\cos\theta}$

39. $r=\dfrac{25}{10-5\cos\theta}$ **40.** $r=\dfrac{4}{2-2\cos\theta}$

41. $r=\dfrac{400}{16+8\sin\theta}$ **42.** $r=\dfrac{12}{3+3\sin\theta}$

43. $r=\dfrac{8}{2-2\sin\theta}$ **44.** $r=\dfrac{4}{2-\sin\theta}$

Graphing Inequalities

Sketch the regions defined by the inequalities in Exercises 45 and 46.

45. $0 \le r \le 2\cos\theta$ **46.** $-3\cos\theta \le r \le 0$

T Grapher Explorations

Graph the lines and conic sections in Exercises 47–56.

47. $r = 3\sec(\theta - \pi/3)$ **48.** $r = 4\sec(\theta + \pi/6)$

49. $r = 4\sin\theta$ **50.** $r = -2\cos\theta$

51. $r = 8/(4 + \cos\theta)$ **52.** $r = 8/(4 + \sin\theta)$

53. $r = 1/(1 - \sin\theta)$ **54.** $r = 1/(1 + \cos\theta)$

55. $r = 1/(1 + 2\sin\theta)$ **56.** $r = 1/(1 + 2\cos\theta)$

Theory and Examples

57. Perihelion and aphelion A planet travels about its sun in an ellipse whose semimajor axis has length a. (See accompanying figure.)

a. Show that $r = a(1 - e)$ when the planet is closest to the sun and that $r = a(1 + e)$ when the planet is farthest from the sun.

b. Use the data in the table in Exercise 58 to find how close each planet in our solar system comes to the sun and how far away each planet gets from the sun.

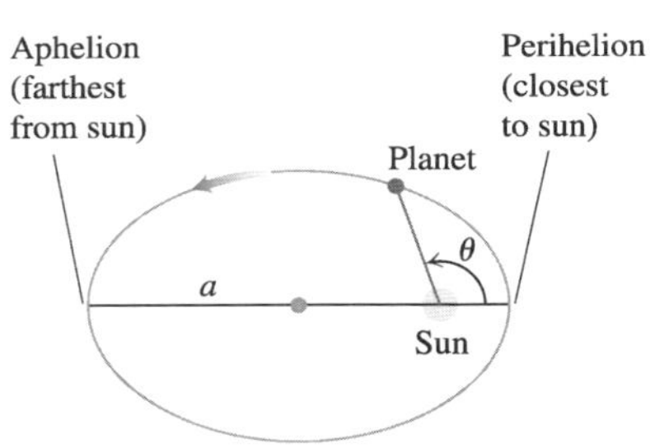

58. Planetary orbits In Example 6, we found a polar equation for the orbit of Pluto. Use the data in the table below to find polar equations for the orbits of the other planets.

Planet	Semimajor axis (astronomical units)	Eccentricity
Mercury	0.3871	0.2056
Venus	0.7233	0.0068
Earth	1.000	0.0167
Mars	1.524	0.0934
Jupiter	5.203	0.0484
Saturn	9.539	0.0543
Uranus	19.18	0.0460
Neptune	30.06	0.0082
Pluto	39.44	0.2481

59. a. Find Cartesian equations for the curves $r = 4\sin\theta$ and $r = \sqrt{3}\sec\theta$.

b. Sketch the curves together and label their points of intersection in both Cartesian and polar coordinates.

60. Repeat Exercise 59 for $r = 8\cos\theta$ and $r = 2\sec\theta$.

61. Find a polar equation for the parabola with focus (0, 0) and directrix $r\cos\theta = 4$.

62. Find a polar equation for the parabola with focus (0, 0) and directrix $r\cos(\theta - \pi/2) = 2$.

63. a. The space engineer's formula for eccentricity The space engineer's formula for the eccentricity of an elliptical orbit is

$$e = \frac{r_{\max} - r_{\min}}{r_{\max} + r_{\min}},$$

where r is the distance from the space vehicle to the attracting focus of the ellipse along which it travels. Why does the formula work?

b. Drawing ellipses with string You have a string with a knot in each end that can be pinned to a drawing board. The string is 10 in. long from the center of one knot to the center of the other. How far apart should the pins be to use the method illustrated in Figure 10.5 (Section 10.1) to draw an ellipse of eccentricity 0.2? The resulting ellipse would resemble the orbit of Mercury.

64. Halley's comet (See Section 10.2, Example 1.)

a. Write an equation for the orbit of Halley's comet in a coordinate system in which the sun lies at the origin and the other focus lies on the negative x-axis, scaled in astronomical units.

b. How close does the comet come to the sun in astronomical units? In kilometers?

c. What is the farthest the comet gets from the sun in astronomical units? In kilometers?

In Exercises 65–68, find a polar equation for the given curve. In each case, sketch a typical curve.

65. $x^2 + y^2 - 2ay = 0$ **66.** $y^2 = 4ax + 4a^2$

67. $x\cos\alpha + y\sin\alpha = p$ (α, p constant)

68. $(x^2 + y^2)^2 + 2ax(x^2 + y^2) - a^2y^2 = 0$

COMPUTER EXPLORATIONS

69. Use a CAS to plot the polar equation

$$r = \frac{ke}{1 + e\cos\theta}$$

for various values of k and e, $-\pi \le \theta \le \pi$. Answer the following questions.

a. Take $k = -2$. Describe what happens to the plots as you take e to be $3/4$, 1, and $5/4$. Repeat for $k = 2$.

b. Take $k = -1$. Describe what happens to the plots as you take e to be $7/6, 5/4, 4/3, 3/2, 2, 3, 5, 10$, and 20. Repeat for $e = 1/2, 1/3, 1/4, 1/10$, and $1/20$.

c. Now keep $e > 0$ fixed and describe what happens as you take k to be $-1, -2, -3, -4$, and -5. Be sure to look at graphs for parabolas, ellipses, and hyperbolas.

70. Use a CAS to plot the polar ellipse

$$r = \frac{a(1 - e^2)}{1 + e\cos\theta}$$

for various values of $a > 0$ and $0 < e < 1$, $-\pi \le \theta \le \pi$.

a. Take $e = 9/10$. Describe what happens to the plots as you let a equal $1, 3/2, 2, 3, 5$, and 10. Repeat with $e = 1/4$.

b. Take $a = 2$. Describe what happens as you take e to be $9/10, 8/10, 7/10, \ldots, 1/10, 1/20$, and $1/50$.

Chapter 10 Questions to Guide Your Review

1. What is a parabola? What are the Cartesian equations for parabolas whose vertices lie at the origin and whose foci lie on the coordinate axes? How can you find the focus and directrix of such a parabola from its equation?
2. What is an ellipse? What are the Cartesian equations for ellipses centered at the origin with foci on one of the coordinate axes? How can you find the foci, vertices, and directrices of such an ellipse from its equation?
3. What is a hyperbola? What are the Cartesian equations for hyperbolas centered at the origin with foci on one of the coordinate axes? How can you find the foci, vertices, and directrices of such an ellipse from its equation?
4. What is the eccentricity of a conic section? How can you classify conic sections by eccentricity? How are an ellipse's shape and eccentricity related?
5. Explain the equation $PF = e \cdot PD$.
6. What is a quadratic curve in the xy-plane? Give examples of degenerate and nondegenerate quadratic curves.
7. How can you find a Cartesian coordinate system in which the new equation for a conic section in the plane has no xy-term? Give an example.
8. How can you tell what kind of graph to expect from a quadratic equation in x and y? Give examples.
9. What are some typical parametrizations for conic sections?
10. What is a cycloid? What are typical parametric equations for cycloids? What physical properties account for the importance of cycloids?
11. What are polar coordinates? What equations relate polar coordinates to Cartesian coordinates? Why might you want to change from one coordinate system to the other?
12. What consequence does the lack of uniqueness of polar coordinates have for graphing? Give an example.
13. How do you graph equations in polar coordinates? Include in your discussion symmetry, slope, behavior at the origin, and the use of Cartesian graphs. Give examples.
14. How do you find the area of a region $0 \le r_1(\theta) \le r \le r_2(\theta)$, $\alpha \le \theta \le \beta$, in the polar coordinate plane? Give examples.
15. Under what conditions can you find the length of a curve $r = f(\theta)$, $\alpha \le \theta \le \beta$, in the polar coordinate plane? Give an example of a typical calculation.
16. Under what conditions can you find the area of the surface generated by revolving a curve $r = f(\theta)$, $\alpha \le \theta \le \beta$, about the x-axis? The y-axis? Give examples of typical calculations.
17. What are the standard equations for lines and conic sections in polar coordinates? Give examples.

Chapter 10 Practice Exercises

Graphing Conic Sections

Sketch the parabolas in Exercises 1–4. Include the focus and directrix in each sketch.

1. $x^2 = -4y$　　**2.** $x^2 = 2y$

3. $y^2 = 3x$　　**4.** $y^2 = -(8/3)x$

Find the eccentricities of the ellipses and hyperbolas in Exercises 5–8. Sketch each conic section. Include the foci, vertices, and asymptotes (as appropriate) in your sketch.

5. $16x^2 + 7y^2 = 112$　　**6.** $x^2 + 2y^2 = 4$

7. $3x^2 - y^2 = 3$　　**8.** $5y^2 - 4x^2 = 20$

Shifting Conic Sections

Exercises 9–14 give equations for conic sections and tell how many units up or down and to the right or left each curve is to be shifted. Find an equation for the new conic section and find the new foci, vertices, centers, and asymptotes, as appropriate. If the curve is a parabola, find the new directrix as well.

9. $x^2 = -12y$, right 2, up 3

10. $y^2 = 10x$, left 1/2, down 1

11. $\frac{x^2}{9} + \frac{y^2}{25} = 1$, left 3, down 5

12. $\frac{x^2}{169} + \frac{y^2}{144} = 1$, right 5, up 12

13. $\frac{y^2}{8} - \frac{x^2}{2} = 1$, right 2, up $2\sqrt{2}$

14. $\frac{x^2}{36} - \frac{y^2}{64} = 1$, left 10, down 3

Identifying Conic Sections

Identify the conic sections in Exercises 15–22 and find their foci, vertices, centers, and asymptotes (as appropriate). If the curve is a parabola, find its directrix as well.

15. $x^2 - 4x - 4y^2 = 0$

16. $4x^2 - y^2 + 4y = 8$

17. $y^2 - 2y + 16x = -49$

18. $x^2 - 2x + 8y = -17$

19. $9x^2 + 16y^2 + 54x - 64y = -1$

20. $25x^2 + 9y^2 - 100x + 54y = 44$

21. $x^2 + y^2 - 2x - 2y = 0$

22. $x^2 + y^2 + 4x + 2y = 1$

Using the Discriminant

What conic sections or degenerate cases do the equations in Exercises 23–28 represent? Give a reason for your answer in each case.

23. $x^2 + xy + y^2 + x + y + 1 = 0$

24. $x^2 + 4xy + 4y^2 + x + y + 1 = 0$

25. $x^2 + 3xy + 2y^2 + x + y + 1 = 0$

26. $x^2 + 2xy - 2y^2 + x + y + 1 = 0$

27. $x^2 - 2xy + y^2 = 0$

28. $x^2 - 3xy + 4y^2 = 0$

Rotating Conic Sections

Identify the conic sections in Exercises 29–32. Then rotate the coordinate axes to find a new equation for the conic section that has no cross product term. (The new equations will vary with the size and direction of the rotations used.)

29. $2x^2 + xy + 2y^2 - 15 = 0$

30. $3x^2 + 2xy + 3y^2 = 19$

31. $x^2 + 2\sqrt{3}\,xy - y^2 + 4 = 0$

32. $x^2 - 3xy + y^2 = 5$

Identifying Parametric Equations in the Plane

Exercises 33–36 give parametric equations and parameter intervals for the motion of a particle in the xy-plane. Identify the particle's path by finding a Cartesian equation for it. Graph the Cartesian equation and indicate the direction of motion and the portion traced by the particle.

33. $x = (1/2)\tan t, \quad y = (1/2)\sec t; \quad -\pi/2 < t < \pi/2$

34. $x = -2\cos t, \quad y = 2\sin t; \quad 0 \le t \le \pi$

35. $x = -\cos t, \quad y = \cos^2 t; \quad 0 \le t \le \pi$

36. $x = 4\cos t, \quad y = 9\sin t; \quad 0 \le t \le 2\pi$

Graphs in the Polar Plane

Sketch the regions defined by the polar coordinate inequalities in Exercises 37 and 38.

37. $0 \le r \le 6\cos\theta$

38. $-4\sin\theta \le r \le 0$

Match each graph in Exercises 39–46 with the appropriate equation (a)–(l). There are more equations than graphs, so some equations will not be matched.

a. $r = \cos 2\theta$

b. $r\cos\theta = 1$

c. $r = \frac{6}{1 - 2\cos\theta}$

d. $r = \sin 2\theta$

e. $r = \theta$

f. $r^2 = \cos 2\theta$

g. $r = 1 + \cos\theta$

h. $r = 1 - \sin\theta$

i. $r = \frac{2}{1 - \cos\theta}$

j. $r^2 = \sin 2\theta$

k. $r = -\sin\theta$

l. $r = 2\cos\theta + 1$

39. Four-leaved rose

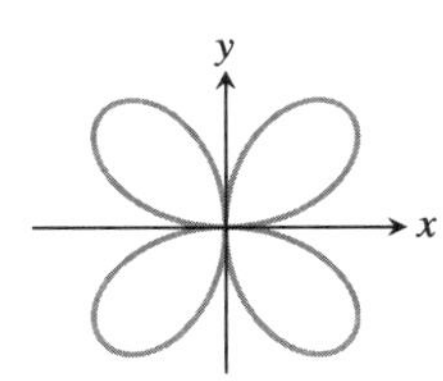

40. Spiral

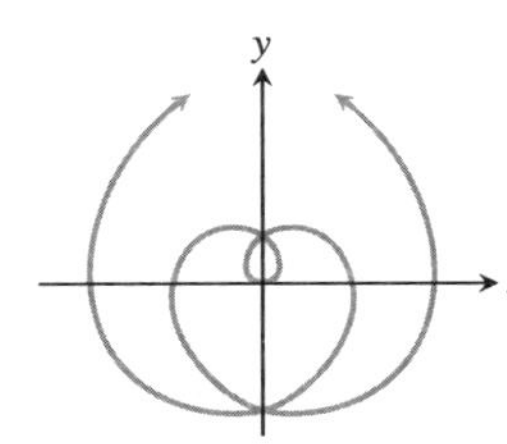

41. Limaçon

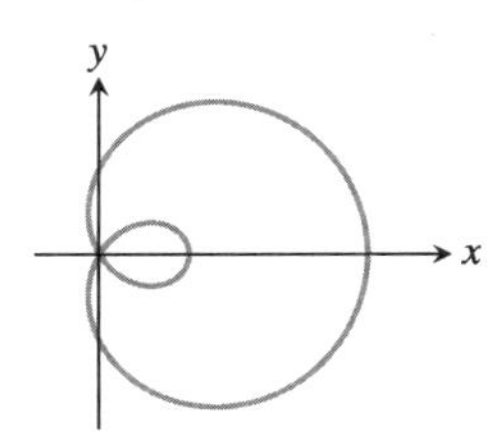

42. Lemniscate

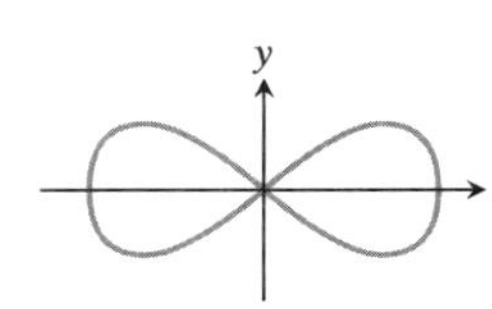

43. Circle

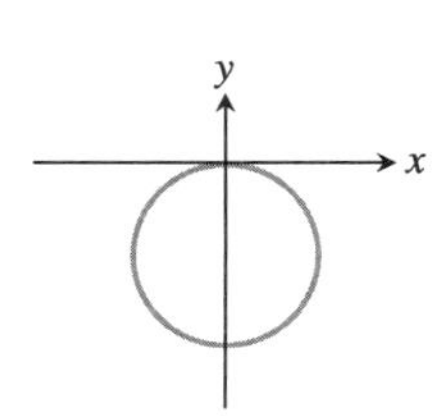

44. Cardioid

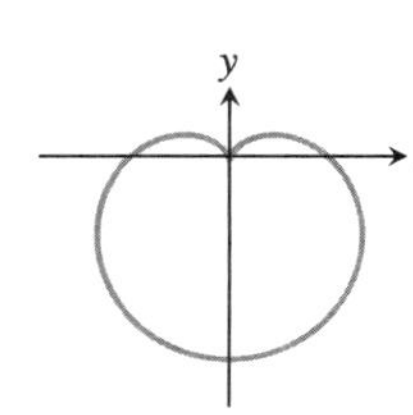

45. Parabola

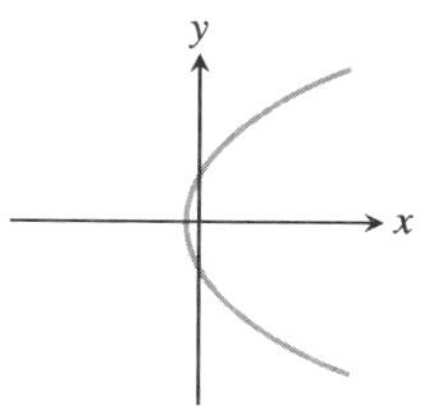

46. Lemniscate

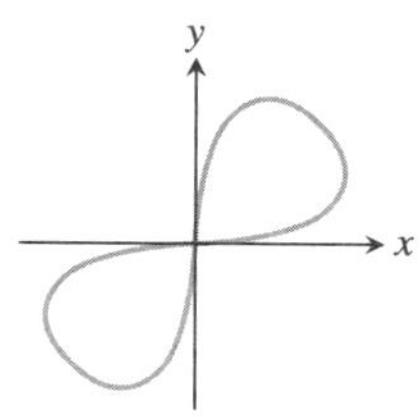

Intersections of Graphs in the Polar Plane

Find the points of intersection of the curves given by the polar coordinate equations in Exercises 47–54.

47. $r = \sin\theta, \quad r = 1 + \sin\theta$ **48.** $r = \cos\theta, \quad r = 1 - \cos\theta$

49. $r = 1 + \cos\theta, \quad r = 1 - \cos\theta$

50. $r = 1 + \sin\theta, \quad r = 1 - \sin\theta$

51. $r = 1 + \sin\theta, \quad r = -1 + \sin\theta$

52. $r = 1 + \cos\theta, \quad r = -1 + \cos\theta$

53. $r = \sec\theta, \quad r = 2\sin\theta$ **54.** $r = -2\csc\theta, \quad r = -4\cos\theta$

Polar to Cartesian Equations

Sketch the lines in Exercises 55–60. Also, find a Cartesian equation for each line.

55. $r\cos\left(\theta + \frac{\pi}{3}\right) = 2\sqrt{3}$ **56.** $r\cos\left(\theta - \frac{3\pi}{4}\right) = \frac{\sqrt{2}}{2}$

57. $r = 2\sec\theta$ **58.** $r = -\sqrt{2}\sec\theta$

59. $r = -(3/2)\csc\theta$ **60.** $r = \left(3\sqrt{3}\right)\csc\theta$

Find Cartesian equations for the circles in Exercises 61–64. Sketch each circle in the coordinate plane and label it with both its Cartesian and polar equations.

61. $r = -4\sin\theta$ **62.** $r = 3\sqrt{3}\sin\theta$

63. $r = 2\sqrt{2}\cos\theta$ **64.** $r = -6\cos\theta$

Cartesian to Polar Equations

Find polar equations for the circles in Exercises 65–68. Sketch each circle in the coordinate plane and label it with both its Cartesian and polar equations.

65. $x^2 + y^2 + 5y = 0$ **66.** $x^2 + y^2 - 2y = 0$

67. $x^2 + y^2 - 3x = 0$ **68.** $x^2 + y^2 + 4x = 0$

Conic Sections in Polar Coordinates

Sketch the conic sections whose polar coordinate equations are given in Exercises 69–72. Give polar coordinates for the vertices and, in the case of ellipses, for the centers as well.

69. $r = \dfrac{2}{1 + \cos\theta}$ **70.** $r = \dfrac{8}{2 + \cos\theta}$

71. $r = \dfrac{6}{1 - 2\cos\theta}$ **72.** $r = \dfrac{12}{3 + \sin\theta}$

Exercises 73–76 give the eccentricities of conic sections with one focus at the origin of the polar coordinate plane, along with the directrix for that focus. Find a polar equation for each conic section.

73. $e = 2, \quad r\cos\theta = 2$ **74.** $e = 1, \quad r\cos\theta = -4$

75. $e = 1/2, \quad r\sin\theta = 2$ **76.** $e = 1/3, \quad r\sin\theta = -6$

Area, Length, and Surface Area in the Polar Plane

Find the areas of the regions in the polar coordinate plane described in Exercises 77–80.

77. Enclosed by the limaçon $r = 2 - \cos\theta$

78. Enclosed by one leaf of the three-leaved rose $r = \sin 3\theta$

79. Inside the "figure eight" $r = 1 + \cos 2\theta$ and outside the circle $r = 1$

80. Inside the cardioid $r = 2(1 + \sin\theta)$ and outside the circle $r = 2\sin\theta$

Find the lengths of the curves given by the polar coordinate equations in Exercises 81–84.

81. $r = -1 + \cos\theta$

82. $r = 2\sin\theta + 2\cos\theta, \quad 0 \le \theta \le \pi/2$

83. $r = 8\sin^3(\theta/3), \quad 0 \le \theta \le \pi/4$

84. $r = \sqrt{1 + \cos 2\theta}, \quad -\pi/2 \le \theta \le \pi/2$

Find the areas of the surfaces generated by revolving the polar coordinate curves in Exercises 85 and 86 about the indicated axes.

85. $r = \sqrt{\cos 2\theta}, \quad 0 \le \theta \le \pi/4, \quad x$-axis

86. $r^2 = \sin 2\theta, \quad y$-axis

Theory and Examples

87. Find the volume of the solid generated by revolving the region enclosed by the ellipse $9x^2 + 4y^2 = 36$ about **(a)** the x-axis, **(b)** the y-axis.

88. The "triangular" region in the first quadrant bounded by the x-axis, the line $x = 4$, and the hyperbola $9x^2 - 4y^2 = 36$ is revolved about the x-axis to generate a solid. Find the volume of the solid.

89. A ripple tank is made by bending a strip of tin around the perimeter of an ellipse for the wall of the tank and soldering a flat bottom onto this. An inch or two of water is put in the tank and you drop a marble into it, right at one focus of the ellipse. Ripples radiate outward through the water, reflect from the strip around the edge of the tank, and a few seconds later a drop of water spurts up at the second focus. Why?

90. LORAN A radio signal was sent simultaneously from towers A and B, located several hundred miles apart on the northern California coast. A ship offshore received the signal from A 1400 microseconds before receiving the signal from B. Assuming that the signals traveled at the rate of 980 ft/microsecond, what can be said about the location of the ship relative to the two towers?

91. On a level plane, at the same instant, you hear the sound of a rifle and that of the bullet hitting the target. What can be said about your location relative to the rifle and target?

92. Archimedes spirals The graph of an equation of the form $r = a\theta$, where a is a nonzero constant, is called an *Archimedes spiral*. Is there anything special about the widths between the successive turns of such a spiral?

93. a. Show that the equations $x = r\cos\theta, y = r\sin\theta$ transform the polar equation

$$r = \frac{k}{1 + e\cos\theta}$$

into the Cartesian equation

$$(1 - e^2)x^2 + y^2 + 2kex - k^2 = 0.$$

b. Then apply the criteria of Section 10.3 to show that

$$\begin{aligned} e = 0 &\Rightarrow \text{circle.} \\ 0 < e < 1 &\Rightarrow \text{ellipse.} \\ e = 1 &\Rightarrow \text{parabola.} \\ e > 1 &\Rightarrow \text{hyperbola.} \end{aligned}$$

94. A satellite orbit A satellite is in an orbit that passes over the North and South Poles of the earth. When it is over the South Pole it is at the highest point of its orbit, 1000 miles above the earth's surface. Above the North Pole it is at the lowest point of its orbit, 300 miles above the earth's surface.

a. Assuming that the orbit is an ellipse with one focus at the center of the earth, find its eccentricity. (Take the diameter of the earth to be 8000 miles.)

b. Using the north–south axis of the earth as the x-axis and the center of the earth as origin, find a polar equation for the orbit.

Chapter 10 Additional and Advanced Exercises

Finding Conic Sections

1. Find an equation for the parabola with focus (4, 0) and directrix $x = 3$. Sketch the parabola together with its vertex, focus, and directrix.

2. Find the vertex, focus, and directrix of the parabola

$$x^2 - 6x - 12y + 9 = 0.$$

3. Find an equation for the curve traced by the point $P(x, y)$ if the distance from P to the vertex of the parabola $x^2 = 4y$ is twice the distance from P to the focus. Identify the curve.

4. A line segment of length $a + b$ runs from the x-axis to the y-axis. The point P on the segment lies a units from one end and b units from the other end. Show that P traces an ellipse as the ends of the segment slide along the axes.

5. The vertices of an ellipse of eccentricity 0.5 lie at the points $(0, \pm 2)$. Where do the foci lie?

6. Find an equation for the ellipse of eccentricity $2/3$ that has the line $x = 2$ as a directrix and the point (4, 0) as the corresponding focus.

7. One focus of a hyperbola lies at the point $(0, -7)$ and the corresponding directrix is the line $y = -1$. Find an equation for the hyperbola if its eccentricity is **(a)** 2, **(b)** 5.

8. Find an equation for the hyperbola with foci $(0, -2)$ and $(0, 2)$ that passes through the point (12, 7).

9. a. Show that the line

$$b^2xx_1 + a^2yy_1 - a^2b^2 = 0$$

is tangent to the ellipse $b^2x^2 + a^2y^2 - a^2b^2 = 0$ at the point (x_1, y_1) on the ellipse.

b. Show that the line

$$b^2xx_1 - a^2yy_1 - a^2b^2 = 0$$

is tangent to the hyperbola $b^2x^2 - a^2y^2 - a^2b^2 = 0$ at the point (x_1, y_1) on the hyperbola.

10. Show that the tangent to the conic section

$$Ax^2 + Bxy + Cy^2 + Dx + Ey + F = 0$$

at a point (x_1, y_1) on it has an equation that may be written in the form

$$Axx_1 + B\left(\frac{x_1y + xy_1}{2}\right) + Cyy_1 + D\left(\frac{x + x_1}{2}\right) + E\left(\frac{y + y_1}{2}\right) + F = 0.$$

Equations and Inequalities

What points in the xy-plane satisfy the equations and inequalities in Exercises 11–18? Draw a figure for each exercise.

11. $(x^2 - y^2 - 1)(x^2 + y^2 - 25)(x^2 + 4y^2 - 4) = 0$

12. $(x + y)(x^2 + y^2 - 1) = 0$

13. $(x^2/9) + (y^2/16) \le 1$

14. $(x^2/9) - (y^2/16) \le 1$

15. $(9x^2 + 4y^2 - 36)(4x^2 + 9y^2 - 16) \le 0$

16. $(9x^2 + 4y^2 - 36)(4x^2 + 9y^2 - 16) > 0$

17. $x^4 - (y^2 - 9)^2 = 0$

18. $x^2 + xy + y^2 < 3$

Parametric Equations and Cycloids

19. Epicycloids When a circle rolls externally along the circumference of a second, fixed circle, any point P on the circumference of the rolling circle describes an *epicycloid*, as shown here. Let the fixed circle have its center at the origin O and have radius a.

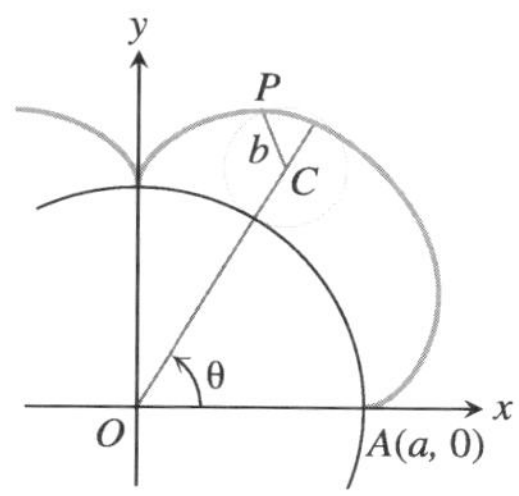

Let the radius of the rolling circle be b and let the initial position of the tracing point P be $A(a, 0)$. Find parametric equations for the epicycloid, using as the parameter the angle θ from the positive x-axis to the line through the circles' centers.

20. a. Find the centroid of the region enclosed by the x-axis and the cycloid arch

$$x = a(t - \sin t), \quad y = a(1 - \cos t); \quad 0 \le t \le 2\pi.$$

b. Find the first moments about the coordinate axes of the curve

$$x = (2/3)t^{3/2}, \quad y = 2\sqrt{t}; \quad 0 \le t \le \sqrt{3}.$$

Polar Coordinates

21. a. Find an equation in polar coordinates for the curve

$$x = e^{2t}\cos t, \quad y = e^{2t}\sin t; \quad -\infty < t < \infty.$$

b. Find the length of the curve from $t = 0$ to $t = 2\pi$.

22. Find the length of the curve $r = 2\sin^3(\theta/3)$, $0 \le \theta \le 3\pi$, in the polar coordinate plane.

23. Find the area of the surface generated by revolving the first-quadrant portion of the cardioid $r = 1 + \cos\theta$ about the x-axis. (*Hint*: Use the identities $1 + \cos\theta = 2\cos^2(\theta/2)$ and $\sin\theta = 2\sin(\theta/2)\cos(\theta/2)$ to simplify the integral.)

24. Sketch the regions enclosed by the curves $r = 2a\cos^2(\theta/2)$ and $r = 2a\sin^2(\theta/2)$, $a > 0$, in the polar coordinate plane and find the area of the portion of the plane they have in common.

Exercises 25–28 give the eccentricities of conic sections with one focus at the origin of the polar coordinate plane, along with the directrix for that focus. Find a polar equation for each conic section.

25. $e = 2, \quad r\cos\theta = 2$

26. $e = 1, \quad r\cos\theta = -4$

27. $e = 1/2, \quad r\sin\theta = 2$

28. $e = 1/3, \quad r\sin\theta = -6$

Theory and Examples

29. A rope with a ring in one end is looped over two pegs in a horizontal line. The free end, after being passed through the ring, has a weight suspended from it to make the rope hang taut. If the rope slips freely over the pegs and through the ring, the weight will descend as far as possible. Assume that the length of the rope is at least four times as great as the distance between the pegs and that the configuration of the rope is symmetric with respect to the line of the vertical part of the rope.

a. Find the angle A formed at the bottom of the loop in the accompanying figure.

b. Show that for each fixed position of the ring on the rope, the possible locations of the ring in space lie on an ellipse with foci at the pegs.

c. Justify the original symmetry assumption by combining the result in part (b) with the assumption that the rope and weight will take a rest position of minimal potential energy.

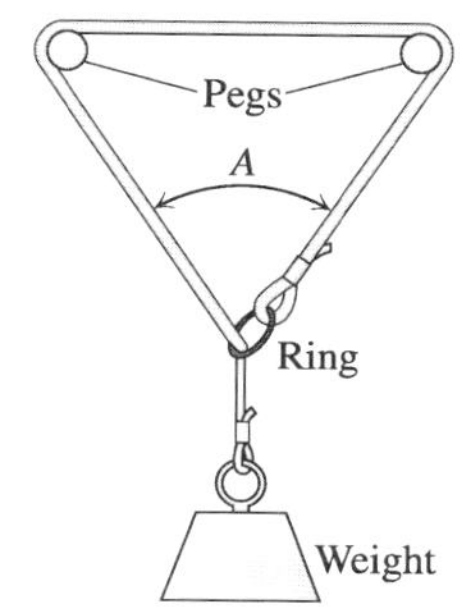

30. Two radar stations lie 20 km apart along an east–west line. A low-flying plane traveling from west to east is known to have a speed of v_0 km/sec. At $t = 0$ a signal is sent from the station at $(-10, 0)$, bounces off the plane, and is received at $(10, 0)$ $30/c$ seconds later (c is the velocity of the signal). When $t = 10/v_0$, another signal is sent out from the station at $(-10, 0)$, reflects off the plane, and is once again received $30/c$ seconds later by the other station. Find the position of the plane when it reflects the second signal under the assumption that v_0 is much less than c.

31. A comet moves in a parabolic orbit with the sun at the focus. When the comet is 4×10^7 miles from the sun, the line from the comet to the sun makes a 60° angle with the orbit's axis, as shown here. How close will the comet come to the sun?

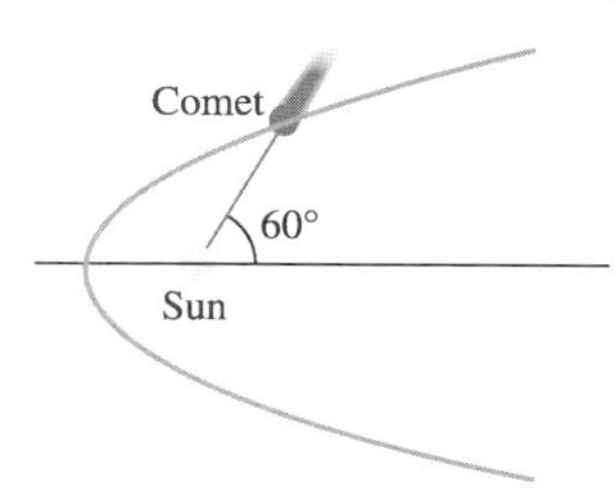

32. Find the points on the parabola $x = 2t, y = t^2, -\infty < t < \infty$, closest to the point $(0, 3)$.

33. Find the eccentricity of the ellipse $x^2 + xy + y^2 = 1$ to the nearest hundredth.

34. Find the eccentricity of the hyperbola $xy = 1$.

35. Is the curve $\sqrt{x} + \sqrt{y} = 1$ part of a conic section? If so, what kind of conic section? If not, why not?

36. Show that the curve $2xy - \sqrt{2}\,y + 2 = 0$ is a hyperbola. Find the hyperbola's center, vertices, foci, axes, and asymptotes.

37. Find a polar coordinate equation for

a. the parabola with focus at the origin and vertex at $(a, \pi/4)$;

b. the ellipse with foci at the origin and (2, 0) and one vertex at (4, 0);

c. the hyperbola with one focus at the origin, center at $(2, \pi/2)$, and a vertex at $(1, \pi/2)$.

38. Any line through the origin will intersect the ellipse $r = 3/(2 + \cos\theta)$ in two points P_1 and P_2. Let d_1 be the distance between P_1 and the origin and let d_2 be the distance between P_2 and the origin. Compute $(1/d_1) + (1/d_2)$.

39. Generating a cardioid with circles Cardioids are special epicycloids (Exercise 18). Show that if you roll a circle of radius a about another circle of radius a in the polar coordinate plane, as in the accompanying figure, the original point of contact P will trace a cardioid. (*Hint:* Start by showing that angles OBC and PAD both have measure θ.)

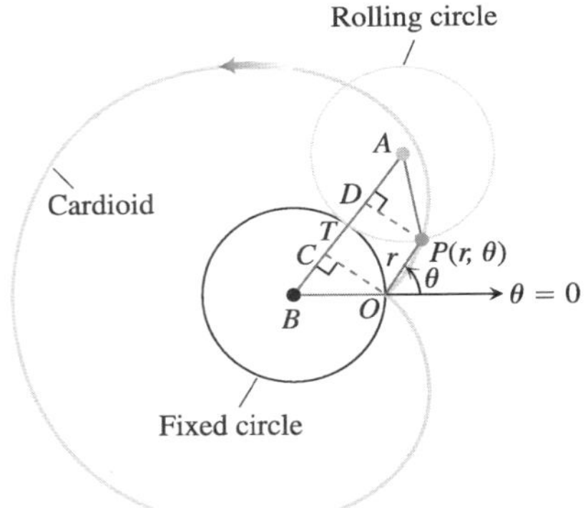

40. A bifold closet door A bifold closet door consists of two 1-ft-wide panels, hinged at point P. The outside bottom corner of one panel rests on a pivot at O (see the accompanying figure). The outside bottom corner of the other panel, denoted by Q, slides along a straight track, shown in the figure as a portion of the x-axis. Assume that as Q moves back and forth, the bottom of the door rubs against a thick carpet. What shape will the door sweep out on the surface of the carpet?

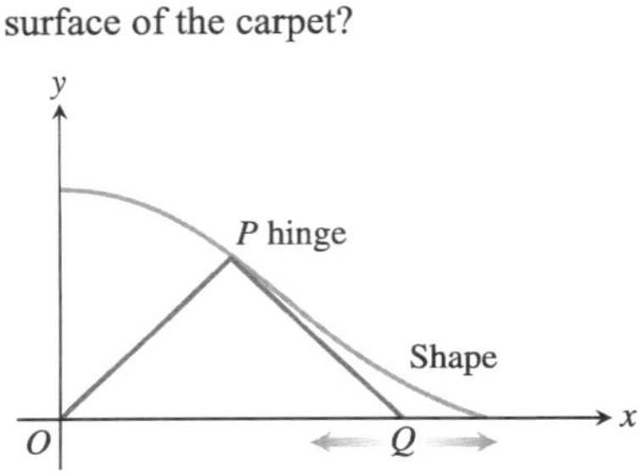

The Angle Between the Radius Vector and the Tangent Line to a Polar Coordinate Curve

In Cartesian coordinates, when we want to discuss the direction of a curve at a point, we use the angle ϕ measured counterclockwise from the positive x-axis to the tangent line. In polar coordinates, it is more convenient to calculate the angle ψ from the *radius vector* to the tangent line (see the accompanying figure). The angle ϕ can then be calculated from the relation

$$\phi = \theta + \psi, \qquad (1)$$

which comes from applying the Exterior Angle Theorem to the triangle in the accompanying figure.

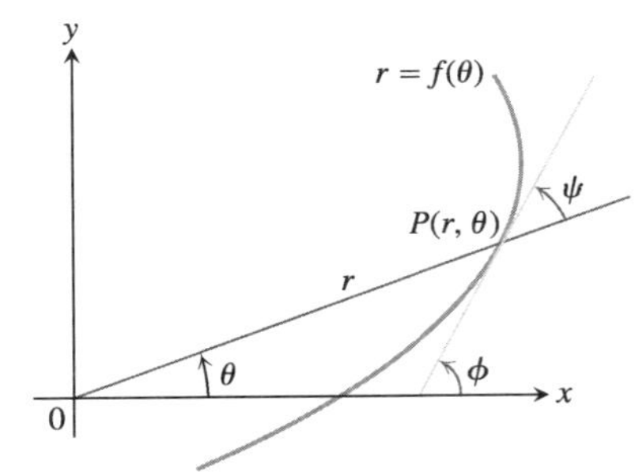

Suppose the equation of the curve is given in the form $r = f(\theta)$, where $f(\theta)$ is a differentiable function of θ. Then

$$x = r\cos\theta \quad \text{and} \quad y = r\sin\theta \qquad (2)$$

are differentiable functions of θ with

$$\begin{aligned} \frac{dx}{d\theta} &= -r\sin\theta + \cos\theta\frac{dr}{d\theta}, \\ \frac{dy}{d\theta} &= r\cos\theta + \sin\theta\frac{dr}{d\theta}. \end{aligned} \qquad (3)$$

Since $\psi = \phi - \theta$ from (1),

$$\tan\psi = \tan(\phi - \theta) = \frac{\tan\phi - \tan\theta}{1 + \tan\phi\tan\theta}.$$

Furthermore,

$$\tan\phi = \frac{dy}{dx} = \frac{dy/d\theta}{dx/d\theta}$$

because $\tan\phi$ is the slope of the curve at P. Also,

$$\tan\theta = \frac{y}{x}.$$

Hence

$$\tan\psi = \frac{\dfrac{dy/d\theta}{dx/d\theta} - \dfrac{y}{x}}{1 + \dfrac{y}{x}\dfrac{dy/d\theta}{dx/d\theta}} = \frac{x\dfrac{dy}{d\theta} - y\dfrac{dx}{d\theta}}{x\dfrac{dx}{d\theta} + y\dfrac{dy}{d\theta}}. \qquad (4)$$

The numerator in the last expression in Equation (4) is found from Equations (2) and (3) to be

$$x\frac{dy}{d\theta} - y\frac{dx}{d\theta} = r^2.$$

Similarly, the denominator is

$$x\frac{dx}{d\theta} + y\frac{dy}{d\theta} = r\frac{dr}{d\theta}.$$

When we substitute these into Equation (4), we obtain

$$\tan\psi = \frac{r}{dr/d\theta}. \tag{5}$$

This is the equation we use for finding ψ as a function of θ.

41. Show, by reference to a figure, that the angle β between the tangents to two curves at a point of intersection may be found from the formula

$$\tan\beta = \frac{\tan\psi_2 - \tan\psi_1}{1 + \tan\psi_2\tan\psi_1}. \tag{6}$$

When will the two curves intersect at right angles?

42. Find the value of $\tan\psi$ for the curve $r = \sin^4(\theta/4)$.

43. Find the angle between the radius vector to the curve $r = 2a\sin 3\theta$ and its tangent when $\theta = \pi/6$.

T **44. a.** Graph the hyperbolic spiral $r\theta = 1$. What appears to happen to ψ as the spiral winds in around the origin?

b. Confirm your finding in part (a) analytically.

45. The circles $r = \sqrt{3}\cos\theta$ and $r = \sin\theta$ intersect at the point $(\sqrt{3}/2, \pi/3)$. Show that their tangents are perpendicular there.

46. Sketch the cardioid $r = a(1 + \cos\theta)$ and circle $r = 3a\cos\theta$ in one diagram and find the angle between their tangents at the point of intersection that lies in the first quadrant.

47. Find the points of intersection of the parabolas

$$r = \frac{1}{1 - \cos\theta} \quad \text{and} \quad r = \frac{3}{1 + \cos\theta}$$

and the angles between their tangents at these points.

48. Find points on the cardioid $r = a(1 + \cos\theta)$ where the tangent line is **(a)** horizontal, **(b)** vertical.

49. Show that parabolas $r = a/(1 + \cos\theta)$ and $r = b/(1 - \cos\theta)$ are orthogonal at each point of intersection $(ab \neq 0)$.

50. Find the angle at which the cardioid $r = a(1 - \cos\theta)$ crosses the ray $\theta = \pi/2$.

51. Find the angle between the line $r = 3\sec\theta$ and the cardioid $r = 4(1 + \cos\theta)$ at one of their intersections.

52. Find the slope of the tangent line to the curve $r = a\tan(\theta/2)$ at $\theta = \pi/2$.

53. Find the angle at which the parabolas $r = 1/(1 - \cos\theta)$ and $r = 1/(1 - \sin\theta)$ intersect in the first quadrant.

54. The equation $r^2 = 2\csc 2\theta$ represents a curve in polar coordinates.

a. Sketch the curve.

b. Find an equivalent Cartesian equation for the curve.

c. Find the angle at which the curve intersects the ray $\theta = \pi/4$.

55. Suppose that the angle ψ from the radius vector to the tangent line of the curve $r = f(\theta)$ has the constant value α.

a. Show that the area bounded by the curve and two rays $\theta = \theta_1$, $\theta = \theta_2$, is proportional to $r_2^2 - r_1^2$, where (r_1, θ_1) and (r_2, θ_2) are polar coordinates of the ends of the arc of the curve between these rays. Find the factor of proportionality.

b. Show that the length of the arc of the curve in part (a) is proportional to $r_2 - r_1$, and find the proportionality constant.

56. Let P be a point on the hyperbola $r^2\sin 2\theta = 2a^2$. Show that the triangle formed by OP, the tangent at P, and the initial line is isosceles.

Chapter 10 Technology Application Projects

Mathematica/Maple Module

Radar Tracking of a Moving Object

Part I: Convert from polar to Cartesian coordinates.

Mathematica/Maple Module

Parametric and Polar Equations with a Figure Skater

Part I: Visualize position, velocity, and acceleration to analyze motion defined by parametric equations.

Part II: Find and analyze the equations of motion for a figure skater tracing a polar plot.

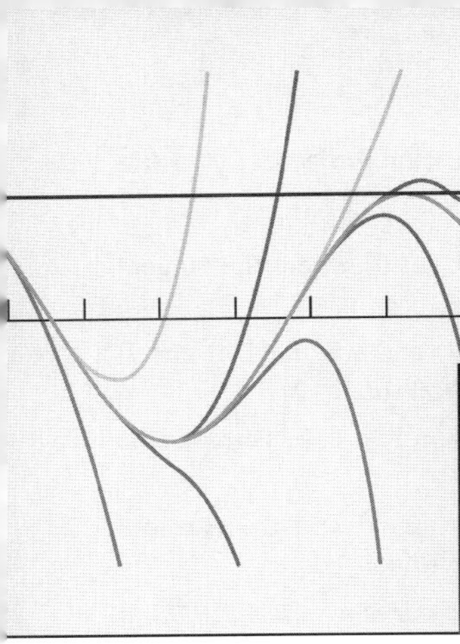

Chapter 11

INFINITE SEQUENCES AND SERIES

OVERVIEW While everyone knows how to add together two numbers, or even several, how to add together infinitely many numbers is not so clear. In this chapter we study such questions, the subject of the theory of infinite series. Infinite series sometimes have a finite sum, as in

$$\frac{1}{2}+\frac{1}{4}+\frac{1}{8}+\frac{1}{16}+\cdots=1.$$

This sum is represented geometrically by the areas of the repeatedly halved unit square shown here. The areas of the small rectangles add together to give the area of the unit square, which they fill. Adding together more and more terms gets us closer and closer to the total.

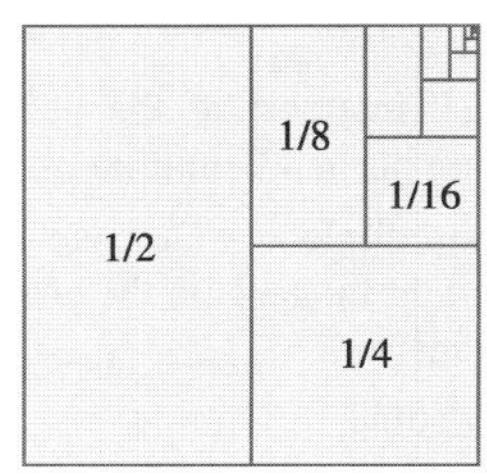

Other infinite series do not have a finite sum, as with

$$1+2+3+4+5+\cdots.$$

The sum of the first few terms gets larger and larger as we add more and more terms. Taking enough terms makes these sums larger than any prechosen constant.

With some infinite series, such as the harmonic series

$$1+\frac{1}{2}+\frac{1}{3}+\frac{1}{4}+\frac{1}{5}+\frac{1}{6}+\cdots$$

it is not obvious whether a finite sum exists. It is unclear whether adding more and more terms gets us closer to some sum, or gives sums that grow without bound.

As we develop the theory of infinite sequences and series, an important application gives a method of representing a differentiable function $f(x)$ as an infinite sum of powers of x. With this method we can extend our knowledge of how to evaluate, differentiate, and integrate polynomials to a class of functions much more general than polynomials. We also investigate a method of representing a function as an infinite sum of sine and cosine functions. This method will yield a powerful tool to study functions.

11.1 Sequences

HISTORICAL ESSAY

Sequences and Series

A sequence is a list of numbers

$$a_1, a_2, a_3, \ldots, a_n, \ldots$$

in a given order. Each of a_1, a_2, a_3 and so on represents a number. These are the **terms** of the sequence. For example the sequence

$$2, 4, 6, 8, 10, 12, \ldots, 2n, \ldots$$

has first term $a_1 = 2$, second term $a_2 = 4$ and nth term $a_n = 2n$. The integer n is called the **index** of a_n, and indicates where a_n occurs in the list. We can think of the sequence

$$a_1, a_2, a_3, \ldots, a_n, \ldots$$

as a function that sends 1 to a_1, 2 to a_2, 3 to a_3, and in general sends the positive integer n to the nth term a_n. This leads to the formal definition of a sequence.

DEFINITION Infinite Sequence

An **infinite sequence** of numbers is a function whose domain is the set of positive integers.

The function associated to the sequence

$$2, 4, 6, 8, 10, 12, \ldots, 2n, \ldots$$

sends 1 to $a_1 = 2$, 2 to $a_2 = 4$, and so on. The general behavior of this sequence is described by the formula

$$a_n = 2n.$$

We can equally well make the domain the integers larger than a given number n_0, and we allow sequences of this type also.

The sequence

$$12, 14, 16, 18, 20, 22 \ldots$$

is described by the formula $a_n = 10 + 2n$. It can also be described by the simpler formula $b_n = 2n$, where the index n starts at 6 and increases. To allow such simpler formulas, we let the first index of the sequence be any integer. In the sequence above, $\{a_n\}$ starts with a_1 while $\{b_n\}$ starts with b_6. Order is important. The sequence $1, 2, 3, 4 \ldots$ is not the same as the sequence $2, 1, 3, 4 \ldots$.

Sequences can be described by writing rules that specify their terms, such as

$$a_n = \sqrt{n},$$

$$b_n = (-1)^{n+1}\frac{1}{n},$$

$$c_n = \frac{n-1}{n},$$

$$d_n = (-1)^{n+1}$$

or by listing terms,

$$\{a_n\} = \{\sqrt{1}, \sqrt{2}, \sqrt{3}, \ldots, \sqrt{n}, \ldots\}$$

$$\{b_n\} = \left\{1, -\frac{1}{2}, \frac{1}{3}, -\frac{1}{4}, \ldots, (-1)^{n+1}\frac{1}{n}, \ldots\right\}$$

$$\{c_n\} = \left\{0, \frac{1}{2}, \frac{2}{3}, \frac{3}{4}, \frac{4}{5}, \ldots, \frac{n-1}{n}, \ldots\right\}$$

$$\{d_n\} = \{1, -1, 1, -1, 1, -1, \ldots, (-1)^{n+1}, \ldots\}.$$

We also sometimes write

$$\{a_n\} = \left\{\sqrt{n}\right\}_{n=1}^{\infty}.$$

Figure 11.1 shows two ways to represent sequences graphically. The first marks the first few points from $a_1, a_2, a_3, \ldots, a_n, \ldots$ on the real axis. The second method shows the graph of the function defining the sequence. The function is defined only on integer inputs, and the graph consists of some points in the xy-plane, located at $(1, a_1)$, $(2, a_2), \ldots, (n, a_n), \ldots$.

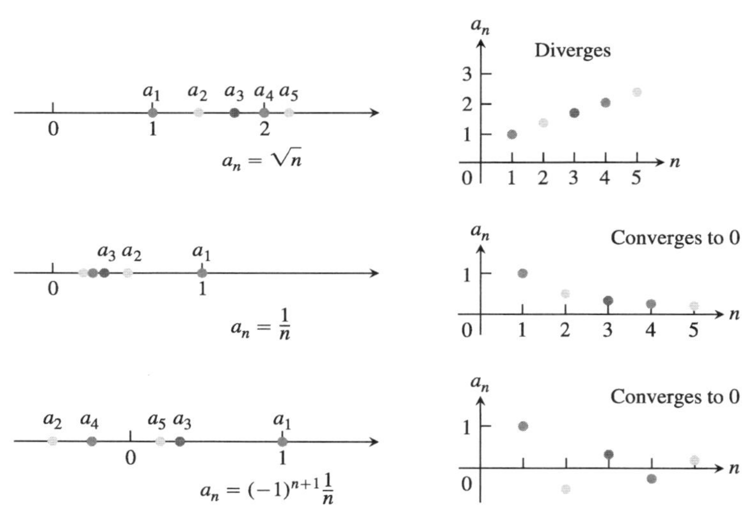

FIGURE 11.1 Sequences can be represented as points on the real line or as points in the plane where the horizontal axis n is the index number of the term and the vertical axis a_n is its value.

Convergence and Divergence

Sometimes the numbers in a sequence approach a single value as the index n increases. This happens in the sequence

$$\left\{1, \frac{1}{2}, \frac{1}{3}, \frac{1}{4}, \ldots, \frac{1}{n}, \ldots\right\}$$

whose terms approach 0 as n gets large, and in the sequence

$$\left\{0, \frac{1}{2}, \frac{2}{3}, \frac{3}{4}, \frac{4}{5}, \ldots, 1 - \frac{1}{n}, \ldots\right\}$$

whose terms approach 1. On the other hand, sequences like

$$\{\sqrt{1}, \sqrt{2}, \sqrt{3}, \ldots, \sqrt{n}, \ldots\}$$

have terms that get larger than any number as n increases, and sequences like

$$\{1, -1, 1, -1, 1, -1, \ldots, (-1)^{n+1}, \ldots\}$$

bounce back and forth between 1 and -1, never converging to a single value. The following definition captures the meaning of having a sequence converge to a limiting value. It says that if we go far enough out in the sequence, by taking the index n to be larger then some value N, the difference between a_n and the limit of the sequence becomes less than any preselected number $\epsilon > 0$.

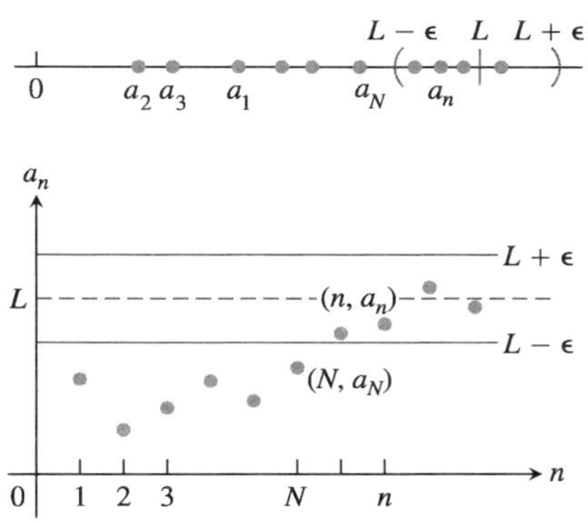

FIGURE 11.2 $a_n \to L$ if $y = L$ is a horizontal asymptote of the sequence of points $\{(n, a_n)\}$. In this figure, all the a_n's after a_N lie within ϵ of L.

DEFINITIONS Converges, Diverges, Limit

The sequence $\{a_n\}$ **converges** to the number L if to every positive number ϵ there corresponds an integer N such that for all n,

$$n > N \quad \Rightarrow \quad |a_n - L| < \epsilon.$$

If no such number L exists, we say that $\{a_n\}$ **diverges**.

If $\{a_n\}$ converges to L, we write $\lim_{n\to\infty} a_n = L$, or simply $a_n \to L$, and call L the **limit** of the sequence (Figure 11.2).

HISTORICAL BIOGRAPHY

Nicole Oresme (ca. 1320–1382)

The definition is very similar to the definition of the limit of a function $f(x)$ as x tends to ∞ ($\lim_{x\to\infty} f(x)$ in Section 2.4). We will exploit this connection to calculate limits of sequences.

EXAMPLE 1 Applying the Definition

Show that

(a) $\lim_{n\to\infty} \frac{1}{n} = 0$ **(b)** $\lim_{n\to\infty} k = k$ (any constant k)

Solution

(a) Let $\epsilon > 0$ be given. We must show that there exists an integer N such that for all n,

$$n > N \quad \Rightarrow \quad \left|\frac{1}{n} - 0\right| < \epsilon.$$

This implication will hold if $(1/n) < \epsilon$ or $n > 1/\epsilon$. If N is any integer greater than $1/\epsilon$, the implication will hold for all $n > N$. This proves that $\lim_{n\to\infty}(1/n) = 0$.

(b) Let $\epsilon > 0$ be given. We must show that there exists an integer N such that for all n,

$$n > N \quad \Rightarrow \quad |k - k| < \epsilon.$$

Since $k - k = 0$, we can use any positive integer for N and the implication will hold. This proves that $\lim_{n\to\infty} k = k$ for any constant k. ■

EXAMPLE 2 A Divergent Sequence

Show that the sequence $\{1, -1, 1, -1, 1, -1, \dots, (-1)^{n+1}, \dots\}$ diverges.

Solution Suppose the sequence converges to some number L. By choosing $\epsilon = 1/2$ in the definition of the limit, all terms a_n of the sequence with index n larger than some N must lie within $\epsilon = 1/2$ of L. Since the number 1 appears repeatedly as every other term of the sequence, we must have that the number 1 lies within the distance $\epsilon = 1/2$ of L. It follows that $|L - 1| < 1/2$, or equivalently, $1/2 < L < 3/2$. Likewise, the number -1 appears repeatedly in the sequence with arbitrarily high index. So we must also have that $|L - (-1)| < 1/2$, or equivalently, $-3/2 < L < -1/2$. But the number L cannot lie in both of the intervals $(1/2, 3/2)$ and $(-3/2, -1/2)$ because they have no overlap. Therefore, no such limit L exists and so the sequence diverges.

Note that the same argument works for any positive number ϵ smaller than 1, not just $1/2$. ■

The sequence $\{\sqrt{n}\}$ also diverges, but for a different reason. As n increases, its terms become larger than any fixed number. We describe the behavior of this sequence by writing

$$\lim_{n\to\infty} \sqrt{n} = \infty.$$

In writing infinity as the limit of a sequence, we are not saying that the differences between the terms a_n and ∞ become small as n increases. Nor are we asserting that there is some number infinity that the sequence approaches. We are merely using a notation that captures the idea that a_n eventually gets and stays larger than any fixed number as n gets large.

DEFINITION Diverges to Infinity

The sequence $\{a_n\}$ **diverges to infinity** if for every number M there is an integer N such that for all n larger than N, $a_n > M$. If this condition holds we write

$$\lim_{n\to\infty} a_n = \infty \qquad \text{or} \qquad a_n \to \infty.$$

Similarly if for every number m there is an integer N such that for all $n > N$ we have $a_n < m$, then we say $\{a_n\}$ **diverges to negative infinity** and write

$$\lim_{n\to\infty} a_n = -\infty \qquad \text{or} \qquad a_n \to -\infty.$$

A sequence may diverge without diverging to infinity or negative infinity. We saw this in Example 2, and the sequences $\{1, -2, 3, -4, 5, -6, 7, -8, \dots\}$ and $\{1, 0, 2, 0, 3, 0, \dots\}$ are also examples of such divergence.

Calculating Limits of Sequences

If we always had to use the formal definition of the limit of a sequence, calculating with ϵ's and N's, then computing limits of sequences would be a formidable task. Fortunately we can derive a few basic examples, and then use these to quickly analyze the limits of many more sequences. We will need to understand how to combine and compare sequences. Since sequences are functions with domain restricted to the positive integers, it is not too surprising that the theorems on limits of functions given in Chapter 2 have versions for sequences.

THEOREM 1

Let $\{a_n\}$ and $\{b_n\}$ be sequences of real numbers and let A and B be real numbers. The following rules hold if $\lim_{n\to\infty} a_n = A$ and $\lim_{n\to\infty} b_n = B$.

1. *Sum Rule:* $\lim_{n\to\infty}(a_n + b_n) = A + B$
2. *Difference Rule:* $\lim_{n\to\infty}(a_n - b_n) = A - B$
3. *Product Rule:* $\lim_{n\to\infty}(a_n \cdot b_n) = A \cdot B$
4. *Constant Multiple Rule:* $\lim_{n\to\infty}(k \cdot b_n) = k \cdot B$ (Any number k)
5. *Quotient Rule:* $\lim_{n\to\infty}\dfrac{a_n}{b_n} = \dfrac{A}{B}$ if $B \neq 0$

The proof is similar to that of Theorem 1 of Section 2.2, and is omitted.

EXAMPLE 3 Applying Theorem 1

By combining Theorem 1 with the limits of Example 1, we have:

(a) $\lim_{n\to\infty}\left(-\frac{1}{n}\right) = -1 \cdot \lim_{n\to\infty}\frac{1}{n} = -1 \cdot 0 = 0$ Constant Multiple Rule and Example 1a

(b) $\lim_{n\to\infty}\left(\frac{n-1}{n}\right) = \lim_{n\to\infty}\left(1 - \frac{1}{n}\right) = \lim_{n\to\infty} 1 - \lim_{n\to\infty}\frac{1}{n} = 1 - 0 = 1$ Difference Rule and Example 1a

(c) $\lim_{n\to\infty}\frac{5}{n^2} = 5 \cdot \lim_{n\to\infty}\frac{1}{n} \cdot \lim_{n\to\infty}\frac{1}{n} = 5 \cdot 0 \cdot 0 = 0$ Product Rule

(d) $\lim_{n\to\infty}\frac{4 - 7n^6}{n^6 + 3} = \lim_{n\to\infty}\frac{(4/n^6) - 7}{1 + (3/n^6)} = \frac{0 - 7}{1 + 0} = -7.$ Sum and Quotient Rules ■

Be cautious in applying Theorem 1. It does not say, for example, that each of the sequences $\{a_n\}$ and $\{b_n\}$ have limits if their sum $\{a_n + b_n\}$ has a limit. For instance, $\{a_n\} = \{1, 2, 3, \dots\}$ and $\{b_n\} = \{-1, -2, -3, \dots\}$ both diverge, but their sum $\{a_n + b_n\} = \{0, 0, 0, \dots\}$ clearly converges to 0.

One consequence of Theorem 1 is that every nonzero multiple of a divergent sequence $\{a_n\}$ diverges. For suppose, to the contrary, that $\{ca_n\}$ converges for some number $c \neq 0$. Then, by taking $k = 1/c$ in the Constant Multiple Rule in Theorem 1, we see that the sequence

$$\left\{\frac{1}{c} \cdot ca_n\right\} = \{a_n\}$$

converges. Thus, $\{ca_n\}$ cannot converge unless $\{a_n\}$ also converges. If $\{a_n\}$ does not converge, then $\{ca_n\}$ does not converge.

The next theorem is the sequence version of the Sandwich Theorem in Section 2.2. You are asked to prove the theorem in Exercise 95.

THEOREM 2 The Sandwich Theorem for Sequences

Let $\{a_n\}$, $\{b_n\}$, and $\{c_n\}$ be sequences of real numbers. If $a_n \leq b_n \leq c_n$ holds for all n beyond some index N, and if $\lim_{n\to\infty} a_n = \lim_{n\to\infty} c_n = L$, then $\lim_{n\to\infty} b_n = L$ also.

An immediate consequence of Theorem 2 is that, if $|b_n| \le c_n$ and $c_n \to 0$, then $b_n \to 0$ because $-c_n \le b_n \le c_n$. We use this fact in the next example.

EXAMPLE 4 Applying the Sandwich Theorem

Since $1/n \to 0$, we know that

(a) $\dfrac{\cos n}{n} \to 0$ because $-\dfrac{1}{n} \le \dfrac{\cos n}{n} \le \dfrac{1}{n}$;

(b) $\dfrac{1}{2^n} \to 0$ because $0 \le \dfrac{1}{2^n} \le \dfrac{1}{n}$;

(c) $(-1)^n \dfrac{1}{n} \to 0$ because $-\dfrac{1}{n} \le (-1)^n \dfrac{1}{n} \le \dfrac{1}{n}$. ■

The application of Theorems 1 and 2 is broadened by a theorem stating that applying a continuous function to a convergent sequence produces a convergent sequence. We state the theorem without proof (Exercise 96).

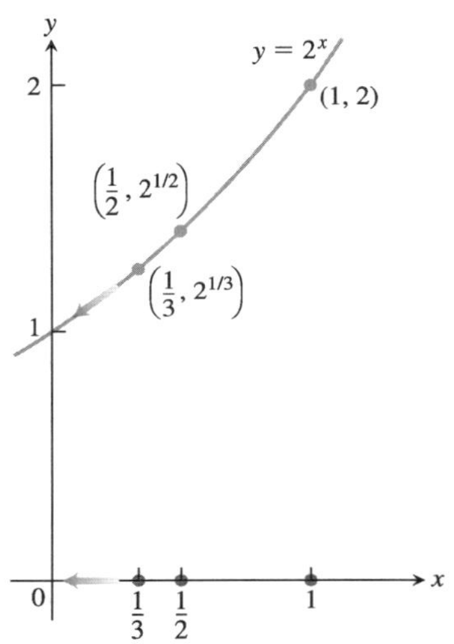

FIGURE 11.3 As $n \to \infty$, $1/n \to 0$ and $2^{1/n} \to 2^0$ (Example 6).

> **THEOREM 3 The Continuous Function Theorem for Sequences**
> Let $\{a_n\}$ be a sequence of real numbers. If $a_n \to L$ and if f is a function that is continuous at L and defined at all a_n, then $f(a_n) \to f(L)$.

EXAMPLE 5 Applying Theorem 3

Show that $\sqrt{(n+1)/n} \to 1$.

Solution We know that $(n+1)/n \to 1$. Taking $f(x) = \sqrt{x}$ and $L = 1$ in Theorem 3 gives $\sqrt{(n+1)/n} \to \sqrt{1} = 1$. ■

EXAMPLE 6 The Sequence $\{2^{1/n}\}$

The sequence $\{1/n\}$ converges to 0. By taking $a_n = 1/n$, $f(x) = 2^x$, and $L = 0$ in Theorem 3, we see that $2^{1/n} = f(1/n) \to f(L) = 2^0 = 1$. The sequence $\{2^{1/n}\}$ converges to 1 (Figure 11.3). ■

Using l'Hôpital's Rule

The next theorem enables us to use l'Hôpital's Rule to find the limits of some sequences. It formalizes the connection between $\lim_{n\to\infty} a_n$ and $\lim_{x\to\infty} f(x)$.

> **THEOREM 4**
> Suppose that $f(x)$ is a function defined for all $x \ge n_0$ and that $\{a_n\}$ is a sequence of real numbers such that $a_n = f(n)$ for $n \ge n_0$. Then
> $$\lim_{x\to\infty} f(x) = L \quad \Rightarrow \quad \lim_{n\to\infty} a_n = L.$$

Proof Suppose that $\lim_{x\to\infty} f(x) = L$. Then for each positive number ϵ there is a number M such that for all x,

$$x > M \quad \Rightarrow \quad |f(x) - L| < \epsilon.$$

Let N be an integer greater than M and greater than or equal to n_0. Then

$$n > N \quad \Rightarrow \quad a_n = f(n) \quad \text{and} \quad |a_n - L| = |f(n) - L| < \epsilon. \qquad \blacksquare$$

EXAMPLE 7 Applying L'Hôpital's Rule

Show that

$$\lim_{n\to\infty} \frac{\ln n}{n} = 0.$$

Solution The function $(\ln x)/x$ is defined for all $x \geq 1$ and agrees with the given sequence at positive integers. Therefore, by Theorem 4, $\lim_{n\to\infty}(\ln n)/n$ will equal $\lim_{x\to\infty}(\ln x)/x$ if the latter exists. A single application of l'Hôpital's Rule shows that

$$\lim_{x\to\infty} \frac{\ln x}{x} = \lim_{x\to\infty} \frac{1/x}{1} = \frac{0}{1} = 0.$$

We conclude that $\lim_{n\to\infty}(\ln n)/n = 0$. ■

When we use l'Hôpital's Rule to find the limit of a sequence, we often treat n as a continuous real variable and differentiate directly with respect to n. This saves us from having to rewrite the formula for a_n as we did in Example 7.

EXAMPLE 8 Applying L'Hôpital's Rule

Find

$$\lim_{n\to\infty} \frac{2^n}{5n}.$$

Solution By l'Hôpital's Rule (differentiating with respect to n),

$$\begin{aligned}\lim_{n\to\infty} \frac{2^n}{5n} &= \lim_{n\to\infty} \frac{2^n \cdot \ln 2}{5} \\ &= \infty.\end{aligned} \qquad \blacksquare$$

EXAMPLE 9 Applying L'Hôpital's Rule to Determine Convergence

Does the sequence whose nth term is

$$a_n = \left(\frac{n+1}{n-1}\right)^n$$

converge? If so, find $\lim_{n\to\infty} a_n$.

Solution The limit leads to the indeterminate form 1^∞. We can apply l'Hôpital's Rule if we first change the form to $\infty \cdot 0$ by taking the natural logarithm of a_n:

$$\begin{aligned}\ln a_n &= \ln\left(\frac{n+1}{n-1}\right)^n \\ &= n \ln\left(\frac{n+1}{n-1}\right).\end{aligned}$$

Then,

$$\begin{aligned}
\lim_{n\to\infty} \ln a_n &= \lim_{n\to\infty} n \ln\left(\frac{n+1}{n-1}\right) && \infty \cdot 0 \\
&= \lim_{n\to\infty} \frac{\ln\left(\frac{n+1}{n-1}\right)}{1/n} && \frac{0}{0} \\
&= \lim_{n\to\infty} \frac{-2/(n^2-1)}{-1/n^2} && \text{l'Hôpital's Rule} \\
&= \lim_{n\to\infty} \frac{2n^2}{n^2-1} = 2.
\end{aligned}$$

Since $\ln a_n \to 2$ and $f(x) = e^x$ is continuous, Theorem 4 tells us that

$$a_n = e^{\ln a_n} \to e^2.$$

The sequence $\{a_n\}$ converges to e^2. ■

Commonly Occurring Limits

The next theorem gives some limits that arise frequently.

THEOREM 5
The following six sequences converge to the limits listed below:

1. $\lim_{n\to\infty} \frac{\ln n}{n} = 0$
2. $\lim_{n\to\infty} \sqrt[n]{n} = 1$
3. $\lim_{n\to\infty} x^{1/n} = 1 \qquad (x > 0)$
4. $\lim_{n\to\infty} x^n = 0 \qquad (|x| < 1)$
5. $\lim_{n\to\infty} \left(1 + \frac{x}{n}\right)^n = e^x \qquad (\text{any } x)$
6. $\lim_{n\to\infty} \frac{x^n}{n!} = 0 \qquad (\text{any } x)$

In Formulas (3) through (6), x remains fixed as $n \to \infty$.

Factorial Notation
The notation $n!$ ("n factorial") means the product $1 \cdot 2 \cdot 3 \cdots n$ of the integers from 1 to n. Notice that $(n+1)! = (n+1) \cdot n!$. Thus, $4! = 1 \cdot 2 \cdot 3 \cdot 4 = 24$ and $5! = 1 \cdot 2 \cdot 3 \cdot 4 \cdot 5 = 5 \cdot 4! = 120$. We define $0!$ to be 1. Factorials grow even faster than exponentials, as the table suggests.

n	e^n (rounded)	$n!$
1	3	1
5	148	120
10	22,026	3,628,800
20	4.9×10^8	2.4×10^{18}

Proof The first limit was computed in Example 7. The next two can be proved by taking logarithms and applying Theorem 4 (Exercises 93 and 94). The remaining proofs are given in Appendix 3. ■

EXAMPLE 10 Applying Theorem 5

(a) $\frac{\ln(n^2)}{n} = \frac{2\ln n}{n} \to 2 \cdot 0 = 0$ Formula 1

(b) $\sqrt[n]{n^2} = n^{2/n} = (n^{1/n})^2 \to (1)^2 = 1$ Formula 2

(c) $\sqrt[n]{3n} = 3^{1/n}(n^{1/n}) \to 1 \cdot 1 = 1$ Formula 3 with $x = 3$ and Formula 2

(d) $\left(-\frac{1}{2}\right)^n \to 0$ Formula 4 with $x = -\frac{1}{2}$

(e) $\left(\frac{n-2}{n}\right)^n = \left(1 + \frac{-2}{n}\right)^n \to e^{-2}$ Formula 5 with $x = -2$

(f) $\frac{100^n}{n!} \to 0$ Formula 6 with $x = 100$ ■

Recursive Definitions

So far, we have calculated each a_n directly from the value of n. But sequences are often defined **recursively** by giving

1. The value(s) of the initial term or terms, and
2. A rule, called a **recursion formula**, for calculating any later term from terms that precede it.

EXAMPLE 11 Sequences Constructed Recursively

(a) The statements $a_1 = 1$ and $a_n = a_{n-1} + 1$ define the sequence $1, 2, 3, \ldots, n, \ldots$ of positive integers. With $a_1 = 1$, we have $a_2 = a_1 + 1 = 2$, $a_3 = a_2 + 1 = 3$, and so on.

(b) The statements $a_1 = 1$ and $a_n = n \cdot a_{n-1}$ define the sequence $1, 2, 6, 24, \ldots, n!, \ldots$ of factorials. With $a_1 = 1$, we have $a_2 = 2 \cdot a_1 = 2$, $a_3 = 3 \cdot a_2 = 6$, $a_4 = 4 \cdot a_3 = 24$, and so on.

(c) The statements $a_1 = 1$, $a_2 = 1$, and $a_{n+1} = a_n + a_{n-1}$ define the sequence $1, 1, 2, 3, 5, \ldots$ of **Fibonacci numbers**. With $a_1 = 1$ and $a_2 = 1$, we have $a_3 = 1 + 1 = 2$, $a_4 = 2 + 1 = 3$, $a_5 = 3 + 2 = 5$, and so on.

(d) As we can see by applying Newton's method, the statements $x_0 = 1$ and $x_{n+1} = x_n - [(\sin x_n - x_n^2)/(\cos x_n - 2x_n)]$ define a sequence that converges to a solution of the equation $\sin x - x^2 = 0$. ■

Bounded Nondecreasing Sequences

The terms of a general sequence can bounce around, sometimes getting larger, sometimes smaller. An important special kind of sequence is one for which each term is at least as large as its predecessor.

> **DEFINITION Nondecreasing Sequence**
> A sequence $\{a_n\}$ with the property that $a_n \le a_{n+1}$ for all n is called a **nondecreasing sequence**.

EXAMPLE 12 Nondecreasing Sequences

(a) The sequence $1, 2, 3, \ldots, n, \ldots$ of natural numbers

(b) The sequence $\frac{1}{2}, \frac{2}{3}, \frac{3}{4}, \ldots, \frac{n}{n+1}, \ldots$

(c) The constant sequence $\{3\}$ ■

There are two kinds of nondecreasing sequences—those whose terms increase beyond any finite bound and those whose terms do not.

> **DEFINITIONS Bounded, Upper Bound, Least Upper Bound**
> A sequence $\{a_n\}$ is **bounded from above** if there exists a number M such that $a_n \leq M$ for all n. The number M is an **upper bound** for $\{a_n\}$. If M is an upper bound for $\{a_n\}$ but no number less than M is an upper bound for $\{a_n\}$, then M is the **least upper bound** for $\{a_n\}$.

EXAMPLE 13 Applying the Definition for Boundedness

(a) The sequence $1, 2, 3, \ldots, n, \ldots$ has no upper bound.

(b) The sequence $\frac{1}{2}, \frac{2}{3}, \frac{3}{4}, \ldots, \frac{n}{n+1}, \ldots$ is bounded above by $M = 1$.

No number less than 1 is an upper bound for the sequence, so 1 is the least upper bound (Exercise 113). ■

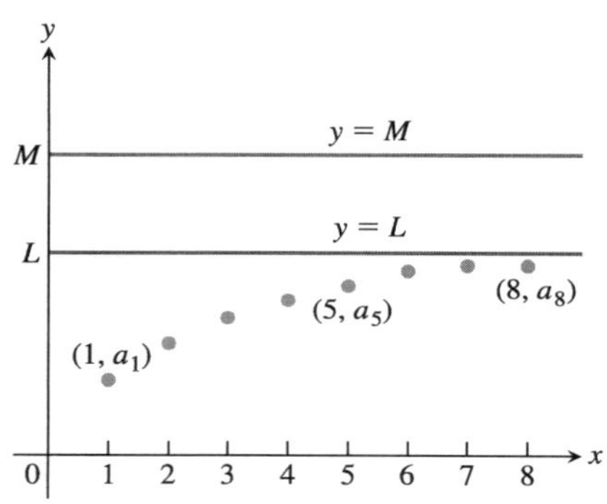

FIGURE 11.4 If the terms of a nondecreasing sequence have an upper bound M, they have a limit $L \leq M$.

A nondecreasing sequence that is bounded from above always has a least upper bound. This is the completeness property of the real numbers, discussed in Appendix 4. We will prove that if L is the least upper bound then the sequence converges to L.

Suppose we plot the points $(1, a_1), (2, a_2), \ldots, (n, a_n), \ldots$ in the xy-plane. If M is an upper bound of the sequence, all these points will lie on or below the line $y = M$ (Figure 11.4). The line $y = L$ is the lowest such line. None of the points (n, a_n) lies above $y = L$, but some do lie above any lower line $y = L - \epsilon$, if ϵ is a positive number. The sequence converges to L because

(a) $a_n \leq L$ for *all* values of n and

(b) given any $\epsilon > 0$, there exists at least one integer N for which $a_N > L - \epsilon$.

The fact that $\{a_n\}$ is nondecreasing tells us further that

$$a_n \geq a_N > L - \epsilon \qquad \text{for all } n \geq N.$$

Thus, *all* the numbers a_n beyond the Nth number lie within ϵ of L. This is precisely the condition for L to be the limit of the sequence $\{a_n\}$.

The facts for nondecreasing sequences are summarized in the following theorem. A similar result holds for nonincreasing sequences (Exercise 107).

> **THEOREM 6 The Nondecreasing Sequence Theorem**
> A nondecreasing sequence of real numbers converges if and only if it is bounded from above. If a nondecreasing sequence converges, it converges to its least upper bound.

Theorem 6 implies that a nondecreasing sequence converges when it is bounded from above. It diverges to infinity if it is not bounded from above.

EXERCISES 11.1

Finding Terms of a Sequence

Each of Exercises 1–6 gives a formula for the nth term a_n of a sequence $\{a_n\}$. Find the values of a_1, a_2, a_3, and a_4.

1. $a_n = \dfrac{1-n}{n^2}$

2. $a_n = \dfrac{1}{n!}$

3. $a_n = \dfrac{(-1)^{n+1}}{2n-1}$

4. $a_n = 2 + (-1)^n$

5. $a_n = \dfrac{2^n}{2^{n+1}}$

6. $a_n = \dfrac{2^n - 1}{2^n}$

Each of Exercises 7–12 gives the first term or two of a sequence along with a recursion formula for the remaining terms. Write out the first ten terms of the sequence.

7. $a_1 = 1, \quad a_{n+1} = a_n + (1/2^n)$

8. $a_1 = 1, \quad a_{n+1} = a_n/(n+1)$

9. $a_1 = 2, \quad a_{n+1} = (-1)^{n+1}a_n/2$

10. $a_1 = -2, \quad a_{n+1} = na_n/(n+1)$

11. $a_1 = a_2 = 1, \quad a_{n+2} = a_{n+1} + a_n$

12. $a_1 = 2, \quad a_2 = -1, \quad a_{n+2} = a_{n+1}/a_n$

Finding a Sequence's Formula

In Exercises 13–22, find a formula for the nth term of the sequence.

13. The sequence $1, -1, 1, -1, 1, \ldots$ — 1's with alternating signs

14. The sequence $-1, 1, -1, 1, -1, \ldots$ — 1's with alternating signs

15. The sequence $1, -4, 9, -16, 25, \ldots$ — Squares of the positive integers; with alternating signs

16. The sequence $1, -\frac{1}{4}, \frac{1}{9}, -\frac{1}{16}, \frac{1}{25}, \ldots$ — Reciprocals of squares of the positive integers, with alternating signs

17. The sequence $0, 3, 8, 15, 24, \ldots$ — Squares of the positive integers diminished by 1

18. The sequence $-3, -2, -1, 0, 1, \ldots$ — Integers beginning with -3

19. The sequence $1, 5, 9, 13, 17, \ldots$ — Every other odd positive integer

20. The sequence $2, 6, 10, 14, 18, \ldots$ — Every other even positive integer

21. The sequence $1, 0, 1, 0, 1, \ldots$ — Alternating 1's and 0's

22. The sequence $0, 1, 1, 2, 2, 3, 3, 4, \ldots$ — Each positive integer repeated

Finding Limits

Which of the sequences $\{a_n\}$ in Exercises 23–84 converge, and which diverge? Find the limit of each convergent sequence.

23. $a_n = 2 + (0.1)^n$

24. $a_n = \dfrac{n + (-1)^n}{n}$

25. $a_n = \dfrac{1-2n}{1+2n}$

26. $a_n = \dfrac{2n+1}{1-3\sqrt{n}}$

27. $a_n = \dfrac{1-5n^4}{n^4+8n^3}$

28. $a_n = \dfrac{n+3}{n^2+5n+6}$

29. $a_n = \dfrac{n^2-2n+1}{n-1}$

30. $a_n = \dfrac{1-n^3}{70-4n^2}$

31. $a_n = 1 + (-1)^n$

32. $a_n = (-1)^n\left(1 - \dfrac{1}{n}\right)$

33. $a_n = \left(\dfrac{n+1}{2n}\right)\left(1 - \dfrac{1}{n}\right)$

34. $a_n = \left(2 - \dfrac{1}{2^n}\right)\left(3 + \dfrac{1}{2^n}\right)$

35. $a_n = \dfrac{(-1)^{n+1}}{2n-1}$

36. $a_n = \left(-\dfrac{1}{2}\right)^n$

37. $a_n = \sqrt{\dfrac{2n}{n+1}}$

38. $a_n = \dfrac{1}{(0.9)^n}$

39. $a_n = \sin\left(\dfrac{\pi}{2} + \dfrac{1}{n}\right)$

40. $a_n = n\pi\cos(n\pi)$

41. $a_n = \dfrac{\sin n}{n}$

42. $a_n = \dfrac{\sin^2 n}{2^n}$

43. $a_n = \dfrac{n}{2^n}$

44. $a_n = \dfrac{3^n}{n^3}$

45. $a_n = \dfrac{\ln(n+1)}{\sqrt{n}}$

46. $a_n = \dfrac{\ln n}{\ln 2n}$

47. $a_n = 8^{1/n}$

48. $a_n = (0.03)^{1/n}$

49. $a_n = \left(1 + \dfrac{7}{n}\right)^n$

50. $a_n = \left(1 - \dfrac{1}{n}\right)^n$

51. $a_n = \sqrt[n]{10n}$

52. $a_n = \sqrt[n]{n^2}$

53. $a_n = \left(\dfrac{3}{n}\right)^{1/n}$

54. $a_n = (n+4)^{1/(n+4)}$

55. $a_n = \dfrac{\ln n}{n^{1/n}}$

56. $a_n = \ln n - \ln(n+1)$

57. $a_n = \sqrt[n]{4^n n}$

58. $a_n = \sqrt[n]{3^{2n+1}}$

59. $a_n = \dfrac{n!}{n^n}$ (*Hint:* Compare with $1/n$.)

60. $a_n = \dfrac{(-4)^n}{n!}$

61. $a_n = \dfrac{n!}{10^{6n}}$

62. $a_n = \dfrac{n!}{2^n \cdot 3^n}$

63. $a_n = \left(\dfrac{1}{n}\right)^{1/(\ln n)}$

64. $a_n = \ln\left(1 + \dfrac{1}{n}\right)^n$

65. $a_n = \left(\dfrac{3n + 1}{3n - 1}\right)^n$

66. $a_n = \left(\dfrac{n}{n + 1}\right)^n$

67. $a_n = \left(\dfrac{x^n}{2n + 1}\right)^{1/n}, \quad x > 0$

68. $a_n = \left(1 - \dfrac{1}{n^2}\right)^n$

69. $a_n = \dfrac{3^n \cdot 6^n}{2^{-n} \cdot n!}$

70. $a_n = \dfrac{(10/11)^n}{(9/10)^n + (11/12)^n}$

71. $a_n = \tanh n$

72. $a_n = \sinh(\ln n)$

73. $a_n = \dfrac{n^2}{2n - 1}\sin\dfrac{1}{n}$

74. $a_n = n\left(1 - \cos\dfrac{1}{n}\right)$

75. $a_n = \tan^{-1} n$

76. $a_n = \dfrac{1}{\sqrt{n}}\tan^{-1} n$

77. $a_n = \left(\dfrac{1}{3}\right)^n + \dfrac{1}{\sqrt{2^n}}$

78. $a_n = \sqrt[n]{n^2 + n}$

79. $a_n = \dfrac{(\ln n)^{200}}{n}$

80. $a_n = \dfrac{(\ln n)^5}{\sqrt{n}}$

81. $a_n = n - \sqrt{n^2 - n}$

82. $a_n = \dfrac{1}{\sqrt{n^2 - 1} - \sqrt{n^2 + n}}$

83. $a_n = \dfrac{1}{n}\displaystyle\int_1^n \dfrac{1}{x}\,dx$

84. $a_n = \displaystyle\int_1^n \dfrac{1}{x^p}\,dx, \quad p > 1$

Theory and Examples

85. The first term of a sequence is $x_1 = 1$. Each succeeding term is the sum of all those that come before it:

$$x_{n+1} = x_1 + x_2 + \cdots + x_n.$$

Write out enough early terms of the sequence to deduce a general formula for x_n that holds for $n \geq 2$.

86. A sequence of rational numbers is described as follows:

$$\frac{1}{1}, \frac{3}{2}, \frac{7}{5}, \frac{17}{12}, \ldots, \frac{a}{b}, \frac{a + 2b}{a + b}, \ldots.$$

Here the numerators form one sequence, the denominators form a second sequence, and their ratios form a third sequence. Let x_n and y_n be, respectively, the numerator and the denominator of the nth fraction $r_n = x_n/y_n$.

a. Verify that $x_1^2 - 2y_1^2 = -1$, $x_2^2 - 2y_2^2 = +1$ and, more generally, that if $a^2 - 2b^2 = -1$ or $+1$, then

$$(a + 2b)^2 - 2(a + b)^2 = +1 \quad \text{or} \quad -1,$$

respectively.

b. The fractions $r_n = x_n/y_n$ approach a limit as n increases. What is that limit? (*Hint:* Use part (a) to show that $r_n^2 - 2 = \pm(1/y_n)^2$ and that y_n is not less than n.)

87. **Newton's method** The following sequences come from the recursion formula for Newton's method,

$$x_{n+1} = x_n - \frac{f(x_n)}{f'(x_n)}.$$

Do the sequences converge? If so, to what value? In each case, begin by identifying the function f that generates the sequence.

a. $x_0 = 1, \quad x_{n+1} = x_n - \dfrac{x_n^2 - 2}{2x_n} = \dfrac{x_n}{2} + \dfrac{1}{x_n}$

b. $x_0 = 1, \quad x_{n+1} = x_n - \dfrac{\tan x_n - 1}{\sec^2 x_n}$

c. $x_0 = 1, \quad x_{n+1} = x_n - 1$

88. **a.** Suppose that $f(x)$ is differentiable for all x in $[0, 1]$ and that $f(0) = 0$. Define the sequence $\{a_n\}$ by the rule $a_n = nf(1/n)$. Show that $\lim_{n\to\infty} a_n = f'(0)$.

Use the result in part (a) to find the limits of the following sequences $\{a_n\}$.

b. $a_n = n\tan^{-1}\dfrac{1}{n}$

c. $a_n = n(e^{1/n} - 1)$

d. $a_n = n\ln\left(1 + \dfrac{2}{n}\right)$

89. **Pythagorean triples** A triple of positive integers a, b, and c is called a **Pythagorean triple** if $a^2 + b^2 = c^2$. Let a be an odd positive integer and let

$$b = \left\lfloor \frac{a^2}{2} \right\rfloor \quad \text{and} \quad c = \left\lceil \frac{a^2}{2} \right\rceil$$

be, respectively, the integer floor and ceiling for $a^2/2$.

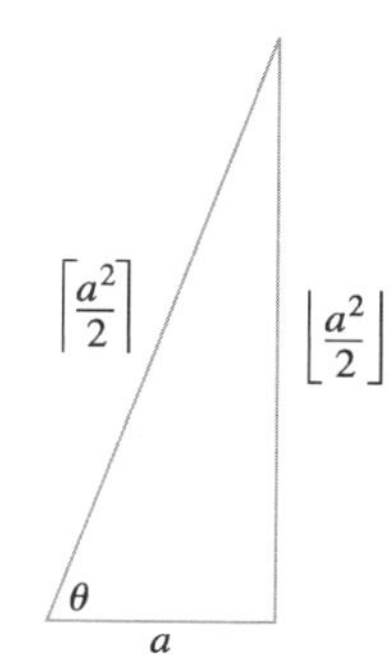

a. Show that $a^2 + b^2 = c^2$. (*Hint:* Let $a = 2n + 1$ and express b and c in terms of n.)

b. By direct calculation, or by appealing to the figure here, find

$$\lim_{a\to\infty}\frac{\left\lfloor \dfrac{a^2}{2}\right\rfloor}{\left\lceil \dfrac{a^2}{2}\right\rceil}.$$

90. The *n*th root of *n*!

a. Show that $\lim_{n\to\infty}(2n\pi)^{1/(2n)} = 1$ and hence, using Stirling's approximation (Chapter 8, Additional Exercise 50a), that

$$\sqrt[n]{n!} \approx \frac{n}{e} \quad \text{for large values of } n.$$

T **b.** Test the approximation in part (a) for $n = 40, 50, 60, \ldots$, as far as your calculator will allow.

91. a. Assuming that $\lim_{n\to\infty}(1/n^c) = 0$ if c is any positive constant, show that

$$\lim_{n\to\infty}\frac{\ln n}{n^c} = 0$$

if c is any positive constant.

b. Prove that $\lim_{n\to\infty}(1/n^c) = 0$ if c is any positive constant. (*Hint:* If $\epsilon = 0.001$ and $c = 0.04$, how large should N be to ensure that $|1/n^c - 0| < \epsilon$ if $n > N$?)

92. The zipper theorem Prove the "zipper theorem" for sequences: If $\{a_n\}$ and $\{b_n\}$ both converge to L, then the sequence

$$a_1, b_1, a_2, b_2, \ldots, a_n, b_n, \ldots$$

converges to L.

93. Prove that $\lim_{n\to\infty}\sqrt[n]{n} = 1$.

94. Prove that $\lim_{n\to\infty}x^{1/n} = 1, (x > 0)$.

95. Prove Theorem 2.

96. Prove Theorem 3.

In Exercises 97–100, determine if the sequence is nondecreasing and if it is bounded from above.

97. $a_n = \dfrac{3n+1}{n+1}$

98. $a_n = \dfrac{(2n+3)!}{(n+1)!}$

99. $a_n = \dfrac{2^n 3^n}{n!}$

100. $a_n = 2 - \dfrac{2}{n} - \dfrac{1}{2^n}$

Which of the sequences in Exercises 101–106 converge, and which diverge? Give reasons for your answers.

101. $a_n = 1 - \dfrac{1}{n}$

102. $a_n = n - \dfrac{1}{n}$

103. $a_n = \dfrac{2^n - 1}{2^n}$

104. $a_n = \dfrac{2^n - 1}{3^n}$

105. $a_n = ((-1)^n + 1)\left(\dfrac{n+1}{n}\right)$

106. The first term of a sequence is $x_1 = \cos(1)$. The next terms are $x_2 = x_1$ or $\cos(2)$, whichever is larger; and $x_3 = x_2$ or $\cos(3)$, whichever is larger (farther to the right). In general,

$$x_{n+1} = \max\{x_n, \cos(n+1)\}.$$

107. Nonincreasing sequences A sequence of numbers $\{a_n\}$ in which $a_n \ge a_{n+1}$ for every n is called a **nonincreasing sequence**. A sequence $\{a_n\}$ is **bounded from below** if there is a number M with $M \le a_n$ for every n. Such a number M is called a **lower bound** for the sequence. Deduce from Theorem 6 that a nonincreasing sequence that is bounded from below converges and that a nonincreasing sequence that is not bounded from below diverges.

(*Continuation of Exercise 107.*) Using the conclusion of Exercise 107, determine which of the sequences in Exercises 108–112 converge and which diverge.

108. $a_n = \dfrac{n+1}{n}$

109. $a_n = \dfrac{1+\sqrt{2n}}{\sqrt{n}}$

110. $a_n = \dfrac{1-4^n}{2^n}$

111. $a_n = \dfrac{4^{n+1}+3^n}{4^n}$

112. $a_1 = 1, \quad a_{n+1} = 2a_n - 3$

113. The sequence $\{n/(n+1)\}$ has a least upper bound of 1 Show that if M is a number less than 1, then the terms of $\{n/(n+1)\}$ eventually exceed M. That is, if $M < 1$ there is an integer N such that $n/(n+1) > M$ whenever $n > N$. Since $n/(n+1) < 1$ for every n, this proves that 1 is a least upper bound for $\{n/(n+1)\}$.

114. Uniqueness of least upper bounds Show that if M_1 and M_2 are least upper bounds for the sequence $\{a_n\}$, then $M_1 = M_2$. That is, a sequence cannot have two different least upper bounds.

115. Is it true that a sequence $\{a_n\}$ of positive numbers must converge if it is bounded from above? Give reasons for your answer.

116. Prove that if $\{a_n\}$ is a convergent sequence, then to every positive number ϵ there corresponds an integer N such that for all m and n,

$$m > N \quad\text{and}\quad n > N \quad \Rightarrow \quad |a_m - a_n| < \epsilon.$$

117. Uniqueness of limits Prove that limits of sequences are unique. That is, show that if L_1 and L_2 are numbers such that $a_n \to L_1$ and $a_n \to L_2$, then $L_1 = L_2$.

118. Limits and subsequences If the terms of one sequence appear in another sequence in their given order, we call the first sequence a **subsequence** of the second. Prove that if two subsequences of a sequence $\{a_n\}$ have different limits $L_1 \ne L_2$, then $\{a_n\}$ diverges.

119. For a sequence $\{a_n\}$ the terms of even index are denoted by a_{2k} and the terms of odd index by a_{2k+1}. Prove that if $a_{2k} \to L$ and $a_{2k+1} \to L$, then $a_n \to L$.

120. Prove that a sequence $\{a_n\}$ converges to 0 if and only if the sequence of absolute values $\{|a_n|\}$ converges to 0.

T Calculator Explorations of Limits

In Exercises 121–124, experiment with a calculator to find a value of N that will make the inequality hold for all $n > N$. Assuming that the inequality is the one from the formal definition of the limit of a sequence, what sequence is being considered in each case and what is its limit?

121. $|\sqrt[n]{0.5} - 1| < 10^{-3}$ **122.** $|\sqrt[n]{n} - 1| < 10^{-3}$

123. $(0.9)^n < 10^{-3}$ **124.** $2^n/n! < 10^{-7}$

125. Sequences generated by Newton's method Newton's method, applied to a differentiable function $f(x)$, begins with a starting value x_0 and constructs from it a sequence of numbers $\{x_n\}$ that under favorable circumstances converges to a zero of f. The recursion formula for the sequence is

$$x_{n+1} = x_n - \frac{f(x_n)}{f'(x_n)}.$$

a. Show that the recursion formula for $f(x) = x^2 - a, a > 0$, can be written as $x_{n+1} = (x_n + a/x_n)/2$.

b. Starting with $x_0 = 1$ and $a = 3$, calculate successive terms of the sequence until the display begins to repeat. What number is being approximated? Explain.

126. (*Continuation of Exercise 125.*) Repeat part (b) of Exercise 125 with $a = 2$ in place of $a = 3$.

127. A recursive definition of $\pi/2$ If you start with $x_1 = 1$ and define the subsequent terms of $\{x_n\}$ by the rule $x_n = x_{n-1} + \cos x_{n-1}$, you generate a sequence that converges rapidly to $\pi/2$. **a.** Try it. **b.** Use the accompanying figure to explain why the convergence is so rapid.

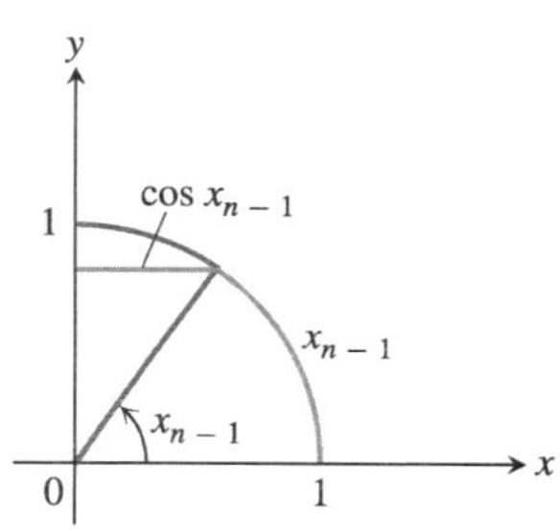

128. According to a front-page article in the December 15, 1992, issue of the *Wall Street Journal*, Ford Motor Company used about $7\frac{1}{4}$ hours of labor to produce stampings for the average vehicle, down from an estimated 15 hours in 1980. The Japanese needed only about $3\frac{1}{2}$ hours.

Ford's improvement since 1980 represents an average decrease of 6% per year. If that rate continues, then n years from 1992 Ford will use about

$$S_n = 7.25(0.94)^n$$

hours of labor to produce stampings for the average vehicle. Assuming that the Japanese continue to spend $3\frac{1}{2}$ hours per vehicle, how many more years will it take Ford to catch up? Find out two ways:

a. Find the first term of the sequence $\{S_n\}$ that is less than or equal to 3.5.

T **b.** Graph $f(x) = 7.25(0.94)^x$ and use Trace to find where the graph crosses the line $y = 3.5$.

COMPUTER EXPLORATIONS

Use a CAS to perform the following steps for the sequences in Exercises 129–140.

a. Calculate and then plot the first 25 terms of the sequence. Does the sequence appear to be bounded from above or below? Does it appear to converge or diverge? If it does converge, what is the limit L?

b. If the sequence converges, find an integer N such that $|a_n - L| \le 0.01$ for $n \ge N$. How far in the sequence do you have to get for the terms to lie within 0.0001 of L?

129. $a_n = \sqrt[n]{n}$ **130.** $a_n = \left(1 + \frac{0.5}{n}\right)^n$

131. $a_1 = 1, \quad a_{n+1} = a_n + \frac{1}{5^n}$

132. $a_1 = 1, \quad a_{n+1} = a_n + (-2)^n$

133. $a_n = \sin n$ **134.** $a_n = n \sin \frac{1}{n}$

135. $a_n = \frac{\sin n}{n}$ **136.** $a_n = \frac{\ln n}{n}$

137. $a_n = (0.9999)^n$ **138.** $a_n = 123456^{1/n}$

139. $a_n = \frac{8^n}{n!}$ **140.** $a_n = \frac{n^{41}}{19^n}$

141. Compound interest, deposits, and withdrawals If you invest an amount of money A_0 at a fixed annual interest rate r compounded m times per year, and if the constant amount b is added to the account at the end of each compounding period (or taken from the account if $b < 0$), then the amount you have after $n + 1$ compounding periods is

$$A_{n+1} = \left(1 + \frac{r}{m}\right)A_n + b. \quad (1)$$

a. If $A_0 = 1000, r = 0.02015, m = 12$, and $b = 50$, calculate and plot the first 100 points (n, A_n). How much money is in your account at the end of 5 years? Does $\{A_n\}$ converge? Is $\{A_n\}$ bounded?

b. Repeat part (a) with $A_0 = 5000, r = 0.0589, m = 12$, and $b = -50$.

c. If you invest 5000 dollars in a certificate of deposit (CD) that pays 4.5% annually, compounded quarterly, and you make no further investments in the CD, approximately how many years will it take before you have 20,000 dollars? What if the CD earns 6.25%?

d. It can be shown that for any $k \geq 0$, the sequence defined recursively by Equation (1) satisfies the relation

$$A_k = \left(1 + \frac{r}{m}\right)^k \left(A_0 + \frac{mb}{r}\right) - \frac{mb}{r}. \quad (2)$$

For the values of the constants A_0, r, m, and b given in part (a), validate this assertion by comparing the values of the first 50 terms of both sequences. Then show by direct substitution that the terms in Equation (2) satisfy the recursion formula in Equation (1).

142. Logistic difference equation The recursive relation

$$a_{n+1} = ra_n(1 - a_n)$$

is called the *logistic difference equation*, and when the initial value a_0 is given the equation defines the *logistic sequence* $\{a_n\}$. Throughout this exercise we choose a_0 in the interval $0 < a_0 < 1$, say $a_0 = 0.3$.

a. Choose $r = 3/4$. Calculate and plot the points (n, a_n) for the first 100 terms in the sequence. Does it appear to converge? What do you guess is the limit? Does the limit seem to depend on your choice of a_0?

b. Choose several values of r in the interval $1 < r < 3$ and repeat the procedures in part (a). Be sure to choose some points near the endpoints of the interval. Describe the behavior of the sequences you observe in your plots.

c. Now examine the behavior of the sequence for values of r near the endpoints of the interval $3 < r < 3.45$. The transition value $r = 3$ is called a **bifurcation value** and the new behavior of the sequence in the interval is called an **attracting 2-cycle**. Explain why this reasonably describes the behavior.

d. Next explore the behavior for r values near the endpoints of each of the intervals $3.45 < r < 3.54$ and $3.54 < r < 3.55$. Plot the first 200 terms of the sequences. Describe in your own words the behavior observed in your plots for each interval. Among how many values does the sequence appear to oscillate for each interval? The values $r = 3.45$ and $r = 3.54$ (rounded to two decimal places) are also called bifurcation values because the behavior of the sequence changes as r crosses over those values.

e. The situation gets even more interesting. There is actually an increasing sequence of bifurcation values $3 < 3.45 < 3.54 < \cdots < c_n < c_{n+1} \cdots$ such that for $c_n < r < c_{n+1}$ the logistic sequence $\{a_n\}$ eventually oscillates steadily among 2^n values, called an **attracting 2^n-cycle**. Moreover, the bifurcation sequence $\{c_n\}$ is bounded above by 3.57 (so it converges). If you choose a value of $r < 3.57$ you will observe a 2^n-cycle of some sort. Choose $r = 3.5695$ and plot 300 points.

f. Let us see what happens when $r > 3.57$. Choose $r = 3.65$ and calculate and plot the first 300 terms of $\{a_n\}$. Observe how the terms wander around in an unpredictable, chaotic fashion. You cannot predict the value of a_{n+1} from previous values of the sequence.

g. For $r = 3.65$ choose two starting values of a_0 that are close together, say, $a_0 = 0.3$ and $a_0 = 0.301$. Calculate and plot the first 300 values of the sequences determined by each starting value. Compare the behaviors observed in your plots. How far out do you go before the corresponding terms of your two sequences appear to depart from each other? Repeat the exploration for $r = 3.75$. Can you see how the plots look different depending on your choice of a_0? We say that the logistic sequence is *sensitive to the initial condition a_0*.

11.2 Infinite Series

An *infinite series* is the sum of an infinite sequence of numbers

$$a_1 + a_2 + a_3 + \cdots + a_n + \cdots$$

The goal of this section is to understand the meaning of such an infinite sum and to develop methods to calculate it. Since there are infinitely many terms to add in an infinite series, we cannot just keep adding to see what comes out. Instead we look at what we get by summing the first n terms of the sequence and stopping. The sum of the first n terms

$$s_n = a_1 + a_2 + a_3 + \cdots + a_n$$

is an ordinary finite sum and can be calculated by normal addition. It is called the *nth partial sum*. As n gets larger, we expect the partial sums to get closer and closer to a limiting value in the same sense that the terms of a sequence approach a limit, as discussed in Section 11.1.

For example, to assign meaning to an expression like

$$1 + \frac{1}{2} + \frac{1}{4} + \frac{1}{8} + \frac{1}{16} + \cdots$$

we add the terms one at a time from the beginning and look for a pattern in how these partial sums grow.

Partial sum		**Suggestive expression for partial sum**	**Value**
First:	$s_1 = 1$	$2 - 1$	1
Second:	$s_2 = 1 + \frac{1}{2}$	$2 - \frac{1}{2}$	$\frac{3}{2}$
Third:	$s_3 = 1 + \frac{1}{2} + \frac{1}{4}$	$2 - \frac{1}{4}$	$\frac{7}{4}$
⋮	⋮	⋮	⋮
nth:	$s_n = 1 + \frac{1}{2} + \frac{1}{4} + \cdots + \frac{1}{2^{n-1}}$	$2 - \frac{1}{2^{n-1}}$	$\frac{2^n - 1}{2^{n-1}}$

Indeed there is a pattern. The partial sums form a sequence whose nth term is

$$s_n = 2 - \frac{1}{2^{n-1}}.$$

This sequence of partial sums converges to 2 because $\lim_{n\to\infty}(1/2^n) = 0$. We say

$$\text{“the sum of the infinite series } 1 + \frac{1}{2} + \frac{1}{4} + \cdots + \frac{1}{2^{n-1}} + \cdots \text{ is 2.”}$$

Is the sum of any finite number of terms in this series equal to 2? No. Can we actually add an infinite number of terms one by one? No. But we can still define their sum by defining it to be the limit of the sequence of partial sums as $n \to \infty$, in this case 2 (Figure 11.5). Our knowledge of sequences and limits enables us to break away from the confines of finite sums.

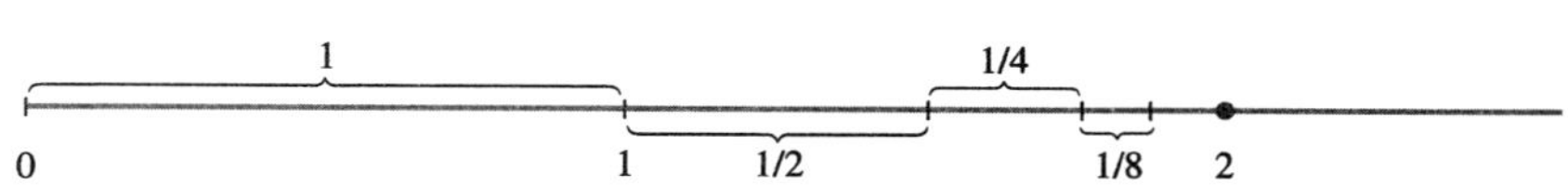

FIGURE 11.5 As the lengths 1, $^1/_2$, $^1/_4$, $^1/_8$, ... are added one by one, the sum approaches 2.

HISTORICAL BIOGRAPHY

Blaise Pascal
(1623–1662)

DEFINITIONS Infinite Series, *n*th Term, Partial Sum, Converges, Sum

Given a sequence of numbers $\{a_n\}$, an expression of the form

$$a_1 + a_2 + a_3 + \cdots + a_n + \cdots$$

is an **infinite series**. The number a_n is the ***n*th term** of the series. The sequence $\{s_n\}$ defined by

$$\begin{aligned} s_1 &= a_1 \\ s_2 &= a_1 + a_2 \\ &\vdots \\ s_n &= a_1 + a_2 + \cdots + a_n = \sum_{k=1}^{n} a_k \\ &\vdots \end{aligned}$$

is the **sequence of partial sums** of the series, the number s_n being the ***n*th partial sum**. If the sequence of partial sums converges to a limit L, we say that the series **converges** and that its **sum** is L. In this case, we also write

$$a_1 + a_2 + \cdots + a_n + \cdots = \sum_{n=1}^{\infty} a_n = L.$$

If the sequence of partial sums of the series does not converge, we say that the series **diverges**.

When we begin to study a given series $a_1 + a_2 + \cdots + a_n + \cdots$, we might not know whether it converges or diverges. In either case, it is convenient to use sigma notation to write the series as

$$\sum_{n=1}^{\infty} a_n, \quad \sum_{k=1}^{\infty} a_k, \quad \text{or} \quad \sum a_n$$

A useful shorthand when summation from 1 to ∞ is understood

Geometric Series

Geometric series are series of the form

$$a + ar + ar^2 + \cdots + ar^{n-1} + \cdots = \sum_{n=1}^{\infty} ar^{n-1}$$

in which a and r are fixed real numbers and $a \neq 0$. The series can also be written as $\sum_{n=0}^{\infty} ar^n$. The **ratio** r can be positive, as in

$$1 + \frac{1}{2} + \frac{1}{4} + \cdots + \left(\frac{1}{2}\right)^{n-1} + \cdots,$$

or negative, as in

$$1 - \frac{1}{3} + \frac{1}{9} - \cdots + \left(-\frac{1}{3}\right)^{n-1} + \cdots.$$

If $r = 1$, the nth partial sum of the geometric series is

$$s_n = a + a(1) + a(1)^2 + \cdots + a(1)^{n-1} = na,$$

and the series diverges because $\lim_{n\to\infty} s_n = \pm\infty$, depending on the sign of a. If $r = -1$, the series diverges because the nth partial sums alternate between a and 0. If $|r| \neq 1$, we can determine the convergence or divergence of the series in the following way:

$$\begin{aligned} s_n &= a + ar + ar^2 + \cdots + ar^{n-1} \\ rs_n &= ar + ar^2 + \cdots + ar^{n-1} + ar^n && \text{Multiply } s_n \text{ by } r. \\ s_n - rs_n &= a - ar^n && \text{Subtract } rs_n \text{ from } s_n\text{. Most of the terms on the right cancel.} \\ s_n(1-r) &= a(1-r^n) && \text{Factor.} \\ s_n &= \frac{a(1-r^n)}{1-r}, \quad (r \neq 1). && \text{We can solve for } s_n \text{ if } r \neq 1. \end{aligned}$$

If $|r| < 1$, then $r^n \to 0$ as $n \to \infty$ (as in Section 11.1) and $s_n \to a/(1-r)$. If $|r| > 1$, then $|r^n| \to \infty$ and the series diverges.

> If $|r| < 1$, the geometric series $a + ar + ar^2 + \cdots + ar^{n-1} + \cdots$ converges to $a/(1-r)$:
>
> $$\sum_{n=1}^{\infty} ar^{n-1} = \frac{a}{1-r}, \qquad |r| < 1.$$
>
> If $|r| \geq 1$, the series diverges.

We have determined when a geometric series converges or diverges, and to what value. Often we can determine that a series converges without knowing the value to which it converges, as we will see in the next several sections. The formula $a/(1-r)$ for the sum of a geometric series applies *only* when the summation index begins with $n = 1$ in the expression $\sum_{n=1}^{\infty} ar^{n-1}$ (or with the index $n = 0$ if we write the series as $\sum_{n=0}^{\infty} ar^n$).

EXAMPLE 1 Index Starts with $n = 1$

The geometric series with $a = 1/9$ and $r = 1/3$ is

$$\frac{1}{9} + \frac{1}{27} + \frac{1}{81} + \cdots = \sum_{n=1}^{\infty} \frac{1}{9}\left(\frac{1}{3}\right)^{n-1} = \frac{1/9}{1-(1/3)} = \frac{1}{6}.$$ ■

EXAMPLE 2 Index Starts with $n = 0$

The series

$$\sum_{n=0}^{\infty} \frac{(-1)^n 5}{4^n} = 5 - \frac{5}{4} + \frac{5}{16} - \frac{5}{64} + \cdots$$

is a geometric series with $a = 5$ and $r = -1/4$. It converges to

$$\frac{a}{1-r} = \frac{5}{1+(1/4)} = 4.$$ ■

EXAMPLE 3 A Bouncing Ball

You drop a ball from a meters above a flat surface. Each time the ball hits the surface after falling a distance h, it rebounds a distance rh, where r is positive but less than 1. Find the total distance the ball travels up and down (Figure 11.6).

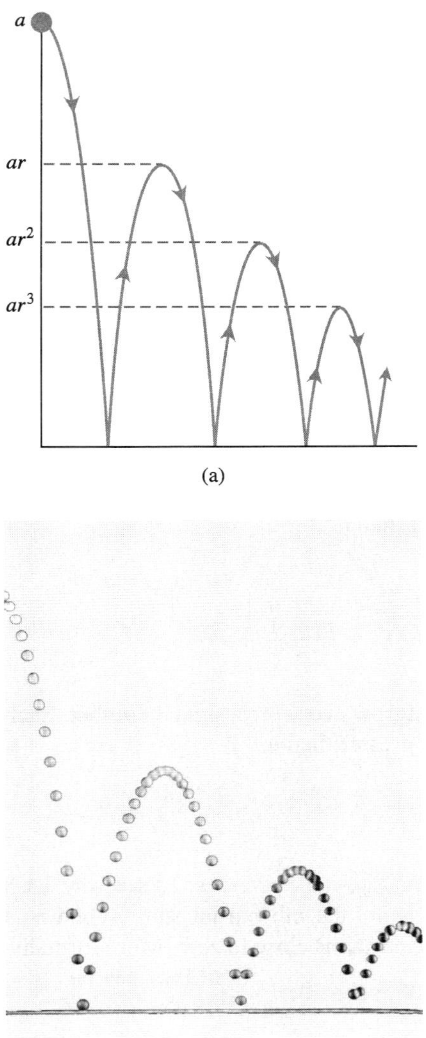

(a)

(b)

FIGURE 11.6 (a) Example 3 shows how to use a geometric series to calculate the total vertical distance traveled by a bouncing ball if the height of each rebound is reduced by the factor r. (b) A stroboscopic photo of a bouncing ball.

Solution The total distance is

$$s = a + \underbrace{2ar + 2ar^2 + 2ar^3 + \cdots}_{\text{This sum is } 2ar/(1-r).} = a + \frac{2ar}{1-r} = a\frac{1+r}{1-r}.$$

If $a = 6$ m and $r = 2/3$, for instance, the distance is

$$s = 6\frac{1 + (2/3)}{1 - (2/3)} = 6\left(\frac{5/3}{1/3}\right) = 30 \text{ m}.$$

EXAMPLE 4 Repeating Decimals

Express the repeating decimal 5.232323 . . . as the ratio of two integers.

Solution

$$\begin{aligned} 5.232323\ldots &= 5 + \frac{23}{100} + \frac{23}{(100)^2} + \frac{23}{(100)^3} + \cdots \\ &= 5 + \frac{23}{100}\underbrace{\left(1 + \frac{1}{100} + \left(\frac{1}{100}\right)^2 + \cdots\right)}_{1/(1-0.01)} \qquad a = 1,\ r = 1/100 \\ &= 5 + \frac{23}{100}\left(\frac{1}{0.99}\right) = 5 + \frac{23}{99} = \frac{518}{99} \end{aligned}$$

Unfortunately, formulas like the one for the sum of a convergent geometric series are rare and we usually have to settle for an estimate of a series' sum (more about this later). The next example, however, is another case in which we can find the sum exactly.

EXAMPLE 5 A Nongeometric but Telescoping Series

Find the sum of the series $\sum_{n=1}^{\infty} \frac{1}{n(n+1)}$.

Solution We look for a pattern in the sequence of partial sums that might lead to a formula for s_k. The key observation is the partial fraction decomposition

$$\frac{1}{n(n+1)} = \frac{1}{n} - \frac{1}{n+1},$$

so

$$\sum_{n=1}^{k} \frac{1}{n(n+1)} = \sum_{n=1}^{k}\left(\frac{1}{n} - \frac{1}{n+1}\right)$$

and

$$s_k = \left(\frac{1}{1} - \frac{1}{2}\right) + \left(\frac{1}{2} - \frac{1}{3}\right) + \left(\frac{1}{3} - \frac{1}{4}\right) + \cdots + \left(\frac{1}{k} - \frac{1}{k+1}\right).$$

Removing parentheses and canceling adjacent terms of opposite sign collapses the sum to

$$s_k = 1 - \frac{1}{k+1}.$$

We now see that $s_k \to 1$ as $k \to \infty$. The series converges, and its sum is 1:

$$\sum_{n=1}^{\infty} \frac{1}{n(n+1)} = 1.$$

■

Divergent Series

One reason that a series may fail to converge is that its terms don't become small.

EXAMPLE 6 Partial Sums Outgrow Any Number

(a) The series

$$\sum_{n=1}^{\infty} n^2 = 1 + 4 + 9 + \cdots + n^2 + \cdots$$

diverges because the partial sums grow beyond every number L. After $n = 1$, the partial sum $s_n = 1 + 4 + 9 + \cdots + n^2$ is greater than n^2.

(b) The series

$$\sum_{n=1}^{\infty} \frac{n+1}{n} = \frac{2}{1} + \frac{3}{2} + \frac{4}{3} + \cdots + \frac{n+1}{n} + \cdots$$

diverges because the partial sums eventually outgrow every preassigned number. Each term is greater than 1, so the sum of n terms is greater than n. ■

The nth-Term Test for Divergence

Observe that $\lim_{n\to\infty} a_n$ must equal zero if the series $\sum_{n=1}^{\infty} a_n$ converges. To see why, let S represent the series' sum and $s_n = a_1 + a_2 + \cdots + a_n$ the nth partial sum. When n is large, both s_n and s_{n-1} are close to S, so their difference, a_n, is close to zero. More formally,

$$a_n = s_n - s_{n-1} \quad \to \quad S - S = 0. \qquad \text{Difference Rule for sequences}$$

This establishes the following theorem.

Caution
Theorem 7 *does not say* that $\sum_{n=1}^{\infty} a_n$ converges if $a_n \to 0$. It is possible for a series to diverge when $a_n \to 0$.

THEOREM 7

If $\sum_{n=1}^{\infty} a_n$ converges, then $a_n \to 0$.

Theorem 7 leads to a test for detecting the kind of divergence that occurred in Example 6.

The nth-Term Test for Divergence

$\sum_{n=1}^{\infty} a_n$ diverges if $\lim_{n\to\infty} a_n$ fails to exist or is different from zero.

EXAMPLE 7 Applying the *n*th-Term Test

(a) $\sum_{n=1}^{\infty} n^2$ diverges because $n^2 \to \infty$

(b) $\sum_{n=1}^{\infty} \frac{n+1}{n}$ diverges because $\frac{n+1}{n} \to 1$

(c) $\sum_{n=1}^{\infty} (-1)^{n+1}$ diverges because $\lim_{n\to\infty}(-1)^{n+1}$ does not exist

(d) $\sum_{n=1}^{\infty} \frac{-n}{2n+5}$ diverges because $\lim_{n\to\infty} \frac{-n}{2n+5} = -\frac{1}{2} \neq 0.$ ■

EXAMPLE 8 $a_n \to 0$ but the Series Diverges

The series

$$1 + \underbrace{\frac{1}{2} + \frac{1}{2}}_{\text{2 terms}} + \underbrace{\frac{1}{4} + \frac{1}{4} + \frac{1}{4} + \frac{1}{4}}_{\text{4 terms}} + \cdots + \underbrace{\frac{1}{2^n} + \frac{1}{2^n} + \cdots + \frac{1}{2^n}}_{2^n \text{ terms}} + \cdots$$

diverges because the terms are grouped into clusters that add to 1, so the partial sums increase without bound. However, the terms of the series form a sequence that converges to 0. Example 1 of Section 11.3 shows that the harmonic series also behaves in this manner. ■

Combining Series

Whenever we have two convergent series, we can add them term by term, subtract them term by term, or multiply them by constants to make new convergent series.

THEOREM 8

If $\sum a_n = A$ and $\sum b_n = B$ are convergent series, then

1. *Sum Rule:* $\sum(a_n + b_n) = \sum a_n + \sum b_n = A + B$
2. *Difference Rule:* $\sum(a_n - b_n) = \sum a_n - \sum b_n = A - B$
3. *Constant Multiple Rule:* $\sum ka_n = k\sum a_n = kA$ (Any number k).

Proof The three rules for series follow from the analogous rules for sequences in Theorem 1, Section 11.1. To prove the Sum Rule for series, let

$$A_n = a_1 + a_2 + \cdots + a_n, \quad B_n = b_1 + b_2 + \cdots + b_n.$$

Then the partial sums of $\sum(a_n + b_n)$ are

$$\begin{aligned} s_n &= (a_1 + b_1) + (a_2 + b_2) + \cdots + (a_n + b_n) \\ &= (a_1 + \cdots + a_n) + (b_1 + \cdots + b_n) \\ &= A_n + B_n. \end{aligned}$$

Since $A_n \to A$ and $B_n \to B$, we have $s_n \to A + B$ by the Sum Rule for sequences. The proof of the Difference Rule is similar.

To prove the Constant Multiple Rule for series, observe that the partial sums of $\sum ka_n$ form the sequence

$$s_n = ka_1 + ka_2 + \cdots + ka_n = k(a_1 + a_2 + \cdots + a_n) = kA_n,$$

which converges to kA by the Constant Multiple Rule for sequences. ■

As corollaries of Theorem 8, we have

1. Every nonzero constant multiple of a divergent series diverges.
2. If $\sum a_n$ converges and $\sum b_n$ diverges, then $\sum(a_n + b_n)$ and $\sum(a_n - b_n)$ both diverge.

We omit the proofs.

CAUTION Remember that $\sum(a_n + b_n)$ can converge when $\sum a_n$ and $\sum b_n$ both diverge. For example, $\sum a_n = 1 + 1 + 1 + \cdots$ and $\sum b_n = (-1) + (-1) + (-1) + \cdots$ diverge, whereas $\sum(a_n + b_n) = 0 + 0 + 0 + \cdots$ converges to 0.

EXAMPLE 9 Find the sums of the following series.

(a)
$$\begin{aligned}\sum_{n=1}^{\infty} \frac{3^{n-1} - 1}{6^{n-1}} &= \sum_{n=1}^{\infty} \left(\frac{1}{2^{n-1}} - \frac{1}{6^{n-1}}\right) \\ &= \sum_{n=1}^{\infty} \frac{1}{2^{n-1}} - \sum_{n=1}^{\infty} \frac{1}{6^{n-1}} && \text{Difference Rule} \\ &= \frac{1}{1 - (1/2)} - \frac{1}{1 - (1/6)} && \text{Geometric series with } a = 1 \text{ and } r = 1/2,\ 1/6 \\ &= 2 - \frac{6}{5} \\ &= \frac{4}{5}\end{aligned}$$

(b)
$$\begin{aligned}\sum_{n=0}^{\infty} \frac{4}{2^n} &= 4\sum_{n=0}^{\infty} \frac{1}{2^n} && \text{Constant Multiple Rule} \\ &= 4\left(\frac{1}{1 - (1/2)}\right) && \text{Geometric series with } a = 1,\ r = 1/2 \\ &= 8\end{aligned}$$
■

Adding or Deleting Terms

We can add a finite number of terms to a series or delete a finite number of terms without altering the series' convergence or divergence, although in the case of convergence this will usually change the sum. If $\sum_{n=1}^{\infty} a_n$ converges, then $\sum_{n=k}^{\infty} a_n$ converges for any $k > 1$ and

$$\sum_{n=1}^{\infty} a_n = a_1 + a_2 + \cdots + a_{k-1} + \sum_{n=k}^{\infty} a_n.$$

Conversely, if $\sum_{n=k}^{\infty} a_n$ converges for any $k > 1$, then $\sum_{n=1}^{\infty} a_n$ converges. Thus,

$$\sum_{n=1}^{\infty} \frac{1}{5^n} = \frac{1}{5} + \frac{1}{25} + \frac{1}{125} + \sum_{n=4}^{\infty} \frac{1}{5^n}$$

and

$$\sum_{n=4}^{\infty} \frac{1}{5^n} = \left(\sum_{n=1}^{\infty} \frac{1}{5^n}\right) - \frac{1}{5} - \frac{1}{25} - \frac{1}{125}.$$

Reindexing

HISTORICAL BIOGRAPHY

Richard Dedekind
(1831–1916)

As long as we preserve the order of its terms, we can reindex any series without altering its convergence. To raise the starting value of the index h units, replace the n in the formula for a_n by $n - h$:

$$\sum_{n=1}^{\infty} a_n = \sum_{n=1+h}^{\infty} a_{n-h} = a_1 + a_2 + a_3 + \cdots.$$

To lower the starting value of the index h units, replace the n in the formula for a_n by $n + h$:

$$\sum_{n=1}^{\infty} a_n = \sum_{n=1-h}^{\infty} a_{n+h} = a_1 + a_2 + a_3 + \cdots.$$

It works like a horizontal shift. We saw this in starting a geometric series with the index $n = 0$ instead of the index $n = 1$, but we can use any other starting index value as well. We usually give preference to indexings that lead to simple expressions.

EXAMPLE 10 Reindexing a Geometric Series

We can write the geometric series

$$\sum_{n=1}^{\infty} \frac{1}{2^{n-1}} = 1 + \frac{1}{2} + \frac{1}{4} + \cdots$$

as

$$\sum_{n=0}^{\infty} \frac{1}{2^n}, \qquad \sum_{n=5}^{\infty} \frac{1}{2^{n-5}}, \qquad \text{or even} \qquad \sum_{n=-4}^{\infty} \frac{1}{2^{n+4}}.$$

The partial sums remain the same no matter what indexing we choose. ■

EXERCISES 11.2

Finding nth Partial Sums

In Exercises 1–6, find a formula for the nth partial sum of each series and use it to find the series' sum if the series converges.

1. $2 + \frac{2}{3} + \frac{2}{9} + \frac{2}{27} + \cdots + \frac{2}{3^{n-1}} + \cdots$

2. $\frac{9}{100} + \frac{9}{100^2} + \frac{9}{100^3} + \cdots + \frac{9}{100^n} + \cdots$

3. $1 - \frac{1}{2} + \frac{1}{4} - \frac{1}{8} + \cdots + (-1)^{n-1}\frac{1}{2^{n-1}} + \cdots$

4. $1 - 2 + 4 - 8 + \cdots + (-1)^{n-1}2^{n-1} + \cdots$

5. $\frac{1}{2\cdot 3} + \frac{1}{3\cdot 4} + \frac{1}{4\cdot 5} + \cdots + \frac{1}{(n+1)(n+2)} + \cdots$

6. $\frac{5}{1\cdot 2} + \frac{5}{2\cdot 3} + \frac{5}{3\cdot 4} + \cdots + \frac{5}{n(n+1)} + \cdots$

Series with Geometric Terms

In Exercises 7–14, write out the first few terms of each series to show how the series starts. Then find the sum of the series.

7. $\sum_{n=0}^{\infty} \frac{(-1)^n}{4^n}$

8. $\sum_{n=2}^{\infty} \frac{1}{4^n}$

9. $\sum_{n=1}^{\infty} \frac{7}{4^n}$

10. $\sum_{n=0}^{\infty} (-1)^n \frac{5}{4^n}$

11. $\sum_{n=0}^{\infty} \left(\frac{5}{2^n} + \frac{1}{3^n}\right)$

12. $\sum_{n=0}^{\infty} \left(\frac{5}{2^n} - \frac{1}{3^n}\right)$

13. $\sum_{n=0}^{\infty} \left(\frac{1}{2^n} + \frac{(-1)^n}{5^n}\right)$

14. $\sum_{n=0}^{\infty} \left(\frac{2^{n+1}}{5^n}\right)$

Telescoping Series

Find the sum of each series in Exercises 15–22.

15. $\sum_{n=1}^{\infty} \frac{4}{(4n-3)(4n+1)}$

16. $\sum_{n=1}^{\infty} \frac{6}{(2n-1)(2n+1)}$

17. $\sum_{n=1}^{\infty} \frac{40n}{(2n-1)^2(2n+1)^2}$

18. $\sum_{n=1}^{\infty} \frac{2n+1}{n^2(n+1)^2}$

19. $\sum_{n=1}^{\infty} \left(\frac{1}{\sqrt{n}} - \frac{1}{\sqrt{n+1}}\right)$

20. $\sum_{n=1}^{\infty} \left(\frac{1}{2^{1/n}} - \frac{1}{2^{1/(n+1)}}\right)$

21. $\sum_{n=1}^{\infty} \left(\frac{1}{\ln(n+2)} - \frac{1}{\ln(n+1)}\right)$

22. $\sum_{n=1}^{\infty} (\tan^{-1}(n) - \tan^{-1}(n+1))$

Convergence or Divergence

Which series in Exercises 23–40 converge, and which diverge? Give reasons for your answers. If a series converges, find its sum.

23. $\sum_{n=0}^{\infty} \left(\frac{1}{\sqrt{2}}\right)^n$

24. $\sum_{n=0}^{\infty} (\sqrt{2})^n$

25. $\sum_{n=1}^{\infty} (-1)^{n+1} \frac{3}{2^n}$

26. $\sum_{n=1}^{\infty} (-1)^{n+1} n$

27. $\sum_{n=0}^{\infty} \cos n\pi$

28. $\sum_{n=0}^{\infty} \frac{\cos n\pi}{5^n}$

29. $\sum_{n=0}^{\infty} e^{-2n}$

30. $\sum_{n=1}^{\infty} \ln \frac{1}{n}$

31. $\sum_{n=1}^{\infty} \frac{2}{10^n}$

32. $\sum_{n=0}^{\infty} \frac{1}{x^n}, \quad |x| > 1$

33. $\sum_{n=0}^{\infty} \frac{2^n - 1}{3^n}$

34. $\sum_{n=1}^{\infty} \left(1 - \frac{1}{n}\right)^n$

35. $\sum_{n=0}^{\infty} \frac{n!}{1000^n}$

36. $\sum_{n=1}^{\infty} \frac{n^n}{n!}$

37. $\sum_{n=1}^{\infty} \ln\left(\frac{n}{n+1}\right)$

38. $\sum_{n=1}^{\infty} \ln\left(\frac{n}{2n+1}\right)$

39. $\sum_{n=0}^{\infty} \left(\frac{e}{\pi}\right)^n$

40. $\sum_{n=0}^{\infty} \frac{e^{n\pi}}{\pi^{ne}}$

Geometric Series

In each of the geometric series in Exercises 41–44, write out the first few terms of the series to find a and r, and find the sum of the series. Then express the inequality $|r| < 1$ in terms of x and find the values of x for which the inequality holds and the series converges.

41. $\sum_{n=0}^{\infty} (-1)^n x^n$

42. $\sum_{n=0}^{\infty} (-1)^n x^{2n}$

43. $\sum_{n=0}^{\infty} 3\left(\frac{x-1}{2}\right)^n$

44. $\sum_{n=0}^{\infty} \frac{(-1)^n}{2} \left(\frac{1}{3 + \sin x}\right)^n$

In Exercises 45–50, find the values of x for which the given geometric series converges. Also, find the sum of the series (as a function of x) for those values of x.

45. $\sum_{n=0}^{\infty} 2^n x^n$

46. $\sum_{n=0}^{\infty} (-1)^n x^{-2n}$

47. $\sum_{n=0}^{\infty} (-1)^n (x+1)^n$

48. $\sum_{n=0}^{\infty} \left(-\frac{1}{2}\right)^n (x-3)^n$

49. $\sum_{n=0}^{\infty} \sin^n x$

50. $\sum_{n=0}^{\infty} (\ln x)^n$

Repeating Decimals

Express each of the numbers in Exercises 51–58 as the ratio of two integers.

51. $0.\overline{23} = 0.23\ 23\ 23\ldots$

52. $0.\overline{234} = 0.234\ 234\ 234\ldots$

53. $0.\overline{7} = 0.7777\ldots$

54. $0.\overline{d} = 0.dddd\ldots$, where d is a digit

55. $0.0\overline{6} = 0.06666\ldots$

56. $1.\overline{414} = 1.414\ 414\ 414\ldots$

57. $1.24\overline{123} = 1.24\ 123\ 123\ 123\ldots$

58. $3.\overline{142857} = 3.142857\ 142857\ldots$

Theory and Examples

59. The series in Exercise 5 can also be written as

$$\sum_{n=1}^{\infty} \frac{1}{(n+1)(n+2)} \quad \text{and} \quad \sum_{n=-1}^{\infty} \frac{1}{(n+3)(n+4)}.$$

Write it as a sum beginning with **(a)** $n = -2$, **(b)** $n = 0$, **(c)** $n = 5$.

60. The series in Exercise 6 can also be written as

$$\sum_{n=1}^{\infty} \frac{5}{n(n+1)} \quad \text{and} \quad \sum_{n=0}^{\infty} \frac{5}{(n+1)(n+2)}.$$

Write it as a sum beginning with **(a)** $n = -1$, **(b)** $n = 3$, **(c)** $n = 20$.

61. Make up an infinite series of nonzero terms whose sum is

a. 1 **b.** -3 **c.** 0.

62. (*Continuation of Exercise 61.*) Can you make an infinite series of nonzero terms that converges to any number you want? Explain.

63. Show by example that $\sum(a_n/b_n)$ may diverge even though $\sum a_n$ and $\sum b_n$ converge and no b_n equals 0.

64. Find convergent geometric series $A = \sum a_n$ and $B = \sum b_n$ that illustrate the fact that $\sum a_n b_n$ may converge without being equal to AB.

65. Show by example that $\sum(a_n/b_n)$ may converge to something other than A/B even when $A = \sum a_n$, $B = \sum b_n \neq 0$, and no b_n equals 0.

66. If $\sum a_n$ converges and $a_n > 0$ for all n, can anything be said about $\sum(1/a_n)$? Give reasons for your answer.

67. What happens if you add a finite number of terms to a divergent series or delete a finite number of terms from a divergent series? Give reasons for your answer.

68. If $\sum a_n$ converges and $\sum b_n$ diverges, can anything be said about their term-by-term sum $\sum(a_n + b_n)$? Give reasons for your answer.

69. Make up a geometric series $\sum ar^{n-1}$ that converges to the number 5 if

a. $a = 2$ **b.** $a = 13/2$.

70. Find the value of b for which

$$1 + e^b + e^{2b} + e^{3b} + \cdots = 9.$$

71. For what values of r does the infinite series

$$1 + 2r + r^2 + 2r^3 + r^4 + 2r^5 + r^6 + \cdots$$

converge? Find the sum of the series when it converges.

72. Show that the error $(L - s_n)$ obtained by replacing a convergent geometric series with one of its partial sums s_n is $ar^n/(1 - r)$.

73. A ball is dropped from a height of 4 m. Each time it strikes the pavement after falling from a height of h meters it rebounds to a height of $0.75h$ meters. Find the total distance the ball travels up and down.

74. (*Continuation of Exercise 73.*) Find the total number of seconds the ball in Exercise 73 is traveling. (*Hint:* The formula $s = 4.9t^2$ gives $t = \sqrt{s/4.9}$.)

75. The accompanying figure shows the first five of a sequence of squares. The outermost square has an area of 4 m^2. Each of the other squares is obtained by joining the midpoints of the sides of the squares before it. Find the sum of the areas of all the squares.

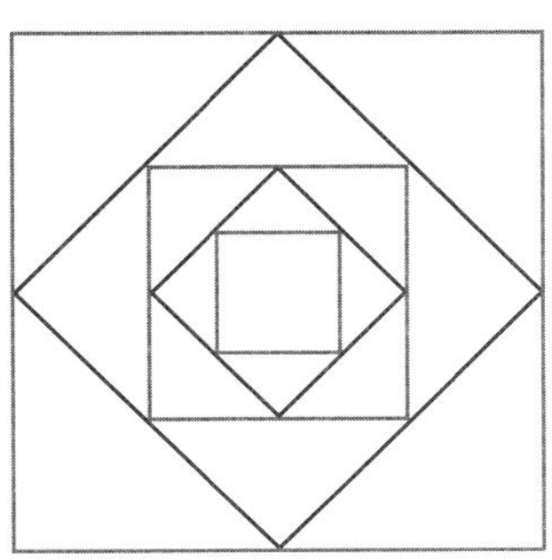

76. The accompanying figure shows the first three rows and part of the fourth row of a sequence of rows of semicircles. There are 2^n semicircles in the nth row, each of radius $1/2^n$. Find the sum of the areas of all the semicircles.

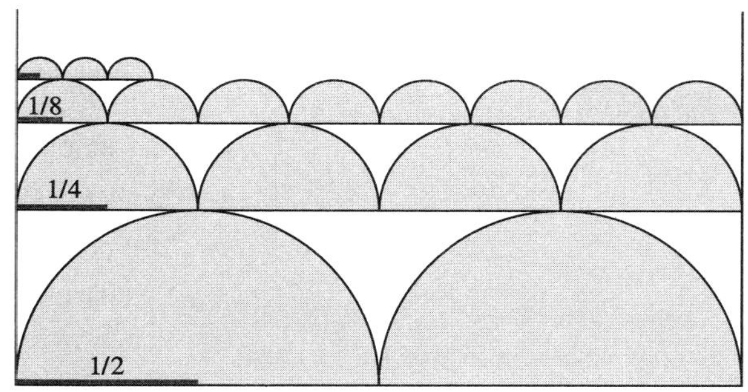

77. Helga von Koch's snowflake curve Helga von Koch's snowflake is a curve of infinite length that encloses a region of finite area. To see why this is so, suppose the curve is generated by starting with an equilateral triangle whose sides have length 1.

a. Find the length L_n of the nth curve C_n and show that $\lim_{n\to\infty} L_n = \infty$.

b. Find the area A_n of the region enclosed by C_n and calculate $\lim_{n\to\infty} A_n$.

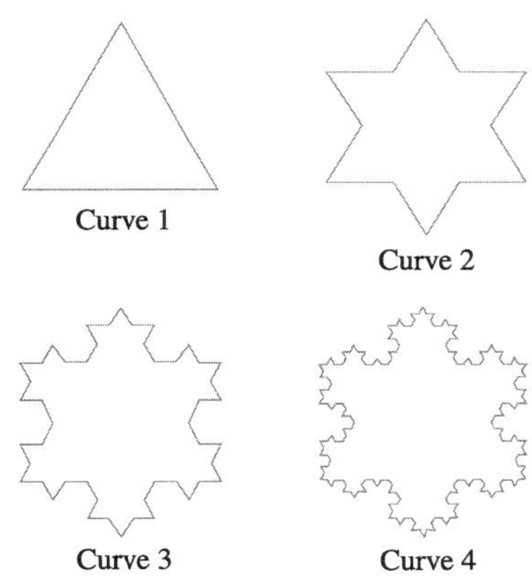

78. The accompanying figure provides an informal proof that $\sum_{n=1}^{\infty}(1/n^2)$ is less than 2. Explain what is going on. (*Source:* "Convergence with Pictures" by P. J. Rippon, *American Mathematical Monthly*, Vol. 93, No. 6, 1986, pp. 476–478.)

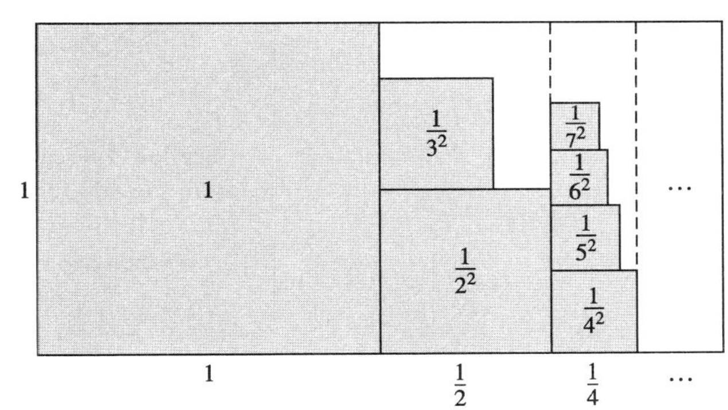

11.3 The Integral Test

Given a series $\sum a_n$, we have two questions:

1. Does the series converge?
2. If it converges, what is its sum?

Much of the rest of this chapter is devoted to the first question, and in this section we answer that question by making a connection to the convergence of the improper integral $\int_1^\infty f(x)\,dx$. However, as a practical matter the second question is also important, and we will return to it later.

In this section and the next two, we study series that do not have negative terms. The reason for this restriction is that the partial sums of these series form nondecreasing sequences, and nondecreasing sequences that are bounded from above always converge (Theorem 6, Section 11.1). To show that a series of nonnegative terms converges, we need only show that its partial sums are bounded from above.

It may at first seem to be a drawback that this approach establishes the fact of convergence without producing the sum of the series in question. Surely it would be better to compute sums of series directly from formulas for their partial sums. But in most cases such formulas are not available, and in their absence we have to turn instead to the two-step procedure of first establishing convergence and then approximating the sum.

Nondecreasing Partial Sums

Suppose that $\sum_{n=1}^{\infty} a_n$ is an infinite series with $a_n \geq 0$ for all n. Then each partial sum is greater than or equal to its predecessor because $s_{n+1} = s_n + a_n$:

$$s_1 \leq s_2 \leq s_3 \leq \cdots \leq s_n \leq s_{n+1} \leq \cdots.$$

Since the partial sums form a nondecreasing sequence, the Nondecreasing Sequence Theorem (Theorem 6, Section 11.1) tells us that the series will converge if and only if the partial sums are bounded from above.

Corollary of Theorem 6

A series $\sum_{n=1}^{\infty} a_n$ of nonnegative terms converges if and only if its partial sums are bounded from above.

HISTORICAL BIOGRAPHY

Nicole Oresme
(1320–1382)

EXAMPLE 1 The Harmonic Series

The series

$$\sum_{n=1}^{\infty} \frac{1}{n} = 1 + \frac{1}{2} + \frac{1}{3} + \cdots + \frac{1}{n} + \cdots$$

is called the **harmonic series**. The harmonic series is divergent, but this doesn't follow from the nth-Term Test. The nth term $1/n$ does go to zero, but the series still diverges. The reason it diverges is because there is no upper bound for its partial sums. To see why, group the terms of the series in the following way:

$$1 + \frac{1}{2} + \underbrace{\left(\frac{1}{3} + \frac{1}{4}\right)}_{>\frac{2}{4}=\frac{1}{2}} + \underbrace{\left(\frac{1}{5} + \frac{1}{6} + \frac{1}{7} + \frac{1}{8}\right)}_{>\frac{4}{8}=\frac{1}{2}} + \underbrace{\left(\frac{1}{9} + \frac{1}{10} + \cdots + \frac{1}{16}\right)}_{>\frac{8}{16}=\frac{1}{2}} + \cdots.$$

The sum of the first two terms is 1.5. The sum of the next two terms is $1/3 + 1/4$, which is greater than $1/4 + 1/4 = 1/2$. The sum of the next four terms is $1/5 + 1/6 + 1/7 + 1/8$, which is greater than $1/8 + 1/8 + 1/8 + 1/8 = 1/2$. The sum of the next eight terms is $1/9 + 1/10 + 1/11 + 1/12 + 1/13 + 1/14 + 1/15 + 1/16$, which is greater than $8/16 = 1/2$. The sum of the next 16 terms is greater than $16/32 = 1/2$, and so on. In general, the sum of 2^n terms ending with $1/2^{n+1}$ is greater than $2^n/2^{n+1} = 1/2$. The sequence of partial sums is not bounded from above: If $n = 2^k$, the partial sum s_n is greater than $k/2$. The harmonic series diverges. ■

The Integral Test

We introduce the Integral Test with a series that is related to the harmonic series, but whose nth term is $1/n^2$ instead of $1/n$.

EXAMPLE 2 Does the following series converge?

$$\sum_{n=1}^{\infty} \frac{1}{n^2} = 1 + \frac{1}{4} + \frac{1}{9} + \frac{1}{16} + \cdots + \frac{1}{n^2} + \cdots$$

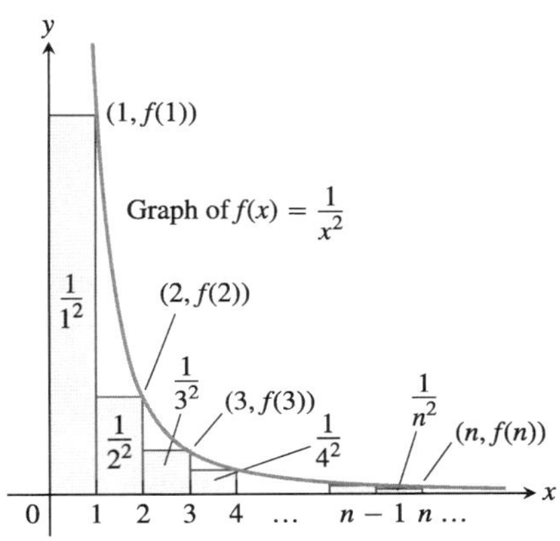

FIGURE 11.7 The sum of the areas of the rectangles under the graph of $f(x) = 1/x^2$ is less than the area under the graph (Example 2).

Solution We determine the convergence of $\sum_{n=1}^{\infty}(1/n^2)$ by comparing it with $\int_1^{\infty}(1/x^2)\,dx$. To carry out the comparison, we think of the terms of the series as values of the function $f(x) = 1/x^2$ and interpret these values as the areas of rectangles under the curve $y = 1/x^2$.

As Figure 11.7 shows,

$$\begin{aligned} s_n &= \frac{1}{1^2} + \frac{1}{2^2} + \frac{1}{3^2} + \cdots + \frac{1}{n^2} \\ &= f(1) + f(2) + f(3) + \cdots + f(n) \\ &< f(1) + \int_1^n \frac{1}{x^2}\,dx \\ &< 1 + \int_1^{\infty} \frac{1}{x^2}\,dx \\ &< 1 + 1 = 2. \end{aligned}$$

As in Section 8.8, Example 3, $\int_1^{\infty}(1/x^2)\,dx = 1$.

Thus the partial sums of $\sum_{n=1}^{\infty} 1/n^2$ are bounded from above (by 2) and the series converges. The sum of the series is known to be $\pi^2/6 \approx 1.64493$. (See Exercise 16 in Section 11.11.) ■

Caution
The series and integral need not have the same value in the convergent case. As we noted in Example 2, $\sum_{n=1}^{\infty}(1/n^2) = \pi^2/6$ while $\int_1^{\infty}(1/x^2)\,dx = 1$.

THEOREM 9 The Integral Test
Let $\{a_n\}$ be a sequence of positive terms. Suppose that $a_n = f(n)$, where f is a continuous, positive, decreasing function of x for all $x \geq N$ (N a positive integer). Then the series $\sum_{n=N}^{\infty} a_n$ and the integral $\int_N^{\infty} f(x)\,dx$ both converge or both diverge.

Proof We establish the test for the case $N = 1$. The proof for general N is similar.

We start with the assumption that f is a decreasing function with $f(n) = a_n$ for every n. This leads us to observe that the rectangles in Figure 11.8a, which have areas

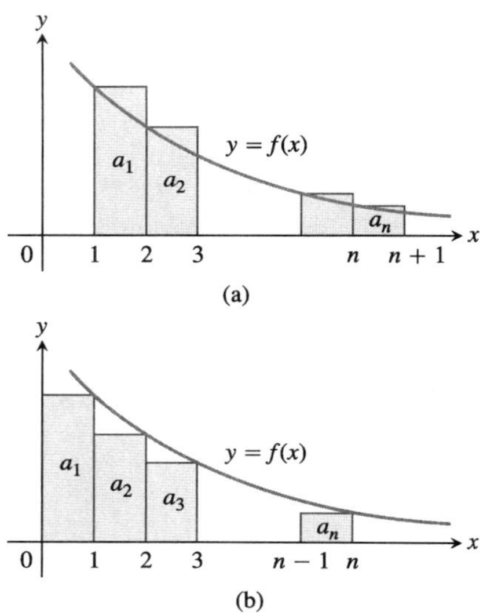

FIGURE 11.8 Subject to the conditions of the Integral Test, the series $\sum_{n=1}^{\infty} a_n$ and the integral $\int_1^{\infty} f(x)\,dx$ both converge or both diverge.

$a_1, a_2, \ldots, a_n$, collectively enclose more area than that under the curve $y = f(x)$ from $x = 1$ to $x = n + 1$. That is,

$$\int_1^{n+1} f(x)\,dx \le a_1 + a_2 + \cdots + a_n.$$

In Figure 11.8b the rectangles have been faced to the left instead of to the right. If we momentarily disregard the first rectangle, of area a_1, we see that

$$a_2 + a_3 + \cdots + a_n \le \int_1^n f(x)\,dx.$$

If we include a_1, we have

$$a_1 + a_2 + \cdots + a_n \le a_1 + \int_1^n f(x)\,dx.$$

Combining these results gives

$$\int_1^{n+1} f(x)\,dx \le a_1 + a_2 + \cdots + a_n \le a_1 + \int_1^n f(x)\,dx.$$

These inequalities hold for each n, and continue to hold as $n \to \infty$.

If $\int_1^{\infty} f(x)\,dx$ is finite, the right-hand inequality shows that $\sum a_n$ is finite. If $\int_1^{\infty} f(x)\,dx$ is infinite, the left-hand inequality shows that $\sum a_n$ is infinite. Hence the series and the integral are both finite or both infinite. ■

EXAMPLE 3 The p-Series

Show that the ***p*-series**

$$\sum_{n=1}^{\infty} \frac{1}{n^p} = \frac{1}{1^p} + \frac{1}{2^p} + \frac{1}{3^p} + \cdots + \frac{1}{n^p} + \cdots$$

(p a real constant) converges if $p > 1$, and diverges if $p \le 1$.

Solution If $p > 1$, then $f(x) = 1/x^p$ is a positive decreasing function of x. Since

$$\begin{aligned}\int_1^{\infty} \frac{1}{x^p}\,dx &= \int_1^{\infty} x^{-p}\,dx = \lim_{b\to\infty}\left[\frac{x^{-p+1}}{-p+1}\right]_1^b \\ &= \frac{1}{1-p}\lim_{b\to\infty}\left(\frac{1}{b^{p-1}} - 1\right) \\ &= \frac{1}{1-p}(0-1) = \frac{1}{p-1},\end{aligned}$$

$b^{p-1} \to \infty$ as $b \to \infty$ because $p - 1 > 0$.

the series converges by the Integral Test. We emphasize that the sum of the p-series is *not* $1/(p-1)$. The series converges, but we don't know the value it converges to.

If $p < 1$, then $1 - p > 0$ and

$$\int_1^{\infty} \frac{1}{x^p}\,dx = \frac{1}{1-p}\lim_{b\to\infty}\left(b^{1-p} - 1\right) = \infty.$$

The series diverges by the Integral Test.

If $p = 1$, we have the (divergent) harmonic series

$$1 + \frac{1}{2} + \frac{1}{3} + \cdots + \frac{1}{n} + \cdots.$$

We have convergence for $p > 1$ but divergence for every other value of p. ■

The p-series with $p = 1$ is the **harmonic series** (Example 1). The p-Series Test shows that the harmonic series is just *barely* divergent; if we increase p to 1.000000001, for instance, the series converges!

The slowness with which the partial sums of the harmonic series approaches infinity is impressive. For instance, it takes about 178,482,301 terms of the harmonic series to move the partial sums beyond 20. It would take your calculator several weeks to compute a sum with this many terms. (See also Exercise 33b.)

EXAMPLE 4 A Convergent Series

The series

$$\sum_{n=1}^{\infty} \frac{1}{n^2 + 1}$$

converges by the Integral Test. The function $f(x) = 1/(x^2 + 1)$ is positive, continuous, and decreasing for $x \geq 1$, and

$$\begin{aligned}\int_1^{\infty} \frac{1}{x^2 + 1}\,dx &= \lim_{b\to\infty} \Big[\arctan x\Big]_1^b \\ &= \lim_{b\to\infty} [\arctan b - \arctan 1] \\ &= \frac{\pi}{2} - \frac{\pi}{4} = \frac{\pi}{4}.\end{aligned}$$

Again we emphasize that $\pi/4$ is *not* the sum of the series. The series converges, but we do not know the value of its sum. ■

Convergence of the series in Example 4 can also be verified by comparison with the series $\sum 1/n^2$. Comparison tests are studied in the next section.

EXERCISES 11.3

Determining Convergence or Divergence

Which of the series in Exercises 1–30 converge, and which diverge? Give reasons for your answers. (When you check an answer, remember that there may be more than one way to determine the series' convergence or divergence.)

1. $\sum_{n=1}^{\infty} \frac{1}{10^n}$
2. $\sum_{n=1}^{\infty} e^{-n}$
3. $\sum_{n=1}^{\infty} \frac{n}{n+1}$
4. $\sum_{n=1}^{\infty} \frac{5}{n+1}$
5. $\sum_{n=1}^{\infty} \frac{3}{\sqrt{n}}$
6. $\sum_{n=1}^{\infty} \frac{-2}{n\sqrt{n}}$
7. $\sum_{n=1}^{\infty} -\frac{1}{8^n}$
8. $\sum_{n=1}^{\infty} \frac{-8}{n}$
9. $\sum_{n=2}^{\infty} \frac{\ln n}{n}$
10. $\sum_{n=2}^{\infty} \frac{\ln n}{\sqrt{n}}$
11. $\sum_{n=1}^{\infty} \frac{2^n}{3^n}$
12. $\sum_{n=1}^{\infty} \frac{5^n}{4^n + 3}$
13. $\sum_{n=0}^{\infty} \frac{-2}{n+1}$
14. $\sum_{n=1}^{\infty} \frac{1}{2n-1}$
15. $\sum_{n=1}^{\infty} \frac{2^n}{n+1}$
16. $\sum_{n=1}^{\infty} \frac{1}{\sqrt{n}(\sqrt{n}+1)}$
17. $\sum_{n=2}^{\infty} \frac{\sqrt{n}}{\ln n}$
18. $\sum_{n=1}^{\infty} \left(1 + \frac{1}{n}\right)^n$
19. $\sum_{n=1}^{\infty} \frac{1}{(\ln 2)^n}$
20. $\sum_{n=1}^{\infty} \frac{1}{(\ln 3)^n}$
21. $\sum_{n=3}^{\infty} \frac{(1/n)}{(\ln n)\sqrt{\ln^2 n - 1}}$
22. $\sum_{n=1}^{\infty} \frac{1}{n(1 + \ln^2 n)}$

23. $\sum_{n=1}^{\infty} n \sin \frac{1}{n}$

24. $\sum_{n=1}^{\infty} n \tan \frac{1}{n}$

25. $\sum_{n=1}^{\infty} \frac{e^n}{1 + e^{2n}}$

26. $\sum_{n=1}^{\infty} \frac{2}{1 + e^n}$

27. $\sum_{n=1}^{\infty} \frac{8 \tan^{-1} n}{1 + n^2}$

28. $\sum_{n=1}^{\infty} \frac{n}{n^2 + 1}$

29. $\sum_{n=1}^{\infty} \operatorname{sech} n$

30. $\sum_{n=1}^{\infty} \operatorname{sech}^2 n$

Theory and Examples

For what values of a, if any, do the series in Exercises 31 and 32 converge?

31. $\sum_{n=1}^{\infty} \left(\frac{a}{n + 2} - \frac{1}{n + 4} \right)$

32. $\sum_{n=3}^{\infty} \left(\frac{1}{n - 1} - \frac{2a}{n + 1} \right)$

33. **a.** Draw illustrations like those in Figures 11.7 and 11.8 to show that the partial sums of the harmonic series satisfy the inequalities

$$\ln (n + 1) = \int_1^{n+1} \frac{1}{x}\, dx \le 1 + \frac{1}{2} + \cdots + \frac{1}{n}$$

$$\le 1 + \int_1^{n} \frac{1}{x}\, dx = 1 + \ln n.$$

T **b.** There is absolutely no empirical evidence for the divergence of the harmonic series even though we know it diverges. The partial sums just grow too slowly. To see what we mean, suppose you had started with $s_1 = 1$ the day the universe was formed, 13 billion years ago, and added a new term every *second*. About how large would the partial sum s_n be today, assuming a 365-day year?

34. Are there any values of x for which $\sum_{n=1}^{\infty}(1/(nx))$ converges? Give reasons for your answer.

35. Is it true that if $\sum_{n=1}^{\infty} a_n$ is a divergent series of positive numbers then there is also a divergent series $\sum_{n=1}^{\infty} b_n$ of positive numbers with $b_n < a_n$ for every n? Is there a "smallest" divergent series of positive numbers? Give reasons for your answers.

36. (*Continuation of Exercise 35.*) Is there a "largest" convergent series of positive numbers? Explain.

37. **The Cauchy condensation test** The Cauchy condensation test says: Let $\{a_n\}$ be a nonincreasing sequence ($a_n \ge a_{n+1}$ for all n) of positive terms that converges to 0. Then $\sum a_n$ converges if and only if $\sum 2^n a_{2^n}$ converges. For example, $\sum(1/n)$ diverges because $\sum 2^n \cdot (1/2^n) = \sum 1$ diverges. Show why the test works.

38. Use the Cauchy condensation test from Exercise 37 to show that

a. $\sum_{n=2}^{\infty} \frac{1}{n \ln n}$ diverges;

b. $\sum_{n=1}^{\infty} \frac{1}{n^p}$ converges if $p > 1$ and diverges if $p \le 1$.

39. **Logarithmic *p*-series**

a. Show that

$$\int_2^{\infty} \frac{dx}{x(\ln x)^p} \quad (p \text{ a positive constant})$$

converges if and only if $p > 1$.

b. What implications does the fact in part (a) have for the convergence of the series

$$\sum_{n=2}^{\infty} \frac{1}{n(\ln n)^p}?$$

Give reasons for your answer.

40. (*Continuation of Exercise 39.*) Use the result in Exercise 39 to determine which of the following series converge and which diverge. Support your answer in each case.

a. $\sum_{n=2}^{\infty} \frac{1}{n(\ln n)}$

b. $\sum_{n=2}^{\infty} \frac{1}{n(\ln n)^{1.01}}$

c. $\sum_{n=2}^{\infty} \frac{1}{n \ln (n^3)}$

d. $\sum_{n=2}^{\infty} \frac{1}{n(\ln n)^3}$

41. **Euler's constant** Graphs like those in Figure 11.8 suggest that as n increases there is little change in the difference between the sum

$$1 + \frac{1}{2} + \cdots + \frac{1}{n}$$

and the integral

$$\ln n = \int_1^n \frac{1}{x}\, dx.$$

To explore this idea, carry out the following steps.

a. By taking $f(x) = 1/x$ in the proof of Theorem 9, show that

$$\ln (n + 1) \le 1 + \frac{1}{2} + \cdots + \frac{1}{n} \le 1 + \ln n$$

or

$$0 < \ln (n + 1) - \ln n \le 1 + \frac{1}{2} + \cdots + \frac{1}{n} - \ln n \le 1.$$

Thus, the sequence

$$a_n = 1 + \frac{1}{2} + \cdots + \frac{1}{n} - \ln n$$

is bounded from below and from above.

b. Show that

$$\frac{1}{n + 1} < \int_n^{n+1} \frac{1}{x}\, dx = \ln (n + 1) - \ln n,$$

and use this result to show that the sequence $\{a_n\}$ in part (a) is decreasing.

Since a decreasing sequence that is bounded from below converges (Exercise 107 in Section 11.1), the numbers a_n defined in part (a) converge:

$$1 + \frac{1}{2} + \cdots + \frac{1}{n} - \ln n \rightarrow \gamma.$$

The number γ, whose value is $0.5772\ldots$, is called *Euler's constant*. In contrast to other special numbers like π and e, no other expression with a simple law of formulation has ever been found for γ.

42. Use the integral test to show that

$$\sum_{n=0}^{\infty} e^{-n^2}$$

converges.

11.4 Comparison Tests

We have seen how to determine the convergence of geometric series, p-series, and a few others. We can test the convergence of many more series by comparing their terms to those of a series whose convergence is known.

THEOREM 10 The Comparison Test

Let $\sum a_n$ be a series with no negative terms.

(a) $\sum a_n$ converges if there is a convergent series $\sum c_n$ with $a_n \leq c_n$ for all $n > N$, for some integer N.

(b) $\sum a_n$ diverges if there is a divergent series of nonnegative terms $\sum d_n$ with $a_n \geq d_n$ for all $n > N$, for some integer N.

HISTORICAL BIOGRAPHY

Albert of Saxony
(ca. 1316–1390)

Proof In Part (a), the partial sums of $\sum a_n$ are bounded above by

$$M = a_1 + a_2 + \cdots + a_N + \sum_{n=N+1}^{\infty} c_n.$$

They therefore form a nondecreasing sequence with a limit $L \leq M$.

In Part (b), the partial sums of $\sum a_n$ are not bounded from above. If they were, the partial sums for $\sum d_n$ would be bounded by

$$M^* = d_1 + d_2 + \cdots + d_N + \sum_{n=N+1}^{\infty} a_n$$

and $\sum d_n$ would have to converge instead of diverge. ■

EXAMPLE 1 Applying the Comparison Test

(a) The series

$$\sum_{n=1}^{\infty} \frac{5}{5n-1}$$

diverges because its nth term

$$\frac{5}{5n-1} = \frac{1}{n - \frac{1}{5}} > \frac{1}{n}$$

is greater than the nth term of the divergent harmonic series.

(b) The series

$$\sum_{n=0}^{\infty} \frac{1}{n!} = 1 + \frac{1}{1!} + \frac{1}{2!} + \frac{1}{3!} + \cdots$$

converges because its terms are all positive and less than or equal to the corresponding terms of

$$1 + \sum_{n=0}^{\infty} \frac{1}{2^n} = 1 + 1 + \frac{1}{2} + \frac{1}{2^2} + \cdots.$$

The geometric series on the left converges and we have

$$1 + \sum_{n=0}^{\infty} \frac{1}{2^n} = 1 + \frac{1}{1 - (1/2)} = 3.$$

The fact that 3 is an upper bound for the partial sums of $\sum_{n=0}^{\infty}(1/n!)$ does not mean that the series converges to 3. As we will see in Section 11.9, the series converges to e.

(c) The series

$$5 + \frac{2}{3} + \frac{1}{7} + 1 + \frac{1}{2 + \sqrt{1}} + \frac{1}{4 + \sqrt{2}} + \frac{1}{8 + \sqrt{3}} + \cdots + \frac{1}{2^n + \sqrt{n}} + \cdots$$

converges. To see this, we ignore the first three terms and compare the remaining terms with those of the convergent geometric series $\sum_{n=0}^{\infty}(1/2^n)$. The term $1/(2^n + \sqrt{n})$ of the truncated sequence is less than the corresponding term $1/2^n$ of the geometric series. We see that term by term we have the comparison,

$$1 + \frac{1}{2 + \sqrt{1}} + \frac{1}{4 + \sqrt{2}} + \frac{1}{8 + \sqrt{3}} + \cdots \le 1 + \frac{1}{2} + \frac{1}{4} + \frac{1}{8} + \cdots$$

So the truncated series and the original series converge by an application of the Comparison Test. ■

The Limit Comparison Test

We now introduce a comparison test that is particularly useful for series in which a_n is a rational function of n.

THEOREM 11 Limit Comparison Test
Suppose that $a_n > 0$ and $b_n > 0$ for all $n \ge N$ (N an integer).

1. If $\lim_{n\to\infty} \frac{a_n}{b_n} = c > 0$, then $\sum a_n$ and $\sum b_n$ both converge or both diverge.
2. If $\lim_{n\to\infty} \frac{a_n}{b_n} = 0$ and $\sum b_n$ converges, then $\sum a_n$ converges.
3. If $\lim_{n\to\infty} \frac{a_n}{b_n} = \infty$ and $\sum b_n$ diverges, then $\sum a_n$ diverges.

Proof We will prove Part 1. Parts 2 and 3 are left as Exercises 37(a) and (b).

Since $c/2 > 0$, there exists an integer N such that for all n

$$n > N \Rightarrow \left|\frac{a_n}{b_n} - c\right| < \frac{c}{2}.$$

Limit definition with $\epsilon = c/2, L = c$, and a_n replaced by a_n/b_n

Thus, for $n > N$,

$$-\frac{c}{2} < \frac{a_n}{b_n} - c < \frac{c}{2},$$

$$\frac{c}{2} < \frac{a_n}{b_n} < \frac{3c}{2},$$

$$\left(\frac{c}{2}\right)b_n < a_n < \left(\frac{3c}{2}\right)b_n.$$

If Σb_n converges, then $\Sigma(3c/2)b_n$ converges and Σa_n converges by the Direct Comparison Test. If Σb_n diverges, then $\Sigma(c/2)b_n$ diverges and Σa_n diverges by the Direct Comparison Test. ■

EXAMPLE 2 Using the Limit Comparison Test

Which of the following series converge, and which diverge?

(a) $\frac{3}{4} + \frac{5}{9} + \frac{7}{16} + \frac{9}{25} + \cdots = \sum_{n=1}^{\infty} \frac{2n + 1}{(n + 1)^2} = \sum_{n=1}^{\infty} \frac{2n + 1}{n^2 + 2n + 1}$

(b) $\frac{1}{1} + \frac{1}{3} + \frac{1}{7} + \frac{1}{15} + \cdots = \sum_{n=1}^{\infty} \frac{1}{2^n - 1}$

(c) $\frac{1 + 2\ln 2}{9} + \frac{1 + 3\ln 3}{14} + \frac{1 + 4\ln 4}{21} + \cdots = \sum_{n=2}^{\infty} \frac{1 + n\ln n}{n^2 + 5}$

Solution

(a) Let $a_n = (2n + 1)/(n^2 + 2n + 1)$. For large n, we expect a_n to behave like $2n/n^2 = 2/n$ since the leading terms dominate for large n, so we let $b_n = 1/n$. Since

$$\sum_{n=1}^{\infty} b_n = \sum_{n=1}^{\infty} \frac{1}{n} \text{ diverges}$$

and

$$\lim_{n\to\infty} \frac{a_n}{b_n} = \lim_{n\to\infty} \frac{2n^2 + n}{n^2 + 2n + 1} = 2,$$

Σa_n diverges by Part 1 of the Limit Comparison Test. We could just as well have taken $b_n = 2/n$, but $1/n$ is simpler.

(b) Let $a_n = 1/(2^n - 1)$. For large n, we expect a_n to behave like $1/2^n$, so we let $b_n = 1/2^n$. Since

$$\sum_{n=1}^{\infty} b_n = \sum_{n=1}^{\infty} \frac{1}{2^n} \text{ converges}$$

and

$$\begin{aligned} \lim_{n\to\infty} \frac{a_n}{b_n} &= \lim_{n\to\infty} \frac{2^n}{2^n - 1} \\ &= \lim_{n\to\infty} \frac{1}{1 - (1/2^n)} \\ &= 1, \end{aligned}$$

Σa_n converges by Part 1 of the Limit Comparison Test.

(c) Let $a_n = (1 + n\ln n)/(n^2 + 5)$. For large n, we expect a_n to behave like $(n \ln n)/n^2 = (\ln n)/n$, which is greater than $1/n$ for $n \geq 3$, so we take $b_n = 1/n$. Since

$$\sum_{n=2}^{\infty} b_n = \sum_{n=2}^{\infty} \frac{1}{n} \text{ diverges}$$

and

$$\begin{aligned} \lim_{n\to\infty} \frac{a_n}{b_n} &= \lim_{n\to\infty} \frac{n + n^2 \ln n}{n^2 + 5} \\ &= \infty, \end{aligned}$$

Σa_n diverges by Part 3 of the Limit Comparison Test. ■

EXAMPLE 3 Does $\displaystyle\sum_{n=1}^{\infty} \frac{\ln n}{n^{3/2}}$ converge?

Solution Because $\ln n$ grows more slowly than n^c for any positive constant c (Section 11.1, Exercise 91), we would expect to have

$$\frac{\ln n}{n^{3/2}} < \frac{n^{1/4}}{n^{3/2}} = \frac{1}{n^{5/4}}$$

for n sufficiently large. Indeed, taking $a_n = (\ln n)/n^{3/2}$ and $b_n = 1/n^{5/4}$, we have

$$\begin{aligned} \lim_{n\to\infty} \frac{a_n}{b_n} &= \lim_{n\to\infty} \frac{\ln n}{n^{1/4}} \\ &= \lim_{n\to\infty} \frac{1/n}{(1/4)n^{-3/4}} && \text{l'Hôpital's Rule} \\ &= \lim_{n\to\infty} \frac{4}{n^{1/4}} = 0. \end{aligned}$$

Since $\Sigma b_n = \Sigma(1/n^{5/4})$ (a p-series with $p > 1$) converges, Σa_n converges by Part 2 of the Limit Comparison Test. ■

EXERCISES 11.4

Determining Convergence or Divergence

Which of the series in Exercises 1–36 converge, and which diverge? Give reasons for your answers.

1. $\sum_{n=1}^{\infty} \frac{1}{2\sqrt{n} + \sqrt[3]{n}}$
2. $\sum_{n=1}^{\infty} \frac{3}{n + \sqrt{n}}$
3. $\sum_{n=1}^{\infty} \frac{\sin^2 n}{2^n}$
4. $\sum_{n=1}^{\infty} \frac{1 + \cos n}{n^2}$
5. $\sum_{n=1}^{\infty} \frac{2n}{3n - 1}$
6. $\sum_{n=1}^{\infty} \frac{n + 1}{n^2\sqrt{n}}$
7. $\sum_{n=1}^{\infty} \left(\frac{n}{3n + 1}\right)^n$
8. $\sum_{n=1}^{\infty} \frac{1}{\sqrt{n^3 + 2}}$
9. $\sum_{n=3}^{\infty} \frac{1}{\ln(\ln n)}$
10. $\sum_{n=2}^{\infty} \frac{1}{(\ln n)^2}$
11. $\sum_{n=1}^{\infty} \frac{(\ln n)^2}{n^3}$
12. $\sum_{n=1}^{\infty} \frac{(\ln n)^3}{n^3}$
13. $\sum_{n=2}^{\infty} \frac{1}{\sqrt{n}\ln n}$
14. $\sum_{n=1}^{\infty} \frac{(\ln n)^2}{n^{3/2}}$
15. $\sum_{n=1}^{\infty} \frac{1}{1 + \ln n}$
16. $\sum_{n=1}^{\infty} \frac{1}{(1 + \ln n)^2}$
17. $\sum_{n=2}^{\infty} \frac{\ln(n + 1)}{n + 1}$
18. $\sum_{n=1}^{\infty} \frac{1}{(1 + \ln^2 n)}$
19. $\sum_{n=2}^{\infty} \frac{1}{n\sqrt{n^2 - 1}}$
20. $\sum_{n=1}^{\infty} \frac{\sqrt{n}}{n^2 + 1}$
21. $\sum_{n=1}^{\infty} \frac{1 - n}{n2^n}$
22. $\sum_{n=1}^{\infty} \frac{n + 2^n}{n^2 2^n}$
23. $\sum_{n=1}^{\infty} \frac{1}{3^{n-1} + 1}$
24. $\sum_{n=1}^{\infty} \frac{3^{n-1} + 1}{3^n}$
25. $\sum_{n=1}^{\infty} \sin\frac{1}{n}$
26. $\sum_{n=1}^{\infty} \tan\frac{1}{n}$
27. $\sum_{n=1}^{\infty} \frac{10n + 1}{n(n + 1)(n + 2)}$
28. $\sum_{n=3}^{\infty} \frac{5n^3 - 3n}{n^2(n - 2)(n^2 + 5)}$
29. $\sum_{n=1}^{\infty} \frac{\tan^{-1} n}{n^{1.1}}$
30. $\sum_{n=1}^{\infty} \frac{\sec^{-1} n}{n^{1.3}}$
31. $\sum_{n=1}^{\infty} \frac{\coth n}{n^2}$
32. $\sum_{n=1}^{\infty} \frac{\tanh n}{n^2}$
33. $\sum_{n=1}^{\infty} \frac{1}{n\sqrt[n]{n}}$
34. $\sum_{n=1}^{\infty} \frac{\sqrt[n]{n}}{n^2}$
35. $\sum_{n=1}^{\infty} \frac{1}{1 + 2 + 3 + \cdots + n}$
36. $\sum_{n=1}^{\infty} \frac{1}{1 + 2^2 + 3^2 + \cdots + n^2}$

Theory and Examples

37. Prove **(a)** Part 2 and **(b)** Part 3 of the Limit Comparison Test.

38. If $\sum_{n=1}^{\infty} a_n$ is a convergent series of nonnegative numbers, can anything be said about $\sum_{n=1}^{\infty}(a_n/n)$? Explain.

39. Suppose that $a_n > 0$ and $b_n > 0$ for $n \geq N$ (N an integer). If $\lim_{n\to\infty}(a_n/b_n) = \infty$ and $\sum a_n$ converges, can anything be said about $\sum b_n$? Give reasons for your answer.

40. Prove that if $\sum a_n$ is a convergent series of nonnegative terms, then $\sum a_n{}^2$ converges.

COMPUTER EXPLORATION

41. It is not yet known whether the series

$$\sum_{n=1}^{\infty} \frac{1}{n^3 \sin^2 n}$$

converges or diverges. Use a CAS to explore the behavior of the series by performing the following steps.

a. Define the sequence of partial sums

$$s_k = \sum_{n=1}^{k} \frac{1}{n^3 \sin^2 n}.$$

What happens when you try to find the limit of s_k as $k \to \infty$? Does your CAS find a closed form answer for this limit?

b. Plot the first 100 points (k, s_k) for the sequence of partial sums. Do they appear to converge? What would you estimate the limit to be?

c. Next plot the first 200 points (k, s_k). Discuss the behavior in your own words.

d. Plot the first 400 points (k, s_k). What happens when $k = 355$? Calculate the number $355/113$. Explain from your calculation what happened at $k = 355$. For what values of k would you guess this behavior might occur again?

You will find an interesting discussion of this series in Chapter 72 of *Mazes for the Mind* by Clifford A. Pickover, St. Martin's Press, Inc., New York, 1992.

11.5 The Ratio and Root Tests

The Ratio Test measures the rate of growth (or decline) of a series by examining the ratio a_{n+1}/a_n. For a geometric series $\sum ar^n$, this rate is a constant $((ar^{n+1})/(ar^n) = r)$, and the series converges if and only if its ratio is less than 1 in absolute value. The Ratio Test is a powerful rule extending that result. We prove it on the next page using the Comparison Test.

THEOREM 12 The Ratio Test
Let $\sum a_n$ be a series with positive terms and suppose that

$$\lim_{n\to\infty} \frac{a_{n+1}}{a_n} = \rho.$$

Then

(a) the series *converges* if $\rho < 1$,
(b) the series *diverges* if $\rho > 1$ or ρ is infinite,
(c) the test is *inconclusive* if $\rho = 1$.

Proof

(a) $\boldsymbol{\rho < 1}$. Let r be a number between ρ and 1. Then the number $\epsilon = r - \rho$ is positive. Since

$$\frac{a_{n+1}}{a_n} \to \rho,$$

a_{n+1}/a_n must lie within ϵ of ρ when n is large enough, say for all $n \geq N$. In particular

$$\frac{a_{n+1}}{a_n} < \rho + \epsilon = r, \qquad \text{when } n \geq N.$$

That is,

$$\begin{aligned} a_{N+1} &< ra_N, \\ a_{N+2} &< ra_{N+1} < r^2 a_N, \\ a_{N+3} &< ra_{N+2} < r^3 a_N, \\ &\vdots \\ a_{N+m} &< ra_{N+m-1} < r^m a_N. \end{aligned}$$

These inequalities show that the terms of our series, after the Nth term, approach zero more rapidly than the terms in a geometric series with ratio $r < 1$. More precisely, consider the series $\sum c_n$, where $c_n = a_n$ for $n = 1, 2, \ldots, N$ and $c_{N+1} = ra_N$, $c_{N+2} = r^2 a_N, \ldots, c_{N+m} = r^m a_N, \ldots$. Now $a_n \leq c_n$ for all n, and

$$\begin{aligned} \sum_{n=1}^{\infty} c_n &= a_1 + a_2 + \cdots + a_{N-1} + a_N + ra_N + r^2 a_N + \cdots \\ &= a_1 + a_2 + \cdots + a_{N-1} + a_N(1 + r + r^2 + \cdots). \end{aligned}$$

The geometric series $1 + r + r^2 + \cdots$ converges because $|r| < 1$, so $\sum c_n$ converges. Since $a_n \leq c_n$, $\sum a_n$ also converges.

(b) $\boldsymbol{1 < \rho \leq \infty}$. From some index M on,

$$\frac{a_{n+1}}{a_n} > 1 \qquad \text{and} \qquad a_M < a_{M+1} < a_{M+2} < \cdots.$$

The terms of the series do not approach zero as n becomes infinite, and the series diverges by the nth-Term Test.

(c) $\rho = 1$**.** The two series

$$\sum_{n=1}^{\infty} \frac{1}{n} \quad \text{and} \quad \sum_{n=1}^{\infty} \frac{1}{n^2}$$

show that some other test for convergence must be used when $\rho = 1$.

$$\text{For } \sum_{n=1}^{\infty} \frac{1}{n}: \qquad \frac{a_{n+1}}{a_n} = \frac{1/(n+1)}{1/n} = \frac{n}{n+1} \to 1.$$

$$\text{For } \sum_{n=1}^{\infty} \frac{1}{n^2}: \qquad \frac{a_{n+1}}{a_n} = \frac{1/(n+1)^2}{1/n^2} = \left(\frac{n}{n+1}\right)^2 \to 1^2 = 1.$$

In both cases, $\rho = 1$, yet the first series diverges, whereas the second converges. ■

The Ratio Test is often effective when the terms of a series contain factorials of expressions involving n or expressions raised to a power involving n.

EXAMPLE 1 Applying the Ratio Test

Investigate the convergence of the following series.

(a) $\displaystyle\sum_{n=0}^{\infty} \frac{2^n + 5}{3^n}$ **(b)** $\displaystyle\sum_{n=1}^{\infty} \frac{(2n)!}{n!n!}$ **(c)** $\displaystyle\sum_{n=1}^{\infty} \frac{4^n n! n!}{(2n)!}$

Solution

(a) For the series $\sum_{n=0}^{\infty} (2^n + 5)/3^n$,

$$\frac{a_{n+1}}{a_n} = \frac{(2^{n+1} + 5)/3^{n+1}}{(2^n + 5)/3^n} = \frac{1}{3} \cdot \frac{2^{n+1} + 5}{2^n + 5} = \frac{1}{3} \cdot \left(\frac{2 + 5 \cdot 2^{-n}}{1 + 5 \cdot 2^{-n}}\right) \to \frac{1}{3} \cdot \frac{2}{1} = \frac{2}{3}.$$

The series converges because $\rho = 2/3$ is less than 1. This does *not* mean that 2/3 is the sum of the series. In fact,

$$\sum_{n=0}^{\infty} \frac{2^n + 5}{3^n} = \sum_{n=0}^{\infty} \left(\frac{2}{3}\right)^n + \sum_{n=0}^{\infty} \frac{5}{3^n} = \frac{1}{1 - (2/3)} + \frac{5}{1 - (1/3)} = \frac{21}{2}.$$

(b) If $a_n = \dfrac{(2n)!}{n!n!}$, then $a_{n+1} = \dfrac{(2n+2)!}{(n+1)!(n+1)!}$ and

$$\begin{aligned}\frac{a_{n+1}}{a_n} &= \frac{n!n!(2n+2)(2n+1)(2n)!}{(n+1)!(n+1)!(2n)!} \\ &= \frac{(2n+2)(2n+1)}{(n+1)(n+1)} = \frac{4n+2}{n+1} \to 4.\end{aligned}$$

The series diverges because $\rho = 4$ is greater than 1.

(c) If $a_n = 4^n n! n!/(2n)!$, then

$$\begin{aligned}\frac{a_{n+1}}{a_n} &= \frac{4^{n+1}(n+1)!(n+1)!}{(2n+2)(2n+1)(2n)!} \cdot \frac{(2n)!}{4^n n! n!} \\ &= \frac{4(n+1)(n+1)}{(2n+2)(2n+1)} = \frac{2(n+1)}{2n+1} \to 1.\end{aligned}$$

Because the limit is $\rho = 1$, we cannot decide from the Ratio Test whether the series converges. When we notice that $a_{n+1}/a_n = (2n + 2)/(2n + 1)$, we conclude that a_{n+1} is always greater than a_n because $(2n + 2)/(2n + 1)$ is always greater than 1. Therefore, all terms are greater than or equal to $a_1 = 2$, and the nth term does not approach zero as $n \to \infty$. The series diverges. ■

The Root Test

The convergence tests we have so far for $\sum a_n$ work best when the formula for a_n is relatively simple. But consider the following.

EXAMPLE 2 Let $a_n = \begin{cases} n/2^n, & n \text{ odd} \\ 1/2^n, & n \text{ even.} \end{cases}$ Does $\sum a_n$ converge?

Solution We write out several terms of the series:

$$\sum_{n=1}^{\infty} a_n = \frac{1}{2^1} + \frac{1}{2^2} + \frac{3}{2^3} + \frac{1}{2^4} + \frac{5}{2^5} + \frac{1}{2^6} + \frac{7}{2^7} + \cdots$$

$$= \frac{1}{2} + \frac{1}{4} + \frac{3}{8} + \frac{1}{16} + \frac{5}{32} + \frac{1}{64} + \frac{7}{128} + \cdots.$$

Clearly, this is not a geometric series. The nth term approaches zero as $n \to \infty$, so we do not know if the series diverges. The Integral Test does not look promising. The Ratio Test produces

$$\frac{a_{n+1}}{a_n} = \begin{cases} \dfrac{1}{2n}, & n \text{ odd} \\[2ex] \dfrac{n+1}{2}, & n \text{ even.} \end{cases}$$

As $n \to \infty$, the ratio is alternately small and large and has no limit.

A test that will answer the question (the series converges) is the Root Test. ■

THEOREM 13 The Root Test

Let $\sum a_n$ be a series with $a_n \geq 0$ for $n \geq N$, and suppose that

$$\lim_{n \to \infty} \sqrt[n]{a_n} = \rho.$$

Then

(a) the series *converges* if $\rho < 1$,

(b) the series *diverges* if $\rho > 1$ or ρ is infinite,

(c) the test is *inconclusive* if $\rho = 1$.

Proof

(a) $\boldsymbol{\rho < 1}$**.** Choose an $\epsilon > 0$ so small that $\rho + \epsilon < 1$. Since $\sqrt[n]{a_n} \to \rho$, the terms $\sqrt[n]{a_n}$ eventually get closer than ϵ to ρ. In other words, there exists an index $M \geq N$ such that

$$\sqrt[n]{a_n} < \rho + \epsilon \qquad \text{when } n \geq M.$$

Then it is also true that

$$a_n < (\rho + \epsilon)^n \qquad \text{for } n \geq M.$$

Now, $\sum_{n=M}^{\infty} (\rho + \epsilon)^n$, a geometric series with ratio $(\rho + \epsilon) < 1$, converges. By comparison, $\sum_{n=M}^{\infty} a_n$ converges, from which it follows that

$$\sum_{n=1}^{\infty} a_n = a_1 + \cdots + a_{M-1} + \sum_{n=M}^{\infty} a_n$$

converges.

(b) $\mathbf{1 < \rho \leq \infty}$**.** For all indices beyond some integer M, we have $\sqrt[n]{a_n} > 1$, so that $a_n > 1$ for $n > M$. The terms of the series do not converge to zero. The series diverges by the nth-Term Test.

(c) $\boldsymbol{\rho} = \mathbf{1}$**.** The series $\sum_{n=1}^{\infty} (1/n)$ and $\sum_{n=1}^{\infty} (1/n^2)$ show that the test is not conclusive when $\rho = 1$. The first series diverges and the second converges, but in both cases $\sqrt[n]{a_n} \to 1$. ■

EXAMPLE 3 Applying the Root Test

Which of the following series converges, and which diverges?

(a) $\displaystyle\sum_{n=1}^{\infty} \frac{n^2}{2^n}$ **(b)** $\displaystyle\sum_{n=1}^{\infty} \frac{2^n}{n^2}$ **(c)** $\displaystyle\sum_{n=1}^{\infty} \left(\frac{1}{1 + n}\right)^n$

Solution

(a) $\displaystyle\sum_{n=1}^{\infty} \frac{n^2}{2^n}$ converges because $\displaystyle\sqrt[n]{\frac{n^2}{2^n}} = \frac{\sqrt[n]{n^2}}{\sqrt[n]{2^n}} = \frac{\left(\sqrt[n]{n}\right)^2}{2} \to \frac{1}{2} < 1.$

(b) $\displaystyle\sum_{n=1}^{\infty} \frac{2^n}{n^2}$ diverges because $\displaystyle\sqrt[n]{\frac{2^n}{n^2}} = \frac{2}{\left(\sqrt[n]{n}\right)^2} \to \frac{2}{1} > 1.$

(c) $\displaystyle\sum_{n=1}^{\infty} \left(\frac{1}{1 + n}\right)^n$ converges because $\displaystyle\sqrt[n]{\left(\frac{1}{1 + n}\right)^n} = \frac{1}{1 + n} \to 0 < 1.$ ■

EXAMPLE 2 Revisited

Let $a_n = \begin{cases} n/2^n, & n \text{ odd} \\ 1/2^n, & n \text{ even.} \end{cases}$ Does $\sum a_n$ converge?

Solution We apply the Root Test, finding that

$$\sqrt[n]{a_n} = \begin{cases} \sqrt[n]{n}/2, & n \text{ odd} \\ 1/2, & n \text{ even.} \end{cases}$$

Therefore,

$$\frac{1}{2} \leq \sqrt[n]{a_n} \leq \frac{\sqrt[n]{n}}{2}.$$

Since $\sqrt[n]{n} \to 1$ (Section 11.1, Theorem 5), we have $\lim_{n\to\infty} \sqrt[n]{a_n} = 1/2$ by the Sandwich Theorem. The limit is less than 1, so the series converges by the Root Test. ■

EXERCISES 11.5

Determining Convergence or Divergence

Which of the series in Exercises 1–26 converge, and which diverge? Give reasons for your answers. (When checking your answers, remember there may be more than one way to determine a series' convergence or divergence.)

1. $\sum_{n=1}^{\infty} \frac{n^{\sqrt{2}}}{2^n}$

2. $\sum_{n=1}^{\infty} n^2 e^{-n}$

3. $\sum_{n=1}^{\infty} n! e^{-n}$

4. $\sum_{n=1}^{\infty} \frac{n!}{10^n}$

5. $\sum_{n=1}^{\infty} \frac{n^{10}}{10^n}$

6. $\sum_{n=1}^{\infty} \left(\frac{n-2}{n}\right)^n$

7. $\sum_{n=1}^{\infty} \frac{2+(-1)^n}{1.25^n}$

8. $\sum_{n=1}^{\infty} \frac{(-2)^n}{3^n}$

9. $\sum_{n=1}^{\infty} \left(1-\frac{3}{n}\right)^n$

10. $\sum_{n=1}^{\infty} \left(1-\frac{1}{3n}\right)^n$

11. $\sum_{n=1}^{\infty} \frac{\ln n}{n^3}$

12. $\sum_{n=1}^{\infty} \frac{(\ln n)^n}{n^n}$

13. $\sum_{n=1}^{\infty} \left(\frac{1}{n}-\frac{1}{n^2}\right)$

14. $\sum_{n=1}^{\infty} \left(\frac{1}{n}-\frac{1}{n^2}\right)^n$

15. $\sum_{n=1}^{\infty} \frac{\ln n}{n}$

16. $\sum_{n=1}^{\infty} \frac{n \ln n}{2^n}$

17. $\sum_{n=1}^{\infty} \frac{(n+1)(n+2)}{n!}$

18. $\sum_{n=1}^{\infty} e^{-n}(n^3)$

19. $\sum_{n=1}^{\infty} \frac{(n+3)!}{3!n!3^n}$

20. $\sum_{n=1}^{\infty} \frac{n2^n(n+1)!}{3^n n!}$

21. $\sum_{n=1}^{\infty} \frac{n!}{(2n+1)!}$

22. $\sum_{n=1}^{\infty} \frac{n!}{n^n}$

23. $\sum_{n=2}^{\infty} \frac{n}{(\ln n)^n}$

24. $\sum_{n=2}^{\infty} \frac{n}{(\ln n)^{(n/2)}}$

25. $\sum_{n=1}^{\infty} \frac{n! \ln n}{n(n+2)!}$

26. $\sum_{n=1}^{\infty} \frac{3^n}{n^3 2^n}$

Which of the series $\sum_{n=1}^{\infty} a_n$ defined by the formulas in Exercises 27–38 converge, and which diverge? Give reasons for your answers.

27. $a_1 = 2, \quad a_{n+1} = \frac{1+\sin n}{n} a_n$

28. $a_1 = 1, \quad a_{n+1} = \frac{1+\tan^{-1} n}{n} a_n$

29. $a_1 = \frac{1}{3}, \quad a_{n+1} = \frac{3n-1}{2n+5} a_n$

30. $a_1 = 3, \quad a_{n+1} = \frac{n}{n+1} a_n$

31. $a_1 = 2, \quad a_{n+1} = \frac{2}{n} a_n$

32. $a_1 = 5, \quad a_{n+1} = \frac{\sqrt[n]{n}}{2} a_n$

33. $a_1 = 1, \quad a_{n+1} = \frac{1+\ln n}{n} a_n$

34. $a_1 = \frac{1}{2}, \quad a_{n+1} = \frac{n+\ln n}{n+10} a_n$

35. $a_1 = \frac{1}{3}, \quad a_{n+1} = \sqrt[n]{a_n}$

36. $a_1 = \frac{1}{2}, \quad a_{n+1} = (a_n)^{n+1}$

37. $a_n = \frac{2^n n! n!}{(2n)!}$

38. $a_n = \frac{(3n)!}{n!(n+1)!(n+2)!}$

Which of the series in Exercises 39–44 converge, and which diverge? Give reasons for your answers.

39. $\sum_{n=1}^{\infty} \frac{(n!)^n}{(n^n)^2}$

40. $\sum_{n=1}^{\infty} \frac{(n!)^n}{n^{(n^2)}}$

41. $\sum_{n=1}^{\infty} \frac{n^n}{2^{(n^2)}}$

42. $\sum_{n=1}^{\infty} \frac{n^n}{(2^n)^2}$

43. $\sum_{n=1}^{\infty} \frac{1 \cdot 3 \cdot \cdots \cdot (2n-1)}{4^n 2^n n!}$

44. $\sum_{n=1}^{\infty} \frac{1 \cdot 3 \cdot \cdots \cdot (2n-1)}{[2 \cdot 4 \cdot \cdots \cdot (2n)](3^n+1)}$

Theory and Examples

45. Neither the Ratio nor the Root Test helps with p-series. Try them on

$$\sum_{n=1}^{\infty} \frac{1}{n^p}$$

and show that both tests fail to provide information about convergence.

46. Show that neither the Ratio Test nor the Root Test provides information about the convergence of

$$\sum_{n=2}^{\infty} \frac{1}{(\ln n)^p} \quad (p \text{ constant}).$$

47. Let $a_n = \begin{cases} n/2^n, & \text{if } n \text{ is a prime number} \\ 1/2^n, & \text{otherwise.} \end{cases}$

Does $\sum a_n$ converge? Give reasons for your answer.

11.6 Alternating Series, Absolute and Conditional Convergence

A series in which the terms are alternately positive and negative is an **alternating series**.

Here are three examples:

$$1-\frac{1}{2}+\frac{1}{3}-\frac{1}{4}+\frac{1}{5}-\cdots+\frac{(-1)^{n+1}}{n}+\cdots \tag{1}$$

$$-2+1-\frac{1}{2}+\frac{1}{4}-\frac{1}{8}+\cdots+\frac{(-1)^{n}4}{2^{n}}+\cdots \tag{2}$$

$$1-2+3-4+5-6+\cdots+(-1)^{n+1}n+\cdots \tag{3}$$

Series (1), called the **alternating harmonic series**, converges, as we will see in a moment. Series (2) a geometric series with ratio $r=-1/2$, converges to $-2/[1+(1/2)]=-4/3$. Series (3) diverges because the nth term does not approach zero.

We prove the convergence of the alternating harmonic series by applying the Alternating Series Test.

THEOREM 14 The Alternating Series Test (Leibniz's Theorem)

The series

$$\sum_{n=1}^{\infty}(-1)^{n+1}u_n=u_1-u_2+u_3-u_4+\cdots$$

converges if all three of the following conditions are satisfied:

1. The u_n's are all positive.
2. $u_n \geq u_{n+1}$ for all $n \geq N$, for some integer N.
3. $u_n \to 0$.

Proof Assume $N=1$. If n is an even integer, say $n=2m$, then the sum of the first n terms is

$$\begin{aligned} s_{2m}&=(u_1-u_2)+(u_3-u_4)+\cdots+(u_{2m-1}-u_{2m})\\ &=u_1-(u_2-u_3)-(u_4-u_5)-\cdots-(u_{2m-2}-u_{2m-1})-u_{2m}. \end{aligned}$$

The first equality shows that s_{2m} is the sum of m nonnegative terms, since each term in parentheses is positive or zero. Hence $s_{2m+2}\geq s_{2m}$, and the sequence $\{s_{2m}\}$ is nondecreasing. The second equality shows that $s_{2m}\leq u_1$. Since $\{s_{2m}\}$ is nondecreasing and bounded from above, it has a limit, say

$$\lim_{m\to\infty} s_{2m}=L. \tag{4}$$

If n is an odd integer, say $n=2m+1$, then the sum of the first n terms is $s_{2m+1}=s_{2m}+u_{2m+1}$. Since $u_n\to 0$,

$$\lim_{m\to\infty} u_{2m+1}=0$$

and, as $m\to\infty$,

$$s_{2m+1}=s_{2m}+u_{2m+1}\to L+0=L. \tag{5}$$

Combining the results of Equations (4) and (5) gives $\lim_{n\to\infty} s_n=L$ (Section 11.1, Exercise 119). ■

EXAMPLE 1 The alternating harmonic series

$$\sum_{n=1}^{\infty}(-1)^{n+1}\frac{1}{n} = 1 - \frac{1}{2} + \frac{1}{3} - \frac{1}{4} + \cdots$$

satisfies the three requirements of Theorem 14 with $N = 1$; it therefore converges. ■

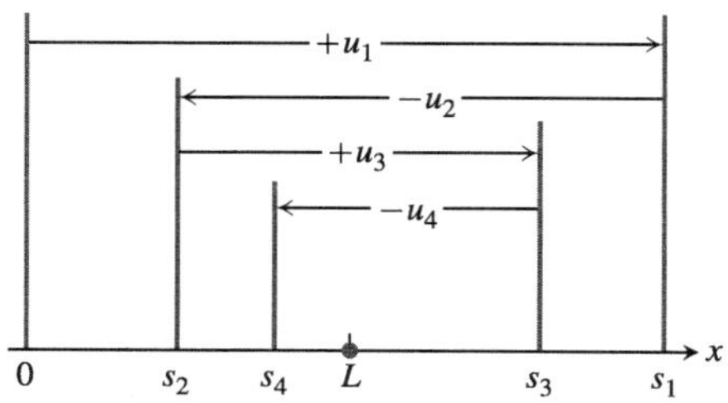

FIGURE 11.9 The partial sums of an alternating series that satisfies the hypotheses of Theorem 14 for $N = 1$ straddle the limit from the beginning.

A graphical interpretation of the partial sums (Figure 11.9) shows how an alternating series converges to its limit L when the three conditions of Theorem 14 are satisfied with $N = 1$. (Exercise 63 asks you to picture the case $N > 1$.) Starting from the origin of the x-axis, we lay off the positive distance $s_1 = u_1$. To find the point corresponding to $s_2 = u_1 - u_2$, we back up a distance equal to u_2. Since $u_2 \le u_1$, we do not back up any farther than the origin. We continue in this seesaw fashion, backing up or going forward as the signs in the series demand. But for $n \ge N$, each forward or backward step is shorter than (or at most the same size as) the preceding step, because $u_{n+1} \le u_n$. And since the nth term approaches zero as n increases, the size of step we take forward or backward gets smaller and smaller. We oscillate across the limit L, and the amplitude of oscillation approaches zero. The limit L lies between any two successive sums s_n and s_{n+1} and hence differs from s_n by an amount less than u_{n+1}.

Because

$$|L - s_n| < u_{n+1} \qquad \text{for } n \ge N,$$

we can make useful estimates of the sums of convergent alternating series.

THEOREM 15 The Alternating Series Estimation Theorem
If the alternating series $\sum_{n=1}^{\infty}(-1)^{n+1}u_n$ satisfies the three conditions of Theorem 14, then for $n \ge N$,

$$s_n = u_1 - u_2 + \cdots + (-1)^{n+1}u_n$$

approximates the sum L of the series with an error whose absolute value is less than u_{n+1}, the numerical value of the first unused term. Furthermore, the remainder, $L - s_n$, has the same sign as the first unused term.

We leave the verification of the sign of the remainder for Exercise 53.

EXAMPLE 2 We try Theorem 15 on a series whose sum we know:

$$\sum_{n=0}^{\infty}(-1)^n\frac{1}{2^n} = 1 - \frac{1}{2} + \frac{1}{4} - \frac{1}{8} + \frac{1}{16} - \frac{1}{32} + \frac{1}{64} - \frac{1}{128} \;\Big|\; + \frac{1}{256} - \cdots.$$

The theorem says that if we truncate the series after the eighth term, we throw away a total that is positive and less than $1/256$. The sum of the first eight terms is 0.6640625. The sum of the series is

$$\frac{1}{1 - (-1/2)} = \frac{1}{3/2} = \frac{2}{3}.$$

The difference, $(2/3) - 0.6640625 = 0.0026041666\ldots$, is positive and less than $(1/256) = 0.00390625$. ■

Absolute and Conditional Convergence

DEFINITION Absolutely Convergent

A series $\sum a_n$ **converges absolutely** (is **absolutely convergent**) if the corresponding series of absolute values, $\sum |a_n|$, converges.

The geometric series

$$1 - \frac{1}{2} + \frac{1}{4} - \frac{1}{8} + \cdots$$

converges absolutely because the corresponding series of absolute values

$$1 + \frac{1}{2} + \frac{1}{4} + \frac{1}{8} + \cdots$$

converges. The alternating harmonic series does not converge absolutely. The corresponding series of absolute values is the (divergent) harmonic series.

DEFINITION Conditionally Convergent

A series that converges but does not converge absolutely **converges conditionally**.

The alternating harmonic series converges conditionally.

Absolute convergence is important for two reasons. First, we have good tests for convergence of series of positive terms. Second, if a series converges absolutely, then it converges. That is the thrust of the next theorem.

THEOREM 16 The Absolute Convergence Test

If $\sum_{n=1}^{\infty} |a_n|$ converges, then $\sum_{n=1}^{\infty} a_n$ converges.

Proof For each n,

$$-|a_n| \le a_n \le |a_n|, \qquad \text{so} \qquad 0 \le a_n + |a_n| \le 2|a_n|.$$

If $\sum_{n=1}^{\infty} |a_n|$ converges, then $\sum_{n=1}^{\infty} 2|a_n|$ converges and, by the Direct Comparison Test, the nonnegative series $\sum_{n=1}^{\infty} (a_n + |a_n|)$ converges. The equality $a_n = (a_n + |a_n|) - |a_n|$ now lets us express $\sum_{n=1}^{\infty} a_n$ as the difference of two convergent series:

$$\sum_{n=1}^{\infty} a_n = \sum_{n=1}^{\infty} (a_n + |a_n| - |a_n|) = \sum_{n=1}^{\infty} (a_n + |a_n|) - \sum_{n=1}^{\infty} |a_n|.$$

Therefore, $\sum_{n=1}^{\infty} a_n$ converges. ■

CAUTION We can rephrase Theorem 16 to say that every absolutely convergent series converges. However, the converse statement is false: Many convergent series do not converge absolutely (such as the alternating harmonic series in Example 1).

EXAMPLE 3 Applying the Absolute Convergence Test

(a) For $\sum_{n=1}^{\infty}(-1)^{n+1}\frac{1}{n^2} = 1 - \frac{1}{4} + \frac{1}{9} - \frac{1}{16} + \cdots$, the corresponding series of absolute values is the convergent series

$$\sum_{n=1}^{\infty}\frac{1}{n^2} = 1 + \frac{1}{4} + \frac{1}{9} + \frac{1}{16} + \cdots.$$

The original series converges because it converges absolutely.

(b) For $\sum_{n=1}^{\infty}\frac{\sin n}{n^2} = \frac{\sin 1}{1} + \frac{\sin 2}{4} + \frac{\sin 3}{9} + \cdots$, the corresponding series of absolute values is

$$\sum_{n=1}^{\infty}\left|\frac{\sin n}{n^2}\right| = \frac{|\sin 1|}{1} + \frac{|\sin 2|}{4} + \cdots,$$

which converges by comparison with $\sum_{n=1}^{\infty}(1/n^2)$ because $|\sin n| \le 1$ for every n. The original series converges absolutely; therefore it converges. ■

EXAMPLE 4 Alternating p-Series

If p is a positive constant, the sequence $\{1/n^p\}$ is a decreasing sequence with limit zero. Therefore the alternating p-series

$$\sum_{n=1}^{\infty}\frac{(-1)^{n-1}}{n^p} = 1 - \frac{1}{2^p} + \frac{1}{3^p} - \frac{1}{4^p} + \cdots, \qquad p > 0$$

converges.

If $p > 1$, the series converges absolutely. If $0 < p \le 1$, the series converges conditionally.

$$\text{Conditional convergence:} \qquad 1 - \frac{1}{\sqrt{2}} + \frac{1}{\sqrt{3}} - \frac{1}{\sqrt{4}} + \cdots$$

$$\text{Absolute convergence:} \qquad 1 - \frac{1}{2^{3/2}} + \frac{1}{3^{3/2}} - \frac{1}{4^{3/2}} + \cdots$$

■

Rearranging Series

THEOREM 17 The Rearrangement Theorem for Absolutely Convergent Series

If $\sum_{n=1}^{\infty} a_n$ converges absolutely, and $b_1, b_2, \ldots, b_n, \ldots$ is any arrangement of the sequence $\{a_n\}$, then $\sum b_n$ converges absolutely and

$$\sum_{n=1}^{\infty} b_n = \sum_{n=1}^{\infty} a_n.$$

(For an outline of the proof, see Exercise 60.)

EXAMPLE 5 Applying the Rearrangement Theorem

As we saw in Example 3, the series

$$1-\frac{1}{4}+\frac{1}{9}-\frac{1}{16}+\cdots+(-1)^{n-1}\frac{1}{n^2}+\cdots$$

converges absolutely. A possible rearrangement of the terms of the series might start with a positive term, then two negative terms, then three positive terms, then four negative terms, and so on: After k terms of one sign, take $k+1$ terms of the opposite sign. The first ten terms of such a series look like this:

$$1-\frac{1}{4}-\frac{1}{16}+\frac{1}{9}+\frac{1}{25}+\frac{1}{49}-\frac{1}{36}-\frac{1}{64}-\frac{1}{100}-\frac{1}{144}+\cdots.$$

The Rearrangement Theorem says that both series converge to the same value. In this example, if we had the second series to begin with, we would probably be glad to exchange it for the first, if we knew that we could. We can do even better: The sum of either series is also equal to

$$\sum_{n=1}^{\infty}\frac{1}{(2n-1)^2}-\sum_{n=1}^{\infty}\frac{1}{(2n)^2}.$$

(See Exercise 61.) ■

If we rearrange infinitely many terms of a conditionally convergent series, we can get results that are far different from the sum of the original series. Here is an example.

EXAMPLE 6 Rearranging the Alternating Harmonic Series

The alternating harmonic series

$$\frac{1}{1}-\frac{1}{2}+\frac{1}{3}-\frac{1}{4}+\frac{1}{5}-\frac{1}{6}+\frac{1}{7}-\frac{1}{8}+\frac{1}{9}-\frac{1}{10}+\frac{1}{11}-\cdots$$

can be rearranged to diverge or to reach any preassigned sum.

(a) *Rearranging* $\sum_{n=1}^{\infty}(-1)^{n+1}/n$ *to diverge.* The series of terms $\sum[1/(2n-1)]$ diverges to $+\infty$ and the series of terms $\sum(-1/2n)$ diverges to $-\infty$. No matter how far out in the sequence of odd-numbered terms we begin, we can always add enough positive terms to get an arbitrarily large sum. Similarly, with the negative terms, no matter how far out we start, we can add enough consecutive even-numbered terms to get a negative sum of arbitrarily large absolute value. If we wished to do so, we could start adding odd-numbered terms until we had a sum greater than $+3$, say, and then follow that with enough consecutive negative terms to make the new total less than -4. We could then add enough positive terms to make the total greater than $+5$ and follow with consecutive unused negative terms to make a new total less than -6, and so on. In this way, we could make the swings arbitrarily large in either direction.

(b) *Rearranging* $\sum_{n=1}^{\infty}(-1)^{n+1}/n$ *to converge to* 1. Another possibility is to focus on a particular limit. Suppose we try to get sums that converge to 1. We start with the first term, $1/1$, and then subtract $1/2$. Next we add $1/3$ and $1/5$, which brings the total back to 1 or above. Then we add consecutive negative terms until the total is less than 1. We continue in this manner: When the sum is less than 1, add positive terms until the total is 1 or more; then subtract (add negative) terms until the total is again less than 1. This process can be continued indefinitely. Because both the odd-numbered terms and the even-numbered terms of the original series approach zero as $n \to \infty$, the amount by which our partial sums exceed 1 or fall below it approaches zero. So the new series converges to 1. The rearranged series starts like this:

$$\frac{1}{1}-\frac{1}{2}+\frac{1}{3}+\frac{1}{5}-\frac{1}{4}+\frac{1}{7}+\frac{1}{9}-\frac{1}{6}+\frac{1}{11}+\frac{1}{13}-\frac{1}{8}+\frac{1}{15}+\frac{1}{17}-\frac{1}{10}$$
$$+\frac{1}{19}+\frac{1}{21}-\frac{1}{12}+\frac{1}{23}+\frac{1}{25}-\frac{1}{14}+\frac{1}{27}-\frac{1}{16}+\cdots$$

The kind of behavior illustrated by the series in Example 6 is typical of what can happen with any conditionally convergent series. Therefore we must always add the terms of a conditionally convergent series in the order given.

We have now developed several tests for convergence and divergence of series. In summary:

1. **The nth-Term Test:** Unless $a_n \to 0$, the series diverges.
2. **Geometric series:** $\sum ar^n$ converges if $|r| < 1$; otherwise it diverges.
3. **p-series:** $\sum 1/n^p$ converges if $p > 1$; otherwise it diverges.
4. **Series with nonnegative terms:** Try the Integral Test, Ratio Test, or Root Test. Try comparing to a known series with the Comparison Test.
5. **Series with some negative terms:** Does $\sum |a_n|$ converge? If yes, so does $\sum a_n$, since absolute convergence implies convergence.
6. **Alternating series:** $\sum a_n$ converges if the series satisfies the conditions of the Alternating Series Test.

EXERCISES 11.6

Determining Convergence or Divergence

Which of the alternating series in Exercises 1–10 converge, and which diverge? Give reasons for your answers.

1. $\sum_{n=1}^{\infty}(-1)^{n+1}\frac{1}{n^2}$

2. $\sum_{n=1}^{\infty}(-1)^{n+1}\frac{1}{n^{3/2}}$

3. $\sum_{n=1}^{\infty}(-1)^{n+1}\left(\frac{n}{10}\right)^n$

4. $\sum_{n=1}^{\infty}(-1)^{n+1}\frac{10^n}{n^{10}}$

5. $\sum_{n=2}^{\infty}(-1)^{n+1}\frac{1}{\ln n}$

6. $\sum_{n=1}^{\infty}(-1)^{n+1}\frac{\ln n}{n}$

7. $\sum_{n=2}^{\infty}(-1)^{n+1}\frac{\ln n}{\ln n^2}$

8. $\sum_{n=1}^{\infty}(-1)^{n}\ln\left(1+\frac{1}{n}\right)$

9. $\sum_{n=1}^{\infty}(-1)^{n+1}\frac{\sqrt{n}+1}{n+1}$

10. $\sum_{n=1}^{\infty}(-1)^{n+1}\frac{3\sqrt{n+1}}{\sqrt{n}+1}$

Absolute Convergence

Which of the series in Exercises 11–44 converge absolutely, which converge, and which diverge? Give reasons for your answers.

11. $\sum_{n=1}^{\infty}(-1)^{n+1}(0.1)^n$

12. $\sum_{n=1}^{\infty}(-1)^{n+1}\frac{(0.1)^n}{n}$

13. $\sum_{n=1}^{\infty}(-1)^{n}\frac{1}{\sqrt{n}}$

14. $\sum_{n=1}^{\infty}\frac{(-1)^n}{1+\sqrt{n}}$

15. $\sum_{n=1}^{\infty}(-1)^{n+1}\frac{n}{n^3+1}$

16. $\sum_{n=1}^{\infty}(-1)^{n+1}\frac{n!}{2^n}$

17. $\sum_{n=1}^{\infty}(-1)^{n}\frac{1}{n+3}$

18. $\sum_{n=1}^{\infty}(-1)^{n}\frac{\sin n}{n^2}$

19. $\sum_{n=1}^{\infty}(-1)^{n+1}\frac{3+n}{5+n}$

20. $\sum_{n=2}^{\infty}(-1)^{n}\frac{1}{\ln(n^3)}$

21. $\sum_{n=1}^{\infty}(-1)^{n+1}\frac{1+n}{n^2}$

22. $\sum_{n=1}^{\infty}\frac{(-2)^{n+1}}{n+5^n}$

23. $\sum_{n=1}^{\infty}(-1)^{n}n^2(2/3)^n$

24. $\sum_{n=1}^{\infty}(-1)^{n+1}\left(\sqrt[n]{10}\right)$

25. $\sum_{n=1}^{\infty}(-1)^{n}\frac{\tan^{-1} n}{n^2+1}$

26. $\sum_{n=2}^{\infty}(-1)^{n+1}\frac{1}{n\ln n}$

27. $\sum_{n=1}^{\infty}(-1)^n \frac{n}{n+1}$

28. $\sum_{n=1}^{\infty}(-1)^n \frac{\ln n}{n-\ln n}$

29. $\sum_{n=1}^{\infty} \frac{(-100)^n}{n!}$

30. $\sum_{n=1}^{\infty}(-5)^{-n}$

31. $\sum_{n=1}^{\infty} \frac{(-1)^{n-1}}{n^2+2n+1}$

32. $\sum_{n=2}^{\infty}(-1)^n \left(\frac{\ln n}{\ln n^2}\right)^n$

33. $\sum_{n=1}^{\infty} \frac{\cos n\pi}{n\sqrt{n}}$

34. $\sum_{n=1}^{\infty} \frac{\cos n\pi}{n}$

35. $\sum_{n=1}^{\infty} \frac{(-1)^n(n+1)^n}{(2n)^n}$

36. $\sum_{n=1}^{\infty} \frac{(-1)^{n+1}(n!)^2}{(2n)!}$

37. $\sum_{n=1}^{\infty}(-1)^n \frac{(2n)!}{2^n n! n}$

38. $\sum_{n=1}^{\infty}(-1)^n \frac{(n!)^2 3^n}{(2n+1)!}$

39. $\sum_{n=1}^{\infty}(-1)^n \left(\sqrt{n+1}-\sqrt{n}\right)$

40. $\sum_{n=1}^{\infty}(-1)^n \left(\sqrt{n^2+n}-n\right)$

41. $\sum_{n=1}^{\infty}(-1)^n \left(\sqrt{n+\sqrt{n}}-\sqrt{n}\right)$

42. $\sum_{n=1}^{\infty} \frac{(-1)^n}{\sqrt{n}+\sqrt{n+1}}$

43. $\sum_{n=1}^{\infty}(-1)^n \operatorname{sech} n$

44. $\sum_{n=1}^{\infty}(-1)^n \operatorname{csch} n$

Error Estimation

In Exercises 45–48, estimate the magnitude of the error involved in using the sum of the first four terms to approximate the sum of the entire series.

45. $\sum_{n=1}^{\infty}(-1)^{n+1} \frac{1}{n}$ It can be shown that the sum is ln 2.

46. $\sum_{n=1}^{\infty}(-1)^{n+1} \frac{1}{10^n}$

47. $\sum_{n=1}^{\infty}(-1)^{n+1} \frac{(0.01)^n}{n}$ As you will see in Section 11.7, the sum is ln (1.01).

48. $\frac{1}{1+t}=\sum_{n=0}^{\infty}(-1)^n t^n, \quad 0<t<1$

T Approximate the sums in Exercises 49 and 50 with an error of magnitude less than 5×10^{-6}.

49. $\sum_{n=0}^{\infty}(-1)^n \frac{1}{(2n)!}$ As you will see in Section 11.9, the sum is cos 1, the cosine of 1 radian.

50. $\sum_{n=0}^{\infty}(-1)^n \frac{1}{n!}$ As you will see in Section 11.9, the sum is e^{-1}.

Theory and Examples

51. **a.** The series

$$\frac{1}{3}-\frac{1}{2}+\frac{1}{9}-\frac{1}{4}+\frac{1}{27}-\frac{1}{8}+\cdots+\frac{1}{3^n}-\frac{1}{2^n}+\cdots$$

does not meet one of the conditions of Theorem 14. Which one?

b. Find the sum of the series in part (a).

T 52. The limit L of an alternating series that satisfies the conditions of Theorem 14 lies between the values of any two consecutive partial sums. This suggests using the average

$$\frac{s_n+s_{n+1}}{2}=s_n+\frac{1}{2}(-1)^{n+2}a_{n+1}$$

to estimate L. Compute

$$s_{20}+\frac{1}{2}\cdot\frac{1}{21}$$

as an approximation to the sum of the alternating harmonic series. The exact sum is $\ln 2=0.6931\ldots$.

53. **The sign of the remainder of an alternating series that satisfies the conditions of Theorem 14** Prove the assertion in Theorem 15 that whenever an alternating series satisfying the conditions of Theorem 14 is approximated with one of its partial sums, then the remainder (sum of the unused terms) has the same sign as the first unused term. (*Hint:* Group the remainder's terms in consecutive pairs.)

54. Show that the sum of the first $2n$ terms of the series

$$1-\frac{1}{2}+\frac{1}{2}-\frac{1}{3}+\frac{1}{3}-\frac{1}{4}+\frac{1}{4}-\frac{1}{5}+\frac{1}{5}-\frac{1}{6}+\cdots$$

is the same as the sum of the first n terms of the series

$$\frac{1}{1\cdot 2}+\frac{1}{2\cdot 3}+\frac{1}{3\cdot 4}+\frac{1}{4\cdot 5}+\frac{1}{5\cdot 6}+\cdots.$$

Do these series converge? What is the sum of the first $2n+1$ terms of the first series? If the series converge, what is their sum?

55. Show that if $\sum_{n=1}^{\infty} a_n$ diverges, then $\sum_{n=1}^{\infty}|a_n|$ diverges.

56. Show that if $\sum_{n=1}^{\infty} a_n$ converges absolutely, then

$$\left|\sum_{n=1}^{\infty} a_n\right| \leq \sum_{n=1}^{\infty}|a_n|.$$

57. Show that if $\sum_{n=1}^{\infty} a_n$ and $\sum_{n=1}^{\infty} b_n$ both converge absolutely, then so does

a. $\sum_{n=1}^{\infty}(a_n+b_n)$ **b.** $\sum_{n=1}^{\infty}(a_n-b_n)$

c. $\sum_{n=1}^{\infty} k a_n$ (k any number)

58. Show by example that $\sum_{n=1}^{\infty} a_n b_n$ may diverge even if $\sum_{n=1}^{\infty} a_n$ and $\sum_{n=1}^{\infty} b_n$ both converge.

T 59. In Example 6, suppose the goal is to arrange the terms to get a new series that converges to $-1/2$. Start the new arrangement with the first negative term, which is $-1/2$. Whenever you have a sum that is less than or equal to $-1/2$, start introducing positive terms, taken in order, until the new total is greater than $-1/2$. Then add negative terms until the total is less than or equal to $-1/2$ again. Continue this process until your partial sums have been above the target at least three times and finish at or below it. If s_n is the sum of the first n terms of your new series, plot the points (n, s_n) to illustrate how the sums are behaving.

60. Outline of the proof of the Rearrangement Theorem (Theorem 17)

a. Let ϵ be a positive real number, let $L = \sum_{n=1}^{\infty} a_n$, and let $s_k = \sum_{n=1}^{k} a_n$. Show that for some index N_1 and for some index $N_2 \geq N_1$,

$$\sum_{n=N_1}^{\infty} |a_n| < \frac{\epsilon}{2} \quad \text{and} \quad |s_{N_2} - L| < \frac{\epsilon}{2}.$$

Since all the terms $a_1, a_2, \ldots, a_{N_2}$ appear somewhere in the sequence $\{b_n\}$, there is an index $N_3 \geq N_2$ such that if $n \geq N_3$, then $\left(\sum_{k=1}^{n} b_k\right) - s_{N_2}$ is at most a sum of terms a_m with $m \geq N_1$. Therefore, if $n \geq N_3$,

$$\begin{aligned} \left|\sum_{k=1}^{n} b_k - L\right| &\leq \left|\sum_{k=1}^{n} b_k - s_{N_2}\right| + |s_{N_2} - L| \\ &\leq \sum_{k=N_1}^{\infty} |a_k| + |s_{N_2} - L| < \epsilon. \end{aligned}$$

b. The argument in part (a) shows that if $\sum_{n=1}^{\infty} a_n$ converges absolutely then $\sum_{n=1}^{\infty} b_n$ converges and $\sum_{n=1}^{\infty} b_n = \sum_{n=1}^{\infty} a_n$. Now show that because $\sum_{n=1}^{\infty} |a_n|$ converges, $\sum_{n=1}^{\infty} |b_n|$ converges to $\sum_{n=1}^{\infty} |a_n|$.

61. Unzipping absolutely convergent series

a. Show that if $\sum_{n=1}^{\infty} |a_n|$ converges and

$$b_n = \begin{cases} a_n, & \text{if } a_n \geq 0 \\ 0, & \text{if } a_n < 0, \end{cases}$$

then $\sum_{n=1}^{\infty} b_n$ converges.

b. Use the results in part (a) to show likewise that if $\sum_{n=1}^{\infty} |a_n|$ converges and

$$c_n = \begin{cases} 0, & \text{if } a_n \geq 0 \\ a_n, & \text{if } a_n < 0, \end{cases}$$

then $\sum_{n=1}^{\infty} c_n$ converges.

In other words, if a series converges absolutely, its positive terms form a convergent series, and so do its negative terms. Furthermore,

$$\sum_{n=1}^{\infty} a_n = \sum_{n=1}^{\infty} b_n + \sum_{n=1}^{\infty} c_n$$

because $b_n = (a_n + |a_n|)/2$ and $c_n = (a_n - |a_n|)/2$.

62. What is wrong here?:

Multiply both sides of the alternating harmonic series

$$S = 1 - \frac{1}{2} + \frac{1}{3} - \frac{1}{4} + \frac{1}{5} - \frac{1}{6} + \frac{1}{7} - \frac{1}{8} + \frac{1}{9} - \frac{1}{10} + \frac{1}{11} - \frac{1}{12} + \cdots$$

by 2 to get

$$2S = 2 - 1 + \frac{2}{3} - \frac{1}{2} + \frac{2}{5} - \frac{1}{3} + \frac{2}{7} - \frac{1}{4} + \frac{2}{9} - \frac{1}{5} + \frac{2}{11} - \frac{1}{6} + \cdots.$$

Collect terms with the same denominator, as the arrows indicate, to arrive at

$$2S = 1 - \frac{1}{2} + \frac{1}{3} - \frac{1}{4} + \frac{1}{5} - \frac{1}{6} + \cdots.$$

The series on the right-hand side of this equation is the series we started with. Therefore, $2S = S$, and dividing by S gives $2 = 1$. (*Source:* "Riemann's Rearrangement Theorem" by Stewart Galanor, *Mathematics Teacher*, Vol. 80, No. 8, 1987, pp. 675–681.)

63. Draw a figure similar to Figure 11.9 to illustrate the convergence of the series in Theorem 14 when $N > 1$.

11.7 Power Series

Now that we can test infinite series for convergence we can study the infinite polynomials mentioned at the beginning of this chapter. We call these polynomials power series because they are defined as infinite series of powers of some variable, in our case x. Like polynomials, power series can be added, subtracted, multiplied, differentiated, and integrated to give new power series.

Power Series and Convergence

We begin with the formal definition.

DEFINITIONS Power Series, Center, Coefficients

A **power series about $x = 0$** is a series of the form

$$\sum_{n=0}^{\infty} c_n x^n = c_0 + c_1 x + c_2 x^2 + \cdots + c_n x^n + \cdots. \tag{1}$$

A **power series about $x = a$** is a series of the form

$$\sum_{n=0}^{\infty} c_n (x-a)^n = c_0 + c_1(x-a) + c_2(x-a)^2 + \cdots + c_n(x-a)^n + \cdots \tag{2}$$

in which the **center** a and the **coefficients** $c_0, c_1, c_2, \ldots, c_n, \ldots$ are constants.

Equation (1) is the special case obtained by taking $a = 0$ in Equation (2).

EXAMPLE 1 A Geometric Series

Taking all the coefficients to be 1 in Equation (1) gives the geometric power series

$$\sum_{n=0}^{\infty} x^n = 1 + x + x^2 + \cdots + x^n + \cdots.$$

This is the geometric series with first term 1 and ratio x. It converges to $1/(1-x)$ for $|x| < 1$. We express this fact by writing

$$\frac{1}{1-x} = 1 + x + x^2 + \cdots + x^n + \cdots, \qquad -1 < x < 1. \tag{3}$$

■

Up to now, we have used Equation (3) as a formula for the sum of the series on the right. We now change the focus: We think of the partial sums of the series on the right as polynomials $P_n(x)$ that approximate the function on the left. For values of x near zero, we need take only a few terms of the series to get a good approximation. As we move toward $x = 1$, or -1, we must take more terms. Figure 11.10 shows the graphs of $f(x) = 1/(1-x)$, and the approximating polynomials $y_n = P_n(x)$ for $n = 0, 1, 2$, and 8. The function $f(x) = 1/(1-x)$ is not continuous on intervals containing $x = 1$, where it has a vertical asymptote. The approximations do not apply when $x \geq 1$.

EXAMPLE 2 A Geometric Series

The power series

$$1 - \frac{1}{2}(x-2) + \frac{1}{4}(x-2)^2 + \cdots + \left(-\frac{1}{2}\right)^n (x-2)^n + \cdots \tag{4}$$

matches Equation (2) with $a = 2$, $c_0 = 1$, $c_1 = -1/2$, $c_2 = 1/4, \ldots, c_n = (-1/2)^n$. This is a geometric series with first term 1 and ratio $r = -\dfrac{x-2}{2}$. The series converges for

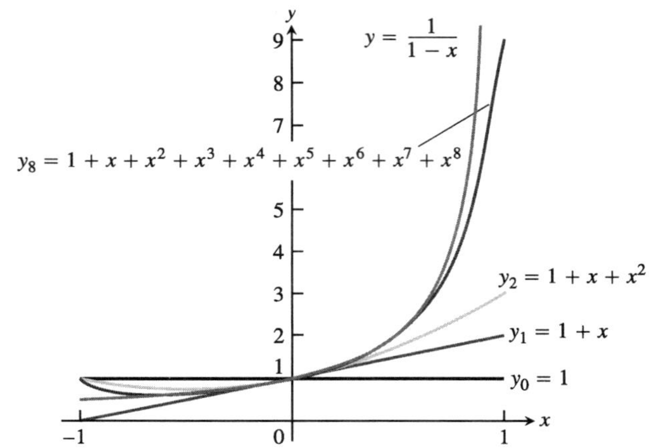

FIGURE 11.10 The graphs of $f(x) = 1/(1 - x)$ and four of its polynomial approximations (Example 1).

$\left|\frac{x-2}{2}\right| < 1$ or $0 < x < 4$. The sum is

$$\frac{1}{1-r} = \frac{1}{1 + \frac{x-2}{2}} = \frac{2}{x},$$

so

$$\frac{2}{x} = 1 - \frac{(x-2)}{2} + \frac{(x-2)^2}{4} - \cdots + \left(-\frac{1}{2}\right)^n (x-2)^n + \cdots, \qquad 0 < x < 4.$$

Series (4) generates useful polynomial approximations of $f(x) = 2/x$ for values of x near 2:

$$P_0(x) = 1$$

$$P_1(x) = 1 - \frac{1}{2}(x-2) = 2 - \frac{x}{2}$$

$$P_2(x) = 1 - \frac{1}{2}(x-2) + \frac{1}{4}(x-2)^2 = 3 - \frac{3x}{2} + \frac{x^2}{4},$$

and so on (Figure 11.11). ■

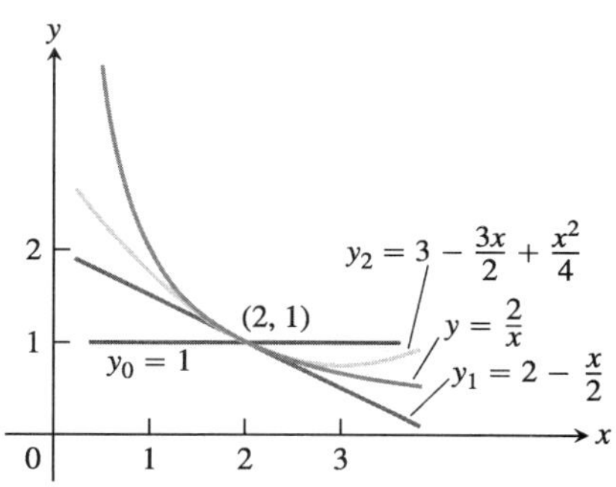

FIGURE 11.11 The graphs of $f(x) = 2/x$ and its first three polynomial approximations (Example 2).

EXAMPLE 3 Testing for Convergence Using the Ratio Test

For what values of x do the following power series converge?

(a) $\displaystyle\sum_{n=1}^{\infty}(-1)^{n-1}\frac{x^n}{n} = x - \frac{x^2}{2} + \frac{x^3}{3} - \cdots$

(b) $\displaystyle\sum_{n=1}^{\infty}(-1)^{n-1}\frac{x^{2n-1}}{2n-1} = x - \frac{x^3}{3} + \frac{x^5}{5} - \cdots$

(c) $\displaystyle\sum_{n=0}^{\infty}\frac{x^n}{n!} = 1 + x + \frac{x^2}{2!} + \frac{x^3}{3!} + \cdots$

(d) $\displaystyle\sum_{n=0}^{\infty}n!x^n = 1 + x + 2!x^2 + 3!x^3 + \cdots$

Solution Apply the Ratio Test to the series $\sum|u_n|$, where u_n is the nth term of the series in question.

(a) $\left|\dfrac{u_{n+1}}{u_n}\right| = \dfrac{n}{n+1}|x| \rightarrow |x|.$

The series converges absolutely for $|x| < 1$. It diverges if $|x| > 1$ because the nth term does not converge to zero. At $x = 1$, we get the alternating harmonic series $1 - 1/2 + 1/3 - 1/4 + \cdots$, which converges. At $x = -1$ we get $-1 - 1/2 - 1/3 - 1/4 - \cdots$, the negative of the harmonic series; it diverges. Series (a) converges for $-1 < x \leq 1$ and diverges elsewhere.

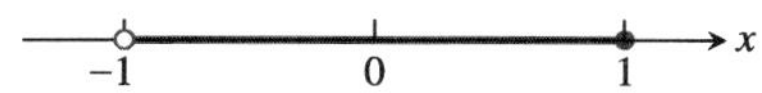

(b) $\left|\dfrac{u_{n+1}}{u_n}\right| = \dfrac{2n-1}{2n+1}x^2 \rightarrow x^2.$

The series converges absolutely for $x^2 < 1$. It diverges for $x^2 > 1$ because the nth term does not converge to zero. At $x = 1$ the series becomes $1 - 1/3 + 1/5 - 1/7 + \cdots$, which converges by the Alternating Series Theorem. It also converges at $x = -1$ because it is again an alternating series that satisfies the conditions for convergence. The value at $x = -1$ is the negative of the value at $x = 1$. Series (b) converges for $-1 \leq x \leq 1$ and diverges elsewhere.

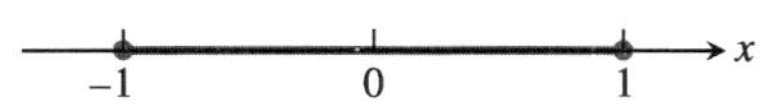

(c) $\left|\dfrac{u_{n+1}}{u_n}\right| = \left|\dfrac{x^{n+1}}{(n+1)!}\cdot\dfrac{n!}{x^n}\right| = \dfrac{|x|}{n+1} \rightarrow 0$ for every x.

The series converges absolutely for all x.

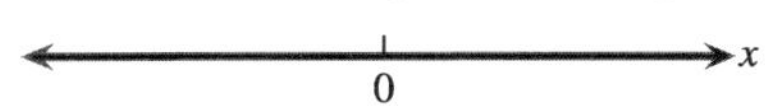

(d) $\left|\dfrac{u_{n+1}}{u_n}\right| = \left|\dfrac{(n+1)!x^{n+1}}{n!x^n}\right| = (n+1)|x| \rightarrow \infty$ unless $x = 0$.

The series diverges for all values of x except $x = 0$.

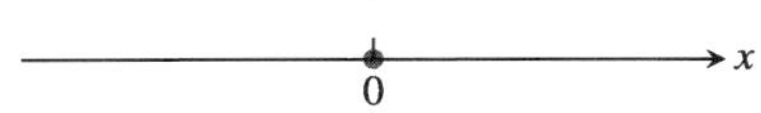

■

Example 3 illustrates how we usually test a power series for convergence, and the possible results.

THEOREM 18 The Convergence Theorem for Power Series

If the power series $\sum_{n=0}^{\infty} a_n x^n = a_0 + a_1 x + a_2 x^2 + \cdots$ converges for $x = c \neq 0$, then it converges absolutely for all x with $|x| < |c|$. If the series diverges for $x = d$, then it diverges for all x with $|x| > |d|$.

Proof Suppose the series $\sum_{n=0}^{\infty} a_n c^n$ converges. Then $\lim_{n\to\infty} a_n c^n = 0$. Hence, there is an integer N such that $|a_n c^n| < 1$ for all $n \geq N$. That is,

$$|a_n| < \frac{1}{|c|^n} \qquad \text{for } n \geq N. \tag{5}$$

Now take any x such that $|x| < |c|$ and consider

$$|a_0| + |a_1 x| + \cdots + |a_{N-1}x^{N-1}| + |a_N x^N| + |a_{N+1}x^{N+1}| + \cdots .$$

There are only a finite number of terms prior to $|a_N x^N|$, and their sum is finite. Starting with $|a_N x^N|$ and beyond, the terms are less than

$$\left|\frac{x}{c}\right|^N + \left|\frac{x}{c}\right|^{N+1} + \left|\frac{x}{c}\right|^{N+2} + \cdots \tag{6}$$

because of Inequality (5). But Series (6) is a geometric series with ratio $r = |x/c|$, which is less than 1, since $|x| < |c|$. Hence Series (6) converges, so the original series converges absolutely. This proves the first half of the theorem.

The second half of the theorem follows from the first. If the series diverges at $x = d$ and converges at a value x_0 with $|x_0| > |d|$, we may take $c = x_0$ in the first half of the theorem and conclude that the series converges absolutely at d. But the series cannot converge absolutely and diverge at one and the same time. Hence, if it diverges at d, it diverges for all x with $|x| > |d|$. ■

To simplify the notation, Theorem 18 deals with the convergence of series of the form $\sum a_n x^n$. For series of the form $\sum a_n(x-a)^n$ we can replace $x - a$ by x' and apply the results to the series $\sum a_n(x')^n$.

The Radius of Convergence of a Power Series

The theorem we have just proved and the examples we have studied lead to the conclusion that a power series $\sum c_n(x-a)^n$ behaves in one of three possible ways. It might converge only at $x = a$, or converge everywhere, or converge on some interval of radius R centered at $x = a$. We prove this as a Corollary to Theorem 18.

COROLLARY TO THEOREM 18

The convergence of the series $\sum c_n(x-a)^n$ is described by one of the following three possibilities:

1. There is a positive number R such that the series diverges for x with $|x - a| > R$ but converges absolutely for x with $|x - a| < R$. The series may or may not converge at either of the endpoints $x = a - R$ and $x = a + R$.
2. The series converges absolutely for every x $(R = \infty)$.
3. The series converges at $x = a$ and diverges elsewhere $(R = 0)$.

Proof We assume first that $a = 0$, so that the power series is centered at 0. If the series converges everywhere we are in Case 2. If it converges only at $x = 0$ we are in Case 3. Otherwise there is a nonzero number d such that $\sum c_n d^n$ diverges. The set S of values of x for which the series $\sum c_n x^n$ converges is nonempty because it contains 0 and a positive number p as well. By Theorem 18, the series diverges for all x with $|x| > |d|$, so $|x| \le |d|$ for all $x \in S$, and S is a bounded set. By the Completeness Property of the real numbers (see Appendix 4) a nonempty, bounded set has a least upper bound R. (The least upper bound is the smallest number with the property that the elements $x \in S$ satisfy $x \le R$.) If $|x| > R \ge p$, then $x \notin S$ so the series $\sum c_n x^n$ diverges. If $|x| < R$, then $|x|$ is not an upper bound for S (because it's smaller than the least upper bound) so there is a number $b \in S$ such that $b > |x|$. Since $b \in S$, the series $\sum c_n b^n$ converges and therefore the series $\sum c_n |x|^n$ converges by Theorem 18. This proves the Corollary for power series centered at $a = 0$.

For a power series centered at $a \ne 0$, we set $x' = (x - a)$ and repeat the argument with x'. Since $x' = 0$ when $x = a$, a radius R interval of convergence for $\sum c_n (x')^n$ centered at $x' = 0$ is the same as a radius R interval of convergence for $\sum c_n (x - a)^n$ centered at $x = a$. This establishes the Corollary for the general case. ■

R is called the **radius of convergence** of the power series and the interval of radius R centered at $x = a$ is called the **interval of convergence**. The interval of convergence may be open, closed, or half-open, depending on the particular series. At points x with $|x - a| < R$, the series converges absolutely. If the series converges for all values of x, we say its radius of convergence is infinite. If it converges only at $x = a$, we say its radius of convergence is zero.

How to Test a Power Series for Convergence

1. *Use the Ratio Test (or nth-Root Test) to find the interval where the series converges absolutely.* Ordinarily, this is an open interval

$$|x - a| < R \qquad \text{or} \qquad a - R < x < a + R.$$

2. *If the interval of absolute convergence is finite, test for convergence or divergence at each endpoint*, as in Examples 3a and b. Use a Comparison Test, the Integral Test, or the Alternating Series Test.
3. *If the interval of absolute convergence is $a - R < x < a + R$, the series diverges for $|x - a| > R$* (it does not even converge conditionally), because the nth term does not approach zero for those values of x.

Term-by-Term Differentiation

A theorem from advanced calculus says that a power series can be differentiated term by term at each interior point of its interval of convergence.

THEOREM 19 The Term-by-Term Differentiation Theorem

If $\sum c_n(x-a)^n$ converges for $a-R<x<a+R$ for some $R>0$, it defines a function f:

$$f(x)=\sum_{n=0}^{\infty} c_n(x-a)^n, \qquad a-R<x<a+R.$$

Such a function f has derivatives of all orders inside the interval of convergence. We can obtain the derivatives by differentiating the original series term by term:

$$f'(x)=\sum_{n=1}^{\infty} nc_n(x-a)^{n-1}$$

$$f''(x)=\sum_{n=2}^{\infty} n(n-1)c_n(x-a)^{n-2},$$

and so on. Each of these derived series converges at every interior point of the interval of convergence of the original series.

EXAMPLE 4 Applying Term-by-Term Differentiation

Find series for $f'(x)$ and $f''(x)$ if

$$f(x)=\frac{1}{1-x}=1+x+x^2+x^3+x^4+\cdots+x^n+\cdots$$

$$=\sum_{n=0}^{\infty} x^n, \qquad -1<x<1$$

Solution

$$f'(x)=\frac{1}{(1-x)^2}=1+2x+3x^2+4x^3+\cdots+nx^{n-1}+\cdots$$

$$=\sum_{n=1}^{\infty} nx^{n-1}, \qquad -1<x<1$$

$$f''(x)=\frac{2}{(1-x)^3}=2+6x+12x^2+\cdots+n(n-1)x^{n-2}+\cdots$$

$$=\sum_{n=2}^{\infty} n(n-1)x^{n-2}, \qquad -1<x<1$$ ■

CAUTION Term-by-term differentiation might not work for other kinds of series. For example, the trigonometric series

$$\sum_{n=1}^{\infty} \frac{\sin(n!x)}{n^2}$$

converges for all x. But if we differentiate term by term we get the series

$$\sum_{n=1}^{\infty} \frac{n!\cos(n!x)}{n^2},$$

which diverges for all x. This is not a power series, since it is not a sum of positive integer powers of x.

Term-by-Term Integration

Another advanced calculus theorem states that a power series can be integrated term by term throughout its interval of convergence.

THEOREM 20 The Term-by-Term Integration Theorem

Suppose that

$$f(x) = \sum_{n=0}^{\infty} c_n(x-a)^n$$

converges for $a - R < x < a + R$ $(R > 0)$. Then

$$\sum_{n=0}^{\infty} c_n \frac{(x-a)^{n+1}}{n+1}$$

converges for $a - R < x < a + R$ and

$$\int f(x)\,dx = \sum_{n=0}^{\infty} c_n \frac{(x-a)^{n+1}}{n+1} + C$$

for $a - R < x < a + R$.

EXAMPLE 5 A Series for $\tan^{-1} x$, $-1 \le x \le 1$

Identify the function

$$f(x) = x - \frac{x^3}{3} + \frac{x^5}{5} - \cdots, \qquad -1 \le x \le 1.$$

Solution We differentiate the original series term by term and get

$$f'(x) = 1 - x^2 + x^4 - x^6 + \cdots, \qquad -1 < x < 1.$$

This is a geometric series with first term 1 and ratio $-x^2$, so

$$f'(x) = \frac{1}{1-(-x^2)} = \frac{1}{1+x^2}.$$

We can now integrate $f'(x) = 1/(1+x^2)$ to get

$$\int f'(x)\,dx = \int \frac{dx}{1+x^2} = \tan^{-1} x + C.$$

The series for $f(x)$ is zero when $x = 0$, so $C = 0$. Hence

$$f(x) = x - \frac{x^3}{3} + \frac{x^5}{5} - \frac{x^7}{7} + \cdots = \tan^{-1} x, \qquad -1 < x < 1. \tag{7}$$

In Section 11.10, we will see that the series also converges to $\tan^{-1} x$ at $x = \pm 1$. ■

Notice that the original series in Example 5 converges at both endpoints of the original interval of convergence, but Theorem 20 can guarantee the convergence of the differentiated series only inside the interval.

EXAMPLE 6 A Series for $\ln(1+x)$, $-1 < x \le 1$

The series

$$\frac{1}{1+t} = 1 - t + t^2 - t^3 + \cdots$$

converges on the open interval $-1 < t < 1$. Therefore,

$$\ln(1+x) = \int_0^x \frac{1}{1+t}\,dt = t - \frac{t^2}{2} + \frac{t^3}{3} - \frac{t^4}{4} + \cdots\Big]_0^x \qquad \text{Theorem 20}$$

$$= x - \frac{x^2}{2} + \frac{x^3}{3} - \frac{x^4}{4} + \cdots, \qquad -1 < x < 1.$$

It can also be shown that the series converges at $x = 1$ to the number $\ln 2$, but that was not guaranteed by the theorem. ■

USING TECHNOLOGY **Study of Series**

Series are in many ways analogous to integrals. Just as the number of functions with explicit antiderivatives in terms of elementary functions is small compared to the number of integrable functions, the number of power series in x that agree with explicit elementary functions on x-intervals is small compared to the number of power series that converge on some x-interval. Graphing utilities can aid in the study of such series in much the same way that numerical integration aids in the study of definite integrals. The ability to study power series at particular values of x is built into most Computer Algebra Systems.

If a series converges rapidly enough, CAS exploration might give us an idea of the sum. For instance, in calculating the early partial sums of the series $\sum_{k=1}^{\infty}[1/(2^{k-1})]$ (Section 11.4, Example 2b), Maple returns $S_n = 1.6066\,95152$ for $31 \le n \le 200$. This suggests that the sum of the series is 1.6066 95152 to 10 digits. Indeed,

$$\sum_{k=201}^{\infty}\frac{1}{2^k-1} = \sum_{k=201}^{\infty}\frac{1}{2^{k-1}(2-(1/2^{k-1}))} < \sum_{k=201}^{\infty}\frac{1}{2^{k-1}} = \frac{1}{2^{199}} < 1.25\times 10^{-60}.$$

The remainder after 200 terms is negligible.

However, CAS and calculator exploration cannot do much for us if the series converges or diverges very slowly, and indeed can be downright misleading. For example, try calculating the partial sums of the series $\sum_{k=1}^{\infty}[1/(10^{10}k)]$. The terms are tiny in comparison to the numbers we normally work with and the partial sums, even for hundreds of terms, are miniscule. We might well be fooled into thinking that the series converges. In fact, it diverges, as we can see by writing it as $(1/10^{10})\sum_{k=1}^{\infty}(1/k)$, a constant times the harmonic series.

We will know better how to interpret numerical results after studying error estimates in Section 11.9.

Multiplication of Power Series

Another theorem from advanced calculus states that absolutely converging power series can be multiplied the way we multiply polynomials. We omit the proof.

THEOREM 21 The Series Multiplication Theorem for Power Series
If $A(x) = \sum_{n=0}^{\infty} a_n x^n$ and $B(x) = \sum_{n=0}^{\infty} b_n x^n$ converge absolutely for $|x| < R$, and

$$c_n = a_0 b_n + a_1 b_{n-1} + a_2 b_{n-2} + \cdots + a_{n-1} b_1 + a_n b_0 = \sum_{k=0}^{n} a_k b_{n-k},$$

then $\sum_{n=0}^{\infty} c_n x^n$ converges absolutely to $A(x)B(x)$ for $|x| < R$:

$$\left(\sum_{n=0}^{\infty} a_n x^n\right) \cdot \left(\sum_{n=0}^{\infty} b_n x^n\right) = \sum_{n=0}^{\infty} c_n x^n.$$

EXAMPLE 7 Multiply the geometric series

$$\sum_{n=0}^{\infty} x^n = 1 + x + x^2 + \cdots + x^n + \cdots = \frac{1}{1-x}, \qquad \text{for } |x| < 1,$$

by itself to get a power series for $1/(1-x)^2$, for $|x| < 1$.

Solution Let

$$A(x) = \sum_{n=0}^{\infty} a_n x^n = 1 + x + x^2 + \cdots + x^n + \cdots = 1/(1-x)$$

$$B(x) = \sum_{n=0}^{\infty} b_n x^n = 1 + x + x^2 + \cdots + x^n + \cdots = 1/(1-x)$$

and

$$c_n = \underbrace{a_0 b_n + a_1 b_{n-1} + \cdots + a_k b_{n-k} + \cdots + a_n b_0}_{n+1 \text{ terms}}$$

$$= \underbrace{1 + 1 + \cdots + 1}_{n+1 \text{ ones}} = n + 1.$$

Then, by the Series Multiplication Theorem,

$$A(x) \cdot B(x) = \sum_{n=0}^{\infty} c_n x^n = \sum_{n=0}^{\infty} (n+1) x^n$$

$$= 1 + 2x + 3x^2 + 4x^3 + \cdots + (n+1)x^n + \cdots$$

is the series for $1/(1-x)^2$. The series all converge absolutely for $|x| < 1$.

Notice that Example 4 gives the same answer because

$$\frac{d}{dx}\left(\frac{1}{1-x}\right) = \frac{1}{(1-x)^2}.$$ ■

EXERCISES 11.7

Intervals of Convergence

In Exercises 1–32, **(a)** find the series' radius and interval of convergence. For what values of x does the series converge **(b)** absolutely, **(c)** conditionally?

1. $\sum_{n=0}^{\infty} x^n$
2. $\sum_{n=0}^{\infty} (x+5)^n$
3. $\sum_{n=0}^{\infty} (-1)^n(4x+1)^n$
4. $\sum_{n=1}^{\infty} \frac{(3x-2)^n}{n}$
5. $\sum_{n=0}^{\infty} \frac{(x-2)^n}{10^n}$
6. $\sum_{n=0}^{\infty} (2x)^n$
7. $\sum_{n=0}^{\infty} \frac{nx^n}{n+2}$
8. $\sum_{n=1}^{\infty} \frac{(-1)^n(x+2)^n}{n}$
9. $\sum_{n=1}^{\infty} \frac{x^n}{n\sqrt{n}\,3^n}$
10. $\sum_{n=1}^{\infty} \frac{(x-1)^n}{\sqrt{n}}$
11. $\sum_{n=0}^{\infty} \frac{(-1)^n x^n}{n!}$
12. $\sum_{n=0}^{\infty} \frac{3^n x^n}{n!}$
13. $\sum_{n=0}^{\infty} \frac{x^{2n+1}}{n!}$
14. $\sum_{n=0}^{\infty} \frac{(2x+3)^{2n+1}}{n!}$
15. $\sum_{n=0}^{\infty} \frac{x^n}{\sqrt{n^2+3}}$
16. $\sum_{n=0}^{\infty} \frac{(-1)^n x^n}{\sqrt{n^2+3}}$
17. $\sum_{n=0}^{\infty} \frac{n(x+3)^n}{5^n}$
18. $\sum_{n=0}^{\infty} \frac{nx^n}{4^n(n^2+1)}$
19. $\sum_{n=0}^{\infty} \frac{\sqrt{n}x^n}{3^n}$
20. $\sum_{n=1}^{\infty} \sqrt[n]{n}(2x+5)^n$
21. $\sum_{n=1}^{\infty} \left(1+\frac{1}{n}\right)^n x^n$
22. $\sum_{n=1}^{\infty} (\ln n)x^n$
23. $\sum_{n=1}^{\infty} n^n x^n$
24. $\sum_{n=0}^{\infty} n!(x-4)^n$
25. $\sum_{n=1}^{\infty} \frac{(-1)^{n+1}(x+2)^n}{n2^n}$
26. $\sum_{n=0}^{\infty} (-2)^n(n+1)(x-1)^n$
27. $\sum_{n=2}^{\infty} \frac{x^n}{n(\ln n)^2}$ Get the information you need about $\sum 1/(n(\ln n)^2)$ from Section 11.3, Exercise 39.
28. $\sum_{n=2}^{\infty} \frac{x^n}{n\ln n}$ Get the information you need about $\sum 1/(n\ln n)$ from Section 11.3, Exercise 38.
29. $\sum_{n=1}^{\infty} \frac{(4x-5)^{2n+1}}{n^{3/2}}$
30. $\sum_{n=1}^{\infty} \frac{(3x+1)^{n+1}}{2n+2}$
31. $\sum_{n=1}^{\infty} \frac{(x+\pi)^n}{\sqrt{n}}$
32. $\sum_{n=0}^{\infty} \frac{(x-\sqrt{2})^{2n+1}}{2^n}$

In Exercises 33–38, find the series' interval of convergence and, within this interval, the sum of the series as a function of x.

33. $\sum_{n=0}^{\infty} \frac{(x-1)^{2n}}{4^n}$
34. $\sum_{n=0}^{\infty} \frac{(x+1)^{2n}}{9^n}$
35. $\sum_{n=0}^{\infty} \left(\frac{\sqrt{x}}{2}-1\right)^n$
36. $\sum_{n=0}^{\infty} (\ln x)^n$
37. $\sum_{n=0}^{\infty} \left(\frac{x^2+1}{3}\right)^n$
38. $\sum_{n=0}^{\infty} \left(\frac{x^2-1}{2}\right)^n$

Theory and Examples

39. For what values of x does the series

$$1-\frac{1}{2}(x-3)+\frac{1}{4}(x-3)^2+\cdots+\left(-\frac{1}{2}\right)^n(x-3)^n+\cdots$$

converge? What is its sum? What series do you get if you differentiate the given series term by term? For what values of x does the new series converge? What is its sum?

40. If you integrate the series in Exercise 39 term by term, what new series do you get? For what values of x does the new series converge, and what is another name for its sum?

41. The series

$$\sin x = x-\frac{x^3}{3!}+\frac{x^5}{5!}-\frac{x^7}{7!}+\frac{x^9}{9!}-\frac{x^{11}}{11!}+\cdots$$

converges to $\sin x$ for all x.

a. Find the first six terms of a series for $\cos x$. For what values of x should the series converge?

b. By replacing x by $2x$ in the series for $\sin x$, find a series that converges to $\sin 2x$ for all x.

c. Using the result in part (a) and series multiplication, calculate the first six terms of a series for $2\sin x\cos x$. Compare your answer with the answer in part (b).

42. The series

$$e^x = 1+x+\frac{x^2}{2!}+\frac{x^3}{3!}+\frac{x^4}{4!}+\frac{x^5}{5!}+\cdots$$

converges to e^x for all x.

a. Find a series for $(d/dx)e^x$. Do you get the series for e^x? Explain your answer.

b. Find a series for $\int e^x\,dx$. Do you get the series for e^x? Explain your answer.

c. Replace x by $-x$ in the series for e^x to find a series that converges to e^{-x} for all x. Then multiply the series for e^x and e^{-x} to find the first six terms of a series for $e^{-x}\cdot e^x$.

43. The series

$$\tan x = x + \frac{x^3}{3} + \frac{2x^5}{15} + \frac{17x^7}{315} + \frac{62x^9}{2835} + \cdots$$

converges to $\tan x$ for $-\pi/2 < x < \pi/2$.

a. Find the first five terms of the series for $\ln|\sec x|$. For what values of x should the series converge?

b. Find the first five terms of the series for $\sec^2 x$. For what values of x should this series converge?

c. Check your result in part (b) by squaring the series given for $\sec x$ in Exercise 44.

44. The series

$$\sec x = 1 + \frac{x^2}{2} + \frac{5}{24}x^4 + \frac{61}{720}x^6 + \frac{277}{8064}x^8 + \cdots$$

converges to $\sec x$ for $-\pi/2 < x < \pi/2$.

a. Find the first five terms of a power series for the function $\ln|\sec x + \tan x|$. For what values of x should the series converge?

b. Find the first four terms of a series for $\sec x \tan x$. For what values of x should the series converge?

c. Check your result in part (b) by multiplying the series for $\sec x$ by the series given for $\tan x$ in Exercise 43.

45. Uniqueness of convergent power series

a. Show that if two power series $\sum_{n=0}^{\infty} a_n x^n$ and $\sum_{n=0}^{\infty} b_n x^n$ are convergent and equal for all values of x in an open interval $(-c, c)$, then $a_n = b_n$ for every n. (*Hint:* Let $f(x) = \sum_{n=0}^{\infty} a_n x^n = \sum_{n=0}^{\infty} b_n x^n$. Differentiate term by term to show that a_n and b_n both equal $f^{(n)}(0)/(n!)$.)

b. Show that if $\sum_{n=0}^{\infty} a_n x^n = 0$ for all x in an open interval $(-c, c)$, then $a_n = 0$ for every n.

46. The sum of the series $\sum_{n=0}^{\infty} (n^2/2^n)$ To find the sum of this series, express $1/(1-x)$ as a geometric series, differentiate both sides of the resulting equation with respect to x, multiply both sides of the result by x, differentiate again, multiply by x again, and set x equal to $1/2$. What do you get? (*Source*: David E. Dobbs' letter to the editor, *Illinois Mathematics Teacher*, Vol. 33, Issue 4, 1982, p. 27.)

47. Convergence at endpoints Show by examples that the convergence of a power series at an endpoint of its interval of convergence may be either conditional or absolute.

48. Make up a power series whose interval of convergence is

a. $(-3, 3)$ **b.** $(-2, 0)$ **c.** $(1, 5)$.

11.8 Taylor and Maclaurin Series

This section shows how functions that are infinitely differentiable generate power series called Taylor series. In many cases, these series can provide useful polynomial approximations of the generating functions.

Series Representations

We know from Theorem 19 that within its interval of convergence the sum of a power series is a continuous function with derivatives of all orders. But what about the other way around? If a function $f(x)$ has derivatives of all orders on an interval I, can it be expressed as a power series on I? And if it can, what will its coefficients be?

We can answer the last question readily if we assume that $f(x)$ is the sum of a power series

$$\begin{aligned} f(x) &= \sum_{n=0}^{\infty} a_n (x-a)^n \\ &= a_0 + a_1(x-a) + a_2(x-a)^2 + \cdots + a_n(x-a)^n + \cdots \end{aligned}$$

with a positive radius of convergence. By repeated term-by-term differentiation within the interval of convergence I we obtain

$$\begin{aligned} f'(x) &= a_1 + 2a_2(x-a) + 3a_3(x-a)^2 + \cdots + na_n(x-a)^{n-1} + \cdots \\ f''(x) &= 1\cdot 2a_2 + 2\cdot 3a_3(x-a) + 3\cdot 4a_4(x-a)^2 + \cdots \\ f'''(x) &= 1\cdot 2\cdot 3a_3 + 2\cdot 3\cdot 4a_4(x-a) + 3\cdot 4\cdot 5a_5(x-a)^2 + \cdots, \end{aligned}$$

with the nth derivative, for all n, being

$$f^{(n)}(x) = n!a_n + \text{a sum of terms with } (x - a) \text{ as a factor.}$$

Since these equations all hold at $x = a$, we have

$$\begin{aligned} f'(a) &= a_1, \\ f''(a) &= 1 \cdot 2a_2, \\ f'''(a) &= 1 \cdot 2 \cdot 3a_3, \end{aligned}$$

and, in general,

$$f^{(n)}(a) = n!a_n.$$

These formulas reveal a pattern in the coefficients of any power series $\sum_{n=0}^{\infty} a_n(x - a)^n$ that converges to the values of f on I ("represents f on I"). If there *is* such a series (still an open question), then there is only one such series and its nth coefficient is

$$a_n = \frac{f^{(n)}(a)}{n!}.$$

If f has a series representation, then the series must be

$$f(x) = f(a) + f'(a)(x - a) + \frac{f''(a)}{2!}(x - a)^2 + \cdots + \frac{f^{(n)}(a)}{n!}(x - a)^n + \cdots. \tag{1}$$

But if we start with an arbitrary function f that is infinitely differentiable on an interval I centered at $x = a$ and use it to generate the series in Equation (1), will the series then converge to $f(x)$ at each x in the interior of I? The answer is maybe—for some functions it will but for other functions it will not, as we will see.

Taylor and Maclaurin Series

HISTORICAL BIOGRAPHIES

Brook Taylor (1685–1731)

Colin Maclaurin (1698–1746)

DEFINITIONS Taylor Series, Maclaurin Series

Let f be a function with derivatives of all orders throughout some interval containing a as an interior point. Then the **Taylor series generated by f at $x = a$ is**

$$\sum_{k=0}^{\infty} \frac{f^{(k)}(a)}{k!}(x - a)^k = f(a) + f'(a)(x - a) + \frac{f''(a)}{2!}(x - a)^2 + \cdots + \frac{f^{(n)}(a)}{n!}(x - a)^n + \cdots.$$

The **Maclaurin series generated by f is**

$$\sum_{k=0}^{\infty} \frac{f^{(k)}(0)}{k!}x^k = f(0) + f'(0)x + \frac{f''(0)}{2!}x^2 + \cdots + \frac{f^{(n)}(0)}{n!}x^n + \cdots,$$

the Taylor series generated by f at $x = 0$.

The Maclaurin series generated by f is often just called the Taylor series of f.

EXAMPLE 1 Finding a Taylor Series

Find the Taylor series generated by $f(x) = 1/x$ at $a = 2$. Where, if anywhere, does the series converge to $1/x$?

Solution We need to find $f(2), f'(2), f''(2), \ldots$. Taking derivatives we get

$$\begin{aligned}
f(x) &= x^{-1}, & f(2) &= 2^{-1} = \frac{1}{2},\\
f'(x) &= -x^{-2}, & f'(2) &= -\frac{1}{2^2},\\
f''(x) &= 2!x^{-3}, & \frac{f''(2)}{2!} &= 2^{-3} = \frac{1}{2^3},\\
f'''(x) &= -3!x^{-4}, & \frac{f'''(2)}{3!} &= -\frac{1}{2^4},\\
&\vdots & &\vdots\\
f^{(n)}(x) &= (-1)^n n! x^{-(n+1)}, & \frac{f^{(n)}(2)}{n!} &= \frac{(-1)^n}{2^{n+1}}.
\end{aligned}$$

The Taylor series is

$$\begin{aligned}
f(2) &+ f'(2)(x-2) + \frac{f''(2)}{2!}(x-2)^2 + \cdots + \frac{f^{(n)}(2)}{n!}(x-2)^n + \cdots\\
&= \frac{1}{2} - \frac{(x-2)}{2^2} + \frac{(x-2)^2}{2^3} - \cdots + (-1)^n \frac{(x-2)^n}{2^{n+1}} + \cdots.
\end{aligned}$$

This is a geometric series with first term $1/2$ and ratio $r = -(x-2)/2$. It converges absolutely for $|x-2| < 2$ and its sum is

$$\frac{1/2}{1 + (x-2)/2} = \frac{1}{2 + (x-2)} = \frac{1}{x}.$$

In this example the Taylor series generated by $f(x) = 1/x$ at $a = 2$ converges to $1/x$ for $|x-2| < 2$ or $0 < x < 4$. ■

Taylor Polynomials

The linearization of a differentiable function f at a point a is the polynomial of degree one given by

$$P_1(x) = f(a) + f'(a)(x-a).$$

In Section 3.8 we used this linearization to approximate $f(x)$ at values of x near a. If f has derivatives of higher order at a, then it has higher-order polynomial approximations as well, one for each available derivative. These polynomials are called the Taylor polynomials of f.

> **DEFINITION Taylor Polynomial of Order n**
>
> Let f be a function with derivatives of order k for $k = 1, 2, \ldots, N$ in some interval containing a as an interior point. Then for any integer n from 0 through N, the **Taylor polynomial of order n** generated by f at $x = a$ is the polynomial
>
> $$P_n(x) = f(a) + f'(a)(x-a) + \frac{f''(a)}{2!}(x-a)^2 + \cdots + \frac{f^{(k)}(a)}{k!}(x-a)^k + \cdots + \frac{f^{(n)}(a)}{n!}(x-a)^n.$$

We speak of a Taylor polynomial of *order n* rather than *degree n* because $f^{(n)}(a)$ may be zero. The first two Taylor polynomials of $f(x) = \cos x$ at $x = 0$, for example, are $P_0(x) = 1$ and $P_1(x) = 1$. The first-order Taylor polynomial has degree zero, not one.

Just as the linearization of f at $x = a$ provides the best linear approximation of f in the neighborhood of a, the higher-order Taylor polynomials provide the best polynomial approximations of their respective degrees. (See Exercise 32.)

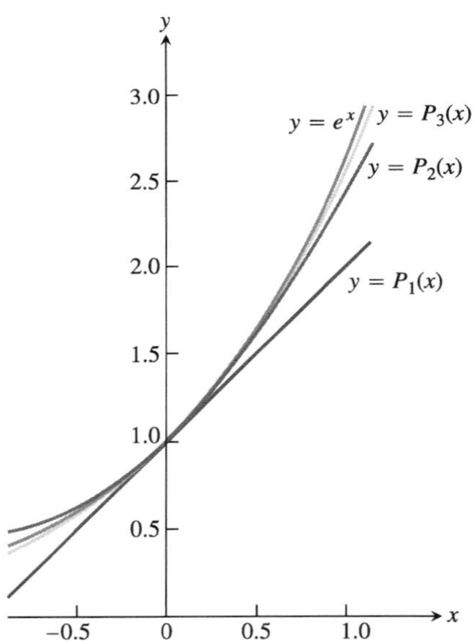

FIGURE 11.12 The graph of $f(x) = e^x$ and its Taylor polynomials
$P_1(x) = 1 + x$
$P_2(x) = 1 + x + (x^2/2!)$
$P_3(x) = 1 + x + (x^2/2!) + (x^3/3!)$.
Notice the very close agreement near the center $x = 0$ (Example 2).

EXAMPLE 2 Finding Taylor Polynomials for e^x

Find the Taylor series and the Taylor polynomials generated by $f(x) = e^x$ at $x = 0$.

Solution Since

$$f(x) = e^x, \quad f'(x) = e^x, \quad \ldots, \quad f^{(n)}(x) = e^x, \quad \ldots,$$

we have

$$f(0) = e^0 = 1, \quad f'(0) = 1, \quad \ldots, \quad f^{(n)}(0) = 1, \quad \ldots.$$

The Taylor series generated by f at $x = 0$ is

$$\begin{aligned} f(0) + f'(0)x + \frac{f''(0)}{2!}x^2 + \cdots + \frac{f^{(n)}(0)}{n!}x^n + \cdots &= 1 + x + \frac{x^2}{2} + \cdots + \frac{x^n}{n!} + \cdots \\ &= \sum_{k=0}^{\infty} \frac{x^k}{k!}. \end{aligned}$$

This is also the Maclaurin series for e^x. In Section 11.9 we will see that the series converges to e^x at every x.

The Taylor polynomial of order n at $x = 0$ is

$$P_n(x) = 1 + x + \frac{x^2}{2} + \cdots + \frac{x^n}{n!}.$$

See Figure 11.12. ■

EXAMPLE 3 Finding Taylor Polynomials for $\cos x$

Find the Taylor series and Taylor polynomials generated by $f(x) = \cos x$ at $x = 0$.

Solution The cosine and its derivatives are

$$\begin{aligned} f(x) &= \cos x, & f'(x) &= -\sin x, \\ f''(x) &= -\cos x, & f^{(3)}(x) &= \sin x, \\ &\vdots & &\vdots \\ f^{(2n)}(x) &= (-1)^n \cos x, & f^{(2n+1)}(x) &= (-1)^{n+1} \sin x. \end{aligned}$$

At $x = 0$, the cosines are 1 and the sines are 0, so

$$f^{(2n)}(0) = (-1)^n, \qquad f^{(2n+1)}(0) = 0.$$

The Taylor series generated by f at 0 is

$$\begin{aligned} f(0) + f'(0)x + \frac{f''(0)}{2!}x^2 + \frac{f'''(0)}{3!}x^3 + \cdots + \frac{f^{(n)}(0)}{n!}x^n + \cdots \\ = 1 + 0 \cdot x - \frac{x^2}{2!} + 0 \cdot x^3 + \frac{x^4}{4!} + \cdots + (-1)^n \frac{x^{2n}}{(2n)!} + \cdots \\ = \sum_{k=0}^{\infty} \frac{(-1)^k x^{2k}}{(2k)!}. \end{aligned}$$

This is also the Maclaurin series for $\cos x$. In Section 11.9, we will see that the series converges to $\cos x$ at every x.

Because $f^{(2n+1)}(0) = 0$, the Taylor polynomials of orders $2n$ and $2n + 1$ are identical:

$$P_{2n}(x) = P_{2n+1}(x) = 1 - \frac{x^2}{2!} + \frac{x^4}{4!} - \cdots + (-1)^n \frac{x^{2n}}{(2n)!}.$$

Figure 11.13 shows how well these polynomials approximate $f(x) = \cos x$ near $x = 0$. Only the right-hand portions of the graphs are given because the graphs are symmetric about the y-axis. ■

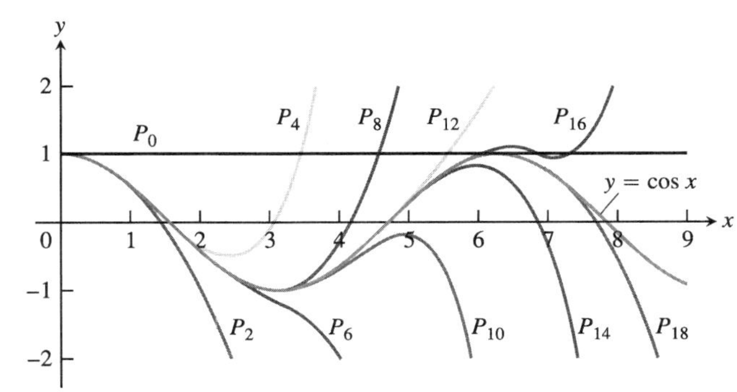

FIGURE 11.13 The polynomials

$$P_{2n}(x) = \sum_{k=0}^{n} \frac{(-1)^k x^{2k}}{(2k)!}$$

converge to $\cos x$ as $n \to \infty$. We can deduce the behavior of $\cos x$ arbitrarily far away solely from knowing the values of the cosine and its derivatives at $x = 0$ (Example 3).

EXAMPLE 4 A Function f Whose Taylor Series Converges at Every x but Converges to $f(x)$ Only at $x = 0$

It can be shown (though not easily) that

$$f(x) = \begin{cases} 0, & x = 0 \\ e^{-1/x^2}, & x \neq 0 \end{cases}$$

(Figure 11.14) has derivatives of all orders at $x = 0$ and that $f^{(n)}(0) = 0$ for all n. This means that the Taylor series generated by f at $x = 0$ is

$$\begin{aligned} f(0) + f'(0)x + \frac{f''(0)}{2!}x^2 + \cdots + \frac{f^{(n)}(0)}{n!}x^n + \cdots \\ = 0 + 0\cdot x + 0\cdot x^2 + \cdots + 0\cdot x^n + \cdots \\ = 0 + 0 + \cdots + 0 + \cdots. \end{aligned}$$

The series converges for every x (its sum is 0) but converges to $f(x)$ only at $x = 0$. ■

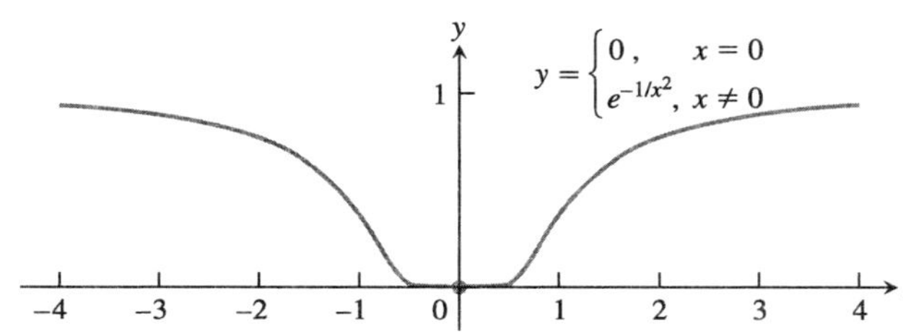

FIGURE 11.14 The graph of the continuous extension of $y = e^{-1/x^2}$ is so flat at the origin that all of its derivatives there are zero (Example 4).

Two questions still remain.

1. For what values of x can we normally expect a Taylor series to converge to its generating function?
2. How accurately do a function's Taylor polynomials approximate the function on a given interval?

The answers are provided by a theorem of Taylor in the next section.

EXERCISES 11.8

Finding Taylor Polynomials

In Exercises 1–8, find the Taylor polynomials of orders 0, 1, 2, and 3 generated by f at a.

1. $f(x) = \ln x, \quad a = 1$
2. $f(x) = \ln(1 + x), \quad a = 0$
3. $f(x) = 1/x, \quad a = 2$
4. $f(x) = 1/(x + 2), \quad a = 0$
5. $f(x) = \sin x, \quad a = \pi/4$
6. $f(x) = \cos x, \quad a = \pi/4$
7. $f(x) = \sqrt{x}, \quad a = 4$
8. $f(x) = \sqrt{x + 4}, \quad a = 0$

Finding Taylor Series at $x = 0$ (Maclaurin Series)

Find the Maclaurin series for the functions in Exercises 9–20.

9. e^{-x}
10. $e^{x/2}$
11. $\dfrac{1}{1 + x}$
12. $\dfrac{1}{1 - x}$
13. $\sin 3x$
14. $\sin \dfrac{x}{2}$

15. $7\cos(-x)$

16. $5\cos \pi x$

17. $\cosh x = \dfrac{e^x + e^{-x}}{2}$

18. $\sinh x = \dfrac{e^x - e^{-x}}{2}$

19. $x^4 - 2x^3 - 5x + 4$

20. $(x+1)^2$

Finding Taylor Series

In Exercises 21–28, find the Taylor series generated by f at $x = a$.

21. $f(x) = x^3 - 2x + 4, \quad a = 2$

22. $f(x) = 2x^3 + x^2 + 3x - 8, \quad a = 1$

23. $f(x) = x^4 + x^2 + 1, \quad a = -2$

24. $f(x) = 3x^5 - x^4 + 2x^3 + x^2 - 2, \quad a = -1$

25. $f(x) = 1/x^2, \quad a = 1$

26. $f(x) = x/(1-x), \quad a = 0$

27. $f(x) = e^x, \quad a = 2$

28. $f(x) = 2^x, \quad a = 1$

Theory and Examples

29. Use the Taylor series generated by e^x at $x = a$ to show that

$$e^x = e^a\left[1 + (x-a) + \frac{(x-a)^2}{2!} + \cdots\right].$$

30. (*Continuation of Exercise 29.*) Find the Taylor series generated by e^x at $x = 1$. Compare your answer with the formula in Exercise 29.

31. Let $f(x)$ have derivatives through order n at $x = a$. Show that the Taylor polynomial of order n and its first n derivatives have the same values that f and its first n derivatives have at $x = a$.

32. Of all polynomials of degree $\le n$, the Taylor polynomial of order n gives the best approximation Suppose that $f(x)$ is differentiable on an interval centered at $x = a$ and that $g(x) = b_0 + b_1(x-a) + \cdots + b_n(x-a)^n$ is a polynomial of degree n with constant coefficients $b_0, \ldots, b_n$. Let $E(x) = f(x) - g(x)$. Show that if we impose on g the conditions

a. $E(a) = 0$ — The approximation error is zero at $x = a$.

b. $\displaystyle\lim_{x\to a}\frac{E(x)}{(x-a)^n} = 0,$ — The error is negligible when compared to $(x-a)^n$.

then

$$g(x) = f(a) + f'(a)(x-a) + \frac{f''(a)}{2!}(x-a)^2 + \cdots + \frac{f^{(n)}(a)}{n!}(x-a)^n.$$

Thus, the Taylor polynomial $P_n(x)$ is the only polynomial of degree less than or equal to n whose error is both zero at $x = a$ and negligible when compared with $(x-a)^n$.

Quadratic Approximations

The Taylor polynomial of order 2 generated by a twice-differentiable function $f(x)$ at $x = a$ is called the **quadratic approximation** of f at $x = a$. In Exercises 33–38, find the **(a)** linearization (Taylor polynomial of order 1) and **(b)** quadratic approximation of f at $x = 0$.

33. $f(x) = \ln(\cos x)$

34. $f(x) = e^{\sin x}$

35. $f(x) = 1/\sqrt{1-x^2}$

36. $f(x) = \cosh x$

37. $f(x) = \sin x$

38. $f(x) = \tan x$

11.9 Convergence of Taylor Series; Error Estimates

This section addresses the two questions left unanswered by Section 11.8:

1. When does a Taylor series converge to its generating function?
2. How accurately do a function's Taylor polynomials approximate the function on a given interval?

Taylor's Theorem

We answer these questions with the following theorem.

THEOREM 22 Taylor's Theorem

If f and its first n derivatives $f', f'', \ldots, f^{(n)}$ are continuous on the closed interval between a and b, and $f^{(n)}$ is differentiable on the open interval between a and b, then there exists a number c between a and b such that

$$f(b) = f(a) + f'(a)(b - a) + \frac{f''(a)}{2!}(b - a)^2 + \cdots$$
$$+ \frac{f^{(n)}(a)}{n!}(b - a)^n + \frac{f^{(n+1)}(c)}{(n + 1)!}(b - a)^{n+1}.$$

Taylor's Theorem is a generalization of the Mean Value Theorem (Exercise 39). There is a proof of Taylor's Theorem at the end of this section.

When we apply Taylor's Theorem, we usually want to hold a fixed and treat b as an independent variable. Taylor's formula is easier to use in circumstances like these if we change b to x. Here is a version of the theorem with this change.

Taylor's Formula

If f has derivatives of all orders in an open interval I containing a, then for each positive integer n and for each x in I,

$$f(x) = f(a) + f'(a)(x - a) + \frac{f''(a)}{2!}(x - a)^2 + \cdots$$
$$+ \frac{f^{(n)}(a)}{n!}(x - a)^n + R_n(x), \qquad (1)$$

where

$$R_n(x) = \frac{f^{(n+1)}(c)}{(n + 1)!}(x - a)^{n+1} \quad \text{for some } c \text{ between } a \text{ and } x. \qquad (2)$$

When we state Taylor's theorem this way, it says that for each $x \in I$,

$$f(x) = P_n(x) + R_n(x).$$

The function $R_n(x)$ is determined by the value of the $(n + 1)$st derivative $f^{(n+1)}$ at a point c that depends on both a and x, and which lies somewhere between them. For any value of n we want, the equation gives both a polynomial approximation of f of that order and a formula for the error involved in using that approximation over the interval I.

Equation (1) is called **Taylor's formula**. The function $R_n(x)$ is called the **remainder of order n** or the **error term** for the approximation of f by $P_n(x)$ over I. If $R_n(x) \to 0$ as $n \to \infty$ for all $x \in I$, we say that the Taylor series generated by f at $x = a$ **converges** to f on I, and we write

$$f(x) = \sum_{k=0}^{\infty} \frac{f^{(k)}(a)}{k!}(x - a)^k.$$

Often we can estimate R_n without knowing the value of c, as the following example illustrates.

EXAMPLE 1 The Taylor Series for e^x Revisited

Show that the Taylor series generated by $f(x) = e^x$ at $x = 0$ converges to $f(x)$ for every real value of x.

Solution The function has derivatives of all orders throughout the interval $I = (-\infty, \infty)$. Equations (1) and (2) with $f(x) = e^x$ and $a = 0$ give

$$e^x = 1 + x + \frac{x^2}{2!} + \cdots + \frac{x^n}{n!} + R_n(x) \qquad \text{Polynomial from Section 11.8, Example 2}$$

and

$$R_n(x) = \frac{e^c}{(n+1)!}x^{n+1} \qquad \text{for some } c \text{ between 0 and } x.$$

Since e^x is an increasing function of x, e^c lies between $e^0 = 1$ and e^x. When x is negative, so is c, and $e^c < 1$. When x is zero, $e^x = 1$ and $R_n(x) = 0$. When x is positive, so is c, and $e^c < e^x$. Thus,

$$|R_n(x)| \le \frac{|x|^{n+1}}{(n+1)!} \qquad \text{when } x \le 0,$$

and

$$|R_n(x)| < e^x \frac{x^{n+1}}{(n+1)!} \qquad \text{when } x > 0.$$

Finally, because

$$\lim_{n\to\infty} \frac{x^{n+1}}{(n+1)!} = 0 \qquad \text{for every } x, \qquad \text{Section 11.1}$$

$\lim_{n\to\infty} R_n(x) = 0$, and the series converges to e^x for every x. Thus,

$$e^x = \sum_{k=0}^{\infty} \frac{x^k}{k!} = 1 + x + \frac{x^2}{2!} + \cdots + \frac{x^k}{k!} + \cdots. \tag{3}$$

■

Estimating the Remainder

It is often possible to estimate $R_n(x)$ as we did in Example 1. This method of estimation is so convenient that we state it as a theorem for future reference.

THEOREM 23 The Remainder Estimation Theorem
If there is a positive constant M such that $|f^{(n+1)}(t)| \le M$ for all t between x and a, inclusive, then the remainder term $R_n(x)$ in Taylor's Theorem satisfies the inequality

$$|R_n(x)| \le M\frac{|x-a|^{n+1}}{(n+1)!}.$$

If this condition holds for every n and the other conditions of Taylor's Theorem are satisfied by f, then the series converges to $f(x)$.

We are now ready to look at some examples of how the Remainder Estimation Theorem and Taylor's Theorem can be used together to settle questions of convergence. As you will see, they can also be used to determine the accuracy with which a function is approximated by one of its Taylor polynomials.

EXAMPLE 2 The Taylor Series for $\sin x$ at $x = 0$

Show that the Taylor series for $\sin x$ at $x = 0$ converges for all x.

Solution The function and its derivatives are

$$\begin{aligned} f(x) &= \sin x, & f'(x) &= \cos x, \\ f''(x) &= -\sin x, & f'''(x) &= -\cos x, \\ &\vdots & &\vdots \\ f^{(2k)}(x) &= (-1)^k \sin x, & f^{(2k+1)}(x) &= (-1)^k \cos x, \end{aligned}$$

so

$$f^{(2k)}(0) = 0 \quad \text{and} \quad f^{(2k+1)}(0) = (-1)^k.$$

The series has only odd-powered terms and, for $n = 2k + 1$, Taylor's Theorem gives

$$\sin x = x - \frac{x^3}{3!} + \frac{x^5}{5!} - \cdots + \frac{(-1)^k x^{2k+1}}{(2k+1)!} + R_{2k+1}(x).$$

All the derivatives of $\sin x$ have absolute values less than or equal to 1, so we can apply the Remainder Estimation Theorem with $M = 1$ to obtain

$$|R_{2k+1}(x)| \le 1 \cdot \frac{|x|^{2k+2}}{(2k+2)!}.$$

Since $(|x|^{2k+2}/(2k+2)!) \to 0$ as $k \to \infty$, whatever the value of x, $R_{2k+1}(x) \to 0$, and the Maclaurin series for $\sin x$ converges to $\sin x$ for every x. Thus,

$$\sin x = \sum_{k=0}^{\infty} \frac{(-1)^k x^{2k+1}}{(2k+1)!} = x - \frac{x^3}{3!} + \frac{x^5}{5!} - \frac{x^7}{7!} + \cdots. \tag{4}$$

■

EXAMPLE 3 The Taylor Series for $\cos x$ at $x = 0$ Revisited

Show that the Taylor series for $\cos x$ at $x = 0$ converges to $\cos x$ for every value of x.

Solution We add the remainder term to the Taylor polynomial for $\cos x$ (Section 11.8, Example 3) to obtain Taylor's formula for $\cos x$ with $n = 2k$:

$$\cos x = 1 - \frac{x^2}{2!} + \frac{x^4}{4!} - \cdots + (-1)^k \frac{x^{2k}}{(2k)!} + R_{2k}(x).$$

Because the derivatives of the cosine have absolute value less than or equal to 1, the Remainder Estimation Theorem with $M = 1$ gives

$$|R_{2k}(x)| \leq 1 \cdot \frac{|x|^{2k+1}}{(2k+1)!}.$$

For every value of x, $R_{2k} \to 0$ as $k \to \infty$. Therefore, the series converges to $\cos x$ for every value of x. Thus,

$$\cos x = \sum_{k=0}^{\infty} \frac{(-1)^k x^{2k}}{(2k)!} = 1 - \frac{x^2}{2!} + \frac{x^4}{4!} - \frac{x^6}{6!} + \cdots. \tag{5}$$

■

EXAMPLE 4 Finding a Taylor Series by Substitution

Find the Taylor series for $\cos 2x$ at $x = 0$.

Solution We can find the Taylor series for $\cos 2x$ by substituting $2x$ for x in the Taylor series for $\cos x$:

$$\cos 2x = \sum_{k=0}^{\infty} \frac{(-1)^k (2x)^{2k}}{(2k)!} = 1 - \frac{(2x)^2}{2!} + \frac{(2x)^4}{4!} - \frac{(2x)^6}{6!} + \cdots \qquad \text{Equation (5) with } 2x \text{ for } x$$

$$= 1 - \frac{2^2x^2}{2!} + \frac{2^4x^4}{4!} - \frac{2^6x^6}{6!} + \cdots$$

$$= \sum_{k=0}^{\infty} (-1)^k \frac{2^{2k}x^{2k}}{(2k)!}.$$

Equation (5) holds for $-\infty < x < \infty$, implying that it holds for $-\infty < 2x < \infty$, so the newly created series converges for all x. Exercise 45 explains why the series is in fact the Taylor series for $\cos 2x$. ■

EXAMPLE 5 Finding a Taylor Series by Multiplication

Find the Taylor series for $x \sin x$ at $x = 0$.

Solution We can find the Taylor series for $x \sin x$ by multiplying the Taylor series for $\sin x$ (Equation 4) by x:

$$x \sin x = x\left(x - \frac{x^3}{3!} + \frac{x^5}{5!} - \frac{x^7}{7!} + \cdots\right)$$

$$= x^2 - \frac{x^4}{3!} + \frac{x^6}{5!} - \frac{x^8}{7!} + \cdots.$$

The new series converges for all x because the series for $\sin x$ converges for all x. Exercise 45 explains why the series is the Taylor series for $x \sin x$. ■

Truncation Error

The Taylor series for e^x at $x = 0$ converges to e^x for all x. But we still need to decide how many terms to use to approximate e^x to a given degree of accuracy. We get this information from the Remainder Estimation Theorem.

EXAMPLE 6 Calculate e with an error of less than 10^{-6}.

Solution We can use the result of Example 1 with $x = 1$ to write

$$e = 1 + 1 + \frac{1}{2!} + \cdots + \frac{1}{n!} + R_n(1),$$

with

$$R_n(1) = e^c \frac{1}{(n+1)!} \qquad \text{for some } c \text{ between 0 and 1.}$$

For the purposes of this example, we assume that we know that $e < 3$. Hence, we are certain that

$$\frac{1}{(n+1)!} < R_n(1) < \frac{3}{(n+1)!}$$

because $1 < e^c < 3$ for $0 < c < 1$.

By experiment we find that $1/9! > 10^{-6}$, while $3/10! < 10^{-6}$. Thus we should take $(n + 1)$ to be at least 10, or n to be at least 9. With an error of less than 10^{-6},

$$e = 1 + 1 + \frac{1}{2} + \frac{1}{3!} + \cdots + \frac{1}{9!} \approx 2.718282. \qquad \blacksquare$$

EXAMPLE 7 For what values of x can we replace $\sin x$ by $x - (x^3/3!)$ with an error of magnitude no greater than 3×10^{-4}?

Solution Here we can take advantage of the fact that the Taylor series for $\sin x$ is an alternating series for every nonzero value of x. According to the Alternating Series Estimation Theorem (Section 11.6), the error in truncating

$$\sin x = x - \frac{x^3}{3!} \;\Big|\; + \frac{x^5}{5!} - \cdots$$

after $(x^3/3!)$ is no greater than

$$\left|\frac{x^5}{5!}\right| = \frac{|x|^5}{120}.$$

Therefore the error will be less than or equal to 3×10^{-4} if

$$\frac{|x|^5}{120} < 3 \times 10^{-4} \qquad \text{or} \qquad |x| < \sqrt[5]{360 \times 10^{-4}} \approx 0.514. \qquad \text{Rounded down, to be safe}$$

The Alternating Series Estimation Theorem tells us something that the Remainder Estimation Theorem does not: namely, that the estimate $x - (x^3/3!)$ for $\sin x$ is an underestimate when x is positive because then $x^5/120$ is positive.

Figure 11.15 shows the graph of $\sin x$, along with the graphs of a number of its approximating Taylor polynomials. The graph of $P_3(x) = x - (x^3/3!)$ is almost indistinguishable from the sine curve when $-1 \le x \le 1$.

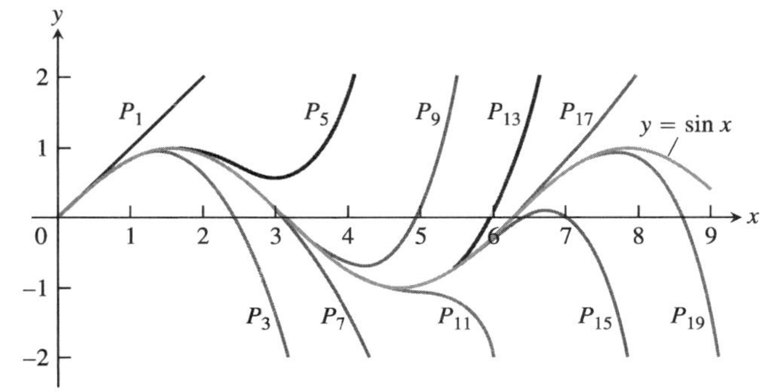

FIGURE 11.15 The polynomials

$$P_{2n+1}(x) = \sum_{k=0}^{n} \frac{(-1)^k x^{2k+1}}{(2k+1)!}$$

converge to $\sin x$ as $n \to \infty$. Notice how closely $P_3(x)$ approximates the sine curve for $x < 1$ (Example 7).

You might wonder how the estimate given by the Remainder Estimation Theorem compares with the one just obtained from the Alternating Series Estimation Theorem. If we write

$$\sin x = x - \frac{x^3}{3!} + R_3,$$

then the Remainder Estimation Theorem gives

$$|R_3| \le 1 \cdot \frac{|x|^4}{4!} = \frac{|x|^4}{24},$$

which is not as good. But if we recognize that $x - (x^3/3!) = 0 + x + 0x^2 - (x^3/3!) + 0x^4$ is the Taylor polynomial of order 4 as well as of order 3, then

$$\sin x = x - \frac{x^3}{3!} + 0 + R_4,$$

and the Remainder Estimation Theorem with $M = 1$ gives

$$|R_4| \le 1 \cdot \frac{|x|^5}{5!} = \frac{|x|^5}{120}.$$

This is what we had from the Alternating Series Estimation Theorem. ■

Combining Taylor Series

On the intersection of their intervals of convergence, Taylor series can be added, subtracted, and multiplied by constants, and the results are once again Taylor series. The Taylor series for $f(x) + g(x)$ is the sum of the Taylor series for $f(x)$ and $g(x)$ because the nth derivative of $f + g$ is $f^{(n)} + g^{(n)}$, and so on. Thus we obtain the Taylor series for $(1 + \cos 2x)/2$ by adding 1 to the Taylor series for $\cos 2x$ and dividing the combined results by 2, and the Taylor series for $\sin x + \cos x$ is the term-by-term sum of the Taylor series for $\sin x$ and $\cos x$.

Euler's Identity

As you may recall, a complex number is a number of the form $a + bi$, where a and b are real numbers and $i = \sqrt{-1}$. If we substitute $x = i\theta$ (θ real) in the Taylor series for e^x and use the relations

$$i^2 = -1, \qquad i^3 = i^2 i = -i, \qquad i^4 = i^2 i^2 = 1, \qquad i^5 = i^4 i = i,$$

and so on, to simplify the result, we obtain

$$\begin{aligned} e^{i\theta} &= 1 + \frac{i\theta}{1!} + \frac{i^2\theta^2}{2!} + \frac{i^3\theta^3}{3!} + \frac{i^4\theta^4}{4!} + \frac{i^5\theta^5}{5!} + \frac{i^6\theta^6}{6!} + \cdots \\ &= \left(1 - \frac{\theta^2}{2!} + \frac{\theta^4}{4!} - \frac{\theta^6}{6!} + \cdots\right) + i\left(\theta - \frac{\theta^3}{3!} + \frac{\theta^5}{5!} - \cdots\right) = \cos\theta + i\sin\theta. \end{aligned}$$

This does not *prove* that $e^{i\theta} = \cos\theta + i\sin\theta$ because we have not yet defined what it means to raise e to an imaginary power. Rather, it says how to define $e^{i\theta}$ to be consistent with other things we know.

DEFINITION

For any real number θ, $e^{i\theta} = \cos\theta + i\sin\theta$. (6)

Equation (6), called **Euler's identity**, enables us to define e^{a+bi} to be $e^a \cdot e^{bi}$ for any complex number $a + bi$. One consequence of the identity is the equation

$$e^{i\pi} = -1.$$

When written in the form $e^{i\pi} + 1 = 0$, this equation combines five of the most important constants in mathematics.

A Proof of Taylor's Theorem

We prove Taylor's theorem assuming $a < b$. The proof for $a > b$ is nearly the same.

The Taylor polynomial

$$P_n(x) = f(a) + f'(a)(x - a) + \frac{f''(a)}{2!}(x - a)^2 + \cdots + \frac{f^{(n)}(a)}{n!}(x - a)^n$$

and its first n derivatives match the function f and its first n derivatives at $x = a$. We do not disturb that matching if we add another term of the form $K(x - a)^{n+1}$, where K is any constant, because such a term and its first n derivatives are all equal to zero at $x = a$. The new function

$$\phi_n(x) = P_n(x) + K(x - a)^{n+1}$$

and its first n derivatives still agree with f and its first n derivatives at $x = a$.

We now choose the particular value of K that makes the curve $y = \phi_n(x)$ agree with the original curve $y = f(x)$ at $x = b$. In symbols,

$$f(b) = P_n(b) + K(b - a)^{n+1}, \qquad \text{or} \qquad K = \frac{f(b) - P_n(b)}{(b - a)^{n+1}}. \tag{7}$$

With K defined by Equation (7), the function

$$F(x) = f(x) - \phi_n(x)$$

measures the difference between the original function f and the approximating function ϕ_n for each x in $[a, b]$.

We now use Rolle's Theorem (Section 4.2). First, because $F(a) = F(b) = 0$ and both F and F' are continuous on $[a, b]$, we know that

$$F'(c_1) = 0 \qquad \text{for some } c_1 \text{ in } (a, b).$$

Next, because $F'(a) = F'(c_1) = 0$ and both F' and F'' are continuous on $[a, c_1]$, we know that

$$F''(c_2) = 0 \qquad \text{for some } c_2 \text{ in } (a, c_1).$$

Rolle's Theorem, applied successively to $F'', F''', \dots, F^{(n-1)}$ implies the existence of

$$\begin{array}{lll} c_3 & \text{in } (a, c_2) & \text{such that } F'''(c_3) = 0, \\ c_4 & \text{in } (a, c_3) & \text{such that } F^{(4)}(c_4) = 0, \\ \vdots & & \\ c_n & \text{in } (a, c_{n-1}) & \text{such that } F^{(n)}(c_n) = 0. \end{array}$$

Finally, because $F^{(n)}$ is continuous on $[a, c_n]$ and differentiable on (a, c_n), and $F^{(n)}(a) = F^{(n)}(c_n) = 0$, Rolle's Theorem implies that there is a number c_{n+1} in (a, c_n) such that

$$F^{(n+1)}(c_{n+1}) = 0. \tag{8}$$

If we differentiate $F(x) = f(x) - P_n(x) - K(x - a)^{n+1}$ a total of $n + 1$ times, we get

$$F^{(n+1)}(x) = f^{(n+1)}(x) - 0 - (n + 1)!K. \tag{9}$$

Equations (8) and (9) together give

$$K = \frac{f^{(n+1)}(c)}{(n + 1)!} \qquad \text{for some number } c = c_{n+1} \text{ in } (a, b). \tag{10}$$

Equations (7) and (10) give

$$f(b) = P_n(b) + \frac{f^{(n+1)}(c)}{(n + 1)!}(b - a)^{n+1}.$$

This concludes the proof. ■

EXERCISES 11.9

Taylor Series by Substitution

Use substitution (as in Example 4) to find the Taylor series at $x = 0$ of the functions in Exercises 1–6.

1. e^{-5x} **2.** $e^{-x/2}$ **3.** $5\sin(-x)$

4. $\sin\left(\frac{\pi x}{2}\right)$ **5.** $\cos\sqrt{x + 1}$ **6.** $\cos\left(x^{3/2}/\sqrt{2}\right)$

More Taylor Series

Find Taylor series at $x = 0$ for the functions in Exercises 7–18.

7. xe^x **8.** $x^2 \sin x$ **9.** $\frac{x^2}{2} - 1 + \cos x$

10. $\sin x - x + \frac{x^3}{3!}$ **11.** $x\cos\pi x$ **12.** $x^2\cos(x^2)$

13. $\cos^2 x$ (*Hint:* $\cos^2 x = (1 + \cos 2x)/2$.)

14. $\sin^2 x$

15. $\dfrac{x^2}{1 - 2x}$

16. $x \ln(1 + 2x)$

17. $\dfrac{1}{(1 - x)^2}$

18. $\dfrac{2}{(1 - x)^3}$

Error Estimates

19. For approximately what values of x can you replace $\sin x$ by $x - (x^3/6)$ with an error of magnitude no greater than 5×10^{-4}? Give reasons for your answer.

20. If $\cos x$ is replaced by $1 - (x^2/2)$ and $|x| < 0.5$, what estimate can be made of the error? Does $1 - (x^2/2)$ tend to be too large, or too small? Give reasons for your answer.

21. How close is the approximation $\sin x = x$ when $|x| < 10^{-3}$? For which of these values of x is $x < \sin x$?

22. The estimate $\sqrt{1 + x} = 1 + (x/2)$ is used when x is small. Estimate the error when $|x| < 0.01$.

23. The approximation $e^x = 1 + x + (x^2/2)$ is used when x is small. Use the Remainder Estimation Theorem to estimate the error when $|x| < 0.1$.

24. (*Continuation of Exercise 23.*) When $x < 0$, the series for e^x is an alternating series. Use the Alternating Series Estimation Theorem to estimate the error that results from replacing e^x by $1 + x + (x^2/2)$ when $-0.1 < x < 0$. Compare your estimate with the one you obtained in Exercise 23.

25. Estimate the error in the approximation $\sinh x = x + (x^3/3!)$ when $|x| < 0.5$. (*Hint:* Use R_4, not R_3.)

26. When $0 \le h \le 0.01$, show that e^h may be replaced by $1 + h$ with an error of magnitude no greater than 0.6% of h. Use $e^{0.01} = 1.01$.

27. For what positive values of x can you replace $\ln(1 + x)$ by x with an error of magnitude no greater than 1% of the value of x?

28. You plan to estimate $\pi/4$ by evaluating the Maclaurin series for $\tan^{-1} x$ at $x = 1$. Use the Alternating Series Estimation Theorem to determine how many terms of the series you would have to add to be sure the estimate is good to two decimal places.

29. **a.** Use the Taylor series for $\sin x$ and the Alternating Series Estimation Theorem to show that

$$1 - \frac{x^2}{6} < \frac{\sin x}{x} < 1, \quad x \neq 0.$$

T **b.** Graph $f(x) = (\sin x)/x$ together with the functions $y = 1 - (x^2/6)$ and $y = 1$ for $-5 \le x \le 5$. Comment on the relationships among the graphs.

30. **a.** Use the Taylor series for $\cos x$ and the Alternating Series Estimation Theorem to show that

$$\frac{1}{2} - \frac{x^2}{24} < \frac{1 - \cos x}{x^2} < \frac{1}{2}, \quad x \neq 0.$$

(This is the inequality in Section 2.2, Exercise 52.)

T **b.** Graph $f(x) = (1 - \cos x)/x^2$ together with $y = (1/2) - (x^2/24)$ and $y = 1/2$ for $-9 \le x \le 9$. Comment on the relationships among the graphs.

Finding and Identifying Maclaurin Series

Recall that the Maclaurin series is just another name for the Taylor series at $x = 0$. Each of the series in Exercises 31–34 is the value of the Maclaurin series of a function $f(x)$ at some point. What function and what point? What is the sum of the series?

31. $(0.1) - \dfrac{(0.1)^3}{3!} + \dfrac{(0.1)^5}{5!} - \cdots + \dfrac{(-1)^k(0.1)^{2k+1}}{(2k + 1)!} + \cdots$

32. $1 - \dfrac{\pi^2}{4^2 \cdot 2!} + \dfrac{\pi^4}{4^4 \cdot 4!} - \cdots + \dfrac{(-1)^k(\pi)^{2k}}{4^{2k} \cdot (2k!)} + \cdots$

33. $\dfrac{\pi}{3} - \dfrac{\pi^3}{3^3 \cdot 3} + \dfrac{\pi^5}{3^5 \cdot 5} - \cdots + \dfrac{(-1)^k \pi^{2k+1}}{3^{2k+1}(2k + 1)} + \cdots$

34. $(\pi/4) - \dfrac{(\pi/4)^2}{2} + \dfrac{(\pi/4)^3}{3} - \cdots + (-1)^{k-1}\dfrac{(\pi/4)^k}{k} + \cdots$

35. Multiply the Maclaurin series for e^x and $\sin x$ together to find the first five nonzero terms of the Maclaurin series for $e^x \sin x$.

36. Multiply the Maclaurin series for e^x and $\cos x$ together to find the first five nonzero terms of the Maclaurin series for $e^x \cos x$.

37. Use the identity $\sin^2 x = (1 - \cos 2x)/2$ to obtain the Maclaurin series for $\sin^2 x$. Then differentiate this series to obtain the Maclaurin series for $2 \sin x \cos x$. Check that this is the series for $\sin 2x$.

38. (*Continuation of Exercise 37.*) Use the identity $\cos^2 x = \cos 2x + \sin^2 x$ to obtain a power series for $\cos^2 x$.

Theory and Examples

39. **Taylor's Theorem and the Mean Value Theorem** Explain how the Mean Value Theorem (Section 4.2, Theorem 4) is a special case of Taylor's Theorem.

40. **Linearizations at inflection points** Show that if the graph of a twice-differentiable function $f(x)$ has an inflection point at $x = a$, then the linearization of f at $x = a$ is also the quadratic approximation of f at $x = a$. This explains why tangent lines fit so well at inflection points.

41. **The (second) second derivative test** Use the equation

$$f(x) = f(a) + f'(a)(x - a) + \frac{f''(c_2)}{2}(x - a)^2$$

to establish the following test.

Let f have continuous first and second derivatives and suppose that $f'(a) = 0$. Then

a. f has a local maximum at a if $f'' \le 0$ throughout an interval whose interior contains a;

b. f has a local minimum at a if $f'' \ge 0$ throughout an interval whose interior contains a.

42. A cubic approximation Use Taylor's formula with $a = 0$ and $n = 3$ to find the standard cubic approximation of $f(x) = 1/(1 - x)$ at $x = 0$. Give an upper bound for the magnitude of the error in the approximation when $|x| \le 0.1$.

43. **a.** Use Taylor's formula with $n = 2$ to find the quadratic approximation of $f(x) = (1 + x)^k$ at $x = 0$ (k a constant).

b. If $k = 3$, for approximately what values of x in the interval $[0, 1]$ will the error in the quadratic approximation be less than $1/100$?

44. Improving approximations to π

a. Let P be an approximation of π accurate to n decimals. Show that $P + \sin P$ gives an approximation correct to $3n$ decimals. (*Hint:* Let $P = \pi + x$.)

T **b.** Try it with a calculator.

45. The Taylor series generated by $f(x) = \sum_{n=0}^{\infty} a_n x^n$ is $\sum_{n=0}^{\infty} a_n x^n$ A function defined by a power series $\sum_{n=0}^{\infty} a_n x^n$ with a radius of convergence $c > 0$ has a Taylor series that converges to the function at every point of $(-c, c)$. Show this by showing that the Taylor series generated by $f(x) = \sum_{n=0}^{\infty} a_n x^n$ is the series $\sum_{n=0}^{\infty} a_n x^n$ itself.

An immediate consequence of this is that series like

$$x \sin x = x^2 - \frac{x^4}{3!} + \frac{x^6}{5!} - \frac{x^8}{7!} + \cdots$$

and

$$x^2 e^x = x^2 + x^3 + \frac{x^4}{2!} + \frac{x^5}{3!} + \cdots,$$

obtained by multiplying Taylor series by powers of x, as well as series obtained by integration and differentiation of convergent power series, are themselves the Taylor series generated by the functions they represent.

46. Taylor series for even functions and odd functions (*Continuation of Section 11.7, Exercise 45.*) Suppose that $f(x) = \sum_{n=0}^{\infty} a_n x^n$ converges for all x in an open interval $(-c, c)$. Show that

a. If f is even, then $a_1 = a_3 = a_5 = \cdots = 0$, i.e., the Taylor series for f at $x = 0$ contains only even powers of x.

b. If f is odd, then $a_0 = a_2 = a_4 = \cdots = 0$, i.e., the Taylor series for f at $x = 0$ contains only odd powers of x.

47. Taylor polynomials of periodic functions

a. Show that every continuous periodic function $f(x)$, $-\infty < x < \infty$, is bounded in magnitude by showing that there exists a positive constant M such that $|f(x)| \le M$ for all x.

b. Show that the graph of every Taylor polynomial of positive degree generated by $f(x) = \cos x$ must eventually move away from the graph of $\cos x$ as $|x|$ increases. You can see this in Figure 11.13. The Taylor polynomials of $\sin x$ behave in a similar way (Figure 11.15).

T **48.** **a.** Graph the curves $y = (1/3) - (x^2)/5$ and $y = (x - \tan^{-1} x)/x^3$ together with the line $y = 1/3$.

b. Use a Taylor series to explain what you see. What is

$$\lim_{x \to 0} \frac{x - \tan^{-1} x}{x^3} ?$$

Euler's Identity

49. Use Equation (6) to write the following powers of e in the form $a + bi$.

a. $e^{-i\pi}$ **b.** $e^{i\pi/4}$ **c.** $e^{-i\pi/2}$

50. Use Equation (6) to show that

$$\cos \theta = \frac{e^{i\theta} + e^{-i\theta}}{2} \quad \text{and} \quad \sin \theta = \frac{e^{i\theta} - e^{-i\theta}}{2i}.$$

51. Establish the equations in Exercise 50 by combining the formal Taylor series for $e^{i\theta}$ and $e^{-i\theta}$.

52. Show that

a. $\cosh i\theta = \cos \theta$, **b.** $\sinh i\theta = i \sin \theta$.

53. By multiplying the Taylor series for e^x and $\sin x$, find the terms through x^5 of the Taylor series for $e^x \sin x$. This series is the imaginary part of the series for

$$e^x \cdot e^{ix} = e^{(1+i)x}.$$

Use this fact to check your answer. For what values of x should the series for $e^x \sin x$ converge?

54. When a and b are real, we define $e^{(a+ib)x}$ with the equation

$$e^{(a+ib)x} = e^{ax} \cdot e^{ibx} = e^{ax}(\cos bx + i \sin bx).$$

Differentiate the right-hand side of this equation to show that

$$\frac{d}{dx} e^{(a+ib)x} = (a + ib)e^{(a+ib)x}.$$

Thus the familiar rule $(d/dx)e^{kx} = ke^{kx}$ holds for k complex as well as real.

55. Use the definition of $e^{i\theta}$ to show that for any real numbers θ, θ_1, and θ_2,

a. $e^{i\theta_1} e^{i\theta_2} = e^{i(\theta_1 + \theta_2)}$, **b.** $e^{-i\theta} = 1/e^{i\theta}$.

56. Two complex numbers $a + ib$ and $c + id$ are equal if and only if $a = c$ and $b = d$. Use this fact to evaluate

$$\int e^{ax} \cos bx \, dx \quad \text{and} \quad \int e^{ax} \sin bx \, dx$$

from

$$\int e^{(a+ib)x} \, dx = \frac{a - ib}{a^2 + b^2} e^{(a+ib)x} + C,$$

where $C = C_1 + iC_2$ is a complex constant of integration.

COMPUTER EXPLORATIONS

Linear, Quadratic, and Cubic Approximations

Taylor's formula with $n = 1$ and $a = 0$ gives the linearization of a function at $x = 0$. With $n = 2$ and $n = 3$ we obtain the standard quadratic and cubic approximations. In these exercises we explore the errors associated with these approximations. We seek answers to two questions:

a. For what values of x can the function be replaced by each approximation with an error less than 10^{-2}?

b. What is the maximum error we could expect if we replace the function by each approximation over the specified interval?

Using a CAS, perform the following steps to aid in answering questions (a) and (b) for the functions and intervals in Exercises 57–62.

Step 1: Plot the function over the specified interval.

Step 2: Find the Taylor polynomials $P_1(x)$, $P_2(x)$, and $P_3(x)$ at $x = 0$.

Step 3: Calculate the $(n + 1)$st derivative $f^{(n+1)}(c)$ associated with the remainder term for each Taylor polynomial. Plot the derivative as a function of c over the specified interval and estimate its maximum absolute value, M.

Step 4: Calculate the remainder $R_n(x)$ for each polynomial. Using the estimate M from Step 3 in place of $f^{(n+1)}(c)$, plot $R_n(x)$ over the specified interval. Then estimate the values of x that answer question (a).

Step 5: Compare your estimated error with the actual error $E_n(x) = |f(x) - P_n(x)|$ by plotting $E_n(x)$ over the specified interval. This will help answer question (b).

Step 6: Graph the function and its three Taylor approximations together. Discuss the graphs in relation to the information discovered in Steps 4 and 5.

57. $f(x) = \dfrac{1}{\sqrt{1 + x}}, \quad |x| \le \dfrac{3}{4}$

58. $f(x) = (1 + x)^{3/2}, \quad -\dfrac{1}{2} \le x \le 2$

59. $f(x) = \dfrac{x}{x^2 + 1}, \quad |x| \le 2$

60. $f(x) = (\cos x)(\sin 2x), \quad |x| \le 2$

61. $f(x) = e^{-x}\cos 2x, \quad |x| \le 1$

62. $f(x) = e^{x/3}\sin 2x, \quad |x| \le 2$

11.10 Applications of Power Series

This section introduces the binomial series for estimating powers and roots and shows how series are sometimes used to approximate the solution of an initial value problem, to evaluate nonelementary integrals, and to evaluate limits that lead to indeterminate forms. We provide a self-contained derivation of the Taylor series for $\tan^{-1} x$ and conclude with a reference table of frequently used series.

The Binomial Series for Powers and Roots

The Taylor series generated by $f(x) = (1 + x)^m$, when m is constant, is

$$1 + mx + \frac{m(m-1)}{2!}x^2 + \frac{m(m-1)(m-2)}{3!}x^3 + \cdots + \frac{m(m-1)(m-2)\cdots(m-k+1)}{k!}x^k + \cdots. \qquad (1)$$

This series, called the **binomial series**, converges absolutely for $|x| < 1$. To derive the series, we first list the function and its derivatives:

$$\begin{aligned} f(x) &= (1+x)^m \\ f'(x) &= m(1+x)^{m-1} \\ f''(x) &= m(m-1)(1+x)^{m-2} \\ f'''(x) &= m(m-1)(m-2)(1+x)^{m-3} \\ &\vdots \\ f^{(k)}(x) &= m(m-1)(m-2)\cdots(m-k+1)(1+x)^{m-k}. \end{aligned}$$

We then evaluate these at $x = 0$ and substitute into the Taylor series formula to obtain Series (1).

If m is an integer greater than or equal to zero, the series stops after $(m+1)$ terms because the coefficients from $k = m + 1$ on are zero.

If m is not a positive integer or zero, the series is infinite and converges for $|x| < 1$. To see why, let u_k be the term involving x^k. Then apply the Ratio Test for absolute convergence to see that

$$\left|\frac{u_{k+1}}{u_k}\right| = \left|\frac{m-k}{k+1}x\right| \to |x| \qquad \text{as } k \to \infty.$$

Our derivation of the binomial series shows only that it is generated by $(1+x)^m$ and converges for $|x| < 1$. The derivation does not show that the series converges to $(1+x)^m$. It does, but we omit the proof.

The Binomial Series

For $-1 < x < 1$,

$$(1+x)^m = 1 + \sum_{k=1}^{\infty} \binom{m}{k} x^k,$$

where we define

$$\binom{m}{1} = m, \qquad \binom{m}{2} = \frac{m(m-1)}{2!},$$

and

$$\binom{m}{k} = \frac{m(m-1)(m-2)\cdots(m-k+1)}{k!} \qquad \text{for } k \ge 3.$$

EXAMPLE 1 Using the Binomial Series

If $m = -1$,

$$\binom{-1}{1} = -1, \qquad \binom{-1}{2} = \frac{-1(-2)}{2!} = 1,$$

and

$$\binom{-1}{k} = \frac{-1(-2)(-3)\cdots(-1-k+1)}{k!} = (-1)^k\left(\frac{k!}{k!}\right) = (-1)^k.$$

With these coefficient values and with x replaced by $-x$, the binomial series formula gives the familiar geometric series

$$(1+x)^{-1} = 1 + \sum_{k=1}^{\infty}(-1)^k x^k = 1 - x + x^2 - x^3 + \cdots + (-1)^k x^k + \cdots.$$

EXAMPLE 2 Using the Binomial Series

We know from Section 3.8, Example 1, that $\sqrt{1+x} \approx 1 + (x/2)$ for $|x|$ small. With $m = 1/2$, the binomial series gives quadratic and higher-order approximations as well, along with error estimates that come from the Alternating Series Estimation Theorem:

$$\begin{aligned}(1+x)^{1/2} &= 1 + \frac{x}{2} + \frac{\left(\frac{1}{2}\right)\left(-\frac{1}{2}\right)}{2!}x^2 + \frac{\left(\frac{1}{2}\right)\left(-\frac{1}{2}\right)\left(-\frac{3}{2}\right)}{3!}x^3 \\ &\quad + \frac{\left(\frac{1}{2}\right)\left(-\frac{1}{2}\right)\left(-\frac{3}{2}\right)\left(-\frac{5}{2}\right)}{4!}x^4 + \cdots \\ &= 1 + \frac{x}{2} - \frac{x^2}{8} + \frac{x^3}{16} - \frac{5x^4}{128} + \cdots.\end{aligned}$$

Substitution for x gives still other approximations. For example,

$$\sqrt{1-x^2} \approx 1 - \frac{x^2}{2} - \frac{x^4}{8} \qquad \text{for } |x^2| \text{ small}$$

$$\sqrt{1-\frac{1}{x}} \approx 1 - \frac{1}{2x} - \frac{1}{8x^2} \qquad \text{for } \left|\frac{1}{x}\right| \text{ small, that is, } |x| \text{ large}.$$

Power Series Solutions of Differential Equations and Initial Value Problems

When we cannot find a relatively simple expression for the solution of an initial value problem or differential equation, we try to get information about the solution in other ways. One way is to try to find a power series representation for the solution. If we can do so, we immediately have a source of polynomial approximations of the solution, which may be all that we really need. The first example (Example 3) deals with a first-order linear differential equation that could be solved with the methods of Section 9.2. The example shows how, not knowing this, we can solve the equation with power series. The second example (Example 4) deals with an equation that cannot be solved analytically by previous methods.

EXAMPLE 3 Series Solution of an Initial Value Problem

Solve the initial value problem

$$y' - y = x, \qquad y(0) = 1.$$

Solution We assume that there is a solution of the form

$$y = a_0 + a_1 x + a_2 x^2 + \cdots + a_{n-1}x^{n-1} + a_n x^n + \cdots. \tag{2}$$

Our goal is to find values for the coefficients a_k that make the series and its first derivative

$$y' = a_1 + 2a_2x + 3a_3x^2 + \cdots + na_nx^{n-1} + \cdots \tag{3}$$

satisfy the given differential equation and initial condition. The series $y' - y$ is the difference of the series in Equations (2) and (3):

$$\begin{aligned} y' - y = (a_1 - a_0) &+ (2a_2 - a_1)x + (3a_3 - a_2)x^2 + \cdots \\ &+ (na_n - a_{n-1})x^{n-1} + \cdots. \end{aligned} \tag{4}$$

If y is to satisfy the equation $y' - y = x$, the series in Equation (4) must equal x. Since power series representations are unique (Exercise 45 in Section 11.7), the coefficients in Equation (4) must satisfy the equations

$$\begin{aligned} a_1 - a_0 &= 0 && \text{Constant terms} \\ 2a_2 - a_1 &= 1 && \text{Coefficients of } x \\ 3a_3 - a_2 &= 0 && \text{Coefficients of } x^2 \\ &\vdots && \vdots \\ na_n - a_{n-1} &= 0 && \text{Coefficients of } x^{n-1} \\ &\vdots && \vdots \end{aligned}$$

We can also see from Equation (2) that $y = a_0$ when $x = 0$, so that $a_0 = 1$ (this being the initial condition). Putting it all together, we have

$$a_0 = 1, \qquad a_1 = a_0 = 1, \qquad a_2 = \frac{1 + a_1}{2} = \frac{1 + 1}{2} = \frac{2}{2},$$

$$a_3 = \frac{a_2}{3} = \frac{2}{3 \cdot 2} = \frac{2}{3!}, \ldots, \qquad a_n = \frac{a_{n-1}}{n} = \frac{2}{n!}, \ldots$$

Substituting these coefficient values into the equation for y (Equation (2)) gives

$$\begin{aligned} y &= 1 + x + 2 \cdot \frac{x^2}{2!} + 2 \cdot \frac{x^3}{3!} + \cdots + 2 \cdot \frac{x^n}{n!} + \cdots \\ &= 1 + x + 2 \underbrace{\left(\frac{x^2}{2!} + \frac{x^3}{3!} + \cdots + \frac{x^n}{n!} + \cdots \right)}_{\text{the Taylor series for } e^x - 1 - x} \\ &= 1 + x + 2(e^x - 1 - x) = 2e^x - 1 - x. \end{aligned}$$

The solution of the initial value problem is $y = 2e^x - 1 - x$.

As a check, we see that

$$y(0) = 2e^0 - 1 - 0 = 2 - 1 = 1$$

and

$$y' - y = (2e^x - 1) - (2e^x - 1 - x) = x.$$

■

EXAMPLE 4 Solving a Differential Equation

Find a power series solution for

$$y'' + x^2y = 0. \tag{5}$$

Solution We assume that there is a solution of the form

$$y = a_0 + a_1 x + a_2 x^2 + \cdots + a_n x^n + \cdots, \tag{6}$$

and find what the coefficients a_k have to be to make the series and its second derivative

$$y'' = 2a_2 + 3 \cdot 2a_3 x + \cdots + n(n-1)a_n x^{n-2} + \cdots \tag{7}$$

satisfy Equation (5). The series for $x^2 y$ is x^2 times the right-hand side of Equation (6):

$$x^2 y = a_0 x^2 + a_1 x^3 + a_2 x^4 + \cdots + a_n x^{n+2} + \cdots. \tag{8}$$

The series for $y'' + x^2 y$ is the sum of the series in Equations (7) and (8):

$$\begin{aligned} y'' + x^2 y &= 2a_2 + 6a_3 x + (12a_4 + a_0)x^2 + (20a_5 + a_1)x^3 \\ &\quad + \cdots + (n(n-1)a_n + a_{n-4})x^{n-2} + \cdots. \end{aligned} \tag{9}$$

Notice that the coefficient of x^{n-2} in Equation (8) is a_{n-4}. If y and its second derivative y'' are to satisfy Equation (5), the coefficients of the individual powers of x on the right-hand side of Equation (9) must all be zero:

$$2a_2 = 0, \qquad 6a_3 = 0, \qquad 12a_4 + a_0 = 0, \qquad 20a_5 + a_1 = 0, \tag{10}$$

and for all $n \geq 4$,

$$n(n-1)a_n + a_{n-4} = 0. \tag{11}$$

We can see from Equation (6) that

$$a_0 = y(0), \qquad a_1 = y'(0).$$

In other words, the first two coefficients of the series are the values of y and y' at $x = 0$. Equations in (10) and the recursion formula in Equation (11) enable us to evaluate all the other coefficients in terms of a_0 and a_1.

The first two of Equations (10) give

$$a_2 = 0, \qquad a_3 = 0.$$

Equation (11) shows that if $a_{n-4} = 0$, then $a_n = 0$; so we conclude that

$$a_6 = 0, \qquad a_7 = 0, \qquad a_{10} = 0, \qquad a_{11} = 0,$$

and whenever $n = 4k + 2$ or $4k + 3$, a_n is zero. For the other coefficients we have

$$a_n = \frac{-a_{n-4}}{n(n-1)}$$

so that

$$a_4 = \frac{-a_0}{4 \cdot 3}, \qquad a_8 = \frac{-a_4}{8 \cdot 7} = \frac{a_0}{3 \cdot 4 \cdot 7 \cdot 8}$$

$$a_{12} = \frac{-a_8}{11 \cdot 12} = \frac{-a_0}{3 \cdot 4 \cdot 7 \cdot 8 \cdot 11 \cdot 12}$$

and

$$a_5 = \frac{-a_1}{5 \cdot 4}, \qquad a_9 = \frac{-a_5}{9 \cdot 8} = \frac{a_1}{4 \cdot 5 \cdot 8 \cdot 9}$$

$$a_{13} = \frac{-a_9}{12 \cdot 13} = \frac{-a_1}{4 \cdot 5 \cdot 8 \cdot 9 \cdot 12 \cdot 13}.$$

The answer is best expressed as the sum of two separate series—one multiplied by a_0, the other by a_1:

$$y = a_0\left(1 - \frac{x^4}{3\cdot 4} + \frac{x^8}{3\cdot 4\cdot 7\cdot 8} - \frac{x^{12}}{3\cdot 4\cdot 7\cdot 8\cdot 11\cdot 12} + \cdots\right)$$
$$+ a_1\left(x - \frac{x^5}{4\cdot 5} + \frac{x^9}{4\cdot 5\cdot 8\cdot 9} - \frac{x^{13}}{4\cdot 5\cdot 8\cdot 9\cdot 12\cdot 13} + \cdots\right).$$

Both series converge absolutely for all x, as is readily seen by the Ratio Test. ■

Evaluating Nonelementary Integrals

Taylor series can be used to express nonelementary integrals in terms of series. Integrals like $\int \sin x^2\,dx$ arise in the study of the diffraction of light.

EXAMPLE 5 Express $\int \sin x^2\,dx$ as a power series.

Solution From the series for $\sin x$ we obtain

$$\sin x^2 = x^2 - \frac{x^6}{3!} + \frac{x^{10}}{5!} - \frac{x^{14}}{7!} + \frac{x^{18}}{9!} - \cdots.$$

Therefore,

$$\int \sin x^2\,dx = C + \frac{x^3}{3} - \frac{x^7}{7\cdot 3!} + \frac{x^{11}}{11\cdot 5!} - \frac{x^{15}}{15\cdot 7!} + \frac{x^{10}}{19\cdot 9!} - \cdots. \quad ■$$

EXAMPLE 6 **Estimating a Definite Integral**

Estimate $\int_0^1 \sin x^2\,dx$ with an error of less than 0.001.

Solution From the indefinite integral in Example 5,

$$\int_0^1 \sin x^2\,dx = \frac{1}{3} - \frac{1}{7\cdot 3!} + \frac{1}{11\cdot 5!} - \frac{1}{15\cdot 7!} + \frac{1}{19\cdot 9!} - \cdots.$$

The series alternates, and we find by experiment that

$$\frac{1}{11\cdot 5!} \approx 0.00076$$

is the first term to be numerically less than 0.001. The sum of the preceding two terms gives

$$\int_0^1 \sin x^2\,dx \approx \frac{1}{3} - \frac{1}{42} \approx 0.310.$$

With two more terms we could estimate

$$\int_0^1 \sin x^2\,dx \approx 0.310268$$

with an error of less than 10^{-6}. With only one term beyond that we have

$$\int_0^1 \sin x^2\,dx \approx \frac{1}{3} - \frac{1}{42} + \frac{1}{1320} - \frac{1}{75600} + \frac{1}{6894720} \approx 0.310268303,$$

with an error of about 1.08×10^{-9}. To guarantee this accuracy with the error formula for the Trapezoidal Rule would require using about 8000 subintervals. ■

Arctangents

In Section 11.7, Example 5, we found a series for $\tan^{-1} x$ by differentiating to get

$$\frac{d}{dx}\tan^{-1} x = \frac{1}{1+x^2} = 1 - x^2 + x^4 - x^6 + \cdots$$

and integrating to get

$$\tan^{-1} x = x - \frac{x^3}{3} + \frac{x^5}{5} - \frac{x^7}{7} + \cdots.$$

However, we did not prove the term-by-term integration theorem on which this conclusion depended. We now derive the series again by integrating both sides of the finite formula

$$\frac{1}{1+t^2} = 1 - t^2 + t^4 - t^6 + \cdots + (-1)^n t^{2n} + \frac{(-1)^{n+1}t^{2n+2}}{1+t^2}, \tag{12}$$

in which the last term comes from adding the remaining terms as a geometric series with first term $a = (-1)^{n+1}t^{2n+2}$ and ratio $r = -t^2$. Integrating both sides of Equation (12) from $t = 0$ to $t = x$ gives

$$\tan^{-1} x = x - \frac{x^3}{3} + \frac{x^5}{5} - \frac{x^7}{7} + \cdots + (-1)^n \frac{x^{2n+1}}{2n+1} + R_n(x),$$

where

$$R_n(x) = \int_0^x \frac{(-1)^{n+1}t^{2n+2}}{1+t^2}\,dt.$$

The denominator of the integrand is greater than or equal to 1; hence

$$|R_n(x)| \le \int_0^{|x|} t^{2n+2}\,dt = \frac{|x|^{2n+3}}{2n+3}.$$

If $|x| \le 1$, the right side of this inequality approaches zero as $n \to \infty$. Therefore $\lim_{n\to\infty} R_n(x) = 0$ if $|x| \le 1$ and

$$\begin{aligned} \tan^{-1} x &= \sum_{n=0}^{\infty} \frac{(-1)^n x^{2n+1}}{2n+1}, \qquad |x| \le 1. \\ \tan^{-1} x &= x - \frac{x^3}{3} + \frac{x^5}{5} - \frac{x^7}{7} + \cdots, \qquad |x| \le 1 \end{aligned} \tag{13}$$

We take this route instead of finding the Taylor series directly because the formulas for the higher-order derivatives of $\tan^{-1} x$ are unmanageable. When we put $x = 1$ in Equation (13), we get **Leibniz's formula**:

$$\frac{\pi}{4} = 1 - \frac{1}{3} + \frac{1}{5} - \frac{1}{7} + \frac{1}{9} - \cdots + \frac{(-1)^n}{2n+1} + \cdots.$$

Because this series converges very slowly, it is not used in approximating π to many decimal places. The series for $\tan^{-1} x$ converges most rapidly when x is near zero. For that reason, people who use the series for $\tan^{-1} x$ to compute π use various trigonometric identities.

For example, if

$$\alpha = \tan^{-1}\frac{1}{2} \qquad \text{and} \qquad \beta = \tan^{-1}\frac{1}{3},$$

then

$$\tan(\alpha + \beta) = \frac{\tan\alpha + \tan\beta}{1 - \tan\alpha\tan\beta} = \frac{\frac{1}{2} + \frac{1}{3}}{1 - \frac{1}{6}} = 1 = \tan\frac{\pi}{4}$$

and

$$\frac{\pi}{4} = \alpha + \beta = \tan^{-1}\frac{1}{2} + \tan^{-1}\frac{1}{3}.$$

Now Equation (13) may be used with $x = 1/2$ to evaluate $\tan^{-1}(1/2)$ and with $x = 1/3$ to give $\tan^{-1}(1/3)$. The sum of these results, multiplied by 4, gives π.

Evaluating Indeterminate Forms

We can sometimes evaluate indeterminate forms by expressing the functions involved as Taylor series.

EXAMPLE 7 Limits Using Power Series

Evaluate

$$\lim_{x \to 1} \frac{\ln x}{x - 1}.$$

Solution We represent $\ln x$ as a Taylor series in powers of $x - 1$. This can be accomplished by calculating the Taylor series generated by $\ln x$ at $x = 1$ directly or by replacing x by $x - 1$ in the series for $\ln(1 + x)$ in Section 11.7, Example 6. Either way, we obtain

$$\ln x = (x - 1) - \frac{1}{2}(x - 1)^2 + \cdots,$$

from which we find that

$$\lim_{x \to 1} \frac{\ln x}{x - 1} = \lim_{x \to 1}\left(1 - \frac{1}{2}(x - 1) + \cdots\right) = 1.$$

■

EXAMPLE 8 Limits Using Power Series

Evaluate

$$\lim_{x \to 0} \frac{\sin x - \tan x}{x^3}.$$

Solution The Taylor series for $\sin x$ and $\tan x$, to terms in x^5, are

$$\sin x = x - \frac{x^3}{3!} + \frac{x^5}{5!} - \cdots, \qquad \tan x = x + \frac{x^3}{3} + \frac{2x^5}{15} + \cdots.$$

Hence,

$$\sin x - \tan x = -\frac{x^3}{2} - \frac{x^5}{8} - \cdots = x^3\left(-\frac{1}{2} - \frac{x^2}{8} - \cdots\right)$$

and

$$\begin{aligned}\lim_{x\to 0}\frac{\sin x - \tan x}{x^3} &= \lim_{x\to 0}\left(-\frac{1}{2} - \frac{x^2}{8} - \cdots\right)\\ &= -\frac{1}{2}.\end{aligned}$$

■

If we apply series to calculate $\lim_{x\to 0}((1/\sin x) - (1/x))$, we not only find the limit successfully but also discover an approximation formula for $\csc x$.

EXAMPLE 9 Approximation Formula for csc *x*

Find $\lim_{x\to 0}\left(\frac{1}{\sin x} - \frac{1}{x}\right)$.

Solution

$$\begin{aligned}\frac{1}{\sin x} - \frac{1}{x} = \frac{x - \sin x}{x\sin x} &= \frac{x - \left(x - \frac{x^3}{3!} + \frac{x^5}{5!} - \cdots\right)}{x\cdot\left(x - \frac{x^3}{3!} + \frac{x^5}{5!} - \cdots\right)}\\ &= \frac{x^3\left(\frac{1}{3!} - \frac{x^2}{5!} + \cdots\right)}{x^2\left(1 - \frac{x^2}{3!} + \cdots\right)} = x\frac{\frac{1}{3!} - \frac{x^2}{5!} + \cdots}{1 - \frac{x^2}{3!} + \cdots}.\end{aligned}$$

Therefore,

$$\lim_{x\to 0}\left(\frac{1}{\sin x} - \frac{1}{x}\right) = \lim_{x\to 0}\left(x\frac{\frac{1}{3!} - \frac{x^2}{5!} + \cdots}{1 - \frac{x^2}{3!} + \cdots}\right) = 0.$$

From the quotient on the right, we can see that if $|x|$ is small, then

$$\frac{1}{\sin x} - \frac{1}{x} \approx x\cdot\frac{1}{3!} = \frac{x}{6} \quad\text{or}\quad \csc x \approx \frac{1}{x} + \frac{x}{6}.$$

■

TABLE 11.1 Frequently used Taylor series

$$\frac{1}{1-x} = 1 + x + x^2 + \cdots + x^n + \cdots = \sum_{n=0}^{\infty} x^n, \quad |x| < 1$$

$$\frac{1}{1+x} = 1 - x + x^2 - \cdots + (-x)^n + \cdots = \sum_{n=0}^{\infty} (-1)^n x^n, \quad |x| < 1$$

$$e^x = 1 + x + \frac{x^2}{2!} + \cdots + \frac{x^n}{n!} + \cdots = \sum_{n=0}^{\infty} \frac{x^n}{n!}, \quad |x| < \infty$$

$$\sin x = x - \frac{x^3}{3!} + \frac{x^5}{5!} - \cdots + (-1)^n \frac{x^{2n+1}}{(2n+1)!} + \cdots = \sum_{n=0}^{\infty} \frac{(-1)^n x^{2n+1}}{(2n+1)!}, \quad |x| < \infty$$

$$\cos x = 1 - \frac{x^2}{2!} + \frac{x^4}{4!} - \cdots + (-1)^n \frac{x^{2n}}{(2n)!} + \cdots = \sum_{n=0}^{\infty} \frac{(-1)^n x^{2n}}{(2n)!}, \quad |x| < \infty$$

$$\ln(1+x) = x - \frac{x^2}{2} + \frac{x^3}{3} - \cdots + (-1)^{n-1} \frac{x^n}{n} + \cdots = \sum_{n=1}^{\infty} \frac{(-1)^{n-1} x^n}{n}, \quad -1 < x \le 1$$

$$\ln \frac{1+x}{1-x} = 2 \tanh^{-1} x = 2\left(x + \frac{x^3}{3} + \frac{x^5}{5} + \cdots + \frac{x^{2n+1}}{2n+1} + \cdots\right) = 2\sum_{n=0}^{\infty} \frac{x^{2n+1}}{2n+1}, \quad |x| < 1$$

$$\tan^{-1} x = x - \frac{x^3}{3} + \frac{x^5}{5} - \cdots + (-1)^n \frac{x^{2n+1}}{2n+1} + \cdots = \sum_{n=0}^{\infty} \frac{(-1)^n x^{2n+1}}{2n+1}, \quad |x| \le 1$$

Binomial Series

$$(1+x)^m = 1 + mx + \frac{m(m-1)x^2}{2!} + \frac{m(m-1)(m-2)x^3}{3!} + \cdots + \frac{m(m-1)(m-2)\cdots(m-k+1)x^k}{k!} + \cdots$$

$$= 1 + \sum_{k=1}^{\infty} \binom{m}{k} x^k, \quad |x| < 1,$$

where

$$\binom{m}{1} = m, \quad \binom{m}{2} = \frac{m(m-1)}{2!}, \quad \binom{m}{k} = \frac{m(m-1)\cdots(m-k+1)}{k!} \quad \text{for } k \ge 3.$$

Note: To write the binomial series compactly, it is customary to define $\binom{m}{0}$ to be 1 and to take $x^0 = 1$ (even in the usually excluded case where $x = 0$), yielding $(1+x)^m = \sum_{k=0}^{\infty} \binom{m}{k} x^k$. If m is a *positive integer*, the series terminates at x^m and the result converges for all x.

EXERCISES 11.10

Binomial Series

Find the first four terms of the binomial series for the functions in Exercises 1–10.

1. $(1+x)^{1/2}$ **2.** $(1+x)^{1/3}$ **3.** $(1-x)^{-1/2}$

4. $(1-2x)^{1/2}$ **5.** $\left(1+\frac{x}{2}\right)^{-2}$ **6.** $\left(1-\frac{x}{2}\right)^{-2}$

7. $(1+x^3)^{-1/2}$ **8.** $(1+x^2)^{-1/3}$

9. $\left(1+\frac{1}{x}\right)^{1/2}$ **10.** $\left(1-\frac{2}{x}\right)^{1/3}$

Find the binomial series for the functions in Exercises 11–14.

11. $(1+x)^4$ **12.** $(1+x^2)^3$

13. $(1-2x)^3$ **14.** $\left(1-\frac{x}{2}\right)^4$

Initial Value Problems

Find series solutions for the initial value problems in Exercises 15–32.

15. $y'+y=0,\quad y(0)=1$ **16.** $y'-2y=0,\quad y(0)=1$

17. $y'-y=1,\quad y(0)=0$ **18.** $y'+y=1,\quad y(0)=2$

19. $y'-y=x,\quad y(0)=0$ **20.** $y'+y=2x,\quad y(0)=-1$

21. $y'-xy=0,\quad y(0)=1$ **22.** $y'-x^2y=0,\quad y(0)=1$

23. $(1-x)y'-y=0,\quad y(0)=2$

24. $(1+x^2)y'+2xy=0,\quad y(0)=3$

25. $y''-y=0,\quad y'(0)=1$ and $y(0)=0$

26. $y''+y=0,\quad y'(0)=0$ and $y(0)=1$

27. $y''+y=x,\quad y'(0)=1$ and $y(0)=2$

28. $y''-y=x,\quad y'(0)=2$ and $y(0)=-1$

29. $y''-y=-x,\quad y'(2)=-2$ and $y(2)=0$

30. $y''-x^2y=0,\quad y'(0)=b$ and $y(0)=a$

31. $y''+x^2y=x,\quad y'(0)=b$ and $y(0)=a$

32. $y''-2y'+y=0,\quad y'(0)=1$ and $y(0)=0$

Approximations and Nonelementary Integrals

T In Exercises 33–36, use series to estimate the integrals' values with an error of magnitude less than 10^{-3}. (The answer section gives the integrals' values rounded to five decimal places.)

33. $\int_0^{0.2}\sin x^2\,dx$ **34.** $\int_0^{0.2}\frac{e^{-x}-1}{x}\,dx$

35. $\int_0^{0.1}\frac{1}{\sqrt{1+x^4}}\,dx$ **36.** $\int_0^{0.25}\sqrt[3]{1+x^2}\,dx$

T Use series to approximate the values of the integrals in Exercises 37–40 with an error of magnitude less than 10^{-8}.

37. $\int_0^{0.1}\frac{\sin x}{x}\,dx$ **38.** $\int_0^{0.1}e^{-x^2}\,dx$

39. $\int_0^{0.1}\sqrt{1+x^4}\,dx$ **40.** $\int_0^{1}\frac{1-\cos x}{x^2}\,dx$

41. Estimate the error if $\cos t^2$ is approximated by $1-\frac{t^4}{2}+\frac{t^8}{4!}$ in the integral $\int_0^1\cos t^2\,dt$.

42. Estimate the error if $\cos\sqrt{t}$ is approximated by $1-\frac{t}{2}+\frac{t^2}{4!}-\frac{t^3}{6!}$ in the integral $\int_0^1\cos\sqrt{t}\,dt$.

In Exercises 43–46, find a polynomial that will approximate $F(x)$ throughout the given interval with an error of magnitude less than 10^{-3}.

43. $F(x)=\int_0^x\sin t^2\,dt,\quad [0,1]$

44. $F(x)=\int_0^x t^2e^{-t^2}\,dt,\quad [0,1]$

45. $F(x)=\int_0^x\tan^{-1}t\,dt,\quad$ **(a)** $[0,0.5]$ **(b)** $[0,1]$

46. $F(x)=\int_0^x\frac{\ln(1+t)}{t}\,dt,\quad$ **(a)** $[0,0.5]$ **(b)** $[0,1]$

Indeterminate Forms

Use series to evaluate the limits in Exercises 47–56.

47. $\lim_{x\to0}\frac{e^x-(1+x)}{x^2}$ **48.** $\lim_{x\to0}\frac{e^x-e^{-x}}{x}$

49. $\lim_{t\to0}\frac{1-\cos t-(t^2/2)}{t^4}$ **50.** $\lim_{\theta\to0}\frac{\sin\theta-\theta+(\theta^3/6)}{\theta^5}$

51. $\lim_{y\to0}\frac{y-\tan^{-1}y}{y^3}$ **52.** $\lim_{y\to0}\frac{\tan^{-1}y-\sin y}{y^3\cos y}$

53. $\lim_{x\to\infty}x^2(e^{-1/x^2}-1)$ **54.** $\lim_{x\to\infty}(x+1)\sin\frac{1}{x+1}$

55. $\lim_{x\to0}\frac{\ln(1+x^2)}{1-\cos x}$ **56.** $\lim_{x\to2}\frac{x^2-4}{\ln(x-1)}$

Theory and Examples

57. Replace x by $-x$ in the Taylor series for $\ln(1+x)$ to obtain a series for $\ln(1-x)$. Then subtract this from the Taylor series for $\ln(1+x)$ to show that for $|x|<1$,

$$\ln\frac{1+x}{1-x}=2\left(x+\frac{x^3}{3}+\frac{x^5}{5}+\cdots\right).$$

58. How many terms of the Taylor series for $\ln(1+x)$ should you add to be sure of calculating $\ln(1.1)$ with an error of magnitude less than 10^{-8}? Give reasons for your answer.

59. According to the Alternating Series Estimation Theorem, how many terms of the Taylor series for $\tan^{-1}1$ would you have to add to be sure of finding $\pi/4$ with an error of magnitude less than 10^{-3}? Give reasons for your answer.

60. Show that the Taylor series for $f(x)=\tan^{-1}x$ diverges for $|x|>1$.

T **61. Estimating Pi** About how many terms of the Taylor series for $\tan^{-1}x$ would you have to use to evaluate each term on the right-hand side of the equation

$$\pi=48\tan^{-1}\frac{1}{18}+32\tan^{-1}\frac{1}{57}-20\tan^{-1}\frac{1}{239}$$

with an error of magnitude less than 10^{-6}? In contrast, the convergence of $\sum_{n=1}^{\infty}(1/n^2)$ to $\pi^2/6$ is so slow that even 50 terms will not yield two-place accuracy.

62. Integrate the first three nonzero terms of the Taylor series for $\tan t$ from 0 to x to obtain the first three nonzero terms of the Taylor series for $\ln\sec x$.

63. a. Use the binomial series and the fact that

$$\frac{d}{dx}\sin^{-1}x = (1 - x^2)^{-1/2}$$

to generate the first four nonzero terms of the Taylor series for $\sin^{-1}x$. What is the radius of convergence?

b. Series for $\cos^{-1}x$ Use your result in part (a) to find the first five nonzero terms of the Taylor series for $\cos^{-1}x$.

64. a. Series for $\sinh^{-1}x$ Find the first four nonzero terms of the Taylor series for

$$\sinh^{-1}x = \int_0^x \frac{dt}{\sqrt{1+t^2}}.$$

T **b.** Use the first *three* terms of the series in part (a) to estimate $\sinh^{-1} 0.25$. Give an upper bound for the magnitude of the estimation error.

65. Obtain the Taylor series for $1/(1 + x)^2$ from the series for $-1/(1 + x)$.

66. Use the Taylor series for $1/(1 - x^2)$ to obtain a series for $2x/(1 - x^2)^2$.

T **67. Estimating Pi** The English mathematician Wallis discovered the formula

$$\frac{\pi}{4} = \frac{2\cdot 4\cdot 4\cdot 6\cdot 6\cdot 8\cdot\cdots}{3\cdot 3\cdot 5\cdot 5\cdot 7\cdot 7\cdot\cdots}.$$

Find π to two decimal places with this formula.

T **68.** Construct a table of natural logarithms $\ln n$ for $n = 1, 2, 3, \ldots, 10$ by using the formula in Exercise 57, but taking advantage of the relationships $\ln 4 = 2\ln 2$, $\ln 6 = \ln 2 + \ln 3$, $\ln 8 = 3\ln 2$, $\ln 9 = 2\ln 3$, and $\ln 10 = \ln 2 + \ln 5$ to reduce the job to the calculation of relatively few logarithms by series. Start by using the following values for x in Exercise 57:

$$\frac{1}{3},\ \frac{1}{5},\ \frac{1}{9},\ \frac{1}{13}.$$

69. Series for $\sin^{-1}x$ Integrate the binomial series for $(1 - x^2)^{-1/2}$ to show that for $|x| < 1$,

$$\sin^{-1}x = x + \sum_{n=1}^{\infty}\frac{1\cdot 3\cdot 5\cdot\cdots\cdot(2n-1)}{2\cdot 4\cdot 6\cdot\cdots\cdot(2n)}\,\frac{x^{2n+1}}{2n+1}.$$

70. Series for $\tan^{-1}x$ for $|x| > 1$ Derive the series

$$\tan^{-1}x = \frac{\pi}{2} - \frac{1}{x} + \frac{1}{3x^3} - \frac{1}{5x^5} + \cdots, \quad x > 1$$

$$\tan^{-1}x = -\frac{\pi}{2} - \frac{1}{x} + \frac{1}{3x^3} - \frac{1}{5x^5} + \cdots, \quad x < -1,$$

by integrating the series

$$\frac{1}{1+t^2} = \frac{1}{t^2}\cdot\frac{1}{1+(1/t^2)} = \frac{1}{t^2} - \frac{1}{t^4} + \frac{1}{t^6} - \frac{1}{t^8} + \cdots$$

in the first case from x to ∞ and in the second case from $-\infty$ to x.

71. The value of $\sum_{n=1}^{\infty}\tan^{-1}(2/n^2)$

a. Use the formula for the tangent of the difference of two angles to show that

$$\tan(\tan^{-1}(n+1) - \tan^{-1}(n-1)) = \frac{2}{n^2}$$

b. Show that

$$\sum_{n=1}^{N}\tan^{-1}\frac{2}{n^2} = \tan^{-1}(N+1) + \tan^{-1}N - \frac{\pi}{4}.$$

c. Find the value of $\sum_{n=1}^{\infty}\tan^{-1}\frac{2}{n^2}$.

11.11 Fourier Series

HISTORICAL BIOGRAPHY

Jean-Baptiste Joseph Fourier (1768–1830)

We have seen how Taylor series can be used to approximate a function f by polynomials. The Taylor polynomials give a close fit to f near a particular point $x = a$, but the error in the approximation can be large at points that are far away. There is another method that often gives good approximations on wide intervals, and often works with discontinuous functions for which Taylor polynomials fail. Introduced by Joseph Fourier, this method approximates functions with sums of sine and cosine functions. It is well suited for analyzing periodic functions, such as radio signals and alternating currents, for solving heat transfer problems, and for many other problems in science and engineering.

Suppose we wish to approximate a function f on the interval $[0, 2\pi]$ by a sum of sine and cosine functions,

$$\begin{aligned} f_n(x) = a_0 &+ (a_1 \cos x + b_1 \sin x) + (a_2 \cos 2x + b_2 \sin 2x) + \cdots \\ &+ (a_n \cos nx + b_n \sin nx) \end{aligned}$$

or, in sigma notation,

$$f_n(x) = a_0 + \sum_{k=1}^{n} (a_k \cos kx + b_k \sin kx). \tag{1}$$

We would like to choose values for the constants $a_0, a_1, a_2, \ldots, a_n$ and $b_1, b_2, \ldots, b_n$ that make $f_n(x)$ a "best possible" approximation to $f(x)$. The notion of "best possible" is defined as follows:

1. $f_n(x)$ and $f(x)$ give the same value when integrated from 0 to 2π.
2. $f_n(x) \cos kx$ and $f(x) \cos kx$ give the same value when integrated from 0 to 2π $(k = 1, \ldots, n)$.
3. $f_n(x) \sin kx$ and $f(x) \sin kx$ give the same value when integrated from 0 to 2π $(k = 1, \ldots, n)$.

Altogether we impose $2n + 1$ conditions on f_n:

$$\int_0^{2\pi} f_n(x)\,dx = \int_0^{2\pi} f(x)\,dx,$$

$$\int_0^{2\pi} f_n(x)\cos kx\,dx = \int_0^{2\pi} f(x)\cos kx\,dx, \qquad k = 1, \ldots, n,$$

$$\int_0^{2\pi} f_n(x)\sin kx\,dx = \int_0^{2\pi} f(x)\sin kx\,dx, \qquad k = 1, \ldots, n.$$

It is possible to choose $a_0, a_1, a_2, \ldots a_n$ and $b_1, b_2, \ldots, b_n$ so that all these conditions are satisfied, by proceeding as follows. Integrating both sides of Equation (1) from 0 to 2π gives

$$\int_0^{2\pi} f_n(x)\,dx = 2\pi a_0$$

since the integral over $[0, 2\pi]$ of $\cos kx$ equals zero when $k \geq 1$, as does the integral of $\sin kx$. Only the constant term a_0 contributes to the integral of f_n over $[0, 2\pi]$. A similar calculation applies with each of the other terms. If we multiply both sides of Equation (1) by $\cos x$ and integrate from 0 to 2π then we obtain

$$\int_0^{2\pi} f_n(x)\cos x\,dx = \pi a_1.$$

This follows from the fact that

$$\int_0^{2\pi} \cos px \cos px\,dx = \pi$$

and

$$\int_0^{2\pi} \cos px \cos qx\,dx = \int_0^{2\pi} \cos px \sin mx\,dx = \int_0^{2\pi} \sin px \sin qx\,dx = 0$$

whenever p, q and m are integers and p is not equal to q (Exercises 9–13). If we multiply Equation (1) by $\sin x$ and integrate from 0 to 2π we obtain

$$\int_0^{2\pi} f_n(x)\sin x\,dx = \pi b_1.$$

Proceeding in a similar fashion with

$$\cos 2x, \sin 2x, \ldots, \cos nx, \sin nx$$

we obtain only one nonzero term each time, the term with a sine-squared or cosine-squared term. To summarize,

$$\int_0^{2\pi} f_n(x)\,dx = 2\pi a_0$$

$$\int_0^{2\pi} f_n(x)\cos kx\,dx = \pi a_k, \qquad k = 1, \ldots, n$$

$$\int_0^{2\pi} f_n(x)\sin kx\,dx = \pi b_k, \qquad k = 1, \ldots, n$$

We chose f_n so that the integrals on the left remain the same when f_n is replaced by f, so we can use these equations to find $a_0, a_1, a_2, \ldots a_n$ and $b_1, b_2, \ldots, b_n$ from f:

$$a_0 = \frac{1}{2\pi}\int_0^{2\pi} f(x)\,dx \tag{2}$$

$$a_k = \frac{1}{\pi}\int_0^{2\pi} f(x)\cos kx\,dx, \qquad k = 1, \ldots, n \tag{3}$$

$$b_k = \frac{1}{\pi}\int_0^{2\pi} f(x)\sin kx\,dx, \qquad k = 1, \ldots, n \tag{4}$$

The only condition needed to find these coefficients is that the integrals above must exist. If we let $n \to \infty$ and use these rules to get the coefficients of an infinite series, then the resulting sum is called the **Fourier series for $f(x)$**,

$$a_0 + \sum_{k=1}^{\infty}(a_k\cos kx + b_k\sin kx). \tag{5}$$

EXAMPLE 1 Finding a Fourier Series Expansion

Fourier series can be used to represent some functions that cannot be represented by Taylor series; for example, the step function f shown in Figure 11.16a.

$$f(x) = \begin{cases} 1, & \text{if } 0 \le x \le \pi \\ 2, & \text{if } \pi < x \le 2\pi. \end{cases}$$

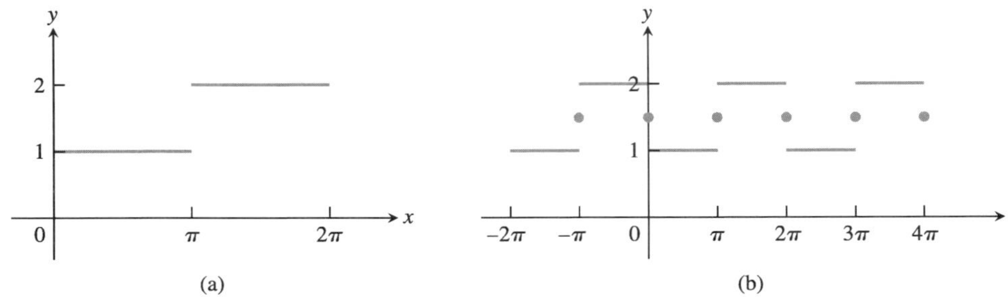

FIGURE 11.16 (a) The step function

$$f(x) = \begin{cases} 1, & 0 \le x \le \pi \\ 2, & \pi < x \le 2\pi \end{cases}$$

(b) The graph of the Fourier series for f is periodic and has the value $3/2$ at each point of discontinuity (Example 1).

The coefficients of the Fourier series of f are computed using Equations (2), (3), and (4).

$$\begin{aligned} a_0 &= \frac{1}{2\pi}\int_0^{2\pi} f(x)\,dx \\ &= \frac{1}{2\pi}\left(\int_0^{\pi} 1\,dx + \int_{\pi}^{2\pi} 2\,dx\right) = \frac{3}{2} \end{aligned}$$

$$\begin{aligned} a_k &= \frac{1}{\pi}\int_0^{2\pi} f(x)\cos kx\,dx \\ &= \frac{1}{\pi}\left(\int_0^{\pi} \cos kx\,dx + \int_{\pi}^{2\pi} 2\cos kx\,dx\right) \\ &= \frac{1}{\pi}\left(\left[\frac{\sin kx}{k}\right]_0^{\pi} + \left[\frac{2\sin kx}{k}\right]_{\pi}^{2\pi}\right) = 0, \qquad k \ge 1 \end{aligned}$$

$$\begin{aligned} b_k &= \frac{1}{\pi}\int_0^{2\pi} f(x)\sin kx\,dx \\ &= \frac{1}{\pi}\left(\int_0^{\pi} \sin kx\,dx + \int_{\pi}^{2\pi} 2\sin kx\,dx\right) \\ &= \frac{1}{\pi}\left(\left[-\frac{\cos kx}{k}\right]_0^{\pi} + \left[-\frac{2\cos kx}{k}\right]_{\pi}^{2\pi}\right) \\ &= \frac{\cos k\pi - 1}{k\pi} = \frac{(-1)^k - 1}{k\pi}. \end{aligned}$$

So

$$a_0 = \frac{3}{2}, \quad a_1 = a_2 = \cdots = 0,$$

and

$$b_1 = -\frac{2}{\pi}, \quad b_2 = 0, \quad b_3 = -\frac{2}{3\pi}, \quad b_4 = 0, \quad b_5 = -\frac{2}{5\pi}, \quad b_6 = 0, \ldots$$

The Fourier series is

$$\frac{3}{2} - \frac{2}{\pi}\left(\sin x + \frac{\sin 3x}{3} + \frac{\sin 5x}{5} + \cdots\right).$$

Notice that at $x = \pi$, where the function $f(x)$ jumps from 1 to 2, all the sine terms vanish, leaving $3/2$ as the value of the series. This is not the value of f at π, since $f(\pi) = 1$. The Fourier series also sums to $3/2$ at $x = 0$ and $x = 2\pi$. In fact, all terms in the Fourier series are periodic, of period 2π, and the value of the series at $x + 2\pi$ is the same as its value at x. The series we obtained represents the periodic function graphed in Figure 11.16b, with domain the entire real line and a pattern that repeats over every interval of width 2π. The function jumps discontinuously at $x = n\pi, n = 0, \pm 1, \pm 2, \ldots$ and at these points has value $3/2$, the average value of the one-sided limits from each side. The convergence of the Fourier series of f is indicated in Figure 11.17. ■

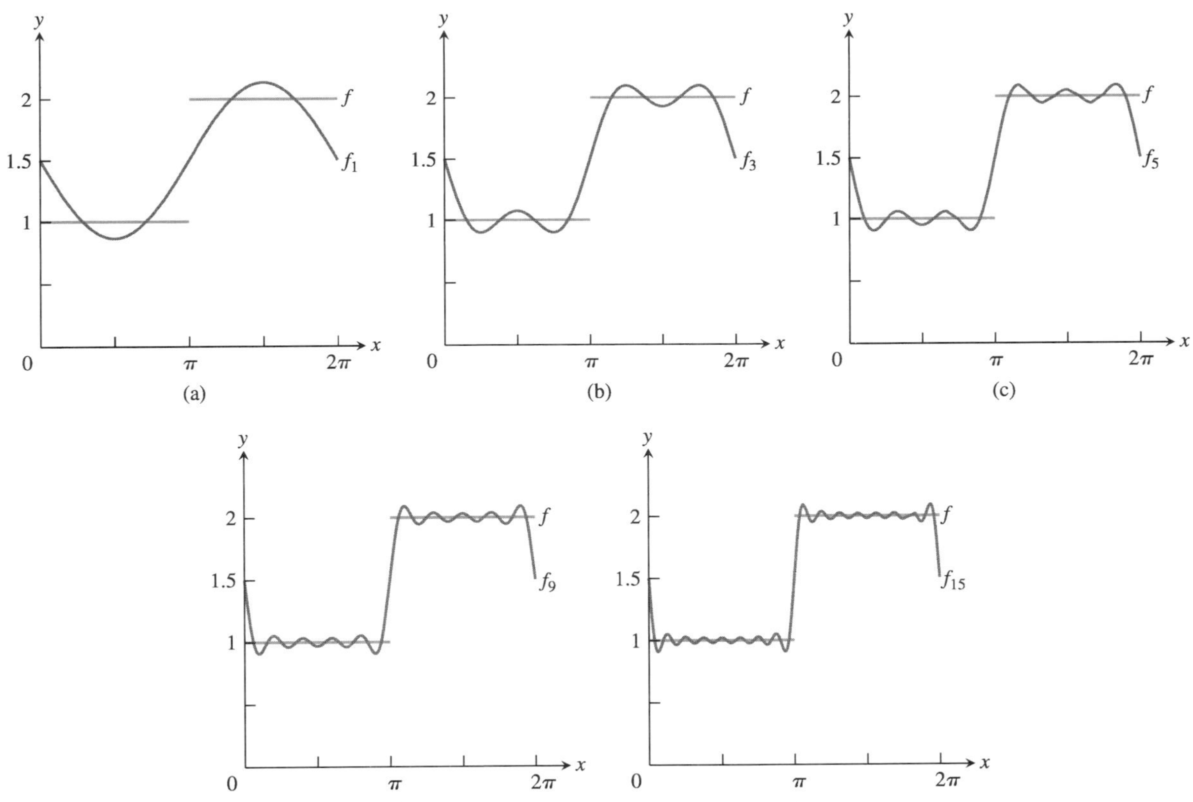

FIGURE 11.17 The Fourier approximation functions f_1, f_3, f_5, f_9, and f_{15} of the function $f(x) = \begin{cases} 1, & 0 \le x \le \pi \\ 2, & \pi < x \le 2\pi \end{cases}$ in Example 1.

Convergence of Fourier Series

Taylor series are computed from the value of a function and its derivatives at a single point $x = a$, and cannot reflect the behavior of a discontinuous function such as f in Example 1 past a discontinuity. The reason that a Fourier series can be used to represent such functions is that the Fourier series of a function depends on the existence of certain *integrals*, whereas the Taylor series depends on derivatives of a function near a single point. A function can be fairly "rough," even discontinuous, and still be integrable.

The coefficients used to construct Fourier series are precisely those one should choose to minimize the integral of the square of the error in approximating f by f_n. That is,

$$\int_0^{2\pi} [f(x) - f_n(x)]^2\, dx$$

is minimized by choosing $a_0, a_1, a_2, \ldots a_n$ and $b_1, b_2, \ldots, b_n$ as we did. While Taylor series are useful to approximate a function and its derivatives near a point, Fourier series minimize an error which is distributed over an interval.

We state without proof a result concerning the convergence of Fourier series. A function is **piecewise continuous** over an interval I if it has finitely many discontinuities on the interval, and at these discontinuities one-sided limits exist from each side. (See Chapter 5, Additional Exercises 11–18.)

THEOREM 24 Let $f(x)$ be a function such that f and f' are piecewise continuous on the interval $[0, 2\pi]$. Then f is equal to its Fourier series at all points where f is continuous. At a point c where f has a discontinuity, the Fourier series converges to

$$\frac{f(c^+) + f(c^-)}{2}$$

where $f(c^+)$ and $f(c^-)$ are the right- and left-hand limits of f at c.

EXERCISES 11.11

Finding Fourier Series

In Exercises 1–8, find the Fourier series associated with the given functions. Sketch each function.

1. $f(x) = 1 \quad 0 \le x \le 2\pi.$

2. $f(x) = \begin{cases} 1, & 0 \le x \le \pi \\ -1, & \pi < x \le 2\pi \end{cases}$

3. $f(x) = \begin{cases} x, & 0 \le x \le \pi \\ x - 2\pi, & \pi < x \le 2\pi \end{cases}$

4. $f(x) = \begin{cases} x^2, & 0 \le x \le \pi \\ 0, & \pi < x \le 2\pi \end{cases}$

5. $f(x) = e^x \quad 0 \le x \le 2\pi.$

6. $f(x) = \begin{cases} e^x, & 0 \le x \le \pi \\ 0, & \pi < x \le 2\pi \end{cases}$

7. $f(x) = \begin{cases} \cos x, & 0 \le x \le \pi \\ 0, & \pi < x \le 2\pi \end{cases}$

8. $f(x) = \begin{cases} 2, & 0 \le x \le \pi \\ -x, & \pi < x \le 2\pi \end{cases}$

Theory and Examples

Establish the results in Exercises 9–13, where p and q are positive integers.

9. $\displaystyle\int_0^{2\pi} \cos px\, dx = 0$ for all p.

10. $\int_0^{2\pi} \sin px\, dx = 0$ for all p.

11. $\int_0^{2\pi} \cos px \cos qx\, dx = \begin{cases} 0, & \text{if } p \neq q \\ \pi, & \text{if } p = q \end{cases}$.

(*Hint:* $\cos A \cos B = (1/2)[\cos(A + B) + \cos(A - B)]$.)

12. $\int_0^{2\pi} \sin px \sin qx\, dx = \begin{cases} 0, & \text{if } p \neq q \\ \pi, & \text{if } p = q \end{cases}$.

(*Hint:* $\sin A \sin B = (1/2)[\cos(A - B) - \cos(A + B)]$.)

13. $\int_0^{2\pi} \sin px \cos qx\, dx = 0$ for all p and q.

(*Hint*: $\sin A \cos B = (1/2)[\sin(A + B) + \sin(A - B)]$.)

14. **Fourier series of sums of functions** If f and g both satisfy the conditions of Theorem 24, is the Fourier series of $f + g$ on $[0, 2\pi]$ the sum of the Fourier series of f and the Fourier series of g? Give reasons for your answer.

15. **Term-by-term differentiation**
    a. Use Theorem 24 to verify that the Fourier series for $f(x)$ in Exercise 3 converges to $f(x)$ for $0 < x < 2\pi$.
    b. Although $f'(x) = 1$, show that the series obtained by term-by-term differentiation of the Fourier series in part (a) diverges.

16. Use Theorem 24 to find the Value of the Fourier series determined in Exercise 4 and show that $\frac{\pi^2}{6} = \sum_{n=1}^{\infty} \frac{1}{n^2}$.

Chapter 11 Questions to Guide Your Review

1. What is an infinite sequence? What does it mean for such a sequence to converge? To diverge? Give examples.
2. What is a nondecreasing sequence? Under what circumstances does such a sequence have a limit? Give examples.
3. What theorems are available for calculating limits of sequences? Give examples.
4. What theorem sometimes enables us to use l'Hôpital's Rule to calculate the limit of a sequence? Give an example.
5. What six sequence limits are likely to arise when you work with sequences and series?
6. What is an infinite series? What does it mean for such a series to converge? To diverge? Give examples.
7. What is a geometric series? When does such a series converge? Diverge? When it does converge, what is its sum? Give examples.
8. Besides geometric series, what other convergent and divergent series do you know?
9. What is the nth-Term Test for Divergence? What is the idea behind the test?
10. What can be said about term-by-term sums and differences of convergent series? About constant multiples of convergent and divergent series?
11. What happens if you add a finite number of terms to a convergent series? A divergent series? What happens if you delete a finite number of terms from a convergent series? A divergent series?
12. How do you reindex a series? Why might you want to do this?
13. Under what circumstances will an infinite series of nonnegative terms converge? Diverge? Why study series of nonnegative terms?
14. What is the Integral Test? What is the reasoning behind it? Give an example of its use.
15. When do p-series converge? Diverge? How do you know? Give examples of convergent and divergent p-series.
16. What are the Direct Comparison Test and the Limit Comparison Test? What is the reasoning behind these tests? Give examples of their use.
17. What are the Ratio and Root Tests? Do they always give you the information you need to determine convergence or divergence? Give examples.
18. What is an alternating series? What theorem is available for determining the convergence of such a series?
19. How can you estimate the error involved in approximating the sum of an alternating series with one of the series' partial sums? What is the reasoning behind the estimate?
20. What is absolute convergence? Conditional convergence? How are the two related?
21. What do you know about rearranging the terms of an absolutely convergent series? Of a conditionally convergent series? Give examples.
22. What is a power series? How do you test a power series for convergence? What are the possible outcomes?
23. What are the basic facts about
    a. term-by-term differentiation of power series?
    b. term-by-term integration of power series?
    c. multiplication of power series?

    Give examples.
24. What is the Taylor series generated by a function $f(x)$ at a point $x = a$? What information do you need about f to construct the series? Give an example.
25. What is a Maclaurin series?

26. Does a Taylor series always converge to its generating function? Explain.
27. What are Taylor polynomials? Of what use are they?
28. What is Taylor's formula? What does it say about the errors involved in using Taylor polynomials to approximate functions? In particular, what does Taylor's formula say about the error in a linearization? A quadratic approximation?
29. What is the binomial series? On what interval does it converge? How is it used?
30. How can you sometimes use power series to solve initial value problems?
31. How can you sometimes use power series to estimate the values of nonelementary definite integrals?
32. What are the Taylor series for $1/(1-x)$, $1/(1+x)$, e^x, $\sin x$, $\cos x$, $\ln(1+x)$, $\ln[(1+x)/(1-x)]$, and $\tan^{-1} x$? How do you estimate the errors involved in replacing these series with their partial sums?
33. What is a Fourier series? How do you calculate the Fourier coefficients $a_0, a_1, a_2, \ldots$ and $b_1, b_2, \ldots$ for a function $f(x)$ defined on the interval $[0, 2\pi]$?
34. State the theorem on convergence of the Fourier series for $f(x)$ when f and f' are piecewise continuous on $[0, 2\pi]$.

Chapter 11 Practice Exercises

Convergent or Divergent Sequences

Which of the sequences whose nth terms appear in Exercises 1–18 converge, and which diverge? Find the limit of each convergent sequence.

1. $a_n = 1 + \dfrac{(-1)^n}{n}$
2. $a_n = \dfrac{1-(-1)^n}{\sqrt{n}}$
3. $a_n = \dfrac{1-2^n}{2^n}$
4. $a_n = 1 + (0.9)^n$
5. $a_n = \sin \dfrac{n\pi}{2}$
6. $a_n = \sin n\pi$
7. $a_n = \dfrac{\ln(n^2)}{n}$
8. $a_n = \dfrac{\ln(2n+1)}{n}$
9. $a_n = \dfrac{n + \ln n}{n}$
10. $a_n = \dfrac{\ln(2n^3+1)}{n}$
11. $a_n = \left(\dfrac{n-5}{n}\right)^n$
12. $a_n = \left(1 + \dfrac{1}{n}\right)^{-n}$
13. $a_n = \sqrt[n]{\dfrac{3^n}{n}}$
14. $a_n = \left(\dfrac{3}{n}\right)^{1/n}$
15. $a_n = n(2^{1/n} - 1)$
16. $a_n = \sqrt[n]{2n+1}$
17. $a_n = \dfrac{(n+1)!}{n!}$
18. $a_n = \dfrac{(-4)^n}{n!}$

Convergent Series

Find the sums of the series in Exercises 19–24.

19. $\displaystyle\sum_{n=3}^{\infty} \frac{1}{(2n-3)(2n-1)}$
20. $\displaystyle\sum_{n=2}^{\infty} \frac{-2}{n(n+1)}$
21. $\displaystyle\sum_{n=1}^{\infty} \frac{9}{(3n-1)(3n+2)}$
22. $\displaystyle\sum_{n=3}^{\infty} \frac{-8}{(4n-3)(4n+1)}$
23. $\displaystyle\sum_{n=0}^{\infty} e^{-n}$
24. $\displaystyle\sum_{n=1}^{\infty} (-1)^n \frac{3}{4^n}$

Convergent or Divergent Series

Which of the series in Exercises 25–40 converge absolutely, which converge conditionally, and which diverge? Give reasons for your answers.

25. $\displaystyle\sum_{n=1}^{\infty} \frac{1}{\sqrt{n}}$
26. $\displaystyle\sum_{n=1}^{\infty} \frac{-5}{n}$
27. $\displaystyle\sum_{n=1}^{\infty} \frac{(-1)^n}{\sqrt{n}}$
28. $\displaystyle\sum_{n=1}^{\infty} \frac{1}{2n^3}$
29. $\displaystyle\sum_{n=1}^{\infty} \frac{(-1)^n}{\ln(n+1)}$
30. $\displaystyle\sum_{n=2}^{\infty} \frac{1}{n(\ln n)^2}$
31. $\displaystyle\sum_{n=1}^{\infty} \frac{\ln n}{n^3}$
32. $\displaystyle\sum_{n=3}^{\infty} \frac{\ln n}{\ln(\ln n)}$
33. $\displaystyle\sum_{n=1}^{\infty} \frac{(-1)^n}{n\sqrt{n^2+1}}$
34. $\displaystyle\sum_{n=1}^{\infty} \frac{(-1)^n 3n^2}{n^3+1}$
35. $\displaystyle\sum_{n=1}^{\infty} \frac{n+1}{n!}$
36. $\displaystyle\sum_{n=1}^{\infty} \frac{(-1)^n(n^2+1)}{2n^2+n-1}$
37. $\displaystyle\sum_{n=1}^{\infty} \frac{(-3)^n}{n!}$
38. $\displaystyle\sum_{n=1}^{\infty} \frac{2^n 3^n}{n^n}$
39. $\displaystyle\sum_{n=1}^{\infty} \frac{1}{\sqrt{n(n+1)(n+2)}}$
40. $\displaystyle\sum_{n=2}^{\infty} \frac{1}{n\sqrt{n^2-1}}$

Power Series

In Exercises 41–50, **(a)** find the series' radius and interval of convergence. Then identify the values of x for which the series converges **(b)** absolutely and **(c)** conditionally.

41. $\displaystyle\sum_{n=1}^{\infty} \frac{(x+4)^n}{n3^n}$
42. $\displaystyle\sum_{n=1}^{\infty} \frac{(x-1)^{2n-2}}{(2n-1)!}$
43. $\displaystyle\sum_{n=1}^{\infty} \frac{(-1)^{n-1}(3x-1)^n}{n^2}$
44. $\displaystyle\sum_{n=0}^{\infty} \frac{(n+1)(2x+1)^n}{(2n+1)2^n}$
45. $\displaystyle\sum_{n=1}^{\infty} \frac{x^n}{n^n}$
46. $\displaystyle\sum_{n=1}^{\infty} \frac{x^n}{\sqrt{n}}$

47. $\sum_{n=0}^{\infty} \frac{(n+1)x^{2n-1}}{3^n}$

48. $\sum_{n=0}^{\infty} \frac{(-1)^n(x-1)^{2n+1}}{2n+1}$

49. $\sum_{n=1}^{\infty} (\operatorname{csch} n)x^n$

50. $\sum_{n=1}^{\infty} (\coth n)x^n$

Maclaurin Series

Each of the series in Exercises 51–56 is the value of the Taylor series at $x = 0$ of a function $f(x)$ at a particular point. What function and what point? What is the sum of the series?

51. $1 - \frac{1}{4} + \frac{1}{16} - \cdots + (-1)^n \frac{1}{4^n} + \cdots$

52. $\frac{2}{3} - \frac{4}{18} + \frac{8}{81} - \cdots + (-1)^{n-1} \frac{2^n}{n3^n} + \cdots$

53. $\pi - \frac{\pi^3}{3!} + \frac{\pi^5}{5!} - \cdots + (-1)^n \frac{\pi^{2n+1}}{(2n+1)!} + \cdots$

54. $1 - \frac{\pi^2}{9 \cdot 2!} + \frac{\pi^4}{81 \cdot 4!} - \cdots + (-1)^n \frac{\pi^{2n}}{3^{2n}(2n)!} + \cdots$

55. $1 + \ln 2 + \frac{(\ln 2)^2}{2!} + \cdots + \frac{(\ln 2)^n}{n!} + \cdots$

56. $\frac{1}{\sqrt{3}} - \frac{1}{9\sqrt{3}} + \frac{1}{45\sqrt{3}} - \cdots + (-1)^{n-1} \frac{1}{(2n-1)\left(\sqrt{3}\right)^{2n-1}} + \cdots$

Find Taylor series at $x = 0$ for the functions in Exercises 57–64.

57. $\frac{1}{1-2x}$

58. $\frac{1}{1+x^3}$

59. $\sin \pi x$

60. $\sin \frac{2x}{3}$

61. $\cos (x^{5/2})$

62. $\cos \sqrt{5x}$

63. $e^{(\pi x/2)}$

64. e^{-x^2}

Taylor Series

In Exercises 65–68, find the first four nonzero terms of the Taylor series generated by f at $x = a$.

65. $f(x) = \sqrt{3 + x^2}$ at $x = -1$

66. $f(x) = 1/(1 - x)$ at $x = 2$

67. $f(x) = 1/(x + 1)$ at $x = 3$

68. $f(x) = 1/x$ at $x = a > 0$

Initial Value Problems

Use power series to solve the initial value problems in Exercises 69–76.

69. $y' + y = 0, \quad y(0) = -1$

70. $y' - y = 0, \quad y(0) = -3$

71. $y' + 2y = 0, \quad y(0) = 3$

72. $y' + y = 1, \quad y(0) = 0$

73. $y' - y = 3x, \quad y(0) = -1$

74. $y' + y = x, \quad y(0) = 0$

75. $y' - y = x, \quad y(0) = 1$

76. $y' - y = -x, \quad y(0) = 2$

Nonelementary Integrals

Use series to approximate the values of the integrals in Exercises 77–80 with an error of magnitude less than 10^{-8}. (The answer section gives the integrals' values rounded to 10 decimal places.)

77. $\int_0^{1/2} e^{-x^3}\, dx$

78. $\int_0^1 x \sin (x^3)\, dx$

79. $\int_0^{1/2} \frac{\tan^{-1} x}{x}\, dx$

80. $\int_0^{1/64} \frac{\tan^{-1} x}{\sqrt{x}}\, dx$

Indeterminate Forms

In Exercises 81–86:

a. Use power series to evaluate the limit.

T b. Then use a grapher to support your calculation.

81. $\lim_{x \to 0} \frac{7 \sin x}{e^{2x} - 1}$

82. $\lim_{\theta \to 0} \frac{e^\theta - e^{-\theta} - 2\theta}{\theta - \sin \theta}$

83. $\lim_{t \to 0} \left(\frac{1}{2 - 2\cos t} - \frac{1}{t^2}\right)$

84. $\lim_{h \to 0} \frac{(\sin h)/h - \cos h}{h^2}$

85. $\lim_{z \to 0} \frac{1 - \cos^2 z}{\ln (1 - z) + \sin z}$

86. $\lim_{y \to 0} \frac{y^2}{\cos y - \cosh y}$

87. Use a series representation of $\sin 3x$ to find values of r and s for which

$$\lim_{x \to 0} \left(\frac{\sin 3x}{x^3} + \frac{r}{x^2} + s\right) = 0.$$

88. **a.** Show that the approximation $\csc x \approx 1/x + x/6$ in Section 11.10, Example 9, leads to the approximation $\sin x \approx 6x/(6 + x^2)$.

T b. Compare the accuracies of the approximations $\sin x \approx x$ and $\sin x \approx 6x/(6 + x^2)$ by comparing the graphs of $f(x) = \sin x - x$ and $g(x) = \sin x - (6x/(6 + x^2))$. Describe what you find.

Theory and Examples

89. **a.** Show that the series

$$\sum_{n=1}^{\infty} \left(\sin \frac{1}{2n} - \sin \frac{1}{2n+1}\right)$$

converges.

T b. Estimate the magnitude of the error involved in using the sum of the sines through $n = 20$ to approximate the sum of the series. Is the approximation too large, or too small? Give reasons for your answer.

90. **a.** Show that the series $\sum_{n=1}^{\infty} \left(\tan \frac{1}{2n} - \tan \frac{1}{2n+1}\right)$ converges.

T b. Estimate the magnitude of the error in using the sum of the tangents through $-\tan (1/41)$ to approximate the sum of the series. Is the approximation too large, or too small? Give reasons for your answer.

91. Find the radius of convergence of the series

$$\sum_{n=1}^{\infty} \frac{2 \cdot 5 \cdot 8 \cdot \cdots \cdot (3n-1)}{2 \cdot 4 \cdot 6 \cdot \cdots \cdot (2n)} x^n.$$

92. Find the radius of convergence of the series

$$\sum_{n=1}^{\infty} \frac{3 \cdot 5 \cdot 7 \cdot \cdots \cdot (2n+1)}{4 \cdot 9 \cdot 14 \cdot \cdots \cdot (5n-1)} (x-1)^n.$$

93. Find a closed-form formula for the nth partial sum of the series $\sum_{n=2}^{\infty} \ln(1 - (1/n^2))$ and use it to determine the convergence or divergence of the series.

94. Evaluate $\sum_{k=2}^{\infty} (1/(k^2 - 1))$ by finding the limits as $n \to \infty$ of the series' nth partial sum.

95. **a.** Find the interval of convergence of the series

$$y = 1 + \frac{1}{6}x^3 + \frac{1}{180}x^6 + \cdots + \frac{1 \cdot 4 \cdot 7 \cdot \cdots \cdot (3n-2)}{(3n)!} x^{3n} + \cdots.$$

b. Show that the function defined by the series satisfies a differential equation of the form

$$\frac{d^2y}{dx^2} = x^a y + b$$

and find the values of the constants a and b.

96. **a.** Find the Maclaurin series for the function $x^2/(1 + x)$.

b. Does the series converge at $x = 1$? Explain.

97. If $\sum_{n=1}^{\infty} a_n$ and $\sum_{n=1}^{\infty} b_n$ are convergent series of nonnegative numbers, can anything be said about $\sum_{n=1}^{\infty} a_n b_n$? Give reasons for your answer.

98. If $\sum_{n=1}^{\infty} a_n$ and $\sum_{n=1}^{\infty} b_n$ are divergent series of nonnegative numbers, can anything be said about $\sum_{n=1}^{\infty} a_n b_n$? Give reasons for your answer.

99. Prove that the sequence $\{x_n\}$ and the series $\sum_{k=1}^{\infty} (x_{k+1} - x_k)$ both converge or both diverge.

100. Prove that $\sum_{n=1}^{\infty} (a_n/(1 + a_n))$ converges if $a_n > 0$ for all n and $\sum_{n=1}^{\infty} a_n$ converges.

101. (*Continuation of Section 4.7, Exercise 27.*) If you did Exercise 27 in Section 4.7, you saw that in practice Newton's method stopped too far from the root of $f(x) = (x-1)^{40}$ to give a useful estimate of its value, $x = 1$. Prove that nevertheless, for any starting value $x_0 \neq 1$, the sequence $x_0, x_1, x_2, \ldots, x_n, \ldots$ of approximations generated by Newton's method really does converge to 1.

102. Suppose that $a_1, a_2, a_3, \ldots, a_n$ are positive numbers satisfying the following conditions:

i. $a_1 \geq a_2 \geq a_3 \geq \cdots$;

ii. the series $a_2 + a_4 + a_8 + a_{16} + \cdots$ diverges.

Show that the series

$$\frac{a_1}{1} + \frac{a_2}{2} + \frac{a_3}{3} + \cdots$$

diverges.

103. Use the result in Exercise 102 to show that

$$1 + \sum_{n=2}^{\infty} \frac{1}{n \ln n}$$

diverges.

104. Suppose you wish to obtain a quick estimate for the value of $\int_0^1 x^2 e^x \, dx$. There are several ways to do this.

a. Use the Trapezoidal Rule with $n = 2$ to estimate $\int_0^1 x^2 e^x \, dx$.

b. Write out the first three nonzero terms of the Taylor series at $x = 0$ for $x^2 e^x$ to obtain the fourth Taylor polynomial $P(x)$ for $x^2 e^x$. Use $\int_0^1 P(x)\, dx$ to obtain another estimate for $\int_0^1 x^2 e^x \, dx$.

c. The second derivative of $f(x) = x^2 e^x$ is positive for all $x > 0$. Explain why this enables you to conclude that the Trapezoidal Rule estimate obtained in part (a) is too large. (*Hint:* What does the second derivative tell you about the graph of a function? How does this relate to the trapezoidal approximation of the area under this graph?)

d. All the derivatives of $f(x) = x^2 e^x$ are positive for $x > 0$. Explain why this enables you to conclude that all Maclaurin polynomial approximations to $f(x)$ for x in $[0, 1]$ will be too small. (*Hint:* $f(x) = P_n(x) + R_n(x)$.)

e. Use integration by parts to evaluate $\int_0^1 x^2 e^x \, dx$.

Fourier Series

Find the Fourier series for the functions in Exercises 105–108. Sketch each function.

105. $f(x) = \begin{cases} 0, & 0 \leq x \leq \pi \\ 1, & \pi < x \leq 2\pi \end{cases}$

106. $f(x) = \begin{cases} x, & 0 \leq x \leq \pi \\ 1, & \pi < x \leq 2\pi \end{cases}$

107. $f(x) = \begin{cases} \pi - x, & 0 \leq x \leq \pi \\ x - 2\pi, & \pi < x \leq 2\pi \end{cases}$

108. $f(x) = |\sin x|, \quad 0 \leq x \leq 2\pi$

Chapter 11 Additional and Advanced Exercises

Convergence or Divergence

Which of the series $\sum_{n=1}^{\infty} a_n$ defined by the formulas in Exercises 1–4 converge, and which diverge? Give reasons for your answers.

1. $\displaystyle\sum_{n=1}^{\infty} \frac{1}{(3n-2)^{n+(1/2)}}$

2. $\displaystyle\sum_{n=1}^{\infty} \frac{(\tan^{-1} n)^2}{n^2+1}$

3. $\displaystyle\sum_{n=1}^{\infty} (-1)^n \tanh n$

4. $\displaystyle\sum_{n=2}^{\infty} \frac{\log_n (n!)}{n^3}$

Which of the series $\sum_{n=1}^{\infty} a_n$ defined by the formulas in Exercises 5–8 converge, and which diverge? Give reasons for your answers.

5. $a_1 = 1, \quad a_{n+1} = \dfrac{n(n+1)}{(n+2)(n+3)} a_n$

   (*Hint:* Write out several terms, see which factors cancel, and then generalize.)

6. $a_1 = a_2 = 7, \quad a_{n+1} = \dfrac{n}{(n-1)(n+1)} a_n \quad \text{if } n \geq 2$

7. $a_1 = a_2 = 1, \quad a_{n+1} = \dfrac{1}{1+a_n} \quad \text{if } n \geq 2$

8. $a_n = 1/3^n \quad \text{if } n \text{ is odd}, \quad a_n = n/3^n \quad \text{if } n \text{ is even}$

Choosing Centers for Taylor Series

Taylor's formula

$$f(x) = f(a) + f'(a)(x-a) + \frac{f''(a)}{2!}(x-a)^2 + \cdots + \frac{f^{(n)}(a)}{n!}(x-a)^n + \frac{f^{(n+1)}(c)}{(n+1)!}(x-a)^{n+1}$$

expresses the value of f at x in terms of the values of f and its derivatives at $x = a$. In numerical computations, we therefore need a to be a point where we know the values of f and its derivatives. We also need a to be close enough to the values of f we are interested in to make $(x-a)^{n+1}$ so small we can neglect the remainder.

In Exercises 9–14, what Taylor series would you choose to represent the function near the given value of x? (There may be more than one good answer.) Write out the first four nonzero terms of the series you choose.

9. $\cos x$ near $x = 1$

10. $\sin x$ near $x = 6.3$

11. e^x near $x = 0.4$

12. $\ln x$ near $x = 1.3$

13. $\cos x$ near $x = 69$

14. $\tan^{-1} x$ near $x = 2$

Theory and Examples

15. Let a and b be constants with $0 < a < b$. Does the sequence $\{(a^n + b^n)^{1/n}\}$ converge? If it does converge, what is the limit?

16. Find the sum of the infinite series

$$1 + \frac{2}{10} + \frac{3}{10^2} + \frac{7}{10^3} + \frac{2}{10^4} + \frac{3}{10^5} + \frac{7}{10^6} + \frac{2}{10^7} + \frac{3}{10^8} + \frac{7}{10^9} + \cdots.$$

17. Evaluate

$$\sum_{n=0}^{\infty} \int_n^{n+1} \frac{1}{1+x^2}\, dx.$$

18. Find all values of x for which

$$\sum_{n=1}^{\infty} \frac{nx^n}{(n+1)(2x+1)^n}$$

converges absolutely.

19. **Generalizing Euler's constant** The accompanying figure shows the graph of a positive twice-differentiable decreasing function f whose second derivative is positive on $(0, \infty)$. For each n, the number A_n is the area of the lunar region between the curve and the line segment joining the points $(n, f(n))$ and $(n+1, f(n+1))$.

    a. Use the figure to show that $\sum_{n=1}^{\infty} A_n < (1/2)(f(1) - f(2))$.

    b. Then show the existence of

$$\lim_{n\to\infty} \left[\sum_{k=1}^{n} f(k) - \frac{1}{2}(f(1) + f(n)) - \int_1^n f(x)\, dx \right].$$

    c. Then show the existence of

$$\lim_{n\to\infty} \left[\sum_{k=1}^{n} f(k) - \int_1^n f(x)\, dx \right].$$

If $f(x) = 1/x$, the limit in part (c) is Euler's constant (Section 11.3, Exercise 41). (*Source:* "Convergence with Pictures" by P. J. Rippon, *American Mathematical Monthly*, Vol. 93, No. 6, 1986, pp. 476–478.)

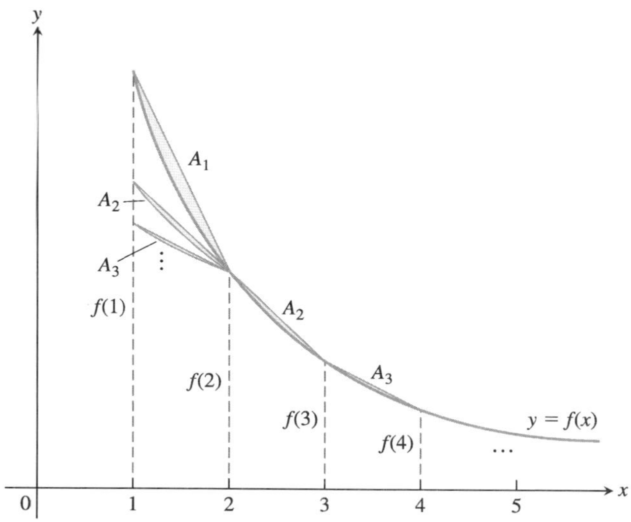

20. This exercise refers to the "right side up" equilateral triangle with sides of length $2b$ in the accompanying figure. "Upside down" equilateral triangles are removed from the original triangle as the sequence of pictures suggests. The sum of the areas removed from the original triangle forms an infinite series.

a. Find this infinite series.

b. Find the sum of this infinite series and hence find the total area removed from the original triangle.

c. Is every point on the original triangle removed? Explain why or why not.

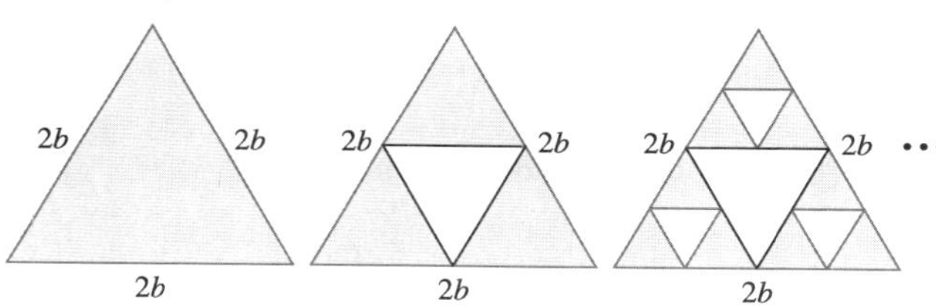

T **21. a.** Does the value of

$$\lim_{n\to\infty}\left(1-\frac{\cos(a/n)}{n}\right)^n, \quad a \text{ constant},$$

appear to depend on the value of a? If so, how?

b. Does the value of

$$\lim_{n\to\infty}\left(1-\frac{\cos(a/n)}{bn}\right)^n, \quad a \text{ and } b \text{ constant, } b \neq 0,$$

appear to depend on the value of b? If so, how?

c. Use calculus to confirm your findings in parts (a) and (b).

22. Show that if $\sum_{n=1}^{\infty} a_n$ converges, then

$$\sum_{n=1}^{\infty}\left(\frac{1+\sin(a_n)}{2}\right)^n$$

converges.

23. Find a value for the constant b that will make the radius of convergence of the power series

$$\sum_{n=2}^{\infty}\frac{b^n x^n}{\ln n}$$

equal to 5.

24. How do you know that the functions $\sin x$, $\ln x$, and e^x are not polynomials? Give reasons for your answer.

25. Find the value of a for which the limit

$$\lim_{x\to 0}\frac{\sin(ax)-\sin x - x}{x^3}$$

is finite and evaluate the limit.

26. Find values of a and b for which

$$\lim_{x\to 0}\frac{\cos(ax)-b}{2x^2} = -1.$$

27. Raabe's (or Gauss's) test The following test, which we state without proof, is an extension of the Ratio Test.

Raabe's test: If $\sum_{n=1}^{\infty} u_n$ is a series of positive constants and there exist constants C, K, and N such that

$$\frac{u_n}{u_{n+1}} = 1 + \frac{C}{n} + \frac{f(n)}{n^2}, \tag{1}$$

where $|f(n)| < K$ for $n \geq N$, then $\sum_{n=1}^{\infty} u_n$ converges if $C > 1$ and diverges if $C \leq 1$.

Show that the results of Raabe's test agree with what you know about the series $\sum_{n=1}^{\infty}(1/n^2)$ and $\sum_{n=1}^{\infty}(1/n)$.

28. (*Continuation of Exercise 27.*) Suppose that the terms of $\sum_{n=1}^{\infty} u_n$ are defined recursively by the formulas

$$u_1 = 1, \quad u_{n+1} = \frac{(2n-1)^2}{(2n)(2n+1)}u_n.$$

Apply Raabe's test to determine whether the series converges.

29. If $\sum_{n=1}^{\infty} a_n$ converges, and if $a_n \neq 1$ and $a_n > 0$ for all n,

a. Show that $\sum_{n=1}^{\infty} a_n^2$ converges.

b. Does $\sum_{n=1}^{\infty} a_n/(1-a_n)$ converge? Explain.

30. (*Continuation of Exercise 29.*) If $\sum_{n=1}^{\infty} a_n$ converges, and if $1 > a_n > 0$ for all n, show that $\sum_{n=1}^{\infty}\ln(1-a_n)$ converges.

(*Hint:* First show that $|\ln(1-a_n)| \leq a_n/(1-a_n)$.)

31. Nicole Oresme's Theorem Prove Nicole Oresme's Theorem that

$$1 + \frac{1}{2}\cdot 2 + \frac{1}{4}\cdot 3 + \cdots + \frac{n}{2^{n-1}} + \cdots = 4.$$

(*Hint:* Differentiate both sides of the equation $1/(1-x) = 1 + \sum_{n=1}^{\infty} x^n$.)

32. a. Show that

$$\sum_{n=1}^{\infty} \frac{n(n+1)}{x^n} = \frac{2x^2}{(x-1)^3}$$

for $|x| > 1$ by differentiating the identity

$$\sum_{n=1}^{\infty} x^{n+1} = \frac{x^2}{1-x}$$

twice, multiplying the result by x, and then replacing x by $1/x$.

b. Use part (a) to find the real solution greater than 1 of the equation

$$x = \sum_{n=1}^{\infty} \frac{n(n+1)}{x^n}.$$

33. A fast estimate of $\pi/2$ As you saw if you did Exercise 127 in Section 11.1, the sequence generated by starting with $x_0 = 1$ and applying the recursion formula $x_{n+1} = x_n + \cos x_n$ converges rapidly to $\pi/2$. To explain the speed of the convergence, let $\epsilon_n = (\pi/2) - x_n$. (See the accompanying figure.) Then

$$\begin{aligned}\epsilon_{n+1} &= \frac{\pi}{2} - x_n - \cos x_n \\ &= \epsilon_n - \cos\left(\frac{\pi}{2} - \epsilon_n\right) \\ &= \epsilon_n - \sin \epsilon_n \\ &= \frac{1}{3!}(\epsilon_n)^3 - \frac{1}{5!}(\epsilon_n)^5 + \cdots.\end{aligned}$$

Use this equality to show that

$$0 < \epsilon_{n+1} < \frac{1}{6}(\epsilon_n)^3.$$

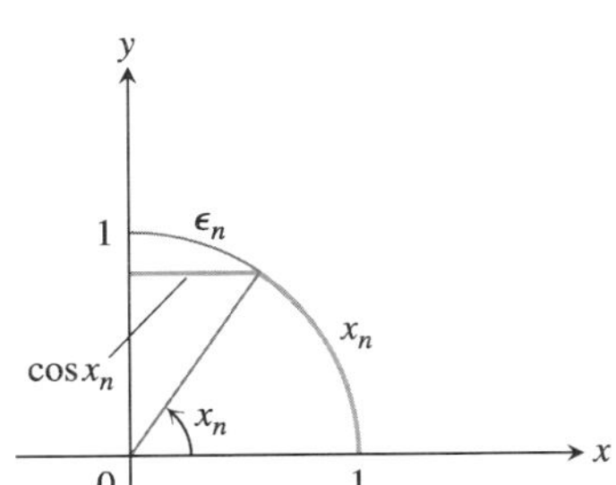

34. If $\sum_{n=1}^{\infty} a_n$ is a convergent series of positive numbers, can anything be said about the convergence of $\sum_{n=1}^{\infty} \ln(1 + a_n)$? Give reasons for your answer.

35. Quality control

a. Differentiate the series

$$\frac{1}{1-x} = 1 + x + x^2 + \cdots + x^n + \cdots$$

to obtain a series for $1/(1-x)^2$.

b. In one throw of two dice, the probability of getting a roll of 7 is $p = 1/6$. If you throw the dice repeatedly, the probability that a 7 will appear for the first time at the nth throw is $q^{n-1}p$, where $q = 1 - p = 5/6$. The expected number of throws until a 7 first appears is $\sum_{n=1}^{\infty} nq^{n-1}p$. Find the sum of this series.

c. As an engineer applying statistical control to an industrial operation, you inspect items taken at random from the assembly line. You classify each sampled item as either "good" or "bad." If the probability of an item's being good is p and of an item's being bad is $q = 1 - p$, the probability that the first bad item found is the nth one inspected is $p^{n-1}q$. The average number inspected up to and including the first bad item found is $\sum_{n=1}^{\infty} np^{n-1}q$. Evaluate this sum, assuming $0 < p < 1$.

36. Expected value Suppose that a random variable X may assume the values 1, 2, 3, ..., with probabilities $p_1, p_2, p_3, \ldots$, where p_k is the probability that X equals k ($k = 1, 2, 3, \ldots$). Suppose also that $p_k \geq 0$ and that $\sum_{k=1}^{\infty} p_k = 1$. The **expected value** of X, denoted by $E(X)$, is the number $\sum_{k=1}^{\infty} kp_k$, provided the series converges. In each of the following cases, show that $\sum_{k=1}^{\infty} p_k = 1$ and find $E(X)$ if it exists. (*Hint:* See Exercise 35.)

a. $p_k = 2^{-k}$ **b.** $p_k = \dfrac{5^{k-1}}{6^k}$

c. $p_k = \dfrac{1}{k(k+1)} = \dfrac{1}{k} - \dfrac{1}{k+1}$

T 37. Safe and effective dosage The concentration in the blood resulting from a single dose of a drug normally decreases with time as the drug is eliminated from the body. Doses may therefore need to be repeated periodically to keep the concentration from dropping below some particular level. One model for the effect of repeated doses gives the residual concentration just before the $(n + 1)$st dose as

$$R_n = C_0 e^{-kt_0} + C_0 e^{-2kt_0} + \cdots + C_0 e^{-nkt_0},$$

where C_0 = the change in concentration achievable by a single dose (mg/mL), k = the *elimination constant* (h^{-1}), and t_0 = time between doses (h). See the accompanying figure.

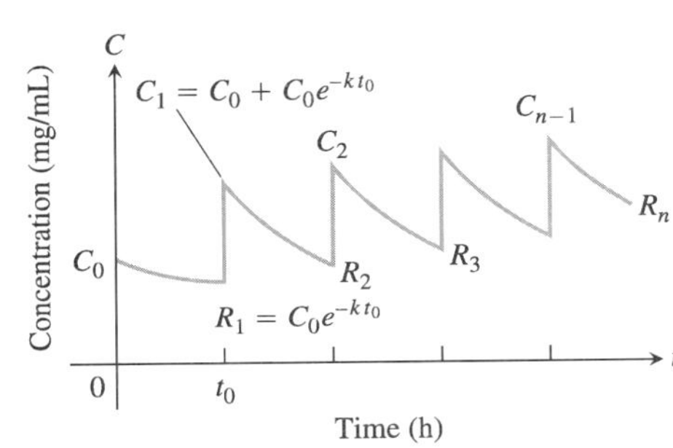

a. Write R_n in closed form as a single fraction, and find $R = \lim_{n\to\infty} R_n$.

b. Calculate R_1 and R_{10} for $C_0 = 1$ mg/mL, $k = 0.1\ \text{h}^{-1}$, and $t_0 = 10$ h. How good an estimate of R is R_{10}?

c. If $k = 0.01\ \text{h}^{-1}$ and $t_0 = 10$ h, find the smallest n such that $R_n > (1/2)R$.

(Source: Prescribing Safe and Effective Dosage, B. Horelick and S. Koont, COMAP, Inc., Lexington, MA.)

38. Time between drug doses *(Continuation of Exercise 37.)* If a drug is known to be ineffective below a concentration C_L and harmful above some higher concentration C_H, one needs to find values of C_0 and t_0 that will produce a concentration that is safe (not above C_H) but effective (not below C_L). See the accompanying figure. We therefore want to find values for C_0 and t_0 for which

$$R = C_L \quad \text{and} \quad C_0 + R = C_H.$$

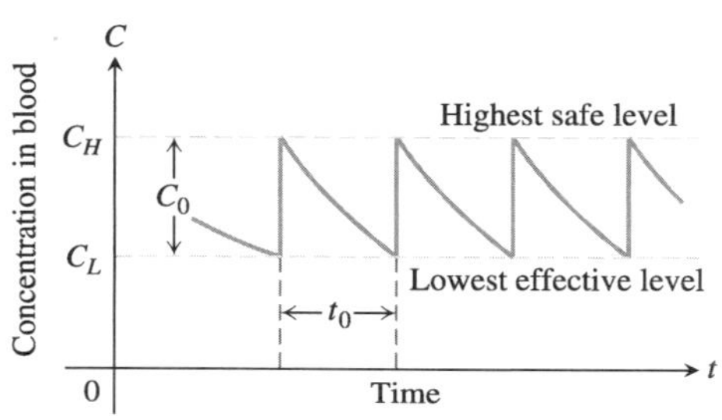

Thus $C_0 = C_H - C_L$. When these values are substituted in the equation for R obtained in part (a) of Exercise 37, the resulting equation simplifies to

$$t_0 = \frac{1}{k}\ln\frac{C_H}{C_L}.$$

To reach an effective level rapidly, one might administer a "loading" dose that would produce a concentration of C_H mg/mL. This could be followed every t_0 hours by a dose that raises the concentration by $C_0 = C_H - C_L$ mg/mL.

a. Verify the preceding equation for t_0.

b. If $k = 0.05\ \text{h}^{-1}$ and the highest safe concentration is e times the lowest effective concentration, find the length of time between doses that will assure safe and effective concentrations.

c. Given $C_H = 2$ mg/mL, $C_L = 0.5$ mg/mL, and $k = 0.02\ \text{h}^{-1}$, determine a scheme for administering the drug.

d. Suppose that $k = 0.2\ \text{h}^{-1}$ and that the smallest effective concentration is 0.03 mg/mL. A single dose that produces a concentration of 0.1 mg/mL is administered. About how long will the drug remain effective?

39. An infinite product The infinite product

$$\prod_{n=1}^{\infty}(1 + a_n) = (1 + a_1)(1 + a_2)(1 + a_3)\cdots$$

is said to converge if the series

$$\sum_{n=1}^{\infty}\ln(1 + a_n),$$

obtained by taking the natural logarithm of the product, converges. Prove that the product converges if $a_n > -1$ for every n and if $\sum_{n=1}^{\infty}|a_n|$ converges. (*Hint:* Show that

$$|\ln(1 + a_n)| \le \frac{|a_n|}{1 - |a_n|} \le 2|a_n|$$

when $|a_n| < 1/2$.)

40. If p is a constant, show that the series

$$1 + \sum_{n=3}^{\infty}\frac{1}{n \cdot \ln n \cdot [\ln(\ln n)]^p}$$

a. converges if $p > 1$, **b.** diverges if $p \le 1$. In general, if $f_1(x) = x$, $f_{n+1}(x) = \ln(f_n(x))$, and n takes on the values $1, 2, 3, \ldots$, we find that $f_2(x) = \ln x$, $f_3(x) = \ln(\ln x)$, and so on. If $f_n(a) > 1$, then

$$\int_a^{\infty}\frac{dx}{f_1(x)f_2(x)\cdots f_n(x)(f_{n+1}(x))^p}$$

converges if $p > 1$ and diverges if $p \le 1$.

41. a. Prove the following theorem: If $\{c_n\}$ is a sequence of numbers such that every sum $t_n = \sum_{k=1}^{n} c_k$ is bounded, then the series $\sum_{n=1}^{\infty} c_n/n$ converges and is equal to $\sum_{n=1}^{\infty} t_n/(n(n + 1))$.

Outline of proof: Replace c_1 by t_1 and c_n by $t_n - t_{n-1}$ for $n \ge 2$. If $s_{2n+1} = \sum_{k=1}^{2n+1} c_k/k$, show that

$$\begin{aligned} s_{2n+1} &= t_1\left(1 - \frac{1}{2}\right) + t_2\left(\frac{1}{2} - \frac{1}{3}\right) \\ &\quad + \cdots + t_{2n}\left(\frac{1}{2n} - \frac{1}{2n + 1}\right) + \frac{t_{2n+1}}{2n + 1} \\ &= \sum_{k=1}^{2n}\frac{t_k}{k(k + 1)} + \frac{t_{2n+1}}{2n + 1}. \end{aligned}$$

Because $|t_k| < M$ for some constant M, the series

$$\sum_{k=1}^{\infty}\frac{t_k}{k(k + 1)}$$

converges absolutely and s_{2n+1} has a limit as $n \to \infty$. Finally, if $s_{2n} = \sum_{k=1}^{2n} c_k/k$, then $s_{2n+1} - s_{2n} = c_{2n+1}/(2n + 1)$ approaches zero as $n \to \infty$ because $|c_{2n+1}| = |t_{2n+1} - t_{2n}| < 2M$. Hence the sequence of partial sums of the series $\sum c_k/k$ converges and the limit is $\sum_{k=1}^{\infty} t_k/(k(k + 1))$.

b. Show how the foregoing theorem applies to the alternating harmonic series

$$1-\frac{1}{2}+\frac{1}{3}-\frac{1}{4}+\frac{1}{5}-\frac{1}{6}+\cdots.$$

c. Show that the series

$$1-\frac{1}{2}-\frac{1}{3}+\frac{1}{4}+\frac{1}{5}-\frac{1}{6}-\frac{1}{7}+\cdots.$$

converges. (After the first term, the signs are two negative, two positive, two negative, two positive, and so on in that pattern.)

42. The convergence of $\sum_{n=1}^{\infty}[(-1)^{n-1}x^n]/n$ to $\ln(1+x)$ for $-1<x\le 1$

a. Show by long division or otherwise that

$$\frac{1}{1+t}=1-t+t^2-t^3+\cdots+(-1)^n t^n+\frac{(-1)^{n+1}t^{n+1}}{1+t}.$$

b. By integrating the equation of part (a) with respect to t from 0 to x, show that

$$\ln(1+x)=x-\frac{x^2}{2}+\frac{x^3}{3}-\frac{x^4}{4}+\cdots+(-1)^n\frac{x^{n+1}}{n+1}+R_{n+1}$$

where

$$R_{n+1}=(-1)^{n+1}\int_0^x\frac{t^{n+1}}{1+t}\,dt.$$

c. If $x\ge 0$, show that

$$|R_{n+1}|\le\int_0^x t^{n+1}\,dt=\frac{x^{n+2}}{n+2}.$$

(*Hint:* As t varies from 0 to x,

$$1+t\ge 1\quad\text{and}\quad t^{n+1}/(1+t)\le t^{n+1},$$

and

$$\left|\int_0^x f(t)\,dt\right|\le\int_0^x|f(t)|\,dt.\Big)$$

d. If $-1<x<0$, show that

$$|R_{n+1}|\le\left|\int_0^x\frac{t^{n+1}}{1-|x|}\,dt\right|=\frac{|x|^{n+2}}{(n+2)(1-|x|)}.$$

(*Hint:* If $x<t\le 0$, then $|1+t|\ge 1-|x|$ and

$$\left|\frac{t^{n+1}}{1+t}\right|\le\frac{|t|^{n+1}}{1-|x|}.\Big)$$

e. Use the foregoing results to prove that the series

$$x-\frac{x^2}{2}+\frac{x^3}{3}-\frac{x^4}{4}+\cdots+\frac{(-1)^n x^{n+1}}{n+1}+\cdots$$

converges to $\ln(1+x)$ for $-1<x\le 1$.

Chapter 11 Technology Application Projects

Mathematica/Maple Module

Bouncing Ball

The model predicts the height of a bouncing ball, and the time until it stops bouncing.

Mathematica/Maple Module

Taylor Polynomial Approximations of a Function

A graphical animation shows the convergence of the Taylor polynomials to functions having derivatives of all orders over an interval in their domains.

Chapter

12 VECTORS AND THE GEOMETRY OF SPACE

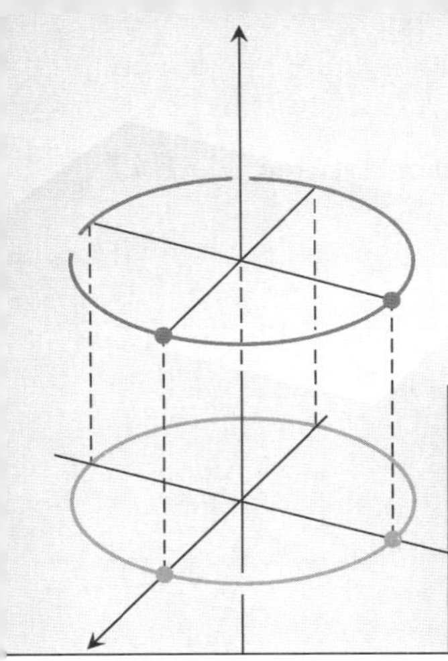

OVERVIEW To apply calculus in many real-world situations and in higher mathematics, we need a mathematical description of three-dimensional space. In this chapter we introduce three-dimensional coordinate systems and vectors. Building on what we already know about coordinates in the *xy*-plane, we establish coordinates in space by adding a third axis that measures distance above and below the *xy*-plane. Vectors are used to study the analytic geometry of space, where they give simple ways to describe lines, planes, surfaces, and curves in space. We use these geometric ideas in the rest of the book to study motion in space and the calculus of functions of several variables, with their many important applications in science, engineering, economics, and higher mathematics.

12.1 Three-Dimensional Coordinate Systems

To locate a point in space, we use three mutually perpendicular coordinate axes, arranged as in Figure 12.1. The axes shown there make a *right-handed* coordinate frame. When you hold your right hand so that the fingers curl from the positive x-axis toward the positive y-axis, your thumb points along the positive z-axis. So when you look down on the xy-plane from the positive direction of the z-axis, positive angles in the plane are measured counterclockwise from the positive x-axis and around the positive z-axis. (In a *left-handed* coordinate frame, the z-axis would point downward in Figure 12.1 and angles in the plane would be positive when measured clockwise from the positive x-axis. This is not the convention we have used for measuring angles in the xy-plane. Right-handed and left-handed coordinate frames are not equivalent.)

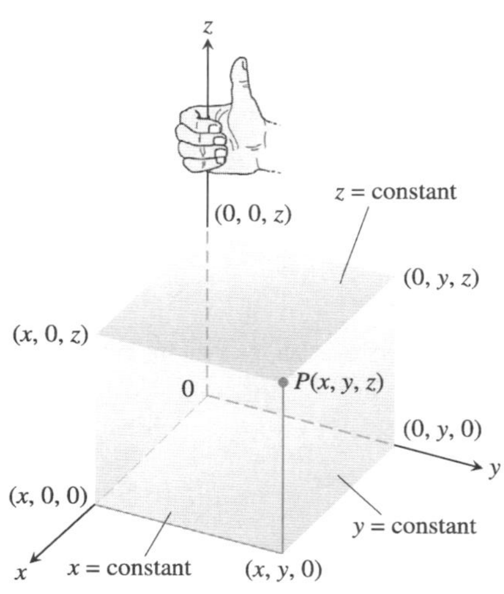

FIGURE 12.1 The Cartesian coordinate system is right-handed.

The Cartesian coordinates (x, y, z) of a point P in space are the numbers at which the planes through P perpendicular to the axes cut the axes. Cartesian coordinates for space are also called **rectangular coordinates** because the axes that define them meet at right angles. Points on the x-axis have y- and z-coordinates equal to zero. That is, they have coordinates of the form $(x, 0, 0)$. Similarly, points on the y-axis have coordinates of the form $(0, y, 0)$, and points on the z-axis have coordinates of the form $(0, 0, z)$.

The planes determined by the coordinates axes are the ***xy*-plane**, whose standard equation is $z = 0$; the ***yz*-plane**, whose standard equation is $x = 0$; and the ***xz*-plane**, whose standard equation is $y = 0$. They meet at the **origin** $(0, 0, 0)$ (Figure 12.2). The origin is also identified by simply 0 or sometimes the letter O.

The three **coordinate planes** $x = 0, y = 0$, and $z = 0$ divide space into eight cells called **octants**. The octant in which the point coordinates are all positive is called the **first octant**; there is no conventional numbering for the other seven octants.

The points in a plane perpendicular to the x-axis all have the same x-coordinate, this being the number at which that plane cuts the x-axis. The y- and z-coordinates can be any numbers. Similarly, the points in a plane perpendicular to the y-axis have a common y-coordinate and the points in a plane perpendicular to the z-axis have a common z-coordinate. To write equations for these planes, we name the common coordinate's value. The plane $x = 2$ is the plane perpendicular to the x-axis at $x = 2$. The plane $y = 3$ is the plane perpendicular to the y-axis at $y = 3$. The plane $z = 5$ is the plane perpendicular to the z-axis at $z = 5$. Figure 12.3 shows the planes $x = 2$, $y = 3$, and $z = 5$, together with their intersection point (2, 3, 5).

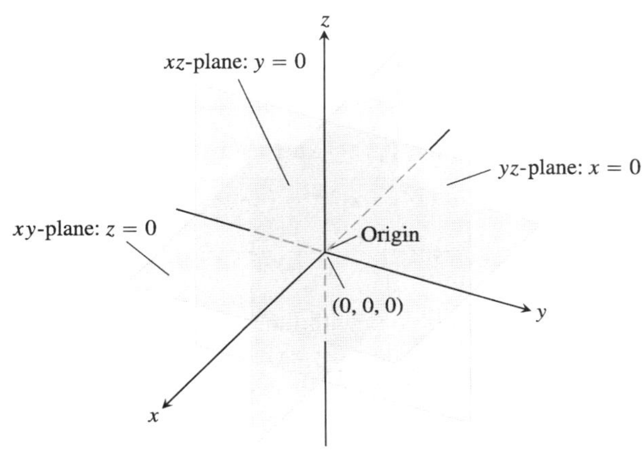

FIGURE 12.2 The planes $x = 0, y = 0$, and $z = 0$ divide space into eight octants.

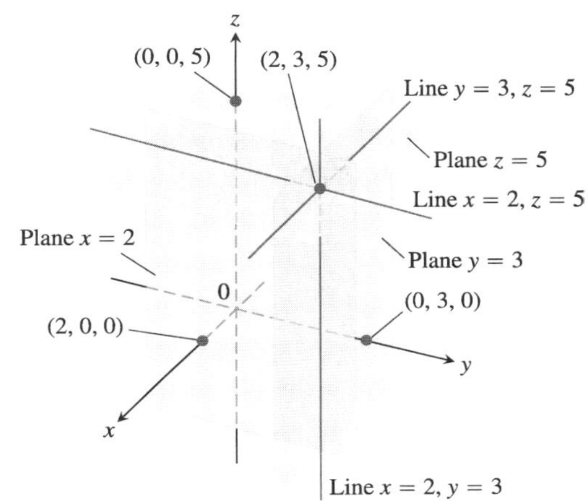

FIGURE 12.3 The planes $x = 2, y = 3$, and $z = 5$ determine three lines through the point (2, 3, 5).

The planes $x = 2$ and $y = 3$ in Figure 12.3 intersect in a line parallel to the z-axis. This line is described by the *pair* of equations $x = 2, y = 3$. A point (x, y, z) lies on the line if and only if $x = 2$ and $y = 3$. Similarly, the line of intersection of the planes $y = 3$ and $z = 5$ is described by the equation pair $y = 3, z = 5$. This line runs parallel to the x-axis. The line of intersection of the planes $x = 2$ and $z = 5$, parallel to the y-axis, is described by the equation pair $x = 2, z = 5$.

In the following examples, we match coordinate equations and inequalities with the sets of points they define in space.

EXAMPLE 1 Interpreting Equations and Inequalities Geometrically

(a) $z \geq 0$ — The half-space consisting of the points on and above the xy-plane.

(b) $x = -3$ — The plane perpendicular to the x-axis at $x = -3$. This plane lies parallel to the yz-plane and 3 units behind it.

(c) $z = 0, x \leq 0, y \geq 0$ — The second quadrant of the xy-plane.

(d) $x \geq 0, y \geq 0, z \geq 0$ — The first octant.

(e) $-1 \leq y \leq 1$ — The slab between the planes $y = -1$ and $y = 1$ (planes included).

(f) $y = -2, z = 2$ — The line in which the planes $y = -2$ and $z = 2$ intersect. Alternatively, the line through the point $(0, -2, 2)$ parallel to the x-axis. ■

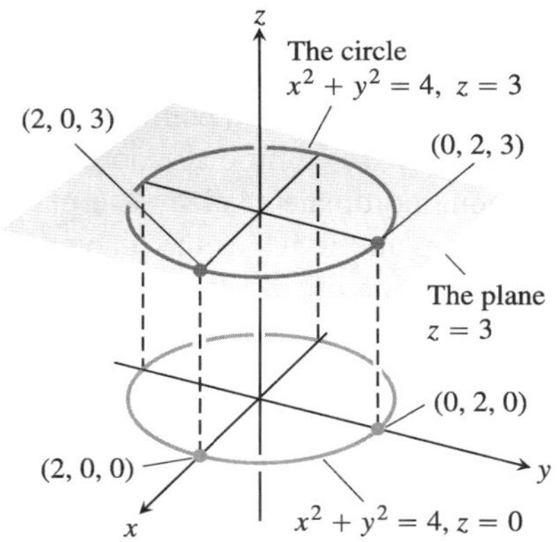

FIGURE 12.4 The circle $x^2 + y^2 = 4$ in the plane $z = 3$ (Example 2).

EXAMPLE 2 Graphing Equations

What points $P(x, y, z)$ satisfy the equations

$$x^2 + y^2 = 4 \quad \text{and} \quad z = 3?$$

Solution The points lie in the horizontal plane $z = 3$ and, in this plane, make up the circle $x^2 + y^2 = 4$. We call this set of points "the circle $x^2 + y^2 = 4$ in the plane $z = 3$" or, more simply, "the circle $x^2 + y^2 = 4, z = 3$" (Figure 12.4). ■

Distance and Spheres in Space

The formula for the distance between two points in the xy-plane extends to points in space.

> **The Distance Between $P_1(x_1, y_1, z_1)$ and $P_2(x_2, y_2, z_2)$ is**
>
> $$|P_1P_2| = \sqrt{(x_2 - x_1)^2 + (y_2 - y_1)^2 + (z_2 - z_1)^2}$$

Proof We construct a rectangular box with faces parallel to the coordinate planes and the points P_1 and P_2 at opposite corners of the box (Figure 12.5). If $A(x_2, y_1, z_1)$ and $B(x_2, y_2, z_1)$ are the vertices of the box indicated in the figure, then the three box edges P_1A, AB, and BP_2 have lengths

$$|P_1A| = |x_2 - x_1|, \qquad |AB| = |y_2 - y_1|, \qquad |BP_2| = |z_2 - z_1|.$$

Because triangles P_1BP_2 and P_1AB are both right-angled, two applications of the Pythagorean theorem give

$$|P_1P_2|^2 = |P_1B|^2 + |BP_2|^2 \quad \text{and} \quad |P_1B|^2 = |P_1A|^2 + |AB|^2$$

(see Figure 12.5).

So

$$\begin{aligned}
|P_1P_2|^2 &= |P_1B|^2 + |BP_2|^2 \\
&= |P_1A|^2 + |AB|^2 + |BP_2|^2 && \text{Substitute } |P_1B|^2 = |P_1A|^2 + |AB|^2. \\
&= |x_2 - x_1|^2 + |y_2 - y_1|^2 + |z_2 - z_1|^2 \\
&= (x_2 - x_1)^2 + (y_2 - y_1)^2 + (z_2 - z_1)^2
\end{aligned}$$

Therefore

$$|P_1P_2| = \sqrt{(x_2 - x_1)^2 + (y_2 - y_1)^2 + (z_2 - z_1)^2}$$ ■

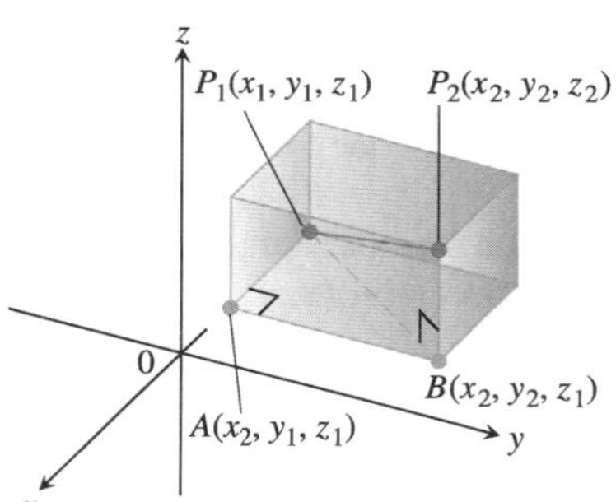

FIGURE 12.5 We find the distance between P_1 and P_2 by applying the Pythagorean theorem to the right triangles P_1AB and P_1BP_2.

EXAMPLE 3 Finding the Distance Between Two Points

The distance between $P_1(2, 1, 5)$ and $P_2(-2, 3, 0)$ is

$$\begin{aligned}
|P_1P_2| &= \sqrt{(-2 - 2)^2 + (3 - 1)^2 + (0 - 5)^2} \\
&= \sqrt{16 + 4 + 25} \\
&= \sqrt{45} \approx 6.708.
\end{aligned}$$ ■

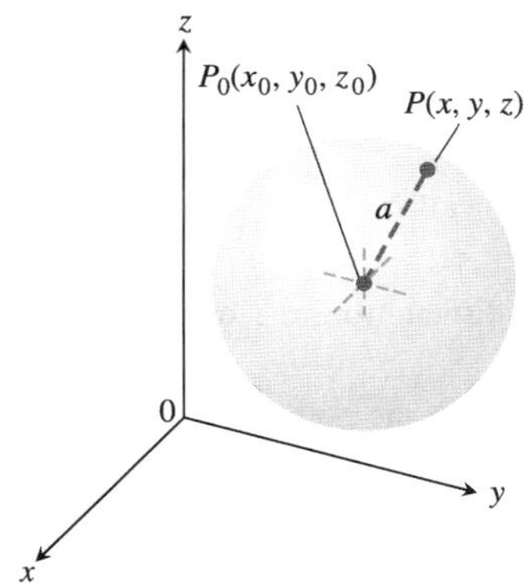

FIGURE 12.6 The standard equation of the sphere of radius a centered at the point (x_0, y_0, z_0) is

$$(x - x_0)^2 + (y - y_0)^2 + (z - z_0)^2 = a^2.$$

We can use the distance formula to write equations for spheres in space (Figure 12.6). A point $P(x, y, z)$ lies on the sphere of radius a centered at $P_0(x_0, y_0, z_0)$ precisely when $|P_0P| = a$ or

$$(x - x_0)^2 + (y - y_0)^2 + (z - z_0)^2 = a^2.$$

The Standard Equation for the Sphere of Radius a and Center (x_0, y_0, z_0)

$$(x - x_0)^2 + (y - y_0)^2 + (z - z_0)^2 = a^2$$

EXAMPLE 4 Finding the Center and Radius of a Sphere

Find the center and radius of the sphere

$$x^2 + y^2 + z^2 + 3x - 4z + 1 = 0.$$

Solution We find the center and radius of a sphere the way we find the center and radius of a circle: Complete the squares on the x-, y-, and z-terms as necessary and write each quadratic as a squared linear expression. Then, from the equation in standard form, read off the center and radius. For the sphere here, we have

$$x^2 + y^2 + z^2 + 3x - 4z + 1 = 0$$

$$(x^2 + 3x) + y^2 + (z^2 - 4z) = -1$$

$$\left(x^2 + 3x + \left(\frac{3}{2}\right)^2\right) + y^2 + \left(z^2 - 4z + \left(\frac{-4}{2}\right)^2\right) = -1 + \left(\frac{3}{2}\right)^2 + \left(\frac{-4}{2}\right)^2$$

$$\left(x + \frac{3}{2}\right)^2 + y^2 + (z - 2)^2 = -1 + \frac{9}{4} + 4 = \frac{21}{4}.$$

From this standard form, we read that $x_0 = -3/2$, $y_0 = 0$, $z_0 = 2$, and $a = \sqrt{21}/2$. The center is $(-3/2, 0, 2)$. The radius is $\sqrt{21}/2$. ■

EXAMPLE 5 Interpreting Equations and Inequalities

(a) $x^2 + y^2 + z^2 < 4$ The interior of the sphere $x^2 + y^2 + z^2 = 4$.

(b) $x^2 + y^2 + z^2 \le 4$ The solid ball bounded by the sphere $x^2 + y^2 + z^2 = 4$. Alternatively, the sphere $x^2 + y^2 + z^2 = 4$ together with its interior.

(c) $x^2 + y^2 + z^2 > 4$ The exterior of the sphere $x^2 + y^2 + z^2 = 4$.

(d) $x^2 + y^2 + z^2 = 4, z \le 0$ The lower hemisphere cut from the sphere $x^2 + y^2 + z^2 = 4$ by the xy-plane (the plane $z = 0$). ■

Just as polar coordinates give another way to locate points in the xy-plane (Section 10.5), alternative coordinate systems, different from the Cartesian coordinate system developed here, exist for three-dimensional space. We examine two of these coordinate systems in Section 15.6.

EXERCISES 12.1

Sets, Equations, and Inequalities

In Exercises 1–12, give a geometric description of the set of points in space whose coordinates satisfy the given pairs of equations.

1. $x = 2, \quad y = 3$ **2.** $x = -1, \quad z = 0$

3. $y = 0, \quad z = 0$ **4.** $x = 1, \quad y = 0$

5. $x^2 + y^2 = 4, \quad z = 0$ **6.** $x^2 + y^2 = 4, \quad z = -2$

7. $x^2 + z^2 = 4, \quad y = 0$ **8.** $y^2 + z^2 = 1, \quad x = 0$

9. $x^2 + y^2 + z^2 = 1, \quad x = 0$

10. $x^2 + y^2 + z^2 = 25, \quad y = -4$

11. $x^2 + y^2 + (z + 3)^2 = 25, \quad z = 0$

12. $x^2 + (y - 1)^2 + z^2 = 4, \quad y = 0$

In Exercises 13–18, describe the sets of points in space whose coordinates satisfy the given inequalities or combinations of equations and inequalities.

13. a. $x \ge 0, \quad y \ge 0, \quad z = 0$ **b.** $x \ge 0, \quad y \le 0, \quad z = 0$

14. a. $0 \le x \le 1$ **b.** $0 \le x \le 1, \quad 0 \le y \le 1$

c. $0 \le x \le 1, \quad 0 \le y \le 1, \quad 0 \le z \le 1$

15. a. $x^2 + y^2 + z^2 \le 1$ **b.** $x^2 + y^2 + z^2 > 1$

16. a. $x^2 + y^2 \le 1, \quad z = 0$ **b.** $x^2 + y^2 \le 1, \quad z = 3$

c. $x^2 + y^2 \le 1$, no restriction on z

17. a. $x^2 + y^2 + z^2 = 1, \quad z \ge 0$

b. $x^2 + y^2 + z^2 \le 1, \quad z \ge 0$

18. a. $x = y, \quad z = 0$ **b.** $x = y$, no restriction on z

In Exercises 19–28, describe the given set with a single equation or with a pair of equations.

19. The plane perpendicular to the

a. x-axis at $(3, 0, 0)$ **b.** y-axis at $(0, -1, 0)$

c. z-axis at $(0, 0, -2)$

20. The plane through the point $(3, -1, 2)$ perpendicular to the

a. x-axis **b.** y-axis **c.** z-axis

21. The plane through the point $(3, -1, 1)$ parallel to the

a. xy-plane **b.** yz-plane **c.** xz-plane

22. The circle of radius 2 centered at $(0, 0, 0)$ and lying in the

a. xy-plane **b.** yz-plane **c.** xz-plane

23. The circle of radius 2 centered at $(0, 2, 0)$ and lying in the

a. xy-plane **b.** yz-plane **c.** plane $y = 2$

24. The circle of radius 1 centered at $(-3, 4, 1)$ and lying in a plane parallel to the

a. xy-plane **b.** yz-plane **c.** xz-plane

25. The line through the point $(1, 3, -1)$ parallel to the

a. x-axis **b.** y-axis **c.** z-axis

26. The set of points in space equidistant from the origin and the point $(0, 2, 0)$

27. The circle in which the plane through the point $(1, 1, 3)$ perpendicular to the z-axis meets the sphere of radius 5 centered at the origin

28. The set of points in space that lie 2 units from the point $(0, 0, 1)$ and, at the same time, 2 units from the point $(0, 0, -1)$

Write inequalities to describe the sets in Exercises 29–34.

29. The slab bounded by the planes $z = 0$ and $z = 1$ (planes included)

30. The solid cube in the first octant bounded by the coordinate planes and the planes $x = 2, y = 2$, and $z = 2$

31. The half-space consisting of the points on and below the xy-plane

32. The upper hemisphere of the sphere of radius 1 centered at the origin

33. The **(a)** interior and **(b)** exterior of the sphere of radius 1 centered at the point $(1, 1, 1)$

34. The closed region bounded by the spheres of radius 1 and radius 2 centered at the origin. (*Closed* means the spheres are to be included. Had we wanted the spheres left out, we would have asked for the *open* region bounded by the spheres. This is analogous to the way we use *closed* and *open* to describe intervals: *closed* means endpoints included, *open* means endpoints left out. Closed sets include boundaries; open sets leave them out.)

Distance

In Exercises 35–40, find the distance between points P_1 and P_2.

35. $P_1(1, 1, 1), \quad P_2(3, 3, 0)$

36. $P_1(-1, 1, 5), \quad P_2(2, 5, 0)$

37. $P_1(1, 4, 5), \quad P_2(4, -2, 7)$

38. $P_1(3, 4, 5), \quad P_2(2, 3, 4)$

39. $P_1(0, 0, 0), \quad P_2(2, -2, -2)$

40. $P_1(5, 3, -2), \quad P_2(0, 0, 0)$

Spheres

Find the centers and radii of the spheres in Exercises 41–44.

41. $(x + 2)^2 + y^2 + (z - 2)^2 = 8$

42. $\left(x + \frac{1}{2}\right)^2 + \left(y + \frac{1}{2}\right)^2 + \left(z + \frac{1}{2}\right)^2 = \frac{21}{4}$

43. $\left(x - \sqrt{2}\right)^2 + \left(y - \sqrt{2}\right)^2 + \left(z + \sqrt{2}\right)^2 = 2$

44. $x^2 + \left(y + \frac{1}{3}\right)^2 + \left(z - \frac{1}{3}\right)^2 = \frac{29}{9}$

Find equations for the spheres whose centers and radii are given in Exercises 45–48.

	Center	Radius
45.	(1, 2, 3)	$\sqrt{14}$
46.	(0, −1, 5)	2
47.	(−2, 0, 0)	$\sqrt{3}$
48.	(0, −7, 0)	7

Find the centers and radii of the spheres in Exercises 49–52.

49. $x^2 + y^2 + z^2 + 4x - 4z = 0$

50. $x^2 + y^2 + z^2 - 6y + 8z = 0$

51. $2x^2 + 2y^2 + 2z^2 + x + y + z = 9$

52. $3x^2 + 3y^2 + 3z^2 + 2y - 2z = 9$

Theory and Examples

53. Find a formula for the distance from the point $P(x, y, z)$ to the

a. x-axis **b.** y-axis **c.** z-axis

54. Find a formula for the distance from the point $P(x, y, z)$ to the

a. xy-plane **b.** yz-plane **c.** xz-plane

55. Find the perimeter of the triangle with vertices $A(-1, 2, 1)$, $B(1, -1, 3)$, and $C(3, 4, 5)$.

56. Show that the point $P(3, 1, 2)$ is equidistant from the points $A(2, -1, 3)$ and $B(4, 3, 1)$.

12.2 Vectors

Some of the things we measure are determined simply by their magnitudes. To record mass, length, or time, for example, we need only write down a number and name an appropriate unit of measure. We need more information to describe a force, displacement, or velocity. To describe a force, we need to record the direction in which it acts as well as how large it is. To describe a body's displacement, we have to say in what direction it moved as well as how far. To describe a body's velocity, we have to know where the body is headed as well as how fast it is going.

Component Form

A quantity such as force, displacement, or velocity is called a *vector* and is represented by a **directed line segment** (Figure 12.7). The arrow points in the direction of the action and its length gives the magnitude of the action in terms of a suitably chosen unit. For example, a force vector points in the direction in which the force acts; its length is a measure of the force's strength; a velocity vector points in the direction of motion and its length is the speed of the moving object. Figure 12.8 displays the velocity vector **v** at a specific location for a particle moving along a path in the plane or in space. (This application of vectors is studied in Chapter 13.)

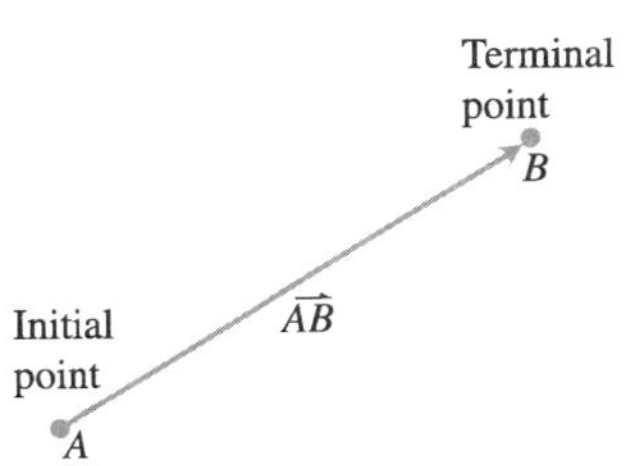

FIGURE 12.7 The directed line segment $\overrightarrow{AB}$.

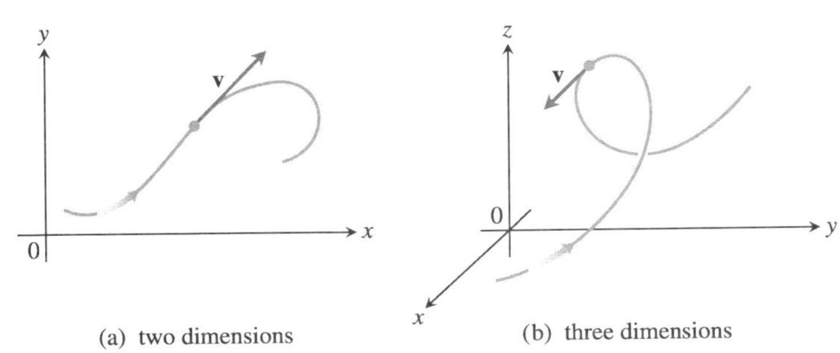

FIGURE 12.8 The velocity vector of a particle moving along a path (a) in the plane (b) in space. The arrowhead on the path indicates the direction of motion of the particle.

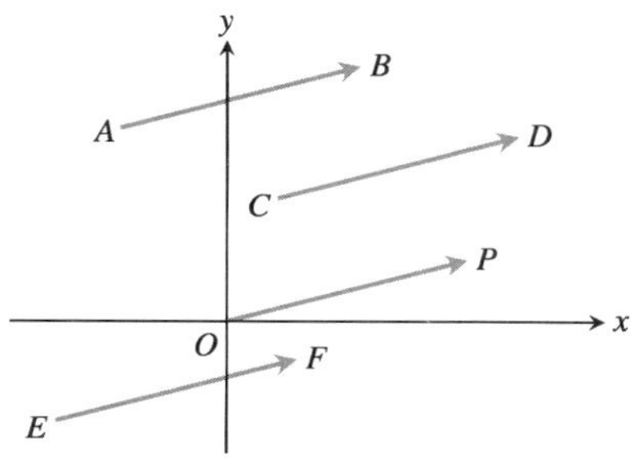

FIGURE 12.9 The four arrows in the plane (directed line segments) shown here have the same length and direction. They therefore represent the same vector, and we write $\overrightarrow{AB} = \overrightarrow{CD} = \overrightarrow{OP} = \overrightarrow{EF}$.

DEFINITIONS Vector, Initial and Terminal Point, Length

A **vector** is a directed line segment. The directed line segment $\overrightarrow{AB}$ has **initial point** A and **terminal point** B; its **length** is denoted by $|\overrightarrow{AB}|$. Two vectors are **equal** if they have the same length and direction.

The arrows we use when we draw vectors are understood to represent the same vector if they have the same length, are parallel, and point in the same direction (Figure 12.9) regardless of the initial point.

In textbooks, vectors are usually written in lowercase, boldface letters, for example **u**, **v**, and **w**. Sometimes we use uppercase boldface letters, such as **F**, to denote a force vector. In handwritten form, it is customary to draw small arrows above the letters, for example $\vec{u}$, $\vec{v}$, $\vec{w}$, and $\vec{F}$.

We need a way to represent vectors algebraically so that we can be more precise about the direction of a vector.

Let $\mathbf{v} = \overrightarrow{PQ}$. There is one directed line segment equal to $\overrightarrow{PQ}$ whose initial point is the origin (Figure 12.10). It is the representative of **v** in **standard position** and is the vector we normally use to represent **v**. We can specify **v** by writing the coordinates of its terminal point (v_1, v_2, v_3) when **v** is in standard position. If **v** is a vector in the plane its terminal point (v_1, v_2) has two coordinates.

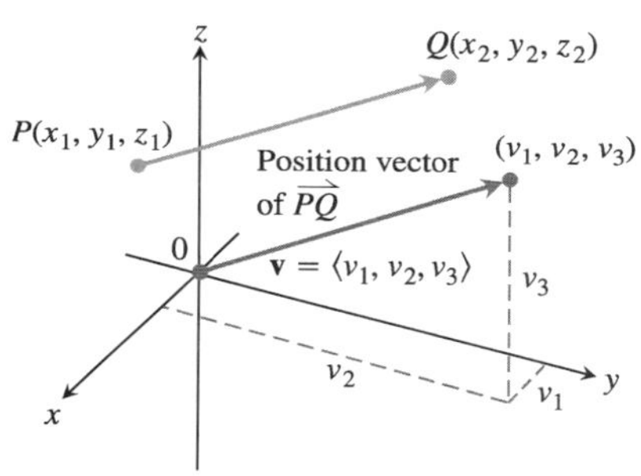

FIGURE 12.10 A vector $\overrightarrow{PQ}$ in standard position has its initial point at the origin. The directed line segments $\overrightarrow{PQ}$ and **v** are parallel and have the same length.

DEFINITION Component Form

If **v** is a **two-dimensional** vector in the plane equal to the vector with initial point at the origin and terminal point (v_1, v_2), then the **component form** of **v** is

$$\mathbf{v} = \langle v_1, v_2 \rangle .$$

If **v** is a **three-dimensional** vector equal to the vector with initial point at the origin and terminal point (v_1, v_2, v_3), then the **component form** of **v** is

$$\mathbf{v} = \langle v_1, v_2, v_3 \rangle .$$

So a two-dimensional vector is an ordered pair $\mathbf{v} = \langle v_1, v_2 \rangle$ of real numbers, and a three-dimensional vector is an ordered triple $\mathbf{v} = \langle v_1, v_2, v_3 \rangle$ of real numbers. The numbers v_1, v_2, and v_3 are called the **components** of **v**.

Observe that if $\mathbf{v} = \langle v_1, v_2, v_3 \rangle$ is represented by the directed line segment $\overrightarrow{PQ}$, where the initial point is $P(x_1, y_1, z_1)$ and the terminal point is $Q(x_2, y_2, z_2)$, then $x_1 + v_1 = x_2, y_1 + v_2 = y_2$, and $z_1 + v_3 = z_2$ (see Figure 12.10). Thus, $v_1 = x_2 - x_1, v_2 = y_2 - y_1$, and $v_3 = z_2 - z_1$ are the components of $\overrightarrow{PQ}$.

In summary, given the points $P(x_1, y_1, z_1)$ and $Q(x_2, y_2, z_2)$, the standard position vector $\mathbf{v} = \langle v_1, v_2, v_3 \rangle$ equal to $\overrightarrow{PQ}$ is

$$\mathbf{v} = \langle x_2 - x_1, y_2 - y_1, z_2, -z_1 \rangle .$$

If **v** is two-dimensional with $P(x_1, y_1)$ and $Q(x_2, y_2)$ as points in the plane, then $\mathbf{v} = \langle x_2 - x_1, y_2 - y_1 \rangle$. There is no third component for planar vectors. With this understanding, we will develop the algebra of three-dimensional vectors and simply drop the third component when the vector is two-dimensional (a planar vector).

Two vectors are equal if and only if their standard position vectors are identical. Thus $\langle u_1, u_2, u_3\rangle$ and $\langle v_1, v_2, v_3\rangle$ are equal if and only if $u_1 = v_1$, $u_2 = v_2$, and $u_3 = v_3$.

The **magnitude** or **length** of the vector $\overrightarrow{PQ}$ is the length of any of its equivalent directed line segment representations. In particular, if $\mathbf{v} = \langle x_2 - x_1, y_2 - y_1, z_2 - z_1\rangle$ is the standard position vector for $\overrightarrow{PQ}$, then the distance formula gives the magnitude or length of $\mathbf{v}$, denoted by the symbol $|\mathbf{v}|$ or $\|\mathbf{v}\|$.

> The **magnitude** or **length** of the vector $\mathbf{v} = \overrightarrow{PQ}$ is the nonnegative number
>
> $$|\mathbf{v}| = \sqrt{v_1^2 + v_2^2 + v_3^2} = \sqrt{(x_2 - x_1)^2 + (y_2 - y_1)^2 + (z_2 - z_1)^2}$$
>
> (See Figure 12.10.)

The only vector with length 0 is the **zero vector** $\mathbf{0} = \langle 0, 0\rangle$ or $\mathbf{0} = \langle 0, 0, 0\rangle$. This vector is also the only vector with no specific direction.

EXAMPLE 1 Component Form and Length of a Vector

Find the **(a)** component form and **(b)** length of the vector with initial point $P(-3, 4, 1)$ and terminal point $Q(-5, 2, 2)$.

Solution

(a) The standard position vector $\mathbf{v}$ representing $\overrightarrow{PQ}$ has components

$$v_1 = x_2 - x_1 = -5 - (-3) = -2, \qquad v_2 = y_2 - y_1 = 2 - 4 = -2,$$

and

$$v_3 = z_2 - z_1 = 2 - 1 = 1.$$

The component form of $\overrightarrow{PQ}$ is

$$\mathbf{v} = \langle -2, -2, 1\rangle.$$

(b) The length or magnitude of $\mathbf{v} = \overrightarrow{PQ}$ is

$$|\mathbf{v}| = \sqrt{(-2)^2 + (-2)^2 + (1)^2} = \sqrt{9} = 3.$$ ■

EXAMPLE 2 Force Moving a Cart

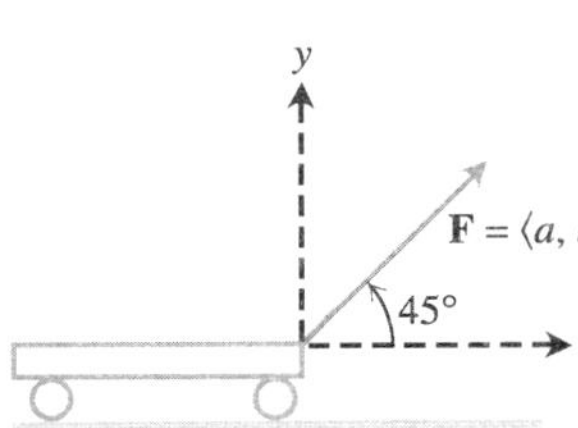

FIGURE 12.11 The force pulling the cart forward is represented by the vector **F** of magnitude 20 (pounds) making an angle of 45° with the horizontal ground (positive x-axis) (Example 2).

A small cart is being pulled along a smooth horizontal floor with a 20-lb force **F** making a 45° angle to the floor (Figure 12.11). What is the *effective* force moving the cart forward?

Solution The effective force is the horizontal component of $\mathbf{F} = \langle a, b\rangle$, given by

$$a = |\mathbf{F}| \cos 45° = (20)\left(\frac{\sqrt{2}}{2}\right) \approx 14.14 \text{ lb}.$$

Notice that **F** is a two-dimensional vector. ■

Vector Algebra Operations

Two principal operations involving vectors are *vector addition* and *scalar multiplication*. A **scalar** is simply a real number, and is called such when we want to draw attention to its differences from vectors. Scalars can be positive, negative, or zero.

DEFINITIONS Vector Addition and Multiplication of a Vector by a Scalar

Let $\mathbf{u} = \langle u_1, u_2, u_3 \rangle$ and $\mathbf{v} = \langle v_1, v_2, v_3 \rangle$ be vectors with k a scalar.

Addition: $\mathbf{u} + \mathbf{v} = \langle u_1 + v_1, u_2 + v_2, u_3 + v_3 \rangle$

Scalar multiplication: $k\mathbf{u} = \langle ku_1, ku_2, ku_3 \rangle$

We add vectors by adding the corresponding components of the vectors. We multiply a vector by a scalar by multiplying each component by the scalar. The definitions apply to planar vectors except there are only two components, $\langle u_1, u_2 \rangle$ and $\langle v_1, v_2 \rangle$.

The definition of vector addition is illustrated geometrically for planar vectors in Figure 12.12a, where the initial point of one vector is placed at the terminal point of the other. Another interpretation is shown in Figure 12.12b (called the **parallelogram law** of addition), where the sum, called the **resultant vector**, is the diagonal of the parallelogram. In physics, forces add vectorially as do velocities, accelerations, and so on. So the force acting on a particle subject to electric and gravitational forces is obtained by adding the two force vectors.

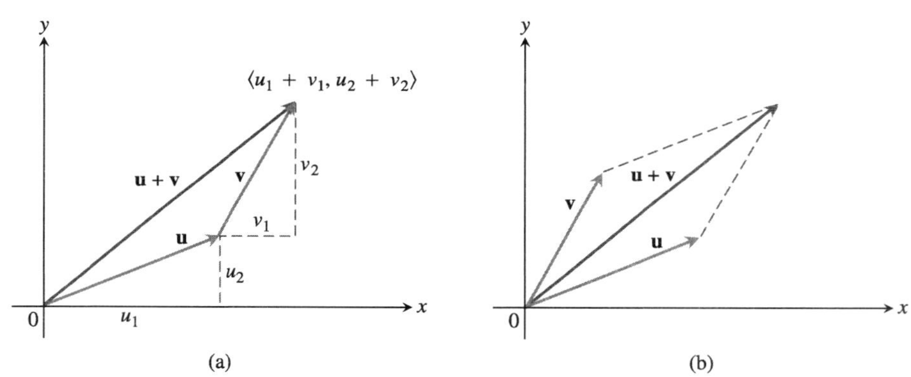

FIGURE 12.12 (a) Geometric interpretation of the vector sum. (b) The parallelogram law of vector addition.

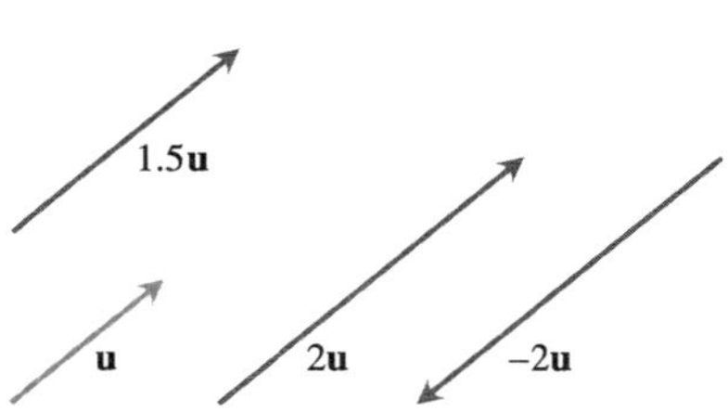

FIGURE 12.13 Scalar multiples of **u**.

Figure 12.13 displays a geometric interpretation of the product $k\mathbf{u}$ of the scalar k and vector $\mathbf{u}$. If $k > 0$, then $k\mathbf{u}$ has the same direction as $\mathbf{u}$; if $k < 0$, then the direction of $k\mathbf{u}$ is opposite to that of $\mathbf{u}$. Comparing the lengths of $\mathbf{u}$ and $k\mathbf{u}$, we see that

$$\begin{aligned} |k\mathbf{u}| &= \sqrt{(ku_1)^2 + (ku_2)^2 + (ku_3)^2} = \sqrt{k^2(u_1{}^2 + u_2{}^2 + u_3{}^2)} \\ &= \sqrt{k^2}\sqrt{u_1{}^2 + u_2{}^2 + u_3{}^2} = |k|\,|\mathbf{u}|. \end{aligned}$$

The length of $k\mathbf{u}$ is the absolute value of the scalar k times the length of $\mathbf{u}$. The vector $(-1)\mathbf{u} = -\mathbf{u}$ has the same length as $\mathbf{u}$ but points in the opposite direction.

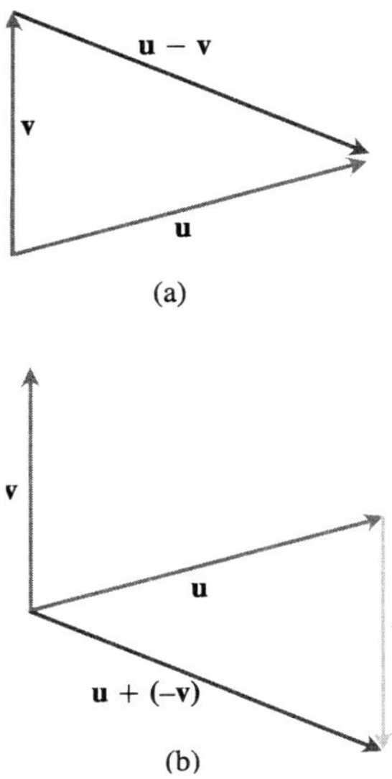

FIGURE 12.14 (a) The vector $\mathbf{u} - \mathbf{v}$, when added to $\mathbf{v}$, gives $\mathbf{u}$. (b) $\mathbf{u} - \mathbf{v} = \mathbf{u} + (-\mathbf{v})$.

By the **difference** $\mathbf{u} - \mathbf{v}$ of two vectors, we mean

$$\mathbf{u} - \mathbf{v} = \mathbf{u} + (-\mathbf{v}).$$

If $\mathbf{u} = \langle u_1, u_2, u_3 \rangle$ and $\mathbf{v} = \langle v_1, v_2, v_3 \rangle$, then

$$\mathbf{u} - \mathbf{v} = \langle u_1 - v_1, u_2 - v_2, u_3 - v_3 \rangle.$$

Note that $(\mathbf{u} - \mathbf{v}) + \mathbf{v} = \mathbf{u}$, so adding the vector $(\mathbf{u} - \mathbf{v})$ to $\mathbf{v}$ gives $\mathbf{u}$ (Figure 12.14a). Figure 12.14b shows the difference $\mathbf{u} - \mathbf{v}$ as the sum $\mathbf{u} + (-\mathbf{v})$.

EXAMPLE 3 Performing Operations on Vectors

Let $\mathbf{u} = \langle -1, 3, 1 \rangle$ and $\mathbf{v} = \langle 4, 7, 0 \rangle$. Find

(a) $2\mathbf{u} + 3\mathbf{v}$ **(b)** $\mathbf{u} - \mathbf{v}$ **(c)** $\left|\frac{1}{2}\mathbf{u}\right|$.

Solution

(a) $2\mathbf{u} + 3\mathbf{v} = 2\langle -1, 3, 1 \rangle + 3\langle 4, 7, 0 \rangle = \langle -2, 6, 2 \rangle + \langle 12, 21, 0 \rangle = \langle 10, 27, 2 \rangle$

(b) $\mathbf{u} - \mathbf{v} = \langle -1, 3, 1 \rangle - \langle 4, 7, 0 \rangle = \langle -1 - 4, 3 - 7, 1 - 0 \rangle = \langle -5, -4, 1 \rangle$

(c) $\left|\frac{1}{2}\mathbf{u}\right| = \left|\left\langle -\frac{1}{2}, \frac{3}{2}, \frac{1}{2} \right\rangle\right| = \sqrt{\left(-\frac{1}{2}\right)^2 + \left(\frac{3}{2}\right)^2 + \left(\frac{1}{2}\right)^2} = \frac{1}{2}\sqrt{11}.$ ∎

Vector operations have many of the properties of ordinary arithmetic. These properties are readily verified using the definitions of vector addition and multiplication by a scalar.

Properties of Vector Operations

Let $\mathbf{u}$, $\mathbf{v}$, $\mathbf{w}$ be vectors and a, b be scalars.

1. $\mathbf{u} + \mathbf{v} = \mathbf{v} + \mathbf{u}$	**2.** $(\mathbf{u} + \mathbf{v}) + \mathbf{w} = \mathbf{u} + (\mathbf{v} + \mathbf{w})$
3. $\mathbf{u} + \mathbf{0} = \mathbf{u}$	**4.** $\mathbf{u} + (-\mathbf{u}) = \mathbf{0}$
5. $0\mathbf{u} = \mathbf{0}$	**6.** $1\mathbf{u} = \mathbf{u}$
7. $a(b\mathbf{u}) = (ab)\mathbf{u}$	**8.** $a(\mathbf{u} + \mathbf{v}) = a\mathbf{u} + a\mathbf{v}$
9. $(a + b)\mathbf{u} = a\mathbf{u} + b\mathbf{u}$	

An important application of vectors occurs in navigation.

EXAMPLE 4 Finding Ground Speed and Direction

A Boeing® 767® airplane, flying due east at 500 mph in still air, encounters a 70-mph tailwind blowing in the direction 60° north of east. The airplane holds its compass heading due east but, because of the wind, acquires a new ground speed and direction. What are they?

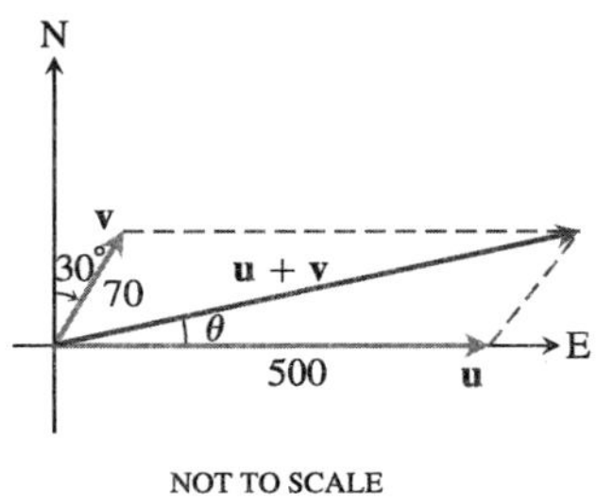

FIGURE 12.15 Vectors representing the velocities of the airplane **u** and tailwind **v** in Example 4.

Solution If **u** = the velocity of the airplane alone and **v** = the velocity of the tailwind, then $|\mathbf{u}| = 500$ and $|\mathbf{v}| = 70$ (Figure 12.15). The velocity of the airplane with respect to the ground is given by the magnitude and direction of the *resultant vector* $\mathbf{u} + \mathbf{v}$. If we let the positive x-axis represent east and the positive y-axis represent north, then the component forms of **u** and **v** are

$$\mathbf{u} = \langle 500, 0 \rangle \quad \text{and} \quad \mathbf{v} = \langle 70 \cos 60°, 70 \sin 60° \rangle = \langle 35, 35\sqrt{3} \rangle.$$

Therefore,

$$\mathbf{u} + \mathbf{v} = \langle 535, 35\sqrt{3} \rangle$$
$$|\mathbf{u} + \mathbf{v}| = \sqrt{535^2 + (35\sqrt{3})^2} \approx 538.4$$

and

$$\theta = \tan^{-1} \frac{35\sqrt{3}}{535} \approx 6.5°. \qquad \text{Figure 12.15}$$

The new ground speed of the airplane is about 538.4 mph, and its new direction is about 6.5° north of east. ■

Unit Vectors

A vector **v** of length 1 is called a **unit vector**. The **standard unit vectors** are

$$\mathbf{i} = \langle 1, 0, 0 \rangle, \quad \mathbf{j} = \langle 0, 1, 0 \rangle, \quad \text{and} \quad \mathbf{k} = \langle 0, 0, 1 \rangle.$$

Any vector $\mathbf{v} = \langle v_1, v_2, v_3 \rangle$ can be written as a *linear combination* of the standard unit vectors as follows:

$$\begin{aligned}\mathbf{v} = \langle v_1, v_2, v_3 \rangle &= \langle v_1, 0, 0 \rangle + \langle 0, v_2, 0 \rangle + \langle 0, 0, v_3 \rangle \\ &= v_1\langle 1, 0, 0 \rangle + v_2\langle 0, 1, 0 \rangle + v_3\langle 0, 0, 1 \rangle \\ &= v_1\mathbf{i} + v_2\mathbf{j} + v_3\mathbf{k}.\end{aligned}$$

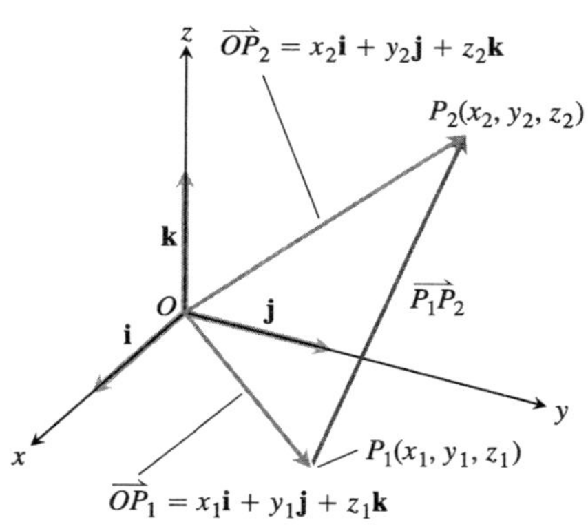

FIGURE 12.16 The vector from P_1 to P_2 is $\overrightarrow{P_1P_2} = (x_2 - x_1)\mathbf{i} + (y_2 - y_1)\mathbf{j} + (z_2 - z_1)\mathbf{k}$.

We call the scalar (or number) v_1 the **i-component** of the vector **v**, v_2 the **j-component**, and v_3 the **k-component**. In component form, the vector from $P_1(x_1, y_1, z_1)$ to $P_2(x_2, y_2, z_2)$ is

$$\overrightarrow{P_1P_2} = (x_2 - x_1)\mathbf{i} + (y_2 - y_1)\mathbf{j} + (z_2 - z_1)\mathbf{k}$$

(Figure 12.16).

Whenever $\mathbf{v} \neq \mathbf{0}$, its length $|\mathbf{v}|$ is not zero and

$$\left| \frac{1}{|\mathbf{v}|}\mathbf{v} \right| = \frac{1}{|\mathbf{v}|}|\mathbf{v}| = 1.$$

That is, $\mathbf{v}/|\mathbf{v}|$ is a unit vector in the direction of **v**, called **the direction** of the nonzero vector **v**.

EXAMPLE 5 Finding a Vector's Direction

Find a unit vector **u** in the direction of the vector from $P_1(1, 0, 1)$ to $P_2(3, 2, 0)$.

Solution We divide $\overrightarrow{P_1P_2}$ by its length:

$$\overrightarrow{P_1P_2} = (3-1)\mathbf{i} + (2-0)\mathbf{j} + (0-1)\mathbf{k} = 2\mathbf{i} + 2\mathbf{j} - \mathbf{k}$$

$$|\overrightarrow{P_1P_2}| = \sqrt{(2)^2 + (2)^2 + (-1)^2} = \sqrt{4+4+1} = \sqrt{9} = 3$$

$$\mathbf{u} = \frac{\overrightarrow{P_1P_2}}{|\overrightarrow{P_1P_2}|} = \frac{2\mathbf{i} + 2\mathbf{j} - \mathbf{k}}{3} = \frac{2}{3}\mathbf{i} + \frac{2}{3}\mathbf{j} - \frac{1}{3}\mathbf{k}.$$

The unit vector $\mathbf{u}$ is the direction of $\overrightarrow{P_1P_2}$. ■

EXAMPLE 6 Expressing Velocity as Speed Times Direction

If $\mathbf{v} = 3\mathbf{i} - 4\mathbf{j}$ is a velocity vector, express $\mathbf{v}$ as a product of its speed times a unit vector in the direction of motion.

Solution Speed is the magnitude (length) of $\mathbf{v}$:

$$|\mathbf{v}| = \sqrt{(3)^2 + (-4)^2} = \sqrt{9+16} = 5.$$

HISTORICAL BIOGRAPHY

Hermann Grassmann (1809–1877)

The unit vector $\mathbf{v}/|\mathbf{v}|$ has the same direction as $\mathbf{v}$:

$$\frac{\mathbf{v}}{|\mathbf{v}|} = \frac{3\mathbf{i} - 4\mathbf{j}}{5} = \frac{3}{5}\mathbf{i} - \frac{4}{5}\mathbf{j}.$$

So

$$\mathbf{v} = 3\mathbf{i} - 4\mathbf{j} = \underbrace{5}_{\text{Length (speed)}}\underbrace{\left(\frac{3}{5}\mathbf{i} - \frac{4}{5}\mathbf{j}\right)}_{\text{Direction of motion}}.$$ ■

In summary, we can express any nonzero vector $\mathbf{v}$ in terms of its two important features, length and direction, by writing $\mathbf{v} = |\mathbf{v}|\dfrac{\mathbf{v}}{|\mathbf{v}|}$.

> If $\mathbf{v} \neq \mathbf{0}$, then
>
> **1.** $\dfrac{\mathbf{v}}{|\mathbf{v}|}$ is a unit vector in the direction of $\mathbf{v}$;
>
> **2.** the equation $\mathbf{v} = |\mathbf{v}|\dfrac{\mathbf{v}}{|\mathbf{v}|}$ expresses $\mathbf{v}$ in terms of its length and direction.

EXAMPLE 7 A Force Vector

A force of 6 newtons is applied in the direction of the vector $\mathbf{v} = 2\mathbf{i} + 2\mathbf{j} - \mathbf{k}$. Express the force $\mathbf{F}$ as a product of its magnitude and direction.

Solution The force vector has magnitude 6 and direction $\dfrac{\mathbf{v}}{|\mathbf{v}|}$, so

$$\mathbf{F} = 6\frac{\mathbf{v}}{|\mathbf{v}|} = 6\frac{2\mathbf{i} + 2\mathbf{j} - \mathbf{k}}{\sqrt{2^2 + 2^2 + (-1)^2}} = 6\frac{2\mathbf{i} + 2\mathbf{j} - \mathbf{k}}{3}$$

$$= 6\left(\frac{2}{3}\mathbf{i} + \frac{2}{3}\mathbf{j} - \frac{1}{3}\mathbf{k}\right).$$ ■

Midpoint of a Line Segment

Vectors are often useful in geometry. For example, the coordinates of the midpoint of a line segment are found by averaging.

> The **midpoint** M of the line segment joining points $P_1(x_1, y_1, z_1)$ and $P_2(x_2, y_2, z_2)$ is the point
>
> $$\left(\frac{x_1 + x_2}{2}, \frac{y_1 + y_2}{2}, \frac{z_1 + z_2}{2}\right).$$

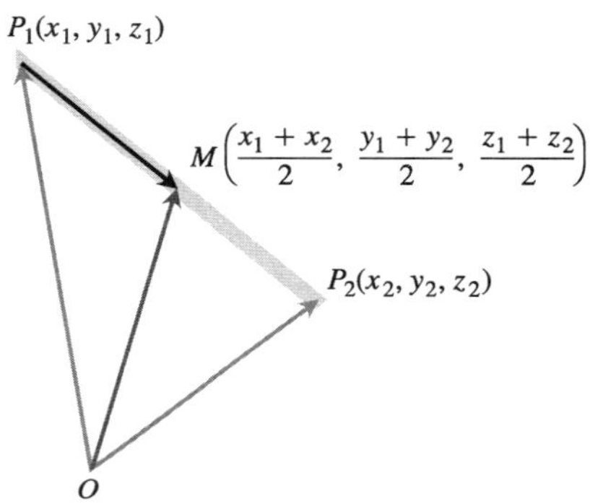

FIGURE 12.17 The coordinates of the midpoint are the averages of the coordinates of P_1 and P_2.

To see why, observe (Figure 12.17) that

$$\begin{aligned}\overrightarrow{OM} &= \overrightarrow{OP_1} + \frac{1}{2}(\overrightarrow{P_1P_2}) = \overrightarrow{OP_1} + \frac{1}{2}(\overrightarrow{OP_2} - \overrightarrow{OP_1})\\ &= \frac{1}{2}(\overrightarrow{OP_1} + \overrightarrow{OP_2})\\ &= \frac{x_1 + x_2}{2}\mathbf{i} + \frac{y_1 + y_2}{2}\mathbf{j} + \frac{z_1 + z_2}{2}\mathbf{k}.\end{aligned}$$

EXAMPLE 8 Finding Midpoints

The midpoint of the segment joining $P_1(3, -2, 0)$ and $P_2(7, 4, 4)$ is

$$\left(\frac{3 + 7}{2}, \frac{-2 + 4}{2}, \frac{0 + 4}{2}\right) = (5, 1, 2).$$ ■

EXERCISES 12.2

Vectors in the Plane

In Exercises 1–8, let $\mathbf{u} = \langle 3, -2\rangle$ and $\mathbf{v} = \langle -2, 5\rangle$. Find the **(a)** component form and **(b)** magnitude (length) of the vector.

1. $3\mathbf{u}$

2. $-2\mathbf{v}$

3. $\mathbf{u} + \mathbf{v}$

4. $\mathbf{u} - \mathbf{v}$

5. $2\mathbf{u} - 3\mathbf{v}$

6. $-2\mathbf{u} + 5\mathbf{v}$

7. $\frac{3}{5}\mathbf{u} + \frac{4}{5}\mathbf{v}$

8. $-\frac{5}{13}\mathbf{u} + \frac{12}{13}\mathbf{v}$

In Exercises 9–16, find the component form of the vector.

9. The vector $\overrightarrow{PQ}$, where $P = (1, 3)$ and $Q = (2, -1)$

10. The vector $\overrightarrow{OP}$ where O is the origin and P is the midpoint of segment RS, where $R = (2, -1)$ and $S = (-4, 3)$

11. The vector from the point $A = (2, 3)$ to the origin

12. The sum of $\overrightarrow{AB}$ and $\overrightarrow{CD}$, where $A = (1, -1)$, $B = (2, 0)$, $C = (-1, 3)$, and $D = (-2, 2)$

13. The unit vector that makes an angle $\theta = 2\pi/3$ with the positive x-axis

14. The unit vector that makes an angle $\theta = -3\pi/4$ with the positive x-axis

15. The unit vector obtained by rotating the vector $\langle 0, 1\rangle$ 120° counterclockwise about the origin

16. The unit vector obtained by rotating the vector $\langle 1, 0\rangle$ 135° counterclockwise about the origin

Vectors in Space

In Exercises 17–22, express each vector in the form $\mathbf{v} = v_1\mathbf{i} + v_2\mathbf{j} + v_3\mathbf{k}$.

17. $\overrightarrow{P_1P_2}$ if P_1 is the point $(5, 7, -1)$ and P_2 is the point $(2, 9, -2)$

18. $\overrightarrow{P_1P_2}$ if P_1 is the point $(1, 2, 0)$ and P_2 is the point $(-3, 0, 5)$

19. $\overrightarrow{AB}$ if A is the point $(-7, -8, 1)$ and B is the point $(-10, 8, 1)$

20. $\overrightarrow{AB}$ if A is the point $(1, 0, 3)$ and B is the point $(-1, 4, 5)$

21. $5\mathbf{u} - \mathbf{v}$ if $\mathbf{u} = \langle 1, 1, -1 \rangle$ and $\mathbf{v} = \langle 2, 0, 3 \rangle$

22. $-2\mathbf{u} + 3\mathbf{v}$ if $\mathbf{u} = \langle -1, 0, 2 \rangle$ and $\mathbf{v} = \langle 1, 1, 1 \rangle$

Geometry and Calculation

In Exercises 23 and 24, copy vectors **u**, **v**, and **w** head to tail as needed to sketch the indicated vector.

23.

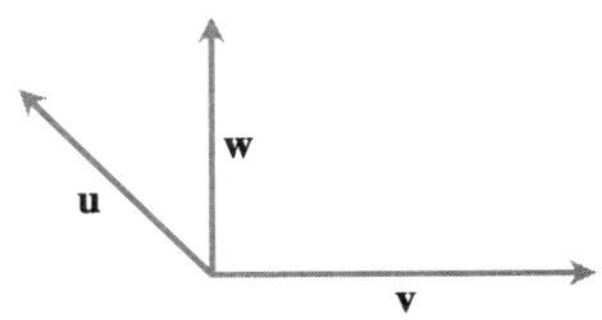

a. $\mathbf{u} + \mathbf{v}$ **b.** $\mathbf{u} + \mathbf{v} + \mathbf{w}$

c. $\mathbf{u} - \mathbf{v}$ **d.** $\mathbf{u} - \mathbf{w}$

24.

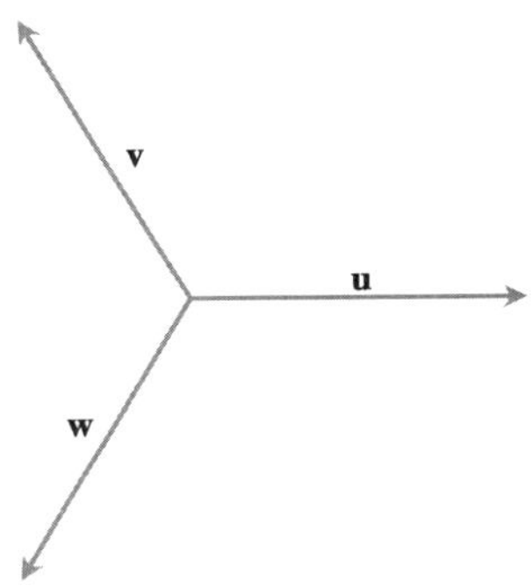

a. $\mathbf{u} - \mathbf{v}$ **b.** $\mathbf{u} - \mathbf{v} + \mathbf{w}$

c. $2\mathbf{u} - \mathbf{v}$ **d.** $\mathbf{u} + \mathbf{v} + \mathbf{w}$

Length and Direction

In Exercises 25–30, express each vector as a product of its length and direction.

25. $2\mathbf{i} + \mathbf{j} - 2\mathbf{k}$

26. $9\mathbf{i} - 2\mathbf{j} + 6\mathbf{k}$

27. $5\mathbf{k}$

28. $\frac{3}{5}\mathbf{i} + \frac{4}{5}\mathbf{k}$

29. $\frac{1}{\sqrt{6}}\mathbf{i} - \frac{1}{\sqrt{6}}\mathbf{j} - \frac{1}{\sqrt{6}}\mathbf{k}$

30. $\frac{\mathbf{i}}{\sqrt{3}} + \frac{\mathbf{j}}{\sqrt{3}} + \frac{\mathbf{k}}{\sqrt{3}}$

31. Find the vectors whose lengths and directions are given. Try to do the calculations without writing.

Length	Direction
a. 2	$\mathbf{i}$
b. $\sqrt{3}$	$-\mathbf{k}$
c. $\frac{1}{2}$	$\frac{3}{5}\mathbf{j} + \frac{4}{5}\mathbf{k}$
d. 7	$\frac{6}{7}\mathbf{i} - \frac{2}{7}\mathbf{j} + \frac{3}{7}\mathbf{k}$

32. Find the vectors whose lengths and directions are given. Try to do the calculations without writing.

Length	Direction
a. 7	$-\mathbf{j}$
b. $\sqrt{2}$	$-\frac{3}{5}\mathbf{i} - \frac{4}{5}\mathbf{k}$
c. $\frac{13}{12}$	$\frac{3}{13}\mathbf{i} - \frac{4}{13}\mathbf{j} - \frac{12}{13}\mathbf{k}$
d. $a > 0$	$\frac{1}{\sqrt{2}}\mathbf{i} + \frac{1}{\sqrt{3}}\mathbf{j} - \frac{1}{\sqrt{6}}\mathbf{k}$

33. Find a vector of magnitude 7 in the direction of $\mathbf{v} = 12\mathbf{i} - 5\mathbf{k}$.

34. Find a vector of magnitude 3 in the direction opposite to the direction of $\mathbf{v} = (1/2)\mathbf{i} - (1/2)\mathbf{j} - (1/2)\mathbf{k}$.

Vectors Determined by Points; Midpoints

In Exercises 35–38, find

a. the direction of $\overrightarrow{P_1P_2}$ and

b. the midpoint of line segment P_1P_2.

35. $P_1(-1, 1, 5)$ $P_2(2, 5, 0)$

36. $P_1(1, 4, 5)$ $P_2(4, -2, 7)$

37. $P_1(3, 4, 5)$ $P_2(2, 3, 4)$

38. $P_1(0, 0, 0)$ $P_2(2, -2, -2)$

39. If $\overrightarrow{AB} = \mathbf{i} + 4\mathbf{j} - 2\mathbf{k}$ and B is the point $(5, 1, 3)$, find A.

40. If $\overrightarrow{AB} = -7\mathbf{i} + 3\mathbf{j} + 8\mathbf{k}$ and A is the point $(-2, -3, 6)$, find B.

Theory and Applications

41. Linear combination Let $\mathbf{u} = 2\mathbf{i} + \mathbf{j}$, $\mathbf{v} = \mathbf{i} + \mathbf{j}$, and $\mathbf{w} = \mathbf{i} - \mathbf{j}$. Find scalars a and b such that $\mathbf{u} = a\mathbf{v} + b\mathbf{w}$.

42. Linear combination Let $\mathbf{u} = \mathbf{i} - 2\mathbf{j}$, $\mathbf{v} = 2\mathbf{i} + 3\mathbf{j}$, and $\mathbf{w} = \mathbf{i} + \mathbf{j}$. Write $\mathbf{u} = \mathbf{u}_1 + \mathbf{u}_2$, where $\mathbf{u}_1$ is parallel to **v** and $\mathbf{u}_2$ is parallel to **w**. (See Exercise 41.)

43. Force vector You are pulling on a suitcase with a force **F** (pictured here) whose magnitude is $|\mathbf{F}| = 10$ lb. Find the **i**- and **j**-components of **F**.

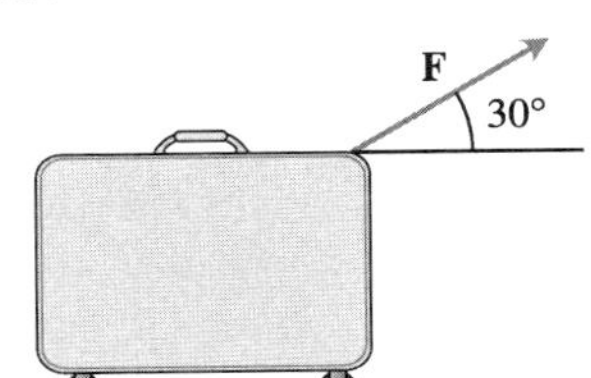

44. Force vector A kite string exerts a 12-lb pull ($|\mathbf{F}| = 12$) on a kite and makes a 45° angle with the horizontal. Find the horizontal and vertical components of **F**.

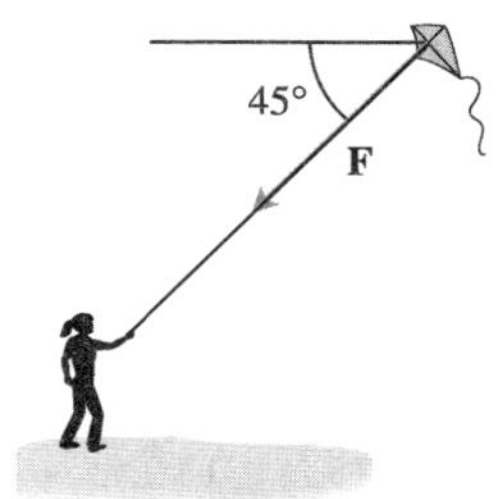

45. **Velocity** An airplane is flying in the direction 25° west of north at 800 km/h. Find the component form of the velocity of the airplane, assuming that the positive x-axis represents due east and the positive y-axis represents due north.

46. **Velocity** An airplane is flying in the direction 10° east of south at 600 km/h. Find the component form of the velocity of the airplane, assuming that the positive x-axis represents due east and the positive y-axis represents due north.

47. **Location** A bird flies from its nest 5 km in the direction 60° north of east, where it stops to rest on a tree. It then flies 10 km in the direction due southeast and lands atop a telephone pole. Place an xy-coordinate system so that the origin is the bird's nest, the x-axis points east, and the y-axis points north.

    a. At what point is the tree located?

    b. At what point is the telephone pole?

48. Use similar triangles to find the coordinates of the point Q that divides the segment from $P_1(x_1, y_1, z_1)$ to $P_2(x_2, y_2, z_2)$ into two lengths whose ratio is $p/q = r$.

49. **Medians of a triangle** Suppose that A, B, and C are the corner points of the thin triangular plate of constant density shown here.

    a. Find the vector from C to the midpoint M of side AB.

    b. Find the vector from C to the point that lies two-thirds of the way from C to M on the median CM.

    c. Find the coordinates of the point in which the medians of ΔABC intersect. According to Exercise 29, Section 6.4, this point is the plate's center of mass.

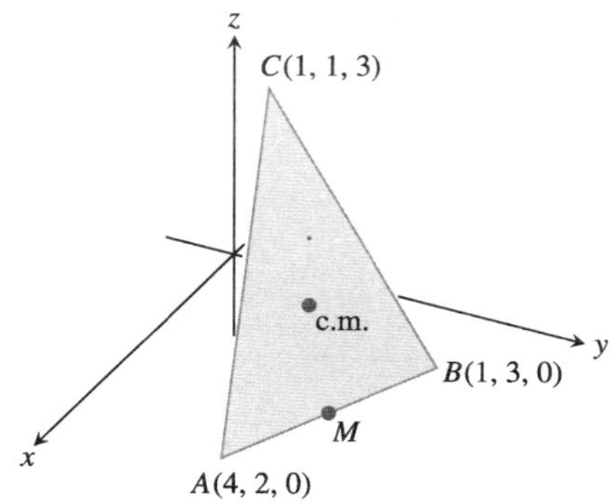

50. Find the vector from the origin to the point of intersection of the medians of the triangle whose vertices are

$$A(1, -1, 2), \quad B(2, 1, 3), \quad \text{and} \quad C(-1, 2, -1).$$

51. Let $ABCD$ be a general, not necessarily planar, quadrilateral in space. Show that the two segments joining the midpoints of opposite sides of $ABCD$ bisect each other. (*Hint:* Show that the segments have the same midpoint.)

52. Vectors are drawn from the center of a regular n-sided polygon in the plane to the vertices of the polygon. Show that the sum of the vectors is zero. (*Hint:* What happens to the sum if you rotate the polygon about its center?)

53. Suppose that A, B, and C are vertices of a triangle and that a, b, and c are, respectively, the midpoints of the opposite sides. Show that $\overrightarrow{Aa} + \overrightarrow{Bb} + \overrightarrow{Cc} = \mathbf{0}$.

54. **Unit vectors in the plane** Show that a unit vector in the plane can be expressed as $\mathbf{u} = (\cos\theta)\mathbf{i} + (\sin\theta)\mathbf{j}$, obtained by rotating $\mathbf{i}$ through an angle θ in the counterclockwise direction. Explain why this form gives *every* unit vector in the plane.

12.3 The Dot Product

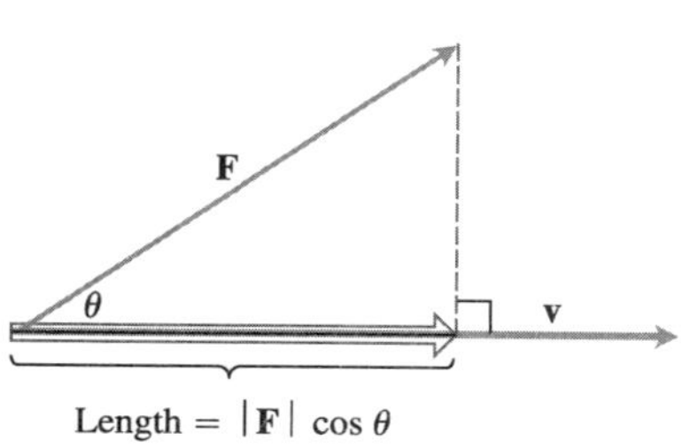

FIGURE 12.18 The magnitude of the force $\mathbf{F}$ in the direction of vector $\mathbf{v}$ is the length $|\mathbf{F}|\cos\theta$ of the projection of $\mathbf{F}$ onto $\mathbf{v}$.

If a force $\mathbf{F}$ is applied to a particle moving along a path, we often need to know the magnitude of the force in the direction of motion. If $\mathbf{v}$ is parallel to the tangent line to the path at the point where $\mathbf{F}$ is applied, then we want the magnitude of $\mathbf{F}$ in the direction of $\mathbf{v}$. Figure 12.18 shows that the scalar quantity we seek is the length $|\mathbf{F}|\cos\theta$, where θ is the angle between the two vectors $\mathbf{F}$ and $\mathbf{v}$.

In this section, we show how to calculate easily the angle between two vectors directly from their components. A key part of the calculation is an expression called the *dot product.* Dot products are also called *inner* or *scalar* products because the product results in a scalar, not a vector. After investigating the dot product, we apply it to finding the projection of one vector onto another (as displayed in Figure 12.18) and to finding the work done by a constant force acting through a displacement.

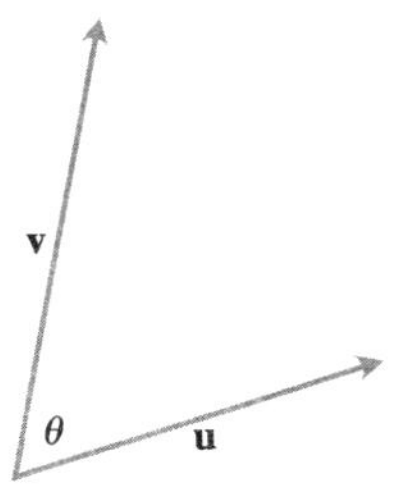

FIGURE 12.19 The angle between **u** and **v**.

Angle Between Vectors

When two nonzero vectors **u** and **v** are placed so their initial points coincide, they form an angle θ of measure $0 \le \theta \le \pi$ (Figure 12.19). If the vectors do not lie along the same line, the angle θ is measured in the plane containing both of them. If they do lie along the same line, the angle between them is 0 if they point in the same direction, and π if they point in opposite directions. The angle θ is the **angle between u and v**. Theorem 1 gives a formula to determine this angle.

THEOREM 1 Angle Between Two Vectors
The angle θ between two nonzero vectors $\mathbf{u} = \langle u_1, u_2, u_3\rangle$ and $\mathbf{v} = \langle v_1, v_2, v_3\rangle$ is given by

$$\theta = \cos^{-1}\left(\frac{u_1v_1 + u_2v_2 + u_3v_3}{|\mathbf{u}||\mathbf{v}|}\right).$$

Before proving Theorem 1 (which is a consequence of the law of cosines), let's focus attention on the expression $u_1v_1 + u_2v_2 + u_3v_3$ in the calculation for θ.

DEFINITION Dot Product
The **dot product u · v** ("**u** dot **v**") of vectors $\mathbf{u} = \langle u_1, u_2, u_3\rangle$ and $\mathbf{v} = \langle v_1, v_2, v_3\rangle$ is

$$\mathbf{u}\cdot\mathbf{v} = u_1v_1 + u_2v_2 + u_3v_3.$$

EXAMPLE 1 Finding Dot Products

(a) $$\begin{aligned}\langle 1, -2, -1\rangle\cdot\langle -6, 2, -3\rangle &= (1)(-6) + (-2)(2) + (-1)(-3)\\ &= -6 - 4 + 3 = -7\end{aligned}$$

(b) $$\left(\frac{1}{2}\mathbf{i} + 3\mathbf{j} + \mathbf{k}\right)\cdot(4\mathbf{i} - \mathbf{j} + 2\mathbf{k}) = \left(\frac{1}{2}\right)(4) + (3)(-1) + (1)(2) = 1$$ ■

The dot product of a pair of two-dimensional vectors is defined in a similar fashion:

$$\langle u_1, u_2\rangle\cdot\langle v_1, v_2\rangle = u_1v_1 + u_2v_2.$$

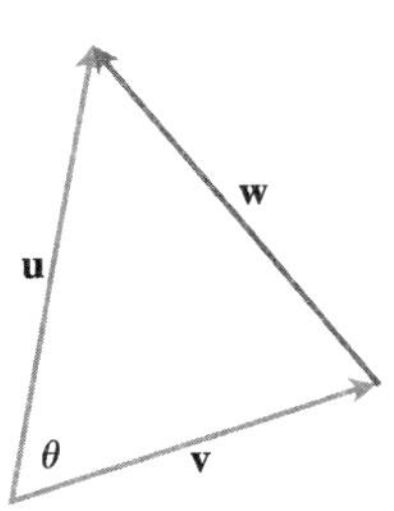

FIGURE 12.20 The parallelogram law of addition of vectors gives $\mathbf{w} = \mathbf{u} - \mathbf{v}$.

Proof of Theorem 1 Applying the law of cosines (Equation (6), Section 1.6) to the triangle in Figure 12.20, we find that

$$|\mathbf{w}|^2 = |\mathbf{u}|^2 + |\mathbf{v}|^2 - 2|\mathbf{u}||\mathbf{v}|\cos\theta \qquad \text{Law of cosines}$$

$$2|\mathbf{u}||\mathbf{v}|\cos\theta = |\mathbf{u}|^2 + |\mathbf{v}|^2 - |\mathbf{w}|^2.$$

Because $\mathbf{w} = \mathbf{u} - \mathbf{v}$, the component form of $\mathbf{w}$ is $\langle u_1 - v_1, u_2 - v_2, u_3 - v_3 \rangle$. So

$$|\mathbf{u}|^2 = \left(\sqrt{u_1^2 + u_2^2 + u_3^2}\right)^2 = u_1^2 + u_2^2 + u_3^2$$

$$|\mathbf{v}|^2 = \left(\sqrt{v_1^2 + v_2^2 + v_3^2}\right)^2 = v_1^2 + v_2^2 + v_3^2$$

$$\begin{aligned}|\mathbf{w}|^2 &= \left(\sqrt{(u_1 - v_1)^2 + (u_2 - v_2)^2 + (u_3 - v_3)^2}\right)^2 \\ &= (u_1 - v_1)^2 + (u_2 - v_2)^2 + (u_3 - v_3)^2 \\ &= u_1^2 - 2u_1v_1 + v_1^2 + u_2^2 - 2u_2v_2 + v_2^2 + u_3^2 - 2u_3v_3 + v_3^2\end{aligned}$$

and

$$|\mathbf{u}|^2 + |\mathbf{v}|^2 - |\mathbf{w}|^2 = 2(u_1v_1 + u_2v_2 + u_3v_3).$$

Therefore,

$$\begin{aligned}2|\mathbf{u}||\mathbf{v}|\cos\theta &= |\mathbf{u}|^2 + |\mathbf{v}|^2 - |\mathbf{w}|^2 = 2(u_1v_1 + u_2v_2 + u_3v_3) \\ |\mathbf{u}||\mathbf{v}|\cos\theta &= u_1v_1 + u_2v_2 + u_3v_3 \\ \cos\theta &= \frac{u_1v_1 + u_2v_2 + u_3v_3}{|\mathbf{u}||\mathbf{v}|}\end{aligned}$$

So

$$\theta = \cos^{-1}\left(\frac{u_1v_1 + u_2v_2 + u_3v_3}{|\mathbf{u}||\mathbf{v}|}\right)$$ ■

With the notation of the dot product, the angle between two vectors $\mathbf{u}$ and $\mathbf{v}$ can be written as

$$\theta = \cos^{-1}\left(\frac{\mathbf{u}\cdot\mathbf{v}}{|\mathbf{u}||\mathbf{v}|}\right).$$

EXAMPLE 2 Finding the Angle Between Two Vectors in Space

Find the angle between $\mathbf{u} = \mathbf{i} - 2\mathbf{j} - 2\mathbf{k}$ and $\mathbf{v} = 6\mathbf{i} + 3\mathbf{j} + 2\mathbf{k}$.

Solution We use the formula above:

$$\mathbf{u}\cdot\mathbf{v} = (1)(6) + (-2)(3) + (-2)(2) = 6 - 6 - 4 = -4$$

$$|\mathbf{u}| = \sqrt{(1)^2 + (-2)^2 + (-2)^2} = \sqrt{9} = 3$$

$$|\mathbf{v}| = \sqrt{(6)^2 + (3)^2 + (2)^2} = \sqrt{49} = 7$$

$$\begin{aligned}\theta &= \cos^{-1}\left(\frac{\mathbf{u}\cdot\mathbf{v}}{|\mathbf{u}||\mathbf{v}|}\right) \\ &= \cos^{-1}\left(\frac{-4}{(3)(7)}\right) \approx 1.76 \text{ radians}.\end{aligned}$$ ■

The angle formula applies to two-dimensional vectors as well.

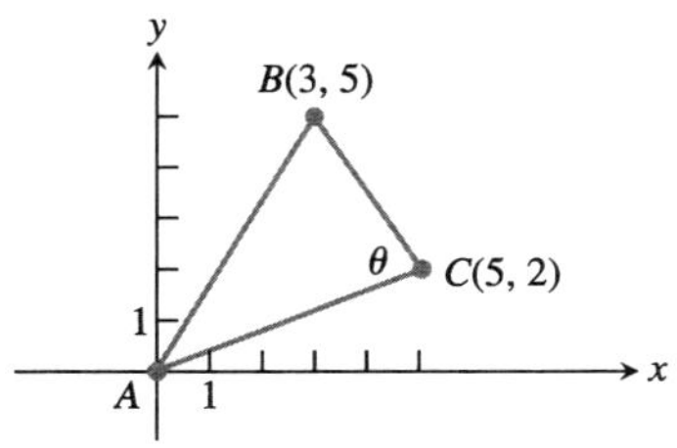

FIGURE 12.21 The triangle in Example 3.

EXAMPLE 3 Finding an Angle of a Triangle

Find the angle θ in the triangle ABC determined by the vertices $A = (0, 0)$, $B = (3, 5)$, and $C = (5, 2)$ (Figure 12.21).

Solution The angle θ is the angle between the vectors $\overrightarrow{CA}$ and $\overrightarrow{CB}$. The component forms of these two vectors are

$$\overrightarrow{CA} = \langle -5, -2 \rangle \qquad \text{and} \qquad \overrightarrow{CB} = \langle -2, 3 \rangle.$$

First we calculate the dot product and magnitudes of these two vectors.

$$\begin{aligned}
\overrightarrow{CA} \cdot \overrightarrow{CB} &= (-5)(-2) + (-2)(3) = 4 \\
|\overrightarrow{CA}| &= \sqrt{(-5)^2 + (-2)^2} = \sqrt{29} \\
|\overrightarrow{CB}| &= \sqrt{(-2)^2 + (3)^2} = \sqrt{13}
\end{aligned}$$

Then applying the angle formula, we have

$$\begin{aligned}
\theta &= \cos^{-1}\left(\frac{\overrightarrow{CA} \cdot \overrightarrow{CB}}{|\overrightarrow{CA}|\,|\overrightarrow{CB}|}\right) \\
&= \cos^{-1}\left(\frac{4}{\left(\sqrt{29}\right)\left(\sqrt{13}\right)}\right) \\
&\approx 78.1^\circ \qquad \text{or} \qquad 1.36 \text{ radians}.
\end{aligned}$$

■

Perpendicular (Orthogonal) Vectors

Two nonzero vectors **u** and **v** are perpendicular or **orthogonal** if the angle between them is $\pi/2$. For such vectors, we have $\mathbf{u} \cdot \mathbf{v} = 0$ because $\cos(\pi/2) = 0$. The converse is also true. If **u** and **v** are nonzero vectors with $\mathbf{u} \cdot \mathbf{v} = |\mathbf{u}|\,|\mathbf{v}| \cos\theta = 0$, then $\cos\theta = 0$ and $\theta = \cos^{-1} 0 = \pi/2$.

> **DEFINITION Orthogonal Vectors**
> Vectors **u** and **v** are **orthogonal** (or **perpendicular**) if and only if $\mathbf{u} \cdot \mathbf{v} = 0$.

EXAMPLE 4 Applying the Definition of Orthogonality

(a) $\mathbf{u} = \langle 3, -2 \rangle$ and $\mathbf{v} = \langle 4, 6 \rangle$ are orthogonal because $\mathbf{u} \cdot \mathbf{v} = (3)(4) + (-2)(6) = 0$.

(b) $\mathbf{u} = 3\mathbf{i} - 2\mathbf{j} + \mathbf{k}$ and $\mathbf{v} = 2\mathbf{j} + 4\mathbf{k}$ are orthogonal because $\mathbf{u} \cdot \mathbf{v} = (3)(0) + (-2)(2) + (1)(4) = 0$.

(c) **0** is orthogonal to every vector **u** since

$$\begin{aligned}
\mathbf{0} \cdot \mathbf{u} &= \langle 0, 0, 0 \rangle \cdot \langle u_1, u_2, u_3 \rangle \\
&= (0)(u_1) + (0)(u_2) + (0)(u_3) \\
&= 0.
\end{aligned}$$

■

Dot Product Properties and Vector Projections

The dot product obeys many of the laws that hold for ordinary products of real numbers (scalars).

Properties of the Dot Product

If $\mathbf{u}$, $\mathbf{v}$, and $\mathbf{w}$ are any vectors and c is a scalar, then

1. $\mathbf{u} \cdot \mathbf{v} = \mathbf{v} \cdot \mathbf{u}$
2. $(c\mathbf{u}) \cdot \mathbf{v} = \mathbf{u} \cdot (c\mathbf{v}) = c(\mathbf{u} \cdot \mathbf{v})$
3. $\mathbf{u} \cdot (\mathbf{v} + \mathbf{w}) = \mathbf{u} \cdot \mathbf{v} + \mathbf{u} \cdot \mathbf{w}$
4. $\mathbf{u} \cdot \mathbf{u} = |\mathbf{u}|^2$
5. $\mathbf{0} \cdot \mathbf{u} = 0$.

HISTORICAL BIOGRAPHY

Carl Friedrich Gauss
(1777–1855)

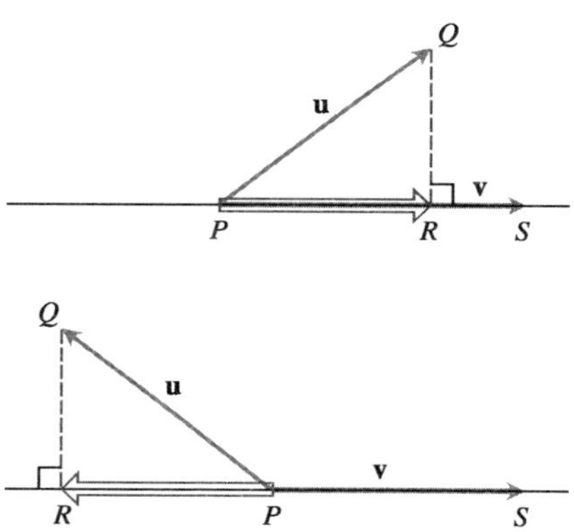

FIGURE 12.22 The vector projection of $\mathbf{u}$ onto $\mathbf{v}$.

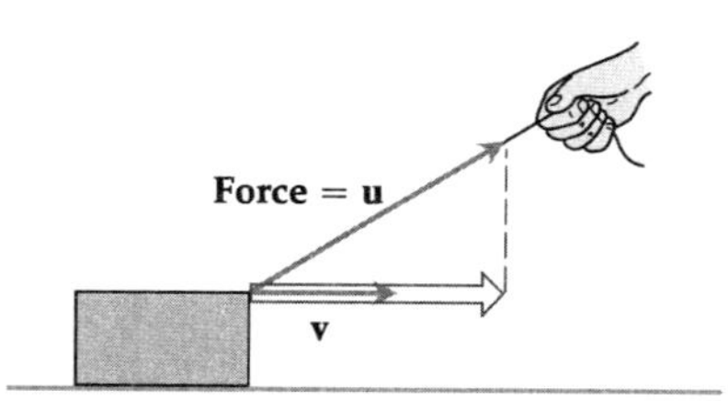

FIGURE 12.23 If we pull on the box with force $\mathbf{u}$, the effective force moving the box forward in the direction $\mathbf{v}$ is the projection of $\mathbf{u}$ onto $\mathbf{v}$.

Proofs of Properties 1 and 3 The properties are easy to prove using the definition. For instance, here are the proofs of Properties 1 and 3.

1. $\mathbf{u} \cdot \mathbf{v} = u_1v_1 + u_2v_2 + u_3v_3 = v_1u_1 + v_2u_2 + v_3u_3 = \mathbf{v} \cdot \mathbf{u}$

3.
$$\begin{aligned}\mathbf{u} \cdot (\mathbf{v} + \mathbf{w}) &= \langle u_1, u_2, u_3 \rangle \cdot \langle v_1 + w_1, v_2 + w_2, v_3 + w_3 \rangle \\ &= u_1(v_1 + w_1) + u_2(v_2 + w_2) + u_3(v_3 + w_3) \\ &= u_1v_1 + u_1w_1 + u_2v_2 + u_2w_2 + u_3v_3 + u_3w_3 \\ &= (u_1v_1 + u_2v_2 + u_3v_3) + (u_1w_1 + u_2w_2 + u_3w_3) \\ &= \mathbf{u} \cdot \mathbf{v} + \mathbf{u} \cdot \mathbf{w}\end{aligned}$$

■

We now return to the problem of projecting one vector onto another, posed in the opening to this section. The **vector projection** of $\mathbf{u} = \overrightarrow{PQ}$ onto a nonzero vector $\mathbf{v} = \overrightarrow{PS}$ (Figure 12.22) is the vector $\overrightarrow{PR}$ determined by dropping a perpendicular from Q to the line PS. The notation for this vector is

$$\text{proj}_{\mathbf{v}}\,\mathbf{u} \qquad \text{("the vector projection of } \mathbf{u} \text{ onto } \mathbf{v}\text{")}.$$

If $\mathbf{u}$ represents a force, then $\text{proj}_{\mathbf{v}}\,\mathbf{u}$ represents the effective force in the direction of $\mathbf{v}$ (Figure 12.23).

If the angle θ between $\mathbf{u}$ and $\mathbf{v}$ is acute, $\text{proj}_{\mathbf{v}}\,\mathbf{u}$ has length $|\mathbf{u}|\cos\theta$ and direction $\mathbf{v}/|\mathbf{v}|$ (Figure 12.24). If θ is obtuse, $\cos\theta < 0$ and $\text{proj}_{\mathbf{v}}\,\mathbf{u}$ has length $-|\mathbf{u}|\cos\theta$ and direction $-\mathbf{v}/|\mathbf{v}|$. In both cases,

$$\begin{aligned}\text{proj}_{\mathbf{v}}\,\mathbf{u} &= (|\mathbf{u}|\cos\theta)\frac{\mathbf{v}}{|\mathbf{v}|} \\ &= \left(\frac{\mathbf{u}\cdot\mathbf{v}}{|\mathbf{v}|}\right)\frac{\mathbf{v}}{|\mathbf{v}|} \qquad |\mathbf{u}|\cos\theta = \frac{|\mathbf{u}||\mathbf{v}|\cos\theta}{|\mathbf{v}|} = \frac{\mathbf{u}\cdot\mathbf{v}}{|\mathbf{v}|} \\ &= \left(\frac{\mathbf{u}\cdot\mathbf{v}}{|\mathbf{v}|^2}\right)\mathbf{v}.\end{aligned}$$

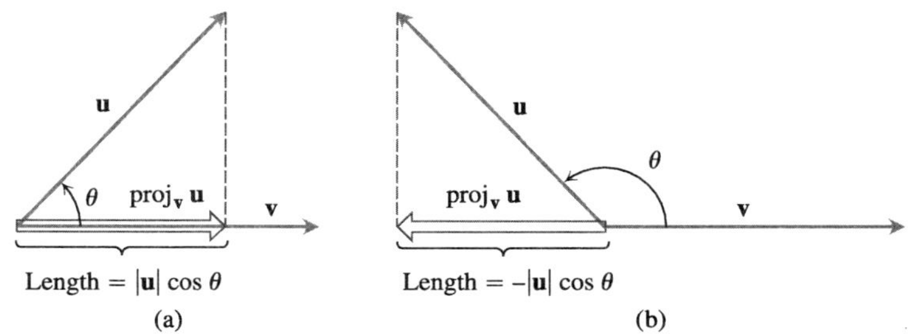

FIGURE 12.24 The length of $\text{proj}_{\mathbf{v}}\mathbf{u}$ is (a) $|\mathbf{u}|\cos\theta$ if $\cos\theta \geq 0$ and (b) $-|\mathbf{u}|\cos\theta$ if $\cos\theta < 0$.

The number $|\mathbf{u}|\cos\theta$ is called the **scalar component of u in the direction of v**. To summarize,

Vector projection of **u** onto **v**:

$$\text{proj}_{\mathbf{v}}\mathbf{u} = \left(\frac{\mathbf{u}\cdot\mathbf{v}}{|\mathbf{v}|^2}\right)\mathbf{v} \tag{1}$$

Scalar component of **u** in the direction of **v**:

$$|\mathbf{u}|\cos\theta = \frac{\mathbf{u}\cdot\mathbf{v}}{|\mathbf{v}|} = \mathbf{u}\cdot\frac{\mathbf{v}}{|\mathbf{v}|} \tag{2}$$

Note that both the vector projection of **u** onto **v** and the scalar component of **u** onto **v** depend only on the direction of the vector **v** and not its length (because we dot **u** with $\mathbf{v}/|\mathbf{v}|$, which is the direction of **v**).

EXAMPLE 5 Finding the Vector Projection

Find the vector projection of $\mathbf{u} = 6\mathbf{i} + 3\mathbf{j} + 2\mathbf{k}$ onto $\mathbf{v} = \mathbf{i} - 2\mathbf{j} - 2\mathbf{k}$ and the scalar component of **u** in the direction of **v**.

Solution We find $\text{proj}_{\mathbf{v}}\mathbf{u}$ from Equation (1):

$$\begin{aligned}\text{proj}_{\mathbf{v}}\mathbf{u} &= \frac{\mathbf{u}\cdot\mathbf{v}}{\mathbf{v}\cdot\mathbf{v}}\mathbf{v} = \frac{6-6-4}{1+4+4}(\mathbf{i} - 2\mathbf{j} - 2\mathbf{k}) \\ &= -\frac{4}{9}(\mathbf{i} - 2\mathbf{j} - 2\mathbf{k}) = -\frac{4}{9}\mathbf{i} + \frac{8}{9}\mathbf{j} + \frac{8}{9}\mathbf{k}.\end{aligned}$$

We find the scalar component of **u** in the direction of **v** from Equation (2):

$$\begin{aligned}|\mathbf{u}|\cos\theta &= \mathbf{u}\cdot\frac{\mathbf{v}}{|\mathbf{v}|} = (6\mathbf{i} + 3\mathbf{j} + 2\mathbf{k})\cdot\left(\frac{1}{3}\mathbf{i} - \frac{2}{3}\mathbf{j} - \frac{2}{3}\mathbf{k}\right) \\ &= 2 - 2 - \frac{4}{3} = -\frac{4}{3}.\end{aligned}$$

■

Equations (1) and (2) also apply to two-dimensional vectors.

EXAMPLE 6 Finding Vector Projections and Scalar Components

Find the vector projection of a force $\mathbf{F} = 5\mathbf{i} + 2\mathbf{j}$ onto $\mathbf{v} = \mathbf{i} - 3\mathbf{j}$ and the scalar component of $\mathbf{F}$ in the direction of $\mathbf{v}$.

Solution The vector projection is

$$\begin{aligned}\text{proj}_{\mathbf{v}}\,\mathbf{F} &= \left(\frac{\mathbf{F}\cdot\mathbf{v}}{|\mathbf{v}|^2}\right)\mathbf{v}\\ &= \frac{5-6}{1+9}(\mathbf{i}-3\mathbf{j}) = -\frac{1}{10}(\mathbf{i}-3\mathbf{j})\\ &= -\frac{1}{10}\mathbf{i} + \frac{3}{10}\mathbf{j}.\end{aligned}$$

The scalar component of $\mathbf{F}$ in the direction of $\mathbf{v}$ is

$$|\mathbf{F}|\cos\theta = \frac{\mathbf{F}\cdot\mathbf{v}}{|\mathbf{v}|} = \frac{5-6}{\sqrt{1+9}} = -\frac{1}{\sqrt{10}}.$$

■

Work

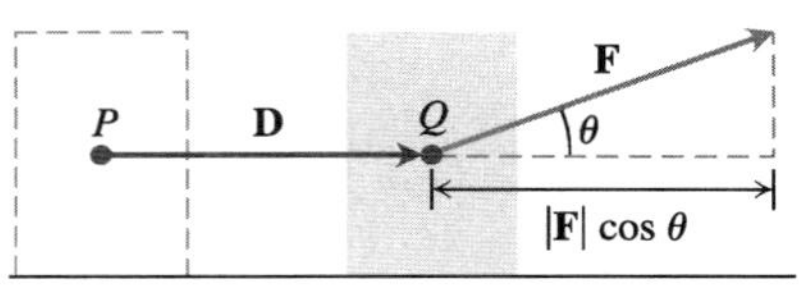

FIGURE 12.25 The work done by a constant force $\mathbf{F}$ during a displacement $\mathbf{D}$ is $(|\mathbf{F}|\cos\theta)|\mathbf{D}|$.

In Chapter 6, we calculated the work done by a constant force of magnitude F in moving an object through a distance d as $W = Fd$. That formula holds only if the force is directed along the line of motion. If a force $\mathbf{F}$ moving an object through a displacement $\mathbf{D} = \overrightarrow{PQ}$ has some other direction, the work is performed by the component of $\mathbf{F}$ in the direction of $\mathbf{D}$. If θ is the angle between $\mathbf{F}$ and $\mathbf{D}$ (Figure 12.25), then

$$\begin{aligned}\text{Work} &= \begin{pmatrix}\text{scalar component of } \mathbf{F}\\ \text{in the direction of } \mathbf{D}\end{pmatrix}(\text{length of } \mathbf{D})\\ &= (|\mathbf{F}|\cos\theta)|\mathbf{D}|\\ &= \mathbf{F}\cdot\mathbf{D}.\end{aligned}$$

DEFINITION **Work by Constant Force**

The **work** done by a constant force $\mathbf{F}$ acting through a displacement $\mathbf{D} = \overrightarrow{PQ}$ is

$$W = \mathbf{F}\cdot\mathbf{D} = |\mathbf{F}||\mathbf{D}|\cos\theta,$$

where θ is the angle between $\mathbf{F}$ and $\mathbf{D}$.

EXAMPLE 7 Applying the Definition of Work

If $|\mathbf{F}| = 40$ N (newtons), $|\mathbf{D}| = 3$ m, and $\theta = 60°$, the work done by $\mathbf{F}$ in acting from P to Q is

$$\begin{aligned}\text{Work} &= |\mathbf{F}||\mathbf{D}|\cos\theta && \text{Definition}\\ &= (40)(3)\cos 60° && \text{Given values}\\ &= (120)(1/2)\\ &= 60 \text{ J (joules)}.\end{aligned}$$

■

We encounter more challenging work problems in Chapter 16 when we learn to find the work done by a variable force along a *path* in space.

Writing a Vector as a Sum of Orthogonal Vectors

We know one way to write a vector $\mathbf{u} = \langle u_1, u_2 \rangle$ or $\mathbf{u} = \langle u_1, u_2, u_3 \rangle$ as a sum of two orthogonal vectors:

$$\mathbf{u} = u_1\mathbf{i} + u_2\mathbf{j} \qquad \text{or} \qquad \mathbf{u} = u_1\mathbf{i} + (u_2\mathbf{j} + u_3\mathbf{k})$$

(since $\mathbf{i}\cdot\mathbf{j} = \mathbf{i}\cdot\mathbf{k} = \mathbf{j}\cdot\mathbf{k} = 0$).

Sometimes, however, it is more informative to express **u** as a different sum. In mechanics, for instance, we often need to write a vector **u** as a sum of a vector parallel to a given vector **v** and a vector orthogonal to **v**. As an example, in studying the motion of a particle moving along a path in the plane (or space), it is desirable to know the components of the acceleration vector in the direction of the tangent to the path (at a point) and of the normal to the path. (These *tangential* and *normal components* of acceleration are investigated in Section 13.4.) The acceleration vector can then be expressed as the sum of its (vector) tangential and normal components (which reflect important geometric properties about the nature of the path itself, such as *curvature*). Velocity and acceleration vectors are studied in the next chapter.

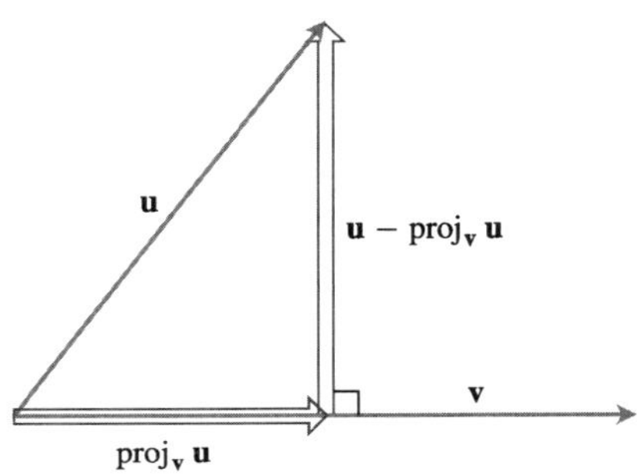

FIGURE 12.26 Writing **u** as the sum of vectors parallel and orthogonal to **v**.

Generally, for vectors **u** and **v**, it is easy to see from Figure 12.26 that the vector

$$\mathbf{u} - \operatorname{proj}_{\mathbf{v}} \mathbf{u}$$

is orthogonal to the projection vector $\operatorname{proj}_{\mathbf{v}} \mathbf{u}$ (which has the same direction as **v**). The following calculation verifies this observation:

$$\begin{aligned}
(\mathbf{u} - \operatorname{proj}_{\mathbf{v}} \mathbf{u})\cdot\operatorname{proj}_{\mathbf{v}} \mathbf{u} &= \left(\mathbf{u} - \left(\frac{\mathbf{u}\cdot\mathbf{v}}{|\mathbf{v}|^2}\right)\mathbf{v}\right)\cdot\left(\frac{\mathbf{u}\cdot\mathbf{v}}{|\mathbf{v}|^2}\right)\mathbf{v} && \text{Equation (1)}\\
&= \left(\frac{\mathbf{u}\cdot\mathbf{v}}{|\mathbf{v}|^2}\right)(\mathbf{u}\cdot\mathbf{v}) - \left(\frac{\mathbf{u}\cdot\mathbf{v}}{|\mathbf{v}|^2}\right)^2(\mathbf{v}\cdot\mathbf{v}) && \text{Dot product properties 2 and 3}\\
&= \frac{(\mathbf{u}\cdot\mathbf{v})^2}{|\mathbf{v}|^2} - \frac{(\mathbf{u}\cdot\mathbf{v})^2}{|\mathbf{v}|^2} && \mathbf{v}\cdot\mathbf{v} = |\mathbf{v}|^2 \text{ cancels}\\
&= 0.
\end{aligned}$$

So the equation

$$\mathbf{u} = \operatorname{proj}_{\mathbf{v}} \mathbf{u} + (\mathbf{u} - \operatorname{proj}_{\mathbf{v}} \mathbf{u})$$

expresses **u** as a sum of orthogonal vectors.

How to Write u as a Vector Parallel to v Plus a Vector Orthogonal to v

$$\begin{aligned}
\mathbf{u} &= \operatorname{proj}_{\mathbf{v}} \mathbf{u} + (\mathbf{u} - \operatorname{proj}_{\mathbf{v}} \mathbf{u})\\
&= \underbrace{\left(\frac{\mathbf{u}\cdot\mathbf{v}}{|\mathbf{v}|^2}\right)\mathbf{v}}_{\text{Parallel to } \mathbf{v}} + \underbrace{\left(\mathbf{u} - \left(\frac{\mathbf{u}\cdot\mathbf{v}}{|\mathbf{v}|^2}\right)\mathbf{v}\right)}_{\text{Orthogonal to } \mathbf{v}}
\end{aligned}$$

EXAMPLE 8 Force on a Spacecraft

A force $\mathbf{F} = 2\mathbf{i} + \mathbf{j} - 3\mathbf{k}$ is applied to a spacecraft with velocity vector $\mathbf{v} = 3\mathbf{i} - \mathbf{j}$. Express $\mathbf{F}$ as a sum of a vector parallel to $\mathbf{v}$ and a vector orthogonal to $\mathbf{v}$.

Solution

$$\begin{aligned}\mathbf{F} &= \text{proj}_{\mathbf{v}}\mathbf{F} + (\mathbf{F} - \text{proj}_{\mathbf{v}}\mathbf{F})\\ &= \frac{\mathbf{F}\cdot\mathbf{v}}{\mathbf{v}\cdot\mathbf{v}}\mathbf{v} + \left(\mathbf{F} - \frac{\mathbf{F}\cdot\mathbf{v}}{\mathbf{v}\cdot\mathbf{v}}\mathbf{v}\right)\\ &= \left(\frac{6-1}{9+1}\right)\mathbf{v} + \left(\mathbf{F} - \left(\frac{6-1}{9+1}\right)\mathbf{v}\right)\\ &= \frac{5}{10}(3\mathbf{i} - \mathbf{j}) + \left(2\mathbf{i} + \mathbf{j} - 3\mathbf{k} - \frac{5}{10}(3\mathbf{i} - \mathbf{j})\right)\\ &= \left(\frac{3}{2}\mathbf{i} - \frac{1}{2}\mathbf{j}\right) + \left(\frac{1}{2}\mathbf{i} + \frac{3}{2}\mathbf{j} - 3\mathbf{k}\right).\end{aligned}$$

The force $(3/2)\mathbf{i} - (1/2)\mathbf{j}$ is the effective force parallel to the velocity $\mathbf{v}$. The force $(1/2)\mathbf{i} + (3/2)\mathbf{j} - 3\mathbf{k}$ is orthogonal to $\mathbf{v}$. To check that this vector is orthogonal to $\mathbf{v}$, we find the dot product:

$$\left(\frac{1}{2}\mathbf{i} + \frac{3}{2}\mathbf{j} - 3\mathbf{k}\right)\cdot(3\mathbf{i} - \mathbf{j}) = \frac{3}{2} - \frac{3}{2} = 0.$$

■

EXERCISES 12.3

Dot Product and Projections

In Exercises 1–8, find

a. $\mathbf{v}\cdot\mathbf{u}$, $|\mathbf{v}|$, $|\mathbf{u}|$

b. the cosine of the angle between $\mathbf{v}$ and $\mathbf{u}$

c. the scalar component of $\mathbf{u}$ in the direction of $\mathbf{v}$

d. the vector $\text{proj}_{\mathbf{v}}\mathbf{u}$.

1. $\mathbf{v} = 2\mathbf{i} - 4\mathbf{j} + \sqrt{5}\mathbf{k}$, $\mathbf{u} = -2\mathbf{i} + 4\mathbf{j} - \sqrt{5}\mathbf{k}$

2. $\mathbf{v} = (3/5)\mathbf{i} + (4/5)\mathbf{k}$, $\mathbf{u} = 5\mathbf{i} + 12\mathbf{j}$

3. $\mathbf{v} = 10\mathbf{i} + 11\mathbf{j} - 2\mathbf{k}$, $\mathbf{u} = 3\mathbf{j} + 4\mathbf{k}$

4. $\mathbf{v} = 2\mathbf{i} + 10\mathbf{j} - 11\mathbf{k}$, $\mathbf{u} = 2\mathbf{i} + 2\mathbf{j} + \mathbf{k}$

5. $\mathbf{v} = 5\mathbf{j} - 3\mathbf{k}$, $\mathbf{u} = \mathbf{i} + \mathbf{j} + \mathbf{k}$

6. $\mathbf{v} = -\mathbf{i} + \mathbf{j}$, $\mathbf{u} = \sqrt{2}\mathbf{i} + \sqrt{3}\mathbf{j} + 2\mathbf{k}$

7. $\mathbf{v} = 5\mathbf{i} + \mathbf{j}$, $\mathbf{u} = 2\mathbf{i} + \sqrt{17}\mathbf{j}$

8. $\mathbf{v} = \left\langle \frac{1}{\sqrt{2}}, \frac{1}{\sqrt{3}} \right\rangle$, $\mathbf{u} = \left\langle \frac{1}{\sqrt{2}}, -\frac{1}{\sqrt{3}} \right\rangle$

T Angles Between Vectors

Find the angles between the vectors in Exercises 9–12 to the nearest hundredth of a radian.

9. $\mathbf{u} = 2\mathbf{i} + \mathbf{j}$, $\mathbf{v} = \mathbf{i} + 2\mathbf{j} - \mathbf{k}$

10. $\mathbf{u} = 2\mathbf{i} - 2\mathbf{j} + \mathbf{k}$, $\mathbf{v} = 3\mathbf{i} + 4\mathbf{k}$

11. $\mathbf{u} = \sqrt{3}\mathbf{i} - 7\mathbf{j}$, $\mathbf{v} = \sqrt{3}\mathbf{i} + \mathbf{j} - 2\mathbf{k}$

12. $\mathbf{u} = \mathbf{i} + \sqrt{2}\mathbf{j} - \sqrt{2}\mathbf{k}$, $\mathbf{v} = -\mathbf{i} + \mathbf{j} + \mathbf{k}$

13. Triangle Find the measures of the angles of the triangle whose vertices are $A = (-1, 0)$, $B = (2, 1)$, and $C = (1, -2)$.

14. Rectangle Find the measures of the angles between the diagonals of the rectangle whose vertices are $A = (1, 0)$, $B = (0, 3)$, $C = (3, 4)$, and $D = (4, 1)$.

15. Direction angles and direction cosines The *direction angles* α, β, and γ of a vector $\mathbf{v} = a\mathbf{i} + b\mathbf{j} + c\mathbf{k}$ are defined as follows:

α is the angle between $\mathbf{v}$ and the positive x-axis $(0 \le \alpha \le \pi)$

β is the angle between $\mathbf{v}$ and the positive y-axis $(0 \le \beta \le \pi)$

γ is the angle between $\mathbf{v}$ and the positive z-axis $(0 \le \gamma \le \pi)$.

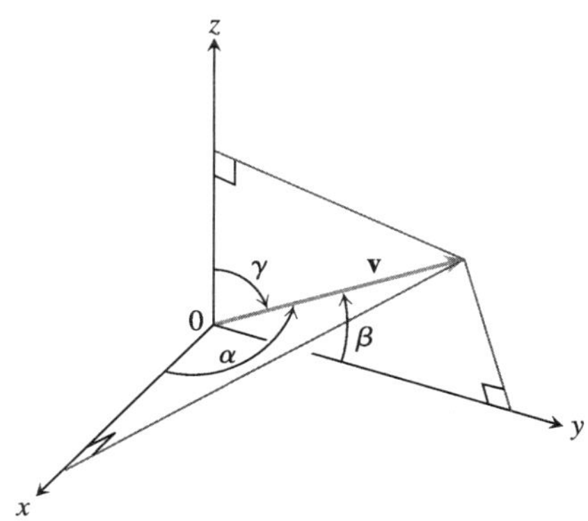

a. Show that

$$\cos\alpha = \frac{a}{|\mathbf{v}|}, \qquad \cos\beta = \frac{b}{|\mathbf{v}|}, \qquad \cos\gamma = \frac{c}{|\mathbf{v}|},$$

and $\cos^2\alpha + \cos^2\beta + \cos^2\gamma = 1$. These cosines are called the *direction cosines* of **v**.

b. Unit vectors are built from direction cosines Show that if $\mathbf{v} = a\mathbf{i} + b\mathbf{j} + c\mathbf{k}$ is a unit vector, then a, b, and c are the direction cosines of **v**.

16. Water main construction A water main is to be constructed with a 20% grade in the north direction and a 10% grade in the east direction. Determine the angle θ required in the water main for the turn from north to east.

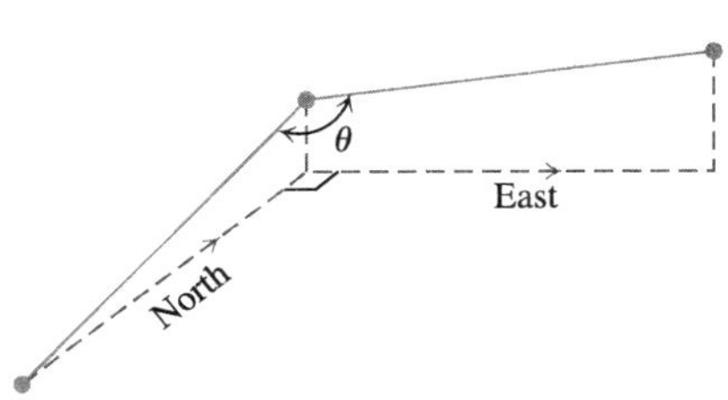

Decomposing Vectors

In Exercises 17–19, write **u** as the sum of a vector parallel to **v** and a vector orthogonal to **v**.

17. $\mathbf{u} = 3\mathbf{j} + 4\mathbf{k}, \quad \mathbf{v} = \mathbf{i} + \mathbf{j}$

18. $\mathbf{u} = \mathbf{j} + \mathbf{k}, \quad \mathbf{v} = \mathbf{i} + \mathbf{j}$

19. $\mathbf{u} = 8\mathbf{i} + 4\mathbf{j} - 12\mathbf{k}, \quad \mathbf{v} = \mathbf{i} + 2\mathbf{j} - \mathbf{k}$

20. Sum of vectors $\mathbf{u} = \mathbf{i} + (\mathbf{j} + \mathbf{k})$ is already the sum of a vector parallel to **i** and a vector orthogonal to **i**. If you use $\mathbf{v} = \mathbf{i}$, in the decomposition $\mathbf{u} = \text{proj}_{\mathbf{v}}\,\mathbf{u} + (\mathbf{u} - \text{proj}_{\mathbf{v}}\,\mathbf{u})$, do you get $\text{proj}_{\mathbf{v}}\,\mathbf{u} = \mathbf{i}$ and $(\mathbf{u} - \text{proj}_{\mathbf{v}}\,\mathbf{u}) = \mathbf{j} + \mathbf{k}$? Try it and find out.

Geometry and Examples

21. Sums and differences In the accompanying figure, it looks as if $\mathbf{v}_1 + \mathbf{v}_2$ and $\mathbf{v}_1 - \mathbf{v}_2$ are orthogonal. Is this mere coincidence, or are there circumstances under which we may expect the sum of two vectors to be orthogonal to their difference? Give reasons for your answer.

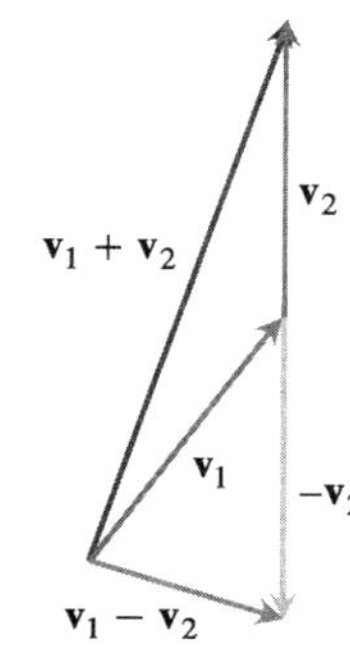

22. Orthogonality on a circle Suppose that AB is the diameter of a circle with center O and that C is a point on one of the two arcs joining A and B. Show that $\overrightarrow{CA}$ and $\overrightarrow{CB}$ are orthogonal.

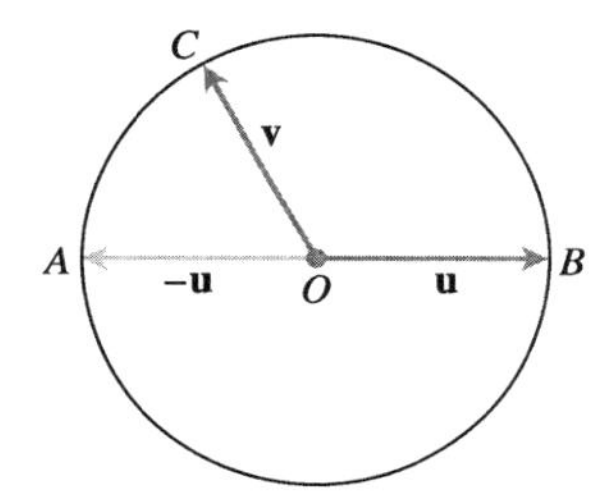

23. Diagonals of a rhombus Show that the diagonals of a rhombus (parallelogram with sides of equal length) are perpendicular.

24. Perpendicular diagonals Show that squares are the only rectangles with perpendicular diagonals.

25. When parallelograms are rectangles Prove that a parallelogram is a rectangle if and only if its diagonals are equal in length. (This fact is often exploited by carpenters.)

26. Diagonal of parallelogram Show that the indicated diagonal of the parallelogram determined by vectors **u** and **v** bisects the angle between **u** and **v** if $|\mathbf{u}| = |\mathbf{v}|$.

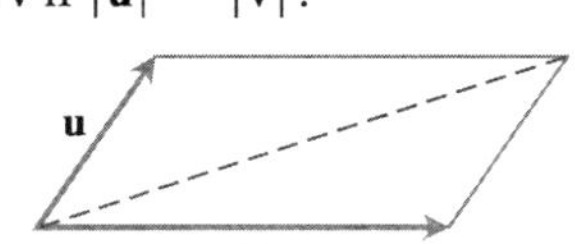

27. Projectile motion A gun with muzzle velocity of 1200 ft/sec is fired at an angle of 8° above the horizontal. Find the horizontal and vertical components of the velocity.

28. Inclined plane Suppose that a box is being towed up an inclined plane as shown in the figure. Find the force **w** needed to make the component of the force parallel to the inclined plane equal to 2.5 lb.

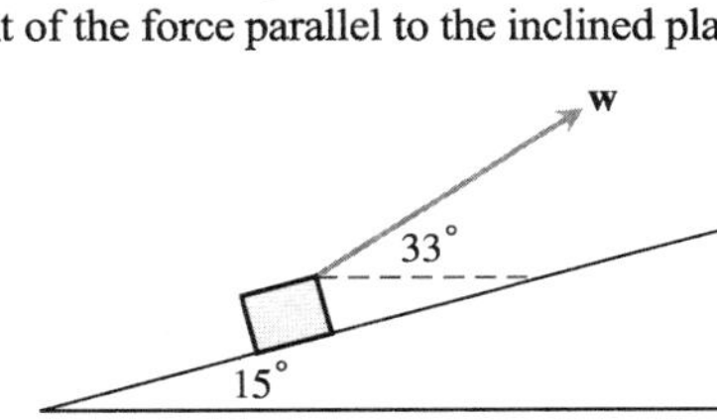

Theory and Examples

29. a. Cauchy-Schwartz inequality Use the fact that $\mathbf{u}\cdot\mathbf{v} = |\mathbf{u}||\mathbf{v}|\cos\theta$ to show that the inequality $|\mathbf{u}\cdot\mathbf{v}| \le |\mathbf{u}||\mathbf{v}|$ holds for any vectors **u** and **v**.

b. Under what circumstances, if any, does $|\mathbf{u}\cdot\mathbf{v}|$ equal $|\mathbf{u}||\mathbf{v}|$? Give reasons for your answer.

30. Copy the axes and vector shown here. Then shade in the points (x, y) for which $(x\mathbf{i} + y\mathbf{j})\cdot\mathbf{v} \le 0$. Justify your answer.

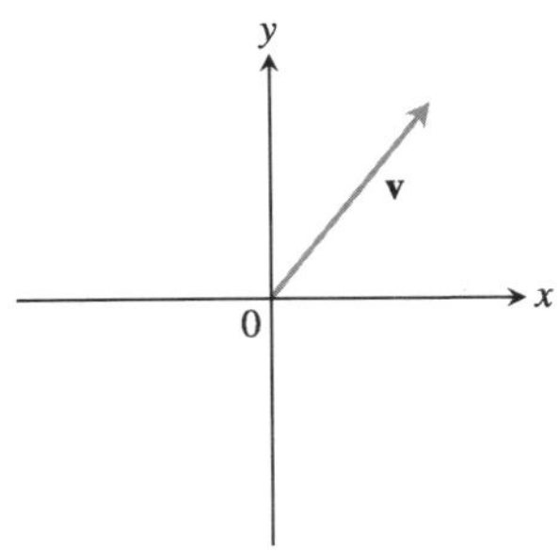

31. Orthogonal unit vectors If $\mathbf{u}_1$ and $\mathbf{u}_2$ are orthogonal unit vectors and $\mathbf{v} = a\mathbf{u}_1 + b\mathbf{u}_2$, find $\mathbf{v}\cdot\mathbf{u}_1$.

32. Cancellation in dot products In real-number multiplication, if $uv_1 = uv_2$ and $u \ne 0$, we can cancel the u and conclude that $v_1 = v_2$. Does the same rule hold for the dot product: If $\mathbf{u}\cdot\mathbf{v}_1 = \mathbf{u}\cdot\mathbf{v}_2$ and $\mathbf{u} \ne \mathbf{0}$, can you conclude that $\mathbf{v}_1 = \mathbf{v}_2$? Give reasons for your answer.

Equations for Lines in the Plane

33. Line perpendicular to a vector Show that the vector $\mathbf{v} = a\mathbf{i} + b\mathbf{j}$ is perpendicular to the line $ax + by = c$ by establishing that the slope of **v** is the negative reciprocal of the slope of the given line.

34. Line parallel to a vector Show that the vector $\mathbf{v} = a\mathbf{i} + b\mathbf{j}$ is parallel to the line $bx - ay = c$ by establishing that the slope of the line segment representing **v** is the same as the slope of the given line.

In Exercises 35–38, use the result of Exercise 33 to find an equation for the line through P perpendicular to **v**. Then sketch the line. Include **v** in your sketch *as a vector starting at the origin.*

35. $P(2, 1)$, $\mathbf{v} = \mathbf{i} + 2\mathbf{j}$

36. $P(-1, 2)$, $\mathbf{v} = -2\mathbf{i} - \mathbf{j}$

37. $P(-2, -7)$, $\mathbf{v} = -2\mathbf{i} + \mathbf{j}$

38. $P(11, 10)$, $\mathbf{v} = 2\mathbf{i} - 3\mathbf{j}$

In Exercises 39–42, use the result of Exercise 34 to find an equation for the line through P parallel to **v**. Then sketch the line. Include **v** in your sketch *as a vector starting at the origin.*

39. $P(-2, 1)$, $\mathbf{v} = \mathbf{i} - \mathbf{j}$

40. $P(0, -2)$, $\mathbf{v} = 2\mathbf{i} + 3\mathbf{j}$

41. $P(1, 2)$, $\mathbf{v} = -\mathbf{i} - 2\mathbf{j}$

42. $P(1, 3)$, $\mathbf{v} = 3\mathbf{i} - 2\mathbf{j}$

Work

43. Work along a line Find the work done by a force $\mathbf{F} = 5\mathbf{i}$ (magnitude 5 N) in moving an object along the line from the origin to the point $(1, 1)$ (distance in meters).

44. Locomotive The union Pacific's *Big Boy* locomotive could pull 6000-ton trains with a tractive effort (pull) of 602,148 N (135,375 lb). At this level of effort, about how much work did *Big Boy* do on the (approximately straight) 605-km journey from San Francisco to Los Angeles?

45. Inclined plane How much work does it take to slide a crate 20 m along a loading dock by pulling on it with a 200 N force at an angle of 30° from the horizontal?

46. Sailboat The wind passing over a boat's sail exerted a 1000-lb magnitude force **F** as shown here. How much work did the wind perform in moving the boat forward 1 mi? Answer in foot-pounds.

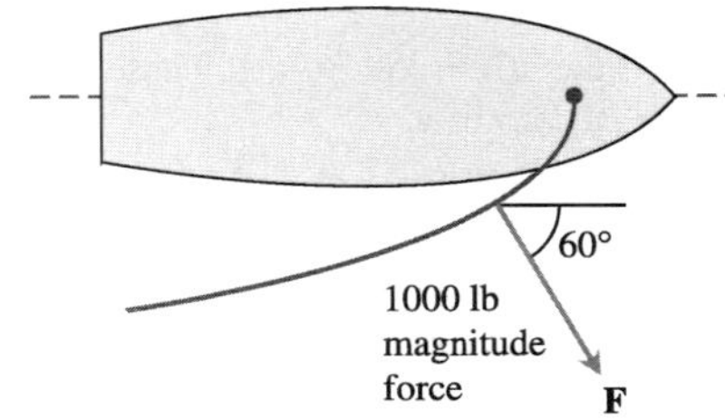

Angles Between Lines in the Plane

The acute angle between intersecting lines that do not cross at right angles is the same as the angle determined by vectors normal to the lines or by the vectors parallel to the lines.

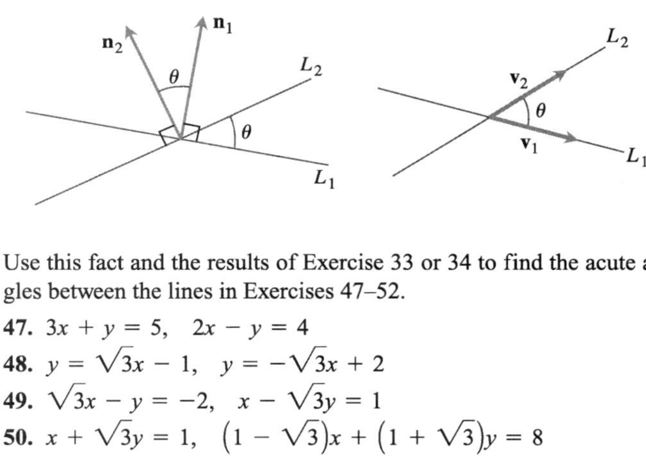

Use this fact and the results of Exercise 33 or 34 to find the acute angles between the lines in Exercises 47–52.

47. $3x + y = 5$, $2x - y = 4$

48. $y = \sqrt{3}x - 1$, $y = -\sqrt{3}x + 2$

49. $\sqrt{3}x - y = -2$, $x - \sqrt{3}y = 1$

50. $x + \sqrt{3}y = 1$, $\left(1 - \sqrt{3}\right)x + \left(1 + \sqrt{3}\right)y = 8$

51. $3x - 4y = 3$, $x - y = 7$

52. $12x + 5y = 1$, $2x - 2y = 3$

Angles Between Differentiable Curves

The angles between two differentiable curves at a point of intersection are the angles between the curves' tangent lines at these points. Find the angles between the curves in Exercises 53–56. Note that if $\mathbf{v} = a\mathbf{i} + b\mathbf{j}$ is a vector in the plane, then the vector has slope b/a provided $a \neq 0$.

53. $y = (3/2) - x^2, \quad y = x^2$ (two points of intersection)

54. $x = (3/4) - y^2, \quad x = y^2 - (3/4)$ (two points of intersection)

55. $y = x^3, \quad x = y^2$ (two points of intersection)

56. $y = -x^2, \quad y = \sqrt{x}$ (two points of intersection)

12.4 The Cross Product

In studying lines in the plane, when we needed to describe how a line was tilting, we used the notions of slope and angle of inclination. In space, we want a way to describe how a *plane* is tilting. We accomplish this by multiplying two vectors in the plane together to get a third vector perpendicular to the plane. The direction of this third vector tells us the "inclination" of the plane. The product we use to multiply the vectors together is the *vector* or *cross product*, the second of the two vector multiplication methods we study in calculus.

Cross products are widely used to describe the effects of forces in studies of electricity, magnetism, fluid flows, and orbital mechanics. This section presents the mathematical properties that account for the use of cross products in these fields.

The Cross Product of Two Vectors in Space

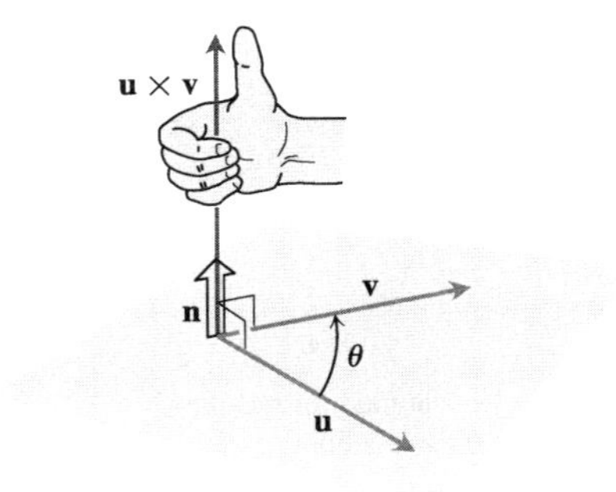

FIGURE 12.27 The construction of $\mathbf{u} \times \mathbf{v}$.

We start with two nonzero vectors **u** and **v** in space. If **u** and **v** are not parallel, they determine a plane. We select a unit vector **n** perpendicular to the plane by the **right-hand rule**. This means that we choose **n** to be the unit (normal) vector that points the way your right thumb points when your fingers curl through the angle θ from **u** to **v** (Figure 12.27). Then the **cross product u × v** ("**u** cross **v**") is the *vector* defined as follows.

> **DEFINITION** **Cross Product**
>
> $$\mathbf{u} \times \mathbf{v} = (|\mathbf{u}||\mathbf{v}| \sin\theta)\, \mathbf{n}$$

Unlike the dot product, the cross product is a vector. For this reason it's also called the **vector product** of **u** and **v**, and applies *only* to vectors in space. The vector $\mathbf{u} \times \mathbf{v}$ is orthogonal to both **u** and **v** because it is a scalar multiple of **n**.

Since the sines of 0 and π are both zero, it makes sense to define the cross product of two parallel nonzero vectors to be **0**. If one or both of **u** and **v** are zero, we also define $\mathbf{u} \times \mathbf{v}$ to be zero. This way, the cross product of two vectors **u** and **v** is zero if and only if **u** and **v** are parallel or one or both of them are zero.

> **Parallel Vectors**
>
> Nonzero vectors **u** and **v** are parallel if and only if $\mathbf{u} \times \mathbf{v} = \mathbf{0}$.

The cross product obeys the following laws.

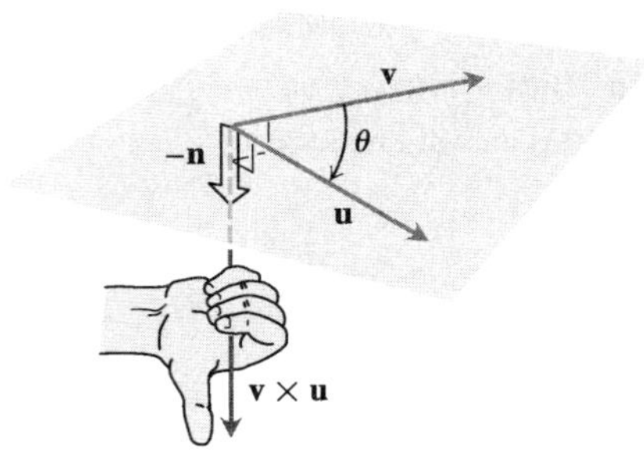

FIGURE 12.28 The construction of $\mathbf{v} \times \mathbf{u}$.

> **Properties of the Cross Product**
> If $\mathbf{u}$, $\mathbf{v}$, and $\mathbf{w}$ are any vectors and r, s are scalars, then
> 1. $(r\mathbf{u}) \times (s\mathbf{v}) = (rs)(\mathbf{u} \times \mathbf{v})$
> 2. $\mathbf{u} \times (\mathbf{v} + \mathbf{w}) = \mathbf{u} \times \mathbf{v} + \mathbf{u} \times \mathbf{w}$
> 3. $(\mathbf{v} + \mathbf{w}) \times \mathbf{u} = \mathbf{v} \times \mathbf{u} + \mathbf{w} \times \mathbf{u}$
> 4. $\mathbf{v} \times \mathbf{u} = -(\mathbf{u} \times \mathbf{v})$
> 5. $\mathbf{0} \times \mathbf{u} = \mathbf{0}$

To visualize Property 4, for example, notice that when the fingers of a right hand curl through the angle θ from $\mathbf{v}$ to $\mathbf{u}$, the thumb points the opposite way and the unit vector we choose in forming $\mathbf{v} \times \mathbf{u}$ is the negative of the one we choose in forming $\mathbf{u} \times \mathbf{v}$ (Figure 12.28).

Property 1 can be verified by applying the definition of cross product to both sides of the equation and comparing the results. Property 2 is proved in Appendix 6. Property 3 follows by multiplying both sides of the equation in Property 2 by -1 and reversing the order of the products using Property 4. Property 5 is a definition. As a rule, cross product multiplication is *not associative* so $(\mathbf{u} \times \mathbf{v}) \times \mathbf{w}$ does not generally equal $\mathbf{u} \times (\mathbf{v} \times \mathbf{w})$. (See Additional Exercise 15.)

When we apply the definition to calculate the pairwise cross products of $\mathbf{i}$, $\mathbf{j}$, and $\mathbf{k}$, we find (Figure 12.29)

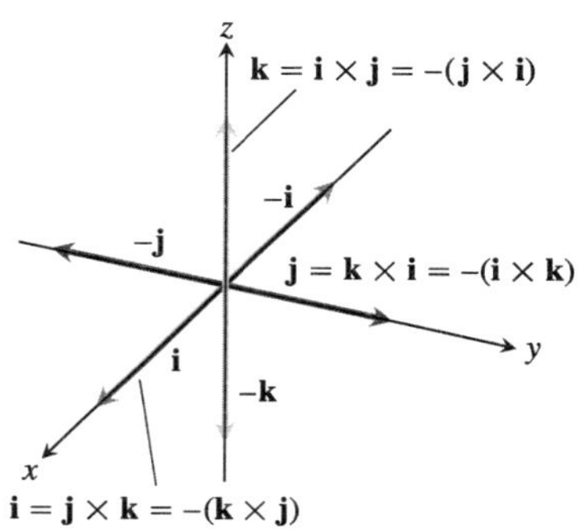

FIGURE 12.29 The pairwise cross products of $\mathbf{i}$, $\mathbf{j}$, and $\mathbf{k}$.

$$\mathbf{i} \times \mathbf{j} = -(\mathbf{j} \times \mathbf{i}) = \mathbf{k}$$

$$\mathbf{j} \times \mathbf{k} = -(\mathbf{k} \times \mathbf{j}) = \mathbf{i}$$

$$\mathbf{k} \times \mathbf{i} = -(\mathbf{i} \times \mathbf{k}) = \mathbf{j}$$

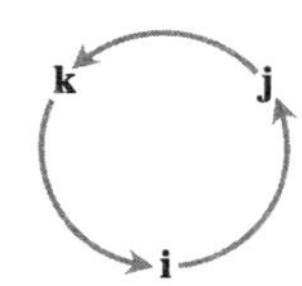

Diagram for recalling these products

and

$$\mathbf{i} \times \mathbf{i} = \mathbf{j} \times \mathbf{j} = \mathbf{k} \times \mathbf{k} = \mathbf{0}.$$

$|\mathbf{u} \times \mathbf{v}|$ Is the Area of a Parallelogram

Because $\mathbf{n}$ is a unit vector, the magnitude of $\mathbf{u} \times \mathbf{v}$ is

$$|\mathbf{u} \times \mathbf{v}| = |\mathbf{u}||\mathbf{v}|\,|\sin\theta|\,|\mathbf{n}| = |\mathbf{u}||\mathbf{v}|\sin\theta.$$

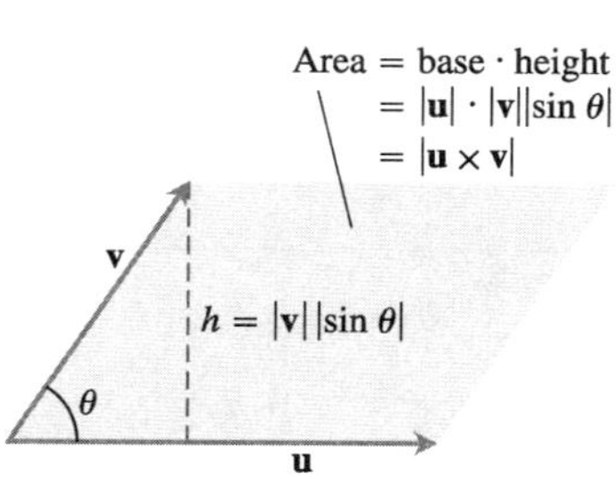

FIGURE 12.30 The parallelogram determined by $\mathbf{u}$ and $\mathbf{v}$.

This is the area of the parallelogram determined by $\mathbf{u}$ and $\mathbf{v}$ (Figure 12.30), $|\mathbf{u}|$ being the base of the parallelogram and $|\mathbf{v}||\sin\theta|$ the height.

Determinant Formula for $\mathbf{u} \times \mathbf{v}$

Our next objective is to calculate $\mathbf{u} \times \mathbf{v}$ from the components of $\mathbf{u}$ and $\mathbf{v}$ relative to a Cartesian coordinate system.

Determinants

2×2 and 3×3 determinants are evaluated as follows:

$$\begin{vmatrix} a & b \\ c & d \end{vmatrix} = ad - bc$$

EXAMPLE

$$\begin{vmatrix} 2 & 1 \\ -4 & 3 \end{vmatrix} = (2)(3) - (1)(-4) = 6 + 4 = 10$$

$$\begin{vmatrix} a_1 & a_2 & a_3 \\ b_1 & b_2 & b_3 \\ c_1 & c_2 & c_3 \end{vmatrix} = a_1 \begin{vmatrix} b_2 & b_3 \\ c_2 & c_3 \end{vmatrix} - a_2 \begin{vmatrix} b_1 & b_3 \\ c_1 & c_3 \end{vmatrix} + a_3 \begin{vmatrix} b_1 & b_2 \\ c_1 & c_2 \end{vmatrix}$$

EXAMPLE

$$\begin{vmatrix} -5 & 3 & 1 \\ 2 & 1 & 1 \\ -4 & 3 & 1 \end{vmatrix} = (-5)\begin{vmatrix} 1 & 1 \\ 3 & 1 \end{vmatrix} - (3)\begin{vmatrix} 2 & 1 \\ -4 & 1 \end{vmatrix} + (1)\begin{vmatrix} 2 & 1 \\ -4 & 3 \end{vmatrix}$$
$$= -5(1 - 3) - 3(2 + 4) + 1(6 + 4)$$
$$= 10 - 18 + 10 = 2$$

(For more information, see the Web site at **www.aw-bc.com/thomas.**)

Suppose that

$$\mathbf{u} = u_1\mathbf{i} + u_2\mathbf{j} + u_3\mathbf{k}, \qquad \mathbf{v} = v_1\mathbf{i} + v_2\mathbf{j} + v_3\mathbf{k}.$$

Then the distributive laws and the rules for multiplying **i**, **j**, and **k** tell us that

$$\begin{aligned} \mathbf{u} \times \mathbf{v} &= (u_1\mathbf{i} + u_2\mathbf{j} + u_3\mathbf{k}) \times (v_1\mathbf{i} + v_2\mathbf{j} + v_3\mathbf{k}) \\ &= u_1v_1\mathbf{i}\times\mathbf{i} + u_1v_2\mathbf{i}\times\mathbf{j} + u_1v_3\mathbf{i}\times\mathbf{k} \\ &\quad + u_2v_1\mathbf{j}\times\mathbf{i} + u_2v_2\mathbf{j}\times\mathbf{j} + u_2v_3\mathbf{j}\times\mathbf{k} \\ &\quad + u_3v_1\mathbf{k}\times\mathbf{i} + u_3v_2\mathbf{k}\times\mathbf{j} + u_3v_3\mathbf{k}\times\mathbf{k} \\ &= (u_2v_3 - u_3v_2)\mathbf{i} - (u_1v_3 - u_3v_1)\mathbf{j} + (u_1v_2 - u_2v_1)\mathbf{k}. \end{aligned}$$

The terms in the last line are the same as the terms in the expansion of the symbolic determinant

$$\begin{vmatrix} \mathbf{i} & \mathbf{j} & \mathbf{k} \\ u_1 & u_2 & u_3 \\ v_1 & v_2 & v_3 \end{vmatrix}.$$

We therefore have the following rule.

> **Calculating Cross Products Using Determinants**
>
> If $\mathbf{u} = u_1\mathbf{i} + u_2\mathbf{j} + u_3\mathbf{k}$ and $\mathbf{v} = v_1\mathbf{i} + v_2\mathbf{j} + v_3\mathbf{k}$, then
>
> $$\mathbf{u} \times \mathbf{v} = \begin{vmatrix} \mathbf{i} & \mathbf{j} & \mathbf{k} \\ u_1 & u_2 & u_3 \\ v_1 & v_2 & v_3 \end{vmatrix}.$$

EXAMPLE 1 Calculating Cross Products with Determinants

Find $\mathbf{u} \times \mathbf{v}$ and $\mathbf{v} \times \mathbf{u}$ if $\mathbf{u} = 2\mathbf{i} + \mathbf{j} + \mathbf{k}$ and $\mathbf{v} = -4\mathbf{i} + 3\mathbf{j} + \mathbf{k}$.

Solution

$$\mathbf{u} \times \mathbf{v} = \begin{vmatrix} \mathbf{i} & \mathbf{j} & \mathbf{k} \\ 2 & 1 & 1 \\ -4 & 3 & 1 \end{vmatrix} = \begin{vmatrix} 1 & 1 \\ 3 & 1 \end{vmatrix}\mathbf{i} - \begin{vmatrix} 2 & 1 \\ -4 & 1 \end{vmatrix}\mathbf{j} + \begin{vmatrix} 2 & 1 \\ -4 & 3 \end{vmatrix}\mathbf{k}$$
$$= -2\mathbf{i} - 6\mathbf{j} + 10\mathbf{k}$$
$$\mathbf{v} \times \mathbf{u} = -(\mathbf{u} \times \mathbf{v}) = 2\mathbf{i} + 6\mathbf{j} - 10\mathbf{k}$$

■

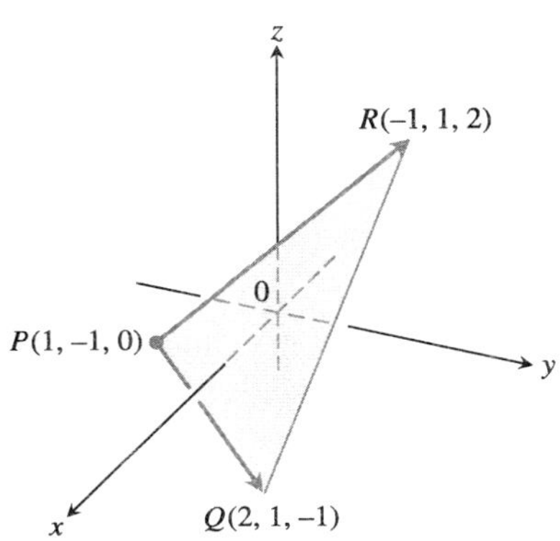

FIGURE 12.31 The area of triangle PQR is half of $|\overrightarrow{PQ} \times \overrightarrow{PR}|$ (Example 2).

EXAMPLE 2 Finding Vectors Perpendicular to a Plane

Find a vector perpendicular to the plane of $P(1, -1, 0)$, $Q(2, 1, -1)$, and $R(-1, 1, 2)$ (Figure 12.31).

Solution The vector $\overrightarrow{PQ} \times \overrightarrow{PR}$ is perpendicular to the plane because it is perpendicular to both vectors. In terms of components,

$$\overrightarrow{PQ} = (2-1)\mathbf{i} + (1+1)\mathbf{j} + (-1-0)\mathbf{k} = \mathbf{i} + 2\mathbf{j} - \mathbf{k}$$

$$\overrightarrow{PR} = (-1-1)\mathbf{i} + (1+1)\mathbf{j} + (2-0)\mathbf{k} = -2\mathbf{i} + 2\mathbf{j} + 2\mathbf{k}$$

$$\overrightarrow{PQ} \times \overrightarrow{PR} = \begin{vmatrix} \mathbf{i} & \mathbf{j} & \mathbf{k} \\ 1 & 2 & -1 \\ -2 & 2 & 2 \end{vmatrix} = \begin{vmatrix} 2 & -1 \\ 2 & 2 \end{vmatrix}\mathbf{i} - \begin{vmatrix} 1 & -1 \\ -2 & 2 \end{vmatrix}\mathbf{j} + \begin{vmatrix} 1 & 2 \\ -2 & 2 \end{vmatrix}\mathbf{k}$$

$$= 6\mathbf{i} + 6\mathbf{k}.$$

■

EXAMPLE 3 Finding the Area of a Triangle

Find the area of the triangle with vertices $P(1, -1, 0)$, $Q(2, 1, -1)$, and $R(-1, 1, 2)$ (Figure 12.31).

Solution The area of the parallelogram determined by P, Q, and R is

$$|\overrightarrow{PQ} \times \overrightarrow{PR}| = |6\mathbf{i} + 6\mathbf{k}| \qquad \text{Values from Example 2.}$$

$$= \sqrt{(6)^2 + (6)^2} = \sqrt{2 \cdot 36} = 6\sqrt{2}.$$

The triangle's area is half of this, or $3\sqrt{2}$. ■

EXAMPLE 4 Finding a Unit Normal to a Plane

Find a unit vector perpendicular to the plane of $P(1, -1, 0)$, $Q(2, 1, -1)$, and $R(-1, 1, 2)$.

Solution Since $\overrightarrow{PQ} \times \overrightarrow{PR}$ is perpendicular to the plane, its direction $\mathbf{n}$ is a unit vector perpendicular to the plane. Taking values from Examples 2 and 3, we have

$$\mathbf{n} = \frac{\overrightarrow{PQ} \times \overrightarrow{PR}}{|\overrightarrow{PQ} \times \overrightarrow{PR}|} = \frac{6\mathbf{i} + 6\mathbf{k}}{6\sqrt{2}} = \frac{1}{\sqrt{2}}\mathbf{i} + \frac{1}{\sqrt{2}}\mathbf{k}.$$

■

For ease in calculating the cross product using determinants, we usually write vectors in the form $\mathbf{v} = v_1\mathbf{i} + v_2\mathbf{j} + v_3\mathbf{k}$ rather than as ordered triples $\mathbf{v} = \langle v_1, v_2, v_3 \rangle$.

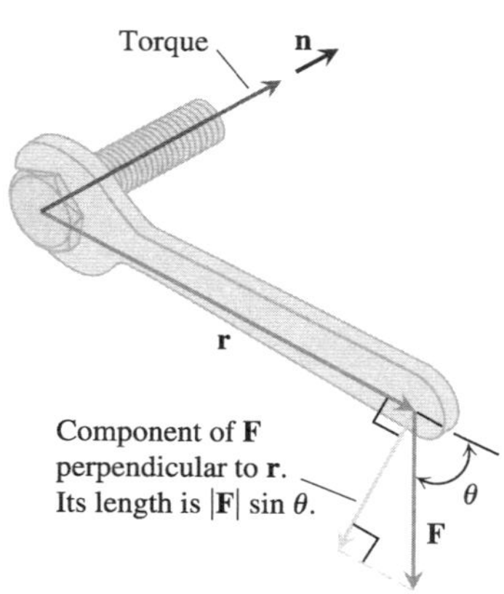

FIGURE 12.32 The torque vector describes the tendency of the force $\mathbf{F}$ to drive the bolt forward.

Torque

When we turn a bolt by applying a force $\mathbf{F}$ to a wrench (Figure 12.32), the torque we produce acts along the axis of the bolt to drive the bolt forward. The magnitude of the torque depends on how far out on the wrench the force is applied and on how much of the force is perpendicular to the wrench at the point of application. The number we use to measure the torque's magnitude is the product of the length of the lever arm $\mathbf{r}$ and the scalar component of $\mathbf{F}$ perpendicular to $\mathbf{r}$. In the notation of Figure 12.32,

$$\text{Magnitude of torque vector} = |\mathbf{r}||\mathbf{F}| \sin\theta,$$

or $|\mathbf{r} \times \mathbf{F}|$. If we let $\mathbf{n}$ be a unit vector along the axis of the bolt in the direction of the torque, then a complete description of the torque vector is $\mathbf{r} \times \mathbf{F}$, or

$$\text{Torque vector} = (|\mathbf{r}||\mathbf{F}| \sin\theta)\,\mathbf{n}.$$

Recall that we defined $\mathbf{u} \times \mathbf{v}$ to be $\mathbf{0}$ when $\mathbf{u}$ and $\mathbf{v}$ are parallel. This is consistent with the torque interpretation as well. If the force $\mathbf{F}$ in Figure 12.32 is parallel to the wrench, meaning that we are trying to turn the bolt by pushing or pulling along the line of the wrench's handle, the torque produced is zero.

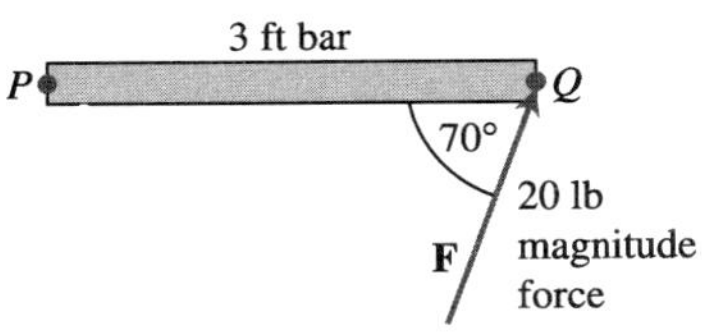

FIGURE 12.33 The magnitude of the torque exerted by **F** at P is about 56.4 ft-lb (Example 5).

EXAMPLE 5 Finding the Magnitude of a Torque

The magnitude of the torque generated by force $\mathbf{F}$ at the pivot point P in Figure 12.33 is

$$\begin{aligned} |\overrightarrow{PQ} \times \mathbf{F}| &= |\overrightarrow{PQ}||\mathbf{F}| \sin 70^\circ \\ &\approx (3)(20)(0.94) \\ &\approx 56.4 \text{ ft-lb}. \end{aligned}$$

■

Triple Scalar or Box Product

The product $(\mathbf{u} \times \mathbf{v}) \cdot \mathbf{w}$ is called the **triple scalar product** of $\mathbf{u}$, $\mathbf{v}$, and $\mathbf{w}$ (in that order). As you can see from the formula

$$|(\mathbf{u} \times \mathbf{v}) \cdot \mathbf{w}| = |\mathbf{u} \times \mathbf{v}||\mathbf{w}||\cos\theta|,$$

the absolute value of the product is the volume of the parallelepiped (parallelogram-sided box) determined by $\mathbf{u}$, $\mathbf{v}$, and $\mathbf{w}$ (Figure 12.34). The number $|\mathbf{u} \times \mathbf{v}|$ is the area of the base parallelogram. The number $|\mathbf{w}||\cos\theta|$ is the parallelepiped's height. Because of this geometry, $(\mathbf{u} \times \mathbf{v}) \cdot \mathbf{w}$ is also called the **box product** of $\mathbf{u}$, $\mathbf{v}$, and $\mathbf{w}$.

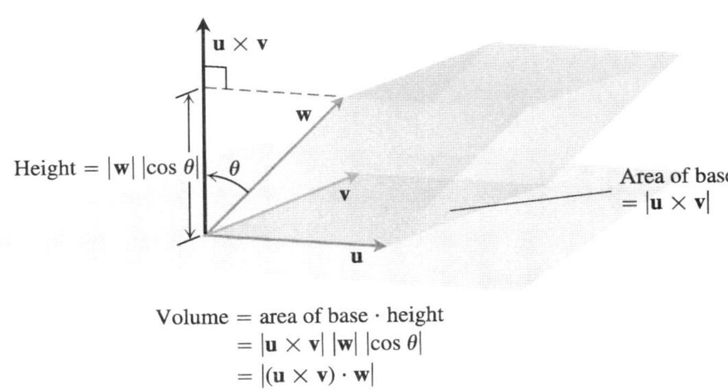

FIGURE 12.34 The number $|(\mathbf{u} \times \mathbf{v}) \cdot \mathbf{w}|$ is the volume of a parallelepiped.

The dot and cross may be interchanged in a triple scalar product without altering its value.

By treating the planes of $\mathbf{v}$ and $\mathbf{w}$ and of $\mathbf{w}$ and $\mathbf{u}$ as the base planes of the parallelepiped determined by $\mathbf{u}$, $\mathbf{v}$, and $\mathbf{w}$, we see that

$$(\mathbf{u} \times \mathbf{v}) \cdot \mathbf{w} = (\mathbf{v} \times \mathbf{w}) \cdot \mathbf{u} = (\mathbf{w} \times \mathbf{u}) \cdot \mathbf{v}.$$

Since the dot product is commutative, we also have

$$(\mathbf{u} \times \mathbf{v}) \cdot \mathbf{w} = \mathbf{u} \cdot (\mathbf{v} \times \mathbf{w}).$$

The triple scalar product can be evaluated as a determinant:

$$(\mathbf{u}\times\mathbf{v})\cdot\mathbf{w} = \left[\begin{vmatrix} u_2 & u_3 \\ v_2 & v_3 \end{vmatrix}\mathbf{i} - \begin{vmatrix} u_1 & u_3 \\ v_1 & v_3 \end{vmatrix}\mathbf{j} + \begin{vmatrix} u_1 & u_2 \\ v_1 & v_2 \end{vmatrix}\mathbf{k}\right]\cdot\mathbf{w}$$

$$= w_1\begin{vmatrix} u_2 & u_3 \\ v_2 & v_3 \end{vmatrix} - w_2\begin{vmatrix} u_1 & u_3 \\ v_1 & v_3 \end{vmatrix} + w_3\begin{vmatrix} u_1 & u_2 \\ v_1 & v_2 \end{vmatrix}$$

$$= \begin{vmatrix} u_1 & u_2 & u_3 \\ v_1 & v_2 & v_3 \\ w_1 & w_2 & w_3 \end{vmatrix}.$$

Calculating the Triple Scalar Product

$$(\mathbf{u}\times\mathbf{v})\cdot\mathbf{w} = \begin{vmatrix} u_1 & u_2 & u_3 \\ v_1 & v_2 & v_3 \\ w_1 & w_2 & w_3 \end{vmatrix}$$

EXAMPLE 6 Finding the Volume of a Parallelepiped

Find the volume of the box (parallelepiped) determined by $\mathbf{u} = \mathbf{i} + 2\mathbf{j} - \mathbf{k}$, $\mathbf{v} = -2\mathbf{i} + 3\mathbf{k}$, and $\mathbf{w} = 7\mathbf{j} - 4\mathbf{k}$.

Solution Using the rule for calculating determinants, we find

$$(\mathbf{u}\times\mathbf{v})\cdot\mathbf{w} = \begin{vmatrix} 1 & 2 & -1 \\ -2 & 0 & 3 \\ 0 & 7 & -4 \end{vmatrix} = -23.$$

The volume is $|(\mathbf{u}\times\mathbf{v})\cdot\mathbf{w}| = 23$ units cubed. ■

EXERCISES 12.4

Cross Product Calculations

In Exercises 1–8, find the length and direction (when defined) of $\mathbf{u}\times\mathbf{v}$ and $\mathbf{v}\times\mathbf{u}$.

1. $\mathbf{u} = 2\mathbf{i} - 2\mathbf{j} - \mathbf{k}, \quad \mathbf{v} = \mathbf{i} - \mathbf{k}$
2. $\mathbf{u} = 2\mathbf{i} + 3\mathbf{j}, \quad \mathbf{v} = -\mathbf{i} + \mathbf{j}$
3. $\mathbf{u} = 2\mathbf{i} - 2\mathbf{j} + 4\mathbf{k}, \quad \mathbf{v} = -\mathbf{i} + \mathbf{j} - 2\mathbf{k}$
4. $\mathbf{u} = \mathbf{i} + \mathbf{j} - \mathbf{k}, \quad \mathbf{v} = \mathbf{0}$
5. $\mathbf{u} = 2\mathbf{i}, \quad \mathbf{v} = -3\mathbf{j}$
6. $\mathbf{u} = \mathbf{i}\times\mathbf{j}, \quad \mathbf{v} = \mathbf{j}\times\mathbf{k}$
7. $\mathbf{u} = -8\mathbf{i} - 2\mathbf{j} - 4\mathbf{k}, \quad \mathbf{v} = 2\mathbf{i} + 2\mathbf{j} + \mathbf{k}$
8. $\mathbf{u} = \frac{3}{2}\mathbf{i} - \frac{1}{2}\mathbf{j} + \mathbf{k}, \quad \mathbf{v} = \mathbf{i} + \mathbf{j} + 2\mathbf{k}$

In Exercises 9–14, sketch the coordinate axes and then include the vectors $\mathbf{u}$, $\mathbf{v}$ and $\mathbf{u}\times\mathbf{v}$ as vectors starting at the origin.

9. $\mathbf{u} = \mathbf{i}, \quad \mathbf{v} = \mathbf{j}$
10. $\mathbf{u} = \mathbf{i} - \mathbf{k}, \quad \mathbf{v} = \mathbf{j}$
11. $\mathbf{u} = \mathbf{i} - \mathbf{k}, \quad \mathbf{v} = \mathbf{j} + \mathbf{k}$
12. $\mathbf{u} = 2\mathbf{i} - \mathbf{j}, \quad \mathbf{v} = \mathbf{i} + 2\mathbf{j}$
13. $\mathbf{u} = \mathbf{i} + \mathbf{j}, \quad \mathbf{v} = \mathbf{i} - \mathbf{j}$
14. $\mathbf{u} = \mathbf{j} + 2\mathbf{k}, \quad \mathbf{v} = \mathbf{i}$

Triangles in Space

In Exercises 15–18,

a. Find the area of the triangle determined by the points P, Q, and R.

b. Find a unit vector perpendicular to plane PQR.

15. $P(1, -1, 2)$, $Q(2, 0, -1)$, $R(0, 2, 1)$
16. $P(1, 1, 1)$, $Q(2, 1, 3)$, $R(3, -1, 1)$
17. $P(2, -2, 1)$, $Q(3, -1, 2)$, $R(3, -1, 1)$
18. $P(-2, 2, 0)$, $Q(0, 1, -1)$, $R(-1, 2, -2)$

Triple Scalar Products

In Exercises 19–22, verify that $(\mathbf{u} \times \mathbf{v}) \cdot \mathbf{w} = (\mathbf{v} \times \mathbf{w}) \cdot \mathbf{u} = (\mathbf{w} \times \mathbf{u}) \cdot \mathbf{v}$ and find the volume of the parallelepiped (box) determined by **u**, **v**, and **w**.

	u	v	w
19.	$2\mathbf{i}$	$2\mathbf{j}$	$2\mathbf{k}$
20.	$\mathbf{i} - \mathbf{j} + \mathbf{k}$	$2\mathbf{i} + \mathbf{j} - 2\mathbf{k}$	$-\mathbf{i} + 2\mathbf{j} - \mathbf{k}$
21.	$2\mathbf{i} + \mathbf{j}$	$2\mathbf{i} - \mathbf{j} + \mathbf{k}$	$\mathbf{i} + 2\mathbf{k}$
22.	$\mathbf{i} + \mathbf{j} - 2\mathbf{k}$	$-\mathbf{i} - \mathbf{k}$	$2\mathbf{i} + 4\mathbf{j} - 2\mathbf{k}$

Theory and Examples

23. **Parallel and perpendicular vectors** Let $\mathbf{u} = 5\mathbf{i} - \mathbf{j} + \mathbf{k}$, $\mathbf{v} = \mathbf{j} - 5\mathbf{k}$, $\mathbf{w} = -15\mathbf{i} + 3\mathbf{j} - 3\mathbf{k}$. Which vectors, if any, are **(a)** perpendicular? **(b)** Parallel? Give reasons for your answers.

24. **Parallel and perpendicular vectors** Let $\mathbf{u} = \mathbf{i} + 2\mathbf{j} - \mathbf{k}$, $\mathbf{v} = -\mathbf{i} + \mathbf{j} + \mathbf{k}$, $\mathbf{w} = \mathbf{i} + \mathbf{k}$, $\mathbf{r} = -(\pi/2)\mathbf{i} - \pi\mathbf{j} + (\pi/2)\mathbf{k}$. Which vectors, if any, are **(a)** perpendicular? **(b)** Parallel? Give reasons for your answers.

In Exercises 39 and 40, find the magnitude of the torque exerted by **F** on the bolt at P if $|\overrightarrow{PQ}| = 8$ in. and $|\mathbf{F}| = 30$ lb. Answer in foot-pounds.

25.

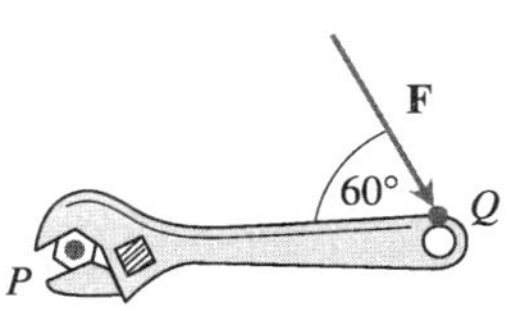

26.

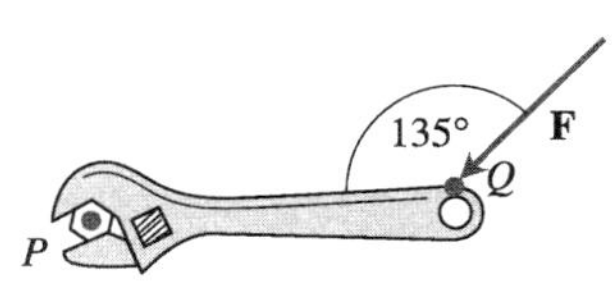

27. Which of the following are *always true*, and which are *not always true*? Give reasons for your answers.
   a. $|\mathbf{u}| = \sqrt{\mathbf{u} \cdot \mathbf{u}}$
   b. $\mathbf{u} \cdot \mathbf{u} = |\mathbf{u}|$
   c. $\mathbf{u} \times \mathbf{0} = \mathbf{0} \times \mathbf{u} = \mathbf{0}$
   d. $\mathbf{u} \times (-\mathbf{u}) = \mathbf{0}$
   e. $\mathbf{u} \times \mathbf{v} = \mathbf{v} \times \mathbf{u}$
   f. $\mathbf{u} \times (\mathbf{v} + \mathbf{w}) = \mathbf{u} \times \mathbf{v} + \mathbf{u} \times \mathbf{w}$
   g. $(\mathbf{u} \times \mathbf{v}) \cdot \mathbf{v} = 0$
   h. $(\mathbf{u} \times \mathbf{v}) \cdot \mathbf{w} = \mathbf{u} \cdot (\mathbf{v} \times \mathbf{w})$

28. Which of the following are *always true*, and which are *not always true*? Give reasons for your answers.
   a. $\mathbf{u} \cdot \mathbf{v} = \mathbf{v} \cdot \mathbf{u}$
   b. $\mathbf{u} \times \mathbf{v} = -(\mathbf{v} \times \mathbf{u})$
   c. $(-\mathbf{u}) \times \mathbf{v} = -(\mathbf{u} \times \mathbf{v})$
   d. $(c\mathbf{u}) \cdot \mathbf{v} = \mathbf{u} \cdot (c\mathbf{v}) = c(\mathbf{u} \cdot \mathbf{v})$ (any number c)
   e. $c(\mathbf{u} \times \mathbf{v}) = (c\mathbf{u}) \times \mathbf{v} = \mathbf{u} \times (c\mathbf{v})$ (any number c)
   f. $\mathbf{u} \cdot \mathbf{u} = |\mathbf{u}|^2$
   g. $(\mathbf{u} \times \mathbf{u}) \cdot \mathbf{u} = 0$
   h. $(\mathbf{u} \times \mathbf{v}) \cdot \mathbf{u} = \mathbf{v} \cdot (\mathbf{u} \times \mathbf{v})$

29. Given nonzero vectors **u**, **v**, and **w**, use dot product and cross product notation, as appropriate, to describe the following.
   a. The vector projection of **u** onto **v**
   b. A vector orthogonal to **u** and **v**
   c. A vector orthogonal to $\mathbf{u} \times \mathbf{v}$ and **w**
   d. The volume of the parallelepiped determined by **u**, **v**, and **w**

30. Given nonzero vectors **u**, **v**, and **w**, use dot product and cross product notation to describe the following.
   a. A vector orthogonal to $\mathbf{u} \times \mathbf{v}$ and $\mathbf{u} \times \mathbf{w}$
   b. A vector orthogonal to $\mathbf{u} + \mathbf{v}$ and $\mathbf{u} - \mathbf{v}$
   c. A vector of length $|\mathbf{u}|$ in the direction of **v**
   d. The area of the parallelogram determined by **u** and **w**

31. Let **u**, **v**, and **w** be vectors. Which of the following make sense, and which do not? Give reasons for your answers.
   a. $(\mathbf{u} \times \mathbf{v}) \cdot \mathbf{w}$
   b. $\mathbf{u} \times (\mathbf{v} \cdot \mathbf{w})$
   c. $\mathbf{u} \times (\mathbf{v} \times \mathbf{w})$
   d. $\mathbf{u} \cdot (\mathbf{v} \cdot \mathbf{w})$

32. **Cross products of three vectors** Show that except in degenerate cases, $(\mathbf{u} \times \mathbf{v}) \times \mathbf{w}$ lies in the plane of **u** and **v**, whereas $\mathbf{u} \times (\mathbf{v} \times \mathbf{w})$ lies in the plane of **v** and **w**. What *are* the degenerate cases?

33. **Cancellation in cross products** If $\mathbf{u} \times \mathbf{v} = \mathbf{u} \times \mathbf{w}$ and $\mathbf{u} \neq \mathbf{0}$, then does $\mathbf{v} = \mathbf{w}$? Give reasons for your answer.

34. **Double cancellation** If $\mathbf{u} \neq \mathbf{0}$ and if $\mathbf{u} \times \mathbf{v} = \mathbf{u} \times \mathbf{w}$ and $\mathbf{u} \cdot \mathbf{v} = \mathbf{u} \cdot \mathbf{w}$, then does $\mathbf{v} = \mathbf{w}$? Give reasons for your answer.

Area in the Plane

Find the areas of the parallelograms whose vertices are given in Exercises 35–38.

35. $A(1, 0)$, $B(0, 1)$, $C(-1, 0)$, $D(0, -1)$
36. $A(0, 0)$, $B(7, 3)$, $C(9, 8)$, $D(2, 5)$
37. $A(-1, 2)$, $B(2, 0)$, $C(7, 1)$, $D(4, 3)$
38. $A(-6, 0)$, $B(1, -4)$, $C(3, 1)$, $D(-4, 5)$

Find the areas of the triangles whose vertices are given in Exercises 39–42.

39. $A(0, 0)$, $B(-2, 3)$, $C(3, 1)$
40. $A(-1, -1)$, $B(3, 3)$, $C(2, 1)$
41. $A(-5, 3)$, $B(1, -2)$, $C(6, -2)$
42. $A(-6, 0)$, $B(10, -5)$, $C(-2, 4)$

43. **Triangle area** Find a formula for the area of the triangle in the xy-plane with vertices at $(0, 0)$, (a_1, a_2), and (b_1, b_2). Explain your work.

44. **Triangle area** Find a concise formula for the area of a triangle with vertices (a_1, a_2), (b_1, b_2), and (c_1, c_2).

12.5 Lines and Planes in Space

In the calculus of functions of a single variable, we used our knowledge of lines to study curves in the plane. We investigated tangents and found that, when highly magnified, differentiable curves were effectively linear.

To study the calculus of functions of more than one variable in the next chapter, we start with planes and use our knowledge of planes to study the surfaces that are the graphs of functions in space.

This section shows how to use scalar and vector products to write equations for lines, line segments, and planes in space.

Lines and Line Segments in Space

In the plane, a line is determined by a point and a number giving the slope of the line. In space a line is determined by a point and a *vector* giving the direction of the line.

Suppose that L is a line in space passing through a point $P_0(x_0, y_0, z_0)$ parallel to a vector $\mathbf{v} = v_1\mathbf{i} + v_2\mathbf{j} + v_3\mathbf{k}$. Then L is the set of all points $P(x, y, z)$ for which $\overrightarrow{P_0P}$ is parallel to $\mathbf{v}$ (Figure 12.35). Thus, $\overrightarrow{P_0P} = t\mathbf{v}$ for some scalar parameter t. The value of t depends on the location of the point P along the line, and the domain of t is $(-\infty, \infty)$. The expanded form of the equation $\overrightarrow{P_0P} = t\mathbf{v}$ is

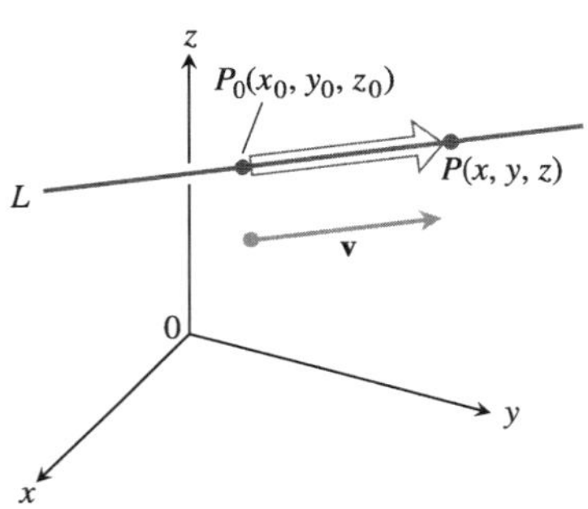

FIGURE 12.35 A point P lies on L through P_0 parallel to $\mathbf{v}$ if and only if $\overrightarrow{P_0P}$ is a scalar multiple of $\mathbf{v}$.

$$(x - x_0)\mathbf{i} + (y - y_0)\mathbf{j} + (z - z_0)\mathbf{k} = t(v_1\mathbf{i} + v_2\mathbf{j} + v_3\mathbf{k}),$$

which can be rewritten as

$$x\mathbf{i} + y\mathbf{j} + z\mathbf{k} = x_0\mathbf{i} + y_0\mathbf{j} + z_0\mathbf{k} + t(v_1\mathbf{i} + v_2\mathbf{j} + v_3\mathbf{k}). \tag{1}$$

If $\mathbf{r}(t)$ is the position vector of a point $P(x, y, z)$ on the line and $\mathbf{r}_0$ is the position vector of the point $P_0(x_0, y_0, z_0)$, then Equation (1) gives the following vector form for the equation of a line in space.

> **Vector Equation for a Line**
> **A vector equation for the line L through $P_0(x_0, y_0, z_0)$ parallel to $\mathbf{v}$** is
>
> $$\mathbf{r}(t) = \mathbf{r}_0 + t\mathbf{v}, \qquad -\infty < t < \infty, \tag{2}$$
>
> where $\mathbf{r}$ is the position vector of a point $P(x, y, z)$ on L and $\mathbf{r}_0$ is the position vector of $P_0(x_0, y_0, z_0)$.

Equating the corresponding components of the two sides of Equation (1) gives three scalar equations involving the parameter t:

$$x = x_0 + tv_1, \qquad y = y_0 + tv_2, \qquad z = z_0 + tv_3.$$

These equations give us the standard parametrization of the line for the parameter interval $-\infty < t < \infty$.

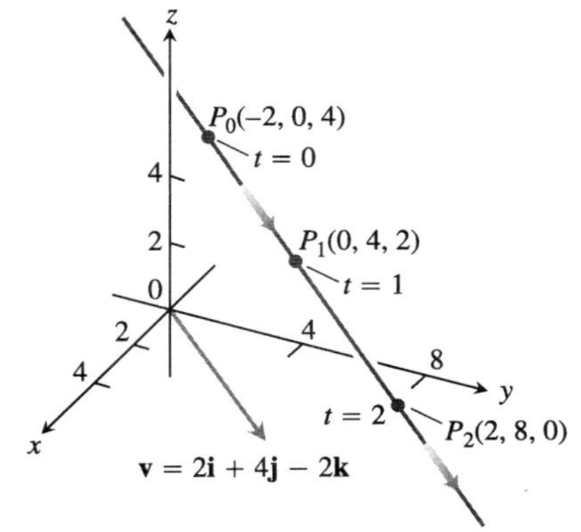

FIGURE 12.36 Selected points and parameter values on the line $x = -2 + 2t, y = 4t, z = 4 - 2t$. The arrows show the direction of increasing t (Example 1).

> **Parametric Equations for a Line**
> **The standard parametrization of the line through $P_0(x_0, y_0, z_0)$ parallel to $\mathbf{v} = v_1\mathbf{i} + v_2\mathbf{j} + v_3\mathbf{k}$ is**
>
> $$x = x_0 + tv_1, \quad y = y_0 + tv_2, \quad z = z_0 + tv_3, \quad -\infty < t < \infty \tag{3}$$

EXAMPLE 1 Parametrizing a Line Through a Point Parallel to a Vector

Find parametric equations for the line through $(-2, 0, 4)$ parallel to $\mathbf{v} = 2\mathbf{i} + 4\mathbf{j} - 2\mathbf{k}$ (Figure 12.36).

Solution With $P_0(x_0, y_0, z_0)$ equal to $(-2, 0, 4)$ and $v_1\mathbf{i} + v_2\mathbf{j} + v_3\mathbf{k}$ equal to $2\mathbf{i} + 4\mathbf{j} - 2\mathbf{k}$, Equations (3) become

$$x = -2 + 2t, \qquad y = 4t, \qquad z = 4 - 2t.$$ ■

EXAMPLE 2 Parametrizing a Line Through Two Points

Find parametric equations for the line through $P(-3, 2, -3)$ and $Q(1, -1, 4)$.

Solution The vector

$$\begin{aligned} \overrightarrow{PQ} &= (1 - (-3))\mathbf{i} + (-1 - 2)\mathbf{j} + (4 - (-3))\mathbf{k} \\ &= 4\mathbf{i} - 3\mathbf{j} + 7\mathbf{k} \end{aligned}$$

is parallel to the line, and Equations (3) with $(x_0, y_0, z_0) = (-3, 2, -3)$ give

$$x = -3 + 4t, \qquad y = 2 - 3t, \qquad z = -3 + 7t.$$

We could have chosen $Q(1, -1, 4)$ as the "base point" and written

$$x = 1 + 4t, \quad y = -1 - 3t, \quad z = 4 + 7t.$$

These equations serve as well as the first; they simply place you at a different point on the line for a given value of t. ■

Notice that parametrizations are not unique. Not only can the "base point" change, but so can the parameter. The equations $x = -3 + 4t^3, y = 2 - 3t^3$, and $z = -3 + 7t^3$ also parametrize the line in Example 2.

To parametrize a line segment joining two points, we first parametrize the line through the points. We then find the t-values for the endpoints and restrict t to lie in the closed interval bounded by these values. The line equations together with this added restriction parametrize the segment.

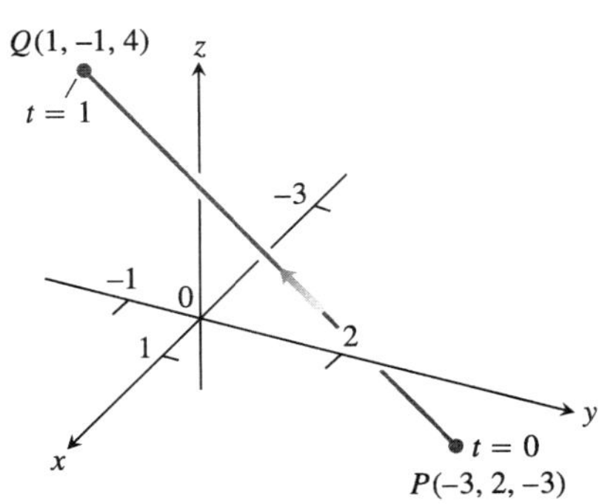

FIGURE 12.37 Example 3 derives a parametrization of line segment PQ. The arrow shows the direction of increasing t.

EXAMPLE 3 Parametrizing a Line Segment

Parametrize the line segment joining the points $P(-3, 2, -3)$ and $Q(1, -1, 4)$ (Figure 12.37).

Solution We begin with equations for the line through P and Q, taking them, in this case, from Example 2:

$$x = -3 + 4t, \qquad y = 2 - 3t, \qquad z = -3 + 7t.$$

We observe that the point

$$(x, y, z) = (-3 + 4t, 2 - 3t, -3 + 7t)$$

on the line passes through $P(-3, 2, -3)$ at $t = 0$ and $Q(1, -1, 4)$ at $t = 1$. We add the restriction $0 \le t \le 1$ to parametrize the segment:

$$x = -3 + 4t, \qquad y = 2 - 3t, \qquad z = -3 + 7t, \qquad 0 \le t \le 1. \qquad \blacksquare$$

The vector form (Equation (2)) for a line in space is more revealing if we think of a line as the path of a particle starting at position $P_0(x_0, y_0, z_0)$ and moving in the direction of vector $\mathbf{v}$. Rewriting Equation (2), we have

$$\begin{aligned} \mathbf{r}(t) &= \mathbf{r}_0 + t\mathbf{v} \\ &= \underbrace{\mathbf{r}_0}_{\text{Initial position}} + \underbrace{t}_{\text{Time}}\underbrace{|\mathbf{v}|}_{\text{Speed}}\underbrace{\frac{\mathbf{v}}{|\mathbf{v}|}}_{\text{Direction}}. \end{aligned} \tag{4}$$

In other words, the position of the particle at time t is its initial position plus its distance moved (speed $\times$ time) in the direction $\mathbf{v}/|\mathbf{v}|$ of its straight-line motion.

EXAMPLE 4 Flight of a Helicopter

A helicopter is to fly directly from a helipad at the origin in the direction of the point (1, 1, 1) at a speed of 60 ft/sec. What is the position of the helicopter after 10 sec?

Solution We place the origin at the starting position (helipad) of the helicopter. Then the unit vector

$$\mathbf{u} = \frac{1}{\sqrt{3}}\mathbf{i} + \frac{1}{\sqrt{3}}\mathbf{j} + \frac{1}{\sqrt{3}}\mathbf{k}$$

gives the flight direction of the helicopter. From Equation (4), the position of the helicopter at any time t is

$$\begin{aligned} \mathbf{r}(t) &= \mathbf{r}_0 + t(\text{speed})\mathbf{u} \\ &= \mathbf{0} + t(60)\left(\frac{1}{\sqrt{3}}\mathbf{i} + \frac{1}{\sqrt{3}}\mathbf{j} + \frac{1}{\sqrt{3}}\mathbf{k}\right) \\ &= 20\sqrt{3}t(\mathbf{i} + \mathbf{j} + \mathbf{k}). \end{aligned}$$

When $t = 10$ sec,

$$\begin{aligned} \mathbf{r}(10) &= 200\sqrt{3}\,(\mathbf{i} + \mathbf{j} + \mathbf{k}) \\ &= \left\langle 200\sqrt{3}, 200\sqrt{3}, 200\sqrt{3} \right\rangle. \end{aligned}$$

After 10 sec of flight from the origin toward (1, 1, 1), the helicopter is located at the point $(200\sqrt{3}, 200\sqrt{3}, 200\sqrt{3})$ in space. It has traveled a distance of (60 ft/sec)(10 sec) = 600 ft, which is the length of the vector $\mathbf{r}(10)$. $\blacksquare$

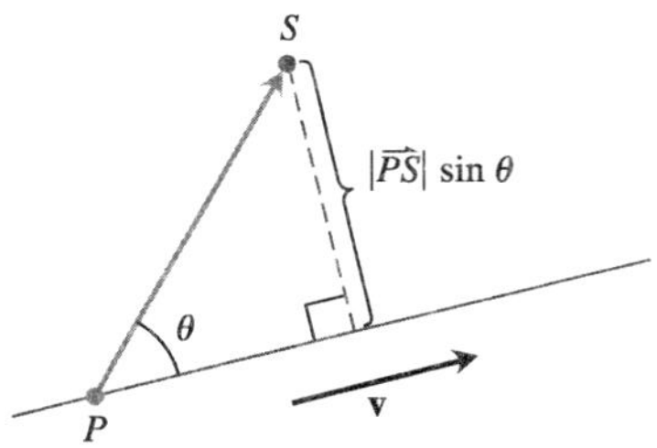

FIGURE 12.38 The distance from S to the line through P parallel to $\mathbf{v}$ is $|\overrightarrow{PS}| \sin\theta$, where θ is the angle between $\overrightarrow{PS}$ and $\mathbf{v}$.

The Distance from a Point to a Line in Space

To find the distance from a point S to a line that passes through a point P parallel to a vector $\mathbf{v}$, we find the absolute value of the scalar component of $\overrightarrow{PS}$ in the direction of a vector normal to the line (Figure 12.38). In the notation of the figure, the absolute value of the scalar component is, $|\overrightarrow{PS}| \sin\theta$, which is $\dfrac{|\overrightarrow{PS} \times \mathbf{v}|}{|\mathbf{v}|}$.

Distance from a Point S to a Line Through P Parallel to v

$$d = \frac{|\overrightarrow{PS} \times \mathbf{v}|}{|\mathbf{v}|} \tag{5}$$

EXAMPLE 5 Finding Distance from a Point to a Line

Find the distance from the point $S(1, 1, 5)$ to the line

$$L: \quad x = 1 + t, \quad y = 3 - t, \quad z = 2t.$$

Solution We see from the equations for L that L passes through $P(1, 3, 0)$ parallel to $\mathbf{v} = \mathbf{i} - \mathbf{j} + 2\mathbf{k}$. With

$$\overrightarrow{PS} = (1 - 1)\mathbf{i} + (1 - 3)\mathbf{j} + (5 - 0)\mathbf{k} = -2\mathbf{j} + 5\mathbf{k}$$

and

$$\overrightarrow{PS} \times \mathbf{v} = \begin{vmatrix} \mathbf{i} & \mathbf{j} & \mathbf{k} \\ 0 & -2 & 5 \\ 1 & -1 & 2 \end{vmatrix} = \mathbf{i} + 5\mathbf{j} + 2\mathbf{k},$$

Equation (5) gives

$$d = \frac{|\overrightarrow{PS} \times \mathbf{v}|}{|\mathbf{v}|} = \frac{\sqrt{1 + 25 + 4}}{\sqrt{1 + 1 + 4}} = \frac{\sqrt{30}}{\sqrt{6}} = \sqrt{5}.$$ ■

An Equation for a Plane in Space

A plane in space is determined by knowing a point on the plane and its "tilt" or orientation. This "tilt" is defined by specifying a vector that is perpendicular or normal to the plane.

Suppose that plane M passes through a point $P_0(x_0, y_0, z_0)$ and is normal to the nonzero vector $\mathbf{n} = A\mathbf{i} + B\mathbf{j} + C\mathbf{k}$. Then M is the set of all points $P(x, y, z)$ for which $\overrightarrow{P_0P}$ is orthogonal to $\mathbf{n}$ (Figure 12.39). Thus, the dot product $\mathbf{n} \cdot \overrightarrow{P_0P} = 0$. This equation is equivalent to

$$(A\mathbf{i} + B\mathbf{j} + C\mathbf{k}) \cdot [(x - x_0)\mathbf{i} + (y - y_0)\mathbf{j} + (z - z_0)\mathbf{k}] = 0$$

or

$$A(x - x_0) + B(y - y_0) + C(z - z_0) = 0.$$

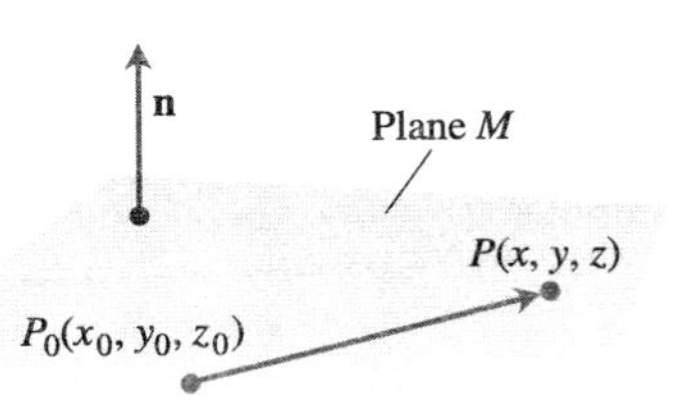

FIGURE 12.39 The standard equation for a plane in space is defined in terms of a vector normal to the plane: A point P lies in the plane through P_0 normal to $\mathbf{n}$ if and only if $\mathbf{n} \cdot \overrightarrow{P_0P} = 0$.

Equation for a Plane
The plane through $P_0(x_0, y_0, z_0)$ normal to $\mathbf{n} = A\mathbf{i} + B\mathbf{j} + C\mathbf{k}$ has

Vector equation:	$\mathbf{n} \cdot \overrightarrow{P_0P} = 0$
Component equation:	$A(x - x_0) + B(y - y_0) + C(z - z_0) = 0$
Component equation simplified:	$Ax + By + Cz = D,$ where $D = Ax_0 + By_0 + Cz_0$

EXAMPLE 6 Finding an Equation for a Plane

Find an equation for the plane through $P_0(-3, 0, 7)$ perpendicular to $\mathbf{n} = 5\mathbf{i} + 2\mathbf{j} - \mathbf{k}$.

Solution The component equation is

$$5(x - (-3)) + 2(y - 0) + (-1)(z - 7) = 0.$$

Simplifying, we obtain

$$\begin{aligned} 5x + 15 + 2y - z + 7 &= 0 \\ 5x + 2y - z &= -22. \end{aligned}$$

■

Notice in Example 6 how the components of $\mathbf{n} = 5\mathbf{i} + 2\mathbf{j} - \mathbf{k}$ became the coefficients of x, y, and z in the equation $5x + 2y - z = -22$. The vector $\mathbf{n} = A\mathbf{i} + B\mathbf{j} + C\mathbf{k}$ is normal to the plane $Ax + By + Cz = D$.

EXAMPLE 7 Finding an Equation for a Plane Through Three Points

Find an equation for the plane through $A(0, 0, 1)$, $B(2, 0, 0)$, and $C(0, 3, 0)$.

Solution We find a vector normal to the plane and use it with one of the points (it does not matter which) to write an equation for the plane.

The cross product

$$\overrightarrow{AB} \times \overrightarrow{AC} = \begin{vmatrix} \mathbf{i} & \mathbf{j} & \mathbf{k} \\ 2 & 0 & -1 \\ 0 & 3 & -1 \end{vmatrix} = 3\mathbf{i} + 2\mathbf{j} + 6\mathbf{k}$$

is normal to the plane. We substitute the components of this vector and the coordinates of A(0, 0, 1) into the component form of the equation to obtain

$$\begin{aligned} 3(x - 0) + 2(y - 0) + 6(z - 1) &= 0 \\ 3x + 2y + 6z &= 6. \end{aligned}$$

■

Lines of Intersection

Just as lines are parallel if and only if they have the same direction, two planes are **parallel** if and only if their normals are parallel, or $\mathbf{n}_1 = k\mathbf{n}_2$ for some scalar k. Two planes that are not parallel intersect in a line.

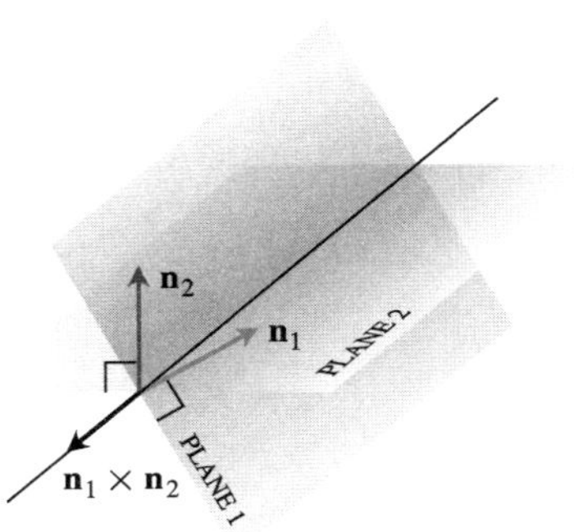

FIGURE 12.40 How the line of intersection of two planes is related to the planes' normal vectors (Example 8).

EXAMPLE 8 Finding a Vector Parallel to the Line of Intersection of Two Planes

Find a vector parallel to the line of intersection of the planes $3x - 6y - 2z = 15$ and $2x + y - 2z = 5$.

Solution The line of intersection of two planes is perpendicular to both planes' normal vectors $\mathbf{n}_1$ and $\mathbf{n}_2$ (Figure 12.40) and therefore parallel to $\mathbf{n}_1 \times \mathbf{n}_2$. Turning this around, $\mathbf{n}_1 \times \mathbf{n}_2$ is a vector parallel to the planes' line of intersection. In our case,

$$\mathbf{n}_1 \times \mathbf{n}_2 = \begin{vmatrix} \mathbf{i} & \mathbf{j} & \mathbf{k} \\ 3 & -6 & -2 \\ 2 & 1 & -2 \end{vmatrix} = 14\mathbf{i} + 2\mathbf{j} + 15\mathbf{k}.$$

Any nonzero scalar multiple of $\mathbf{n}_1 \times \mathbf{n}_2$ will do as well. ■

EXAMPLE 9 Parametrizing the Line of Intersection of Two Planes

Find parametric equations for the line in which the planes $3x - 6y - 2z = 15$ and $2x + y - 2z = 5$ intersect.

Solution We find a vector parallel to the line and a point on the line and use Equations (3).

Example 8 identifies $\mathbf{v} = 14\mathbf{i} + 2\mathbf{j} + 15\mathbf{k}$ as a vector parallel to the line. To find a point on the line, we can take any point common to the two planes. Substituting $z = 0$ in the plane equations and solving for x and y simultaneously identifies one of these points as $(3, -1, 0)$. The line is

$$x = 3 + 14t, \qquad y = -1 + 2t, \qquad z = 15t.$$

The choice $z = 0$ is arbitrary and we could have chosen $z = 1$ or $z = -1$ just as well. Or we could have let $x = 0$ and solved for y and z. The different choices would simply give different parametrizations of the same line. ■

Sometimes we want to know where a line and a plane intersect. For example, if we are looking at a flat plate and a line segment passes through it, we may be interested in knowing what portion of the line segment is hidden from our view by the plate. This application is used in computer graphics (Exercise 74).

EXAMPLE 10 Finding the Intersection of a Line and a Plane

Find the point where the line

$$x = \frac{8}{3} + 2t, \qquad y = -2t, \qquad z = 1 + t$$

intersects the plane $3x + 2y + 6z = 6$.

Solution The point

$$\left(\frac{8}{3} + 2t, -2t, 1 + t\right)$$

lies in the plane if its coordinates satisfy the equation of the plane, that is, if

$$\begin{aligned} 3\left(\frac{8}{3} + 2t\right) + 2(-2t) + 6(1 + t) &= 6 \\ 8 + 6t - 4t + 6 + 6t &= 6 \\ 8t &= -8 \\ t &= -1. \end{aligned}$$

The point of intersection is

$$(x, y, z)\big|_{t=-1} = \left(\frac{8}{3} - 2, 2, 1 - 1\right) = \left(\frac{2}{3}, 2, 0\right).$$

■

The Distance from a Point to a Plane

If P is a point on a plane with normal $\mathbf{n}$, then the distance from any point S to the plane is the length of the vector projection of $\overrightarrow{PS}$ onto $\mathbf{n}$. That is, the distance from S to the plane is

$$d = \left|\overrightarrow{PS} \cdot \frac{\mathbf{n}}{|\mathbf{n}|}\right| \tag{6}$$

where $\mathbf{n} = A\mathbf{i} + B\mathbf{j} + C\mathbf{k}$ is normal to the plane.

EXAMPLE 11 Finding the Distance from a Point to a Plane

Find the distance from $S(1, 1, 3)$ to the plane $3x + 2y + 6z = 6$.

Solution We find a point P in the plane and calculate the length of the vector projection of $\overrightarrow{PS}$ onto a vector $\mathbf{n}$ normal to the plane (Figure 12.41). The coefficients in the equation $3x + 2y + 6z = 6$ give

$$\mathbf{n} = 3\mathbf{i} + 2\mathbf{j} + 6\mathbf{k}.$$

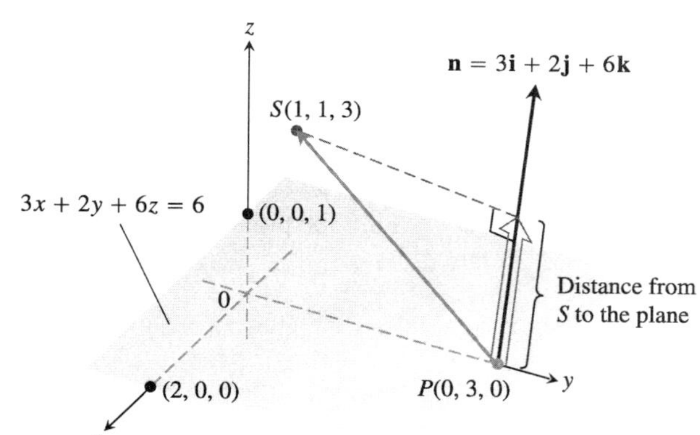

FIGURE 12.41 The distance from S to the plane is the length of the vector projection of $\overrightarrow{PS}$ onto $\mathbf{n}$ (Example 11).

The points on the plane easiest to find from the plane's equation are the intercepts. If we take P to be the y-intercept $(0, 3, 0)$, then

$$\begin{aligned}\overrightarrow{PS} &= (1-0)\mathbf{i} + (1-3)\mathbf{j} + (3-0)\mathbf{k}\\ &= \mathbf{i} - 2\mathbf{j} + 3\mathbf{k},\end{aligned}$$

$$|\mathbf{n}| = \sqrt{(3)^2 + (2)^2 + (6)^2} = \sqrt{49} = 7.$$

The distance from S to the plane is

$$\begin{aligned}d &= \left|\overrightarrow{PS}\cdot\frac{\mathbf{n}}{|\mathbf{n}|}\right| \qquad \text{length of } \mathrm{proj}_{\mathbf{n}}\overrightarrow{PS}\\ &= \left|(\mathbf{i} - 2\mathbf{j} + 3\mathbf{k})\cdot\left(\frac{3}{7}\mathbf{i} + \frac{2}{7}\mathbf{j} + \frac{6}{7}\mathbf{k}\right)\right|\\ &= \left|\frac{3}{7} - \frac{4}{7} + \frac{18}{7}\right| = \frac{17}{7}.\end{aligned}$$

■

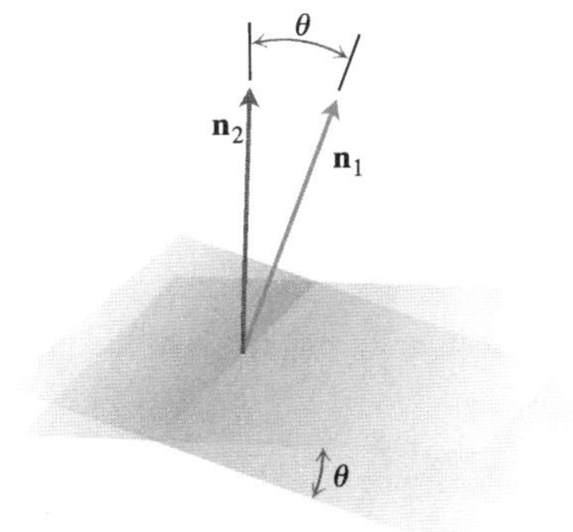

FIGURE 12.42 The angle between two planes is obtained from the angle between their normals.

Angles Between Planes

The angle between two intersecting planes is defined to be the (acute) angle determined by their normal vectors (Figure 12.42).

EXAMPLE 12 Find the angle between the planes $3x - 6y - 2z = 15$ and $2x + y - 2z = 5$.

Solution The vectors

$$\mathbf{n}_1 = 3\mathbf{i} - 6\mathbf{j} - 2\mathbf{k}, \qquad \mathbf{n}_2 = 2\mathbf{i} + \mathbf{j} - 2\mathbf{k}$$

are normals to the planes. The angle between them is

$$\begin{aligned}\theta &= \cos^{-1}\left(\frac{\mathbf{n}_1\cdot\mathbf{n}_2}{|\mathbf{n}_1||\mathbf{n}_2|}\right)\\ &= \cos^{-1}\left(\frac{4}{21}\right)\\ &\approx 1.38 \text{ radians.} \qquad \text{About 79 deg}\end{aligned}$$

■

EXERCISES 12.5

Lines and Line Segments

Find parametric equations for the lines in Exercises 1–12.

1. The line through the point $P(3, -4, -1)$ parallel to the vector $\mathbf{i} + \mathbf{j} + \mathbf{k}$
2. The line through $P(1, 2, -1)$ and $Q(-1, 0, 1)$
3. The line through $P(-2, 0, 3)$ and $Q(3, 5, -2)$
4. The line through $P(1, 2, 0)$ and $Q(1, 1, -1)$
5. The line through the origin parallel to the vector $2\mathbf{j} + \mathbf{k}$
6. The line through the point $(3, -2, 1)$ parallel to the line $x = 1 + 2t, y = 2 - t, z = 3t$
7. The line through $(1, 1, 1)$ parallel to the z-axis
8. The line through $(2, 4, 5)$ perpendicular to the plane $3x + 7y - 5z = 21$
9. The line through $(0, -7, 0)$ perpendicular to the plane $x + 2y + 2z = 13$

10. The line through (2, 3, 0) perpendicular to the vectors $\mathbf{u} = \mathbf{i} + 2\mathbf{j} + 3\mathbf{k}$ and $\mathbf{v} = 3\mathbf{i} + 4\mathbf{j} + 5\mathbf{k}$

11. The x-axis

12. The z-axis

Find parametrizations for the line segments joining the points in Exercises 13–20. Draw coordinate axes and sketch each segment, indicating the direction of increasing t for your parametrization.

13. $(0, 0, 0)$, $(1, 1, 3/2)$

14. $(0, 0, 0)$, $(1, 0, 0)$

15. $(1, 0, 0)$, $(1, 1, 0)$

16. $(1, 1, 0)$, $(1, 1, 1)$

17. $(0, 1, 1)$, $(0, -1, 1)$

18. $(0, 2, 0)$, $(3, 0, 0)$

19. $(2, 0, 2)$, $(0, 2, 0)$

20. $(1, 0, -1)$, $(0, 3, 0)$

Planes

Find equations for the planes in Exercises 21–26.

21. The plane through $P_0(0, 2, -1)$ normal to $\mathbf{n} = 3\mathbf{i} - 2\mathbf{j} - \mathbf{k}$

22. The plane through $(1, -1, 3)$ parallel to the plane

$$3x + y + z = 7$$

23. The plane through $(1, 1, -1)$, $(2, 0, 2)$, and $(0, -2, 1)$

24. The plane through $(2, 4, 5)$, $(1, 5, 7)$, and $(-1, 6, 8)$

25. The plane through $P_0(2, 4, 5)$ perpendicular to the line

$$x = 5 + t, \quad y = 1 + 3t, \quad z = 4t$$

26. The plane through $A(1, -2, 1)$ perpendicular to the vector from the origin to A

27. Find the point of intersection of the lines $x = 2t + 1$, $y = 3t + 2$, $z = 4t + 3$, and $x = s + 2$, $y = 2s + 4$, $z = -4s - 1$, and then find the plane determined by these lines.

28. Find the point of intersection of the lines $x = t$, $y = -t + 2$, $z = t + 1$, and $x = 2s + 2$, $y = s + 3$, $z = 5s + 6$, and then find the plane determined by these lines.

In Exercises 29 and 30, find the plane determined by the intersecting lines.

29. $L1$: $x = -1 + t$, $y = 2 + t$, $z = 1 - t$; $-\infty < t < \infty$
$L2$: $x = 1 - 4s$, $y = 1 + 2s$, $z = 2 - 2s$; $-\infty < s < \infty$

30. $L1$: $x = t$, $y = 3 - 3t$, $z = -2 - t$; $-\infty < t < \infty$
$L2$: $x = 1 + s$, $y = 4 + s$, $z = -1 + s$; $-\infty < s < \infty$

31. Find a plane through $P_0(2, 1, -1)$ and perpendicular to the line of intersection of the planes $2x + y - z = 3$, $x + 2y + z = 2$.

32. Find a plane through the points $P_1(1, 2, 3)$, $P_2(3, 2, 1)$ and perpendicular to the plane $4x - y + 2z = 7$.

Distances

In Exercises 33–38, find the distance from the point to the line.

33. $(0, 0, 12)$; $x = 4t$, $y = -2t$, $z = 2t$

34. $(0, 0, 0)$; $x = 5 + 3t$, $y = 5 + 4t$, $z = -3 - 5t$

35. $(2, 1, 3)$; $x = 2 + 2t$, $y = 1 + 6t$, $z = 3$

36. $(2, 1, -1)$; $x = 2t$, $y = 1 + 2t$, $z = 2t$

37. $(3, -1, 4)$; $x = 4 - t$, $y = 3 + 2t$, $z = -5 + 3t$

38. $(-1, 4, 3)$; $x = 10 + 4t$, $y = -3$, $z = 4t$

In Exercises 39–44, find the distance from the point to the plane.

39. $(2, -3, 4)$, $x + 2y + 2z = 13$

40. $(0, 0, 0)$, $3x + 2y + 6z = 6$

41. $(0, 1, 1)$, $4y + 3z = -12$

42. $(2, 2, 3)$, $2x + y + 2z = 4$

43. $(0, -1, 0)$, $2x + y + 2z = 4$

44. $(1, 0, -1)$, $-4x + y + z = 4$

45. Find the distance from the plane $x + 2y + 6z = 1$ to the plane $x + 2y + 6z = 10$.

46. Find the distance from the line $x = 2 + t$, $y = 1 + t$, $z = -(1/2) - (1/2)t$ to the plane $x + 2y + 6z = 10$.

Angles

Find the angles between the planes in Exercises 47 and 48.

47. $x + y = 1$, $2x + y - 2z = 2$

48. $5x + y - z = 10$, $x - 2y + 3z = -1$

T Use a calculator to find the acute angles between the planes in Exercises 49–52 to the nearest hundredth of a radian.

49. $2x + 2y + 2z = 3$, $2x - 2y - z = 5$

50. $x + y + z = 1$, $z = 0$ (the xy-plane)

51. $2x + 2y - z = 3$, $x + 2y + z = 2$

52. $4y + 3z = -12$, $3x + 2y + 6z = 6$

Intersecting Lines and Planes

In Exercises 53–56, find the point in which the line meets the plane.

53. $x = 1 - t$, $y = 3t$, $z = 1 + t$; $2x - y + 3z = 6$

54. $x = 2$, $y = 3 + 2t$, $z = -2 - 2t$; $6x + 3y - 4z = -12$

55. $x = 1 + 2t$, $y = 1 + 5t$, $z = 3t$; $x + y + z = 2$

56. $x = -1 + 3t$, $y = -2$, $z = 5t$; $2x - 3z = 7$

Find parametrizations for the lines in which the planes in Exercises 57–60 intersect.

57. $x + y + z = 1$, $x + y = 2$

58. $3x - 6y - 2z = 3$, $2x + y - 2z = 2$

59. $x - 2y + 4z = 2$, $x + y - 2z = 5$

60. $5x - 2y = 11$, $4y - 5z = -17$

Given two lines in space, either they are parallel, or they intersect, or they are skew (imagine, for example, the flight paths of two planes in the sky). Exercises 61 and 62 each give three lines. In each exercise, determine whether the lines, taken two at a time, are parallel, intersect, or are skew. If they intersect, find the point of intersection.

61. $L1$: $x = 3 + 2t,\ y = -1 + 4t,\ z = 2 - t;\ -\infty < t < \infty$
$L2$: $x = 1 + 4s,\ y = 1 + 2s,\ z = -3 + 4s;\ -\infty < s < \infty$
$L3$: $x = 3 + 2r,\ y = 2 + r,\ z = -2 + 2r;\ -\infty < r < \infty$

62. $L1$: $x = 1 + 2t,\quad y = -1 - t,\quad z = 3t;\quad -\infty < t < \infty$
$L2$: $x = 2 - s,\quad y = 3s,\quad z = 1 + s;\quad -\infty < s < \infty$
$L3$: $x = 5 + 2r,\quad y = 1 - r,\quad z = 8 + 3r;\ -\infty < r < \infty$

Theory and Examples

63. Use Equations (3) to generate a parametrization of the line through $P(2, -4, 7)$ parallel to $\mathbf{v}_1 = 2\mathbf{i} - \mathbf{j} + 3\mathbf{k}$. Then generate another parametrization of the line using the point $P_2(-2, -2, 1)$ and the vector $\mathbf{v}_2 = -\mathbf{i} + (1/2)\mathbf{j} - (3/2)\mathbf{k}$.

64. Use the component form to generate an equation for the plane through $P_1(4, 1, 5)$ normal to $\mathbf{n}_1 = \mathbf{i} - 2\mathbf{j} + \mathbf{k}$. Then generate another equation for the same plane using the point $P_2(3, -2, 0)$ and the normal vector $\mathbf{n}_2 = -\sqrt{2}\mathbf{i} + 2\sqrt{2}\mathbf{j} - \sqrt{2}\mathbf{k}$.

65. Find the points in which the line $x = 1 + 2t, y = -1 - t, z = 3t$ meets the coordinate planes. Describe the reasoning behind your answer.

66. Find equations for the line in the plane $z = 3$ that makes an angle of $\pi/6$ rad with $\mathbf{i}$ and an angle of $\pi/3$ rad with $\mathbf{j}$. Describe the reasoning behind your answer.

67. Is the line $x = 1 - 2t, y = 2 + 5t, z = -3t$ parallel to the plane $2x + y - z = 8$? Give reasons for your answer.

68. How can you tell when two planes $A_1x + B_1y + C_1z = D_1$ and $A_2x + B_2y + C_2z = D_2$ are parallel? Perpendicular? Give reasons for your answer.

69. Find two different planes whose intersection is the line $x = 1 + t, y = 2 - t, z = 3 + 2t$. Write equations for each plane in the form $Ax + By + Cz = D$.

70. Find a plane through the origin that meets the plane M: $2x + 3y + z = 12$ in a right angle. How do you know that your plane is perpendicular to M?

71. For any nonzero numbers a, b, and c, the graph of $(x/a) + (y/b) + (z/c) = 1$ is a plane. Which planes have an equation of this form?

72. Suppose L_1 and L_2 are disjoint (nonintersecting) nonparallel lines. Is it possible for a nonzero vector to be perpendicular to both L_1 and L_2? Give reasons for your answer.

Computer Graphics

73. **Perspective in computer graphics** In computer graphics and perspective drawing, we need to represent objects seen by the eye in space as images on a two-dimensional plane. Suppose that the eye is at $E(x_0, 0, 0)$ as shown here and that we want to represent a point $P_1(x_1, y_1, z_1)$ as a point on the yz-plane. We do this by projecting P_1 onto the plane with a ray from E. The point P_1 will be portrayed as the point $P(0, y, z)$. The problem for us as graphics designers is to find y and z given E and P_1.

    a. Write a vector equation that holds between $\overrightarrow{EP}$ and $\overrightarrow{EP_1}$. Use the equation to express y and z in terms of x_0, x_1, y_1, and z_1.

    b. Test the formulas obtained for y and z in part (a) by investigating their behavior at $x_1 = 0$ and $x_1 = x_0$ and by seeing what happens as $x_0 \to \infty$. What do you find?

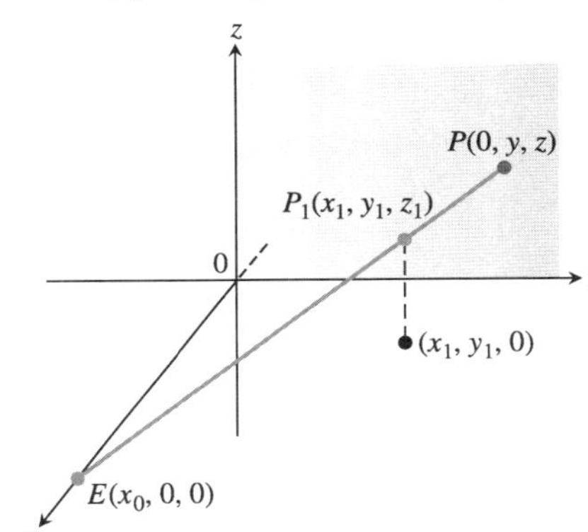

74. **Hidden lines** Here is another typical problem in computer graphics. Your eye is at (4, 0, 0). You are looking at a triangular plate whose vertices are at (1, 0, 1), (1, 1, 0), and (−2, 2, 2). The line segment from (1, 0, 0) to (0, 2, 2) passes through the plate. What portion of the line segment is hidden from your view by the plate? (This is an exercise in finding intersections of lines and planes.)

12.6 Cylinders and Quadric Surfaces

Up to now, we have studied two special types of surfaces: spheres and planes. In this section, we extend our inventory to include a variety of cylinders and quadric surfaces. Quadric surfaces are surfaces defined by second-degree equations in x, y, and z. Spheres are quadric surfaces, but there are others of equal interest.

Cylinders

A **cylinder** is a surface that is generated by moving a straight line along a given planar curve while holding the line parallel to a given fixed line. The curve is called a **generating curve** for the cylinder (Figure 12.43). In solid geometry, where *cylinder* means *circular* *cylinder*, the generating curves are circles, but now we allow generating curves of any kind. The cylinder in our first example is generated by a parabola.

When graphing a cylinder or other surface by hand or analyzing one generated by a computer, it helps to look at the curves formed by intersecting the surface with planes parallel to the coordinate planes. These curves are called **cross-sections** or **traces**.

EXAMPLE 1 The Parabolic Cylinder $y = x^2$

Find an equation for the cylinder made by the lines parallel to the z-axis that pass through the parabola $y = x^2, z = 0$ (Figure 12.44).

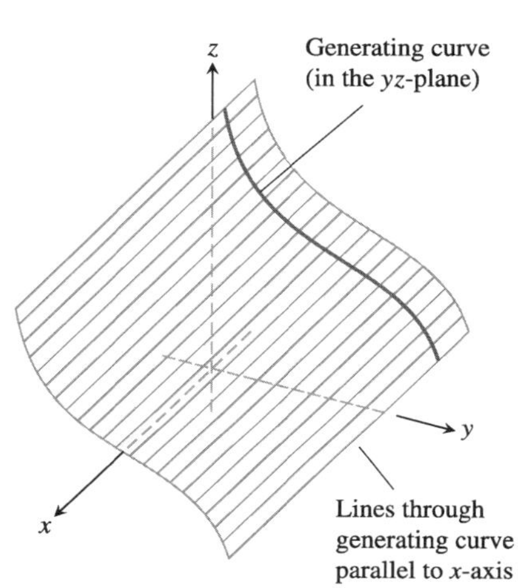

FIGURE 12.43 A cylinder and generating curve.

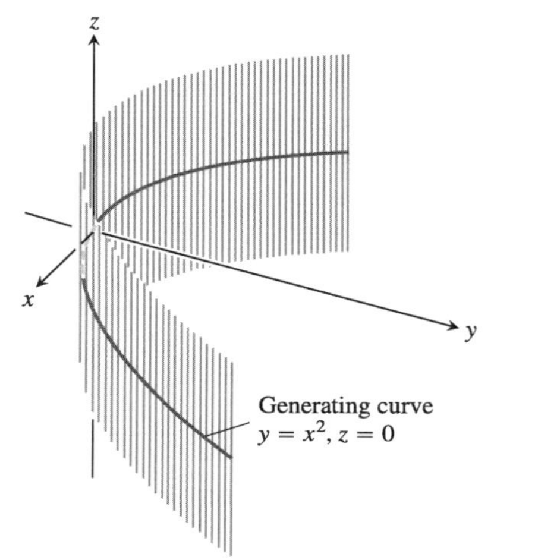

FIGURE 12.44 The cylinder of lines passing through the parabola $y = x^2$ in the xy-plane parallel to the z-axis (Example 1).

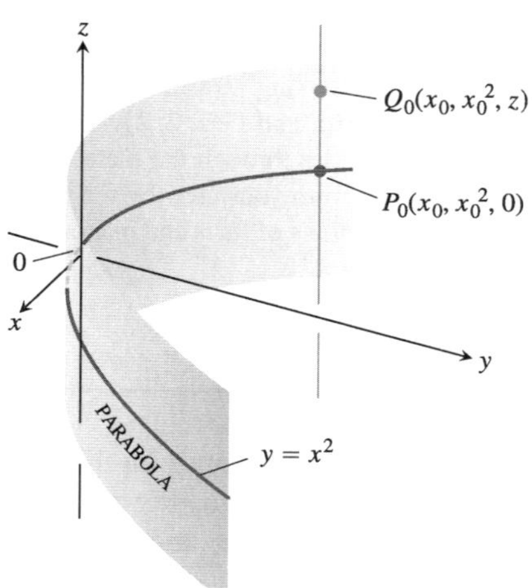

FIGURE 12.45 Every point of the cylinder in Figure 12.44 has coordinates of the form (x_0, x_0^2, z). We call it "the cylinder $y = x^2$."

Solution Suppose that the point $P_0(x_0, x_0^2, 0)$ lies on the parabola $y = x^2$ in the xy-plane. Then, for any value of z, the point $Q(x_0, x_0^2, z)$ will lie on the cylinder because it lies on the line $x = x_0, y = x_0^2$ through P_0 parallel to the z-axis. Conversely, any point $Q(x_0, x_0^2, z)$ whose y-coordinate is the square of its x-coordinate lies on the cylinder because it lies on the line $x = x_0, y = x_0^2$ through P_0 parallel to the z-axis (Figure 12.45).

Regardless of the value of z, therefore, the points on the surface are the points whose coordinates satisfy the equation $y = x^2$. This makes $y = x^2$ an equation for the cylinder. Because of this, we call the cylinder "the cylinder $y = x^2$." ■

As Example 1 suggests, any curve $f(x, y) = c$ in the xy-plane defines a cylinder parallel to the z-axis whose equation is also $f(x, y) = c$. The equation $x^2 + y^2 = 1$ defines the circular cylinder made by the lines parallel to the z-axis that pass through the circle $x^2 + y^2 = 1$ in the xy-plane. The equation $x^2 + 4y^2 = 9$ defines the elliptical cylinder made by the lines parallel to the z-axis that pass through the ellipse $x^2 + 4y^2 = 9$ in the xy-plane.

In a similar way, any curve $g(x, z) = c$ in the xz-plane defines a cylinder parallel to the y-axis whose space equation is also $g(x, z) = c$ (Figure 12.46). Any curve $h(y, z) = c$

defines a cylinder parallel to the x-axis whose space equation is also $h(y, z) = c$ (Figure 12.47). The axis of a cylinder need not be parallel to a coordinate axis, however.

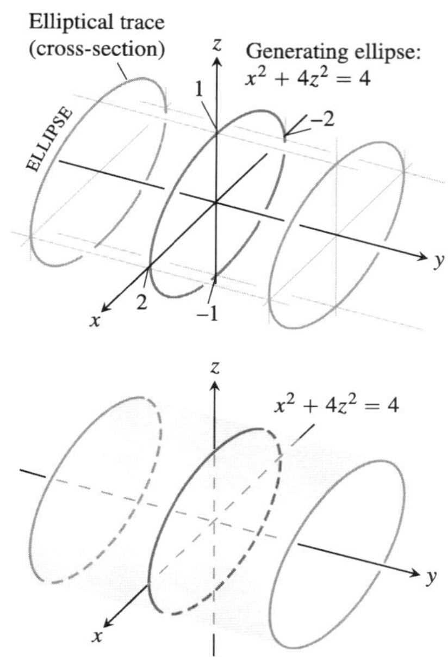

FIGURE 12.46 The elliptical cylinder $x^2 + 4z^2 = 4$ is made of lines parallel to the y-axis and passing through the ellipse $x^2 + 4z^2 = 4$ in the xz-plane. The cross-sections or "traces" of the cylinder in planes perpendicular to the y-axis are ellipses congruent to the generating ellipse. The cylinder extends along the entire y-axis.

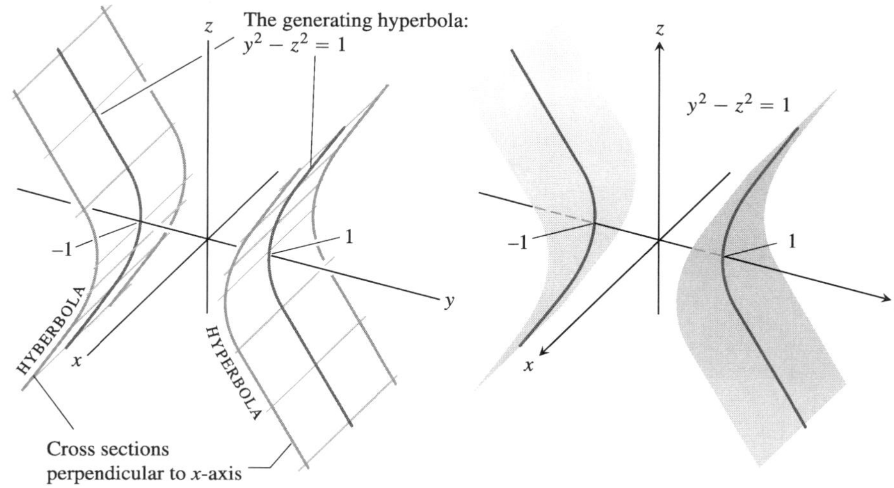

FIGURE 12.47 The hyperbolic cylinder $y^2 - z^2 = 1$ is made of lines parallel to the x-axis and passing through the hyperbola $y^2 - z^2 = 1$ in the yz-plane. The cross-sections of the cylinder in planes perpendicular to the x-axis are hyperbolas congruent to the generating hyperbola.

Quadric Surfaces

The next type of surface we examine is a *quadric* surface. These surfaces are the three-dimensional analogues of ellipses, parabolas, and hyperbolas.

A **quadric surface** is the graph in space of a second-degree equation in x, y, and z. The most general form is

$$Ax^2 + By^2 + Cz^2 + Dxy + Eyz + Fxz + Gx + Hy + Jz + K = 0,$$

where A, B, C, and so on are constants. However, this equation can be simplified by translation and rotation, as in the two-dimensional case. We will study only the simpler equations. Although defined differently, the cylinders in Figures 12.45 through 12.47 were also examples of quadric surfaces. The basic quadric surfaces are **ellipsoids**, **paraboloids**, **elliptical cones**, and **hyperboloids**. (We think of spheres as special ellipsoids.) We now present examples of each type.

EXAMPLE 2 Ellipsoids

The **ellipsoid**

$$\frac{x^2}{a^2} + \frac{y^2}{b^2} + \frac{z^2}{c^2} = 1 \tag{1}$$

(Figure 12.48) cuts the coordinate axes at $(\pm a, 0, 0)$, $(0, \pm b, 0)$, and $(0, 0, \pm c)$. It lies within the rectangular box defined by the inequalities $|x| \le a$, $|y| \le b$, and $|z| \le c$. The surface is symmetric with respect to each of the coordinate planes because each variable in the defining equation is squared.

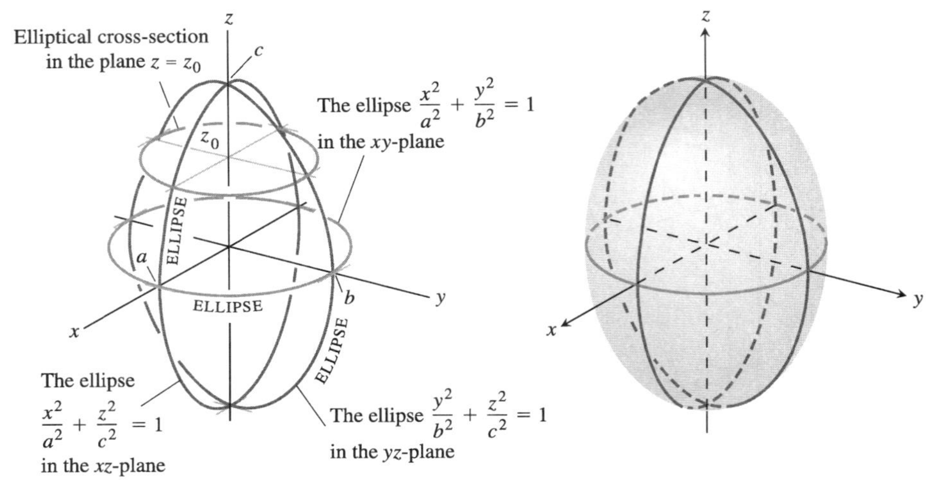

FIGURE 12.48 The ellipsoid

$$\frac{x^2}{a^2} + \frac{y^2}{b^2} + \frac{z^2}{c^2} = 1$$

in Example 2 has elliptical cross-sections in each of the three coordinate planes.

The curves in which the three coordinate planes cut the surface are ellipses. For example,

$$\frac{x^2}{a^2} + \frac{y^2}{b^2} = 1 \qquad \text{when} \qquad z = 0.$$

The section cut from the surface by the plane $z = z_0$, $|z_0| < c$, is the ellipse

$$\frac{x^2}{a^2(1 - (z_0/c)^2)} + \frac{y^2}{b^2(1 - (z_0/c)^2)} = 1.$$

If any two of the semiaxes a, b, and c are equal, the surface is an **ellipsoid of revolution**. If all three are equal, the surface is a sphere. ■

EXAMPLE 3 Paraboloids

The **elliptical paraboloid**

$$\frac{x^2}{a^2} + \frac{y^2}{b^2} = \frac{z}{c} \tag{2}$$

is symmetric with respect to the planes $x = 0$ and $y = 0$ (Figure 12.49). The only intercept on the axes is the origin. Except for this point, the surface lies above (if $c > 0$) or entirely below (if $c < 0$) the xy-plane, depending on the sign of c. The sections cut by the coordinate planes are

$x = 0$: the parabola $z = \frac{c}{b^2}y^2$

$y = 0$: the parabola $z = \frac{c}{a^2}x^2$

$z = 0$: the point $(0, 0, 0)$.

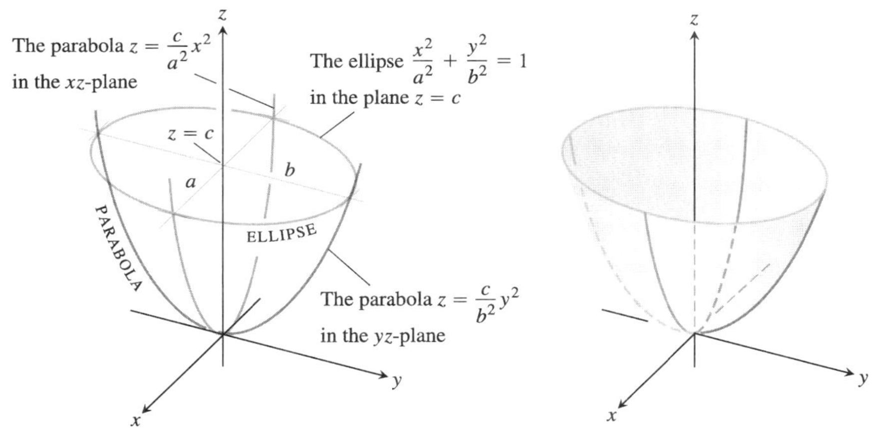

FIGURE 12.49 The elliptical paraboloid $(x^2/a^2) + (y^2/b^2) = z/c$ in Example 3, shown for $c > 0$. The cross-sections perpendicular to the z-axis above the xy-plane are ellipses. The cross-sections in the planes that contain the z-axis are parabolas.

Each plane $z = z_0$ above the xy-plane cuts the surface in the ellipse

$$\frac{x^2}{a^2} + \frac{y^2}{b^2} = \frac{z_0}{c}.$$

EXAMPLE 4 Cones

The **elliptical cone**

$$\frac{x^2}{a^2} + \frac{y^2}{b^2} = \frac{z^2}{c^2} \tag{3}$$

is symmetric with respect to the three coordinate planes (Figure 12.50). The sections cut

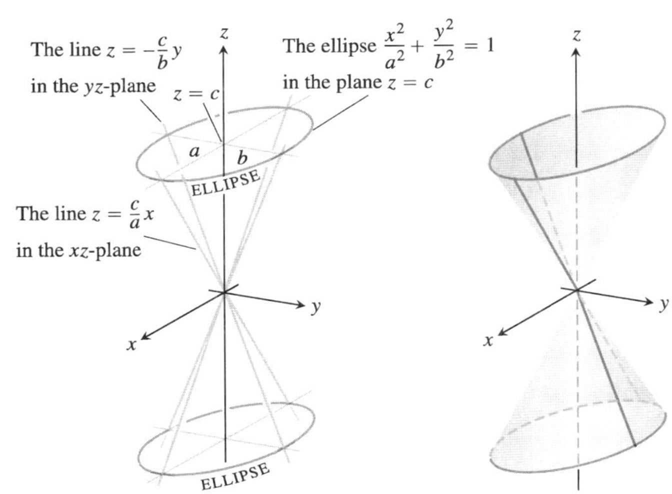

FIGURE 12.50 The elliptical cone $(x^2/a^2) + (y^2/b^2) = (z^2/c^2)$ in Example 4. Planes perpendicular to the z-axis cut the cone in ellipses above and below the xy-plane. Vertical planes that contain the z-axis cut it in pairs of intersecting lines.

by the coordinate planes are

$$x = 0: \quad \text{the lines } z = \pm\frac{c}{b}y$$

$$y = 0: \quad \text{the lines } z = \pm\frac{c}{a}x$$

$$z = 0: \quad \text{the point } (0, 0, 0).$$

The sections cut by planes $z = z_0$ above and below the xy-plane are ellipses whose centers lie on the z-axis and whose vertices lie on the lines given above.

If $a = b$, the cone is a right circular cone. ∎

EXAMPLE 5 Hyperboloids

The **hyperboloid of one sheet**

$$\frac{x^2}{a^2} + \frac{y^2}{b^2} - \frac{z^2}{c^2} = 1 \tag{4}$$

is symmetric with respect to each of the three coordinate planes (Figure 12.51).

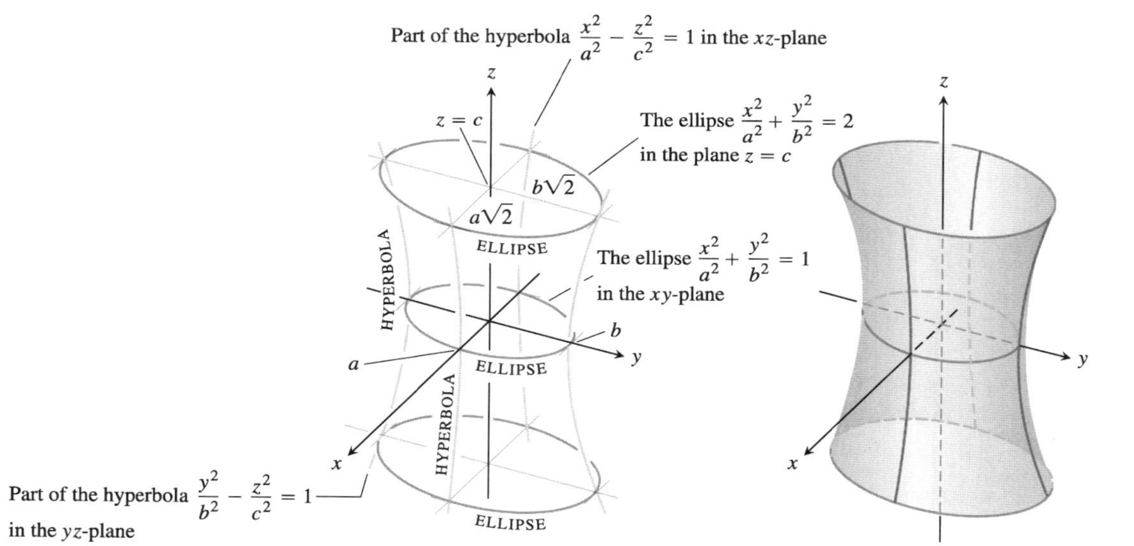

FIGURE 12.51 The hyperboloid $(x^2/a^2) + (y^2/b^2) - (z^2/c^2) = 1$ in Example 5. Planes perpendicular to the z-axis cut it in ellipses. Vertical planes containing the z-axis cut it in hyperbolas.

The sections cut out by the coordinate planes are

$$x = 0: \quad \text{the hyperbola } \frac{y^2}{b^2} - \frac{z^2}{c^2} = 1$$

$$y = 0: \quad \text{the hyperbola } \frac{x^2}{a^2} - \frac{z^2}{c^2} = 1$$

$$z = 0: \quad \text{the ellipse } \frac{x^2}{a^2} + \frac{y^2}{b^2} = 1.$$

The plane $z = z_0$ cuts the surface in an ellipse with center on the z-axis and vertices on one of the hyperbolic sections above.

The surface is connected, meaning that it is possible to travel from one point on it to any other without leaving the surface. For this reason, it is said to have *one* sheet, in contrast to the hyperboloid in the next example, which has two sheets.

If $a = b$, the hyperboloid is a surface of revolution. ■

EXAMPLE 6 Hyperboloids

The **hyperboloid of two sheets**

$$\frac{z^2}{c^2} - \frac{x^2}{a^2} - \frac{y^2}{b^2} = 1 \tag{5}$$

is symmetric with respect to the three coordinate planes (Figure 12.52). The plane $z = 0$ does not intersect the surface; in fact, for a horizontal plane to intersect the surface, we must have $|z| \geq c$. The hyperbolic sections

$$x = 0: \quad \frac{z^2}{c^2} - \frac{y^2}{b^2} = 1$$

$$y = 0: \quad \frac{z^2}{c^2} - \frac{x^2}{a^2} = 1$$

have their vertices and foci on the z-axis. The surface is separated into two portions, one above the plane $z = c$ and the other below the plane $z = -c$. This accounts for its name.

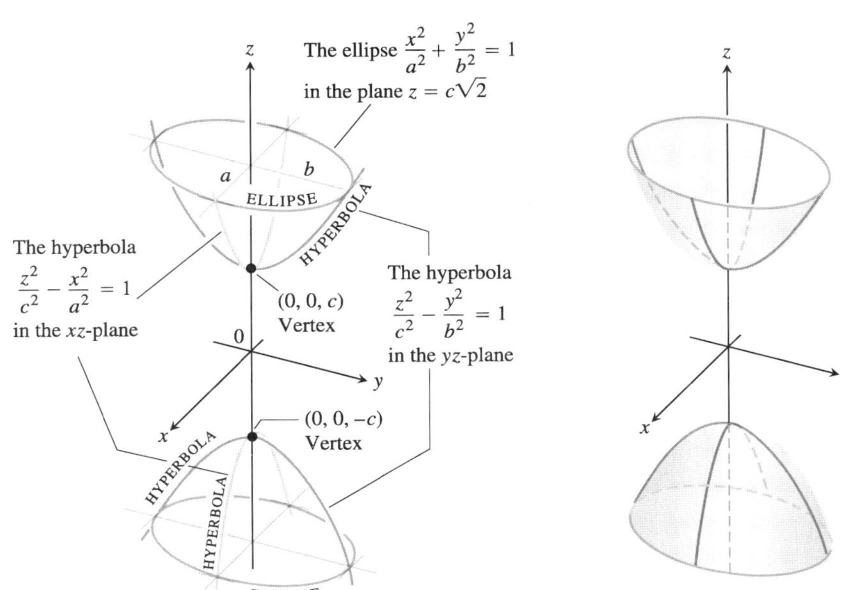

FIGURE 12.52 The hyperboloid $(z^2/c^2) - (x^2/a^2) - (y^2/b^2) = 1$ in Example 6. Planes perpendicular to the z-axis above and below the vertices cut it in ellipses. Vertical planes containing the z-axis cut it in hyperbolas.

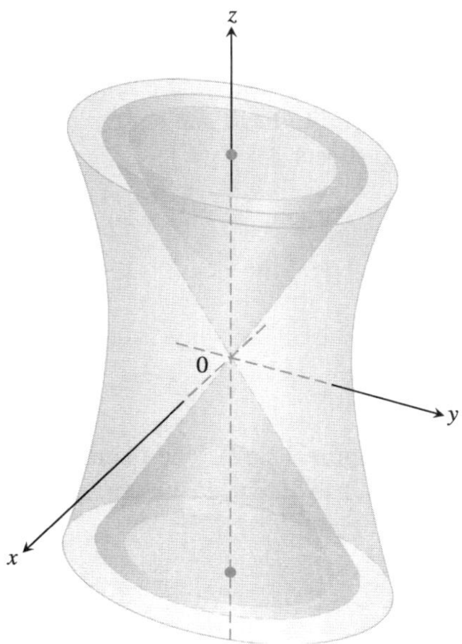

FIGURE 12.53 Both hyperboloids are asymptotic to the cone (Example 6).

Equations (4) and (5) have different numbers of negative terms. The number in each case is the same as the number of sheets of the hyperboloid. If we replace the 1 on the right side of either Equation (4) or Equation (5) by 0, we obtain the equation

$$\frac{x^2}{a^2} + \frac{y^2}{b^2} = \frac{z^2}{c^2}$$

for an elliptical cone (Equation 3). The hyperboloids are asymptotic to this cone (Figure 12.53) in the same way that the hyperbolas

$$\frac{x^2}{a^2} - \frac{y^2}{b^2} = \pm 1$$

are asymptotic to the lines

$$\frac{x^2}{a^2} - \frac{y^2}{b^2} = 0$$

in the xy-plane. ■

EXAMPLE 7 A Saddle Point

The **hyperbolic paraboloid**

$$\frac{y^2}{b^2} - \frac{x^2}{a^2} = \frac{z}{c}, \qquad c > 0 \tag{6}$$

has symmetry with respect to the planes $x = 0$ and $y = 0$ (Figure 12.54). The sections in these planes are

$$x = 0: \quad \text{the parabola } z = \frac{c}{b^2}y^2. \tag{7}$$

$$y = 0: \quad \text{the parabola } z = -\frac{c}{a^2}x^2. \tag{8}$$

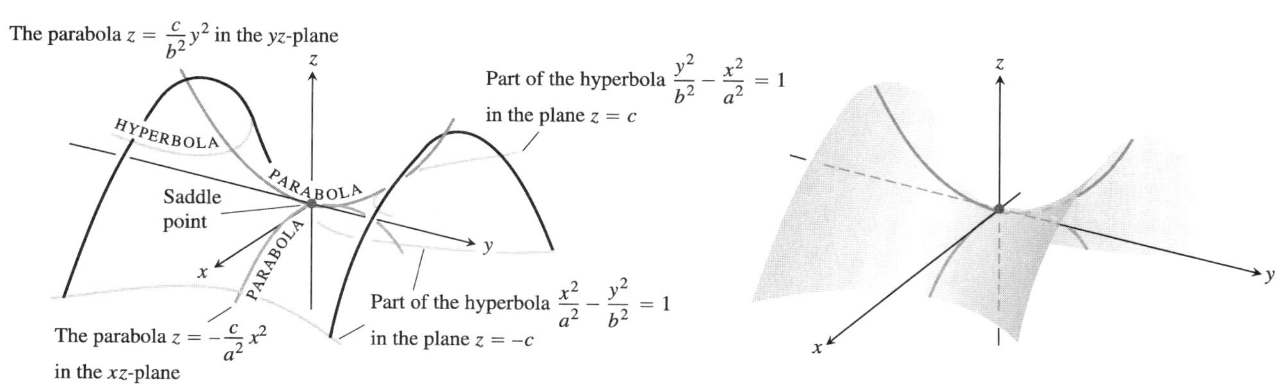

FIGURE 12.54 The hyperbolic paraboloid $(y^2/b^2) - (x^2/a^2) = z/c$, $c > 0$. The cross-sections in planes perpendicular to the z-axis above and below the xy-plane are hyperbolas. The cross-sections in planes perpendicular to the other axes are parabolas.

In the plane $x = 0$, the parabola opens upward from the origin. The parabola in the plane $y = 0$ opens downward.

If we cut the surface by a plane $z = z_0 > 0$, the section is a hyperbola,

$$\frac{y^2}{b^2} - \frac{x^2}{a^2} = \frac{z_0}{c},$$

with its focal axis parallel to the y-axis and its vertices on the parabola in Equation (7). If z_0 is negative, the focal axis is parallel to the x-axis and the vertices lie on the parabola in Equation (8).

Near the origin, the surface is shaped like a saddle or mountain pass. To a person traveling along the surface in the yz-plane the origin looks like a minimum. To a person traveling in the xz-plane the origin looks like a maximum. Such a point is called a **saddle point** of a surface. ■

USING TECHNOLOGY Visualizing in Space

A CAS or other graphing utility can help in visualizing surfaces in space. It can draw traces in different planes, and many computer graphing systems can rotate a figure so you can see it as if it were a physical model you could turn in your hand. Hidden-line algorithms (see Exercise 74, Section 12.5) are used to block out portions of the surface that you would not see from your current viewing angle. A system may require surfaces to be entered in parametric form, as discussed in Section 16.6 (see also CAS Exercises 57 through 60 in Section 14.1). Sometimes you may have to manipulate the grid mesh to see all portions of a surface.

EXERCISES 12.6

Matching Equations with Surfaces

In Exercises 1–12, match the equation with the surface it defines. Also, identify each surface by type (paraboloid, ellipsoid, etc.) The surfaces are labeled (a)–(l).

1. $x^2 + y^2 + 4z^2 = 10$
2. $z^2 + 4y^2 - 4x^2 = 4$
3. $9y^2 + z^2 = 16$
4. $y^2 + z^2 = x^2$
5. $x = y^2 - z^2$
6. $x = -y^2 - z^2$
7. $x^2 + 2z^2 = 8$
8. $z^2 + x^2 - y^2 = 1$
9. $x = z^2 - y^2$
10. $z = -4x^2 - y^2$
11. $x^2 + 4z^2 = y^2$
12. $9x^2 + 4y^2 + 2z^2 = 36$

a.

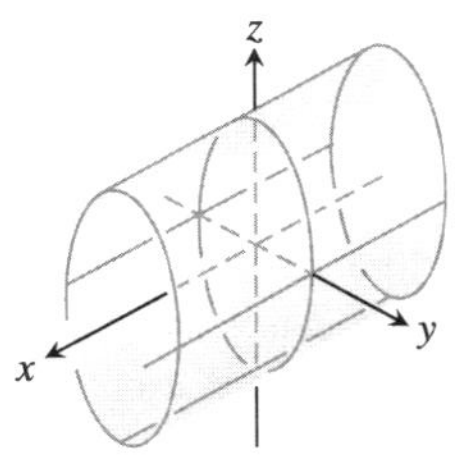

b.

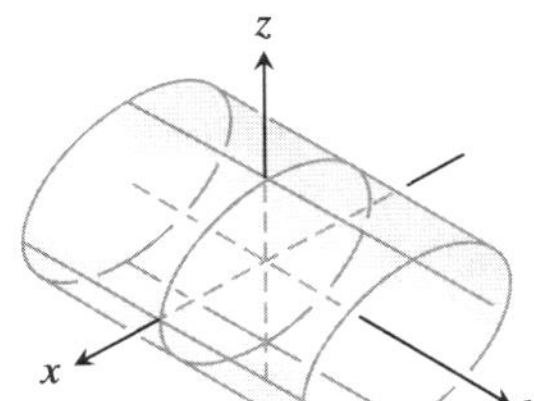

c.

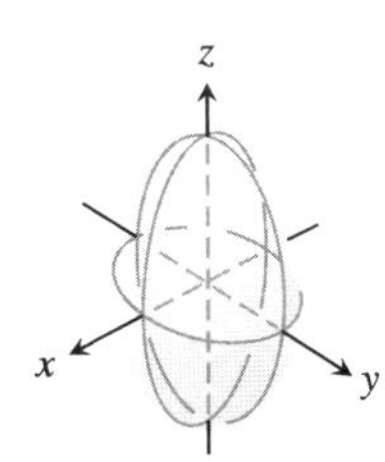

d.

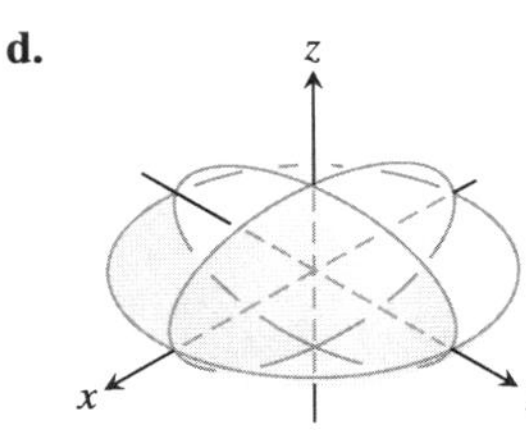

e.

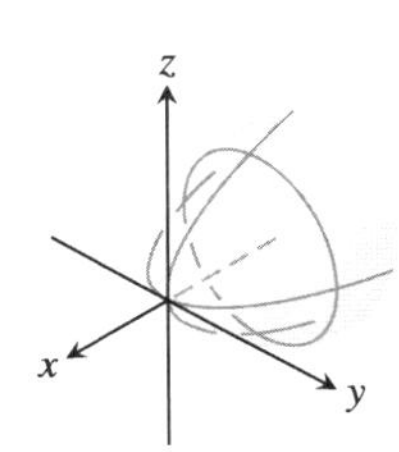

f.

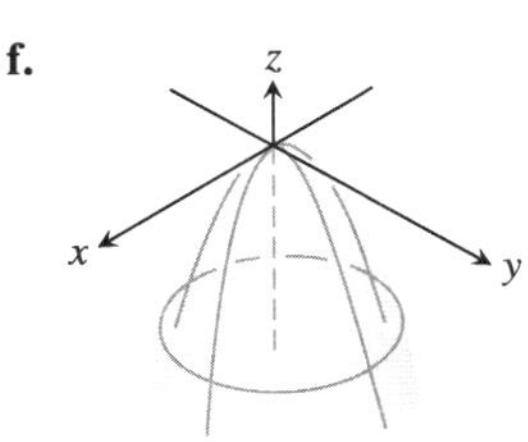

g.

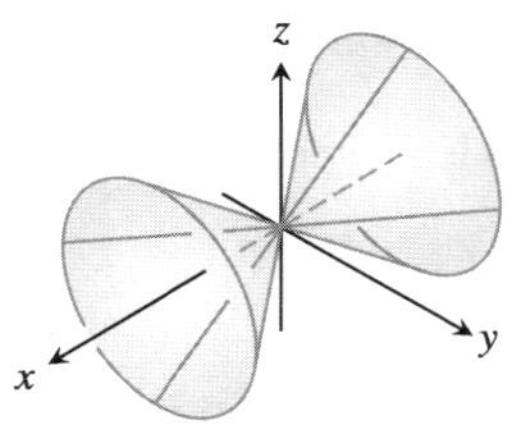

h.

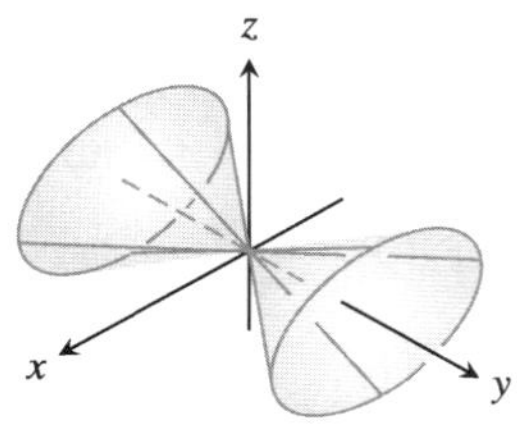

i.

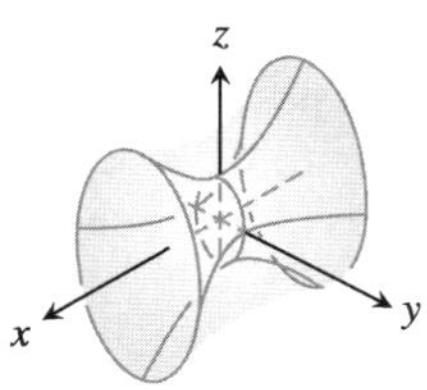

j.

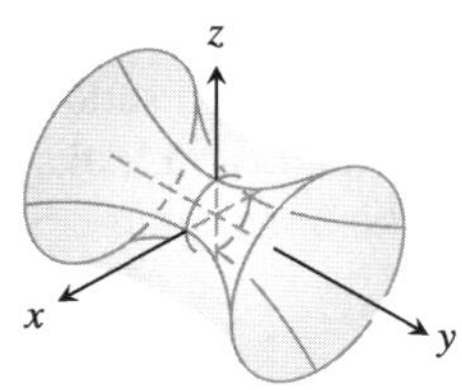

k.

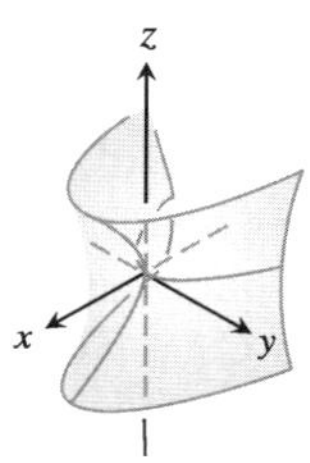

l.

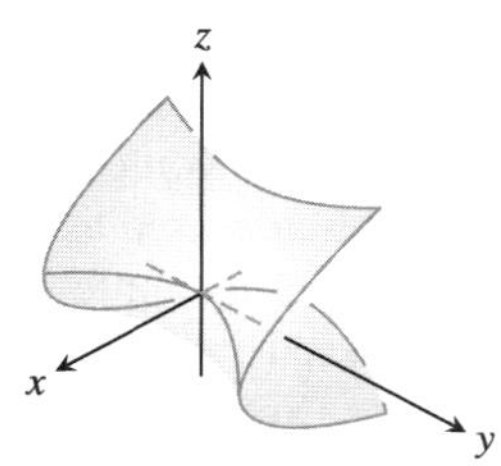

Drawing

Sketch the surfaces in Exercises 13–76.

CYLINDERS

13. $x^2 + y^2 = 4$ **14.** $x^2 + z^2 = 4$

15. $z = y^2 - 1$ **16.** $x = y^2$

17. $x^2 + 4z^2 = 16$ **18.** $4x^2 + y^2 = 36$

19. $z^2 - y^2 = 1$ **20.** $yz = 1$

ELLIPSOIDS

21. $9x^2 + y^2 + z^2 = 9$ **22.** $4x^2 + 4y^2 + z^2 = 16$

23. $4x^2 + 9y^2 + 4z^2 = 36$ **24.** $9x^2 + 4y^2 + 36z^2 = 36$

PARABOLOIDS

25. $z = x^2 + 4y^2$ **26.** $z = x^2 + 9y^2$

27. $z = 8 - x^2 - y^2$ **28.** $z = 18 - x^2 - 9y^2$

29. $x = 4 - 4y^2 - z^2$ **30.** $y = 1 - x^2 - z^2$

CONES

31. $x^2 + y^2 = z^2$ **32.** $y^2 + z^2 = x^2$

33. $4x^2 + 9z^2 = 9y^2$ **34.** $9x^2 + 4y^2 = 36z^2$

HYPERBOLOIDS

35. $x^2 + y^2 - z^2 = 1$ **36.** $y^2 + z^2 - x^2 = 1$

37. $(y^2/4) + (z^2/9) - (x^2/4) = 1$

38. $(x^2/4) + (y^2/4) - (z^2/9) = 1$

39. $z^2 - x^2 - y^2 = 1$ **40.** $(y^2/4) - (x^2/4) - z^2 = 1$

41. $x^2 - y^2 - (z^2/4) = 1$ **42.** $(x^2/4) - y^2 - (z^2/4) = 1$

HYPERBOLIC PARABOLOIDS

43. $y^2 - x^2 = z$ **44.** $x^2 - y^2 = z$

ASSORTED

45. $x^2 + y^2 + z^2 = 4$ **46.** $4x^2 + 4y^2 = z^2$

47. $z = 1 + y^2 - x^2$ **48.** $y^2 - z^2 = 4$

49. $y = -(x^2 + z^2)$ **50.** $z^2 - 4x^2 - 4y^2 = 4$

51. $16x^2 + 4y^2 = 1$ **52.** $z = x^2 + y^2 + 1$

53. $x^2 + y^2 - z^2 = 4$ **54.** $x = 4 - y^2$

55. $x^2 + z^2 = y$ **56.** $z^2 - (x^2/4) - y^2 = 1$

57. $x^2 + z^2 = 1$ **58.** $4x^2 + 4y^2 + z^2 = 4$

59. $16y^2 + 9z^2 = 4x^2$ **60.** $z = x^2 - y^2 - 1$

61. $9x^2 + 4y^2 + z^2 = 36$ **62.** $4x^2 + 9z^2 = y^2$

63. $x^2 + y^2 - 16z^2 = 16$ **64.** $z^2 + 4y^2 = 9$

65. $z = -(x^2 + y^2)$ **66.** $y^2 - x^2 - z^2 = 1$

67. $x^2 - 4y^2 = 1$ **68.** $z = 4x^2 + y^2 - 4$

69. $4y^2 + z^2 - 4x^2 = 4$ **70.** $z = 1 - x^2$

71. $x^2 + y^2 = z$ **72.** $(x^2/4) + y^2 - z^2 = 1$

73. $yz = 1$ **74.** $36x^2 + 9y^2 + 4z^2 = 36$

75. $9x^2 + 16y^2 = 4z^2$ **76.** $4z^2 - x^2 - y^2 = 4$

Theory and Examples

77. a. Express the area A of the cross-section cut from the ellipsoid

$$x^2 + \frac{y^2}{4} + \frac{z^2}{9} = 1$$

by the plane $z = c$ as a function of c. (The area of an ellipse with semiaxes a and b is πab.)

b. Use slices perpendicular to the z-axis to find the volume of the ellipsoid in part (a).

c. Now find the volume of the ellipsoid

$$\frac{x^2}{a^2} + \frac{y^2}{b^2} + \frac{z^2}{c^2} = 1.$$

Does your formula give the volume of a sphere of radius a if $a = b = c$?

78. The barrel shown here is shaped like an ellipsoid with equal pieces cut from the ends by planes perpendicular to the z-axis. The cross-sections perpendicular to the z-axis are circular. The barrel is $2h$ units high, its midsection radius is R, and its end radii are both r. Find a formula for the barrel's volume. Then check two things. First, suppose the sides of the barrel are straightened to turn the barrel into a cylinder of radius R and height $2h$. Does your formula give the cylinder's volume? Second, suppose $r = 0$ and $h = R$ so the barrel is a sphere. Does your formula give the sphere's volume?

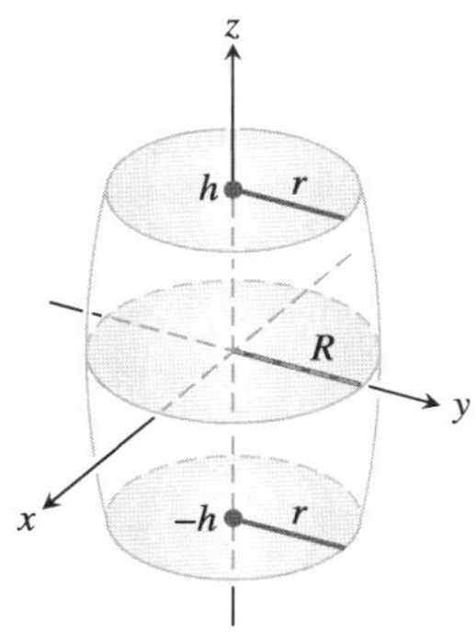

79. Show that the volume of the segment cut from the paraboloid

$$\frac{x^2}{a^2} + \frac{y^2}{b^2} = \frac{z}{c}$$

by the plane $z = h$ equals half the segment's base times its altitude. (Figure 12.49 shows the segment for the special case $h = c$.)

80. a. Find the volume of the solid bounded by the hyperboloid

$$\frac{x^2}{a^2} + \frac{y^2}{b^2} - \frac{z^2}{c^2} = 1$$

and the planes $z = 0$ and $z = h$, $h > 0$.

b. Express your answer in part (a) in terms of h and the areas A_0 and A_h of the regions cut by the hyperboloid from the planes $z = 0$ and $z = h$.

c. Show that the volume in part (a) is also given by the formula

$$V = \frac{h}{6}(A_0 + 4A_m + A_h),$$

where A_m is the area of the region cut by the hyperboloid from the plane $z = h/2$.

81. If the hyperbolic paraboloid $(y^2/b^2) - (x^2/a^2) = z/c$ is cut by the plane $y = y_1$, the resulting curve is a parabola. Find its vertex and focus.

82. Suppose you set $z = 0$ in the equation

$$Ax^2 + By^2 + Cz^2 + Dxy + Eyz + Fxz + Gx + Hy + Jz + K = 0$$

to obtain a curve in the xy-plane. What will the curve be like? Give reasons for your answer.

83. Every time we found the trace of a quadric surface in a plane parallel to one of the coordinate planes, it turned out to be a conic section. Was this mere coincidence? Did it have to happen? Give reasons for your answer.

84. Suppose you intersect a quadric surface with a plane that is *not* parallel to one of the coordinate planes. What will the trace in the plane be like? Give reasons for your answer.

T Computer Grapher Explorations

Plot the surfaces in Exercises 85–88 over the indicated domains. If you can, rotate the surface into different viewing positions.

85. $z = y^2, \quad -2 \le x \le 2, \quad -0.5 \le y \le 2$

86. $z = 1 - y^2, \quad -2 \le x \le 2, \quad -2 \le y \le 2$

87. $z = x^2 + y^2, \quad -3 \le x \le 3, \quad -3 \le y \le 3$

88. $z = x^2 + 2y^2$ over

a. $-3 \le x \le 3, \quad -3 \le y \le 3$

b. $-1 \le x \le 1, \quad -2 \le y \le 3$

c. $-2 \le x \le 2, \quad -2 \le y \le 2$

d. $-2 \le x \le 2, \quad -1 \le y \le 1$

COMPUTER EXPLORATIONS

Surface Plots

Use a CAS to plot the surfaces in Exercises 89–94. Identify the type of quadric surface from your graph.

89. $\dfrac{x^2}{9} + \dfrac{y^2}{36} = 1 - \dfrac{z^2}{25}$

90. $\dfrac{x^2}{9} - \dfrac{z^2}{9} = 1 - \dfrac{y^2}{16}$

91. $5x^2 = z^2 - 3y^2$

92. $\dfrac{y^2}{16} = 1 - \dfrac{x^2}{9} + z$

93. $\dfrac{x^2}{9} - 1 = \dfrac{y^2}{16} + \dfrac{z^2}{2}$

94. $y - \sqrt{4 - z^2} = 0$

Chapter 12 Questions to Guide Your Review

1. When do directed line segments in the plane represent the same vector?
2. How are vectors added and subtracted geometrically? Algebraically?
3. How do you find a vector's magnitude and direction?
4. If a vector is multiplied by a positive scalar, how is the result related to the original vector? What if the scalar is zero? Negative?

5. Define the *dot product* (*scalar product*) of two vectors. Which algebraic laws are satisfied by dot products? Give examples. When is the dot product of two vectors equal to zero?
6. What geometric interpretation does the dot product have? Give examples.
7. What is the vector projection of a vector **u** onto a vector **v**? How do you write **u** as the sum of a vector parallel to **v** and a vector orthogonal to **v**?
8. Define the *cross product* (*vector product*) of two vectors. Which algebraic laws are satisfied by cross products, and which are not? Give examples. When is the cross product of two vectors equal to zero?
9. What geometric or physical interpretations do cross products have? Give examples.
10. What is the determinant formula for calculating the cross product of two vectors relative to the Cartesian **i**, **j**, **k**-coordinate system? Use it in an example.
11. How do you find equations for lines, line segments, and planes in space? Give examples. Can you express a line in space by a single equation? A plane?
12. How do you find the distance from a point to a line in space? From a point to a plane? Give examples.
13. What are box products? What significance do they have? How are they evaluated? Give an example.
14. How do you find equations for spheres in space? Give examples.
15. How do you find the intersection of two lines in space? A line and a plane? Two planes? Give examples.
16. What is a cylinder? Give examples of equations that define cylinders in Cartesian coordinates.
17. What are quadric surfaces? Give examples of different kinds of ellipsoids, paraboloids, cones, and hyperboloids (equations and sketches).

Chapter 12 Practice Exercises

Vector Calculations in Two Dimensions

In Exercises 1–4, let $\mathbf{u} = \langle -3, 4\rangle$ and $\mathbf{v} = \langle 2, -5\rangle$. Find **(a)** the component form of the vector and **(b)** its magnitude.

1. $3\mathbf{u} - 4\mathbf{v}$
2. $\mathbf{u} + \mathbf{v}$
3. $-2\mathbf{u}$
4. $5\mathbf{v}$

In Exercises 5–8, find the component form of the vector.

5. The vector obtained by rotating $\langle 0, 1\rangle$ through an angle of $2\pi/3$ radians
6. The unit vector that makes an angle of $\pi/6$ radian with the positive x-axis
7. The vector 2 units long in the direction $4\mathbf{i} - \mathbf{j}$
8. The vector 5 units long in the direction opposite to the direction of $(3/5)\mathbf{i} + (4/5)\mathbf{j}$

Express the vectors in Exercises 9–12 in terms of their lengths and directions.

9. $\sqrt{2}\mathbf{i} + \sqrt{2}\mathbf{j}$
10. $-\mathbf{i} - \mathbf{j}$
11. Velocity vector $\mathbf{v} = (-2\sin t)\mathbf{i} + (2\cos t)\mathbf{j}$ when $t = \pi/2$.
12. Velocity vector $\mathbf{v} = (e^t\cos t - e^t\sin t)\mathbf{i} + (e^t\sin t + e^t\cos t)\mathbf{j}$ when $t = \ln 2$.

Vector Calculations in Three Dimensions

Express the vectors in Exercises 13 and 14 in terms of their lengths and directions.

13. $2\mathbf{i} - 3\mathbf{j} + 6\mathbf{k}$
14. $\mathbf{i} + 2\mathbf{j} - \mathbf{k}$
15. Find a vector 2 units long in the direction of $\mathbf{v} = 4\mathbf{i} - \mathbf{j} + 4\mathbf{k}$.
16. Find a vector 5 units long in the direction opposite to the direction of $\mathbf{v} = (3/5)\mathbf{i} + (4/5)\mathbf{k}$.

In Exercises 17 and 18, find $|\mathbf{v}|$, $|\mathbf{u}|$, $\mathbf{v}\cdot\mathbf{u}$, $\mathbf{u}\cdot\mathbf{v}$, $\mathbf{v}\times\mathbf{u}$, $\mathbf{u}\times\mathbf{v}$, $|\mathbf{v}\times\mathbf{u}|$, the angle between **v** and **u**, the scalar component of **u** in the direction of **v**, and the vector projection of **u** onto **v**.

17. $\mathbf{v} = \mathbf{i} + \mathbf{j}$
 $\mathbf{u} = 2\mathbf{i} + \mathbf{j} - 2\mathbf{k}$
18. $\mathbf{v} = \mathbf{i} + \mathbf{j} + 2\mathbf{k}$
 $\mathbf{u} = -\mathbf{i} - \mathbf{k}$

In Exercises 19 and 20, write **u** as the sum of a vector parallel to **v** and a vector orthogonal to **v**.

19. $\mathbf{v} = 2\mathbf{i} + \mathbf{j} - \mathbf{k}$
 $\mathbf{u} = \mathbf{i} + \mathbf{j} - 5\mathbf{k}$
20. $\mathbf{u} = \mathbf{i} - 2\mathbf{j}$
 $\mathbf{v} = \mathbf{i} + \mathbf{j} + \mathbf{k}$

In Exercises 21 and 22, draw coordinate axes and then sketch **u**, **v**, and $\mathbf{u}\times\mathbf{v}$ as vectors at the origin.

21. $\mathbf{u} = \mathbf{i}$, $\mathbf{v} = \mathbf{i} + \mathbf{j}$
22. $\mathbf{u} = \mathbf{i} - \mathbf{j}$, $\mathbf{v} = \mathbf{i} + \mathbf{j}$
23. If $|\mathbf{v}| = 2$, $|\mathbf{w}| = 3$, and the angle between **v** and **w** is $\pi/3$, find $|\mathbf{v} - 2\mathbf{w}|$.
24. For what value or values of a will the vectors $\mathbf{u} = 2\mathbf{i} + 4\mathbf{j} - 5\mathbf{k}$ and $\mathbf{v} = -4\mathbf{i} - 8\mathbf{j} + a\mathbf{k}$ be parallel?

In Exercises 25 and 26, find **(a)** the area of the parallelogram determined by vectors **u** and **v** and **(b)** the volume of the parallelepiped determined by the vectors **u**, **v**, and **w**.

25. $\mathbf{u} = \mathbf{i} + \mathbf{j} - \mathbf{k}$, $\mathbf{v} = 2\mathbf{i} + \mathbf{j} + \mathbf{k}$, $\mathbf{w} = -\mathbf{i} - 2\mathbf{j} + 3\mathbf{k}$
26. $\mathbf{u} = \mathbf{i} + \mathbf{j}$, $\mathbf{v} = \mathbf{j}$, $\mathbf{w} = \mathbf{i} + \mathbf{j} + \mathbf{k}$

Lines, Planes, and Distances

27. Suppose that **n** is normal to a plane and that **v** is parallel to the plane. Describe how you would find a vector **n** that is both perpendicular to **v** and parallel to the plane.

28. Find a vector in the plane parallel to the line $ax + by = c$.

In Exercises 29 and 30, find the distance from the point to the line.

29. $(2, 2, 0)$; $x = -t, \quad y = t, \quad z = -1 + t$

30. $(0, 4, 1)$; $x = 2 + t, \quad y = 2 + t, \quad z = t$

31. Parametrize the line that passes through the point $(1, 2, 3)$ parallel to the vector $\mathbf{v} = -3\mathbf{i} + 7\mathbf{k}$.

32. Parametrize the line segment joining the points $P(1, 2, 0)$ and $Q(1, 3, -1)$.

In Exercises 33 and 34, find the distance from the point to the plane.

33. $(6, 0, -6), \quad x - y = 4$

34. $(3, 0, 10), \quad 2x + 3y + z = 2$

35. Find an equation for the plane that passes through the point $(3, -2, 1)$ normal to the vector $\mathbf{n} = 2\mathbf{i} + \mathbf{j} + \mathbf{k}$.

36. Find an equation for the plane that passes through the point $(-1, 6, 0)$ perpendicular to the line $x = -1 + t, y = 6 - 2t, z = 3t$.

In Exercises 37 and 38, find an equation for the plane through points P, Q, and R.

37. $P(1, -1, 2), \quad Q(2, 1, 3), \quad R(-1, 2, -1)$

38. $P(1, 0, 0), \quad Q(0, 1, 0), \quad R(0, 0, 1)$

39. Find the points in which the line $x = 1 + 2t, y = -1 - t, z = 3t$ meets the three coordinate planes.

40. Find the point in which the line through the origin perpendicular to the plane $2x - y - z = 4$ meets the plane $3x - 5y + 2z = 6$.

41. Find the acute angle between the planes $x = 7$ and $x + y + \sqrt{2}z = -3$.

42. Find the acute angle between the planes $x + y = 1$ and $y + z = 1$.

43. Find parametric equations for the line in which the planes $x + 2y + z = 1$ and $x - y + 2z = -8$ intersect.

44. Show that the line in which the planes

$$x + 2y - 2z = 5 \quad \text{and} \quad 5x - 2y - z = 0$$

intersect is parallel to the line

$$x = -3 + 2t, \quad y = 3t, \quad z = 1 + 4t.$$

45. The planes $3x + 6z = 1$ and $2x + 2y - z = 3$ intersect in a line.

a. Show that the planes are orthogonal.

b. Find equations for the line of intersection.

46. Find an equation for the plane that passes through the point $(1, 2, 3)$ parallel to $\mathbf{u} = 2\mathbf{i} + 3\mathbf{j} + \mathbf{k}$ and $\mathbf{v} = \mathbf{i} - \mathbf{j} + 2\mathbf{k}$.

47. Is $\mathbf{v} = 2\mathbf{i} - 4\mathbf{j} + \mathbf{k}$ related in any special way to the plane $2x + y = 5$? Give reasons for your answer.

48. The equation $\mathbf{n} \cdot \overrightarrow{P_0P} = 0$ represents the plane through P_0 normal to $\mathbf{n}$. What set does the inequality $\mathbf{n} \cdot \overrightarrow{P_0P} > 0$ represent?

49. Find the distance from the point $P(1, 4, 0)$ to the plane through $A(0, 0, 0)$, $B(2, 0, -1)$ and $C(2, -1, 0)$.

50. Find the distance from the point $(2, 2, 3)$ to the plane $2x + 3y + 5z = 0$.

51. Find a vector parallel to the plane $2x - y - z = 4$ and orthogonal to $\mathbf{i} + \mathbf{j} + \mathbf{k}$.

52. Find a unit vector orthogonal to **A** in the plane of **B** and **C** if $\mathbf{A} = 2\mathbf{i} - \mathbf{j} + \mathbf{k}$, $\mathbf{B} = \mathbf{i} + 2\mathbf{j} + \mathbf{k}$, and $\mathbf{C} = \mathbf{i} + \mathbf{j} - 2\mathbf{k}$.

53. Find a vector of magnitude 2 parallel to the line of intersection of the planes $x + 2y + z - 1 = 0$ and $x - y + 2z + 7 = 0$.

54. Find the point in which the line through the origin perpendicular to the plane $2x - y - z = 4$ meets the plane $3x - 5y + 2z = 6$.

55. Find the point in which the line through $P(3, 2, 1)$ normal to the plane $2x - y + 2z = -2$ meets the plane.

56. What angle does the line of intersection of the planes $2x + y - z = 0$ and $x + y + 2z = 0$ make with the positive x-axis?

57. The line

$$L: \quad x = 3 + 2t, \quad y = 2t, \quad z = t$$

intersects the plane $x + 3y - z = -4$ in a point P. Find the coordinates of P and find equations for the line in the plane through P perpendicular to L.

58. Show that for every real number k the plane

$$x - 2y + z + 3 + k(2x - y - z + 1) = 0$$

contains the line of intersection of the planes

$$x - 2y + z + 3 = 0 \quad \text{and} \quad 2x - y - z + 1 = 0.$$

59. Find an equation for the plane through $A(-2, 0, -3)$ and $B(1, -2, 1)$ that lies parallel to the line through $C(-2, -13/5, 26/5)$ and $D(16/5, -13/5, 0)$.

60. Is the line $x = 1 + 2t, y = -2 + 3t, z = -5t$ related in any way to the plane $-4x - 6y + 10z = 9$? Give reasons for your answer.

61. Which of the following are equations for the plane through the points $P(1, 1, -1)$, $Q(3, 0, 2)$, and $R(-2, 1, 0)$?

a. $(2\mathbf{i} - 3\mathbf{j} + 3\mathbf{k}) \cdot ((x + 2)\mathbf{i} + (y - 1)\mathbf{j} + z\mathbf{k}) = 0$

b. $x = 3 - t, \quad y = -11t, \quad z = 2 - 3t$

c. $(x + 2) + 11(y - 1) = 3z$

d. $(2\mathbf{i} - 3\mathbf{j} + 3\mathbf{k}) \times ((x + 2)\mathbf{i} + (y - 1)\mathbf{j} + z\mathbf{k}) = \mathbf{0}$

e. $(2\mathbf{i} - \mathbf{j} + 3\mathbf{k}) \times (-3\mathbf{i} + \mathbf{k}) \cdot ((x + 2)\mathbf{i} + (y - 1)\mathbf{j} + z\mathbf{k}) = 0$

62. The parallelogram shown on page 902 has vertices at $A(2, -1, 4)$, $B(1, 0, -1)$, $C(1, 2, 3)$, and D. Find

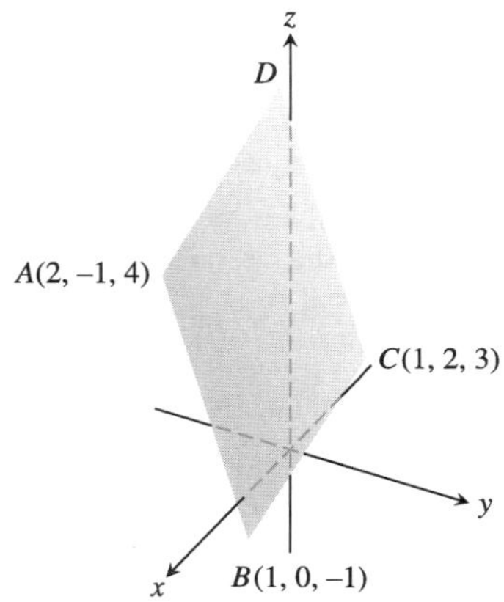

a. the coordinates of D,

b. the cosine of the interior angle at B,

c. the vector projection of $\overrightarrow{BA}$ onto $\overrightarrow{BC}$,

d. the area of the parallelogram,

e. an equation for the plane of the parallelogram,

f. the areas of the orthogonal projections of the parallelogram on the three coordinate planes.

63. Distance between lines Find the distance between the line L_1 through the points $A(1, 0, -1)$ and $B(-1, 1, 0)$ and the line L_2 through the points $C(3, 1, -1)$ and $D(4, 5, -2)$. The distance is to be measured along the line perpendicular to the two lines. First find a vector **n** perpendicular to both lines. Then project $\overrightarrow{AC}$ onto **n**.

64. (*Continuation of Exercise 63.*) Find the distance between the line through $A(4, 0, 2)$ and $B(2, 4, 1)$ and the line through $C(1, 3, 2)$ and $D(2, 2, 4)$.

Quadric Surfaces

Identify and sketch the surfaces in Exercises 65–76.

65. $x^2 + y^2 + z^2 = 4$

66. $x^2 + (y - 1)^2 + z^2 = 1$

67. $4x^2 + 4y^2 + z^2 = 4$

68. $36x^2 + 9y^2 + 4z^2 = 36$

69. $z = -(x^2 + y^2)$

70. $y = -(x^2 + z^2)$

71. $x^2 + y^2 = z^2$

72. $x^2 + z^2 = y^2$

73. $x^2 + y^2 - z^2 = 4$

74. $4y^2 + z^2 - 4x^2 = 4$

75. $y^2 - x^2 - z^2 = 1$

76. $z^2 - x^2 - y^2 = 1$

Chapter 12 Additional and Advanced Exercises

1. Submarine hunting Two surface ships on maneuvers are trying to determine a submarine's course and speed to prepare for an aircraft intercept. As shown here, ship A is located at $(4, 0, 0)$, whereas ship B is located at $(0, 5, 0)$. All coordinates are given in thousands of feet. Ship A locates the submarine in the direction of the vector $2\mathbf{i} + 3\mathbf{j} - (1/3)\mathbf{k}$, and ship B locates it in the direction of the vector $18\mathbf{i} - 6\mathbf{j} - \mathbf{k}$. Four minutes ago, the submarine was located at $(2, -1, -1/3)$. The aircraft is due in 20 min. Assuming that the submarine moves in a straight line at a constant speed, to what position should the surface ships direct the aircraft?

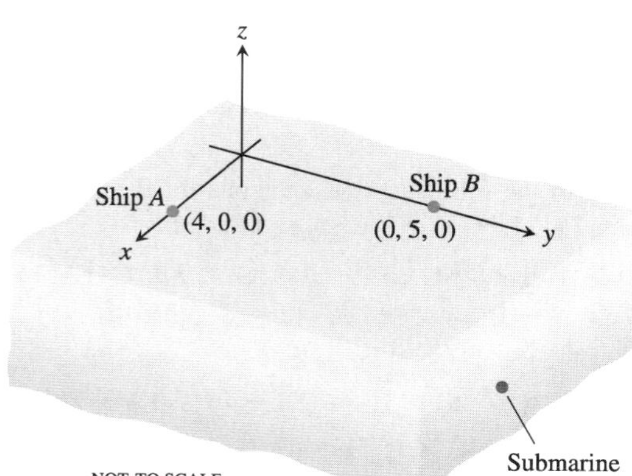

2. A helicopter rescue Two helicopters, H_1 and H_2, are traveling together. At time $t = 0$, they separate and follow different straight-line paths given by

$$H_1: \quad x = 6 + 40t, \quad y = -3 + 10t, \quad z = -3 + 2t$$
$$H_2: \quad x = 6 + 110t, \quad y = -3 + 4t, \quad z = -3 + t.$$

Time t is measured in hours and all coordinates are measured in miles. Due to system malfunctions, H_2 stops its flight at $(446, 13, 1)$ and, in a negligible amount of time, lands at $(446, 13, 0)$. Two hours later, H_1 is advised of this fact and heads toward H_2 at 150 mph. How long will it take H_1 to reach H_2?

3. Torque The operator's manual for the Toro® 21 in. lawnmower says "tighten the spark plug to 15 ft-lb (20.4 N·m)." If you are installing the plug with a 10.5-in. socket wrench that places the center of your hand 9 in. from the axis of the spark plug, about how hard should you pull? Answer in pounds.

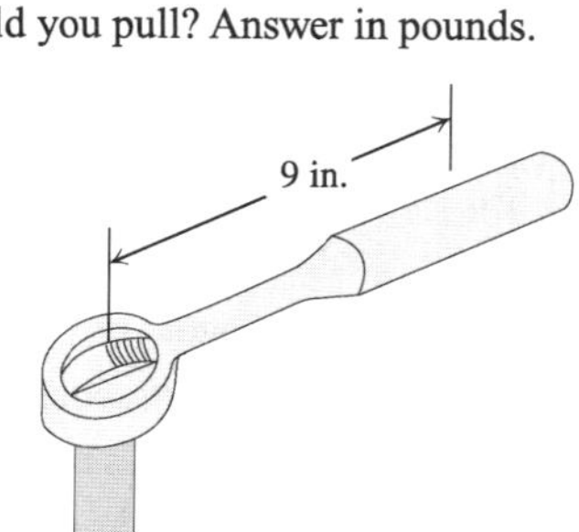

4. Rotating body The line through the origin and the point $A(1, 1, 1)$ is the axis of rotation of a right body rotating with a constant angular speed of $3/2$ rad/sec. The rotation appears to be clockwise when we look toward the origin from A. Find the velocity $\mathbf{v}$ of the point of the body that is at the position $B(1, 3, 2)$.

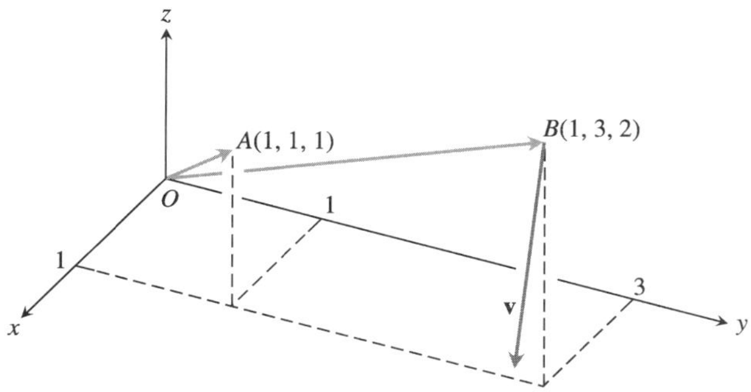

5. Determinants and planes

a. Show that

$$\begin{vmatrix} x_1 - x & y_1 - y & z_1 - z \\ x_2 - x & y_2 - y & z_2 - z \\ x_3 - x & y_3 - y & z_3 - z \end{vmatrix} = 0$$

is an equation for the plane through the three noncollinear points $P_1(x_1, y_1, z_1)$, $P_2(x_2, y_2, z_2)$, and $P_3(x_3, y_3, z_3)$.

b. What set of points in space is described by the equation

$$\begin{vmatrix} x & y & z & 1 \\ x_1 & y_1 & z_1 & 1 \\ x_2 & y_2 & z_2 & 1 \\ x_3 & y_3 & z_3 & 1 \end{vmatrix} = 0?$$

6. Determinants and lines Show that the lines

$$x = a_1 s + b_1, y = a_2 s + b_2, z = a_3 s + b_3, -\infty < s < \infty,$$

and

$$x = c_1 t + d_1, y = c_2 t + d_2, z = c_3 t + d_3, -\infty < t < \infty,$$

intersect or are parallel if and only if

$$\begin{vmatrix} a_1 & c_1 & b_1 - d_1 \\ a_2 & c_2 & b_2 - d_2 \\ a_3 & c_3 & b_3 - d_3 \end{vmatrix} = 0.$$

7. Parallelogram The accompanying figure shows parallelogram $ABCD$ and the midpoint P of diagonal BD.

a. Express $\overrightarrow{BD}$ in terms of $\overrightarrow{AB}$ and $\overrightarrow{AD}$.

b. Express $\overrightarrow{AP}$ in terms of $\overrightarrow{AB}$ and $\overrightarrow{AD}$.

c. Prove that P is also the midpoint of diagonal AC.

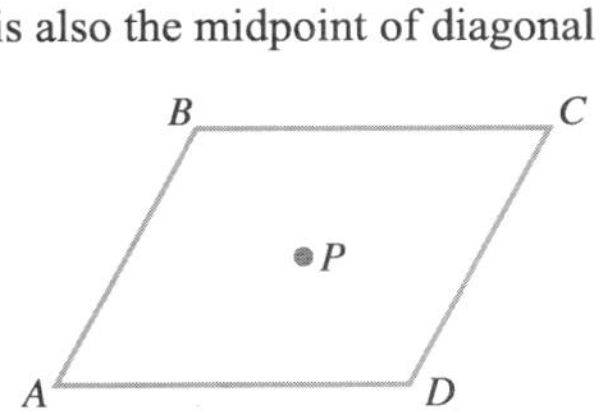

8. In the figure here, D is the midpoint of side AB of triangle ABC, and E is one-third of the way between C and B. Use vectors to prove that F is the midpoint of line segment CD.

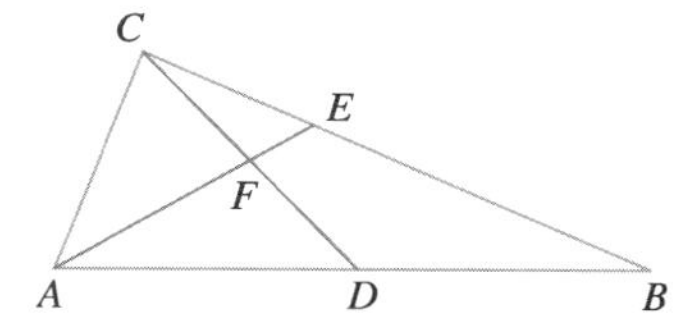

9. Use vectors to show that the distance from $P_1(x_1, y_1)$ to the line $ax + by = c$ is

$$d = \frac{|ax_1 + by_1 - c|}{\sqrt{a^2 + b^2}}.$$

10. a. Use vectors to show that the distance from $P_1(x_1, y_1, z_1)$ to the plane $Ax + By + Cz = D$ is

$$d = \frac{|Ax_1 + By_1 + Cz_1 - D|}{\sqrt{A^2 + B^2 + C^2}}.$$

b. Find an equation for the sphere that is tangent to the planes $x + y + z = 3$ and $x + y + z = 9$ if the planes $2x - y = 0$ and $3x - z = 0$ pass through the center of the sphere.

11. a. Show that the distance between the parallel planes $Ax + By + Cz = D_1$ and $Ax + By + Cz = D_2$ is

$$d = \frac{|D_1 - D_2|}{|A\mathbf{i} + B\mathbf{j} + C\mathbf{k}|}.$$

b. Find the distance between the planes $2x + 3y - z = 6$ and $2x + 3y - z = 12$.

c. Find an equation for the plane parallel to the plane $2x - y + 2z = -4$ if the point $(3, 2, -1)$ is equidistant from the two planes.

d. Write equations for the planes that lie parallel to and 5 units away from the plane $x - 2y + z = 3$.

12. Prove that four points A, B, C, and D are coplanar (lie in a common plane) if and only if $\overrightarrow{AD} \cdot (\overrightarrow{AB} \times \overrightarrow{BC}) = 0$.

13. The projection of a vector on a plane Let P be a plane in space and let $\mathbf{v}$ be a vector. The vector projection of $\mathbf{v}$ onto the plane P, $\text{proj}_P \mathbf{v}$, can be defined informally as follows. Suppose the sun is shining so that its rays are normal to the plane P. Then $\text{proj}_P \mathbf{v}$ is the "shadow" of $\mathbf{v}$ onto P. If P is the plane $x + 2y + 6z = 6$ and $\mathbf{v} = \mathbf{i} + \mathbf{j} + \mathbf{k}$, find $\text{proj}_P \mathbf{v}$.

14. The accompanying figure shows nonzero vectors $\mathbf{v}$, $\mathbf{w}$, and $\mathbf{z}$, with $\mathbf{z}$ orthogonal to the line L, and $\mathbf{v}$ and $\mathbf{w}$ making equal angles β with L. Assuming $|\mathbf{v}| = |\mathbf{w}|$, find $\mathbf{w}$ in terms of $\mathbf{v}$ and $\mathbf{z}$.

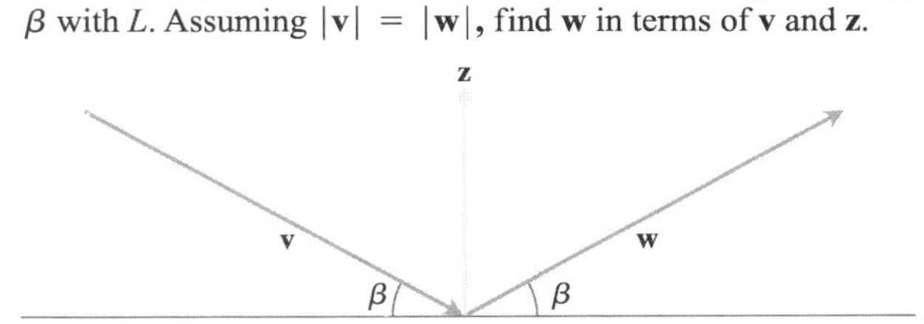

15. Triple vector products The *triple vector products* $(\mathbf{u} \times \mathbf{v}) \times \mathbf{w}$ and $\mathbf{u} \times (\mathbf{v} \times \mathbf{w})$ are usually not equal, although the formulas for evaluating them from components are similar:

$$(\mathbf{u} \times \mathbf{v}) \times \mathbf{w} = (\mathbf{u} \cdot \mathbf{w})\mathbf{v} - (\mathbf{v} \cdot \mathbf{w})\mathbf{u}.$$
$$\mathbf{u} \times (\mathbf{v} \times \mathbf{w}) = (\mathbf{u} \cdot \mathbf{w})\mathbf{v} - (\mathbf{u} \cdot \mathbf{v})\mathbf{w}.$$

Verify each formula for the following vectors by evaluating its two sides and comparing the results.

u	**v**	**w**
a. $2\mathbf{i}$	$2\mathbf{j}$	$2\mathbf{k}$
b. $\mathbf{i} - \mathbf{j} + \mathbf{k}$	$2\mathbf{i} + \mathbf{j} - 2\mathbf{k}$	$-\mathbf{i} + 2\mathbf{j} - \mathbf{k}$
c. $2\mathbf{i} + \mathbf{j}$	$2\mathbf{i} - \mathbf{j} + \mathbf{k}$	$\mathbf{i} + 2\mathbf{k}$
d. $\mathbf{i} + \mathbf{j} - 2\mathbf{k}$	$-\mathbf{i} - \mathbf{k}$	$2\mathbf{i} + 4\mathbf{j} - 2\mathbf{k}$

16. Cross and dot products Show that if **u**, **v**, **w**, and **r** are any vectors, then

a. $\mathbf{u} \times (\mathbf{v} \times \mathbf{w}) + \mathbf{v} \times (\mathbf{w} \times \mathbf{u}) + \mathbf{w} \times (\mathbf{u} \times \mathbf{v}) = \mathbf{0}$

b. $\mathbf{u} \times \mathbf{v} = (\mathbf{u} \cdot \mathbf{v} \times \mathbf{i})\mathbf{i} + (\mathbf{u} \cdot \mathbf{v} \times \mathbf{j})\mathbf{j} + (\mathbf{u} \cdot \mathbf{v} \times \mathbf{k})\mathbf{k}$

c. $(\mathbf{u} \times \mathbf{v}) \cdot (\mathbf{w} \times \mathbf{r}) = \begin{vmatrix} \mathbf{u} \cdot \mathbf{w} & \mathbf{v} \cdot \mathbf{w} \\ \mathbf{u} \cdot \mathbf{r} & \mathbf{v} \cdot \mathbf{r} \end{vmatrix}.$

17. Cross and dot products Prove or disprove the formula

$$\mathbf{u} \times (\mathbf{u} \times (\mathbf{u} \times \mathbf{v})) \cdot \mathbf{w} = -|\mathbf{u}|^2 \mathbf{u} \cdot \mathbf{v} \times \mathbf{w}.$$

18. By forming the cross product of two appropriate vectors, derive the trigonometric identity

$$\sin (A - B) = \sin A \cos B - \cos A \sin B.$$

19. Use vectors to prove that

$$(a^2 + b^2)(c^2 + d^2) \geq (ac + bd)^2$$

for any four numbers a, b, c, and d. (*Hint:* Let $\mathbf{u} = a\mathbf{i} + b\mathbf{j}$ and $\mathbf{v} = c\mathbf{i} + d\mathbf{j}$.)

20. Suppose that vectors **u** and **v** are not parallel and that $\mathbf{u} = \mathbf{w} + \mathbf{r}$, where **w** is parallel to **v** and **r** is orthogonal to **v**. Express **w** and **r** in terms of **u** and **v**.

21. Show that $|\mathbf{u} + \mathbf{v}| \leq |\mathbf{u}| + |\mathbf{v}|$ for any vectors **u** and **v**.

22. Show that $\mathbf{w} = |\mathbf{v}|\mathbf{u} + |\mathbf{u}|\mathbf{v}$ bisects the angle between **u** and **v**.

23. Show that $|\mathbf{v}|\mathbf{u} + |\mathbf{u}|\mathbf{v}$ and $|\mathbf{v}|\mathbf{u} - |\mathbf{u}|\mathbf{v}$ are orthogonal.

24. Dot multiplication is positive definite Show that dot multiplication of vectors is *positive definite*; that is, show that $\mathbf{u} \cdot \mathbf{u} \geq 0$ for every vector **u** and that $\mathbf{u} \cdot \mathbf{u} = 0$ if and only if $\mathbf{u} = \mathbf{0}$.

25. Point masses and gravitation In physics, the law of gravitation says that if P and Q are (point) masses with mass M and m, respectively, then P is attracted to Q by the force

$$\mathbf{F} = \frac{GMm\mathbf{r}}{|\mathbf{r}|^3},$$

where **r** is the vector from P to Q and G is the universal gravitational constant. Moreover, if $Q_1, \ldots, Q_k$ are (point) masses with mass $m_1, \ldots, m_k$, respectively, then the force on P due to all the Q_i's is

$$\mathbf{F} = \sum_{i=1}^{k} \frac{GMm_i}{|\mathbf{r}_i|^3}\mathbf{r}_i,$$

where $\mathbf{r}_i$ is the vector from P to Q_i.

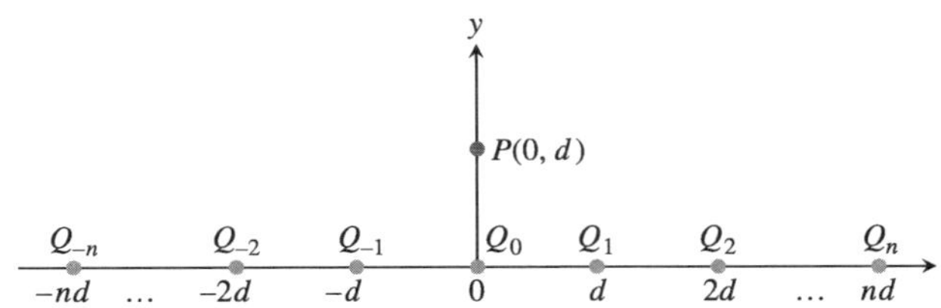

a. Let point P with mass M be located at the point $(0, d)$, $d > 0$, in the coordinate plane. For $i = -n, -n + 1, \ldots, -1, 0, 1, \ldots, n$, let Q_i be located at the point $(id, 0)$ and have mass mi. Find the magnitude of the gravitational force on P due to all the Q_i's.

b. Is the limit as $n \to \infty$ of the magnitude of the force on P finite? Why, or why not?

26. Relativistic sums Einstein's special theory of relativity roughly says that with respect to a reference frame (coordinate system) no material object can travel as fast as c, the speed of light. So, if $\vec{x}$ and $\vec{y}$ are two velocities such that $|\vec{x}| < c$ and $|\vec{y}| < c$, then the *relativistic sum* $\vec{x} \oplus \vec{y}$ of $\vec{x}$ and $\vec{y}$ must have length less than c. Einstein's special theory of relativity says that

$$\vec{x} \oplus \vec{y} = \frac{\vec{x} + \vec{y}}{1 + \dfrac{\vec{x} \cdot \vec{y}}{c^2}} + \frac{1}{c^2} \cdot \frac{\gamma_x}{\gamma_x + 1} \cdot \frac{\vec{x} \times (\vec{x} \times \vec{y})}{1 + \dfrac{\vec{x} \cdot \vec{y}}{c^2}},$$

where

$$\gamma_x = \frac{1}{\sqrt{1 - \dfrac{\vec{x} \cdot \vec{x}}{c^2}}}.$$

It can be shown that if $|\vec{x}| < c$ and $|\vec{y}| < c$, then $|\vec{x} \oplus \vec{y}| < c$. This exercise deals with two special cases.

a. Prove that if $\vec{x}$ and $\vec{y}$ are orthogonal, $|\vec{x}| < c$, $|\vec{y}| < c$, then $|\vec{x} \oplus \vec{y}| < c$.

b. Prove that if $\vec{x}$ and $\vec{y}$ are parallel, $|\vec{x}| < c$, $|\vec{y}| < c$, then $|\vec{x} \oplus \vec{y}| < c$.

c. Compute $\lim_{c \to \infty} \vec{x} \oplus \vec{y}$.

Chapter 12 Technology Application Projects

Mathematica/Maple Module
Using Vectors to Represent Lines and Find Distances

Parts I and II: Learn the advantages of interpreting lines as vectors.

Part III: Use vectors to find the distance from a point to a line.

Mathematica/Maple Module
Putting a Scene in Three Dimensions onto a Two-Dimensional Canvas

Use the concept of planes in space to obtain a two-dimensional image.

Mathematica/Maple Module
Getting Started in Plotting in 3D

Part I: Use the vector definition of lines and planes to generate graphs and equations, and to compare different forms for the equations of a single line.

Part II: Plot functions that are defined implicitly.

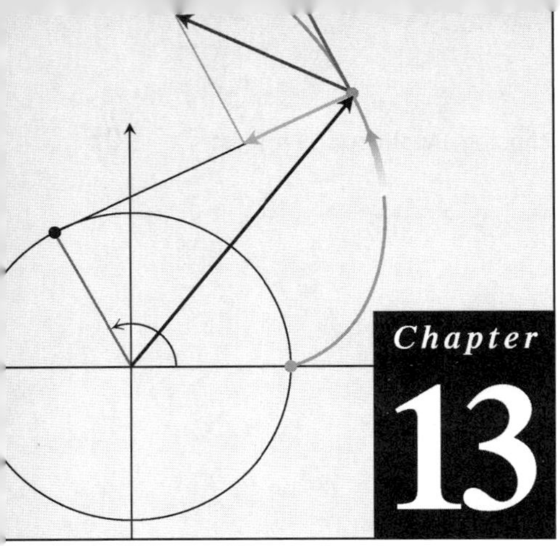

Chapter 13

VECTOR-VALUED FUNCTIONS AND MOTION IN SPACE

OVERVIEW When a body (or object) travels through space, the equations $x = f(t)$, $y = g(t)$, and $z = h(t)$ that give the body's coordinates as functions of time serve as parametric equations for the body's motion and path. With vector notation, we can condense these into a single equation $\mathbf{r}(t) = f(t)\mathbf{i} + g(t)\mathbf{j} + h(t)\mathbf{k}$ that gives the body's position as a vector function of time. For an object moving in the xy-plane, the component function $h(t)$ is zero for all time (that is, identically zero).

In this chapter, we use calculus to study the paths, velocities, and accelerations of moving bodies. As we go along, we will see how our work answers the standard questions about the paths and motions of projectiles, planets, and satellites. In the final section, we use our new vector calculus to derive Kepler's laws of planetary motion from Newton's laws of motion and gravitation.

13.1 Vector Functions

When a particle moves through space during a time interval I, we think of the particle's coordinates as functions defined on I:

$$x = f(t), \qquad y = g(t), \qquad z = h(t), \qquad t \in I. \tag{1}$$

The points $(x, y, z) = (f(t), g(t), h(t))$, $t \in I$, make up the **curve** in space that we call the particle's **path**. The equations and interval in Equation (1) **parametrize** the curve. A curve in space can also be represented in vector form. The vector

$$\mathbf{r}(t) = \overrightarrow{OP} = f(t)\mathbf{i} + g(t)\mathbf{j} + h(t)\mathbf{k} \tag{2}$$

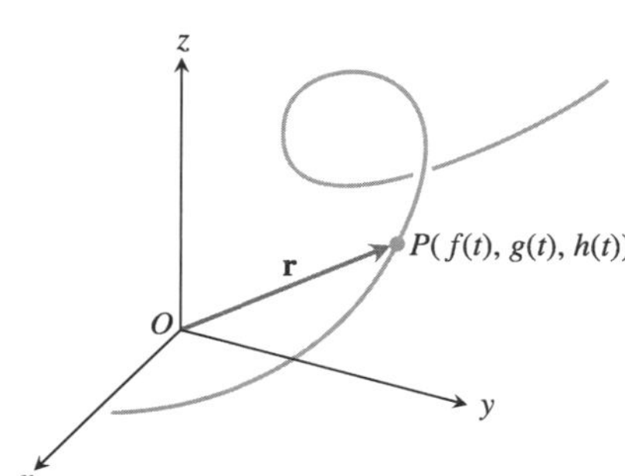

FIGURE 13.1 The position vector $\mathbf{r} = \overrightarrow{OP}$ of a particle moving through space is a function of time.

from the origin to the particle's **position** $P(f(t), g(t), h(t))$ at time t is the particle's **position vector** (Figure 13.1). The functions f, g, and h are the **component functions (components)** of the position vector. We think of the particle's path as the **curve traced by r** during the time interval I. Figure 13.2 displays several space curves generated by a computer graphing program. It would not be easy to plot these curves by hand.

Equation (2) defines $\mathbf{r}$ as a vector function of the real variable t on the interval I. More generally, a **vector function** or **vector-valued function** on a domain set D is a rule that assigns a vector in space to each element in D. For now, the domains will be intervals of real numbers resulting in a space curve. Later, in Chapter 16, the domains will be regions in the plane. Vector functions will then represent surfaces in space. Vector functions on a domain in the plane or space also give rise to "vector fields," which are important to the study of the flow of a fluid, gravitational fields, and electromagnetic phenomena. We investigate vector fields and their applications in Chapter 16.

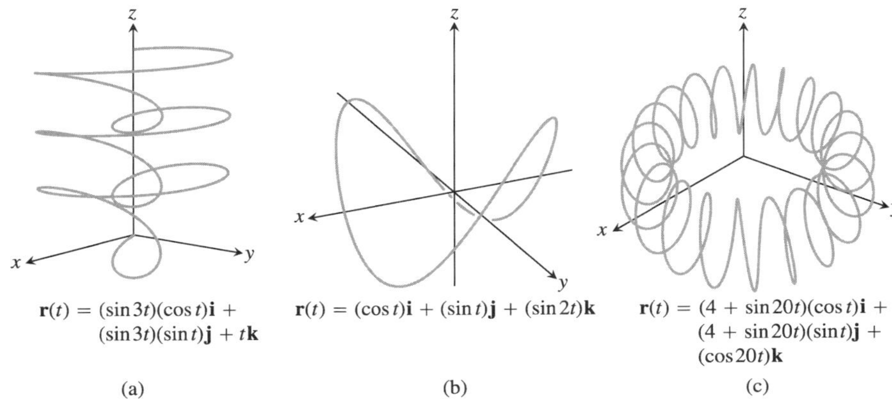

FIGURE 13.2 Computer-generated space curves are defined by the position vectors $\mathbf{r}(t)$.

We refer to real-valued functions as **scalar functions** to distinguish them from vector functions. The components of $\mathbf{r}$ are scalar functions of t. When we define a vector-valued function by giving its component functions, we assume the vector function's domain to be the common domain of the components.

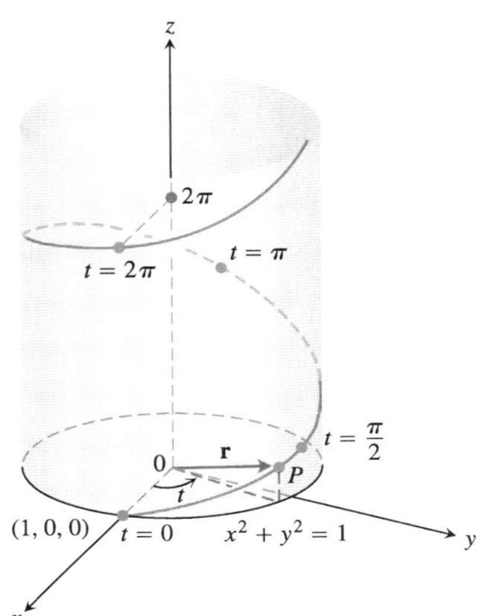

FIGURE 13.3 The upper half of the helix $\mathbf{r}(t) = (\cos t)\mathbf{i} + (\sin t)\mathbf{j} + t\mathbf{k}$ (Example 1).

EXAMPLE 1 Graphing a Helix

Graph the vector function

$$\mathbf{r}(t) = (\cos t)\mathbf{i} + (\sin t)\mathbf{j} + t\mathbf{k}.$$

Solution The vector function

$$\mathbf{r}(t) = (\cos t)\mathbf{i} + (\sin t)\mathbf{j} + t\mathbf{k}$$

is defined for all real values of t. The curve traced by $\mathbf{r}$ is a helix (from an old Greek word for "spiral") that winds around the circular cylinder $x^2 + y^2 = 1$ (Figure 13.3). The curve lies on the cylinder because the $\mathbf{i}$- and $\mathbf{j}$-components of $\mathbf{r}$, being the x- and y-coordinates of the tip of $\mathbf{r}$, satisfy the cylinder's equation:

$$x^2 + y^2 = (\cos t)^2 + (\sin t)^2 = 1.$$

The curve rises as the $\mathbf{k}$-component $z = t$ increases. Each time t increases by 2π, the curve completes one turn around the cylinder. The equations

$$x = \cos t, \qquad y = \sin t, \qquad z = t$$

parametrize the helix, the interval $-\infty < t < \infty$ being understood. You will find more helices in Figure 13.4. ■

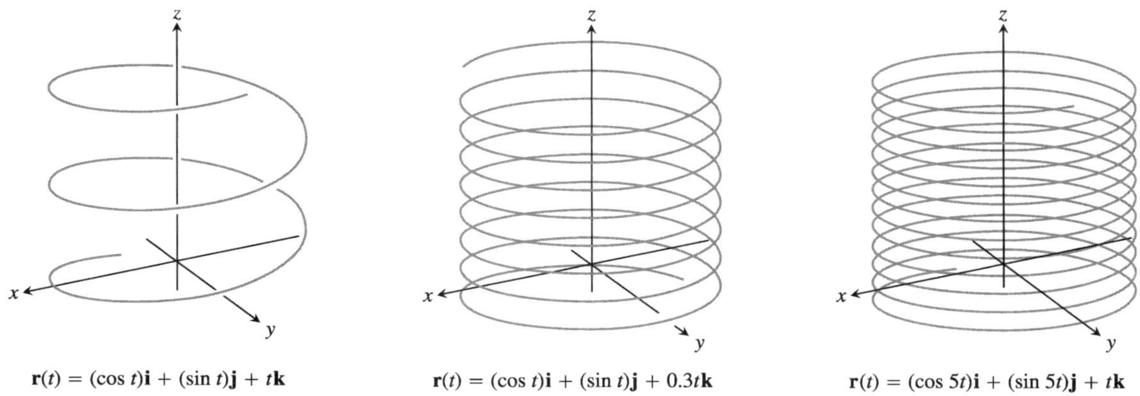

FIGURE 13.4 Helices drawn by computer.

Limits and Continuity

The way we define limits of vector-valued functions is similar to the way we define limits of real-valued functions.

DEFINITION Limit of Vector Functions

Let $\mathbf{r}(t) = f(t)\mathbf{i} + g(t)\mathbf{j} + h(t)\mathbf{k}$ be a vector function and $\mathbf{L}$ a vector. We say that $\mathbf{r}$ has **limit L** as t approaches t_0 and write

$$\lim_{t \to t_0} \mathbf{r}(t) = \mathbf{L}$$

if, for every number $\epsilon > 0$, there exists a corresponding number $\delta > 0$ such that for all t

$$0 < |t - t_0| < \delta \quad \Rightarrow \quad |\mathbf{r}(t) - \mathbf{L}| < \epsilon.$$

If $\mathbf{L} = L_1\mathbf{i} + L_2\mathbf{j} + L_3\mathbf{k}$, then $\lim_{t \to t_0} \mathbf{r}(t) = \mathbf{L}$ precisely when

$$\lim_{t \to t_0} f(t) = L_1, \qquad \lim_{t \to t_0} g(t) = L_2, \qquad \text{and} \qquad \lim_{t \to t_0} h(t) = L_3.$$

The equation

$$\lim_{t \to t_0} \mathbf{r}(t) = \left(\lim_{t \to t_0} f(t)\right)\mathbf{i} + \left(\lim_{t \to t_0} g(t)\right)\mathbf{j} + \left(\lim_{t \to t_0} h(t)\right)\mathbf{k} \tag{3}$$

provides a practical way to calculate limits of vector functions.

EXAMPLE 2 Finding Limits of Vector Functions

If $\mathbf{r}(t) = (\cos t)\mathbf{i} + (\sin t)\mathbf{j} + t\mathbf{k}$, then

$$\begin{aligned}\lim_{t \to \pi/4} \mathbf{r}(t) &= \left(\lim_{t \to \pi/4} \cos t\right)\mathbf{i} + \left(\lim_{t \to \pi/4} \sin t\right)\mathbf{j} + \left(\lim_{t \to \pi/4} t\right)\mathbf{k} \\ &= \frac{\sqrt{2}}{2}\mathbf{i} + \frac{\sqrt{2}}{2}\mathbf{j} + \frac{\pi}{4}\mathbf{k}.\end{aligned}$$

■

We define continuity for vector functions the same way we define continuity for scalar functions.

> **DEFINITION Continuous at a Point**
>
> A vector function $\mathbf{r}(t)$ is **continuous at a point** $t = t_0$ in its domain if $\lim_{t\to t_0} \mathbf{r}(t) = \mathbf{r}(t_0)$. The function is **continuous** if it is continuous at every point in its domain.

From Equation (3), we see that $\mathbf{r}(t)$ is continuous at $t = t_0$ if and only if each component function is continuous there.

EXAMPLE 3 Continuity of Space Curves

(a) All the space curves shown in Figures 13.2 and 13.4 are continuous because their component functions are continuous at every value of t in $(-\infty, \infty)$.

(b) The function

$$\mathbf{g}(t) = (\cos t)\mathbf{i} + (\sin t)\mathbf{j} + \lfloor t \rfloor \mathbf{k}$$

is discontinuous at every integer, where the greatest integer function $\lfloor t \rfloor$ is discontinuous. ■

Derivatives and Motion

Suppose that $\mathbf{r}(t) = f(t)\mathbf{i} + g(t)\mathbf{j} + h(t)\mathbf{k}$ is the position vector of a particle moving along a curve in space and that f, g, and h are differentiable functions of t. Then the difference between the particle's positions at time t and time $t + \Delta t$ is

$$\Delta\mathbf{r} = \mathbf{r}(t + \Delta t) - \mathbf{r}(t)$$

(Figure 13.5a). In terms of components,

$$\begin{aligned}\Delta\mathbf{r} &= \mathbf{r}(t + \Delta t) - \mathbf{r}(t)\\ &= [f(t + \Delta t)\mathbf{i} + g(t + \Delta t)\mathbf{j} + h(t + \Delta t)\mathbf{k}]\\ &\quad - [f(t)\mathbf{i} + g(t)\mathbf{j} + h(t)\mathbf{k}]\\ &= [f(t + \Delta t) - f(t)]\mathbf{i} + [g(t + \Delta t) - g(t)]\mathbf{j} + [h(t + \Delta t) - h(t)]\mathbf{k}.\end{aligned}$$

As Δt approaches zero, three things seem to happen simultaneously. First, Q approaches P along the curve. Second, the secant line PQ seems to approach a limiting position tangent to the curve at P. Third, the quotient $\Delta\mathbf{r}/\Delta t$ (Figure 13.5b) approaches the limit

$$\begin{aligned}\lim_{\Delta t\to 0}\frac{\Delta\mathbf{r}}{\Delta t} &= \left[\lim_{\Delta t\to 0}\frac{f(t+\Delta t)-f(t)}{\Delta t}\right]\mathbf{i} + \left[\lim_{\Delta t\to 0}\frac{g(t+\Delta t)-g(t)}{\Delta t}\right]\mathbf{j}\\ &\quad + \left[\lim_{\Delta t\to 0}\frac{h(t+\Delta t)-h(t)}{\Delta t}\right]\mathbf{k}\\ &= \left[\frac{df}{dt}\right]\mathbf{i} + \left[\frac{dg}{dt}\right]\mathbf{j} + \left[\frac{dh}{dt}\right]\mathbf{k}.\end{aligned}$$

We are therefore led by past experience to the following definition.

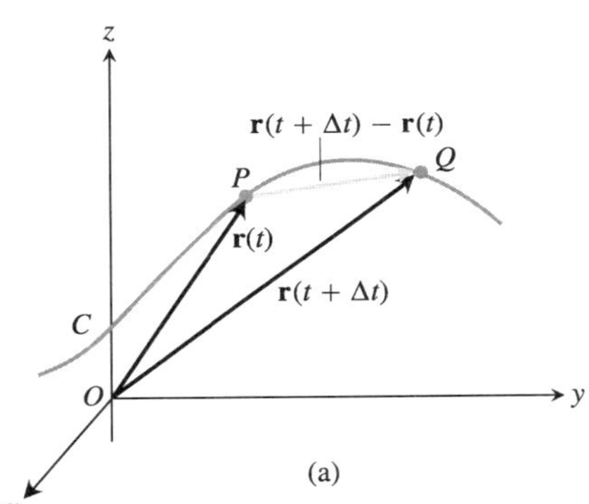

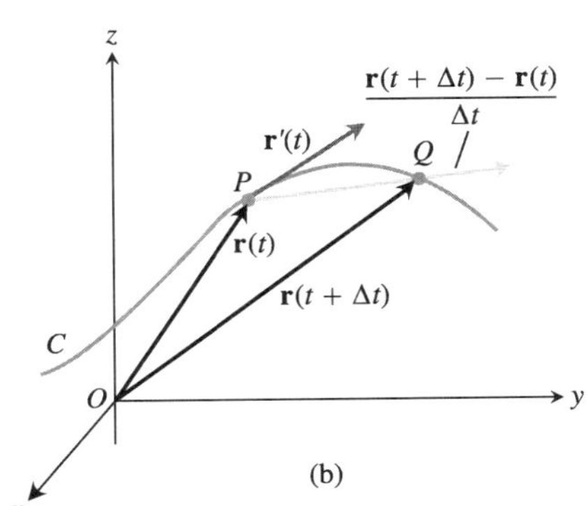

FIGURE 13.5 As $\Delta t \to 0$, the point Q approaches the point P along the curve C. In the limit, the vector $\overrightarrow{PQ}/\Delta t$ becomes the tangent vector $\mathbf{r}'(t)$.

DEFINITION Derivative

The vector function $\mathbf{r}(t) = f(t)\mathbf{i} + g(t)\mathbf{j} + h(t)\mathbf{k}$ has a **derivative (is differentiable) at t** if f, g, and h have derivatives at t. The derivative is the vector function

$$\mathbf{r}'(t) = \frac{d\mathbf{r}}{dt} = \lim_{\Delta t \to 0} \frac{\mathbf{r}(t + \Delta t) - \mathbf{r}(t)}{\Delta t} = \frac{df}{dt}\mathbf{i} + \frac{dg}{dt}\mathbf{j} + \frac{dh}{dt}\mathbf{k}.$$

A vector function $\mathbf{r}$ is **differentiable** if it is differentiable at every point of its domain. The curve traced by $\mathbf{r}$ is **smooth** if $d\mathbf{r}/dt$ is continuous and never $\mathbf{0}$, that is, if f, g, and h have continuous first derivatives that are not simultaneously 0.

The geometric significance of the definition of derivative is shown in Figure 13.5. The points P and Q have position vectors $\mathbf{r}(t)$ and $\mathbf{r}(t + \Delta t)$, and the vector $\overrightarrow{PQ}$ is represented by $\mathbf{r}(t + \Delta t) - \mathbf{r}(t)$. For $\Delta t > 0$, the scalar multiple $(1/\Delta t)(\mathbf{r}(t + \Delta t) - \mathbf{r}(t))$ points in the same direction as the vector $\overrightarrow{PQ}$. As $\Delta t \to 0$, this vector approaches a vector that is tangent to the curve at P (Figure 13.5b). The vector $\mathbf{r}'(t)$, when different from $\mathbf{0}$, is defined to be the vector **tangent** to the curve at P. The **tangent line** to the curve at a point $(f(t_0), g(t_0), h(t_0))$ is defined to be the line through the point parallel to $\mathbf{r}'(t_0)$. We require $d\mathbf{r}/dt \neq \mathbf{0}$ for a smooth curve to make sure the curve has a continuously turning tangent at each point. On a smooth curve, there are no sharp corners or cusps.

A curve that is made up of a finite number of smooth curves pieced together in a continuous fashion is called **piecewise smooth** (Figure 13.6).

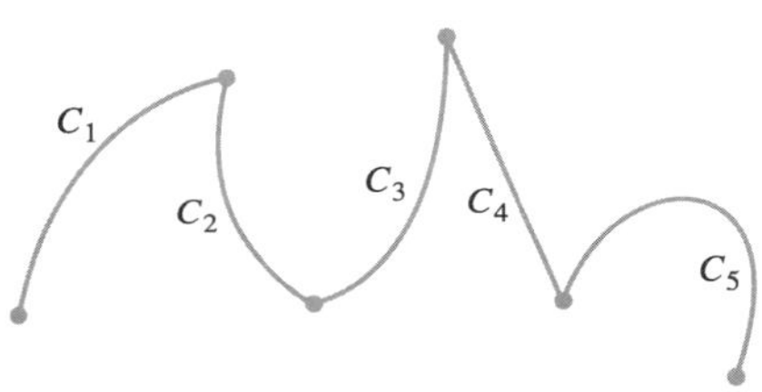

FIGURE 13.6 A piecewise smooth curve made up of five smooth curves connected end to end in continuous fashion.

Look once again at Figure 13.5. We drew the figure for Δt positive, so $\Delta\mathbf{r}$ points forward, in the direction of the motion. The vector $\Delta\mathbf{r}/\Delta t$, having the same direction as $\Delta\mathbf{r}$, points forward too. Had Δt been negative, $\Delta\mathbf{r}$ would have pointed backward, against the direction of motion. The quotient $\Delta\mathbf{r}/\Delta t$, however, being a negative scalar multiple of $\Delta\mathbf{r}$, would once again have pointed forward. No matter how $\Delta\mathbf{r}$ points, $\Delta\mathbf{r}/\Delta t$ points forward and we expect the vector $d\mathbf{r}/dt = \lim_{\Delta t \to 0} \Delta\mathbf{r}/\Delta t$, when different from $\mathbf{0}$, to do the same. This means that the derivative $d\mathbf{r}/dt$ is just what we want for modeling a particle's velocity. It points in the direction of motion and gives the rate of change of position with respect to time. For a smooth curve, the velocity is never zero; the particle does not stop or reverse direction.

DEFINITIONS Velocity, Direction, Speed, Acceleration

If $\mathbf{r}$ is the position vector of a particle moving along a smooth curve in space, then

$$\mathbf{v}(t) = \frac{d\mathbf{r}}{dt}$$

is the particle's **velocity vector**, tangent to the curve. At any time t, the direction of $\mathbf{v}$ is the **direction of motion**, the magnitude of $\mathbf{v}$ is the particle's **speed**, and the derivative $\mathbf{a} = d\mathbf{v}/dt$, when it exists, is the particle's **acceleration vector**. In summary,

1. Velocity is the derivative of position: $\mathbf{v} = \dfrac{d\mathbf{r}}{dt}$.
2. Speed is the magnitude of velocity: Speed $= |\mathbf{v}|$.
3. Acceleration is the derivative of velocity: $\mathbf{a} = \dfrac{d\mathbf{v}}{dt} = \dfrac{d^2\mathbf{r}}{dt^2}$.
4. The unit vector $\mathbf{v}/|\mathbf{v}|$ is the direction of motion at time t.

We can express the velocity of a moving particle as the product of its speed and direction:

$$\text{Velocity} = |\mathbf{v}|\left(\frac{\mathbf{v}}{|\mathbf{v}|}\right) = (\text{speed})(\text{direction}).$$

In Section 12.5, Example 4 we found this expression for velocity useful in locating, for example, the position of a helicopter moving along a straight line in space. Now let's look at an example of an object moving along a (nonlinear) space curve.

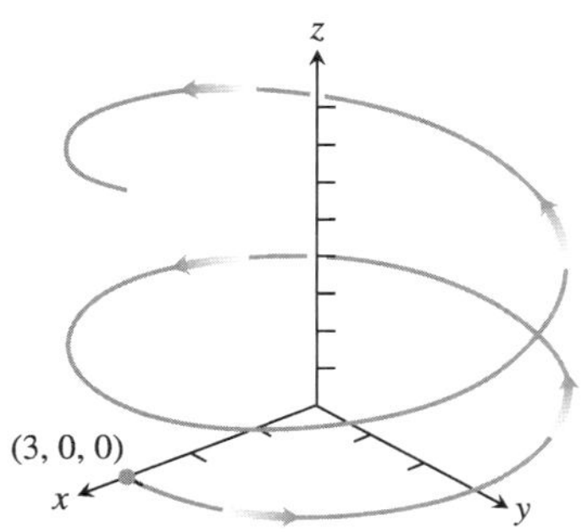

FIGURE 13.7 The path of a hang glider with position vector $\mathbf{r}(t) = (3\cos t)\mathbf{i} + (3\sin t)\mathbf{j} + t^2\mathbf{k}$ (Example 4).

EXAMPLE 4 Flight of a Hang Glider

A person on a hang glider is spiraling upward due to rapidly rising air on a path having position vector $\mathbf{r}(t) = (3\cos t)\mathbf{i} + (3\sin t)\mathbf{j} + t^2\mathbf{k}$. The path is similar to that of a helix (although it's *not* a helix, as you will see in Section 13.4) and is shown in Figure 13.7 for $0 \le t \le 4\pi$. Find

(a) the velocity and acceleration vectors,

(b) the glider's speed at any time t,

(c) the times, if any, when the glider's acceleration is orthogonal to its velocity.

Solution

(a) $\mathbf{r} = (3\cos t)\mathbf{i} + (3\sin t)\mathbf{j} + t^2\mathbf{k}$

$$\mathbf{v} = \frac{d\mathbf{r}}{dt} = -(3\sin t)\mathbf{i} + (3\cos t)\mathbf{j} + 2t\mathbf{k}$$

$$\mathbf{a} = \frac{d^2\mathbf{r}}{dt^2} = -(3\cos t)\mathbf{i} - (3\sin t)\mathbf{j} + 2\mathbf{k}$$

(b) Speed is the magnitude of $\mathbf{v}$:

$$\begin{aligned}|\mathbf{v}(t)| &= \sqrt{(-3\sin t)^2 + (3\cos t)^2 + (2t)^2}\\ &= \sqrt{9\sin^2 t + 9\cos^2 t + 4t^2}\\ &= \sqrt{9 + 4t^2}.\end{aligned}$$

The glider is moving faster and faster as it rises along its path.

(c) To find the times when $\mathbf{v}$ and $\mathbf{a}$ are orthogonal, we look for values of t for which

$$\mathbf{v}\cdot\mathbf{a} = 9\sin t\cos t - 9\cos t\sin t + 4t = 4t = 0.$$

Thus, the only time the acceleration vector is orthogonal to $\mathbf{v}$ is when $t = 0$. We study acceleration for motions along paths in more detail in Section 13.5. There we discover how the acceleration vector reveals the curving nature and tendency of the path to "twist" out of a certain plane containing the velocity vector. ■

Differentiation Rules

Because the derivatives of vector functions may be computed component by component, the rules for differentiating vector functions have the same form as the rules for differentiating scalar functions.

Differentiation Rules for Vector Functions

Let **u** and **v** be differentiable vector functions of t, **C** a constant vector, c any scalar, and f any differentiable scalar function.

1. *Constant Function Rule:* $\frac{d}{dt}\mathbf{C} = \mathbf{0}$
2. *Scalar Multiple Rules:* $\frac{d}{dt}[c\mathbf{u}(t)] = c\mathbf{u}'(t)$

   $\frac{d}{dt}[f(t)\mathbf{u}(t)] = f'(t)\mathbf{u}(t) + f(t)\mathbf{u}'(t)$
3. *Sum Rule:* $\frac{d}{dt}[\mathbf{u}(t) + \mathbf{v}(t)] = \mathbf{u}'(t) + \mathbf{v}'(t)$
4. *Difference Rule:* $\frac{d}{dt}[\mathbf{u}(t) - \mathbf{v}(t)] = \mathbf{u}'(t) - \mathbf{v}'(t)$
5. *Dot Product Rule:* $\frac{d}{dt}[\mathbf{u}(t)\cdot\mathbf{v}(t)] = \mathbf{u}'(t)\cdot\mathbf{v}(t) + \mathbf{u}(t)\cdot\mathbf{v}'(t)$
6. *Cross Product Rule:* $\frac{d}{dt}[\mathbf{u}(t)\times\mathbf{v}(t)] = \mathbf{u}'(t)\times\mathbf{v}(t) + \mathbf{u}(t)\times\mathbf{v}'(t)$
7. *Chain Rule:* $\frac{d}{dt}[\mathbf{u}(f(t))] = f'(t)\mathbf{u}'(f(t))$

When you use the Cross Product Rule, remember to preserve the order of the factors. If **u** comes first on the left side of the equation, it must also come first on the right or the signs will be wrong.

We will prove the product rules and Chain Rule but leave the rules for constants, scalar multiples, sums, and differences as exercises.

Proof of the Dot Product Rule Suppose that

$$\mathbf{u} = u_1(t)\mathbf{i} + u_2(t)\mathbf{j} + u_3(t)\mathbf{k}$$

and

$$\mathbf{v} = v_1(t)\mathbf{i} + v_2(t)\mathbf{j} + v_3(t)\mathbf{k}.$$

Then

$$\begin{aligned}\frac{d}{dt}(\mathbf{u}\cdot\mathbf{v}) &= \frac{d}{dt}(u_1v_1 + u_2v_2 + u_3v_3)\\ &= \underbrace{u_1'v_1 + u_2'v_2 + u_3'v_3}_{\mathbf{u}'\cdot\mathbf{v}} + \underbrace{u_1v_1' + u_2v_2' + u_3v_3'}_{\mathbf{u}\cdot\mathbf{v}'}.\end{aligned}$$

■

Proof of the Cross Product Rule We model the proof after the proof of the Product Rule for scalar functions. According to the definition of derivative,

$$\frac{d}{dt}(\mathbf{u}\times\mathbf{v}) = \lim_{h\to 0}\frac{\mathbf{u}(t+h)\times\mathbf{v}(t+h) - \mathbf{u}(t)\times\mathbf{v}(t)}{h}.$$

To change this fraction into an equivalent one that contains the difference quotients for the derivatives of **u** and **v**, we subtract and add $\mathbf{u}(t) \times \mathbf{v}(t+h)$ in the numerator. Then

$$\begin{aligned}
&\frac{d}{dt}(\mathbf{u}\times\mathbf{v})\\
&= \lim_{h\to 0} \frac{\mathbf{u}(t+h)\times\mathbf{v}(t+h) - \mathbf{u}(t)\times\mathbf{v}(t+h) + \mathbf{u}(t)\times\mathbf{v}(t+h) - \mathbf{u}(t)\times\mathbf{v}(t)}{h}\\
&= \lim_{h\to 0} \left[\frac{\mathbf{u}(t+h)-\mathbf{u}(t)}{h}\times\mathbf{v}(t+h) + \mathbf{u}(t)\times\frac{\mathbf{v}(t+h)-\mathbf{v}(t)}{h}\right]\\
&= \lim_{h\to 0} \frac{\mathbf{u}(t+h)-\mathbf{u}(t)}{h}\times\lim_{h\to 0}\mathbf{v}(t+h) + \lim_{h\to 0}\mathbf{u}(t)\times\lim_{h\to 0}\frac{\mathbf{v}(t+h)-\mathbf{v}(t)}{h}.
\end{aligned}$$

The last of these equalities holds because the limit of the cross product of two vector functions is the cross product of their limits if the latter exist (Exercise 52). As h approaches zero, $\mathbf{v}(t+h)$ approaches $\mathbf{v}(t)$ because **v**, being differentiable at t, is continuous at t (Exercise 53). The two fractions approach the values of $d\mathbf{u}/dt$ and $d\mathbf{v}/dt$ at t. In short,

$$\frac{d}{dt}(\mathbf{u}\times\mathbf{v}) = \frac{d\mathbf{u}}{dt}\times\mathbf{v} + \mathbf{u}\times\frac{d\mathbf{v}}{dt}.$$ ■

As an algebraic convenience, we sometimes write the product of a scalar c and a vector **v** as $\mathbf{v}c$ instead of $c\mathbf{v}$. This permits us, for instance, to write the Chain Rule in a familiar form:

$$\frac{d\mathbf{u}}{dt} = \frac{d\mathbf{u}}{ds}\frac{ds}{dt},$$

where $s = f(t)$.

Proof of the Chain Rule Suppose that $\mathbf{u}(s) = a(s)\mathbf{i} + b(s)\mathbf{j} + c(s)\mathbf{k}$ is a differentiable vector function of s and that $s = f(t)$ is a differentiable scalar function of t. Then a, b, and c are differentiable functions of t, and the Chain Rule for differentiable real-valued functions gives

$$\begin{aligned}
\frac{d}{dt}[\mathbf{u}(s)] &= \frac{da}{dt}\mathbf{i} + \frac{db}{dt}\mathbf{j} + \frac{dc}{dt}\mathbf{k}\\
&= \frac{da}{ds}\frac{ds}{dt}\mathbf{i} + \frac{db}{ds}\frac{ds}{dt}\mathbf{j} + \frac{dc}{ds}\frac{ds}{dt}\mathbf{k}\\
&= \frac{ds}{dt}\left(\frac{da}{ds}\mathbf{i} + \frac{db}{ds}\mathbf{j} + \frac{dc}{ds}\mathbf{k}\right)\\
&= \frac{ds}{dt}\frac{d\mathbf{u}}{ds}\\
&= f'(t)\mathbf{u}'(f(t)). \qquad s = f(t)
\end{aligned}$$ ■

Vector Functions of Constant Length

When we track a particle moving on a sphere centered at the origin (Figure 13.8), the position vector has a constant length equal to the radius of the sphere. The velocity vector $d\mathbf{r}/dt$, tangent to the path of motion, is tangent to the sphere and hence perpendicular to **r**. This is always the case for a differentiable vector function of constant length: The vector and its first derivative are orthogonal. With the length constant, the change in the function is a change in direction only, and direction changes take place at right angles. We can also obtain this result by direct calculation:

$$\begin{aligned}
\mathbf{r}(t)\cdot\mathbf{r}(t) &= c^2 && |\mathbf{r}(t)| = c \text{ is constant.}\\
\frac{d}{dt}[\mathbf{r}(t)\cdot\mathbf{r}(t)] &= 0 && \text{Differentiate both sides.}\\
\mathbf{r}'(t)\cdot\mathbf{r}(t) + \mathbf{r}(t)\cdot\mathbf{r}'(t) &= 0 && \text{Rule 5 with } \mathbf{r}(t) = \mathbf{u}(t) = \mathbf{v}(t)\\
2\mathbf{r}'(t)\cdot\mathbf{r}(t) &= 0.
\end{aligned}$$

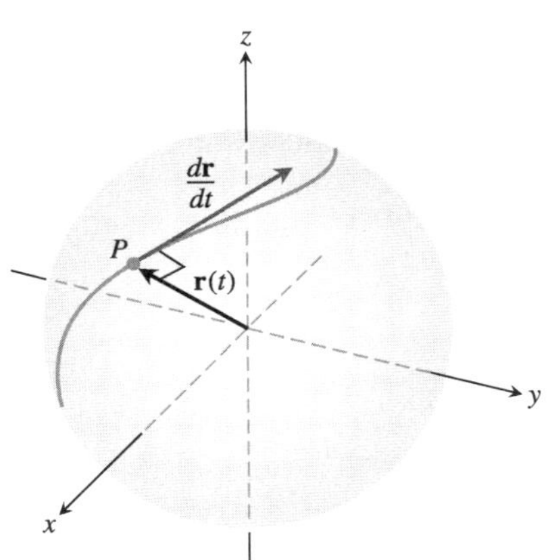

FIGURE 13.8 If a particle moves on a sphere in such a way that its position **r** is a differentiable function of time, then $\mathbf{r}\cdot(d\mathbf{r}/dt) = 0$.

The vectors $\mathbf{r}'(t)$ and $\mathbf{r}(t)$ are orthogonal because their dot product is 0. In summary,

> If $\mathbf{r}$ is a differentiable vector function of t of constant length, then
>
> $$\mathbf{r}\cdot\frac{d\mathbf{r}}{dt} = 0. \tag{4}$$

We will use this observation repeatedly in Section 13.4.

EXAMPLE 5 Supporting Equation (4)

Show that $\mathbf{r}(t) = (\sin t)\mathbf{i} + (\cos t)\mathbf{j} + \sqrt{3}\mathbf{k}$ has constant length and is orthogonal to its derivative.

Solution

$$\begin{aligned}
\mathbf{r}(t) &= (\sin t)\mathbf{i} + (\cos t)\mathbf{j} + \sqrt{3}\mathbf{k} \\
|\mathbf{r}(t)| &= \sqrt{(\sin t)^2 + (\cos t)^2 + \left(\sqrt{3}\right)^2} = \sqrt{1+3} = 2 \\
\frac{d\mathbf{r}}{dt} &= (\cos t)\mathbf{i} - (\sin t)\mathbf{j} \\
\mathbf{r}\cdot\frac{d\mathbf{r}}{dt} &= \sin t\cos t - \sin t\cos t = 0
\end{aligned}$$

■

Integrals of Vector Functions

A differentiable vector function $\mathbf{R}(t)$ is an **antiderivative** of a vector function $\mathbf{r}(t)$ on an interval I if $d\mathbf{R}/dt = \mathbf{r}$ at each point of I. If $\mathbf{R}$ is an antiderivative of $\mathbf{r}$ on I, it can be shown, working one component at a time, that every antiderivative of $\mathbf{r}$ on I has the form $\mathbf{R} + \mathbf{C}$ for some constant vector $\mathbf{C}$ (Exercise 56). The set of all antiderivatives of $\mathbf{r}$ on I is the **indefinite integral** of $\mathbf{r}$ on I.

> **DEFINITION** Indefinite Integral
>
> The **indefinite integral** of $\mathbf{r}$ with respect to t is the set of all antiderivatives of $\mathbf{r}$, denoted by $\int \mathbf{r}(t)\,dt$. If $\mathbf{R}$ is any antiderivative of $\mathbf{r}$, then
>
> $$\int \mathbf{r}(t)\,dt = \mathbf{R}(t) + \mathbf{C}.$$

The usual arithmetic rules for indefinite integrals apply.

EXAMPLE 6 Finding Indefinite Integrals

$$\int ((\cos t)\mathbf{i} + \mathbf{j} - 2t\mathbf{k})\,dt = \left(\int \cos t\,dt\right)\mathbf{i} + \left(\int dt\right)\mathbf{j} - \left(\int 2t\,dt\right)\mathbf{k} \tag{5}$$

$$= (\sin t + C_1)\mathbf{i} + (t + C_2)\mathbf{j} - (t^2 + C_3)\mathbf{k} \tag{6}$$

$$= (\sin t)\mathbf{i} + t\mathbf{j} - t^2\mathbf{k} + \mathbf{C} \qquad \mathbf{C} = C_1\mathbf{i} + C_2\mathbf{j} - C_3\mathbf{k}$$

As in the integration of scalar functions, we recommend that you skip the steps in Equations (5) and (6) and go directly to the final form. Find an antiderivative for each component and add a constant vector at the end. ■

Definite integrals of vector functions are best defined in terms of components.

DEFINITION Definite Integral
If the components of $\mathbf{r}(t) = f(t)\mathbf{i} + g(t)\mathbf{j} + h(t)\mathbf{k}$ are integrable over $[a, b]$, then so is $\mathbf{r}$, and the **definite integral** of $\mathbf{r}$ from a to b is

$$\int_a^b \mathbf{r}(t)\,dt = \left(\int_a^b f(t)\,dt\right)\mathbf{i} + \left(\int_a^b g(t)\,dt\right)\mathbf{j} + \left(\int_a^b h(t)\,dt\right)\mathbf{k}.$$

EXAMPLE 7 Evaluating Definite Integrals

$$\begin{aligned}\int_0^\pi ((\cos t)\mathbf{i} + \mathbf{j} - 2t\mathbf{k})\,dt &= \left(\int_0^\pi \cos t\,dt\right)\mathbf{i} + \left(\int_0^\pi dt\right)\mathbf{j} - \left(\int_0^\pi 2t\,dt\right)\mathbf{k}\\ &= \Big[\sin t\Big]_0^\pi \mathbf{i} + \Big[t\Big]_0^\pi \mathbf{j} - \Big[t^2\Big]_0^\pi \mathbf{k}\\ &= [0 - 0]\mathbf{i} + [\pi - 0]\mathbf{j} - [\pi^2 - 0^2]\mathbf{k}\\ &= \pi\mathbf{j} - \pi^2\mathbf{k}\end{aligned}$$ ■

The Fundamental Theorem of Calculus for continuous vector functions says that

$$\int_a^b \mathbf{r}(t)\,dt = \mathbf{R}(t)\Big]_a^b = \mathbf{R}(b) - \mathbf{R}(a)$$

where $\mathbf{R}$ is any antiderivative of $\mathbf{r}$, so that $\mathbf{R}'(t) = \mathbf{r}(t)$ (Exercise 57).

EXAMPLE 8 Revisiting the Flight of a Glider

Suppose that we did not know the path of the glider in Example 4, but only its acceleration vector $\mathbf{a}(t) = -(3\cos t)\mathbf{i} - (3\sin t)\mathbf{j} + 2\mathbf{k}$. We also know that initially (at time $t = 0$), the glider departed from the point $(3, 0, 0)$ with velocity $\mathbf{v}(0) = 3\mathbf{j}$. Find the glider's position as a function of t.

Solution Our goal is to find $\mathbf{r}(t)$ knowing

The differential equation: $\mathbf{a} = \dfrac{d^2\mathbf{r}}{dt^2} = -(3\cos t)\mathbf{i} - (3\sin t)\mathbf{j} + 2\mathbf{k}$

The initial conditions: $\mathbf{v}(0) = 3\mathbf{j}$ and $\mathbf{r}(0) = 3\mathbf{i} + 0\mathbf{j} + 0\mathbf{k}$.

Integrating both sides of the differential equation with respect to t gives

$$\mathbf{v}(t) = -(3\sin t)\mathbf{i} + (3\cos t)\mathbf{j} + 2t\mathbf{k} + \mathbf{C}_1.$$

We use $\mathbf{v}(0) = 3\mathbf{j}$ to find $\mathbf{C}_1$:

$$\begin{aligned}3\mathbf{j} &= -(3\sin 0)\mathbf{i} + (3\cos 0)\mathbf{j} + (0)\mathbf{k} + \mathbf{C}_1\\ 3\mathbf{j} &= 3\mathbf{j} + \mathbf{C}_1\\ \mathbf{C}_1 &= \mathbf{0}.\end{aligned}$$

The glider's velocity as a function of time is

$$\frac{d\mathbf{r}}{dt} = \mathbf{v}(t) = -(3\sin t)\mathbf{i} + (3\cos t)\mathbf{j} + 2t\mathbf{k}.$$

Integrating both sides of this last differential equation gives

$$\mathbf{r}(t) = (3\cos t)\mathbf{i} + (3\sin t)\mathbf{j} + t^2\mathbf{k} + \mathbf{C}_2.$$

We then use the initial condition $\mathbf{r}(0) = 3\mathbf{i}$ to find $\mathbf{C}_2$:

$$\begin{aligned} 3\mathbf{i} &= (3\cos 0)\mathbf{i} + (3\sin 0)\mathbf{j} + (0^2)\mathbf{k} + \mathbf{C}_2 \\ 3\mathbf{i} &= 3\mathbf{i} + (0)\mathbf{j} + (0)\mathbf{k} + \mathbf{C}_2 \\ \mathbf{C}_2 &= \mathbf{0}. \end{aligned}$$

The glider's position as a function of t is

$$\mathbf{r}(t) = (3\cos t)\mathbf{i} + (3\sin t)\mathbf{j} + t^2\mathbf{k}.$$

This is the path of the glider we know from Example 4 and is shown in Figure 13.7.

Note: It was peculiar to this example that both of the constant vectors of integration, $\mathbf{C}_1$ and $\mathbf{C}_2$, turned out to be $\mathbf{0}$. Exercises 31 and 32 give different results for these constants. ■

EXERCISES 13.1

Motion in the *xy*-plane

In Exercises 1–4, $\mathbf{r}(t)$ is the position of a particle in the xy-plane at time t. Find an equation in x and y whose graph is the path of the particle. Then find the particle's velocity and acceleration vectors at the given value of t.

1. $\mathbf{r}(t) = (t+1)\mathbf{i} + (t^2-1)\mathbf{j}, \quad t = 1$
2. $\mathbf{r}(t) = (t^2+1)\mathbf{i} + (2t-1)\mathbf{j}, \quad t = 1/2$
3. $\mathbf{r}(t) = e^t\mathbf{i} + \frac{2}{9}e^{2t}\mathbf{j}, \quad t = \ln 3$
4. $\mathbf{r}(t) = (\cos 2t)\mathbf{i} + (3\sin 2t)\mathbf{j}, \quad t = 0$

Exercises 5–8 give the position vectors of particles moving along various curves in the xy-plane. In each case, find the particle's velocity and acceleration vectors at the stated times and sketch them as vectors on the curve.

5. **Motion on the circle $x^2 + y^2 = 1$**

$$\mathbf{r}(t) = (\sin t)\mathbf{i} + (\cos t)\mathbf{j}; \quad t = \pi/4 \text{ and } \pi/2$$

6. **Motion on the circle $x^2 + y^2 = 16$**

$$\mathbf{r}(t) = \left(4\cos\frac{t}{2}\right)\mathbf{i} + \left(4\sin\frac{t}{2}\right)\mathbf{j}; \quad t = \pi \text{ and } 3\pi/2$$

7. **Motion on the cycloid $x = t - \sin t,\ y = 1 - \cos t$**

$$\mathbf{r}(t) = (t - \sin t)\mathbf{i} + (1 - \cos t)\mathbf{j}; \quad t = \pi \text{ and } 3\pi/2$$

8. **Motion on the parabola $y = x^2 + 1$**

$$\mathbf{r}(t) = t\mathbf{i} + (t^2+1)\mathbf{j}; \quad t = -1, 0, \text{ and } 1$$

Velocity and Acceleration in Space

In Exercises 9–14, $\mathbf{r}(t)$ is the position of a particle in space at time t. Find the particle's velocity and acceleration vectors. Then find the particle's speed and direction of motion at the given value of t. Write the particle's velocity at that time as the product of its speed and direction.

9. $\mathbf{r}(t) = (t+1)\mathbf{i} + (t^2-1)\mathbf{j} + 2t\mathbf{k}, \quad t = 1$
10. $\mathbf{r}(t) = (1+t)\mathbf{i} + \frac{t^2}{\sqrt{2}}\mathbf{j} + \frac{t^3}{3}\mathbf{k}, \quad t = 1$
11. $\mathbf{r}(t) = (2\cos t)\mathbf{i} + (3\sin t)\mathbf{j} + 4t\mathbf{k}, \quad t = \pi/2$
12. $\mathbf{r}(t) = (\sec t)\mathbf{i} + (\tan t)\mathbf{j} + \frac{4}{3}t\mathbf{k}, \quad t = \pi/6$
13. $\mathbf{r}(t) = (2\ln(t+1))\mathbf{i} + t^2\mathbf{j} + \frac{t^2}{2}\mathbf{k}, \quad t = 1$
14. $\mathbf{r}(t) = (e^{-t})\mathbf{i} + (2\cos 3t)\mathbf{j} + (2\sin 3t)\mathbf{k}, \quad t = 0$

In Exercises 15–18, $\mathbf{r}(t)$ is the position of a particle in space at time t. Find the angle between the velocity and acceleration vectors at time $t = 0$.

15. $\mathbf{r}(t) = (3t + 1)\mathbf{i} + \sqrt{3}t\mathbf{j} + t^2\mathbf{k}$

16. $\mathbf{r}(t) = \left(\frac{\sqrt{2}}{2}t\right)\mathbf{i} + \left(\frac{\sqrt{2}}{2}t - 16t^2\right)\mathbf{j}$

17. $\mathbf{r}(t) = (\ln(t^2 + 1))\mathbf{i} + (\tan^{-1} t)\mathbf{j} + \sqrt{t^2 + 1}\,\mathbf{k}$

18. $\mathbf{r}(t) = \frac{4}{9}(1 + t)^{3/2}\mathbf{i} + \frac{4}{9}(1 - t)^{3/2}\mathbf{j} + \frac{1}{3}t\mathbf{k}$

In Exercises 19 and 20, $\mathbf{r}(t)$ is the position vector of a particle in space at time t. Find the time or times in the given time interval when the velocity and acceleration vectors are orthogonal.

19. $\mathbf{r}(t) = (t - \sin t)\mathbf{i} + (1 - \cos t)\mathbf{j}, \quad 0 \le t \le 2\pi$

20. $\mathbf{r}(t) = (\sin t)\mathbf{i} + t\mathbf{j} + (\cos t)\mathbf{k}, \quad t \ge 0$

Integrating Vector-Valued Functions

Evaluate the integrals in Exercises 21–26.

21. $\int_0^1 [t^3\mathbf{i} + 7\mathbf{j} + (t + 1)\mathbf{k}]\,dt$

22. $\int_1^2 \left[(6 - 6t)\mathbf{i} + 3\sqrt{t}\mathbf{j} + \left(\frac{4}{t^2}\right)\mathbf{k}\right] dt$

23. $\int_{-\pi/4}^{\pi/4} [(\sin t)\mathbf{i} + (1 + \cos t)\mathbf{j} + (\sec^2 t)\mathbf{k}]\,dt$

24. $\int_0^{\pi/3} [(\sec t \tan t)\mathbf{i} + (\tan t)\mathbf{j} + (2 \sin t \cos t)\mathbf{k}]\,dt$

25. $\int_1^4 \left[\frac{1}{t}\mathbf{i} + \frac{1}{5 - t}\mathbf{j} + \frac{1}{2t}\mathbf{k}\right] dt$

26. $\int_0^1 \left[\frac{2}{\sqrt{1 - t^2}}\mathbf{i} + \frac{\sqrt{3}}{1 + t^2}\mathbf{k}\right] dt$

Initial Value Problems for Vector-Valued Functions

Solve the initial value problems in Exercises 27–32 for $\mathbf{r}$ as a vector function of t.

27. Differential equation: $\frac{d\mathbf{r}}{dt} = -t\mathbf{i} - t\mathbf{j} - t\mathbf{k}$

Initial condition: $\mathbf{r}(0) = \mathbf{i} + 2\mathbf{j} + 3\mathbf{k}$

28. Differential equation: $\frac{d\mathbf{r}}{dt} = (180t)\mathbf{i} + (180t - 16t^2)\mathbf{j}$

Initial condition: $\mathbf{r}(0) = 100\mathbf{j}$

29. Differential equation: $\frac{d\mathbf{r}}{dt} = \frac{3}{2}(t + 1)^{1/2}\mathbf{i} + e^{-t}\mathbf{j} + \frac{1}{t + 1}\mathbf{k}$

Initial condition: $\mathbf{r}(0) = \mathbf{k}$

30. Differential equation: $\frac{d\mathbf{r}}{dt} = (t^3 + 4t)\mathbf{i} + t\mathbf{j} + 2t^2\mathbf{k}$

Initial condition: $\mathbf{r}(0) = \mathbf{i} + \mathbf{j}$

31. Differential equation: $\frac{d^2\mathbf{r}}{dt^2} = -32\mathbf{k}$

Initial conditions: $\mathbf{r}(0) = 100\mathbf{k}$ and $\left.\frac{d\mathbf{r}}{dt}\right|_{t=0} = 8\mathbf{i} + 8\mathbf{j}$

32. Differential equation: $\frac{d^2\mathbf{r}}{dt^2} = -(\mathbf{i} + \mathbf{j} + \mathbf{k})$

Initial conditions: $\mathbf{r}(0) = 10\mathbf{i} + 10\mathbf{j} + 10\mathbf{k}$ and $\left.\frac{d\mathbf{r}}{dt}\right|_{t=0} = \mathbf{0}$

Tangent Lines to Smooth Curves

As mentioned in the text, the tangent line to a smooth curve $\mathbf{r}(t) = f(t)\mathbf{i} + g(t)\mathbf{j} + h(t)\mathbf{k}$ at $t = t_0$ is the line that passes through the point $(f(t_0), g(t_0), h(t_0))$ parallel to $\mathbf{v}(t_0)$, the curve's velocity vector at t_0. In Exercises 33–36, find parametric equations for the line that is tangent to the given curve at the given parameter value $t = t_0$.

33. $\mathbf{r}(t) = (\sin t)\mathbf{i} + (t^2 - \cos t)\mathbf{j} + e^t\mathbf{k}, \quad t_0 = 0$

34. $\mathbf{r}(t) = (2 \sin t)\mathbf{i} + (2 \cos t)\mathbf{j} + 5t\mathbf{k}, \quad t_0 = 4\pi$

35. $\mathbf{r}(t) = (a \sin t)\mathbf{i} + (a \cos t)\mathbf{j} + bt\mathbf{k}, \quad t_0 = 2\pi$

36. $\mathbf{r}(t) = (\cos t)\mathbf{i} + (\sin t)\mathbf{j} + (\sin 2t)\mathbf{k}, \quad t_0 = \frac{\pi}{2}$

Motion on Circular Paths

37. Each of the following equations in parts (a)–(e) describes the motion of a particle having the same path, namely the unit circle $x^2 + y^2 = 1$. Although the path of each particle in parts (a)–(e) is the same, the behavior, or "dynamics," of each particle is different. For each particle, answer the following questions.

i. Does the particle have constant speed? If so, what is its constant speed?

ii. Is the particle's acceleration vector always orthogonal to its velocity vector?

iii. Does the particle move clockwise or counterclockwise around the circle?

iv. Does the particle begin at the point (1, 0)?

a. $\mathbf{r}(t) = (\cos t)\mathbf{i} + (\sin t)\mathbf{j}, \quad t \ge 0$

b. $\mathbf{r}(t) = \cos(2t)\mathbf{i} + \sin(2t)\mathbf{j}, \quad t \ge 0$

c. $\mathbf{r}(t) = \cos(t - \pi/2)\mathbf{i} + \sin(t - \pi/2)\mathbf{j}, \quad t \ge 0$

d. $\mathbf{r}(t) = (\cos t)\mathbf{i} - (\sin t)\mathbf{j}, \quad t \ge 0$

e. $\mathbf{r}(t) = \cos(t^2)\mathbf{i} + \sin(t^2)\mathbf{j}, \quad t \ge 0$

38. Show that the vector-valued function

$$\mathbf{r}(t) = (2\mathbf{i} + 2\mathbf{j} + \mathbf{k}) + \cos t\left(\frac{1}{\sqrt{2}}\mathbf{i} - \frac{1}{\sqrt{2}}\mathbf{j}\right) + \sin t\left(\frac{1}{\sqrt{3}}\mathbf{i} + \frac{1}{\sqrt{3}}\mathbf{j} + \frac{1}{\sqrt{3}}\mathbf{k}\right)$$

describes the motion of a particle moving in the circle of radius 1 centered at the point (2, 2, 1) and lying in the plane $x + y - 2z = 2$.

Motion Along a Straight Line

39. At time $t = 0$, a particle is located at the point (1, 2, 3). It travels in a straight line to the point (4, 1, 4), has speed 2 at (1, 2, 3) and constant acceleration $3\mathbf{i} - \mathbf{j} + \mathbf{k}$. Find an equation for the position vector $\mathbf{r}(t)$ of the particle at time t.

40. A particle traveling in a straight line is located at the point $(1, -1, 2)$ and has speed 2 at time $t = 0$. The particle moves toward the point (3, 0, 3) with constant acceleration $2\mathbf{i} + \mathbf{j} + \mathbf{k}$. Find its position vector $\mathbf{r}(t)$ at time t.

Theory and Examples

41. Motion along a parabola A particle moves along the top of the parabola $y^2 = 2x$ from left to right at a constant speed of 5 units per second. Find the velocity of the particle as it moves through the point (2, 2).

42. Motion along a cycloid A particle moves in the xy-plane in such a way that its position at time t is

$$\mathbf{r}(t) = (t - \sin t)\mathbf{i} + (1 - \cos t)\mathbf{j}.$$

T **a.** Graph $\mathbf{r}(t)$. The resulting curve is a cycloid.

b. Find the maximum and minimum values of $|\mathbf{v}|$ and $|\mathbf{a}|$. (*Hint:* Find the extreme values of $|\mathbf{v}|^2$ and $|\mathbf{a}|^2$ first and take square roots later.)

43. Motion along an ellipse A particle moves around the ellipse $(y/3)^2 + (z/2)^2 = 1$ in the yz-plane in such a way that its position at time t is

$$\mathbf{r}(t) = (3\cos t)\mathbf{j} + (2\sin t)\mathbf{k}.$$

Find the maximum and minimum values of $|\mathbf{v}|$ and $|\mathbf{a}|$. (*Hint:* Find the extreme values of $|\mathbf{v}|^2$ and $|\mathbf{a}|^2$ first and take square roots later.)

44. A satellite in circular orbit A satellite of mass m is revolving at a constant speed v around a body of mass M (Earth, for example) in a circular orbit of radius r_0 (measured from the body's center of mass). Determine the satellite's orbital period T (the time to complete one full orbit), as follows:

a. Coordinatize the orbital plane by placing the origin at the body's center of mass, with the satellite on the x-axis at $t = 0$ and moving counterclockwise, as in the accompanying figure.

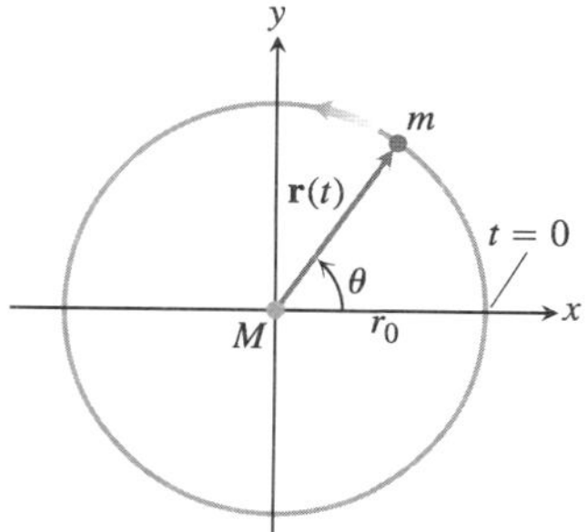

Let $\mathbf{r}(t)$ be the satellite's position vector at time t. Show that $\theta = vt/r_0$ and hence that

$$\mathbf{r}(t) = \left(r_0 \cos \frac{vt}{r_0}\right)\mathbf{i} + \left(r_0 \sin \frac{vt}{r_0}\right)\mathbf{j}.$$

b. Find the acceleration of the satellite.

c. According to Newton's law of gravitation, the gravitational force exerted on the satellite is directed toward M and is given by

$$\mathbf{F} = \left(-\frac{GmM}{r_0^2}\right)\frac{\mathbf{r}}{r_0},$$

where G is the universal constant of gravitation. Using Newton's second law, $\mathbf{F} = m\mathbf{a}$, show that $v^2 = GM/r_0$.

d. Show that the orbital period T satisfies $vT = 2\pi r_0$.

e. From parts (c) and (d), deduce that

$$T^2 = \frac{4\pi^2}{GM}r_0^3.$$

That is, the square of the period of a satellite in circular orbit is proportional to the cube of the radius from the orbital center.

45. Let $\mathbf{v}$ be a differentiable vector function of t. Show that if $\mathbf{v} \cdot (d\mathbf{v}/dt) = 0$ for all t, then $|\mathbf{v}|$ is constant.

46. Derivatives of triple scalar products

a. Show that if $\mathbf{u}$, $\mathbf{v}$, and $\mathbf{w}$ are differentiable vector functions of t, then

$$\frac{d}{dt}(\mathbf{u} \cdot \mathbf{v} \times \mathbf{w}) = \frac{d\mathbf{u}}{dt} \cdot \mathbf{v} \times \mathbf{w} + \mathbf{u} \cdot \frac{d\mathbf{v}}{dt} \times \mathbf{w} + \mathbf{u} \cdot \mathbf{v} \times \frac{d\mathbf{w}}{dt}. \qquad (7)$$

b. Show that Equation (7) is equivalent to

$$\frac{d}{dt}\begin{vmatrix} u_1 & u_2 & u_3 \\ v_1 & v_2 & v_3 \\ w_1 & w_2 & w_3 \end{vmatrix} = \begin{vmatrix} \frac{du_1}{dt} & \frac{du_2}{dt} & \frac{du_3}{dt} \\ v_1 & v_2 & v_3 \\ w_1 & w_2 & w_3 \end{vmatrix} + \begin{vmatrix} u_1 & u_2 & u_3 \\ \frac{dv_1}{dt} & \frac{dv_2}{dt} & \frac{dv_3}{dt} \\ w_1 & w_2 & w_3 \end{vmatrix} + \begin{vmatrix} u_1 & u_2 & u_3 \\ v_1 & v_2 & v_3 \\ \frac{dw_1}{dt} & \frac{dw_2}{dt} & \frac{dw_3}{dt} \end{vmatrix}. \qquad (8)$$

Equation (8) says that the derivative of a 3 by 3 determinant of differentiable functions is the sum of the three determinants obtained from the original by differentiating one row at a time. The result extends to determinants of any order.

47. (*Continuation of Exercise 46.*) Suppose that $\mathbf{r}(t) = f(t)\mathbf{i} + g(t)\mathbf{j} + h(t)\mathbf{k}$ and that f, g, and h have derivatives through order three. Use Equation (7) or (8) to show that

$$\frac{d}{dt}\left(\mathbf{r}\cdot\frac{d\mathbf{r}}{dt}\times\frac{d^2\mathbf{r}}{dt^2}\right) = \mathbf{r}\cdot\left(\frac{d\mathbf{r}}{dt}\times\frac{d^3\mathbf{r}}{dt^3}\right). \qquad (9)$$

(*Hint:* Differentiate on the left and look for vectors whose products are zero.)

48. Constant Function Rule Prove that if $\mathbf{u}$ is the vector function with the constant value $\mathbf{C}$, then $d\mathbf{u}/dt = \mathbf{0}$.

49. Scalar Multiple Rules

a. Prove that if $\mathbf{u}$ is a differentiable function of t and c is any real number, then

$$\frac{d(c\mathbf{u})}{dt} = c\frac{d\mathbf{u}}{dt}.$$

b. Prove that if $\mathbf{u}$ is a differentiable function of t and f is a differentiable scalar function of t, then

$$\frac{d}{dt}(f\mathbf{u}) = \frac{df}{dt}\mathbf{u} + f\frac{d\mathbf{u}}{dt}.$$

50. Sum and Difference Rules Prove that if $\mathbf{u}$ and $\mathbf{v}$ are differentiable functions of t, then

$$\frac{d}{dt}(\mathbf{u} + \mathbf{v}) = \frac{d\mathbf{u}}{dt} + \frac{d\mathbf{v}}{dt}$$

and

$$\frac{d}{dt}(\mathbf{u} - \mathbf{v}) = \frac{d\mathbf{u}}{dt} - \frac{d\mathbf{v}}{dt}.$$

51. Component Test for Continuity at a Point Show that the vector function $\mathbf{r}$ defined by $\mathbf{r}(t) = f(t)\mathbf{i} + g(t)\mathbf{j} + h(t)\mathbf{k}$ is continuous at $t = t_0$ if and only if f, g, and h are continuous at t_0.

52. Limits of cross products of vector functions Suppose that $\mathbf{r}_1(t) = f_1(t)\mathbf{i} + f_2(t)\mathbf{j} + f_3(t)\mathbf{k}$, $\mathbf{r}_2(t) = g_1(t)\mathbf{i} + g_2(t)\mathbf{j} + g_3(t)\mathbf{k}$, $\lim_{t\to t_0}\mathbf{r}_1(t) = \mathbf{A}$, and $\lim_{t\to t_0}\mathbf{r}_2(t) = \mathbf{B}$. Use the determinant formula for cross products and the Limit Product Rule for scalar functions to show that

$$\lim_{t\to t_0}(\mathbf{r}_1(t)\times\mathbf{r}_2(t)) = \mathbf{A}\times\mathbf{B}$$

53. Differentiable vector functions are continuous Show that if $\mathbf{r}(t) = f(t)\mathbf{i} + g(t)\mathbf{j} + h(t)\mathbf{k}$ is differentiable at $t = t_0$, then it is continuous at t_0 as well.

54. Establish the following properties of integrable vector functions.

a. The *Constant Scalar Multiple Rule:*

$$\int_a^b k\mathbf{r}(t)\,dt = k\int_a^b \mathbf{r}(t)\,dt \quad \text{(any scalar } k\text{)}$$

The *Rule for Negatives,*

$$\int_a^b (-\mathbf{r}(t))\,dt = -\int_a^b \mathbf{r}(t)\,dt,$$

is obtained by taking $k = -1$.

b. The *Sum and Difference Rules:*

$$\int_a^b (\mathbf{r}_1(t) \pm \mathbf{r}_2(t))\,dt = \int_a^b \mathbf{r}_1(t)\,dt \pm \int_a^b \mathbf{r}_2(t)\,dt$$

c. The *Constant Vector Multiple Rules:*

$$\int_a^b \mathbf{C}\cdot\mathbf{r}(t)\,dt = \mathbf{C}\cdot\int_a^b \mathbf{r}(t)\,dt \quad \text{(any constant vector } \mathbf{C}\text{)}$$

and

$$\int_a^b \mathbf{C}\times\mathbf{r}(t)\,dt = \mathbf{C}\times\int_a^b \mathbf{r}(t)\,dt \quad \text{(any constant vector } \mathbf{C}\text{)}$$

55. Products of scalar and vector functions Suppose that the scalar function $u(t)$ and the vector function $\mathbf{r}(t)$ are both defined for $a \le t \le b$.

a. Show that $u\mathbf{r}$ is continuous on $[a, b]$ if u and $\mathbf{r}$ are continuous on $[a, b]$.

b. If u and $\mathbf{r}$ are both differentiable on $[a, b]$, show that $u\mathbf{r}$ is differentiable on $[a, b]$ and that

$$\frac{d}{dt}(u\mathbf{r}) = u\frac{d\mathbf{r}}{dt} + \mathbf{r}\frac{du}{dt}.$$

56. Antiderivatives of vector functions

a. Use Corollary 2 of the Mean Value Theorem for scalar functions to show that if two vector functions $\mathbf{R}_1(t)$ and $\mathbf{R}_2(t)$ have identical derivatives on an interval I, then the functions differ by a constant vector value throughout I.

b. Use the result in part (a) to show that if $\mathbf{R}(t)$ is any antiderivative of $\mathbf{r}(t)$ on I, then any other antiderivative of $\mathbf{r}$ on I equals $\mathbf{R}(t) + \mathbf{C}$ for some constant vector $\mathbf{C}$.

57. The Fundamental Theorem of Calculus The Fundamental Theorem of Calculus for scalar functions of a real variable holds for vector functions of a real variable as well. Prove this by using the theorem for scalar functions to show first that if a vector function $\mathbf{r}(t)$ is continuous for $a \le t \le b$, then

$$\frac{d}{dt}\int_a^t \mathbf{r}(\tau)\,d\tau = \mathbf{r}(t)$$

at every point t of (a, b). Then use the conclusion in part (b) of Exercise 56 to show that if $\mathbf{R}$ is any antiderivative of $\mathbf{r}$ on $[a, b]$ then

$$\int_a^b \mathbf{r}(t)\,dt = \mathbf{R}(b) - \mathbf{R}(a).$$

COMPUTER EXPLORATIONS

Drawing Tangents to Space Curves

Use a CAS to perform the following steps in Exercises 58–61.

a. Plot the space curve traced out by the position vector $\mathbf{r}$.

b. Find the components of the velocity vector $d\mathbf{r}/dt$.

c. Evaluate $d\mathbf{r}/dt$ at the given point t_0 and determine the equation of the tangent line to the curve at $\mathbf{r}(t_0)$.

d. Plot the tangent line together with the curve over the given interval.

58. $\mathbf{r}(t) = (\sin t - t\cos t)\mathbf{i} + (\cos t + t\sin t)\mathbf{j} + t^2\mathbf{k}$, $0 \le t \le 6\pi$, $t_0 = 3\pi/2$

59. $\mathbf{r}(t) = \sqrt{2}t\mathbf{i} + e^t\mathbf{j} + e^{-t}\mathbf{k}$, $-2 \le t \le 3$, $t_0 = 1$

60. $\mathbf{r}(t) = (\sin 2t)\mathbf{i} + (\ln(1 + t))\mathbf{j} + t\mathbf{k}$, $0 \le t \le 4\pi$, $t_0 = \pi/4$

61. $\mathbf{r}(t) = (\ln(t^2 + 2))\mathbf{i} + (\tan^{-1} 3t)\mathbf{j} + \sqrt{t^2 + 1}\,\mathbf{k}$, $-3 \le t \le 5$, $t_0 = 3$

In Exercises 62 and 63, you will explore graphically the behavior of the helix

$$\mathbf{r}(t) = (\cos at)\mathbf{i} + (\sin at)\mathbf{j} + bt\mathbf{k}.$$

as you change the values of the constants a and b. Use a CAS to perform the steps in each exercise.

62. Set $b = 1$. Plot the helix $\mathbf{r}(t)$ together with the tangent line to the curve at $t = 3\pi/2$ for $a = 1, 2, 4,$ and 6 over the interval $0 \le t \le 4\pi$. Describe in your own words what happens to the graph of the helix and the position of the tangent line as a increases through these positive values.

63. Set $a = 1$. Plot the helix $\mathbf{r}(t)$ together with the tangent line to the curve at $t = 3\pi/2$ for $b = 1/4, 1/2, 2,$ and 4 over the interval $0 \le t \le 4\pi$. Describe in your own words what happens to the graph of the helix and the position of the tangent line as b increases through these positive values.

13.2 Modeling Projectile Motion

When we shoot a projectile into the air we usually want to know beforehand how far it will go (will it reach the target?), how high it will rise (will it clear the hill?), and when it will land (when do we get results?). We get this information from the direction and magnitude of the projectile's initial velocity vector, using Newton's second law of motion.

The Vector and Parametric Equations for Ideal Projectile Motion

To derive equations for projectile motion, we assume that the projectile behaves like a particle moving in a vertical coordinate plane and that the only force acting on the projectile during its flight is the constant force of gravity, which always points straight down. In practice, none of these assumptions really holds. The ground moves beneath the projectile as the earth turns, the air creates a frictional force that varies with the projectile's speed and altitude, and the force of gravity changes as the projectile moves along. All this must be taken into account by applying corrections to the predictions of the *ideal* equations we are about to derive. The corrections, however, are not the subject of this section.

We assume that the projectile is launched from the origin at time $t = 0$ into the first quadrant with an initial velocity $\mathbf{v}_0$ (Figure 13.9). If $\mathbf{v}_0$ makes an angle α with the horizontal, then

$$\mathbf{v}_0 = (|\mathbf{v}_0|\cos\alpha)\mathbf{i} + (|\mathbf{v}_0|\sin\alpha)\mathbf{j}.$$

If we use the simpler notation v_0 for the initial speed $|\mathbf{v}_0|$, then

$$\mathbf{v}_0 = (v_0\cos\alpha)\mathbf{i} + (v_0\sin\alpha)\mathbf{j}. \tag{1}$$

The projectile's initial position is

$$\mathbf{r}_0 = 0\mathbf{i} + 0\mathbf{j} = \mathbf{0}. \tag{2}$$

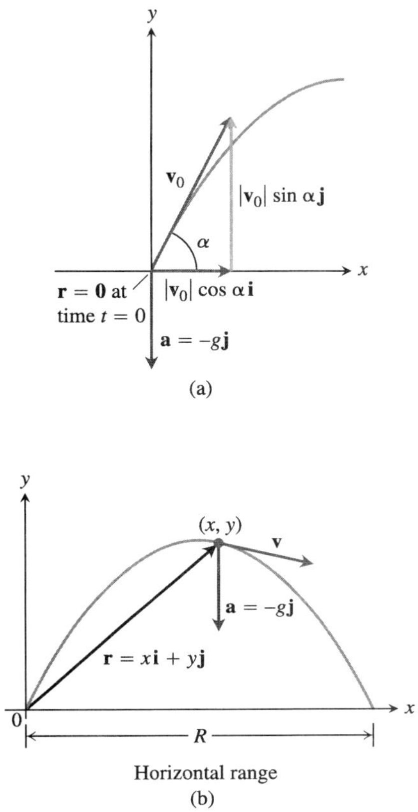

FIGURE 13.9 (a) Position, velocity, acceleration, and launch angle at $t = 0$. (b) Position, velocity, and acceleration at a later time t.

Newton's second law of motion says that the force acting on the projectile is equal to the projectile's mass m times its acceleration, or $m(d^2\mathbf{r}/dt^2)$ if $\mathbf{r}$ is the projectile's position vector and t is time. If the force is solely the gravitational force $-mg\mathbf{j}$, then

$$m\frac{d^2\mathbf{r}}{dt^2} = -mg\mathbf{j} \quad \text{and} \quad \frac{d^2\mathbf{r}}{dt^2} = -g\mathbf{j}.$$

We find $\mathbf{r}$ as a function of t by solving the following initial value problem.

$$\text{Differential equation:} \quad \frac{d^2\mathbf{r}}{dt^2} = -g\mathbf{j}$$

$$\text{Initial conditions:} \quad \mathbf{r} = \mathbf{r}_0 \quad \text{and} \quad \frac{d\mathbf{r}}{dt} = \mathbf{v}_0 \quad \text{when } t = 0$$

The first integration gives

$$\frac{d\mathbf{r}}{dt} = -(gt)\mathbf{j} + \mathbf{v}_0.$$

A second integration gives

$$\mathbf{r} = -\frac{1}{2}gt^2\mathbf{j} + \mathbf{v}_0 t + \mathbf{r}_0.$$

Substituting the values of $\mathbf{v}_0$ and $\mathbf{r}_0$ from Equations (1) and (2) gives

$$\mathbf{r} = -\frac{1}{2}gt^2\mathbf{j} + \underbrace{(v_0\cos\alpha)t\mathbf{i} + (v_0\sin\alpha)t\mathbf{j}}_{\mathbf{v}_0 t} + \mathbf{0}$$

Collecting terms, we have

Ideal Projectile Motion Equation

$$\mathbf{r} = (v_0\cos\alpha)t\mathbf{i} + \left((v_0\sin\alpha)t - \frac{1}{2}gt^2\right)\mathbf{j}. \tag{3}$$

Equation (3) is the *vector equation* for ideal projectile motion. The angle α is the projectile's **launch angle** (**firing angle**, **angle of elevation**), and v_0, as we said before, is the projectile's **initial speed**. The components of $\mathbf{r}$ give the parametric equations

$$x = (v_0\cos\alpha)t \quad \text{and} \quad y = (v_0\sin\alpha)t - \frac{1}{2}gt^2, \tag{4}$$

where x is the distance downrange and y is the height of the projectile at time $t \geq 0$.

EXAMPLE 1 Firing an Ideal Projectile

A projectile is fired from the origin over horizontal ground at an initial speed of 500 m/sec and a launch angle of 60°. Where will the projectile be 10 sec later?

Solution We use Equation (3) with $v_0 = 500$, $\alpha = 60°$, $g = 9.8$, and $t = 10$ to find the projectile's components 10 sec after firing.

$$\begin{aligned}\mathbf{r} &= (v_0 \cos\alpha)t\mathbf{i} + \left((v_0 \sin\alpha)t - \frac{1}{2}gt^2\right)\mathbf{j} \\ &= (500)\left(\frac{1}{2}\right)(10)\mathbf{i} + \left((500)\left(\frac{\sqrt{3}}{2}\right)10 - \left(\frac{1}{2}\right)(9.8)(100)\right)\mathbf{j} \\ &\approx 2500\mathbf{i} + 3840\mathbf{j}.\end{aligned}$$

Ten seconds after firing, the projectile is about 3840 m in the air and 2500 m downrange. ■

Height, Flight Time, and Range

Equation (3) enables us to answer most questions about the ideal motion for a projectile fired from the origin.

The projectile reaches its highest point when its vertical velocity component is zero, that is, when

$$\frac{dy}{dt} = v_0 \sin\alpha - gt = 0, \qquad \text{or} \qquad t = \frac{v_0 \sin\alpha}{g}.$$

For this value of t, the value of y is

$$y_{\max} = (v_0 \sin\alpha)\left(\frac{v_0 \sin\alpha}{g}\right) - \frac{1}{2}g\left(\frac{v_0 \sin\alpha}{g}\right)^2 = \frac{(v_0 \sin\alpha)^2}{2g}.$$

To find when the projectile lands when fired over horizontal ground, we set the vertical component equal to zero in Equation (3) and solve for t.

$$\begin{aligned}(v_0 \sin\alpha)t - \frac{1}{2}gt^2 &= 0 \\ t\left(v_0 \sin\alpha - \frac{1}{2}gt\right) &= 0 \\ t = 0, \qquad t &= \frac{2v_0 \sin\alpha}{g}\end{aligned}$$

Since 0 is the time the projectile is fired, $(2v_0 \sin\alpha)/g$ must be the time when the projectile strikes the ground.

To find the projectile's **range** R, the distance from the origin to the point of impact on horizontal ground, we find the value of the horizontal component when $t = (2v_0 \sin\alpha)/g$.

$$\begin{aligned}x &= (v_0 \cos\alpha)t \\ R &= (v_0 \cos\alpha)\left(\frac{2v_0 \sin\alpha}{g}\right) = \frac{v_0^2}{g}(2\sin\alpha\cos\alpha) = \frac{v_0^2}{g}\sin 2\alpha\end{aligned}$$

The range is largest when $\sin 2\alpha = 1$ or $\alpha = 45°$.

Height, Flight Time, and Range for Ideal Projectile Motion
For ideal projectile motion when an object is launched from the origin over a horizontal surface with initial speed v_0 and launch angle α:

$$\textit{Maximum height:} \quad y_{max} = \frac{(v_0 \sin\alpha)^2}{2g}$$

$$\textit{Flight time:} \quad t = \frac{2v_0 \sin\alpha}{g}$$

$$\textit{Range:} \quad R = \frac{v_0^2}{g}\sin 2\alpha.$$

EXAMPLE 2 Investigating Ideal Projectile Motion

Find the maximum height, flight time, and range of a projectile fired from the origin over horizontal ground at an initial speed of 500 m/sec and a launch angle of 60° (same projectile as Example 1).

Solution

$$\text{Maximum height:} \quad y_{max} = \frac{(v_0 \sin\alpha)^2}{2g} = \frac{(500\sin 60°)^2}{2(9.8)} \approx 9566 \text{ m}$$

$$\text{Flight time:} \quad t = \frac{2v_0 \sin\alpha}{g} = \frac{2(500)\sin 60°}{9.8} \approx 88.4 \text{ sec}$$

$$\text{Range:} \quad R = \frac{v_0^2}{g}\sin 2\alpha = \frac{(500)^2 \sin 120°}{9.8} \approx 22{,}092 \text{ m}$$

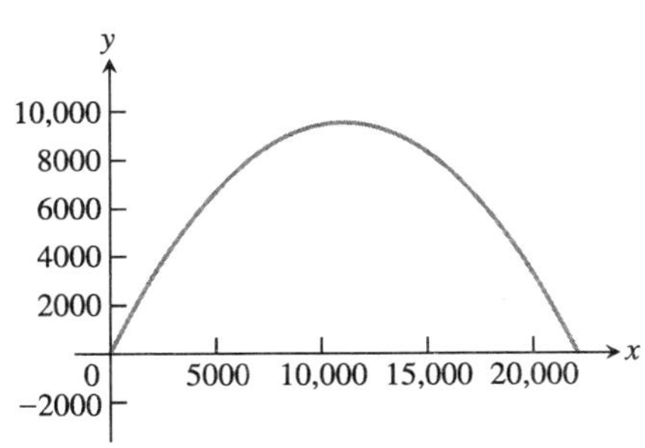

FIGURE 13.10 The graph of the projectile described in Example 2.

From Equation (3), the position vector of the projectile is

$$\begin{aligned}\mathbf{r} &= (v_0\cos\alpha)t\mathbf{i} + \left((v_0\sin\alpha)t - \frac{1}{2}gt^2\right)\mathbf{j}\\ &= (500\cos 60°)t\mathbf{i} + \left((500\sin 60°)t - \frac{1}{2}(9.8)t^2\right)\mathbf{j}\\ &= 250t\mathbf{i} + \left(\left(250\sqrt{3}\right)t - 4.9t^2\right)\mathbf{j}.\end{aligned}$$

A graph of the projectile's path is shown in Figure 13.10. ■

Ideal Trajectories Are Parabolic

It is often claimed that water from a hose traces a parabola in the air, but anyone who looks closely enough will see this is not so. The air slows the water down, and its forward progress is too slow at the end to keep pace with the rate at which it falls.

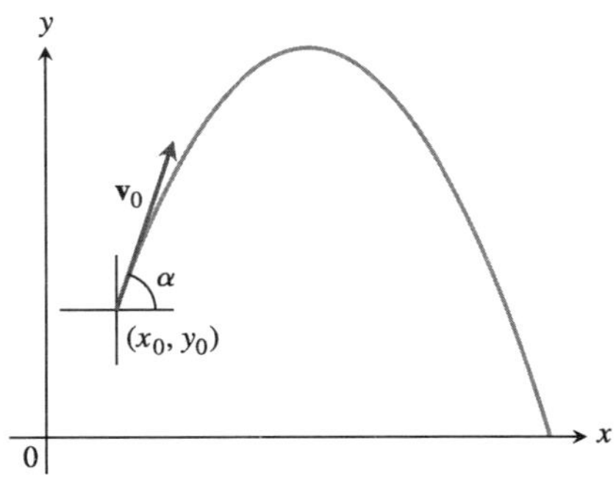

FIGURE 13.11 The path of a projectile fired from (x_0, y_0) with an initial velocity $\mathbf{v}_0$ at an angle of α degrees with the horizontal.

What is really being claimed is that ideal projectiles move along parabolas, and this we can see from Equations (4). If we substitute $t = x/(v_0 \cos \alpha)$ from the first equation into the second, we obtain the Cartesian-coordinate equation

$$y = -\left(\frac{g}{2v_0^2 \cos^2 \alpha}\right)x^2 + (\tan \alpha)x.$$

This equation has the form $y = ax^2 + bx$, so its graph is a parabola.

Firing from (x_0, y_0)

If we fire our ideal projectile from the point (x_0, y_0) instead of the origin (Figure 13.11), the position vector for the path of motion is

$$\mathbf{r} = (x_0 + (v_0 \cos \alpha)t)\mathbf{i} + \left(y_0 + (v_0 \sin \alpha)t - \frac{1}{2}gt^2\right)\mathbf{j}, \tag{5}$$

as you are asked to show in Exercise 19.

EXAMPLE 3 Firing a Flaming Arrow

To open the 1992 Summer Olympics in Barcelona, bronze medalist archer Antonio Rebollo lit the Olympic torch with a flaming arrow (Figure 13.12). Suppose that Rebollo shot the arrow at a height of 6 ft above ground level 90 ft from the 70-ft-high cauldron, and he wanted the arrow to reach maximum height exactly 4 ft above the center of the cauldron (Figure 13.12).

FIGURE 13.12 Spanish archer Antonio Rebollo lights the Olympic torch in Barcelona with a flaming arrow.

(a) Express y_{max} in terms of the initial speed v_0 and firing angle α.

(b) Use $y_{max} = 74$ ft (Figure 13.13) and the result from part (a) to find the value of $v_0 \sin \alpha$.

(c) Find the value of $v_0 \cos \alpha$.

(d) Find the initial firing angle of the arrow.

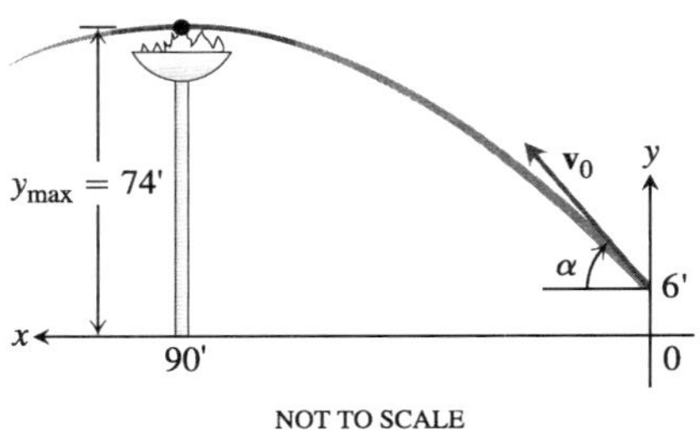

FIGURE 13.13 Ideal path of the arrow that lit the Olympic torch (Example 3).

Solution

(a) We use a coordinate system in which the positive x-axis lies along the ground toward the left (to match the second photograph in Figure 13.12) and the coordinates of the flaming arrow at $t = 0$ are $x_0 = 0$ and $y_0 = 6$ (Figure 13.13). We have

$$y = y_0 + (v_0 \sin\alpha)t - \frac{1}{2}gt^2 \qquad \text{Equation (5), } \mathbf{j}\text{-component}$$

$$= 6 + (v_0 \sin\alpha)t - \frac{1}{2}gt^2. \qquad y_0 = 6$$

We find the time when the arrow reaches its highest point by setting $dy/dt = 0$ and solving for t, obtaining

$$t = \frac{v_0 \sin\alpha}{g}.$$

For this value of t, the value of y is

$$y_{max} = 6 + (v_0 \sin\alpha)\left(\frac{v_0 \sin\alpha}{g}\right) - \frac{1}{2}g\left(\frac{v_0 \sin\alpha}{g}\right)^2$$

$$= 6 + \frac{(v_0 \sin\alpha)^2}{2g}.$$

(b) Using $y_{max} = 74$ and $g = 32$, we see from the preceeding equation in part (a) that

$$74 = 6 + \frac{(v_0 \sin\alpha)^2}{2(32)}$$

or

$$v_0 \sin\alpha = \sqrt{(68)(64)}.$$

(c) When the arrow reaches y_{max}, the horizontal distance traveled to the center of the cauldron is $x = 90$ ft. We substitute the time to reach y_{max} from part (a) and the horizontal distance $x = 90$ ft into the **i**-component of Equation (5) to obtain

$$x = x_0 + (v_0 \cos\alpha)t \qquad \text{Equation (5), } \mathbf{i}\text{-component}$$

$$90 = 0 + (v_0 \cos\alpha)t \qquad x = 90,\ x_0 = 0$$

$$= (v_0 \cos\alpha)\left(\frac{v_0 \sin\alpha}{g}\right). \qquad t = (v_0 \sin\alpha)/g$$

Solving this equation for $v_0 \cos\alpha$ and using $g = 32$ and the result from part (b), we have

$$v_0 \cos\alpha = \frac{90g}{v_0 \sin\alpha} = \frac{(90)(32)}{\sqrt{(68)(64)}}.$$

(d) Parts (b) and (c) together tell us that

$$\tan\alpha = \frac{v_0 \sin\alpha}{v_0 \cos\alpha} = \frac{\left(\sqrt{(68)(64)}\right)^2}{(90)(32)} = \frac{68}{45}$$

or

$$\alpha = \tan^{-1}\left(\frac{68}{45}\right) \approx 56.5°.$$

This is Rebollo's firing angle. ■

Projectile Motion with Wind Gusts

The next example shows how to account for another force acting on a projectile. We also assume that the path of the baseball in Example 4 lies in a vertical plane.

EXAMPLE 4 Hitting a Baseball

A baseball is hit when it is 3 ft above the ground. It leaves the bat with initial speed of 152 ft/sec, making an angle of 20° with the horizontal. At the instant the ball is hit, an instantaneous gust of wind blows in the horizontal direction directly opposite the direction the ball is taking toward the outfield, adding a component of $-8.8\mathbf{i}$ (ft/sec) to the ball's initial velocity (8.8 ft/sec = 6 mph).

(a) Find a vector equation (position vector) for the path of the baseball.

(b) How high does the baseball go, and when does it reach maximum height?

(c) Assuming that the ball is not caught, find its range and flight time.

Solution

(a) Using Equation (1) and accounting for the gust of wind, the initial velocity of the baseball is

$$\begin{aligned}\mathbf{v}_0 &= (v_0 \cos \alpha)\mathbf{i} + (v_0 \sin \alpha)\mathbf{j} - 8.8\mathbf{i}\\ &= (152 \cos 20°)\mathbf{i} + (152 \sin 20°)\mathbf{j} - (8.8)\mathbf{i}\\ &= (152 \cos 20° - 8.8)\mathbf{i} + (152 \sin 20°)\mathbf{j}.\end{aligned}$$

The initial position is $\mathbf{r}_0 = 0\mathbf{i} + 3\mathbf{j}$. Integration of $d^2\mathbf{r}/dt^2 = -g\mathbf{j}$ gives

$$\frac{d\mathbf{r}}{dt} = -(gt)\mathbf{j} + \mathbf{v}_0.$$

A second integration gives

$$\mathbf{r} = -\frac{1}{2}gt^2\mathbf{j} + \mathbf{v}_0 t + \mathbf{r}_0.$$

Substituting the values of $\mathbf{v}_0$ and $\mathbf{r}_0$ into the last equation gives the position vector of the baseball.

$$\begin{aligned}\mathbf{r} &= -\frac{1}{2}gt^2\mathbf{j} + \mathbf{v}_0 t + \mathbf{r}_0\\ &= -16t^2\mathbf{j} + (152 \cos 20° - 8.8)t\mathbf{i} + (152 \sin 20°)t\mathbf{j} + 3\mathbf{j}\\ &= (152 \cos 20° - 8.8)t\mathbf{i} + \left(3 + (152 \sin 20°)t - 16t^2\right)\mathbf{j}.\end{aligned}$$

(b) The baseball reaches its highest point when the vertical component of velocity is zero, or

$$\frac{dy}{dt} = 152 \sin 20° - 32t = 0.$$

Solving for t we find

$$t = \frac{152 \sin 20°}{32} \approx 1.62 \text{ sec}.$$

Substituting this time into the vertical component for $\mathbf{r}$ gives the maximum height

$$\begin{aligned} y_{\max} &= 3 + (152 \sin 20°)(1.62) - 16(1.62)^2 \\ &\approx 45.2 \text{ ft}. \end{aligned}$$

That is, the maximum height of the baseball is about 45.2 ft, reached about 1.6 sec after leaving the bat.

(c) To find when the baseball lands, we set the vertical component for $\mathbf{r}$ equal to 0 and solve for t:

$$\begin{aligned} 3 + (152 \sin 20°)t - 16t^2 &= 0 \\ 3 + (51.99)t - 16t^2 &= 0. \end{aligned}$$

The solution values are about $t = 3.3$ sec and $t = -0.06$ sec. Substituting the positive time into the horizontal component for $\mathbf{r}$, we find the range

$$\begin{aligned} R &= (152 \cos 20° - 8.8)(3.3) \\ &\approx 442 \text{ ft}. \end{aligned}$$

Thus, the horizontal range is about 442 ft, and the flight time is about 3.3 sec. ■

In Exercises 29 through 31, we consider projectile motion when there is air resistance slowing down the flight.

EXERCISES 13.2

Projectile flights in the following exercises are to be treated as ideal unless stated otherwise. All launch angles are assumed to be measured from the horizontal. All projectiles are assumed to be launched from the origin over a horizontal surface unless stated otherwise.

1. **Travel time** A projectile is fired at a speed of 840 m/sec at an angle of 60°. How long will it take to get 21 km downrange?

2. **Finding muzzle speed** Find the muzzle speed of a gun whose maximum range is 24.5 km.

3. **Flight time and height** A projectile is fired with an initial speed of 500 m/sec at an angle of elevation of 45°.

   a. When and how far away will the projectile strike?

   b. How high overhead will the projectile be when it is 5 km downrange?

   c. What is the greatest height reached by the projectile?

4. **Throwing a baseball** A baseball is thrown from the stands 32 ft above the field at an angle of 30° up from the horizontal. When and how far away will the ball strike the ground if its initial speed is 32 ft/sec?

5. **Shot put** An athlete puts a 16-lb shot at an angle of 45° to the horizontal from 6.5 ft above the ground at an initial speed of 44 ft/sec as suggested in the accompanying figure. How long after launch and how far from the inner edge of the stopboard does the shot land?

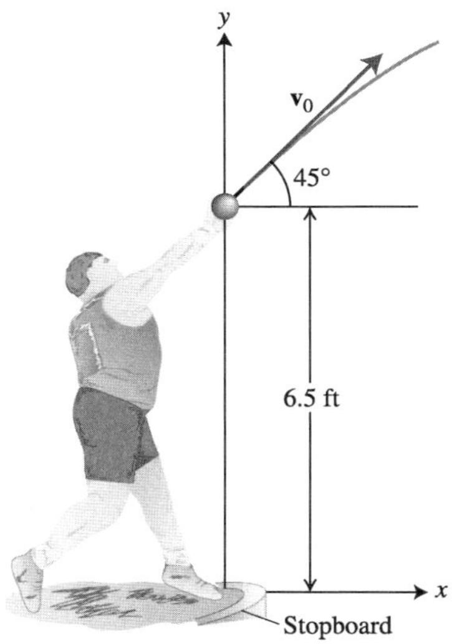

6. (*Continuation of Exercise* 5.) Because of its initial elevation, the shot in Exercise 5 would have gone slightly farther if it had been launched at a 40° angle. How much farther? Answer in inches.

7. **Firing golf balls** A spring gun at ground level fires a golf ball at an angle of 45°. The ball lands 10 m away.
   a. What was the ball's initial speed?
   b. For the same initial speed, find the two firing angles that make the range 6 m.

8. **Beaming electrons** An electron in a TV tube is beamed horizontally at a speed of 5×10^6 m/sec toward the face of the tube 40 cm away. About how far will the electron drop before it hits?

9. **Finding golf ball speed** Laboratory tests designed to find how far golf balls of different hardness go when hit with a driver showed that a 100-compression ball hit with a club-head speed of 100 mph at a launch angle of 9° carried 248.8 yd. What was the launch speed of the ball? (It was more than 100 mph. At the same time the club head was moving forward, the compressed ball was kicking away from the club face, adding to the ball's forward speed.)

10. A *human cannonball* is to be fired with an initial speed of $v_0 = 80\sqrt{10/3}$ ft/sec. The circus performer (of the right caliber, naturally) hopes to land on a special cushion located 200 ft downrange at the same height as the muzzle of the cannon. The circus is being held in a large room with a flat ceiling 75 ft higher than the muzzle. Can the performer be fired to the cushion without striking the ceiling? If so, what should the cannon's angle of elevation be?

11. A golf ball leaves the ground at a 30° angle at a speed of 90 ft/sec. Will it clear the top of a 30-ft tree that is in the way, 135 ft down the fairway? Explain.

12. **Elevated green** A golf ball is hit with an initial speed of 116 ft/sec at an angle of elevation of 45° from the tee to a green that is elevated 45 ft above the tee as shown in the diagram. Assuming that the pin, 369 ft downrange, does not get in the way, where will the ball land in relation to the pin?

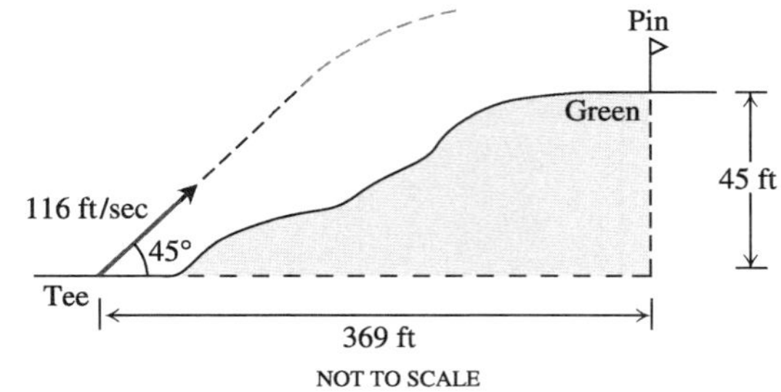

13. **The Green Monster** A baseball hit by a Boston Red Sox player at a 20° angle from 3 ft above the ground just cleared the left end of the "Green Monster," the left-field wall in Fenway Park. This wall is 37 ft high and 315 ft from home plate (see the accompanying figure).
   a. What was the initial speed of the ball?
   b. How long did it take the ball to reach the wall?

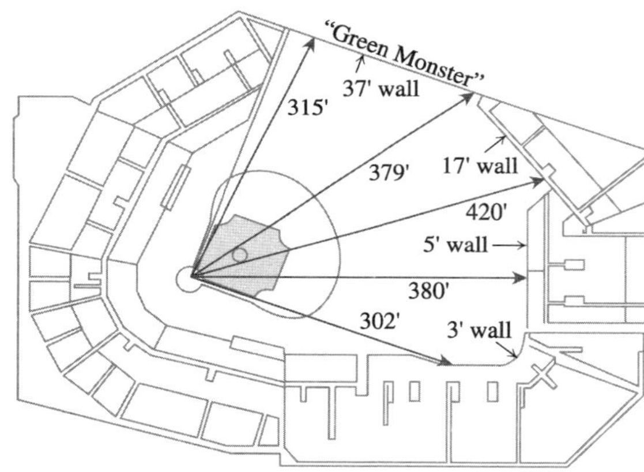

14. **Equal-range firing angles** Show that a projectile fired at an angle of α degrees, $0 < \alpha < 90$, has the same range as a projectile fired at the same speed at an angle of $(90 - \alpha)$ degrees. (In models that take air resistance into account, this symmetry is lost.)

15. **Equal-range firing angles** What two angles of elevation will enable a projectile to reach a target 16 km downrange on the same level as the gun if the projectile's initial speed is 400 m/sec?

16. **Range and height versus speed**
   a. Show that doubling a projectile's initial speed at a given launch angle multiplies its range by 4.
   b. By about what percentage should you increase the initial speed to double the height and range?

17. **Shot put** In Moscow in 1987, Natalya Lisouskaya set a women's world record by putting an 8 lb 13 oz shot 73 ft 10 in. Assuming that she launched the shot at a 40° angle to the horizontal from 6.5 ft above the ground, what was the shot's initial speed?

18. Height versus time Show that a projectile attains three-quarters of its maximum height in half the time it takes to reach the maximum height.

19. Firing from (x_0, y_0) Derive the equations

$$x = x_0 + (v_0 \cos \alpha)t,$$

$$y = y_0 + (v_0 \sin \alpha)t - \frac{1}{2}gt^2,$$

(see Equation (5) in the text) by solving the following initial value problem for a vector $\mathbf{r}$ in the plane.

Differential equation: $\quad \dfrac{d^2\mathbf{r}}{dt^2} = -g\mathbf{j}$

Initial conditions: $\quad \mathbf{r}(0) = x_0\mathbf{i} + y_0\mathbf{j}$

$$\frac{d\mathbf{r}}{dt}(0) = (v_0 \cos \alpha)\mathbf{i} + (v_0 \sin \alpha)\mathbf{j}$$

20. Flaming arrow Using the firing angle found in Example 3, find the speed at which the flaming arrow left Rebollo's bow. See Figure 13.13.

21. Flaming arrow The cauldron in Example 3 is 12 ft in diameter. Using Equation (5) and Example 3c, find how long it takes the flaming arrow to cover the horizontal distance to the rim. How high is the arrow at this time?

22. Describe the path of a projectile given by Equations (4) when $\alpha = 90°$.

23. Model train The accompanying multiflash photograph shows a model train engine moving at a constant speed on a straight horizontal track. As the engine moved along, a marble was fired into the air by a spring in the engine's smokestack. The marble, which continued to move with the same forward speed as the engine, rejoined the engine 1 sec after it was fired. Measure the angle the marble's path made with the horizontal and use the information to find how high the marble went and how fast the engine was moving.

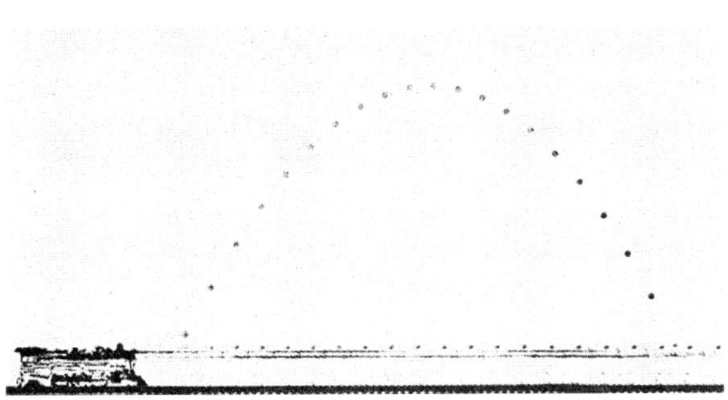

24. Colliding marbles The figure shows an experiment with two marbles. Marble A was launched toward marble B with launch angle α and initial speed v_0. At the same instant, marble B was released to fall from rest at $R \tan \alpha$ units directly above a spot R units downrange from A. The marbles were found to collide regardless of the value of v_0. Was this mere coincidence, or must this happen? Give reasons for your answer.

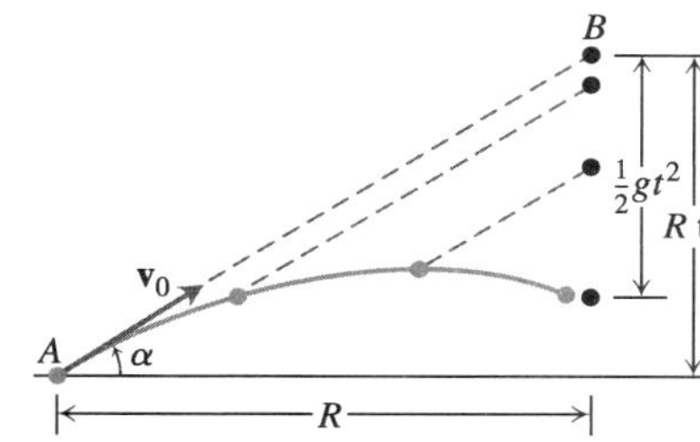

25. Launching downhill An ideal projectile is launched straight down an inclined plane as shown in the accompanying figure.

a. Show that the greatest downhill range is achieved when the initial velocity vector bisects angle AOR.

b. If the projectile were fired uphill instead of down, what launch angle would maximize its range? Give reasons for your answer.

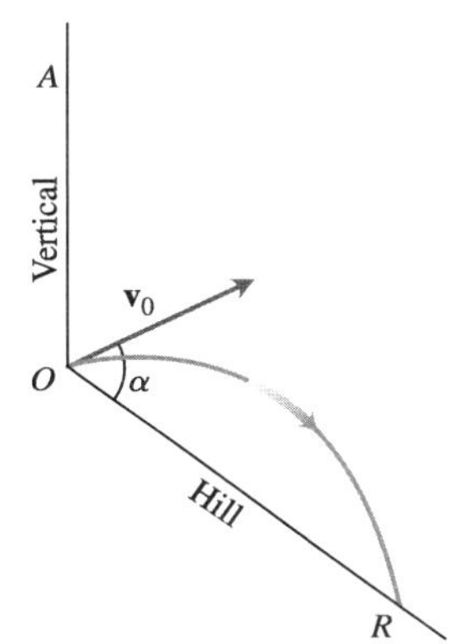

26. Hitting a baseball under a wind gust A baseball is hit when it is 2.5 ft above the ground. It leaves the bat with an initial velocity of 145 ft/sec at a launch angle of 23°. At the instant the ball is hit, an instantaneous gust of wind blows against the ball, adding a component of $-14\mathbf{i}$ (ft/sec) to the ball's initial velocity. A 15-ft-high fence lies 300 ft from home plate in the direction of the flight.

a. Find a vector equation for the path of the baseball.

b. How high does the baseball go, and when does it reach maximum height?

c. Find the range and flight time of the baseball, assuming that the ball is not caught.

d. When is the baseball 20 ft high? How far (ground distance) is the baseball from home plate at that height?

e. Has the batter hit a home run? Explain.

27. Volleyball A volleyball is hit when it is 4 ft above the ground and 12 ft from a 6-ft-high net. It leaves the point of impact with an initial velocity of 35 ft/sec at an angle of 27° and slips by the opposing team untouched.

a. Find a vector equation for the path of the volleyball.

b. How high does the volleyball go, and when does it reach maximum height?

c. Find its range and flight time.

d. When is the volleyball 7 ft above the ground? How far (ground distance) is the volleyball from where it will land?

e. Suppose that the net is raised to 8 ft. Does this change things? Explain.

28. Where trajectories crest For a projectile fired from the ground at launch angle α with initial speed v_0, consider α as a variable and v_0 as a fixed constant. For each α, $0 < \alpha < \pi/2$, we obtain a parabolic trajectory as shown in the accompanying figure. Show that the points in the plane that give the maximum heights of these parabolic trajectories all lie on the ellipse

$$x^2 + 4\left(y - \frac{v_0^2}{4g}\right)^2 = \frac{v_0^4}{4g^2},$$

where $x \geq 0$.

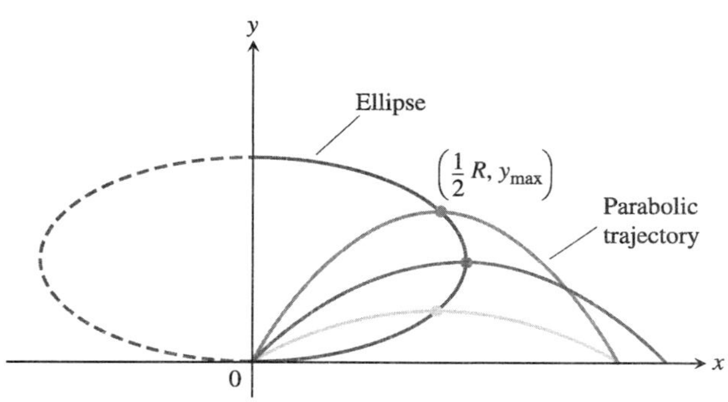

Projectile Motion with Linear Drag

The main force affecting the motion of a projectile, other than gravity, is air resistance. This slowing down force is **drag force**, and it acts in a direction *opposite* to the velocity of the projectile (see accompanying figure). For projectiles moving through the air at relatively low speeds, however, the drag force is (very nearly) proportional to the speed (to the first power) and so is called **linear**.

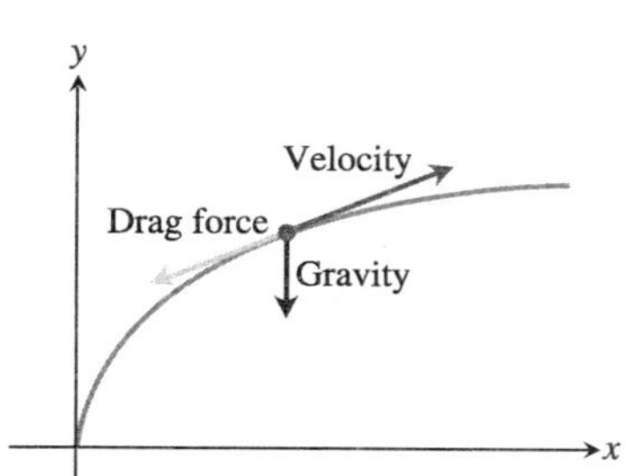

29. Linear drag Derive the equations

$$x = \frac{v_0}{k}(1 - e^{-kt})\cos\alpha$$

$$y = \frac{v_0}{k}(1 - e^{-kt})(\sin\alpha) + \frac{g}{k^2}(1 - kt - e^{-kt})$$

by solving the following initial value problem for a vector **r** in the plane.

Differential equation: $\dfrac{d^2\mathbf{r}}{dt^2} = -g\mathbf{j} - k\mathbf{v} = -g\mathbf{j} - k\dfrac{d\mathbf{r}}{dt}$

Initial conditions: $\mathbf{r}(0) = \mathbf{0}$

$$\left.\frac{d\mathbf{r}}{dt}\right|_{t=0} = \mathbf{v}_0 = (v_0\cos\alpha)\mathbf{i} + (v_0\sin\alpha)\mathbf{j}$$

The **drag coefficient** k is a positive constant representing resistance due to air density, v_0 and α are the projectile's initial speed and launch angle, and g is the acceleration of gravity.

30. Hitting a baseball with linear drag Consider the baseball problem in Example 4 when there is linear drag (see Exercise 29). Assume a drag coefficient $k = 0.12$, but no gust of wind.

a. From Exercise 29, find a vector form for the path of the baseball.

b. How high does the baseball go, and when does it reach maximum height?

c. Find the range and flight time of the baseball.

d. When is the baseball 30 ft high? How far (ground distance) is the baseball from home plate at that height?

e. A 10-ft-high outfield fence is 340 ft from home plate in the direction of the flight of the baseball. The outfielder can jump and catch any ball up to 11 ft off the ground to stop it from going over the fence. Has the batter hit a home run?

31. Hitting a baseball with linear drag under a wind gust Consider again the baseball problem in Example 4. This time assume a drag coefficient of 0.08 *and* an instantaneous gust of wind that adds a component of $-17.6\mathbf{i}$ (ft/sec) to the initial velocity at the instant the baseball is hit.

a. Find a vector equation for the path of the baseball.

b. How high does the baseball go, and when does it reach maximum height?

c. Find the range and flight time of the baseball.

d. When is the baseball 35 ft high? How far (ground distance) is the baseball from home plate at that height?

e. A 20-ft-high outfield fence is 380 ft from home plate in the direction of the flight of the baseball. Has the batter hit a home run? If "yes," what change in the horizontal component of the ball's initial velocity would have kept the ball in the park? If "no," what change would have allowed it to be a home run?

13.3 Arc Length and the Unit Tangent Vector T

Imagine the motions you might experience traveling at high speeds along a path through the air or space. Specifically, imagine the motions of turning to your left or right and the up-and-down motions tending to lift you from, or pin you down to, your seat. Pilots flying through the atmosphere, turning and twisting in flight acrobatics, certainly experience these motions. Turns that are too tight, descents or climbs that are too steep, or either one coupled with high and increasing speed can cause an aircraft to spin out of control, possibly even to break up in midair, and crash to Earth.

In this and the next two sections, we study the features of a curve's shape that describe mathematically the sharpness of its turning and its twisting perpendicular to the forward motion.

Arc Length Along a Space Curve

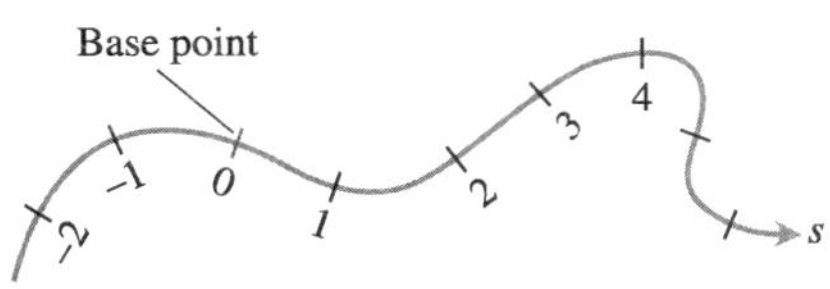

FIGURE 13.14 Smooth curves can be scaled like number lines, the coordinate of each point being its directed distance along the curve from a preselected base point.

One of the features of smooth space curves is that they have a measurable length. This enables us to locate points along these curves by giving their directed distance s along the curve from some **base point**, the way we locate points on coordinate axes by giving their directed distance from the origin (Figure 13.14). Time is the natural parameter for describing a moving body's velocity and acceleration, but s is the natural parameter for studying a curve's shape. Both parameters appear in analyses of space flight.

To measure distance along a smooth curve in space, we add a z-term to the formula we use for curves in the plane.

DEFINITION Length of a Smooth Curve

The **length** of a smooth curve $\mathbf{r}(t) = x(t)\mathbf{i} + y(t)\mathbf{j} + z(t)\mathbf{k}$, $a \le t \le b$, that is traced exactly once as t increases from $t = a$ to $t = b$, is

$$L = \int_a^b \sqrt{\left(\frac{dx}{dt}\right)^2 + \left(\frac{dy}{dt}\right)^2 + \left(\frac{dz}{dt}\right)^2}\, dt. \tag{1}$$

Just as for plane curves, we can calculate the length of a curve in space from any convenient parametrization that meets the stated conditions. We omit the proof.

The square root in Equation (1) is $|\mathbf{v}|$, the length of a velocity vector $d\mathbf{r}/dt$. This enables us to write the formula for length a shorter way.

Arc Length Formula

$$L = \int_a^b |\mathbf{v}|\, dt \tag{2}$$

EXAMPLE 1 Distance Traveled by a Glider

A glider is soaring upward along the helix $\mathbf{r}(t) = (\cos t)\mathbf{i} + (\sin t)\mathbf{j} + t\mathbf{k}$. How far does the glider travel along its path from $t = 0$ to $t = 2\pi \approx 6.28$ sec?

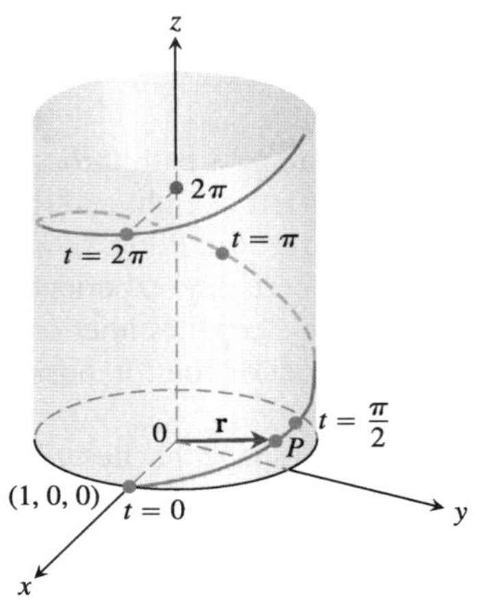

FIGURE 13.15 The helix $\mathbf{r}(t) = (\cos t)\mathbf{i} + (\sin t)\mathbf{j} + t\mathbf{k}$ in Example 1.

Solution The path segment during this time corresponds to one full turn of the helix (Figure 13.15). The length of this portion of the curve is

$$L = \int_a^b |\mathbf{v}|\,dt = \int_0^{2\pi} \sqrt{(-\sin t)^2 + (\cos t)^2 + (1)^2}\,dt$$

$$= \int_0^{2\pi} \sqrt{2}\,dt = 2\pi\sqrt{2} \text{ units of length.}$$

This is $\sqrt{2}$ times the length of the circle in the xy-plane over which the helix stands. ■

If we choose a base point $P(t_0)$ on a smooth curve C parametrized by t, each value of t determines a point $P(t) = (x(t), y(t), z(t))$ on C and a "directed distance"

$$s(t) = \int_{t_0}^{t} |\mathbf{v}(\tau)|\,d\tau,$$

measured along C from the base point (Figure 13.16). If $t > t_0$, $s(t)$ is the distance from $P(t_0)$ to $P(t)$. If $t < t_0$, $s(t)$ is the negative of the distance. Each value of s determines a point on C and this parametrizes C with respect to s. We call s an **arc length parameter** for the curve. The parameter's value increases in the direction of increasing t. The arc length parameter is particularly effective for investigating the turning and twisting nature of a space curve.

We use the Greek letter τ ("tau") as the variable of integration because the letter t is already in use as the upper limit.

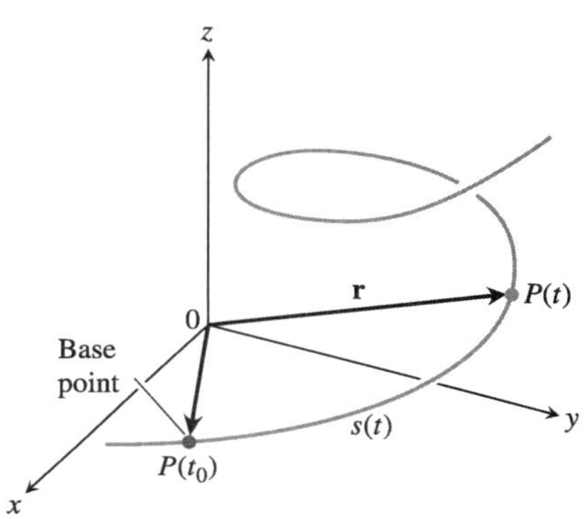

FIGURE 13.16 The directed distance along the curve from $P(t_0)$ to any point $P(t)$ is

$$s(t) = \int_{t_0}^{t} |\mathbf{v}(\tau)|\,d\tau.$$

Arc Length Parameter with Base Point $P(t_0)$

$$s(t) = \int_{t_0}^{t} \sqrt{[x'(\tau)]^2 + [y'(\tau)]^2 + [z'(\tau)]^2}\,d\tau = \int_{t_0}^{t} |\mathbf{v}(\tau)|\,d\tau \qquad (3)$$

If a curve $\mathbf{r}(t)$ is already given in terms of some parameter t and $s(t)$ is the arc length function given by Equation (3), then we may be able to solve for t as a function of s: $t = t(s)$. Then the curve can be reparametrized in terms of s by substituting for t: $\mathbf{r} = \mathbf{r}(t(s))$.

EXAMPLE 2 Finding an Arc Length Parametrization

If $t_0 = 0$, the arc length parameter along the helix

$$\mathbf{r}(t) = (\cos t)\mathbf{i} + (\sin t)\mathbf{j} + t\mathbf{k}$$

from t_0 to t is

$$s(t) = \int_{t_0}^{t} |\mathbf{v}(\tau)|\,d\tau \qquad \text{Equation (3)}$$

$$= \int_0^t \sqrt{2}\,d\tau \qquad \text{Value from Example 1}$$

$$= \sqrt{2}\,t.$$

Solving this equation for t gives $t = s/\sqrt{2}$. Substituting into the position vector $\mathbf{r}$ gives the following arc length parametrization for the helix:

$$\mathbf{r}(t(s)) = \left(\cos\frac{s}{\sqrt{2}}\right)\mathbf{i} + \left(\sin\frac{s}{\sqrt{2}}\right)\mathbf{j} + \frac{s}{\sqrt{2}}\mathbf{k}. \qquad \blacksquare$$

Unlike Example 2, the arc length parametrization is generally difficult to find analytically for a curve already given in terms of some other parameter t. Fortunately, however, we rarely need an exact formula for $s(t)$ or its inverse $t(s)$.

EXAMPLE 3 Distance Along a Line

Show that if $\mathbf{u} = u_1\mathbf{i} + u_2\mathbf{j} + u_3\mathbf{k}$ is a unit vector, then the arc length parameter along the line

$$\mathbf{r}(t) = (x_0 + tu_1)\mathbf{i} + (y_0 + tu_2)\mathbf{j} + (z_0 + tu_3)\mathbf{k}$$

from the point $P_0(x_0, y_0, z_0)$ where $t = 0$ is t itself.

Solution

$$\mathbf{v} = \frac{d}{dt}(x_0 + tu_1)\mathbf{i} + \frac{d}{dt}(y_0 + tu_2)\mathbf{j} + \frac{d}{dt}(z_0 + tu_3)\mathbf{k} = u_1\mathbf{i} + u_2\mathbf{j} + u_3\mathbf{k} = \mathbf{u},$$

so

$$s(t) = \int_0^t |\mathbf{v}|\,d\tau = \int_0^t |\mathbf{u}|\,d\tau = \int_0^t 1\,d\tau = t. \qquad \blacksquare$$

HISTORICAL BIOGRAPHY

Josiah Willard Gibbs (1839–1903)

Speed on a Smooth Curve

Since the derivatives beneath the radical in Equation (3) are continuous (the curve is smooth), the Fundamental Theorem of Calculus tells us that s is a differentiable function of t with derivative

$$\frac{ds}{dt} = |\mathbf{v}(t)|. \tag{4}$$

As we already knew, the speed with which a particle moves along its path is the magnitude of $\mathbf{v}$.

Notice that although the base point $P(t_0)$ plays a role in defining s in Equation (3), it plays no role in Equation (4). The rate at which a moving particle covers distance along its path is independent of how far away it is from the base point.

Notice also that $ds/dt > 0$ since, by definition, $|\mathbf{v}|$ is never zero for a smooth curve. We see once again that s is an increasing function of t.

Unit Tangent Vector T

We already know the velocity vector $\mathbf{v} = d\mathbf{r}/dt$ is tangent to the curve and that the vector

$$\mathbf{T} = \frac{\mathbf{v}}{|\mathbf{v}|}$$

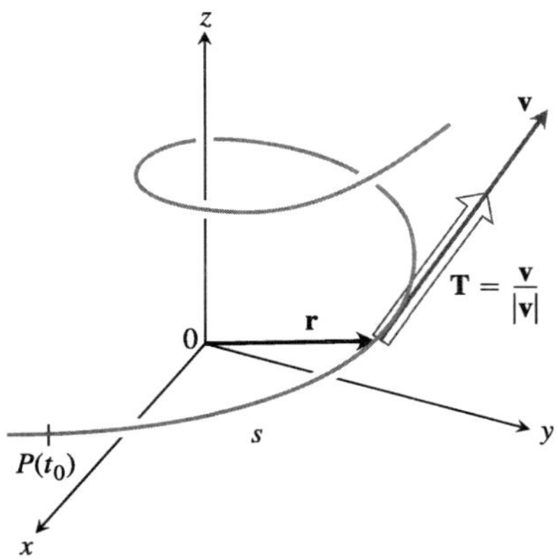

FIGURE 13.17 We find the unit tangent vector $\mathbf{T}$ by dividing $\mathbf{v}$ by $|\mathbf{v}|$.

is therefore a unit vector tangent to the (smooth) curve. Since $ds/dt > 0$ for the curves we are considering, s is one-to-one and has an inverse that gives t as a differentiable function of s (Section 7.1). The derivative of the inverse is

$$\frac{dt}{ds} = \frac{1}{ds/dt} = \frac{1}{|\mathbf{v}|}.$$

This makes $\mathbf{r}$ a differentiable function of s whose derivative can be calculated with the Chain Rule to be

$$\frac{d\mathbf{r}}{ds} = \frac{d\mathbf{r}}{dt}\frac{dt}{ds} = \mathbf{v}\frac{1}{|\mathbf{v}|} = \frac{\mathbf{v}}{|\mathbf{v}|} = \mathbf{T}.$$

This equation says that $d\mathbf{r}/ds$ is the unit tangent vector in the direction of the velocity vector $\mathbf{v}$ (Figure 13.17).

DEFINITION Unit Tangent Vector

The **unit tangent vector** of a smooth curve $\mathbf{r}(t)$ is

$$\mathbf{T} = \frac{d\mathbf{r}}{ds} = \frac{d\mathbf{r}/dt}{ds/dt} = \frac{\mathbf{v}}{|\mathbf{v}|}. \quad (5)$$

The unit tangent vector $\mathbf{T}$ is a differentiable function of t whenever $\mathbf{v}$ is a differentiable function of t. As we see in Section 13.5, $\mathbf{T}$ is one of three unit vectors in a traveling reference frame that is used to describe the motion of space vehicles and other bodies traveling in three dimensions.

EXAMPLE 4 Finding the Unit Tangent Vector T

Find the unit tangent vector of the curve

$$\mathbf{r}(t) = (3\cos t)\mathbf{i} + (3\sin t)\mathbf{j} + t^2\mathbf{k}$$

representing the path of the glider in Example 4, Section 13.1.

Solution In that example, we found

$$\mathbf{v} = \frac{d\mathbf{r}}{dt} = -(3\sin t)\mathbf{i} + (3\cos t)\mathbf{j} + 2t\mathbf{k}$$

and

$$|\mathbf{v}| = \sqrt{9 + 4t^2}.$$

Thus,

$$\mathbf{T} = \frac{\mathbf{v}}{|\mathbf{v}|} = -\frac{3\sin t}{\sqrt{9+4t^2}}\mathbf{i} + \frac{3\cos t}{\sqrt{9+4t^2}}\mathbf{j} + \frac{2t}{\sqrt{9+4t^2}}\mathbf{k}.$$ ■

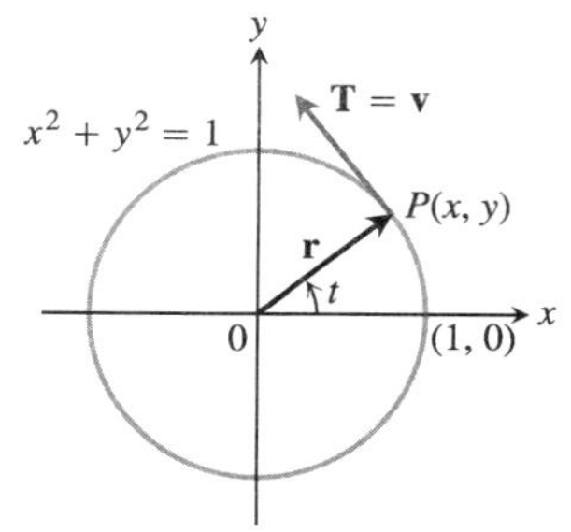

FIGURE 13.18 The motion $\mathbf{r}(t) = (\cos t)\mathbf{i} + (\sin t)\mathbf{j}$ (Example 5).

EXAMPLE 5 Motion on the Unit Circle

For the counterclockwise motion

$$\mathbf{r}(t) = (\cos t)\mathbf{i} + (\sin t)\mathbf{j}$$

around the unit circle,

$$\mathbf{v} = (-\sin t)\mathbf{i} + (\cos t)\mathbf{j}$$

is already a unit vector, so $\mathbf{T} = \mathbf{v}$ (Figure 13.18). ■

EXERCISES 13.3

Finding Unit Tangent Vectors and Lengths of Curves

In Exercises 1–8, find the curve's unit tangent vector. Also, find the length of the indicated portion of the curve.

1. $\mathbf{r}(t) = (2\cos t)\mathbf{i} + (2\sin t)\mathbf{j} + \sqrt{5}t\mathbf{k}, \quad 0 \le t \le \pi$
2. $\mathbf{r}(t) = (6\sin 2t)\mathbf{i} + (6\cos 2t)\mathbf{j} + 5t\mathbf{k}, \quad 0 \le t \le \pi$
3. $\mathbf{r}(t) = t\mathbf{i} + (2/3)t^{3/2}\mathbf{k}, \quad 0 \le t \le 8$
4. $\mathbf{r}(t) = (2 + t)\mathbf{i} - (t + 1)\mathbf{j} + t\mathbf{k}, \quad 0 \le t \le 3$
5. $\mathbf{r}(t) = (\cos^3 t)\mathbf{j} + (\sin^3 t)\mathbf{k}, \quad 0 \le t \le \pi/2$
6. $\mathbf{r}(t) = 6t^3\mathbf{i} - 2t^3\mathbf{j} - 3t^3\mathbf{k}, \quad 1 \le t \le 2$
7. $\mathbf{r}(t) = (t\cos t)\mathbf{i} + (t\sin t)\mathbf{j} + \left(2\sqrt{2}/3\right)t^{3/2}\mathbf{k}, \quad 0 \le t \le \pi$
8. $\mathbf{r}(t) = (t\sin t + \cos t)\mathbf{i} + (t\cos t - \sin t)\mathbf{j}, \quad \sqrt{2} \le t \le 2$
9. Find the point on the curve
$$\mathbf{r}(t) = (5\sin t)\mathbf{i} + (5\cos t)\mathbf{j} + 12t\mathbf{k}$$
at a distance 26π units along the curve from the point (0, 5, 0) in the direction of increasing arc length.
10. Find the point on the curve
$$\mathbf{r}(t) = (12\sin t)\mathbf{i} - (12\cos t)\mathbf{j} + 5t\mathbf{k}$$
at a distance 13π units along the curve from the point $(0, -12, 0)$ in the direction opposite to the direction of increasing arc length.

Arc Length Parameter

In Exercises 11–14, find the arc length parameter along the curve from the point where $t = 0$ by evaluating the integral

$$s = \int_0^t |\mathbf{v}(\tau)|\, d\tau$$

from Equation (3). Then find the length of the indicated portion of the curve.

11. $\mathbf{r}(t) = (4\cos t)\mathbf{i} + (4\sin t)\mathbf{j} + 3t\mathbf{k}, \quad 0 \le t \le \pi/2$
12. $\mathbf{r}(t) = (\cos t + t\sin t)\mathbf{i} + (\sin t - t\cos t)\mathbf{j}, \quad \pi/2 \le t \le \pi$
13. $\mathbf{r}(t) = (e^t\cos t)\mathbf{i} + (e^t\sin t)\mathbf{j} + e^t\mathbf{k}, \quad -\ln 4 \le t \le 0$
14. $\mathbf{r}(t) = (1 + 2t)\mathbf{i} + (1 + 3t)\mathbf{j} + (6 - 6t)\mathbf{k}, \quad -1 \le t \le 0$

Theory and Examples

15. **Arc length** Find the length of the curve
$$\mathbf{r}(t) = \left(\sqrt{2}t\right)\mathbf{i} + \left(\sqrt{2}t\right)\mathbf{j} + (1 - t^2)\mathbf{k}$$
from (0, 0, 1) to $\left(\sqrt{2}, \sqrt{2}, 0\right)$.
16. **Length of helix** The length $2\pi\sqrt{2}$ of the turn of the helix in Example 1 is also the length of the diagonal of a square 2π units on a side. Show how to obtain this square by cutting away and flattening a portion of the cylinder around which the helix winds.
17. **Ellipse**
    a. Show that the curve $\mathbf{r}(t) = (\cos t)\mathbf{i} + (\sin t)\mathbf{j} + (1 - \cos t)\mathbf{k}$, $0 \le t \le 2\pi$, is an ellipse by showing that it is the intersection of a right circular cylinder and a plane. Find equations for the cylinder and plane.
    b. Sketch the ellipse on the cylinder. Add to your sketch the unit tangent vectors at $t = 0, \pi/2, \pi$, and $3\pi/2$.
    c. Show that the acceleration vector always lies parallel to the plane (orthogonal to a vector normal to the plane). Thus, if you draw the acceleration as a vector attached to the ellipse, it will lie in the plane of the ellipse. Add the acceleration vectors for $t = 0, \pi/2, \pi$, and $3\pi/2$ to your sketch.
    d. Write an integral for the length of the ellipse. Do not try to evaluate the integral; it is nonelementary.

    T e. **Numerical integrator** Estimate the length of the ellipse to two decimal places.
18. **Length is independent of parametrization** To illustrate that the length of a smooth space curve does not depend on

the parametrization you use to compute it, calculate the length of one turn of the helix in Example 1 with the following parametrizations.

a. $\mathbf{r}(t) = (\cos 4t)\mathbf{i} + (\sin 4t)\mathbf{j} + 4t\mathbf{k}, \quad 0 \le t \le \pi/2$

b. $\mathbf{r}(t) = [\cos (t/2)]\mathbf{i} + [\sin (t/2)]\mathbf{j} + (t/2)\mathbf{k}, \quad 0 \le t \le 4\pi$

c. $\mathbf{r}(t) = (\cos t)\mathbf{i} - (\sin t)\mathbf{j} - t\mathbf{k}, \quad -2\pi \le t \le 0$

19. The involute of a circle If a string wound around a fixed circle is unwound while held taut in the plane of the circle, its end P traces an *involute* of the circle. In the accompanying figure, the circle in question is the circle $x^2 + y^2 = 1$ and the tracing point starts at $(1, 0)$. The unwound portion of the string is tangent to the circle at Q, and t is the radian measure of the angle from the positive x-axis to segment OQ. Derive the parametric equations

$$x = \cos t + t\sin t, \quad y = \sin t - t\cos t, \quad t > 0$$

of the point $P(x, y)$ for the involute.

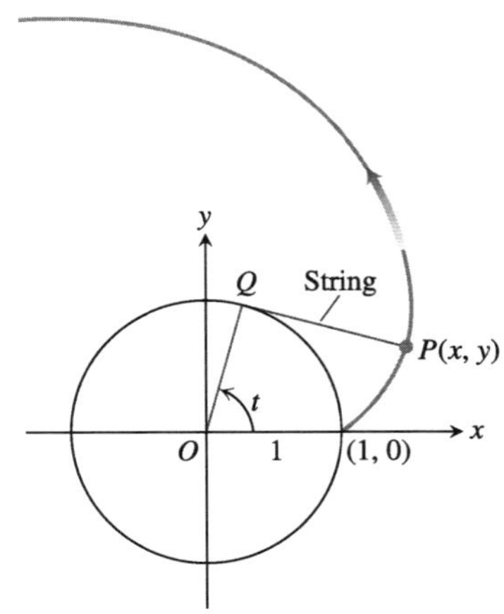

20. (*Continuation of Exercise 19.*) Find the unit tangent vector to the involute of the circle at the point $P(x, y)$.

13.4 Curvature and the Unit Normal Vector N

In this section we study how a curve turns or bends. We look first at curves in the coordinate plane, and then at curves in space.

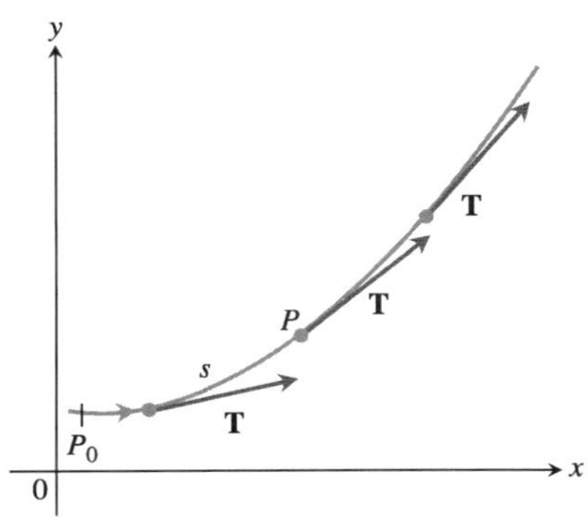

FIGURE 13.19 As P moves along the curve in the direction of increasing arc length, the unit tangent vector turns. The value of $|d\mathbf{T}/ds|$ at P is called the *curvature* of the curve at P.

Curvature of a Plane Curve

As a particle moves along a smooth curve in the plane, $\mathbf{T} = d\mathbf{r}/ds$ turns as the curve bends. Since $\mathbf{T}$ is a unit vector, its length remains constant and only its direction changes as the particle moves along the curve. The rate at which $\mathbf{T}$ turns per unit of length along the curve is called the *curvature* (Figure 13.19). The traditional symbol for the curvature function is the Greek letter κ ("kappa").

> **DEFINITION** Curvature
>
> If $\mathbf{T}$ is the unit vector of a smooth curve, the **curvature** function of the curve is
>
> $$\kappa = \left|\frac{d\mathbf{T}}{ds}\right|.$$

If $|d\mathbf{T}/ds|$ is large, $\mathbf{T}$ turns sharply as the particle passes through P, and the curvature at P is large. If $|d\mathbf{T}/ds|$ is close to zero, $\mathbf{T}$ turns more slowly and the curvature at P is smaller.

If a smooth curve $\mathbf{r}(t)$ is already given in terms of some parameter t other than the arc length parameter s, we can calculate the curvature as

$$\begin{aligned}\kappa &= \left|\frac{d\mathbf{T}}{ds}\right| = \left|\frac{d\mathbf{T}}{dt}\frac{dt}{ds}\right| && \text{Chain Rule}\\ &= \frac{1}{|ds/dt|}\left|\frac{d\mathbf{T}}{dt}\right| \\ &= \frac{1}{|\mathbf{v}|}\left|\frac{d\mathbf{T}}{dt}\right|. && \frac{ds}{dt} = |\mathbf{v}|\end{aligned}$$

Formula for Calculating Curvature
If $\mathbf{r}(t)$ is a smooth curve, then the curvature is

$$\kappa = \frac{1}{|\mathbf{v}|}\left|\frac{d\mathbf{T}}{dt}\right|, \tag{1}$$

where $\mathbf{T} = \mathbf{v}/|\mathbf{v}|$ is the unit tangent vector.

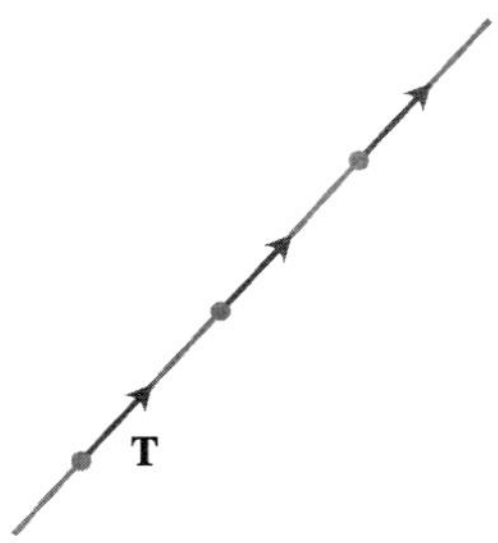

FIGURE 13.20 Along a straight line, **T** always points in the same direction. The curvature, $|d\mathbf{T}/ds|$, is zero (Example 1).

Testing the definition, we see in Examples 1 and 2 below that the curvature is constant for straight lines and circles.

EXAMPLE 1 The Curvature of a Straight Line Is Zero

On a straight line, the unit tangent vector **T** always points in the same direction, so its components are constants. Therefore, $|d\mathbf{T}/ds| = |\mathbf{0}| = 0$ (Figure 13.20). ■

EXAMPLE 2 The Curvature of a Circle of Radius a is $1/a$

To see why, we begin with the parametrization

$$\mathbf{r}(t) = (a\cos t)\mathbf{i} + (a\sin t)\mathbf{j}$$

of a circle of radius a. Then,

$$\mathbf{v} = \frac{d\mathbf{r}}{dt} = -(a\sin t)\mathbf{i} + (a\cos t)\mathbf{j}$$

$$|\mathbf{v}| = \sqrt{(-a\sin t)^2 + (a\cos t)^2} = \sqrt{a^2} = |a| = a.$$

Since $a > 0$, $|a| = a$.

From this we find

$$\mathbf{T} = \frac{\mathbf{v}}{|\mathbf{v}|} = -(\sin t)\mathbf{i} + (\cos t)\mathbf{j}$$

$$\frac{d\mathbf{T}}{dt} = -(\cos t)\mathbf{i} - (\sin t)\mathbf{j}$$

$$\left|\frac{d\mathbf{T}}{dt}\right| = \sqrt{\cos^2 t + \sin^2 t} = 1.$$

Hence, for any value of the parameter t,

$$\kappa = \frac{1}{|\mathbf{v}|}\left|\frac{d\mathbf{T}}{dt}\right| = \frac{1}{a}(1) = \frac{1}{a}.$$ ■

Although the formula for calculating κ in Equation (1) is also valid for space curves, in the next section we find a computational formula that is usually more convenient to apply.

Among the vectors orthogonal to the unit tangent vector **T** is one of particular significance because it points in the direction in which the curve is turning. Since **T** has constant length (namely, 1), the derivative $d\mathbf{T}/ds$ is orthogonal to **T** (Section 13.1). Therefore, if we divide $d\mathbf{T}/ds$ by its length κ, we obtain a *unit* vector **N** orthogonal to **T** (Figure 13.21).

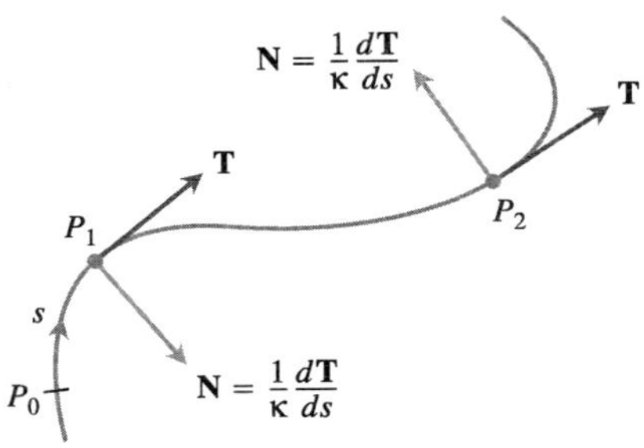

FIGURE 13.21 The vector $d\mathbf{T}/ds$, normal to the curve, always points in the direction in which $\mathbf{T}$ is turning. The unit normal vector $\mathbf{N}$ is the direction of $d\mathbf{T}/ds$.

> **DEFINITION Principal Unit Normal**
> At a point where $\kappa \neq 0$, the **principal unit normal** vector for a smooth curve in the plane is
> $$\mathbf{N} = \frac{1}{\kappa}\frac{d\mathbf{T}}{ds}.$$

The vector $d\mathbf{T}/ds$ points in the direction in which $\mathbf{T}$ turns as the curve bends. Therefore, if we face in the direction of increasing arc length, the vector $d\mathbf{T}/ds$ points toward the right if $\mathbf{T}$ turns clockwise and toward the left if $\mathbf{T}$ turns counterclockwise. In other words, the principal normal vector $\mathbf{N}$ will point toward the concave side of the curve (Figure 13.21).

If a smooth curve $\mathbf{r}(t)$ is already given in terms of some parameter t other than the arc length parameter s, we can use the Chain Rule to calculate $\mathbf{N}$ directly:

$$\begin{aligned}\mathbf{N} &= \frac{d\mathbf{T}/ds}{|d\mathbf{T}/ds|} \\ &= \frac{(d\mathbf{T}/dt)(dt/ds)}{|d\mathbf{T}/dt||dt/ds|} \\ &= \frac{d\mathbf{T}/dt}{|d\mathbf{T}/dt|}. \qquad \frac{dt}{ds} = \frac{1}{ds/dt} > 0 \text{ cancels}\end{aligned}$$

This formula enables us to find $\mathbf{N}$ without having to find κ and s first.

> **Formula for Calculating N**
> If $\mathbf{r}(t)$ is a smooth curve, then the principal unit normal is
> $$\mathbf{N} = \frac{d\mathbf{T}/dt}{|d\mathbf{T}/dt|}, \qquad (2)$$
> where $\mathbf{T} = \mathbf{v}/|\mathbf{v}|$ is the unit tangent vector.

EXAMPLE 3 Finding T and N

Find $\mathbf{T}$ and $\mathbf{N}$ for the circular motion

$$\mathbf{r}(t) = (\cos 2t)\mathbf{i} + (\sin 2t)\mathbf{j}.$$

Solution We first find $\mathbf{T}$:

$$\begin{aligned}\mathbf{v} &= -(2\sin 2t)\mathbf{i} + (2\cos 2t)\mathbf{j} \\ |\mathbf{v}| &= \sqrt{4\sin^2 2t + 4\cos^2 2t} = 2 \\ \mathbf{T} &= \frac{\mathbf{v}}{|\mathbf{v}|} = -(\sin 2t)\mathbf{i} + (\cos 2t)\mathbf{j}.\end{aligned}$$

From this we find

$$\frac{d\mathbf{T}}{dt} = -(2\cos 2t)\mathbf{i} - (2\sin 2t)\mathbf{j}$$

$$\left|\frac{d\mathbf{T}}{dt}\right| = \sqrt{4\cos^2 2t + 4\sin^2 2t} = 2$$

and

$$\mathbf{N} = \frac{d\mathbf{T}/dt}{|d\mathbf{T}/dt|}$$

$$= -(\cos 2t)\mathbf{i} - (\sin 2t)\mathbf{j}. \qquad \text{Equation (2)}$$

Notice that $\mathbf{T}\cdot\mathbf{N} = 0$, verifying that **N** is orthogonal to **T**. Notice too, that for the circular motion here, **N** points from $\mathbf{r}(t)$ towards the circle's center at the origin. ■

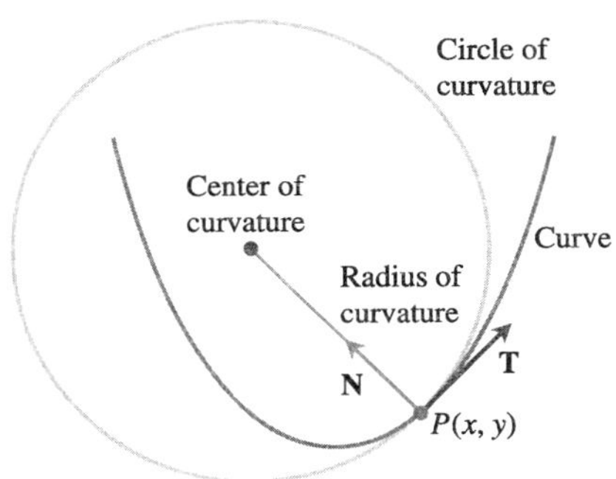

FIGURE 13.22 The osculating circle at $P(x, y)$ lies toward the inner side of the curve.

Circle of Curvature for Plane Curves

The **circle of curvature** or **osculating circle** at a point P on a plane curve where $\kappa \neq 0$ is the circle in the plane of the curve that

1. is tangent to the curve at P (has the same tangent line the curve has)
2. has the same curvature the curve has at P
3. lies toward the concave or inner side of the curve (as in Figure 13.22).

The **radius of curvature** of the curve at P is the radius of the circle of curvature, which, according to Example 2, is

$$\text{Radius of curvature} = \rho = \frac{1}{\kappa}.$$

To find ρ, we find κ and take the reciprocal. The **center of curvature** of the curve at P is the center of the circle of curvature.

EXAMPLE 4 Finding the Osculating Circle for a Parabola

Find and graph the osculating circle of the parabola $y = x^2$ at the origin.

Solution We parametrize the parabola using the parameter $t = x$ (Section 10.4, Example 1)

$$\mathbf{r}(t) = t\mathbf{i} + t^2\mathbf{j}.$$

First we find the curvature of the parabola at the origin, using Equation (1):

$$\mathbf{v} = \frac{d\mathbf{r}}{dt} = \mathbf{i} + 2t\mathbf{j}$$

$$|\mathbf{v}| = \sqrt{1 + 4t^2}$$

so that

$$\mathbf{T} = \frac{\mathbf{v}}{|\mathbf{v}|} = (1 + 4t^2)^{-1/2}\mathbf{i} + 2t(1 + 4t^2)^{-1/2}\mathbf{j}.$$

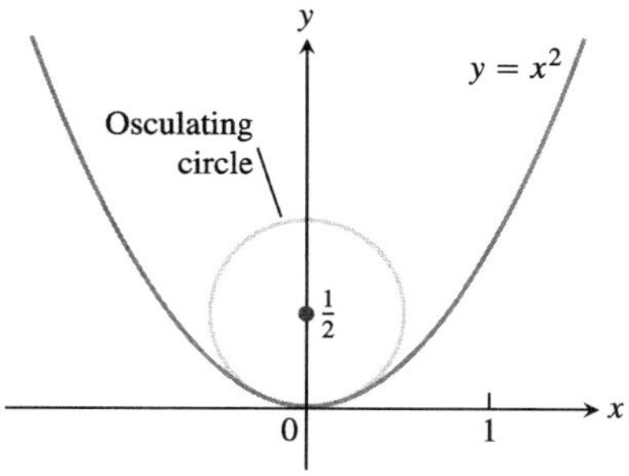

FIGURE 13.23 The osculating circle for the parabola $y = x^2$ at the origin (Example 4).

From this we find

$$\frac{d\mathbf{T}}{dt} = -4t(1 + 4t^2)^{-3/2}\mathbf{i} + [2(1 + 4t^2)^{-1/2} - 8t^2(1 + 4t^2)^{-3/2}]\mathbf{j}.$$

At the origin, $t = 0$, so the curvature is

$$\begin{aligned} \kappa(0) &= \frac{1}{|\mathbf{v}(0)|}\left|\frac{d\mathbf{T}}{dt}(0)\right| && \text{Equation (1)} \\ &= \frac{1}{\sqrt{1}}|0\mathbf{i} + 2\mathbf{j}| \\ &= (1)\sqrt{0^2 + 2^2} = 2. \end{aligned}$$

Therefore, the radius of curvature is $1/\kappa = 1/2$ and the center of the circle is $(0, 1/2)$ (see Figure 13.23). The equation of the osculating circle is

$$(x - 0)^2 + \left(y - \frac{1}{2}\right)^2 = \left(\frac{1}{2}\right)^2$$

or

$$x^2 + \left(y - \frac{1}{2}\right)^2 = \frac{1}{4}.$$

You can see from Figure 13.23 that the osculating circle is a better approximation to the parabola at the origin than is the tangent line approximation $y = 0$. ■

Curvature and Normal Vectors for Space Curves

If a smooth curve in space is specified by the position vector $\mathbf{r}(t)$ as a function of some parameter t, and if s is the arc length parameter of the curve, then the unit tangent vector $\mathbf{T}$ is $d\mathbf{r}/ds = \mathbf{v}/|\mathbf{v}|$. The **curvature** in space is then defined to be

$$\kappa = \left|\frac{d\mathbf{T}}{ds}\right| = \frac{1}{|\mathbf{v}|}\left|\frac{d\mathbf{T}}{dt}\right| \tag{3}$$

just as for plane curves. The vector $d\mathbf{T}/ds$ is orthogonal to $\mathbf{T}$, and we define the **principal unit normal** to be

$$\mathbf{N} = \frac{1}{\kappa}\frac{d\mathbf{T}}{ds} = \frac{d\mathbf{T}/dt}{|d\mathbf{T}/dt|}. \tag{4}$$

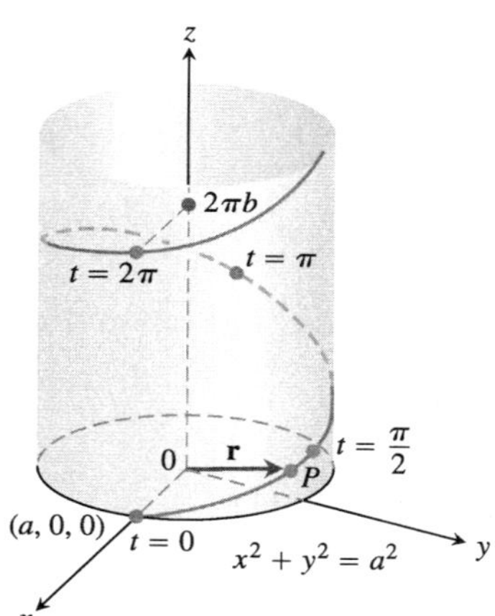

FIGURE 13.24 The helix

$$\mathbf{r}(t) = (a\cos t)\mathbf{i} + (a\sin t)\mathbf{j} + bt\mathbf{k},$$

drawn with a and b positive and $t \geq 0$ (Example 5).

EXAMPLE 5 Finding Curvature

Find the curvature for the helix (Figure 13.24)

$$\mathbf{r}(t) = (a\cos t)\mathbf{i} + (a\sin t)\mathbf{j} + bt\mathbf{k}, \qquad a, b \geq 0, \qquad a^2 + b^2 \neq 0.$$

Solution We calculate **T** from the velocity vector **v**:

$$\mathbf{v} = -(a \sin t)\mathbf{i} + (a \cos t)\mathbf{j} + b\mathbf{k}$$

$$|\mathbf{v}| = \sqrt{a^2 \sin^2 t + a^2 \cos^2 t + b^2} = \sqrt{a^2 + b^2}$$

$$\mathbf{T} = \frac{\mathbf{v}}{|\mathbf{v}|} = \frac{1}{\sqrt{a^2 + b^2}}[-(a \sin t)\mathbf{i} + (a \cos t)\mathbf{j} + b\mathbf{k}].$$

Then using Equation (3),

$$\begin{aligned}
\kappa &= \frac{1}{|\mathbf{v}|}\left|\frac{d\mathbf{T}}{dt}\right| \\
&= \frac{1}{\sqrt{a^2 + b^2}}\left|\frac{1}{\sqrt{a^2 + b^2}}[-(a \cos t)\mathbf{i} - (a \sin t)\mathbf{j}]\right| \\
&= \frac{a}{a^2 + b^2}\left|-(\cos t)\mathbf{i} - (\sin t)\mathbf{j}\right| \\
&= \frac{a}{a^2 + b^2}\sqrt{(\cos t)^2 + (\sin t)^2} = \frac{a}{a^2 + b^2}.
\end{aligned}$$

From this equation, we see that increasing b for a fixed a decreases the curvature. Decreasing a for a fixed b eventually decreases the curvature as well. Stretching a spring tends to straighten it.

If $b = 0$, the helix reduces to a circle of radius a and its curvature reduces to $1/a$, as it should. If $a = 0$, the helix becomes the z-axis, and its curvature reduces to 0, again as it should. ■

EXAMPLE 6 Finding the Principal Unit Normal Vector N

Find **N** for the helix in Example 5.

Solution We have

$$\frac{d\mathbf{T}}{dt} = -\frac{1}{\sqrt{a^2 + b^2}}[(a \cos t)\mathbf{i} + (a \sin t)\mathbf{j}] \qquad \text{Example 5}$$

$$\left|\frac{d\mathbf{T}}{dt}\right| = \frac{1}{\sqrt{a^2 + b^2}}\sqrt{a^2 \cos^2 t + a^2 \sin^2 t} = \frac{a}{\sqrt{a^2 + b^2}}$$

$$\begin{aligned}
\mathbf{N} &= \frac{d\mathbf{T}/dt}{|d\mathbf{T}/dt|} \qquad \text{Equatiion (4)} \\
&= -\frac{\sqrt{a^2 + b^2}}{a} \cdot \frac{1}{\sqrt{a^2 + b^2}}[(a \cos t)\mathbf{i} + (a \sin t)\mathbf{j}] \\
&= -(\cos t)\mathbf{i} - (\sin t)\mathbf{j}.
\end{aligned}$$

■

EXERCISES 13.4

Plane Curves

Find **T**, **N**, and κ for the plane curves in Exercises 1–4.

1. $\mathbf{r}(t) = t\mathbf{i} + (\ln \cos t)\mathbf{j}, \quad -\pi/2 < t < \pi/2$
2. $\mathbf{r}(t) = (\ln \sec t)\mathbf{i} + t\mathbf{j}, \quad -\pi/2 < t < \pi/2$
3. $\mathbf{r}(t) = (2t + 3)\mathbf{i} + (5 - t^2)\mathbf{j}$
4. $\mathbf{r}(t) = (\cos t + t \sin t)\mathbf{i} + (\sin t - t \cos t)\mathbf{j}, \quad t > 0$
5. **A formula for the curvature of the graph of a function in the *xy*-plane**
   a. The graph $y = f(x)$ in the xy-plane automatically has the parametrization $x = x$, $y = f(x)$, and the vector formula $\mathbf{r}(x) = x\mathbf{i} + f(x)\mathbf{j}$. Use this formula to show that if f is a twice-differentiable function of x, then

$$\kappa(x) = \frac{|f''(x)|}{\left[1 + (f'(x))^2\right]^{3/2}}.$$

   b. Use the formula for κ in part (a) to find the curvature of $y = \ln(\cos x)$, $-\pi/2 < x < \pi/2$. Compare your answer with the answer in Exercise 1.
   c. Show that the curvature is zero at a point of inflection.
6. **A formula for the curvature of a parametrized plane curve**
   a. Show that the curvature of a smooth curve $\mathbf{r}(t) = f(t)\mathbf{i} + g(t)\mathbf{j}$ defined by twice-differentiable functions $x = f(t)$ and $y = g(t)$ is given by the formula

$$\kappa = \frac{|\dot{x}\ddot{y} - \dot{y}\ddot{x}|}{(\dot{x}^2 + \dot{y}^2)^{3/2}}.$$

   Apply the formula to find the curvatures of the following curves.
   b. $\mathbf{r}(t) = t\mathbf{i} + (\ln \sin t)\mathbf{j}, \quad 0 < t < \pi$
   c. $\mathbf{r}(t) = [\tan^{-1}(\sinh t)]\mathbf{i} + (\ln \cosh t)\mathbf{j}.$
7. **Normals to plane curves**
   a. Show that $\mathbf{n}(t) = -g'(t)\mathbf{i} + f'(t)\mathbf{j}$ and $-\mathbf{n}(t) = g'(t)\mathbf{i} - f'(t)\mathbf{j}$ are both normal to the curve $\mathbf{r}(t) = f(t)\mathbf{i} + g(t)\mathbf{j}$ at the point $(f(t), g(t))$.

   To obtain **N** for a particular plane curve, we can choose the one of **n** or $-$**n** from part (a) that points toward the concave side of the curve, and make it into a unit vector. (See Figure 13.21.) Apply this method to find **N** for the following curves.
   b. $\mathbf{r}(t) = t\mathbf{i} + e^{2t}\mathbf{j}$
   c. $\mathbf{r}(t) = \sqrt{4 - t^2}\,\mathbf{i} + t\mathbf{j}, \quad -2 \le t \le 2$
8. (*Continuation of Exercise 7.*)
   a. Use the method of Exercise 7 to find **N** for the curve $\mathbf{r}(t) = t\mathbf{i} + (1/3)t^3\mathbf{j}$ when $t < 0$; when $t > 0$.
   b. Calculate

$$\mathbf{N} = \frac{d\mathbf{T}/dt}{|d\mathbf{T}/dt|}, \quad t \ne 0,$$

   for the curve in part (a). Does **N** exist at $t = 0$? Graph the curve and explain what is happening to **N** as t passes from negative to positive values.

Space Curves

Find **T**, **N**, and κ for the space curves in Exercises 9–16.

9. $\mathbf{r}(t) = (3 \sin t)\mathbf{i} + (3 \cos t)\mathbf{j} + 4t\mathbf{k}$
10. $\mathbf{r}(t) = (\cos t + t \sin t)\mathbf{i} + (\sin t - t \cos t)\mathbf{j} + 3\mathbf{k}$
11. $\mathbf{r}(t) = (e^t \cos t)\mathbf{i} + (e^t \sin t)\mathbf{j} + 2\mathbf{k}$
12. $\mathbf{r}(t) = (6 \sin 2t)\mathbf{i} + (6 \cos 2t)\mathbf{j} + 5t\mathbf{k}$
13. $\mathbf{r}(t) = (t^3/3)\mathbf{i} + (t^2/2)\mathbf{j}, \quad t > 0$
14. $\mathbf{r}(t) = (\cos^3 t)\mathbf{i} + (\sin^3 t)\mathbf{j}, \quad 0 < t < \pi/2$
15. $\mathbf{r}(t) = t\mathbf{i} + (a \cosh(t/a))\mathbf{j}, \quad a > 0$
16. $\mathbf{r}(t) = (\cosh t)\mathbf{i} - (\sinh t)\mathbf{j} + t\mathbf{k}$

More on Curvature

17. Show that the parabola $y = ax^2$, $a \ne 0$, has its largest curvature at its vertex and has no minimum curvature. (*Note:* Since the curvature of a curve remains the same if the curve is translated or rotated, this result is true for any parabola.)
18. Show that the ellipse $x = a \cos t$, $y = b \sin t$, $a > b > 0$, has its largest curvature on its major axis and its smallest curvature on its minor axis. (As in Exercise 17, the same is true for any ellipse.)
19. **Maximizing the curvature of a helix** In Example 5, we found the curvature of the helix $\mathbf{r}(t) = (a \cos t)\mathbf{i} + (a \sin t)\mathbf{j} + bt\mathbf{k}$ $(a, b \ge 0)$ to be $\kappa = a/(a^2 + b^2)$. What is the largest value κ can have for a given value of b? Give reasons for your answer.
20. **Total curvature** We find the **total curvature** of the portion of a smooth curve that runs from $s = s_0$ to $s = s_1 > s_0$ by integrating κ from s_0 to s_1. If the curve has some other parameter, say t, then the total curvature is

$$K = \int_{s_0}^{s_1} \kappa\, ds = \int_{t_0}^{t_1} \kappa \frac{ds}{dt}\, dt = \int_{t_0}^{t_1} \kappa |\mathbf{v}|\, dt,$$

   where t_0 and t_1 correspond to s_0 and s_1. Find the total curvatures of
   a. The portion of the helix $\mathbf{r}(t) = (3 \cos t)\mathbf{i} + (3 \sin t)\mathbf{j} + t\mathbf{k}$, $0 \le t \le 4\pi$.
   b. The parabola $y = x^2$, $-\infty < x < \infty$.
21. Find an equation for the circle of curvature of the curve $\mathbf{r}(t) = t\mathbf{i} + (\sin t)\mathbf{j}$ at the point $(\pi/2, 1)$. (The curve parametrizes the graph of $y = \sin x$ in the xy-plane.)

22. Find an equation for the circle of curvature of the curve $\mathbf{r}(t) = (2 \ln t)\mathbf{i} - [t + (1/t)]\mathbf{j}, e^{-2} \le t \le e^2$, at the point $(0, -2)$, where $t = 1$.

T Grapher Explorations

The formula

$$\kappa(x) = \frac{|f''(x)|}{\left[1 + (f'(x))^2\right]^{3/2}},$$

derived in Exercise 5, expresses the curvature $\kappa(x)$ of a twice-differentiable plane curve $y = f(x)$ as a function of x. Find the curvature function of each of the curves in Exercises 23–26. Then graph $f(x)$ together with $\kappa(x)$ over the given interval. You will find some surprises.

23. $y = x^2, \quad -2 \le x \le 2$ **24.** $y = x^4/4, \quad -2 \le x \le 2$

25. $y = \sin x, \quad 0 \le x \le 2\pi$ **26.** $y = e^x, \quad -1 \le x \le 2$

COMPUTER EXPLORATIONS

Circles of Curvature

In Exercises 27–34 you will use a CAS to explore the osculating circle at a point P on a plane curve where $\kappa \ne 0$. Use a CAS to perform the following steps:

a. Plot the plane curve given in parametric or function form over the specified interval to see what it looks like.

b. Calculate the curvature κ of the curve at the given value t_0 using the appropriate formula from Exercise 5 or 6. Use the parametrization $x = t$ and $y = f(t)$ if the curve is given as a function $y = f(x)$.

c. Find the unit normal vector $\mathbf{N}$ at t_0. Notice that the signs of the components of $\mathbf{N}$ depend on whether the unit tangent vector $\mathbf{T}$ is turning clockwise or counterclockwise at $t = t_0$. (See Exercise 7.)

d. If $\mathbf{C} = a\mathbf{i} + b\mathbf{j}$ is the vector from the origin to the center (a, b) of the osculating circle, find the center $\mathbf{C}$ from the vector equation

$$\mathbf{C} = \mathbf{r}(t_0) + \frac{1}{\kappa(t_0)}\mathbf{N}(t_0).$$

The point $P(x_0, y_0)$ on the curve is given by the position vector $\mathbf{r}(t_0)$.

e. Plot implicitly the equation $(x - a)^2 + (y - b)^2 = 1/\kappa^2$ of the osculating circle. Then plot the curve and osculating circle together. You may need to experiment with the size of the viewing window, but be sure it is square.

27. $\mathbf{r}(t) = (3 \cos t)\mathbf{i} + (5 \sin t)\mathbf{j}, \quad 0 \le t \le 2\pi, \quad t_0 = \pi/4$

28. $\mathbf{r}(t) = (\cos^3 t)\mathbf{i} + (\sin^3 t)\mathbf{j}, \quad 0 \le t \le 2\pi, \quad t_0 = \pi/4$

29. $\mathbf{r}(t) = t^2\mathbf{i} + (t^3 - 3t)\mathbf{j}, \quad -4 \le t \le 4, \quad t_0 = 3/5$

30. $\mathbf{r}(t) = (t^3 - 2t^2 - t)\mathbf{i} + \dfrac{3t}{\sqrt{1 + t^2}}\mathbf{j}, \quad -2 \le t \le 5, \quad t_0 = 1$

31. $\mathbf{r}(t) = (2t - \sin t)\mathbf{i} + (2 - 2 \cos t)\mathbf{j}, \quad 0 \le t \le 3\pi, \quad t_0 = 3\pi/2$

32. $\mathbf{r}(t) = (e^{-t} \cos t)\mathbf{i} + (e^{-t} \sin t)\mathbf{j}, \quad 0 \le t \le 6\pi, \quad t_0 = \pi/4$

33. $y = x^2 - x, \quad -2 \le x \le 5, \quad x_0 = 1$

34. $y = x(1 - x)^{2/5}, \quad -1 \le x \le 2, \quad x_0 = 1/2$

13.5 Torsion and the Unit Binormal Vector B

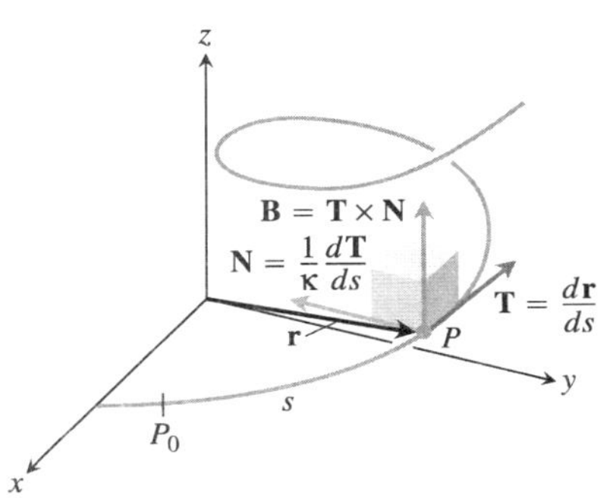

FIGURE 13.25 The **TNB** frame of mutually orthogonal unit vectors traveling along a curve in space.

If you are traveling along a space curve, the Cartesian **i**, **j**, and **k** coordinate system for representing the vectors describing your motion are not truly relevant to you. What is meaningful instead are the vectors representative of your forward direction (the unit tangent vector **T**), the direction in which your path is turning (the unit normal vector **N**), and the tendency of your motion to "twist" out of the plane created by these vectors in the direction perpendicular to this plane (defined by the *unit binormal vector* $\mathbf{B} = \mathbf{T} \times \mathbf{N}$). Expressing the acceleration vector along the curve as a linear combination of this **TNB** frame of mutually orthogonal unit vectors traveling with the motion (Figure 13.25) is particularly revealing of the nature of the path and motion along it.

Torsion

The **binormal vector** of a curve in space is $\mathbf{B} = \mathbf{T} \times \mathbf{N}$, a unit vector orthogonal to both **T** and **N** (Figure 13.26). Together **T**, **N**, and **B** define a moving right-handed vector frame that plays a significant role in calculating the paths of particles moving through space. It is

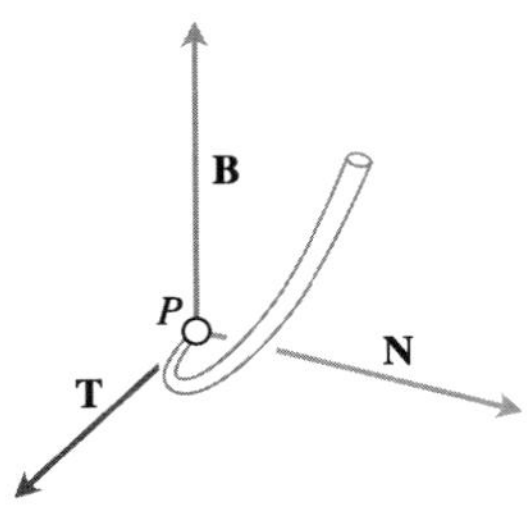

FIGURE 13.26 The vectors **T**, **N**, and **B** (in that order) make a right-handed frame of mutually orthogonal unit vectors in space.

called the **Frenet** ("fre-*nay*") **frame** (after Jean-Frédéric Frenet, 1816–1900), or the **TNB frame**.

How does $d\mathbf{B}/ds$ behave in relation to **T**, **N**, and **B**? From the rule for differentiating a cross product, we have

$$\frac{d\mathbf{B}}{ds} = \frac{d\mathbf{T}}{ds} \times \mathbf{N} + \mathbf{T} \times \frac{d\mathbf{N}}{ds}.$$

Since **N** is the direction of $d\mathbf{T}/ds$, $(d\mathbf{T}/ds) \times \mathbf{N} = \mathbf{0}$ and

$$\frac{d\mathbf{B}}{ds} = \mathbf{0} + \mathbf{T} \times \frac{d\mathbf{N}}{ds} = \mathbf{T} \times \frac{d\mathbf{N}}{ds}.$$

From this we see that $d\mathbf{B}/ds$ is orthogonal to **T** since a cross product is orthogonal to its factors.

Since $d\mathbf{B}/ds$ is also orthogonal to **B** (the latter has constant length), it follows that $d\mathbf{B}/ds$ is orthogonal to the plane of **B** and **T**. In other words, $d\mathbf{B}/ds$ is parallel to **N**, so $d\mathbf{B}/ds$ is a scalar multiple of **N**. In symbols,

$$\frac{d\mathbf{B}}{ds} = -\tau\mathbf{N}.$$

The negative sign in this equation is traditional. The scalar τ is called the *torsion* along the curve. Notice that

$$\frac{d\mathbf{B}}{ds}\cdot\mathbf{N} = -\tau\mathbf{N}\cdot\mathbf{N} = -\tau(1) = -\tau,$$

so that

$$\tau = -\frac{d\mathbf{B}}{ds}\cdot\mathbf{N}.$$

DEFINITION Torsion

Let $\mathbf{B} = \mathbf{T} \times \mathbf{N}$. The **torsion** function of a smooth curve is

$$\tau = -\frac{d\mathbf{B}}{ds}\cdot\mathbf{N}. \qquad (1)$$

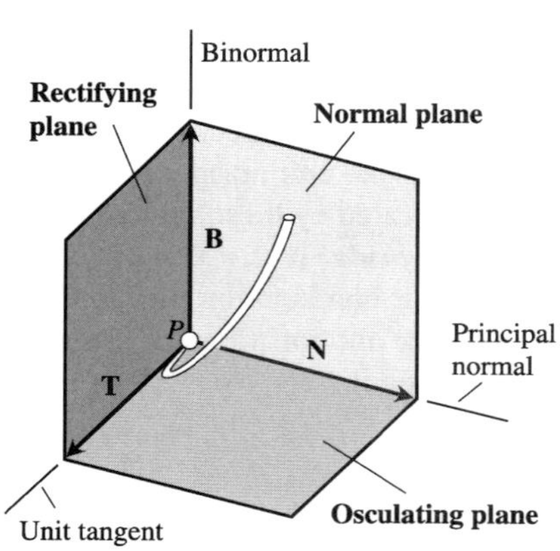

FIGURE 13.27 The names of the three planes determined by **T**, **N**, and **B**.

Unlike the curvature κ, which is never negative, the torsion τ may be positive, negative, or zero.

The three planes determined by **T**, **N**, and **B** are named and shown in Figure 13.27. The curvature $\kappa = |d\mathbf{T}/ds|$ can be thought of as the rate at which the normal plane turns as the point P moves along its path. Similarly, the torsion $\tau = -(d\mathbf{B}/ds)\cdot\mathbf{N}$ is the rate at which the osculating plane turns about **T** as P moves along the curve. Torsion measures how the curve twists.

If we think of the curve as the path of a moving body, then $|d\mathbf{T}/ds|$ tells how much the path turns to the left or right as the object moves along; it is called the *curvature* of the object's path. The number $-(d\mathbf{B}/ds)\cdot\mathbf{N}$ tells how much a body's path rotates or twists out of its plane of motion as the object moves along; it is called the *torsion* of the body's path. Look at Figure 13.28. If P is a train climbing up a curved track, the rate at which the headlight turns from side to side per unit distance is the curvature of the track. The rate at which the engine tends to twist out of the plane formed by **T** and **N** is the torsion.

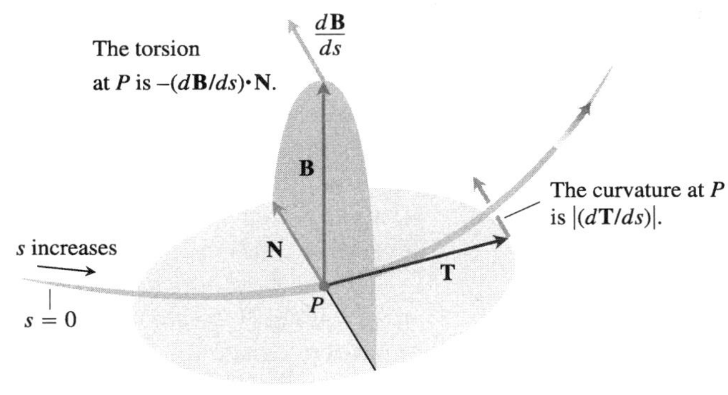

FIGURE 13.28 Every moving body travels with a **TNB** frame that characterizes the geometry of its path of motion.

Tangential and Normal Components of Acceleration

When a body is accelerated by gravity, brakes, a combination of rocket motors, or whatever, we usually want to know how much of the acceleration acts in the direction of motion, in the tangential direction **T**. We can calculate this using the Chain Rule to rewrite **v** as

$$\mathbf{v} = \frac{d\mathbf{r}}{dt} = \frac{d\mathbf{r}}{ds}\frac{ds}{dt} = \mathbf{T}\frac{ds}{dt}$$

and differentiating both ends of this string of equalities to get

$$\begin{aligned}\mathbf{a} &= \frac{d\mathbf{v}}{dt} = \frac{d}{dt}\left(\mathbf{T}\frac{ds}{dt}\right) = \frac{d^2s}{dt^2}\mathbf{T} + \frac{ds}{dt}\frac{d\mathbf{T}}{dt}\\ &= \frac{d^2s}{dt^2}\mathbf{T} + \frac{ds}{dt}\left(\frac{d\mathbf{T}}{ds}\frac{ds}{dt}\right) = \frac{d^2s}{dt^2}\mathbf{T} + \frac{ds}{dt}\left(\kappa\mathbf{N}\frac{ds}{dt}\right) \qquad \frac{d\mathbf{T}}{ds} = \kappa\mathbf{N}\\ &= \frac{d^2s}{dt^2}\mathbf{T} + \kappa\left(\frac{ds}{dt}\right)^2\mathbf{N}.\end{aligned}$$

DEFINITION **Tangential and Normal Components of Acceleration**

$$\mathbf{a} = a_{\mathrm{T}}\mathbf{T} + a_{\mathrm{N}}\mathbf{N}, \tag{2}$$

where

$$a_{\mathrm{T}} = \frac{d^2s}{dt^2} = \frac{d}{dt}|\mathbf{v}| \quad \text{and} \quad a_{\mathrm{N}} = \kappa\left(\frac{ds}{dt}\right)^2 = \kappa|\mathbf{v}|^2 \tag{3}$$

are the **tangential** and **normal** scalar components of acceleration.

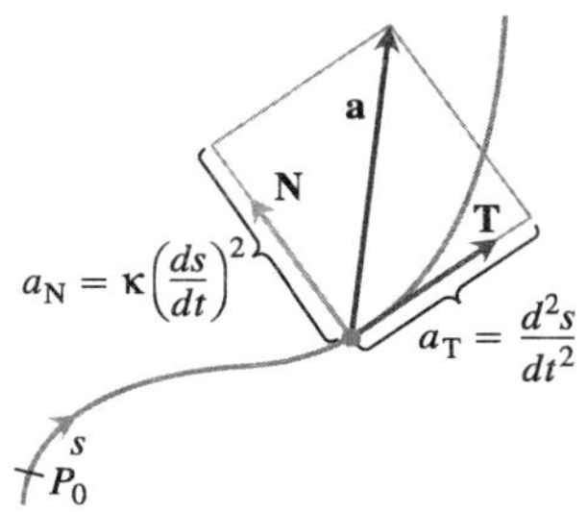

FIGURE 13.29 The tangential and normal components of acceleration. The acceleration **a** always lies in the plane of **T** and **N**, orthogonal to **B**.

Notice that the binormal vector **B** does not appear in Equation (2). No matter how the path of the moving body we are watching may appear to twist and turn in space, the acceleration **a** *always lies in the plane of* **T** and **N** orthogonal to **B**. The equation also tells us exactly how much of the acceleration takes place tangent to the motion (d^2s/dt^2) and how much takes place normal to the motion $[\kappa(ds/dt)^2]$ (Figure 13.29).

What information can we glean from Equations (3)? By definition, acceleration **a** is the rate of change of velocity **v**, and in general, both the length and direction of **v** change as a body moves along its path. The tangential component of acceleration a_T measures the rate of change of the *length* of **v** (that is, the change in the speed). The normal component of acceleration a_N measures the rate of change of the *direction* of **v**.

Notice that the normal scalar component of the acceleration is the curvature times the *square* of the speed. This explains why you have to hold on when your car makes a sharp (large κ), high-speed (large $|\mathbf{v}|$) turn. If you double the speed of your car, you will experience four times the normal component of acceleration for the same curvature.

If a body moves in a circle at a constant speed, d^2s/dt^2 is zero and all the acceleration points along **N** toward the circle's center. If the body is speeding up or slowing down, **a** has a nonzero tangential component (Figure 13.30).

To calculate a_N, we usually use the formula $a_N = \sqrt{|\mathbf{a}|^2 - a_T^2}$, which comes from solving the equation $|\mathbf{a}|^2 = \mathbf{a}\cdot\mathbf{a} = a_T^2 + a_N^2$ for a_N. With this formula, we can find a_N without having to calculate κ first.

Formula for Calculating the Normal Component of Acceleration

$$a_N = \sqrt{|\mathbf{a}|^2 - a_T^2} \qquad (4)$$

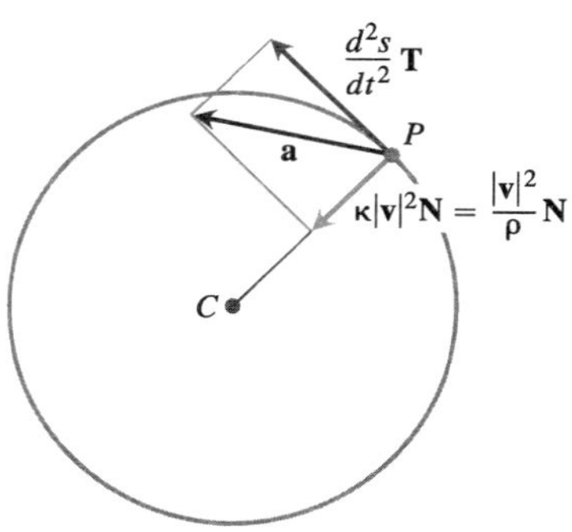

FIGURE 13.30 The tangential and normal components of the acceleration of a body that is speeding up as it moves counterclockwise around a circle of radius ρ.

EXAMPLE 1 Finding the Acceleration Scalar Components a_T, a_N

Without finding **T** and **N**, write the acceleration of the motion

$$\mathbf{r}(t) = (\cos t + t\sin t)\mathbf{i} + (\sin t - t\cos t)\mathbf{j}, \qquad t > 0$$

in the form $\mathbf{a} = a_T\mathbf{T} + a_N\mathbf{N}$. (The path of the motion is the involute of the circle in Figure 13.31.)

Solution We use the first of Equations (3) to find a_T:

$$\mathbf{v} = \frac{d\mathbf{r}}{dt} = (-\sin t + \sin t + t\cos t)\mathbf{i} + (\cos t - \cos t + t\sin t)\mathbf{j}$$
$$= (t\cos t)\mathbf{i} + (t\sin t)\mathbf{j}$$
$$|\mathbf{v}| = \sqrt{t^2\cos^2 t + t^2\sin^2 t} = \sqrt{t^2} = |t| = t \qquad t > 0$$
$$a_T = \frac{d}{dt}|\mathbf{v}| = \frac{d}{dt}(t) = 1. \qquad \text{Equation (3)}$$

Knowing a_T, we use Equation (4) to find a_N:

$$\mathbf{a} = (\cos t - t\sin t)\mathbf{i} + (\sin t + t\cos t)\mathbf{j}$$
$$|\mathbf{a}|^2 = t^2 + 1 \qquad \text{After some algebra}$$
$$a_N = \sqrt{|\mathbf{a}|^2 - a_T^2}$$
$$= \sqrt{(t^2 + 1) - (1)} = \sqrt{t^2} = t.$$

We then use Equation (2) to find **a**:

$$\mathbf{a} = a_{\mathrm{T}}\mathbf{T} + a_{\mathrm{N}}\mathbf{N} = (1)\mathbf{T} + (t)\mathbf{N} = \mathbf{T} + t\mathbf{N}.$$

■

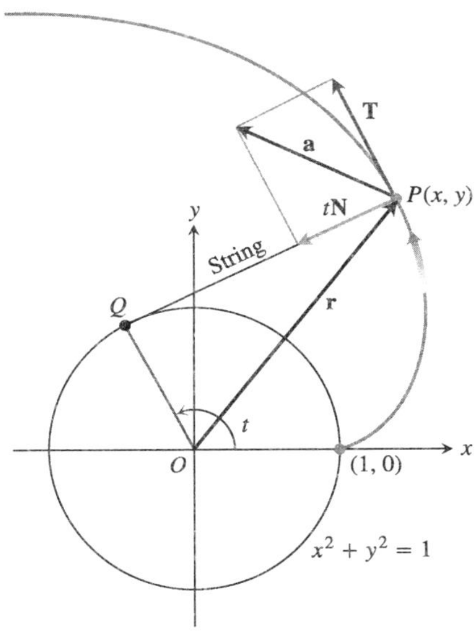

FIGURE 13.31 The tangential and normal components of the acceleration of the motion $\mathbf{r}(t) = (\cos t + t\sin t)\mathbf{i} + (\sin t - t\cos t)\mathbf{j}$, for $t > 0$. If a string wound around a fixed circle is unwound while held taut in the plane of the circle, its end P traces an involute of the circle (Example 1).

Formulas for Computing Curvature and Torsion

We now give some easy-to-use formulas for computing the curvature and torsion of a smooth curve. From Equation (2), we have

$$\begin{aligned}\mathbf{v} \times \mathbf{a} &= \left(\frac{ds}{dt}\mathbf{T}\right) \times \left[\frac{d^2s}{dt^2}\mathbf{T} + \kappa\left(\frac{ds}{dt}\right)^2\mathbf{N}\right] && \mathbf{v} = d\mathbf{r}/dt = (ds/dt)\mathbf{T} \\ &= \left(\frac{ds}{dt}\frac{d^2s}{dt^2}\right)(\mathbf{T} \times \mathbf{T}) + \kappa\left(\frac{ds}{dt}\right)^3(\mathbf{T} \times \mathbf{N}) \\ &= \kappa\left(\frac{ds}{dt}\right)^3\mathbf{B}. && \mathbf{T} \times \mathbf{T} = \mathbf{0} \text{ and } \mathbf{T} \times \mathbf{N} = \mathbf{B}\end{aligned}$$

It follows that

$$|\mathbf{v} \times \mathbf{a}| = \kappa\left|\frac{ds}{dt}\right|^3|\mathbf{B}| = \kappa|\mathbf{v}|^3. \qquad \frac{ds}{dt} = |\mathbf{v}| \text{ and } |\mathbf{B}| = 1$$

Solving for κ gives the following formula.

Vector Formula for Curvature

$$\kappa = \frac{|\mathbf{v} \times \mathbf{a}|}{|\mathbf{v}|^3} \tag{5}$$

Equation (5) calculates the curvature, a geometric property of the curve, from the velocity and acceleration of any vector representation of the curve in which $|\mathbf{v}|$ is different from zero. Take a moment to think about how remarkable this really is: From any formula for motion along a curve, no matter how variable the motion may be (as long as **v** is never zero), we can calculate a physical property of the curve that seems to have nothing to do with the way the curve is traversed.

The most widely used formula for torsion, derived in more advanced texts, is

$$\tau = \frac{\begin{vmatrix} \dot{x} & \dot{y} & \dot{z} \\ \ddot{x} & \ddot{y} & \ddot{z} \\ \dddot{x} & \dddot{y} & \dddot{z} \end{vmatrix}}{|\mathbf{v} \times \mathbf{a}|^2} \qquad (\text{if } \mathbf{v} \times \mathbf{a} \neq \mathbf{0}). \tag{6}$$

Newton's Dot Notation for Derivatives

The dots in Equation (6) denote differentiation with respect to t, one derivative for each dot. Thus, $\dot{x}$ ("x dot") means dx/dt, $\ddot{x}$ ("x double dot") means d^2x/dt^2, and $\dddot{x}$ ("x triple dot") means d^3x/dt^3. Similarly, $\dot{y} = dy/dt$, and so on.

This formula calculates the torsion directly from the derivatives of the component functions $x = f(t), y = g(t), z = h(t)$ that make up $\mathbf{r}$. The determinant's first row comes from $\mathbf{v}$, the second row comes from $\mathbf{a}$, and the third row comes from $\dot{\mathbf{a}} = d\mathbf{a}/dt$.

EXAMPLE 2 Finding Curvature and Torsion

Use Equations (5) and (6) to find κ and τ for the helix

$$\mathbf{r}(t) = (a \cos t)\mathbf{i} + (a \sin t)\mathbf{j} + bt\mathbf{k}, \qquad a, b \geq 0, \qquad a^2 + b^2 \neq 0.$$

Solution We calculate the curvature with Equation (5):

$$\mathbf{v} = -(a \sin t)\mathbf{i} + (a \cos t)\mathbf{j} + b\mathbf{k}$$

$$\mathbf{a} = -(a \cos t)\mathbf{i} - (a \sin t)\mathbf{j}$$

$$\mathbf{v} \times \mathbf{a} = \begin{vmatrix} \mathbf{i} & \mathbf{j} & \mathbf{k} \\ -a \sin t & a \cos t & b \\ -a \cos t & -a \sin t & 0 \end{vmatrix}$$

$$= (ab \sin t)\mathbf{i} - (ab \cos t)\mathbf{j} + a^2\mathbf{k}$$

$$\kappa = \frac{|\mathbf{v} \times \mathbf{a}|}{|\mathbf{v}|^3} = \frac{\sqrt{a^2b^2 + a^4}}{(a^2 + b^2)^{3/2}} = \frac{a\sqrt{a^2 + b^2}}{(a^2 + b^2)^{3/2}} = \frac{a}{a^2 + b^2}. \tag{7}$$

Notice that Equation (7) agrees with the result in Example 5 in Section 13.4, where we calculated the curvature directly from its definition.

To evaluate Equation (6) for the torsion, we find the entries in the determinant by differentiating $\mathbf{r}$ with respect to t. We already have $\mathbf{v}$ and $\mathbf{a}$, and

$$\dot{\mathbf{a}} = \frac{d\mathbf{a}}{dt} = (a \sin t)\mathbf{i} - (a \cos t)\mathbf{j}.$$

Hence,

$$\tau = \frac{\begin{vmatrix} \dot{x} & \dot{y} & \dot{z} \\ \ddot{x} & \ddot{y} & \ddot{z} \\ \dddot{x} & \dddot{y} & \dddot{z} \end{vmatrix}}{|\mathbf{v} \times \mathbf{a}|^2} = \frac{\begin{vmatrix} -a \sin t & a \cos t & b \\ -a \cos t & -a \sin t & 0 \\ a \sin t & -a \cos t & 0 \end{vmatrix}}{\left(a\sqrt{a^2 + b^2}\right)^2}$$

Value of $|\mathbf{v} \times \mathbf{a}|$ from Equation (7)

$$= \frac{b(a^2 \cos^2 t + a^2 \sin^2 t)}{a^2(a^2 + b^2)}$$

$$= \frac{b}{a^2 + b^2}.$$

From this last equation we see that the torsion of a helix about a circular cylinder is constant. In fact, constant curvature and constant torsion characterize the helix among all curves in space. ■

Formulas for Curves in Space

Unit tangent vector:	$\mathbf{T} = \dfrac{\mathbf{v}}{\lvert\mathbf{v}\rvert}$
Principal unit normal vector:	$\mathbf{N} = \dfrac{d\mathbf{T}/dt}{\lvert d\mathbf{T}/dt\rvert}$
Binormal vector:	$\mathbf{B} = \mathbf{T} \times \mathbf{N}$
Curvature:	$\kappa = \left\lvert \dfrac{d\mathbf{T}}{ds} \right\rvert = \dfrac{\lvert \mathbf{v} \times \mathbf{a} \rvert}{\lvert\mathbf{v}\rvert^3}$
Torsion:	$\tau = -\dfrac{d\mathbf{B}}{ds} \cdot \mathbf{N} = \dfrac{\begin{vmatrix} \dot{x} & \dot{y} & \dot{z} \\ \ddot{x} & \ddot{y} & \ddot{z} \\ \dddot{x} & \dddot{y} & \dddot{z} \end{vmatrix}}{\lvert \mathbf{v} \times \mathbf{a} \rvert^2}$
Tangential and normal scalar components of acceleration:	$\mathbf{a} = a_{\mathrm{T}}\mathbf{T} + a_{\mathrm{N}}\mathbf{N}$ $a_{\mathrm{T}} = \dfrac{d}{dt}\lvert\mathbf{v}\rvert$ $a_{\mathrm{N}} = \kappa\lvert\mathbf{v}\rvert^2 = \sqrt{\lvert\mathbf{a}\rvert^2 - a_{\mathrm{T}}^2}$

EXERCISES 13.5

Finding Torsion and the Binormal Vector

For Exercises 1–8 you found **T**, **N**, and κ in Section 13.4 (Exercises 9–16). Find now **B** and τ for these space curves.

1. $\mathbf{r}(t) = (3\sin t)\mathbf{i} + (3\cos t)\mathbf{j} + 4t\mathbf{k}$
2. $\mathbf{r}(t) = (\cos t + t\sin t)\mathbf{i} + (\sin t - t\cos t)\mathbf{j} + 3\mathbf{k}$
3. $\mathbf{r}(t) = (e^t\cos t)\mathbf{i} + (e^t\sin t)\mathbf{j} + 2\mathbf{k}$
4. $\mathbf{r}(t) = (6\sin 2t)\mathbf{i} + (6\cos 2t)\mathbf{j} + 5t\mathbf{k}$
5. $\mathbf{r}(t) = (t^3/3)\mathbf{i} + (t^2/2)\mathbf{j}, \quad t > 0$
6. $\mathbf{r}(t) = (\cos^3 t)\mathbf{i} + (\sin^3 t)\mathbf{j}, \quad 0 < t < \pi/2$
7. $\mathbf{r}(t) = t\mathbf{i} + (a\cosh(t/a))\mathbf{j}, \quad a > 0$
8. $\mathbf{r}(t) = (\cosh t)\mathbf{i} - (\sinh t)\mathbf{j} + t\mathbf{k}$

Tangential and Normal Components of Acceleration

In Exercises 9 and 10, write **a** in the form $a_{\mathrm{T}}\mathbf{T} + a_{\mathrm{N}}\mathbf{N}$ without finding **T** and **N**.

9. $\mathbf{r}(t) = (a\cos t)\mathbf{i} + (a\sin t)\mathbf{j} + bt\mathbf{k}$
10. $\mathbf{r}(t) = (1 + 3t)\mathbf{i} + (t - 2)\mathbf{j} - 3t\mathbf{k}$

In Exercises 11–14, write **a** in the form $\mathbf{a} = a_{\mathrm{T}}\mathbf{T} + a_{\mathrm{N}}\mathbf{N}$ at the given value of t without finding **T** and **N**.

11. $\mathbf{r}(t) = (t + 1)\mathbf{i} + 2t\mathbf{j} + t^2\mathbf{k}, \quad t = 1$
12. $\mathbf{r}(t) = (t\cos t)\mathbf{i} + (t\sin t)\mathbf{j} + t^2\mathbf{k}, \quad t = 0$
13. $\mathbf{r}(t) = t^2\mathbf{i} + (t + (1/3)t^3)\mathbf{j} + (t - (1/3)t^3)\mathbf{k}, \quad t = 0$
14. $\mathbf{r}(t) = (e^t\cos t)\mathbf{i} + (e^t\sin t)\mathbf{j} + \sqrt{2}e^t\mathbf{k}, \quad t = 0$

In Exercises 15 and 16, find **r**, **T**, **N**, and **B** at the given value of t. Then find equations for the osculating, normal, and rectifying planes at that value of t.

15. $\mathbf{r}(t) = (\cos t)\mathbf{i} + (\sin t)\mathbf{j} - \mathbf{k}, \quad t = \pi/4$
16. $\mathbf{r}(t) = (\cos t)\mathbf{i} + (\sin t)\mathbf{j} + t\mathbf{k}, \quad t = 0$

Physical Applications

17. The speedometer on your car reads a steady 35 mph. Could you be accelerating? Explain.
18. Can anything be said about the acceleration of a particle that is moving at a constant speed? Give reasons for your answer.
19. Can anything be said about the speed of a particle whose acceleration is always orthogonal to its velocity? Give reasons for your answer.

20. An object of mass m travels along the parabola $y = x^2$ with a constant speed of 10 units/sec. What is the force on the object due to its acceleration at (0, 0)? at $(2^{1/2}, 2)$? Write your answers in terms of **i** and **j**. (Remember Newton's law, $\mathbf{F} = m\mathbf{a}$.)

21. The following is a quotation from an article in *The American Mathematical Monthly*, titled "Curvature in the Eighties" by Robert Osserman (October 1990, page 731):

> Curvature also plays a key role in physics. The magnitude of a force required to move an object at constant speed along a curved path is, according to Newton's laws, a constant multiple of the curvature of the trajectories.

Explain mathematically why the second sentence of the quotation is true.

22. Show that a moving particle will move in a straight line if the normal component of its acceleration is zero.

23. A sometime shortcut to curvature If you already know $|a_N|$ and $|\mathbf{v}|$, then the formula $a_N = \kappa|\mathbf{v}|^2$ gives a convenient way to find the curvature. Use it to find the curvature and radius of curvature of the curve

$$\mathbf{r}(t) = (\cos t + t\sin t)\mathbf{i} + (\sin t - t\cos t)\mathbf{j}, \quad t > 0.$$

(Take a_N and $|\mathbf{v}|$ from Example 1.)

24. Show that κ and τ are both zero for the line

$$\mathbf{r}(t) = (x_0 + At)\mathbf{i} + (y_0 + Bt)\mathbf{j} + (z_0 + Ct)\mathbf{k}.$$

Theory and Examples

25. What can be said about the torsion of a smooth plane curve $\mathbf{r}(t) = f(t)\mathbf{i} + g(t)\mathbf{j}$? Give reasons for your answer.

26. The torsion of a helix In Example 2, we found the torsion of the helix

$$\mathbf{r}(t) = (a\cos t)\mathbf{i} + (a\sin t)\mathbf{j} + bt\mathbf{k}, \quad a, b \geq 0$$

to be $\tau = b/(a^2 + b^2)$. What is the largest value τ can have for a given value of a? Give reasons for your answer.

27. Differentiable curves with zero torsion lie in planes That a sufficiently differentiable curve with zero torsion lies in a plane is a special case of the fact that a particle whose velocity remains perpendicular to a fixed vector **C** moves in a plane perpendicular to **C**. This, in turn, can be viewed as the solution of the following problem in calculus.

Suppose $\mathbf{r}(t) = f(t)\mathbf{i} + g(t)\mathbf{j} + h(t)\mathbf{k}$ is twice differentiable for all t in an interval $[a, b]$, that $\mathbf{r} = 0$ when $t = a$, and that $\mathbf{v}\cdot\mathbf{k} = 0$ for all t in $[a, b]$. Then $h(t) = 0$ for all t in $[a, b]$.

Solve this problem. (*Hint:* Start with $\mathbf{a} = d^2\mathbf{r}/dt^2$ and apply the initial conditions in reverse order.)

28. A formula that calculates τ from B and v If we start with the definition $\tau = -(d\mathbf{B}/ds)\cdot\mathbf{N}$ and apply the Chain Rule to rewrite $d\mathbf{B}/ds$ as

$$\frac{d\mathbf{B}}{ds} = \frac{d\mathbf{B}}{dt}\frac{dt}{ds} = \frac{d\mathbf{B}}{dt}\frac{1}{|\mathbf{v}|},$$

we arrive at the formula

$$\tau = -\frac{1}{|\mathbf{v}|}\left(\frac{d\mathbf{B}}{dt}\cdot\mathbf{N}\right).$$

The advantage of this formula over Equation (6) is that it is easier to derive and state. The disadvantage is that it can take a lot of work to evaluate without a computer. Use the new formula to find the torsion of the helix in Example 2.

COMPUTER EXPLORATIONS

Curvature, Torsion, and the TNB Frame

Rounding the answers to four decimal places, use a CAS to find **v**, **a**, speed, **T**, **N**, **B**, κ, τ, and the tangential and normal components of acceleration for the curves in Exercises 29–32 at the given values of t.

29. $\mathbf{r}(t) = (t\cos t)\mathbf{i} + (t\sin t)\mathbf{j} + t\mathbf{k}, \quad t = \sqrt{3}$

30. $\mathbf{r}(t) = (e^t\cos t)\mathbf{i} + (e^t\sin t)\mathbf{j} + e^t\mathbf{k}, \quad t = \ln 2$

31. $\mathbf{r}(t) = (t - \sin t)\mathbf{i} + (1 - \cos t)\mathbf{j} + \sqrt{-t}\,\mathbf{k}, \quad t = -3\pi$

32. $\mathbf{r}(t) = (3t - t^2)\mathbf{i} + (3t^2)\mathbf{j} + (3t + t^3)\mathbf{k}, \quad t = 1$

13.6 Planetary Motion and Satellites

In this section, we derive Kepler's laws of planetary motion from Newton's laws of motion and gravitation and discuss the orbits of Earth satellites. The derivation of Kepler's laws from Newton's is one of the triumphs of calculus. It draws on almost everything we have studied so far, including the algebra and geometry of vectors in space, the calculus of vector functions, the solutions of differential equations and initial value problems, and the polar coordinate description of conic sections.

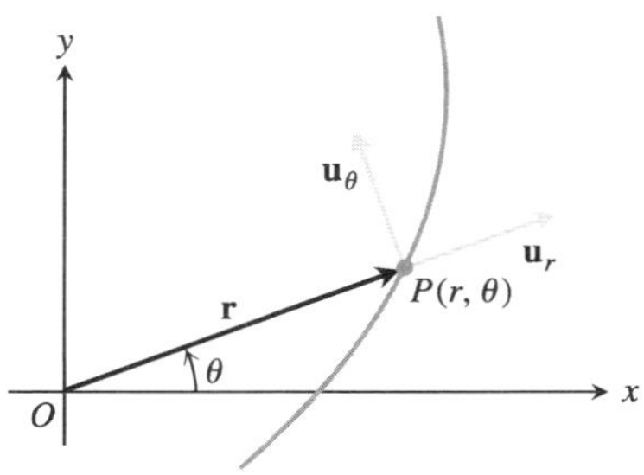

FIGURE 13.32 The length of $\mathbf{r}$ is the positive polar coordinate r of the point P. Thus, $\mathbf{u}_r$, which is $\mathbf{r}/|\mathbf{r}|$, is also $\mathbf{r}/r$. Equations (1) express $\mathbf{u}_r$ and $\mathbf{u}_\theta$ in terms of $\mathbf{i}$ and $\mathbf{j}$.

Motion in Polar and Cylindrical Coordinates

When a particle moves along a curve in the polar coordinate plane, we express its position, velocity, and acceleration in terms of the moving unit vectors

$$\mathbf{u}_r = (\cos\theta)\mathbf{i} + (\sin\theta)\mathbf{j}, \qquad \mathbf{u}_\theta = -(\sin\theta)\mathbf{i} + (\cos\theta)\mathbf{j}, \tag{1}$$

shown in Figure 13.32. The vector $\mathbf{u}_r$ points along the position vector $\overrightarrow{OP}$, so $\mathbf{r} = r\mathbf{u}_r$. The vector $\mathbf{u}_\theta$, orthogonal to $\mathbf{u}_r$, points in the direction of increasing θ.

We find from Equations (1) that

$$\begin{aligned}\frac{d\mathbf{u}_r}{d\theta} &= -(\sin\theta)\mathbf{i} + (\cos\theta)\mathbf{j} = \mathbf{u}_\theta \\ \frac{d\mathbf{u}_\theta}{d\theta} &= -(\cos\theta)\mathbf{i} - (\sin\theta)\mathbf{j} = -\mathbf{u}_r.\end{aligned} \tag{2}$$

When we differentiate $\mathbf{u}_r$ and $\mathbf{u}_\theta$ with respect to t to find how they change with time, the Chain Rule gives

$$\dot{\mathbf{u}}_r = \frac{d\mathbf{u}_r}{d\theta}\dot{\theta} = \dot{\theta}\mathbf{u}_\theta, \qquad \dot{\mathbf{u}}_\theta = \frac{d\mathbf{u}_\theta}{d\theta}\dot{\theta} = -\dot{\theta}\mathbf{u}_r. \tag{3}$$

Hence,

$$\mathbf{v} = \dot{\mathbf{r}} = \frac{d}{dt}\left(r\mathbf{u}_r\right) = \dot{r}\mathbf{u}_r + r\dot{\mathbf{u}}_r = \dot{r}\mathbf{u}_r + r\dot{\theta}\mathbf{u}_\theta. \tag{4}$$

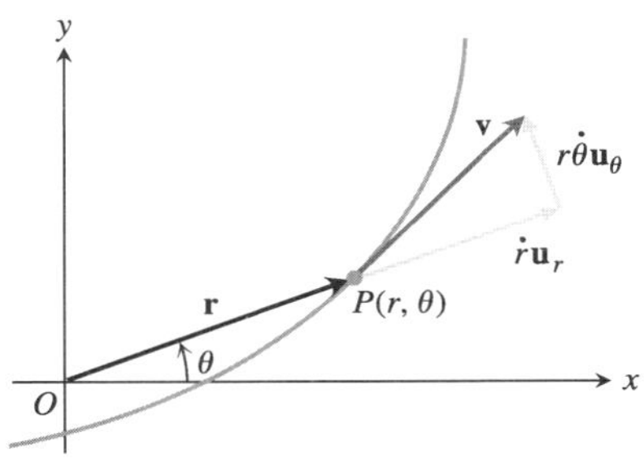

FIGURE 13.33 In polar coordinates, the velocity vector is

$$\mathbf{v} = \dot{r}\mathbf{u}_r + r\dot{\theta}\mathbf{u}_\theta$$

See Figure 13.33. As in the previous section, we use Newton's dot notation for time derivatives to keep the formulas as simple as we can: $\dot{\mathbf{u}}_r$ means $d\mathbf{u}_r/dt$, $\dot{\theta}$ means $d\theta/dt$, and so on.

The acceleration is

$$\mathbf{a} = \dot{\mathbf{v}} = (\ddot{r}\mathbf{u}_r + \dot{r}\dot{\mathbf{u}}_r) + (\dot{r}\dot{\theta}\mathbf{u}_\theta + r\ddot{\theta}\mathbf{u}_\theta + r\dot{\theta}\dot{\mathbf{u}}_\theta). \tag{5}$$

When Equations (3) are used to evaluate $\dot{\mathbf{u}}_r$ and $\dot{\mathbf{u}}_\theta$ and the components are separated, the equation for acceleration becomes

$$\mathbf{a} = (\ddot{r} - r\dot{\theta}^2)\mathbf{u}_r + (r\ddot{\theta} + 2\dot{r}\dot{\theta})\mathbf{u}_\theta. \tag{6}$$

To extend these equations of motion to space, we add $z\mathbf{k}$ to the right-hand side of the equation $\mathbf{r} = r\mathbf{u}_r$. Then, in these *cylindrical coordinates*,

Notice that $|\mathbf{r}| \neq r$ if $z \neq 0$.

$$\begin{aligned}\mathbf{r} &= r\mathbf{u}_r + z\mathbf{k} \\ \mathbf{v} &= \dot{r}\mathbf{u}_r + r\dot{\theta}\mathbf{u}_\theta + \dot{z}\mathbf{k} \\ \mathbf{a} &= (\ddot{r} - r\dot{\theta}^2)\mathbf{u}_r + (r\ddot{\theta} + 2\dot{r}\dot{\theta})\mathbf{u}_\theta + \ddot{z}\mathbf{k}.\end{aligned} \tag{7}$$

The vectors $\mathbf{u}_r$, $\mathbf{u}_\theta$, and $\mathbf{k}$ make a right-handed frame (Figure 13.34) in which

$$\mathbf{u}_r \times \mathbf{u}_\theta = \mathbf{k}, \qquad \mathbf{u}_\theta \times \mathbf{k} = \mathbf{u}_r, \qquad \mathbf{k} \times \mathbf{u}_r = \mathbf{u}_\theta. \tag{8}$$

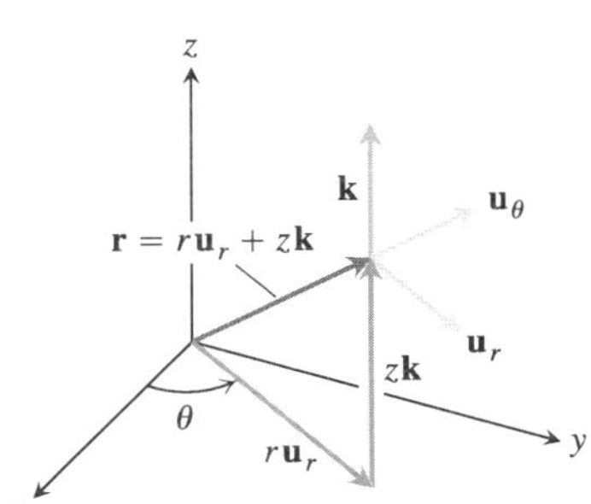

FIGURE 13.34 Position vector and basic unit vectors in cylindrical coordinates.

Planets Move in Planes

Newton's law of gravitation says that if $\mathbf{r}$ is the radius vector from the center of a sun of mass M to the center of a planet of mass m, then the force $\mathbf{F}$ of the gravitational attraction between the planet and sun is

$$\mathbf{F} = -\frac{GmM}{|\mathbf{r}|^2}\frac{\mathbf{r}}{|\mathbf{r}|} \tag{9}$$

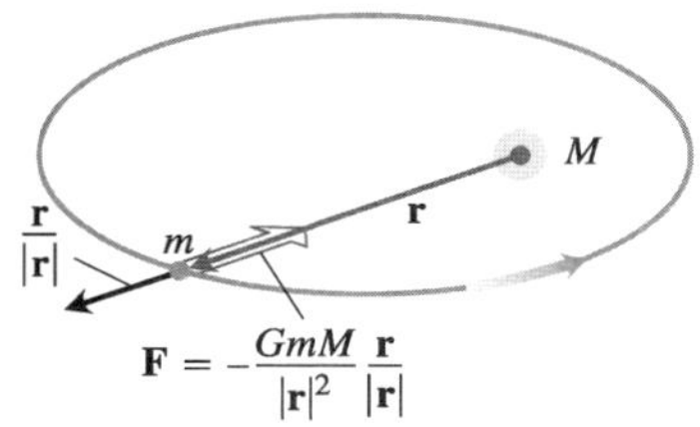

FIGURE 13.35 The force of gravity is directed along the line joining the centers of mass.

(Figure 13.35). The number G is the **universal gravitational constant.** If we measure mass in kilograms, force in newtons, and distance in meters, G is about $6.6726 \times 10^{-11}\ \mathrm{Nm^2\,kg^{-2}}$.

Combining Equation (9) with Newton's second law, $\mathbf{F} = m\ddot{\mathbf{r}}$, for the force acting on the planet gives

$$m\ddot{\mathbf{r}} = -\frac{GmM}{|\mathbf{r}|^2}\frac{\mathbf{r}}{|\mathbf{r}|},$$

$$\ddot{\mathbf{r}} = -\frac{GM}{|\mathbf{r}|^2}\frac{\mathbf{r}}{|\mathbf{r}|}. \tag{10}$$

The planet is accelerated toward the sun's center at all times.

Equation (10) says that $\ddot{\mathbf{r}}$ is a scalar multiple of $\mathbf{r}$, so that

$$\mathbf{r} \times \ddot{\mathbf{r}} = \mathbf{0}. \tag{11}$$

A routine calculation shows $\mathbf{r} \times \ddot{\mathbf{r}}$ to be the derivative of $\mathbf{r} \times \dot{\mathbf{r}}$:

$$\frac{d}{dt}(\mathbf{r} \times \dot{\mathbf{r}}) = \underbrace{\dot{\mathbf{r}} \times \dot{\mathbf{r}}}_{\mathbf{0}} + \mathbf{r} \times \ddot{\mathbf{r}} = \mathbf{r} \times \ddot{\mathbf{r}}. \tag{12}$$

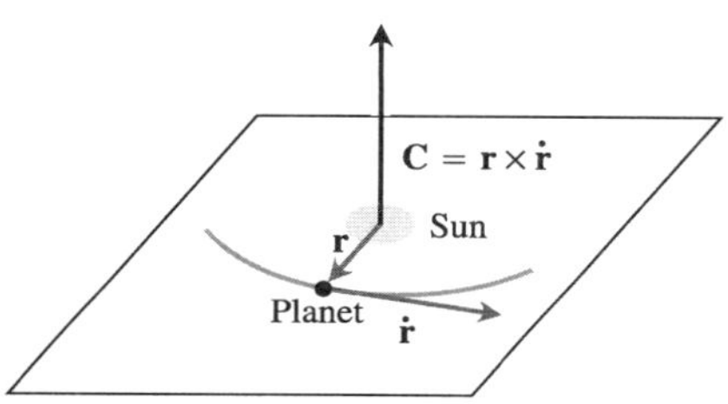

FIGURE 13.36 A planet that obeys Newton's laws of gravitation and motion travels in the plane through the sun's center of mass perpendicular to $\mathbf{C} = \mathbf{r} \times \dot{\mathbf{r}}$.

Hence Equation (11) is equivalent to

$$\frac{d}{dt}(\mathbf{r} \times \dot{\mathbf{r}}) = \mathbf{0}, \tag{13}$$

which integrates to

$$\mathbf{r} \times \dot{\mathbf{r}} = \mathbf{C} \tag{14}$$

for some constant vector $\mathbf{C}$.

Equation (14) tells us that $\mathbf{r}$ and $\dot{\mathbf{r}}$ always lie in a plane perpendicular to $\mathbf{C}$. Hence, the planet moves in a fixed plane through the center of its sun (Figure 13.36).

Coordinates and Initial Conditions

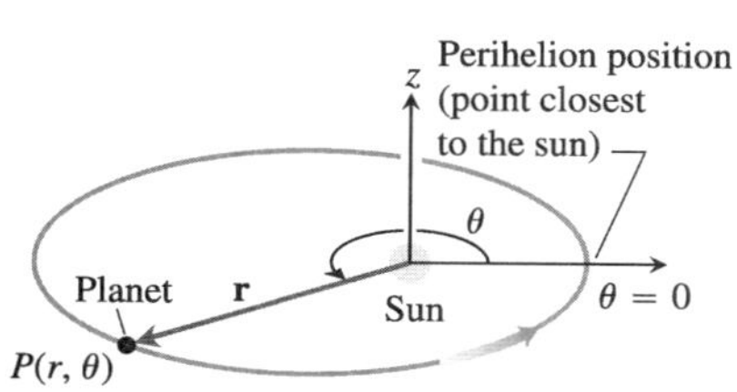

FIGURE 13.37 The coordinate system for planetary motion. The motion is counterclockwise when viewed from above, as it is here, and $\dot{\theta} > 0$.

We now introduce coordinates in a way that places the origin at the sun's center of mass and makes the plane of the planet's motion the polar coordinate plane. This makes $\mathbf{r}$ the planet's polar coordinate position vector and makes $|\mathbf{r}|$ equal to r and $\mathbf{r}/|\mathbf{r}|$ equal to $\mathbf{u}_r$. We also position the z-axis in a way that makes $\mathbf{k}$ the direction of $\mathbf{C}$. Thus, $\mathbf{k}$ has the same right-hand relation to $\mathbf{r} \times \dot{\mathbf{r}}$ that $\mathbf{C}$ does, and the planet's motion is counterclockwise when viewed from the positive z-axis. This makes θ increase with t, so that $\dot{\theta} > 0$ for all t. Finally, we rotate the polar coordinate plane about the z-axis, if necessary, to make the initial ray coincide with the direction $\mathbf{r}$ has when the planet is closest to the sun. This runs the ray through the planet's **perihelion** position (Figure 13.37).

If we measure time so that $t = 0$ at perihelion, we have the following initial conditions for the planet's motion.

1. $r = r_0$, the minimum radius, when $t = 0$
2. $\dot{r} = 0$ when $t = 0$ (because r has a minimum value then)
3. $\theta = 0$ when $t = 0$
4. $|\mathbf{v}| = v_0$ when $t = 0$

Since

$$
\begin{aligned}
v_0 &= |\mathbf{v}|_{t=0} \\
&= |\dot{r}\mathbf{u}_r + r\dot{\theta}\mathbf{u}_\theta|_{t=0} && \text{Equation (4)} \\
&= |r\dot{\theta}\mathbf{u}_\theta|_{t=0} && \dot{r} = 0 \text{ when } t = 0 \\
&= (|r\dot{\theta}||\mathbf{u}_\theta|)_{t=0} \\
&= |r\dot{\theta}|_{t=0} && |\mathbf{u}_\theta| = 1 \\
&= (r\dot{\theta})_{t=0}, && r \text{ and } \dot{\theta} \text{ both positive}
\end{aligned}
$$

we also know that

5. $r\dot{\theta} = v_0$ when $t = 0$.

HISTORICAL BIOGRAPHY

Johannes Kepler (1571–1630)

Kepler's First Law (The Conic Section Law)

Kepler's first law says that a planet's path is a conic section with the sun at one focus. The eccentricity of the conic is

$$e = \frac{r_0 v_0^2}{GM} - 1 \tag{15}$$

and the polar equation is

$$r = \frac{(1 + e)r_0}{1 + e\cos\theta}. \tag{16}$$

The derivation uses Kepler's second law, so we will state and prove the second law before proving the first law.

Kepler's Second Law (The Equal Area Law)

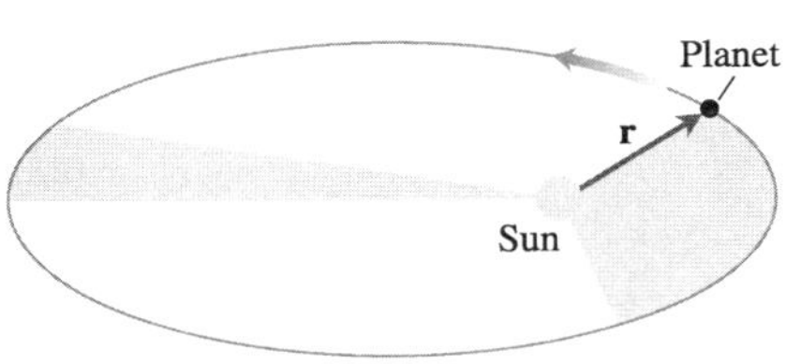

FIGURE 13.38 The line joining a planet to its sun sweeps over equal areas in equal times.

Kepler's second law says that the radius vector from the sun to a planet (the vector $\mathbf{r}$ in our model) sweeps out equal areas in equal times (Figure 13.38). To derive the law, we use Equation (4) to evaluate the cross product $\mathbf{C} = \mathbf{r} \times \dot{\mathbf{r}}$ from Equation (14):

$$
\begin{aligned}
\mathbf{C} &= \mathbf{r} \times \dot{\mathbf{r}} = \mathbf{r} \times \mathbf{v} \\
&= r\mathbf{u}_r \times (\dot{r}\mathbf{u}_r + r\dot{\theta}\mathbf{u}_\theta) && \text{Equation (4)} \\
&= r\dot{r}\underbrace{(\mathbf{u}_r \times \mathbf{u}_r)}_{\mathbf{0}} + r(r\dot{\theta})\underbrace{(\mathbf{u}_r \times \mathbf{u}_\theta)}_{\mathbf{k}} \\
&= r(r\dot{\theta})\mathbf{k}.
\end{aligned} \tag{17}
$$

Setting t equal to zero shows that

$$\mathbf{C} = [r(r\dot{\theta})]_{t=0}\,\mathbf{k} = r_0 v_0 \mathbf{k}. \tag{18}$$

Substituting this value for $\mathbf{C}$ in Equation (17) gives

$$r_0 v_0 \mathbf{k} = r^2\dot{\theta}\mathbf{k}, \quad \text{or} \quad r^2\dot{\theta} = r_0 v_0. \tag{19}$$

This is where the area comes in. The area differential in polar coordinates is

$$dA = \frac{1}{2}r^2\,d\theta$$

(Section 10.7). Accordingly, dA/dt has the constant value

$$\frac{dA}{dt} = \frac{1}{2}r^2\dot{\theta} = \frac{1}{2}r_0 v_0. \tag{20}$$

So dA/dt is constant, giving Kepler's second law.

For Earth, r_0 is about 150,000,000 km, v_0 is about 30 km/sec, and dA/dt is about 2,250,000,000 km^2/sec. Every time your heart beats, Earth advances 30 km along its orbit, and the radius joining Earth to the sun sweeps out 2,250,000,000 km^2 of area.

Proof of Kepler's First Law

To prove that a planet moves along a conic section with one focus at its sun, we need to express the planet's radius r as a function of θ. This requires a long sequence of calculations and some substitutions that are not altogether obvious.

We begin with the equation that comes from equating the coefficients of $\mathbf{u}_r = \mathbf{r}/|\mathbf{r}|$ in Equations (6) and (10):

$$\ddot{r} - r\dot{\theta}^2 = -\frac{GM}{r^2}. \tag{21}$$

We eliminate $\dot{\theta}$ temporarily by replacing it with $r_0 v_0 / r^2$ from Equation (19) and rearrange the resulting equation to get

$$\ddot{r} = \frac{r_0{}^2 v_0{}^2}{r^3} - \frac{GM}{r^2}. \tag{22}$$

We change this into a first-order equation by a change of variable. With

$$p = \frac{dr}{dt}, \qquad \frac{d^2r}{dt^2} = \frac{dp}{dt} = \frac{dp}{dr}\frac{dr}{dt} = p\frac{dp}{dr}, \qquad \text{Chain Rule}$$

Equation (22) becomes

$$p\frac{dp}{dr} = \frac{r_0{}^2 v_0{}^2}{r^3} - \frac{GM}{r^2}. \tag{23}$$

Multiplying through by 2 and integrating with respect to r gives

$$p^2 = (\dot{r})^2 = -\frac{r_0{}^2 v_0{}^2}{r^2} + \frac{2GM}{r} + C_1. \tag{24}$$

The initial conditions that $r = r_0$ and $\dot{r} = 0$ when $t = 0$ determine the value of C_1 to be

$$C_1 = v_0{}^2 - \frac{2GM}{r_0}.$$

Accordingly, Equation (24), after a suitable rearrangement, becomes

$$\dot{r}^2 = v_0{}^2\left(1 - \frac{r_0{}^2}{r^2}\right) + 2GM\left(\frac{1}{r} - \frac{1}{r_0}\right). \tag{25}$$

The effect of going from Equation (21) to Equation (25) has been to replace a second-order differential equation in r by a first-order differential equation in r. Our goal is still to express r in terms of θ, so we now bring θ back into the picture. To accomplish this, we divide both sides of Equation (25) by the squares of the corresponding sides of the equation $r^2\dot{\theta} = r_0 v_0$ (Equation 19) and use the fact that $\dot{r}/\dot{\theta} = (dr/dt)/(d\theta/dt) = dr/d\theta$ to get

$$\begin{aligned} \frac{1}{r^4}\left(\frac{dr}{d\theta}\right)^2 &= \frac{1}{r_0{}^2} - \frac{1}{r^2} + \frac{2GM}{r_0{}^2 v_0{}^2}\left(\frac{1}{r} - \frac{1}{r_0}\right) \\ &= \frac{1}{r_0{}^2} - \frac{1}{r^2} + 2h\left(\frac{1}{r} - \frac{1}{r_0}\right). \qquad h = \frac{GM}{r_0{}^2 v_0^2} \end{aligned} \tag{26}$$

To simplify further, we substitute

$$u = \frac{1}{r}, \qquad u_0 = \frac{1}{r_0}, \qquad \frac{du}{d\theta} = -\frac{1}{r^2}\frac{dr}{d\theta}, \qquad \left(\frac{du}{d\theta}\right)^2 = \frac{1}{r^4}\left(\frac{dr}{d\theta}\right)^2,$$

obtaining

$$\left(\frac{du}{d\theta}\right)^2 = u_0{}^2 - u^2 + 2hu - 2hu_0 = (u_0 - h)^2 - (u - h)^2, \tag{27}$$

$$\frac{du}{d\theta} = \pm\sqrt{(u_0 - h)^2 - (u - h)^2}. \tag{28}$$

Which sign do we take? We know that $\dot{\theta} = r_0 v_0/r^2$ is positive. Also, r starts from a minimum value at $t = 0$, so it cannot immediately decrease, and $\dot{r} \geq 0$, at least for early positive values of t. Therefore,

$$\frac{dr}{d\theta} = \frac{\dot{r}}{\dot{\theta}} \geq 0 \qquad \text{and} \qquad \frac{du}{d\theta} = -\frac{1}{r^2}\frac{dr}{d\theta} \leq 0.$$

The correct sign for Equation (28) is the negative sign. With this determined, we rearrange Equation (28) and integrate both sides with respect to θ:

$$\begin{aligned} \frac{-1}{\sqrt{(u_0 - h)^2 - (u - h)^2}}\frac{du}{d\theta} &= 1 \\ \cos^{-1}\left(\frac{u - h}{u_0 - h}\right) &= \theta + C_2. \end{aligned} \tag{29}$$

The constant C_2 is zero because $u = u_0$ when $\theta = 0$ and $\cos^{-1}(1) = 0$. Therefore,

$$\frac{u - h}{u_0 - h} = \cos\theta$$

and

$$\frac{1}{r} = u = h + (u_0 - h)\cos\theta. \tag{30}$$

A few more algebraic maneuvers produce the final equation

$$r = \frac{(1 + e)r_0}{1 + e\cos\theta}, \tag{31}$$

where

$$e = \frac{1}{r_0 h} - 1 = \frac{r_0 v_0{}^2}{GM} - 1. \tag{32}$$

Together, Equations (31) and (32) say that the path of the planet is a conic section with one focus at the sun and with eccentricity $(r_0 v_0^2/GM) - 1$. This is the modern formulation of Kepler's first law.

Kepler's Third Law (The Time–Distance Law)

The time T it takes a planet to go around its sun once is the planet's **orbital period**. *Kepler's third law* says that T and the orbit's semimajor axis a are related by the equation

$$\frac{T^2}{a^3} = \frac{4\pi^2}{GM}. \tag{33}$$

Since the right-hand side of this equation is constant within a given solar system, the ratio of T^2 to a^3 *is the same for every planet in the system.*

Kepler's third law is the starting point for working out the size of our solar system. It allows the semimajor axis of each planetary orbit to be expressed in astronomical units, Earth's semimajor axis being one unit. The distance between any two planets at any time can then be predicted in astronomical units and all that remains is to find one of these distances in kilometers. This can be done by bouncing radar waves off Venus, for example. The astronomical unit is now known, after a series of such measurements, to be 149,597,870 km.

We derive Kepler's third law by combining two formulas for the area enclosed by the planet's elliptical orbit:

Formula 1: $\quad \text{Area} = \pi ab \qquad$ The geometry formula in which a is the semimajor axis and b is the semiminor axis

Formula 2:
$$\begin{aligned} \text{Area} &= \int_0^T dA \\ &= \int_0^T \frac{1}{2} r_0 v_0 \, dt \qquad \text{Equation (20)} \\ &= \frac{1}{2} T r_0 v_0. \end{aligned}$$

Equating these gives

$$T = \frac{2\pi ab}{r_0 v_0} = \frac{2\pi a^2}{r_0 v_0}\sqrt{1 - e^2}. \qquad \text{For any ellipse, } b = a\sqrt{1 - e^2} \tag{34}$$

It remains only to express a and e in terms of r_0, v_0, G, and M. Equation (32) does this for e. For a, we observe that setting θ equal to π in Equation (31) gives

$$r_{\max} = r_0 \frac{1 + e}{1 - e}.$$

Hence,

$$2a = r_0 + r_{\max} = \frac{2r_0}{1 - e} = \frac{2r_0 GM}{2GM - r_0 v_0^2}. \tag{35}$$

Squaring both sides of Equation (34) and substituting the results of Equations (32) and (35) now produces Kepler's third law (Exercise 15).

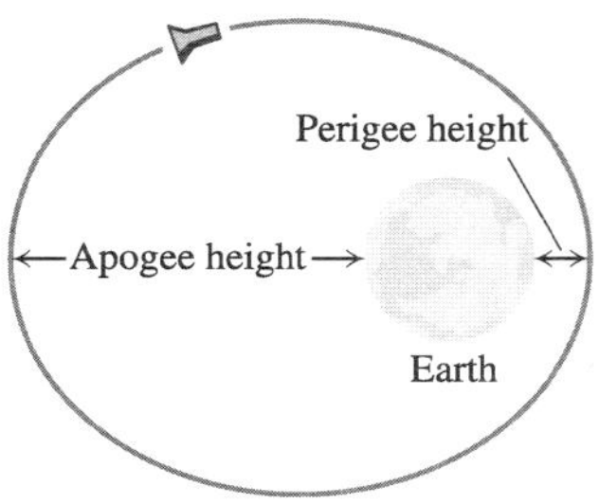

FIGURE 13.39 The orbit of an Earth satellite: $2a$ = diameter of Earth + perigee height + apogee height.

Orbit Data

Although Kepler discovered his laws empirically and stated them only for the six planets known at the time, the modern derivations of Kepler's laws show that they apply to any body driven by a force that obeys an inverse square law like Equation (9). They apply to Halley's comet and the asteroid Icarus. They apply to the moon's orbit about Earth, and they applied to the orbit of the spacecraft *Apollo 8* about the moon.

Tables 13.1 through 13.3 give additional data for planetary orbits and for the orbits of seven of Earth's artificial satellites (Figure 13.39). *Vanguard 1* sent back data that revealed differences between the levels of Earth's oceans and provided the first determination of the precise locations of some of the more isolated Pacific islands. The data also verified that the gravitation of the sun and moon would affect the orbits of Earth's satellites and that solar radiation could exert enough pressure to deform an orbit.

TABLE 13.1 Values of a, e, and T for the major planets

Planet	Semimajor axis a^*	Eccentricity e	Period T
Mercury	57.95	0.2056	87.967 days
Venus	108.11	0.0068	224.701 days
Earth	149.57	0.0167	365.256 days
Mars	227.84	0.0934	1.8808 years
Jupiter	778.14	0.0484	11.8613 years
Saturn	1427.0	0.0543	29.4568 years
Uranus	2870.3	0.0460	84.0081 years
Neptune	4499.9	0.0082	164.784 years
Pluto	5909	0.2481	248.35 years

*Millions of kilometers.

TABLE 13.2 Data on Earth's satellites

Name	Launch date	Time or expected time aloft	Mass at launch (kg)	Period (min)	Perigee height (km)	Apogee height (km)	Semimajor axis a (km)	Eccentricity
Sputnik 1	Oct. 1957	57.6 days	83.6	96.2	215	939	6955	0.052
Vanguard 1	Mar. 1958	300 years	1.47	138.5	649	4340	8872	0.208
Syncom 3	Aug. 1964	$>10^6$ years	39	1436.2	35,718	35,903	42,189	0.002
Skylab 4	Nov. 1973	84.06 days	13,980	93.11	422	437	6808	0.001
Tiros II	Oct. 1978	500 years	734	102.12	850	866	7236	0.001
GOES 4	Sept. 1980	$>10^6$ years	627	1436.2	35,776	35,800	42,166	0.0003
Intelsat 5	Dec. 1980	$>10^6$ years	1928	1417.67	35,143	35,707	41,803	0.007

TABLE 13.3 Numerical data

Universal gravitational constant:	$G = 6.6726 \times 10^{-11}$ Nm^2 kg^{-2}
Sun's mass:	1.99×10^{30} kg
Earth's mass:	5.975×10^{24} kg
Equatorial radius of Earth:	6378.533 km
Polar radius of Earth:	6356.912 km
Earth's rotational period:	1436.1 min
Earth's orbital period:	1 year = 365.256 days

Syncom 3 is one of a series of U.S. Department of Defense telecommunications satellites. *Tiros II* (for "television infrared observation satellite") is one of a series of weather satellites. *GOES 4* (for "geostationary operational environmental satellite") is one of a series of satellites designed to gather information about Earth's atmosphere. Its orbital period, 1436.2 min, is nearly the same as Earth's rotational period of 1436.1 min, and its orbit is nearly circular ($e = 0.0003$). *Intelsat 5* is a heavy-capacity commercial telecommunications satellite.

EXERCISES 13.6

Reminder: When a calculation involves the gravitational constant G, express force in newtons, distance in meters, mass in kilograms, and time in seconds.

1. **Period of *Skylab 4*** Since the orbit of *Skylab 4* had a semimajor axis of $a = 6808$ km, Kepler's third law with M equal to Earth's mass should give the period. Calculate it. Compare your result with the value in Table 13.2.

2. **Earth's velocity at perihelion** Earth's distance from the sun at perihelion is approximately 149,577,000 km, and the eccentricity of Earth's orbit about the sun is 0.0167. Find the velocity v_0 of Earth in its orbit at perihelion. (Use Equation (15).)

3. **Semimajor axis of *Proton I*** In July 1965, the USSR launched *Proton I*, weighing 12,200 kg (at launch), with a perigee height of 183 km, an apogee height of 589 km, and a period of 92.25 min. Using the relevant data for the mass of Earth and the gravitational constant G, find the semimajor axis a of the orbit from Equation (3). Compare your answer with the number you get by adding the perigee and apogee heights to the diameter of the Earth.

4. **Semimajor axis of *Viking I*** The *Viking I* orbiter, which surveyed Mars from August 1975 to June 1976, had a period of 1639 min. Use this and the mass of Mars, 6.418×10^{23} kg, to find the semimajor axis of the *Viking I* orbit.

5. **Average diameter of Mars** (*Continuation of Exercise 4.*) The *Viking I* orbiter was 1499 km from the surface of Mars at its closest point and 35,800 km from the surface at its farthest point. Use this information together with the value you obtained in Exercise 4 to estimate the average diameter of Mars.

6. **Period of *Viking 2*** The *Viking 2* orbiter, which surveyed Mars from September 1975 to August 1976, moved in an ellipse whose semimajor axis was 22,030 km. What was the orbital period? (Express your answer in minutes.)

7. **Geosynchronous orbits** Several satellites in Earth's equatorial plane have nearly circular orbits whose periods are the same as Earth's rotational period. Such orbits are *geosynchronous* or *geostationary* because they hold the satellite over the same spot on the Earth's surface.
   a. Approximately what is the semimajor axis of a geosynchronous orbit? Give reasons for your answer.
   b. About how high is a geosynchronous orbit above Earth's surface?
   c. Which of the satellites in Table 13.2 have (nearly) geosynchronous orbits?

8. The mass of Mars is 6.418×10^{23} kg. If a satellite revolving about Mars is to hold a stationary orbit (have the same period as

the period of Mars's rotation, which is 1477.4 min), what must the semimajor axis of its orbit be? Give reasons for your answer.

9. **Distance from Earth to the moon** The period of the moon's rotation about Earth is 2.36055×10^6 sec. About how far away is the moon?

10. **Finding satellite speed** A satellite moves around Earth in a circular orbit. Express the satellite's speed as a function of the orbit's radius.

11. **Orbital period** If T is measured in seconds and a in meters, what is the value of T^2/a^3 for planets in our solar system? For satellites orbiting Earth? For satellites orbiting the moon? (The moon's mass is 7.354×10^{22} kg.)

12. **Type of orbit** For what values of v_0 in Equation (15) is the orbit in Equation (16) a circle? An ellipse? A parabola? A hyperbola?

13. **Circular orbits** Show that a planet in a circular orbit moves with a constant speed. (*Hint:* This is a consequence of one of Kepler's laws.)

14. Suppose that $\mathbf{r}$ is the position vector of a particle moving along a plane curve and dA/dt is the rate at which the vector sweeps out area. Without introducing coordinates, and assuming the necessary derivatives exist, give a geometric argument based on increments and limits for the validity of the equation

$$\frac{dA}{dt} = \frac{1}{2}|\mathbf{r} \times \dot{\mathbf{r}}|.$$

15. **Kepler's third law** Complete the derivation of Kepler's third law (the part following Equation (34)).

In Exercises 16 and 17, two planets, planet A and planet B, are orbiting their sun in circular orbits with A being the inner planet and B being farther away from the sun. Suppose the positions of A and B at time t are

$$\mathbf{r}_A(t) = 2\cos(2\pi t)\mathbf{i} + 2\sin(2\pi t)\mathbf{j}$$

and

$$\mathbf{r}_B(t) = 3\cos(\pi t)\mathbf{i} + 3\sin(\pi t)\mathbf{j},$$

respectively, where the sun is assumed to be located at the origin and distance is measured in astronomical units. (Notice that planet A moves faster than planet B.)

The people on planet A regard their planet, not the sun, as the center of their planetary system (their solar system).

16. Using planet A as the origin of a new coordinate system, give parametric equations for the location of planet B at time t. Write your answer in terms of $\cos(\pi t)$ and $\sin(\pi t)$.

T 17. Using planet A as the origin, graph the path of planet B.

This exercise illustrates the difficulty that people before Kepler's time, with an earth-centered (planet A) view of our solar system, had in understanding the motions of the planets (i.e., planet B = Mars). See D. G. Saari's article in the *American Mathematical Monthly*, Vol. 97 (Feb. 1990), pp. 105–119.

18. Kepler discovered that the path of Earth around the sun is an ellipse with the sun at one of the foci. Let $\mathbf{r}(t)$ be the position vector from the center of the sun to the center of Earth at time t. Let $\mathbf{w}$ be the vector from Earth's South Pole to North Pole. It is known that $\mathbf{w}$ is constant and not orthogonal to the plane of the ellipse (Earth's axis is tilted). In terms of $\mathbf{r}(t)$ and $\mathbf{w}$, give the mathematical meaning of (i) perihelion, (ii) aphelion, (iii) equinox, (iv) summer solstice, (v) winter solstice.

Chapter 13 Questions to Guide Your Review

1. State the rules for differentiating and integrating vector functions. Give examples.
2. How do you define and calculate the velocity, speed, direction of motion, and acceleration of a body moving along a sufficiently differentiable space curve? Give an example.
3. What is special about the derivatives of vector functions of constant length? Give an example.
4. What are the vector and parametric equations for ideal projectile motion? How do you find a projectile's maximum height, flight time, and range? Give examples.
5. How do you define and calculate the length of a segment of a smooth space curve? Give an example. What mathematical assumptions are involved in the definition?
6. How do you measure distance along a smooth curve in space from a preselected base point? Give an example.
7. What is a differentiable curve's unit tangent vector? Give an example.
8. Define curvature, circle of curvature (osculating circle), center of curvature, and radius of curvature for twice-differentiable curves in the plane. Give examples. What curves have zero curvature? Constant curvature?
9. What is a plane curve's principal normal vector? When is it defined? Which way does it point? Give an example.
10. How do you define $\mathbf{N}$ and κ for curves in space? How are these quantities related? Give examples.

11. What is a curve's binormal vector? Give an example. How is this vector related to the curve's torsion? Give an example.

12. What formulas are available for writing a moving body's acceleration as a sum of its tangential and normal components? Give an example. Why might one want to write the acceleration this way? What if the body moves at a constant speed? At a constant speed around a circle?

13. State Kepler's laws. To what phenomena do they apply?

Chapter 13 Practice Exercises

Motion in a Cartesian Plane

In Exercises 1 and 2, graph the curves and sketch their velocity and acceleration vectors at the given values of t. Then write $\mathbf{a}$ in the form $\mathbf{a} = a_T\mathbf{T} + a_N\mathbf{N}$ without finding $\mathbf{T}$ and $\mathbf{N}$, and find the value of κ at the given values of t.

1. $\mathbf{r}(t) = (4\cos t)\mathbf{i} + \left(\sqrt{2}\sin t\right)\mathbf{j}, \quad t = 0 \text{ and } \pi/4$

2. $\mathbf{r}(t) = \left(\sqrt{3}\sec t\right)\mathbf{i} + \left(\sqrt{3}\tan t\right)\mathbf{j}, \quad t = 0$

3. The position of a particle in the plane at time t is

$$\mathbf{r} = \frac{1}{\sqrt{1+t^2}}\mathbf{i} + \frac{t}{\sqrt{1+t^2}}\mathbf{j}.$$

Find the particle's highest speed.

4. Suppose $\mathbf{r}(t) = (e^t\cos t)\mathbf{i} + (e^t\sin t)\mathbf{j}$. Show that the angle between $\mathbf{r}$ and $\mathbf{a}$ never changes. What *is* the angle?

5. **Finding curvature** At point P, the velocity and acceleration of a particle moving in the plane are $\mathbf{v} = 3\mathbf{i} + 4\mathbf{j}$ and $\mathbf{a} = 5\mathbf{i} + 15\mathbf{j}$. Find the curvature of the particle's path at P.

6. Find the point on the curve $y = e^x$ where the curvature is greatest.

7. A particle moves around the unit circle in the xy-plane. Its position at time t is $\mathbf{r} = x\mathbf{i} + y\mathbf{j}$, where x and y are differentiable functions of t. Find dy/dt if $\mathbf{v}\cdot\mathbf{i} = y$. Is the motion clockwise, or counterclockwise?

8. You send a message through a pneumatic tube that follows the curve $9y = x^3$ (distance in meters). At the point $(3, 3)$, $\mathbf{v}\cdot\mathbf{i} = 4$ and $\mathbf{a}\cdot\mathbf{i} = -2$. Find the values of $\mathbf{v}\cdot\mathbf{j}$ and $\mathbf{a}\cdot\mathbf{j}$ at $(3, 3)$.

9. **Characterizing circular motion** A particle moves in the plane so that its velocity and position vectors are always orthogonal. Show that the particle moves in a circle centered at the origin.

10. **Speed along a cycloid** A circular wheel with radius 1 ft and center C rolls to the right along the x-axis at a half-turn per second. (See the accompanying figure.) At time t seconds, the position vector of the point P on the wheel's circumference is

$$\mathbf{r} = (\pi t - \sin\pi t)\mathbf{i} + (1 - \cos\pi t)\mathbf{j}.$$

a. Sketch the curve traced by P during the interval $0 \le t \le 3$.

b. Find $\mathbf{v}$ and $\mathbf{a}$ at $t = 0, 1, 2,$ and 3 and add these vectors to your sketch.

c. At any given time, what is the forward speed of the topmost point of the wheel? Of C?

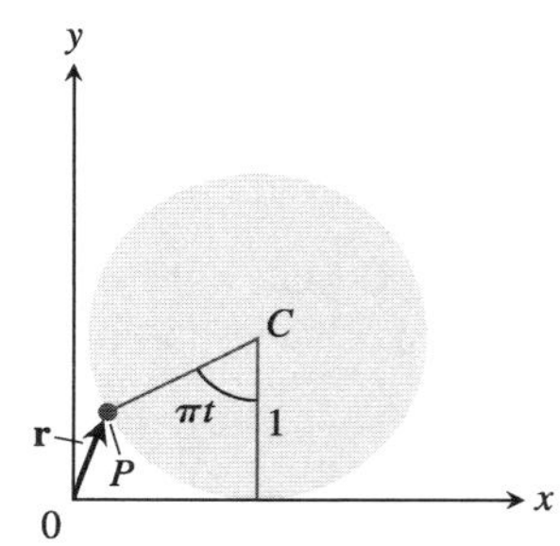

Projectile Motion and Motion in a Plane

11. **Shot put** A shot leaves the thrower's hand 6.5 ft above the ground at a 45° angle at 44 ft/sec. Where is it 3 sec later?

12. **Javelin** A javelin leaves the thrower's hand 7 ft above the ground at a 45° angle at 80 ft/sec. How high does it go?

13. A golf ball is hit with an initial speed v_0 at an angle α to the horizontal from a point that lies at the foot of a straight-sided hill that is inclined at an angle ϕ to the horizontal, where

$$0 < \phi < \alpha < \frac{\pi}{2}.$$

Show that the ball lands at a distance

$$\frac{2v_0^2\cos\alpha}{g\cos^2\phi}\sin(\alpha - \phi),$$

measured up the face of the hill. Hence, show that the greatest range that can be achieved for a given v_0 occurs when $\alpha = (\phi/2) + (\pi/4)$, i.e., when the initial velocity vector bisects the angle between the vertical and the hill.

14. The Dictator The Civil War mortar Dictator weighed so much (17,120 lb) that it had to be mounted on a railroad car. It had a 13-in. bore and used a 20-lb powder charge to fire a 200-lb shell. The mortar was made by Mr. Charles Knapp in his ironworks in Pittsburgh, Pennsylvania, and was used by the Union army in 1864 in the siege of Petersburg, Virginia. How far did it shoot? Here we have a difference of opinion. The ordnance manual claimed 4325 yd, while field officers claimed 4752 yd. Assuming a 45° firing angle, what muzzle speeds are involved here?

15. The World's record for popping a champagne cork

a. Until 1988, the world's record for popping a champagne cork was 109 ft. 6 in., once held by Captain Michael Hill of the British Royal Artillery (of course). Assuming Cpt. Hill held the bottle neck at ground level at a 45° angle, and the cork behaved like an ideal projectile, how fast was the cork going as it left the bottle?

b. A new world record of 177 ft. 9 in. was set on June 5, 1988, by Prof. Emeritus Heinrich of Rensselaer Polytechnic Institute, firing from 4 ft. above ground level at the Woodbury Vineyards Winery, New York. Assuming an ideal trajectory, what was the cork's initial speed?

16. Javelin In Potsdam in 1988, Petra Felke of (then) East Germany set a women's world record by throwing a javelin 262 ft 5 in.

a. Assuming that Felke launched the javelin at a 40° angle to the horizontal 6.5 ft above the ground, what was the javelin's initial speed?

b. How high did the javelin go?

17. Synchronous curves By eliminating α from the ideal projectile equations

$$x = (v_0 \cos\alpha)t, \quad y = (v_0 \sin\alpha)t - \frac{1}{2}gt^2,$$

show that $x^2 + (y + gt^2/2)^2 = v_0{}^2 t^2$. This shows that projectiles launched simultaneously from the origin at the same initial speed will, at any given instant, all lie on the circle of radius $v_0 t$ centered at $(0, -gt^2/2)$, regardless of their launch angle. These circles are the *synchronous curves* of the launching.

18. Radius of curvature Show that the radius of curvature of a twice-differentiable plane curve $\mathbf{r}(t) = f(t)\mathbf{i} + g(t)\mathbf{j}$ is given by the formula

$$\rho = \frac{\dot{x}^2 + \dot{y}^2}{\sqrt{\ddot{x}^2 + \ddot{y}^2 - \ddot{s}^2}}, \quad \text{where} \quad \ddot{s} = \frac{d}{dt}\sqrt{\dot{x}^2 + \dot{y}^2}.$$

19. Curvature Express the curvature of the curve

$$\mathbf{r}(t) = \left(\int_0^t \cos\left(\frac{1}{2}\pi\theta^2\right) d\theta\right)\mathbf{i} + \left(\int_0^t \sin\left(\frac{1}{2}\pi\theta^2\right) d\theta\right)\mathbf{j}$$

as a function of the directed distance s measured along the curve from the origin. (See the accompanying figure.)

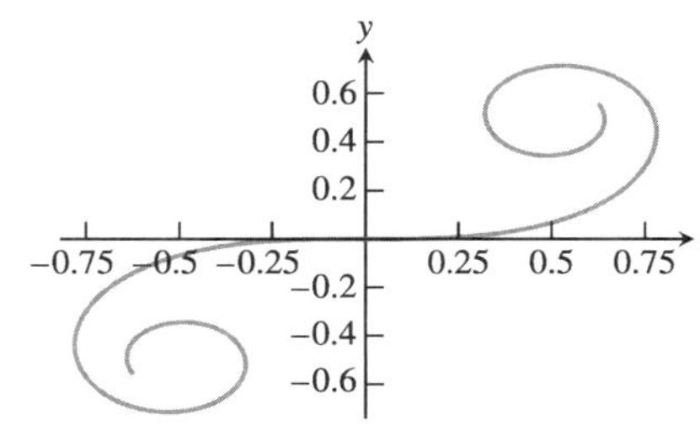

20. An alternative definition of curvature in the plane An alternative definition gives the curvature of a sufficiently differentiable plane curve to be $|d\phi/ds|$, where ϕ is the angle between $\mathbf{T}$ and $\mathbf{i}$ (Figure 13.40a). Figure 13.40b shows the distance s measured counterclockwise around the circle $x^2 + y^2 = a^2$ from the point $(a, 0)$ to a point P, along with the angle ϕ at P. Calculate the circle's curvature using the alternative definition. (*Hint:* $\phi = \theta + \pi/2$.)

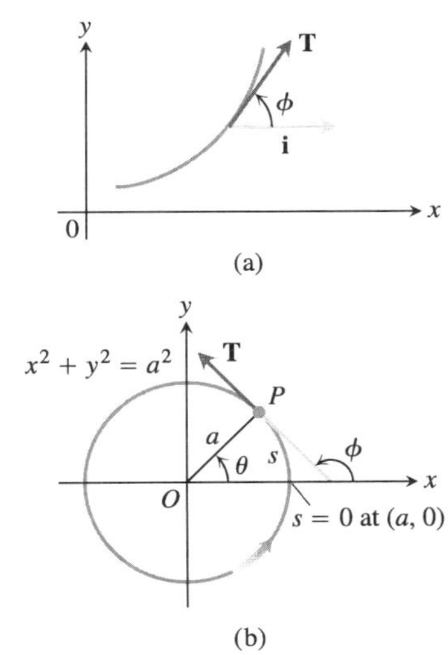

FIGURE 13.40 Figures for Exercise 20.

Motion in Space

Find the lengths of the curves in Exercises 21 and 22.

21. $\mathbf{r}(t) = (2\cos t)\mathbf{i} + (2\sin t)\mathbf{j} + t^2\mathbf{k}, \quad 0 \le t \le \pi/4$

22. $\mathbf{r}(t) = (3\cos t)\mathbf{i} + (3\sin t)\mathbf{j} + 2t^{3/2}\mathbf{k}, \quad 0 \le t \le 3$

In Exercises 23–26, find $\mathbf{T}$, $\mathbf{N}$, $\mathbf{B}$, κ, and τ at the given value of t.

23. $\mathbf{r}(t) = \frac{4}{9}(1 + t)^{3/2}\mathbf{i} + \frac{4}{9}(1 - t)^{3/2}\mathbf{j} + \frac{1}{3}t\mathbf{k}, \quad t = 0$

24. $\mathbf{r}(t) = (e^t \sin 2t)\mathbf{i} + (e^t \cos 2t)\mathbf{j} + 2e^t\mathbf{k}, \quad t = 0$

25. $\mathbf{r}(t) = t\mathbf{i} + \frac{1}{2}e^{2t}\mathbf{j}, \quad t = \ln 2$

26. $\mathbf{r}(t) = (3\cosh 2t)\mathbf{i} + (3\sinh 2t)\mathbf{j} + 6t\mathbf{k}, \quad t = \ln 2$

In Exercises 27 and 28, write $\mathbf{a}$ in the form $\mathbf{a} = a_{\mathrm{T}}\mathbf{T} + a_{\mathrm{N}}\mathbf{N}$ at $t = 0$ without finding $\mathbf{T}$ and $\mathbf{N}$.

27. $\mathbf{r}(t) = (2 + 3t + 3t^2)\mathbf{i} + (4t + 4t^2)\mathbf{j} - (6\cos t)\mathbf{k}$

28. $\mathbf{r}(t) = (2 + t)\mathbf{i} + (t + 2t^2)\mathbf{j} + (1 + t^2)\mathbf{k}$

29. Find $\mathbf{T}$, $\mathbf{N}$, $\mathbf{B}$, κ, and τ as functions of t if $\mathbf{r}(t) = (\sin t)\mathbf{i} + (\sqrt{2}\cos t)\mathbf{j} + (\sin t)\mathbf{k}$.

30. At what times in the interval $0 \le t \le \pi$ are the velocity and acceleration vectors of the motion $\mathbf{r}(t) = \mathbf{i} + (5\cos t)\mathbf{j} + (3\sin t)\mathbf{k}$ orthogonal?

31. The position of a particle moving in space at time $t \ge 0$ is

$$\mathbf{r}(t) = 2\mathbf{i} + \left(4\sin\frac{t}{2}\right)\mathbf{j} + \left(3 - \frac{t}{\pi}\right)\mathbf{k}.$$

Find the first time $\mathbf{r}$ is orthogonal to the vector $\mathbf{i} - \mathbf{j}$.

32. Find equations for the osculating, normal, and rectifying planes of the curve $\mathbf{r}(t) = t\mathbf{i} + t^2\mathbf{j} + t^3\mathbf{k}$ at the point $(1, 1, 1)$.

33. Find parametric equations for the line that is tangent to the curve $\mathbf{r}(t) = e^t\mathbf{i} + (\sin t)\mathbf{j} + \ln(1 - t)\mathbf{k}$ at $t = 0$.

34. Find parametric equations for the line tangent to the helix $\mathbf{r}(t) = (\sqrt{2}\cos t)\mathbf{i} + (\sqrt{2}\sin t)\mathbf{j} + t\mathbf{k}$ at the point where $t = \pi/4$.

35. The view from *Skylab 4* What percentage of Earth's surface area could the astronauts see when *Skylab 4* was at its apogee height, 437 km above the surface? To find out, model the visible surface as the surface generated by revolving the circular arc GT, shown here, about the y-axis. Then carry out these steps:

1. Use similar triangles in the figure to show that $y_0/6380 = 6380/(6380 + 437)$. Solve for y_0.
2. To four significant digits, calculate the visible area as

$$VA = \int_{y_0}^{6380} 2\pi x\sqrt{1 + \left(\frac{dx}{dy}\right)^2}\, dy.$$

3. Express the result as a percentage of Earth's surface area.

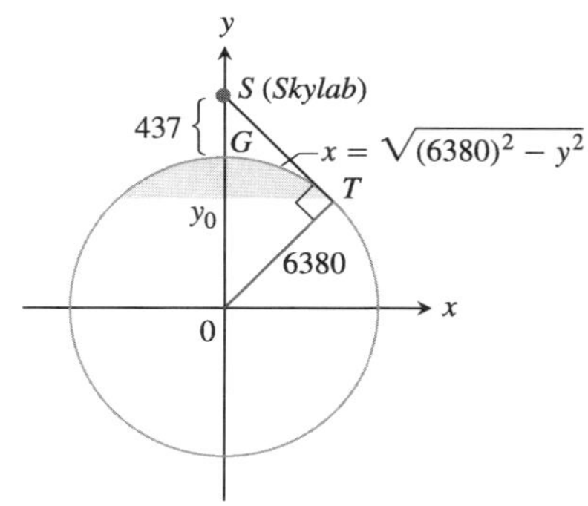

Chapter 13 Additional and Advanced Exercises

Applications

1. A straight river is 100 m wide. A rowboat leaves the far shore at time $t = 0$. The person in the boat rows at a rate of 20 m/min, always toward the near shore. The velocity of the river at (x, y) is

$$\mathbf{v} = \left(-\frac{1}{250}(y - 50)^2 + 10\right)\mathbf{i}\ \text{m/min}, \quad 0 < y < 100.$$

a. Given that $\mathbf{r}(0) = 0\mathbf{i} + 100\mathbf{j}$, what is the position of the boat at time t?

b. How far downstream will the boat land on the near shore?

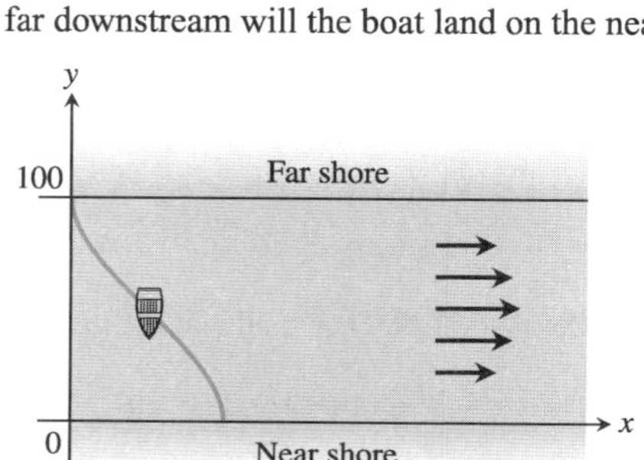

2. A straight river is 20 m wide. The velocity of the river at (x, y) is

$$\mathbf{v} = -\frac{3x(20 - x)}{100}\mathbf{j}\ \text{m/min}, \quad 0 \le x \le 20.$$

A boat leaves the shore at $(0, 0)$ and travels through the water with a constant velocity. It arrives at the opposite shore at $(20, 0)$. The speed of the boat is always $\sqrt{20}$ m/min.

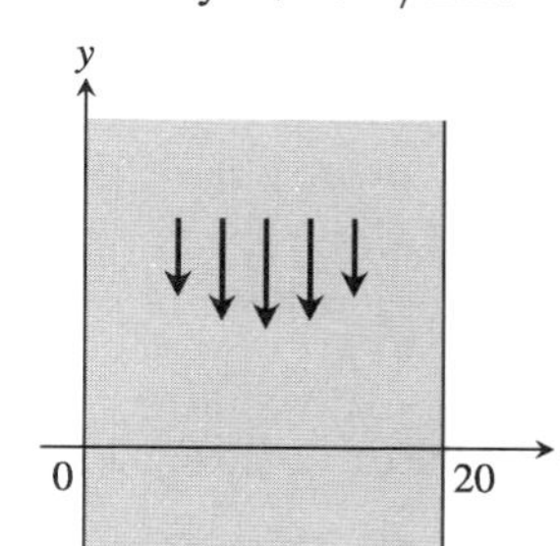

a. Find the velocity of the boat.

b. Find the location of the boat at time t.

c. Sketch the path of the boat.

3. A frictionless particle P, starting from rest at time $t = 0$ at the point $(a, 0, 0)$, slides down the helix

$$\mathbf{r}(\theta) = (a\cos\theta)\mathbf{i} + (a\sin\theta)\mathbf{j} + b\theta\mathbf{k} \quad (a, b > 0)$$

under the influence of gravity, as in the accompanying figure. The θ in this equation is the cylindrical coordinate θ and the helix is the curve $r = a, z = b\theta, \theta \ge 0$, in cylindrical coordinates. We assume θ to be a differentiable function of t for the motion. The law of conservation of energy tells us that the particle's speed after it has fallen straight down a distance z is $\sqrt{2gz}$, where g is the constant acceleration of gravity.

a. Find the angular velocity $d\theta/dt$ when $\theta = 2\pi$.

b. Express the particle's θ- and z-coordinates as functions of t.

c. Express the tangential and normal components of the velocity $d\mathbf{r}/dt$ and acceleration $d^2\mathbf{r}/dt^2$ as functions of t. Does the acceleration have any nonzero component in the direction of the binormal vector $\mathbf{B}$?

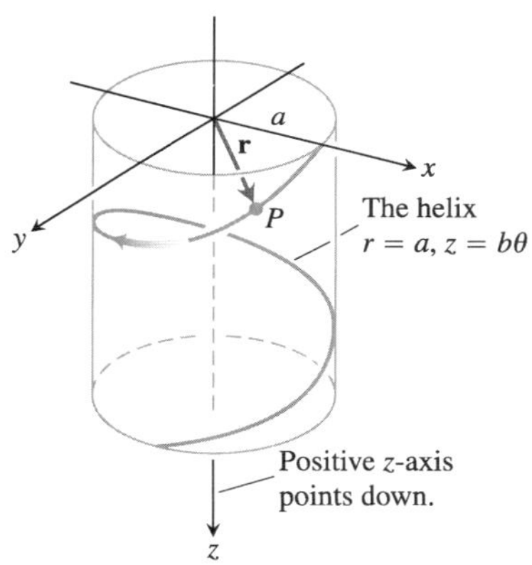

4. Suppose the curve in Exercise 3 is replaced by the conical helix $r = a\theta, z = b\theta$ shown in the accompanying figure.

a. Express the angular velocity $d\theta/dt$ as a function of θ.

b. Express the distance the particle travels along the helix as a function of θ.

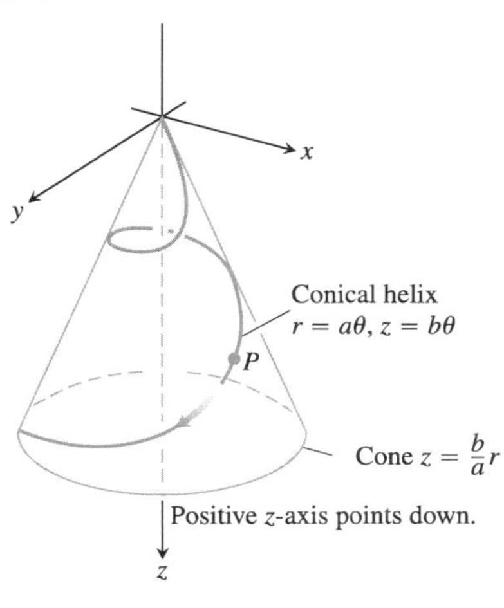

Polar Coordinate Systems and Motion in Space

5. Deduce from the orbit equation

$$r = \frac{(1 + e)r_0}{1 + e\cos\theta}$$

that a planet is closest to its sun when $\theta = 0$ and show that $r = r_0$ at that time.

T 6. **A Kepler equation** The problem of locating a planet in its orbit at a given time and date eventually leads to solving "Kepler" equations of the form

$$f(x) = x - 1 - \frac{1}{2}\sin x = 0.$$

a. Show that this particular equation has a solution between $x = 0$ and $x = 2$.

b. With your computer or calculator in radian mode, use Newton's method to find the solution to as many places as you can.

7. In Section 13.6, we found the velocity of a particle moving in the plane to be

$$\mathbf{v} = \dot{x}\,\mathbf{i} + \dot{y}\,\mathbf{j} = \dot{r}\,\mathbf{u}_r + r\dot{\theta}\,\mathbf{u}_\theta.$$

a. Express $\dot{x}$ and $\dot{y}$ in terms of $\dot{r}$ and $r\dot{\theta}$ by evaluating the dot products $\mathbf{v}\cdot\mathbf{i}$ and $\mathbf{v}\cdot\mathbf{j}$.

b. Express $\dot{r}$ and $r\dot{\theta}$ in terms of $\dot{x}$ and $\dot{y}$ by evaluating the dot products $\mathbf{v}\cdot\mathbf{u}_r$ and $\mathbf{v}\cdot\mathbf{u}_\theta$.

8. Express the curvature of a twice-differentiable curve $r = f(\theta)$ in the polar coordinate plane in terms of f and its derivatives.

9. A slender rod through the origin of the polar coordinate plane rotates (in the plane) about the origin at the rate of 3 rad/min. A beetle starting from the point (2, 0) crawls along the rod toward the origin at the rate of 1 in./min.

a. Find the beetle's acceleration and velocity in polar form when it is halfway to (1 in. from) the origin.

T **b.** To the nearest tenth of an inch, what will be the length of the path the beetle has traveled by the time it reaches the origin?

10. **Conservation of angular momentum** Let $\mathbf{r}(t)$ denote the position in space of a moving object at time t. Suppose the force acting on the object at time t is

$$\mathbf{F}(t) = -\frac{c}{|\mathbf{r}(t)|^3}\mathbf{r}(t),$$

where c is a constant. In physics the **angular momentum** of an object at time t is defined to be $\mathbf{L}(t) = \mathbf{r}(t) \times m\mathbf{v}(t)$, where m is the mass of the object and $\mathbf{v}(t)$ is the velocity. Prove that angular momentum is a conserved quantity; i.e., prove that $\mathbf{L}(t)$ is a constant vector, independent of time. Remember Newton's law $\mathbf{F} = m\mathbf{a}$. (This is a calculus problem, not a physics problem.)

Cylindrical Coordinate Systems

11. Unit vectors for position and motion in cylindrical coordinates When the position of a particle moving in space is given in cylindrical coordinates, the unit vectors we use to describe its position and motion are

$$\mathbf{u}_r = (\cos\theta)\mathbf{i} + (\sin\theta)\mathbf{j}, \qquad \mathbf{u}_\theta = -(\sin\theta)\mathbf{i} + (\cos\theta)\mathbf{j},$$

and $\mathbf{k}$ (see accompanying figure). The particle's position vector is then $\mathbf{r} = r\,\mathbf{u}_r + z\,\mathbf{k}$, where r is the positive polar distance coordinate of the particle's position.

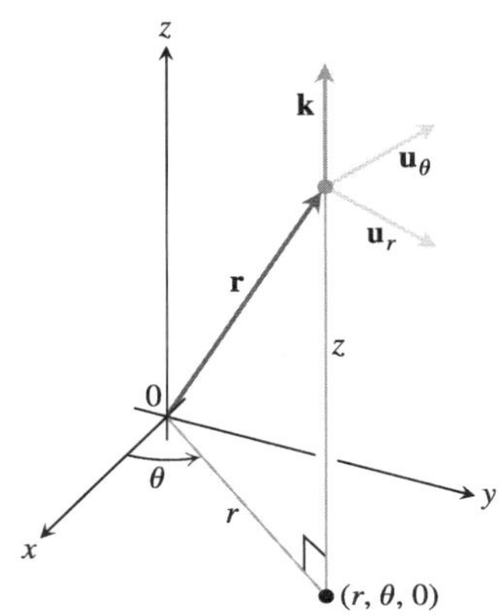

a. Show that $\mathbf{u}_r$, $\mathbf{u}_\theta$, and $\mathbf{k}$, in this order, form a right-handed frame of unit vectors.

b. Show that

$$\frac{d\mathbf{u}_r}{d\theta} = \mathbf{u}_\theta \quad \text{and} \quad \frac{d\mathbf{u}_\theta}{d\theta} = -\mathbf{u}_r.$$

c. Assuming that the necessary derivatives with respect to t exist, express $\mathbf{v} = \dot{\mathbf{r}}$ and $\mathbf{a} = \ddot{\mathbf{r}}$ in terms of $\mathbf{u}_r$, $\mathbf{u}_\theta$, $\mathbf{k}$, $\dot{r}$, and $\dot{\theta}$. (The dots indicate derivatives with respect to t: $\dot{\mathbf{r}}$ means $d\mathbf{r}/dt$, $\ddot{\mathbf{r}}$ means $d^2\mathbf{r}/dt^2$, and so on.) Section 13.6 derives these formulas and shows how the vectors mentioned here are used in describing planetary motion.

12. Arc length in cylindrical coordinates

a. Show that when you express $ds^2 = dx^2 + dy^2 + dz^2$ in terms of cylindrical coordinates, you get $ds^2 = dr^2 + r^2\,d\theta^2 + dz^2$.

b. Interpret this result geometrically in terms of the edges and a diagonal of a box. Sketch the box.

c. Use the result in part (a) to find the length of the curve $r = e^\theta, z = e^\theta, 0 \le \theta \le \theta \ln 8$.

Chapter 13 Technology Application Projects

Mathematica/Maple Module
Radar Tracking of a Moving Object
Visualize position, velocity, and acceleration vectors to analyze motion.

Mathematica/Maple Module
Parametric and Polar Equations with a Figure Skater
Visualize position, velocity, and acceleration vectors to analyze motion.

Mathematica/Maple Module
Moving in Three Dimensions
Compute distance traveled, speed, curvature, and torsion for motion along a space curve. Visualize and compute the tangential, normal, and binormal vectors associated with motion along a space curve.

Chapter

14 PARTIAL DERIVATIVES

OVERVIEW In studying a real-world phenomenon, a quantity being investigated usually depends on two or more independent variables. So we need to extend the basic ideas of the calculus of functions of a single variable to functions of several variables. Although the calculus rules remain essentially the same, the calculus is even richer. The derivatives of functions of several variables are more varied and more interesting because of the different ways in which the variables can interact. Their integrals lead to a greater variety of applications. The studies of probability, statistics, fluid dynamics, and electricity, to mention only a few, all lead in natural ways to functions of more than one variable.

14.1 Functions of Several Variables

Many functions depend on more than one independent variable. The function $V = \pi r^2 h$ calculates the volume of a right circular cylinder from its radius and height. The function $f(x, y) = x^2 + y^2$ calculates the height of the paraboloid $z = x^2 + y^2$ above the point $P(x, y)$ from the two coordinates of P. The temperature T of a point on Earth's surface depends on its latitude x and longitude y, expressed by writing $T = f(x, y)$. In this section, we define functions of more than one independent variable and discuss ways to graph them.

Real-valued functions of several independent real variables are defined much the way you would imagine from the single-variable case. The domains are sets of ordered pairs (triples, quadruples, n-tuples) of real numbers, and the ranges are sets of real numbers of the kind we have worked with all along.

DEFINITIONS Function of n Independent Variables

Suppose D is a set of n-tuples of real numbers $(x_1, x_2, \ldots, x_n)$. A **real-valued function** f on D is a rule that assigns a unique (single) real number

$$w = f(x_1, x_2, \ldots, x_n)$$

to each element in D. The set D is the function's **domain**. The set of w-values taken on by f is the function's **range**. The symbol w is the **dependent variable** of f, and f is said to be a function of the n **independent variables** x_1 to x_n. We also call the x_j's the function's **input variables** and call w the function's **output variable**.

If f is a function of two independent variables, we usually call the independent variables x and y and picture the domain of f as a region in the xy-plane. If f is a function of three independent variables, we call the variables x, y, and z and picture the domain as a region in space.

In applications, we tend to use letters that remind us of what the variables stand for. To say that the volume of a right circular cylinder is a function of its radius and height, we might write $V = f(r, h)$. To be more specific, we might replace the notation $f(r, h)$ by the formula that calculates the value of V from the values of r and h, and write $V = \pi r^2 h$. In either case, r and h would be the independent variables and V the dependent variable of the function.

As usual, we evaluate functions defined by formulas by substituting the values of the independent variables in the formula and calculating the corresponding value of the dependent variable.

EXAMPLE 1 Evaluating a Function

The value of $f(x, y, z) = \sqrt{x^2 + y^2 + z^2}$ at the point (3, 0, 4) is

$$f(3, 0, 4) = \sqrt{(3)^2 + (0)^2 + (4)^2} = \sqrt{25} = 5.$$

From Section 12.1, we recognize f as the distance function from the origin to the point (x, y, z) in Cartesian space coordinates. ■

Domains and Ranges

In defining a function of more than one variable, we follow the usual practice of excluding inputs that lead to complex numbers or division by zero. If $f(x, y) = \sqrt{y - x^2}$, y cannot be less than x^2. If $f(x, y) = 1/(xy)$, xy cannot be zero. The domain of a function is assumed to be the largest set for which the defining rule generates real numbers, unless the domain is otherwise specified explicitly. The range consists of the set of output values for the dependent variable.

EXAMPLE 2 (a) Functions of Two Variables

Function	Domain	Range
$w = \sqrt{y - x^2}$	$y \geq x^2$	$[0, \infty)$
$w = \dfrac{1}{xy}$	$xy \neq 0$	$(-\infty, 0) \cup (0, \infty)$
$w = \sin xy$	Entire plane	$[-1, 1]$

(b) Functions of Three Variables

Function	Domain	Range
$w = \sqrt{x^2 + y^2 + z^2}$	Entire space	$[0, \infty)$
$w = \dfrac{1}{x^2 + y^2 + z^2}$	$(x, y, z) \neq (0, 0, 0)$	$(0, \infty)$
$w = xy \ln z$	Half-space $z > 0$	$(-\infty, \infty)$

■

Functions of Two Variables

Regions in the plane can have interior points and boundary points just like intervals on the real line. Closed intervals $[a, b]$ include their boundary points, open intervals (a, b) don't include their boundary points, and intervals such as $[a, b)$ are neither open nor closed.

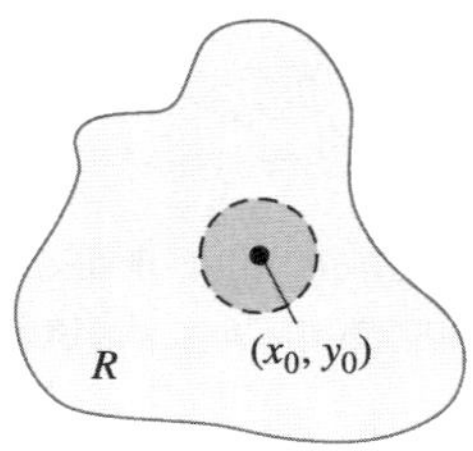

(a) Interior point

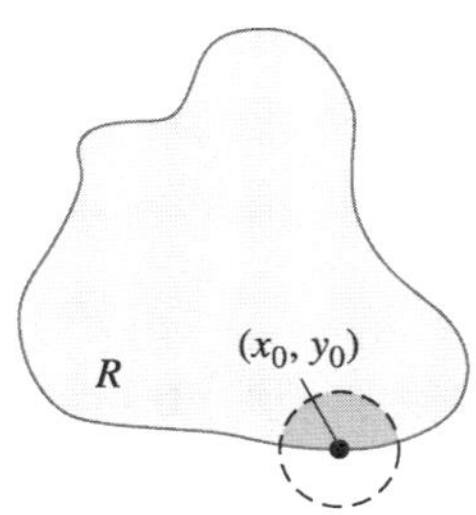

(b) Boundary point

FIGURE 14.1 Interior points and boundary points of a plane region R. An interior point is necessarily a point of R. A boundary point of R need not belong to R.

> **DEFINITIONS Interior and Boundary Points, Open, Closed**
>
> A point (x_0, y_0) in a region (set) R in the xy-plane is an **interior point** of R if it is the center of a disk of positive radius that lies entirely in R (Figure 14.1). A point (x_0, y_0) is a **boundary point** of R if every disk centered at (x_0, y_0) contains points that lie outside of R as well as points that lie in R. (The boundary point itself need not belong to R.)
>
> The interior points of a region, as a set, make up the **interior** of the region. The region's boundary points make up its **boundary**. A region is **open** if it consists entirely of interior points. A region is **closed** if it contains all its boundary points (Figure 14.2).

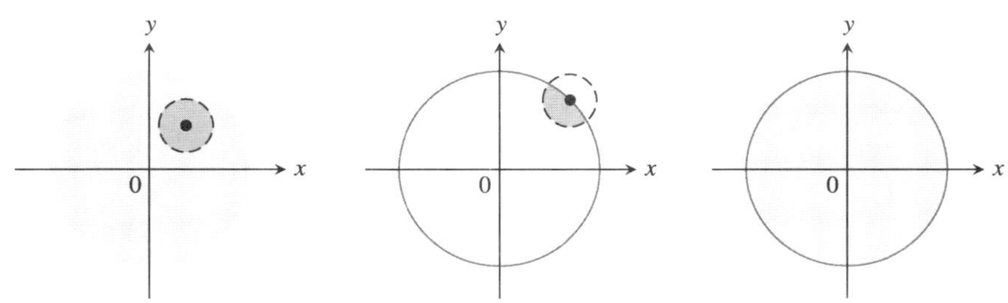

$\{(x, y) \mid x^2 + y^2 < 1\}$ Open unit disk. Every point an interior point.

$\{(x, y) \mid x^2 + y^2 = 1\}$ Boundary of unit disk. (The unit circle.)

$\{(x, y) \mid x^2 + y^2 \le 1\}$ Closed unit disk. Contains all boundary points.

FIGURE 14.2 Interior points and boundary points of the unit disk in the plane.

As with intervals of real numbers, some regions in the plane are neither open nor closed. If you start with the open disk in Figure 14.2 and add to it some of but not all its boundary points, the resulting set is neither open nor closed. The boundary points that *are* there keep the set from being open. The absence of the remaining boundary points keeps the set from being closed.

> **DEFINITIONS Bounded and Unbounded Regions in the Plane**
>
> A region in the plane is **bounded** if it lies inside a disk of fixed radius. A region is **unbounded** if it is not bounded.

Examples of *bounded* sets in the plane include line segments, triangles, interiors of triangles, rectangles, circles, and disks. Examples of *unbounded* sets in the plane include lines, coordinate axes, the graphs of functions defined on infinite intervals, quadrants, half-planes, and the plane itself.

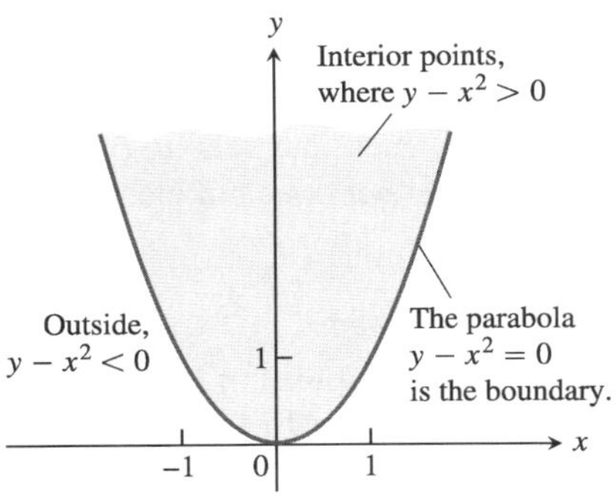

FIGURE 14.3 The domain of $f(x, y) = \sqrt{y - x^2}$ consists of the shaded region and its bounding parabola $y = x^2$ (Example 3).

EXAMPLE 3 Describing the Domain of a Function of Two Variables

Describe the domain of the function $f(x, y) = \sqrt{y - x^2}$.

Solution Since f is defined only where $y - x^2 \geq 0$, the domain is the closed, unbounded region shown in Figure 14.3. The parabola $y = x^2$ is the boundary of the domain. The points above the parabola make up the domain's interior. ■

Graphs, Level Curves, and Contours of Functions of Two Variables

There are two standard ways to picture the values of a function $f(x, y)$. One is to draw and label curves in the domain on which f has a constant value. The other is to sketch the surface $z = f(x, y)$ in space.

> **DEFINITIONS** Level Curve, Graph, Surface
>
> The set of points in the plane where a function $f(x, y)$ has a constant value $f(x, y) = c$ is called a **level curve** of f. The set of all points $(x, y, f(x, y))$ in space, for (x, y) in the domain of f, is called the **graph** of f. The graph of f is also called the **surface** $z = f(x, y)$.

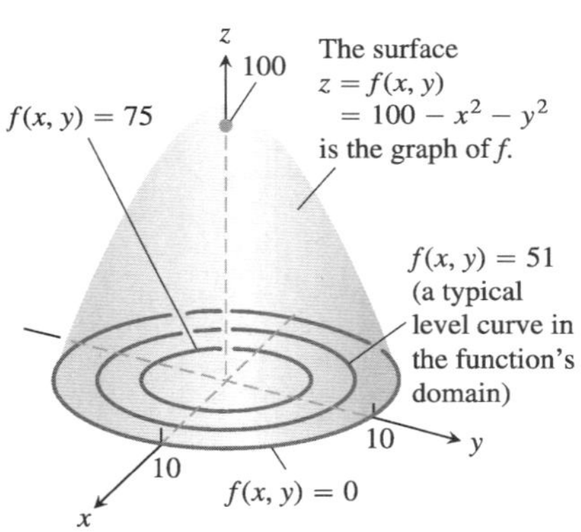

FIGURE 14.4 The graph and selected level curves of the function $f(x, y) = 100 - x^2 - y^2$ (Example 4).

EXAMPLE 4 Graphing a Function of Two Variables

Graph $f(x, y) = 100 - x^2 - y^2$ and plot the level curves $f(x, y) = 0$, $f(x, y) = 51$, and $f(x, y) = 75$ in the domain of f in the plane.

Solution The domain of f is the entire xy-plane, and the range of f is the set of real numbers less than or equal to 100. The graph is the paraboloid $z = 100 - x^2 - y^2$, a portion of which is shown in Figure 14.4.

The level curve $f(x, y) = 0$ is the set of points in the xy-plane at which

$$f(x, y) = 100 - x^2 - y^2 = 0, \qquad \text{or} \qquad x^2 + y^2 = 100,$$

which is the circle of radius 10 centered at the origin. Similarly, the level curves $f(x, y) = 51$ and $f(x, y) = 75$ (Figure 14.4) are the circles

$$f(x, y) = 100 - x^2 - y^2 = 51, \qquad \text{or} \qquad x^2 + y^2 = 49$$

$$f(x, y) = 100 - x^2 - y^2 = 75, \qquad \text{or} \qquad x^2 + y^2 = 25.$$

The level curve $f(x, y) = 100$ consists of the origin alone. (It is still a level curve.) ■

The curve in space in which the plane $z = c$ cuts a surface $z = f(x, y)$ is made up of the points that represent the function value $f(x, y) = c$. It is called the **contour curve** $f(x, y) = c$ to distinguish it from the level curve $f(x, y) = c$ in the domain of f. Figure 14.5 shows the contour curve $f(x, y) = 75$ on the surface $z = 100 - x^2 - y^2$ defined by the function $f(x, y) = 100 - x^2 - y^2$. The contour curve lies directly above the circle $x^2 + y^2 = 25$, which is the level curve $f(x, y) = 75$ in the function's domain.

Not everyone makes this distinction, however, and you may wish to call both kinds of curves by a single name and rely on context to convey which one you have in mind. On most maps, for example, the curves that represent constant elevation (height above sea level) are called contours, not level curves (Figure 14.6).

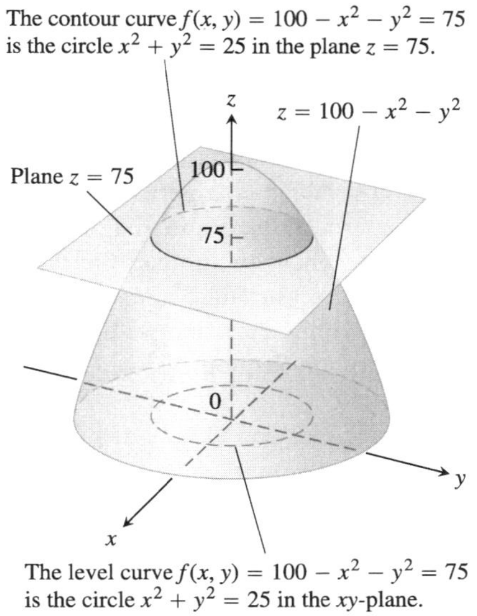

FIGURE 14.5 A plane $z = c$ parallel to the xy-plane intersecting a surface $z = f(x, y)$ produces a contour curve.

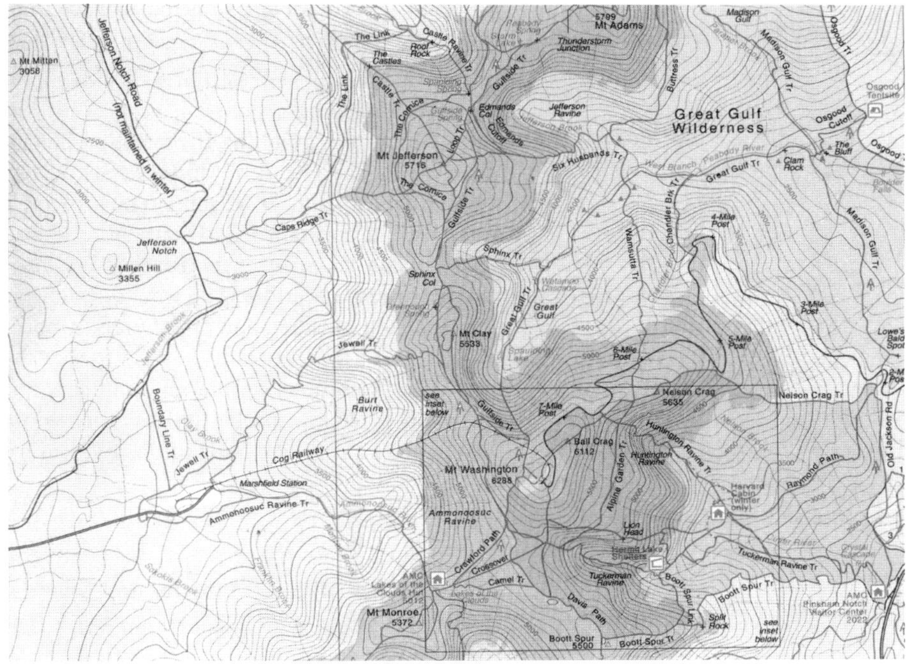

FIGURE 14.6 Contours on Mt. Washington in New Hampshire. (Reproduced by permission from the Appalachian Mountain Club.)

Functions of Three Variables

In the plane, the points where a function of two independent variables has a constant value $f(x, y) = c$ make a curve in the function's domain. In space, the points where a function of three independent variables has a constant value $f(x, y, z) = c$ make a surface in the function's domain.

DEFINITION Level Surface

The set of points (x, y, z) in space where a function of three independent variables has a constant value $f(x, y, z) = c$ is called a **level surface** of f.

Since the graphs of functions of three variables consist of points $(x, y, z, f(x, y, z))$ lying in a four-dimensional space, we cannot sketch them effectively in our three-dimensional frame of reference. We can see how the function behaves, however, by looking at its three-dimensional level surfaces.

EXAMPLE 5 Describing Level Surfaces of a Function of Three Variables

Describe the level surfaces of the function

$$f(x, y, z) = \sqrt{x^2 + y^2 + z^2}.$$

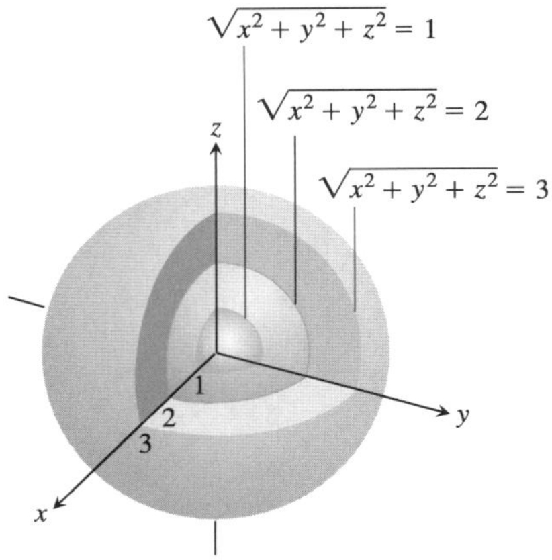

FIGURE 14.7 The level surfaces of $f(x, y, z) = \sqrt{x^2 + y^2 + z^2}$ are concentric spheres (Example 5).

Solution The value of f is the distance from the origin to the point (x, y, z). Each level surface $\sqrt{x^2 + y^2 + z^2} = c, c > 0$, is a sphere of radius c centered at the origin. Figure 14.7 shows a cutaway view of three of these spheres. The level surface $\sqrt{x^2 + y^2 + z^2} = 0$ consists of the origin alone.

We are not graphing the function here; we are looking at level surfaces in the function's domain. The level surfaces show how the function's values change as we move through its domain. If we remain on a sphere of radius c centered at the origin, the function maintains a constant value, namely c. If we move from one sphere to another, the function's value changes. It increases if we move away from the origin and decreases if we move toward the origin. The way the values change depends on the direction we take. The dependence of change on direction is important. We return to it in Section 14.5. ■

The definitions of interior, boundary, open, closed, bounded, and unbounded for regions in space are similar to those for regions in the plane. To accommodate the extra dimension, we use solid balls of positive radius instead of disks.

DEFINITIONS Interior and Boundary Points for Space Regions

A point (x_0, y_0, z_0) in a region R in space is an **interior point** of R if it is the center of a solid ball that lies entirely in R (Figure 14.8a). A point (x_0, y_0, z_0) is a **boundary point** of R if every sphere centered at (x_0, y_0, z_0) encloses points that lie outside of R as well as points that lie inside R (Figure 14.8b). The **interior** of R is the set of interior points of R. The **boundary** of R is the set of boundary points of R.

A region is **open** if it consists entirely of interior points. A region is **closed** if it contains its entire boundary.

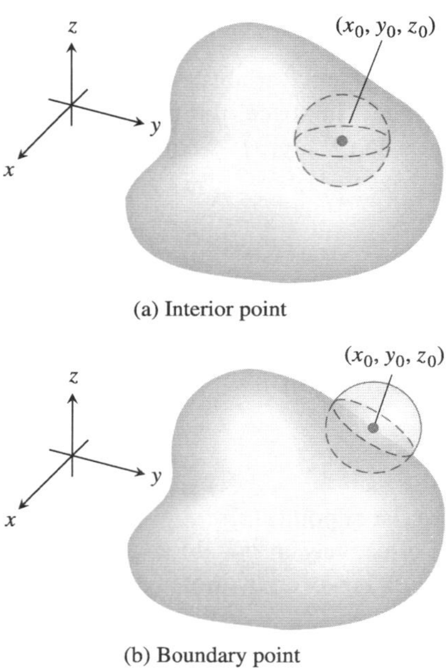

FIGURE 14.8 Interior points and boundary points of a region in space.

Examples of *open* sets in space include the interior of a sphere, the open half-space $z > 0$, the first octant (where x, y, and z are all positive), and space itself.

Examples of *closed* sets in space include lines, planes, the closed half-space $z \geq 0$, the first octant together with its bounding planes, and space itself (since it has no boundary points).

A solid sphere with part of its boundary removed or a solid cube with a missing face, edge, or corner point would be *neither open nor closed*.

Functions of more than three independent variables are also important. For example, the temperature on a surface in space may depend not only on the location of the point $P(x, y, z)$ on the surface, but also on time t when it is visited, so we would write $T = f(x, y, z, t)$.

Computer Graphing

Three-dimensional graphing programs for computers and calculators make it possible to graph functions of two variables with only a few keystrokes. We can often get information more quickly from a graph than from a formula.

EXAMPLE 6 Modeling Temperature Beneath Earth's Surface

The temperature beneath the Earth's surface is a function of the depth x beneath the surface and the time t of the year. If we measure x in feet and t as the number of days elapsed from the expected date of the yearly highest surface temperature, we can model the variation in temperature with the function

$$w = \cos(1.7 \times 10^{-2}t - 0.2x)e^{-0.2x}.$$

(The temperature at 0 ft is scaled to vary from $+1$ to -1, so that the variation at x feet can be interpreted as a fraction of the variation at the surface.)

Figure 14.9 shows a computer-generated graph of the function. At a depth of 15 ft, the variation (change in vertical amplitude in the figure) is about 5% of the surface variation. At 30 ft, there is almost no variation during the year.

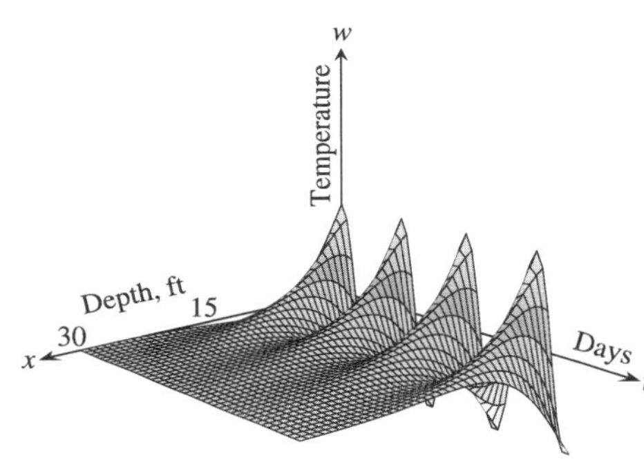

FIGURE 14.9 This computer-generated graph of

$$w = \cos(1.7 \times 10^{-2}t - 0.2x)e^{-0.2x}$$

shows the seasonal variation of the temperature belowground as a fraction of surface temperature. At $x = 15$ ft, the variation is only 5% of the variation at the surface. At $x = 30$ ft, the variation is less than 0.25% of the surface variation (Example 6). (Adapted from art provided by Norton Starr.)

The graph also shows that the temperature 15 ft below the surface is about half a year out of phase with the surface temperature. When the temperature is lowest on the surface (late January, say), it is at its highest 15 ft below. Fifteen feet below the ground, the seasons are reversed. ■

Figure 14.10 shows computer-generated graphs of a number of functions of two variables together with their level curves.

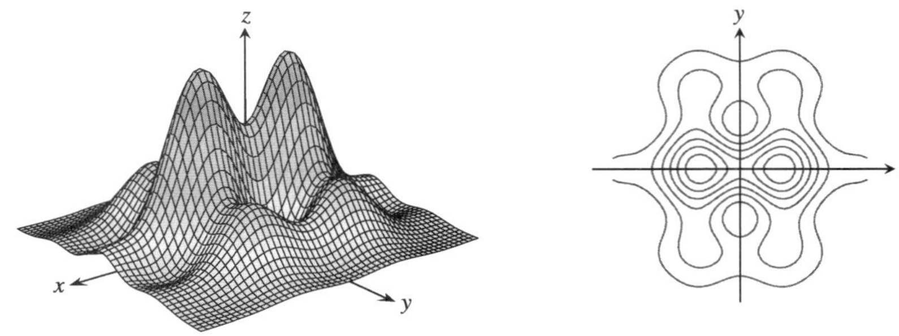

(a) $z = e^{-(x^2 + y^2)/8}(\sin x^2 + \cos y^2)$

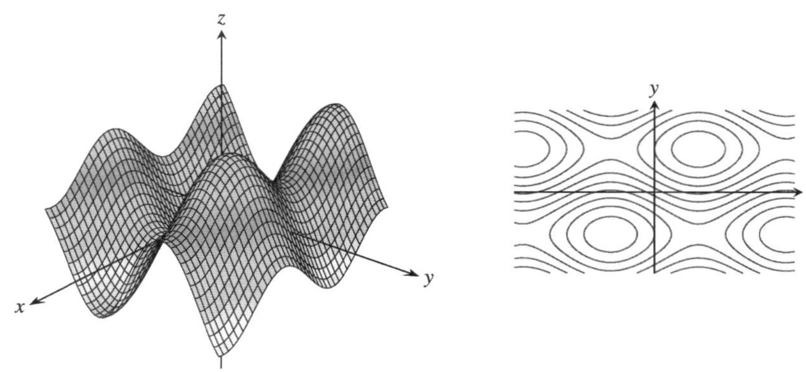

(b) $z = \sin x + 2 \sin y$

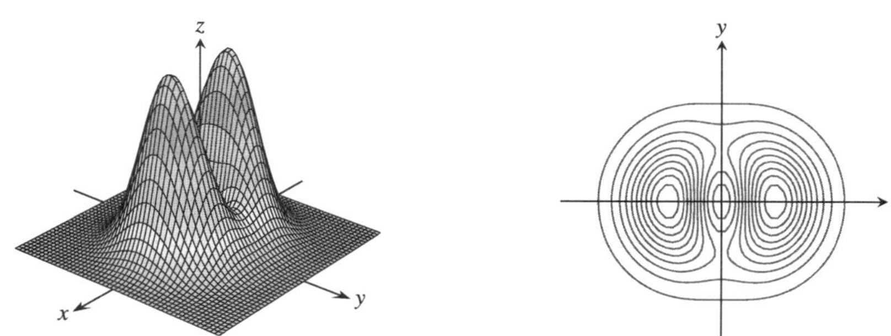

(c) $z = (4x^2 + y^2)e^{-x^2-y^2}$

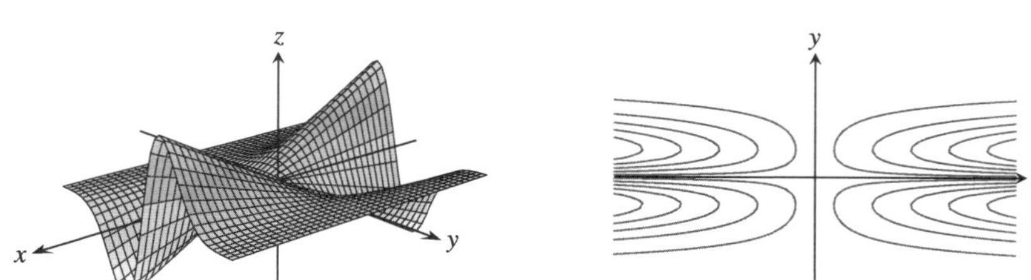

(d) $z = xye^{-y^2}$

FIGURE 14.10 Computer-generated graphs and level curves of typical functions of two variables.

EXERCISES 14.1

Domain, Range, and Level Curves

In Exercises 1–12, **(a)** find the function's domain, **(b)** find the function's range, **(c)** describe the function's level curves, **(d)** find the boundary of the function's domain, **(e)** determine if the domain is an open region, a closed region, or neither, and **(f)** decide if the domain is bounded or unbounded.

1. $f(x, y) = y - x$

2. $f(x, y) = \sqrt{y - x}$

3. $f(x, y) = 4x^2 + 9y^2$

4. $f(x, y) = x^2 - y^2$

5. $f(x, y) = xy$

6. $f(x, y) = y/x^2$

7. $f(x, y) = \dfrac{1}{\sqrt{16 - x^2 - y^2}}$

8. $f(x, y) = \sqrt{9 - x^2 - y^2}$

9. $f(x, y) = \ln(x^2 + y^2)$

10. $f(x, y) = e^{-(x^2+y^2)}$

11. $f(x, y) = \sin^{-1}(y - x)$

12. $f(x, y) = \tan^{-1}\left(\dfrac{y}{x}\right)$

Identifying Surfaces and Level Curves

Exercises 13–18 show level curves for the functions graphed in (a)–(f). Match each set of curves with the appropriate function.

13.

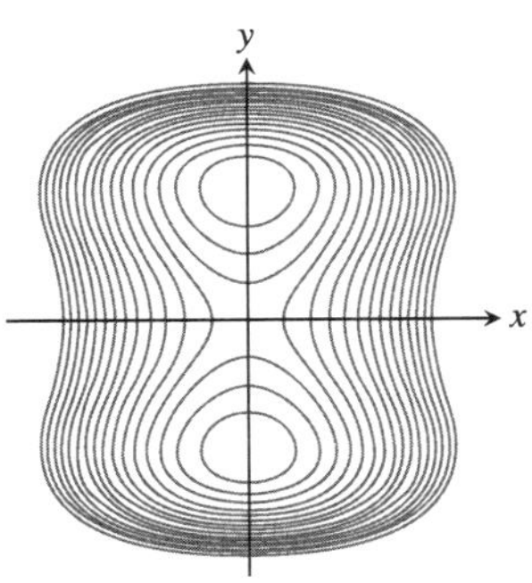

14.

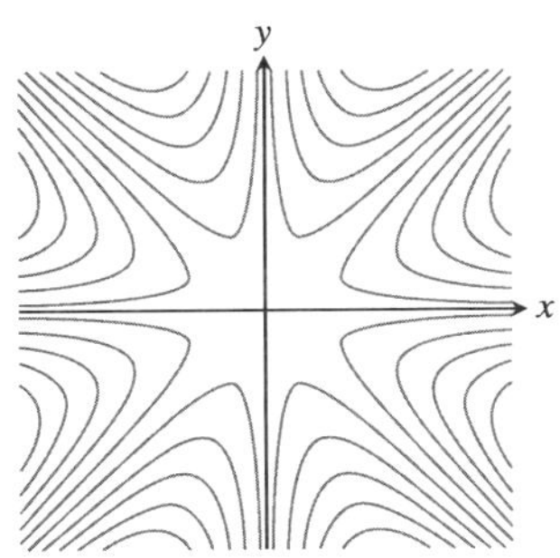

15.

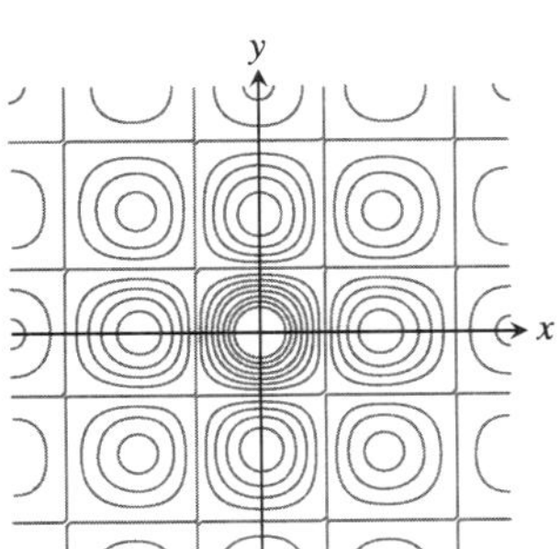

16.

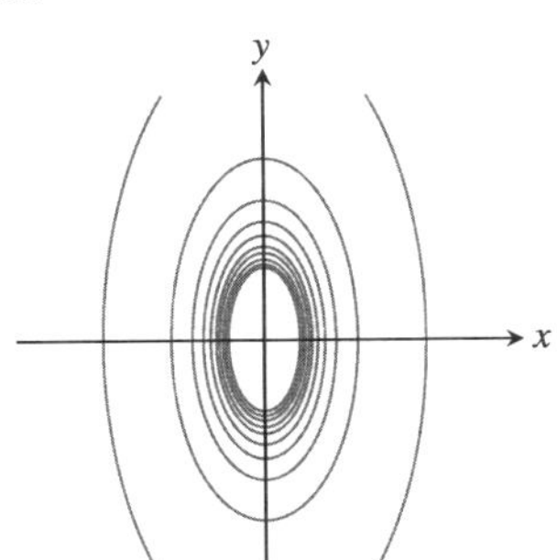

17.

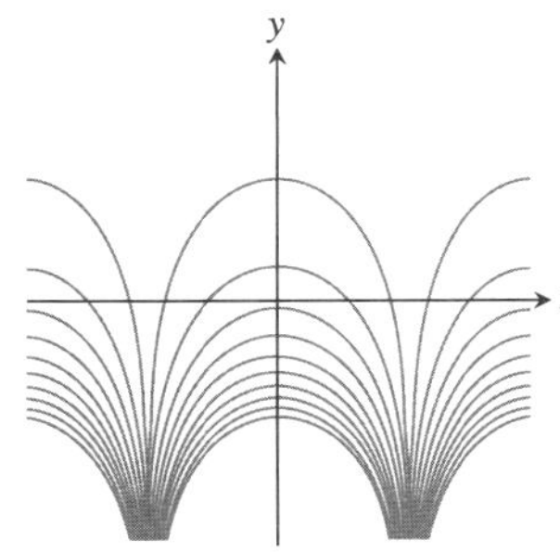

18.

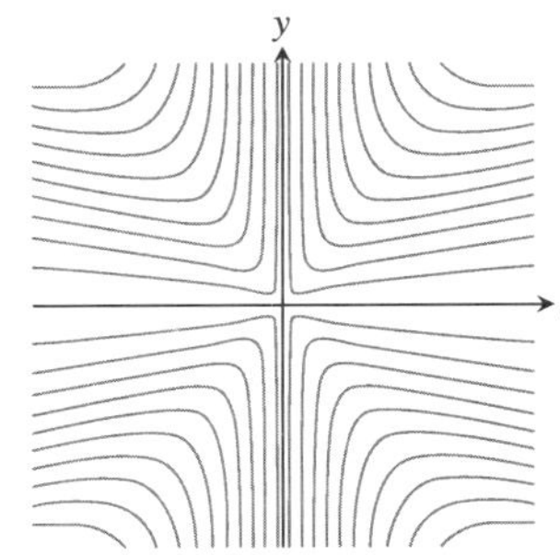

a.

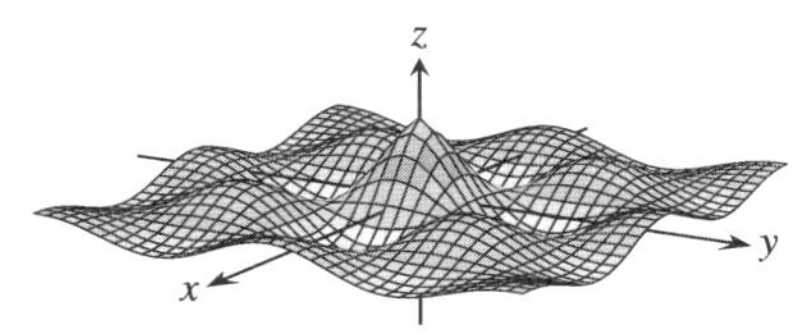

$z = (\cos x)(\cos y)\, e^{-\sqrt{x^2 + y^2}/4}$

b.

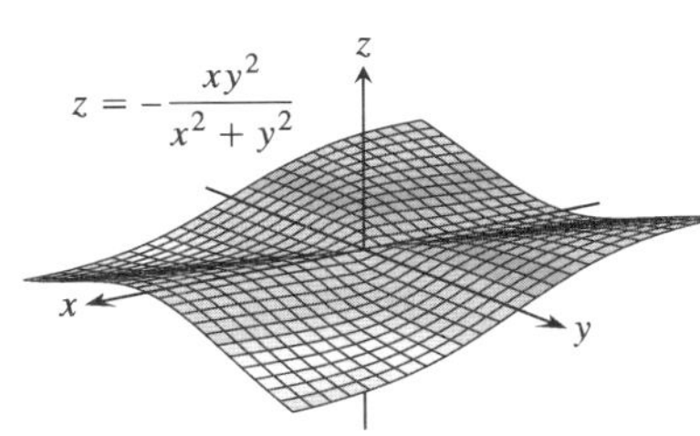

$z = -\dfrac{xy^2}{x^2 + y^2}$

c.

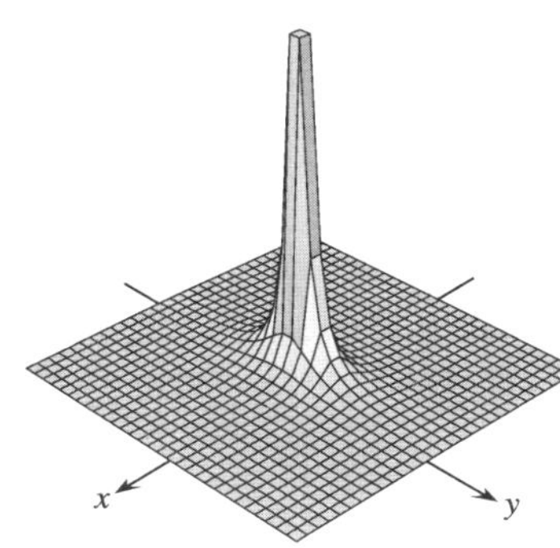

$z = \dfrac{1}{4x^2 + y^2}$

d.

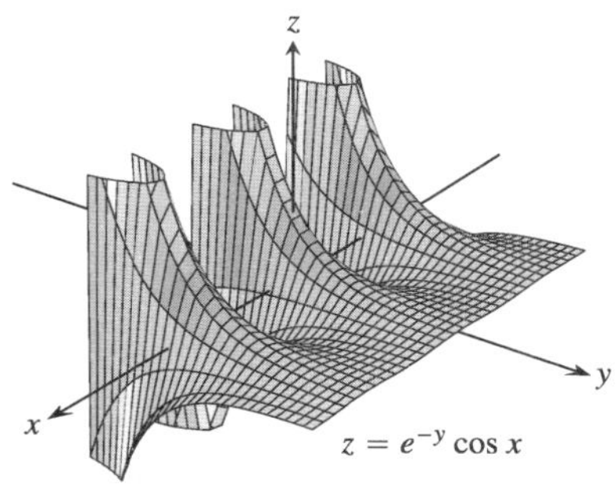

e.

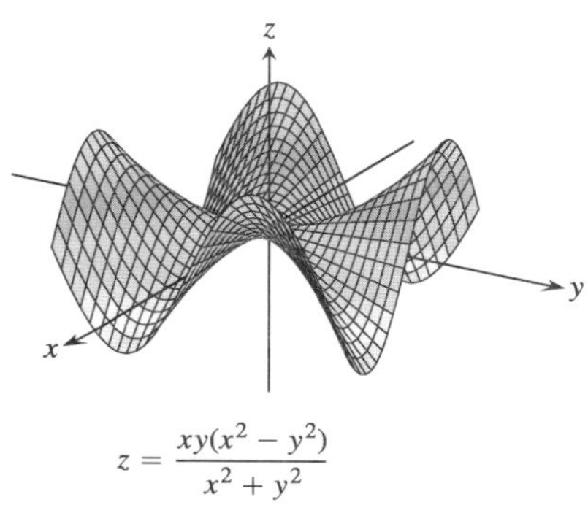

f.

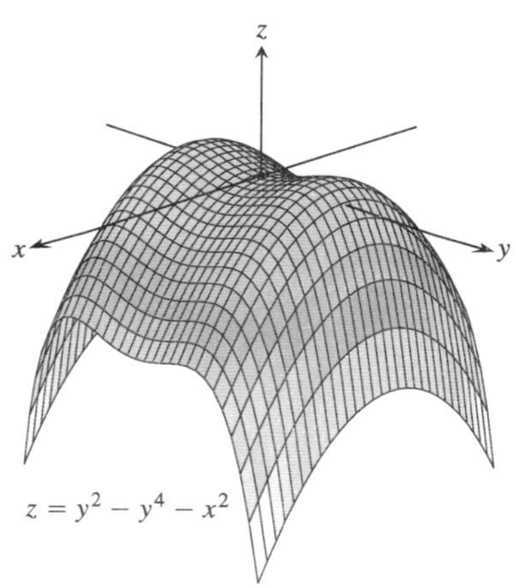

Identifying Functions of Two Variables

Display the values of the functions in Exercises 19–28 in two ways: **(a)** by sketching the surface $z = f(x, y)$ and **(b)** by drawing an assortment of level curves in the function's domain. Label each level curve with its function value.

19. $f(x, y) = y^2$ **20.** $f(x, y) = 4 - y^2$

21. $f(x, y) = x^2 + y^2$ **22.** $f(x, y) = \sqrt{x^2 + y^2}$

23. $f(x, y) = -(x^2 + y^2)$ **24.** $f(x, y) = 4 - x^2 - y^2$

25. $f(x, y) = 4x^2 + y^2$ **26.** $f(x, y) = 4x^2 + y^2 + 1$

27. $f(x, y) = 1 - |y|$ **28.** $f(x, y) = 1 - |x| - |y|$

Finding a Level Curve

In Exercises 29–32, find an equation for the level curve of the function $f(x, y)$ that passes through the given point.

29. $f(x, y) = 16 - x^2 - y^2, \quad \left(2\sqrt{2}, \sqrt{2}\right)$

30. $f(x, y) = \sqrt{x^2 - 1}, \quad (1, 0)$

31. $f(x, y) = \displaystyle\int_x^y \frac{dt}{1 + t^2}, \quad \left(-\sqrt{2}, \sqrt{2}\right)$

32. $f(x, y) = \displaystyle\sum_{n=0}^{\infty} \left(\frac{x}{y}\right)^n, \quad (1, 2)$

Sketching Level Surfaces

In Exercises 33–40, sketch a typical level surface for the function.

33. $f(x, y, z) = x^2 + y^2 + z^2$ **34.** $f(x, y, z) = \ln(x^2 + y^2 + z^2)$

35. $f(x, y, z) = x + z$ **36.** $f(x, y, z) = z$

37. $f(x, y, z) = x^2 + y^2$ **38.** $f(x, y, z) = y^2 + z^2$

39. $f(x, y, z) = z - x^2 - y^2$

40. $f(x, y, z) = (x^2/25) + (y^2/16) + (z^2/9)$

Finding a Level Surface

In Exercises 41–44, find an equation for the level surface of the function through the given point.

41. $f(x, y, z) = \sqrt{x - y} - \ln z, \quad (3, -1, 1)$

42. $f(x, y, z) = \ln(x^2 + y + z^2), \quad (-1, 2, 1)$

43. $g(x, y, z) = \displaystyle\sum_{n=0}^{\infty} \frac{(x + y)^n}{n!z^n}, \quad (\ln 2, \ln 4, 3)$

44. $g(x, y, z) = \displaystyle\int_x^y \frac{d\theta}{\sqrt{1 - \theta^2}} + \int_{\sqrt{2}}^z \frac{dt}{t\sqrt{t^2 - 1}}, \quad (0, 1/2, 2)$

Theory and Examples

45. The maximum value of a function on a line in space Does the function $f(x, y, z) = xyz$ have a maximum value on the line $x = 20 - t, y = t, z = 20$? If so, what is it? Give reasons for your answer. (*Hint:* Along the line, $w = f(x, y, z)$ is a differentiable function of t.)

46. The minimum value of a function on a line in space Does the function $f(x, y, z) = xy - z$ have a minimum value on the line $x = t - 1, y = t - 2, z = t + 7$? If so, what is it? Give reasons for your answer. (*Hint:* Along the line, $w = f(x, y, z)$ is a differentiable function of t.)

47. The Concorde's sonic booms Sound waves from the *Concorde* bend as the temperature changes above and below the altitude at which the plane flies. The sonic boom carpet is the region on the ground that receives shock waves directly from the plane, not reflected from the atmosphere or diffracted along the ground. The carpet is determined by the grazing rays striking the ground from the point directly under the plane. (See accompanying figure.)

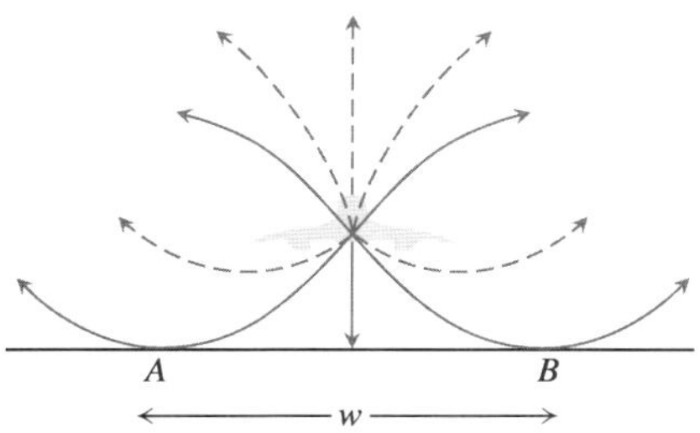

Sonic boom carpet

The width w of the region in which people on the ground hear the *Concorde*'s sonic boom directly, not reflected from a layer in the atmosphere, is a function of

T = air temperature at ground level (in degrees Kelvin)

h = the *Concorde*'s altitude (in kilometers)

d = the vertical temperature gradient (temperature drop in degrees Kelvin per kilometer).

The formula for w is

$$w = 4\left(\frac{Th}{d}\right)^{1/2}.$$

The Washington-bound *Concorde* approached the United States from Europe on a course that took it south of Nantucket Island at an altitude of 16.8 km. If the surface temperature is 290 K and the vertical temperature gradient is 5 K/km, how many kilometers south of Nantucket did the plane have to be flown to keep its sonic boom carpet away from the island? (From "Concorde Sonic Booms as an Atmospheric Probe" by N. K. Balachandra, W. L. Donn, and D. H. Rind, *Science*, Vol. 197 (July 1, 1977), pp. 47–49.)

48. As you know, the graph of a real-valued function of a single real variable is a set in a two-coordinate space. The graph of a real-valued function of two independent real variables is a set in a three-coordinate space. The graph of a real-valued function of three independent real variables is a set in a four-coordinate space. How would you define the graph of a real-valued function $f(x_1, x_2, x_3, x_4)$ of four independent real variables? How would you define the graph of a real-valued function $f(x_1, x_2, x_3, \ldots, x_n)$ of n independent real variables?

COMPUTER EXPLORATIONS

Explicit Surfaces

Use a CAS to perform the following steps for each of the functions in Exercises 49–52.

a. Plot the surface over the given rectangle.

b. Plot several level curves in the rectangle.

c. Plot the level curve of f through the given point.

49. $f(x, y) = x \sin\frac{y}{2} + y \sin 2x, \quad 0 \le x \le 5\pi \quad 0 \le y \le 5\pi,$ $P(3\pi, 3\pi)$

50. $f(x, y) = (\sin x)(\cos y)e^{\sqrt{x^2+y^2}/8}, \quad 0 \le x \le 5\pi,$ $0 \le y \le 5\pi, \quad P(4\pi, 4\pi)$

51. $f(x, y) = \sin(x + 2\cos y), \quad -2\pi \le x \le 2\pi,$ $-2\pi \le y \le 2\pi, \quad P(\pi, \pi)$

52. $f(x, y) = e^{(x^{0.1}-y)} \sin(x^2 + y^2), \quad 0 \le x \le 2\pi,$ $-2\pi \le y \le \pi, \quad P(\pi, -\pi)$

Implicit Surfaces

Use a CAS to plot the level surfaces in Exercises 53–56.

53. $4 \ln(x^2 + y^2 + z^2) = 1$ **54.** $x^2 + z^2 = 1$

55. $x + y^2 - 3z^2 = 1$

56. $\sin\left(\frac{x}{2}\right) - (\cos y)\sqrt{x^2 + z^2} = 2$

Parametrized Surfaces

Just as you describe curves in the plane parametrically with a pair of equations $x = f(t), y = g(t)$ defined on some parameter interval I, you can sometimes describe surfaces in space with a triple of equations $x = f(u, v), y = g(u, v), z = h(u, v)$ defined on some parameter rectangle $a \le u \le b, c \le v \le d$. Many computer algebra systems permit you to plot such surfaces in *parametric mode*. (Parametrized surfaces are discussed in detail in Section 16.6.) Use a CAS to plot the surfaces in Exercises 57–60. Also plot several level curves in the xy-plane.

57. $x = u\cos v, \quad y = u\sin v, \quad z = u, \quad 0 \le u \le 2,$ $0 \le v \le 2\pi$

58. $x = u\cos v, \quad y = u\sin v, \quad z = v, \quad 0 \le u \le 2,$ $0 \le v \le 2\pi$

59. $x = (2 + \cos u)\cos v, \quad y = (2 + \cos u)\sin v, \quad z = \sin u,$ $0 \le u \le 2\pi, \quad 0 \le v \le 2\pi$

60. $x = 2\cos u\cos v, \quad y = 2\cos u\sin v, \quad z = 2\sin u,$ $0 \le u \le 2\pi, \quad 0 \le v \le \pi$

14.2 Limits and Continuity in Higher Dimensions

This section treats limits and continuity for multivariable functions. The definition of the limit of a function of two or three variables is similar to the definition of the limit of a function of a single variable but with a crucial difference, as we now see.

Limits

If the values of $f(x, y)$ lie arbitrarily close to a fixed real number L for all points (x, y) sufficiently close to a point (x_0, y_0), we say that f approaches the limit L as (x, y) approaches (x_0, y_0). This is similar to the informal definition for the limit of a function of a single variable. Notice, however, that if (x_0, y_0) lies in the interior of f's domain, (x, y) can approach (x_0, y_0) from any direction. The direction of approach can be an issue, as in some of the examples that follow.

DEFINITION Limit of a Function of Two Variables

We say that a function $f(x, y)$ approaches the **limit** L as (x, y) approaches (x_0, y_0), and write

$$\lim_{(x, y)\to(x_0, y_0)} f(x, y) = L$$

if, for every number $\epsilon > 0$, there exists a corresponding number $\delta > 0$ such that for all (x, y) in the domain of f,

$$|f(x, y) - L| < \epsilon \qquad \text{whenever} \qquad 0 < \sqrt{(x - x_0)^2 + (y - y_0)^2} < \delta.$$

The definition of limit says that the distance between $f(x, y)$ and L becomes arbitrarily small whenever the distance from (x, y) to (x_0, y_0) is made sufficiently small (but not 0).

The definition of limit applies to boundary points (x_0, y_0) as well as interior points of the domain of f. The only requirement is that the point (x, y) remain in the domain at all times. It can be shown, as for functions of a single variable, that

$$\lim_{(x, y)\to(x_0, y_0)} x = x_0$$

$$\lim_{(x, y)\to(x_0, y_0)} y = y_0$$

$$\lim_{(x, y)\to(x_0, y_0)} k = k \qquad \text{(any number } k).$$

For example, in the first limit statement above, $f(x, y) = x$ and $L = x_0$. Using the definition of limit, suppose that $\epsilon > 0$ is chosen. If we let δ equal this ϵ, we see that

$$0 < \sqrt{(x - x_0)^2 + (y - y_0)^2} < \delta = \epsilon$$

implies

$$0 < \sqrt{(x - x_0)^2} < \epsilon \qquad (x - x_0)^2 \le (x - x_0)^2 + (y - y_0)^2$$

$$|x - x_0| < \epsilon \qquad \sqrt{a^2} = |a|$$

$$|f(x, y) - x_0| < \epsilon \qquad x = f(x, y)$$

That is,

$$|f(x, y) - x_0| < \epsilon \qquad \text{whenever} \qquad 0 < \sqrt{(x - x_0)^2 + (y - y_0)^2} < \delta.$$

So

$$\lim_{(x, y) \to (x_0, y_0)} f(x, y) = \lim_{(x, y) \to (x_0, y_0)} x = x_0.$$

It can also be shown that the limit of the sum of two functions is the sum of their limits (when they both exist), with similar results for the limits of the differences, products, constant multiples, quotients, and powers.

THEOREM 1 Properties of Limits of Functions of Two Variables

The following rules hold if L, M, and k are real numbers and

$$\lim_{(x, y) \to (x_0, y_0)} f(x, y) = L \qquad \text{and} \qquad \lim_{(x, y) \to (x_0, y_0)} g(x, y) = M.$$

1. *Sum Rule:* $\lim_{(x, y) \to (x_0, y_0)} (f(x, y) + g(x, y)) = L + M$
2. *Difference Rule:* $\lim_{(x, y) \to (x_0, y_0)} (f(x, y) - g(x, y)) = L - M$
3. *Product Rule:* $\lim_{(x, y) \to (x_0, y_0)} (f(x, y) \cdot g(x, y)) = L \cdot M$
4. *Constant Multiple Rule:* $\lim_{(x, y) \to (x_0, y_0)} (kf(x, y)) = kL$ (any number k)
5. *Quotient Rule:* $\lim_{(x, y) \to (x_0, y_0)} \dfrac{f(x, y)}{g(x, y)} = \dfrac{L}{M}$ $\quad M \neq 0$
6. *Power Rule:* If r and s are integers with no common factors, and $s \neq 0$, then

$$\lim_{(x, y) \to (x_0, y_0)} (f(x, y))^{r/s} = L^{r/s}$$

provided $L^{r/s}$ is a real number. (If s is even, we assume that $L > 0$.)

While we won't prove Theorem 1 here, we give an informal discussion of why it's true. If (x, y) is sufficiently close to (x_0, y_0), then $f(x, y)$ is close to L and $g(x, y)$ is close to M (from the informal interpretation of limits). It is then reasonable that $f(x, y) + g(x, y)$ is close to $L + M$; $f(x, y) - g(x, y)$ is close to $L - M$; $f(x, y)g(x, y)$ is close to LM; $kf(x, y)$ is close to kL; and that $f(x, y)/g(x, y)$ is close to L/M if $M \neq 0$.

When we apply Theorem 1 to polynomials and rational functions, we obtain the useful result that the limits of these functions as $(x, y) \to (x_0, y_0)$ can be calculated by evaluating the functions at (x_0, y_0). The only requirement is that the rational functions be defined at (x_0, y_0).

EXAMPLE 1 Calculating Limits

(a) $$\lim_{(x, y) \to (0,1)} \frac{x - xy + 3}{x^2y + 5xy - y^3} = \frac{0 - (0)(1) + 3}{(0)^2(1) + 5(0)(1) - (1)^3} = -3$$

(b) $$\lim_{(x, y) \to (3, -4)} \sqrt{x^2 + y^2} = \sqrt{(3)^2 + (-4)^2} = \sqrt{25} = 5$$

■

EXAMPLE 2 Calculating Limits

Find

$$\lim_{(x,y)\to(0,0)} \frac{x^2 - xy}{\sqrt{x} - \sqrt{y}}.$$

Solution Since the denominator $\sqrt{x} - \sqrt{y}$ approaches 0 as $(x, y) \to (0, 0)$, we cannot use the Quotient Rule from Theorem 1. If we multiply numerator and denominator by $\sqrt{x} + \sqrt{y}$, however, we produce an equivalent fraction whose limit we *can* find:

$$\begin{aligned}
\lim_{(x,y)\to(0,0)} \frac{x^2 - xy}{\sqrt{x} - \sqrt{y}} &= \lim_{(x,y)\to(0,0)} \frac{\left(x^2 - xy\right)\left(\sqrt{x} + \sqrt{y}\right)}{\left(\sqrt{x} - \sqrt{y}\right)\left(\sqrt{x} + \sqrt{y}\right)} \\
&= \lim_{(x,y)\to(0,0)} \frac{x(x - y)\left(\sqrt{x} + \sqrt{y}\right)}{x - y} && \text{Algebra} \\
&= \lim_{(x,y)\to(0,0)} x\left(\sqrt{x} + \sqrt{y}\right) && \text{Cancel the nonzero factor } (x - y). \\
&= 0\left(\sqrt{0} + \sqrt{0}\right) = 0
\end{aligned}$$

We can cancel the factor $(x - y)$ because the path $y = x$ (along which $x - y = 0$) is *not* in the domain of the function

$$\frac{x^2 - xy}{\sqrt{x} - \sqrt{y}}.$$

■

EXAMPLE 3 Applying the Limit Definition

Find $\displaystyle\lim_{(x,y)\to(0,0)} \frac{4xy^2}{x^2 + y^2}$ if it exists.

Solution We first observe that along the line $x = 0$, the function always has value 0 when $y \neq 0$. Likewise, along the line $y = 0$, the function has value 0 provided $x \neq 0$. So if the limit does exist as (x, y) approaches $(0, 0)$, the value of the limit must be 0. To see if this is true, we apply the definition of limit.

Let $\epsilon > 0$ be given, but arbitrary. We want to find a $\delta > 0$ such that

$$\left| \frac{4xy^2}{x^2 + y^2} - 0 \right| < \epsilon \quad \text{whenever} \quad 0 < \sqrt{x^2 + y^2} < \delta$$

or

$$\frac{4|x|y^2}{x^2 + y^2} < \epsilon \quad \text{whenever} \quad 0 < \sqrt{x^2 + y^2} < \delta.$$

Since $y^2 \leq x^2 + y^2$ we have that

$$\frac{4|x|y^2}{x^2 + y^2} \leq 4|x| = 4\sqrt{x^2} \leq 4\sqrt{x^2 + y^2}.$$

So if we choose $\delta = \epsilon/4$ and let $0 < \sqrt{x^2 + y^2} < \delta$, we get

$$\left|\frac{4xy^2}{x^2 + y^2} - 0\right| \le 4\sqrt{x^2 + y^2} < 4\delta = 4\left(\frac{\epsilon}{4}\right) = \epsilon.$$

It follows from the definition that

$$\lim_{(x, y)\to(0,0)} \frac{4xy^2}{x^2 + y^2} = 0.$$

Continuity

As with functions of a single variable, continuity is defined in terms of limits.

DEFINITION Continuous Function of Two Variables

A function $f(x, y)$ is **continuous at the point (x_0, y_0)** if

1. f is defined at (x_0, y_0),
2. $\lim_{(x, y)\to(x_0, y_0)} f(x, y)$ exists,
3. $\lim_{(x, y)\to(x_0, y_0)} f(x, y) = f(x_0, y_0)$.

A function is **continuous** if it is continuous at every point of its domain.

As with the definition of limit, the definition of continuity applies at boundary points as well as interior points of the domain of f. The only requirement is that the point (x, y) remain in the domain at all times.

As you may have guessed, one of the consequences of Theorem 1 is that algebraic combinations of continuous functions are continuous at every point at which all the functions involved are defined. This means that sums, differences, products, constant multiples, quotients, and powers of continuous functions are continuous where defined. In particular, polynomials and rational functions of two variables are continuous at every point at which they are defined.

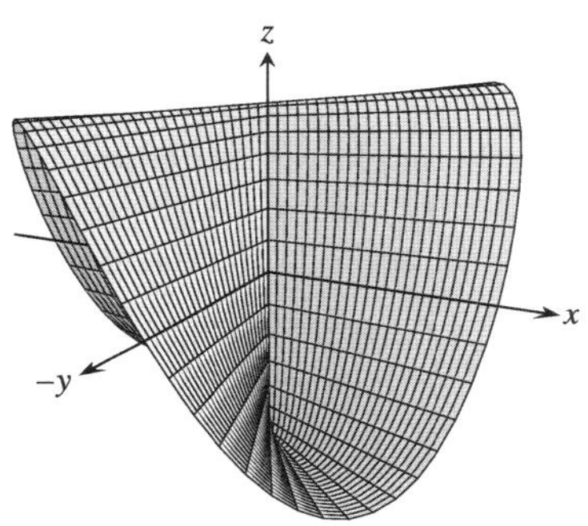

(a)

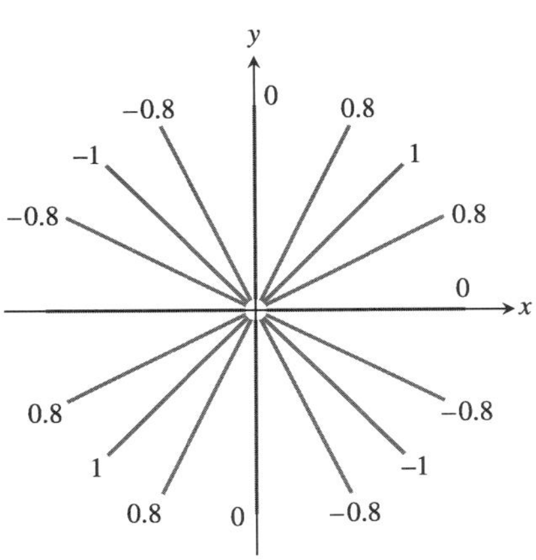

(b)

FIGURE 14.11 (a) The graph of

$$f(x, y) = \begin{cases} \dfrac{2xy}{x^2 + y^2}, & (x, y) \ne (0, 0) \\ 0, & (x, y) = (0, 0). \end{cases}$$

The function is continuous at every point except the origin. (b) The level curves of f (Example 4).

EXAMPLE 4 A Function with a Single Point of Discontinuity

Show that

$$f(x, y) = \begin{cases} \dfrac{2xy}{x^2 + y^2}, & (x, y) \ne (0, 0) \\ 0, & (x, y) = (0, 0) \end{cases}$$

is continuous at every point except the origin (Figure 14.11).

Solution The function f is continuous at any point $(x, y) \ne (0, 0)$ because its values are then given by a rational function of x and y.

At (0, 0), the value of f is defined, but f, we claim, has no limit as $(x, y) \to (0, 0)$. The reason is that different paths of approach to the origin can lead to different results, as we now see.

For every value of m, the function f has a constant value on the "punctured" line $y = mx, x \neq 0$, because

$$f(x, y)\bigg|_{y=mx} = \frac{2xy}{x^2 + y^2}\bigg|_{y=mx} = \frac{2x(mx)}{x^2 + (mx)^2} = \frac{2mx^2}{x^2 + m^2x^2} = \frac{2m}{1 + m^2}.$$

Therefore, f has this number as its limit as (x, y) approaches $(0, 0)$ along the line:

$$\lim_{\substack{(x, y)\to(0,0) \\ \text{along } y=mx}} f(x, y) = \lim_{(x, y)\to(0,0)} \left[f(x, y)\bigg|_{y=mx} \right] = \frac{2m}{1 + m^2}.$$

This limit changes with m. There is therefore no single number we may call the limit of f as (x, y) approaches the origin. The limit fails to exist, and the function is not continuous. ■

Example 4 illustrates an important point about limits of functions of two variables (or even more variables, for that matter). For a limit to exist at a point, the limit must be the same along every approach path. This result is analogous to the single-variable case where both the left- and right-sided limits had to have the same value; therefore, for functions of two or more variables, if we ever find paths with different limits, we know the function has no limit at the point they approach.

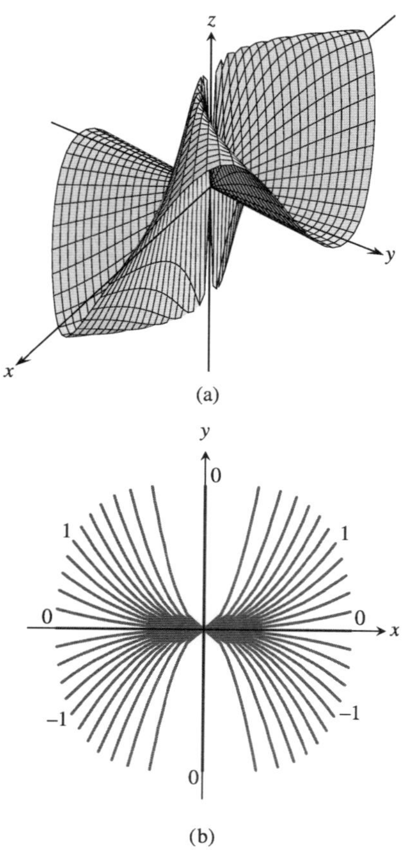

FIGURE 14.12 (a) The graph of $f(x, y) = 2x^2y/(x^4 + y^2)$. As the graph suggests and the level-curve values in part (b) confirm, $\lim_{(x, y)\to(0,0)} f(x, y)$ does not exist (Example 5).

> **Two-Path Test for Nonexistence of a Limit**
> If a function $f(x, y)$ has different limits along two different paths as (x, y) approaches (x_0, y_0), then $\lim_{(x, y)\to(x_0, y_0)} f(x, y)$ does not exist.

EXAMPLE 5 Applying the Two-Path Test

Show that the function

$$f(x, y) = \frac{2x^2y}{x^4 + y^2}$$

(Figure 14.12) has no limit as (x, y) approaches $(0, 0)$.

Solution The limit cannot be found by direct substitution, which gives the form $0/0$. We examine the values of f along curves that end at $(0, 0)$. Along the curve $y = kx^2, x \neq 0$, the function has the constant value

$$f(x, y)\bigg|_{y=kx^2} = \frac{2x^2y}{x^4 + y^2}\bigg|_{y=kx^2} = \frac{2x^2(kx^2)}{x^4 + (kx^2)^2} = \frac{2kx^4}{x^4 + k^2x^4} = \frac{2k}{1 + k^2}.$$

Therefore,

$$\lim_{\substack{(x, y)\to(0,0) \\ \text{along } y=kx^2}} f(x, y) = \lim_{(x, y)\to(0,0)} \left[f(x, y)\bigg|_{y=kx^2} \right] = \frac{2k}{1 + k^2}.$$

This limit varies with the path of approach. If (x, y) approaches $(0, 0)$ along the parabola $y = x^2$, for instance, $k = 1$ and the limit is 1. If (x, y) approaches $(0, 0)$ along the x-axis, $k = 0$ and the limit is 0. By the two-path test, f has no limit as (x, y) approaches $(0, 0)$.

The language here may seem contradictory. You might well ask, "What do you mean f has no limit as (x, y) approaches the origin—it has lots of limits." But that is the point. There is no *single* path-independent limit, and therefore, by the definition, $\lim_{(x, y)\to(0,0)} f(x, y)$ does not exist. ■

Compositions of continuous functions are also continuous. The proof, omitted here, is similar to that for functions of a single variable (Theorem 10 in Section 2.6).

Continuity of Composites
If f is continuous at (x_0, y_0) and g is a single-variable function continuous at $f(x_0, y_0)$, then the composite function $h = g \circ f$ defined by $h(x, y) = g(f(x, y))$ is continuous at (x_0, y_0).

For example, the composite functions

$$e^{x-y}, \qquad \cos\frac{xy}{x^2+1}, \qquad \ln(1+x^2y^2)$$

are continuous at every point (x, y).

As with functions of a single variable, the general rule is that composites of continuous functions are continuous. The only requirement is that each function be continuous where it is applied.

Functions of More Than Two Variables

The definitions of limit and continuity for functions of two variables and the conclusions about limits and continuity for sums, products, quotients, powers, and composites all extend to functions of three or more variables. Functions like

$$\ln(x+y+z) \qquad \text{and} \qquad \frac{y\sin z}{x-1}$$

are continuous throughout their domains, and limits like

$$\lim_{P\to(1,0,-1)} \frac{e^{x+z}}{z^2+\cos\sqrt{xy}} = \frac{e^{1-1}}{(-1)^2+\cos 0} = \frac{1}{2},$$

where P denotes the point (x, y, z), may be found by direct substitution.

Extreme Values of Continuous Functions on Closed, Bounded Sets

We have seen that a function of a single variable that is continuous throughout a closed, bounded interval $[a, b]$ takes on an absolute maximum value and an absolute minimum value at least once in $[a, b]$. The same is true of a function $z = f(x, y)$ that is continuous on a closed, bounded set R in the plane (like a line segment, a disk, or a filled-in triangle). The function takes on an absolute maximum value at some point in R and an absolute minimum value at some point in R.

Theorems similar to these and other theorems of this section hold for functions of three or more variables. A continuous function $w = f(x, y, z)$, for example, must take on absolute maximum and minimum values on any closed, bounded set (solid ball or cube, spherical shell, rectangular solid) on which it is defined.

We learn how to find these extreme values in Section 14.7, but first we need to study derivatives in higher dimensions. That is the topic of the next section.

EXERCISES 14.2

Limits with Two Variables

Find the limits in Exercises 1–12.

1. $\lim\limits_{(x,y)\to(0,0)} \dfrac{3x^2 - y^2 + 5}{x^2 + y^2 + 2}$

2. $\lim\limits_{(x,y)\to(0,4)} \dfrac{x}{\sqrt{y}}$

3. $\lim\limits_{(x,y)\to(3,4)} \sqrt{x^2 + y^2 - 1}$

4. $\lim\limits_{(x,y)\to(2,-3)} \left(\dfrac{1}{x} + \dfrac{1}{y}\right)^2$

5. $\lim\limits_{(x,y)\to(0,\pi/4)} \sec x \tan y$

6. $\lim\limits_{(x,y)\to(0,0)} \cos \dfrac{x^2 + y^3}{x + y + 1}$

7. $\lim\limits_{(x,y)\to(0,\ln 2)} e^{x-y}$

8. $\lim\limits_{(x,y)\to(1,1)} \ln|1 + x^2y^2|$

9. $\lim\limits_{(x,y)\to(0,0)} \dfrac{e^y \sin x}{x}$

10. $\lim\limits_{(x,y)\to(1,1)} \cos \sqrt[3]{|xy| - 1}$

11. $\lim\limits_{(x,y)\to(1,0)} \dfrac{x \sin y}{x^2 + 1}$

12. $\lim\limits_{(x,y)\to(\pi/2,0)} \dfrac{\cos y + 1}{y - \sin x}$

Limits of Quotients

Find the limits in Exercises 13–20 by rewriting the fractions first.

13. $\lim\limits_{\substack{(x,y)\to(1,1)\\ x\neq y}} \dfrac{x^2 - 2xy + y^2}{x - y}$

14. $\lim\limits_{\substack{(x,y)\to(1,1)\\ x\neq y}} \dfrac{x^2 - y^2}{x - y}$

15. $\lim\limits_{\substack{(x,y)\to(1,1)\\ x\neq 1}} \dfrac{xy - y - 2x + 2}{x - 1}$

16. $\lim\limits_{\substack{(x,y)\to(2,-4)\\ y\neq -4,\, x\neq x^2}} \dfrac{y + 4}{x^2y - xy + 4x^2 - 4x}$

17. $\lim\limits_{\substack{(x,y)\to(0,0)\\ x\neq y}} \dfrac{x - y + 2\sqrt{x} - 2\sqrt{y}}{\sqrt{x} - \sqrt{y}}$

18. $\lim\limits_{\substack{(x,y)\to(2,2)\\ x+y\neq 4}} \dfrac{x + y - 4}{\sqrt{x + y} - 2}$

19. $\lim\limits_{\substack{(x,y)\to(2,0)\\ 2x-y\neq 4}} \dfrac{\sqrt{2x - y} - 2}{2x - y - 4}$

20. $\lim\limits_{\substack{(x,y)\to(4,3)\\ x\neq y+1}} \dfrac{\sqrt{x} - \sqrt{y + 1}}{x - y - 1}$

Limits with Three Variables

Find the limits in Exercises 21–26.

21. $\lim\limits_{P\to(1,3,4)} \left(\dfrac{1}{x} + \dfrac{1}{y} + \dfrac{1}{z}\right)$

22. $\lim\limits_{P\to(1,-1,-1)} \dfrac{2xy + yz}{x^2 + z^2}$

23. $\lim\limits_{P\to(3,3,0)} (\sin^2 x + \cos^2 y + \sec^2 z)$

24. $\lim\limits_{P\to(-1/4,\pi/2,2)} \tan^{-1} xyz$

25. $\lim\limits_{P\to(\pi,0,3)} ze^{-2y} \cos 2x$

26. $\lim\limits_{P\to(0,-2,0)} \ln\sqrt{x^2 + y^2 + z^2}$

Continuity in the Plane

At what points (x, y) in the plane are the functions in Exercises 27–30 continuous?

27. a. $f(x, y) = \sin(x + y)$ b. $f(x, y) = \ln(x^2 + y^2)$

28. a. $f(x, y) = \dfrac{x + y}{x - y}$ b. $f(x, y) = \dfrac{y}{x^2 + 1}$

29. a. $g(x, y) = \sin \dfrac{1}{xy}$ b. $g(x, y) = \dfrac{x + y}{2 + \cos x}$

30. a. $g(x, y) = \dfrac{x^2 + y^2}{x^2 - 3x + 2}$ b. $g(x, y) = \dfrac{1}{x^2 - y}$

Continuity in Space

At what points (x, y, z) in space are the functions in Exercises 31–34 continuous?

31. a. $f(x, y, z) = x^2 + y^2 - 2z^2$
    b. $f(x, y, z) = \sqrt{x^2 + y^2 - 1}$

32. a. $f(x, y, z) = \ln xyz$ b. $f(x, y, z) = e^{x+y} \cos z$

33. a. $h(x, y, z) = xy \sin \dfrac{1}{z}$ b. $h(x, y, z) = \dfrac{1}{x^2 + z^2 - 1}$

34. a. $h(x, y, z) = \dfrac{1}{|y| + |z|}$ b. $h(x, y, z) = \dfrac{1}{|xy| + |z|}$

No Limit at a Point

By considering different paths of approach, show that the functions in Exercises 35–42 have no limit as $(x, y) \to (0, 0)$.

35. $f(x, y) = -\dfrac{x}{\sqrt{x^2 + y^2}}$

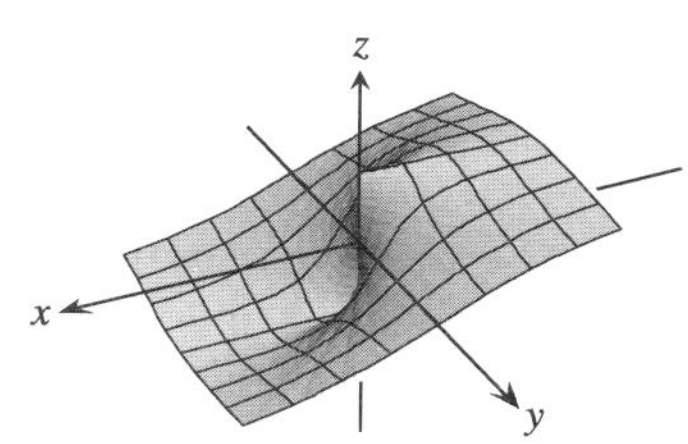

36. $f(x, y) = \dfrac{x^4}{x^4 + y^2}$

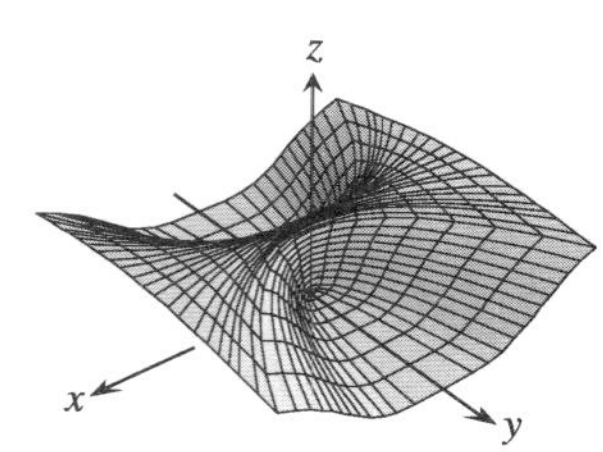

37. $f(x, y) = \dfrac{x^4 - y^2}{x^4 + y^2}$

38. $f(x, y) = \dfrac{xy}{|xy|}$

39. $g(x, y) = \dfrac{x - y}{x + y}$

40. $g(x, y) = \dfrac{x + y}{x - y}$

41. $h(x, y) = \dfrac{x^2 + y}{y}$

42. $h(x, y) = \dfrac{x^2}{x^2 - y}$

Theory and Examples

43. If $\lim_{(x,y)\to(x_0,y_0)} f(x,y) = L$, must f be defined at (x_0, y_0)? Give reasons for your answer.

44. If $f(x_0, y_0) = 3$, what can you say about

$$\lim_{(x,y)\to(x_0,y_0)} f(x,y)$$

if f is continuous at (x_0, y_0)? If f is not continuous at (x_0, y_0)? Give reasons for your answer.

The Sandwich Theorem for functions of two variables states that if $g(x,y) \le f(x,y) \le h(x,y)$ for all $(x,y) \ne (x_0,y_0)$ in a disk centered at (x_0, y_0) and if g and h have the same finite limit L as $(x,y) \to (x_0,y_0)$, then

$$\lim_{(x,y)\to(x_0,y_0)} f(x,y) = L.$$

Use this result to support your answers to the questions in Exercises 45–48.

45. Does knowing that

$$1 - \frac{x^2y^2}{3} < \frac{\tan^{-1} xy}{xy} < 1$$

tell you anything about

$$\lim_{(x,y)\to(0,0)} \frac{\tan^{-1} xy}{xy}?$$

Give reasons for your answer.

46. Does knowing that

$$2|xy| - \frac{x^2y^2}{6} < 4 - 4\cos\sqrt{|xy|} < 2|xy|$$

tell you anything about

$$\lim_{(x,y)\to(0,0)} \frac{4 - 4\cos\sqrt{|xy|}}{|xy|}?$$

Give reasons for your answer.

47. Does knowing that $|\sin(1/x)| \le 1$ tell you anything about

$$\lim_{(x,y)\to(0,0)} y \sin\frac{1}{x}?$$

Give reasons for your answer.

48. Does knowing that $|\cos(1/y)| \le 1$ tell you anything about

$$\lim_{(x,y)\to(0,0)} x \cos\frac{1}{y}?$$

Give reasons for your answer.

49. *(Continuation of Example 4.)*

a. Reread Example 4. Then substitute $m = \tan\theta$ into the formula

$$f(x,y)\bigg|_{y=mx} = \frac{2m}{1+m^2}$$

and simplify the result to show how the value of f varies with the line's angle of inclination.

b. Use the formula you obtained in part (a) to show that the limit of f as $(x,y) \to (0,0)$ along the line $y = mx$ varies from -1 to 1 depending on the angle of approach.

50. Continuous extension Define $f(0,0)$ in a way that extends

$$f(x,y) = xy\frac{x^2 - y^2}{x^2 + y^2}$$

to be continuous at the origin.

Changing to Polar Coordinates

If you cannot make any headway with $\lim_{(x,y)\to(0,0)} f(x,y)$ in rectangular coordinates, try changing to polar coordinates. Substitute $x = r\cos\theta$, $y = r\sin\theta$, and investigate the limit of the resulting expression as $r \to 0$. In other words, try to decide whether there exists a number L satisfying the following criterion:

Given $\epsilon > 0$, there exists a $\delta > 0$ such that for all r and θ,

$$|r| < \delta \quad\Rightarrow\quad |f(r,\theta) - L| < \epsilon. \tag{1}$$

If such an L exists, then

$$\lim_{(x,y)\to(0,0)} f(x,y) = \lim_{r\to 0} f(r,\theta) = L.$$

For instance,

$$\lim_{(x,y)\to(0,0)} \frac{x^3}{x^2+y^2} = \lim_{r\to 0} \frac{r^3\cos^3\theta}{r^2} = \lim_{r\to 0} r\cos^3\theta = 0.$$

To verify the last of these equalities, we need to show that Equation (1) is satisfied with $f(r,\theta) = r\cos^3\theta$ and $L = 0$. That is, we need to show that given any $\epsilon > 0$ there exists a $\delta > 0$ such that for all r and θ,

$$|r| < \delta \quad\Rightarrow\quad |r\cos^3\theta - 0| < \epsilon.$$

Since

$$|r\cos^3\theta| = |r||\cos^3\theta| \le |r|\cdot 1 = |r|,$$

the implication holds for all r and θ if we take $\delta = \epsilon$.

In contrast,

$$\frac{x^2}{x^2+y^2} = \frac{r^2\cos^2\theta}{r^2} = \cos^2\theta$$

takes on all values from 0 to 1 regardless of how small $|r|$ is, so that $\lim_{(x,y)\to(0,0)} x^2/(x^2+y^2)$ does not exist.

In each of these instances, the existence or nonexistence of the limit as $r \to 0$ is fairly clear. Shifting to polar coordinates does not always help, however, and may even tempt us to false conclusions. For example, the limit may exist along every straight line (or ray) $\theta =$ constant and yet fail to exist in the broader sense. Example 4 illustrates this point. In polar coordinates, $f(x,y) = (2x^2y)/(x^4+y^2)$ becomes

$$f(r\cos\theta, r\sin\theta) = \frac{r\cos\theta\sin 2\theta}{r^2\cos^4\theta + \sin^2\theta}$$

for $r \neq 0$. If we hold θ constant and let $r \to 0$, the limit is 0. On the path $y = x^2$, however, we have $r \sin\theta = r^2\cos^2\theta$ and

$$f(r\cos\theta, r\sin\theta) = \frac{r\cos\theta\sin 2\theta}{r^2\cos^4\theta + (r\cos^2\theta)^2}$$

$$= \frac{2r\cos^2\theta\sin\theta}{2r^2\cos^4\theta} = \frac{r\sin\theta}{r^2\cos^2\theta} = 1.$$

In Exercises 51–56, find the limit of f as $(x, y) \to (0, 0)$ or show that the limit does not exist.

51. $f(x, y) = \dfrac{x^3 - xy^2}{x^2 + y^2}$

52. $f(x, y) = \cos\left(\dfrac{x^3 - y^3}{x^2 + y^2}\right)$

53. $f(x, y) = \dfrac{y^2}{x^2 + y^2}$

54. $f(x, y) = \dfrac{2x}{x^2 + x + y^2}$

55. $f(x, y) = \tan^{-1}\left(\dfrac{|x| + |y|}{x^2 + y^2}\right)$

56. $f(x, y) = \dfrac{x^2 - y^2}{x^2 + y^2}$

In Exercises 57 and 58, define $f(0, 0)$ in a way that extends f to be continuous at the origin.

57. $f(x, y) = \ln\left(\dfrac{3x^2 - x^2y^2 + 3y^2}{x^2 + y^2}\right)$

58. $f(x, y) = \dfrac{3x^2y}{x^2 + y^2}$

Using the δ-ϵ Definition

Each of Exercises 59–62 gives a function $f(x, y)$ and a positive number ϵ. In each exercise, show that there exists a $\delta > 0$ such that for all (x, y),

$$\sqrt{x^2 + y^2} < \delta \quad \Rightarrow \quad |f(x, y) - f(0, 0)| < \epsilon.$$

59. $f(x, y) = x^2 + y^2, \quad \epsilon = 0.01$

60. $f(x, y) = y/(x^2 + 1), \quad \epsilon = 0.05$

61. $f(x, y) = (x + y)/(x^2 + 1), \quad \epsilon = 0.01$

62. $f(x, y) = (x + y)/(2 + \cos x), \quad \epsilon = 0.02$

Each of Exercises 63–66 gives a function $f(x, y, z)$ and a positive number ϵ. In each exercise, show that there exists a $\delta > 0$ such that for all (x, y, z),

$$\sqrt{x^2 + y^2 + z^2} < \delta \quad \Rightarrow \quad |f(x, y, z) - f(0, 0, 0)| < \epsilon.$$

63. $f(x, y, z) = x^2 + y^2 + z^2, \quad \epsilon = 0.015$

64. $f(x, y, z) = xyz, \quad \epsilon = 0.008$

65. $f(x, y, z) = \dfrac{x + y + z}{x^2 + y^2 + z^2 + 1}, \quad \epsilon = 0.015$

66. $f(x, y, z) = \tan^2 x + \tan^2 y + \tan^2 z, \quad \epsilon = 0.03$

67. Show that $f(x, y, z) = x + y - z$ is continuous at every point (x_0, y_0, z_0).

68. Show that $f(x, y, z) = x^2 + y^2 + z^2$ is continuous at the origin.

14.3 Partial Derivatives

The calculus of several variables is basically single-variable calculus applied to several variables one at a time. When we hold all but one of the independent variables of a function constant and differentiate with respect to that one variable, we get a "partial" derivative. This section shows how partial derivatives are defined and interpreted geometrically, and how to calculate them by applying the rules for differentiating functions of a single variable.

Partial Derivatives of a Function of Two Variables

If (x_0, y_0) is a point in the domain of a function $f(x, y)$, the vertical plane $y = y_0$ will cut the surface $z = f(x, y)$ in the curve $z = f(x, y_0)$ (Figure 14.13). This curve is the graph of the function $z = f(x, y_0)$ in the plane $y = y_0$. The horizontal coordinate in this plane is x; the vertical coordinate is z. The y-value is held constant at y_0, so y is not a variable.

We define the partial derivative of f with respect to x at the point (x_0, y_0) as the ordinary derivative of $f(x, y_0)$ with respect to x at the point $x = x_0$. To distinguish partial derivatives from ordinary derivatives we use the symbol ∂ rather than the d previously used.

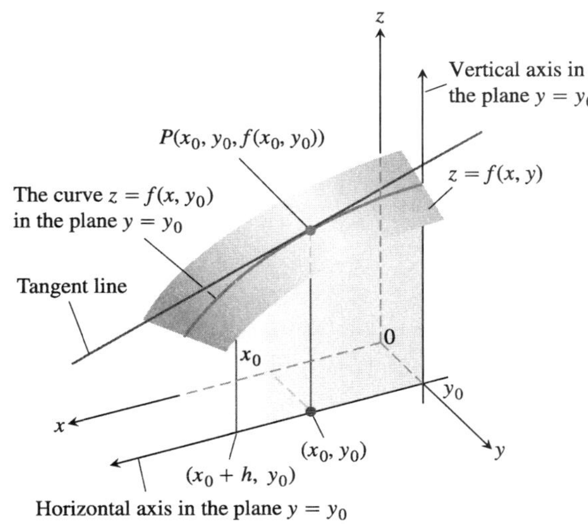

FIGURE 14.13 The intersection of the plane $y = y_0$ with the surface $z = f(x, y)$, viewed from above the first quadrant of the xy-plane.

DEFINITION Partial Derivative with Respect to x

The **partial derivative of $f(x, y)$ with respect to x** at the point (x_0, y_0) is

$$\left.\frac{\partial f}{\partial x}\right|_{(x_0, y_0)} = \lim_{h \to 0} \frac{f(x_0 + h, y_0) - f(x_0, y_0)}{h},$$

provided the limit exists.

An equivalent expression for the partial derivative is

$$\left.\frac{d}{dx} f(x, y_0)\right|_{x=x_0}.$$

The slope of the curve $z = f(x, y_0)$ at the point $P(x_0, y_0, f(x_0, y_0))$ in the plane $y = y_0$ is the value of the partial derivative of f with respect to x at (x_0, y_0). The tangent line to the curve at P is the line in the plane $y = y_0$ that passes through P with this slope. The partial derivative $\partial f/\partial x$ at (x_0, y_0) gives the rate of change of f with respect to x when y is held fixed at the value y_0. This is the rate of change of f in the direction of **i** at (x_0, y_0).

The notation for a partial derivative depends on what we want to emphasize:

$\frac{\partial f}{\partial x}(x_0, y_0)$ or $f_x(x_0, y_0)$ "Partial derivative of f with respect to x at (x_0, y_0)" or "f sub x at (x_0, y_0)." Convenient for stressing the point (x_0, y_0).

$\left.\frac{\partial z}{\partial x}\right|_{(x_0, y_0)}$ "Partial derivative of z with respect to x at (x_0, y_0)." Common in science and engineering when you are dealing with variables and do not mention the function explicitly.

$f_x, \frac{\partial f}{\partial x}, z_x$, or $\frac{\partial z}{\partial x}$ "Partial derivative of f (or z) with respect to x." Convenient when you regard the partial derivative as a function in its own right.

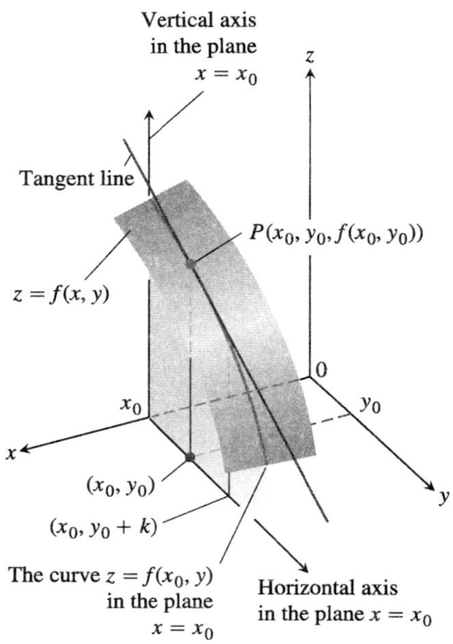

FIGURE 14.14 The intersection of the plane $x = x_0$ with the surface $z = f(x, y)$, viewed from above the first quadrant of the xy-plane.

The definition of the partial derivative of $f(x, y)$ with respect to y at a point (x_0, y_0) is similar to the definition of the partial derivative of f with respect to x. We hold x fixed at the value x_0 and take the ordinary derivative of $f(x_0, y)$ with respect to y at y_0.

DEFINITION Partial Derivative with Respect to *y*

The **partial derivative of *f*(*x*, *y*) with respect to *y*** at the point (x_0, y_0) is

$$\left.\frac{\partial f}{\partial y}\right|_{(x_0, y_0)} = \left.\frac{d}{dy} f(x_0, y)\right|_{y=y_0} = \lim_{h \to 0} \frac{f(x_0, y_0 + h) - f(x_0, y_0)}{h},$$

provided the limit exists.

The slope of the curve $z = f(x_0, y)$ at the point $P(x_0, y_0, f(x_0, y_0))$ in the vertical plane $x = x_0$ (Figure 14.14) is the partial derivative of f with respect to y at (x_0, y_0). The tangent line to the curve at P is the line in the plane $x = x_0$ that passes through P with this slope. The partial derivative gives the rate of change of f with respect to y at (x_0, y_0) when x is held fixed at the value x_0. This is the rate of change of f in the direction of $\mathbf{j}$ at (x_0, y_0).

The partial derivative with respect to y is denoted the same way as the partial derivative with respect to x:

$$\frac{\partial f}{\partial y}(x_0, y_0), \qquad f_y(x_0, y_0), \qquad \frac{\partial f}{\partial y}, \qquad f_y.$$

Notice that we now have two tangent lines associated with the surface $z = f(x, y)$ at the point $P(x_0, y_0, f(x_0, y_0))$ (Figure 14.15). Is the plane they determine tangent to the surface at P? We will see that it is, but we have to learn more about partial derivatives before we can find out why.

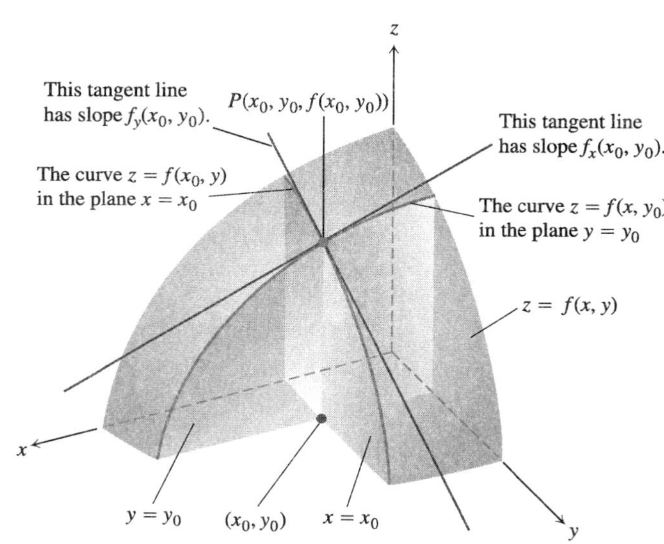

FIGURE 14.15 Figures 14.13 and 14.14 combined. The tangent lines at the point $(x_0, y_0, f(x_0, y_0))$ determine a plane that, in this picture at least, appears to be tangent to the surface.

Calculations

The definitions of $\partial f/\partial x$ and $\partial f/\partial y$ give us two different ways of differentiating f at a point: with respect to x in the usual way while treating y as a constant and with respect to y in the usual way while treating x as constant. As the following examples show, the values of these partial derivatives are usually different at a given point (x_0, y_0).

EXAMPLE 1 Finding Partial Derivatives at a Point

Find the values of $\partial f/\partial x$ and $\partial f/\partial y$ at the point $(4, -5)$ if

$$f(x, y) = x^2 + 3xy + y - 1.$$

Solution To find $\partial f/\partial x$, we treat y as a constant and differentiate with respect to x:

$$\frac{\partial f}{\partial x} = \frac{\partial}{\partial x}(x^2 + 3xy + y - 1) = 2x + 3\cdot 1\cdot y + 0 - 0 = 2x + 3y.$$

The value of $\partial f/\partial x$ at $(4, -5)$ is $2(4) + 3(-5) = -7$.

To find $\partial f/\partial y$, we treat x as a constant and differentiate with respect to y:

$$\frac{\partial f}{\partial y} = \frac{\partial}{\partial y}(x^2 + 3xy + y - 1) = 0 + 3\cdot x\cdot 1 + 1 - 0 = 3x + 1.$$

The value of $\partial f/\partial y$ at $(4, -5)$ is $3(4) + 1 = 13$. ■

EXAMPLE 2 Finding a Partial Derivative as a Function

Find $\partial f/\partial y$ if $f(x, y) = y \sin xy$.

Solution We treat x as a constant and f as a product of y and $\sin xy$:

$$\begin{aligned}\frac{\partial f}{\partial y} &= \frac{\partial}{\partial y}(y \sin xy) = y\frac{\partial}{\partial y}\sin xy + (\sin xy)\frac{\partial}{\partial y}(y)\\ &= (y \cos xy)\frac{\partial}{\partial y}(xy) + \sin xy = xy \cos xy + \sin xy.\end{aligned}$$ ■

USING TECHNOLOGY Partial Differentiation

A simple grapher can support your calculations even in multiple dimensions. If you specify the values of all but one independent variable, the grapher can calculate partial derivatives and can plot traces with respect to that remaining variable. Typically, a CAS can compute partial derivatives symbolically and numerically as easily as it can compute simple derivatives. Most systems use the same command to differentiate a function, regardless of the number of variables. (Simply specify the variable with which differentiation is to take place).

EXAMPLE 3 Partial Derivatives May Be Different Functions

Find f_x and f_y if

$$f(x, y) = \frac{2y}{y + \cos x}.$$

Solution We treat f as a quotient. With y held constant, we get

$$f_x = \frac{\partial}{\partial x}\left(\frac{2y}{y + \cos x}\right) = \frac{(y + \cos x)\frac{\partial}{\partial x}(2y) - 2y\frac{\partial}{\partial x}(y + \cos x)}{(y + \cos x)^2}$$

$$= \frac{(y + \cos x)(0) - 2y(-\sin x)}{(y + \cos x)^2} = \frac{2y \sin x}{(y + \cos x)^2}.$$

With x held constant, we get

$$f_y = \frac{\partial}{\partial y}\left(\frac{2y}{y + \cos x}\right) = \frac{(y + \cos x)\frac{\partial}{\partial y}(2y) - 2y\frac{\partial}{dy}(y + \cos x)}{(y + \cos x)^2}$$

$$= \frac{(y + \cos x)(2) - 2y(1)}{(y + \cos x)^2} = \frac{2 \cos x}{(y + \cos x)^2}.$$ ■

Implicit differentiation works for partial derivatives the way it works for ordinary derivatives, as the next example illustrates.

EXAMPLE 4 Implicit Partial Differentiation

Find $\partial z/\partial x$ if the equation

$$yz - \ln z = x + y$$

defines z as a function of the two independent variables x and y and the partial derivative exists.

Solution We differentiate both sides of the equation with respect to x, holding y constant and treating z as a differentiable function of x:

$$\frac{\partial}{\partial x}(yz) - \frac{\partial}{\partial x}\ln z = \frac{\partial x}{\partial x} + \frac{\partial y}{\partial x}$$

$$y\frac{\partial z}{\partial x} - \frac{1}{z}\frac{\partial z}{\partial x} = 1 + 0$$

With y constant, $\frac{\partial}{\partial x}(yz) = y\frac{\partial z}{\partial x}$.

$$\left(y - \frac{1}{z}\right)\frac{\partial z}{\partial x} = 1$$

$$\frac{\partial z}{\partial x} = \frac{z}{yz - 1}.$$ ■

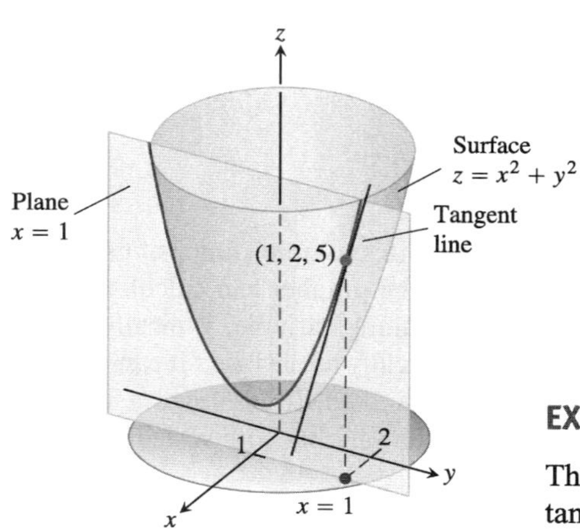

FIGURE 14.16 The tangent to the curve of intersection of the plane $x = 1$ and surface $z = x^2 + y^2$ at the point $(1, 2, 5)$ (Example 5).

EXAMPLE 5 Finding the Slope of a Surface in the y-Direction

The plane $x = 1$ intersects the paraboloid $z = x^2 + y^2$ in a parabola. Find the slope of the tangent to the parabola at $(1, 2, 5)$ (Figure 14.16).

Solution The slope is the value of the partial derivative $\partial z/\partial y$ at $(1, 2)$:

$$\left.\frac{\partial z}{\partial y}\right|_{(1,2)} = \left.\frac{\partial}{\partial y}(x^2 + y^2)\right|_{(1,2)} = \left.2y\right|_{(1,2)} = 2(2) = 4.$$

As a check, we can treat the parabola as the graph of the single-variable function $z = (1)^2 + y^2 = 1 + y^2$ in the plane $x = 1$ and ask for the slope at $y = 2$. The slope, calculated now as an ordinary derivative, is

$$\left.\frac{dz}{dy}\right|_{y=2} = \left.\frac{d}{dy}(1 + y^2)\right|_{y=2} = \left.2y\right|_{y=2} = 4.$$

■

Functions of More Than Two Variables

The definitions of the partial derivatives of functions of more than two independent variables are like the definitions for functions of two variables. They are ordinary derivatives with respect to one variable, taken while the other independent variables are held constant.

EXAMPLE 6 A Function of Three Variables

If x, y, and z are independent variables and

$$f(x, y, z) = x \sin(y + 3z),$$

then

$$\begin{aligned}\frac{\partial f}{\partial z} &= \frac{\partial}{\partial z}[x \sin(y + 3z)] = x \frac{\partial}{\partial z} \sin(y + 3z) \\ &= x \cos(y + 3z) \frac{\partial}{\partial z}(y + 3z) = 3x \cos(y + 3z).\end{aligned}$$

■

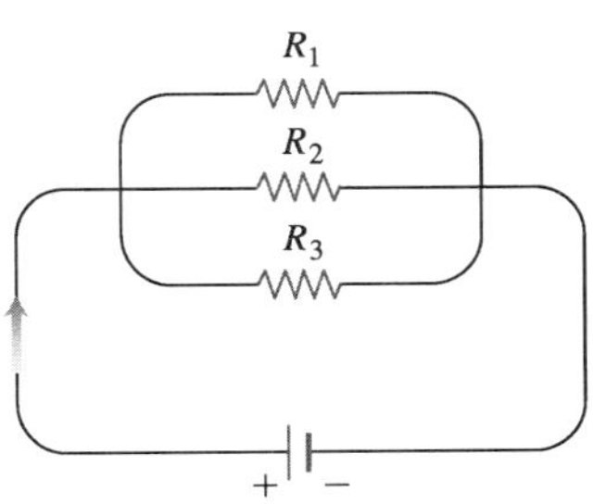

FIGURE 14.17 Resistors arranged this way are said to be connected in parallel (Example 7). Each resistor lets a portion of the current through. Their equivalent resistance R is calculated with the formula

$$\frac{1}{R} = \frac{1}{R_1} + \frac{1}{R_2} + \frac{1}{R_3}.$$

EXAMPLE 7 Electrical Resistors in Parallel

If resistors of R_1, R_2, and R_3 ohms are connected in parallel to make an R-ohm resistor, the value of R can be found from the equation

$$\frac{1}{R} = \frac{1}{R_1} + \frac{1}{R_2} + \frac{1}{R_3}$$

(Figure 14.17). Find the value of $\partial R/\partial R_2$ when $R_1 = 30$, $R_2 = 45$, and $R_3 = 90$ ohms.

Solution To find $\partial R/\partial R_2$, we treat R_1 and R_3 as constants and, using implicit differentiation, differentiate both sides of the equation with respect to R_2:

$$\begin{aligned}\frac{\partial}{\partial R_2}\left(\frac{1}{R}\right) &= \frac{\partial}{\partial R_2}\left(\frac{1}{R_1} + \frac{1}{R_2} + \frac{1}{R_3}\right) \\ -\frac{1}{R^2}\frac{\partial R}{\partial R_2} &= 0 - \frac{1}{R_2^2} + 0 \\ \frac{\partial R}{\partial R_2} &= \frac{R^2}{R_2^2} = \left(\frac{R}{R_2}\right)^2.\end{aligned}$$

When $R_1 = 30$, $R_2 = 45$, and $R_3 = 90$,

$$\frac{1}{R} = \frac{1}{30} + \frac{1}{45} + \frac{1}{90} = \frac{3 + 2 + 1}{90} = \frac{6}{90} = \frac{1}{15},$$

so $R = 15$ and

$$\frac{\partial R}{\partial R_2} = \left(\frac{15}{45}\right)^2 = \left(\frac{1}{3}\right)^2 = \frac{1}{9}.$$

Partial Derivatives and Continuity

A function $f(x, y)$ can have partial derivatives with respect to both x and y at a point without the function being continuous there. This is different from functions of a single variable, where the existence of a derivative implies continuity. If the partial derivatives of $f(x, y)$ exist and are continuous throughout a disk centered at (x_0, y_0), however, then f *is* continuous at (x_0, y_0), as we see at the end of this section.

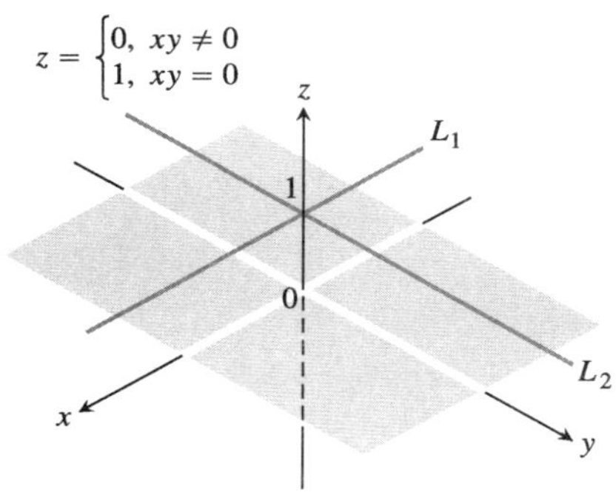

FIGURE 14.18 The graph of

$$f(x, y) = \begin{cases} 0, & xy \neq 0 \\ 1, & xy = 0 \end{cases}$$

consists of the lines L_1 and L_2 and the four open quadrants of the xy-plane. The function has partial derivatives at the origin but is not continuous there (Example 8).

EXAMPLE 8 Partials Exist, But f Discontinuous

Let

$$f(x, y) = \begin{cases} 0, & xy \neq 0 \\ 1, & xy = 0 \end{cases}$$

(Figure 14.18).

(a) Find the limit of f as (x, y) approaches $(0, 0)$ along the line $y = x$.

(b) Prove that f is not continuous at the origin.

(c) Show that both partial derivatives $\partial f/\partial x$ and $\partial f/\partial y$ exist at the origin.

Solution

(a) Since $f(x, y)$ is constantly zero along the line $y = x$ (except at the origin), we have

$$\lim_{(x,y)\to(0,0)} f(x, y)\Big|_{y=x} = \lim_{(x,y)\to(0,0)} 0 = 0.$$

(b) Since $f(0, 0) = 1$, the limit in part (a) proves that f is not continuous at $(0, 0)$.

(c) To find $\partial f/\partial x$ at $(0, 0)$, we hold y fixed at $y = 0$. Then $f(x, y) = 1$ for all x, and the graph of f is the line L_1 in Figure 14.18. The slope of this line at any x is $\partial f/\partial x = 0$. In particular, $\partial f/\partial x = 0$ at $(0, 0)$. Similarly, $\partial f/\partial y$ is the slope of line L_2 at any y, so $\partial f/\partial y = 0$ at $(0, 0)$.

Example 8 notwithstanding, it is still true in higher dimensions that *differentiability* at a point implies continuity. What Example 8 suggests is that we need a stronger requirement for differentiability in higher dimensions than the mere existence of the partial derivatives. We define differentiability for functions of two variables at the end of this section and revisit the connection to continuity.

Second-Order Partial Derivatives

When we differentiate a function $f(x, y)$ twice, we produce its second-order derivatives. These derivatives are usually denoted by

$\dfrac{\partial^2 f}{\partial x^2}$	"d squared fdx squared"	or	f_{xx}	"f sub xx"
$\dfrac{\partial^2 f}{\partial y^2}$	"d squared fdy squared"	or	f_{yy}	"f sub yy"

$\frac{\partial^2 f}{\partial x \partial y}$ "*d* squared *fdx dy*" or f_{yx} "*f* sub *yx*"

$\frac{\partial^2 f}{\partial y \partial x}$ "*d* squared *fdy dx*" or f_{xy} "*f* sub *xy*"

The defining equations are

$$\frac{\partial^2 f}{\partial x^2} = \frac{\partial}{\partial x}\left(\frac{\partial f}{\partial x}\right), \qquad \frac{\partial^2 f}{\partial x \partial y} = \frac{\partial}{\partial x}\left(\frac{\partial f}{\partial y}\right),$$

and so on. Notice the order in which the derivatives are taken:

$\frac{\partial^2 f}{\partial x \partial y}$ Differentiate first with respect to y, then with respect to x.

$f_{yx} = (f_y)_x$ Means the same thing.

HISTORICAL BIOGRAPHY

Pierre-Simon Laplace (1749–1827)

EXAMPLE 9 Finding Second-Order Partial Derivatives

If $f(x, y) = x\cos y + ye^x$, find

$$\frac{\partial^2 f}{\partial x^2}, \quad \frac{\partial^2 f}{\partial y \partial x}, \quad \frac{\partial^2 f}{\partial y^2}, \quad \text{and} \quad \frac{\partial^2 f}{\partial x \partial y}.$$

Solution

$$\frac{\partial f}{\partial x} = \frac{\partial}{\partial x}(x\cos y + ye^x) = \cos y + ye^x$$

So

$$\frac{\partial^2 f}{\partial y \partial x} = \frac{\partial}{\partial y}\left(\frac{\partial f}{\partial x}\right) = -\sin y + e^x$$

$$\frac{\partial^2 f}{\partial x^2} = \frac{\partial}{\partial x}\left(\frac{\partial f}{\partial x}\right) = ye^x.$$

$$\frac{\partial f}{\partial y} = \frac{\partial}{\partial y}(x\cos y + ye^x) = -x\sin y + e^x$$

So

$$\frac{\partial^2 f}{\partial x \partial y} = \frac{\partial}{\partial x}\left(\frac{\partial f}{\partial y}\right) = -\sin y + e^x$$

$$\frac{\partial^2 f}{\partial y^2} = \frac{\partial}{\partial y}\left(\frac{\partial f}{\partial y}\right) = -x\cos y.$$

■

The Mixed Derivative Theorem

You may have noticed that the "mixed" second-order partial derivatives

$$\frac{\partial^2 f}{\partial y \partial x} \quad \text{and} \quad \frac{\partial^2 f}{\partial x \partial y}$$

in Example 9 were equal. This was not a coincidence. They must be equal whenever f, f_x, f_y, f_{xy}, and f_{yx} are continuous, as stated in the following theorem.

THEOREM 2 The Mixed Derivative Theorem

If $f(x, y)$ and its partial derivatives f_x, f_y, f_{xy}, and f_{yx} are defined throughout an open region containing a point (a, b) and are all continuous at (a, b), then

$$f_{xy}(a, b) = f_{yx}(a, b).$$

HISTORICAL BIOGRAPHY

Alexis Clairaut
(1713–1765)

Theorem 2 is also known as Clairaut's Theorem, named after the French mathematician Alexis Clairaut who discovered it. A proof is given in Appendix 7. Theorem 2 says that to calculate a mixed second-order derivative, we may differentiate in either order, provided the continuity conditions are satisfied. This can work to our advantage.

EXAMPLE 10 Choosing the Order of Differentiation

Find $\partial^2 w/\partial x \partial y$ if

$$w = xy + \frac{e^y}{y^2 + 1}.$$

Solution The symbol $\partial^2 w/\partial x \partial y$ tells us to differentiate first with respect to y and then with respect to x. If we postpone the differentiation with respect to y and differentiate first with respect to x, however, we get the answer more quickly. In two steps,

$$\frac{\partial w}{\partial x} = y \qquad \text{and} \qquad \frac{\partial^2 w}{\partial y \partial x} = 1.$$

If we differentiate first with respect to y, we obtain $\partial^2 w/\partial x \partial y = 1$ as well. ■

Partial Derivatives of Still Higher Order

Although we will deal mostly with first- and second-order partial derivatives, because these appear the most frequently in applications, there is no theoretical limit to how many times we can differentiate a function as long as the derivatives involved exist. Thus, we get third- and fourth-order derivatives denoted by symbols like

$$\frac{\partial^3 f}{\partial x \partial y^2} = f_{yyx}$$

$$\frac{\partial^4 f}{\partial x^2 \partial y^2} = f_{yyxx},$$

and so on. As with second-order derivatives, the order of differentiation is immaterial as long as all the derivatives through the order in question are continuous.

EXAMPLE 11 Calculating a Partial Derivative of Fourth-Order

Find f_{yxyz} if $f(x, y, z) = 1 - 2xy^2z + x^2y$.

Solution We first differentiate with respect to the variable y, then x, then y again, and finally with respect to z:

$$f_y = -4xyz + x^2$$

$$f_{yx} = -4yz + 2x$$

$$f_{yxy} = -4z$$

$$f_{yxyz} = -4$$

■

Differentiability

The starting point for differentiability is not Fermat's difference quotient but rather the idea of increment. You may recall from our work with functions of a single variable in Section 3.8 that if $y = f(x)$ is differentiable at $x = x_0$, then the change in the value of f that results from changing x from x_0 to $x_0 + \Delta x$ is given by an equation of the form

$$\Delta y = f'(x_0)\Delta x + \epsilon \Delta x$$

in which $\epsilon \to 0$ as $\Delta x \to 0$. For functions of two variables, the analogous property becomes the definition of differentiability. The Increment Theorem (from advanced calculus) tells us when to expect the property to hold.

THEOREM 3 The Increment Theorem for Functions of Two Variables

Suppose that the first partial derivatives of $f(x, y)$ are defined throughout an open region R containing the point (x_0, y_0) and that f_x and f_y are continuous at (x_0, y_0). Then the change

$$\Delta z = f(x_0 + \Delta x, y_0 + \Delta y) - f(x_0, y_0)$$

in the value of f that results from moving from (x_0, y_0) to another point $(x_0 + \Delta x, y_0 + \Delta y)$ in R satisfies an equation of the form

$$\Delta z = f_x(x_0, y_0)\Delta x + f_y(x_0, y_0)\Delta y + \epsilon_1 \Delta x + \epsilon_2 \Delta y,$$

in which each of $\epsilon_1, \epsilon_2 \to 0$ as both $\Delta x, \Delta y \to 0$.

You can see where the epsilons come from in the proof in Appendix 7. You will also see that similar results hold for functions of more than two independent variables.

DEFINITION Differentiable Function

A function $z = f(x, y)$ is **differentiable at** (x_0, y_0) if $f_x(x_0, y_0)$ and $f_y(x_0, y_0)$ exist and Δz satisfies an equation of the form

$$\Delta z = f_x(x_0, y_0)\Delta x + f_y(x_0, y_0)\Delta y + \epsilon_1 \Delta x + \epsilon_2 \Delta y,$$

in which each of $\epsilon_1, \epsilon_2 \to 0$ as both $\Delta x, \Delta y \to 0$. We call f **differentiable** if it is differentiable at every point in its domain.

In light of this definition, we have the immediate corollary of Theorem 3 that a function is differentiable if its first partial derivatives are *continuous*.

COROLLARY OF THEOREM 3 Continuity of Partial Derivatives Implies Differentiability

If the partial derivatives f_x and f_y of a function $f(x, y)$ are continuous throughout an open region R, then f is differentiable at every point of R.

If $z = f(x, y)$ is differentiable, then the definition of differentiability assures that $\Delta z = f(x_0 + \Delta x, y_0 + \Delta y) - f(x_0, y_0)$ approaches 0 as Δx and Δy approach 0. This tells us that a function of two variables is continuous at every point where it is differentiable.

THEOREM 4 Differentiability Implies Continuity
If a function $f(x, y)$ is differentiable at (x_0, y_0), then f is continuous at (x_0, y_0).

As we can see from Theorems 3 and 4, a function $f(x, y)$ must be continuous at a point (x_0, y_0) if f_x and f_y are continuous throughout an open region containing (x_0, y_0). Remember, however, that it is still possible for a function of two variables to be discontinuous at a point where its first partial derivatives exist, as we saw in Example 8. Existence alone of the partial derivative at a point is not enough.

EXERCISES 14.3

Calculating First-Order Partial Derivatives

In Exercises 1–22, find $\partial f/\partial x$ and $\partial f/\partial y$.

1. $f(x, y) = 2x^2 - 3y - 4$ **2.** $f(x, y) = x^2 - xy + y^2$

3. $f(x, y) = (x^2 - 1)(y + 2)$

4. $f(x, y) = 5xy - 7x^2 - y^2 + 3x - 6y + 2$

5. $f(x, y) = (xy - 1)^2$ **6.** $f(x, y) = (2x - 3y)^3$

7. $f(x, y) = \sqrt{x^2 + y^2}$ **8.** $f(x, y) = (x^3 + (y/2))^{2/3}$

9. $f(x, y) = 1/(x + y)$ **10.** $f(x, y) = x/(x^2 + y^2)$

11. $f(x, y) = (x + y)/(xy - 1)$ **12.** $f(x, y) = \tan^{-1}(y/x)$

13. $f(x, y) = e^{(x+y+1)}$ **14.** $f(x, y) = e^{-x}\sin(x + y)$

15. $f(x, y) = \ln(x + y)$ **16.** $f(x, y) = e^{xy}\ln y$

17. $f(x, y) = \sin^2(x - 3y)$ **18.** $f(x, y) = \cos^2(3x - y^2)$

19. $f(x, y) = x^y$ **20.** $f(x, y) = \log_y x$

21. $f(x, y) = \int_x^y g(t)\,dt$ (g continuous for all t)

22. $f(x, y) = \sum_{n=0}^{\infty}(xy)^n \quad (|xy| < 1)$

In Exercises 23–34, find f_x, f_y, and f_z.

23. $f(x, y, z) = 1 + xy^2 - 2z^2$ **24.** $f(x, y, z) = xy + yz + xz$

25. $f(x, y, z) = x - \sqrt{y^2 + z^2}$

26. $f(x, y, z) = (x^2 + y^2 + z^2)^{-1/2}$

27. $f(x, y, z) = \sin^{-1}(xyz)$ **28.** $f(x, y, z) = \sec^{-1}(x + yz)$

29. $f(x, y, z) = \ln(x + 2y + 3z)$

30. $f(x, y, z) = yz\ln(xy)$ **31.** $f(x, y, z) = e^{-(x^2+y^2+z^2)}$

32. $f(x, y, z) = e^{-xyz}$

33. $f(x, y, z) = \tanh(x + 2y + 3z)$

34. $f(x, y, z) = \sinh(xy - z^2)$

In Exercises 35–40, find the partial derivative of the function with respect to each variable.

35. $f(t, \alpha) = \cos(2\pi t - \alpha)$ **36.** $g(u, v) = v^2 e^{(2u/v)}$

37. $h(\rho, \phi, \theta) = \rho\sin\phi\cos\theta$ **38.** $g(r, \theta, z) = r(1 - \cos\theta) - z$

39. Work done by the heart (Section 3.8, Exercise 51)

$$W(P, V, \delta, v, g) = PV + \frac{V\delta v^2}{2g}$$

40. Wilson lot size formula (Section 4.5, Exercise 45)

$$A(c, h, k, m, q) = \frac{km}{q} + cm + \frac{hq}{2}$$

Calculating Second-Order Partial Derivatives

Find all the second-order partial derivatives of the functions in Exercises 41–46.

41. $f(x, y) = x + y + xy$ **42.** $f(x, y) = \sin xy$

43. $g(x, y) = x^2y + \cos y + y \sin x$

44. $h(x, y) = xe^y + y + 1$

45. $r(x, y) = \ln(x + y)$

46. $s(x, y) = \tan^{-1}(y/x)$

Mixed Partial Derivatives

In Exercises 47–50, verify that $w_{xy} = w_{yx}$.

47. $w = \ln(2x + 3y)$

48. $w = e^x + x \ln y + y \ln x$

49. $w = xy^2 + x^2y^3 + x^3y^4$

50. $w = x \sin y + y \sin x + xy$

51. Which order of differentiation will calculate f_{xy} faster: x first or y first? Try to answer without writing anything down.

a. $f(x, y) = x \sin y + e^y$

b. $f(x, y) = 1/x$

c. $f(x, y) = y + (x/y)$

d. $f(x, y) = y + x^2y + 4y^3 - \ln(y^2 + 1)$

e. $f(x, y) = x^2 + 5xy + \sin x + 7e^x$

f. $f(x, y) = x \ln xy$

52. The fifth-order partial derivative $\partial^5 f/\partial x^2 \partial y^3$ is zero for each of the following functions. To show this as quickly as possible, which variable would you differentiate with respect to first: x or y? Try to answer without writing anything down.

a. $f(x, y) = y^2x^4e^x + 2$

b. $f(x, y) = y^2 + y(\sin x - x^4)$

c. $f(x, y) = x^2 + 5xy + \sin x + 7e^x$

d. $f(x, y) = xe^{y^2/2}$

Using the Partial Derivative Definition

In Exercises 53 and 54, use the limit definition of partial derivative to compute the partial derivatives of the functions at the specified points.

53. $f(x, y) = 1 - x + y - 3x^2y, \quad \dfrac{\partial f}{\partial x}$ and $\dfrac{\partial f}{\partial y}$ at $(1, 2)$

54. $f(x, y) = 4 + 2x - 3y - xy^2, \quad \dfrac{\partial f}{\partial x}$ and $\dfrac{\partial f}{\partial y}$ at $(-2, 1)$

55. **Three variables** Let $w = f(x, y, z)$ be a function of three independent variables and write the formal definition of the partial derivative $\partial f/\partial z$ at (x_0, y_0, z_0). Use this definition to find $\partial f/\partial z$ at $(1, 2, 3)$ for $f(x, y, z) = x^2yz^2$.

56. **Three variables** Let $w = f(x, y, z)$ be a function of three independent variables and write the formal definition of the partial derivative $\partial f/\partial y$ at (x_0, y_0, z_0). Use this definition to find $\partial f/\partial y$ at $(-1, 0, 3)$ for $f(x, y, z) = -2xy^2 + yz^2$.

Differentiating Implicitly

57. Find the value of $\partial z/\partial x$ at the point $(1, 1, 1)$ if the equation

$$xy + z^3x - 2yz = 0$$

defines z as a function of the two independent variables x and y and the partial derivative exists.

58. Find the value of $\partial x/\partial z$ at the point $(1, -1, -3)$ if the equation

$$xz + y \ln x - x^2 + 4 = 0$$

defines x as a function of the two independent variables y and z and the partial derivative exists.

Exercises 59 and 60 are about the triangle shown here.

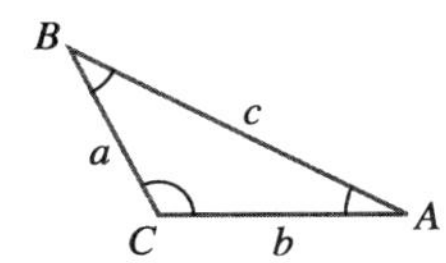

59. Express A implicitly as a function of a, b, and c and calculate $\partial A/\partial a$ and $\partial A/\partial b$.

60. Express a implicitly as a function of A, b, and B and calculate $\partial a/\partial A$ and $\partial a/\partial B$.

61. **Two dependent variables** Express v_x in terms of u and v if the equations $x = v \ln u$ and $y = u \ln v$ define u and v as functions of the independent variables x and y, and if v_x exists. (*Hint:* Differentiate both equations with respect to x and solve for v_x by eliminating u_x.)

62. **Two dependent variables** Find $\partial x/\partial u$ and $\partial y/\partial u$ if the equations $u = x^2 - y^2$ and $v = x^2 - y$ define x and y as functions of the independent variables u and v, and the partial derivatives exist. (See the hint in Exercise 61.) Then let $s = x^2 + y^2$ and find $\partial s/\partial u$.

Laplace Equations

The **three-dimensional Laplace equation**

$$\frac{\partial^2 f}{\partial x^2} + \frac{\partial^2 f}{\partial y^2} + \frac{\partial^2 f}{\partial z^2} = 0$$

is satisfied by steady-state temperature distributions $T = f(x, y, z)$ in space, by gravitational potentials, and by electrostatic potentials. The **two-dimensional Laplace equation**

$$\frac{\partial^2 f}{\partial x^2} + \frac{\partial^2 f}{\partial y^2} = 0,$$

obtained by dropping the $\partial^2 f/\partial z^2$ term from the previous equation, describes potentials and steady-state temperature distributions in a plane (see the accompanying figure). The plane (a) may be treated as a thin slice of the solid (b) perpendicular to the z-axis.

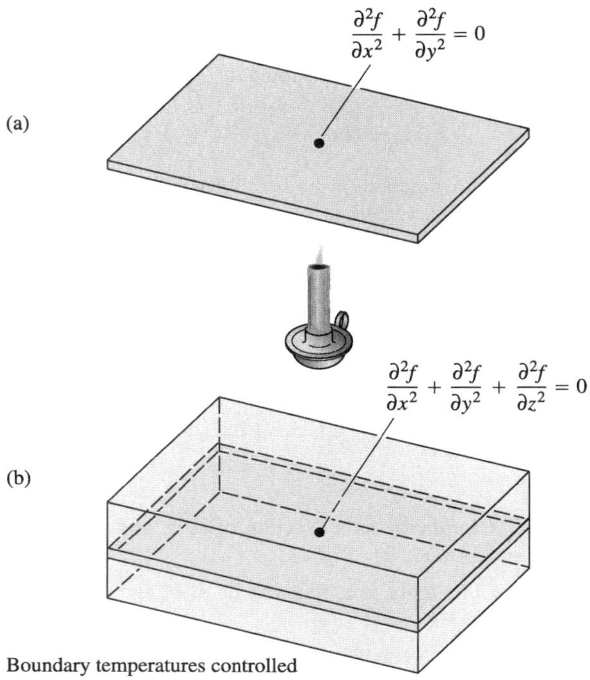

Show that each function in Exercises 63–68 satisfies a Laplace equation.

63. $f(x, y, z) = x^2 + y^2 - 2z^2$

64. $f(x, y, z) = 2z^3 - 3(x^2 + y^2)z$

65. $f(x, y) = e^{-2y} \cos 2x$

66. $f(x, y) = \ln \sqrt{x^2 + y^2}$

67. $f(x, y, z) = (x^2 + y^2 + z^2)^{-1/2}$

68. $f(x, y, z) = e^{3x+4y} \cos 5z$

The Wave Equation

If we stand on an ocean shore and take a snapshot of the waves, the picture shows a regular pattern of peaks and valleys in an instant of time. We see periodic vertical motion in space, with respect to distance. If we stand in the water, we can feel the rise and fall of the water as the waves go by. We see periodic vertical motion in time. In physics, this beautiful symmetry is expressed by the **one-dimensional wave equation**

$$\frac{\partial^2 w}{\partial t^2} = c^2 \frac{\partial^2 w}{\partial x^2},$$

where w is the wave height, x is the distance variable, t is the time variable, and c is the velocity with which the waves are propagated.

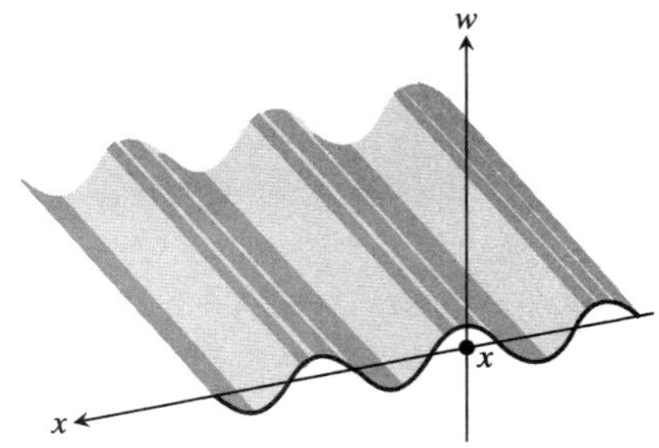

In our example, x is the distance across the ocean's surface, but in other applications, x might be the distance along a vibrating string, distance through air (sound waves), or distance through space (light waves). The number c varies with the medium and type of wave.

Show that the functions in Exercises 69–75 are all solutions of the wave equation.

69. $w = \sin (x + ct)$

70. $w = \cos (2x + 2ct)$

71. $w = \sin (x + ct) + \cos (2x + 2ct)$

72. $w = \ln (2x + 2ct)$

73. $w = \tan (2x - 2ct)$

74. $w = 5 \cos (3x + 3ct) + e^{x+ct}$

75. $w = f(u)$, where f is a differentiable function of u, and $u = a(x + ct)$, where a is a constant

Continuous Partial Derivatives

76. Does a function $f(x, y)$ with continuous first partial derivatives throughout an open region R have to be continuous on R? Give reasons for your answer.

77. If a function $f(x, y)$ has continuous second partial derivatives throughout an open region R, must the first-order partial derivatives of f be continuous on R? Give reasons for your answer.

14.4 The Chain Rule

The Chain Rule for functions of a single variable studied in Section 3.5 said that when $w = f(x)$ was a differentiable function of x and $x = g(t)$ was a differentiable function of t, w became a differentiable function of t and dw/dt could be calculated with the formula

$$\frac{dw}{dt} = \frac{dw}{dx}\frac{dx}{dt}.$$

For functions of two or more variables the Chain Rule has several forms. The form depends on how many variables are involved but works like the Chain Rule in Section 3.5 once we account for the presence of additional variables.

Functions of Two Variables

The Chain Rule formula for a function $w = f(x, y)$ when $x = x(t)$ and $y = y(t)$ are both differentiable functions of t is given in the following theorem.

> **THEOREM 5 Chain Rule for Functions of Two Independent Variables**
> If $w = f(x, y)$ has continuous partial derivatives f_x and f_y and if $x = x(t)$, $y = y(t)$ are differentiable functions of t, then the composite $w = f(x(t), y(t))$ is a differentiable function of t and
>
> $$\frac{df}{dt} = f_x(x(t), y(t)) \cdot x'(t) + f_y(x(t), y(t)) \cdot y'(t),$$
>
> or
>
> $$\frac{dw}{dt} = \frac{\partial f}{\partial x}\frac{dx}{dt} + \frac{\partial f}{\partial y}\frac{dy}{dt}.$$

Proof The proof consists of showing that if x and y are differentiable at $t = t_0$, then w is differentiable at t_0 and

$$\left(\frac{dw}{dt}\right)_{t_0} = \left(\frac{\partial w}{\partial x}\right)_{P_0}\left(\frac{dx}{dt}\right)_{t_0} + \left(\frac{\partial w}{\partial y}\right)_{P_0}\left(\frac{dy}{dt}\right)_{t_0},$$

where $P_0 = (x(t_0), y(t_0))$. The subscripts indicate where each of the derivatives are to be evaluated.

Let Δx, Δy, and Δw be the increments that result from changing t from t_0 to $t_0 + \Delta t$. Since f is differentiable (see the definition in Section 14.3),

To remember the Chain Rule picture the diagram below. To find dw/dt, start at w and read down each route to t, multiplying derivatives along the way. Then add the products.

Chain Rule

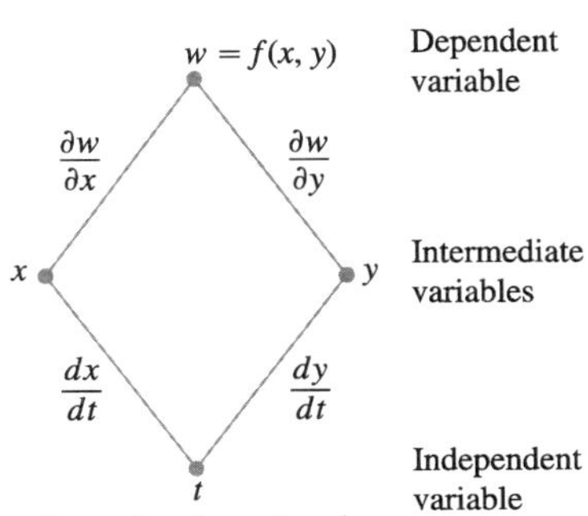

$$\frac{dw}{dt} = \frac{\partial w}{\partial x}\frac{dx}{dt} + \frac{\partial w}{\partial y}\frac{dy}{dt}$$

$$\Delta w = \left(\frac{\partial w}{\partial x}\right)_{P_0}\Delta x + \left(\frac{\partial w}{\partial y}\right)_{P_0}\Delta y + \epsilon_1\Delta x + \epsilon_2\Delta y,$$

where $\epsilon_1, \epsilon_2 \to 0$ as $\Delta x, \Delta y \to 0$. To find dw/dt, we divide this equation through by Δt and let Δt approach zero. The division gives

$$\frac{\Delta w}{\Delta t} = \left(\frac{\partial w}{\partial x}\right)_{P_0}\frac{\Delta x}{\Delta t} + \left(\frac{\partial w}{\partial y}\right)_{P_0}\frac{\Delta y}{\Delta t} + \epsilon_1\frac{\Delta x}{\Delta t} + \epsilon_2\frac{\Delta y}{\Delta t}.$$

Letting Δt approach zero gives

$$\begin{aligned}\left(\frac{dw}{dt}\right)_{t_0} &= \lim_{\Delta t \to 0}\frac{\Delta w}{\Delta t}\\ &= \left(\frac{\partial w}{\partial x}\right)_{P_0}\left(\frac{dx}{dt}\right)_{t_0} + \left(\frac{\partial w}{\partial y}\right)_{P_0}\left(\frac{dy}{dt}\right)_{t_0} + 0\cdot\left(\frac{dx}{dt}\right)_{t_0} + 0\cdot\left(\frac{dy}{dt}\right)_{t_0}.\end{aligned}$$ ■

The **tree diagram** in the margin provides a convenient way to remember the Chain Rule. From the diagram, you see that when $t = t_0$, the derivatives dx/dt and dy/dt are evaluated at t_0. The value of t_0 then determines the value x_0 for the differentiable function x and the value y_0 for the differentiable function y. The partial derivatives $\partial w/\partial x$ and $\partial w/\partial y$ (which are themselves functions of x and y) are evaluated at the point $P_0(x_0, y_0)$ corresponding to t_0. The "true" independent variable is t, whereas x and y are *intermediate variables* (controlled by t) and w is the dependent variable.

A more precise notation for the Chain Rule shows how the various derivatives in Theorem 5 are evaluated:

$$\frac{dw}{dt}(t_0) = \frac{\partial f}{\partial x}(x_0, y_0) \cdot \frac{dx}{dt}(t_0) + \frac{\partial f}{\partial y}(x_0, y_0) \cdot \frac{dy}{dt}(t_0).$$

EXAMPLE 1 Applying the Chain Rule

Use the Chain Rule to find the derivative of

$$w = xy$$

with respect to t along the path $x = \cos t, y = \sin t$. What is the derivative's value at $t = \pi/2$?

Solution We apply the Chain Rule to find dw/dt as follows:

$$\begin{aligned}
\frac{dw}{dt} &= \frac{\partial w}{\partial x}\frac{dx}{dt} + \frac{\partial w}{\partial y}\frac{dy}{dt} \\
&= \frac{\partial(xy)}{\partial x} \cdot \frac{d}{dt}(\cos t) + \frac{\partial(xy)}{\partial y} \cdot \frac{d}{dt}(\sin t) \\
&= (y)(-\sin t) + (x)(\cos t) \\
&= (\sin t)(-\sin t) + (\cos t)(\cos t) \\
&= -\sin^2 t + \cos^2 t \\
&= \cos 2t.
\end{aligned}$$

In this example, we can check the result with a more direct calculation. As a function of t,

$$w = xy = \cos t \sin t = \frac{1}{2}\sin 2t,$$

so

$$\frac{dw}{dt} = \frac{d}{dt}\left(\frac{1}{2}\sin 2t\right) = \frac{1}{2} \cdot 2\cos 2t = \cos 2t.$$

In either case, at the given value of t,

$$\left(\frac{dw}{dt}\right)_{t=\pi/2} = \cos\left(2 \cdot \frac{\pi}{2}\right) = \cos \pi = -1.$$

■

Functions of Three Variables

You can probably predict the Chain Rule for functions of three variables, as it only involves adding the expected third term to the two-variable formula.

> **THEOREM 6 Chain Rule for Functions of Three Independent Variables**
> If $w = f(x, y, z)$ is differentiable and x, y, and z are differentiable functions of t, then w is a differentiable function of t and
> $$\frac{dw}{dt} = \frac{\partial f}{\partial x}\frac{dx}{dt} + \frac{\partial f}{\partial y}\frac{dy}{dt} + \frac{\partial f}{\partial z}\frac{dz}{dt}.$$

Here we have three routes from w to t instead of two, but finding dw/dt is still the same. Read down each route, multiplying derivatives along the way; then add.

Chain Rule

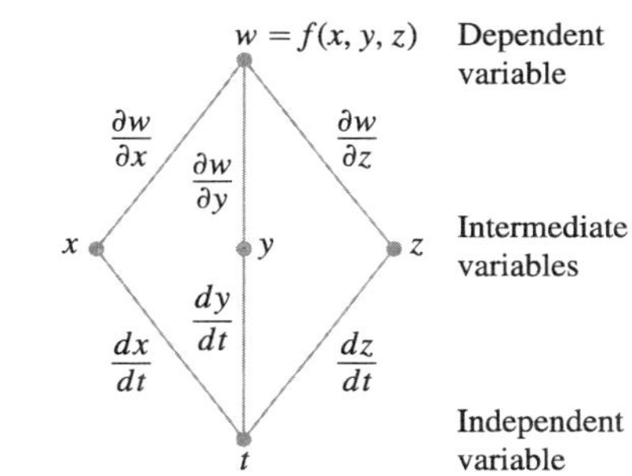

$$\frac{dw}{dt} = \frac{\partial w}{\partial x}\frac{dx}{dt} + \frac{\partial w}{\partial y}\frac{dy}{dt} + \frac{\partial w}{\partial z}\frac{dz}{dt}$$

The proof is identical with the proof of Theorem 5 except that there are now three intermediate variables instead of two. The diagram we use for remembering the new equation is similar as well, with three routes from w to t.

EXAMPLE 2 Changes in a Function's Values Along a Helix

Find dw/dt if

$$w = xy + z, \qquad x = \cos t, \qquad y = \sin t, \qquad z = t.$$

In this example the values of w are changing along the path of a helix (Section 13.1). What is the derivative's value at $t = 0$?

Solution

$$\begin{aligned}\frac{dw}{dt} &= \frac{\partial w}{\partial x}\frac{dx}{dt} + \frac{\partial w}{\partial y}\frac{dy}{dt} + \frac{\partial w}{\partial z}\frac{dz}{dt}\\ &= (y)(-\sin t) + (x)(\cos t) + (1)(1)\\ &= (\sin t)(-\sin t) + (\cos t)(\cos t) + 1 \qquad \text{Substitute for the intermediate variables.}\\ &= -\sin^2 t + \cos^2 t + 1 = 1 + \cos 2t.\end{aligned}$$

$$\left(\frac{dw}{dt}\right)_{t=0} = 1 + \cos(0) = 2.$$ ■

Here is a physical interpretation of change along a curve. If $w = T(x, y, z)$ is the temperature at each point (x, y, z) along a curve C with parametric equations $x = x(t)$, $y = y(t)$, and $z = z(t)$, then the composite function $w = T(x(t), y(t), z(t))$ represents the temperature relative to t along the curve. The derivative dw/dt is then the instantaneous rate of change of temperature along the curve, as calculated in Theorem 6.

Functions Defined on Surfaces

If we are interested in the temperature $w = f(x, y, z)$ at points (x, y, z) on a globe in space, we might prefer to think of x, y, and z as functions of the variables r and s that give the points' longitudes and latitudes. If $x = g(r, s)$, $y = h(r, s)$, and $z = k(r, s)$, we could then express the temperature as a function of r and s with the composite function

$$w = f(g(r, s), h(r, s), k(r, s)).$$

Under the right conditions, w would have partial derivatives with respect to both r and s that could be calculated in the following way.

THEOREM 7 Chain Rule for Two Independent Variables and Three Intermediate Variables

Suppose that $w = f(x, y, z)$, $x = g(r, s)$, $y = h(r, s)$, and $z = k(r, s)$. If all four functions are differentiable, then w has partial derivatives with respect to r and s, given by the formulas

$$\frac{\partial w}{\partial r} = \frac{\partial w}{\partial x}\frac{\partial x}{\partial r} + \frac{\partial w}{\partial y}\frac{\partial y}{\partial r} + \frac{\partial w}{\partial z}\frac{\partial z}{\partial r}$$

$$\frac{\partial w}{\partial s} = \frac{\partial w}{\partial x}\frac{\partial x}{\partial s} + \frac{\partial w}{\partial y}\frac{\partial y}{\partial s} + \frac{\partial w}{\partial z}\frac{\partial z}{\partial s}.$$

The first of these equations can be derived from the Chain Rule in Theorem 6 by holding s fixed and treating r as t. The second can be derived in the same way, holding r fixed and treating s as t. The tree diagrams for both equations are shown in Figure 14.19.

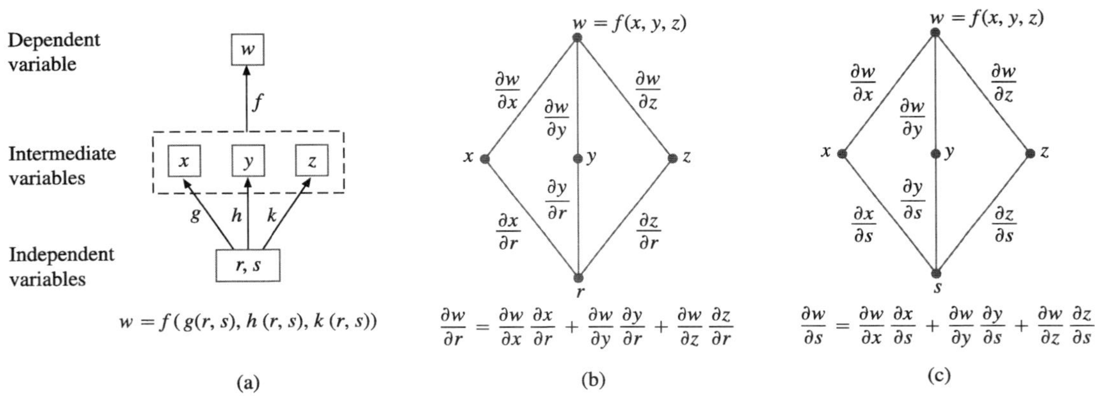

FIGURE 14.19 Composite function and tree diagrams for Theorem 7.

EXAMPLE 3 Partial Derivatives Using Theorem 7

Express $\partial w/\partial r$ and $\partial w/\partial s$ in terms of r and s if

$$w = x + 2y + z^2, \qquad x = \frac{r}{s}, \qquad y = r^2 + \ln s, \qquad z = 2r.$$

Solution

$$\begin{aligned}\frac{\partial w}{\partial r} &= \frac{\partial w}{\partial x}\frac{\partial x}{\partial r} + \frac{\partial w}{\partial y}\frac{\partial y}{\partial r} + \frac{\partial w}{\partial z}\frac{\partial z}{\partial r}\\ &= (1)\left(\frac{1}{s}\right) + (2)(2r) + (2z)(2)\\ &= \frac{1}{s} + 4r + (4r)(2) = \frac{1}{s} + 12r \qquad \text{Substitute for intermediate variable } z.\end{aligned}$$

$$\begin{aligned}\frac{\partial w}{\partial s} &= \frac{\partial w}{\partial x}\frac{\partial x}{\partial s} + \frac{\partial w}{\partial y}\frac{\partial y}{\partial s} + \frac{\partial w}{\partial z}\frac{\partial z}{\partial s}\\ &= (1)\left(-\frac{r}{s^2}\right) + (2)\left(\frac{1}{s}\right) + (2z)(0) = \frac{2}{s} - \frac{r}{s^2}\end{aligned}$$

■

Chain Rule

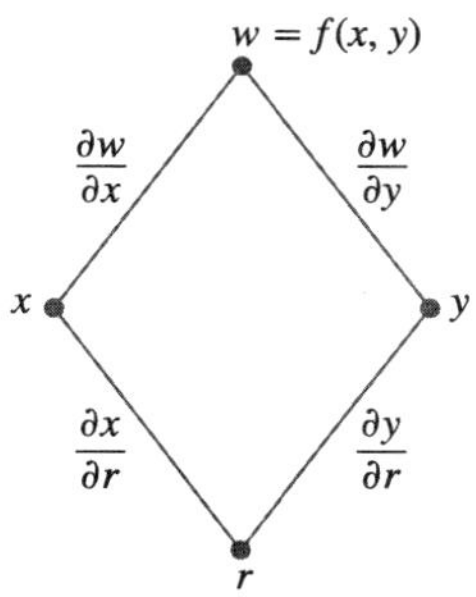

$$\frac{\partial w}{\partial r} = \frac{\partial w}{\partial x}\frac{\partial x}{\partial r} + \frac{\partial w}{\partial y}\frac{\partial y}{\partial r}$$

FIGURE 14.20 Tree diagram for the equation

$$\frac{\partial w}{\partial r} = \frac{\partial w}{\partial x}\frac{\partial x}{\partial r} + \frac{\partial w}{\partial y}\frac{\partial y}{\partial r}.$$

If f is a function of two variables instead of three, each equation in Theorem 7 becomes correspondingly one term shorter.

> If $w = f(x, y)$, $x = g(r, s)$, and $y = h(r, s)$, then
>
> $$\frac{\partial w}{\partial r} = \frac{\partial w}{\partial x}\frac{\partial x}{\partial r} + \frac{\partial w}{\partial y}\frac{\partial y}{\partial r} \quad \text{and} \quad \frac{\partial w}{\partial s} = \frac{\partial w}{\partial x}\frac{\partial x}{\partial s} + \frac{\partial w}{\partial y}\frac{\partial y}{\partial s}.$$

Figure 14.20 shows the tree diagram for the first of these equations. The diagram for the second equation is similar; just replace r with s.

EXAMPLE 4 More Partial Derivatives

Express $\partial w/\partial r$ and $\partial w/\partial s$ in terms of r and s if

$$w = x^2 + y^2, \qquad x = r - s, \qquad y = r + s.$$

Solution

$$\begin{aligned} \frac{\partial w}{\partial r} &= \frac{\partial w}{\partial x}\frac{\partial x}{\partial r} + \frac{\partial w}{\partial y}\frac{\partial y}{\partial r} \\ &= (2x)(1) + (2y)(1) \\ &= 2(r - s) + 2(r + s) \\ &= 4r \end{aligned} \qquad \begin{aligned} \frac{\partial w}{\partial s} &= \frac{\partial w}{\partial x}\frac{\partial x}{\partial s} + \frac{\partial w}{\partial y}\frac{\partial y}{\partial s} \\ &= (2x)(-1) + (2y)(1) \\ &= -2(r - s) + 2(r + s) \\ &= 4s \end{aligned}$$

Substitute for the intermediate variables.

■

If f is a function of x alone, our equations become even simpler.

Chain Rule

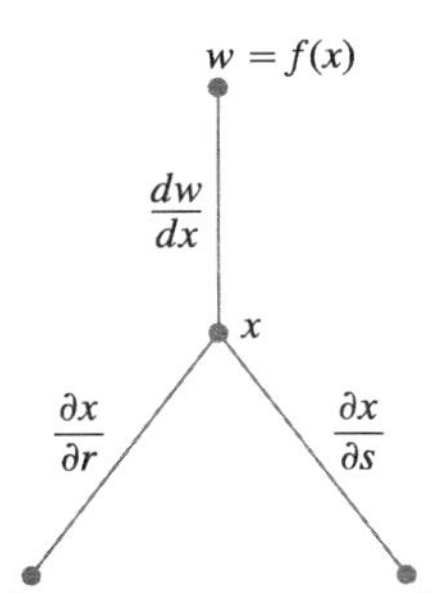

$$\frac{\partial w}{\partial r} = \frac{dw}{dx}\frac{\partial x}{\partial r}$$

$$\frac{\partial w}{\partial s} = \frac{dw}{dx}\frac{\partial x}{\partial s}$$

FIGURE 14.21 Tree diagram for differentiating f as a composite function of r and s with one intermediate variable.

> If $w = f(x)$ and $x = g(r, s)$, then
>
> $$\frac{\partial w}{\partial r} = \frac{dw}{dx}\frac{\partial x}{\partial r} \quad \text{and} \quad \frac{\partial w}{\partial s} = \frac{dw}{dx}\frac{\partial x}{\partial s}.$$

In this case, we can use the ordinary (single-variable) derivative, dw/dx. The tree diagram is shown in Figure 14.21.

Implicit Differentiation Revisited

The two-variable Chain Rule in Theorem 5 leads to a formula that takes most of the work out of implicit differentiation. Suppose that

1. The function $F(x, y)$ is differentiable and
2. The equation $F(x, y) = 0$ defines y implicitly as a differentiable function of x, say $y = h(x)$.

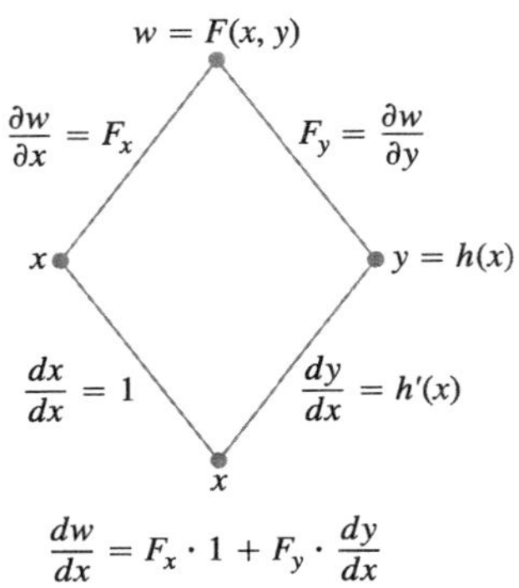

FIGURE 14.22 Tree diagram for differentiating $w = F(x, y)$ with respect to x. Setting $dw/dx = 0$ leads to a simple computational formula for implicit differentiation (Theorem 8).

Since $w = F(x, y) = 0$, the derivative dw/dx must be zero. Computing the derivative from the Chain Rule (tree diagram in Figure 14.22), we find

$$0 = \frac{dw}{dx} = F_x \frac{dx}{dx} + F_y \frac{dy}{dx} \qquad \text{Theorem 5 with } t = x \text{ and } f = F$$

$$= F_x \cdot 1 + F_y \cdot \frac{dy}{dx}.$$

If $F_y = \partial w/\partial y \neq 0$, we can solve this equation for dy/dx to get

$$\frac{dy}{dx} = -\frac{F_x}{F_y}.$$

This relationship gives a surprisingly simple shortcut to finding derivatives of implicitly defined functions, which we state here as a theorem.

> **THEOREM 8 A Formula for Implicit Differentiation**
> Suppose that $F(x, y)$ is differentiable and that the equation $F(x, y) = 0$ defines y as a differentiable function of x. Then at any point where $F_y \neq 0$,
>
> $$\frac{dy}{dx} = -\frac{F_x}{F_y}.$$

EXAMPLE 5 Implicit Differentiation

Use Theorem 8 to find dy/dx if $y^2 - x^2 - \sin xy = 0$.

Solution Take $F(x, y) = y^2 - x^2 - \sin xy$. Then

$$\frac{dy}{dx} = -\frac{F_x}{F_y} = -\frac{-2x - y\cos xy}{2y - x\cos xy}$$

$$= \frac{2x + y\cos xy}{2y - x\cos xy}.$$

This calculation is significantly shorter than the single-variable calculation with which we found dy/dx in Section 3.6, Example 3. ■

Functions of Many Variables

We have seen several different forms of the Chain Rule in this section, but you do not have to memorize them all if you can see them as special cases of the same general formula. When solving particular problems, it may help to draw the appropriate tree diagram by placing the dependent variable on top, the intermediate variables in the middle, and the selected independent variable at the bottom. To find the derivative of the dependent variable with respect to the selected independent variable, start at the dependent variable and read down each route of the tree to the independent variable, calculating and multiplying the derivatives along each route. Then add the products you found for the different routes.

In general, suppose that $w = f(x, y, \ldots, v)$ is a differentiable function of the variables $x, y, \ldots, v$ (a finite set) and the $x, y, \ldots, v$ are differentiable functions of $p, q, \ldots, t$ (another finite set). Then w is a differentiable function of the variables p through t and the partial derivatives of w with respect to these variables are given by equations of the form

$$\frac{\partial w}{\partial p} = \frac{\partial w}{\partial x}\frac{\partial x}{\partial p} + \frac{\partial w}{\partial y}\frac{\partial y}{\partial p} + \cdots + \frac{\partial w}{\partial v}\frac{\partial v}{\partial p}.$$

The other equations are obtained by replacing p by $q, \ldots, t$, one at a time.

One way to remember this equation is to think of the right-hand side as the dot product of two vectors with components

$$\underbrace{\left(\frac{\partial w}{\partial x}, \frac{\partial w}{\partial y}, \ldots, \frac{\partial w}{\partial v}\right)}_{\substack{\text{Derivatives of } w \text{ with} \\ \text{respect to the} \\ \text{intermediate variables}}} \quad \text{and} \quad \underbrace{\left(\frac{\partial x}{\partial p}, \frac{\partial y}{\partial p}, \ldots, \frac{\partial v}{\partial p}\right)}_{\substack{\text{Derivatives of the intermediate} \\ \text{variables with respect to the} \\ \text{selected independent variable}}}.$$

EXERCISES 14.4

Chain Rule: One Independent Variable

In Exercises 1–6, **(a)** express dw/dt as a function of t, both by using the Chain Rule and by expressing w in terms of t and differentiating directly with respect to t. Then **(b)** evaluate dw/dt at the given value of t.

1. $w = x^2 + y^2, \quad x = \cos t, \quad y = \sin t; \quad t = \pi$

2. $w = x^2 + y^2, \quad x = \cos t + \sin t, \quad y = \cos t - \sin t; \quad t = 0$

3. $w = \dfrac{x}{z} + \dfrac{y}{z}, \quad x = \cos^2 t, \quad y = \sin^2 t, \quad z = 1/t; \quad t = 3$

4. $w = \ln(x^2 + y^2 + z^2), \quad x = \cos t, \quad y = \sin t, \quad z = 4\sqrt{t};$ $t = 3$

5. $w = 2ye^x - \ln z, \quad x = \ln(t^2 + 1), \quad y = \tan^{-1} t, \quad z = e^t;$ $t = 1$

6. $w = z - \sin xy, \quad x = t, \quad y = \ln t, \quad z = e^{t-1}; \quad t = 1$

Chain Rule: Two and Three Independent Variables

In Exercises 7 and 8, **(a)** express $\partial z/\partial u$ and $\partial z/\partial v$ as functions of u and v both by using the Chain Rule and by expressing z directly in terms of u and v before differentiating. Then **(b)** evaluate $\partial z/\partial u$ and $\partial z/\partial v$ at the given point (u, v).

7. $z = 4e^x \ln y, \quad x = \ln(u \cos v), \quad y = u \sin v;$ $(u, v) = (2, \pi/4)$

8. $z = \tan^{-1}(x/y), \quad x = u \cos v, \quad y = u \sin v;$ $(u, v) = (1.3, \pi/6)$

In Exercises 9 and 10, **(a)** express $\partial w/\partial u$ and $\partial w/\partial v$ as functions of u and v both by using the Chain Rule and by expressing w directly in terms of u and v before differentiating. Then **(b)** evaluate $\partial w/\partial u$ and $\partial w/\partial v$ at the given point (u, v).

9. $w = xy + yz + xz, \quad x = u + v, \quad y = u - v, \quad z = uv;$ $(u, v) = (1/2, 1)$

10. $w = \ln(x^2 + y^2 + z^2), \quad x = ue^v \sin u, \quad y = ue^v \cos u,$ $z = ue^v; \quad (u, v) = (-2, 0)$

In Exercises 11 and 12, **(a)** express $\partial u/\partial x$, $\partial u/\partial y$, and $\partial u/\partial z$ as functions of x, y, and z both by using the Chain Rule and by expressing u directly in terms of x, y, and z before differentiating. Then **(b)** evaluate $\partial u/\partial x$, $\partial u/\partial y$, and $\partial u/\partial z$ at the given point (x, y, z).

11. $u = \dfrac{p - q}{q - r}, \quad p = x + y + z, \quad q = x - y + z,$ $r = x + y - z; \quad (x, y, z) = \left(\sqrt{3}, 2, 1\right)$

12. $u = e^{qr} \sin^{-1} p, \quad p = \sin x, \quad q = z^2 \ln y, \quad r = 1/z;$ $(x, y, z) = (\pi/4, 1/2, -1/2)$

Using a Tree Diagram

In Exercises 13–24, draw a tree diagram and write a Chain Rule formula for each derivative.

13. $\dfrac{dz}{dt}$ for $z = f(x, y), \quad x = g(t), \quad y = h(t)$

14. $\dfrac{dz}{dt}$ for $z = f(u, v, w), \quad u = g(t), \quad v = h(t), \quad w = k(t)$

15. $\dfrac{\partial w}{\partial u}$ and $\dfrac{\partial w}{\partial v}$ for $w = h(x, y, z), \quad x = f(u, v), \quad y = g(u, v),$ $z = k(u, v)$

16. $\dfrac{\partial w}{\partial x}$ and $\dfrac{\partial w}{\partial y}$ for $w = f(r, s, t), \quad r = g(x, y), \quad s = h(x, y),$
$t = k(x, y)$

17. $\dfrac{\partial w}{\partial u}$ and $\dfrac{\partial w}{\partial v}$ for $w = g(x, y), \quad x = h(u, v), \quad y = k(u, v)$

18. $\dfrac{\partial w}{\partial x}$ and $\dfrac{\partial w}{\partial y}$ for $w = g(u, v), \quad u = h(x, y), \quad v = k(x, y)$

19. $\dfrac{\partial z}{\partial t}$ and $\dfrac{\partial z}{\partial s}$ for $z = f(x, y), \quad x = g(t, s), \quad y = h(t, s)$

20. $\dfrac{\partial y}{\partial r}$ for $y = f(u), \quad u = g(r, s)$

21. $\dfrac{\partial w}{\partial s}$ and $\dfrac{\partial w}{\partial t}$ for $w = g(u), \quad u = h(s, t)$

22. $\dfrac{\partial w}{\partial p}$ for $w = f(x, y, z, v), \quad x = g(p, q), \quad y = h(p, q),$
$z = j(p, q), \quad v = k(p, q)$

23. $\dfrac{\partial w}{\partial r}$ and $\dfrac{\partial w}{\partial s}$ for $w = f(x, y), \quad x = g(r), \quad y = h(s)$

24. $\dfrac{\partial w}{\partial s}$ for $w = g(x, y), \quad x = h(r, s, t), \quad y = k(r, s, t)$

Implicit Differentiation

Assuming that the equations in Exercises 25–28 define y as a differentiable function of x, use Theorem 8 to find the value of dy/dx at the given point.

25. $x^3 - 2y^2 + xy = 0, \quad (1, 1)$

26. $xy + y^2 - 3x - 3 = 0, \quad (-1, 1)$

27. $x^2 + xy + y^2 - 7 = 0, \quad (1, 2)$

28. $xe^y + \sin xy + y - \ln 2 = 0, \quad (0, \ln 2)$

Three-Variable Implicit Differentiation

Theorem 8 can be generalized to functions of three variables and even more. The three-variable version goes like this: If the equation $F(x, y, z) = 0$ determines z as a differentiable function of x and y, then, at points where $F_z \neq 0$,

$$\frac{\partial z}{\partial x} = -\frac{F_x}{F_z} \quad \text{and} \quad \frac{\partial z}{\partial y} = -\frac{F_y}{F_z}.$$

Use these equations to find the values of $\partial z/\partial x$ and $\partial z/\partial y$ at the points in Exercises 29–32.

29. $z^3 - xy + yz + y^3 - 2 = 0, \quad (1, 1, 1)$

30. $\dfrac{1}{x} + \dfrac{1}{y} + \dfrac{1}{z} - 1 = 0, \quad (2, 3, 6)$

31. $\sin(x + y) + \sin(y + z) + \sin(x + z) = 0, \quad (\pi, \pi, \pi)$

32. $xe^y + ye^z + 2\ln x - 2 - 3\ln 2 = 0, \quad (1, \ln 2, \ln 3)$

Finding Specified Partial Derivatives

33. Find $\partial w/\partial r$ when $r = 1, s = -1$ if $w = (x + y + z)^2$, $x = r - s, y = \cos(r + s), z = \sin(r + s)$.

34. Find $\partial w/\partial v$ when $u = -1, v = 2$ if $w = xy + \ln z$, $x = v^2/u, y = u + v, z = \cos u$.

35. Find $\partial w/\partial v$ when $u = 0, v = 0$ if $w = x^2 + (y/x)$, $x = u - 2v + 1, y = 2u + v - 2$.

36. Find $\partial z/\partial u$ when $u = 0, v = 1$ if $z = \sin xy + x\sin y$, $x = u^2 + v^2, y = uv$.

37. Find $\partial z/\partial u$ and $\partial z/\partial v$ when $u = \ln 2, v = 1$ if $z = 5\tan^{-1}x$ and $x = e^u + \ln v$.

38. Find $\partial z/\partial u$ and $\partial z/\partial v$ when $u = 1$ and $v = -2$ if $z = \ln q$ and $q = \sqrt{v + 3}\tan^{-1}u$.

Theory and Examples

39. **Changing voltage in a circuit** The voltage V in a circuit that satisfies the law $V = IR$ is slowly dropping as the battery wears out. At the same time, the resistance R is increasing as the resistor heats up. Use the equation

$$\frac{dV}{dt} = \frac{\partial V}{\partial I}\frac{dI}{dt} + \frac{\partial V}{\partial R}\frac{dR}{dt}$$

to find how the current is changing at the instant when $R = 600$ ohms, $I = 0.04$ amp, $dR/dt = 0.5$ ohm/sec, and $dV/dt = -0.01$ volt/sec.

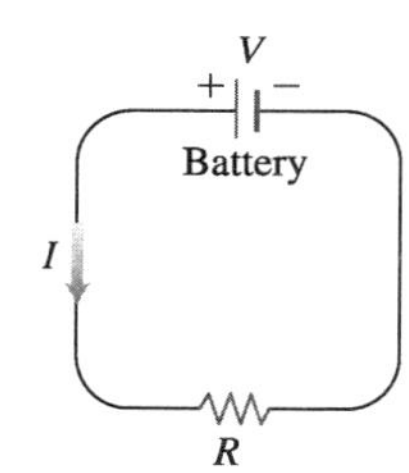

40. **Changing dimensions in a box** The lengths a, b, and c of the edges of a rectangular box are changing with time. At the instant in question, $a = 1$ m, $b = 2$ m, $c = 3$ m, $da/dt = db/dt = 1$ m/sec, and $dc/dt = -3$ m/sec. At what rates are the box's volume V and surface area S changing at that instant? Are the box's interior diagonals increasing in length or decreasing?

41. If $f(u, v, w)$ is differentiable and $u = x - y, v = y - z$, and $w = z - x$, show that

$$\frac{\partial f}{\partial x} + \frac{\partial f}{\partial y} + \frac{\partial f}{\partial z} = 0.$$

42. **Polar coordinates** Suppose that we substitute polar coordinates $x = r\cos\theta$ and $y = r\sin\theta$ in a differentiable function $w = f(x, y)$.

a. Show that

$$\frac{\partial w}{\partial r} = f_x \cos\theta + f_y \sin\theta$$

and

$$\frac{1}{r}\frac{\partial w}{\partial \theta} = -f_x \sin\theta + f_y \cos\theta .$$

b. Solve the equations in part (a) to express f_x and f_y in terms of $\partial w/\partial r$ and $\partial w/\partial \theta$.

c. Show that

$$(f_x)^2 + (f_y)^2 = \left(\frac{\partial w}{\partial r}\right)^2 + \frac{1}{r^2}\left(\frac{\partial w}{\partial \theta}\right)^2.$$

43. Laplace equations Show that if $w = f(u, v)$ satisfies the Laplace equation $f_{uu} + f_{vv} = 0$ and if $u = (x^2 - y^2)/2$ and $v = xy$, then w satisfies the Laplace equation $w_{xx} + w_{yy} = 0$.

44. Laplace equations Let $w = f(u) + g(v)$, where $u = x + iy$ and $v = x - iy$ and $i = \sqrt{-1}$. Show that w satisfies the Laplace equation $w_{xx} + w_{yy} = 0$ if all the necessary functions are differentiable.

Changes in Functions Along Curves

45. Extreme values on a helix Suppose that the partial derivatives of a function $f(x, y, z)$ at points on the helix $x = \cos t$, $y = \sin t$, $z = t$ are

$$f_x = \cos t, \qquad f_y = \sin t, \qquad f_z = t^2 + t - 2.$$

At what points on the curve, if any, can f take on extreme values?

46. A space curve Let $w = x^2 e^{2y} \cos 3z$. Find the value of dw/dt at the point $(1, \ln 2, 0)$ on the curve $x = \cos t$, $y = \ln(t + 2)$, $z = t$.

47. Temperature on a circle Let $T = f(x, y)$ be the temperature at the point (x, y) on the circle $x = \cos t$, $y = \sin t$, $0 \le t \le 2\pi$ and suppose that

$$\frac{\partial T}{\partial x} = 8x - 4y, \qquad \frac{\partial T}{\partial y} = 8y - 4x.$$

a. Find where the maximum and minimum temperatures on the circle occur by examining the derivatives dT/dt and d^2T/dt^2.

b. Suppose that $T = 4x^2 - 4xy + 4y^2$. Find the maximum and minimum values of T on the circle.

48. Temperature on an ellipse Let $T = g(x, y)$ be the temperature at the point (x, y) on the ellipse

$$x = 2\sqrt{2}\cos t, \qquad y = \sqrt{2}\sin t, \qquad 0 \le t \le 2\pi,$$

and suppose that

$$\frac{\partial T}{\partial x} = y, \qquad \frac{\partial T}{\partial y} = x.$$

a. Locate the maximum and minimum temperatures on the ellipse by examining dT/dt and d^2T/dt^2.

b. Suppose that $T = xy - 2$. Find the maximum and minimum values of T on the ellipse.

Differentiating Integrals

Under mild continuity restrictions, it is true that if

$$F(x) = \int_a^b g(t, x)\, dt,$$

then $F'(x) = \int_a^b g_x(t, x)\, dt$. Using this fact and the Chain Rule, we can find the derivative of

$$F(x) = \int_a^{f(x)} g(t, x)\, dt$$

by letting

$$G(u, x) = \int_a^u g(t, x)\, dt,$$

where $u = f(x)$. Find the derivatives of the functions in Exercises 49 and 50.

49. $F(x) = \int_0^{x^2} \sqrt{t^4 + x^3}\, dt$

50. $F(x) = \int_{x^2}^1 \sqrt{t^3 + x^2}\, dt$

14.5 Directional Derivatives and Gradient Vectors

If you look at the map (Figure 14.23) showing contours on the West Point Area along the Hudson River in New York, you will notice that the tributary streams flow perpendicular to the contours. The streams are following paths of steepest descent so the waters reach the Hudson as quickly as possible. Therefore, the instantaneous rate of change in a stream's altitude above sea level has a particular direction. In this section, you see why this direction, called the "downhill" direction, is perpendicular to the contours.

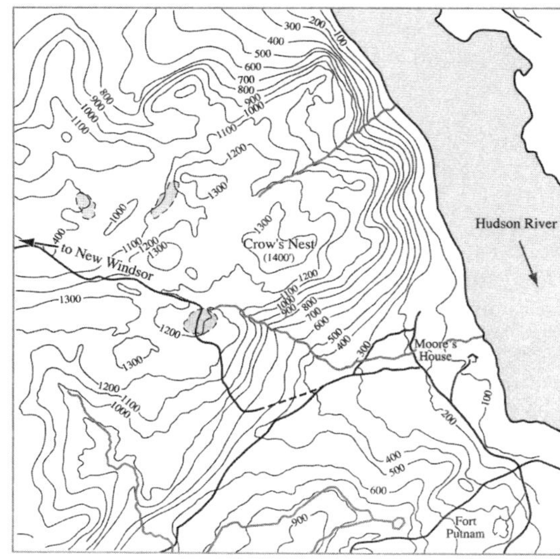

FIGURE 14.23 Contours of the West Point Area in New York show streams, which follow paths of steepest descent, running perpendicular to the contours.

Directional Derivatives in the Plane

We know from Section 14.4 that if $f(x, y)$ is differentiable, then the rate at which f changes with respect to t along a differentiable curve $x = g(t), y = h(t)$ is

$$\frac{df}{dt} = \frac{\partial f}{\partial x}\frac{dx}{dt} + \frac{\partial f}{\partial y}\frac{dy}{dt}.$$

At any point $P_0(x_0, y_0) = P_0(g(t_0), h(t_0))$, this equation gives the rate of change of f with respect to increasing t and therefore depends, among other things, on the direction of motion along the curve. If the curve is a straight line and t is the arc length parameter along the line measured from P_0 in the direction of a given unit vector $\mathbf{u}$, then df/dt is the rate of change of f with respect to distance in its domain in the direction of $\mathbf{u}$. By varying $\mathbf{u}$, we find the rates at which f changes with respect to distance as we move through P_0 in different directions. We now define this idea more precisely.

Suppose that the function $f(x, y)$ is defined throughout a region R in the xy-plane, that $P_0(x_0, y_0)$ is a point in R, and that $\mathbf{u} = u_1\mathbf{i} + u_2\mathbf{j}$ is a unit vector. Then the equations

$$x = x_0 + su_1, \qquad y = y_0 + su_2$$

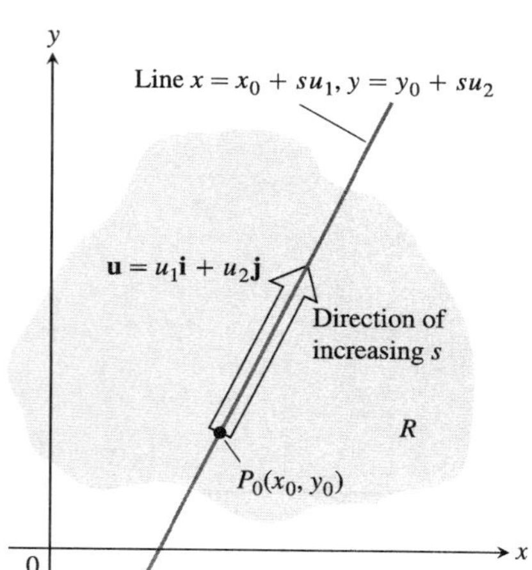

FIGURE 14.24 The rate of change of f in the direction of $\mathbf{u}$ at a point P_0 is the rate at which f changes along this line at P_0.

parametrize the line through P_0 parallel to $\mathbf{u}$. If the parameter s measures arc length from P_0 in the direction of $\mathbf{u}$, we find the rate of change of f at P_0 in the direction of $\mathbf{u}$ by calculating df/ds at P_0 (Figure 14.24).

DEFINITION Directional Derivative

The **derivative of f at $P_0(x_0, y_0)$ in the direction of the unit vector $\mathbf{u} = u_1\mathbf{i} + u_2\mathbf{j}$** is the number

$$\left(\frac{df}{ds}\right)_{\mathbf{u},P_0} = \lim_{s\to 0}\frac{f(x_0 + su_1, y_0 + su_2) - f(x_0, y_0)}{s}, \tag{1}$$

provided the limit exists.

The directional derivative is also denoted by

$$(D_{\mathbf{u}}f)_{P_0}. \qquad \text{"The derivative of } f \text{ at } P_0 \text{ in the direction of } \mathbf{u}\text{"}$$

EXAMPLE 1 Finding a Directional Derivative Using the Definition

Find the derivative of

$$f(x, y) = x^2 + xy$$

at $P_0(1, 2)$ in the direction of the unit vector $\mathbf{u} = \left(1/\sqrt{2}\right)\mathbf{i} + \left(1/\sqrt{2}\right)\mathbf{j}$.

Solution

$$\begin{aligned}
\left(\frac{df}{ds}\right)_{\mathbf{u},P_0} &= \lim_{s\to 0}\frac{f(x_0 + su_1, y_0 + su_2) - f(x_0, y_0)}{s} \qquad \text{Equation (1)}\\
&= \lim_{s\to 0}\frac{f\left(1 + s\cdot\frac{1}{\sqrt{2}}, 2 + s\cdot\frac{1}{\sqrt{2}}\right) - f(1, 2)}{s}\\
&= \lim_{s\to 0}\frac{\left(1 + \frac{s}{\sqrt{2}}\right)^2 + \left(1 + \frac{s}{\sqrt{2}}\right)\left(2 + \frac{s}{\sqrt{2}}\right) - (1^2 + 1\cdot 2)}{s}\\
&= \lim_{s\to 0}\frac{\left(1 + \frac{2s}{\sqrt{2}} + \frac{s^2}{2}\right) + \left(2 + \frac{3s}{\sqrt{2}} + \frac{s^2}{2}\right) - 3}{s}\\
&= \lim_{s\to 0}\frac{\frac{5s}{\sqrt{2}} + s^2}{s} = \lim_{s\to 0}\left(\frac{5}{\sqrt{2}} + s\right) = \left(\frac{5}{\sqrt{2}} + 0\right) = \frac{5}{\sqrt{2}}.
\end{aligned}$$

The rate of change of $f(x, y) = x^2 + xy$ at $P_0(1, 2)$ in the direction $\mathbf{u} = \left(1/\sqrt{2}\right)\mathbf{i} + \left(1/\sqrt{2}\right)\mathbf{j}$ is $5/\sqrt{2}$. ■

Interpretation of the Directional Derivative

The equation $z = f(x, y)$ represents a surface S in space. If $z_0 = f(x_0, y_0)$, then the point $P(x_0, y_0, z_0)$ lies on S. The vertical plane that passes through P and $P_0(x_0, y_0)$ parallel to $\mathbf{u}$

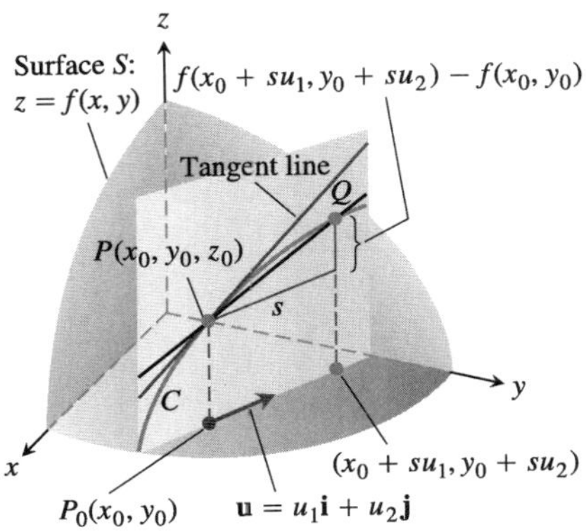

FIGURE 14.25 The slope of curve C at P_0 is $\lim_{Q \to P}$ slope (PQ); this is the directional derivative

$$\left(\frac{df}{ds}\right)_{\mathbf{u},P_0} = (D_{\mathbf{u}}f)_{P_0}.$$

intersects S in a curve C (Figure 14.25). The rate of change of f in the direction of $\mathbf{u}$ is the slope of the tangent to C at P.

When $\mathbf{u} = \mathbf{i}$, the directional derivative at P_0 is $\partial f/\partial x$ evaluated at (x_0, y_0). When $\mathbf{u} = \mathbf{j}$, the directional derivative at P_0 is $\partial f/\partial y$ evaluated at (x_0, y_0). The directional derivative generalizes the two partial derivatives. We can now ask for the rate of change of f in any direction $\mathbf{u}$, not just the directions $\mathbf{i}$ and $\mathbf{j}$.

Here's a physical interpretation of the directional derivative. Suppose that $T = f(x, y)$ is the temperature at each point (x, y) over a region in the plane. Then $f(x_0, y_0)$ is the temperature at the point $P_0(x_0, y_0)$ and $(D_{\mathbf{u}}f)_{P_0}$ is the instantaneous rate of change of the temperature at P_0 stepping off in the direction $\mathbf{u}$.

Calculation and Gradients

We now develop an efficient formula to calculate the directional derivative for a differentiable function f. We begin with the line

$$x = x_0 + su_1, \qquad y = y_0 + su_2, \tag{2}$$

through $P_0(x_0, y_0)$, parametrized with the arc length parameter s increasing in the direction of the unit vector $\mathbf{u} = u_1\mathbf{i} + u_2\mathbf{j}$. Then

$$\left(\frac{df}{ds}\right)_{\mathbf{u},P_0} = \left(\frac{\partial f}{\partial x}\right)_{P_0}\frac{dx}{ds} + \left(\frac{\partial f}{\partial y}\right)_{P_0}\frac{dy}{ds} \qquad \text{Chain Rule for differentiable } f$$

$$= \left(\frac{\partial f}{\partial x}\right)_{P_0} \cdot u_1 + \left(\frac{\partial f}{\partial y}\right)_{P_0} \cdot u_2 \qquad \text{From Equations (2), } dx/ds = u_1 \text{ and } dy/ds = u_2$$

$$= \underbrace{\left[\left(\frac{\partial f}{\partial x}\right)_{P_0}\mathbf{i} + \left(\frac{\partial f}{\partial y}\right)_{P_0}\mathbf{j}\right]}_{\text{Gradient of } f \text{ at } P_0} \cdot \underbrace{\left[u_1\mathbf{i} + u_2\mathbf{j}\right]}_{\text{Direction } \mathbf{u}}. \tag{3}$$

DEFINITION Gradient Vector

The **gradient vector (gradient)** of $f(x, y)$ at a point $P_0(x_0, y_0)$ is the vector

$$\nabla f = \frac{\partial f}{\partial x}\mathbf{i} + \frac{\partial f}{\partial y}\mathbf{j}$$

obtained by evaluating the partial derivatives of f at P_0.

The notation ∇f is read "grad f" as well as "gradient of f" and "del f." The symbol ∇ by itself is read "del." Another notation for the gradient is grad f, read the way it is written.

Equation (3) says that the derivative of a differentiable function f in the direction of $\mathbf{u}$ at P_0 is the dot product of $\mathbf{u}$ with the gradient of f at P_0.

THEOREM 9 The Directional Derivative Is a Dot Product

If $f(x, y)$ is differentiable in an open region containing $P_0(x_0, y_0)$, then

$$\left(\frac{df}{ds}\right)_{\mathbf{u},P_0} = (\nabla f)_{P_0} \cdot \mathbf{u}, \tag{4}$$

the dot product of the gradient f at P_0 and $\mathbf{u}$.

EXAMPLE 2 Finding the Directional Derivative Using the Gradient

Find the derivative of $f(x, y) = xe^y + \cos(xy)$ at the point (2, 0) in the direction of $\mathbf{v} = 3\mathbf{i} - 4\mathbf{j}$.

Solution The direction of $\mathbf{v}$ is the unit vector obtained by dividing $\mathbf{v}$ by its length:

$$\mathbf{u} = \frac{\mathbf{v}}{|\mathbf{v}|} = \frac{\mathbf{v}}{5} = \frac{3}{5}\mathbf{i} - \frac{4}{5}\mathbf{j}.$$

The partial derivatives of f are everywhere continuous and at (2, 0) are given by

$$f_x(2, 0) = (e^y - y\sin(xy))_{(2,0)} = e^0 - 0 = 1$$

$$f_y(2, 0) = (xe^y - x\sin(xy))_{(2,0)} = 2e^0 - 2 \cdot 0 = 2.$$

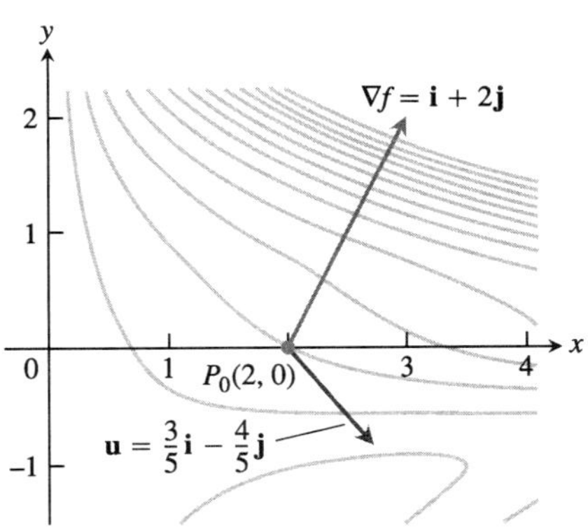

FIGURE 14.26 Picture ∇f as a vector in the domain of f. In the case of $f(x, y) = xe^y + \cos(xy)$, the domain is the entire plane. The rate at which f changes at (2, 0) in the direction $\mathbf{u} = (3/5)\mathbf{i} - (4/5)\mathbf{j}$ is $\nabla f \cdot \mathbf{u} = -1$ (Example 2).

The gradient of f at (2, 0) is

$$\nabla f|_{(2,0)} = f_x(2, 0)\mathbf{i} + f_y(2, 0)\mathbf{j} = \mathbf{i} + 2\mathbf{j}$$

(Figure 14.26). The derivative of f at (2, 0) in the direction of $\mathbf{v}$ is therefore

$$(D_{\mathbf{u}}f)|_{(2,0)} = \nabla f|_{(2,0)} \cdot \mathbf{u} \qquad \text{Equation (4)}$$

$$= (\mathbf{i} + 2\mathbf{j}) \cdot \left(\frac{3}{5}\mathbf{i} - \frac{4}{5}\mathbf{j}\right) = \frac{3}{5} - \frac{8}{5} = -1.$$

■

Evaluating the dot product in the formula

$$D_{\mathbf{u}}f = \nabla f \cdot \mathbf{u} = |\nabla f||\mathbf{u}|\cos\theta = |\nabla f|\cos\theta,$$

where θ is the angle between the vectors $\mathbf{u}$ and ∇f, reveals the following properties.

Properties of the Directional Derivative $D_{\mathbf{u}}f = \nabla f \cdot \mathbf{u} = |\nabla f|\cos\theta$

1. The function f increases most rapidly when $\cos\theta = 1$ or when $\mathbf{u}$ is the direction of ∇f. That is, at each point P in its domain, f increases most rapidly in the direction of the gradient vector ∇f at P. The derivative in this direction is
$$D_{\mathbf{u}}f = |\nabla f|\cos(0) = |\nabla f|.$$
2. Similarly, f decreases most rapidly in the direction of $-\nabla f$. The derivative in this direction is $D_{\mathbf{u}}f = |\nabla f|\cos(\pi) = -|\nabla f|$.
3. Any direction $\mathbf{u}$ orthogonal to a gradient $\nabla f \neq 0$ is a direction of zero change in f because θ then equals $\pi/2$ and
$$D_{\mathbf{u}}f = |\nabla f|\cos(\pi/2) = |\nabla f| \cdot 0 = 0.$$

As we discuss later, these properties hold in three dimensions as well as two.

EXAMPLE 3 Finding Directions of Maximal, Minimal, and Zero Change

Find the directions in which $f(x, y) = (x^2/2) + (y^2/2)$

(a) Increases most rapidly at the point (1, 1)

(b) Decreases most rapidly at (1, 1).

(c) What are the directions of zero change in f at (1, 1)?

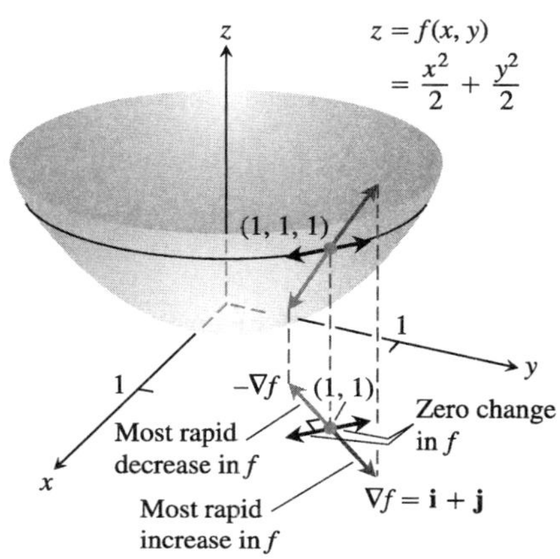

FIGURE 14.27 The direction in which $f(x, y) = (x^2/2) + (y^2/2)$ increases most rapidly at (1, 1) is the direction of $\nabla f|_{(1,1)} = \mathbf{i} + \mathbf{j}$. It corresponds to the direction of steepest ascent on the surface at (1, 1, 1) (Example 3).

Solution

(a) The function increases most rapidly in the direction of ∇f at (1, 1). The gradient there is

$$(\nabla f)_{(1,1)} = (x\mathbf{i} + y\mathbf{j})_{(1,1)} = \mathbf{i} + \mathbf{j}.$$

Its direction is

$$\mathbf{u} = \frac{\mathbf{i}+\mathbf{j}}{|\mathbf{i}+\mathbf{j}|} = \frac{\mathbf{i}+\mathbf{j}}{\sqrt{(1)^2+(1)^2}} = \frac{1}{\sqrt{2}}\mathbf{i} + \frac{1}{\sqrt{2}}\mathbf{j}.$$

(b) The function decreases most rapidly in the direction of $-\nabla f$ at (1, 1), which is

$$-\mathbf{u} = -\frac{1}{\sqrt{2}}\mathbf{i} - \frac{1}{\sqrt{2}}\mathbf{j}.$$

(c) The directions of zero change at (1, 1) are the directions orthogonal to ∇f:

$$\mathbf{n} = -\frac{1}{\sqrt{2}}\mathbf{i} + \frac{1}{\sqrt{2}}\mathbf{j} \quad \text{and} \quad -\mathbf{n} = \frac{1}{\sqrt{2}}\mathbf{i} - \frac{1}{\sqrt{2}}\mathbf{j}.$$

See Figure 14.27. ■

Gradients and Tangents to Level Curves

If a differentiable function $f(x, y)$ has a constant value c along a smooth curve $\mathbf{r} = g(t)\mathbf{i} + h(t)\mathbf{j}$ (making the curve a level curve of f), then $f(g(t), h(t)) = c$. Differentiating both sides of this equation with respect to t leads to the equations

$$\frac{d}{dt}f(g(t), h(t)) = \frac{d}{dt}(c)$$

$$\frac{\partial f}{\partial x}\frac{dg}{dt} + \frac{\partial f}{\partial y}\frac{dh}{dt} = 0 \qquad \text{Chain Rule}$$

$$\underbrace{\left(\frac{\partial f}{\partial x}\mathbf{i} + \frac{\partial f}{\partial y}\mathbf{j}\right)}_{\nabla f} \cdot \underbrace{\left(\frac{dg}{dt}\mathbf{i} + \frac{dh}{dt}\mathbf{j}\right)}_{\frac{d\mathbf{r}}{dt}} = 0. \tag{5}$$

Equation (5) says that ∇f is normal to the tangent vector $d\mathbf{r}/dt$, so it is normal to the curve.

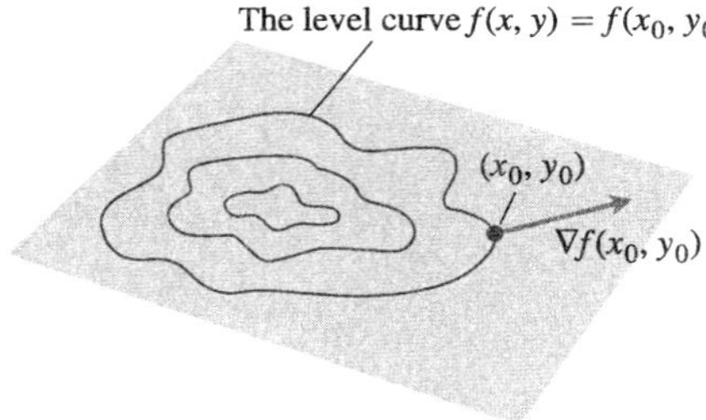

FIGURE 14.28 The gradient of a differentiable function of two variables at a point is always normal to the function's level curve through that point.

> At every point (x_0, y_0) in the domain of a differentiable function $f(x, y)$, the gradient of f is normal to the level curve through (x_0, y_0) (Figure 14.28).

Equation (5) validates our observation that streams flow perpendicular to the contours in topographical maps (see Figure 14.23). Since the downflowing stream will reach its destination in the fastest way, it must flow in the direction of the negative gradient vectors from Property 2 for the directional derivative. Equation (5) tells us these directions are perpendicular to the level curves.

This observation also enables us to find equations for tangent lines to level curves. They are the lines normal to the gradients. The line through a point $P_0(x_0, y_0)$ normal to a vector $\mathbf{N} = A\mathbf{i} + B\mathbf{j}$ has the equation

$$A(x - x_0) + B(y - y_0) = 0$$

(Exercise 35). If $\mathbf{N}$ is the gradient $(\nabla f)_{(x_0, y_0)} = f_x(x_0, y_0)\mathbf{i} + f_y(x_0, y_0)\mathbf{j}$, the equation is the tangent line given by

$$f_x(x_0, y_0)(x - x_0) + f_y(x_0, y_0)(y - y_0) = 0. \tag{6}$$

EXAMPLE 4 Finding the Tangent Line to an Ellipse

Find an equation for the tangent to the ellipse

$$\frac{x^2}{4} + y^2 = 2$$

(Figure 14.29) at the point $(-2, 1)$.

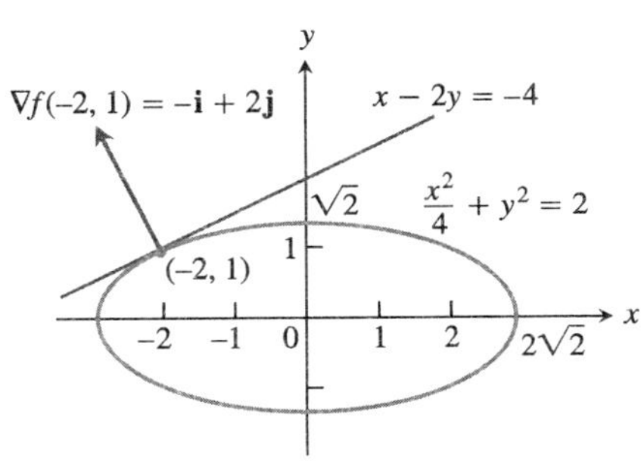

FIGURE 14.29 We can find the tangent to the ellipse $(x^2/4) + y^2 = 2$ by treating the ellipse as a level curve of the function $f(x, y) = (x^2/4) + y^2$ (Example 4).

Solution The ellipse is a level curve of the function

$$f(x, y) = \frac{x^2}{4} + y^2.$$

The gradient of f at $(-2, 1)$ is

$$\nabla f|_{(-2,1)} = \left(\frac{x}{2}\mathbf{i} + 2y\mathbf{j}\right)_{(-2,1)} = -\mathbf{i} + 2\mathbf{j}.$$

The tangent is the line

$$(-1)(x + 2) + (2)(y - 1) = 0 \qquad \text{Equation (6)}$$
$$x - 2y = -4.$$
■

If we know the gradients of two functions f and g, we automatically know the gradients of their constant multiples, sum, difference, product, and quotient. You are asked to establish the following rules in Exercise 36. Notice that these rules have the same form as the corresponding rules for derivatives of single-variable functions.

Algebra Rules for Gradients

1. *Constant Multiple Rule:* $\nabla(kf) = k\nabla f$ (any number k)
2. *Sum Rule:* $\nabla(f + g) = \nabla f + \nabla g$
3. *Difference Rule:* $\nabla(f - g) = \nabla f - \nabla g$
4. *Product Rule:* $\nabla(fg) = f\nabla g + g\nabla f$
5. *Quotient Rule:* $\nabla\left(\frac{f}{g}\right) = \frac{g\nabla f - f\nabla g}{g^2}$

EXAMPLE 5 Illustrating the Gradient Rules

We illustrate the rules with

$$f(x, y) = x - y \qquad g(x, y) = 3y$$
$$\nabla f = \mathbf{i} - \mathbf{j} \qquad \nabla g = 3\mathbf{j}.$$

We have

1. $\nabla(2f) = \nabla(2x - 2y) = 2\mathbf{i} - 2\mathbf{j} = 2\nabla f$
2. $\nabla(f + g) = \nabla(x + 2y) = \mathbf{i} + 2\mathbf{j} = \nabla f + \nabla g$
3. $\nabla(f - g) = \nabla(x - 4y) = \mathbf{i} - 4\mathbf{j} = \nabla f - \nabla g$
4. $$\begin{aligned}\nabla(fg) &= \nabla(3xy - 3y^2) = 3y\mathbf{i} + (3x - 6y)\mathbf{j} \\ &= 3y(\mathbf{i} - \mathbf{j}) + 3y\mathbf{j} + (3x - 6y)\mathbf{j} \\ &= 3y(\mathbf{i} - \mathbf{j}) + (3x - 3y)\mathbf{j} \\ &= 3y(\mathbf{i} - \mathbf{j}) + (x - y)3\mathbf{j} = g\nabla f + f\nabla g\end{aligned}$$
5. $$\begin{aligned}\nabla\left(\frac{f}{g}\right) &= \nabla\left(\frac{x - y}{3y}\right) = \nabla\left(\frac{x}{3y} - \frac{1}{3}\right) \\ &= \frac{1}{3y}\mathbf{i} - \frac{x}{3y^2}\mathbf{j} \\ &= \frac{3y\mathbf{i} - 3x\mathbf{j}}{9y^2} = \frac{3y(\mathbf{i} - \mathbf{j}) - (3x - 3y)\mathbf{j}}{9y^2} \\ &= \frac{3y(\mathbf{i} - \mathbf{j}) - (x - y)3\mathbf{j}}{9y^2} = \frac{g\nabla f - f\nabla g}{g^2}.\end{aligned}$$ ■

Functions of Three Variables

For a differentiable function $f(x, y, z)$ and a unit vector $\mathbf{u} = u_1\mathbf{i} + u_2\mathbf{j} + u_3\mathbf{k}$ in space, we have

$$\nabla f = \frac{\partial f}{\partial x}\mathbf{i} + \frac{\partial f}{\partial y}\mathbf{j} + \frac{\partial f}{\partial z}\mathbf{k}$$

and

$$D_{\mathbf{u}}f = \nabla f \cdot \mathbf{u} = \frac{\partial f}{\partial x}u_1 + \frac{\partial f}{\partial y}u_2 + \frac{\partial f}{\partial z}u_3.$$

The directional derivative can once again be written in the form

$$D_{\mathbf{u}}f = \nabla f \cdot \mathbf{u} = |\nabla f||u| \cos\theta = |\nabla f| \cos\theta,$$

so the properties listed earlier for functions of two variables continue to hold. At any given point, f increases most rapidly in the direction of ∇f and decreases most rapidly in the direction of $-\nabla f$. In any direction orthogonal to ∇f, the derivative is zero.

EXAMPLE 6 Finding Directions of Maximal, Minimal, and Zero Change

(a) Find the derivative of $f(x, y, z) = x^3 - xy^2 - z$ at $P_0(1, 1, 0)$ in the direction of $\mathbf{v} = 2\mathbf{i} - 3\mathbf{j} + 6\mathbf{k}$.

(b) In what directions does f change most rapidly at P_0, and what are the rates of change in these directions?

Solution

(a) The direction of $\mathbf{v}$ is obtained by dividing $\mathbf{v}$ by its length:

$$|\mathbf{v}| = \sqrt{(2)^2 + (-3)^2 + (6)^2} = \sqrt{49} = 7$$

$$\mathbf{u} = \frac{\mathbf{v}}{|\mathbf{v}|} = \frac{2}{7}\mathbf{i} - \frac{3}{7}\mathbf{j} + \frac{6}{7}\mathbf{k}.$$

The partial derivatives of f at P_0 are

$$f_x = (3x^2 - y^2)_{(1,1,0)} = 2, \qquad f_y = -2xy|_{(1,1,0)} = -2, \qquad f_z = -1|_{(1,1,0)} = -1.$$

The gradient of f at P_0 is

$$\nabla f|_{(1,1,0)} = 2\mathbf{i} - 2\mathbf{j} - \mathbf{k}.$$

The derivative of f at P_0 in the direction of $\mathbf{v}$ is therefore

$$(D_{\mathbf{u}}f)_{(1,1,0)} = \nabla f|_{(1,1,0)} \cdot \mathbf{u} = (2\mathbf{i} - 2\mathbf{j} - \mathbf{k}) \cdot \left(\frac{2}{7}\mathbf{i} - \frac{3}{7}\mathbf{j} + \frac{6}{7}\mathbf{k}\right)$$

$$= \frac{4}{7} + \frac{6}{7} - \frac{6}{7} = \frac{4}{7}.$$

(b) The function increases most rapidly in the direction of $\nabla f = 2\mathbf{i} - 2\mathbf{j} - \mathbf{k}$ and decreases most rapidly in the direction of $-\nabla f$. The rates of change in the directions are, respectively,

$$|\nabla f| = \sqrt{(2)^2 + (-2)^2 + (-1)^2} = \sqrt{9} = 3 \quad \text{and} \quad -|\nabla f| = -3. \qquad \blacksquare$$

EXERCISES 14.5

Calculating Gradients at Points

In Exercises 1–4, find the gradient of the function at the given point. Then sketch the gradient together with the level curve that passes through the point.

1. $f(x, y) = y - x, \quad (2, 1)$
2. $f(x, y) = \ln(x^2 + y^2), \quad (1, 1)$
3. $g(x, y) = y - x^2, \quad (-1, 0)$
4. $g(x, y) = \frac{x^2}{2} - \frac{y^2}{2}, \quad (\sqrt{2}, 1)$

In Exercises 5–8, find ∇f at the given point.

5. $f(x, y, z) = x^2 + y^2 - 2z^2 + z \ln x, \quad (1, 1, 1)$
6. $f(x, y, z) = 2z^3 - 3(x^2 + y^2)z + \tan^{-1} xz, \quad (1, 1, 1)$

7. $f(x, y, z) = (x^2 + y^2 + z^2)^{-1/2} + \ln(xyz), \quad (-1, 2, -2)$
8. $f(x, y, z) = e^{x+y}\cos z + (y + 1)\sin^{-1} x, \quad (0, 0, \pi/6)$

Finding Directional Derivatives

In Exercises 9–16, find the derivative of the function at P_0 in the direction of **A**.

9. $f(x, y) = 2xy - 3y^2, \quad P_0(5, 5), \quad \mathbf{A} = 4\mathbf{i} + 3\mathbf{j}$
10. $f(x, y) = 2x^2 + y^2, \quad P_0(-1, 1), \quad \mathbf{A} = 3\mathbf{i} - 4\mathbf{j}$
11. $g(x, y) = x - (y^2/x) + \sqrt{3}\sec^{-1}(2xy), \quad P_0(1, 1),$ $\mathbf{A} = 12\mathbf{i} + 5\mathbf{j}$
12. $h(x, y) = \tan^{-1}(y/x) + \sqrt{3}\sin^{-1}(xy/2), \quad P_0(1, 1),$ $\mathbf{A} = 3\mathbf{i} - 2\mathbf{j}$
13. $f(x, y, z) = xy + yz + zx, \quad P_0(1, -1, 2), \quad \mathbf{A} = 3\mathbf{i} + 6\mathbf{j} - 2\mathbf{k}$
14. $f(x, y, z) = x^2 + 2y^2 - 3z^2, \quad P_0(1, 1, 1), \quad \mathbf{A} = \mathbf{i} + \mathbf{j} + \mathbf{k}$
15. $g(x, y, z) = 3e^x\cos yz, \quad P_0(0, 0, 0), \quad \mathbf{A} = 2\mathbf{i} + \mathbf{j} - 2\mathbf{k}$
16. $h(x, y, z) = \cos xy + e^{yz} + \ln zx, \quad P_0(1, 0, 1/2),$ $\mathbf{A} = \mathbf{i} + 2\mathbf{j} + 2\mathbf{k}$

Directions of Most Rapid Increase and Decrease

In Exercises 17–22, find the directions in which the functions increase and decrease most rapidly at P_0. Then find the derivatives of the functions in these directions.

17. $f(x, y) = x^2 + xy + y^2, \quad P_0(-1, 1)$
18. $f(x, y) = x^2y + e^{xy}\sin y, \quad P_0(1, 0)$
19. $f(x, y, z) = (x/y) - yz, \quad P_0(4, 1, 1)$
20. $g(x, y, z) = xe^y + z^2, \quad P_0(1, \ln 2, 1/2)$
21. $f(x, y, z) = \ln xy + \ln yz + \ln xz, \quad P_0(1, 1, 1)$
22. $h(x, y, z) = \ln(x^2 + y^2 - 1) + y + 6z, \quad P_0(1, 1, 0)$

Tangent Lines to Curves

In Exercises 23–26, sketch the curve $f(x, y) = c$ together with ∇f and the tangent line at the given point. Then write an equation for the tangent line.

23. $x^2 + y^2 = 4, \quad (\sqrt{2}, \sqrt{2})$
24. $x^2 - y = 1, \quad (\sqrt{2}, 1)$
25. $xy = -4, \quad (2, -2)$
26. $x^2 - xy + y^2 = 7, \quad (-1, 2)$

Theory and Examples

27. **Zero directional derivative** In what direction is the derivative of $f(x, y) = xy + y^2$ at $P(3, 2)$ equal to zero?
28. **Zero directional derivative** In what directions is the derivative of $f(x, y) = (x^2 - y^2)/(x^2 + y^2)$ at $P(1, 1)$ equal to zero?
29. Is there a direction **u** in which the rate of change of $f(x, y) = x^2 - 3xy - 4y^2$ at $P(1, 2)$ equals 14? Give reasons for your answer.
30. **Changing temperature along a circle** Is there a direction **u** in which the rate of change of the temperature function $T(x, y, z) = 2xy - yz$ (temperature in degrees Celsius, distance in feet) at $P(1, -1, 1)$ is -3°C/ft? Give reasons for your answer.
31. The derivative of $f(x, y)$ at $P_0(1, 2)$ in the direction of $\mathbf{i} + \mathbf{j}$ is $2\sqrt{2}$ and in the direction of $-2\mathbf{j}$ is -3. What is the derivative of f in the direction of $-\mathbf{i} - 2\mathbf{j}$? Give reasons for your answer.
32. The derivative of $f(x, y, z)$ at a point P is greatest in the direction of $\mathbf{v} = \mathbf{i} + \mathbf{j} - \mathbf{k}$. In this direction, the value of the derivative is $2\sqrt{3}$.
    a. What is ∇f at P? Give reasons for your answer.
    b. What is the derivative of f at P in the direction of $\mathbf{i} + \mathbf{j}$?
33. **Directional derivatives and scalar components** How is the derivative of a differentiable function $f(x, y, z)$ at a point P_0 in the direction of a unit vector **u** related to the scalar component of $(\nabla f)_{P_0}$ in the direction of **u**? Give reasons for your answer.
34. **Directional derivatives and partial derivatives** Assuming that the necessary derivatives of $f(x, y, z)$ are defined, how are $D_{\mathbf{i}}f$, $D_{\mathbf{j}}f$, and $D_{\mathbf{k}}f$ related to f_x, f_y, and f_z? Give reasons for your answer.
35. **Lines in the xy-plane** Show that $A(x - x_0) + B(y - y_0) = 0$ is an equation for the line in the xy-plane through the point (x_0, y_0) normal to the vector $\mathbf{N} = A\mathbf{i} + B\mathbf{j}$.
36. **The algebra rules for gradients** Given a constant k and the gradients

$$\nabla f = \frac{\partial f}{\partial x}\mathbf{i} + \frac{\partial f}{\partial y}\mathbf{j} + \frac{\partial f}{\partial z}\mathbf{k}$$

and

$$\nabla g = \frac{\partial g}{\partial x}\mathbf{i} + \frac{\partial g}{\partial y}\mathbf{j} + \frac{\partial g}{\partial z}\mathbf{k},$$

use the scalar equations

$$\frac{\partial}{\partial x}(kf) = k\frac{\partial f}{\partial x}, \qquad \frac{\partial}{\partial x}(f \pm g) = \frac{\partial f}{\partial x} \pm \frac{\partial g}{\partial x},$$

$$\frac{\partial}{\partial x}(fg) = f\frac{\partial g}{\partial x} + g\frac{\partial f}{\partial x}, \qquad \frac{\partial}{\partial x}\left(\frac{f}{g}\right) = \frac{g\frac{\partial f}{\partial x} - f\frac{\partial g}{\partial x}}{g^2},$$

and so on, to establish the following rules.

a. $\nabla(kf) = k\nabla f$
b. $\nabla(f + g) = \nabla f + \nabla g$
c. $\nabla(f - g) = \nabla f - \nabla g$
d. $\nabla(fg) = f\nabla g + g\nabla f$
e. $\nabla\left(\frac{f}{g}\right) = \frac{g\nabla f - f\nabla g}{g^2}$

14.6 Tangent Planes and Differentials

In this section we define the tangent plane at a point on a smooth surface in space. We calculate an equation of the tangent plane from the partial derivatives of the function defining the surface. This idea is similar to the definition of the tangent line at a point on a curve in the coordinate plane for single-variable functions (Section 2.7). We then study the total differential and linearization of functions of several variables.

Tangent Planes and Normal Lines

If $\mathbf{r} = g(t)\mathbf{i} + h(t)\mathbf{j} + k(t)\mathbf{k}$ is a smooth curve on the level surface $f(x, y, z) = c$ of a differentiable function f, then $f(g(t), h(t), k(t)) = c$. Differentiating both sides of this equation with respect to t leads to

$$\frac{d}{dt} f(g(t), h(t), k(t)) = \frac{d}{dt}(c)$$

$$\frac{\partial f}{\partial x}\frac{dg}{dt} + \frac{\partial f}{\partial y}\frac{dh}{dt} + \frac{\partial f}{\partial z}\frac{dk}{dt} = 0 \qquad \text{Chain Rule}$$

$$\underbrace{\left(\frac{\partial f}{\partial x}\mathbf{i} + \frac{\partial f}{\partial y}\mathbf{j} + \frac{\partial f}{\partial z}\mathbf{k}\right)}_{\nabla f} \cdot \underbrace{\left(\frac{dg}{dt}\mathbf{i} + \frac{dh}{dt}\mathbf{j} + \frac{dk}{dt}\mathbf{k}\right)}_{d\mathbf{r}/dt} = 0. \qquad (1)$$

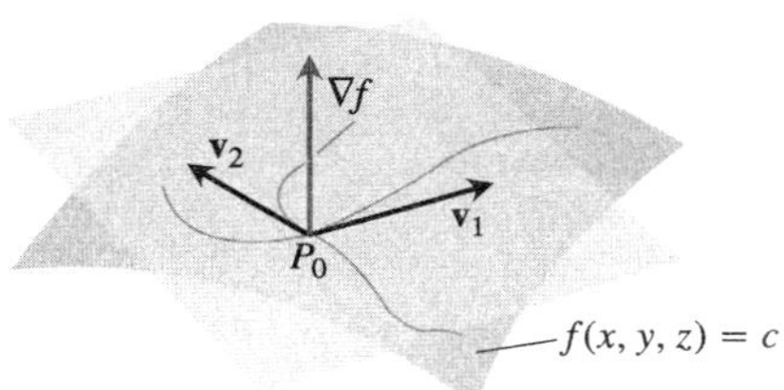

FIGURE 14.30 The gradient ∇f is orthogonal to the velocity vector of every smooth curve in the surface through P_0. The velocity vectors at P_0 therefore lie in a common plane, which we call the tangent plane at P_0.

At every point along the curve, ∇f is orthogonal to the curve's velocity vector.

Now let us restrict our attention to the curves that pass through P_0 (Figure 14.30). All the velocity vectors at P_0 are orthogonal to ∇f at P_0, so the curves' tangent lines all lie in the plane through P_0 normal to ∇f. We call this plane the tangent plane of the surface at P_0. The line through P_0 perpendicular to the plane is the surface's normal line at P_0.

DEFINITIONS Tangent Plane, Normal Line

The **tangent plane** at the point $P_0(x_0, y_0, z_0)$ on the level surface $f(x, y, z) = c$ of a differentiable function f is the plane through P_0 normal to $\nabla f|_{P_0}$.

The **normal line** of the surface at P_0 is the line through P_0 parallel to $\nabla f|_{P_0}$.

Thus, from Section 12.5, the tangent plane and normal line have the following equations:

Tangent Plane to $f(x, y, z) = c$ at $P_0(x_0, y_0, z_0)$

$$f_x(P_0)(x - x_0) + f_y(P_0)(y - y_0) + f_z(P_0)(z - z_0) = 0 \qquad (2)$$

Normal Line to $f(x, y, z) = c$ at $P_0(x_0, y_0, z_0)$

$$x = x_0 + f_x(P_0)t, \qquad y = y_0 + f_y(P_0)t, \qquad z = z_0 + f_z(P_0)t \qquad (3)$$

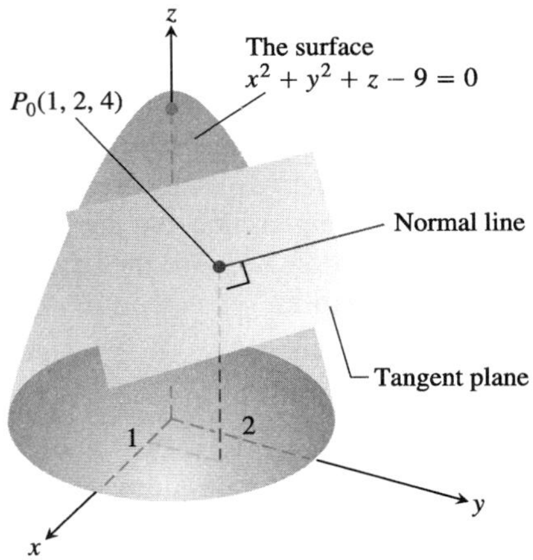

FIGURE 14.31 The tangent plane and normal line to the surface $x^2 + y^2 + z - 9 = 0$ at $P_0(1, 2, 4)$ (Example 1).

EXAMPLE 1 Finding the Tangent Plane and Normal Line

Find the tangent plane and normal line of the surface

$$f(x, y, z) = x^2 + y^2 + z - 9 = 0 \qquad \text{A circular paraboloid}$$

at the point $P_0(1, 2, 4)$.

Solution The surface is shown in Figure 14.31.

The tangent plane is the plane through P_0 perpendicular to the gradient of f at P_0. The gradient is

$$\nabla f|_{P_0} = (2x\mathbf{i} + 2y\mathbf{j} + \mathbf{k})_{(1,2,4)} = 2\mathbf{i} + 4\mathbf{j} + \mathbf{k}.$$

The tangent plane is therefore the plane

$$2(x - 1) + 4(y - 2) + (z - 4) = 0, \qquad \text{or} \qquad 2x + 4y + z = 14.$$

The line normal to the surface at P_0 is

$$x = 1 + 2t, \qquad y = 2 + 4t, \qquad z = 4 + t. \qquad \blacksquare$$

To find an equation for the plane tangent to a smooth surface $z = f(x, y)$ at a point $P_0(x_0, y_0, z_0)$ where $z_0 = f(x_0, y_0)$, we first observe that the equation $z = f(x, y)$ is equivalent to $f(x, y) - z = 0$. The surface $z = f(x, y)$ is therefore the zero level surface of the function $F(x, y, z) = f(x, y) - z$. The partial derivatives of F are

$$F_x = \frac{\partial}{\partial x}(f(x, y) - z) = f_x - 0 = f_x$$

$$F_y = \frac{\partial}{\partial y}(f(x, y) - z) = f_y - 0 = f_y$$

$$F_z = \frac{\partial}{\partial z}(f(x, y) - z) = 0 - 1 = -1.$$

The formula

$$F_x(P_0)(x - x_0) + F_y(P_0)(y - y_0) + F_z(P_0)(z - z_0) = 0$$

for the plane tangent to the level surface at P_0 therefore reduces to

$$f_x(x_0, y_0)(x - x_0) + f_y(x_0, y_0)(y - y_0) - (z - z_0) = 0.$$

> **Plane Tangent to a Surface $z = f(x, y)$ at $(x_0, y_0, f(x_0, y_0))$**
> The plane tangent to the surface $z = f(x, y)$ of a differentiable function f at the point $P_0(x_0, y_0, z_0) = (x_0, y_0, f(x_0, y_0))$ is
>
> $$f_x(x_0, y_0)(x - x_0) + f_y(x_0, y_0)(y - y_0) - (z - z_0) = 0. \qquad (4)$$

EXAMPLE 2 Finding a Plane Tangent to a Surface $z = f(x, y)$

Find the plane tangent to the surface $z = x \cos y - ye^x$ at $(0, 0, 0)$.

Solution We calculate the partial derivatives of $f(x, y) = x\cos y - ye^x$ and use Equation (4):

$$f_x(0, 0) = (\cos y - ye^x)_{(0,0)} = 1 - 0 \cdot 1 = 1$$

$$f_y(0, 0) = (-x\sin y - e^x)_{(0,0)} = 0 - 1 = -1.$$

The tangent plane is therefore

$$1 \cdot (x - 0) - 1 \cdot (y - 0) - (z - 0) = 0, \qquad \text{Equation (4)}$$

or

$$x - y - z = 0.$$

■

EXAMPLE 3 Tangent Line to the Curve of Intersection of Two Surfaces

The surfaces

$$f(x, y, z) = x^2 + y^2 - 2 = 0 \qquad \text{A cylinder}$$

and

$$g(x, y, z) = x + z - 4 = 0 \qquad \text{A plane}$$

meet in an ellipse E (Figure 14.32). Find parametric equations for the line tangent to E at the point $P_0(1, 1, 3)$.

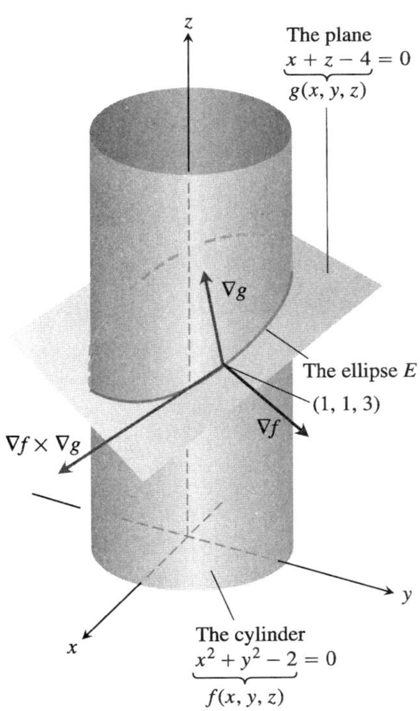

FIGURE 14.32 The cylinder $f(x, y, z) = x^2 + y^2 - 2 = 0$ and the plane $g(x, y, z) = x + z - 4 = 0$ intersect in an ellipse E (Example 3).

Solution The tangent line is orthogonal to both ∇f and ∇g at P_0, and therefore parallel to $\mathbf{v} = \nabla f \times \nabla g$. The components of $\mathbf{v}$ and the coordinates of P_0 give us equations for the line. We have

$$\nabla f|_{(1,1,3)} = (2x\mathbf{i} + 2y\mathbf{j})_{(1,1,3)} = 2\mathbf{i} + 2\mathbf{j}$$

$$\nabla g|_{(1,1,3)} = (\mathbf{i} + \mathbf{k})_{(1,1,3)} = \mathbf{i} + \mathbf{k}$$

$$\mathbf{v} = (2\mathbf{i} + 2\mathbf{j}) \times (\mathbf{i} + \mathbf{k}) = \begin{vmatrix} \mathbf{i} & \mathbf{j} & \mathbf{k} \\ 2 & 2 & 0 \\ 1 & 0 & 1 \end{vmatrix} = 2\mathbf{i} - 2\mathbf{j} - 2\mathbf{k}.$$

The tangent line is

$$x = 1 + 2t, \qquad y = 1 - 2t, \qquad z = 3 - 2t.$$

■

Estimating Change in a Specific Direction

The directional derivative plays the role of an ordinary derivative when we want to estimate how much the value of a function f changes if we move a small distance ds from a point P_0 to another point nearby. If f were a function of a single variable, we would have

$$df = f'(P_0)\, ds. \qquad \text{Ordinary derivative} \times \text{increment}$$

For a function of two or more variables, we use the formula

$$df = (\nabla f|_{P_0} \cdot \mathbf{u})\, ds, \qquad \text{Directional derivative} \times \text{increment}$$

where $\mathbf{u}$ is the direction of the motion away from P_0.

Estimating the Change in f in a Direction u

To estimate the change in the value of a differentiable function f when we move a small distance ds from a point P_0 in a particular direction $\mathbf{u}$, use the formula

$$df = \underbrace{(\nabla f|_{P_0} \cdot \mathbf{u})}_{\text{Directional derivative}} \cdot \underbrace{ds}_{\text{Distance increment}}$$

EXAMPLE 4 Estimating Change in the Value of $f(x, y, z)$

Estimate how much the value of

$$f(x, y, z) = y \sin x + 2yz$$

will change if the point $P(x, y, z)$ moves 0.1 unit from $P_0(0, 1, 0)$ straight toward $P_1(2, 2, -2)$.

Solution We first find the derivative of f at P_0 in the direction of the vector $\overrightarrow{P_0P_1} = 2\mathbf{i} + \mathbf{j} - 2\mathbf{k}$. The direction of this vector is

$$\mathbf{u} = \frac{\overrightarrow{P_0P_1}}{|\overrightarrow{P_0P_1}|} = \frac{\overrightarrow{P_0P_1}}{3} = \frac{2}{3}\mathbf{i} + \frac{1}{3}\mathbf{j} - \frac{2}{3}\mathbf{k}.$$

The gradient of f at P_0 is

$$\nabla f|_{(0,1,0)} = ((y\cos x)\mathbf{i} + (\sin x + 2z)\mathbf{j} + 2y\mathbf{k})_{(0,1,0)} = \mathbf{i} + 2\mathbf{k}.$$

Therefore,

$$\nabla f|_{P_0} \cdot \mathbf{u} = (\mathbf{i} + 2\mathbf{k}) \cdot \left(\frac{2}{3}\mathbf{i} + \frac{1}{3}\mathbf{j} - \frac{2}{3}\mathbf{k}\right) = \frac{2}{3} - \frac{4}{3} = -\frac{2}{3}.$$

The change df in f that results from moving $ds = 0.1$ unit away from P_0 in the direction of $\mathbf{u}$ is approximately

$$df = (\nabla f|_{P_0} \cdot \mathbf{u})(ds) = \left(-\frac{2}{3}\right)(0.1) \approx -0.067 \text{ unit.}$$ ■

How to Linearize a Function of Two Variables

Functions of two variables can be complicated, and we sometimes need to replace them with simpler ones that give the accuracy required for specific applications without being so difficult to work with. We do this in a way that is similar to the way we find linear replacements for functions of a single variable (Section 3.8).

Suppose the function we wish to replace is $z = f(x, y)$ and that we want the replacement to be effective near a point (x_0, y_0) at which we know the values of f, f_x, and f_y and at which f is differentiable. If we move from (x_0, y_0) to any point (x, y) by increments $\Delta x = x - x_0$ and $\Delta y = y - y_0$, then the definition of differentiability from Section 14.3 gives the change

$$f(x, y) - f(x_0, y_0) = f_x(x_0, y_0)\Delta x + f_y(x_0, y_0)\Delta y + \epsilon_1 \Delta x + \epsilon_2 \Delta y,$$

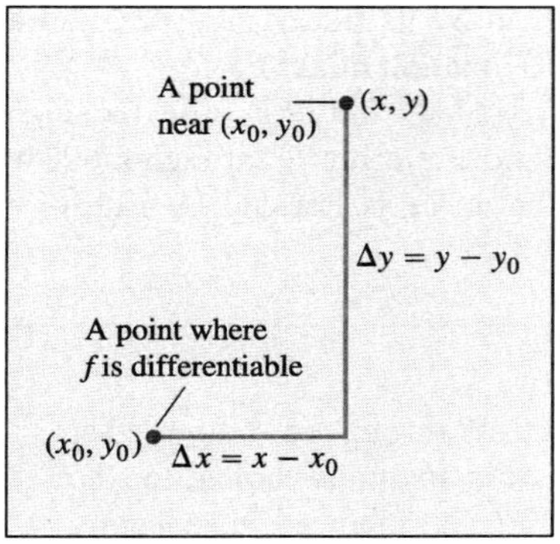

FIGURE 14.33 If f is differentiable at (x_0, y_0), then the value of f at any point (x, y) nearby is approximately $f(x_0, y_0) + f_x(x_0, y_0)\Delta x + f_y(x_0, y_0)\Delta y$.

where $\epsilon_1, \epsilon_2 \to 0$ as $\Delta x, \Delta y \to 0$. If the increments Δx and Δy are small, the products $\epsilon_1 \Delta x$ and $\epsilon_2 \Delta y$ will eventually be smaller still and we will have

$$f(x, y) \approx \underbrace{f(x_0, y_0) + f_x(x_0, y_0)(x - x_0) + f_y(x_0, y_0)(y - y_0)}_{L(x, y)}.$$

In other words, as long as Δx and Δy are small, f will have approximately the same value as the linear function L. If f is hard to use, and our work can tolerate the error involved, we may approximate f by L (Figure 14.33).

DEFINITIONS Linearization, Standard Linear Approximation

The **linearization** of a function $f(x, y)$ at a point (x_0, y_0) where f is differentiable is the function

$$L(x, y) = f(x_0, y_0) + f_x(x_0, y_0)(x - x_0) + f_y(x_0, y_0)(y - y_0). \tag{5}$$

The approximation

$$f(x, y) \approx L(x, y)$$

is the **standard linear approximation** of f at (x_0, y_0).

From Equation (4), we see that the plane $z = L(x, y)$ is tangent to the surface $z = f(x, y)$ at the point (x_0, y_0). Thus, the linearization of a function of two variables is a tangent-*plane* approximation in the same way that the linearization of a function of a single variable is a tangent-*line* approximation.

EXAMPLE 5 Finding a Linearization

Find the linearization of

$$f(x, y) = x^2 - xy + \frac{1}{2}y^2 + 3$$

at the point (3, 2).

Solution We first evaluate f, f_x, and f_y at the point $(x_0, y_0) = (3, 2)$:

$$f(3, 2) = \left(x^2 - xy + \frac{1}{2}y^2 + 3\right)_{(3,2)} = 8$$

$$f_x(3, 2) = \frac{\partial}{\partial x}\left(x^2 - xy + \frac{1}{2}y^2 + 3\right)_{(3,2)} = (2x - y)_{(3,2)} = 4$$

$$f_y(3, 2) = \frac{\partial}{\partial y}\left(x^2 - xy + \frac{1}{2}y^2 + 3\right)_{(3,2)} = (-x + y)_{(3,2)} = -1,$$

giving

$$\begin{aligned} L(x, y) &= f(x_0, y_0) + f_x(x_0, y_0)(x - x_0) + f_y(x_0, y_0)(y - y_0) \\ &= 8 + (4)(x - 3) + (-1)(y - 2) = 4x - y - 2. \end{aligned}$$

The linearization of f at (3, 2) is $L(x, y) = 4x - y - 2$. ■

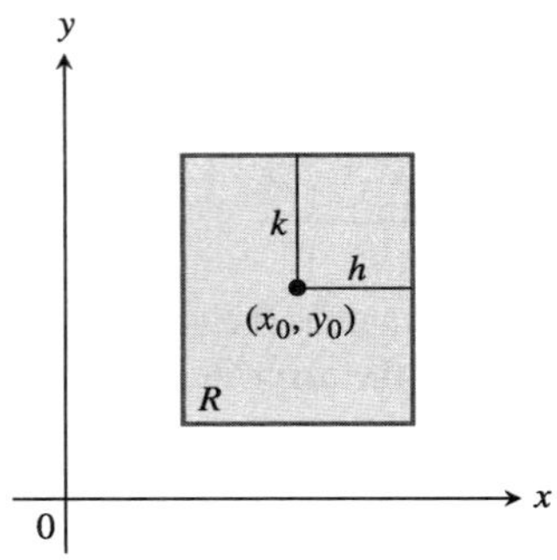

FIGURE 14.34 The rectangular region R: $|x - x_0| \le h, |y - y_0| \le k$ in the xy-plane.

When approximating a differentiable function $f(x, y)$ by its linearization $L(x, y)$ at (x_0, y_0), an important question is how accurate the approximation might be.

If we can find a common upper bound M for $|f_{xx}|, |f_{yy}|$, and $|f_{xy}|$ on a rectangle R centered at (x_0, y_0) (Figure 14.34), then we can bound the error E throughout R by using a simple formula (derived in Section 14.10). The **error** is defined by $E(x, y) = f(x, y) - L(x, y)$.

The Error in the Standard Linear Approximation

If f has continuous first and second partial derivatives throughout an open set containing a rectangle R centered at (x_0, y_0) and if M is any upper bound for the values of $|f_{xx}|, |f_{yy}|$, and $|f_{xy}|$ on R, then the error $E(x, y)$ incurred in replacing $f(x, y)$ on R by its linearization

$$L(x, y) = f(x_0, y_0) + f_x(x_0, y_0)(x - x_0) + f_y(x_0, y_0)(y - y_0)$$

satisfies the inequality

$$|E(x, y)| \le \frac{1}{2}M(|x - x_0| + |y - y_0|)^2.$$

To make $|E(x, y)|$ small for a given M, we just make $|x - x_0|$ and $|y - y_0|$ small.

EXAMPLE 6 Bounding the Error in Example 5

Find an upper bound for the error in the approximation $f(x, y) \approx L(x, y)$ in Example 5 over the rectangle

$$R: \quad |x - 3| \le 0.1, \qquad |y - 2| \le 0.1 .$$

Express the upper bound as a percentage of $f(3, 2)$, the value of f at the center of the rectangle.

Solution We use the inequality

$$|E(x, y)| \le \frac{1}{2}M(|x - x_0| + |y - y_0|)^2 .$$

To find a suitable value for M, we calculate f_{xx}, f_{xy}, and f_{yy}, finding, after a routine differentiation, that all three derivatives are constant, with values

$$|f_{xx}| = |2| = 2, \qquad |f_{xy}| = |-1| = 1, \qquad |f_{yy}| = |1| = 1.$$

The largest of these is 2, so we may safely take M to be 2. With $(x_0, y_0) = (3, 2)$, we then know that, throughout R,

$$|E(x, y)| \le \frac{1}{2}(2)(|x - 3| + |y - 2|)^2 = (|x - 3| + |y - 2|)^2.$$

Finally, since $|x - 3| \le 0.1$ and $|y - 2| \le 0.1$ on R, we have

$$|E(x, y)| \le (0.1 + 0.1)^2 = 0.04.$$

As a percentage of $f(3, 2) = 8$, the error is no greater than

$$\frac{0.04}{8} \times 100 = 0.5\% .$$

■

Differentials

Recall from Section 3.8 that for a function of a single variable, $y = f(x)$, we defined the change in f as x changes from a to $a + \Delta x$ by

$$\Delta f = f(a + \Delta x) - f(a)$$

and the differential of f as

$$df = f'(a)\Delta x.$$

We now consider a function of two variables.

Suppose a differentiable function $f(x, y)$ and its partial derivatives exist at a point (x_0, y_0). If we move to a nearby point $(x_0 + \Delta x, y_0 + \Delta y)$, the change in f is

$$\Delta f = f(x_0 + \Delta x, y_0 + \Delta y) - f(x_0, y_0).$$

A straightforward calculation from the definition of $L(x, y)$, using the notation $x - x_0 = \Delta x$ and $y - y_0 = \Delta y$, shows that the corresponding change in L is

$$\begin{aligned}\Delta L &= L(x_0 + \Delta x, y_0 + \Delta y) - L(x_0, y_0)\\ &= f_x(x_0, y_0)\Delta x + f_y(x_0, y_0)\Delta y.\end{aligned}$$

The **differentials** dx and dy are independent variables, so they can be assigned any values. Often we take $dx = \Delta x = x - x_0$, and $dy = \Delta y = y - y_0$. We then have the following definition of the differential or *total* differential of f.

DEFINITION Total Differential

If we move from (x_0, y_0) to a point $(x_0 + dx, y_0 + dy)$ nearby, the resulting change

$$df = f_x(x_0, y_0)\, dx + f_y(x_0, y_0)\, dy$$

in the linearization of f is called the **total differential of f**.

EXAMPLE 7 Estimating Change in Volume

Suppose that a cylindrical can is designed to have a radius of 1 in. and a height of 5 in., but that the radius and height are off by the amounts $dr = +0.03$ and $dh = -0.1$. Estimate the resulting absolute change in the volume of the can.

Solution To estimate the absolute change in $V = \pi r^2 h$, we use

$$\Delta V \approx dV = V_r(r_0, h_0)\, dr + V_h(r_0, h_0)\, dh.$$

With $V_r = 2\pi rh$ and $V_h = \pi r^2$, we get

$$\begin{aligned}dV &= 2\pi r_0 h_0\, dr + \pi r_0^2\, dh = 2\pi(1)(5)(0.03) + \pi(1)^2(-0.1)\\ &= 0.3\pi - 0.1\pi = 0.2\pi \approx 0.63 \text{ in.}^3\end{aligned}$$

■

Instead of absolute change in the value of a function $f(x, y)$, we can estimate *relative change* or *percentage change* by

$$\frac{df}{f(x_0, y_0)} \quad \text{and} \quad \frac{df}{f(x_0, y_0)} \times 100,$$

respectively. In Example 7, the relative change is estimated by

$$\frac{dV}{V(r_0, h_0)} = \frac{0.2\pi}{\pi r_0^2 h_0} = \frac{0.2\pi}{\pi(1)^2(5)} = 0.04,$$

giving 4% as an estimate of the percentage change.

EXAMPLE 8 Sensitivity to Change

Your company manufactures right circular cylindrical molasses storage tanks that are 25 ft high with a radius of 5 ft. How sensitive are the tanks' volumes to small variations in height and radius?

Solution With $V = \pi r^2 h$, we have the approximation for the change in volume as

$$\begin{aligned} dV &= V_r(5, 25)\, dr + V_h(5, 25)\, dh \\ &= (2\pi rh)_{(5,25)}\, dr + (\pi r^2)_{(5,25)}\, dh \\ &= 250\pi\, dr + 25\pi\, dh. \end{aligned}$$

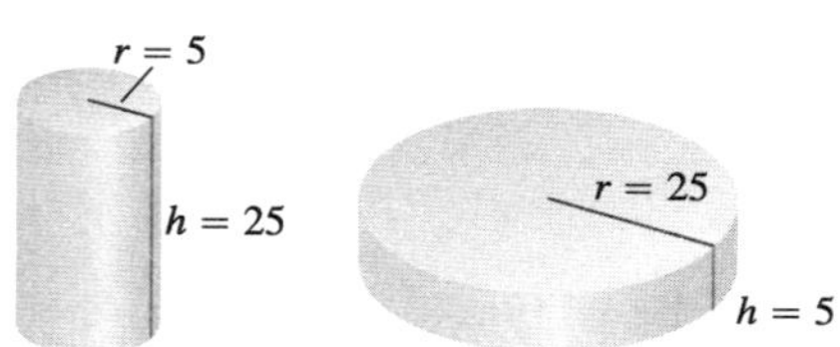

(a) (b)

FIGURE 14.35 The volume of cylinder (a) is more sensitive to a small change in r than it is to an equally small change in h. The volume of cylinder (b) is more sensitive to small changes in h than it is to small changes in r (Example 8).

Thus, a 1-unit change in r will change V by about 250π units. A 1-unit change in h will change V by about 25π units. The tank's volume is 10 times more sensitive to a small change in r than it is to a small change of equal size in h. As a quality control engineer concerned with being sure the tanks have the correct volume, you would want to pay special attention to their radii.

In contrast, if the values of r and h are reversed to make $r = 25$ and $h = 5$, then the total differential in V becomes

$$dV = (2\pi rh)_{(25,5)}\, dr + (\pi r^2)_{(25,5)}\, dh = 250\pi\, dr + 625\pi\, dh.$$

Now the volume is more sensitive to changes in h than to changes in r (Figure 14.35).

The general rule is that functions are most sensitive to small changes in the variables that generate the largest partial derivatives. ■

EXAMPLE 9 Estimating Percentage Error

The volume $V = \pi r^2 h$ of a right circular cylinder is to be calculated from measured values of r and h. Suppose that r is measured with an error of no more than 2% and h with an error of no more than 0.5%. Estimate the resulting possible percentage error in the calculation of V.

Solution We are told that

$$\left|\frac{dr}{r} \times 100\right| \le 2 \quad \text{and} \quad \left|\frac{dh}{h} \times 100\right| \le 0.5.$$

Since

$$\frac{dV}{V} = \frac{2\pi rh\, dr + \pi r^2\, dh}{\pi r^2 h} = \frac{2\, dr}{r} + \frac{dh}{h},$$

we have

$$\begin{aligned}\left|\frac{dV}{V}\right| &= \left|2\frac{dr}{r} + \frac{dh}{h}\right| \\ &\le \left|2\frac{dr}{r}\right| + \left|\frac{dh}{h}\right| \\ &\le 2(0.02) + 0.005 = 0.045.\end{aligned}$$

We estimate the error in the volume calculation to be at most 4.5%. ■

Functions of More Than Two Variables

Analogous results hold for differentiable functions of more than two variables.

1. The **linearization** of $f(x, y, z)$ at a point $P_0(x_0, y_0, z_0)$ is

$$L(x, y, z) = f(P_0) + f_x(P_0)(x - x_0) + f_y(P_0)(y - y_0) + f_z(P_0)(z - z_0).$$

2. Suppose that R is a closed rectangular solid centered at P_0 and lying in an open region on which the second partial derivatives of f are continuous. Suppose also that $|f_{xx}|, |f_{yy}|, |f_{zz}|, |f_{xy}|, |f_{xz}|$, and $|f_{yz}|$ are all less than or equal to M throughout R. Then the **error** $E(x, y, z) = f(x, y, z) - L(x, y, z)$ in the approximation of f by L is bounded throughout R by the inequality

$$|E| \le \frac{1}{2}M(|x - x_0| + |y - y_0| + |z - z_0|)^2.$$

3. If the second partial derivatives of f are continuous and if x, y, and z change from $x_0, y_0,$ and z_0 by small amounts dx, dy, and dz, the **total differential**

$$df = f_x(P_0)\,dx + f_y(P_0)\,dy + f_z(P_0)\,dz$$

gives a good approximation of the resulting change in f.

EXAMPLE 10 Finding a Linear Approximation in 3-Space

Find the linearization $L(x, y, z)$ of

$$f(x, y, z) = x^2 - xy + 3\sin z$$

at the point $(x_0, y_0, z_0) = (2, 1, 0)$. Find an upper bound for the error incurred in replacing f by L on the rectangle

$$R:\quad |x - 2| \le 0.01, \qquad |y - 1| \le 0.02, \qquad |z| \le 0.01.$$

Solution A routine evaluation gives

$$f(2, 1, 0) = 2, \qquad f_x(2, 1, 0) = 3, \qquad f_y(2, 1, 0) = -2, \qquad f_z(2, 1, 0) = 3.$$

Thus,

$$L(x, y, z) = 2 + 3(x - 2) + (-2)(y - 1) + 3(z - 0) = 3x - 2y + 3z - 2.$$

Since

$$\begin{aligned} f_{xx} &= 2, & f_{yy} &= 0, & f_{zz} &= -3\sin z, \\ f_{xy} &= -1, & f_{xz} &= 0, & f_{yz} &= 0, \end{aligned}$$

we may safely take M to be $\max|-3\sin z| = 3$. Hence, the error incurred by replacing f by L on R satisfies

$$|E| \le \frac{1}{2}(3)(0.01 + 0.02 + 0.01)^2 = 0.0024.$$

The error will be no greater than 0.0024. ■

EXERCISES 14.6

Tangent Planes and Normal Lines to Surfaces

In Exercises 1–8, find equations for the

(a) tangent plane and **(b)** normal line at the point P_0 on the given surface.

1. $x^2 + y^2 + z^2 = 3, \quad P_0(1, 1, 1)$
2. $x^2 + y^2 - z^2 = 18, \quad P_0(3, 5, -4)$
3. $2z - x^2 = 0, \quad P_0(2, 0, 2)$
4. $x^2 + 2xy - y^2 + z^2 = 7, \quad P_0(1, -1, 3)$
5. $\cos \pi x - x^2y + e^{xz} + yz = 4, \quad P_0(0, 1, 2)$
6. $x^2 - xy - y^2 - z = 0, \quad P_0(1, 1, -1)$
7. $x + y + z = 1, \quad P_0(0, 1, 0)$
8. $x^2 + y^2 - 2xy - x + 3y - z = -4, \quad P_0(2, -3, 18)$

In Exercises 9–12, find an equation for the plane that is tangent to the given surface at the given point.

9. $z = \ln(x^2 + y^2), \quad (1, 0, 0)$
10. $z = e^{-(x^2+y^2)}, \quad (0, 0, 1)$
11. $z = \sqrt{y - x}, \quad (1, 2, 1)$
12. $z = 4x^2 + y^2, \quad (1, 1, 5)$

Tangent Lines to Curves

In Exercises 13–18, find parametric equations for the line tangent to the curve of intersection of the surfaces at the given point.

13. Surfaces: $x + y^2 + 2z = 4, \quad x = 1$
    Point: $(1, 1, 1)$
14. Surfaces: $xyz = 1, \quad x^2 + 2y^2 + 3z^2 = 6$
    Point: $(1, 1, 1)$
15. Surfaces: $x^2 + 2y + 2z = 4, \quad y = 1$
    Point: $(1, 1, 1/2)$
16. Surfaces: $x + y^2 + z = 2, \quad y = 1$
    Point: $(1/2, 1, 1/2)$
17. Surfaces: $x^3 + 3x^2y^2 + y^3 + 4xy - z^2 = 0, \quad x^2 + y^2 + z^2 = 11$
    Point: $(1, 1, 3)$
18. Surfaces: $x^2 + y^2 = 4, \quad x^2 + y^2 - z = 0$
    Point: $(\sqrt{2}, \sqrt{2}, 4)$

Estimating Change

19. By about how much will
$$f(x, y, z) = \ln\sqrt{x^2 + y^2 + z^2}$$
change if the point $P(x, y, z)$ moves from $P_0(3, 4, 12)$ a distance of $ds = 0.1$ unit in the direction of $3\mathbf{i} + 6\mathbf{j} - 2\mathbf{k}$?
20. By about how much will
$$f(x, y, z) = e^x \cos yz$$
change as the point $P(x, y, z)$ moves from the origin a distance of $ds = 0.1$ unit in the direction of $2\mathbf{i} + 2\mathbf{j} - 2\mathbf{k}$?
21. By about how much will
$$g(x, y, z) = x + x\cos z - y\sin z + y$$
change if the point $P(x, y, z)$ moves from $P_0(2, -1, 0)$ a distance of $ds = 0.2$ unit toward the point $P_1(0, 1, 2)$?
22. By about how much will
$$h(x, y, z) = \cos(\pi xy) + xz^2$$
change if the point $P(x, y, z)$ moves from $P_0(-1, -1, -1)$ a distance of $ds = 0.1$ unit toward the origin?
23. **Temperature change along a circle** Suppose that the Celsius temperature at the point (x, y) in the xy-plane is $T(x, y) = x \sin 2y$ and that distance in the xy-plane is measured in meters. A particle is moving *clockwise* around the circle of radius 1 m centered at the origin at the constant rate of 2 m/sec.
    a. How fast is the temperature experienced by the particle changing in degrees Celsius per meter at the point $P(1/2, \sqrt{3}/2)$?
    b. How fast is the temperature experienced by the particle changing in degrees Celsius per second at P?
24. **Changing temperature along a space curve** The Celsius temperature in a region in space is given by $T(x, y, z) = 2x^2 - xyz$. A particle is moving in this region and its position at time t is given by $x = 2t^2, y = 3t, z = -t^2$, where time is measured in seconds and distance in meters.

a. How fast is the temperature experienced by the particle changing in degrees Celsius per meter when the particle is at the point $P(8, 6, -4)$?

b. How fast is the temperature experienced by the particle changing in degrees Celsius per second at P?

Finding Linearizations

In Exercises 25–30, find the linearization $L(x, y)$ of the function at each point.

25. $f(x, y) = x^2 + y^2 + 1$ at a. $(0, 0)$, b. $(1, 1)$

26. $f(x, y) = (x + y + 2)^2$ at a. $(0, 0)$, b. $(1, 2)$

27. $f(x, y) = 3x - 4y + 5$ at a. $(0, 0)$, b. $(1, 1)$

28. $f(x, y) = x^3y^4$ at a. $(1, 1)$, b. $(0, 0)$

29. $f(x, y) = e^x \cos y$ at a. $(0, 0)$, b. $(0, \pi/2)$

30. $f(x, y) = e^{2y-x}$ at a. $(0, 0)$, b. $(1, 2)$

Upper Bounds for Errors in Linear Approximations

In Exercises 31–36, find the linearization $L(x, y)$ of the function $f(x, y)$ at P_0. Then find an upper bound for the magnitude $|E|$ of the error in the approximation $f(x, y) \approx L(x, y)$ over the rectangle R.

31. $f(x, y) = x^2 - 3xy + 5$ at $P_0(2, 1)$,
R: $|x - 2| \le 0.1$, $|y - 1| \le 0.1$

32. $f(x, y) = (1/2)x^2 + xy + (1/4)y^2 + 3x - 3y + 4$ at $P_0(2, 2)$,
R: $|x - 2| \le 0.1$, $|y - 2| \le 0.1$

33. $f(x, y) = 1 + y + x\cos y$ at $P_0(0, 0)$,
R: $|x| \le 0.2$, $|y| \le 0.2$
(Use $|\cos y| \le 1$ and $|\sin y| \le 1$ in estimating E.)

34. $f(x, y) = xy^2 + y\cos(x - 1)$ at $P_0(1, 2)$,
R: $|x - 1| \le 0.1$, $|y - 2| \le 0.1$

35. $f(x, y) = e^x \cos y$ at $P_0(0, 0)$,
R: $|x| \le 0.1$, $|y| \le 0.1$
(Use $e^x \le 1.11$ and $|\cos y| \le 1$ in estimating E.)

36. $f(x, y) = \ln x + \ln y$ at $P_0(1, 1)$,
R: $|x - 1| \le 0.2$, $|y - 1| \le 0.2$

Functions of Three Variables

Find the linearizations $L(x, y, z)$ of the functions in Exercises 37–42 at the given points.

37. $f(x, y, z) = xy + yz + xz$ at
a. $(1, 1, 1)$ b. $(1, 0, 0)$ c. $(0, 0, 0)$

38. $f(x, y, z) = x^2 + y^2 + z^2$ at
a. $(1, 1, 1)$ b. $(0, 1, 0)$ c. $(1, 0, 0)$

39. $f(x, y, z) = \sqrt{x^2 + y^2 + z^2}$ at
a. $(1, 0, 0)$ b. $(1, 1, 0)$ c. $(1, 2, 2)$

40. $f(x, y, z) = (\sin xy)/z$ at
a. $(\pi/2, 1, 1)$ b. $(2, 0, 1)$

41. $f(x, y, z) = e^x + \cos(y + z)$ at
a. $(0, 0, 0)$ b. $\left(0, \frac{\pi}{2}, 0\right)$ c. $\left(0, \frac{\pi}{4}, \frac{\pi}{4}\right)$

42. $f(x, y, z) = \tan^{-1}(xyz)$ at
a. $(1, 0, 0)$ b. $(1, 1, 0)$ c. $(1, 1, 1)$

In Exercises 43–46, find the linearization $L(x, y, z)$ of the function $f(x, y, z)$ at P_0. Then find an upper bound for the magnitude of the error E in the approximation $f(x, y, z) \approx L(x, y, z)$ over the region R.

43. $f(x, y, z) = xz - 3yz + 2$ at $P_0(1, 1, 2)$
R: $|x - 1| \le 0.01$, $|y - 1| \le 0.01$, $|z - 2| \le 0.02$

44. $f(x, y, z) = x^2 + xy + yz + (1/4)z^2$ at $P_0(1, 1, 2)$
R: $|x - 1| \le 0.01$, $|y - 1| \le 0.01$, $|z - 2| \le 0.08$

45. $f(x, y, z) = xy + 2yz - 3xz$ at $P_0(1, 1, 0)$
R: $|x - 1| \le 0.01$, $|y - 1| \le 0.01$, $|z| \le 0.01$

46. $f(x, y, z) = \sqrt{2}\cos x \sin(y + z)$ at $P_0(0, 0, \pi/4)$
R: $|x| \le 0.01$, $|y| \le 0.01$, $|z - \pi/4| \le 0.01$

Estimating Error; Sensitivity to Change

47. **Estimating maximum error** Suppose that T is to be found from the formula $T = x(e^y + e^{-y})$, where x and y are found to be 2 and ln 2 with maximum possible errors of $|dx| = 0.1$ and $|dy| = 0.02$. Estimate the maximum possible error in the computed value of T.

48. **Estimating volume of a cylinder** About how accurately may $V = \pi r^2 h$ be calculated from measurements of r and h that are in error by 1%?

49. **Maximum percentage error** If $r = 5.0$ cm and $h = 12.0$ cm to the nearest millimeter, what should we expect the maximum percentage error in calculating $V = \pi r^2 h$ to be?

50. **Variation in electrical resistance** The resistance R produced by wiring resistors of R_1 and R_2 ohms in parallel (see accompanying figure) can be calculated from the formula

$$\frac{1}{R} = \frac{1}{R_1} + \frac{1}{R_2}.$$

a. Show that

$$dR = \left(\frac{R}{R_1}\right)^2 dR_1 + \left(\frac{R}{R_2}\right)^2 dR_2.$$

b. You have designed a two-resistor circuit like the one shown on the next page to have resistances of $R_1 = 100$ ohms and $R_2 = 400$ ohms, but there is always some variation in manufacturing and the resistors received by your firm will probably not have these exact values. Will the value of R be more sensitive to variation in R_1 or to variation in R_2? Give reasons for your answer.

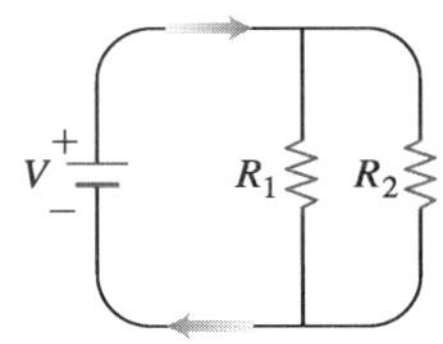

c. In another circuit like the one shown you plan to change R_1 from 20 to 20.1 ohms and R_2 from 25 to 24.9 ohms. By about what percentage will this change R?

51. You plan to calculate the area of a long, thin rectangle from measurements of its length and width. Which dimension should you measure more carefully? Give reasons for your answer.

52. a. Around the point (1, 0), is $f(x, y) = x^2(y + 1)$ more sensitive to changes in x or to changes in y? Give reasons for your answer.

b. What ratio of dx to dy will make df equal zero at (1, 0)?

53. **Error carryover in coordinate changes**

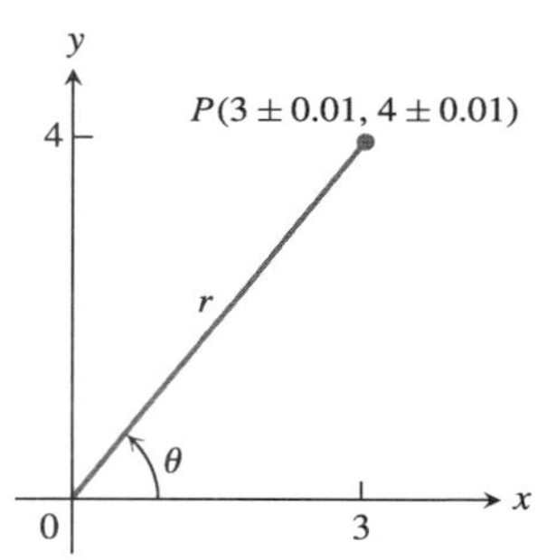

a. If $x = 3 \pm 0.01$ and $y = 4 \pm 0.01$, as shown here, with approximately what accuracy can you calculate the polar coordinates r and θ of the point $P(x, y)$ from the formulas $r^2 = x^2 + y^2$ and $\theta = \tan^{-1}(y/x)$? Express your estimates as percentage changes of the values that r and θ have at the point $(x_0, y_0) = (3, 4)$.

b. At the point $(x_0, y_0) = (3, 4)$, are the values of r and θ more sensitive to changes in x or to changes in y? Give reasons for your answer.

54. **Designing a soda can** A standard 12-fl oz can of soda is essentially a cylinder of radius $r = 1$ in. and height $h = 5$ in.

a. At these dimensions, how sensitive is the can's volume to a small change in radius versus a small change in height?

b. Could you design a soda can that *appears* to hold more soda but in fact holds the same 12-fl oz? What might its dimensions be? (There is more than one correct answer.)

55. **Value of a 2 × 2 determinant** If $|a|$ is much greater than $|b|$, $|c|$, and $|d|$, to which of a, b, c, and d is the value of the determinant

$$f(a, b, c, d) = \begin{vmatrix} a & b \\ c & d \end{vmatrix}$$

most sensitive? Give reasons for your answer.

56. **Estimating maximum error** Suppose that $u = xe^y + y \sin z$ and that x, y, and z can be measured with maximum possible errors of ± 0.2, ± 0.6, and $\pm \pi/180$, respectively. Estimate the maximum possible error in calculating u from the measured values $x = 2$, $y = \ln 3$, $z = \pi/2$.

57. **The Wilson lot size formula** The Wilson lot size formula in economics says that the most economical quantity Q of goods (radios, shoes, brooms, whatever) for a store to order is given by the formula $Q = \sqrt{2KM/h}$, where K is the cost of placing the order, M is the number of items sold per week, and h is the weekly holding cost for each item (cost of space, utilities, security, and so on). To which of the variables K, M, and h is Q most sensitive near the point $(K_0, M_0, h_0) = (2, 20, 0.05)$? Give reasons for your answer.

58. **Surveying a triangular field** The area of a triangle is $(1/2)ab \sin C$, where a and b are the lengths of two sides of the triangle and C is the measure of the included angle. In surveying a triangular plot, you have measured a, b, and C to be 150 ft, 200 ft, and 60°, respectively. By about how much could your area calculation be in error if your values of a and b are off by half a foot each and your measurement of C is off by 2°? See the accompanying figure. Remember to use radians.

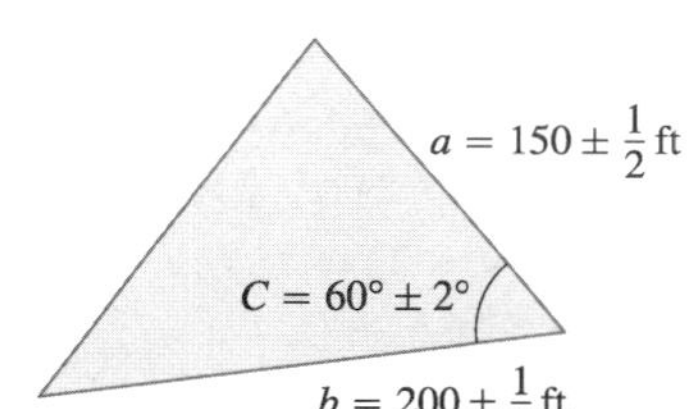

Theory and Examples

59. **The linearization of $f(x, y)$ is a tangent-plane approximation** Show that the tangent plane at the point $P_0(x_0, y_0, f(x_0, y_0))$ on the surface $z = f(x, y)$ defined by a differentiable function f is the plane

$$f_x(x_0, y_0)(x - x_0) + f_y(x_0, y_0)(y - y_0) - (z - f(x_0, y_0)) = 0$$

or

$$z = f(x_0, y_0) + f_x(x_0, y_0)(x - x_0) + f_y(x_0, y_0)(y - y_0).$$

Thus, the tangent plane at P_0 is the graph of the linearization of f at P_0 (see accompanying figure).

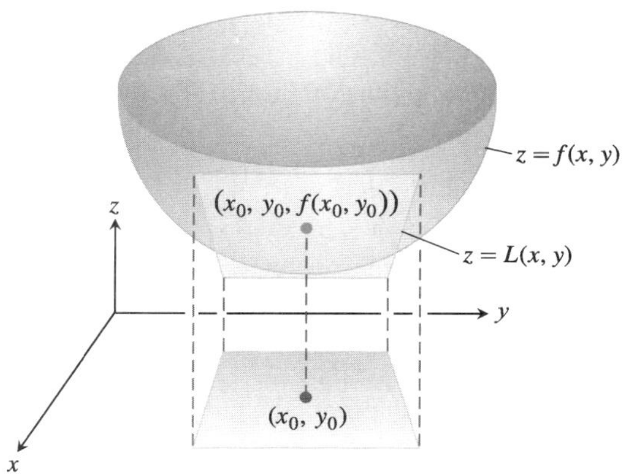

60. **Change along the involute of a circle** Find the derivative of $f(x, y) = x^2 + y^2$ in the direction of the unit tangent vector of the curve

$$\mathbf{r}(t) = (\cos t + t\sin t)\mathbf{i} + (\sin t - t\cos t)\mathbf{j}, \qquad t > 0.$$

61. **Change along a helix** Find the derivative of $f(x, y, z) = x^2 + y^2 + z^2$ in the direction of the unit tangent vector of the helix

$$\mathbf{r}(t) = (\cos t)\mathbf{i} + (\sin t)\mathbf{j} + t\mathbf{k}$$

at the points where $t = -\pi/4, 0,$ and $\pi/4$. The function f gives the square of the distance from a point $P(x, y, z)$ on the helix to the origin. The derivatives calculated here give the rates at which the square of the distance is changing with respect to t as P moves through the points where $t = -\pi/4, 0,$ and $\pi/4$.

62. **Normal curves** A smooth curve is *normal* to a surface $f(x, y, z) = c$ at a point of intersection if the curve's velocity vector is a nonzero scalar multiple of ∇f at the point.

Show that the curve

$$\mathbf{r}(t) = \sqrt{t}\mathbf{i} + \sqrt{t}\mathbf{j} - \frac{1}{4}(t + 3)\mathbf{k}$$

is normal to the surface $x^2 + y^2 - z = 3$ when $t = 1$.

63. **Tangent curves** A smooth curve is *tangent* to the surface at a point of intersection if its velocity vector is orthogonal to ∇f there.

Show that the curve

$$\mathbf{r}(t) = \sqrt{t}\mathbf{i} + \sqrt{t}\mathbf{j} + (2t - 1)\mathbf{k}$$

is tangent to the surface $x^2 + y^2 - z = 1$ when $t = 1$.

14.7 Extreme Values and Saddle Points

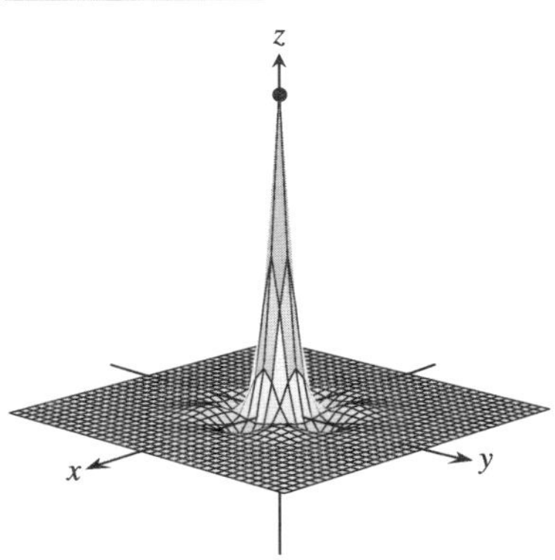

FIGURE 14.36 The function

$$z = (\cos x)(\cos y)e^{-\sqrt{x^2+y^2}}$$

has a maximum value of 1 and a minimum value of about -0.067 on the square region $|x| \le 3\pi/2, |y| \le 3\pi/2$.

Continuous functions of two variables assume extreme values on closed, bounded domains (see Figures 14.36 and 14.37). We see in this section that we can narrow the search for these extreme values by examining the functions' first partial derivatives. A function of two variables can assume extreme values only at domain boundary points or at interior domain points where both first partial derivatives are zero or where one or both of the first partial derivatives fails to exist. However, the vanishing of derivatives at an interior point (a, b) does not always signal the presence of an extreme value. The surface that is the graph of the function might be shaped like a saddle right above (a, b) and cross its tangent plane there.

Derivative Tests for Local Extreme Values

To find the local extreme values of a function of a single variable, we look for points where the graph has a horizontal tangent line. At such points, we then look for local maxima, local minima, and points of inflection. For a function $f(x, y)$ of two variables, we look for points where the surface $z = f(x, y)$ has a horizontal tangent *plane*. At such points, we then look for local maxima, local minima, and saddle points (more about saddle points in a moment).

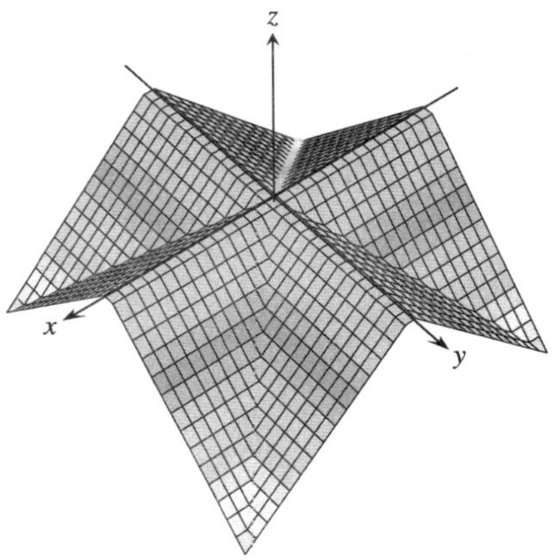

FIGURE 14.37 The "roof surface"

$$z = \frac{1}{2}\left(\left||x| - |y|\right| - |x| - |y|\right)$$

viewed from the point (10, 15, 20). The defining function has a maximum value of 0 and a minimum value of $-a$ on the square region $|x| \le a, |y| \le a$.

DEFINITIONS Local Maximum, Local Minimum

Let $f(x, y)$ be defined on a region R containing the point (a, b). Then

1. $f(a, b)$ is a **local maximum** value of f if $f(a, b) \ge f(x, y)$ for all domain points (x, y) in an open disk centered at (a, b).
2. $f(a, b)$ is a **local minimum** value of f if $f(a, b) \le f(x, y)$ for all domain points (x, y) in an open disk centered at (a, b).

Local maxima correspond to mountain peaks on the surface $z = f(x, y)$ and local minima correspond to valley bottoms (Figure 14.38). At such points the tangent planes, when they exist, are horizontal. Local extrema are also called **relative extrema**.

As with functions of a single variable, the key to identifying the local extrema is a first derivative test.

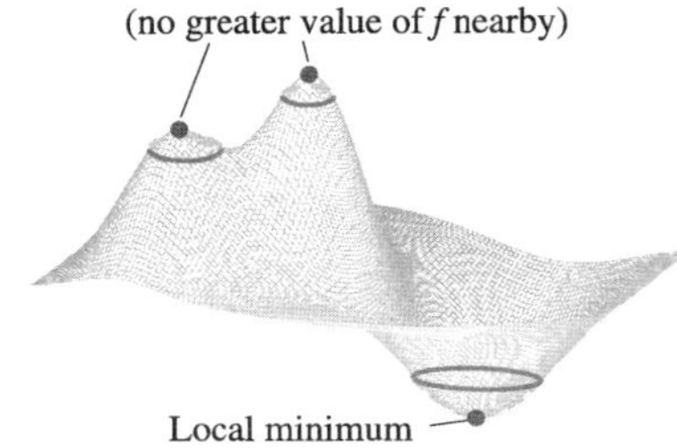

FIGURE 14.38 A local maximum is a mountain peak and a local minimum is a valley low.

HISTORICAL BIOGRAPHY

Siméon-Denis Poisson (1781–1840)

THEOREM 10 First Derivative Test for Local Extreme Values

If $f(x, y)$ has a local maximum or minimum value at an interior point (a, b) of its domain and if the first partial derivatives exist there, then $f_x(a, b) = 0$ and $f_y(a, b) = 0$.

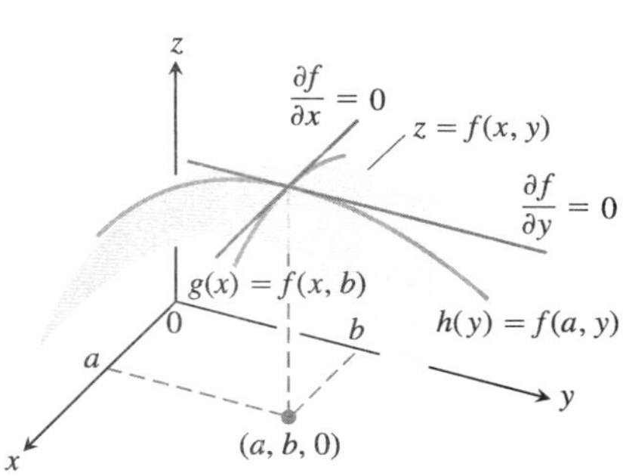

FIGURE 14.39 If a local maximum of f occurs at $x = a, y = b$, then the first partial derivatives $f_x(a, b)$ and $f_y(a, b)$ are both zero.

Proof If f has a local extremum at (a, b), then the function $g(x) = f(x, b)$ has a local extremum at $x = a$ (Figure 14.39). Therefore, $g'(a) = 0$ (Chapter 4, Theorem 2). Now $g'(a) = f_x(a, b)$, so $f_x(a, b) = 0$. A similar argument with the function $h(y) = f(a, y)$ shows that $f_y(a, b) = 0$. ■

If we substitute the values $f_x(a, b) = 0$ and $f_y(a, b) = 0$ into the equation

$$f_x(a, b)(x - a) + f_y(a, b)(y - b) - (z - f(a, b)) = 0$$

for the tangent plane to the surface $z = f(x, y)$ at (a, b), the equation reduces to

$$0 \cdot (x - a) + 0 \cdot (y - b) - z + f(a, b) = 0$$

or

$$z = f(a, b).$$

Thus, Theorem 10 says that the surface does indeed have a horizontal tangent plane at a local extremum, provided there is a tangent plane there.

> **DEFINITION Critical Point**
> An interior point of the domain of a function $f(x, y)$ where both f_x and f_y are zero or where one or both of f_x and f_y do not exist is a **critical point** of f.

Theorem 10 says that the only points where a function $f(x, y)$ can assume extreme values are critical points and boundary points. As with differentiable functions of a single variable, not every critical point gives rise to a local extremum. A differentiable function of a single variable might have a point of inflection. A differentiable function of two variables might have a *saddle point*.

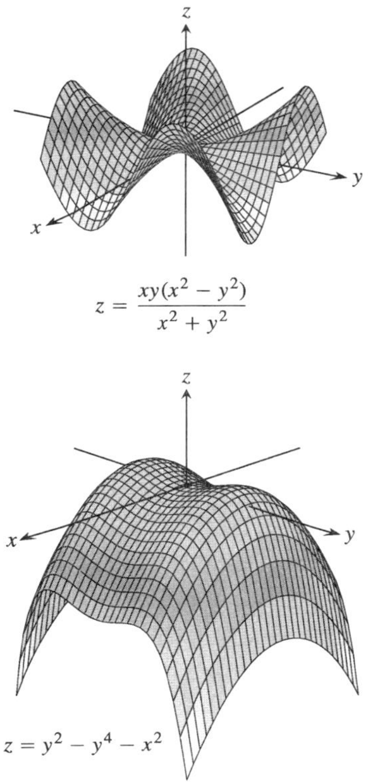

FIGURE 14.40 Saddle points at the origin.

> **DEFINITION Saddle Point**
> A differentiable function $f(x, y)$ has a **saddle point** at a critical point (a, b) if in every open disk centered at (a, b) there are domain points (x, y) where $f(x, y) > f(a, b)$ and domain points (x, y) where $f(x, y) < f(a, b)$. The corresponding point $(a, b, f(a, b))$ on the surface $z = f(x, y)$ is called a saddle point of the surface (Figure 14.40).

EXAMPLE 1 Finding Local Extreme Values

Find the local extreme values of $f(x, y) = x^2 + y^2$.

Solution The domain of f is the entire plane (so there are no boundary points) and the partial derivatives $f_x = 2x$ and $f_y = 2y$ exist everywhere. Therefore, local extreme values can occur only where

$$f_x = 2x = 0 \quad \text{and} \quad f_y = 2y = 0.$$

The only possibility is the origin, where the value of f is zero. Since f is never negative, we see that the origin gives a local minimum (Figure 14.41). ■

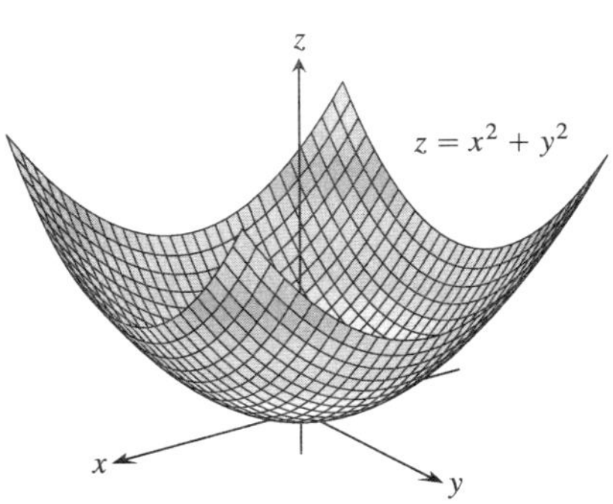

FIGURE 14.41 The graph of the function $f(x, y) = x^2 + y^2$ is the paraboloid $z = x^2 + y^2$. The function has a local minimum value of 0 at the origin (Example 1).

EXAMPLE 2 Identifying a Saddle Point

Find the local extreme values (if any) of $f(x, y) = y^2 - x^2$.

Solution The domain of f is the entire plane (so there are no boundary points) and the partial derivatives $f_x = -2x$ and $f_y = 2y$ exist everywhere. Therefore, local extrema can occur only at the origin $(0, 0)$. Along the positive x-axis, however, f has the value $f(x, 0) = -x^2 < 0$; along the positive y-axis, f has the value $f(0, y) = y^2 > 0$. Therefore, every open disk in the xy-plane centered at $(0, 0)$ contains points where the function is positive and points where it is negative. The function has a saddle point at the origin (Figure 14.42) instead of a local extreme value. We conclude that the function has no local extreme values. ■

That $f_x = f_y = 0$ at an interior point (a, b) of R does not guarantee f has a local extreme value there. If f and its first and second partial derivatives are continuous on R, however, we may be able to learn more from the following theorem, proved in Section 14.10.

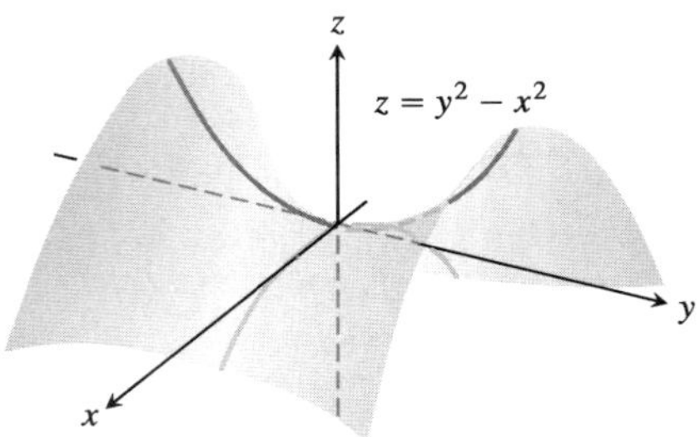

FIGURE 14.42 The origin is a saddle point of the function $f(x, y) = y^2 - x^2$. There are no local extreme values (Example 2).

> **THEOREM 11 Second Derivative Test for Local Extreme Values**
>
> Suppose that $f(x, y)$ and its first and second partial derivatives are continuous throughout a disk centered at (a, b) and that $f_x(a, b) = f_y(a, b) = 0$. Then
>
> **i.** f has a **local maximum** at (a, b) if $f_{xx} < 0$ and $f_{xx}f_{yy} - f_{xy}^2 > 0$ at (a, b).
>
> **ii.** f has a **local minimum** at (a, b) if $f_{xx} > 0$ and $f_{xx}f_{yy} - f_{xy}^2 > 0$ at (a, b).
>
> **iii.** f has a **saddle point** at (a, b) if $f_{xx}f_{yy} - f_{xy}^2 < 0$ at (a, b).
>
> **iv. The test is inconclusive** at (a, b) if $f_{xx}f_{yy} - f_{xy}^2 = 0$ at (a, b). In this case, we must find some other way to determine the behavior of f at (a, b).

The expression $f_{xx}f_{yy} - f_{xy}^2$ is called the **discriminant** or **Hessian** of f. It is sometimes easier to remember it in determinant form,

$$f_{xx}f_{yy} - f_{xy}^2 = \begin{vmatrix} f_{xx} & f_{xy} \\ f_{xy} & f_{yy} \end{vmatrix}.$$

Theorem 11 says that if the discriminant is positive at the point (a, b), then the surface curves the same way in all directions: downward if $f_{xx} < 0$, giving rise to a local maximum, and upward if $f_{xx} > 0$, giving a local minimum. On the other hand, if the discriminant is negative at (a, b), then the surface curves up in some directions and down in others, so we have a saddle point.

EXAMPLE 3 Finding Local Extreme Values

Find the local extreme values of the function

$$f(x, y) = xy - x^2 - y^2 - 2x - 2y + 4.$$

Solution The function is defined and differentiable for all x and y and its domain has no boundary points. The function therefore has extreme values only at the points where f_x and f_y are simultaneously zero. This leads to

$$f_x = y - 2x - 2 = 0, \qquad f_y = x - 2y - 2 = 0,$$

or

$$x = y = -2.$$

Therefore, the point $(-2, -2)$ is the only point where f may take on an extreme value. To see if it does so, we calculate

$$f_{xx} = -2, \qquad f_{yy} = -2, \qquad f_{xy} = 1.$$

The discriminant of f at $(a, b) = (-2, -2)$ is

$$f_{xx}f_{yy} - f_{xy}^2 = (-2)(-2) - (1)^2 = 4 - 1 = 3.$$

The combination

$$f_{xx} < 0 \qquad \text{and} \qquad f_{xx}f_{yy} - f_{xy}^2 > 0$$

tells us that f has a local maximum at $(-2, -2)$. The value of f at this point is $f(-2, -2) = 8$. ■

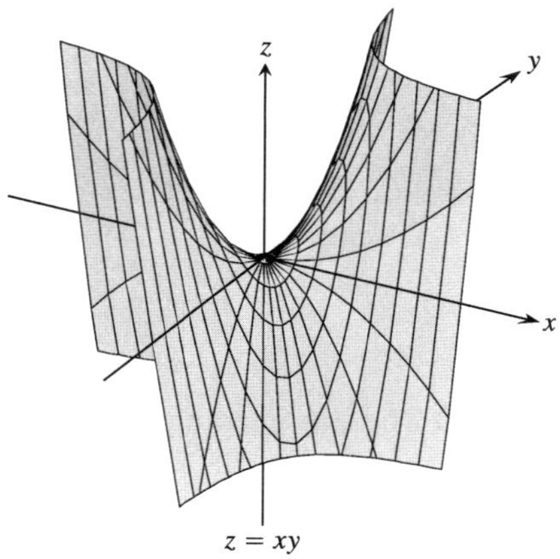

FIGURE 14.43 The surface $z = xy$ has a saddle point at the origin (Example 4).

EXAMPLE 4 Searching for Local Extreme Values

Find the local extreme values of $f(x, y) = xy$.

Solution Since f is differentiable everywhere (Figure 14.43), it can assume extreme values only where

$$f_x = y = 0 \quad \text{and} \quad f_y = x = 0.$$

Thus, the origin is the only point where f might have an extreme value. To see what happens there, we calculate

$$f_{xx} = 0, \qquad f_{yy} = 0, \qquad f_{xy} = 1.$$

The discriminant,

$$f_{xx}f_{yy} - f_{xy}^2 = -1,$$

is negative. Therefore, the function has a saddle point at (0, 0). We conclude that $f(x, y) = xy$ has no local extreme values. ■

Absolute Maxima and Minima on Closed Bounded Regions

We organize the search for the absolute extrema of a continuous function $f(x, y)$ on a closed and bounded region R into three steps.

1. *List the interior points of R* where f may have local maxima and minima and evaluate f at these points. These are the critical points of f.
2. *List the boundary points of R* where f has local maxima and minima and evaluate f at these points. We show how to do this shortly.
3. *Look through the lists* for the maximum and minimum values of f. These will be the absolute maximum and minimum values of f on R. Since absolute maxima and minima are also local maxima and minima, the absolute maximum and minimum values of f appear somewhere in the lists made in Steps 1 and 2.

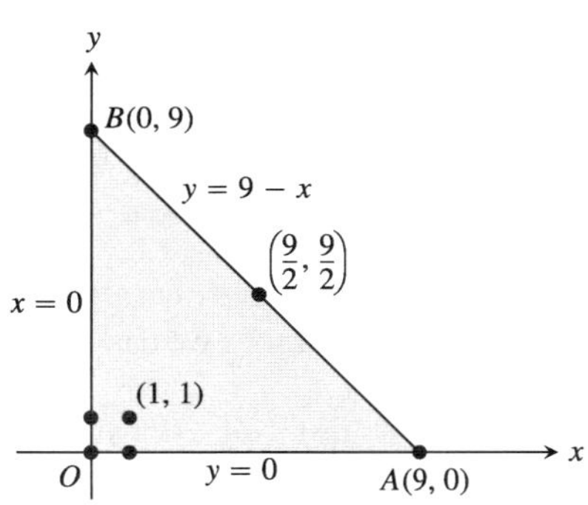

FIGURE 14.44 This triangular region is the domain of the function in Example 5.

EXAMPLE 5 Finding Absolute Extrema

Find the absolute maximum and minimum values of

$$f(x, y) = 2 + 2x + 2y - x^2 - y^2$$

on the triangular region in the first quadrant bounded by the lines $x = 0, y = 0, y = 9 - x$.

Solution Since f is differentiable, the only places where f can assume these values are points inside the triangle (Figure 14.44) where $f_x = f_y = 0$ and points on the boundary.

(a) Interior points. For these we have

$$f_x = 2 - 2x = 0, \qquad f_y = 2 - 2y = 0,$$

yielding the single point $(x, y) = (1, 1)$. The value of f there is

$$f(1, 1) = 4.$$

(b) Boundary points. We take the triangle one side at a time:

(i) On the segment OA, $y = 0$. The function

$$f(x, y) = f(x, 0) = 2 + 2x - x^2$$

may now be regarded as a function of x defined on the closed interval $0 \le x \le 9$. Its extreme values (we know from Chapter 4) may occur at the endpoints

$$x = 0 \quad \text{where} \quad f(0, 0) = 2$$

$$x = 9 \quad \text{where} \quad f(9, 0) = 2 + 18 - 81 = -61$$

and at the interior points where $f'(x, 0) = 2 - 2x = 0$. The only interior point where $f'(x, 0) = 0$ is $x = 1$, where

$$f(x, 0) = f(1, 0) = 3.$$

(ii) On the segment OB, $x = 0$ and

$$f(x, y) = f(0, y) = 2 + 2y - y^2.$$

We know from the symmetry of f in x and y and from the analysis we just carried out that the candidates on this segment are

$$f(0, 0) = 2, \qquad f(0, 9) = -61, \qquad f(0, 1) = 3.$$

(iii) We have already accounted for the values of f at the endpoints of AB, so we need only look at the interior points of AB. With $y = 9 - x$, we have

$$f(x, y) = 2 + 2x + 2(9 - x) - x^2 - (9 - x)^2 = -61 + 18x - 2x^2.$$

Setting $f'(x, 9 - x) = 18 - 4x = 0$ gives

$$x = \frac{18}{4} = \frac{9}{2}.$$

At this value of x,

$$y = 9 - \frac{9}{2} = \frac{9}{2} \quad \text{and} \quad f(x, y) = f\left(\frac{9}{2}, \frac{9}{2}\right) = -\frac{41}{2}.$$

Summary We list all the candidates: $4, 2, -61, 3, -(41/2)$. The maximum is 4, which f assumes at $(1, 1)$. The minimum is -61, which f assumes at $(0, 9)$ and $(9, 0)$. ■

Solving extreme value problems with algebraic constraints on the variables usually requires the method of Lagrange multipliers in the next section. But sometimes we can solve such problems directly, as in the next example.

EXAMPLE 6 Solving a Volume Problem with a Constraint

A delivery company accepts only rectangular boxes the sum of whose length and girth (perimeter of a cross-section) does not exceed 108 in. Find the dimensions of an acceptable box of largest volume.

Solution Let x, y, and z represent the length, width, and height of the rectangular box, respectively. Then the girth is $2y + 2z$. We want to maximize the volume $V = xyz$ of the

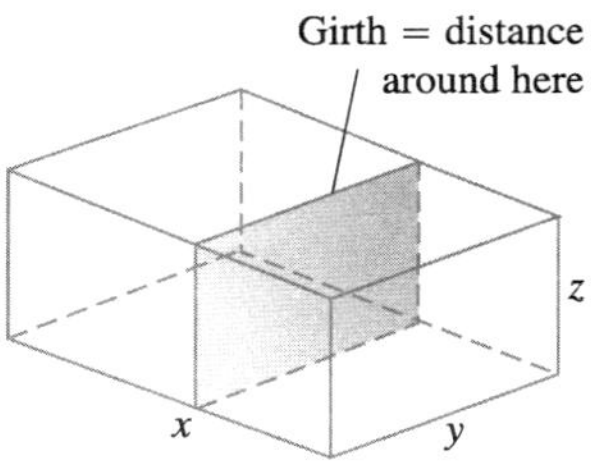

FIGURE 14.45 The box in Example 6.

box (Figure 14.45) satisfying $x + 2y + 2z = 108$ (the largest box accepted by the delivery company). Thus, we can write the volume of the box as a function of two variables.

$$\begin{aligned} V(y, z) &= (108 - 2y - 2z)yz \qquad \begin{matrix} V = xyz \text{ and} \\ x = 108 - 2y - 2z \end{matrix} \\ &= 108yz - 2y^2z - 2yz^2 \end{aligned}$$

Setting the first partial derivatives equal to zero,

$$\begin{aligned} V_y(y, z) &= 108z - 4yz - 2z^2 = (108 - 4y - 2z)z = 0 \\ V_z(y, z) &= 108y - 2y^2 - 4yz = (108 - 2y - 4z)y = 0, \end{aligned}$$

gives the critical points (0, 0), (0, 54), (54, 0), and (18, 18). The volume is zero at (0, 0), (0, 54), (54, 0), which are not maximum values. At the point (18, 18), we apply the Second Derivative Test (Theorem 11):

$$V_{yy} = -4z, \qquad V_{zz} = -4y, \qquad V_{yz} = 108 - 4y - 4z.$$

Then

$$V_{yy}V_{zz} - V_{yz}^2 = 16yz - 16(27 - y - z)^2.$$

Thus,

$$V_{yy}(18, 18) = -4(18) < 0$$

and

$$\left[V_{yy}V_{zz} - V_{yz}^2\right]_{(18,18)} = 16(18)(18) - 16(-9)^2 > 0$$

imply that (18, 18) gives a maximum volume. The dimensions of the package are $x = 108 - 2(18) - 2(18) = 36$ in., $y = 18$ in., and $z = 18$ in. The maximum volume is $V = (36)(18)(18) = 11{,}664$ in.^{3}, or 6.75 ft^3. ■

Despite the power of Theorem 10, we urge you to remember its limitations. It does not apply to boundary points of a function's domain, where it is possible for a function to have extreme values along with nonzero derivatives. Also, it does not apply to points where either f_x or f_y fails to exist.

Summary of Max-Min Tests

The extreme values of $f(x, y)$ can occur only at

i. **boundary points** of the domain of f

ii. **critical points** (interior points where $f_x = f_y = 0$ or points where f_x or f_y fail to exist).

If the first- and second-order partial derivatives of f are continuous throughout a disk centered at a point (a, b) and $f_x(a, b) = f_y(a, b) = 0$, the nature of $f(a, b)$ can be tested with the **Second Derivative Test**:

i. $f_{xx} < 0$ and $f_{xx}f_{yy} - f_{xy}^2 > 0$ at (a, b) $\Rightarrow$ **local maximum**

ii. $f_{xx} > 0$ and $f_{xx}f_{yy} - f_{xy}^2 > 0$ at (a, b) $\Rightarrow$ **local minimum**

iii. $f_{xx}f_{yy} - f_{xy}^2 < 0$ at (a, b) $\Rightarrow$ **saddle point**

iv. $f_{xx}f_{yy} - f_{xy}^2 = 0$ at (a, b) $\Rightarrow$ **test is inconclusive**.

EXERCISES 14.7

Finding Local Extrema

Find all the local maxima, local minima, and saddle points of the functions in Exercises 1–30.

1. $f(x, y) = x^2 + xy + y^2 + 3x - 3y + 4$
2. $f(x, y) = x^2 + 3xy + 3y^2 - 6x + 3y - 6$
3. $f(x, y) = 2xy - 5x^2 - 2y^2 + 4x + 4y - 4$
4. $f(x, y) = 2xy - 5x^2 - 2y^2 + 4x - 4$
5. $f(x, y) = x^2 + xy + 3x + 2y + 5$
6. $f(x, y) = y^2 + xy - 2x - 2y + 2$
7. $f(x, y) = 5xy - 7x^2 + 3x - 6y + 2$
8. $f(x, y) = 2xy - x^2 - 2y^2 + 3x + 4$
9. $f(x, y) = x^2 - 4xy + y^2 + 6y + 2$
10. $f(x, y) = 3x^2 + 6xy + 7y^2 - 2x + 4y$
11. $f(x, y) = 2x^2 + 3xy + 4y^2 - 5x + 2y$
12. $f(x, y) = 4x^2 - 6xy + 5y^2 - 20x + 26y$
13. $f(x, y) = x^2 - y^2 - 2x + 4y + 6$
14. $f(x, y) = x^2 - 2xy + 2y^2 - 2x + 2y + 1$
15. $f(x, y) = x^2 + 2xy$
16. $f(x, y) = 3 + 2x + 2y - 2x^2 - 2xy - y^2$
17. $f(x, y) = x^3 - y^3 - 2xy + 6$
18. $f(x, y) = x^3 + 3xy + y^3$
19. $f(x, y) = 6x^2 - 2x^3 + 3y^2 + 6xy$
20. $f(x, y) = 3y^2 - 2y^3 - 3x^2 + 6xy$
21. $f(x, y) = 9x^3 + y^3/3 - 4xy$
22. $f(x, y) = 8x^3 + y^3 + 6xy$
23. $f(x, y) = x^3 + y^3 + 3x^2 - 3y^2 - 8$
24. $f(x, y) = 2x^3 + 2y^3 - 9x^2 + 3y^2 - 12y$
25. $f(x, y) = 4xy - x^4 - y^4$
26. $f(x, y) = x^4 + y^4 + 4xy$
27. $f(x, y) = \dfrac{1}{x^2 + y^2 - 1}$
28. $f(x, y) = \dfrac{1}{x} + xy + \dfrac{1}{y}$
29. $f(x, y) = y \sin x$
30. $f(x, y) = e^{2x} \cos y$

Finding Absolute Extrema

In Exercises 31–38, find the absolute maxima and minima of the functions on the given domains.

31. $f(x, y) = 2x^2 - 4x + y^2 - 4y + 1$ on the closed triangular plate bounded by the lines $x = 0, y = 2, y = 2x$ in the first quadrant
32. $D(x, y) = x^2 - xy + y^2 + 1$ on the closed triangular plate in the first quadrant bounded by the lines $x = 0, y = 4, y = x$
33. $f(x, y) = x^2 + y^2$ on the closed triangular plate bounded by the lines $x = 0, y = 0, y + 2x = 2$ in the first quadrant
34. $T(x, y) = x^2 + xy + y^2 - 6x$ on the rectangular plate $0 \le x \le 5, -3 \le y \le 3$
35. $T(x, y) = x^2 + xy + y^2 - 6x + 2$ on the rectangular plate $0 \le x \le 5, -3 \le y \le 0$
36. $f(x, y) = 48xy - 32x^3 - 24y^2$ on the rectangular plate $0 \le x \le 1, 0 \le y \le 1$
37. $f(x, y) = (4x - x^2)\cos y$ on the rectangular plate $1 \le x \le 3$, $-\pi/4 \le y \le \pi/4$ (see accompanying figure).

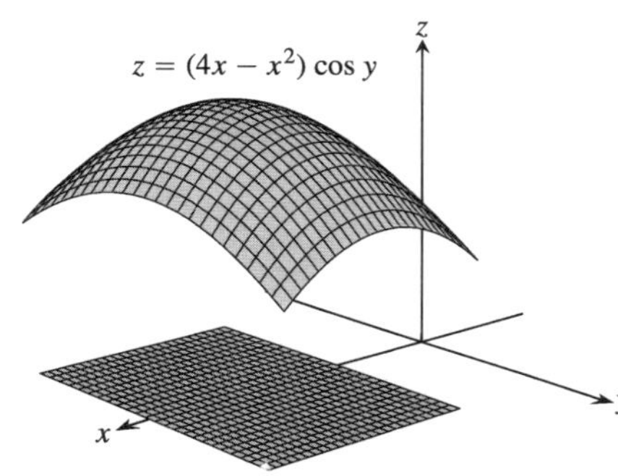

38. $f(x, y) = 4x - 8xy + 2y + 1$ on the triangular plate bounded by the lines $x = 0, y = 0, x + y = 1$ in the first quadrant
39. Find two numbers a and b with $a \le b$ such that
$$\int_a^b (6 - x - x^2)\,dx$$
has its largest value.
40. Find two numbers a and b with $a \le b$ such that
$$\int_a^b (24 - 2x - x^2)^{1/3}\,dx$$
has its largest value.
41. **Temperatures** The flat circular plate in Figure 14.46 has the shape of the region $x^2 + y^2 \le 1$. The plate, including the boundary where $x^2 + y^2 = 1$, is heated so that the temperature at the point (x, y) is
$$T(x, y) = x^2 + 2y^2 - x.$$
Find the temperatures at the hottest and coldest points on the plate.

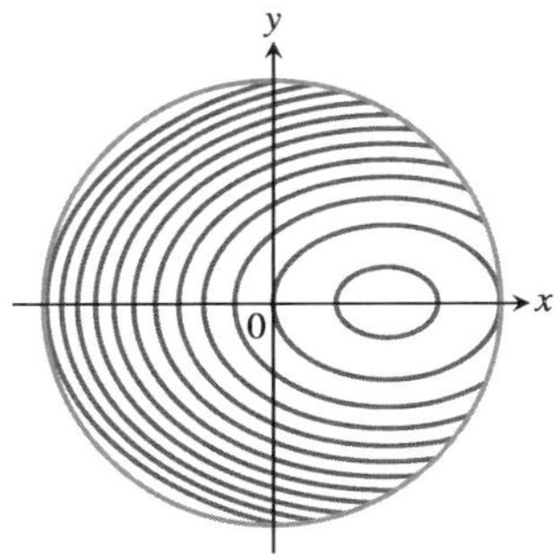

FIGURE 14.46 Curves of constant temperature are called isotherms. The figure shows isotherms of the temperature function $T(x, y) = x^2 + 2y^2 - x$ on the disk $x^2 + y^2 \leq 1$ in the xy-plane. Exercise 41 asks you to locate the extreme temperatures.

42. Find the critical point of

$$f(x, y) = xy + 2x - \ln x^2 y$$

in the open first quadrant $(x > 0, y > 0)$ and show that f takes on a minimum there (Figure 14.47).

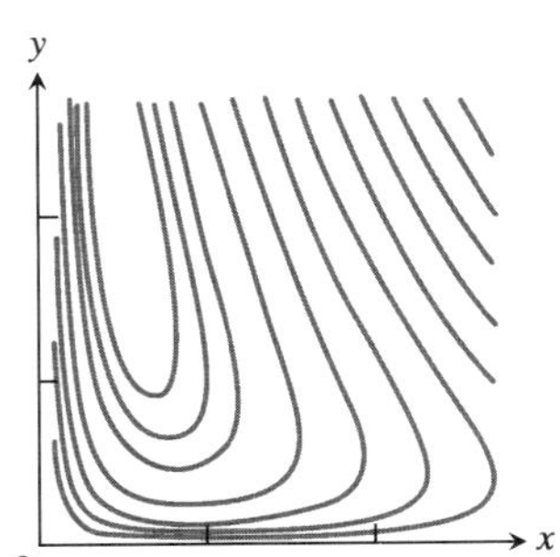

FIGURE 14.47 The function $f(x, y) = xy + 2x - \ln x^2 y$ (selected level curves shown here) takes on a minimum value somewhere in the open first quadrant $x > 0, y > 0$ (Exercise 42).

Theory and Examples

43. Find the maxima, minima, and saddle points of $f(x, y)$, if any, given that

a. $f_x = 2x - 4y$ and $f_y = 2y - 4x$

b. $f_x = 2x - 2$ and $f_y = 2y - 4$

c. $f_x = 9x^2 - 9$ and $f_y = 2y + 4$

Describe your reasoning in each case.

44. The discriminant $f_{xx}f_{yy} - f_{xy}^2$ is zero at the origin for each of the following functions, so the Second Derivative Test fails there. Determine whether the function has a maximum, a minimum, or neither at the origin by imagining what the surface $z = f(x, y)$ looks like. Describe your reasoning in each case.

a. $f(x, y) = x^2y^2$ **b.** $f(x, y) = 1 - x^2y^2$

c. $f(x, y) = xy^2$ **d.** $f(x, y) = x^3y^2$

e. $f(x, y) = x^3y^3$ **f.** $f(x, y) = x^4y^4$

45. Show that $(0, 0)$ is a critical point of $f(x, y) = x^2 + kxy + y^2$ no matter what value the constant k has. (*Hint:* Consider two cases: $k = 0$ and $k \neq 0$.)

46. For what values of the constant k does the Second Derivative Test guarantee that $f(x, y) = x^2 + kxy + y^2$ will have a saddle point at $(0, 0)$? A local minimum at $(0, 0)$? For what values of k is the Second Derivative Test inconclusive? Give reasons for your answers.

47. If $f_x(a, b) = f_y(a, b) = 0$, must f have a local maximum or minimum value at (a, b)? Give reasons for your answer.

48. Can you conclude anything about $f(a, b)$ if f and its first and second partial derivatives are continuous throughout a disk centered at the critical point (a, b) and $f_{xx}(a, b)$ and $f_{yy}(a, b)$ differ in sign? Give reasons for your answer.

49. Among all the points on the graph of $z = 10 - x^2 - y^2$ that lie above the plane $x + 2y + 3z = 0$, find the point farthest from the plane.

50. Find the point on the graph of $z = x^2 + y^2 + 10$ nearest the plane $x + 2y - z = 0$.

51. The function $f(x, y) = x + y$ fails to have an absolute maximum value in the closed first quadrant $x \geq 0$ and $y \geq 0$. Does this contradict the discussion on finding absolute extrema given in the text? Give reasons for your answer.

52. Consider the function $f(x, y) = x^2 + y^2 + 2xy - x - y + 1$ over the square $0 \leq x \leq 1$ and $0 \leq y \leq 1$.

a. Show that f has an absolute minimum along the line segment $2x + 2y = 1$ in this square. What *is* the absolute minimum value?

b. Find the absolute maximum value of f over the square.

Extreme Values on Parametrized Curves

To find the extreme values of a function $f(x, y)$ on a curve $x = x(t), y = y(t)$, we treat f as a function of the single variable t and use the Chain Rule to find where df/dt is zero. As in any other single-variable case, the extreme values of f are then found among the values at the

a. critical points (points where df/dt is zero or fails to exist), and

b. endpoints of the parameter domain.

Find the absolute maximum and minimum values of the following functions on the given curves.

53. Functions:

a. $f(x, y) = x + y$ **b.** $g(x, y) = xy$

c. $h(x, y) = 2x^2 + y^2$

Curves:

i. The semicircle $x^2 + y^2 = 4, \quad y \geq 0$

ii. The quarter circle $x^2 + y^2 = 4, \quad x \geq 0, \quad y \geq 0$

Use the parametric equations $x = 2\cos t, y = 2\sin t$.

54. Functions:

a. $f(x, y) = 2x + 3y$ **b.** $g(x, y) = xy$

c. $h(x, y) = x^2 + 3y^2$

Curves:

i. The semi-ellipse $(x^2/9) + (y^2/4) = 1, \quad y \geq 0$

ii. The quarter ellipse $(x^2/9) + (y^2/4) = 1, \quad x \geq 0, \quad y \geq 0$

Use the parametric equations $x = 3\cos t, y = 2\sin t$.

55. Function: $f(x, y) = xy$

Curves:

i. The line $x = 2t, \quad y = t + 1$

ii. The line segment $x = 2t, \quad y = t + 1, \quad -1 \leq t \leq 0$

iii. The line segment $x = 2t, \quad y = t + 1, \quad 0 \leq t \leq 1$

56. Functions:

a. $f(x, y) = x^2 + y^2$ **b.** $g(x, y) = 1/(x^2 + y^2)$

Curves:

i. The line $x = t, \quad y = 2 - 2t$

ii. The line segment $x = t, \quad y = 2 - 2t, \quad 0 \leq t \leq 1$

Least Squares and Regression Lines

When we try to fit a line $y = mx + b$ to a set of numerical data points $(x_1, y_1), (x_2, y_2), \ldots, (x_n, y_n)$ (Figure 14.48), we usually choose the line that minimizes the sum of the squares of the vertical distances from the points to the line. In theory, this means finding the values of m and b that minimize the value of the function

$$w = (mx_1 + b - y_1)^2 + \cdots + (mx_n + b - y_n)^2. \qquad (1)$$

The values of m and b that do this are found with the First and Second Derivative Tests to be

$$m = \frac{\left(\sum x_k\right)\left(\sum y_k\right) - n\sum x_k y_k}{\left(\sum x_k\right)^2 - n\sum x_k^2}, \qquad (2)$$

$$b = \frac{1}{n}\left(\sum y_k - m\sum x_k\right), \qquad (3)$$

with all sums running from $k = 1$ to $k = n$. Many scientific calculators have these formulas built in, enabling you to find m and b with only a few key strokes after you have entered the data.

The line $y = mx + b$ determined by these values of m and b is called the **least squares line, regression line,** or **trend line** for the data under study. Finding a least squares line lets you

1. summarize data with a simple expression,
2. predict values of y for other, experimentally untried values of x,
3. handle data analytically.

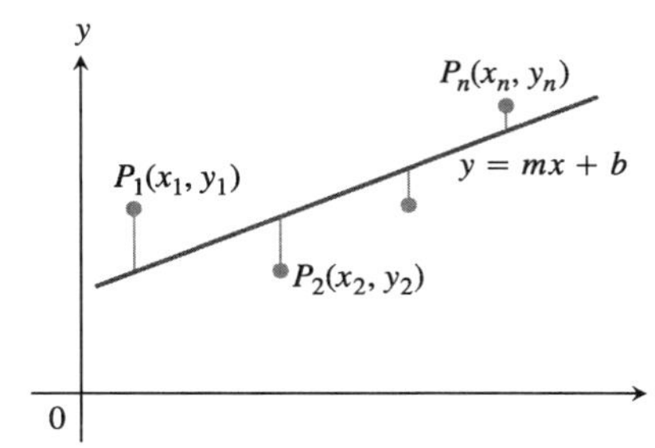

FIGURE 14.48 To fit a line to noncollinear points, we choose the line that minimizes the sum of the squares of the deviations.

EXAMPLE Find the least squares line for the points (0, 1), (1, 3), (2, 2), (3, 4), (4, 5).

Solution We organize the calculations in a table:

k	x_k	y_k	x_k^2	$x_k y_k$
1	0	1	0	0
2	1	3	1	3
3	2	2	4	4
4	3	4	9	12
5	4	5	16	20
Σ	10	15	30	39

Then we find

$$m = \frac{(10)(15) - 5(39)}{(10)^2 - 5(30)} = 0.9$$ Equation (2) with $n = 5$ and data from the table

and use the value of m to find

$$b = \frac{1}{5}\left(15 - (0.9)(10)\right) = 1.2.$$ Equation (3) with $n = 5, m = 0.9$

The least squares line is $y = 0.9x + 1.2$ (Figure 14.49). ■

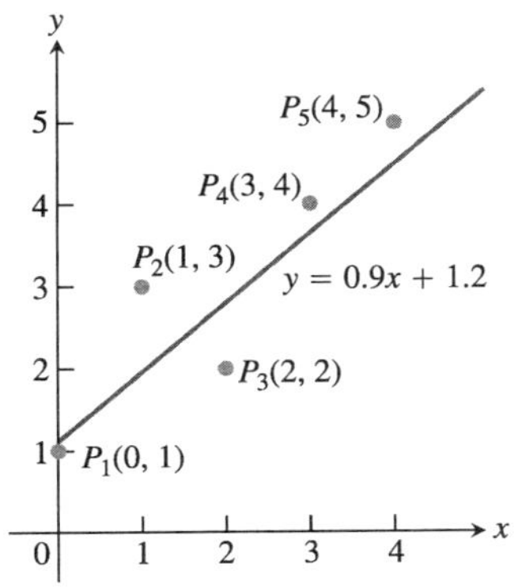

FIGURE 14.49 The least squares line for the data in the example.

In Exercises 57–60, use Equations (2) and (3) to find the least squares line for each set of data points. Then use the linear equation you obtain to predict the value of y that would correspond to $x = 4$.

57. $(-1, 2),\ (0, 1),\ (3, -4)$ **58.** $(-2, 0),\ (0, 2),\ (2, 3)$

59. $(0, 0), (1, 2), (2, 3)$ **60.** $(0, 1), (2, 2), (3, 2)$

T **61.** Write a linear equation for the effect of irrigation on the yield of alfalfa by fitting a least squares line to the data in Table 14.1 (from the University of California Experimental Station, *Bulletin* No. 450, p. 8). Plot the data and draw the line.

TABLE 14.1 Growth of alfalfa

x (total seasonal depth of water applied, in.)	y (average alfalfa yield, tons/acre)
12	5.27
18	5.68
24	6.25
30	7.21
36	8.20
42	8.71

T **62. Craters of Mars** One theory of crater formation suggests that the frequency of large craters should fall off as the square of the diameter (Marcus, *Science*, June 21, 1968, p. 1334). Pictures from *Mariner IV* show the frequencies listed in Table 14.2. Fit a line of the form $F = m(1/D^2) + b$ to the data. Plot the data and draw the line.

TABLE 14.2 Crater sizes on Mars

Diameter in km, D	$1/D^2$ (for left value of class interval)	Frequency, F
32–45	0.001	51
45–64	0.0005	22
64–90	0.00024	14
90–128	0.000123	4

T **63. Köchel numbers** In 1862, the German musicologist Ludwig von Köchel made a chronological list of the musical works of Wolfgang Amadeus Mozart. This list is the source of the Köchel numbers, or "K numbers," that now accompany the titles of Mozart's pieces (Sinfonia Concertante in E-flat major, K.364, for example). Table 14.3 gives the Köchel numbers and composition dates (y) of ten of Mozart's works.

a. Plot y vs. K to show that y is close to being a linear function of K.

b. Find a least squares line $y = m\text{K} + b$ for the data and add the line to your plot in part (a).

c. K.364 was composed in 1779. What date is predicted by the least squares line?

TABLE 14.3 Compositions by Mozart

Köchel number, K	Year composed, y
1	1761
75	1771
155	1772
219	1775
271	1777
351	1780
425	1783
503	1786
575	1789
626	1791

T **64. Submarine sinkings** The data in Table 14.4 show the results of a historical study of German submarines sunk by the U.S. Navy during 16 consecutive months of World War II. The data given for each month are the number of reported sinkings and the number of actual sinkings. The number of submarines sunk was slightly greater than the Navy's reports implied. Find a least squares line for estimating the number of actual sinkings from the number of reported sinkings.

TABLE 14.4 Sinkings of German submarines by U.S. during 16 consecutive months of WWII

Month	Guesses by U.S. (reported sinkings) x	Actual number y
1	3	3
2	2	2
3	4	6
4	2	3
5	5	4
6	5	3
7	9	11
8	12	9
9	8	10
10	13	16
11	14	13
12	3	5
13	4	6
14	13	19
15	10	15
16	16	15
	123	140

COMPUTER EXPLORATIONS

Exploring Local Extrema at Critical Points

In Exercises 65–70, you will explore functions to identify their local extrema. Use a CAS to perform the following steps:

a. Plot the function over the given rectangle.

b. Plot some level curves in the rectangle.

c. Calculate the function's first partial derivatives and use the CAS equation solver to find the critical points. How do the critical points relate to the level curves plotted in part (b)? Which critical points, if any, appear to give a saddle point? Give reasons for your answer.

d. Calculate the function's second partial derivatives and find the discriminant $f_{xx}f_{yy} - f_{xy}^2$.

e. Using the max-min tests, classify the critical points found in part (c). Are your findings consistent with your discussion in part (c)?

65. $f(x, y) = x^2 + y^3 - 3xy, \quad -5 \le x \le 5, \quad -5 \le y \le 5$

66. $f(x, y) = x^3 - 3xy^2 + y^2, \quad -2 \le x \le 2, \quad -2 \le y \le 2$

67. $f(x, y) = x^4 + y^2 - 8x^2 - 6y + 16, \quad -3 \le x \le 3, \quad -6 \le y \le 6$

68. $f(x, y) = 2x^4 + y^4 - 2x^2 - 2y^2 + 3, \quad -3/2 \le x \le 3/2, \quad -3/2 \le y \le 3/2$

69. $f(x, y) = 5x^6 + 18x^5 - 30x^4 + 30xy^2 - 120x^3, \quad -4 \le x \le 3, \quad -2 \le y \le 2$

70. $f(x, y) = \begin{cases} x^5 \ln(x^2 + y^2), & (x, y) \ne (0, 0) \\ 0, & (x, y) = (0, 0) \end{cases}$, $\quad -2 \le x \le 2, \quad -2 \le y \le 2$

14.8 Lagrange Multipliers

HISTORICAL BIOGRAPHY

Joseph Louis Lagrange (1736–1813)

Sometimes we need to find the extreme values of a function whose domain is constrained to lie within some particular subset of the plane—a disk, for example, a closed triangular region, or along a curve. In this section, we explore a powerful method for finding extreme values of constrained functions: the method of *Lagrange multipliers*.

Constrained Maxima and Minima

EXAMPLE 1 Finding a Minimum with Constraint

Find the point $P(x, y, z)$ closest to the origin on the plane $2x + y - z - 5 = 0$.

Solution The problem asks us to find the minimum value of the function

$$\begin{aligned} |\overrightarrow{OP}| &= \sqrt{(x-0)^2 + (y-0)^2 + (z-0)^2} \\ &= \sqrt{x^2 + y^2 + z^2} \end{aligned}$$

subject to the constraint that

$$2x + y - z - 5 = 0.$$

Since $|\overrightarrow{OP}|$ has a minimum value wherever the function

$$f(x, y, z) = x^2 + y^2 + z^2$$

has a minimum value, we may solve the problem by finding the minimum value of $f(x, y, z)$ subject to the constraint $2x + y - z - 5 = 0$ (thus avoiding square roots). If we regard x and y as the independent variables in this equation and write z as

$$z = 2x + y - 5,$$

our problem reduces to one of finding the points (x, y) at which the function

$$h(x, y) = f(x, y, 2x + y - 5) = x^2 + y^2 + (2x + y - 5)^2$$

has its minimum value or values. Since the domain of h is the entire xy-plane, the First Derivative Test of Section 14.7 tells us that any minima that h might have must occur at points where

$$h_x = 2x + 2(2x + y - 5)(2) = 0, \qquad h_y = 2y + 2(2x + y - 5) = 0.$$

This leads to

$$10x + 4y = 20, \qquad 4x + 4y = 10,$$

and the solution

$$x = \frac{5}{3}, \qquad y = \frac{5}{6}.$$

We may apply a geometric argument together with the Second Derivative Test to show that these values minimize h. The z-coordinate of the corresponding point on the plane $z = 2x + y - 5$ is

$$z = 2\left(\frac{5}{3}\right) + \frac{5}{6} - 5 = -\frac{5}{6}.$$

Therefore, the point we seek is

$$\text{Closest point:} \qquad P\left(\frac{5}{3}, \frac{5}{6}, -\frac{5}{6}\right).$$

The distance from P to the origin is $5/\sqrt{6} \approx 2.04$. ■

Attempts to solve a constrained maximum or minimum problem by substitution, as we might call the method of Example 1, do not always go smoothly. This is one of the reasons for learning the new method of this section.

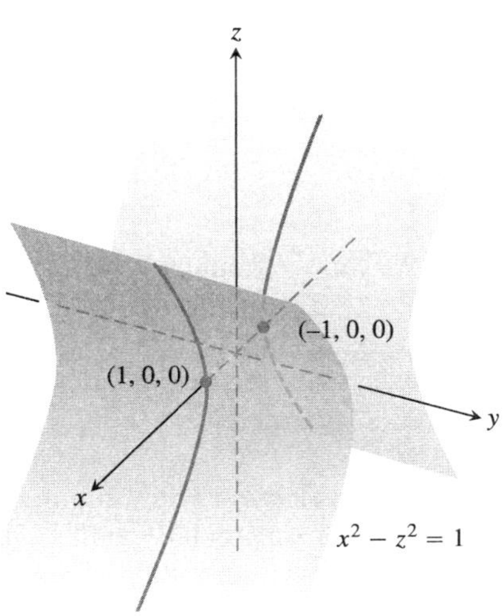

FIGURE 14.50 The hyperbolic cylinder $x^2 - z^2 - 1 = 0$ in Example 2.

EXAMPLE 2 Finding a Minimum with Constraint

Find the points closest to the origin on the hyperbolic cylinder $x^2 - z^2 - 1 = 0$.

Solution 1 The cylinder is shown in Figure 14.50. We seek the points on the cylinder closest to the origin. These are the points whose coordinates minimize the value of the function

$$f(x, y, z) = x^2 + y^2 + z^2 \qquad \text{Square of the distance}$$

subject to the constraint that $x^2 - z^2 - 1 = 0$. If we regard x and y as independent variables in the constraint equation, then

$$z^2 = x^2 - 1$$

and the values of $f(x, y, z) = x^2 + y^2 + z^2$ on the cylinder are given by the function

$$h(x, y) = x^2 + y^2 + (x^2 - 1) = 2x^2 + y^2 - 1.$$

To find the points on the cylinder whose coordinates minimize f, we look for the points in the xy-plane whose coordinates minimize h. The only extreme value of h occurs where

$$h_x = 4x = 0 \qquad \text{and} \qquad h_y = 2y = 0,$$

that is, at the point (0, 0). But there are no points on the cylinder where both x and y are zero. What went wrong?

What happened was that the First Derivative Test found (as it should have) the point *in the domain of h* where h has a minimum value. We, on the other hand, want the points *on the cylinder* where h has a minimum value. Although the domain of h is the entire xy-plane, the domain from which we can select the first two coordinates of the points (x, y, z) on the cylinder is restricted to the "shadow" of the cylinder on the xy-plane; it does not include the band between the lines $x = -1$ and $x = 1$ (Figure 14.51).

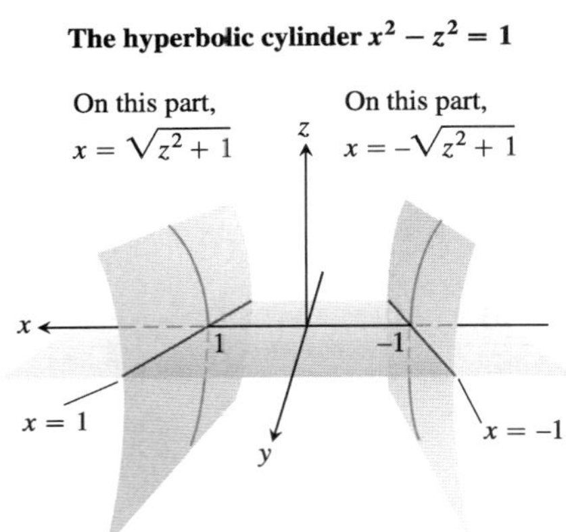

FIGURE 14.51 The region in the xy-plane from which the first two coordinates of the points (x, y, z) on the hyperbolic cylinder $x^2 - z^2 = 1$ are selected excludes the band $-1 < x < 1$ in the xy-plane (Example 2).

We can avoid this problem if we treat y and z as independent variables (instead of x and y) and express x in terms of y and z as

$$x^2 = z^2 + 1.$$

With this substitution, $f(x, y, z) = x^2 + y^2 + z^2$ becomes

$$k(y, z) = (z^2 + 1) + y^2 + z^2 = 1 + y^2 + 2z^2$$

and we look for the points where k takes on its smallest value. The domain of k in the yz-plane now matches the domain from which we select the y- and z-coordinates of the points (x, y, z) on the cylinder. Hence, the points that minimize k in the plane will have corresponding points on the cylinder. The smallest values of k occur where

$$k_y = 2y = 0 \qquad \text{and} \qquad k_z = 4z = 0,$$

or where $y = z = 0$. This leads to

$$x^2 = z^2 + 1 = 1, \qquad x = \pm 1.$$

The corresponding points on the cylinder are $(\pm 1, 0, 0)$. We can see from the inequality

$$k(y, z) = 1 + y^2 + 2z^2 \geq 1$$

that the points $(\pm 1, 0, 0)$ give a minimum value for k. We can also see that the minimum distance from the origin to a point on the cylinder is 1 unit.

Solution 2 Another way to find the points on the cylinder closest to the origin is to imagine a small sphere centered at the origin expanding like a soap bubble until it just touches the cylinder (Figure 14.52). At each point of contact, the cylinder and sphere have the same tangent plane and normal line. Therefore, if the sphere and cylinder are represented as the level surfaces obtained by setting

$$f(x, y, z) = x^2 + y^2 + z^2 - a^2 \qquad \text{and} \qquad g(x, y, z) = x^2 - z^2 - 1$$

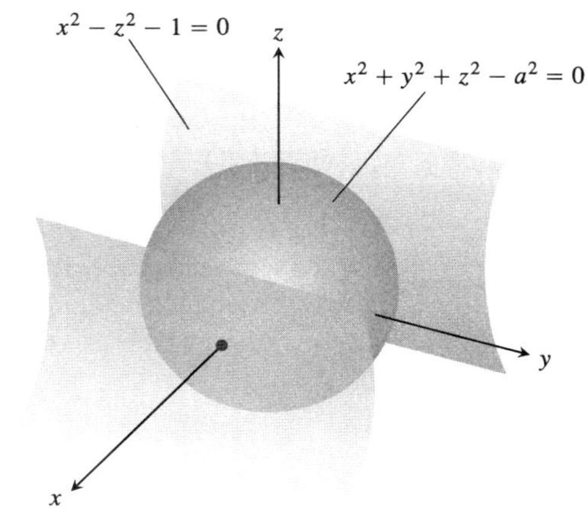

FIGURE 14.52 A sphere expanding like a soap bubble centered at the origin until it just touches the hyperbolic cylinder $x^2 - z^2 - 1 = 0$ (Example 2).

equal to 0, then the gradients ∇f and ∇g will be parallel where the surfaces touch. At any point of contact, we should therefore be able to find a scalar λ ("lambda") such that

$$\nabla f = \lambda \nabla g,$$

or

$$2x\mathbf{i} + 2y\mathbf{j} + 2z\mathbf{k} = \lambda(2x\mathbf{i} - 2z\mathbf{k}).$$

Thus, the coordinates x, y, and z of any point of tangency will have to satisfy the three scalar equations

$$2x = 2\lambda x, \qquad 2y = 0, \qquad 2z = -2\lambda z.$$

For what values of λ will a point (x, y, z) whose coordinates satisfy these scalar equations also lie on the surface $x^2 - z^2 - 1 = 0$? To answer this question, we use our knowledge that no point on the surface has a zero x-coordinate to conclude that $x \neq 0$. Hence, $2x = 2\lambda x$ only if

$$2 = 2\lambda, \qquad \text{or} \qquad \lambda = 1.$$

For $\lambda = 1$, the equation $2z = -2\lambda z$ becomes $2z = -2z$. If this equation is to be satisfied as well, z must be zero. Since $y = 0$ also (from the equation $2y = 0$), we conclude that the points we seek all have coordinates of the form

$$(x, 0, 0).$$

What points on the surface $x^2 - z^2 = 1$ have coordinates of this form? The answer is the points $(x, 0, 0)$ for which

$$x^2 - (0)^2 = 1, \qquad x^2 = 1, \qquad \text{or} \qquad x = \pm 1.$$

The points on the cylinder closest to the origin are the points $(\pm 1, 0, 0)$. ■

The Method of Lagrange Multipliers

In Solution 2 of Example 2, we used the **method of Lagrange multipliers**. The method says that the extreme values of a function $f(x, y, z)$ whose variables are subject to a constraint $g(x, y, z) = 0$ are to be found on the surface $g = 0$ at the points where

$$\nabla f = \lambda \nabla g$$

for some scalar λ (called a **Lagrange multiplier**).

To explore the method further and see why it works, we first make the following observation, which we state as a theorem.

THEOREM 12 The Orthogonal Gradient Theorem
Suppose that $f(x, y, z)$ is differentiable in a region whose interior contains a smooth curve

$$C: \quad \mathbf{r}(t) = g(t)\mathbf{i} + h(t)\mathbf{j} + k(t)\mathbf{k}.$$

If P_0 is a point on C where f has a local maximum or minimum relative to its values on C, then ∇f is orthogonal to C at P_0.

Proof We show that ∇f is orthogonal to the curve's velocity vector at P_0. The values of f on C are given by the composite $f(g(t), h(t), k(t))$, whose derivative with respect to t is

$$\frac{df}{dt} = \frac{\partial f}{\partial x}\frac{dg}{dt} + \frac{\partial f}{\partial y}\frac{dh}{dt} + \frac{\partial f}{\partial z}\frac{dk}{dt} = \nabla f \cdot \mathbf{v}.$$

At any point P_0 where f has a local maximum or minimum relative to its values on the curve, $df/dt = 0$, so

$$\nabla f \cdot \mathbf{v} = 0. \qquad \blacksquare$$

By dropping the z-terms in Theorem 12, we obtain a similar result for functions of two variables.

COROLLARY OF THEOREM 12
At the points on a smooth curve $\mathbf{r}(t) = g(t)\mathbf{i} + h(t)\mathbf{j}$ where a differentiable function $f(x, y)$ takes on its local maxima and minima relative to its values on the curve, $\nabla f \cdot \mathbf{v} = 0$, where $\mathbf{v} = d\mathbf{r}/dt$.

Theorem 12 is the key to the method of Lagrange multipliers. Suppose that $f(x, y, z)$ and $g(x, y, z)$ are differentiable and that P_0 is a point on the surface $g(x, y, z) = 0$ where f has a local maximum or minimum value relative to its other values on the surface. Then f takes on a local maximum or minimum at P_0 relative to its values on every differentiable curve through P_0 on the surface $g(x, y, z) = 0$. Therefore, ∇f is orthogonal to the velocity vector of every such differentiable curve through P_0. So is ∇g, moreover (because ∇g is orthogonal to the level surface $g = 0$, as we saw in Section 14.5). Therefore, at P_0, ∇f is some scalar multiple λ of ∇g.

> **The Method of Lagrange Multipliers**
> Suppose that $f(x, y, z)$ and $g(x, y, z)$ are differentiable and $\nabla g \neq \mathbf{0}$ when $g(x, y, z) = 0$. To find the local maximum and minimum values of f subject to the constraint $g(x, y, z) = 0$ (if these exist), find the values of x, y, z, and λ that simultaneously satisfy the equations
> $$\nabla f = \lambda \nabla g \quad \text{and} \quad g(x, y, z) = 0. \tag{1}$$
> For functions of two independent variables, the condition is similar, but without the variable z.

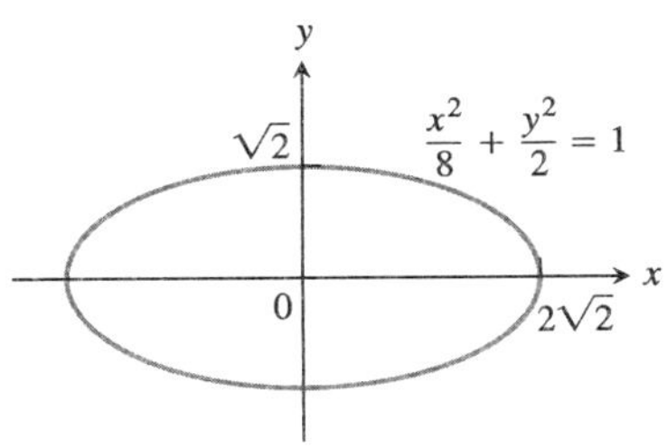

FIGURE 14.53 Example 3 shows how to find the largest and smallest values of the product xy on this ellipse.

EXAMPLE 3 Using the Method of Lagrange Multipliers

Find the greatest and smallest values that the function
$$f(x, y) = xy$$
takes on the ellipse (Figure 14.53)
$$\frac{x^2}{8} + \frac{y^2}{2} = 1.$$

Solution We want the extreme values of $f(x, y) = xy$ subject to the constraint
$$g(x, y) = \frac{x^2}{8} + \frac{y^2}{2} - 1 = 0.$$
To do so, we first find the values of x, y, and λ for which
$$\nabla f = \lambda \nabla g \quad \text{and} \quad g(x, y) = 0.$$
The gradient equation in Equations (1) gives
$$y\mathbf{i} + x\mathbf{j} = \frac{\lambda}{4}x\mathbf{i} + \lambda y\mathbf{j},$$
from which we find
$$y = \frac{\lambda}{4}x, \quad x = \lambda y, \quad \text{and} \quad y = \frac{\lambda}{4}(\lambda y) = \frac{\lambda^2}{4}y,$$
so that $y = 0$ or $\lambda = \pm 2$. We now consider these two cases.

Case 1: If $y = 0$, then $x = y = 0$. But $(0, 0)$ is not on the ellipse. Hence, $y \neq 0$.
Case 2: If $y \neq 0$, then $\lambda = \pm 2$ and $x = \pm 2y$. Substituting this in the equation $g(x, y) = 0$ gives
$$\frac{(\pm 2y)^2}{8} + \frac{y^2}{2} = 1, \quad 4y^2 + 4y^2 = 8 \quad \text{and} \quad y = \pm 1.$$
The function $f(x, y) = xy$ therefore takes on its extreme values on the ellipse at the four points $(\pm 2, 1)$, $(\pm 2, -1)$. The extreme values are $xy = 2$ and $xy = -2$.

The Geometry of the Solution

The level curves of the function $f(x, y) = xy$ are the hyperbolas $xy = c$ (Figure 14.54). The farther the hyperbolas lie from the origin, the larger the absolute value of f. We want

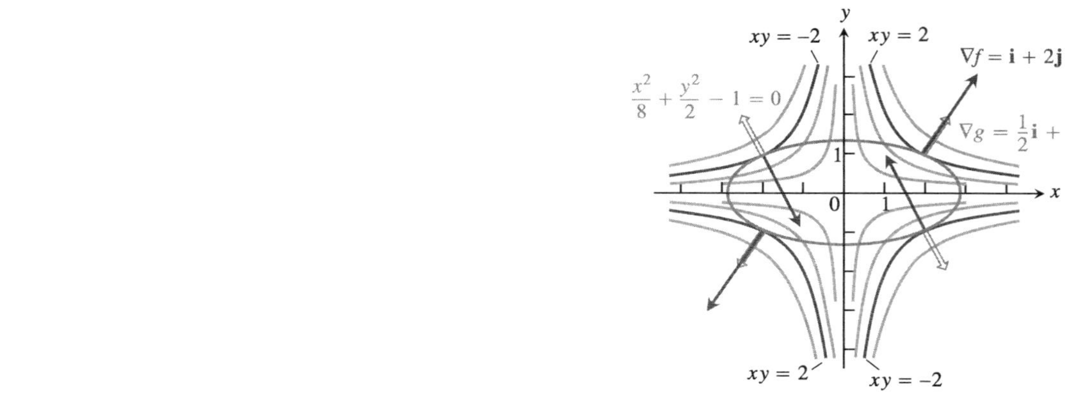

FIGURE 14.54 When subjected to the constraint $g(x, y) = x^2/8 + y^2/2 - 1 = 0$, the function $f(x, y) = xy$ takes on extreme values at the four points $(\pm 2, \pm 1)$. These are the points on the ellipse when ∇f (red) is a scalar multiple of ∇g (blue) (Example 3).

to find the extreme values of $f(x, y)$, given that the point (x, y) also lies on the ellipse $x^2 + 4y^2 = 8$. Which hyperbolas intersecting the ellipse lie farthest from the origin? The hyperbolas that just graze the ellipse, the ones that are tangent to it, are farthest. At these points, any vector normal to the hyperbola is normal to the ellipse, so $\nabla f = y\mathbf{i} + x\mathbf{j}$ is a multiple $(\lambda = \pm 2)$ of $\nabla g = (x/4)\mathbf{i} + y\mathbf{j}$. At the point (2, 1), for example,

$$\nabla f = \mathbf{i} + 2\mathbf{j}, \qquad \nabla g = \frac{1}{2}\mathbf{i} + \mathbf{j}, \qquad \text{and} \qquad \nabla f = 2\nabla g.$$

At the point $(-2, 1)$,

$$\nabla f = \mathbf{i} - 2\mathbf{j}, \qquad \nabla g = -\frac{1}{2}\mathbf{i} + \mathbf{j}, \qquad \text{and} \qquad \nabla f = -2\nabla g.$$ ■

EXAMPLE 4 Finding Extreme Function Values on a Circle

Find the maximum and minimum values of the function $f(x, y) = 3x + 4y$ on the circle $x^2 + y^2 = 1$.

Solution We model this as a Lagrange multiplier problem with

$$f(x, y) = 3x + 4y, \qquad g(x, y) = x^2 + y^2 - 1$$

and look for the values of x, y, and λ that satisfy the equations

$$\nabla f = \lambda \nabla g: \quad 3\mathbf{i} + 4\mathbf{j} = 2x\lambda\mathbf{i} + 2y\lambda\mathbf{j}$$
$$g(x, y) = 0: \quad x^2 + y^2 - 1 = 0.$$

The gradient equation in Equations (1) implies that $\lambda \neq 0$ and gives

$$x = \frac{3}{2\lambda}, \qquad y = \frac{2}{\lambda}.$$

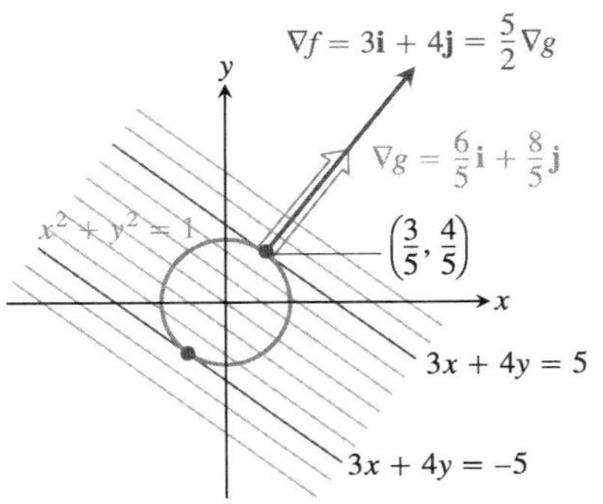

FIGURE 14.55 The function $f(x, y) = 3x + 4y$ takes on its largest value on the unit circle $g(x, y) = x^2 + y^2 - 1 = 0$ at the point $(3/5, 4/5)$ and its smallest value at the point $(-3/5, -4/5)$ (Example 4). At each of these points, ∇f is a scalar multiple of ∇g. The figure shows the gradients at the first point but not the second.

These equations tell us, among other things, that x and y have the same sign. With these values for x and y, the equation $g(x, y) = 0$ gives

$$\left(\frac{3}{2\lambda}\right)^2 + \left(\frac{2}{\lambda}\right)^2 - 1 = 0,$$

so

$$\frac{9}{4\lambda^2} + \frac{4}{\lambda^2} = 1, \qquad 9 + 16 = 4\lambda^2, \qquad 4\lambda^2 = 25, \qquad \text{and} \qquad \lambda = \pm\frac{5}{2}.$$

Thus,

$$x = \frac{3}{2\lambda} = \pm\frac{3}{5}, \qquad y = \frac{2}{\lambda} = \pm\frac{4}{5},$$

and $f(x, y) = 3x + 4y$ has extreme values at $(x, y) = \pm(3/5, 4/5)$.

By calculating the value of $3x + 4y$ at the points $\pm(3/5, 4/5)$, we see that its maximum and minimum values on the circle $x^2 + y^2 = 1$ are

$$3\left(\frac{3}{5}\right) + 4\left(\frac{4}{5}\right) = \frac{25}{5} = 5 \qquad \text{and} \qquad 3\left(-\frac{3}{5}\right) + 4\left(-\frac{4}{5}\right) = -\frac{25}{5} = -5.$$

The Geometry of the Solution

The level curves of $f(x, y) = 3x + 4y$ are the lines $3x + 4y = c$ (Figure 14.55). The farther the lines lie from the origin, the larger the absolute value of f. We want to find the extreme values of $f(x, y)$ given that the point (x, y) also lies on the circle $x^2 + y^2 = 1$. Which lines intersecting the circle lie farthest from the origin? The lines tangent to the circle are farthest. At the points of tangency, any vector normal to the line is normal to the circle, so the gradient $\nabla f = 3\mathbf{i} + 4\mathbf{j}$ is a multiple $(\lambda = \pm 5/2)$ of the gradient $\nabla g = 2x\mathbf{i} + 2y\mathbf{j}$. At the point $(3/5, 4/5)$, for example,

$$\nabla f = 3\mathbf{i} + 4\mathbf{j}, \qquad \nabla g = \frac{6}{5}\mathbf{i} + \frac{8}{5}\mathbf{j}, \qquad \text{and} \qquad \nabla f = \frac{5}{2}\nabla g. \qquad ■$$

Lagrange Multipliers with Two Constraints

Many problems require us to find the extreme values of a differentiable function $f(x, y, z)$ whose variables are subject to two constraints. If the constraints are

$$g_1(x, y, z) = 0 \qquad \text{and} \qquad g_2(x, y, z) = 0$$

and g_1 and g_2 are differentiable, with ∇g_1 not parallel to ∇g_2, we find the constrained local maxima and minima of f by introducing two Lagrange multipliers λ and μ (mu, pronounced "mew"). That is, we locate the points $P(x, y, z)$ where f takes on its constrained extreme values by finding the values of x, y, z, λ, and μ that simultaneously satisfy the equations

$$\boxed{\nabla f = \lambda \nabla g_1 + \mu \nabla g_2, \qquad g_1(x, y, z) = 0, \qquad g_2(x, y, z) = 0} \qquad (2)$$

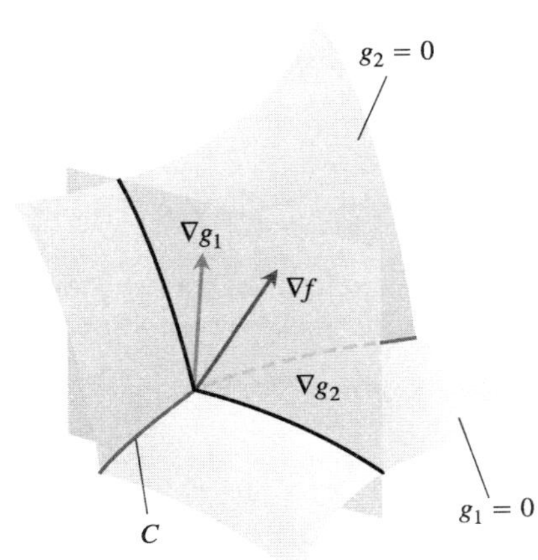

FIGURE 14.56 The vectors ∇g_1 and ∇g_2 lie in a plane perpendicular to the curve C because ∇g_1 is normal to the surface $g_1 = 0$ and ∇g_2 is normal to the surface $g_2 = 0$.

Equations (2) have a nice geometric interpretation. The surfaces $g_1 = 0$ and $g_2 = 0$ (usually) intersect in a smooth curve, say C (Figure 14.56). Along this curve we seek the points where f has local maximum and minimum values relative to its other values on the curve.

These are the points where ∇f is normal to C, as we saw in Theorem 12. But ∇g_1 and ∇g_2 are also normal to C at these points because C lies in the surfaces $g_1 = 0$ and $g_2 = 0$. Therefore, ∇f lies in the plane determined by ∇g_1 and ∇g_2, which means that $\nabla f = \lambda \nabla g_1 + \mu \nabla g_2$ for some λ and μ. Since the points we seek also lie in both surfaces, their coordinates must satisfy the equations $g_1(x, y, z) = 0$ and $g_2(x, y, z) = 0$, which are the remaining requirements in Equations (2).

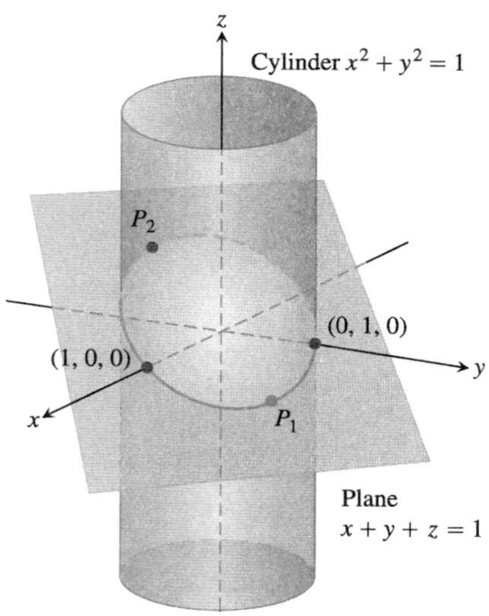

FIGURE 14.57 On the ellipse where the plane and cylinder meet, what are the points closest to and farthest from the origin? (Example 5)

EXAMPLE 5 Finding Extremes of Distance on an Ellipse

The plane $x + y + z = 1$ cuts the cylinder $x^2 + y^2 = 1$ in an ellipse (Figure 14.57). Find the points on the ellipse that lie closest to and farthest from the origin.

Solution We find the extreme values of

$$f(x, y, z) = x^2 + y^2 + z^2$$

(the square of the distance from (x, y, z) to the origin) subject to the constraints

$$g_1(x, y, z) = x^2 + y^2 - 1 = 0 \tag{3}$$

$$g_2(x, y, z) = x + y + z - 1 = 0. \tag{4}$$

The gradient equation in Equations (2) then gives

$$\nabla f = \lambda \nabla g_1 + \mu \nabla g_2$$

$$2x\mathbf{i} + 2y\mathbf{j} + 2z\mathbf{k} = \lambda(2x\mathbf{i} + 2y\mathbf{j}) + \mu(\mathbf{i} + \mathbf{j} + \mathbf{k})$$

$$2x\mathbf{i} + 2y\mathbf{j} + 2z\mathbf{k} = (2\lambda x + \mu)\mathbf{i} + (2\lambda y + \mu)\mathbf{j} + \mu\mathbf{k}$$

or

$$2x = 2\lambda x + \mu, \qquad 2y = 2\lambda y + \mu, \qquad 2z = \mu. \tag{5}$$

The scalar equations in Equations (5) yield

$$\begin{aligned} 2x &= 2\lambda x + 2z \Rightarrow (1 - \lambda)x = z, \\ 2y &= 2\lambda y + 2z \Rightarrow (1 - \lambda)y = z. \end{aligned} \tag{6}$$

Equations (6) are satisfied simultaneously if either $\lambda = 1$ and $z = 0$ or $\lambda \neq 1$ and $x = y = z/(1 - \lambda)$.

If $z = 0$, then solving Equations (3) and (4) simultaneously to find the corresponding points on the ellipse gives the two points $(1, 0, 0)$ and $(0, 1, 0)$. This makes sense when you look at Figure 14.57.

If $x = y$, then Equations (3) and (4) give

$$\begin{aligned} x^2 + x^2 - 1 &= 0 & x + x + z - 1 &= 0 \\ 2x^2 &= 1 & z &= 1 - 2x \\ x &= \pm\frac{\sqrt{2}}{2} & z &= 1 \mp \sqrt{2}. \end{aligned}$$

The corresponding points on the ellipse are

$$P_1 = \left(\frac{\sqrt{2}}{2}, \frac{\sqrt{2}}{2}, 1 - \sqrt{2}\right) \quad \text{and} \quad P_2 = \left(-\frac{\sqrt{2}}{2}, -\frac{\sqrt{2}}{2}, 1 + \sqrt{2}\right).$$

Here we need to be careful, however. Although P_1 and P_2 both give local maxima of f on the ellipse, P_2 is farther from the origin than P_1.

The points on the ellipse closest to the origin are (1, 0, 0) and (0, 1, 0). The point on the ellipse farthest from the origin is P_2. ■

EXERCISES 14.8

Two Independent Variables with One Constraint

1. **Extrema on an ellipse** Find the points on the ellipse $x^2 + 2y^2 = 1$ where $f(x, y) = xy$ has its extreme values.
2. **Extrema on a circle** Find the extreme values of $f(x, y) = xy$ subject to the constraint $g(x, y) = x^2 + y^2 - 10 = 0$.
3. **Maximum on a line** Find the maximum value of $f(x, y) = 49 - x^2 - y^2$ on the line $x + 3y = 10$.
4. **Extrema on a line** Find the local extreme values of $f(x, y) = x^2y$ on the line $x + y = 3$.
5. **Constrained minimum** Find the points on the curve $xy^2 = 54$ nearest the origin.
6. **Constrained minimum** Find the points on the curve $x^2y = 2$ nearest the origin.
7. Use the method of Lagrange multipliers to find
   a. **Minimum on a hyperbola** The minimum value of $x + y$, subject to the constraints $xy = 16, x > 0, y > 0$
   b. **Maximum on a line** The maximum value of xy, subject to the constraint $x + y = 16$.

   Comment on the geometry of each solution.
8. **Extrema on a curve** Find the points on the curve $x^2 + xy + y^2 = 1$ in the xy-plane that are nearest to and farthest from the origin.
9. **Minimum surface area with fixed volume** Find the dimensions of the closed right circular cylindrical can of smallest surface area whose volume is $16\pi\ \text{cm}^3$.
10. **Cylinder in a sphere** Find the radius and height of the open right circular cylinder of largest surface area that can be inscribed in a sphere of radius a. What *is* the largest surface area?
11. **Rectangle of greatest area in an ellipse** Use the method of Lagrange multipliers to find the dimensions of the rectangle of greatest area that can be inscribed in the ellipse $x^2/16 + y^2/9 = 1$ with sides parallel to the coordinate axes.
12. **Rectangle of longest perimeter in an ellipse** Find the dimensions of the rectangle of largest perimeter that can be inscribed in the ellipse $x^2/a^2 + y^2/b^2 = 1$ with sides parallel to the coordinate axes. What *is* the largest perimeter?
13. **Extrema on a circle** Find the maximum and minimum values of $x^2 + y^2$ subject to the constraint $x^2 - 2x + y^2 - 4y = 0$.
14. **Extrema on a circle** Find the maximum and minimum values of $3x - y + 6$ subject to the constraint $x^2 + y^2 = 4$.
15. **Ant on a metal plate** The temperature at a point (x, y) on a metal plate is $T(x, y) = 4x^2 - 4xy + y^2$. An ant on the plate walks around the circle of radius 5 centered at the origin. What are the highest and lowest temperatures encountered by the ant?
16. **Cheapest storage tank** Your firm has been asked to design a storage tank for liquid petroleum gas. The customer's specifications call for a cylindrical tank with hemispherical ends, and the tank is to hold 8000 m^3 of gas. The customer also wants to use the smallest amount of material possible in building the tank. What radius and height do you recommend for the cylindrical portion of the tank?

Three Independent Variables with One Constraint

17. **Minimum distance to a point** Find the point on the plane $x + 2y + 3z = 13$ closest to the point (1, 1, 1).
18. **Maximum distance to a point** Find the point on the sphere $x^2 + y^2 + z^2 = 4$ farthest from the point $(1, -1, 1)$.
19. **Minimum distance to the origin** Find the minimum distance from the surface $x^2 - y^2 - z^2 = 1$ to the origin.
20. **Minimum distance to the origin** Find the point on the surface $z = xy + 1$ nearest the origin.
21. **Minimum distance to the origin** Find the points on the surface $z^2 = xy + 4$ closest to the origin.
22. **Minimum distance to the origin** Find the point(s) on the surface $xyz = 1$ closest to the origin.
23. **Extrema on a sphere** Find the maximum and minimum values of

$$f(x, y, z) = x - 2y + 5z$$

    on the sphere $x^2 + y^2 + z^2 = 30$.
24. **Extrema on a sphere** Find the points on the sphere $x^2 + y^2 + z^2 = 25$ where $f(x, y, z) = x + 2y + 3z$ has its maximum and minimum values.
25. **Minimizing a sum of squares** Find three real numbers whose sum is 9 and the sum of whose squares is as small as possible.
26. **Maximizing a product** Find the largest product the positive numbers x, y, and z can have if $x + y + z^2 = 16$.
27. **Rectangular box of longest volume in a sphere** Find the dimensions of the closed rectangular box with maximum volume that can be inscribed in the unit sphere.

28. **Box with vertex on a plane** Find the volume of the largest closed rectangular box in the first octant having three faces in the coordinate planes and a vertex on the plane $x/a + y/b + z/c = 1$, where $a > 0$, $b > 0$, and $c > 0$.

29. **Hottest point on a space probe** A space probe in the shape of the ellipsoid

$$4x^2 + y^2 + 4z^2 = 16$$

enters Earth's atmosphere and its surface begins to heat. After 1 hour, the temperature at the point (x, y, z) on the probe's surface is

$$T(x, y, z) = 8x^2 + 4yz - 16z + 600.$$

Find the hottest point on the probe's surface.

30. **Extreme temperatures on a sphere** Suppose that the Celsius temperature at the point (x, y, z) on the sphere $x^2 + y^2 + z^2 = 1$ is $T = 400xyz^2$. Locate the highest and lowest temperatures on the sphere.

31. **Maximizing a utility function: an example from economics** In economics, the usefulness or *utility* of amounts x and y of two capital goods G_1 and G_2 is sometimes measured by a function $U(x, y)$. For example, G_1 and G_2 might be two chemicals a pharmaceutical company needs to have on hand and $U(x, y)$ the gain from manufacturing a product whose synthesis requires different amounts of the chemicals depending on the process used. If G_1 costs a dollars per kilogram, G_2 costs b dollars per kilogram, and the total amount allocated for the purchase of G_1 and G_2 together is c dollars, then the company's managers want to maximize $U(x, y)$ given that $ax + by = c$. Thus, they need to solve a typical Lagrange multiplier problem.

Suppose that

$$U(x, y) = xy + 2x$$

and that the equation $ax + by = c$ simplifies to

$$2x + y = 30.$$

Find the maximum value of U and the corresponding values of x and y subject to this latter constraint.

32. **Locating a radio telescope** You are in charge of erecting a radio telescope on a newly discovered planet. To minimize interference, you want to place it where the magnetic field of the planet is weakest. The planet is spherical, with a radius of 6 units. Based on a coordinate system whose origin is at the center of the planet, the strength of the magnetic field is given by $M(x, y, z) = 6x - y^2 + xz + 60$. Where should you locate the radio telescope?

Extreme Values Subject to Two Constraints

33. Maximize the function $f(x, y, z) = x^2 + 2y - z^2$ subject to the constraints $2x - y = 0$ and $y + z = 0$.

34. Minimize the function $f(x, y, z) = x^2 + y^2 + z^2$ subject to the constraints $x + 2y + 3z = 6$ and $x + 3y + 9z = 9$.

35. **Minimum distance to the origin** Find the point closest to the origin on the line of intersection of the planes $y + 2z = 12$ and $x + y = 6$.

36. **Maximum value on line of intersection** Find the maximum value that $f(x, y, z) = x^2 + 2y - z^2$ can have on the line of intersection of the planes $2x - y = 0$ and $y + z = 0$.

37. **Extrema on a curve of intersection** Find the extreme values of $f(x, y, z) = x^2yz + 1$ on the intersection of the plane $z = 1$ with the sphere $x^2 + y^2 + z^2 = 10$.

38. a. **Maximum on line of intersection** Find the maximum value of $w = xyz$ on the line of intersection of the two planes $x + y + z = 40$ and $x + y - z = 0$.

    b. Give a geometric argument to support your claim that you have found a maximum, and not a minimum, value of w.

39. **Extrema on a circle of intersection** Find the extreme values of the function $f(x, y, z) = xy + z^2$ on the circle in which the plane $y - x = 0$ intersects the sphere $x^2 + y^2 + z^2 = 4$.

40. **Minimum distance to the origin** Find the point closest to the origin on the curve of intersection of the plane $2y + 4z = 5$ and the cone $z^2 = 4x^2 + 4y^2$.

Theory and Examples

41. **The condition $\nabla f = \lambda \nabla g$ is not sufficient** Although $\nabla f = \lambda \nabla g$ is a necessary condition for the occurrence of an extreme value of $f(x, y)$ subject to the condition $g(x, y) = 0$, it does not in itself guarantee that one exists. As a case in point, try using the method of Lagrange multipliers to find a maximum value of $f(x, y) = x + y$ subject to the constraint that $xy = 16$. The method will identify the two points $(4, 4)$ and $(-4, -4)$ as candidates for the location of extreme values. Yet the sum $(x + y)$ has no maximum value on the hyperbola $xy = 16$. The farther you go from the origin on this hyperbola in the first quadrant, the larger the sum $f(x, y) = x + y$ becomes.

42. **A least squares plane** The plane $z = Ax + By + C$ is to be "fitted" to the following points (x_k, y_k, z_k):

$$(0, 0, 0), \quad (0, 1, 1), \quad (1, 1, 1), \quad (1, 0, -1).$$

Find the values of A, B, and C that minimize

$$\sum_{k=1}^{4}(Ax_k + By_k + C - z_k)^2,$$

the sum of the squares of the deviations.

43. a. **Maximum on a sphere** Show that the maximum value of $a^2b^2c^2$ on a sphere of radius r centered at the origin of a Cartesian abc-coordinate system is $(r^2/3)^3$.

    b. **Geometric and arithmetic means** Using part (a), show that for nonnegative numbers a, b, and c,

$$(abc)^{1/3} \le \frac{a + b + c}{3};$$

that is, the *geometric mean* of three nonnegative numbers is less than or equal to their *arithmetic mean*.

44. **Sum of products** Let $a_1, a_2, \dots, a_n$ be n positive numbers. Find the maximum of $\Sigma_{i=1}^{n} a_i x_i$ subject to the constraint $\Sigma_{i=1}^{n} x_i^2 = 1$.

COMPUTER EXPLORATIONS

Implementing the Method of Lagrange Multipliers

In Exercises 45–50, use a CAS to perform the following steps implementing the method of Lagrange multipliers for finding constrained extrema:

a. Form the function $h = f - \lambda_1 g_1 - \lambda_2 g_2$, where f is the function to optimize subject to the constraints $g_1 = 0$ and $g_2 = 0$.

b. Determine all the first partial derivatives of h, including the partials with respect to λ_1 and λ_2, and set them equal to 0.

c. Solve the system of equations found in part (b) for all the unknowns, including λ_1 and λ_2.

d. Evaluate f at each of the solution points found in part (c) and select the extreme value subject to the constraints asked for in the exercise.

45. Minimize $f(x, y, z) = xy + yz$ subject to the constraints $x^2 + y^2 - 2 = 0$ and $x^2 + z^2 - 2 = 0$.

46. Minimize $f(x, y, z) = xyz$ subject to the constraints $x^2 + y^2 - 1 = 0$ and $x - z = 0$.

47. Maximize $f(x, y, z) = x^2 + y^2 + z^2$ subject to the constraints $2y + 4z - 5 = 0$ and $4x^2 + 4y^2 - z^2 = 0$.

48. Minimize $f(x, y, z) = x^2 + y^2 + z^2$ subject to the constraints $x^2 - xy + y^2 - z^2 - 1 = 0$ and $x^2 + y^2 - 1 = 0$.

49. Minimize $f(x, y, z, w) = x^2 + y^2 + z^2 + w^2$ subject to the constraints $2x - y + z - w - 1 = 0$ and $x + y - z + w - 1 = 0$.

50. Determine the distance from the line $y = x + 1$ to the parabola $y^2 = x$. (*Hint:* Let (x, y) be a point on the line and (w, z) a point on the parabola. You want to minimize $(x - w)^2 + (y - z)^2$.)

14.9 Partial Derivatives with Constrained Variables

In finding partial derivatives of functions like $w = f(x, y)$, we have assumed x and y to be independent. In many applications, however, this is not the case. For example, the internal energy U of a gas may be expressed as a function $U = f(P, V, T)$ of pressure P, volume V, and temperature T. If the individual molecules of the gas do not interact, however, P, V, and T obey (and are constrained by) the ideal gas law

$$PV = nRT \qquad (n \text{ and } R \text{ constant}),$$

and fail to be independent. In this section we learn how to find partial derivatives in situations like this, which you may encounter in studying economics, engineering, or physics.†

Decide Which Variables Are Dependent and Which Are Independent

If the variables in a function $w = f(x, y, z)$ are constrained by a relation like the one imposed on x, y, and z by the equation $z = x^2 + y^2$, the geometric meanings and the numerical values of the partial derivatives of f will depend on which variables are chosen to be dependent and which are chosen to be independent. To see how this choice can affect the outcome, we consider the calculation of $\partial w/\partial x$ when $w = x^2 + y^2 + z^2$ and $z = x^2 + y^2$.

EXAMPLE 1 Finding a Partial Derivative with Constrained Independent Variables

Find $\partial w/\partial x$ if $w = x^2 + y^2 + z^2$ and $z = x^2 + y^2$.

†This section is based on notes written for MIT by Arthur P. Mattuck.

Solution We are given two equations in the four unknowns x, y, z, and w. Like many such systems, this one can be solved for two of the unknowns (the dependent variables) in terms of the others (the independent variables). In being asked for $\partial w/\partial x$, we are told that w is to be a dependent variable and x an independent variable. The possible choices for the other variables come down to

Dependent	*Independent*
w, z	x, y
w, y	x, z

In either case, we can express w explicitly in terms of the selected independent variables. We do this by using the second equation $z = x^2 + y^2$ to eliminate the remaining dependent variable in the first equation.

In the first case, the remaining dependent variable is z. We eliminate it from the first equation by replacing it by $x^2 + y^2$. The resulting expression for w is

$$\begin{aligned} w &= x^2 + y^2 + z^2 = x^2 + y^2 + (x^2 + y^2)^2 \\ &= x^2 + y^2 + x^4 + 2x^2y^2 + y^4 \end{aligned}$$

and

$$\frac{\partial w}{\partial x} = 2x + 4x^3 + 4xy^2. \tag{1}$$

This is the formula for $\partial w/\partial x$ when x and y are the independent variables.

In the second case, where the independent variables are x and z and the remaining dependent variable is y, we eliminate the dependent variable y in the expression for w by replacing y^2 in the second equation by $z - x^2$. This gives

$$w = x^2 + y^2 + z^2 = x^2 + (z - x^2) + z^2 = z + z^2$$

and

$$\frac{\partial w}{\partial x} = 0. \tag{2}$$

This is the formula for $\partial w/\partial x$ when x and z are the independent variables.

The formulas for $\partial w/\partial x$ in Equations (1) and (2) are genuinely different. We cannot change either formula into the other by using the relation $z = x^2 + y^2$. There is not just one $\partial w/\partial x$, there are two, and we see that the original instruction to find $\partial w/\partial x$ was incomplete. *Which* $\partial w/\partial x$? we ask.

The geometric interpretations of Equations (1) and (2) help to explain why the equations differ. The function $w = x^2 + y^2 + z^2$ measures the square of the distance from the point (x, y, z) to the origin. The condition $z = x^2 + y^2$ says that the point (x, y, z) lies on the paraboloid of revolution shown in Figure 14.58. What does it mean to calculate $\partial w/\partial x$ at a point $P(x, y, z)$ that can move only on this surface? What is the value of $\partial w/\partial x$ when the coordinates of P are, say, $(1, 0, 1)$?

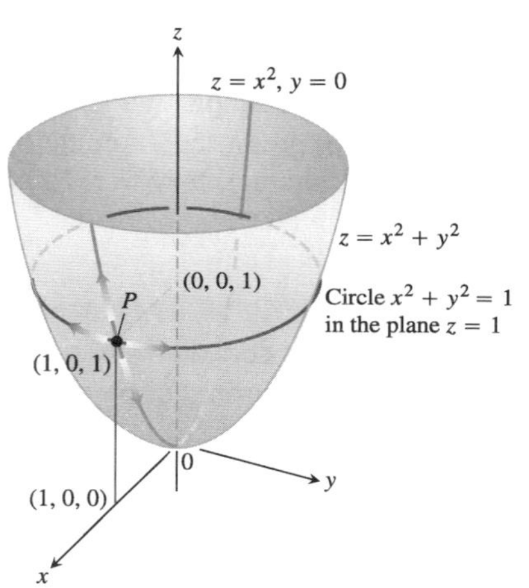

FIGURE 14.58 If P is constrained to lie on the paraboloid $z = x^2 + y^2$, the value of the partial derivative of $w = x^2 + y^2 + z^2$ with respect to x at P depends on the direction of motion (Example 1). (1) As x changes, with $y = 0$, P moves up or down the surface on the parabola $z = x^2$ in the xz-plane with $\partial w/\partial x = 2x + 4x^3$. (2) As x changes, with $z = 1$, P moves on the circle $x^2 + y^2 = 1$, $z = 1$, and $\partial w/\partial x = 0$.

If we take x and y to be independent, then we find $\partial w/\partial x$ by holding y fixed (at $y = 0$ in this case) and letting x vary. Hence, P moves along the parabola $z = x^2$ in the xz-plane. As P moves on this parabola, w, which is the square of the distance from P to the origin, changes. We calculate $\partial w/\partial x$ in this case (our first solution above) to be

$$\frac{\partial w}{\partial x} = 2x + 4x^3 + 4xy^2.$$

At the point $P(1, 0, 1)$, the value of this derivative is

$$\frac{\partial w}{\partial x} = 2 + 4 + 0 = 6.$$

If we take x and z to be independent, then we find $\partial w/\partial x$ by holding z fixed while x varies. Since the z-coordinate of P is 1, varying x moves P along a circle in the plane $z = 1$. As P moves along this circle, its distance from the origin remains constant, and w, being the square of this distance, does not change. That is,

$$\frac{\partial w}{\partial x} = 0,$$

as we found in our second solution. ■

How to Find $\partial w/\partial x$ When the Variables in $w = f(x, y, z)$ Are Constrained by Another Equation

As we saw in Example 1, a typical routine for finding $\partial w/\partial x$ when the variables in the function $w = f(x, y, z)$ are related by another equation has three steps. These steps apply to finding $\partial w/\partial y$ and $\partial w/\partial z$ as well.

1. *Decide* which variables are to be dependent and which are to be independent. (In practice, the decision is based on the physical or theoretical context of our work. In the exercises at the end of this section, we say which variables are which.)
2. *Eliminate* the other dependent variable(s) in the expression for w.
3. *Differentiate* as usual.

If we cannot carry out Step 2 after deciding which variables are dependent, we differentiate the equations as they are and try to solve for $\partial w/\partial x$ afterward. The next example shows how this is done.

EXAMPLE 2 Finding a Partial Derivative with Identified Constrained Independent Variables

Find $\partial w/\partial x$ at the point $(x, y, z) = (2, -1, 1)$ if

$$w = x^2 + y^2 + z^2, \qquad z^3 - xy + yz + y^3 = 1,$$

and x and y are the independent variables.

Solution It is not convenient to eliminate z in the expression for w. We therefore differentiate both equations implicitly with respect to x, treating x and y as independent variables and w and z as dependent variables. This gives

$$\frac{\partial w}{\partial x} = 2x + 2z\frac{\partial z}{\partial x} \tag{3}$$

and

$$3z^2\frac{\partial z}{\partial x} - y + y\frac{\partial z}{\partial x} + 0 = 0. \tag{4}$$

These equations may now be combined to express $\partial w/\partial x$ in terms of x, y, and z. We solve Equation (4) for $\partial z/\partial x$ to get

$$\frac{\partial z}{\partial x} = \frac{y}{y + 3z^2}$$

and substitute into Equation (3) to get

$$\frac{\partial w}{\partial x} = 2x + \frac{2yz}{y + 3z^2}.$$

The value of this derivative at $(x, y, z) = (2, -1, 1)$ is

$$\left(\frac{\partial w}{\partial x}\right)_{(2,-1,1)} = 2(2) + \frac{2(-1)(1)}{-1 + 3(1)^2} = 4 + \frac{-2}{2} = 3.$$

■

HISTORICAL BIOGRAPHY

Sonya Kovalevsky
(1850–1891)

Notation

To show what variables are assumed to be independent in calculating a derivative, we can use the following notation:

$\left(\frac{\partial w}{\partial x}\right)_y$ $\quad\partial w/\partial x$ with x and y independent

$\left(\frac{\partial f}{\partial y}\right)_{x,t}$ $\quad\partial f/\partial y$ with y, x and t independent

EXAMPLE 3 Finding a Partial Derivative with Constrained Variables Notationally Identified

Find $(\partial w/\partial x)_{y,z}$ if $w = x^2 + y - z + \sin t$ and $x + y = t$.

Solution With x, y, z independent, we have

$$t = x + y, \qquad w = x^2 + y - z + \sin(x + y)$$

$$\left(\frac{\partial w}{\partial x}\right)_{y,z} = 2x + 0 - 0 + \cos(x + y)\frac{\partial}{\partial x}(x + y)$$

$$= 2x + \cos(x + y).$$

■

Arrow Diagrams

In solving problems like the one in Example 3, it often helps to start with an arrow diagram that shows how the variables and functions are related. If

$$w = x^2 + y - z + \sin t \qquad \text{and} \qquad x + y = t$$

and we are asked to find $\partial w/\partial x$ when x, y, and z are independent, the appropriate diagram is one like this:

$$\begin{pmatrix} x \\ y \\ z \end{pmatrix} \rightarrow \begin{pmatrix} x \\ y \\ z \\ t \end{pmatrix} \rightarrow w \tag{5}$$

Independent variables — Intermediate variables — Dependent variable

To avoid confusion between the independent and intermediate variables with the same symbolic names in the diagram, it is helpful to rename the intermediate variables (so they are seen as *functions* of the independent variables). Thus, let $u = x$, $v = y$, and $s = z$ denote the renamed intermediate variables. With this notation, the arrow diagram becomes

$$\begin{pmatrix} x \\ y \\ z \end{pmatrix} \rightarrow \begin{pmatrix} u \\ v \\ s \\ t \end{pmatrix} \rightarrow w \tag{6}$$

Independent variables — Intermediate variables and relations $u = x$, $v = y$, $s = z$, $t = x + y$ — Dependent variable

The diagram shows the independent variables on the left, the intermediate variables and their relation to the independent variables in the middle, and the dependent variable on the right. The function w now becomes

$$w = u^2 + v - s + \sin t,$$

where

$$u = x, \qquad v = y, \qquad s = z, \qquad \text{and} \qquad t = x + y.$$

To find $\partial w/\partial x$, we apply the four-variable form of the Chain Rule to w, guided by the arrow diagram in Equation (6):

$$\begin{aligned} \frac{\partial w}{\partial x} &= \frac{\partial w}{\partial u}\frac{\partial u}{\partial x} + \frac{\partial w}{\partial v}\frac{\partial v}{\partial x} + \frac{\partial w}{\partial s}\frac{\partial s}{\partial x} + \frac{\partial w}{\partial t}\frac{\partial t}{\partial x} \\ &= (2u)(1) + (1)(0) + (-1)(0) + (\cos t)(1) \\ &= 2u + \cos t \\ &= 2x + \cos(x + y). \end{aligned}$$

Substituting the original independent variables $u = x$ and $t = x + y$.

EXERCISES 14.9

Finding Partial Derivatives with Constrained Variables

In Exercises 1–3, begin by drawing a diagram that shows the relations among the variables.

1. If $w = x^2 + y^2 + z^2$ and $z = x^2 + y^2$, find

a. $\left(\dfrac{\partial w}{\partial y}\right)_z$ **b.** $\left(\dfrac{\partial w}{\partial z}\right)_x$ **c.** $\left(\dfrac{\partial w}{\partial z}\right)_y$.

2. If $w = x^2 + y - z + \sin t$ and $x + y = t$, find

a. $\left(\dfrac{\partial w}{\partial y}\right)_{x,z}$ **b.** $\left(\dfrac{\partial w}{\partial y}\right)_{z,t}$ **c.** $\left(\dfrac{\partial w}{\partial z}\right)_{x,y}$

d. $\left(\dfrac{\partial w}{\partial z}\right)_{y,t}$ **e.** $\left(\dfrac{\partial w}{\partial t}\right)_{x,z}$ **f.** $\left(\dfrac{\partial w}{\partial t}\right)_{y,z}$.

3. Let $U = f(P, V, T)$ be the internal energy of a gas that obeys the ideal gas law $PV = nRT$ (n and R constant). Find

   a. $\left(\frac{\partial U}{\partial P}\right)_V$ b. $\left(\frac{\partial U}{\partial T}\right)_V$.

4. Find

   a. $\left(\frac{\partial w}{\partial x}\right)_y$ b. $\left(\frac{\partial w}{\partial z}\right)_y$

   at the point $(x, y, z) = (0, 1, \pi)$ if

   $$w = x^2 + y^2 + z^2 \quad \text{and} \quad y \sin z + z \sin x = 0.$$

5. Find

   a. $\left(\frac{\partial w}{\partial y}\right)_x$ b. $\left(\frac{\partial w}{\partial y}\right)_z$

   at the point $(w, x, y, z) = (4, 2, 1, -1)$ if

   $$w = x^2y^2 + yz - z^3 \quad \text{and} \quad x^2 + y^2 + z^2 = 6.$$

6. Find $(\partial u/\partial y)_x$ at the point $(u, v) = \left(\sqrt{2}, 1\right)$, if $x = u^2 + v^2$ and $y = uv$.

7. Suppose that $x^2 + y^2 = r^2$ and $x = r\cos\theta$, as in polar coordinates. Find

   $$\left(\frac{\partial x}{\partial r}\right)_\theta \quad \text{and} \quad \left(\frac{\partial r}{\partial x}\right)_y.$$

8. Suppose that

   $$w = x^2 - y^2 + 4z + t \quad \text{and} \quad x + 2z + t = 25.$$

   Show that the equations

   $$\frac{\partial w}{\partial x} = 2x - 1 \quad \text{and} \quad \frac{\partial w}{\partial x} = 2x - 2$$

   each give $\partial w/\partial x$, depending on which variables are chosen to be dependent and which variables are chosen to be independent. Identify the independent variables in each case.

Partial Derivatives Without Specific Formulas

9. Establish the fact, widely used in hydrodynamics, that if $f(x, y, z) = 0$, then

   $$\left(\frac{\partial x}{\partial y}\right)_z \left(\frac{\partial y}{\partial z}\right)_x \left(\frac{\partial z}{\partial x}\right)_y = -1.$$

   (*Hint:* Express all the derivatives in terms of the formal partial derivatives $\partial f/\partial x$, $\partial f/\partial y$, and $\partial f/\partial z$.)

10. If $z = x + f(u)$, where $u = xy$, show that

    $$x\frac{\partial z}{\partial x} - y\frac{\partial z}{\partial y} = x.$$

11. Suppose that the equation $g(x, y, z) = 0$ determines z as a differentiable function of the independent variables x and y and that $g_z \neq 0$. Show that

    $$\left(\frac{\partial z}{\partial y}\right)_x = -\frac{\partial g/\partial y}{\partial g/\partial z}.$$

12. Suppose that $f(x, y, z, w) = 0$ and $g(x, y, z, w) = 0$ determine z and w as differentiable functions of the independent variables x and y, and suppose that

    $$\frac{\partial f}{\partial z}\frac{\partial g}{\partial w} - \frac{\partial f}{\partial w}\frac{\partial g}{\partial z} \neq 0.$$

    Show that

    $$\left(\frac{\partial z}{\partial x}\right)_y = -\frac{\dfrac{\partial f}{\partial x}\dfrac{\partial g}{\partial w} - \dfrac{\partial f}{\partial w}\dfrac{\partial g}{\partial x}}{\dfrac{\partial f}{\partial z}\dfrac{\partial g}{\partial w} - \dfrac{\partial f}{\partial w}\dfrac{\partial g}{\partial z}}$$

    and

    $$\left(\frac{\partial w}{\partial y}\right)_x = -\frac{\dfrac{\partial f}{\partial z}\dfrac{\partial g}{\partial y} - \dfrac{\partial f}{\partial y}\dfrac{\partial g}{\partial z}}{\dfrac{\partial f}{\partial z}\dfrac{\partial g}{\partial w} - \dfrac{\partial f}{\partial w}\dfrac{\partial g}{\partial z}}.$$

14.10 Taylor's Formula for Two Variables

This section uses Taylor's formula to derive the Second Derivative Test for local extreme values (Section 14.7) and the error formula for linearizations of functions of two independent variables (Section 14.6). The use of Taylor's formula in these derivations leads to an extension of the formula that provides polynomial approximations of all orders for functions of two independent variables.

Derivation of the Second Derivative Test

Let $f(x, y)$ have continuous partial derivatives in an open region R containing a point $P(a, b)$ where $f_x = f_y = 0$ (Figure 14.59). Let h and k be increments small enough to put the

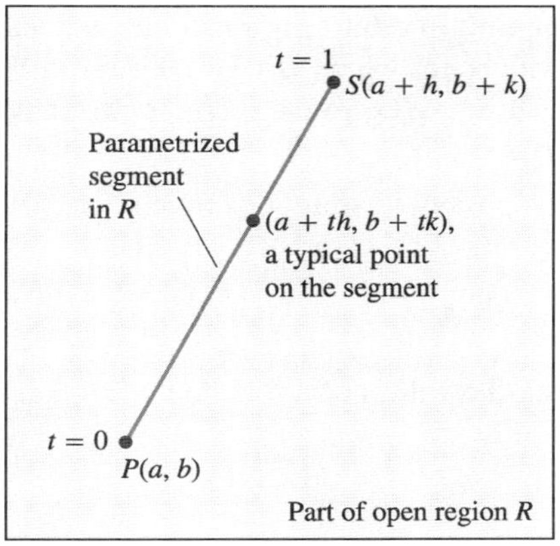

FIGURE 14.59 We begin the derivation of the second derivative test at $P(a, b)$ by parametrizing a typical line segment from P to a point S nearby.

point $S(a + h, b + k)$ and the line segment joining it to P inside R. We parametrize the segment PS as

$$x = a + th, \qquad y = b + tk, \qquad 0 \le t \le 1.$$

If $F(t) = f(a + th, b + tk)$, the Chain Rule gives

$$F'(t) = f_x \frac{dx}{dt} + f_y \frac{dy}{dt} = hf_x + kf_y.$$

Since f_x and f_y are differentiable (they have continuous partial derivatives), F' is a differentiable function of t and

$$\begin{aligned} F'' &= \frac{\partial F'}{\partial x}\frac{dx}{dt} + \frac{\partial F'}{\partial y}\frac{dy}{dt} = \frac{\partial}{\partial x}(hf_x + kf_y)\cdot h + \frac{\partial}{\partial y}(hf_x + kf_y)\cdot k \\ &= h^2 f_{xx} + 2hkf_{xy} + k^2 f_{yy}. \qquad f_{xy} = f_{yx} \end{aligned}$$

Since F and F' are continuous on $[0, 1]$ and F' is differentiable on $(0, 1)$, we can apply Taylor's formula with $n = 2$ and $a = 0$ to obtain

$$\begin{aligned} F(1) &= F(0) + F'(0)(1 - 0) + F''(c)\frac{(1 - 0)^2}{2} \\ F(1) &= F(0) + F'(0) + \frac{1}{2}F''(c) \end{aligned} \tag{1}$$

for some c between 0 and 1. Writing Equation (1) in terms of f gives

$$\begin{aligned} f(a + h, b + k) &= f(a, b) + hf_x(a, b) + kf_y(a, b) \\ &\quad + \frac{1}{2}\left(h^2 f_{xx} + 2hkf_{xy} + k^2 f_{yy}\right)\Big|_{(a+ch,\, b+ck)}. \end{aligned} \tag{2}$$

Since $f_x(a, b) = f_y(a, b) = 0$, this reduces to

$$f(a + h, b + k) - f(a, b) = \frac{1}{2}\left(h^2 f_{xx} + 2hkf_{xy} + k^2 f_{yy}\right)\Big|_{(a+ch,\, b+ck)}. \tag{3}$$

The presence of an extremum of f at (a, b) is determined by the sign of $f(a + h, b + k) - f(a, b)$. By Equation (3), this is the same as the sign of

$$Q(c) = (h^2 f_{xx} + 2hkf_{xy} + k^2 f_{yy})|_{(a+ch, b+ck)}.$$

Now, if $Q(0) \neq 0$, the sign of $Q(c)$ will be the same as the sign of $Q(0)$ for sufficiently small values of h and k. We can predict the sign of

$$Q(0) = h^2 f_{xx}(a, b) + 2hkf_{xy}(a, b) + k^2 f_{yy}(a, b) \tag{4}$$

from the signs of f_{xx} and $f_{xx}f_{yy} - f_{xy}^2$ at (a, b). Multiply both sides of Equation (4) by f_{xx} and rearrange the right-hand side to get

$$f_{xx}Q(0) = (hf_{xx} + kf_{xy})^2 + (f_{xx}f_{yy} - f_{xy}^2)k^2. \tag{5}$$

From Equation (5) we see that

1. If $f_{xx} < 0$ and $f_{xx}f_{yy} - f_{xy}^2 > 0$ at (a, b), then $Q(0) < 0$ for all sufficiently small nonzero values of h and k, and f has a *local maximum* value at (a, b).
2. If $f_{xx} > 0$ and $f_{xx}f_{yy} - f_{xy}^2 > 0$ at (a, b), then $Q(0) > 0$ for all sufficiently small nonzero values of h and k and f has a *local minimum* value at (a, b).

3. If $f_{xx}f_{yy} - f_{xy}^2 < 0$ at (a, b), there are combinations of arbitrarily small nonzero values of h and k for which $Q(0) > 0$, and other values for which $Q(0) < 0$. Arbitrarily close to the point $P_0(a, b, f(a, b))$ on the surface $z = f(x, y)$ there are points above P_0 and points below P_0, so f has a *saddle point* at (a, b).
4. If $f_{xx}f_{yy} - f_{xy}^2 = 0$, another test is needed. The possibility that $Q(0)$ equals zero prevents us from drawing conclusions about the sign of $Q(c)$.

The Error Formula for Linear Approximations

We want to show that the difference $E(x, y)$, between the values of a function $f(x, y)$, and its linearization $L(x, y)$ at (x_0, y_0) satisfies the inequality

$$|E(x, y)| \leq \frac{1}{2}M(|x - x_0| + |y - y_0|)^2.$$

The function f is assumed to have continuous second partial derivatives throughout an open set containing a closed rectangular region R centered at (x_0, y_0). The number M is an upper bound for $|f_{xx}|, |f_{yy}|$, and $|f_{xy}|$ on R.

The inequality we want comes from Equation (2). We substitute x_0 and y_0 for a and b, and $x - x_0$ and $y - y_0$ for h and k, respectively, and rearrange the result as

$$f(x, y) = \underbrace{f(x_0, y_0) + f_x(x_0, y_0)(x - x_0) + f_y(x_0, y_0)(y - y_0)}_{\text{linearization } L(x, y)}$$

$$+ \underbrace{\frac{1}{2}\left((x - x_0)^2 f_{xx} + 2(x - x_0)(y - y_0)f_{xy} + (y - y_0)^2 f_{yy}\right)\Big|_{(x_0+c(x-x_0),\, y_0+c(y-y_0))}}_{\text{error } E(x, y)}.$$

This equation reveals that

$$|E| \leq \frac{1}{2}\left(|x - x_0|^2|f_{xx}| + 2|x - x_0||y - y_0||f_{xy}| + |y - y_0|^2|f_{yy}|\right).$$

Hence, if M is an upper bound for the values of $|f_{xx}|, |f_{xy}|$, and $|f_{yy}|$ on R,

$$\begin{aligned} |E| &\leq \frac{1}{2}\left(|x - x_0|^2 M + 2|x - x_0||y - y_0|M + |y - y_0|^2 M\right) \\ &= \frac{1}{2}M(|x - x_0| + |y - y_0|)^2. \end{aligned}$$

Taylor's Formula for Functions of Two Variables

The formulas derived earlier for F' and F'' can be obtained by applying to $f(x, y)$ the operators

$$\left(h\frac{\partial}{\partial x} + k\frac{\partial}{\partial y}\right) \quad \text{and} \quad \left(h\frac{\partial}{\partial x} + k\frac{\partial}{\partial y}\right)^2 = h^2\frac{\partial^2}{\partial x^2} + 2hk\frac{\partial^2}{\partial x\,\partial y} + k^2\frac{\partial^2}{\partial y^2}.$$

These are the first two instances of a more general formula,

$$F^{(n)}(t) = \frac{d^n}{dt^n}F(t) = \left(h\frac{\partial}{\partial x} + k\frac{\partial}{\partial y}\right)^n f(x, y), \tag{6}$$

which says that applying d^n/dt^n to $F(t)$ gives the same result as applying the operator

$$\left(h\frac{\partial}{\partial x} + k\frac{\partial}{\partial y}\right)^n$$

to $f(x, y)$ after expanding it by the Binomial Theorem.

If partial derivatives of f through order $n + 1$ are continuous throughout a rectangular region centered at (a, b), we may extend the Taylor formula for $F(t)$ to

$$F(t) = F(0) + F'(0)t + \frac{F''(0)}{2!}t^2 + \cdots + \frac{F^{(n)}(0)}{n!}t^{(n)} + \text{remainder},$$

and take $t = 1$ to obtain

$$F(1) = F(0) + F'(0) + \frac{F''(0)}{2!} + \cdots + \frac{F^{(n)}(0)}{n!} + \text{remainder}.$$

When we replace the first n derivatives on the right of this last series by their equivalent expressions from Equation (6) evaluated at $t = 0$ and add the appropriate remainder term, we arrive at the following formula.

Taylor's Formula for $f(x, y)$ at the Point (a, b)

Suppose $f(x, y)$ and its partial derivatives through order $n + 1$ are continuous throughout an open rectangular region R centered at a point (a, b). Then, throughout R,

$$\begin{aligned} f(a+h, b+k) &= f(a, b) + (hf_x + kf_y)|_{(a,b)} + \frac{1}{2!}(h^2 f_{xx} + 2hkf_{xy} + k^2 f_{yy})|_{(a,b)} \\ &\quad + \frac{1}{3!}(h^3 f_{xxx} + 3h^2 k f_{xxy} + 3hk^2 f_{xyy} + k^3 f_{yyy})|_{(a,b)} + \cdots + \frac{1}{n!}\left(h\frac{\partial}{\partial x} + k\frac{\partial}{\partial y}\right)^n f\bigg|_{(a,b)} \\ &\quad + \frac{1}{(n+1)!}\left(h\frac{\partial}{\partial x} + k\frac{\partial}{\partial y}\right)^{n+1} f\bigg|_{(a+ch,b+ck)}. \end{aligned} \tag{7}$$

The first n derivative terms are evaluated at (a, b). The last term is evaluated at some point $(a + ch, b + ck)$ on the line segment joining (a, b) and $(a + h, b + k)$.

If $(a, b) = (0, 0)$ and we treat h and k as independent variables (denoting them now by x and y), then Equation (7) assumes the following simpler form.

Taylor's Formula for $f(x, y)$ at the Origin

$$\begin{aligned} f(x, y) &= f(0, 0) + xf_x + yf_y + \frac{1}{2!}(x^2 f_{xx} + 2xyf_{xy} + y^2 f_{yy}) \\ &\quad + \frac{1}{3!}(x^3 f_{xxx} + 3x^2 y f_{xxy} + 3xy^2 f_{xyy} + y^3 f_{yyy}) + \cdots + \frac{1}{n!}\left(x\frac{\partial}{\partial x} + y\frac{\partial}{\partial y}\right)^n f \\ &\quad + \frac{1}{(n+1)!}\left(x\frac{\partial}{\partial x} + y\frac{\partial}{\partial y}\right)^{n+1} f\bigg|_{(cx,cy)} \end{aligned} \tag{8}$$

The first n derivative terms are evaluated at $(0, 0)$. The last term is evaluated at a point on the line segment joining the origin and (x, y).

Taylor's formula provides polynomial approximations of two-variable functions. The first n derivative terms give the polynomial; the last term gives the approximation error. The first three terms of Taylor's formula give the function's linearization. To improve on the linearization, we add higher power terms.

EXAMPLE 1 Finding a Quadratic Approximation

Find a quadratic approximation to $f(x, y) = \sin x \sin y$ near the origin. How accurate is the approximation if $|x| \leq 0.1$ and $|y| \leq 0.1$?

Solution We take $n = 2$ in Equation (8):

$$f(x, y) = f(0, 0) + (xf_x + yf_y) + \frac{1}{2}(x^2 f_{xx} + 2xyf_{xy} + y^2 f_{yy})$$

$$+ \frac{1}{6}(x^3 f_{xxx} + 3x^2 y f_{xxy} + 3xy^2 f_{xyy} + y^3 f_{yyy})_{(cx,cy)}$$

with

$$f(0, 0) = \sin x \sin y|_{(0,0)} = 0, \qquad f_{xx}(0, 0) = -\sin x \sin y|_{(0,0)} = 0,$$

$$f_x(0, 0) = \cos x \sin y|_{(0,0)} = 0, \qquad f_{xy}(0, 0) = \cos x \cos y|_{(0,0)} = 1,$$

$$f_y(0, 0) = \sin x \cos y|_{(0,0)} = 0, \qquad f_{yy}(0, 0) = -\sin x \sin y|_{(0,0)} = 0,$$

we have

$$\sin x \sin y \approx 0 + 0 + 0 + \frac{1}{2}(x^2(0) + 2xy(1) + y^2(0)),$$

$$\sin x \sin y \approx xy.$$

The error in the approximation is

$$E(x, y) = \frac{1}{6}(x^3 f_{xxx} + 3x^2 y f_{xxy} + 3xy^2 f_{xyy} + y^3 f_{yyy})|_{(cx,cy)}.$$

The third derivatives never exceed 1 in absolute value because they are products of sines and cosines. Also, $|x| \leq 0.1$ and $|y| \leq 0.1$. Hence

$$|E(x, y)| \leq \frac{1}{6}((0.1)^3 + 3(0.1)^3 + 3(0.1)^3 + (0.1)^3) = \frac{8}{6}(0.1)^3 \leq 0.00134$$

(rounded up). The error will not exceed 0.00134 if $|x| \leq 0.1$ and $|y| \leq 0.1$. ■

EXERCISES 14.10

Finding Quadratic and Cubic Approximations

In Exercises 1–10, use Taylor's formula for $f(x, y)$ at the origin to find quadratic and cubic approximations of f near the origin.

1. $f(x, y) = xe^y$
2. $f(x, y) = e^x \cos y$
3. $f(x, y) = y \sin x$
4. $f(x, y) = \sin x \cos y$
5. $f(x, y) = e^x \ln(1 + y)$
6. $f(x, y) = \ln(2x + y + 1)$
7. $f(x, y) = \sin(x^2 + y^2)$
8. $f(x, y) = \cos(x^2 + y^2)$

9. $f(x, y) = \dfrac{1}{1 - x - y}$

10. $f(x, y) = \dfrac{1}{1 - x - y + xy}$

11. Use Taylor's formula to find a quadratic approximation of $f(x, y) = \cos x \cos y$ at the origin. Estimate the error in the approximation if $|x| \le 0.1$ and $|y| \le 0.1$.

12. Use Taylor's formula to find a quadratic approximation of $e^x \sin y$ at the origin. Estimate the error in the approximation if $|x| \le 0.1$ and $|y| \le 0.1$.

Chapter 14 Questions to Guide Your Review

1. What is a real-valued function of two independent variables? Three independent variables? Give examples.
2. What does it mean for sets in the plane or in space to be open? Closed? Give examples. Give examples of sets that are neither open nor closed.
3. How can you display the values of a function $f(x, y)$ of two independent variables graphically? How do you do the same for a function $f(x, y, z)$ of three independent variables?
4. What does it mean for a function $f(x, y)$ to have limit L as $(x, y) \to (x_0, y_0)$? What are the basic properties of limits of functions of two independent variables?
5. When is a function of two (three) independent variables continuous at a point in its domain? Give examples of functions that are continuous at some points but not others.
6. What can be said about algebraic combinations and composites of continuous functions?
7. Explain the two-path test for nonexistence of limits.
8. How are the partial derivatives $\partial f/\partial x$ and $\partial f/\partial y$ of a function $f(x, y)$ defined? How are they interpreted and calculated?
9. How does the relation between first partial derivatives and continuity of functions of two independent variables differ from the relation between first derivatives and continuity for real-valued functions of a single independent variable? Give an example.
10. What is the Mixed Derivative Theorem for mixed second-order partial derivatives? How can it help in calculating partial derivatives of second and higher orders? Give examples.
11. What does it mean for a function $f(x, y)$ to be differentiable? What does the Increment Theorem say about differentiability?
12. How can you sometimes decide from examining f_x and f_y that a function $f(x, y)$ is differentiable? What is the relation between the differentiability of f and the continuity of f at a point?
13. What is the Chain Rule? What form does it take for functions of two independent variables? Three independent variables? Functions defined on surfaces? How do you diagram these different forms? Give examples. What pattern enables one to remember all the different forms?
14. What is the derivative of a function $f(x, y)$ at a point P_0 in the direction of a unit vector $\mathbf{u}$? What rate does it describe? What geometric interpretation does it have? Give examples.
15. What is the gradient vector of a differentiable function $f(x, y)$? How is it related to the function's directional derivatives? State the analogous results for functions of three independent variables.
16. How do you find the tangent line at a point on a level curve of a differentiable function $f(x, y)$? How do you find the tangent plane and normal line at a point on a level surface of a differentiable function $f(x, y, z)$? Give examples.
17. How can you use directional derivatives to estimate change?
18. How do you linearize a function $f(x, y)$ of two independent variables at a point (x_0, y_0) ? Why might you want to do this? How do you linearize a function of three independent variables?
19. What can you say about the accuracy of linear approximations of functions of two (three) independent variables?
20. If (x, y) moves from (x_0, y_0) to a point $(x_0 + dx, y_0 + dy)$ nearby, how can you estimate the resulting change in the value of a differentiable function $f(x, y)$? Give an example.
21. How do you define local maxima, local minima, and saddle points for a differentiable function $f(x, y)$? Give examples.
22. What derivative tests are available for determining the local extreme values of a function $f(x, y)$? How do they enable you to narrow your search for these values? Give examples.
23. How do you find the extrema of a continuous function $f(x, y)$ on a closed bounded region of the xy-plane? Give an example.
24. Describe the method of Lagrange multipliers and give examples.
25. If $w = f(x, y, z)$, where the variables x, y, and z are constrained by an equation $g(x, y, z) = 0$, what is the meaning of the notation $(\partial w/\partial x)_y$? How can an arrow diagram help you calculate this partial derivative with constrained variables? Give examples.
26. How does Taylor's formula for a function $f(x, y)$ generate polynomial approximations and error estimates?

Chapter 14 Practice Exercises

Domain, Range, and Level Curves

In Exercises 1–4, find the domain and range of the given function and identify its level curves. Sketch a typical level curve.

1. $f(x, y) = 9x^2 + y^2$
2. $f(x, y) = e^{x+y}$
3. $g(x, y) = 1/xy$
4. $g(x, y) = \sqrt{x^2 - y}$

In Exercises 5–8, find the domain and range of the given function and identify its level surfaces. Sketch a typical level surface.

5. $f(x, y, z) = x^2 + y^2 - z$
6. $g(x, y, z) = x^2 + 4y^2 + 9z^2$
7. $h(x, y, z) = \dfrac{1}{x^2 + y^2 + z^2}$
8. $k(x, y, z) = \dfrac{1}{x^2 + y^2 + z^2 + 1}$

Evaluating Limits

Find the limits in Exercises 9–14.

9. $\lim\limits_{(x,y)\to(\pi, \ln 2)} e^y \cos x$
10. $\lim\limits_{(x,y)\to(0,0)} \dfrac{2 + y}{x + \cos y}$
11. $\lim\limits_{(x,y)\to(1,1)} \dfrac{x - y}{x^2 - y^2}$
12. $\lim\limits_{(x,y)\to(1,1)} \dfrac{x^3y^3 - 1}{xy - 1}$
13. $\lim\limits_{P\to(1,-1,e)} \ln|x + y + z|$
14. $\lim\limits_{P\to(1,-1,-1)} \tan^{-1}(x + y + z)$

By considering different paths of approach, show that the limits in Exercises 15 and 16 do not exist.

15. $\lim\limits_{\substack{(x,y)\to(0,0)\\ y\neq x^2}} \dfrac{y}{x^2 - y}$
16. $\lim\limits_{\substack{(x,y)\to(0,0)\\ xy\neq 0}} \dfrac{x^2 + y^2}{xy}$

17. **Continuous extension** Let $f(x, y) = (x^2 - y^2)/(x^2 + y^2)$ for $(x, y) \neq (0, 0)$. Is it possible to define $f(0, 0)$ in a way that makes f continuous at the origin? Why?

18. **Continuous extension** Let

$$f(x, y) = \begin{cases} \dfrac{\sin(x - y)}{|x| + |y|}, & |x| + |y| \neq 0 \\ 0, & (x, y) = (0, 0). \end{cases}$$

Is f continuous at the origin? Why?

Partial Derivatives

In Exercises 19–24, find the partial derivative of the function with respect to each variable.

19. $g(r, \theta) = r\cos\theta + r\sin\theta$
20. $f(x, y) = \dfrac{1}{2}\ln(x^2 + y^2) + \tan^{-1}\dfrac{y}{x}$
21. $f(R_1, R_2, R_3) = \dfrac{1}{R_1} + \dfrac{1}{R_2} + \dfrac{1}{R_3}$
22. $h(x, y, z) = \sin(2\pi x + y - 3z)$
23. $P(n, R, T, V) = \dfrac{nRT}{V}$ (the ideal gas law)
24. $f(r, l, T, w) = \dfrac{1}{2rl}\sqrt{\dfrac{T}{\pi w}}$

Second-Order Partials

Find the second-order partial derivatives of the functions in Exercises 25–28.

25. $g(x, y) = y + \dfrac{x}{y}$
26. $g(x, y) = e^x + y\sin x$
27. $f(x, y) = x + xy - 5x^3 + \ln(x^2 + 1)$
28. $f(x, y) = y^2 - 3xy + \cos y + 7e^y$

Chain Rule Calculations

29. Find dw/dt at $t = 0$ if $w = \sin(xy + \pi)$, $x = e^t$, and $y = \ln(t + 1)$.
30. Find dw/dt at $t = 1$ if $w = xe^y + y\sin z - \cos z$, $x = 2\sqrt{t}$, $y = t - 1 + \ln t$, and $z = \pi t$.
31. Find $\partial w/\partial r$ and $\partial w/\partial s$ when $r = \pi$ and $s = 0$ if $w = \sin(2x - y)$, $x = r + \sin s$, $y = rs$.
32. Find $\partial w/\partial u$ and $\partial w/\partial v$ when $u = v = 0$ if $w = \ln\sqrt{1 + x^2} - \tan^{-1}x$ and $x = 2e^u\cos v$.
33. Find the value of the derivative of $f(x, y, z) = xy + yz + xz$ with respect to t on the curve $x = \cos t$, $y = \sin t$, $z = \cos 2t$ at $t = 1$.
34. Show that if $w = f(s)$ is any differentiable function of s and if $s = y + 5x$, then

$$\frac{\partial w}{\partial x} - 5\frac{\partial w}{\partial y} = 0.$$

Implicit Differentiation

Assuming that the equations in Exercises 35 and 36 define y as a differentiable function of x, find the value of dy/dx at point P.

35. $1 - x - y^2 - \sin xy = 0$, $P(0, 1)$
36. $2xy + e^{x+y} - 2 = 0$, $P(0, \ln 2)$

Directional Derivatives

In Exercises 37–40, find the directions in which f increases and decreases most rapidly at P_0 and find the derivative of f in each direction. Also, find the derivative of f at P_0 in the direction of the vector $\mathbf{v}$.

37. $f(x, y) = \cos x\cos y$, $P_0(\pi/4, \pi/4)$, $\mathbf{v} = 3\mathbf{i} + 4\mathbf{j}$
38. $f(x, y) = x^2e^{-2y}$, $P_0(1, 0)$, $\mathbf{v} = \mathbf{i} + \mathbf{j}$
39. $f(x, y, z) = \ln(2x + 3y + 6z)$, $P_0(-1, -1, 1)$, $\mathbf{v} = 2\mathbf{i} + 3\mathbf{j} + 6\mathbf{k}$

40. $f(x, y, z) = x^2 + 3xy - z^2 + 2y + z + 4$, $P_0(0, 0, 0)$, $\mathbf{v} = \mathbf{i} + \mathbf{j} + \mathbf{k}$

41. **Derivative in velocity direction** Find the derivative of $f(x, y, z) = xyz$ in the direction of the velocity vector of the helix

$$\mathbf{r}(t) = (\cos 3t)\mathbf{i} + (\sin 3t)\mathbf{j} + 3t\mathbf{k}$$

at $t = \pi/3$.

42. **Maximum directional derivative** What is the largest value that the directional derivative of $f(x, y, z) = xyz$ can have at the point $(1, 1, 1)$?

43. **Directional derivatives with given values** At the point $(1, 2)$, the function $f(x, y)$ has a derivative of 2 in the direction toward $(2, 2)$ and a derivative of -2 in the direction toward $(1, 1)$.
   a. Find $f_x(1, 2)$ and $f_y(1, 2)$.
   b. Find the derivative of f at $(1, 2)$ in the direction toward the point $(4, 6)$.

44. Which of the following statements are true if $f(x, y)$ is differentiable at (x_0, y_0)? Give reasons for your answers.
   a. If $\mathbf{u}$ is a unit vector, the derivative of f at (x_0, y_0) in the direction of $\mathbf{u}$ is $(f_x(x_0, y_0)\mathbf{i} + f_y(x_0, y_0)\mathbf{j}) \cdot \mathbf{u}$.
   b. The derivative of f at (x_0, y_0) in the direction of $\mathbf{u}$ is a vector.
   c. The directional derivative of f at (x_0, y_0) has its greatest value in the direction of ∇f.
   d. At (x_0, y_0), vector ∇f is normal to the curve $f(x, y) = f(x_0, y_0)$.

Gradients, Tangent Planes, and Normal Lines

In Exercises 45 and 46, sketch the surface $f(x, y, z) = c$ together with ∇f at the given points.

45. $x^2 + y + z^2 = 0$; $(0, -1, \pm 1)$, $(0, 0, 0)$

46. $y^2 + z^2 = 4$; $(2, \pm 2, 0)$, $(2, 0, \pm 2)$

In Exercises 47 and 48, find an equation for the plane tangent to the level surface $f(x, y, z) = c$ at the point P_0. Also, find parametric equations for the line that is normal to the surface at P_0.

47. $x^2 - y - 5z = 0$, $P_0(2, -1, 1)$

48. $x^2 + y^2 + z = 4$, $P_0(1, 1, 2)$

In Exercises 49 and 50, find an equation for the plane tangent to the surface $z = f(x, y)$ at the given point.

49. $z = \ln(x^2 + y^2)$, $(0, 1, 0)$

50. $z = 1/(x^2 + y^2)$, $(1, 1, 1/2)$

In Exercises 51 and 52, find equations for the lines that are tangent and normal to the level curve $f(x, y) = c$ at the point P_0. Then sketch the lines and level curve together with ∇f at P_0.

51. $y - \sin x = 1$, $P_0(\pi, 1)$ 52. $\frac{y^2}{2} - \frac{x^2}{2} = \frac{3}{2}$, $P_0(1, 2)$

Tangent Lines to Curves

In Exercises 53 and 54, find parametric equations for the line that is tangent to the curve of intersection of the surfaces at the given point.

53. Surfaces: $x^2 + 2y + 2z = 4$, $y = 1$
   Point: $(1, 1, 1/2)$

54. Surfaces: $x + y^2 + z = 2$, $y = 1$
   Point: $(1/2, 1, 1/2)$

Linearizations

In Exercises 55 and 56, find the linearization $L(x, y)$ of the function $f(x, y)$ at the point P_0. Then find an upper bound for the magnitude of the error E in the approximation $f(x, y) \approx L(x, y)$ over the rectangle R.

55. $f(x, y) = \sin x \cos y$, $P_0(\pi/4, \pi/4)$
   R: $\left|x - \frac{\pi}{4}\right| \leq 0.1$, $\left|y - \frac{\pi}{4}\right| \leq 0.1$

56. $f(x, y) = xy - 3y^2 + 2$, $P_0(1, 1)$
   R: $|x - 1| \leq 0.1$, $|y - 1| \leq 0.2$

Find the linearizations of the functions in Exercises 57 and 58 at the given points.

57. $f(x, y, z) = xy + 2yz - 3xz$ at $(1, 0, 0)$ and $(1, 1, 0)$

58. $f(x, y, z) = \sqrt{2} \cos x \sin(y + z)$ at $(0, 0, \pi/4)$ and $(\pi/4, \pi/4, 0)$

Estimates and Sensitivity to Change

59. **Measuring the volume of a pipeline** You plan to calculate the volume inside a stretch of pipeline that is about 36 in. in diameter and 1 mile long. With which measurement should you be more careful, the length or the diameter? Why?

60. **Sensitivity to change** Near the point $(1, 2)$, is $f(x, y) = x^2 - xy + y^2 - 3$ more sensitive to changes in x or to changes in y? How do you know?

61. **Change in an electrical circuit** Suppose that the current I (amperes) in an electrical circuit is related to the voltage V (volts) and the resistance R (ohms) by the equation $I = V/R$. If the voltage drops from 24 to 23 volts and the resistance drops from 100 to 80 ohms, will I increase or decrease? By about how much? Is the change in I more sensitive to change in the voltage or to change in the resistance? How do you know?

62. **Maximum error in estimating the area of an ellipse** If $a = 10$ cm and $b = 16$ cm to the nearest millimeter, what should you expect the maximum percentage error to be in the calculated area $A = \pi ab$ of the ellipse $x^2/a^2 + y^2/b^2 = 1$?

63. **Error in estimating a product** Let $y = uv$ and $z = u + v$, where u and v are positive independent variables.
   a. If u is measured with an error of 2% and v with an error of 3%, about what is the percentage error in the calculated value of y?

b. Show that the percentage error in the calculated value of z is less than the percentage error in the value of y.

64. Cardiac index To make different people comparable in studies of cardiac output (Section 3.7, Exercise 25), researchers divide the measured cardiac output by the body surface area to find the *cardiac index* C:

$$C = \frac{\text{cardiac output}}{\text{body surface area}}.$$

The body surface area B of a person with weight w and height h is approximated by the formula

$$B = 71.84w^{0.425}h^{0.725},$$

which gives B in square centimeters when w is measured in kilograms and h in centimeters. You are about to calculate the cardiac index of a person with the following measurements:

Cardiac output:	7 L/min
Weight:	70 kg
Height:	180 cm

Which will have a greater effect on the calculation, a 1-kg error in measuring the weight or a 1-cm error in measuring the height?

Local Extrema

Test the functions in Exercises 65–70 for local maxima and minima and saddle points. Find each function's value at these points.

65. $f(x, y) = x^2 - xy + y^2 + 2x + 2y - 4$

66. $f(x, y) = 5x^2 + 4xy - 2y^2 + 4x - 4y$

67. $f(x, y) = 2x^3 + 3xy + 2y^3$

68. $f(x, y) = x^3 + y^3 - 3xy + 15$

69. $f(x, y) = x^3 + y^3 + 3x^2 - 3y^2$

70. $f(x, y) = x^4 - 8x^2 + 3y^2 - 6y$

Absolute Extrema

In Exercises 71–78, find the absolute maximum and minimum values of f on the region R.

71. $f(x, y) = x^2 + xy + y^2 - 3x + 3y$

R: The triangular region cut from the first quadrant by the line $x + y = 4$

72. $f(x, y) = x^2 - y^2 - 2x + 4y + 1$

R: The rectangular region in the first quadrant bounded by the coordinate axes and the lines $x = 4$ and $y = 2$

73. $f(x, y) = y^2 - xy - 3y + 2x$

R: The square region enclosed by the lines $x = \pm 2$ and $y = \pm 2$

74. $f(x, y) = 2x + 2y - x^2 - y^2$

R: The square region bounded by the coordinate axes and the lines $x = 2, y = 2$ in the first quadrant

75. $f(x, y) = x^2 - y^2 - 2x + 4y$

R: The triangular region bounded below by the x-axis, above by the line $y = x + 2$, and on the right by the line $x = 2$

76. $f(x, y) = 4xy - x^4 - y^4 + 16$

R: The triangular region bounded below by the line $y = -2$, above by the line $y = x$, and on the right by the line $x = 2$

77. $f(x, y) = x^3 + y^3 + 3x^2 - 3y^2$

R: The square region enclosed by the lines $x = \pm 1$ and $y = \pm 1$

78. $f(x, y) = x^3 + 3xy + y^3 + 1$

R: The square region enclosed by the lines $x = \pm 1$ and $y = \pm 1$

Lagrange Multipliers

79. Extrema on a circle Find the extreme values of $f(x, y) = x^3 + y^2$ on the circle $x^2 + y^2 = 1$.

80. Extrema on a circle Find the extreme values of $f(x, y) = xy$ on the circle $x^2 + y^2 = 1$.

81. Extrema in a disk Find the extreme values of $f(x, y) = x^2 + 3y^2 + 2y$ on the unit disk $x^2 + y^2 \le 1$.

82. Extrema in a disk Find the extreme values of $f(x, y) = x^2 + y^2 - 3x - xy$ on the disk $x^2 + y^2 \le 9$.

83. Extrema on a sphere Find the extreme values of $f(x, y, z) = x - y + z$ on the unit sphere $x^2 + y^2 + z^2 = 1$.

84. Minimum distance to origin Find the points on the surface $x^2 - zy = 4$ closest to the origin.

85. Minimizing cost of a box A closed rectangular box is to have volume V cm^3. The cost of the material used in the box is a cents/cm^2 for top and bottom, b cents/cm^2 for front and back, and c cents/cm^2 for the remaining sides. What dimensions minimize the total cost of materials?

86. Least volume Find the plane $x/a + y/b + z/c = 1$ that passes through the point $(2, 1, 2)$ and cuts off the least volume from the first octant.

87. Extrema on curve of intersecting surfaces Find the extreme values of $f(x, y, z) = x(y + z)$ on the curve of intersection of the right circular cylinder $x^2 + y^2 = 1$ and the hyperbolic cylinder $xz = 1$.

88. Minimum distance to origin on curve of intersecting plane and cone Find the point closest to the origin on the curve of intersection of the plane $x + y + z = 1$ and the cone $z^2 = 2x^2 + 2y^2$.

Partial Derivatives with Constrained Variables

In Exercises 89 and 90, begin by drawing a diagram that shows the relations among the variables.

89. If $w = x^2e^{yz}$ and $z = x^2 - y^2$ find

a. $\left(\frac{\partial w}{\partial y}\right)_z$ **b.** $\left(\frac{\partial w}{\partial z}\right)_x$ **c.** $\left(\frac{\partial w}{\partial z}\right)_y$.

90. Let $U = f(P, V, T)$ be the internal energy of a gas that obeys the ideal gas law $PV = nRT$ (n and R constant). Find

a. $\left(\frac{\partial U}{\partial T}\right)_P$ **b.** $\left(\frac{\partial U}{\partial V}\right)_T$.

Theory and Examples

91. Let $w = f(r, \theta)$, $r = \sqrt{x^2 + y^2}$, and $\theta = \tan^{-1}(y/x)$. Find $\partial w/\partial x$ and $\partial w/\partial y$ and express your answers in terms of r and θ.

92. Let $z = f(u, v)$, $u = ax + by$, and $v = ax - by$. Express z_x and z_y in terms of f_u, f_v, and the constants a and b.

93. If a and b are constants, $w = u^3 + \tanh u + \cos u$, and $u = ax + by$, show that

$$a\frac{\partial w}{\partial y} = b\frac{\partial w}{\partial x}.$$

94. Using the Chain Rule If $w = \ln(x^2 + y^2 + 2z)$, $x = r + s$, $y = r - s$, and $z = 2rs$, find w_r and w_s by the Chain Rule. Then check your answer another way.

95. Angle between vectors The equations $e^u \cos v - x = 0$ and $e^u \sin v - y = 0$ define u and v as differentiable functions of x and y. Show that the angle between the vectors

$$\frac{\partial u}{\partial x}\mathbf{i} + \frac{\partial u}{\partial y}\mathbf{j} \quad \text{and} \quad \frac{\partial v}{\partial x}\mathbf{i} + \frac{\partial v}{\partial y}\mathbf{j}$$

is constant.

96. Polar coordinates and second derivatives Introducing polar coordinates $x = r\cos\theta$ and $y = r\sin\theta$ changes $f(x, y)$ to $g(r, \theta)$. Find the value of $\partial^2 g/\partial\theta^2$ at the point $(r, \theta) = (2, \pi/2)$, given that

$$\frac{\partial f}{\partial x} = \frac{\partial f}{\partial y} = \frac{\partial^2 f}{\partial x^2} = \frac{\partial^2 f}{\partial y^2} = 1$$

at that point.

97. Normal line parallel to a plane Find the points on the surface

$$(y + z)^2 + (z - x)^2 = 16$$

where the normal line is parallel to the yz-plane.

98. Tangent plane parallel to xy-plane Find the points on the surface

$$xy + yz + zx - x - z^2 = 0$$

where the tangent plane is parallel to the xy-plane.

99. When gradient is parallel to position vector Suppose that $\nabla f(x, y, z)$ is always parallel to the position vector $x\mathbf{i} + y\mathbf{j} + z\mathbf{k}$. Show that $f(0, 0, a) = f(0, 0, -a)$ for any a.

100. One-sided directional derivative in all directions, but no gradient The one-sided directional derivative of f at $P(x_0, y_0, z_0)$ in the direction $\mathbf{u} = u_1\mathbf{i} + u_2\mathbf{j} + u_3\mathbf{k}$ is the number

$$\lim_{s\to 0^+} \frac{f(x_0 + su_1, y_0 + su_2, z_0 + su_3) - f(x_0, y_0, z_0)}{s}.$$

Show that the one-sided directional derivative of

$$f(x, y, z) = \sqrt{x^2 + y^2 + z^2}$$

at the origin equals 1 in any direction but that f has no gradient vector at the origin.

101. Normal line through origin Show that the line normal to the surface $xy + z = 2$ at the point $(1, 1, 1)$ passes through the origin.

102. Tangent plane and normal line

a. Sketch the surface $x^2 - y^2 + z^2 = 4$.

b. Find a vector normal to the surface at $(2, -3, 3)$. Add the vector to your sketch.

c. Find equations for the tangent plane and normal line at $(2, -3, 3)$.

Chapter 14 Additional and Advanced Exercises

Partial Derivatives

1. Function with saddle at the origin If you did Exercise 50 in Section 14.2, you know that the function

$$f(x, y) = \begin{cases} xy\dfrac{x^2 - y^2}{x^2 + y^2}, & (x, y) \neq (0, 0) \\ 0, & (x, y) = (0, 0) \end{cases}$$

(see the accompanying figure) is continuous at $(0, 0)$. Find $f_{xy}(0, 0)$ and $f_{yx}(0, 0)$.

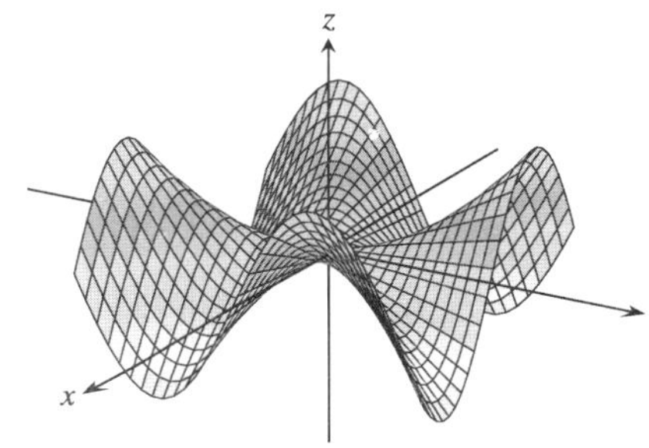

2. **Finding a function from second partials** Find a function $w = f(x, y)$ whose first partial derivatives are $\partial w/\partial x = 1 + e^x \cos y$ and $\partial w/\partial y = 2y - e^x \sin y$ and whose value at the point $(\ln 2, 0)$ is $\ln 2$.

3. **A proof of Leibniz's Rule** Leibniz's Rule says that if f is continuous on $[a, b]$ and if $u(x)$ and $v(x)$ are differentiable functions of x whose values lie in $[a, b]$, then

$$\frac{d}{dx}\int_{u(x)}^{v(x)} f(t)\,dt = f(v(x))\frac{dv}{dx} - f(u(x))\frac{du}{dx}.$$

Prove the rule by setting

$$g(u, v) = \int_u^v f(t)\,dt, \qquad u = u(x), \qquad v = v(x)$$

and calculating dg/dx with the Chain Rule.

4. **Finding a function with constrained second partials** Suppose that f is a twice-differentiable function of r, that $r = \sqrt{x^2 + y^2 + z^2}$, and that

$$f_{xx} + f_{yy} + f_{zz} = 0.$$

Show that for some constants a and b,

$$f(r) = \frac{a}{r} + b.$$

5. **Homogeneous functions** A function $f(x, y)$ is *homogeneous of degree n* (n a nonnegative integer) if $f(tx, ty) = t^n f(x, y)$ for all t, x, and y. For such a function (sufficiently differentiable), prove that

a. $x\dfrac{\partial f}{\partial x} + y\dfrac{\partial f}{\partial y} = nf(x, y)$

b. $x^2\left(\dfrac{\partial^2 f}{\partial x^2}\right) + 2xy\left(\dfrac{\partial^2 f}{\partial x \partial y}\right) + y^2\left(\dfrac{\partial^2 f}{\partial y^2}\right) = n(n-1)f.$

6. **Surface in polar coordinates** Let

$$f(r, \theta) = \begin{cases} \dfrac{\sin 6r}{6r}, & r \neq 0 \\ 1, & r = 0, \end{cases}$$

where r and θ are polar coordinates. Find

a. $\lim_{r \to 0} f(r, \theta)$ **b.** $f_r(0, 0)$ **c.** $f_\theta(r, \theta)$, $r \neq 0$.

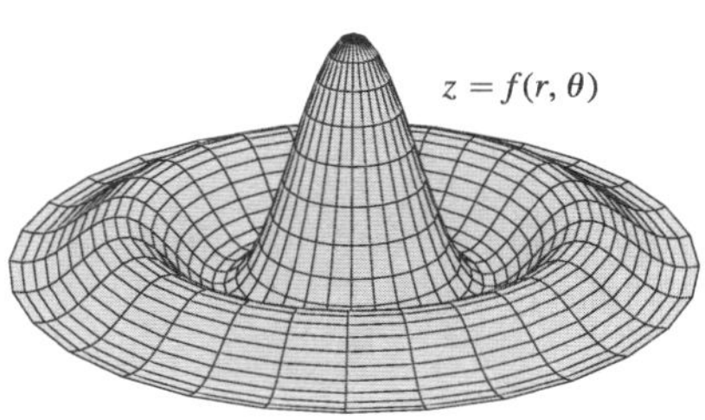

Gradients and Tangents

7. **Properties of position vectors** Let $\mathbf{r} = x\mathbf{i} + y\mathbf{j} + z\mathbf{k}$ and let $r = |\mathbf{r}|$.

a. Show that $\nabla r = \mathbf{r}/r$.

b. Show that $\nabla(r^n) = nr^{n-2}\mathbf{r}$.

c. Find a function whose gradient equals $\mathbf{r}$.

d. Show that $\mathbf{r} \cdot d\mathbf{r} = r\,dr$.

e. Show that $\nabla(\mathbf{A} \cdot \mathbf{r}) = \mathbf{A}$ for any constant vector $\mathbf{A}$.

8. **Gradient orthogonal to tangent** Suppose that a differentiable function $f(x, y)$ has the constant value c along the differentiable curve $x = g(t), y = h(t)$; that is

$$f(g(t), h(t)) = c$$

for all values of t. Differentiate both sides of this equation with respect to t to show that ∇f is orthogonal to the curve's tangent vector at every point on the curve.

9. **Curve tangent to a surface** Show that the curve

$$\mathbf{r}(t) = (\ln t)\mathbf{i} + (t \ln t)\mathbf{j} + t\mathbf{k}$$

is tangent to the surface

$$xz^2 - yz + \cos xy = 1$$

at $(0, 0, 1)$.

10. **Curve tangent to a surface** Show that the curve

$$\mathbf{r}(t) = \left(\frac{t^3}{4} - 2\right)\mathbf{i} + \left(\frac{4}{t} - 3\right)\mathbf{j} + \cos(t - 2)\mathbf{k}$$

is tangent to the surface

$$x^3 + y^3 + z^3 - xyz = 0$$

at $(0, -1, 1)$.

Extreme Values

11. **Extrema on a surface** Show that the only possible maxima and minima of z on the surface $z = x^3 + y^3 - 9xy + 27$ occur at $(0, 0)$ and $(3, 3)$. Show that neither a maximum nor a minimum occurs at $(0, 0)$. Determine whether z has a maximum or a minimum at $(3, 3)$.

12. **Maximum in closed first quadrant** Find the maximum value of $f(x, y) = 6xye^{-(2x+3y)}$ in the closed first quadrant (includes the nonnegative axes).

13. **Minimum volume cut from first octant** Find the minimum volume for a region bounded by the planes $x = 0, y = 0, z = 0$ and a plane tangent to the ellipsoid

$$\frac{x^2}{a^2} + \frac{y^2}{b^2} + \frac{z^2}{c^2} = 1$$

at a point in the first octant.

14. Minimum distance from line to parabola in *xy*-plane By minimizing the function $f(x, y, u, v) = (x - u)^2 + (y - v)^2$ subject to the constraints $y = x + 1$ and $u = v^2$, find the minimum distance in the *xy*-plane from the line $y = x + 1$ to the parabola $y^2 = x$.

Theory and Examples

15. Boundedness of first partials implies continuity Prove the following theorem: If $f(x, y)$ is defined in an open region R of the *xy*-plane and if f_x and f_y are bounded on R, then $f(x, y)$ is continuous on R. (The assumption of boundedness is essential.)

16. Suppose that $\mathbf{r}(t) = g(t)\mathbf{i} + h(t)\mathbf{j} + k(t)\mathbf{k}$ is a smooth curve in the domain of a differentiable function $f(x, y, z)$. Describe the relation between df/dt, ∇f, and $\mathbf{v} = d\mathbf{r}/dt$. What can be said about ∇f and $\mathbf{v}$ at interior points of the curve where f has extreme values relative to its other values on the curve? Give reasons for your answer.

17. Finding functions from partial derivatives Suppose that f and g are functions of x and y such that

$$\frac{\partial f}{\partial y} = \frac{\partial g}{\partial x} \quad \text{and} \quad \frac{\partial f}{\partial x} = \frac{\partial g}{\partial y},$$

and suppose that

$$\frac{\partial f}{\partial x} = 0, \quad f(1, 2) = g(1, 2) = 5 \quad \text{and} \quad f(0, 0) = 4.$$

Find $f(x, y)$ and $g(x, y)$.

18. Rate of change of the rate of change We know that if $f(x, y)$ is a function of two variables and if $\mathbf{u} = a\mathbf{i} + b\mathbf{j}$ is a unit vector, then $D_{\mathbf{u}}f(x, y) = f_x(x, y)a + f_y(x, y)b$ is the rate of change of $f(x, y)$ at (x, y) in the direction of $\mathbf{u}$. Give a similar formula for the rate of change *of the rate of change of* $f(x, y)$ at (x, y) in the direction $\mathbf{u}$.

19. Path of a heat-seeking particle A heat-seeking particle has the property that at any point (x, y) in the plane it moves in the direction of maximum temperature increase. If the temperature at (x, y) is $T(x, y) = -e^{-2y}\cos x$, find an equation $y = f(x)$ for the path of a heat-seeking particle at the point $(\pi/4, 0)$.

20. Velocity after a ricochet A particle traveling in a straight line with constant velocity $\mathbf{i} + \mathbf{j} - 5\mathbf{k}$ passes through the point $(0, 0, 30)$ and hits the surface $z = 2x^2 + 3y^2$. The particle ricochets off the surface, the angle of reflection being equal to the angle of incidence. Assuming no loss of speed, what is the velocity of the particle after the ricochet? Simplify your answer.

21. Directional derivatives tangent to a surface Let S be the surface that is the graph of $f(x, y) = 10 - x^2 - y^2$. Suppose that the temperature in space at each point (x, y, z) is $T(x, y, z) = x^2y + y^2z + 4x + 14y + z$.

a. Among all the possible directions tangential to the surface S at the point $(0, 0, 10)$, which direction will make the rate of change of temperature at $(0, 0, 10)$ a maximum?

b. Which direction tangential to S at the point $(1, 1, 8)$ will make the rate of change of temperature a maximum?

22. Drilling another borehole On a flat surface of land, geologists drilled a borehole straight down and hit a mineral deposit at 1000 ft. They drilled a second borehole 100 ft to the north of the first and hit the mineral deposit at 950 ft. A third borehole 100 ft east of the first borehole struck the mineral deposit at 1025 ft. The geologists have reasons to believe that the mineral deposit is in the shape of a dome, and for the sake of economy, they would like to find where the deposit is closest to the surface. Assuming the surface to be the *xy*-plane, in what direction from the first borehole would you suggest the geologists drill their fourth borehole?

The One-Dimensional Heat Equation

If $w(x, t)$ represents the temperature at position x at time t in a uniform conducting rod with perfectly insulated sides (see the accompanying figure), then the partial derivatives w_{xx} and w_t satisfy a differential equation of the form

$$w_{xx} = \frac{1}{c^2} w_t.$$

This equation is called the **one-dimensional heat equation**. The value of the positive constant c^2 is determined by the material from which the rod is made. It has been determined experimentally for a broad range of materials. For a given application, one finds the appropriate value in a table. For dry soil, for example, $c^2 = 0.19\ \text{ft}^2/\text{day}$.

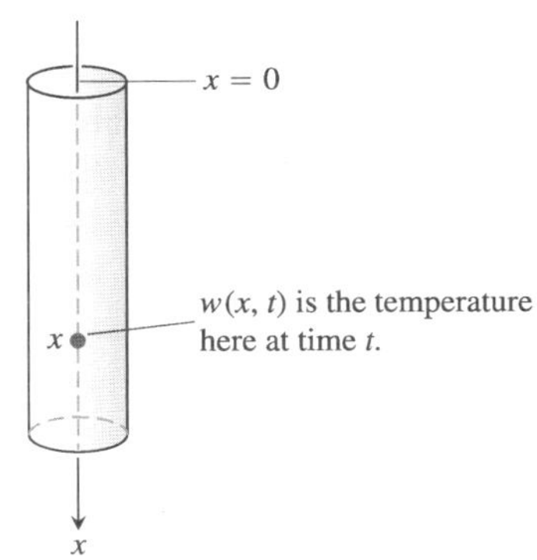

In chemistry and biochemistry, the heat equation is known as the **diffusion equation**. In this context, $w(x, t)$ represents the concentration of a dissolved substance, a salt for instance, diffusing along a tube filled with liquid. The value of $w(x, t)$ is the concentration at point x at time t. In other applications, $w(x, t)$ represents the diffusion of a gas down a long, thin pipe.

In electrical engineering, the heat equation appears in the forms

$$v_{xx} = RCv_t$$

and

$$i_{xx} = RCi_t.$$

These equations describe the voltage υ and the flow of current i in a coaxial cable or in any other cable in which leakage and inductance are negligible. The functions and constants in these equations are

$\upsilon(x, t)$ = voltage at point x at time t

R = resistance per unit length

C = capacitance to ground per unit of cable length

$i(x, t)$ = current at point x at time t.

23. Find all solutions of the one-dimensional heat equation of the form $w = e^{rt} \sin \pi x$, where r is a constant.

24. Find all solutions of the one-dimensional heat equation that have the form $w = e^{rt} \sin kx$ and satisfy the conditions that $w(0, t) = 0$ and $w(L, t) = 0$. What happens to these solutions as $t \to \infty$?

Chapter 14 Technology Application Projects

Mathematica/Maple Module
Plotting Surfaces

Efficiently generate plots of surfaces, contours, and level curves.

Mathematica/Maple Module
Exploring the Mathematics Behind Skateboarding: Analysis of the Directional Derivative

The path of a skateboarder is introduced, first on a level plane, then on a ramp, and finally on a paraboloid. Compute, plot, and analyze the directional derivative in terms of the skateboarder.

Mathematica/Maple Module
Looking for Patterns and Applying the Method of Least Squares to Real Data

Fit a line to a set of numerical data points by choosing the line that minimizes the sum of the squares of the vertical distances from the points to the line.

Mathematica/Maple Module
Lagrange Goes Skateboarding: How High Does He Go?

Revisit and analyze the skateboarders' adventures for maximum and minimum heights from both a graphical and analytic perspective using Lagrange multipliers.

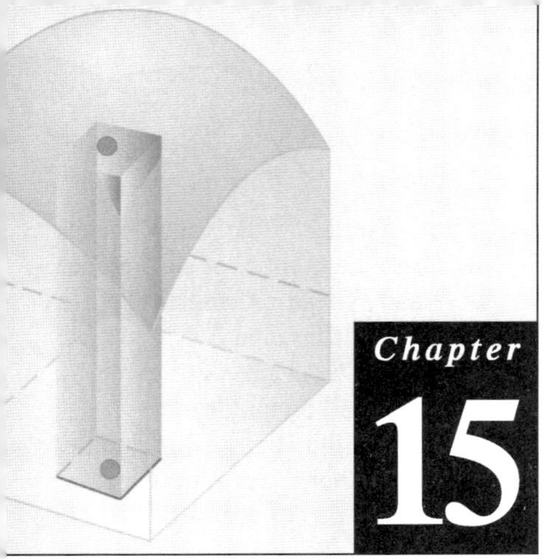

Chapter 15

MULTIPLE INTEGRALS

OVERVIEW In this chapter we consider the integral of a function of two variables $f(x, y)$ over a region in the plane and the integral of a function of three variables $f(x, y, z)$ over a region in space. These integrals are called *multiple integrals* and are defined as the limit of approximating Riemann sums, much like the single-variable integrals presented in Chapter 5. We can use multiple integrals to calculate quantities that vary over two or three dimensions, such as the total mass or the angular momentum of an object of varying density and the volumes of solids with general curved boundaries.

15.1 Double Integrals

In Chapter 5 we defined the definite integral of a continuous function $f(x)$ over an interval $[a, b]$ as a limit of Riemann sums. In this section we extend this idea to define the integral of a continuous function of two variables $f(x, y)$ over a bounded region R in the plane. In both cases the integrals are limits of approximating Riemann sums. The Riemann sums for the integral of a single-variable function $f(x)$ are obtained by partitioning a finite interval into thin subintervals, multiplying the width of each subinterval by the value of f at a point c_k inside that subinterval, and then adding together all the products. A similar method of partitioning, multiplying, and summing is used to construct double integrals. However, this time we pack a planar region R with small rectangles, rather than small subintervals. We then take the product of each small rectangle's area with the value of f at a point inside that rectangle, and finally sum together all these products. When f is continuous, these sums converge to a single number as each of the small rectangles shrinks in both width and height. The limit is the *double integral* of f over R. As with single integrals, we can evaluate multiple integrals via antiderivatives, which frees us from the formidable task of calculating a double integral directly from its definition as a limit of Riemann sums. The major practical problem that arises in evaluating multiple integrals lies in determining the limits of integration. While the integrals of Chapter 5 were evaluated over an interval, which is determined by its two endpoints, multiple integrals are evaluated over a region in the plane or in space. This gives rise to limits of integration which often involve variables, not just constants. Describing the regions of integration is the main new issue that arises in the calculation of multiple integrals.

Double Integrals over Rectangles

We begin our investigation of double integrals by considering the simplest type of planar region, a rectangle. We consider a function $f(x, y)$ defined on a rectangular region R,

$$R: \quad a \le x \le b, \quad c \le y \le d.$$

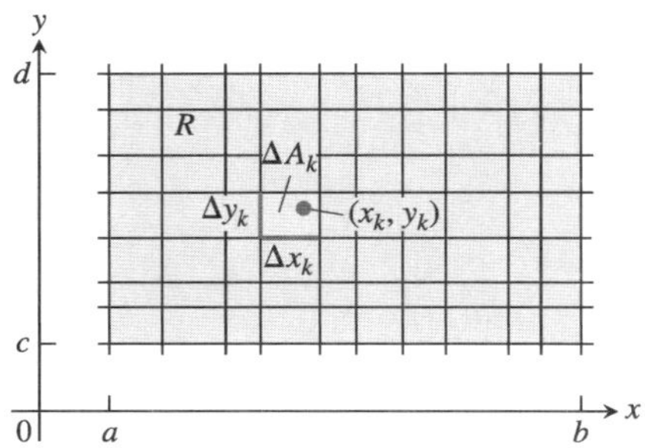

FIGURE 15.1 Rectangular grid partitioning the region R into small rectangles of area $\Delta A_k = \Delta x_k\, \Delta y_k$.

We subdivide R into small rectangles using a network of lines parallel to the x- and y-axes (Figure 15.1). The lines divide R into n rectangular pieces, where the number of such pieces n gets large as the width and height of each piece gets small. These rectangles form a **partition** of R. A small rectangular piece of width Δx and height Δy has area $\Delta A = \Delta x \Delta y$. If we number the small pieces partitioning R in some order, then their areas are given by numbers $\Delta A_1, \Delta A_2, \ldots, \Delta A_n$, where ΔA_k is the area of the kth small rectangle.

To form a Riemann sum over R, we choose a point (x_k, y_k) in the kth small rectangle, multiply the value of f at that point by the area ΔA_k, and add together the products:

$$S_n = \sum_{k=1}^{n} f(x_k, y_k)\, \Delta A_k.$$

Depending on how we pick (x_k, y_k) in the kth small rectangle, we may get different values for S_n.

We are interested in what happens to these Riemann sums as the widths and heights of all the small rectangles in the partition of R approach zero. The **norm** of a partition P, written $\|P\|$, is the largest width or height of any rectangle in the partition. If $\|P\| = 0.1$ then all the rectangles in the partition of R have width at most 0.1 and height at most 0.1. Sometimes the Riemann sums converge as the norm of P goes to zero, written $\|P\| \to 0$. The resulting limit is then written as

$$\lim_{\|P\|\to 0} \sum_{k=1}^{n} f(x_k, y_k)\, \Delta A_k.$$

As $\|P\| \to 0$ and the rectangles get narrow and short, their number n increases, so we can also write this limit as

$$\lim_{n\to\infty} \sum_{k=1}^{n} f(x_k, y_k)\, \Delta A_k.$$

with the understanding that $\Delta A_k \to 0$ as $n \to \infty$ and $\|P\| \to 0$.

There are many choices involved in a limit of this kind. The collection of small rectangles is determined by the grid of vertical and horizontal lines that determine a rectangular partition of R. In each of the resulting small rectangles there is a choice of an arbitrary point (x_k, y_k) at which f is evaluated. These choices together determine a single Riemann sum. To form a limit, we repeat the whole process again and again, choosing partitions whose rectangle widths and heights both go to zero and whose number goes to infinity.

When a limit of the sums S_n exists, giving the same limiting value no matter what choices are made, then the function f is said to be **integrable** and the limit is called the **double integral** of f over R, written as

$$\iint_R f(x, y)\, dA \qquad \text{or} \qquad \iint_R f(x, y)\, dx\, dy.$$

It can be shown that if $f(x, y)$ is a continuous function throughout R, then f is integrable, as in the single-variable case discussed in Chapter 5. Many discontinuous functions are also integrable, including functions which are discontinuous only on a finite number of points or smooth curves. We leave the proof of these facts to a more advanced text.

Double Integrals as Volumes

When $f(x, y)$ is a positive function over a rectangular region R in the xy-plane, we may interpret the double integral of f over R as the volume of the 3-dimensional solid region over the xy-plane bounded below by R and above by the surface $z = f(x, y)$ (Figure 15.2). Each term $f(x_k, y_k)\Delta A_k$ in the sum $S_n = \sum f(x_k, y_k)\Delta A_k$ is the volume of a vertical

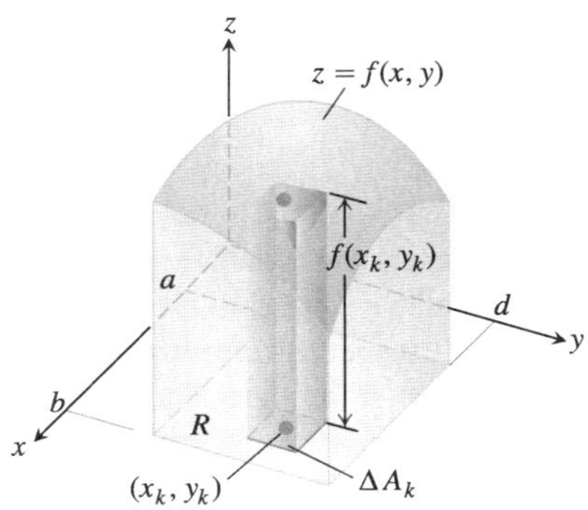

FIGURE 15.2 Approximating solids with rectangular boxes leads us to define the volumes of more general solids as double integrals. The volume of the solid shown here is the double integral of $f(x, y)$ over the base region R.

rectangular box that approximates the volume of the portion of the solid that stands directly above the base ΔA_k. The sum S_n thus approximates what we want to call the total volume of the solid. We *define* this volume to be

$$\text{Volume} = \lim_{n\to\infty} S_n = \iint_R f(x, y)\, dA,$$

where $\Delta A_k \to 0$ as $n \to \infty$.

As you might expect, this more general method of calculating volume agrees with the methods in Chapter 6, but we do not prove this here. Figure 15.3 shows Riemann sum approximations to the volume becoming more accurate as the number n of boxes increases.

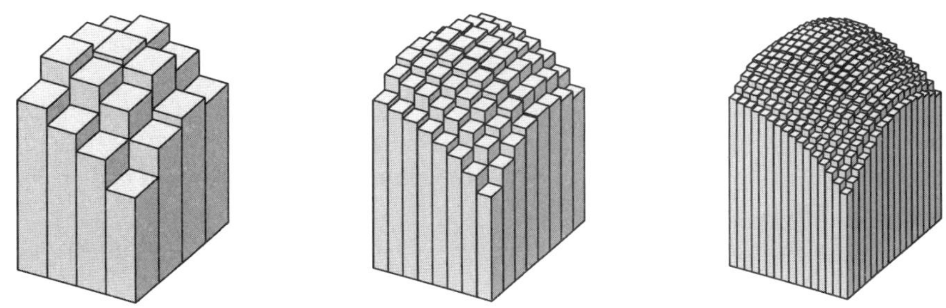

(a) $n = 16$ (b) $n = 64$ (c) $n = 256$

FIGURE 15.3 As n increases, the Riemann sum approximations approach the total volume of the solid shown in Figure 15.2.

Fubini's Theorem for Calculating Double Integrals

Suppose that we wish to calculate the volume under the plane $z = 4 - x - y$ over the rectangular region R: $0 \le x \le 2$, $0 \le y \le 1$ in the xy-plane. If we apply the method of slicing from Section 6.1, with slices perpendicular to the x-axis (Figure 15.4), then the volume is

$$\int_{x=0}^{x=2} A(x)\, dx, \tag{1}$$

where $A(x)$ is the cross-sectional area at x. For each value of x, we may calculate $A(x)$ as the integral

$$A(x) = \int_{y=0}^{y=1} (4 - x - y)\, dy, \tag{2}$$

which is the area under the curve $z = 4 - x - y$ in the plane of the cross-section at x. In calculating $A(x)$, x is held fixed and the integration takes place with respect to y. Combining Equations (1) and (2), we see that the volume of the entire solid is

$$\begin{aligned} \text{Volume} &= \int_{x=0}^{x=2} A(x)\, dx = \int_{x=0}^{x=2} \left(\int_{y=0}^{y=1} (4 - x - y)\, dy \right) dx \\ &= \int_{x=0}^{x=2} \left[4y - xy - \frac{y^2}{2} \right]_{y=0}^{y=1} dx = \int_{x=0}^{x=2} \left(\frac{7}{2} - x \right) dx \\ &= \left[\frac{7}{2}x - \frac{x^2}{2} \right]_0^2 = 5. \end{aligned} \tag{3}$$

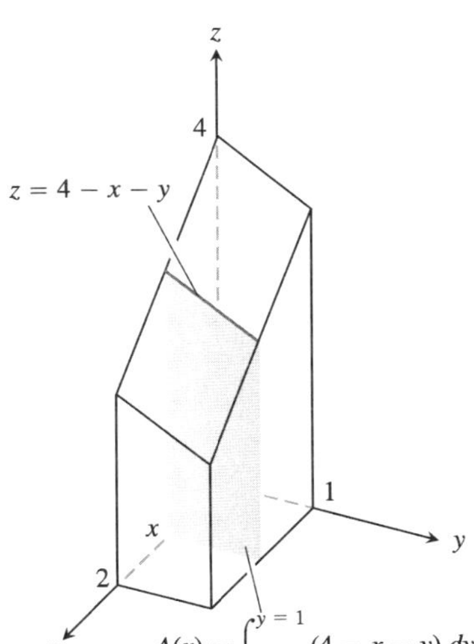

FIGURE 15.4 To obtain the cross-sectional area $A(x)$, we hold x fixed and integrate with respect to y.

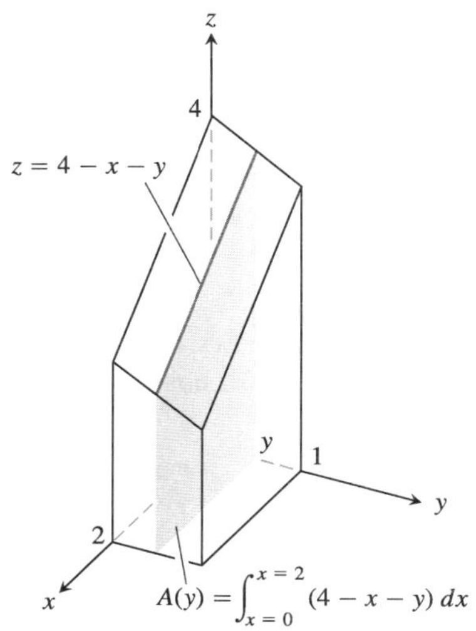

FIGURE 15.5 To obtain the cross-sectional area $A(y)$, we hold y fixed and integrate with respect to x.

If we just wanted to write a formula for the volume, without carrying out any of the integrations, we could write

$$\text{Volume} = \int_0^2 \int_0^1 (4 - x - y)\, dy\, dx.$$

The expression on the right, called an **iterated** or **repeated integral**, says that the volume is obtained by integrating $4 - x - y$ with respect to y from $y = 0$ to $y = 1$, holding x fixed, and then integrating the resulting expression in x with respect to x from $x = 0$ to $x = 2$. The limits of integration 0 and 1 are associated with y, so they are placed on the integral closest to dy. The other limits of integration, 0 and 2, are associated with the variable x, so they are placed on the outside integral symbol that is paired with dx.

What would have happened if we had calculated the volume by slicing with planes perpendicular to the y-axis (Figure 15.5)? As a function of y, the typical cross-sectional area is

$$A(y) = \int_{x=0}^{x=2} (4 - x - y)\, dx = \left[4x - \frac{x^2}{2} - xy\right]_{x=0}^{x=2} = 6 - 2y. \tag{4}$$

The volume of the entire solid is therefore

$$\text{Volume} = \int_{y=0}^{y=1} A(y)\, dy = \int_{y=0}^{y=1} (6 - 2y)\, dy = \left[6y - y^2\right]_0^1 = 5,$$

in agreement with our earlier calculation.

Again, we may give a formula for the volume as an iterated integral by writing

$$\text{Volume} = \int_0^1 \int_0^2 (4 - x - y)\, dx\, dy.$$

The expression on the right says we can find the volume by integrating $4 - x - y$ with respect to x from $x = 0$ to $x = 2$ as in Equation (4) and integrating the result with respect to y from $y = 0$ to $y = 1$. In this iterated integral, the order of integration is first x and then y, the reverse of the order in Equation (3).

What do these two volume calculations with iterated integrals have to do with the double integral

$$\iint_R (4 - x - y)\, dA$$

over the rectangle $R: 0 \le x \le 2, 0 \le y \le 1$? The answer is that both iterated integrals give the value of the double integral. This is what we would reasonably expect, since the double integral measures the volume of the same region as the two iterated integrals. A theorem published in 1907 by Guido Fubini says that the double integral of any continuous function over a rectangle can be calculated as an iterated integral in either order of integration. (Fubini proved his theorem in greater generality, but this is what it says in our setting.)

HISTORICAL BIOGRAPHY

Guido Fubini
(1879–1943)

THEOREM 1 Fubini's Theorem (First Form)
If $f(x, y)$ is continuous throughout the rectangular region $R: a \le x \le b$, $c \le y \le d$, then

$$\iint_R f(x, y)\, dA = \int_c^d \int_a^b f(x, y)\, dx\, dy = \int_a^b \int_c^d f(x, y)\, dy\, dx.$$

Fubini's Theorem says that double integrals over rectangles can be calculated as iterated integrals. Thus, we can evaluate a double integral by integrating with respect to one variable at a time.

Fubini's Theorem also says that we may calculate the double integral by integrating in *either* order, a genuine convenience, as we see in Example 3. When we calculate a volume by slicing, we may use either planes perpendicular to the x-axis or planes perpendicular to the y-axis.

EXAMPLE 1 Evaluating a Double Integral

Calculate $\iint_R f(x, y)\, dA$ for

$$f(x, y) = 1 - 6x^2y \quad \text{and} \quad R:\ 0 \le x \le 2,\quad -1 \le y \le 1.$$

Solution By Fubini's Theorem,

$$\iint_R f(x, y)\, dA = \int_{-1}^{1}\int_{0}^{2} (1 - 6x^2y)\, dx\, dy = \int_{-1}^{1} \Big[x - 2x^3y\Big]_{x=0}^{x=2} dy$$

$$= \int_{-1}^{1} (2 - 16y)\, dy = \Big[2y - 8y^2\Big]_{-1}^{1} = 4.$$

Reversing the order of integration gives the same answer:

$$\int_{0}^{2}\int_{-1}^{1} (1 - 6x^2y)\, dy\, dx = \int_{0}^{2} \Big[y - 3x^2y^2\Big]_{y=-1}^{y=1} dx$$

$$= \int_{0}^{2} [(1 - 3x^2) - (-1 - 3x^2)]\, dx$$

$$= \int_{0}^{2} 2\, dx = 4.$$

■

USING TECHNOLOGY Multiple Integration

Most CAS can calculate both multiple and iterated integrals. The typical procedure is to apply the CAS integrate command in nested iterations according to the order of integration you specify.

Integral	Typical CAS Formulation
$\iint x^2y\, dx\, dy$	int (int (x ^ 2 * y, x), y) ;
$\int_{-\pi/3}^{\pi/4}\int_{0}^{1} x\cos y\, dx\, dy$	int (int (x * cos (y), x = 0 . . 1), y = −Pi/3 . . Pi/4);

If a CAS cannot produce an exact value for a definite integral, it can usually find an approximate value numerically. Setting up a multiple integral for a CAS to solve can be a highly nontrivial task, and requires an understanding of how to describe the boundaries of the region and set up an appropriate integral.

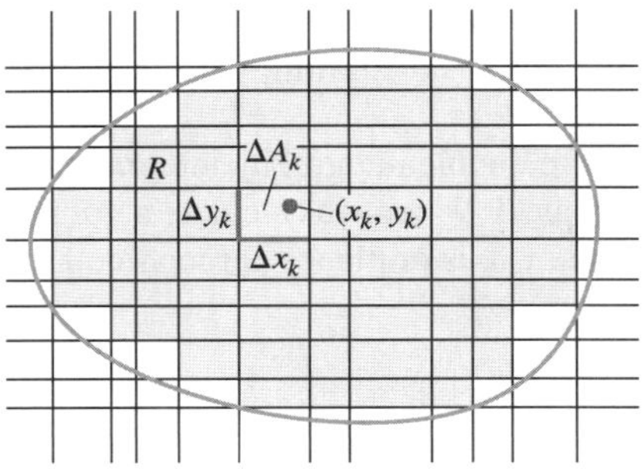

FIGURE 15.6 A rectangular grid partitioning a bounded nonrectangular region into rectangular cells.

Double Integrals over Bounded Nonrectangular Regions

To define the double integral of a function $f(x, y)$ over a bounded, nonrectangular region R, such as the one in Figure 15.6, we again begin by covering R with a grid of small rectangular cells whose union contains all points of R. This time, however, we cannot exactly fill R with a finite number of rectangles lying inside R, since its boundary is curved, and some of the small rectangles in the grid lie partly outside R. A partition of R is formed by taking the rectangles that lie completely inside it, not using any that are either partly or completely outside. For commonly arising regions, more and more of R is included as the norm of a partition (the largest width or height of any rectangle used) approaches zero.

Once we have a partition of R, we number the rectangles in some order from 1 to n and let ΔA_k be the area of the kth rectangle. We then choose a point (x_k, y_k) in the kth rectangle and form the Riemann sum

$$S_n = \sum_{k=1}^{n} f(x_k, y_k)\,\Delta A_k.$$

As the norm of the partition forming S_n goes to zero, $\|P\| \to 0$, the width and height of each enclosed rectangle goes to zero and their number goes to infinity. If $f(x, y)$ is a continuous function, then these Riemann sums converge to a limiting value, not dependent on any of the choices we made. This limit is called the **double integral** of $f(x, y)$ over R:

$$\lim_{\|P\|\to 0} \sum_{k=1}^{n} f(x_k, y_k)\,\Delta A_k = \iint_R f(x, y)\,dA.$$

The nature of the boundary of R introduces issues not found in integrals over an interval. When R has a curved boundary, the n rectangles of a partition lie inside R but do not cover all of R. In order for a partition to approximate R well, the parts of R covered by small rectangles lying partly outside R must become negligible as the norm of the partition approaches zero. This property of being nearly filled in by a partition of small norm is satisfied by all the regions that we will encounter. There is no problem with boundaries made from polygons, circles, ellipses, and from continuous graphs over an interval, joined end to end. A curve with a "fractal" type of shape would be problematic, but such curves are not relevant for most applications. A careful discussion of which type of regions R can be used for computing double integrals is left to a more advanced text.

Double integrals of continuous functions over nonrectangular regions have the same algebraic properties (summarized further on) as integrals over rectangular regions. The domain Additivity Property says that if R is decomposed into nonoverlapping regions R_1 and R_2 with boundaries that are again made of a finite number of line segments or smooth curves (see Figure 15.7 for an example), then

$$\iint_R f(x, y)\,dA = \iint_{R_1} f(x, y)\,dA + \iint_{R_2} f(x, y)\,dA.$$

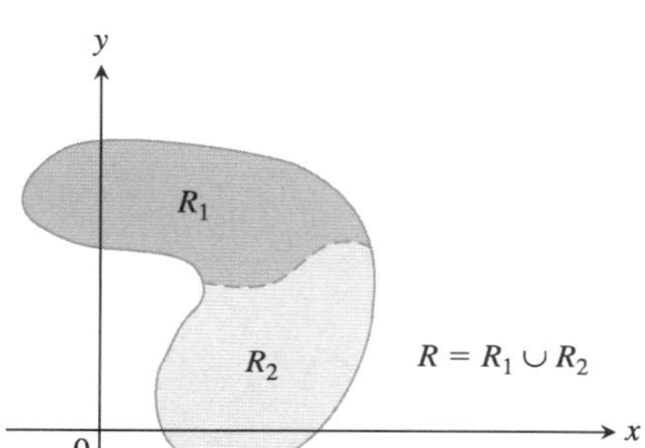

$$\iint_R f(x, y)\,dA = \iint_{R_1} f(x, y)\,dA + \iint_{R_2} f(x, y)\,dA$$

FIGURE 15.7 The Additivity Property for rectangular regions holds for regions bounded by continuous curves.

If $f(x, y)$ is positive and continuous over R we define the volume of the solid region between R and the surface $z = f(x, y)$ to be $\iint_R f(x, y)\,dA$, as before (Figure 15.8).

If R is a region like the one shown in the xy-plane in Figure 15.9, bounded "above" and "below" by the curves $y = g_2(x)$ and $y = g_1(x)$ and on the sides by the lines $x = a$, $x = b$, we may again calculate the volume by the method of slicing. We first calculate the cross-sectional area

$$A(x) = \int_{y=g_1(x)}^{y=g_2(x)} f(x, y)\,dy$$

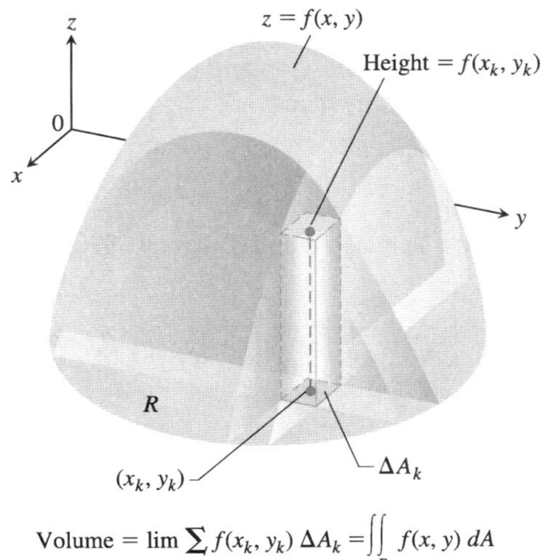

FIGURE 15.8 We define the volumes of solids with curved bases the same way we define the volumes of solids with rectangular bases.

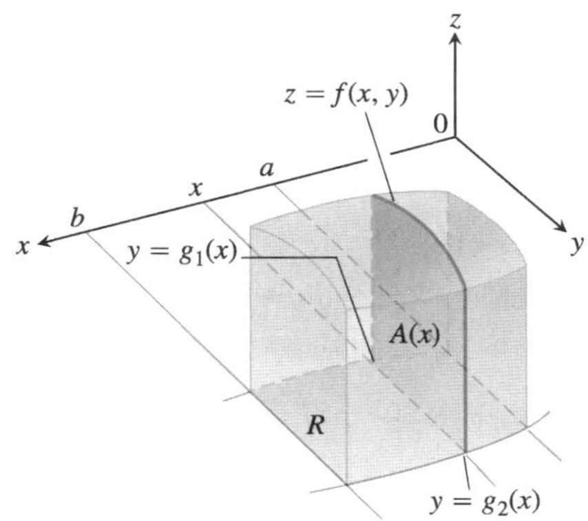

FIGURE 15.9 The area of the vertical slice shown here is

$$A(x) = \int_{g_1(x)}^{g_2(x)} f(x, y)\, dy.$$

To calculate the volume of the solid, we integrate this area from $x = a$ to $x = b$.

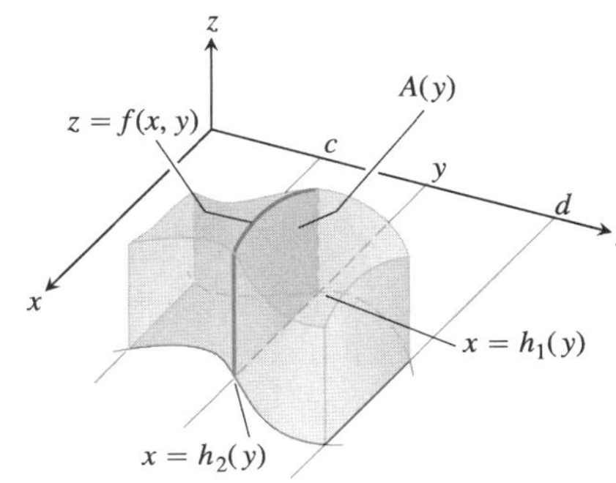

FIGURE 15.10 The volume of the solid shown here is

$$\int_c^d A(y)\, dy = \int_c^d \int_{h_1(y)}^{h_2(y)} f(x, y)\, dx\, dy.$$

and then integrate $A(x)$ from $x = a$ to $x = b$ to get the volume as an iterated integral:

$$V = \int_a^b A(x)\, dx = \int_a^b \int_{g_1(x)}^{g_2(x)} f(x, y)\, dy\, dx. \tag{5}$$

Similarly, if R is a region like the one shown in Figure 15.10, bounded by the curves $x = h_2(y)$ and $x = h_1(y)$ and the lines $y = c$ and $y = d$, then the volume calculated by slicing is given by the iterated integral

$$\text{Volume} = \int_c^d \int_{h_1(y)}^{h_2(y)} f(x, y)\, dx\, dy. \tag{6}$$

That the iterated integrals in Equations (5) and (6) both give the volume that we defined to be the double integral of f over R is a consequence of the following stronger form of Fubini's Theorem.

THEOREM 2 Fubini's Theorem (Stronger Form)

Let $f(x, y)$ be continuous on a region R.

1. If R is defined by $a \le x \le b$, $g_1(x) \le y \le g_2(x)$, with g_1 and g_2 continuous on $[a, b]$, then

$$\iint_R f(x, y)\, dA = \int_a^b \int_{g_1(x)}^{g_2(x)} f(x, y)\, dy\, dx.$$

2. If R is defined by $c \le y \le d$, $h_1(y) \le x \le h_2(y)$, with h_1 and h_2 continuous on $[c, d]$, then

$$\iint_R f(x, y)\, dA = \int_c^d \int_{h_1(y)}^{h_2(y)} f(x, y)\, dx\, dy.$$

EXAMPLE 2 Finding Volume

Find the volume of the prism whose base is the triangle in the xy-plane bounded by the x-axis and the lines $y = x$ and $x = 1$ and whose top lies in the plane

$$z = f(x, y) = 3 - x - y.$$

Solution See Figure 15.11 on page 1075. For any x between 0 and 1, y may vary from $y = 0$ to $y = x$ (Figure 15.11b). Hence,

$$V = \int_0^1 \int_0^x (3 - x - y)\, dy\, dx = \int_0^1 \left[3y - xy - \frac{y^2}{2}\right]_{y=0}^{y=x} dx$$

$$= \int_0^1 \left(3x - \frac{3x^2}{2}\right) dx = \left[\frac{3x^2}{2} - \frac{x^3}{2}\right]_{x=0}^{x=1} = 1.$$

When the order of integration is reversed (Figure 15.11c), the integral for the volume is

$$V = \int_0^1 \int_y^1 (3 - x - y)\, dx\, dy = \int_0^1 \left[3x - \frac{x^2}{2} - xy\right]_{x=y}^{x=1} dy$$

$$= \int_0^1 \left(3 - \frac{1}{2} - y - 3y + \frac{y^2}{2} + y^2\right) dy$$

$$= \int_0^1 \left(\frac{5}{2} - 4y + \frac{3}{2}y^2\right) dy = \left[\frac{5}{2}y - 2y^2 + \frac{y^3}{2}\right]_{y=0}^{y=1} = 1.$$

The two integrals are equal, as they should be. ■

Although Fubini's Theorem assures us that a double integral may be calculated as an iterated integral in either order of integration, the value of one integral may be easier to find than the value of the other. The next example shows how this can happen.

EXAMPLE 3 Evaluating a Double Integral

Calculate

$$\iint_R \frac{\sin x}{x}\, dA,$$

where R is the triangle in the xy-plane bounded by the x-axis, the line $y = x$, and the line $x = 1$.

Solution The region of integration is shown in Figure 15.12. If we integrate first with respect to y and then with respect to x, we find

$$\int_0^1 \left(\int_0^x \frac{\sin x}{x}\, dy\right) dx = \int_0^1 \left(y \frac{\sin x}{x}\bigg]_{y=0}^{y=x}\right) dx = \int_0^1 \sin x\, dx$$

$$= -\cos(1) + 1 \approx 0.46.$$

If we reverse the order of integration and attempt to calculate

$$\int_0^1 \int_y^1 \frac{\sin x}{x}\, dx\, dy,$$

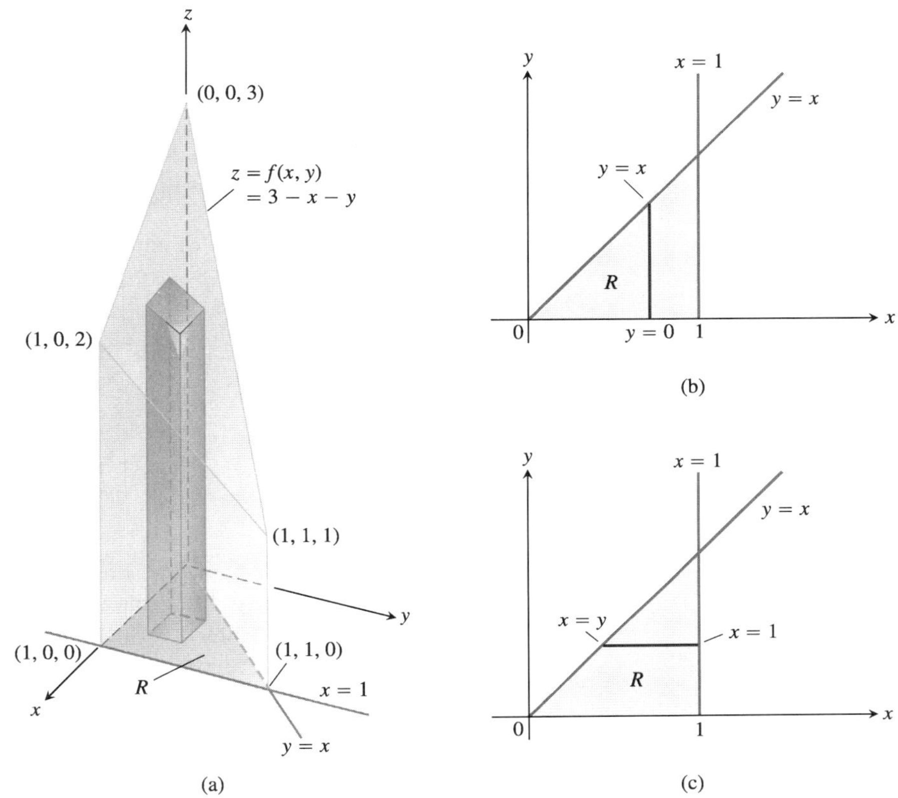

FIGURE 15.11 (a) Prism with a triangular base in the xy-plane. The volume of this prism is defined as a double integral over R. To evaluate it as an iterated integral, we may integrate first with respect to y and then with respect to x, or the other way around (Example 2).
(b) Integration limits of

$$\int_{x=0}^{x=1}\int_{y=0}^{y=x} f(x, y)\, dy\, dx.$$

If we integrate first with respect to y, we integrate along a vertical line through R and then integrate from left to right to include all the vertical lines in R.
(c) Integration limits of

$$\int_{y=0}^{y=1}\int_{x=y}^{x=1} f(x, y)\, dx\, dy.$$

If we integrate first with respect to x, we integrate along a horizontal line through R and then integrate from bottom to top to include all the horizontal lines in R.

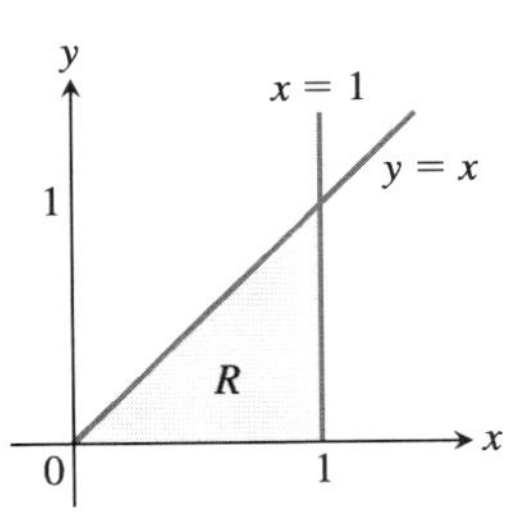

FIGURE 15.12 The region of integration in Example 3.

we run into a problem, because $\int((\sin x)/x)\, dx$ cannot be expressed in terms of elementary functions (there is no simple antiderivative).

There is no general rule for predicting which order of integration will be the good one in circumstances like these. If the order you first choose doesn't work, try the other. Sometimes neither order will work, and then we need to use numerical approximations. ■

Finding Limits of Integration

We now give a procedure for finding limits of integration that applies for many regions in the plane. Regions that are more complicated, and for which this procedure fails, can often be split up into pieces on which the procedure works.

When faced with evaluating $\iint_R f(x, y)\,dA$, integrating first with respect to y and then with respect to x, do the following:

1. *Sketch.* Sketch the region of integration and label the bounding curves.

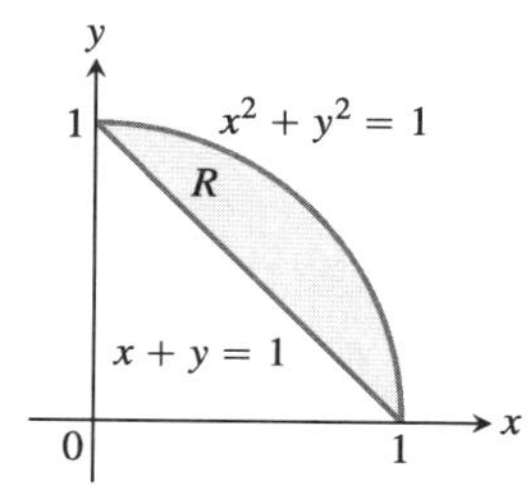

2. *Find the y-limits of integration.* Imagine a vertical line L cutting through R in the direction of increasing y. Mark the y-values where L enters and leaves. These are the y-limits of integration and are usually functions of x (instead of constants).

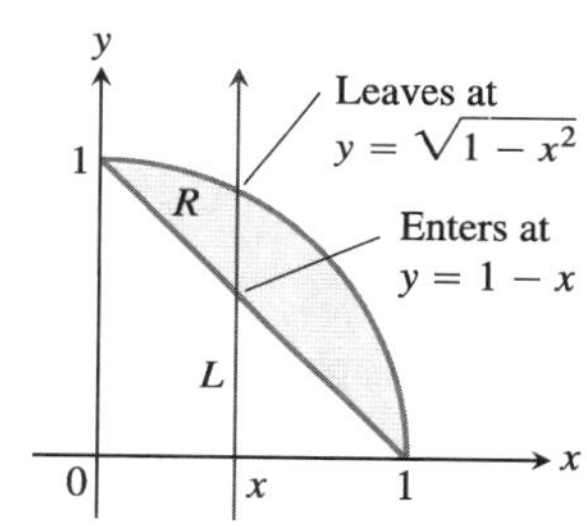

3. *Find the x-limits of integration.* Choose x-limits that include all the vertical lines through R. The integral shown here is

$$\iint_R f(x, y)\,dA =$$

$$\int_{x=0}^{x=1} \int_{y=1-x}^{y=\sqrt{1-x^2}} f(x, y)\,dy\,dx.$$

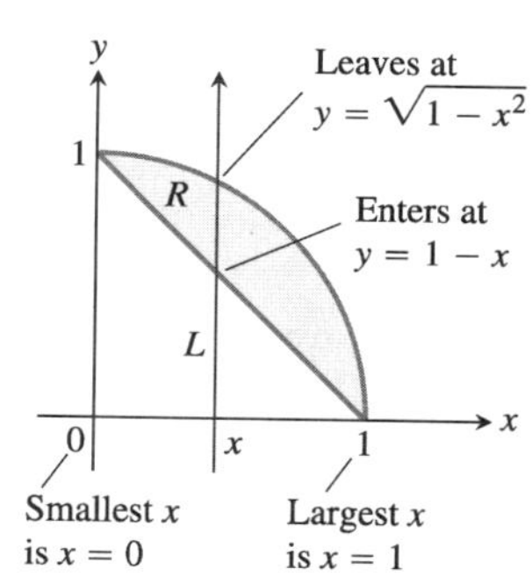

To evaluate the same double integral as an iterated integral with the order of integration reversed, use horizontal lines instead of vertical lines in Steps 2 and 3. The integral is

$$\iint_R f(x, y)\, dA = \int_0^1 \int_{1-y}^{\sqrt{1-y^2}} f(x, y)\, dx\, dy.$$

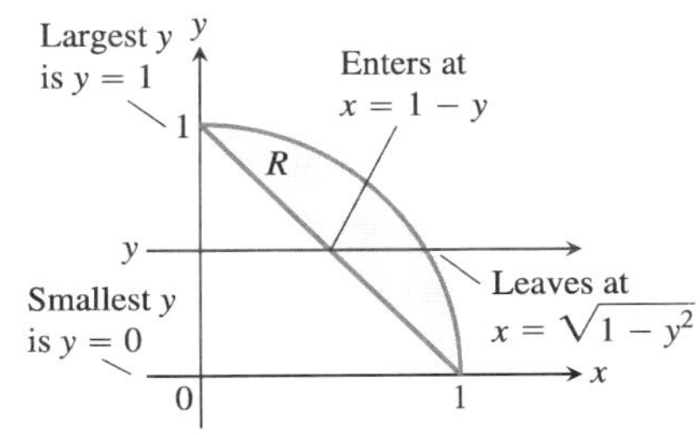

EXAMPLE 4 Reversing the Order of Integration

Sketch the region of integration for the integral

$$\int_0^2 \int_{x^2}^{2x} (4x + 2)\, dy\, dx$$

and write an equivalent integral with the order of integration reversed.

Solution The region of integration is given by the inequalities $x^2 \le y \le 2x$ and $0 \le x \le 2$. It is therefore the region bounded by the curves $y = x^2$ and $y = 2x$ between $x = 0$ and $x = 2$ (Figure 15.13a).

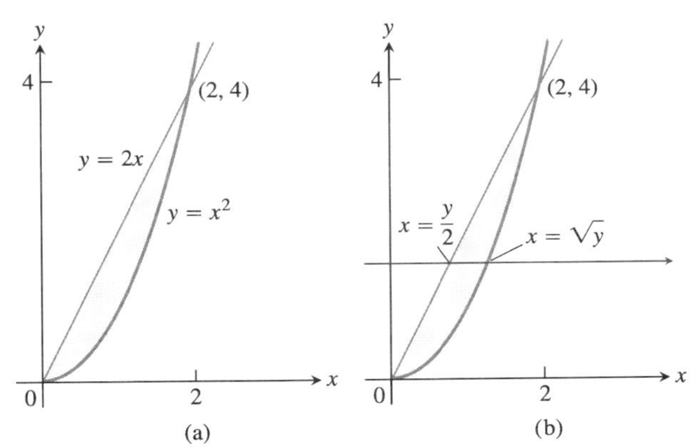

FIGURE 15.13 Region of integration for Example 4.

To find limits for integrating in the reverse order, we imagine a horizontal line passing from left to right through the region. It enters at $x = y/2$ and leaves at $x = \sqrt{y}$. To include all such lines, we let y run from $y = 0$ to $y = 4$ (Figure 15.13b). The integral is

$$\int_0^4 \int_{y/2}^{\sqrt{y}} (4x + 2)\, dx\, dy.$$

The common value of these integrals is 8. ■

Properties of Double Integrals

Like single integrals, double integrals of continuous functions have algebraic properties that are useful in computations and applications.

Properties of Double Integrals

If $f(x, y)$ and $g(x, y)$ are continuous, then

1. *Constant Multiple:* $\displaystyle\iint_R cf(x, y)\, dA = c\iint_R f(x, y)\, dA$ (any number c)

2. *Sum and Difference:*

$$\iint_R (f(x, y) \pm g(x, y))\, dA = \iint_R f(x, y)\, dA \pm \iint_R g(x, y)\, dA$$

3. *Domination:*

(a) $\displaystyle\iint_R f(x, y)\, dA \geq 0 \quad \text{if} \quad f(x, y) \geq 0 \text{ on } R$

(b) $\displaystyle\iint_R f(x, y)\, dA \geq \iint_R g(x, y)\, dA \quad \text{if} \quad f(x, y) \geq g(x, y) \text{ on } R$

4. *Additivity:* $\displaystyle\iint_R f(x, y)\, dA = \iint_{R_1} f(x, y)\, dA + \iint_{R_2} f(x, y)\, dA$

if R is the union of two nonoverlapping regions R_1 and R_2 (Figure 15.7).

The idea behind these properties is that integrals behave like sums. If the function $f(x, y)$ is replaced by its constant multiple $cf(x, y)$, then a Riemann sum for f

$$S_n = \sum_{k=1}^{n} f(x_k, y_k)\, \Delta A_k$$

is replaced by a Riemann sum for cf

$$\sum_{k=1}^{n} cf(x_k, y_k)\, \Delta A_k = c\sum_{k=1}^{n} f(x_k, y_k)\, \Delta A_k = cS_n.$$

Taking limits as $n \rightarrow \infty$ shows that $c\lim_{n\to\infty} S_n = c\iint_R f\, dA$ and $\lim_{n\to\infty} cS_n = \iint_R cf\, dA$ are equal. It follows that the constant multiple property carries over from sums to double integrals.

The other properties are also easy to verify for Riemann sums, and carry over to double integrals for the same reason. While this discussion gives the idea, an actual proof that these properties hold requires a more careful analysis of how Riemann sums converge.

EXERCISES 15.1

Finding Regions of Integration and Double Integrals

In Exercises 1–10, sketch the region of integration and evaluate the integral.

1. $\int_0^3 \int_0^2 (4 - y^2)\, dy\, dx$

2. $\int_0^3 \int_{-2}^0 (x^2y - 2xy)\, dy\, dx$

3. $\int_{-1}^0 \int_{-1}^1 (x + y + 1)\, dx\, dy$

4. $\int_{\pi}^{2\pi} \int_0^{\pi} (\sin x + \cos y)\, dx\, dy$

5. $\int_0^{\pi} \int_0^x x \sin y\, dy\, dx$

6. $\int_0^{\pi} \int_0^{\sin x} y\, dy\, dx$

7. $\int_1^{\ln 8} \int_0^{\ln y} e^{x+y}\, dx\, dy$

8. $\int_1^2 \int_y^{y^2} dx\, dy$

9. $\int_0^1 \int_0^{y^2} 3y^3 e^{xy}\, dx\, dy$

10. $\int_1^4 \int_0^{\sqrt{x}} \frac{3}{2} e^{y/\sqrt{x}}\, dy\, dx$

In Exercises 11–16, integrate f over the given region.

11. **Quadrilateral** $f(x, y) = x/y$ over the region in the first quadrant bounded by the lines $y = x$, $y = 2x$, $x = 1$, $x = 2$

12. **Square** $f(x, y) = 1/(xy)$ over the square $1 \le x \le 2$, $1 \le y \le 2$

13. **Triangle** $f(x, y) = x^2 + y^2$ over the triangular region with vertices $(0, 0)$, $(1, 0)$, and $(0, 1)$

14. **Rectangle** $f(x, y) = y \cos xy$ over the rectangle $0 \le x \le \pi$, $0 \le y \le 1$

15. **Triangle** $f(u, v) = v - \sqrt{u}$ over the triangular region cut from the first quadrant of the uv-plane by the line $u + v = 1$

16. **Curved region** $f(s, t) = e^s \ln t$ over the region in the first quadrant of the st-plane that lies above the curve $s = \ln t$ from $t = 1$ to $t = 2$

Each of Exercises 17–20 gives an integral over a region in a Cartesian coordinate plane. Sketch the region and evaluate the integral.

17. $\int_{-2}^0 \int_v^{-v} 2\, dp\, dv$ (the pv-plane)

18. $\int_0^1 \int_0^{\sqrt{1-s^2}} 8t\, dt\, ds$ (the st-plane)

19. $\int_{-\pi/3}^{\pi/3} \int_0^{\sec t} 3 \cos t\, du\, dt$ (the tu-plane)

20. $\int_0^3 \int_1^{4-2u} \frac{4 - 2u}{v^2}\, dv\, du$ (the uv-plane)

Reversing the Order of Integration

In Exercises 21–30, sketch the region of integration and write an equivalent double integral with the order of integration reversed.

21. $\int_0^1 \int_2^{4-2x} dy\, dx$

22. $\int_0^2 \int_{y-2}^0 dx\, dy$

23. $\int_0^1 \int_y^{\sqrt{y}} dx\, dy$

24. $\int_0^1 \int_{1-x}^{1-x^2} dy\, dx$

25. $\int_0^1 \int_1^{e^x} dy\, dx$

26. $\int_0^{\ln 2} \int_{e^y}^2 dx\, dy$

27. $\int_0^{3/2} \int_0^{9-4x^2} 16x\, dy\, dx$

28. $\int_0^2 \int_0^{4-y^2} y\, dx\, dy$

29. $\int_0^1 \int_{-\sqrt{1-y^2}}^{\sqrt{1-y^2}} 3y\, dx\, dy$

30. $\int_0^2 \int_{-\sqrt{4-x^2}}^{\sqrt{4-x^2}} 6x\, dy\, dx$

Evaluating Double Integrals

In Exercises 31–40, sketch the region of integration, reverse the order of integration, and evaluate the integral.

31. $\int_0^{\pi} \int_x^{\pi} \frac{\sin y}{y}\, dy\, dx$

32. $\int_0^2 \int_x^2 2y^2 \sin xy\, dy\, dx$

33. $\int_0^1 \int_y^1 x^2 e^{xy}\, dx\, dy$

34. $\int_0^2 \int_0^{4-x^2} \frac{xe^{2y}}{4 - y}\, dy\, dx$

35. $\int_0^{2\sqrt{\ln 3}} \int_{y/2}^{\sqrt{\ln 3}} e^{x^2}\, dx\, dy$

36. $\int_0^3 \int_{\sqrt{x/3}}^1 e^{y^3}\, dy\, dx$

37. $\int_0^{1/16} \int_{y^{1/4}}^{1/2} \cos(16\pi x^5)\, dx\, dy$

38. $\int_0^8 \int_{\sqrt[3]{x}}^2 \frac{dy\, dx}{y^4 + 1}$

39. **Square region** $\iint_R (y - 2x^2)\, dA$ where R is the region bounded by the square $|x| + |y| = 1$

40. **Triangular region** $\iint_R xy\, dA$ where R is the region bounded by the lines $y = x$, $y = 2x$, and $x + y = 2$

Volume Beneath a Surface $z = f(x, y)$

41. Find the volume of the region bounded by the paraboloid $z = x^2 + y^2$ and below by the triangle enclosed by the lines $y = x$, $x = 0$, and $x + y = 2$ in the xy-plane.

42. Find the volume of the solid that is bounded above by the cylinder $z = x^2$ and below by the region enclosed by the parabola $y = 2 - x^2$ and the line $y = x$ in the xy-plane.

43. Find the volume of the solid whose base is the region in the xy-plane that is bounded by the parabola $y = 4 - x^2$ and the line $y = 3x$, while the top of the solid is bounded by the plane $z = x + 4$.

44. Find the volume of the solid in the first octant bounded by the coordinate planes, the cylinder $x^2 + y^2 = 4$, and the plane $z + y = 3$.

45. Find the volume of the solid in the first octant bounded by the coordinate planes, the plane $x = 3$, and the parabolic cylinder $z = 4 - y^2$.

46. Find the volume of the solid cut from the first octant by the surface $z = 4 - x^2 - y$.

47. Find the volume of the wedge cut from the first octant by the cylinder $z = 12 - 3y^2$ and the plane $x + y = 2$.

48. Find the volume of the solid cut from the square column $|x| + |y| \leq 1$ by the planes $z = 0$ and $3x + z = 3$.

49. Find the volume of the solid that is bounded on the front and back by the planes $x = 2$ and $x = 1$, on the sides by the cylinders $y = \pm 1/x$, and above and below by the planes $z = x + 1$ and $z = 0$.

50. Find the volume of the solid bounded on the front and back by the planes $x = \pm\pi/3$, on the sides by the cylinders $y = \pm\sec x$, above by the cylinder $z = 1 + y^2$, and below by the xy-plane.

Integrals over Unbounded Regions

Improper double integrals can often be computed similarly to improper integrals of one variable. The first iteration of the following improper integrals is conducted just as if they were proper integrals. One then evaluates an improper integral of a single variable by taking appropriate limits, as in Section 8.8. Evaluate the improper integrals in Exercises 51–54 as iterated integrals.

51. $\displaystyle\int_1^{\infty}\int_{e^{-x}}^{1} \frac{1}{x^3 y}\,dy\,dx$

52. $\displaystyle\int_{-1}^{1}\int_{-1/\sqrt{1-x^2}}^{1/\sqrt{1-x^2}} (2y + 1)\,dy\,dx$

53. $\displaystyle\int_{-\infty}^{\infty}\int_{-\infty}^{\infty} \frac{1}{(x^2 + 1)(y^2 + 1)}\,dx\,dy$

54. $\displaystyle\int_0^{\infty}\int_0^{\infty} xe^{-(x+2y)}\,dx\,dy$

Approximating Double Integrals

In Exercises 55 and 56, approximate the double integral of $f(x, y)$ over the region R partitioned by the given vertical lines $x = a$ and horizontal lines $y = c$. In each subrectangle, use (x_k, y_k) as indicated for your approximation.

$$\iint_R f(x, y)\,dA \approx \sum_{k=1}^{n} f(x_k, y_k)\,\Delta A_k$$

55. $f(x, y) = x + y$ over the region R bounded above by the semicircle $y = \sqrt{1 - x^2}$ and below by the x-axis, using the partition $x = -1, -1/2, 0, 1/4, 1/2, 1$ and $y = 0, 1/2, 1$ with (x_k, y_k) the lower left corner in the kth subrectangle (provided the subrectangle lies within R)

56. $f(x, y) = x + 2y$ over the region R inside the circle $(x - 2)^2 + (y - 3)^2 = 1$ using the partition $x = 1, 3/2, 2, 5/2, 3$ and $y = 2, 5/2, 3, 7/2, 4$ with (x_k, y_k) the center (centroid) in the kth subrectangle (provided the subrectangle lies within R)

Theory and Examples

57. **Circular sector** Integrate $f(x, y) = \sqrt{4 - x^2}$ over the smaller sector cut from the disk $x^2 + y^2 \leq 4$ by the rays $\theta = \pi/6$ and $\theta = \pi/2$.

58. **Unbounded region** Integrate $f(x, y) = 1/[(x^2 - x)(y - 1)^{2/3}]$ over the infinite rectangle $2 \leq x < \infty, 0 \leq y \leq 2$.

59. **Noncircular cylinder** A solid right (noncircular) cylinder has its base R in the xy-plane and is bounded above by the paraboloid $z = x^2 + y^2$. The cylinder's volume is

$$V = \int_0^1\int_0^y (x^2 + y^2)\,dx\,dy + \int_1^2\int_0^{2-y} (x^2 + y^2)\,dx\,dy.$$

Sketch the base region R and express the cylinder's volume as a single iterated integral with the order of integration reversed. Then evaluate the integral to find the volume.

60. **Converting to a double integral** Evaluate the integral

$$\int_0^2 (\tan^{-1}\pi x - \tan^{-1} x)\,dx.$$

(*Hint:* Write the integrand as an integral.)

61. **Maximizing a double integral** What region R in the xy-plane maximizes the value of

$$\iint_R (4 - x^2 - 2y^2)\,dA?$$

Give reasons for your answer.

62. **Minimizing a double integral** What region R in the xy-plane minimizes the value of

$$\iint_R (x^2 + y^2 - 9)\,dA?$$

Give reasons for your answer.

63. Is it possible to evaluate the integral of a continuous function $f(x, y)$ over a rectangular region in the xy-plane and get different answers depending on the order of integration? Give reasons for your answer.

64. How would you evaluate the double integral of a continuous function $f(x, y)$ over the region R in the xy-plane enclosed by the triangle with vertices (0, 1), (2, 0), and (1, 2)? Give reasons for your answer.

65. **Unbounded region** Prove that

$$\int_{-\infty}^{\infty}\int_{-\infty}^{\infty} e^{-x^2-y^2}\,dx\,dy = \lim_{b\to\infty}\int_{-b}^{b}\int_{-b}^{b} e^{-x^2-y^2}\,dx\,dy = 4\left(\int_0^{\infty} e^{-x^2}\,dx\right)^2.$$

66. **Improper double integral** Evaluate the improper integral

$$\int_0^1\int_0^3 \frac{x^2}{(y - 1)^{2/3}}\,dy\,dx.$$

COMPUTER EXPLORATIONS

Evaluating Double Integrals Numerically

Use a CAS double-integral evaluator to estimate the values of the integrals in Exercises 67–70.

67. $\int_1^3 \int_1^x \frac{1}{xy}\, dy\, dx$

68. $\int_0^1 \int_0^1 e^{-(x^2+y^2)}\, dy\, dx$

69. $\int_0^1 \int_0^1 \tan^{-1} xy\, dy\, dx$

70. $\int_{-1}^1 \int_0^{\sqrt{1-x^2}} 3\sqrt{1-x^2-y^2}\, dy\, dx$

Use a CAS double-integral evaluator to find the integrals in Exercises 71–76. Then reverse the order of integration and evaluate, again with a CAS.

71. $\int_0^1 \int_{2y}^4 e^{x^2}\, dx\, dy$

72. $\int_0^3 \int_{x^2}^9 x\cos(y^2)\, dy\, dx$

73. $\int_0^2 \int_{y^3}^{4\sqrt{2y}} (x^2y - xy^2)\, dx\, dy$

74. $\int_0^2 \int_0^{4-y^2} e^{xy}\, dx\, dy$

75. $\int_1^2 \int_0^{x^2} \frac{1}{x+y}\, dy\, dx$

76. $\int_1^2 \int_{y^3}^8 \frac{1}{\sqrt{x^2+y^2}}\, dx\, dy$

15.2 Area, Moments, and Centers of Mass

In this section, we show how to use double integrals to calculate the areas of bounded regions in the plane and to find the average value of a function of two variables. Then we study the physical problem of finding the center of mass of a thin plate covering a region in the plane.

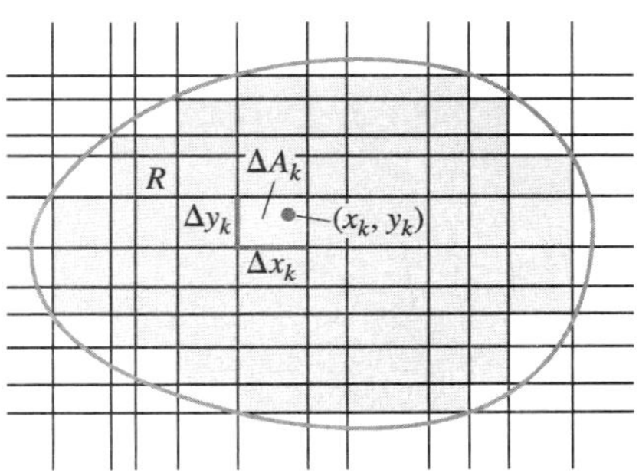

FIGURE 15.14 As the norm of a partition of the region R approaches zero, the sum of the areas ΔA_k gives the area of R defined by the double integral $\iint_R dA$.

Areas of Bounded Regions in the Plane

If we take $f(x, y) = 1$ in the definition of the double integral over a region R in the preceding section, the Riemann sums reduce to

$$S_n = \sum_{k=1}^{n} f(x_k, y_k)\,\Delta A_k = \sum_{k=1}^{n} \Delta A_k. \tag{1}$$

This is simply the sum of the areas of the small rectangles in the partition of R, and approximates what we would like to call the area of R. As the norm of a partition of R approaches zero, the height and width of all rectangles in the partition approach zero, and the coverage of R becomes increasingly complete (Figure 15.14). We define the area of R to be the limit

$$Area = \lim_{\|P\|\to 0} \sum_{k=1}^{n} \Delta A_k = \iint_R dA \tag{2}$$

DEFINITION Area

The **area** of a closed, bounded plane region R is

$$A = \iint_R dA.$$

As with the other definitions in this chapter, the definition here applies to a greater variety of regions than does the earlier single-variable definition of area, but it agrees with the earlier definition on regions to which they both apply. To evaluate the integral in the definition of area, we integrate the constant function $f(x, y) = 1$ over R.

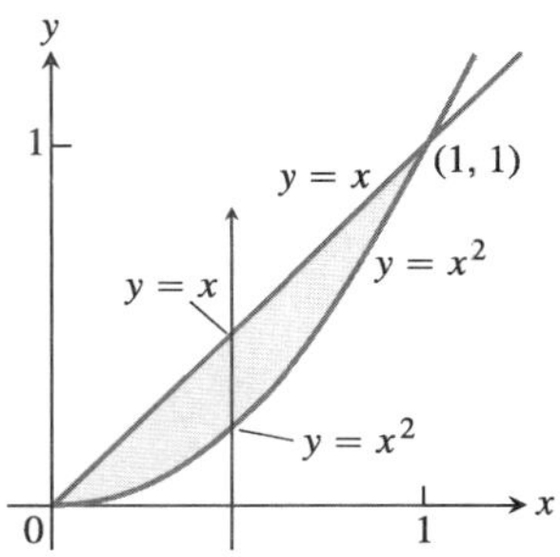

FIGURE 15.15 The region in Example 1.

EXAMPLE 1 Finding Area

Find the area of the region R bounded by $y = x$ and $y = x^2$ in the first quadrant.

Solution We sketch the region (Figure 15.15), noting where the two curves intersect, and calculate the area as

$$A = \int_0^1 \int_{x^2}^{x} dy\, dx = \int_0^1 \Big[y \Big]_{x^2}^{x} dx$$

$$= \int_0^1 (x - x^2)\, dx = \left[\frac{x^2}{2} - \frac{x^3}{3} \right]_0^1 = \frac{1}{6}.$$

Notice that the single integral $\int_0^1 (x - x^2)\, dx$, obtained from evaluating the inside iterated integral, is the integral for the area between these two curves using the method of Section 5.5. ■

EXAMPLE 2 Finding Area

Find the area of the region R enclosed by the parabola $y = x^2$ and the line $y = x + 2$.

Solution If we divide R into the regions R_1 and R_2 shown in Figure 15.16a, we may calculate the area as

$$A = \iint_{R_1} dA + \iint_{R_2} dA = \int_0^1 \int_{-\sqrt{y}}^{\sqrt{y}} dx\, dy + \int_1^4 \int_{y-2}^{\sqrt{y}} dx\, dy.$$

On the other hand, reversing the order of integration (Figure 15.16b) gives

$$A = \int_{-1}^{2} \int_{x^2}^{x+2} dy\, dx.$$

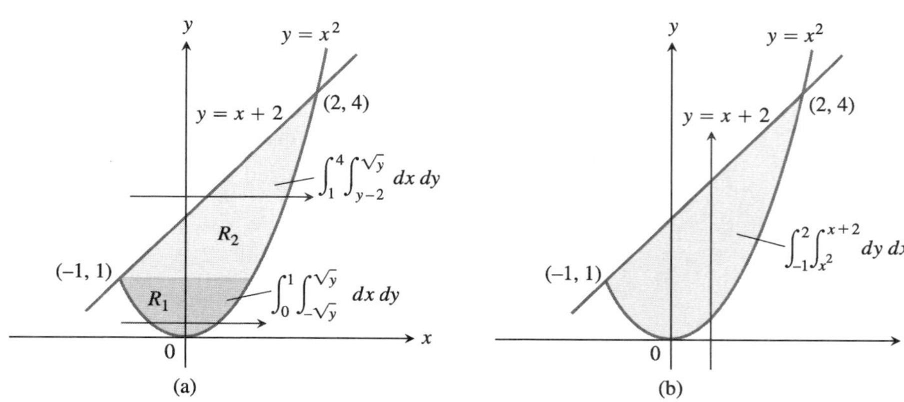

FIGURE 15.16 Calculating this area takes (a) two double integrals if the first integration is with respect to x, but (b) only one if the first integration is with respect to y (Example 2).

This second result, which requires only one integral, is simpler and is the only one we would bother to write down in practice. The area is

$$A = \int_{-1}^{2} \Big[y \Big]_{x^2}^{x+2} dx = \int_{-1}^{2} (x + 2 - x^2)\, dx = \left[\frac{x^2}{2} + 2x - \frac{x^3}{3} \right]_{-1}^{2} = \frac{9}{2}. \qquad ■$$

Average Value

The average value of an integrable function of one variable on a closed interval is the integral of the function over the interval divided by the length of the interval. For an integrable function of two variables defined on a bounded region in the plane, the average value is the integral over the region divided by the area of the region. This can be visualized by thinking of the function as giving the height at one instant of some water sloshing around in a tank whose vertical walls lie over the boundary of the region. The average height of the water in the tank can be found by letting the water settle down to a constant height. The height is then equal to the volume of water in the tank divided by the area of R. We are led to define the average value of an integrable function f over a region R to be

$$\textbf{Average value} \text{ of } f \text{ over } R = \frac{1}{\text{area of } R} \iint_R f\, dA. \qquad (3)$$

If f is the temperature of a thin plate covering R, then the double integral of f over R divided by the area of R is the plate's average temperature. If $f(x, y)$ is the distance from the point (x, y) to a fixed point P, then the average value of f over R is the average distance of points in R from P.

EXAMPLE 3 Finding Average Value

Find the average value of $f(x, y) = x \cos xy$ over the rectangle $R: 0 \le x \le \pi$, $0 \le y \le 1$.

Solution The value of the integral of f over R is

$$\int_0^{\pi} \int_0^{1} x \cos xy\, dy\, dx = \int_0^{\pi} \Big[\sin xy \Big]_{y=0}^{y=1} dx \qquad \int x \cos xy\, dy = \sin xy + C$$

$$= \int_0^{\pi} (\sin x - 0)\, dx = -\cos x \Big]_0^{\pi} = 1 + 1 = 2.$$

The area of R is π. The average value of f over R is $2/\pi$. ■

Moments and Centers of Mass for Thin Flat Plates

In Section 6.4 we introduced the concepts of moments and centers of mass, and we saw how to compute these quantities for thin rods or strips and for plates of constant density. Using multiple integrals we can extend these calculations to a great variety of shapes with varying density. We first consider the problem of finding the center of mass of a thin flat plate: a disk of aluminum, say, or a triangular sheet of metal. We assume the distribution of mass in such a plate to be continuous. A material's *density* function, denoted by $\delta(x, y)$, is the mass per unit area. The *mass* of a plate is obtained by integrating the density function over the region R forming the plate. The first moment about an axis is calculated by integrating over R the distance from the axis times the density. The center of mass is found from the first moments. Table 15.1 gives the double integral formulas for mass, first moments, and center of mass.

TABLE 15.1 Mass and first moment formulas for thin plates covering a region R in the xy-plane

Mass:	$M = \iint_R \delta(x, y)\, dA$	$\delta(x, y)$ is the density at (x, y)
First moments:	$M_x = \iint_R y\delta(x, y)\, dA,$	$M_y = \iint_R x\delta(x, y)\, dA$
Center of mass:	$\bar{x} = \dfrac{M_y}{M},$	$\bar{y} = \dfrac{M_x}{M}$

EXAMPLE 4 Finding the Center of Mass of a Thin Plate of Variable Density

A thin plate covers the triangular region bounded by the x-axis and the lines $x = 1$ and $y = 2x$ in the first quadrant. The plate's density at the point (x, y) is $\delta(x, y) = 6x + 6y + 6$. Find the plate's mass, first moments, and center of mass about the coordinate axes.

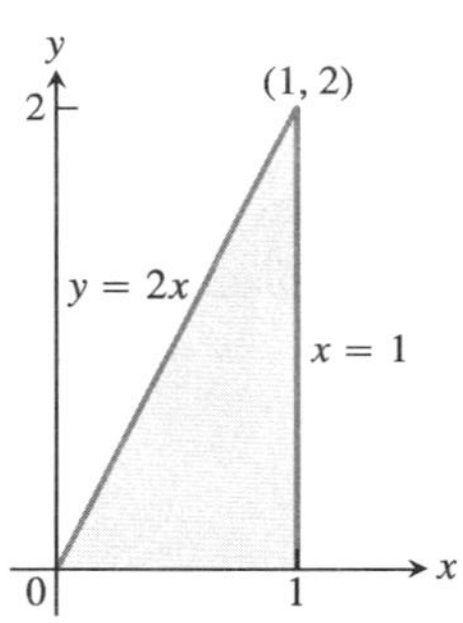

FIGURE 15.17 The triangular region covered by the plate in Example 4.

Solution We sketch the plate and put in enough detail to determine the limits of integration for the integrals we have to evaluate (Figure 15.17).

The plate's mass is

$$M = \int_0^1 \int_0^{2x} \delta(x, y)\, dy\, dx = \int_0^1 \int_0^{2x} (6x + 6y + 6)\, dy\, dx$$

$$= \int_0^1 \left[6xy + 3y^2 + 6y \right]_{y=0}^{y=2x} dx$$

$$= \int_0^1 (24x^2 + 12x)\, dx = \left[8x^3 + 6x^2 \right]_0^1 = 14.$$

The first moment about the x-axis is

$$M_x = \int_0^1 \int_0^{2x} y\delta(x, y)\, dy\, dx = \int_0^1 \int_0^{2x} (6xy + 6y^2 + 6y)\, dy\, dx$$

$$= \int_0^1 \left[3xy^2 + 2y^3 + 3y^2 \right]_{y=0}^{y=2x} dx = \int_0^1 (28x^3 + 12x^2)\, dx$$

$$= \left[7x^4 + 4x^3 \right]_0^1 = 11.$$

A similar calculation gives the moment about the y-axis:

$$M_y = \int_0^1 \int_0^{2x} x\delta(x, y)\, dy\, dx = 10.$$

The coordinates of the center of mass are therefore

$$\bar{x} = \frac{M_y}{M} = \frac{10}{14} = \frac{5}{7}, \qquad \bar{y} = \frac{M_x}{M} = \frac{11}{14}.$$

Moments of Inertia

A body's first moments (Table 15.1) tell us about balance and about the torque the body exerts about different axes in a gravitational field. If the body is a rotating shaft, however, we are more likely to be interested in how much energy is stored in the shaft or about how much energy it will take to accelerate the shaft to a particular angular velocity. This is where the second moment or moment of inertia comes in.

Think of partitioning the shaft into small blocks of mass Δm_k and let r_k denote the distance from the kth block's center of mass to the axis of rotation (Figure 15.18). If the shaft rotates at an angular velocity of $\omega = d\theta/dt$ radians per second, the block's center of mass will trace its orbit at a linear speed of

$$v_k = \frac{d}{dt}(r_k\theta) = r_k\frac{d\theta}{dt} = r_k\omega.$$

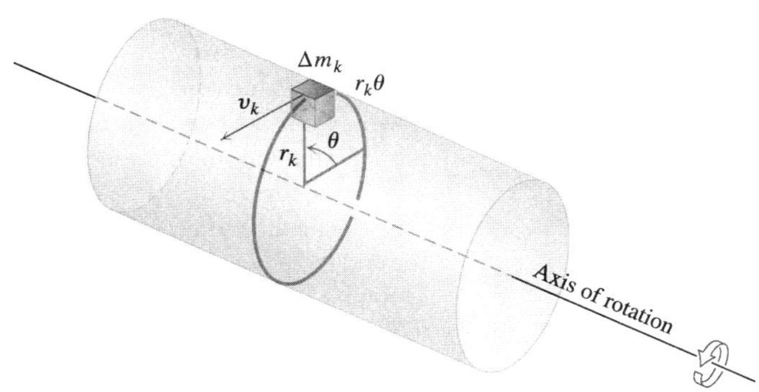

FIGURE 15.18 To find an integral for the amount of energy stored in a rotating shaft, we first imagine the shaft to be partitioned into small blocks. Each block has its own kinetic energy. We add the contributions of the individual blocks to find the kinetic energy of the shaft.

The block's kinetic energy will be approximately

$$\frac{1}{2}\Delta m_k v_k^2 = \frac{1}{2}\Delta m_k(r_k\omega)^2 = \frac{1}{2}\omega^2 r_k^2\, \Delta m_k.$$

The kinetic energy of the shaft will be approximately

$$\sum \frac{1}{2}\omega^2 r_k^2\, \Delta m_k.$$

The integral approached by these sums as the shaft is partitioned into smaller and smaller blocks gives the shaft's kinetic energy:

$$\mathrm{KE}_{\text{shaft}} = \int \frac{1}{2}\omega^2 r^2\, dm = \frac{1}{2}\omega^2 \int r^2\, dm. \tag{4}$$

The factor

$$I = \int r^2\, dm$$

is the *moment of inertia* of the shaft about its axis of rotation, and we see from Equation (4) that the shaft's kinetic energy is

$$\mathrm{KE}_{\text{shaft}} = \frac{1}{2} I\omega^2.$$

The moment of inertia of a shaft resembles in some ways the inertia of a locomotive. To start a locomotive with mass m moving at a linear velocity v, we need to provide a kinetic energy of $\mathrm{KE} = (1/2)mv^2$. To stop the locomotive we have to remove this amount of energy. To start a shaft with moment of inertia I rotating at an angular velocity ω, we need to provide a kinetic energy of $\mathrm{KE} = (1/2)I\omega^2$. To stop the shaft we have to take this amount of energy back out. The shaft's moment of inertia is analogous to the locomotive's mass. What makes the locomotive hard to start or stop is its mass. What makes the shaft hard to start or stop is its moment of inertia. The moment of inertia depends not only on the mass of the shaft, but also its distribution.

The moment of inertia also plays a role in determining how much a horizontal metal beam will bend under a load. The stiffness of the beam is a constant times I, the moment of inertia of a typical cross-section of the beam about the beam's longitudinal axis. The greater the value of I, the stiffer the beam and the less it will bend under a given load. That is why we use I-beams instead of beams whose cross-sections are square. The flanges at the top and bottom of the beam hold most of the beam's mass away from the longitudinal axis to maximize the value of I (Figure 15.19).

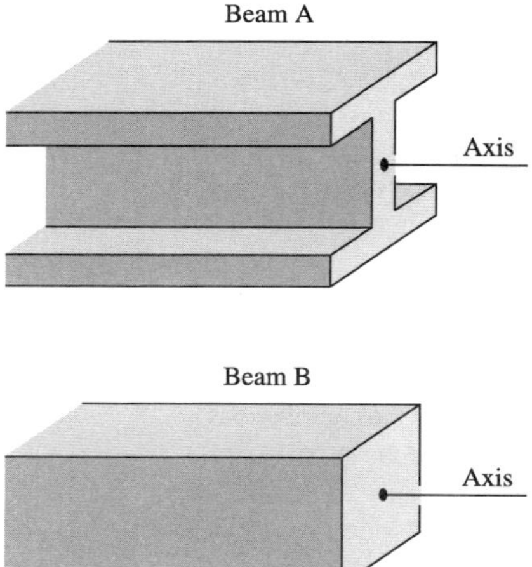

FIGURE 15.19 The greater the polar moment of inertia of the cross-section of a beam about the beam's longitudinal axis, the stiffer the beam. Beams A and B have the same cross-sectional area, but A is stiffer.

To see the moment of inertia at work, try the following experiment. Tape two coins to the ends of a pencil and twiddle the pencil about the center of mass. The moment of inertia accounts for the resistance you feel each time you change the direction of motion. Now move the coins an equal distance toward the center of mass and twiddle the pencil again. The system has the same mass and the same center of mass but now offers less resistance to the changes in motion. The moment of inertia has been reduced. The moment of inertia is what gives a baseball bat, golf club, or tennis racket its "feel." Tennis rackets that weigh the same, look the same, and have identical centers of mass will feel different and behave differently if their masses are not distributed the same way.

Computations of moments of inertia for thin plates in the plane lead to double integral formulas, which are summarized in Table 15.2. A small thin piece of mass Δm is equal to its small area ΔA multiplied by the density of a point in the piece. Computations of moments of inertia for objects occupying a region in space are discussed in Section 15.5.

The mathematical difference between the **first moments** M_x and M_y and the **moments of inertia**, or **second moments**, I_x and I_y is that the second moments use the *squares* of the "lever-arm" distances x and y.

The moment I_0 is also called the **polar moment** of inertia about the origin. It is calculated by integrating the density $\delta(x, y)$ (mass per unit area) times $r^2 = x^2 + y^2$, the square of the distance from a representative point (x, y) to the origin. Notice that $I_0 = I_x + I_y$; once we find two, we get the third automatically. (The moment I_0 is sometimes called I_z, for moment of inertia about the z-axis. The identity $I_z = I_x + I_y$ is then called the **Perpendicular Axis Theorem**.)

The **radius of gyration** R_x is defined by the equation

$$I_x = MR_x^2.$$

It tells how far from the x-axis the entire mass of the plate might be concentrated to give the same I_x. The radius of gyration gives a convenient way to express the moment of inertia in terms of a mass and a length. The radii R_y and R_0 are defined in a similar way, with

$$I_y = MR_y^2 \quad \text{and} \quad I_0 = MR_0^2.$$

We take square roots to get the formulas in Table 15.2, which gives the formulas for moments of inertia (second moments) as well as for radii of gyration.

TABLE 15.2 Second moment formulas for thin plates in the xy-plane

Moments of inertia (second moments):		
About the x-axis:	$I_x = \iint y^2\delta(x, y)\, dA$	
About the y-axis:	$I_y = \iint x^2\delta(x, y)\, dA$	
About a line L:	$I_L = \iint r^2(x, y)\delta(x, y)\, dA,$ where $r(x, y) =$ distance from (x, y) to L	
About the origin (polar moment):	$I_0 = \iint (x^2 + y^2)\delta(x, y)\, dA = I_x + I_y$	
Radii of gyration:	About the x-axis:	$R_x = \sqrt{I_x/M}$
	About the y-axis:	$R_y = \sqrt{I_y/M}$
	About the origin:	$R_0 = \sqrt{I_0/M}$

EXAMPLE 5 Finding Moments of Inertia and Radii of Gyration

For the thin plate in Example 4 (Figure 15.17), find the moments of inertia and radii of gyration about the coordinate axes and the origin.

Solution Using the density function $\delta(x, y) = 6x + 6y + 6$ given in Example 4, the moment of inertia about the x-axis is

$$\begin{aligned} I_x &= \int_0^1 \int_0^{2x} y^2\delta(x, y)\, dy\, dx = \int_0^1 \int_0^{2x} (6xy^2 + 6y^3 + 6y^2)\, dy\, dx \\ &= \int_0^1 \left[2xy^3 + \frac{3}{2}y^4 + 2y^3\right]_{y=0}^{y=2x} dx = \int_0^1 (40x^4 + 16x^3)\, dx \\ &= \left[8x^5 + 4x^4\right]_0^1 = 12. \end{aligned}$$

Similarly, the moment of inertia about the y-axis is

$$I_y = \int_0^1 \int_0^{2x} x^2 \delta(x, y)\, dy\, dx = \frac{39}{5}.$$

Notice that we integrate y^2 times density in calculating I_x and x^2 times density to find I_y.

Since we know I_x and I_y, we do not need to evaluate an integral to find I_0; we can use the equation $I_0 = I_x + I_y$ instead:

$$I_0 = 12 + \frac{39}{5} = \frac{60 + 39}{5} = \frac{99}{5}.$$

The three radii of gyration are

$$R_x = \sqrt{I_x/M} = \sqrt{12/14} = \sqrt{6/7} \approx 0.93$$

$$R_y = \sqrt{I_y/M} = \sqrt{\left(\frac{39}{5}\right)/14} = \sqrt{39/70} \approx 0.75$$

$$R_0 = \sqrt{I_0/M} = \sqrt{\left(\frac{99}{5}\right)/14} = \sqrt{99/70} \approx 1.19.$$

■

Moments are also of importance in statistics. The first moment is used in computing the mean μ of a set of data, and the second moment is used in computing the variance $\left(\Sigma^2\right)$ and the standard deviation $\left(\Sigma\right)$. Third and fourth moments are used for computing statistical quantities known as skewness and kurtosis.

Centroids of Geometric Figures

When the density of an object is constant, it cancels out of the numerator and denominator of the formulas for $\bar{x}$ and $\bar{y}$ in Table 15.1. As far as $\bar{x}$ and $\bar{y}$ are concerned, δ might as well be 1. Thus, when δ is constant, the location of the center of mass becomes a feature of the object's shape and not of the material of which it is made. In such cases, engineers may call the center of mass the **centroid** of the shape. To find a centroid, we set δ equal to 1 and proceed to find $\bar{x}$ and $\bar{y}$ as before, by dividing first moments by masses.

EXAMPLE 6 Finding the Centroid of a Region

Find the centroid of the region in the first quadrant that is bounded above by the line $y = x$ and below by the parabola $y = x^2$.

Solution We sketch the region and include enough detail to determine the limits of integration (Figure 15.20). We then set δ equal to 1 and evaluate the appropriate formulas from Table 15.1:

$$M = \int_0^1 \int_{x^2}^{x} 1\, dy\, dx = \int_0^1 \left[y \right]_{y=x^2}^{y=x} dx = \int_0^1 (x - x^2)\, dx = \left[\frac{x^2}{2} - \frac{x^3}{3} \right]_0^1 = \frac{1}{6}$$

$$M_x = \int_0^1 \int_{x^2}^{x} y\, dy\, dx = \int_0^1 \left[\frac{y^2}{2} \right]_{y=x^2}^{y=x} dx$$

$$= \int_0^1 \left(\frac{x^2}{2} - \frac{x^4}{2} \right) dx = \left[\frac{x^3}{6} - \frac{x^5}{10} \right]_0^1 = \frac{1}{15}$$

$$M_y = \int_0^1 \int_{x^2}^{x} x\, dy\, dx = \int_0^1 \left[xy \right]_{y=x^2}^{y=x} dx = \int_0^1 (x^2 - x^3)\, dx = \left[\frac{x^3}{3} - \frac{x^4}{4} \right]_0^1 = \frac{1}{12}.$$

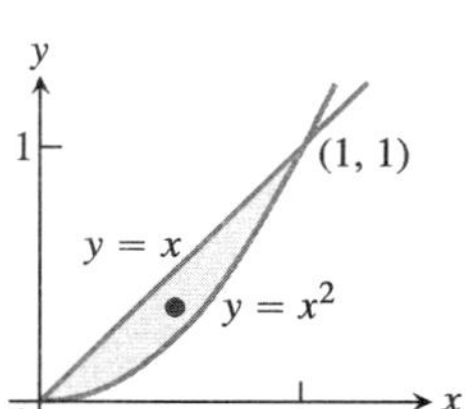

FIGURE 15.20 The centroid of this region is found in Example 6.

From these values of M, M_x, and M_y, we find

$$\bar{x} = \frac{M_y}{M} = \frac{1/12}{1/6} = \frac{1}{2} \quad \text{and} \quad \bar{y} = \frac{M_x}{M} = \frac{1/15}{1/6} = \frac{2}{5}.$$

The centroid is the point $(1/2, 2/5)$. ■

EXERCISES 15.2

Area by Double Integration

In Exercises 1–8, sketch the region bounded by the given lines and curves. Then express the region's area as an iterated double integral and evaluate the integral.

1. The coordinate axes and the line $x + y = 2$
2. The lines $x = 0, y = 2x$, and $y = 4$
3. The parabola $x = -y^2$ and the line $y = x + 2$
4. The parabola $x = y - y^2$ and the line $y = -x$
5. The curve $y = e^x$ and the lines $y = 0, x = 0$, and $x = \ln 2$
6. The curves $y = \ln x$ and $y = 2 \ln x$ and the line $x = e$, in the first quadrant
7. The parabolas $x = y^2$ and $x = 2y - y^2$
8. The parabolas $x = y^2 - 1$ and $x = 2y^2 - 2$

Identifying the Region of Integration

The integrals and sums of integrals in Exercises 9–14 give the areas of regions in the xy-plane. Sketch each region, label each bounding curve with its equation, and give the coordinates of the points where the curves intersect. Then find the area of the region.

9. $\displaystyle\int_0^6 \int_{y^2/3}^{2y} dx\, dy$

10. $\displaystyle\int_0^3 \int_{-x}^{x(2-x)} dy\, dx$

11. $\displaystyle\int_0^{\pi/4} \int_{\sin x}^{\cos x} dy\, dx$

12. $\displaystyle\int_{-1}^2 \int_{y^2}^{y+2} dx\, dy$

13. $\displaystyle\int_{-1}^0 \int_{-2x}^{1-x} dy\, dx + \int_0^2 \int_{-x/2}^{1-x} dy\, dx$

14. $\displaystyle\int_0^2 \int_{x^2-4}^{0} dy\, dx + \int_0^4 \int_0^{\sqrt{x}} dy\, dx$

Average Values

15. Find the average value of $f(x, y) = \sin(x + y)$ over
    a. the rectangle $0 \le x \le \pi, \quad 0 \le y \le \pi$
    b. the rectangle $0 \le x \le \pi, \quad 0 \le y \le \pi/2$
16. Which do you think will be larger, the average value of $f(x, y) = xy$ over the square $0 \le x \le 1, 0 \le y \le 1$, or the average value of f over the quarter circle $x^2 + y^2 \le 1$ in the first quadrant? Calculate them to find out.
17. Find the average height of the paraboloid $z = x^2 + y^2$ over the square $0 \le x \le 2, 0 \le y \le 2$.
18. Find the average value of $f(x, y) = 1/(xy)$ over the square $\ln 2 \le x \le 2 \ln 2, \ln 2 \le y \le 2 \ln 2$.

Constant Density

19. **Finding center of mass** Find a center of mass of a thin plate of density $\delta = 3$ bounded by the lines $x = 0, y = x$, and the parabola $y = 2 - x^2$ in the first quadrant.
20. **Finding moments of inertia and radii of gyration** Find the moments of inertia and radii of gyration about the coordinate axes of a thin rectangular plate of constant density δ bounded by the lines $x = 3$ and $y = 3$ in the first quadrant.
21. **Finding a centroid** Find the centroid of the region in the first quadrant bounded by the x-axis, the parabola $y^2 = 2x$, and the line $x + y = 4$.
22. **Finding a centroid** Find the centroid of the triangular region cut from the first quadrant by the line $x + y = 3$.
23. **Finding a centroid** Find the centroid of the semicircular region bounded by the x-axis and the curve $y = \sqrt{1 - x^2}$.
24. **Finding a centroid** The area of the region in the first quadrant bounded by the parabola $y = 6x - x^2$ and the line $y = x$ is $125/6$ square units. Find the centroid.
25. **Finding a centroid** Find the centroid of the region cut from the first quadrant by the circle $x^2 + y^2 = a^2$.
26. **Finding a centroid** Find the centroid of the region between the x-axis and the arch $y = \sin x, 0 \le x \le \pi$.
27. **Finding moments of inertia** Find the moment of inertia about the x-axis of a thin plate of density $\delta = 1$ bounded by the circle $x^2 + y^2 = 4$. Then use your result to find I_y and I_0 for the plate.
28. **Finding a moment of inertia** Find the moment of inertia with respect to the y-axis of a thin sheet of constant density $\delta = 1$ bounded by the curve $y = (\sin^2 x)/x^2$ and the interval $\pi \le x \le 2\pi$ of the x-axis.
29. **The centroid of an infinite region** Find the centroid of the infinite region in the second quadrant enclosed by the coordinate axes and the curve $y = e^x$. (Use improper integrals in the mass-moment formulas.)

30. **The first moment of an infinite plate** Find the first moment about the y-axis of a thin plate of density $\delta(x, y) = 1$ covering the infinite region under the curve $y = e^{-x^2/2}$ in the first quadrant.

Variable Density

31. **Finding a moment of inertia and radius of gyration** Find the moment of inertia and radius of gyration about the x-axis of a thin plate bounded by the parabola $x = y - y^2$ and the line $x + y = 0$ if $\delta(x, y) = x + y$.

32. **Finding mass** Find the mass of a thin plate occupying the smaller region cut from the ellipse $x^2 + 4y^2 = 12$ by the parabola $x = 4y^2$ if $\delta(x, y) = 5x$.

33. **Finding a center of mass** Find the center of mass of a thin triangular plate bounded by the y-axis and the lines $y = x$ and $y = 2 - x$ if $\delta(x, y) = 6x + 3y + 3$.

34. **Finding a center of mass and moment of inertia** Find the center of mass and moment of inertia about the x-axis of a thin plate bounded by the curves $x = y^2$ and $x = 2y - y^2$ if the density at the point (x, y) is $\delta(x, y) = y + 1$.

35. **Center of mass, moment of inertia, and radius of gyration** Find the center of mass and the moment of inertia and radius of gyration about the y-axis of a thin rectangular plate cut from the first quadrant by the lines $x = 6$ and $y = 1$ if $\delta(x, y) = x + y + 1$.

36. **Center of mass, moment of inertia, and radius of gyration** Find the center of mass and the moment of inertia and radius of gyration about the y-axis of a thin plate bounded by the line $y = 1$ and the parabola $y = x^2$ if the density is $\delta(x, y) = y + 1$.

37. **Center of mass, moment of inertia, and radius of gyration** Find the center of mass and the moment of inertia and radius of gyration about the y-axis of a thin plate bounded by the x-axis, the lines $x = \pm 1$, and the parabola $y = x^2$ if $\delta(x, y) = 7y + 1$.

38. **Center of mass, moment of inertia, and radius of gyration** Find the center of mass and the moment of inertia and radius of gyration about the x-axis of a thin rectangular plate bounded by the lines $x = 0, x = 20, y = -1$, and $y = 1$ if $\delta(x, y) = 1 + (x/20)$.

39. **Center of mass, moments of inertia, and radii of gyration** Find the center of mass, the moment of inertia and radii of gyration about the coordinate axes, and the polar moment of inertia and radius of gyration of a thin triangular plate bounded by the lines $y = x, y = -x$, and $y = 1$ if $\delta(x, y) = y + 1$.

40. **Center of mass, moments of inertia, and radii of gyration** Repeat Exercise 39 for $\delta(x, y) = 3x^2 + 1$.

Theory and Examples

41. **Bacterium population** If $f(x, y) = (10{,}000e^y)/(1 + |x|/2)$ represents the "population density" of a certain bacterium on the xy-plane, where x and y are measured in centimeters, find the total population of bacteria within the rectangle $-5 \le x \le 5$ and $-2 \le y \le 0$.

42. **Regional population** If $f(x, y) = 100\,(y + 1)$ represents the population density of a planar region on Earth, where x and y are measured in miles, find the number of people in the region bounded by the curves $x = y^2$ and $x = 2y - y^2$.

43. **Appliance design** When we design an appliance, one of the concerns is how hard the appliance will be to tip over. When tipped, it will right itself as long as its center of mass lies on the correct side of the *fulcrum*, the point on which the appliance is riding as it tips. Suppose that the profile of an appliance of approximately constant density is parabolic, like an old-fashioned radio. It fills the region $0 \le y \le a(1 - x^2), -1 \le x \le 1$, in the xy-plane (see accompanying figure). What values of a will guarantee that the appliance will have to be tipped more than 45° to fall over?

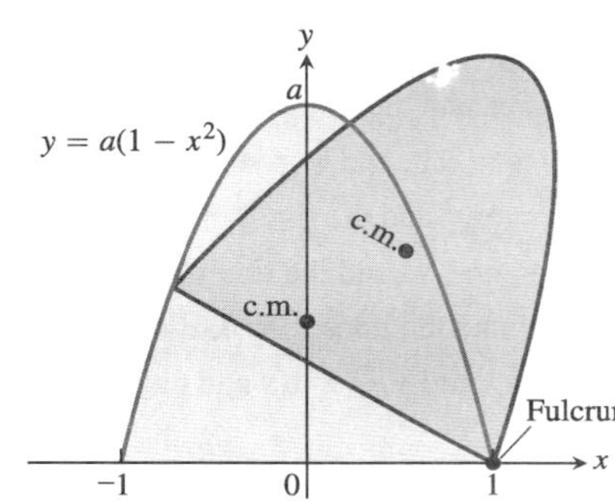

44. **Minimizing a moment of inertia** A rectangular plate of constant density $\delta(x, y) = 1$ occupies the region bounded by the lines $x = 4$ and $y = 2$ in the first quadrant. The moment of inertia I_a of the rectangle about the line $y = a$ is given by the integral

$$I_a = \int_0^4 \int_0^2 (y - a)^2 \, dy \, dx.$$

Find the value of a that minimizes I_a.

45. **Centroid of unbounded region** Find the centroid of the infinite region in the xy-plane bounded by the curves $y = 1/\sqrt{1 - x^2}$, $y = -1/\sqrt{1 - x^2}$, and the lines $x = 0, x = 1$.

46. **Radius of gyration of slender rod** Find the radius of gyration of a slender rod of constant linear density δ gm/cm and length L cm with respect to an axis

   a. through the rod's center of mass perpendicular to the rod's axis.

   b. perpendicular to the rod's axis at one end of the rod.

47. (*Continuation of Exercise 34.*) A thin plate of now constant density δ occupies the region R in the xy-plane bounded by the curves $x = y^2$ and $x = 2y - y^2$.

   a. Constant density Find δ such that the plate has the same mass as the plate in Exercise 34.

   b. Average value Compare the value of δ found in part (a) with the average value of $\delta(x, y) = y + 1$ over R.

48. Average temperature in Texas According to the *Texas Almanac*, Texas has 254 counties and a National Weather Service station in each county. Assume that at time t_0, each of the 254 weather stations recorded the local temperature. Find a formula that would give a reasonable approximation to the average temperature in Texas at time t_0. Your answer should involve information that you would expect to be readily available in the *Texas Almanac*.

The Parallel Axis Theorem

Let $L_{\text{c.m.}}$ be a line in the xy-plane that runs through the center of mass of a thin plate of mass m covering a region in the plane. Let L be a line in the plane parallel to and h units away from $L_{\text{c.m.}}$. The **Parallel Axis Theorem** says that under these conditions the moments of inertia I_L and $I_{\text{c.m.}}$ of the plate about L and $L_{\text{c.m.}}$ satisfy the equation

$$I_L = I_{\text{c.m.}} + mh^2.$$

This equation gives a quick way to calculate one moment when the other moment and the mass are known.

49. Proof of the Parallel Axis Theorem

a. Show that the first moment of a thin flat plate about any line in the plane of the plate through the plate's center of mass is zero. (*Hint:* Place the center of mass at the origin with the line along the y-axis. What does the formula $\bar{x} = M_y/M$ then tell you?)

b. Use the result in part (a) to derive the Parallel Axis Theorem. Assume that the plane is coordinatized in a way that makes $L_{\text{c.m.}}$ the y-axis and L the line $x = h$. Then expand the integrand of the integral for I_L to rewrite the integral as the sum of integrals whose values you recognize.

50. Finding moments of inertia

a. Use the Parallel Axis Theorem and the results of Example 4 to find the moments of inertia of the plate in Example 4 about the vertical and horizontal lines through the plate's center of mass.

b. Use the results in part (a) to find the plate's moments of inertia about the lines $x = 1$ and $y = 2$.

Pappus's Formula

Pappus knew that the centroid of the union of two nonoverlapping plane regions lies on the line segment joining their individual centroids. More specifically, suppose that m_1 and m_2 are the masses of thin plates P_1 and P_2 that cover nonoverlapping regions in the xy-plane. Let $\mathbf{c}_1$ and $\mathbf{c}_2$ be the vectors from the origin to the respective centers of mass of P_1 and P_2. Then the center of mass of the union $P_1 \cup P_2$ of the two plates is determined by the vector

$$\mathbf{c} = \frac{m_1\mathbf{c}_1 + m_2\mathbf{c}_2}{m_1 + m_2}. \tag{5}$$

Equation (5) is known as **Pappus's formula**. For more than two nonoverlapping plates, as long as their number is finite, the formula generalizes to

$$\mathbf{c} = \frac{m_1\mathbf{c}_1 + m_2\mathbf{c}_2 + \cdots + m_n\mathbf{c}_n}{m_1 + m_2 + \cdots + m_n}. \tag{6}$$

This formula is especially useful for finding the centroid of a plate of irregular shape that is made up of pieces of constant density whose centroids we know from geometry. We find the centroid of each piece and apply Equation (6) to find the centroid of the plate.

51. Derive Pappus's formula (Equation (5)). (*Hint:* Sketch the plates as regions in the first quadrant and label their centers of mass as $(\bar{x}_1, \bar{y}_1)$ and $(\bar{x}_2, \bar{y}_2)$. What are the moments of $P_1 \cup P_2$ about the coordinate axes?)

52. Use Equation (5) and mathematical induction to show that Equation (6) holds for any positive integer $n > 2$.

53. Let A, B, and C be the shapes indicated in the accompanying figure. Use Pappus's formula to find the centroid of

a. $A \cup B$ **b.** $A \cup C$

c. $B \cup C$ **d.** $A \cup B \cup C$.

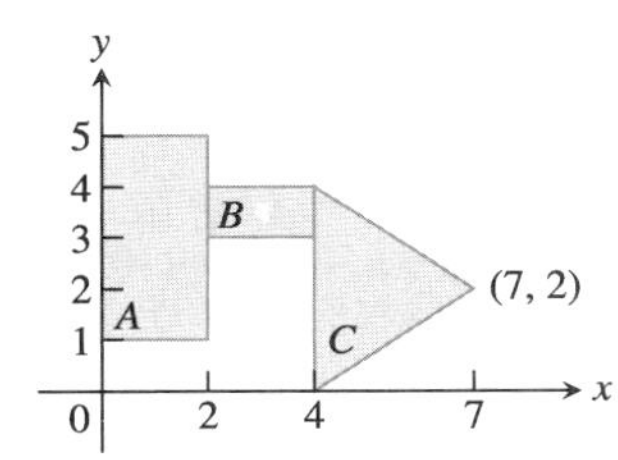

54. Locating center of mass Locate the center of mass of the carpenter's square, shown here.

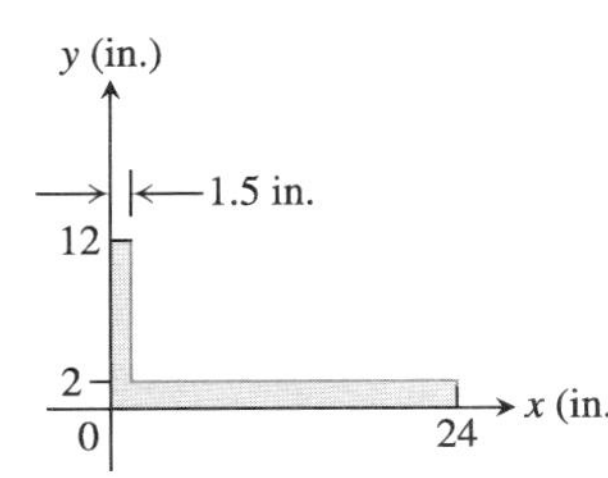

55. An isosceles triangle T has base $2a$ and altitude h. The base lies along the diameter of a semicircular disk D of radius a so that the two together make a shape resembling an ice cream cone. What relation must hold between a and h to place the centroid of $T \cup D$ on the common boundary of T and D? Inside T?

56. An isosceles triangle T of altitude h has as its base one side of a square Q whose edges have length s. (The square and triangle do not overlap.) What relation must hold between h and s to place the centroid of $T \cup Q$ on the base of the triangle? Compare your answer with the answer to Exercise 55.

15.3 Double Integrals in Polar Form

Integrals are sometimes easier to evaluate if we change to polar coordinates. This section shows how to accomplish the change and how to evaluate integrals over regions whose boundaries are given by polar equations.

Integrals in Polar Coordinates

When we defined the double integral of a function over a region R in the xy-plane, we began by cutting R into rectangles whose sides were parallel to the coordinate axes. These were the natural shapes to use because their sides have either constant x-values or constant y-values. In polar coordinates, the natural shape is a "polar rectangle" whose sides have constant r- and θ-values.

Suppose that a function $f(r, \theta)$ is defined over a region R that is bounded by the rays $\theta = \alpha$ and $\theta = \beta$ and by the continuous curves $r = g_1(\theta)$ and $r = g_2(\theta)$. Suppose also that $0 \leq g_1(\theta) \leq g_2(\theta) \leq a$ for every value of θ between α and β. Then R lies in a fan-shaped region Q defined by the inequalities $0 \leq r \leq a$ and $\alpha \leq \theta \leq \beta$. See Figure 15.21.

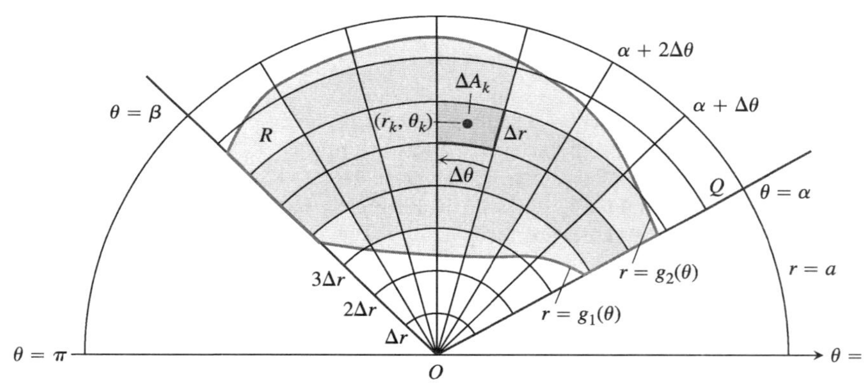

FIGURE 15.21 The region R: $g_1(\theta) \leq r \leq g_2(\theta)$, $\alpha \leq \theta \leq \beta$, is contained in the fan-shaped region Q: $0 \leq r \leq a$, $\alpha \leq \theta \leq \beta$. The partition of Q by circular arcs and rays induces a partition of R.

We cover Q by a grid of circular arcs and rays. The arcs are cut from circles centered at the origin, with radii $\Delta r, 2\Delta r, \ldots, m\Delta r$, where $\Delta r = a/m$. The rays are given by

$$\theta = \alpha, \qquad \theta = \alpha + \Delta\theta, \qquad \theta = \alpha + 2\Delta\theta, \qquad \ldots, \qquad \theta = \alpha + m'\Delta\theta = \beta,$$

where $\Delta\theta = (\beta - \alpha)/m'$. The arcs and rays partition Q into small patches called "polar rectangles."

We number the polar rectangles that lie inside R (the order does not matter), calling their areas $\Delta A_1, \Delta A_2, \ldots, \Delta A_n$. We let (r_k, θ_k) be any point in the polar rectangle whose area is ΔA_k. We then form the sum

$$S_n = \sum_{k=1}^{n} f(r_k, \theta_k)\, \Delta A_k.$$

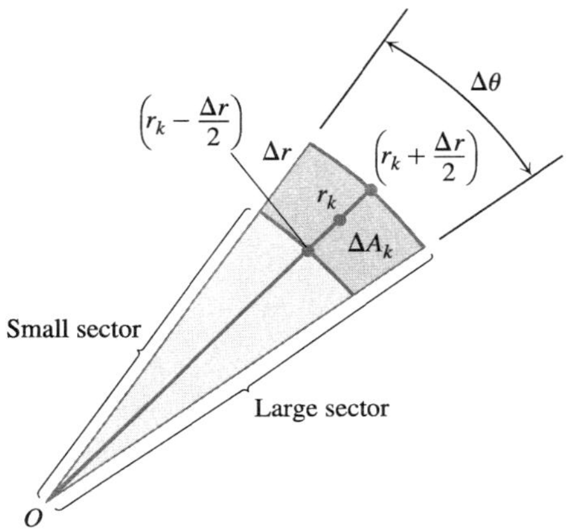

FIGURE 15.22 The observation that

$$\Delta A_k = \begin{pmatrix}\text{area of}\\ \text{large sector}\end{pmatrix} - \begin{pmatrix}\text{area of}\\ \text{small sector}\end{pmatrix}$$

leads to the formula $\Delta A_k = r_k\, \Delta r\, \Delta\theta$.

If f is continuous throughout R, this sum will approach a limit as we refine the grid to make Δr and $\Delta\theta$ go to zero. The limit is called the double integral of f over R. In symbols,

$$\lim_{n\to\infty} S_n = \iint_R f(r, \theta)\, dA.$$

To evaluate this limit, we first have to write the sum S_n in a way that expresses ΔA_k in terms of Δr and $\Delta\theta$. For convenience we choose r_k to be the average of the radii of the inner and outer arcs bounding the kth polar rectangle ΔA_k. The radius of the inner arc bounding ΔA_k is then $r_k - (\Delta r/2)$ (Figure 15.22). The radius of the outer arc is $r_k + (\Delta r/2)$.

The area of a wedge-shaped sector of a circle having radius r and angle θ is

$$A = \frac{1}{2}\theta \cdot r^2,$$

as can be seen by multiplying πr^2, the area of the circle, by $\theta/2\pi$, the fraction of the circle's area contained in the wedge. So the areas of the circular sectors subtended by these arcs at the origin are

$$\text{Inner radius:} \quad \frac{1}{2}\left(r_k - \frac{\Delta r}{2}\right)^2 \Delta\theta$$

$$\text{Outer radius:} \quad \frac{1}{2}\left(r_k + \frac{\Delta r}{2}\right)^2 \Delta\theta.$$

Therefore,

$$\begin{aligned}\Delta A_k &= \text{area of large sector} - \text{area of small sector}\\ &= \frac{\Delta\theta}{2}\left[\left(r_k + \frac{\Delta r}{2}\right)^2 - \left(r_k - \frac{\Delta r}{2}\right)^2\right] = \frac{\Delta\theta}{2}(2r_k\, \Delta r) = r_k\, \Delta r\, \Delta\theta.\end{aligned}$$

Combining this result with the sum defining S_n gives

$$S_n = \sum_{k=1}^{n} f(r_k, \theta_k) r_k\, \Delta r\, \Delta\theta.$$

As $n \to \infty$ and the values of Δr and $\Delta\theta$ approach zero, these sums converge to the double integral

$$\lim_{n\to\infty} S_n = \iint_R f(r, \theta)\, r\, dr\, d\theta.$$

A version of Fubini's Theorem says that the limit approached by these sums can be evaluated by repeated single integrations with respect to r and θ as

$$\iint_R f(r, \theta)\, dA = \int_{\theta=\alpha}^{\theta=\beta} \int_{r=g_1(\theta)}^{r=g_2(\theta)} f(r, \theta)\, r\, dr\, d\theta.$$

Finding Limits of Integration

The procedure for finding limits of integration in rectangular coordinates also works for polar coordinates. To evaluate $\iint_R f(r, \theta)\, dA$ over a region R in polar coordinates, integrating first with respect to r and then with respect to θ, take the following steps.

1. *Sketch*: Sketch the region and label the bounding curves.

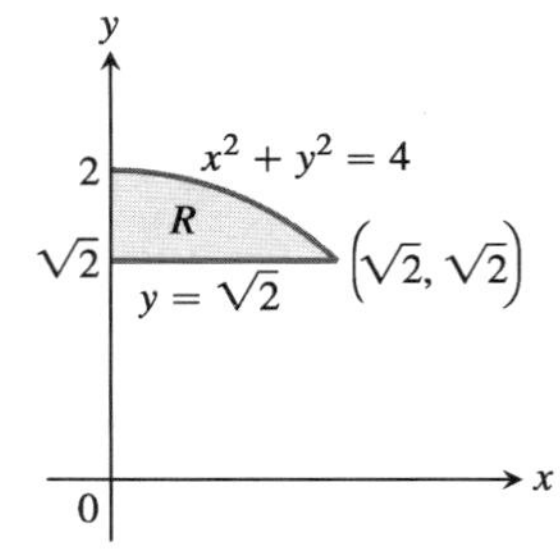

2. *Find the r-limits of integration*: Imagine a ray L from the origin cutting through R in the direction of increasing r. Mark the r-values where L enters and leaves R. These are the r-limits of integration. They usually depend on the angle θ that L makes with the positive x-axis.

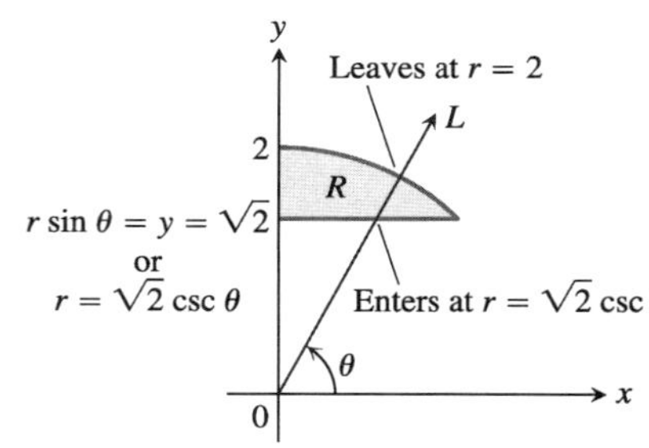

3. *Find the θ-limits of integration*: Find the smallest and largest θ-values that bound R. These are the θ-limits of integration.

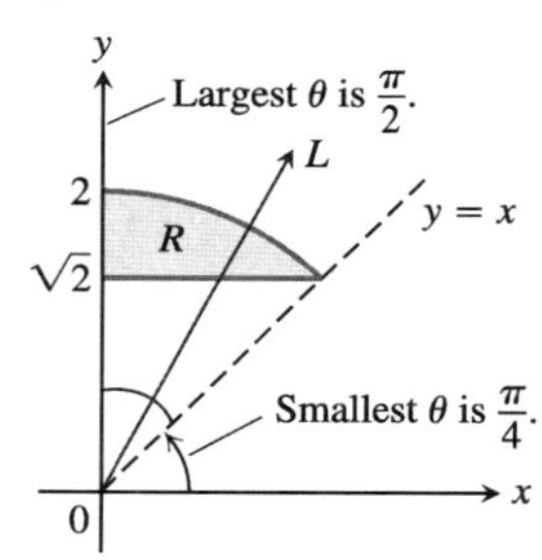

The integral is

$$\iint_R f(r, \theta)\, dA = \int_{\theta=\pi/4}^{\theta=\pi/2} \int_{r=\sqrt{2}\csc\theta}^{r=2} f(r, \theta)\, r\, dr\, d\theta.$$

EXAMPLE 1 Finding Limits of Integration

Find the limits of integration for integrating $f(r, \theta)$ over the region R that lies inside the cardioid $r = 1 + \cos\theta$ and outside the circle $r = 1$.

Solution

1. We first sketch the region and label the bounding curves (Figure 15.23).
2. Next we find the *r-limits of integration*. A typical ray from the origin enters R where $r = 1$ and leaves where $r = 1 + \cos\theta$.

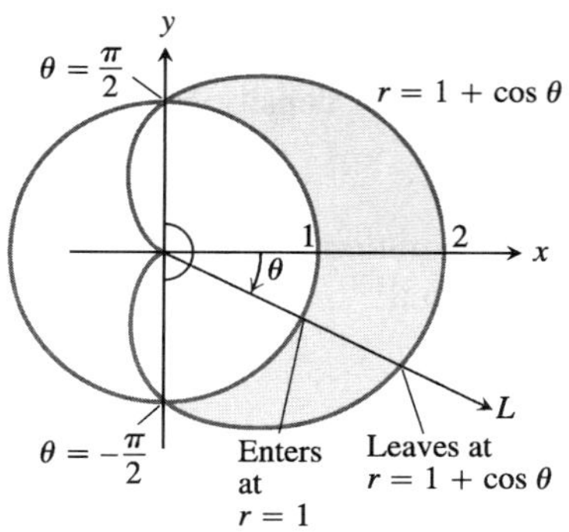

FIGURE 15.23 Finding the limits of integration in polar coordinates for the region in Example 1.

3. Finally we find the *θ-limits of integration*. The rays from the origin that intersect R run from $\theta = -\pi/2$ to $\theta = \pi/2$. The integral is

$$\int_{-\pi/2}^{\pi/2}\int_{1}^{1+\cos\theta} f(r,\theta)\, r\, dr\, d\theta.$$ ■

If $f(r,\theta)$ is the constant function whose value is 1, then the integral of f over R is the area of R.

> **Area in Polar Coordinates**
> The area of a closed and bounded region R in the polar coordinate plane is
> $$A = \iint_R r\, dr\, d\theta.$$

This formula for area is consistent with all earlier formulas, although we do not prove this fact.

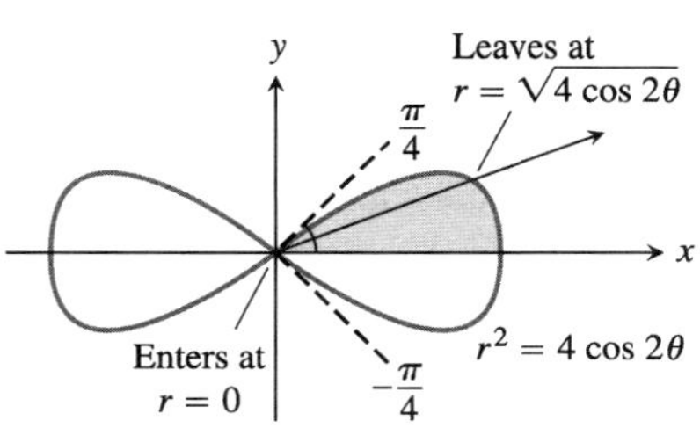

FIGURE 15.24 To integrate over the shaded region, we run r from 0 to $\sqrt{4\cos 2\theta}$ and θ from 0 to $\pi/4$ (Example 2).

EXAMPLE 2 Finding Area in Polar Coordinates

Find the area enclosed by the lemniscate $r^2 = 4\cos 2\theta$.

Solution We graph the lemniscate to determine the limits of integration (Figure 15.24) and see from the symmetry of the region that the total area is 4 times the first-quadrant portion.

$$A = 4\int_0^{\pi/4}\int_0^{\sqrt{4\cos 2\theta}} r\, dr\, d\theta = 4\int_0^{\pi/4}\left[\frac{r^2}{2}\right]_{r=0}^{r=\sqrt{4\cos 2\theta}} d\theta$$

$$= 4\int_0^{\pi/4} 2\cos 2\theta\, d\theta = 4\sin 2\theta\Big]_0^{\pi/4} = 4.$$ ■

Changing Cartesian Integrals into Polar Integrals

The procedure for changing a Cartesian integral $\iint_R f(x,y)\,dx\,dy$ into a polar integral has two steps. First substitute $x = r\cos\theta$ and $y = r\sin\theta$, and replace $dx\,dy$ by $r\,dr\,d\theta$ in the Cartesian integral. Then supply polar limits of integration for the boundary of R.

The Cartesian integral then becomes

$$\iint_R f(x,y)\,dx\,dy = \iint_G f(r\cos\theta, r\sin\theta)\, r\, dr\, d\theta,$$

where G denotes the region of integration in polar coordinates. This is like the substitution method in Chapter 5 except that there are now two variables to substitute for instead of one. Notice that $dx\,dy$ is not replaced by $dr\,d\theta$ but by $r\,dr\,d\theta$. A more general discussion of changes of variables (substitutions) in multiple integrals is given in Section 15.7.

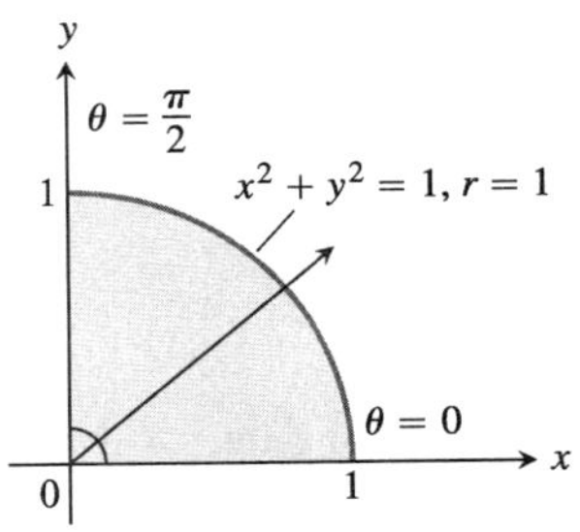

FIGURE 15.25 In polar coordinates, this region is described by simple inequalities:

$$0 \le r \le 1 \quad \text{and} \quad 0 \le \theta \le \pi/2$$

(Example 3).

EXAMPLE 3 Changing Cartesian Integrals to Polar Integrals

Find the polar moment of inertia about the origin of a thin plate of density $\delta(x, y) = 1$ bounded by the quarter circle $x^2 + y^2 = 1$ in the first quadrant.

Solution We sketch the plate to determine the limits of integration (Figure 15.25). In Cartesian coordinates, the polar moment is the value of the integral

$$\int_0^1 \int_0^{\sqrt{1-x^2}} (x^2 + y^2)\, dy\, dx.$$

Integration with respect to y gives

$$\int_0^1 \left(x^2\sqrt{1 - x^2} + \frac{(1 - x^2)^{3/2}}{3} \right) dx,$$

an integral difficult to evaluate without tables.

Things go better if we change the original integral to polar coordinates. Substituting $x = r\cos\theta$, $y = r\sin\theta$ and replacing $dx\,dy$ by $r\,dr\,d\theta$, we get

$$\int_0^1 \int_0^{\sqrt{1-x^2}} (x^2 + y^2)\, dy\, dx = \int_0^{\pi/2} \int_0^1 (r^2)\, r\, dr\, d\theta$$

$$= \int_0^{\pi/2} \left[\frac{r^4}{4} \right]_{r=0}^{r=1} d\theta = \int_0^{\pi/2} \frac{1}{4}\, d\theta = \frac{\pi}{8}.$$

Why is the polar coordinate transformation so effective here? One reason is that $x^2 + y^2$ simplifies to r^2. Another is that the limits of integration become constants. ■

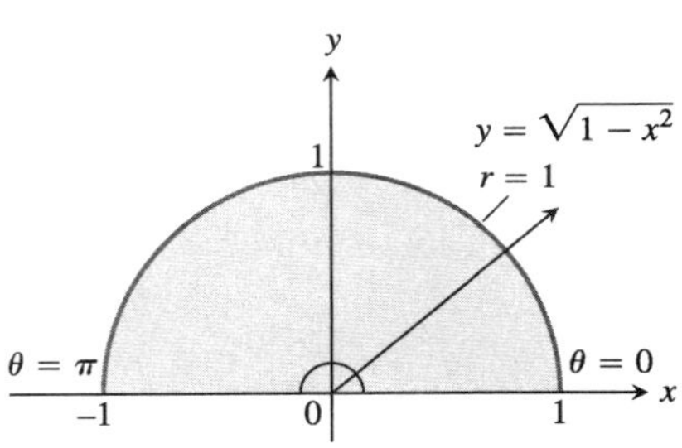

FIGURE 15.26 The semicircular region in Example 4 is the region

$$0 \le r \le 1, \qquad 0 \le \theta \le \pi.$$

EXAMPLE 4 Evaluating Integrals Using Polar Coordinates

Evaluate

$$\iint_R e^{x^2+y^2}\, dy\, dx,$$

where R is the semicircular region bounded by the x-axis and the curve $y = \sqrt{1 - x^2}$ (Figure 15.26).

Solution In Cartesian coordinates, the integral in question is a nonelementary integral and there is no direct way to integrate $e^{x^2+y^2}$ with respect to either x or y. Yet this integral and others like it are important in mathematics—in statistics, for example—and we need to find a way to evaluate it. Polar coordinates save the day. Substituting $x = r\cos\theta$, $y = r\sin\theta$ and replacing $dy\,dx$ by $r\,dr\,d\theta$ enables us to evaluate the integral as

$$\iint_R e^{x^2+y^2}\, dy\, dx = \int_0^{\pi} \int_0^1 e^{r^2}\, r\, dr\, d\theta = \int_0^{\pi} \left[\frac{1}{2} e^{r^2} \right]_0^1 d\theta$$

$$= \int_0^{\pi} \frac{1}{2}(e - 1)\, d\theta = \frac{\pi}{2}(e - 1).$$

The r in the $r\,dr\,d\theta$ was just what we needed to integrate e^{r^2}. Without it, we would have been unable to proceed. ■

EXERCISES 15.3

Evaluating Polar Integrals

In Exercises 1–16, change the Cartesian integral into an equivalent polar integral. Then evaluate the polar integral.

1. $\int_{-1}^{1}\int_{0}^{\sqrt{1-x^2}} dy\,dx$

2. $\int_{-1}^{1}\int_{-\sqrt{1-x^2}}^{\sqrt{1-x^2}} dy\,dx$

3. $\int_{0}^{1}\int_{0}^{\sqrt{1-y^2}} (x^2+y^2)\,dx\,dy$

4. $\int_{-1}^{1}\int_{-\sqrt{1-y^2}}^{\sqrt{1-y^2}} (x^2+y^2)\,dy\,dx$

5. $\int_{-a}^{a}\int_{-\sqrt{a^2-x^2}}^{\sqrt{a^2-x^2}} dy\,dx$

6. $\int_{0}^{2}\int_{0}^{\sqrt{4-y^2}} (x^2+y^2)\,dx\,dy$

7. $\int_{0}^{6}\int_{0}^{y} x\,dx\,dy$

8. $\int_{0}^{2}\int_{0}^{x} y\,dy\,dx$

9. $\int_{-1}^{0}\int_{-\sqrt{1-x^2}}^{0} \frac{2}{1+\sqrt{x^2+y^2}}\,dy\,dx$

10. $\int_{-1}^{1}\int_{-\sqrt{1-y^2}}^{0} \frac{4\sqrt{x^2+y^2}}{1+x^2+y^2}\,dx\,dy$

11. $\int_{0}^{\ln 2}\int_{0}^{\sqrt{(\ln 2)^2-y^2}} e^{\sqrt{x^2+y^2}}\,dx\,dy$

12. $\int_{0}^{1}\int_{0}^{\sqrt{1-x^2}} e^{-(x^2+y^2)}\,dy\,dx$

13. $\int_{0}^{2}\int_{0}^{\sqrt{1-(x-1)^2}} \frac{x+y}{x^2+y^2}\,dy\,dx$

14. $\int_{0}^{2}\int_{-\sqrt{1-(y-1)^2}}^{0} xy^2\,dx\,dy$

15. $\int_{-1}^{1}\int_{-\sqrt{1-y^2}}^{\sqrt{1-y^2}} \ln(x^2+y^2+1)\,dx\,dy$

16. $\int_{-1}^{1}\int_{-\sqrt{1-x^2}}^{\sqrt{1-x^2}} \frac{2}{(1+x^2+y^2)^2}\,dy\,dx$

Finding Area in Polar Coordinates

17. Find the area of the region cut from the first quadrant by the curve $r = 2(2 - \sin 2\theta)^{1/2}$.

18. **Cardioid overlapping a circle** Find the area of the region that lies inside the cardioid $r = 1 + \cos\theta$ and outside the circle $r = 1$.

19. **One leaf of a rose** Find the area enclosed by one leaf of the rose $r = 12\cos 3\theta$.

20. **Snail shell** Find the area of the region enclosed by the positive x-axis and spiral $r = 4\theta/3$, $0 \le \theta \le 2\pi$. The region looks like a snail shell.

21. **Cardioid in the first quadrant** Find the area of the region cut from the first quadrant by the cardioid $r = 1 + \sin\theta$.

22. **Overlapping cardioids** Find the area of the region common to the interiors of the cardioids $r = 1 + \cos\theta$ and $r = 1 - \cos\theta$.

Masses and Moments

23. **First moment of a plate** Find the first moment about the x-axis of a thin plate of constant density $\delta(x, y) = 3$, bounded below by the x-axis and above by the cardioid $r = 1 - \cos\theta$.

24. **Inertial and polar moments of a disk** Find the moment of inertia about the x-axis and the polar moment of inertia about the origin of a thin disk bounded by the circle $x^2 + y^2 = a^2$ if the disk's density at the point (x, y) is $\delta(x, y) = k(x^2 + y^2)$, k a constant.

25. **Mass of a plate** Find the mass of a thin plate covering the region outside the circle $r = 3$ and inside the circle $r = 6\sin\theta$ if the plate's density function is $\delta(x, y) = 1/r$.

26. **Polar moment of a cardioid overlapping circle** Find the polar moment of inertia about the origin of a thin plate covering the region that lies inside the cardioid $r = 1 - \cos\theta$ and outside the circle $r = 1$ if the plate's density function is $\delta(x, y) = 1/r^2$.

27. **Centroid of a cardioid region** Find the centroid of the region enclosed by the cardioid $r = 1 + \cos\theta$.

28. **Polar moment of a cardioid region** Find the polar moment of inertia about the origin of a thin plate enclosed by the cardioid $r = 1 + \cos\theta$ if the plate's density function is $\delta(x, y) = 1$.

Average Values

29. **Average height of a hemisphere** Find the average height of the hemisphere $z = \sqrt{a^2 - x^2 - y^2}$ above the disk $x^2 + y^2 \le a^2$ in the xy-plane.

30. **Average height of a cone** Find the average height of the (single) cone $z = \sqrt{x^2 + y^2}$ above the disk $x^2 + y^2 \le a^2$ in the xy-plane.

31. **Average distance from interior of disk to center** Find the average distance from a point $P(x, y)$ in the disk $x^2 + y^2 \le a^2$ to the origin.

32. **Average distance squared from a point in a disk to a point in its boundary** Find the average value of the *square* of the distance from the point $P(x, y)$ in the disk $x^2 + y^2 \le 1$ to the boundary point $A(1, 0)$.

Theory and Examples

33. **Converting to a polar integral** Integrate $f(x, y) = [\ln(x^2 + y^2)]/\sqrt{x^2 + y^2}$ over the region $1 \le x^2 + y^2 \le e$.

34. **Converting to a polar integral** Integrate $f(x, y) = [\ln(x^2 + y^2)]/(x^2 + y^2)$ over the region $1 \le x^2 + y^2 \le e^2$.

35. **Volume of noncircular right cylinder** The region that lies inside the cardioid $r = 1 + \cos\theta$ and outside the circle $r = 1$ is the base of a solid right cylinder. The top of the cylinder lies in the plane $z = x$. Find the cylinder's volume.

36. Volume of noncircular right cylinder The region enclosed by the lemniscate $r^2 = 2\cos 2\theta$ is the base of a solid right cylinder whose top is bounded by the sphere $z = \sqrt{2 - r^2}$. Find the cylinder's volume.

37. Converting to polar integrals

a. The usual way to evaluate the improper integral $I = \int_0^{\infty} e^{-x^2}\,dx$ is first to calculate its square:

$$I^2 = \left(\int_0^{\infty} e^{-x^2}\,dx\right)\left(\int_0^{\infty} e^{-y^2}\,dy\right) = \int_0^{\infty}\int_0^{\infty} e^{-(x^2+y^2)}\,dx\,dy.$$

Evaluate the last integral using polar coordinates and solve the resulting equation for I.

b. Evaluate

$$\lim_{x\to\infty} \operatorname{erf}(x) = \lim_{x\to\infty}\int_0^{x} \frac{2e^{-t^2}}{\sqrt{\pi}}\,dt.$$

38. Converting to a polar integral Evaluate the integral

$$\int_0^{\infty}\int_0^{\infty} \frac{1}{(1 + x^2 + y^2)^2}\,dx\,dy.$$

39. Existence Integrate the function $f(x, y) = 1/(1 - x^2 - y^2)$ over the disk $x^2 + y^2 \le 3/4$. Does the integral of $f(x, y)$ over the disk $x^2 + y^2 \le 1$ exist? Give reasons for your answer.

40. Area formula in polar coordinates Use the double integral in polar coordinates to derive the formula

$$A = \int_{\alpha}^{\beta} \frac{1}{2} r^2\,d\theta$$

for the area of the fan-shaped region between the origin and polar curve $r = f(\theta)$, $\alpha \le \theta \le \beta$.

41. Average distance to a given point inside a disk Let P_0 be a point inside a circle of radius a and let h denote the distance from P_0 to the center of the circle. Let d denote the distance from an arbitrary point P to P_0. Find the average value of d^2 over the region enclosed by the circle. (*Hint:* Simplify your work by placing the center of the circle at the origin and P_0 on the x-axis.)

42. Area Suppose that the area of a region in the polar coordinate plane is

$$A = \int_{\pi/4}^{3\pi/4}\int_{\csc\theta}^{2\sin\theta} r\,dr\,d\theta.$$

Sketch the region and find its area.

COMPUTER EXPLORATIONS

Coordinate Conversions

In Exercises 43–46, use a CAS to change the Cartesian integrals into an equivalent polar integral and evaluate the polar integral. Perform the following steps in each exercise.

a. Plot the Cartesian region of integration in the xy-plane.

b. Change each boundary curve of the Cartesian region in part (a) to its polar representation by solving its Cartesian equation for r and θ.

c. Using the results in part (b), plot the polar region of integration in the $r\theta$-plane.

d. Change the integrand from Cartesian to polar coordinates. Determine the limits of integration from your plot in part (c) and evaluate the polar integral using the CAS integration utility.

43. $\displaystyle\int_0^1\int_x^1 \frac{y}{x^2 + y^2}\,dy\,dx$

44. $\displaystyle\int_0^1\int_0^{x/2} \frac{x}{x^2 + y^2}\,dy\,dx$

45. $\displaystyle\int_0^1\int_{-y/3}^{y/3} \frac{y}{\sqrt{x^2 + y^2}}\,dx\,dy$

46. $\displaystyle\int_0^1\int_y^{2-y} \sqrt{x + y}\,dx\,dy$

15.4 Triple Integrals in Rectangular Coordinates

Just as double integrals allow us to deal with more general situations than could be handled by single integrals, triple integrals enable us to solve still more general problems. We use triple integrals to calculate the volumes of three-dimensional shapes, the masses and moments of solids of varying density, and the average value of a function over a three-dimensional region. Triple integrals also arise in the study of vector fields and fluid flow in three dimensions, as we will see in Chapter 16.

Triple Integrals

If $F(x, y, z)$ is a function defined on a closed bounded region D in space, such as the region occupied by a solid ball or a lump of clay, then the integral of F over D may be defined in

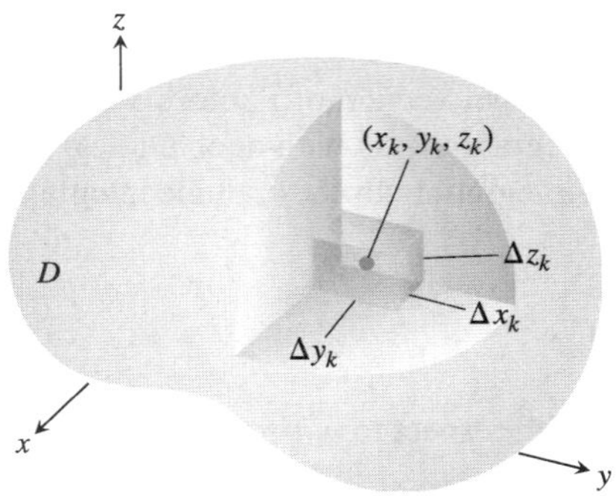

FIGURE 15.27 Partitioning a solid with rectangular cells of volume ΔV_k.

the following way. We partition a rectangular boxlike region containing D into rectangular cells by planes parallel to the coordinate axis (Figure 15.27). We number the cells that lie inside D from 1 to n in some order, the kth cell having dimensions Δx_k by Δy_k by Δz_k and volume $\Delta V_k = \Delta x_k \Delta y_k \Delta z_k$. We choose a point (x_k, y_k, z_k) in each cell and form the sum

$$S_n = \sum_{k=1}^{n} F(x_k, y_k, z_k)\, \Delta V_k. \tag{1}$$

We are interested in what happens as D is partitioned by smaller and smaller cells, so that Δx_k, Δy_k, Δz_k and the norm of the partition $\|P\|$, the largest value among Δx_k, Δy_k, Δz_k, all approach zero. When a single limiting value is attained, no matter how the partitions and points (x_k, y_k, z_k) are chosen, we say that F is **integrable** over D. As before, it can be shown that when F is continuous and the bounding surface of D is formed from finitely many smooth surfaces joined together along finitely many smooth curves, then F is integrable. As $\|P\| \to 0$ and the number of cells n goes to ∞, the sums S_n approach a limit. We call this limit the **triple integral of *F* over *D*** and write

$$\lim_{n\to\infty} S_n = \iiint_D F(x, y, z)\, dV \qquad \text{or} \qquad \lim_{\|P\|\to 0} S_n = \iiint_D F(x, y, z)\, dx\, dy\, dz.$$

The regions D over which continuous functions are integrable are those that can be closely approximated by small rectangular cells. Such regions include those encountered in applications.

Volume of a Region in Space

If F is the constant function whose value is 1, then the sums in Equation (1) reduce to

$$S_n = \sum F(x_k, y_k, z_k)\, \Delta V_k = \sum 1 \cdot \Delta V_k = \sum \Delta V_k.$$

As Δx_k, Δy_k, and Δz_k approach zero, the cells ΔV_k become smaller and more numerous and fill up more and more of D. We therefore define the volume of D to be the triple integral

$$\lim_{n\to\infty} \sum_{k=1}^{n} \Delta V_k = \iiint_D dV.$$

DEFINITION Volume

The **volume** of a closed, bounded region D in space is

$$V = \iiint_D dV.$$

This definition is in agreement with our previous definitions of volume, though we omit the verification of this fact. As we see in a moment, this integral enables us to calculate the volumes of solids enclosed by curved surfaces.

Finding Limits of Integration

We evaluate a triple integral by applying a three-dimensional version of Fubini's Theorem (Section 15.1) to evaluate it by three repeated single integrations. As with double integrals, there is a geometric procedure for finding the limits of integration for these single integrals.

To evaluate

$$\iiint_D F(x, y, z)\, dV$$

over a region D, integrate first with respect to z, then with respect to y, finally with x.

1. *Sketch:* Sketch the region D along with its "shadow" R (vertical projection) in the xy-plane. Label the upper and lower bounding surfaces of D and the upper and lower bounding curves of R.

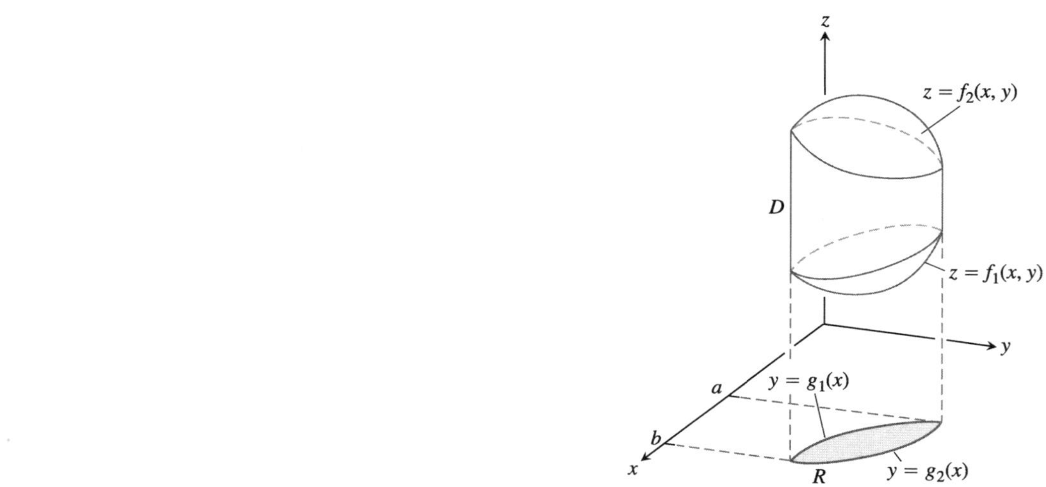

2. *Find the z-limits of integration:* Draw a line M passing through a typical point (x, y) in R parallel to the z-axis. As z increases, M enters D at $z = f_1(x, y)$ and leaves at $z = f_2(x, y)$. These are the z-limits of integration.

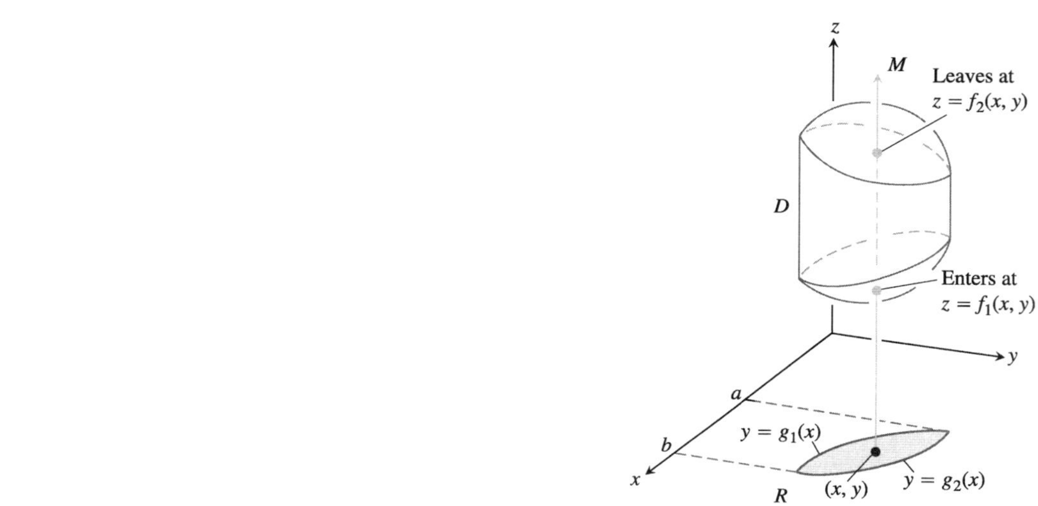

3. *Find the y-limits of integration:* Draw a line L through (x, y) parallel to the y-axis. As y increases, L enters R at $y = g_1(x)$ and leaves at $y = g_2(x)$. These are the y-limits of integration.

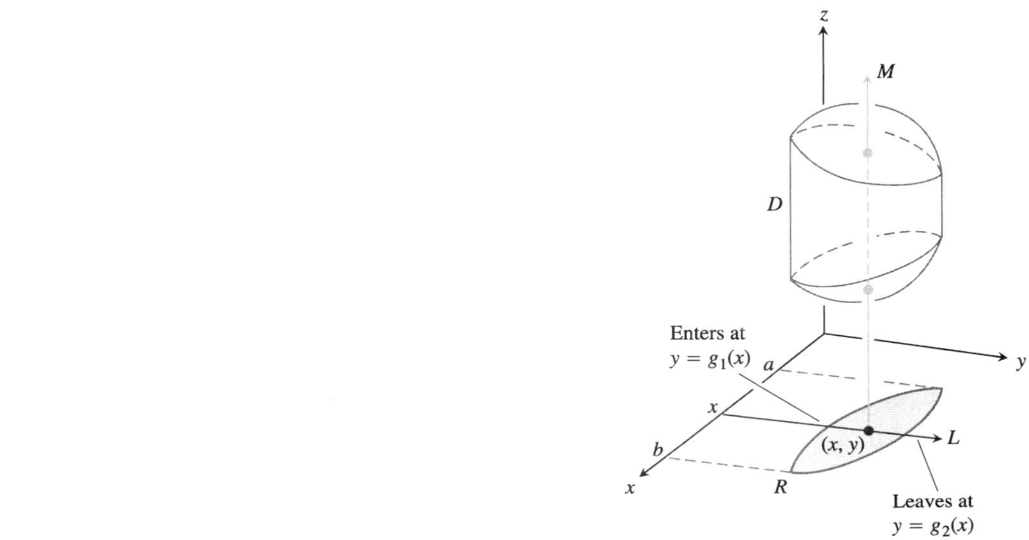

4. *Find the x-limits of integration:* Choose x-limits that include all lines through R parallel to the y-axis ($x = a$ and $x = b$ in the preceding figure). These are the x-limits of integration. The integral is

$$\int_{x=a}^{x=b} \int_{y=g_1(x)}^{y=g_2(x)} \int_{z=f_1(x,y)}^{z=f_2(x,y)} F(x, y, z)\, dz\, dy\, dx.$$

Follow similar procedures if you change the order of integration. The "shadow" of region D lies in the plane of the last two variables with respect to which the iterated integration takes place.

The above procedure applies whenever a solid region D is bounded above and below by a surface, and when the "shadow" region R is bounded by a lower and upper curve. It does not apply to regions with complicated holes through them, although sometimes such regions can be subdivided into simpler regions for which the procedure does apply.

EXAMPLE 1 Finding a Volume

Find the volume of the region D enclosed by the surfaces $z = x^2 + 3y^2$ and $z = 8 - x^2 - y^2$.

Solution The volume is

$$V = \iiint_D dz\, dy\, dx,$$

the integral of $F(x, y, z) = 1$ over D. To find the limits of integration for evaluating the integral, we first sketch the region. The surfaces (Figure 15.28) intersect on the elliptical cylinder $x^2 + 3y^2 = 8 - x^2 - y^2$ or $x^2 + 2y^2 = 4$, $z > 0$. The boundary of the region R, the projection of D onto the xy-plane, is an ellipse with the same equation: $x^2 + 2y^2 = 4$. The "upper" boundary of R is the curve $y = \sqrt{(4 - x^2)/2}$. The lower boundary is the curve $y = -\sqrt{(4 - x^2)/2}$.

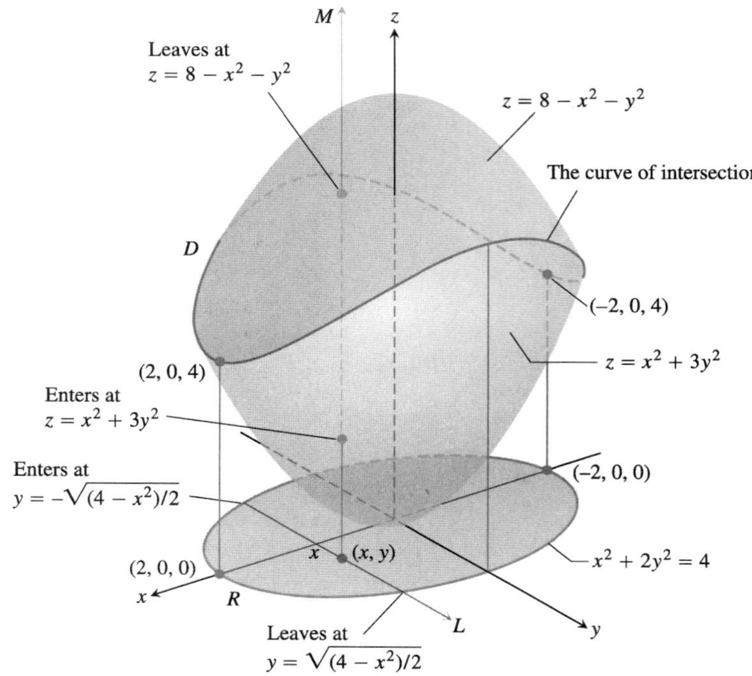

FIGURE 15.28 The volume of the region enclosed by two paraboloids, calculated in Example 1.

Now we find the z-limits of integration. The line M passing through a typical point (x, y) in R parallel to the z-axis enters D at $z = x^2 + 3y^2$ and leaves at $z = 8 - x^2 - y^2$.

Next we find the y-limits of integration. The line L through (x, y) parallel to the y-axis enters R at $y = -\sqrt{(4 - x^2)/2}$ and leaves at $y = \sqrt{(4 - x^2)/2}$.

Finally we find the x-limits of integration. As L sweeps across R, the value of x varies from $x = -2$ at $(-2, 0, 0)$ to $x = 2$ at $(2, 0, 0)$. The volume of D is

$$
\begin{aligned}
V &= \iiint_D dz\,dy\,dx \\
&= \int_{-2}^{2} \int_{-\sqrt{(4-x^2)/2}}^{\sqrt{(4-x^2)/2}} \int_{x^2+3y^2}^{8-x^2-y^2} dz\,dy\,dx \\
&= \int_{-2}^{2} \int_{-\sqrt{(4-x^2)/2}}^{\sqrt{(4-x^2)/2}} (8 - 2x^2 - 4y^2)\,dy\,dx \\
&= \int_{-2}^{2} \left[(8 - 2x^2)y - \frac{4}{3}y^3\right]_{y=-\sqrt{(4-x^2)/2}}^{y=\sqrt{(4-x^2)/2}} dx \\
&= \int_{-2}^{2} \left(2(8 - 2x^2)\sqrt{\frac{4 - x^2}{2}} - \frac{8}{3}\left(\frac{4 - x^2}{2}\right)^{3/2}\right) dx \\
&= \int_{-2}^{2} \left[8\left(\frac{4 - x^2}{2}\right)^{3/2} - \frac{8}{3}\left(\frac{4 - x^2}{2}\right)^{3/2}\right] dx = \frac{4\sqrt{2}}{3}\int_{-2}^{2} (4 - x^2)^{3/2}\,dx \\
&= 8\pi\sqrt{2}. \qquad \text{After integration with the substitution } x = 2\sin u.
\end{aligned}
$$

■

In the next example, we project D onto the xz-plane instead of the xy-plane, to show how to use a different order of integration.

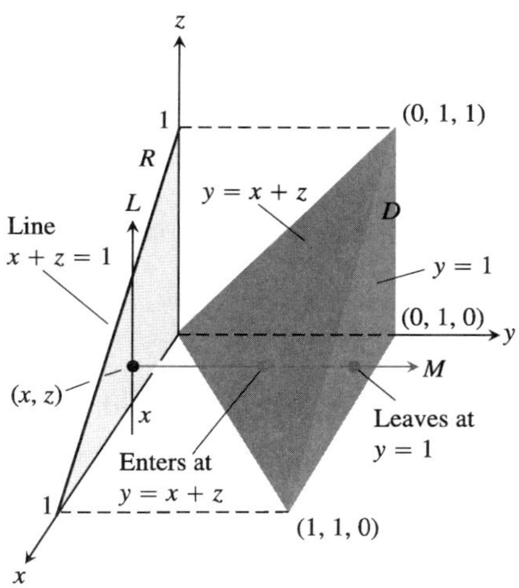

FIGURE 15.29 Finding the limits of integration for evaluating the triple integral of a function defined over the tetrahedron D (Example 2).

EXAMPLE 2 Finding the Limits of Integration in the Order *dy dz dx*

Set up the limits of integration for evaluating the triple integral of a function $F(x, y, z)$ over the tetrahedron D with vertices $(0, 0, 0)$, $(1, 1, 0)$, $(0, 1, 0)$, and $(0, 1, 1)$.

Solution We sketch D along with its "shadow" R in the xz-plane (Figure 15.29). The upper (right-hand) bounding surface of D lies in the plane $y = 1$. The lower (left-hand) bounding surface lies in the plane $y = x + z$. The upper boundary of R is the line $z = 1 - x$. The lower boundary is the line $z = 0$.

First we find the y-limits of integration. The line through a typical point (x, z) in R parallel to the y-axis enters D at $y = x + z$ and leaves at $y = 1$.

Next we find the z-limits of integration. The line L through (x, z) parallel to the z-axis enters R at $z = 0$ and leaves at $z = 1 - x$.

Finally we find the x-limits of integration. As L sweeps across R, the value of x varies from $x = 0$ to $x = 1$. The integral is

$$\int_0^1 \int_0^{1-x} \int_{x+z}^1 F(x, y, z)\, dy\, dz\, dx.$$

■

EXAMPLE 3 Revisiting Example 2 Using the Order *dz dy dx*

To integrate $F(x, y, z)$ over the tetrahedron D in the order $dz\, dy\, dx$, we perform the steps in the following way.

First we find the z-limits of integration. A line parallel to the z-axis through a typical point (x, y) in the xy-plane "shadow" enters the tetrahedron at $z = 0$ and exits through the upper plane where $z = y - x$ (Figure 15.29).

Next we find the y-limits of integration. On the xy-plane, where $z = 0$, the sloped side of the tetrahedron crosses the plane along the line $y = x$. A line through (x, y) parallel to the y-axis enters the shadow in the xy-plane at $y = x$ and exits at $y = 1$.

Finally we find the x-limits of integration. As the line parallel to the y-axis in the previous step sweeps out the shadow, the value of x varies from $x = 0$ to $x = 1$ at the point $(1, 1, 0)$. The integral is

$$\int_0^1 \int_x^1 \int_0^{y-x} F(x, y, z)\, dz\, dy\, dx.$$

For example, if $F(x, y, z) = 1$, we would find the volume of the tetrahedron to be

$$\begin{aligned} V &= \int_0^1 \int_x^1 \int_0^{y-x} dz\, dy\, dx \\ &= \int_0^1 \int_x^1 (y - x)\, dy\, dx \\ &= \int_0^1 \left[\frac{1}{2}y^2 - xy\right]_{y=x}^{y=1} dx \\ &= \int_0^1 \left(\frac{1}{2} - x + \frac{1}{2}x^2\right) dx \\ &= \left[\frac{1}{2}x - \frac{1}{2}x^2 + \frac{1}{6}x^3\right]_0^1 \\ &= \frac{1}{6}. \end{aligned}$$

We get the same result by integrating with the order $dy\,dz\,dx$,

$$V = \int_0^1 \int_0^{1-x} \int_{x+z}^{1} dy\,dz\,dx = \frac{1}{6}.$$

As we have seen, there are sometimes (but not always) two different orders in which the iterated single integrations for evaluating a double integral may be worked. For triple integrals, there can be as many as six, since there are six ways of ordering dx, dy, and dz. Each ordering leads to a different description of the region of integration in space, and to different limits of integration.

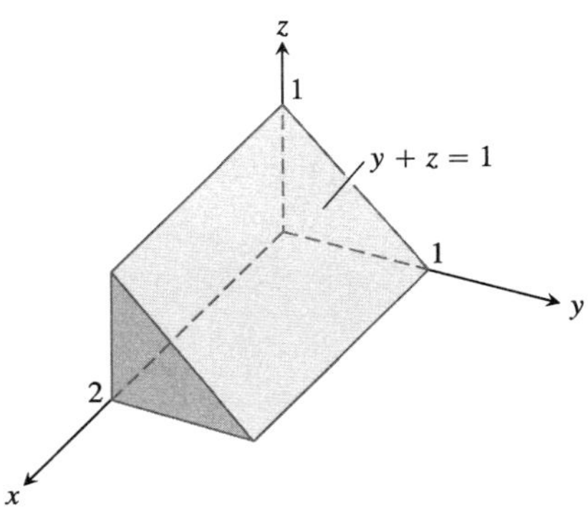

FIGURE 15.30 Example 4 gives six different iterated triple integrals for the volume of this prism.

EXAMPLE 4 Using Different Orders of Integration

Each of the following integrals gives the volume of the solid shown in Figure 15.30.

(a) $\displaystyle\int_0^1 \int_0^{1-z} \int_0^2 dx\,dy\,dz$ **(b)** $\displaystyle\int_0^1 \int_0^{1-y} \int_0^2 dx\,dz\,dy$

(c) $\displaystyle\int_0^1 \int_0^2 \int_0^{1-z} dy\,dx\,dz$ **(d)** $\displaystyle\int_0^2 \int_0^1 \int_0^{1-z} dy\,dz\,dx$

(e) $\displaystyle\int_0^1 \int_0^2 \int_0^{1-y} dz\,dx\,dy$ **(f)** $\displaystyle\int_0^2 \int_0^1 \int_0^{1-y} dz\,dy\,dx$

We work out the integrals in parts (b) and (c):

$$\begin{aligned} V &= \int_0^1 \int_0^{1-y} \int_0^2 dx\,dz\,dy && \text{Integral in part (b)} \\ &= \int_0^1 \int_0^{1-y} 2\,dz\,dy \\ &= \int_0^1 \left[2z\right]_{z=0}^{z=1-y} dy \\ &= \int_0^1 2(1-y)\,dy \\ &= 1. \end{aligned}$$

Also,

$$\begin{aligned} V &= \int_0^1 \int_0^2 \int_0^{1-z} dy\,dx\,dz && \text{Integral in part (c)} \\ &= \int_0^1 \int_0^2 (1-z)\,dx\,dz \\ &= \int_0^1 \left[x - zx\right]_{x=0}^{x=2} dz \end{aligned}$$

$$= \int_0^1 (2 - 2z)\, dz$$

$$= 1.$$

The integrals in parts (a), (d), (e), and (f) also give $V = 1$. ■

Average Value of a Function in Space

The average value of a function F over a region D in space is defined by the formula

$$\textbf{Average value} \text{ of } F \text{ over } D = \frac{1}{\text{volume of } D} \iiint_D F\, dV. \tag{2}$$

For example, if $F(x, y, z) = \sqrt{x^2 + y^2 + z^2}$, then the average value of F over D is the average distance of points in D from the origin. If $F(x, y, z)$ is the temperature at (x, y, z) on a solid that occupies a region D in space, then the average value of F over D is the average temperature of the solid.

EXAMPLE 5 Finding an Average Value

Find the average value of $F(x, y, z) = xyz$ over the cube bounded by the coordinate planes and the planes $x = 2$, $y = 2$, and $z = 2$ in the first octant.

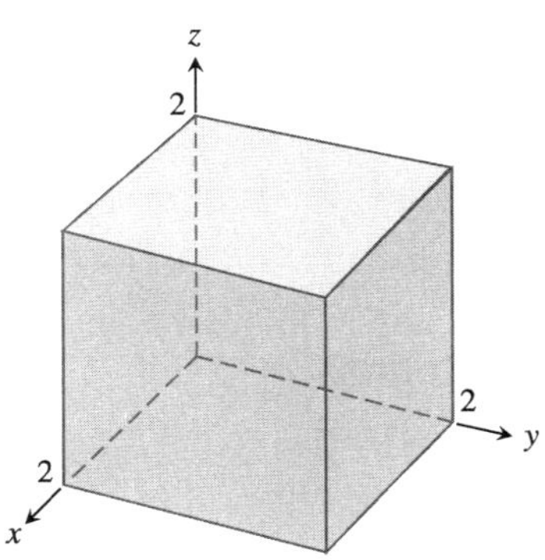

FIGURE 15.31 The region of integration in Example 5.

Solution We sketch the cube with enough detail to show the limits of integration (Figure 15.31). We then use Equation (2) to calculate the average value of F over the cube.

The volume of the cube is $(2)(2)(2) = 8$. The value of the integral of F over the cube is

$$\int_0^2 \int_0^2 \int_0^2 xyz\, dx\, dy\, dz = \int_0^2 \int_0^2 \left[\frac{x^2}{2} yz\right]_{x=0}^{x=2} dy\, dz = \int_0^2 \int_0^2 2yz\, dy\, dz$$

$$= \int_0^2 \left[y^2 z\right]_{y=0}^{y=2} dz = \int_0^2 4z\, dz = \left[2z^2\right]_0^2 = 8.$$

With these values, Equation (2) gives

$$\begin{array}{l}\text{Average value of} \\ xyz \text{ over the cube}\end{array} = \frac{1}{\text{volume}} \iiint_{\text{cube}} xyz\, dV = \left(\frac{1}{8}\right)(8) = 1.$$

In evaluating the integral, we chose the order $dx\, dy\, dz$, but any of the other five possible orders would have done as well. ■

Properties of Triple Integrals

Triple integrals have the same algebraic properties as double and single integrals.

Properties of Triple Integrals

If $F = F(x, y, z)$ and $G = G(x, y, z)$ are continuous, then

1. *Constant Multiple:* $\iiint_D kF\,dV = k\iiint_D F\,dV$ (any number k)

2. *Sum and Difference:* $\iiint_D (F \pm G)\,dV = \iiint_D F\,dV \pm \iiint_D G\,dV$

3. *Domination:*

   (a) $\iiint_D F\,dV \geq 0$ if $F \geq 0$ on D

   (b) $\iiint_D F\,dV \geq \iiint_D G\,dV$ if $F \geq G$ on D

4. *Additivity:* $\iiint_D F\,dV = \iiint_{D_1} E\,dV + \iiint_{D_2} F\,dV$

   if D is the union of two nonoverlapping regions D_1 and D_2.

EXERCISES 15.4

Evaluating Triple Integrals in Different Iterations

1. Evaluate the integral in Example 2 taking $F(x, y, z) = 1$ to find the volume of the tetrahedron.

2. **Volume of rectangular solid** Write six different iterated triple integrals for the volume of the rectangular solid in the first octant bounded by the coordinate planes and the planes $x = 1, y = 2$, and $z = 3$. Evaluate one of the integrals.

3. **Volume of tetrahedron** Write six different iterated triple integrals for the volume of the tetrahedron cut from the first octant by the plane $6x + 3y + 2z = 6$. Evaluate one of the integrals.

4. **Volume of solid** Write six different iterated triple integrals for the volume of the region in the first octant enclosed by the cylinder $x^2 + z^2 = 4$ and the plane $y = 3$. Evaluate one of the integrals.

5. **Volume enclosed by paraboloids** Let D be the region bounded by the paraboloids $z = 8 - x^2 - y^2$ and $z = x^2 + y^2$. Write six different triple iterated integrals for the volume of D. Evaluate one of the integrals.

6. **Volume inside paraboloid beneath a plane** Let D be the region bounded by the paraboloid $z = x^2 + y^2$ and the plane $z = 2y$. Write triple iterated integrals in the order $dz\,dx\,dy$ and $dz\,dy\,dx$ that give the volume of D. Do not evaluate either integral.

Evaluating Triple Iterated Integrals

Evaluate the integrals in Exercises 7–20.

7. $\int_0^1\int_0^1\int_0^1 (x^2 + y^2 + z^2)\,dz\,dy\,dx$

8. $\int_0^{\sqrt{2}}\int_0^{3y}\int_{x^2+3y^2}^{8-x^2-y^2} dz\,dx\,dy$

9. $\int_1^e\int_1^e\int_1^e \frac{1}{xyz}\,dx\,dy\,dz$

10. $\int_0^1\int_0^{3-3x}\int_0^{3-3x-y} dz\,dy\,dx$

11. $\int_0^1\int_0^{\pi}\int_0^{\pi} y\sin z\,dx\,dy\,dz$

12. $\int_{-1}^1\int_{-1}^1\int_{-1}^1 (x + y + z)\,dy\,dx\,dz$

13. $\int_0^3\int_0^{\sqrt{9-x^2}}\int_0^{\sqrt{9-x^2}} dz\,dy\,dx$

14. $\int_0^2\int_{-\sqrt{4-y^2}}^{\sqrt{4-y^2}}\int_0^{2x+y} dz\,dx\,dy$

15. $\int_0^1\int_0^{2-x}\int_0^{2-x-y} dz\,dy\,dx$

16. $\int_0^1\int_0^{1-x^2}\int_3^{4-x^2-y} x\,dz\,dy\,dx$

17. $\int_0^{\pi}\int_0^{\pi}\int_0^{\pi} \cos(u + v + w)\,du\,dv\,dw$ (uvw-space)

18. $\int_1^e\int_1^e\int_1^e \ln r \ln s \ln t\,dt\,dr\,ds$ (rst-space)

19. $\int_0^{\pi/4}\int_0^{\ln\sec v}\int_{-\infty}^{2t} e^x\,dx\,dt\,dv$ (tvx-space)

20. $\displaystyle\int_0^7 \int_0^2 \int_0^{\sqrt{4-q^2}} \frac{q}{r+1}\, dp\, dq\, dr$ (pqr-space)

Volumes Using Triple Integrals

21. Here is the region of integration of the integral

$$\int_{-1}^{1} \int_{x^2}^{1} \int_{0}^{1-y} dz\, dy\, dx .$$

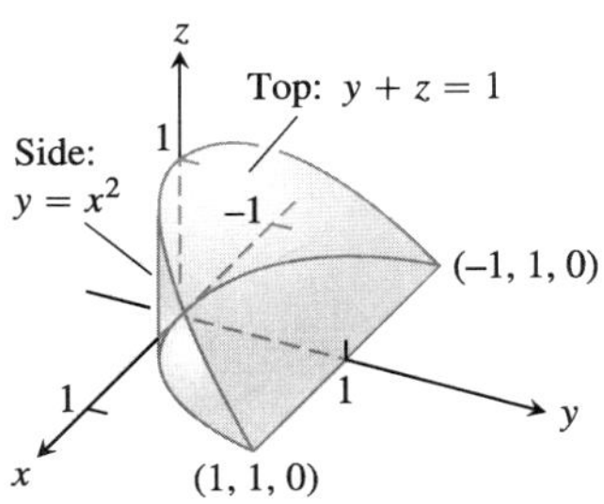

Rewrite the integral as an equivalent iterated integral in the order

a. $dy\, dz\, dx$ **b.** $dy\, dx\, dz$

c. $dx\, dy\, dz$ **d.** $dx\, dz\, dy$

e. $dz\, dx\, dy$.

22. Here is the region of integration of the integral

$$\int_{0}^{1} \int_{-1}^{0} \int_{0}^{y^2} dz\, dy\, dx.$$

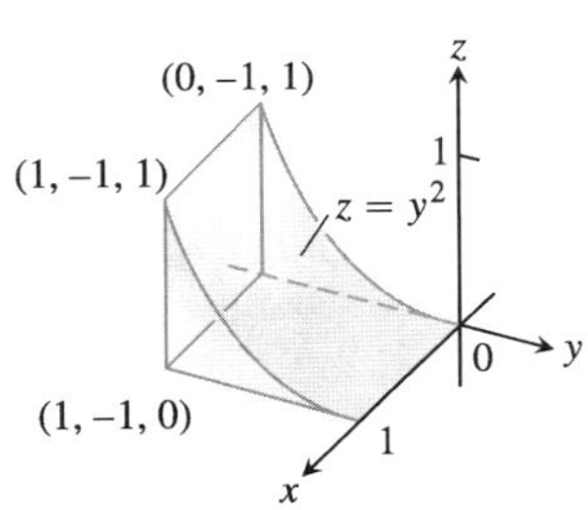

Rewrite the integral as an equivalent iterated integral in the order

a. $dy\, dz\, dx$ **b.** $dy\, dx\, dz$

c. $dx\, dy\, dz$ **d.** $dx\, dz\, dy$

e. $dz\, dx\, dy$.

Find the volumes of the regions in Exercises 23–36.

23. The region between the cylinder $z = y^2$ and the xy-plane that is bounded by the planes $x = 0, x = 1, y = -1, y = 1$

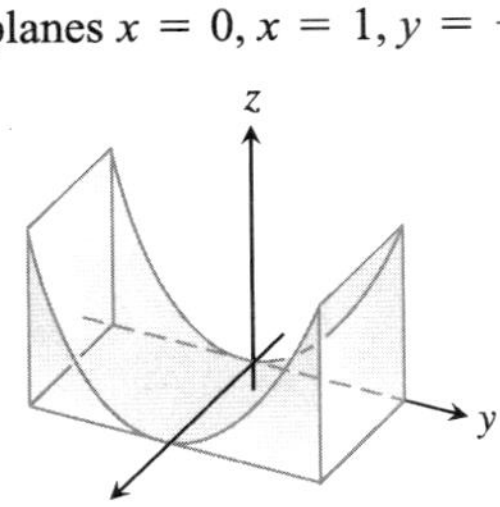

24. The region in the first octant bounded by the coordinate planes and the planes $x + z = 1, y + 2z = 2$

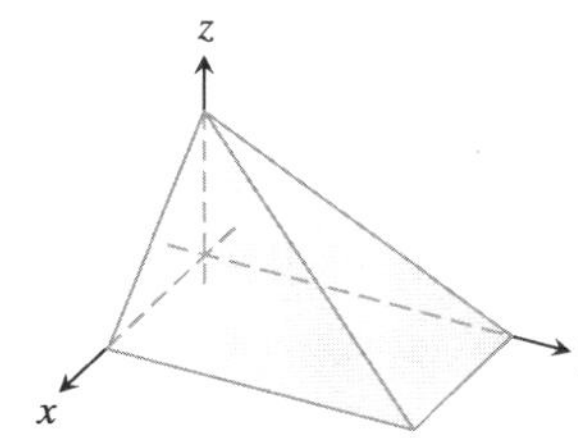

25. The region in the first octant bounded by the coordinate planes, the plane $y + z = 2$, and the cylinder $x = 4 - y^2$

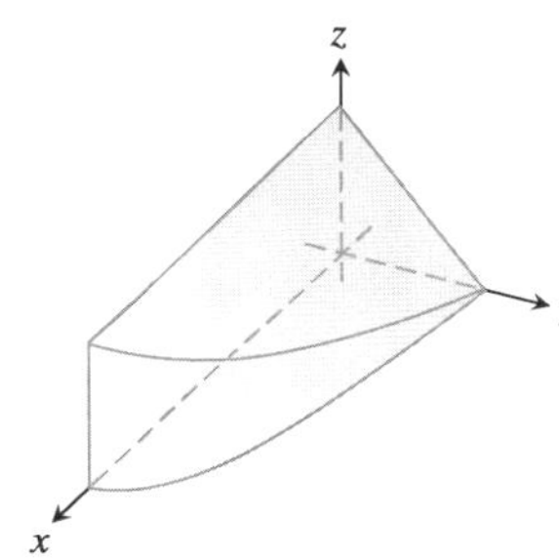

26. The wedge cut from the cylinder $x^2 + y^2 = 1$ by the planes $z = -y$ and $z = 0$

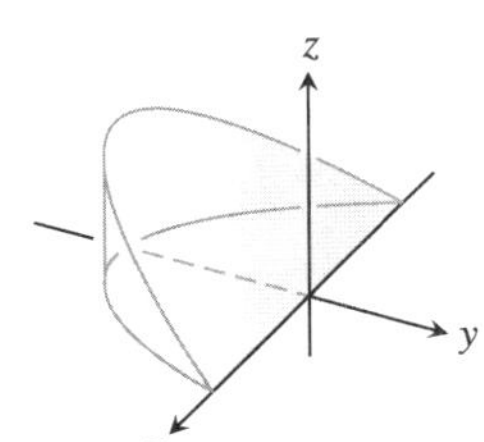

27. The tetrahedron in the first octant bounded by the coordinate planes and the plane passing through (1, 0, 0), (0, 2, 0), and (0, 0, 3).

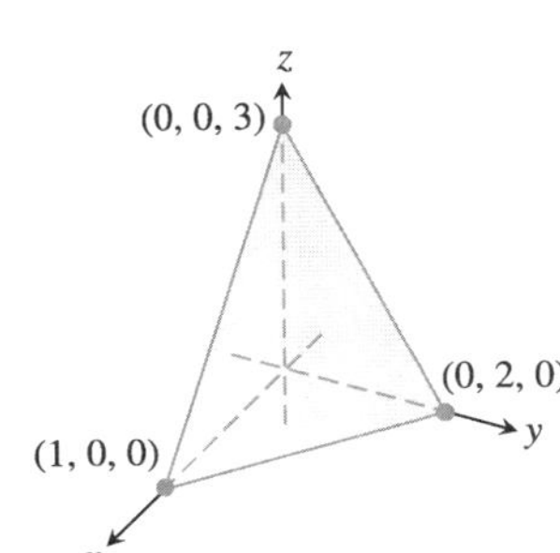

28. The region in the first octant bounded by the coordinate planes, the plane $y = 1 - x$, and the surface $z = \cos(\pi x/2)$, $0 \le x \le 1$

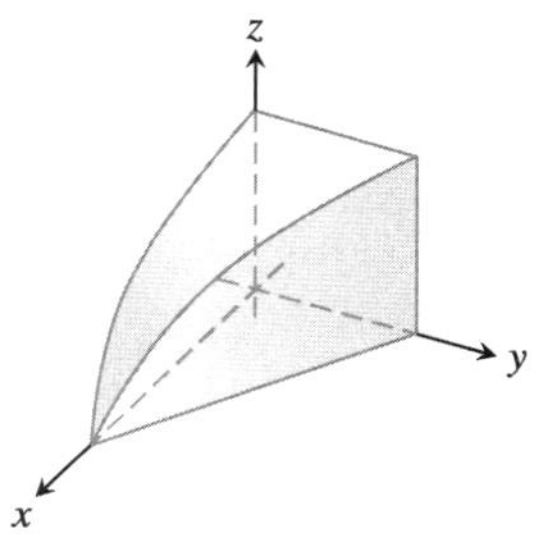

29. The region common to the interiors of the cylinders $x^2 + y^2 = 1$ and $x^2 + z^2 = 1$, one-eighth of which is shown in the accompanying figure.

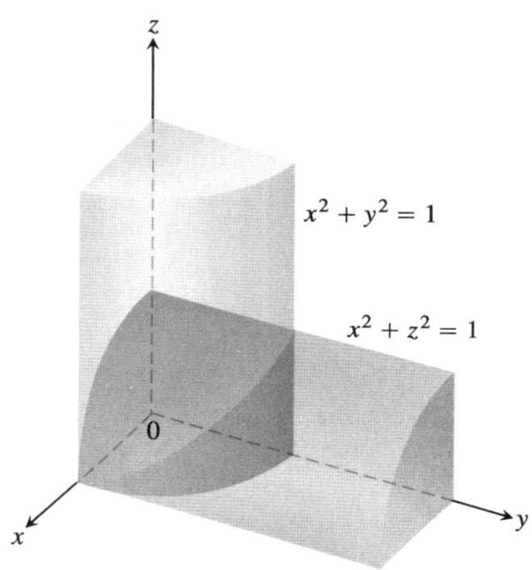

30. The region in the first octant bounded by the coordinate planes and the surface $z = 4 - x^2 - y$

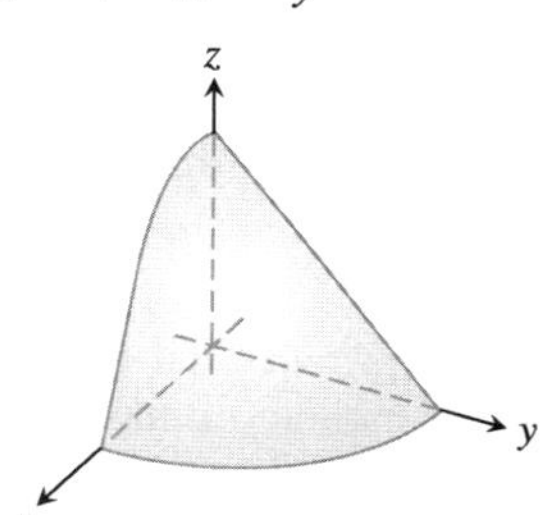

31. The region in the first octant bounded by the coordinate planes, the plane $x + y = 4$, and the cylinder $y^2 + 4z^2 = 16$

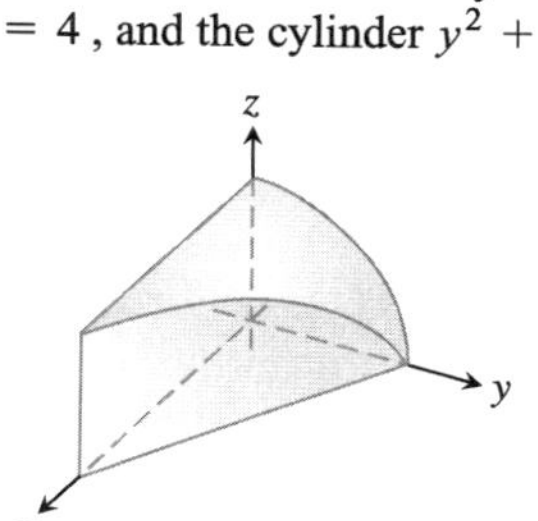

32. The region cut from the cylinder $x^2 + y^2 = 4$ by the plane $z = 0$ and the plane $x + z = 3$

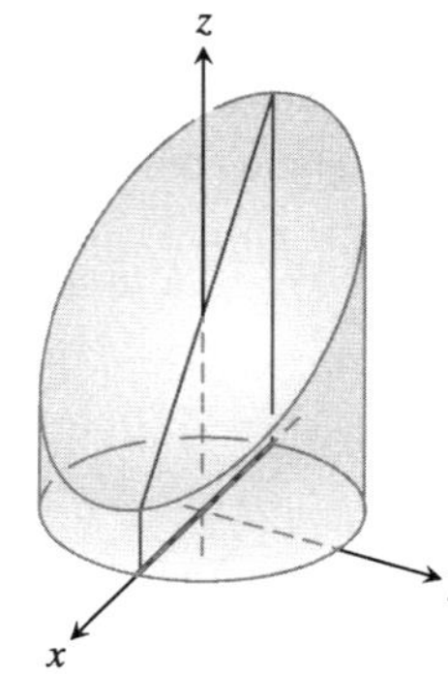

33. The region between the planes $x + y + 2z = 2$ and $2x + 2y + z = 4$ in the first octant

34. The finite region bounded by the planes $z = x$, $x + z = 8$, $z = y$, $y = 8$, and $z = 0$.

35. The region cut from the solid elliptical cylinder $x^2 + 4y^2 \le 4$ by the xy-plane and the plane $z = x + 2$

36. The region bounded in back by the plane $x = 0$, on the front and sides by the parabolic cylinder $x = 1 - y^2$, on the top by the paraboloid $z = x^2 + y^2$, and on the bottom by the xy-plane

Average Values

In Exercises 37–40, find the average value of $F(x, y, z)$ over the given region.

37. $F(x, y, z) = x^2 + 9$ over the cube in the first octant bounded by the coordinate planes and the planes $x = 2$, $y = 2$, and $z = 2$

38. $F(x, y, z) = x + y - z$ over the rectangular solid in the first octant bounded by the coordinate planes and the planes $x = 1$, $y = 1$, and $z = 2$

39. $F(x, y, z) = x^2 + y^2 + z^2$ over the cube in the first octant bounded by the coordinate planes and the planes $x = 1$, $y = 1$, and $z = 1$

40. $F(x, y, z) = xyz$ over the cube in the first octant bounded by the coordinate planes and the planes $x = 2$, $y = 2$, and $z = 2$

Changing the Order of Integration

Evaluate the integrals in Exercises 41–44 by changing the order of integration in an appropriate way.

41. $\displaystyle\int_0^4\int_0^1\int_{2y}^2 \frac{4\cos(x^2)}{2\sqrt{z}}\,dx\,dy\,dz$

42. $\displaystyle\int_0^1\int_0^1\int_{x^2}^1 12xze^{zy^2}\,dy\,dx\,dz$

43. $\displaystyle\int_0^1\int_{\sqrt[3]{z}}^1\int_0^{\ln 3} \frac{\pi e^{2x}\sin \pi y^2}{y^2}\,dx\,dy\,dz$

44. $\displaystyle\int_0^2\int_0^{4-x^2}\int_0^x \frac{\sin 2z}{4-z}\,dy\,dz\,dx$

Theory and Examples

45. Finding upper limit of iterated integral Solve for a:

$$\int_0^1 \int_0^{4-a-x^2} \int_a^{4-x^2-y} dz\, dy\, dx = \frac{4}{15}.$$

46. Ellipsoid For what value of c is the volume of the ellipsoid $x^2 + (y/2)^2 + (z/c)^2 = 1$ equal to 8π?

47. Minimizing a triple integral What domain D in space minimizes the value of the integral

$$\iiint_D (4x^2 + 4y^2 + z^2 - 4)\, dV?$$

Give reasons for your answer.

48. Maximizing a triple integral What domain D in space maximizes the value of the integral

$$\iiint_D (1 - x^2 - y^2 - z^2)\, dV?$$

Give reasons for your answer.

COMPUTER EXPLORATIONS

Numerical Evaluations

In Exercises 49–52, use a CAS integration utility to evaluate the triple integral of the given function over the specified solid region.

49. $F(x, y, z) = x^2y^2z$ over the solid cylinder bounded by $x^2 + y^2 = 1$ and the planes $z = 0$ and $z = 1$

50. $F(x, y, z) = |xyz|$ over the solid bounded below by the paraboloid $z = x^2 + y^2$ and above by the plane $z = 1$

51. $F(x, y, z) = \dfrac{z}{(x^2 + y^2 + z^2)^{3/2}}$ over the solid bounded below by the cone $z = \sqrt{x^2 + y^2}$ and above by the plane $z = 1$

52. $F(x, y, z) = x^4 + y^2 + z^2$ over the solid sphere $x^2 + y^2 + z^2 \le 1$

15.5 Masses and Moments in Three Dimensions

This section shows how to calculate the masses and moments of three-dimensional objects in Cartesian coordinates. The formulas are similar to those for two-dimensional objects. For calculations in spherical and cylindrical coordinates, see Section 15.6.

Masses and Moments

If $\delta(x, y, z)$ is the density of an object occupying a region D in space (mass per unit volume), the integral of δ over D gives the **mass** of the object. To see why, imagine partitioning the object into n mass elements like the one in Figure 15.32. The object's mass is the limit

$$M = \lim_{n\to\infty} \sum_{k=1}^{n} \Delta m_k = \lim_{n\to\infty} \sum_{k=1}^{n} \delta(x_k, y_k, z_k)\, \Delta V_k = \iiint_D \delta(x, y, z)\, dV.$$

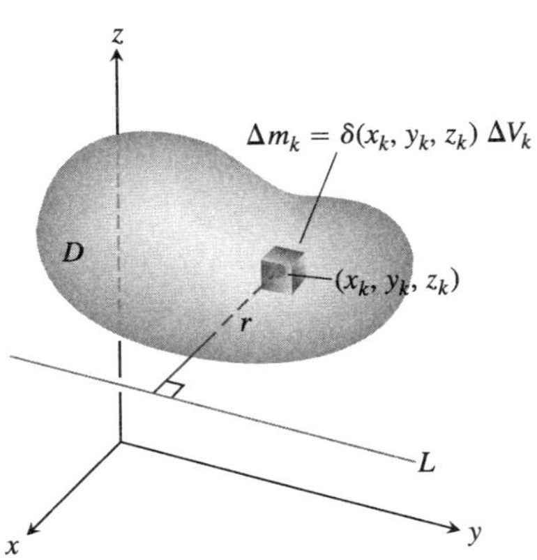

FIGURE 15.32 To define an object's mass and moment of inertia about a line, we first imagine it to be partitioned into a finite number of mass elements Δm_k.

We now derive a formula for the moment of inertia. If $r(x, y, z)$ is the distance from the point (x, y, z) in D to a line L, then the moment of inertia of the mass $\Delta m_k = \delta(x_k, y_k, z_k)\Delta V_k$ about the line L (shown in Figure 15.32) is approximately $\Delta I_k = r^2(x_k, y_k, z_k)\Delta m_k$. **The moment of inertia about L** of the entire object is

$$I_L = \lim_{n\to\infty} \sum_{k=1}^{n} \Delta I_k = \lim_{n\to\infty} \sum_{k=1}^{n} r^2(x_k, y_k, z_k)\, \delta(x_k, y_k, z_k)\, \Delta V_k = \iiint_D r^2 \delta\, dV.$$

If L is the x-axis, then $r^2 = y^2 + z^2$ (Figure 15.33) and

$$I_x = \iiint_D (y^2 + z^2)\, \delta\, dV.$$

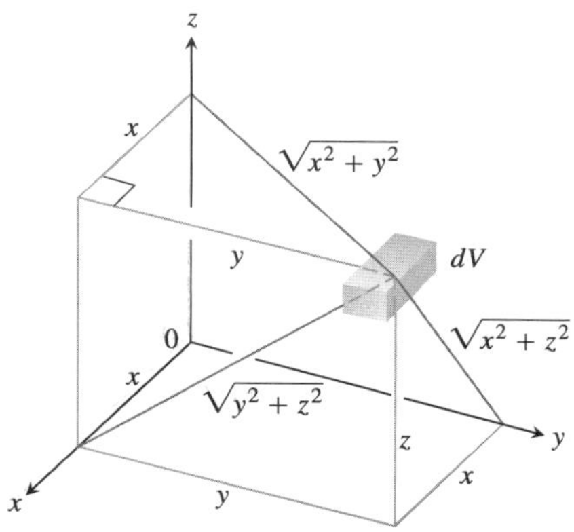

FIGURE 15.33 Distances from dV to the coordinate planes and axes.

Similarly, if L is the y-axis or z-axis we have

$$I_y = \iiint_D (x^2 + z^2)\,\delta\,dV \qquad \text{and} \qquad I_z = \iiint_D (x^2 + y^2)\,\delta\,dV.$$

Likewise, we can obtain the **first moments about the coordinate planes**. For example,

$$M_{yz} = \iiint_D x\delta(x, y, z)\,dV$$

gives the first moment about the yz-plane.

The mass and moment formulas in space analogous to those discussed for planar regions in Section 15.2 are summarized in Table 15.3.

TABLE 15.3 Mass and moment formulas for solid objects in space

Mass: $M = \iiint_D \delta\,dV \qquad (\delta = \delta(x, y, z) = \text{density})$

First moments about the coordinate planes:

$$M_{yz} = \iiint_D x\,\delta\,dV, \qquad M_{xz} = \iiint_D y\,\delta\,dV, \qquad M_{xy} = \iiint_D z\,\delta\,dV$$

Center of mass:

$$\bar{x} = \frac{M_{yz}}{M}, \qquad \bar{y} = \frac{M_{xz}}{M}, \qquad \bar{z} = \frac{M_{xy}}{M}$$

Moments of inertia (second moments) about the coordinate axes:

$$I_x = \iiint (y^2 + z^2)\,\delta\,dV$$

$$I_y = \iiint (x^2 + z^2)\,\delta\,dV$$

$$I_z = \iiint (x^2 + y^2)\,\delta\,dV$$

Moments of inertia about a line *L*:

$$I_L = \iiint r^2\,\delta\,dV \qquad (r(x, y, z) = \text{distance from the point } (x, y, z) \text{ to line } L)$$

Radius of gyration about a line *L*:

$$R_L = \sqrt{I_L/M}$$

EXAMPLE 1 Finding the Center of Mass of a Solid in Space

Find the center of mass of a solid of constant density δ bounded below by the disk R: $x^2 + y^2 \le 4$ in the plane $z = 0$ and above by the paraboloid $z = 4 - x^2 - y^2$ (Figure 15.34).

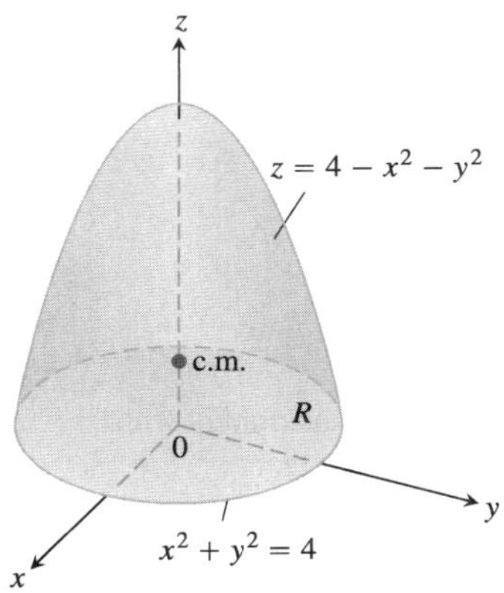

FIGURE 15.34 Finding the center of mass of a solid (Example 1).

Solution By symmetry $\bar{x} = \bar{y} = 0$. To find $\bar{z}$, we first calculate

$$M_{xy} = \iiint_R \int_{z=0}^{z=4-x^2-y^2} z\,\delta\,dz\,dy\,dx = \iint_R \left[\frac{z^2}{2}\right]_{z=0}^{z=4-x^2-y^2} \delta\,dy\,dx$$

$$= \frac{\delta}{2}\iint_R (4 - x^2 - y^2)^2\,dy\,dx$$

$$= \frac{\delta}{2}\int_0^{2\pi}\int_0^2 (4 - r^2)^2\,r\,dr\,d\theta \qquad \text{Polar coordinates}$$

$$= \frac{\delta}{2}\int_0^{2\pi}\left[-\frac{1}{6}(4 - r^2)^3\right]_{r=0}^{r=2} d\theta = \frac{16\delta}{3}\int_0^{2\pi} d\theta = \frac{32\pi\delta}{3}.$$

A similar calculation gives

$$M = \iiint_R \int_0^{4-x^2-y^2} \delta\,dz\,dy\,dx = 8\pi\delta.$$

Therefore $\bar{z} = (M_{xy}/M) = 4/3$ and the center of mass is $(\bar{x}, \bar{y}, \bar{z}) = (0, 0, 4/3)$. ■

When the density of a solid object is constant (as in Example 1), the center of mass is called the **centroid** of the object (as was the case for two-dimensional shapes in Section 15.2).

EXAMPLE 2 Finding the Moments of Inertia About the Coordinate Axes

Find I_x, I_y, I_z for the rectangular solid of constant density δ shown in Figure 15.35.

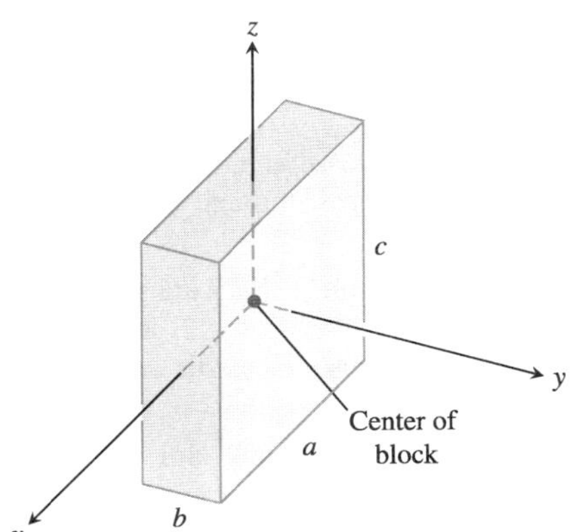

FIGURE 15.35 Finding I_x, I_y, and I_z for the block shown here. The origin lies at the center of the block (Example 2).

Solution The formula for I_x gives

$$I_x = \int_{-c/2}^{c/2}\int_{-b/2}^{b/2}\int_{-a/2}^{a/2} (y^2 + z^2)\,\delta\,dx\,dy\,dz.$$

We can avoid some of the work of integration by observing that $(y^2 + z^2)\delta$ is an even function of x, y, and z. The rectangular solid consists of eight symmetric pieces, one in each octant. We can evaluate the integral on one of these pieces and then multiply by 8 to get the total value.

$$I_x = 8\int_0^{c/2}\int_0^{b/2}\int_0^{a/2} (y^2 + z^2)\,\delta\,dx\,dy\,dz = 4a\delta\int_0^{c/2}\int_0^{b/2} (y^2 + z^2)\,dy\,dz$$

$$= 4a\delta\int_0^{c/2}\left[\frac{y^3}{3} + z^2 y\right]_{y=0}^{y=b/2} dz$$

$$= 4a\delta\int_0^{c/2}\left(\frac{b^3}{24} + \frac{z^2 b}{2}\right) dz$$

$$= 4a\delta\left(\frac{b^3 c}{48} + \frac{c^3 b}{48}\right) = \frac{abc\delta}{12}(b^2 + c^2) = \frac{M}{12}(b^2 + c^2).$$

Similarly,

$$I_y = \frac{M}{12}(a^2 + c^2) \qquad \text{and} \qquad I_z = \frac{M}{12}(a^2 + b^2).$$ ■

EXERCISES 15.5

Constant Density

The solids in Exercises 1–12 all have constant density $\delta = 1$.

1. (*Example 1 Revisited.*) Evaluate the integral for I_x in Table 15.3 directly to show that the shortcut in Example 2 gives the same answer. Use the results in Example 2 to find the radius of gyration of the rectangular solid about each coordinate axis.

2. **Moments of inertia** The coordinate axes in the figure run through the centroid of a solid wedge parallel to the labeled edges. Find I_x, I_y, and I_z if $a = b = 6$ and $c = 4$.

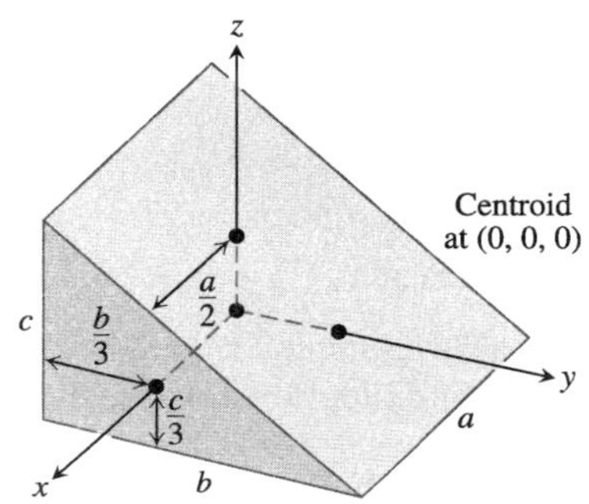

3. **Moments of inertia** Find the moments of inertia of the rectangular solid shown here with respect to its edges by calculating I_x, I_y, and I_z.

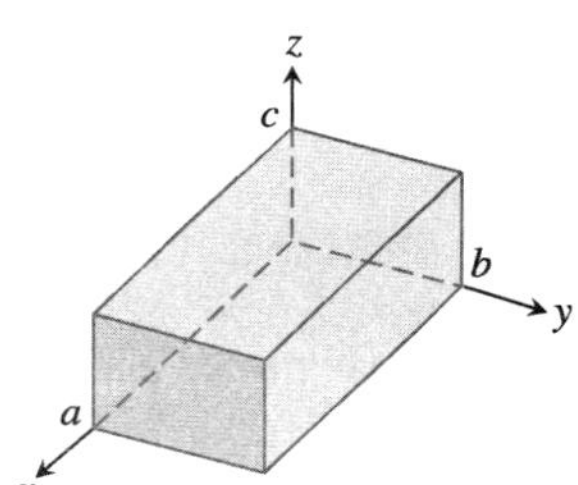

4. **a. Centroid and moments of inertia** Find the centroid and the moments of inertia I_x, I_y, and I_z of the tetrahedron whose vertices are the points (0, 0, 0), (1, 0, 0), (0, 1, 0), and (0, 0, 1).

   b. Radius of gyration Find the radius of gyration of the tetrahedron about the x-axis. Compare it with the distance from the centroid to the x-axis.

5. **Center of mass and moments of inertia** A solid "trough" of constant density is bounded below by the surface $z = 4y^2$, above by the plane $z = 4$, and on the ends by the planes $x = 1$ and $x = -1$. Find the center of mass and the moments of inertia with respect to the three axes.

6. **Center of mass** A solid of constant density is bounded below by the plane $z = 0$, on the sides by the elliptical cylinder $x^2 + 4y^2 = 4$, and above by the plane $z = 2 - x$ (see the accompanying figure).

   a. Find $\bar{x}$ and $\bar{y}$.

   b. Evaluate the integral

$$M_{xy} = \int_{-2}^{2}\int_{-(1/2)\sqrt{4-x^2}}^{(1/2)\sqrt{4-x^2}}\int_{0}^{2-x} z\,dz\,dy\,dx$$

   using integral tables to carry out the final integration with respect to x. Then divide M_{xy} by M to verify that $\bar{z} = 5/4$.

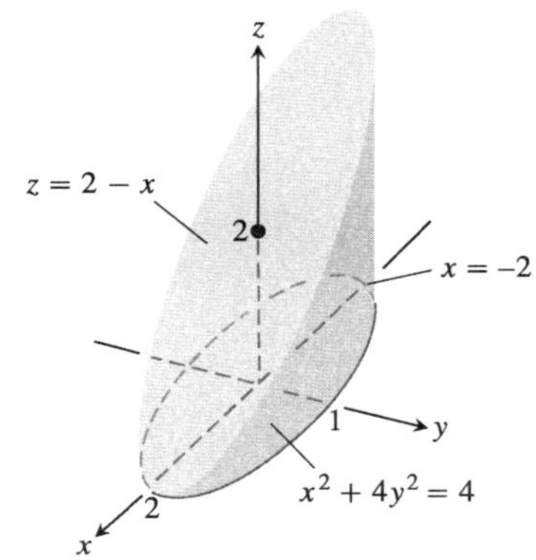

7. **a. Center of mass** Find the center of mass of a solid of constant density bounded below by the paraboloid $z = x^2 + y^2$ and above by the plane $z = 4$.

   b. Find the plane $z = c$ that divides the solid into two parts of equal volume. This plane does not pass through the center of mass.

8. **Moments and radii of gyration** A solid cube, 2 units on a side, is bounded by the planes $x = \pm 1, z = \pm 1, y = 3$, and $y = 5$. Find the center of mass and the moments of inertia and radii of gyration about the coordinate axes.

9. **Moment of inertia and radius of gyration about a line** A wedge like the one in Exercise 2 has $a = 4, b = 6$, and $c = 3$. Make a quick sketch to check for yourself that the square of the distance from a typical point (x, y, z) of the wedge to the line $L: z = 0, y = 6$ is $r^2 = (y - 6)^2 + z^2$. Then calculate the moment of inertia and radius of gyration of the wedge about L.

10. **Moment of inertia and radius of gyration about a line** A wedge like the one in Exercise 2 has $a = 4, b = 6$, and $c = 3$. Make a quick sketch to check for yourself that the square of the distance from a typical point (x, y, z) of the wedge to the line $L: x = 4, y = 0$ is $r^2 = (x - 4)^2 + y^2$. Then calculate the moment of inertia and radius of gyration of the wedge about L.

11. **Moment of inertia and radius of gyration about a line** A solid like the one in Exercise 3 has $a = 4, b = 2$, and $c = 1$. Make a quick sketch to check for yourself that the square of the distance between a typical point (x, y, z) of the solid and the line $L: y = 2, z = 0$ is $r^2 = (y - 2)^2 + z^2$. Then find the moment of inertia and radius of gyration of the solid about L.

12. Moment of inertia and radius of gyration about a line A solid like the one in Exercise 3 has $a = 4, b = 2$, and $c = 1$. Make a quick sketch to check for yourself that the square of the distance between a typical point (x, y, z) of the solid and the line $L: x = 4, y = 0$ is $r^2 = (x - 4)^2 + y^2$. Then find the moment of inertia and radius of gyration of the solid about L.

Variable Density

In Exercises 13 and 14, find

a. the mass of the solid.

b. the center of mass.

13. A solid region in the first octant is bounded by the coordinate planes and the plane $x + y + z = 2$. The density of the solid is $\delta(x, y, z) = 2x$.

14. A solid in the first octant is bounded by the planes $y = 0$ and $z = 0$ and by the surfaces $z = 4 - x^2$ and $x = y^2$ (see the accompanying figure). Its density function is $\delta(x, y, z) = kxy$, k a constant.

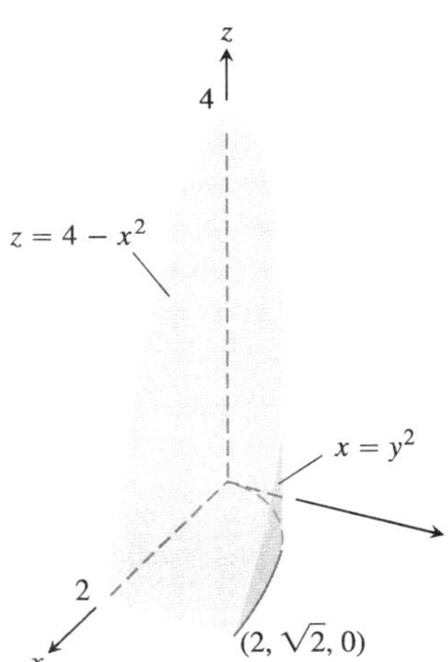

In Exercises 15 and 16, find

a. the mass of the solid.

b. the center of mass.

c. the moments of inertia about the coordinate axes.

d. the radii of gyration about the coordinate axes.

15. A solid cube in the first octant is bounded by the coordinate planes and by the planes $x = 1, y = 1$, and $z = 1$. The density of the cube is $\delta(x, y, z) = x + y + z + 1$.

16. A wedge like the one in Exercise 2 has dimensions $a = 2, b = 6$, and $c = 3$. The density is $\delta(x, y, z) = x + 1$. Notice that if the density is constant, the center of mass will be $(0, 0, 0)$.

17. Mass Find the mass of the solid bounded by the planes $x + z = 1, x - z = -1, y = 0$ and the surface $y = \sqrt{z}$. The density of the solid is $\delta(x, y, z) = 2y + 5$.

18. Mass Find the mass of the solid region bounded by the parabolic surfaces $z = 16 - 2x^2 - 2y^2$ and $z = 2x^2 + 2y^2$ if the density of the solid is $\delta(x, y, z) = \sqrt{x^2 + y^2}$.

Work

In Exercises 19 and 20, calculate the following.

a. The amount of work done by (constant) gravity g in moving the liquid filling in the container to the xy-plane. (*Hint:* Partition the liquid into small volume elements ΔV_i and find the work done (approximately) by gravity on each element. Summation and passage to the limit gives a triple integral to evaluate.)

b. The work done by gravity in moving the center of mass down to the xy-plane.

19. The container is a cubical box in the first octant bounded by the coordinate planes and the planes $x = 1, y = 1$, and $z = 1$. The density of the liquid filling the box is $\delta(x, y, z) = x + y + z + 1$ (see Exercise 15).

20. The container is in the shape of the region bounded by $y = 0, z = 0, z = 4 - x^2$, and $x = y^2$. The density of the liquid filling the region is $\delta(x, y, z) = kxy$, k a constant (see Exercise 14).

The Parallel Axis Theorem

The Parallel Axis Theorem (Exercises 15.2) holds in three dimensions as well as in two. Let $L_{\text{c.m.}}$ be a line through the center of mass of a body of mass m and let L be a parallel line h units away from $L_{\text{c.m.}}$. The **Parallel Axis Theorem** says that the moments of inertia $I_{\text{c.m.}}$ and I_L of the body about $L_{\text{c.m.}}$ and L satisfy the equation

$$I_L = I_{\text{c.m.}} + mh^2. \qquad (1)$$

As in the two-dimensional case, the theorem gives a quick way to calculate one moment when the other moment and the mass are known.

21. Proof of the Parallel Axis Theorem

a. Show that the first moment of a body in space about any plane through the body's center of mass is zero. (*Hint:* Place the body's center of mass at the origin and let the plane be the yz-plane. What does the formula $\bar{x} = M_{yz}/M$ then tell you?)

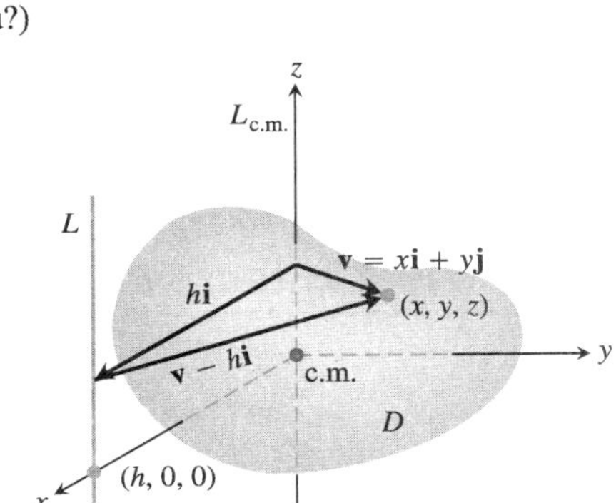

b. To prove the Parallel Axis Theorem, place the body with its center of mass at the origin, with the line $L_{c.m.}$ along the z-axis and the line L perpendicular to the xy-plane at the point $(h, 0, 0)$. Let D be the region of space occupied by the body. Then, in the notation of the figure,

$$I_L = \iiint_D |\mathbf{v} - h\mathbf{i}|^2 \, dm.$$

Expand the integrand in this integral and complete the proof.

22. The moment of inertia about a diameter of a solid sphere of constant density and radius a is $(2/5)ma^2$, where m is the mass of the sphere. Find the moment of inertia about a line tangent to the sphere.

23. The moment of inertia of the solid in Exercise 3 about the z-axis is $I_z = abc(a^2 + b^2)/3$.

a. Use Equation (1) to find the moment of inertia and radius of gyration of the solid about the line parallel to the z-axis through the solid's center of mass.

b. Use Equation (1) and the result in part (a) to find the moment of inertia and radius of gyration of the solid about the line $x = 0, y = 2b$.

24. If $a = b = 6$ and $c = 4$, the moment of inertia of the solid wedge in Exercise 2 about the x-axis is $I_x = 208$. Find the moment of inertia of the wedge about the line $y = 4, z = -4/3$ (the edge of the wedge's narrow end).

Pappus's Formula

Pappus's formula (Exercises 15.2) holds in three dimensions as well as in two. Suppose that bodies B_1 and B_2 of mass m_1 and m_2, respectively, occupy nonoverlapping regions in space and that $\mathbf{c}_1$ and $\mathbf{c}_2$ are the vectors from the origin to the bodies' respective centers of mass. Then the center of mass of the union $B_1 \cup B_2$ of the two bodies is determined by the vector

$$\mathbf{c} = \frac{m_1\mathbf{c}_1 + m_2\mathbf{c}_2}{m_1 + m_2}.$$

As before, this formula is called **Pappus's formula**. As in the two-dimensional case, the formula generalizes to

$$\mathbf{c} = \frac{m_1\mathbf{c}_1 + m_2\mathbf{c}_2 + \cdots + m_n\mathbf{c}_n}{m_1 + m_2 + \cdots + m_n}$$

for n bodies.

25. Derive Pappus's formula. (*Hint:* Sketch B_1 and B_2 as nonoverlapping regions in the first octant and label their centers of mass $(\bar{x}_1, \bar{y}_1, \bar{z}_1)$ and $(\bar{x}_2, \bar{y}_2, \bar{z}_2)$. Express the moments of $B_1 \cup B_2$ about the coordinate planes in terms of the masses m_1 and m_2 and the coordinates of these centers.)

26. The accompanying figure shows a solid made from three rectangular solids of constant density $\delta = 1$. Use Pappus's formula to find the center of mass of

a. $A \cup B$ **b.** $A \cup C$

c. $B \cup C$ **d.** $A \cup B \cup C$.

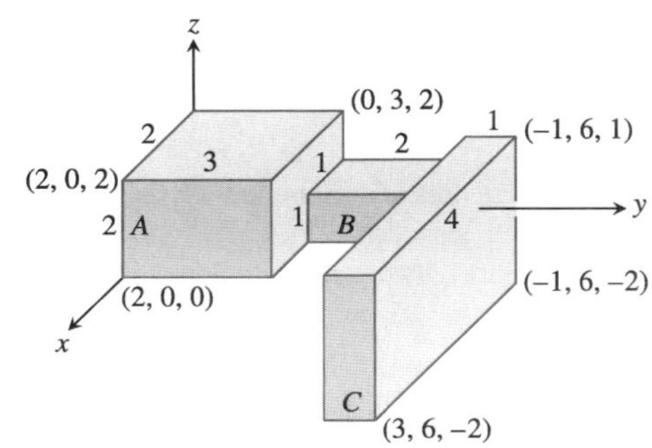

27. a. Suppose that a solid right circular cone C of base radius a and altitude h is constructed on the circular base of a solid hemisphere S of radius a so that the union of the two solids resembles an ice cream cone. The centroid of a solid cone lies one-fourth of the way from the base toward the vertex. The centroid of a solid hemisphere lies three-eighths of the way from the base to the top. What relation must hold between h and a to place the centroid of $C \cup S$ in the common base of the two solids?

b. If you have not already done so, answer the analogous question about a triangle and a semicircle (Section 15.2, Exercise 55). The answers are not the same.

28. A solid pyramid P with height h and four congruent sides is built with its base as one face of a solid cube C whose edges have length s. The centroid of a solid pyramid lies one-fourth of the way from the base toward the vertex. What relation must hold between h and s to place the centroid of $P \cup C$ in the base of the pyramid? Compare your answer with the answer to Exercise 27. Also compare it with the answer to Exercise 56 in Section 15.2.

15.6 Triple Integrals in Cylindrical and Spherical Coordinates

When a calculation in physics, engineering, or geometry involves a cylinder, cone, or sphere, we can often simplify our work by using cylindrical or spherical coordinates, which are introduced in this section. The procedure for transforming to these coordinates and evaluating the resulting triple integrals is similar to the transformation to polar coordinates in the plane studied in Section 15.3.

Integration in Cylindrical Coordinates

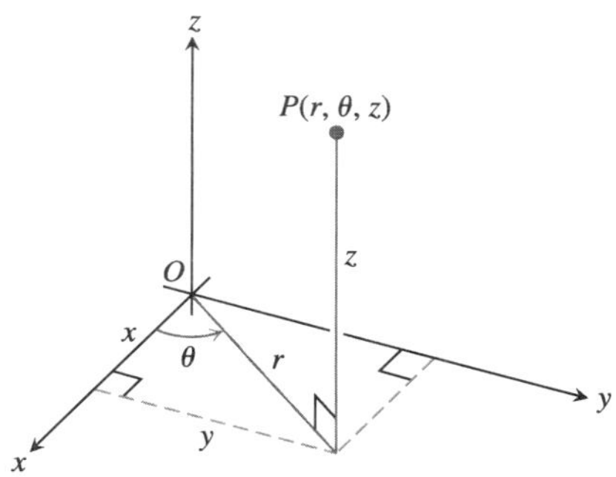

FIGURE 15.36 The cylindrical coordinates of a point in space are r, θ, and z.

We obtain cylindrical coordinates for space by combining polar coordinates in the xy-plane with the usual z-axis. This assigns to every point in space one or more coordinate triples of the form (r, θ, z), as shown in Figure 15.36.

DEFINITION **Cylindrical Coordinates**

Cylindrical coordinates represent a point P in space by ordered triples (r, θ, z) in which

1. r and θ are polar coordinates for the vertical projection of P on the xy-plane
2. z is the rectangular vertical coordinate.

The values of x, y, r, and θ in rectangular and cylindrical coordinates are related by the usual equations.

Equations Relating Rectangular (x, y, z) and Cylindrical (r, θ, z) Coordinates

$$x = r\cos\theta, \qquad y = r\sin\theta, \qquad z = z,$$
$$r^2 = x^2 + y^2, \qquad \tan\theta = y/x$$

In cylindrical coordinates, the equation $r = a$ describes not just a circle in the xy-plane but an entire cylinder about the z-axis (Figure 15.37). The z-axis is given by $r = 0$. The equation $\theta = \theta_0$ describes the plane that contains the z-axis and makes an angle θ_0 with the positive x-axis. And, just as in rectangular coordinates, the equation $z = z_0$ describes a plane perpendicular to the z-axis.

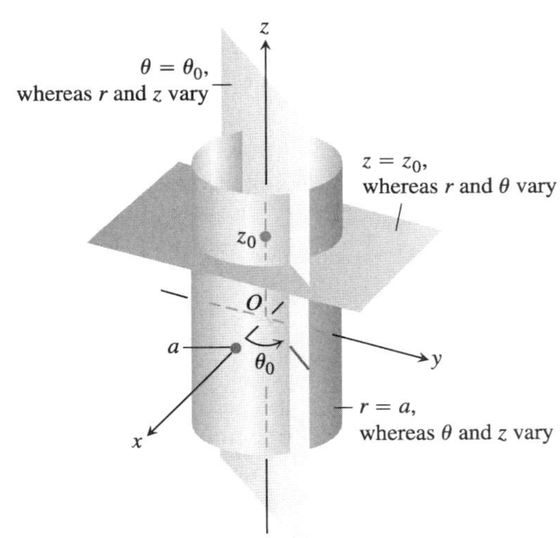

FIGURE 15.37 Constant-coordinate equations in cylindrical coordinates yield cylinders and planes.

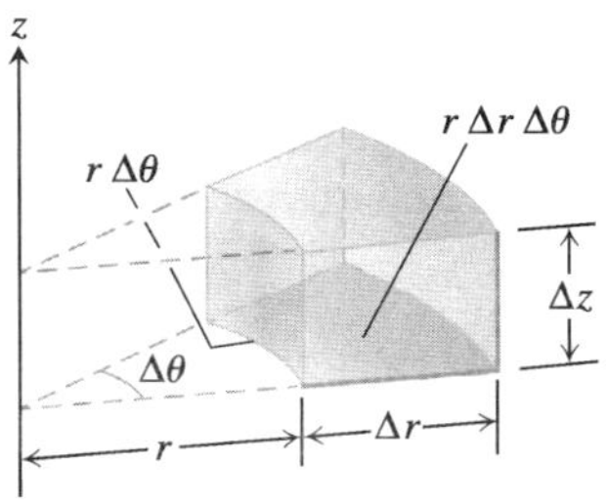

FIGURE 15.38 In cylindrical coordinates the volume of the wedge is approximated by the product $\Delta V = \Delta z\, r\, \Delta r\, \Delta\theta$.

Cylindrical coordinates are good for describing cylinders whose axes run along the z-axis and planes that either contain the z-axis or lie perpendicular to the z-axis. Surfaces like these have equations of constant coordinate value:

$$r = 4. \qquad \text{Cylinder, radius 4, axis the } z\text{-axis}$$

$$\theta = \frac{\pi}{3}. \qquad \text{Plane containing the } z\text{-axis}$$

$$z = 2. \qquad \text{Plane perpendicular to the } z\text{-axis}$$

When computing triple integrals over a region D in cylindrical coordinates, we partition the region into n small cylindrical wedges, rather than into rectangular boxes. In the kth cylindrical wedge, r, θ and z change by Δr_k, $\Delta\theta_k$, and Δz_k, and the largest of these numbers among all the cylindrical wedges is called the **norm** of the partition. We define the triple integral as a limit of Riemann sums using these wedges. The volume of such a cylindrical wedge ΔV_k is obtained by taking the area ΔA_k of its base in the $r\theta$-plane and multiplying by the height Δz (Figure 15.38).

For a point (r_k, θ_k, z_k) in the center of the kth wedge, we calculated in polar coordinates that $\Delta A_k = r_k\, \Delta r_k\, \Delta\theta_k$. So $\Delta V_k = \Delta z_k\, r_k\, \Delta r_k\, \Delta\theta_k$ and a Riemann sum for f over D has the form

$$S_n = \sum_{k=1}^{n} f(r_k, \theta_k, z_k)\, \Delta z_k\, r_k\, \Delta r_k\, \Delta\theta_k.$$

The triple integral of a function f over D is obtained by taking a limit of such Riemann sums with partitions whose norms approach zero

$$\lim_{n\to\infty} S_n = \iiint_D f\, dV = \iiint_D f\, dz\, r\, dr\, d\theta.$$

Triple integrals in cylindrical coordinates are then evaluated as iterated integrals, as in the following example.

EXAMPLE 1 Finding Limits of Integration in Cylindrical Coordinates

Find the limits of integration in cylindrical coordinates for integrating a function $f(r, \theta, z)$ over the region D bounded below by the plane $z = 0$, laterally by the circular cylinder $x^2 + (y-1)^2 = 1$, and above by the paraboloid $z = x^2 + y^2$.

Solution The base of D is also the region's projection R on the xy-plane. The boundary of R is the circle $x^2 + (y-1)^2 = 1$. Its polar coordinate equation is

$$\begin{aligned} x^2 + (y-1)^2 &= 1 \\ x^2 + y^2 - 2y + 1 &= 1 \\ r^2 - 2r\sin\theta &= 0 \\ r &= 2\sin\theta. \end{aligned}$$

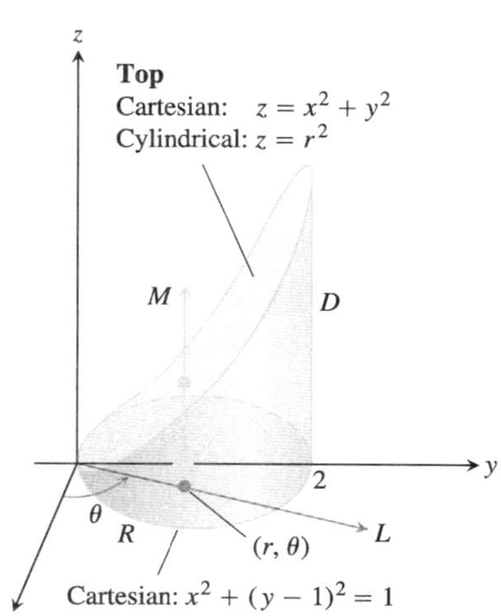

FIGURE 15.39 Finding the limits of integration for evaluating an integral in cylindrical coordinates (Example 1).

The region is sketched in Figure 15.39.

We find the limits of integration, starting with the z-limits. A line M through a typical point (r, θ) in R parallel to the z-axis enters D at $z = 0$ and leaves at $z = x^2 + y^2 = r^2$.

Next we find the r-limits of integration. A ray L through (r, θ) from the origin enters R at $r = 0$ and leaves at $r = 2\sin\theta$.

Finally we find the θ-limits of integration. As L sweeps across R, the angle θ it makes with the positive x-axis runs from $\theta = 0$ to $\theta = \pi$. The integral is

$$\iiint_D f(r, \theta, z)\, dV = \int_0^{\pi} \int_0^{2 \sin \theta} \int_0^{r^2} f(r, \theta, z)\, dz\, r\, dr\, d\theta.$$ ■

Example 1 illustrates a good procedure for finding limits of integration in cylindrical coordinates. The procedure is summarized as follows.

How to Integrate in Cylindrical Coordinates

To evaluate

$$\iiint_D f(r, \theta, z)\, dV$$

over a region D in space in cylindrical coordinates, integrating first with respect to z, then with respect to r, and finally with respect to θ, take the following steps.

1. *Sketch.* Sketch the region D along with its projection R on the xy-plane. Label the surfaces and curves that bound D and R.

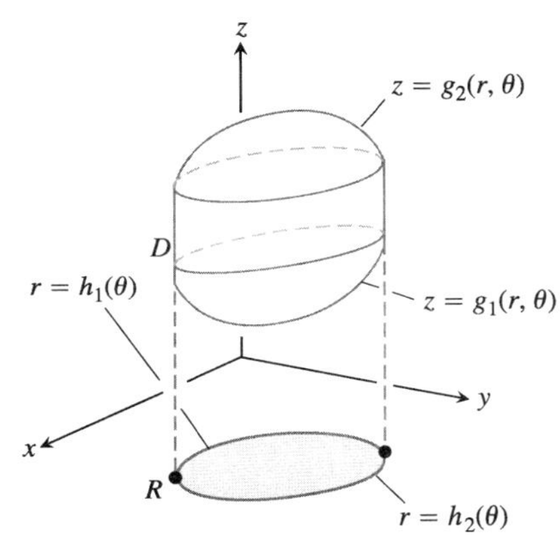

2. *Find the z-limits of integration.* Draw a line M through a typical point (r, θ) of R parallel to the z-axis. As z increases, M enters D at $z = g_1(r, \theta)$ and leaves at $z = g_2(r, \theta)$. These are the z-limits of integration.

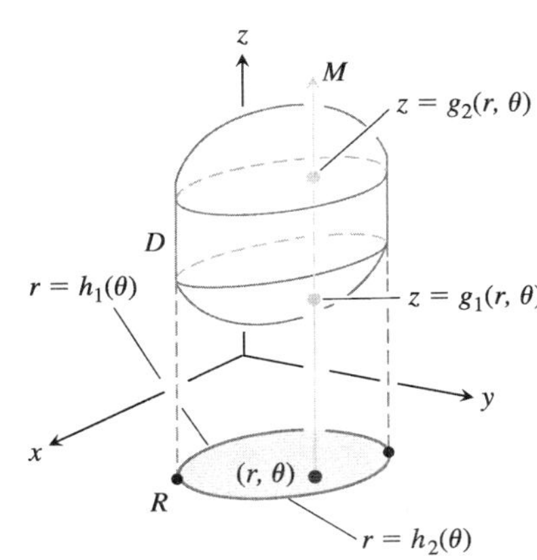

3. *Find the r-limits of integration.* Draw a ray L through (r, θ) from the origin. The ray enters R at $r = h_1(\theta)$ and leaves at $r = h_2(\theta)$. These are the r-limits of integration.

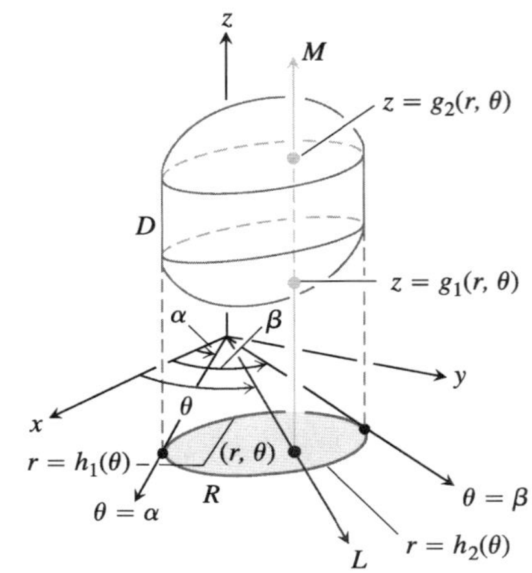

4. *Find the θ-limits of integration.* As L sweeps across R, the angle θ it makes with the positive x-axis runs from $\theta = \alpha$ to $\theta = \beta$. These are the θ-limits of integration. The integral is

$$\iiint_D f(r, \theta, z)\, dV = \int_{\theta=\alpha}^{\theta=\beta} \int_{r=h_1(\theta)}^{r=h_2(\theta)} \int_{z=g_1(r,\theta)}^{z=g_2(r,\theta)} f(r, \theta, z)\, dz\, r\, dr\, d\theta.$$

EXAMPLE 2 Finding a Centroid

Find the centroid ($\delta = 1$) of the solid enclosed by the cylinder $x^2 + y^2 = 4$, bounded above by the paraboloid $z = x^2 + y^2$, and bounded below by the xy-plane.

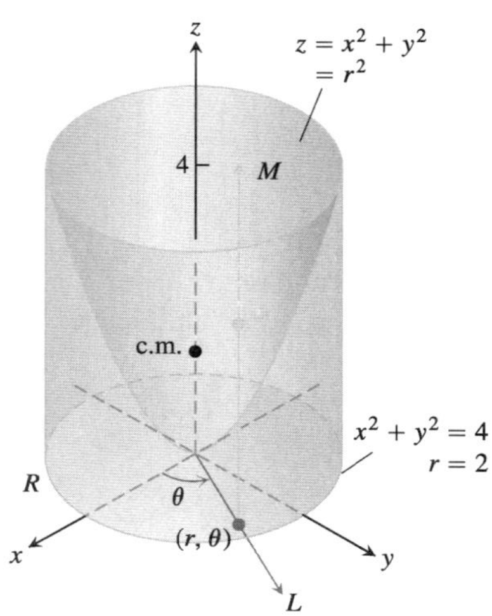

FIGURE 15.40 Example 2 shows how to find the centroid of this solid.

Solution We sketch the solid, bounded above by the paraboloid $z = r^2$ and below by the plane $z = 0$ (Figure 15.40). Its base R is the disk $0 \le r \le 2$ in the xy-plane.

The solid's centroid $(\bar{x}, \bar{y}, \bar{z})$ lies on its axis of symmetry, here the z-axis. This makes $\bar{x} = \bar{y} = 0$. To find $\bar{z}$, we divide the first moment M_{xy} by the mass M.

To find the limits of integration for the mass and moment integrals, we continue with the four basic steps. We completed our initial sketch. The remaining steps give the limits of integration.

The z-limits. A line M through a typical point (r, θ) in the base parallel to the z-axis enters the solid at $z = 0$ and leaves at $z = r^2$.

The r-limits. A ray L through (r, θ) from the origin enters R at $r = 0$ and leaves at $r = 2$.

The θ-limits. As L sweeps over the base like a clock hand, the angle θ it makes with the positive x-axis runs from $\theta = 0$ to $\theta = 2\pi$. The value of M_{xy} is

$$M_{xy} = \int_0^{2\pi} \int_0^2 \int_0^{r^2} z\, dz\, r\, dr\, d\theta = \int_0^{2\pi} \int_0^2 \left[\frac{z^2}{2}\right]_0^{r^2} r\, dr\, d\theta$$

$$= \int_0^{2\pi} \int_0^2 \frac{r^5}{2}\, dr\, d\theta = \int_0^{2\pi} \left[\frac{r^6}{12}\right]_0^2 d\theta = \int_0^{2\pi} \frac{16}{3}\, d\theta = \frac{32\pi}{3}.$$

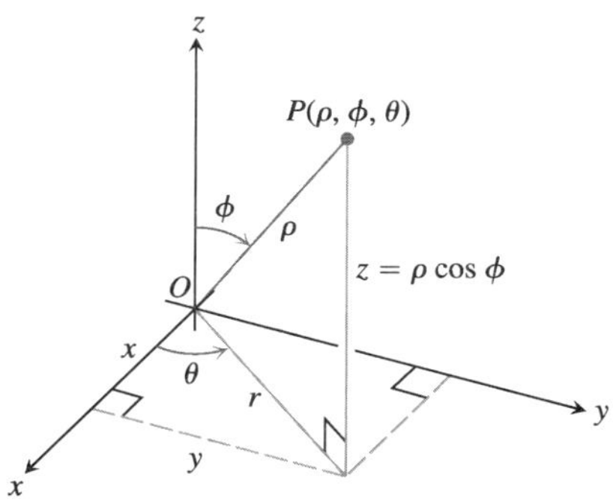

FIGURE 15.41 The spherical coordinates ρ, ϕ, and θ and their relation to x, y, z, and r.

The value of M is

$$M = \int_0^{2\pi}\int_0^2\int_0^{r^2} dz\, r\, dr\, d\theta = \int_0^{2\pi}\int_0^2 \Big[z\Big]_0^{r^2} r\, dr\, d\theta$$

$$= \int_0^{2\pi}\int_0^2 r^3\, dr\, d\theta = \int_0^{2\pi}\left[\frac{r^4}{4}\right]_0^2 d\theta = \int_0^{2\pi} 4\, d\theta = 8\pi.$$

Therefore,

$$\bar{z} = \frac{M_{xy}}{M} = \frac{32\pi}{3}\frac{1}{8\pi} = \frac{4}{3},$$

and the centroid is $(0, 0, 4/3)$. Notice that the centroid lies outside the solid. ■

Spherical Coordinates and Integration

Spherical coordinates locate points in space with two angles and one distance, as shown in Figure 15.41. The first coordinate, $\rho = |\overrightarrow{OP}|$, is the point's distance from the origin. Unlike r, *the variable ρ is never negative*. The second coordinate, ϕ, is the angle $\overrightarrow{OP}$ makes with the positive z-axis. It is required to lie in the interval $[0, \pi]$. The third coordinate is the angle θ as measured in cylindrical coordinates.

DEFINITION Spherical Coordinates

Spherical coordinates represent a point P in space by ordered triples (ρ, ϕ, θ) in which

1. ρ is the distance from P to the origin.
2. ϕ is the angle $\overrightarrow{OP}$ makes with the positive z-axis $(0 \le \phi \le \pi)$.
3. θ is the angle from cylindrical coordinates.

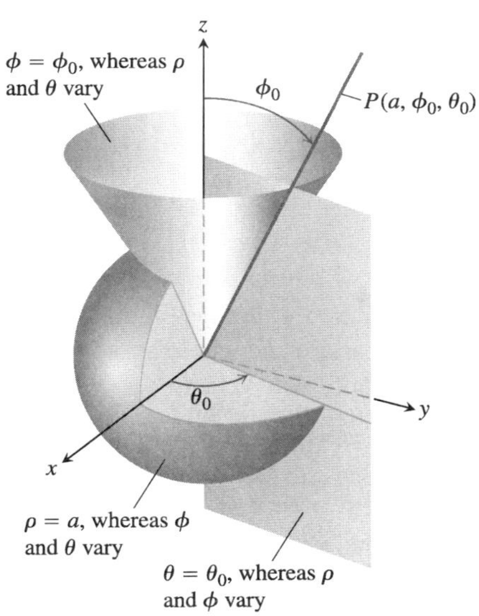

FIGURE 15.42 Constant-coordinate equations in spherical coordinates yield spheres, single cones, and half-planes.

On maps of the Earth, θ is related to the meridian of a point on the Earth and ϕ to its latitude, while ρ is related to elevation above the Earth's surface.

The equation $\rho = a$ describes the sphere of radius a centered at the origin (Figure 15.42). The equation $\phi = \phi_0$ describes a single cone whose vertex lies at the origin and whose axis lies along the z-axis. (We broaden our interpretation to include the xy-plane as the cone $\phi = \pi/2$.) If ϕ_0 is greater than $\pi/2$, the cone $\phi = \phi_0$ opens downward. The equation $\theta = \theta_0$ describes the half-plane that contains the z-axis and makes an angle θ_0 with the positive x-axis.

Equations Relating Spherical Coordinates to Cartesian and Cylindrical Coordinates

$$r = \rho\sin\phi, \qquad x = r\cos\theta = \rho\sin\phi\cos\theta,$$
$$z = \rho\cos\phi, \qquad y = r\sin\theta = \rho\sin\phi\sin\theta, \tag{1}$$
$$\rho = \sqrt{x^2 + y^2 + z^2} = \sqrt{r^2 + z^2}.$$

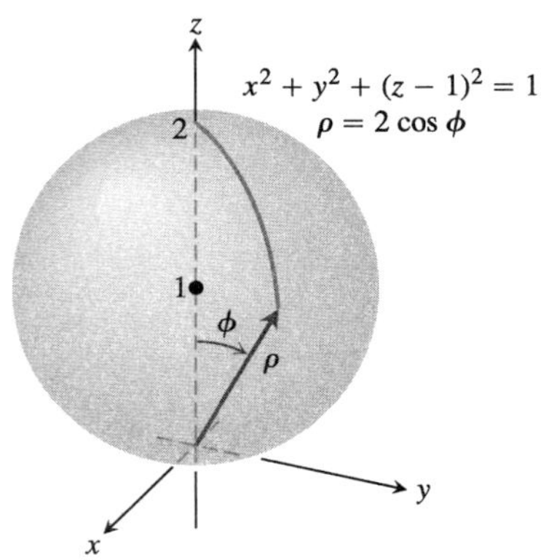

FIGURE 15.43 The sphere in Example 3.

EXAMPLE 3 Converting Cartesian to Spherical

Find a spherical coordinate equation for the sphere $x^2 + y^2 + (z - 1)^2 = 1$.

Solution We use Equations (1) to substitute for x, y, and z:

$$\begin{aligned} x^2 + y^2 + (z-1)^2 &= 1 \\ \rho^2 \sin^2\phi \cos^2\theta + \rho^2 \sin^2\phi \sin^2\theta + (\rho\cos\phi - 1)^2 &= 1 \qquad \text{Equations (1)} \\ \rho^2 \sin^2\phi \underbrace{(\cos^2\theta + \sin^2\theta)}_{1} + \rho^2\cos^2\phi - 2\rho\cos\phi + 1 &= 1 \\ \rho^2 \underbrace{(\sin^2\phi + \cos^2\phi)}_{1} &= 2\rho\cos\phi \\ \rho^2 &= 2\rho\cos\phi \\ \rho &= 2\cos\phi. \end{aligned}$$

See Figure 15.43. ■

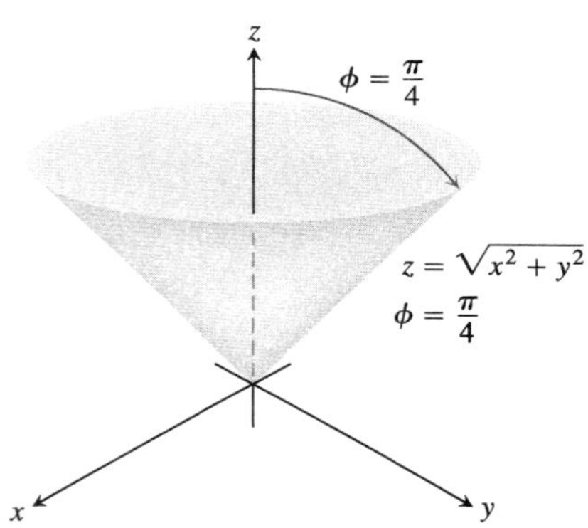

FIGURE 15.44 The cone in Example 4.

EXAMPLE 4 Converting Cartesian to Spherical

Find a spherical coordinate equation for the cone $z = \sqrt{x^2 + y^2}$ (Figure 15.44).

Solution 1 *Use geometry.* The cone is symmetric with respect to the z-axis and cuts the first quadrant of the yz-plane along the line $z = y$. The angle between the cone and the positive z-axis is therefore $\pi/4$ radians. The cone consists of the points whose spherical coordinates have ϕ equal to $\pi/4$, so its equation is $\phi = \pi/4$.

Solution 2 *Use algebra.* If we use Equations (1) to substitute for x, y, and z we obtain the same result:

$$\begin{aligned} z &= \sqrt{x^2 + y^2} \\ \rho\cos\phi &= \sqrt{\rho^2 \sin^2\phi} \qquad \text{Example 3} \\ \rho\cos\phi &= \rho\sin\phi \qquad \rho \ge 0,\ \sin\phi \ge 0 \\ \cos\phi &= \sin\phi \\ \phi &= \frac{\pi}{4}. \qquad 0 \le \phi \le \pi \end{aligned}$$

■

Spherical coordinates are good for describing spheres centered at the origin, half-planes hinged along the z-axis, and cones whose vertices lie at the origin and whose axes lie along the z-axis. Surfaces like these have equations of constant coordinate value:

$$\begin{aligned} \rho &= 4 && \text{Sphere, radius 4, center at origin} \\ \phi &= \frac{\pi}{3} && \text{Cone opening up from the origin, making an angle of } \pi/3 \text{ radians with the positive } z\text{-axis} \\ \theta &= \frac{\pi}{3}. && \text{Half-plane, hinged along the } z\text{-axis, making an angle of } \pi/3 \text{ radians with the positive } x\text{-axis} \end{aligned}$$

When computing triple integrals over a region D in spherical coordinates, we partition the region into n spherical wedges. The size of the kth spherical wedge, which contains a point $(\rho_k, \phi_k, \theta_k)$, is given by changes by $\Delta\rho_k$, $\Delta\theta_k$, and $\Delta\phi_k$ in ρ, θ, and ϕ. Such a spherical wedge has one edge a circular arc of length $\rho_k \, \Delta\phi_k$, another edge a circular arc of

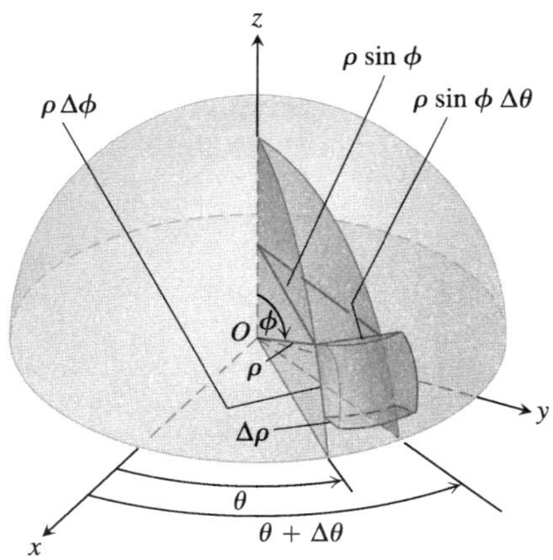

FIGURE 15.45 In spherical coordinates

$$dV = d\rho \cdot \rho\, d\phi \cdot \rho \sin\phi \, d\theta = \rho^2 \sin\phi \, d\rho \, d\phi \, d\theta.$$

length $\rho_k \sin \phi_k \,\Delta\theta_k$, and thickness $\Delta\rho_k$. The spherical wedge closely approximates a cube of these dimensions when $\Delta\rho_k$, $\Delta\theta_k$, and $\Delta\phi_k$ are all small (Figure 15.45). It can be shown that the volume of this spherical wedge ΔV_k is $\Delta V_k = \rho_k^2 \sin\phi_k \,\Delta\rho_k \,\Delta\phi_k \,\Delta\theta_k$ for $(\rho_k, \phi_k, \theta_k)$ a point chosen inside the wedge.

The corresponding Riemann sum for a function $F(\rho, \phi, \theta)$ is

$$S_n = \sum_{k=1}^{n} F(\rho_k, \phi_k, \theta_k)\, \rho_k^2 \sin\phi_k \,\Delta\rho_k \,\Delta\phi_k \,\Delta\theta_k .$$

As the norm of a partition approaches zero, and the spherical wedges get smaller, the Riemann sums have a limit when F is continuous:

$$\lim_{n\to\infty} S_n = \iiint_D F(\rho, \phi, \theta)\, dV = \iiint_D F(\rho, \phi, \theta)\, \rho^2 \sin\phi \, d\rho \, d\phi \, d\theta.$$

In spherical coordinates, we have

$$dV = \rho^2 \sin\phi \, d\rho \, d\phi \, d\theta.$$

To evaluate integrals in spherical coordinates, we usually integrate first with respect to ρ. The procedure for finding the limits of integration is shown below. We restrict our attention to integrating over domains that are solids of revolution about the z-axis (or portions thereof) and for which the limits for θ and ϕ are constant.

How to Integrate in Spherical Coordinates

To evaluate

$$\iiint_D f(\rho, \phi, \theta)\, dV$$

over a region D in space in spherical coordinates, integrating first with respect to ρ, then with respect to ϕ, and finally with respect to θ, take the following steps.

1. *Sketch.* Sketch the region D along with its projection R on the xy-plane. Label the surfaces that bound D.

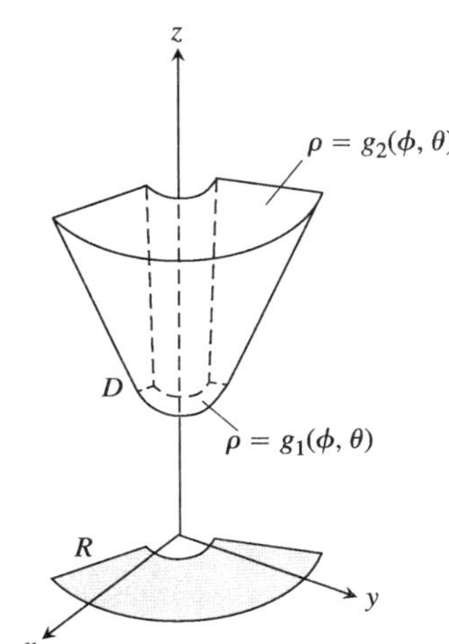

2. *Find the ρ-limits of integration.* Draw a ray M from the origin through D making an angle ϕ with the positive z-axis. Also draw the projection of M on the xy-plane (call the projection L). The ray L makes an angle θ with the positive x-axis. As ρ increases, M enters D at $\rho = g_1(\phi, \theta)$ and leaves at $\rho = g_2(\phi, \theta)$. These are the ρ-limits of integration.

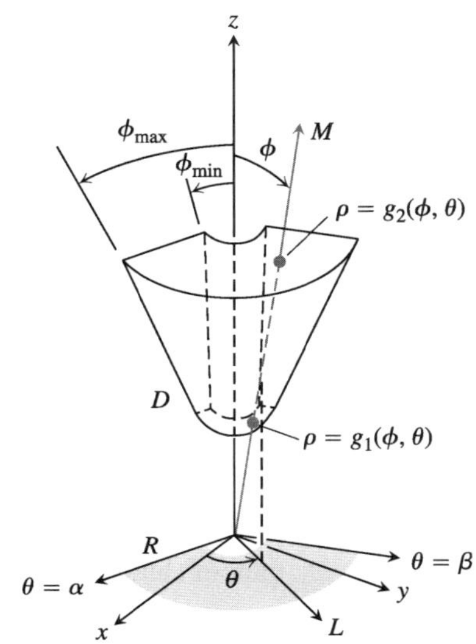

3. *Find the ϕ-limits of integration.* For any given θ, the angle ϕ that M makes with the z-axis runs from $\phi = \phi_{min}$ to $\phi = \phi_{max}$. These are the ϕ-limits of integration.
4. *Find the θ-limits of integration.* The ray L sweeps over R as θ runs from α to β. These are the θ-limits of integration. The integral is

$$\iiint_D f(\rho, \phi, \theta)\, dV = \int_{\theta=\alpha}^{\theta=\beta} \int_{\phi=\phi_{min}}^{\phi=\phi_{max}} \int_{\rho=g_1(\phi,\theta)}^{\rho=g_2(\phi,\theta)} f(\rho, \phi, \theta)\, \rho^2 \sin\phi \, d\rho\, d\phi\, d\theta.$$

EXAMPLE 5 Finding a Volume in Spherical Coordinates

Find the volume of the "ice cream cone" D cut from the solid sphere $\rho \le 1$ by the cone $\phi = \pi/3$.

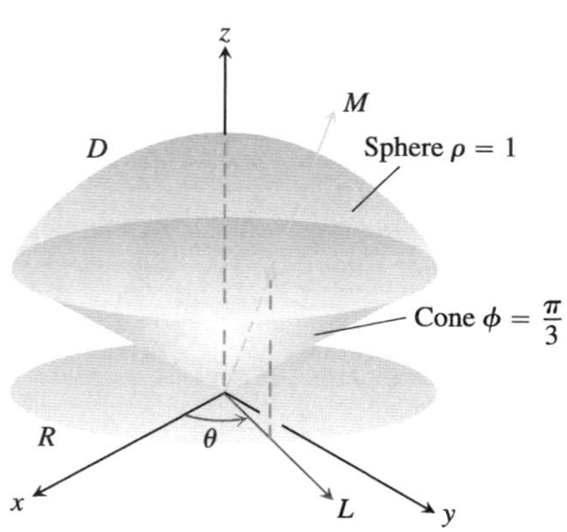

FIGURE 15.46 The ice cream cone in Example 5.

Solution The volume is $V = \iiint_D \rho^2 \sin\phi \, d\rho\, d\phi\, d\theta$, the integral of $f(\rho, \phi, \theta) = 1$ over D.

To find the limits of integration for evaluating the integral, we begin by sketching D and its projection R on the xy-plane (Figure 15.46).

The ρ-limits of integration. We draw a ray M from the origin through D making an angle ϕ with the positive z-axis. We also draw L, the projection of M on the xy-plane, along with the angle θ that L makes with the positive x-axis. Ray M enters D at $\rho = 0$ and leaves at $\rho = 1$.

The ϕ-limits of integration. The cone $\phi = \pi/3$ makes an angle of $\pi/3$ with the positive z-axis. For any given θ, the angle ϕ can run from $\phi = 0$ to $\phi = \pi/3$.

The θ-limits of integration. The ray L sweeps over R as θ runs from 0 to 2π. The volume is

$$V = \iiint_D \rho^2 \sin\phi \, d\rho \, d\phi \, d\theta = \int_0^{2\pi}\int_0^{\pi/3}\int_0^1 \rho^2 \sin\phi \, d\rho \, d\phi \, d\theta$$
$$= \int_0^{2\pi}\int_0^{\pi/3}\left[\frac{\rho^3}{3}\right]_0^1 \sin\phi \, d\phi \, d\theta = \int_0^{2\pi}\int_0^{\pi/3} \frac{1}{3}\sin\phi \, d\phi \, d\theta$$
$$= \int_0^{2\pi}\left[-\frac{1}{3}\cos\phi\right]_0^{\pi/3} d\theta = \int_0^{2\pi}\left(-\frac{1}{6}+\frac{1}{3}\right) d\theta = \frac{1}{6}(2\pi) = \frac{\pi}{3}.$$ ■

EXAMPLE 6 Finding a Moment of Inertia

A solid of constant density $\delta = 1$ occupies the region D in Example 5. Find the solid's moment of inertia about the z-axis.

Solution In rectangular coordinates, the moment is

$$I_z = \iiint (x^2 + y^2) \, dV.$$

In spherical coordinates, $x^2 + y^2 = (\rho \sin\phi \cos\theta)^2 + (\rho \sin\phi \sin\theta)^2 = \rho^2 \sin^2\phi$. Hence,

$$I_z = \iiint (\rho^2 \sin^2\phi)\, \rho^2 \sin\phi \, d\rho \, d\phi \, d\theta = \iiint \rho^4 \sin^3\phi \, d\rho \, d\phi \, d\theta.$$

For the region in Example 5, this becomes

$$I_z = \int_0^{2\pi}\int_0^{\pi/3}\int_0^1 \rho^4 \sin^3\phi \, d\rho \, d\phi \, d\theta = \int_0^{2\pi}\int_0^{\pi/3}\left[\frac{\rho^5}{5}\right]_0^1 \sin^3\phi \, d\phi \, d\theta$$
$$= \frac{1}{5}\int_0^{2\pi}\int_0^{\pi/3} (1 - \cos^2\phi)\sin\phi \, d\phi \, d\theta = \frac{1}{5}\int_0^{2\pi}\left[-\cos\phi + \frac{\cos^3\phi}{3}\right]_0^{\pi/3} d\theta$$
$$= \frac{1}{5}\int_0^{2\pi}\left(-\frac{1}{2} + 1 + \frac{1}{24} - \frac{1}{3}\right) d\theta = \frac{1}{5}\int_0^{2\pi}\frac{5}{24}\, d\theta = \frac{1}{24}(2\pi) = \frac{\pi}{12}.$$ ■

Coordinate Conversion Formulas

CYLINDRICAL TO RECTANGULAR	SPHERICAL TO RECTANGULAR	SPHERICAL TO CYLINDRICAL
$x = r\cos\theta$	$x = \rho\sin\phi\cos\theta$	$r = \rho\sin\phi$
$y = r\sin\theta$	$y = \rho\sin\phi\sin\theta$	$z = \rho\cos\phi$
$z = z$	$z = \rho\cos\phi$	$\theta = \theta$

Corresponding formulas for dV in triple integrals:

$$dV = dx\,dy\,dz$$
$$= dz\,r\,dr\,d\theta$$
$$= \rho^2\sin\phi\,d\rho\,d\phi\,d\theta$$

In the next section we offer a more general procedure for determining dV in cylindrical and spherical coordinates. The results, of course, will be the same.

EXERCISES 15.6

Evaluating Integrals in Cylindrical Coordinates

Evaluate the cylindrical coordinate integrals in Exercises 1–6.

1. $\int_0^{2\pi}\int_0^1\int_r^{\sqrt{2-r^2}} dz\, r\, dr\, d\theta$
2. $\int_0^{2\pi}\int_0^3\int_{r^2/3}^{\sqrt{18-r^2}} dz\, r\, dr\, d\theta$
3. $\int_0^{2\pi}\int_0^{\theta/2\pi}\int_0^{3+24r^2} dz\, r\, dr\, d\theta$
4. $\int_0^{\pi}\int_0^{\theta/\pi}\int_{-\sqrt{4-r^2}}^{3\sqrt{4-r^2}} z\, dz\, r\, dr\, d\theta$
5. $\int_0^{2\pi}\int_0^1\int_r^{1/\sqrt{2-r^2}} 3\, dz\, r\, dr\, d\theta$
6. $\int_0^{2\pi}\int_0^1\int_{-1/2}^{1/2} (r^2\sin^2\theta + z^2)\, dz\, r\, dr\, d\theta$

Changing Order of Integration in Cylindrical Coordinates

The integrals we have seen so far suggest that there are preferred orders of integration for cylindrical coordinates, but other orders usually work well and are occasionally easier to evaluate. Evaluate the integrals in Exercises 7–10.

7. $\int_0^{2\pi}\int_0^3\int_0^{z/3} r^3\, dr\, dz\, d\theta$
8. $\int_{-1}^{1}\int_0^{2\pi}\int_0^{1+\cos\theta} 4r\, dr\, d\theta\, dz$
9. $\int_0^1\int_0^{\sqrt{z}}\int_0^{2\pi} (r^2\cos^2\theta + z^2)\, r\, d\theta\, dr\, dz$
10. $\int_0^2\int_{r-2}^{\sqrt{4-r^2}}\int_0^{2\pi} (r\sin\theta + 1)\, r\, d\theta\, dz\, dr$
11. Let D be the region bounded below by the plane $z = 0$, above by the sphere $x^2 + y^2 + z^2 = 4$, and on the sides by the cylinder $x^2 + y^2 = 1$. Set up the triple integrals in cylindrical coordinates that give the volume of D using the following orders of integration.
   a. $dz\, dr\, d\theta$
   b. $dr\, dz\, d\theta$
   c. $d\theta\, dz\, dr$
12. Let D be the region bounded below by the cone $z = \sqrt{x^2 + y^2}$ and above by the paraboloid $z = 2 - x^2 - y^2$. Set up the triple integrals in cylindrical coordinates that give the volume of D using the following orders of integration.
   a. $dz\, dr\, d\theta$
   b. $dr\, dz\, d\theta$
   c. $d\theta\, dz\, dr$
13. Give the limits of integration for evaluating the integral
$$\iiint f(r, \theta, z)\, dz\, r\, dr\, d\theta$$
as an iterated integral over the region that is bounded below by the plane $z = 0$, on the side by the cylinder $r = \cos\theta$, and on top by the paraboloid $z = 3r^2$.
14. Convert the integral
$$\int_{-1}^{1}\int_0^{\sqrt{1-y^2}}\int_0^{x} (x^2 + y^2)\, dz\, dx\, dy$$
to an equivalent integral in cylindrical coordinates and evaluate the result.

Finding Iterated Integrals in Cylindrical Coordinates

In Exercises 15–20, set up the iterated integral for evaluating $\iiint_D f(r, \theta, z)\, dz\, r\, dr\, d\theta$ over the given region D.

15. D is the right circular cylinder whose base is the circle $r = 2\sin\theta$ in the xy-plane and whose top lies in the plane $z = 4 - y$.

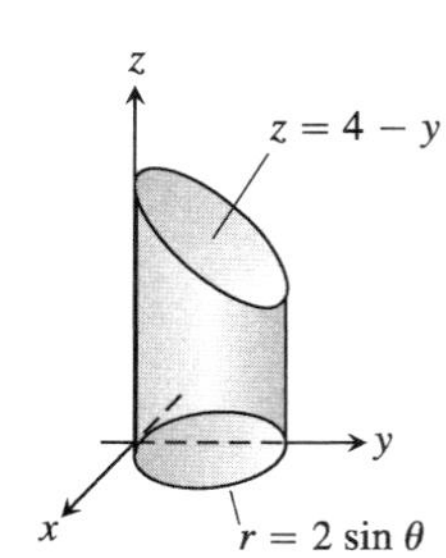

16. D is the right circular cylinder whose base is the circle $r = 3\cos\theta$ and whose top lies in the plane $z = 5 - x$.

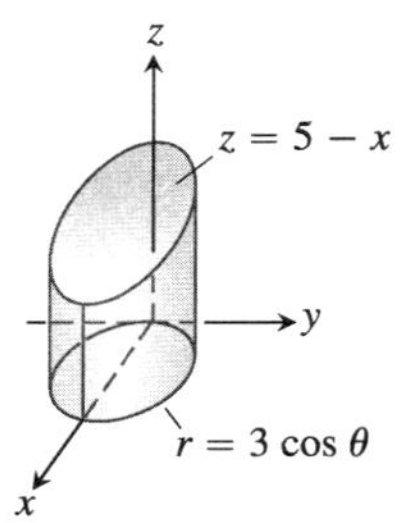

17. D is the solid right cylinder whose base is the region in the xy-plane that lies inside the cardioid $r = 1 + \cos\theta$ and outside the circle $r = 1$ and whose top lies in the plane $z = 4$.

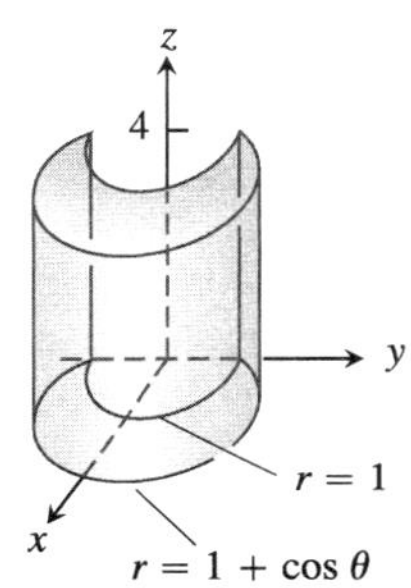

18. D is the solid right cylinder whose base is the region between the circles $r = \cos\theta$ and $r = 2\cos\theta$ and whose top lies in the plane $z = 3 - y$.

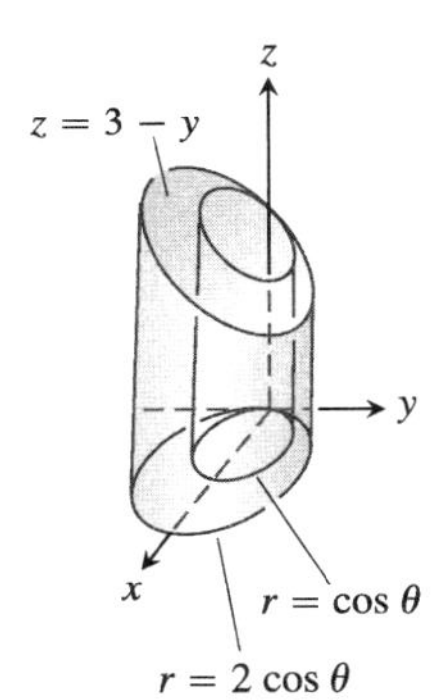

19. D is the prism whose base is the triangle in the xy-plane bounded by the x-axis and the lines $y = x$ and $x = 1$ and whose top lies in the plane $z = 2 - y$.

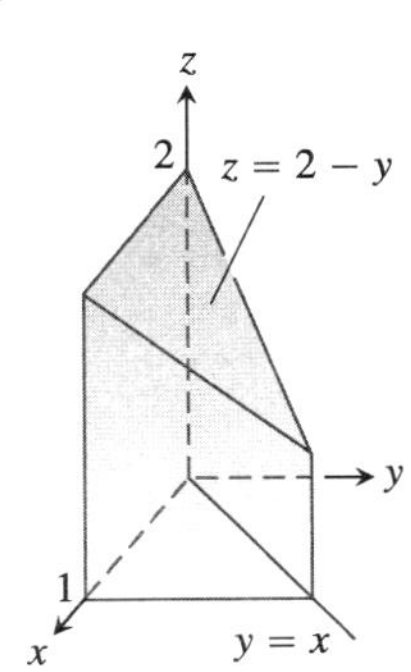

20. D is the prism whose base is the triangle in the xy-plane bounded by the y-axis and the lines $y = x$ and $y = 1$ and whose top lies in the plane $z = 2 - x$.

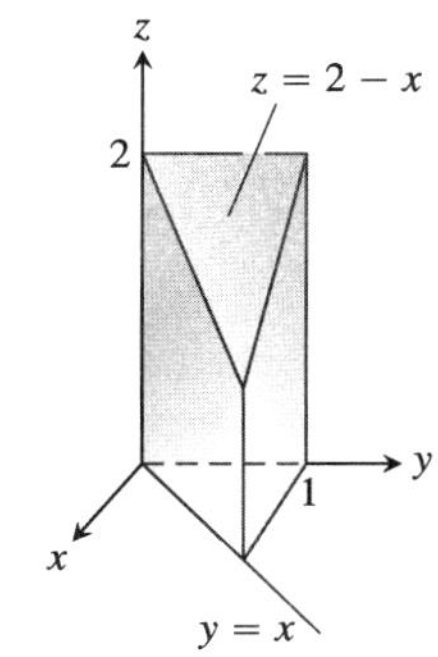

Evaluating Integrals in Spherical Coordinates

Evaluate the spherical coordinate integrals in Exercises 21–26.

21. $\displaystyle\int_0^{\pi}\int_0^{\pi}\int_0^{2\sin\phi} \rho^2 \sin\phi \, d\rho \, d\phi \, d\theta$

22. $\displaystyle\int_0^{2\pi}\int_0^{\pi/4}\int_0^{2} (\rho\cos\phi)\,\rho^2 \sin\phi \, d\rho \, d\phi \, d\theta$

23. $\displaystyle\int_0^{2\pi}\int_0^{\pi}\int_0^{(1-\cos\phi)/2} \rho^2 \sin\phi \, d\rho \, d\phi \, d\theta$

24. $\displaystyle\int_0^{3\pi/2}\int_0^{\pi}\int_0^{1} 5\rho^3 \sin^3\phi \, d\rho \, d\phi \, d\theta$

25. $\displaystyle\int_0^{2\pi}\int_0^{\pi/3}\int_{\sec\phi}^{2} 3\rho^2 \sin\phi \, d\rho \, d\phi \, d\theta$

26. $\displaystyle\int_0^{2\pi}\int_0^{\pi/4}\int_0^{\sec\phi} (\rho\cos\phi)\,\rho^2 \sin\phi \, d\rho \, d\phi \, d\theta$

Changing Order of Integration in Spherical Coordinates

The previous integrals suggest there are preferred orders of integration for spherical coordinates, but other orders are possible and occasionally easier to evaluate. Evaluate the integrals in Exercises 27–30.

27. $\displaystyle\int_0^{2}\int_{-\pi}^{0}\int_{\pi/4}^{\pi/2} \rho^3 \sin 2\phi \, d\phi \, d\theta \, d\rho$

28. $\displaystyle\int_{\pi/6}^{\pi/3}\int_{\csc\phi}^{2\csc\phi}\int_0^{2\pi} \rho^2 \sin\phi \, d\theta \, d\rho \, d\phi$

29. $\displaystyle\int_0^{1}\int_0^{\pi}\int_0^{\pi/4} 12\rho \sin^3\phi \, d\phi \, d\theta \, d\rho$

30. $\displaystyle\int_{\pi/6}^{\pi/2}\int_{-\pi/2}^{\pi/2}\int_{\csc\phi}^{2} 5\rho^4 \sin^3\phi \, d\rho \, d\theta \, d\phi$

31. Let D be the region in Exercise 11. Set up the triple integrals in spherical coordinates that give the volume of D using the following orders of integration.

a. $d\rho \, d\phi \, d\theta$ **b.** $d\phi \, d\rho \, d\theta$

32. Let D be the region bounded below by the cone $z = \sqrt{x^2 + y^2}$ and above by the plane $z = 1$. Set up the triple integrals in spherical coordinates that give the volume of D using the following orders of integration.

a. $d\rho\, d\phi\, d\theta$ **b.** $d\phi\, d\rho\, d\theta$

Finding Iterated Integrals in Spherical Coordinates

In Exercises 33–38, **(a)** find the spherical coordinate limits for the integral that calculates the volume of the given solid and **(b)** then evaluate the integral.

33. The solid between the sphere $\rho = \cos \phi$ and the hemisphere $\rho = 2, z \geq 0$

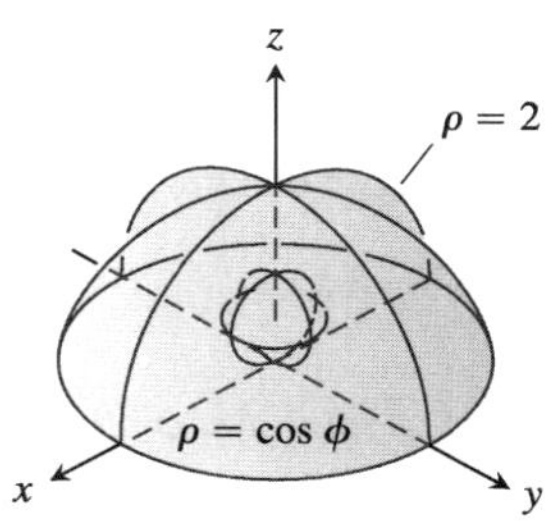

34. The solid bounded below by the hemisphere $\rho = 1, z \geq 0$, and above by the cardioid of revolution $\rho = 1 + \cos \phi$

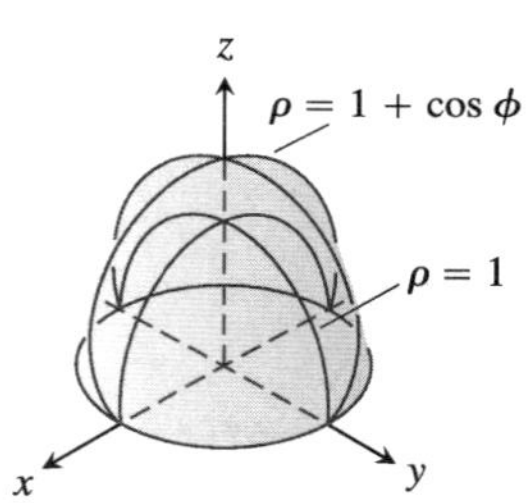

35. The solid enclosed by the cardioid of revolution $\rho = 1 - \cos \phi$

36. The upper portion cut from the solid in Exercise 35 by the xy-plane

37. The solid bounded below by the sphere $\rho = 2 \cos \phi$ and above by the cone $z = \sqrt{x^2 + y^2}$

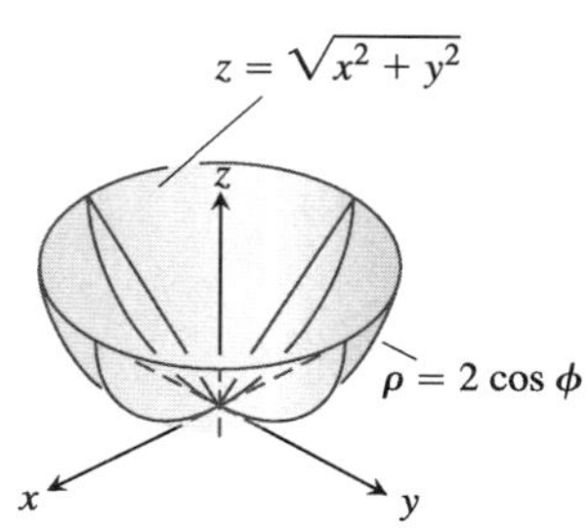

38. The solid bounded below by the xy-plane, on the sides by the sphere $\rho = 2$, and above by the cone $\phi = \pi/3$

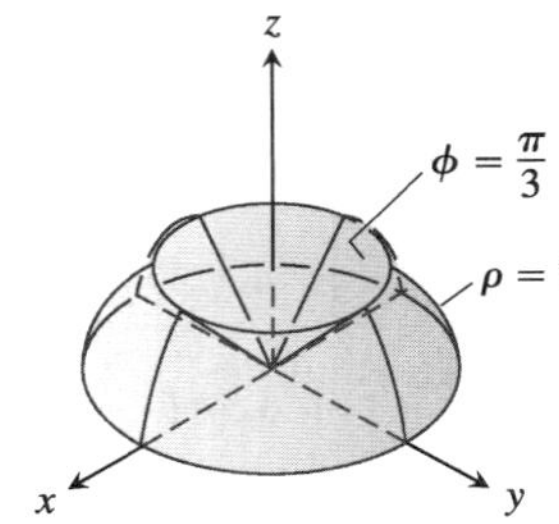

Rectangular, Cylindrical, and Spherical Coordinates

39. Set up triple integrals for the volume of the sphere $\rho = 2$ in **(a)** spherical, **(b)** cylindrical, and **(c)** rectangular coordinates.

40. Let D be the region in the first octant that is bounded below by the cone $\phi = \pi/4$ and above by the sphere $\rho = 3$. Express the volume of D as an iterated triple integral in **(a)** cylindrical and **(b)** spherical coordinates. Then **(c)** find V.

41. Let D be the smaller cap cut from a solid ball of radius 2 units by a plane 1 unit from the center of the sphere. Express the volume of D as an iterated triple integral in **(a)** spherical, **(b)** cylindrical, and **(c)** rectangular coordinates. Then **(d)** find the volume by evaluating one of the three triple integrals.

42. Express the moment of inertia I_z of the solid hemisphere $x^2 + y^2 + z^2 \leq 1, z \geq 0$, as an iterated integral in **(a)** cylindrical and **(b)** spherical coordinates. Then **(c)** find I_z.

Volumes

Find the volumes of the solids in Exercises 43–48.

43.

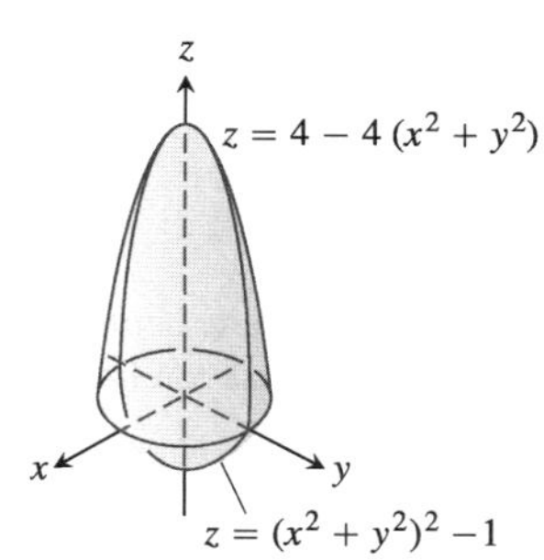

44.

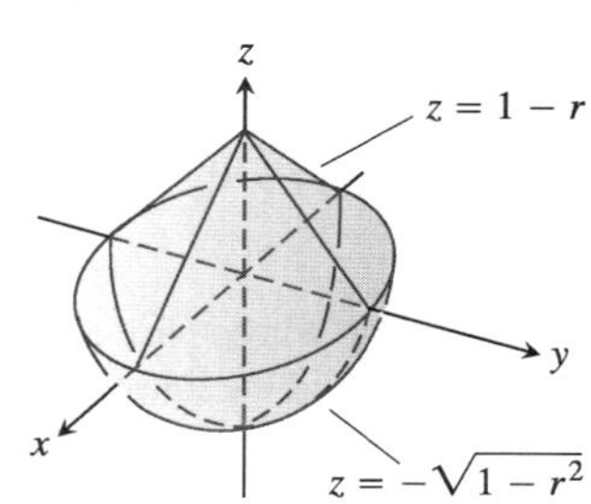

45.

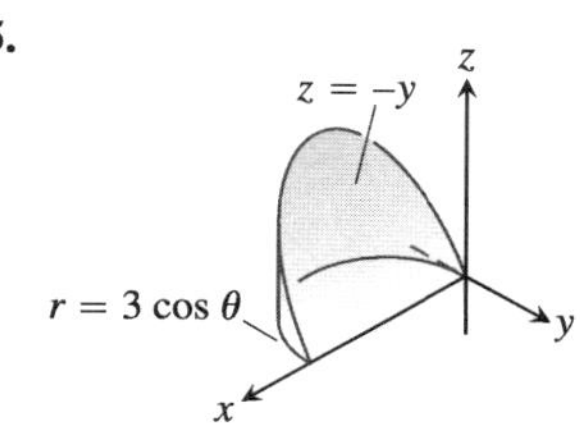

46.

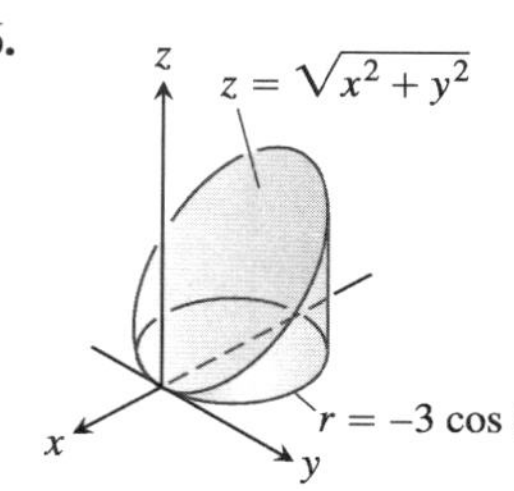

47.

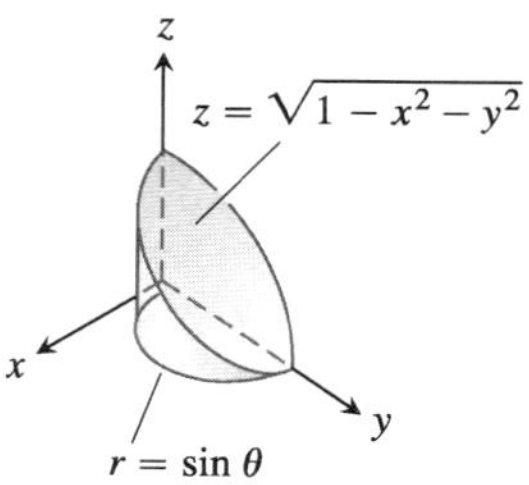

48.

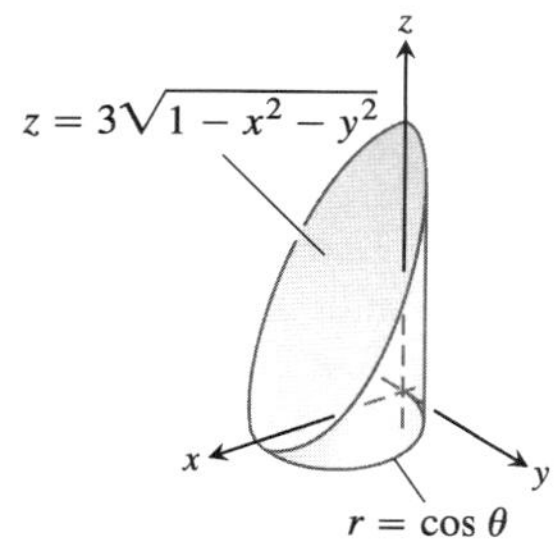

49. Sphere and cones Find the volume of the portion of the solid sphere $\rho \le a$ that lies between the cones $\phi = \pi/3$ and $\phi = 2\pi/3$.

50. Sphere and half-planes Find the volume of the region cut from the solid sphere $\rho \le a$ by the half-planes $\theta = 0$ and $\theta = \pi/6$ in the first octant.

51. Sphere and plane Find the volume of the smaller region cut from the solid sphere $\rho \le 2$ by the plane $z = 1$.

52. Cone and planes Find the volume of the solid enclosed by the cone $z = \sqrt{x^2 + y^2}$ between the planes $z = 1$ and $z = 2$.

53. Cylinder and paraboloid Find the volume of the region bounded below by the plane $z = 0$, laterally by the cylinder $x^2 + y^2 = 1$, and above by the paraboloid $z = x^2 + y^2$.

54. Cylinder and paraboloids Find the volume of the region bounded below by the paraboloid $z = x^2 + y^2$, laterally by the cylinder $x^2 + y^2 = 1$, and above by the paraboloid $z = x^2 + y^2 + 1$.

55. Cylinder and cones Find the volume of the solid cut from the thick-walled cylinder $1 \le x^2 + y^2 \le 2$ by the cones $z = \pm\sqrt{x^2 + y^2}$.

56. Sphere and cylinder Find the volume of the region that lies inside the sphere $x^2 + y^2 + z^2 = 2$ and outside the cylinder $x^2 + y^2 = 1$.

57. Cylinder and planes Find the volume of the region enclosed by the cylinder $x^2 + y^2 = 4$ and the planes $z = 0$ and $y + z = 4$.

58. Cylinder and planes Find the volume of the region enclosed by the cylinder $x^2 + y^2 = 4$ and the planes $z = 0$ and $x + y + z = 4$.

59. Region trapped by paraboloids Find the volume of the region bounded above by the paraboloid $z = 5 - x^2 - y^2$ and below by the paraboloid $z = 4x^2 + 4y^2$.

60. Paraboloid and cylinder Find the volume of the region bounded above by the paraboloid $z = 9 - x^2 - y^2$, below by the xy-plane, and lying *outside* the cylinder $x^2 + y^2 = 1$.

61. Cylinder and sphere Find the volume of the region cut from the solid cylinder $x^2 + y^2 \le 1$ by the sphere $x^2 + y^2 + z^2 = 4$.

62. Sphere and paraboloid Find the volume of the region bounded above by the sphere $x^2 + y^2 + z^2 = 2$ and below by the paraboloid $z = x^2 + y^2$.

Average Values

63. Find the average value of the function $f(r, \theta, z) = r$ over the region bounded by the cylinder $r = 1$ between the planes $z = -1$ and $z = 1$.

64. Find the average value of the function $f(r, \theta, z) = r$ over the solid ball bounded by the sphere $r^2 + z^2 = 1$. (This is the sphere $x^2 + y^2 + z^2 = 1$.)

65. Find the average value of the function $f(\rho, \phi, \theta) = \rho$ over the solid ball $\rho \le 1$.

66. Find the average value of the function $f(\rho, \phi, \theta) = \rho \cos \phi$ over the solid upper ball $\rho \le 1, 0 \le \phi \le \pi/2$.

Masses, Moments, and Centroids

67. Center of mass A solid of constant density is bounded below by the plane $z = 0$, above by the cone $z = r, r \ge 0$, and on the sides by the cylinder $r = 1$. Find the center of mass.

68. Centroid Find the centroid of the region in the first octant that is bounded above by the cone $z = \sqrt{x^2 + y^2}$, below by the plane $z = 0$, and on the sides by the cylinder $x^2 + y^2 = 4$ and the planes $x = 0$ and $y = 0$.

69. Centroid Find the centroid of the solid in Exercise 38.

70. Centroid Find the centroid of the solid bounded above by the sphere $\rho = a$ and below by the cone $\phi = \pi/4$.

71. Centroid Find the centroid of the region that is bounded above by the surface $z = \sqrt{r}$, on the sides by the cylinder $r = 4$, and below by the xy-plane.

72. Centroid Find the centroid of the region cut from the solid ball $r^2 + z^2 \le 1$ by the half-planes $\theta = -\pi/3, r \ge 0$, and $\theta = \pi/3, r \ge 0$.

73. Inertia and radius of gyration Find the moment of inertia and radius of gyration about the z-axis of a thick-walled right circular cylinder bounded on the inside by the cylinder $r = 1$, on the outside by the cylinder $r = 2$, and on the top and bottom by the planes $z = 4$ and $z = 0$. (Take $\delta = 1$.)

74. Moments of inertia of solid circular cylinder Find the moment of inertia of a solid circular cylinder of radius 1 and height 2 **(a)** about the axis of the cylinder and **(b)** about a line through the centroid perpendicular to the axis of the cylinder. (Take $\delta = 1$.)

75. Moment of inertia of solid cone Find the moment of inertia of a right circular cone of base radius 1 and height 1 about an axis through the vertex parallel to the base. (Take $\delta = 1$.)

76. Moment of inertia of solid sphere Find the moment of inertia of a solid sphere of radius a about a diameter. (Take $\delta = 1$.)

77. Moment of inertia of solid cone Find the moment of inertia of a right circular cone of base radius a and height h about its axis. (*Hint:* Place the cone with its vertex at the origin and its axis along the z-axis.)

78. Variable density A solid is bounded on the top by the paraboloid $z = r^2$, on the bottom by the plane $z = 0$, and on the sides by the cylinder $r = 1$. Find the center of mass and the moment of inertia and radius of gyration about the z-axis if the density is

a. $\delta(r, \theta, z) = z$

b. $\delta(r, \theta, z) = r$.

79. Variable density A solid is bounded below by the cone $z = \sqrt{x^2 + y^2}$ and above by the plane $z = 1$. Find the center of mass and the moment of inertia and radius of gyration about the z-axis if the density is

a. $\delta(r, \theta, z) = z$

b. $\delta(r, \theta, z) = z^2$.

80. Variable density A solid ball is bounded by the sphere $\rho = a$. Find the moment of inertia and radius of gyration about the z-axis if the density is

a. $\delta(\rho, \phi, \theta) = \rho^2$

b. $\delta(\rho, \phi, \theta) = r = \rho \sin \phi$.

81. Centroid of solid semiellipsoid Show that the centroid of the solid semiellipsoid of revolution $(r^2/a^2) + (z^2/h^2) \le 1, z \ge 0$, lies on the z-axis three-eighths of the way from the base to the top. The special case $h = a$ gives a solid hemisphere. Thus, the centroid of a solid hemisphere lies on the axis of symmetry three-eighths of the way from the base to the top.

82. Centroid of solid cone Show that the centroid of a solid right circular cone is one-fourth of the way from the base to the vertex. (In general, the centroid of a solid cone or pyramid is one-fourth of the way from the centroid of the base to the vertex.)

83. Variable density A solid right circular cylinder is bounded by the cylinder $r = a$ and the planes $z = 0$ and $z = h, h > 0$. Find the center of mass and the moment of inertia and radius of gyration about the z-axis if the density is $\delta(r, \theta, z) = z + 1$.

84. Mass of planet's atmosphere A spherical planet of radius R has an atmosphere whose density is $\mu = \mu_0 e^{-ch}$, where h is the altitude above the surface of the planet, μ_0 is the density at sea level, and c is a positive constant. Find the mass of the planet's atmosphere.

85. Density of center of a planet A planet is in the shape of a sphere of radius R and total mass M with spherically symmetric density distribution that increases linearly as one approaches its center. What is the density at the center of this planet if the density at its edge (surface) is taken to be zero?

Theory and Examples

86. Vertical circular cylinders in spherical coordinates Find an equation of the form $\rho = f(\phi)$ for the cylinder $x^2 + y^2 = a^2$.

87. Vertical planes in cylindrical coordinates

a. Show that planes perpendicular to the x-axis have equations of the form $r = a \sec \theta$ in cylindrical coordinates.

b. Show that planes perpendicular to the y-axis have equations of the form $r = b \csc \theta$.

88. (*Continuation of Exercise 87.*) Find an equation of the form $r = f(\theta)$ in cylindrical coordinates for the plane $ax + by = c$, $c \ne 0$.

89. Symmetry What symmetry will you find in a surface that has an equation of the form $r = f(z)$ in cylindrical coordinates? Give reasons for your answer.

90. Symmetry What symmetry will you find in a surface that has an equation of the form $\rho = f(\phi)$ in spherical coordinates? Give reasons for your answer.

15.7 Substitutions in Multiple Integrals

This section shows how to evaluate multiple integrals by substitution. As in single integration, the goal of substitution is to replace complicated integrals by ones that are easier to evaluate. Substitutions accomplish this by simplifying the integrand, the limits of integration, or both.

Substitutions in Double Integrals

The polar coordinate substitution of Section 15.3 is a special case of a more general substitution method for double integrals, a method that pictures changes in variables as transformations of regions.

Suppose that a region G in the uv-plane is transformed one-to-one into the region R in the xy-plane by equations of the form

$$x = g(u, v), \qquad y = h(u, v),$$

as suggested in Figure 15.47. We call R the **image** of G under the transformation, and G the **preimage** of R. Any function $f(x, y)$ defined on R can be thought of as a function

$f(g(u, v), h(u, v))$ defined on G as well. How is the integral of $f(x, y)$ over R related to the integral of $f(g(u, v), h(u, v))$ over G?

The answer is: If g, h, and f have continuous partial derivatives and $J(u, v)$ (to be discussed in a moment) is zero only at isolated points, if at all, then

$$\iint_R f(x, y)\, dx\, dy = \iint_G f(g(u, v), h(u, v))\,|J(u, v)|\, du\, dv. \tag{1}$$

HISTORICAL BIOGRAPHY

Carl Gustav Jacob Jacobi (1804–1851)

The factor $J(u, v)$, whose absolute value appears in Equation (1), is the *Jacobian* of the coordinate transformation, named after German mathematician Carl Jacobi. It measures how much the transformation is expanding or contracting the area around a point in G as G is transformed into R.

Definition Jacobian

The **Jacobian determinant** or **Jacobian** of the coordinate transformation $x = g(u, v), y = h(u, v)$ is

$$J(u, v) = \begin{vmatrix} \dfrac{\partial x}{\partial u} & \dfrac{\partial x}{\partial v} \\ \dfrac{\partial y}{\partial u} & \dfrac{\partial y}{\partial v} \end{vmatrix} = \frac{\partial x}{\partial u}\frac{\partial y}{\partial v} - \frac{\partial y}{\partial u}\frac{\partial x}{\partial v}. \tag{2}$$

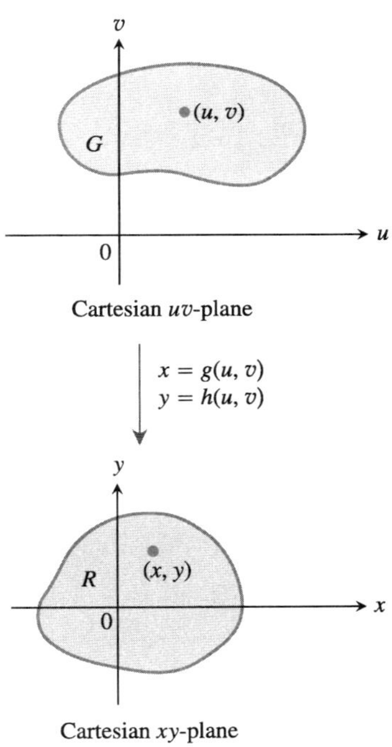

FIGURE 15.47 The equations $x = g(u, v)$ and $y = h(u, v)$ allow us to change an integral over a region R in the xy-plane into an integral over a region G in the uv-plane.

The Jacobian is also denoted by

$$J(u, v) = \frac{\partial(x, y)}{\partial(u, v)}$$

to help remember how the determinant in Equation (2) is constructed from the partial derivatives of x and y. The derivation of Equation (1) is intricate and properly belongs to a course in advanced calculus. We do not give the derivation here.

For polar coordinates, we have r and θ in place of u and v. With $x = r\cos\theta$ and $y = r\sin\theta$, the Jacobian is

$$J(r, \theta) = \begin{vmatrix} \dfrac{\partial x}{\partial r} & \dfrac{\partial x}{\partial \theta} \\ \dfrac{\partial y}{\partial r} & \dfrac{\partial y}{\partial \theta} \end{vmatrix} = \begin{vmatrix} \cos\theta & -r\sin\theta \\ \sin\theta & r\cos\theta \end{vmatrix} = r(\cos^2\theta + \sin^2\theta) = r.$$

Hence, Equation (1) becomes

$$\iint_R f(x, y)\, dx\, dy = \iint_G f(r\cos\theta, r\sin\theta)\,|r|\, dr\, d\theta$$

$$= \iint_G f(r\cos\theta, r\sin\theta)\, r\, dr\, d\theta, \qquad \text{If } r \geq 0 \tag{3}$$

which is the equation found in Section 15.3.

Figure 15.48 shows how the equations $x = r\cos\theta, y = r\sin\theta$ transform the rectangle G: $0 \leq r \leq 1, 0 \leq \theta \leq \pi/2$ into the quarter circle R bounded by $x^2 + y^2 = 1$ in the first quadrant of the xy-plane.

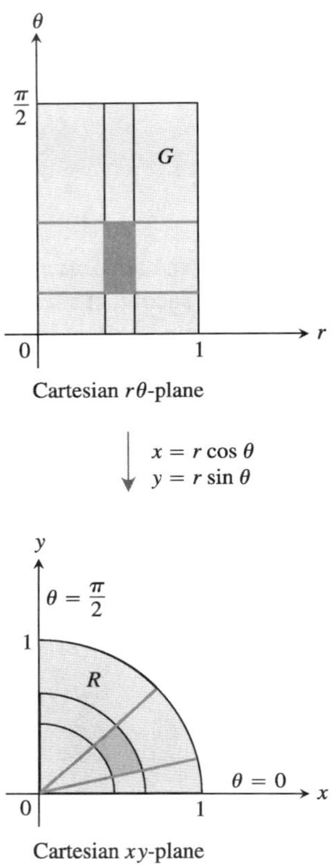

FIGURE 15.48 The equations $x = r\cos\theta$, $y = r\sin\theta$ transform G into R.

Notice that the integral on the right-hand side of Equation (3) is not the integral of $f(r\cos\theta, r\sin\theta)$ over a region in the polar coordinate plane. It is the integral of the product of $f(r\cos\theta, r\sin\theta)$ and r over a region G in the *Cartesian $r\theta$-plane*.

Here is an example of another substitution.

EXAMPLE 1 Applying a Transformation to Integrate

Evaluate

$$\int_0^4 \int_{x=y/2}^{x=(y/2)+1} \frac{2x - y}{2}\, dx\, dy$$

by applying the transformation

$$u = \frac{2x - y}{2}, \qquad v = \frac{y}{2} \tag{4}$$

and integrating over an appropriate region in the uv-plane.

Solution We sketch the region R of integration in the xy-plane and identify its boundaries (Figure 15.49).

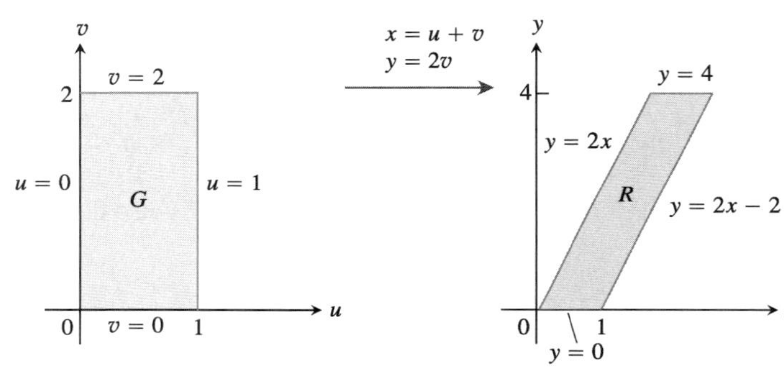

FIGURE 15.49 The equations $x = u + v$ and $y = 2v$ transform G into R. Reversing the transformation by the equations $u = (2x - y)/2$ and $v = y/2$ transforms R into G (Example 1).

To apply Equation (1), we need to find the corresponding uv-region G and the Jacobian of the transformation. To find them, we first solve Equations (4) for x and y in terms of u and v. Routine algebra gives

$$x = u + v \qquad y = 2v. \tag{5}$$

We then find the boundaries of G by substituting these expressions into the equations for the boundaries of R (Figure 15.49).

xy*-equations for the boundary of *R	**Corresponding *uv*-equations for the boundary of *G***	**Simplified *uv*-equations**
$x = y/2$	$u + v = 2v/2 = v$	$u = 0$
$x = (y/2) + 1$	$u + v = (2v/2) + 1 = v + 1$	$u = 1$
$y = 0$	$2v = 0$	$v = 0$
$y = 4$	$2v = 4$	$v = 2$

The Jacobian of the transformation (again from Equations (5)) is

$$J(u, v) = \begin{vmatrix} \dfrac{\partial x}{\partial u} & \dfrac{\partial x}{\partial v} \\ \dfrac{\partial y}{\partial u} & \dfrac{\partial y}{\partial v} \end{vmatrix} = \begin{vmatrix} \dfrac{\partial}{\partial u}(u + v) & \dfrac{\partial}{\partial v}(u + v) \\ \dfrac{\partial}{\partial u}(2v) & \dfrac{\partial}{\partial v}(2v) \end{vmatrix} = \begin{vmatrix} 1 & 1 \\ 0 & 2 \end{vmatrix} = 2.$$

We now have everything we need to apply Equation (1):

$$\int_0^4 \int_{x=y/2}^{x=(y/2)+1} \frac{2x - y}{2}\, dx\, dy = \int_{v=0}^{v=2} \int_{u=0}^{u=1} u\,|J(u, v)|\, du\, dv$$

$$= \int_0^2 \int_0^1 (u)(2)\, du\, dv = \int_0^2 \Big[u^2\Big]_0^1 dv = \int_0^2 dv = 2.$$

■

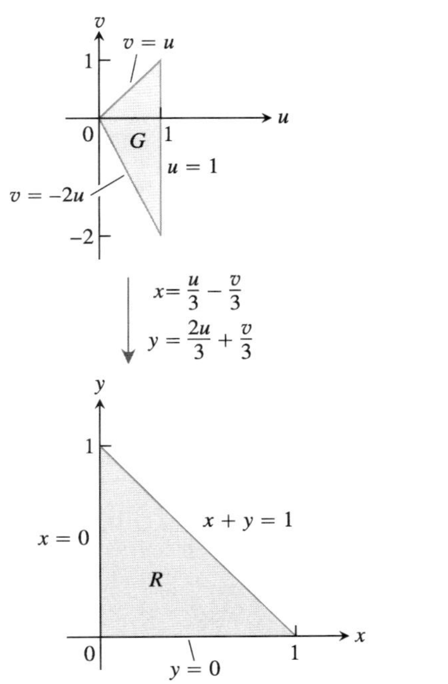

FIGURE 15.50 The equations $x = (u/3) - (v/3)$ and $y = (2u/3) + (v/3)$ transform G into R. Reversing the transformation by the equations $u = x + y$ and $v = y - 2x$ transforms R into G (Example 2).

EXAMPLE 2 Applying a Transformation to Integrate

Evaluate

$$\int_0^1 \int_0^{1-x} \sqrt{x + y}\,(y - 2x)^2\, dy\, dx.$$

Solution We sketch the region R of integration in the xy-plane and identify its boundaries (Figure 15.50). The integrand suggests the transformation $u = x + y$ and $v = y - 2x$. Routine algebra produces x and y as functions of u and v:

$$x = \frac{u}{3} - \frac{v}{3}, \qquad y = \frac{2u}{3} + \frac{v}{3}. \tag{6}$$

From Equations (6), we can find the boundaries of the uv-region G (Figure 15.50).

xy-equations for the boundary of R	Corresponding uv-equations for the boundary of G	Simplified uv-equations
$x + y = 1$	$\left(\frac{u}{3} - \frac{v}{3}\right) + \left(\frac{2u}{3} + \frac{v}{3}\right) = 1$	$u = 1$
$x = 0$	$\frac{u}{3} - \frac{v}{3} = 0$	$v = u$
$y = 0$	$\frac{2u}{3} + \frac{v}{3} = 0$	$v = -2u$

The Jacobian of the transformation in Equations (6) is

$$J(u, v) = \begin{vmatrix} \dfrac{\partial x}{\partial u} & \dfrac{\partial x}{\partial v} \\ \dfrac{\partial y}{\partial u} & \dfrac{\partial y}{\partial v} \end{vmatrix} = \begin{vmatrix} \dfrac{1}{3} & -\dfrac{1}{3} \\ \dfrac{2}{3} & \dfrac{1}{3} \end{vmatrix} = \frac{1}{3}.$$

Applying Equation (1), we evaluate the integral:

$$\int_0^1 \int_0^{1-x} \sqrt{x+y}\,(y-2x)^2\,dy\,dx = \int_{u=0}^{u=1} \int_{v=-2u}^{v=u} u^{1/2} v^2 |J(u,v)|\,dv\,du$$

$$= \int_0^1 \int_{-2u}^{u} u^{1/2} v^2 \left(\frac{1}{3}\right) dv\,du = \frac{1}{3}\int_0^1 u^{1/2}\left[\frac{1}{3}v^3\right]_{v=-2u}^{v=u} du$$

$$= \frac{1}{9}\int_0^1 u^{1/2}(u^3 + 8u^3)\,du = \int_0^1 u^{7/2}\,du = \frac{2}{9}u^{9/2}\Big]_0^1 = \frac{2}{9}.$$

■

Substitutions in Triple Integrals

The cylindrical and spherical coordinate substitutions in Section 15.6 are special cases of a substitution method that pictures changes of variables in triple integrals as transformations of three-dimensional regions. The method is like the method for double integrals except that now we work in three dimensions instead of two.

Suppose that a region G in uvw-space is transformed one-to-one into the region D in xyz-space by differentiable equations of the form

$$x = g(u, v, w), \qquad y = h(u, v, w), \qquad z = k(u, v, w),$$

as suggested in Figure 15.51. Then any function $F(x, y, z)$ defined on D can be thought of as a function

$$F(g(u, v, w), h(u, v, w), k(u, v, w)) = H(u, v, w)$$

defined on G. If g, h, and k have continuous first partial derivatives, then the integral of $F(x, y, z)$ over D is related to the integral of $H(u, v, w)$ over G by the equation

$$\iiint\limits_D F(x, y, z)\,dx\,dy\,dz = \iiint\limits_G H(u, v, w)\,|J(u, v, w)|\,du\,dv\,dw. \tag{7}$$

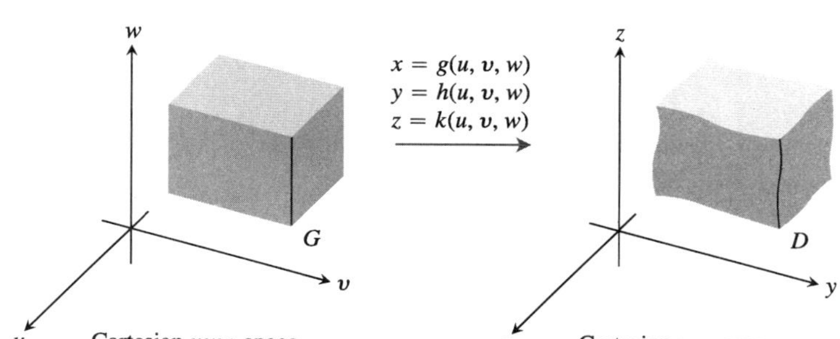

FIGURE 15.51 The equations $x = g(u, v, w)$, $y = h(u, v, w)$, and $z = k(u, v, w)$ allow us to change an integral over a region D in Cartesian xyz-space into an integral over a region G in Cartesian uvw-space.

The factor $J(u, v, w)$, whose absolute value appears in this equation, is the **Jacobian determinant**

$$J(u, v, w) = \begin{vmatrix} \dfrac{\partial x}{\partial u} & \dfrac{\partial x}{\partial v} & \dfrac{\partial x}{\partial w} \\ \dfrac{\partial y}{\partial u} & \dfrac{\partial y}{\partial v} & \dfrac{\partial y}{\partial w} \\ \dfrac{\partial z}{\partial u} & \dfrac{\partial z}{\partial v} & \dfrac{\partial z}{\partial w} \end{vmatrix} = \frac{\partial(x, y, z)}{\partial(u, v, w)}.$$

This determinant measures how much the volume near a point in G is being expanded or contracted by the transformation from (u, v, w) to (x, y, z) coordinates. As in the two-dimensional case, the derivation of the change-of-variable formula in Equation (7) is complicated and we do not go into it here.

For cylindrical coordinates, r, θ, and z take the place of u, v, and w. The transformation from *Cartesian* $r\theta z$-space to Cartesian xyz-space is given by the equations

$$x = r\cos\theta, \qquad y = r\sin\theta, \qquad z = z$$

(Figure 15.52). The Jacobian of the transformation is

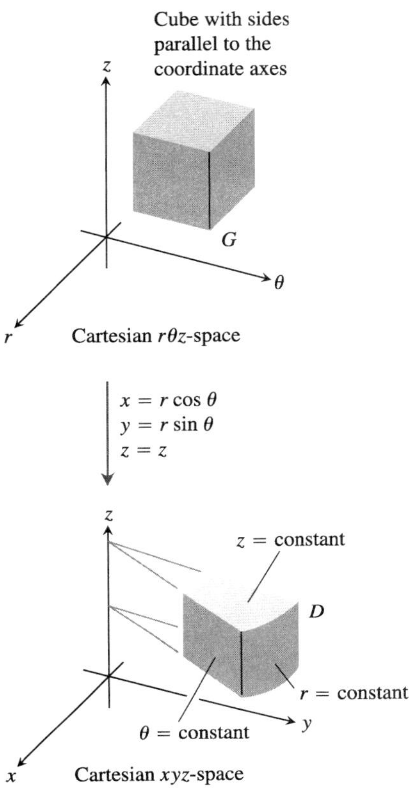

FIGURE 15.52 The equations $x = r\cos\theta$, $y = r\sin\theta$, and $z = z$ transform the cube G into a cylindrical wedge D.

$$J(r, \theta, z) = \begin{vmatrix} \dfrac{\partial x}{\partial r} & \dfrac{\partial x}{\partial \theta} & \dfrac{\partial x}{\partial z} \\ \dfrac{\partial y}{\partial r} & \dfrac{\partial y}{\partial \theta} & \dfrac{\partial y}{\partial z} \\ \dfrac{\partial z}{\partial r} & \dfrac{\partial z}{\partial \theta} & \dfrac{\partial z}{\partial z} \end{vmatrix} = \begin{vmatrix} \cos\theta & -r\sin\theta & 0 \\ \sin\theta & r\cos\theta & 0 \\ 0 & 0 & 1 \end{vmatrix}$$

$$= r\cos^2\theta + r\sin^2\theta = r.$$

The corresponding version of Equation (7) is

$$\iiint\limits_D F(x, y, z)\, dx\, dy\, dz = \iiint\limits_G H(r, \theta, z)\,|r|\, dr\, d\theta\, dz.$$

We can drop the absolute value signs whenever $r \geq 0$.

For spherical coordinates, ρ, ϕ, and θ take the place of u, v, and w. The transformation from Cartesian $\rho\phi\theta$-space to Cartesian xyz-space is given by

$$x = \rho\sin\phi\cos\theta, \qquad y = \rho\sin\phi\sin\theta, \qquad z = \rho\cos\phi$$

(Figure 15.53). The Jacobian of the transformation is

$$J(\rho, \phi, \theta) = \begin{vmatrix} \dfrac{\partial x}{\partial \rho} & \dfrac{\partial x}{\partial \phi} & \dfrac{\partial x}{\partial \theta} \\ \dfrac{\partial y}{\partial \rho} & \dfrac{\partial y}{\partial \phi} & \dfrac{\partial y}{\partial \theta} \\ \dfrac{\partial z}{\partial \rho} & \dfrac{\partial z}{\partial \phi} & \dfrac{\partial z}{\partial \theta} \end{vmatrix} = \rho^2\sin\phi$$

(Exercise 17). The corresponding version of Equation (7) is

$$\iiint_D F(x, y, z)\, dx\, dy\, dz = \iiint_G H(\rho, \phi, \theta)\,|\rho^2 \sin \phi|\, d\rho\, d\phi\, d\theta.$$

We can drop the absolute value signs because $\sin \phi$ is never negative for $0 \le \phi \le \pi$. Note that this is the same result we obtained in Section 15.6.

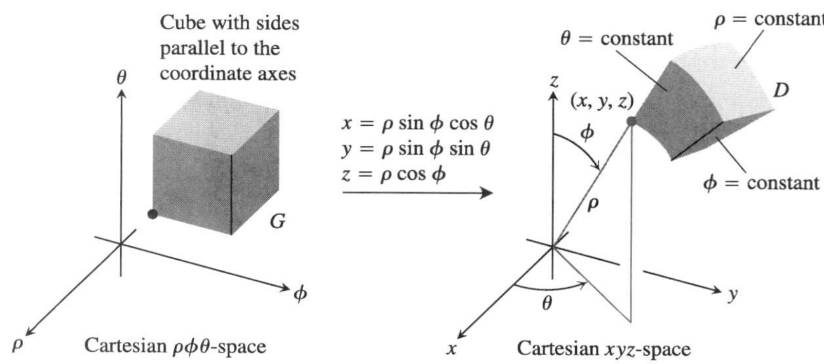

FIGURE 15.53 The equations $x = \rho \sin \phi \cos \theta$, $y = \rho \sin \phi \sin \theta$, and $z = \rho \cos \phi$ transform the cube G into the spherical wedge D.

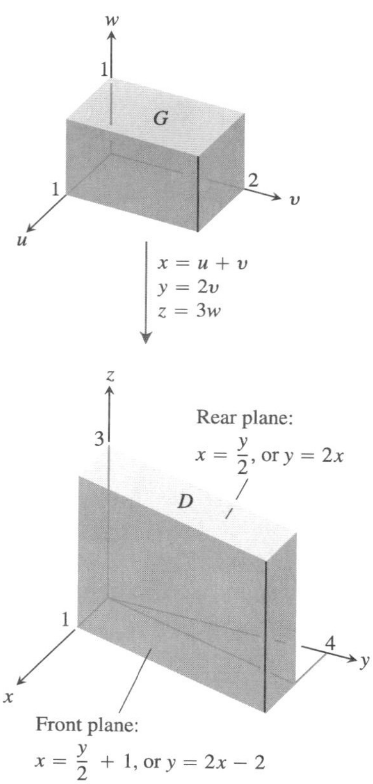

FIGURE 15.54 The equations $x = u + v$, $y = 2v$, and $z = 3w$ transform G into D. Reversing the transformation by the equations $u = (2x - y)/2$, $v = y/2$, and $w = z/3$ transforms D into G (Example 3).

Here is an example of another substitution. Although we could evaluate the integral in this example directly, we have chosen it to illustrate the substitution method in a simple (and fairly intuitive) setting.

EXAMPLE 3 Applying a Transformation to Integrate

Evaluate

$$\int_0^3 \int_0^4 \int_{x=y/2}^{x=(y/2)+1} \left(\frac{2x - y}{2} + \frac{z}{3}\right) dx\, dy\, dz$$

by applying the transformation

$$u = (2x - y)/2, \qquad v = y/2, \qquad w = z/3 \tag{8}$$

and integrating over an appropriate region in uvw-space.

Solution We sketch the region D of integration in xyz-space and identify its boundaries (Figure 15.54). In this case, the bounding surfaces are planes.

To apply Equation (7), we need to find the corresponding uvw-region G and the Jacobian of the transformation. To find them, we first solve Equations (8) for x, y, and z in terms of u, v, and w. Routine algebra gives

$$x = u + v, \qquad y = 2v, \qquad z = 3w. \tag{9}$$

We then find the boundaries of G by substituting these expressions into the equations for the boundaries of D:

xyz-equations for the boundary of D	Corresponding uvw-equations for the boundary of G	Simplified uvw-equations
$x = y/2$	$u + v = 2v/2 = v$	$u = 0$
$x = (y/2) + 1$	$u + v = (2v/2) + 1 = v + 1$	$u = 1$
$y = 0$	$2v = 0$	$v = 0$
$y = 4$	$2v = 4$	$v = 2$
$z = 0$	$3w = 0$	$w = 0$
$z = 3$	$3w = 3$	$w = 1$

The Jacobian of the transformation, again from Equations (9), is

$$J(u, v, w) = \begin{vmatrix} \frac{\partial x}{\partial u} & \frac{\partial x}{\partial v} & \frac{\partial x}{\partial w} \\ \frac{\partial y}{\partial u} & \frac{\partial y}{\partial v} & \frac{\partial y}{\partial w} \\ \frac{\partial z}{\partial u} & \frac{\partial z}{\partial v} & \frac{\partial z}{\partial w} \end{vmatrix} = \begin{vmatrix} 1 & 1 & 0 \\ 0 & 2 & 0 \\ 0 & 0 & 3 \end{vmatrix} = 6.$$

We now have everything we need to apply Equation (7):

$$\int_0^3 \int_0^4 \int_{x=y/2}^{x=(y/2)+1} \left(\frac{2x - y}{2} + \frac{z}{3}\right) dx\, dy\, dz$$

$$= \int_0^1 \int_0^2 \int_0^1 (u + w)|J(u, v, w)|\, du\, dv\, dw$$

$$= \int_0^1 \int_0^2 \int_0^1 (u + w)(6)\, du\, dv\, dw = 6\int_0^1 \int_0^2 \left[\frac{u^2}{2} + uw\right]_0^1 dv\, dw$$

$$= 6\int_0^1 \int_0^2 \left(\frac{1}{2} + w\right) dv\, dw = 6\int_0^1 \left[\frac{v}{2} + vw\right]_0^2 dw = 6\int_0^1 (1 + 2w)\, dw$$

$$= 6\left[w + w^2\right]_0^1 = 6(2) = 12.$$

The goal of this section was to introduce you to the ideas involved in coordinate transformations. A thorough discussion of transformations, the Jacobian, and multivariable substitution is best given in an advanced calculus course after a study of linear algebra.

EXERCISES 15.7

Finding Jacobians and Transformed Regions for Two Variables

1. **a.** Solve the system

$$u = x - y, \qquad v = 2x + y$$

for x and y in terms of u and v. Then find the value of the Jacobian $\partial(x, y)/\partial(u, v)$.

b. Find the image under the transformation $u = x - y$, $v = 2x + y$ of the triangular region with vertices $(0, 0)$, $(1, 1)$, and $(1, -2)$ in the xy-plane. Sketch the transformed region in the uv-plane.

2. **a.** Solve the system

$$u = x + 2y, \qquad v = x - y$$

for x and y in terms of u and v. Then find the value of the Jacobian $\partial(x, y)/\partial(u, v)$.

b. Find the image under the transformation $u = x + 2y$, $v = x - y$ of the triangular region in the xy-plane bounded by the lines $y = 0, y = x$, and $x + 2y = 2$. Sketch the transformed region in the uv-plane.

3. a. Solve the system

$$u = 3x + 2y, \qquad v = x + 4y$$

for x and y in terms of u and v. Then find the value of the Jacobian $\partial(x, y)/\partial(u, v)$.

b. Find the image under the transformation $u = 3x + 2y, v = x + 4y$ of the triangular region in the xy-plane bounded by the x-axis, the y-axis, and the line $x + y = 1$. Sketch the transformed region in the uv-plane.

4. a. Solve the system

$$u = 2x - 3y, \qquad v = -x + y$$

for x and y in terms of u and v. Then find the value of the Jacobian $\partial(x, y)/\partial(u, v)$.

b. Find the image under the transformation $u = 2x - 3y$, $v = -x + y$ of the parallelogram R in the xy-plane with boundaries $x = -3, x = 0, y = x$, and $y = x + 1$. Sketch the transformed region in the uv-plane.

Applying Transformations to Evaluate Double Integrals

5. Evaluate the integral

$$\int_0^4 \int_{x=y/2}^{x=(y/2)+1} \frac{2x - y}{2}\, dx\, dy$$

from Example 1 directly by integration with respect to x and y to confirm that its value is 2.

6. Use the transformation in Exercise 1 to evaluate the integral

$$\iint_R (2x^2 - xy - y^2)\, dx\, dy$$

for the region R in the first quadrant bounded by the lines $y = -2x + 4, y = -2x + 7, y = x - 2$, and $y = x + 1$.

7. Use the transformation in Exercise 3 to evaluate the integral

$$\iint_R (3x^2 + 14xy + 8y^2)\, dx\, dy$$

for the region R in the first quadrant bounded by the lines $y = -(3/2)x + 1, y = -(3/2)x + 3, y = -(1/4)x$, and $y = -(1/4)x + 1$.

8. Use the transformation and parallelogram R in Exercise 4 to evaluate the integral

$$\iint_R 2(x - y)\, dx\, dy.$$

9. Let R be the region in the first quadrant of the xy-plane bounded by the hyperbolas $xy = 1, xy = 9$ and the lines $y = x, y = 4x$. Use the transformation $x = u/v, y = uv$ with $u > 0$ and $v > 0$ to rewrite

$$\iint_R \left(\sqrt{\frac{y}{x}} + \sqrt{xy}\right) dx\, dy$$

as an integral over an appropriate region G in the uv-plane. Then evaluate the uv-integral over G.

10. a. Find the Jacobian of the transformation $x = u, y = uv$, and sketch the region G: $1 \le u \le 2, 1 \le uv \le 2$ in the uv-plane.

b. Then use Equation (1) to transform the integral

$$\int_1^2 \int_1^2 \frac{y}{x}\, dy\, dx$$

into an integral over G, and evaluate both integrals.

11. **Polar moment of inertia of an elliptical plate** A thin plate of constant density covers the region bounded by the ellipse $x^2/a^2 + y^2/b^2 = 1, a > 0, b > 0$, in the xy-plane. Find the first moment of the plate about the origin. (*Hint:* Use the transformation $x = ar\cos\theta, y = br\sin\theta$.)

12. **The area of an ellipse** The area πab of the ellipse $x^2/a^2 + y^2/b^2 = 1$ can be found by integrating the function $f(x, y) = 1$ over the region bounded by the ellipse in the xy-plane. Evaluating the integral directly requires a trigonometric substitution. An easier way to evaluate the integral is to use the transformation $x = au, y = bv$ and evaluate the transformed integral over the disk G: $u^2 + v^2 \le 1$ in the uv-plane. Find the area this way.

13. Use the transformation in Exercise 2 to evaluate the integral

$$\int_0^{2/3} \int_y^{2-2y} (x + 2y)e^{(y-x)}\, dx\, dy$$

by first writing it as an integral over a region G in the uv-plane.

14. Use the transformation $x = u + (1/2)v, y = v$ to evaluate the integral

$$\int_0^2 \int_{y/2}^{(y+4)/2} y^3(2x - y)e^{(2x-y)^2}\, dx\, dy$$

by first writing it as an integral over a region G in the uv-plane.

Finding Jacobian Determinants

15. Find the Jacobian $\partial(x, y)/\partial(u, v)$ for the transformation

a. $x = u\cos v, \quad y = u\sin v$

b. $x = u\sin v, \quad y = u\cos v$.

16. Find the Jacobian $\partial(x, y, z)/\partial(u, v, w)$ of the transformation

a. $x = u\cos v, \quad y = u\sin v, \quad z = w$

b. $x = 2u - 1, \quad y = 3v - 4, \quad z = (1/2)(w - 4)$.

17. Evaluate the appropriate determinant to show that the Jacobian of the transformation from Cartesian $\rho\phi\theta$-space to Cartesian xyz-space is $\rho^2 \sin\phi$.

18. **Substitutions in single integrals** How can substitutions in single definite integrals be viewed as transformations of regions? What is the Jacobian in such a case? Illustrate with an example.

Applying Transformations to Evaluate Triple Integrals

19. Evaluate the integral in Example 3 by integrating with respect to x, y, and z.

20. **Volume of an ellipsoid** Find the volume of the ellipsoid

$$\frac{x^2}{a^2} + \frac{y^2}{b^2} + \frac{z^2}{c^2} = 1.$$

(*Hint:* Let $x = au$, $y = bv$, and $z = cw$. Then find the volume of an appropriate region in uvw-space.)

21. Evaluate

$$\iiint |xyz|\, dx\, dy\, dz$$

over the solid ellipsoid

$$\frac{x^2}{a^2} + \frac{y^2}{b^2} + \frac{z^2}{c^2} \le 1.$$

(*Hint:* Let $x = au$, $y = bv$, and $z = cw$. Then integrate over an appropriate region in uvw-space.)

22. Let D be the region in xyz-space defined by the inequalities

$$1 \le x \le 2, \quad 0 \le xy \le 2, \quad 0 \le z \le 1.$$

Evaluate

$$\iiint_D (x^2y + 3xyz)\, dx\, dy\, dz$$

by applying the transformation

$$u = x, \quad v = xy, \quad w = 3z$$

and integrating over an appropriate region G in uvw-space.

23. **Centroid of a solid semiellipsoid** Assuming the result that the centroid of a solid hemisphere lies on the axis of symmetry three-eighths of the way from the base toward the top, show, by transforming the appropriate integrals, that the center of mass of a solid semiellipsoid $(x^2/a^2) + (y^2/b^2) + (z^2/c^2) \le 1$, $z \ge 0$, lies on the z-axis three-eighths of the way from the base toward the top. (You can do this without evaluating any of the integrals.)

24. **Cylindrical shells** In Section 6.2, we learned how to find the volume of a solid of revolution using the shell method; namely, if the region between the curve $y = f(x)$ and the x-axis from a to b $(0 < a < b)$ is revolved about the y-axis, the volume of the resulting solid is $\int_a^b 2\pi x f(x)\, dx$. Prove that finding volumes by using triple integrals gives the same result. (*Hint:* Use cylindrical coordinates with the roles of y and z changed.)

Chapter 15 Questions to Guide Your Review

1. Define the double integral of a function of two variables over a bounded region in the coordinate plane.
2. How are double integrals evaluated as iterated integrals? Does the order of integration matter? How are the limits of integration determined? Give examples.
3. How are double integrals used to calculate areas, average values, masses, moments, centers of mass, and radii of gyration? Give examples.
4. How can you change a double integral in rectangular coordinates into a double integral in polar coordinates? Why might it be worthwhile to do so? Give an example.
5. Define the triple integral of a function $f(x, y, z)$ over a bounded region in space.
6. How are triple integrals in rectangular coordinates evaluated? How are the limits of integration determined? Give an example.
7. How are triple integrals in rectangular coordinates used to calculate volumes, average values, masses, moments, centers of mass, and radii of gyration? Give examples.
8. How are triple integrals defined in cylindrical and spherical coordinates? Why might one prefer working in one of these coordinate systems to working in rectangular coordinates?
9. How are triple integrals in cylindrical and spherical coordinates evaluated? How are the limits of integration found? Give examples.
10. How are substitutions in double integrals pictured as transformations of two-dimensional regions? Give a sample calculation.
11. How are substitutions in triple integrals pictured as transformations of three-dimensional regions? Give a sample calculation.

Chapter 15 Practice Exercises

Planar Regions of Integration

In Exercises 1–4, sketch the region of integration and evaluate the double integral.

1. $\int_1^{10}\int_0^{1/y} ye^{xy}\,dx\,dy$

2. $\int_0^1\int_0^{x^3} e^{y/x}\,dy\,dx$

3. $\int_0^{3/2}\int_{-\sqrt{9-4t^2}}^{\sqrt{9-4t^2}} t\,ds\,dt$

4. $\int_0^1\int_{\sqrt{y}}^{2-\sqrt{y}} xy\,dx\,dy$

Reversing the Order of Integration

In Exercises 5–8, sketch the region of integration and write an equivalent integral with the order of integration reversed. Then evaluate both integrals.

5. $\int_0^4\int_{-\sqrt{4-y}}^{(y-4)/2} dx\,dy$

6. $\int_0^1\int_{x^2}^{x} \sqrt{x}\,dy\,dx$

7. $\int_0^{3/2}\int_{-\sqrt{9-4y^2}}^{\sqrt{9-4y^2}} y\,dx\,dy$

8. $\int_0^2\int_0^{4-x^2} 2x\,dy\,dx$

Evaluating Double Integrals

Evaluate the integrals in Exercises 9–12.

9. $\int_0^1\int_{2y}^2 4\cos(x^2)\,dx\,dy$

10. $\int_0^2\int_{y/2}^1 e^{x^2}\,dx\,dy$

11. $\int_0^8\int_{\sqrt[3]{x}}^2 \frac{dy\,dx}{y^4+1}$

12. $\int_0^1\int_{\sqrt[3]{y}}^1 \frac{2\pi\sin\pi x^2}{x^2}\,dx\,dy$

Areas and Volumes

13. **Area between line and parabola** Find the area of the region enclosed by the line $y = 2x + 4$ and the parabola $y = 4 - x^2$ in the xy-plane.

14. **Area bounded by lines and parabola** Find the area of the "triangular" region in the xy-plane that is bounded on the right by the parabola $y = x^2$, on the left by the line $x + y = 2$, and above by the line $y = 4$.

15. **Volume of the region under a paraboloid** Find the volume under the paraboloid $z = x^2 + y^2$ above the triangle enclosed by the lines $y = x, x = 0$, and $x + y = 2$ in the xy-plane.

16. **Volume of the region under parabolic cylinder** Find the volume under the parabolic cylinder $z = x^2$ above the region enclosed by the parabola $y = 6 - x^2$ and the line $y = x$ in the xy-plane.

Average Values

Find the average value of $f(x, y) = xy$ over the regions in Exercises 17 and 18.

17. The square bounded by the lines $x = 1, y = 1$ in the first quadrant

18. The quarter circle $x^2 + y^2 \le 1$ in the first quadrant

Masses and Moments

19. **Centroid** Find the centroid of the "triangular" region bounded by the lines $x = 2, y = 2$ and the hyperbola $xy = 2$ in the xy-plane.

20. **Centroid** Find the centroid of the region between the parabola $x + y^2 - 2y = 0$ and the line $x + 2y = 0$ in the xy-plane.

21. **Polar moment** Find the polar moment of inertia about the origin of a thin triangular plate of constant density $\delta = 3$ bounded by the y-axis and the lines $y = 2x$ and $y = 4$ in the xy-plane.

22. **Polar moment** Find the polar moment of inertia about the center of a thin rectangular sheet of constant density $\delta = 1$ bounded by the lines
    a. $x = \pm 2, \quad y = \pm 1$ in the xy-plane
    b. $x = \pm a, \quad y = \pm b$ in the xy-plane.
    (*Hint:* Find I_x. Then use the formula for I_x to find I_y and add the two to find I_0).

23. **Inertial moment and radius of gyration** Find the moment of inertia and radius of gyration about the x-axis of a thin plate of constant density δ covering the triangle with vertices (0, 0), (3, 0), and (3, 2) in the xy-plane.

24. **Plate with variable density** Find the center of mass and the moments of inertia and radii of gyration about the coordinate axes of a thin plate bounded by the line $y = x$ and the parabola $y = x^2$ in the xy-plane if the density is $\delta(x, y) = x + 1$.

25. **Plate with variable density** Find the mass and first moments about the coordinate axes of a thin square plate bounded by the lines $x = \pm 1, y = \pm 1$ in the xy-plane if the density is $\delta(x, y) = x^2 + y^2 + 1/3$.

26. **Triangles with same inertial moment and radius of gyration** Find the moment of inertia and radius of gyration about the x-axis of a thin triangular plate of constant density δ whose base lies along the interval $[0, b]$ on the x-axis and whose vertex lies on the line $y = h$ above the x-axis. As you will see, it does not matter where on the line this vertex lies. All such triangles have the same moment of inertia and radius of gyration about the x-axis.

Polar Coordinates

Evaluate the integrals in Exercises 27 and 28 by changing to polar coordinates.

27. $\int_{-1}^1\int_{-\sqrt{1-x^2}}^{\sqrt{1-x^2}} \frac{2\,dy\,dx}{(1+x^2+y^2)^2}$

28. $\int_{-1}^1\int_{-\sqrt{1-y^2}}^{\sqrt{1-y^2}} \ln(x^2+y^2+1)\,dx\,dy$

29. **Centroid** Find the centroid of the region in the polar coordinate plane defined by the inequalities $0 \le r \le 3, -\pi/3 \le \theta \le \pi/3$.

30. Centroid Find the centroid of the region in the first quadrant bounded by the rays $\theta = 0$ and $\theta = \pi/2$ and the circles $r = 1$ and $r = 3$.

31. a. Centroid Find the centroid of the region in the polar coordinate plane that lies inside the cardioid $r = 1 + \cos\theta$ and outside the circle $r = 1$.

b. Sketch the region and show the centroid in your sketch.

32. a. Centroid Find the centroid of the plane region defined by the polar coordinate inequalities $0 \le r \le a$, $-\alpha \le \theta \le \alpha$ $(0 < \alpha \le \pi)$. How does the centroid move as $\alpha \to \pi^-$?

b. Sketch the region for $\alpha = 5\pi/6$ and show the centroid in your sketch.

33. Integrating over lemniscate Integrate the function $f(x, y) = 1/(1 + x^2 + y^2)^2$ over the region enclosed by one loop of the lemniscate $(x^2 + y^2)^2 - (x^2 - y^2) = 0$.

34. Integrate $f(x, y) = 1/(1 + x^2 + y^2)^2$ over

a. Triangular region The triangle with vertices $(0, 0)$, $(1, 0)$, $(1, \sqrt{3})$.

b. First quadrant The first quadrant of the xy-plane.

Triple Integrals in Cartesian Coordinates

Evaluate the integrals in Exercises 35–38.

35. $\displaystyle\int_0^{\pi}\int_0^{\pi}\int_0^{\pi} \cos(x + y + z)\, dx\, dy\, dz$

36. $\displaystyle\int_{\ln 6}^{\ln 7}\int_0^{\ln 2}\int_{\ln 4}^{\ln 5} e^{(x+y+z)}\, dz\, dy\, dx$

37. $\displaystyle\int_0^{1}\int_0^{x^2}\int_0^{x+y} (2x - y - z)\, dz\, dy\, dx$

38. $\displaystyle\int_1^{e}\int_1^{x}\int_0^{z} \frac{2y}{z^3}\, dy\, dz\, dx$

39. Volume Find the volume of the wedge-shaped region enclosed on the side by the cylinder $x = -\cos y$, $-\pi/2 \le y \le \pi/2$, on the top by the plane $z = -2x$, and below by the xy-plane.

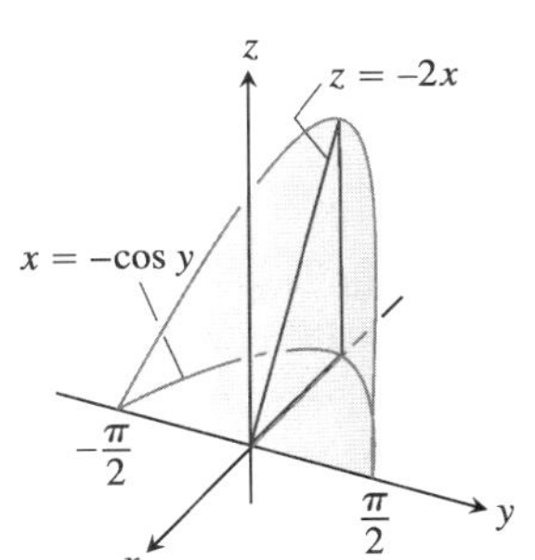

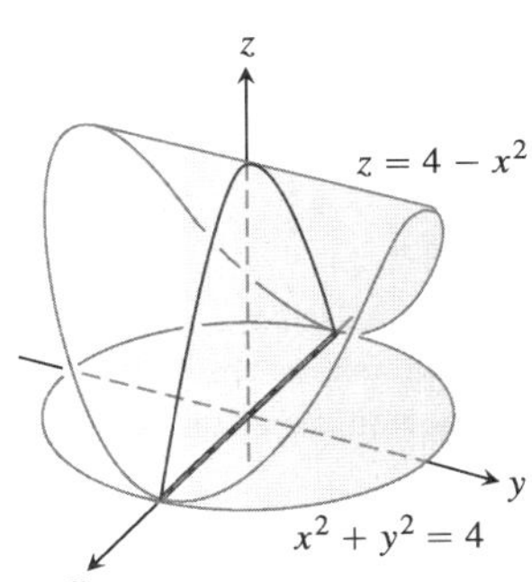

40. Volume Find the volume of the solid that is bounded above by the cylinder $z = 4 - x^2$, on the sides by the cylinder $x^2 + y^2 = 4$, and below by the xy-plane.

41. Average value Find the average value of $f(x, y, z) = 30xz\sqrt{x^2 + y}$ over the rectangular solid in the first octant bounded by the coordinate planes and the planes $x = 1$, $y = 3$, $z = 1$.

42. Average value Find the average value of ρ over the solid sphere $\rho \le a$ (spherical coordinates).

Cylindrical and Spherical Coordinates

43. Cylindrical to rectangular coordinates Convert

$$\int_0^{2\pi}\int_0^{\sqrt{2}}\int_r^{\sqrt{4-r^2}} 3\, dz\, r\, dr\, d\theta, \qquad r \ge 0$$

to **(a)** rectangular coordinates with the order of integration $dz\, dx\, dy$ and **(b)** spherical coordinates. Then **(c)** evaluate one of the integrals.

44. Rectangular to cylindrical coordinates **(a)** Convert to cylindrical coordinates. Then **(b)** evaluate the new integral.

$$\int_0^{1}\int_{-\sqrt{1-x^2}}^{\sqrt{1-x^2}}\int_{-(x^2+y^2)}^{(x^2+y^2)} 21xy^2\, dz\, dy\, dx$$

45. Rectangular to spherical coordinates **(a)** Convert to spherical coordinates. Then **(b)** evaluate the new integral.

$$\int_{-1}^{1}\int_{-\sqrt{1-x^2}}^{\sqrt{1-x^2}}\int_{\sqrt{x^2+y^2}}^{1} dz\, dy\, dx$$

46. Rectangular, cylindrical, and spherical coordinates Write an iterated triple integral for the integral of $f(x, y, z) = 6 + 4y$ over the region in the first octant bounded by the cone $z = \sqrt{x^2 + y^2}$, the cylinder $x^2 + y^2 = 1$, and the coordinate planes in **(a)** rectangular coordinates, **(b)** cylindrical coordinates, and **(c)** spherical coordinates. Then **(d)** find the integral of f by evaluating one of the triple integrals.

47. Cylindrical to rectangular coordinates Set up an integral in rectangular coordinates equivalent to the integral

$$\int_0^{\pi/2}\int_1^{\sqrt{3}}\int_1^{\sqrt{4-r^2}} r^3(\sin\theta\cos\theta)z^2\, dz\, dr\, d\theta.$$

Arrange the order of integration to be z first, then y, then x.

48. Rectangular to cylindrical coordinates The volume of a solid is

$$\int_0^{2}\int_0^{\sqrt{2x-x^2}}\int_{-\sqrt{4-x^2-y^2}}^{\sqrt{4-x^2-y^2}} dz\, dy\, dx.$$

a. Describe the solid by giving equations for the surfaces that form its boundary.

b. Convert the integral to cylindrical coordinates but do not evaluate the integral.

49. Spherical versus cylindrical coordinates Triple integrals involving spherical shapes do not always require spherical coordinates for convenient evaluation. Some calculations may be accomplished more easily with cylindrical coordinates. As a case in point, find the volume of the region bounded above by the sphere $x^2 + y^2 + z^2 = 8$ and below by the plane $z = 2$ by using **(a)** cylindrical coordinates and **(b)** spherical coordinates.

50. **Finding I_z in spherical coordinates** Find the moment of inertia about the z-axis of a solid of constant density $\delta = 1$ that is bounded above by the sphere $\rho = 2$ and below by the cone $\phi = \pi/3$ (spherical coordinates).

51. **Moment of inertia of a "thick" sphere** Find the moment of inertia of a solid of constant density δ bounded by two concentric spheres of radii a and b $(a < b)$ about a diameter.

52. **Moment of inertia of an apple** Find the moment of inertia about the z-axis of a solid of density $\delta = 1$ enclosed by the spherical coordinate surface $\rho = 1 - \cos\phi$. The solid is the red curve rotated about the z-axis in the accompanying figure.

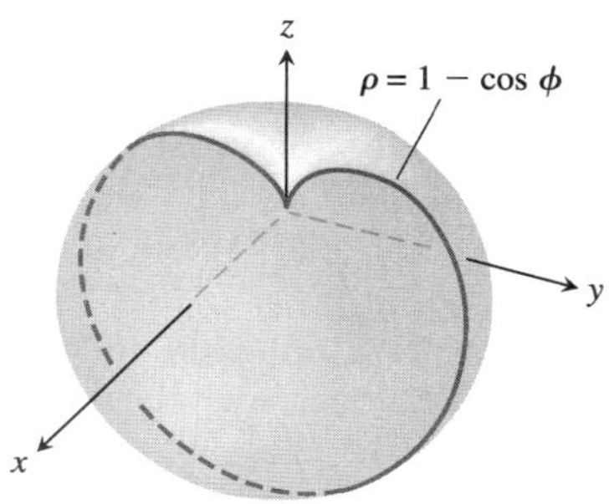

Substitutions

53. Show that if $u = x - y$ and $v = y$, then

$$\int_0^{\infty}\int_0^{x} e^{-sx} f(x - y, y)\, dy\, dx = \int_0^{\infty}\int_0^{\infty} e^{-s(u+v)} f(u, v)\, du\, dv.$$

54. What relationship must hold between the constants a, b, and c to make

$$\int_{-\infty}^{\infty}\int_{-\infty}^{\infty} e^{-(ax^2+2bxy+cy^2)}\, dx\, dy = 1?$$

(*Hint:* Let $s = \alpha x + \beta y$ and $t = \gamma x + \delta y$, where $(\alpha\delta - \beta\gamma)^2 = ac - b^2$. Then $ax^2 + 2bxy + cy^2 = s^2 + t^2$.)

Chapter 15 Additional and Advanced Exercises

Volumes

1. **Sand pile: double and triple integrals** The base of a sand pile covers the region in the xy-plane that is bounded by the parabola $x^2 + y = 6$ and the line $y = x$. The height of the sand above the point (x, y) is x^2. Express the volume of sand as **(a)** a double integral, **(b)** a triple integral. Then **(c)** find the volume.

2. **Water in a hemispherical bowl** A hemispherical bowl of radius 5 cm is filled with water to within 3 cm of the top. Find the volume of water in the bowl.

3. **Solid cylindrical region between two planes** Find the volume of the portion of the solid cylinder $x^2 + y^2 \le 1$ that lies between the planes $z = 0$ and $x + y + z = 2$.

4. **Sphere and paraboloid** Find the volume of the region bounded above by the sphere $x^2 + y^2 + z^2 = 2$ and below by the paraboloid $z = x^2 + y^2$.

5. **Two paraboloids** Find the volume of the region bounded above by the paraboloid $z = 3 - x^2 - y^2$ and below by the paraboloid $z = 2x^2 + 2y^2$.

6. **Spherical coordinates** Find the volume of the region enclosed by the spherical coordinate surface $\rho = 2\sin\phi$ (see accompanying figure).

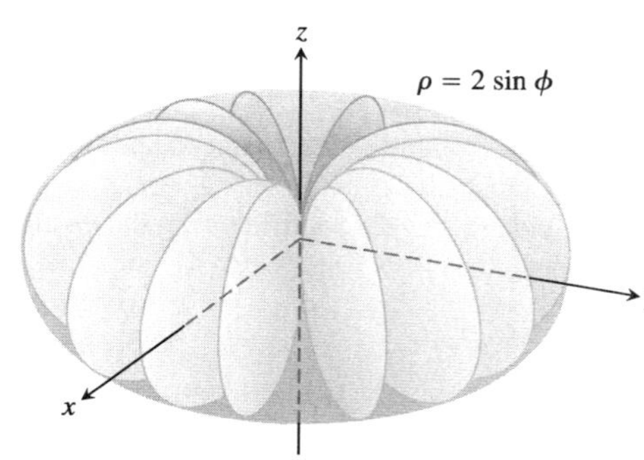

7. **Hole in sphere** A circular cylindrical hole is bored through a solid sphere, the axis of the hole being a diameter of the sphere. The volume of the remaining solid is

$$V = 2\int_0^{2\pi}\int_0^{\sqrt{3}}\int_1^{\sqrt{4-z^2}} r\, dr\, dz\, d\theta.$$

   a. Find the radius of the hole and the radius of the sphere.

   b. Evaluate the integral.

8. **Sphere and cylinder** Find the volume of material cut from the solid sphere $r^2 + z^2 \le 9$ by the cylinder $r = 3\sin\theta$.

9. Two paraboloids Find the volume of the region enclosed by the surfaces $z = x^2 + y^2$ and $z = (x^2 + y^2 + 1)/2$.

10. Cylinder and surface $z = xy$ Find the volume of the region in the first octant that lies between the cylinders $r = 1$ and $r = 2$ and that is bounded below by the xy-plane and above by the surface $z = xy$.

Changing the Order of Integration

11. Evaluate the integral

$$\int_0^{\infty} \frac{e^{-ax} - e^{-bx}}{x}\,dx.$$

(*Hint:* Use the relation

$$\frac{e^{-ax} - e^{-bx}}{x} = \int_a^b e^{-xy}\,dy$$

to form a double integral and evaluate the integral by changing the order of integration.)

12. a. Polar coordinates Show, by changing to polar coordinates, that

$$\int_0^{a \sin \beta} \int_{y \cot \beta}^{\sqrt{a^2 - y^2}} \ln (x^2 + y^2)\,dx\,dy = a^2\beta\left(\ln a - \frac{1}{2}\right),$$

where $a > 0$ and $0 < \beta < \pi/2$.

b. Rewrite the Cartesian integral with the order of integration reversed.

13. Reducing a double to a single integral By changing the order of integration, show that the following double integral can be reduced to a single integral:

$$\int_0^x \int_0^u e^{m(x-t)} f(t)\,dt\,du = \int_0^x (x - t)e^{m(x-t)} f(t)\,dt.$$

Similarly, it can be shown that

$$\int_0^x \int_0^v \int_0^u e^{m(x-t)} f(t)\,dt\,du\,dv = \int_0^x \frac{(x - t)^2}{2} e^{m(x-t)} f(t)\,dt.$$

14. Transforming a double integral to obtain constant limits Sometimes a multiple integral with variable limits can be changed into one with constant limits. By changing the order of integration, show that

$$\int_0^1 f(x)\left(\int_0^x g(x - y)f(y)\,dy\right)dx$$

$$= \int_0^1 f(y)\left(\int_y^1 g(x - y)f(x)\,dx\right)dy$$

$$= \frac{1}{2}\int_0^1 \int_0^1 g(|x - y|)f(x)f(y)\,dx\,dy.$$

Masses and Moments

15. Minimizing polar inertia A thin plate of constant density is to occupy the triangular region in the first quadrant of the xy-plane having vertices $(0, 0)$, $(a, 0)$, and $(a, 1/a)$. What value of a will minimize the plate's polar moment of inertia about the origin?

16. Polar inertia of triangular plate Find the polar moment of inertia about the origin of a thin triangular plate of constant density $\delta = 3$ bounded by the y-axis and the lines $y = 2x$ and $y = 4$ in the xy-plane.

17. Mass and polar inertia of a counterweight The counterweight of a flywheel of constant density 1 has the form of the smaller segment cut from a circle of radius a by a chord at a distance b from the center $(b < a)$. Find the mass of the counterweight and its polar moment of inertia about the center of the wheel.

18. Centroid of boomerang Find the centroid of the boomerang-shaped region between the parabolas $y^2 = -4(x - 1)$ and $y^2 = -2(x - 2)$ in the xy-plane.

Theory and Applications

19. Evaluate

$$\int_0^a \int_0^b e^{\max (b^2x^2,\, a^2y^2)}\,dy\,dx,$$

where a and b are positive numbers and

$$\max (b^2x^2, a^2y^2) = \begin{cases} b^2x^2 & \text{if } b^2x^2 \geq a^2y^2 \\ a^2y^2 & \text{if } b^2x^2 < a^2y^2. \end{cases}$$

20. Show that

$$\iint \frac{\partial^2 F(x, y)}{\partial x\,\partial y}\,dx\,dy$$

over the rectangle $x_0 \leq x \leq x_1$, $y_0 \leq y \leq y_1$, is

$$F(x_1, y_1) - F(x_0, y_1) - F(x_1, y_0) + F(x_0, y_0).$$

21. Suppose that $f(x, y)$ can be written as a product $f(x, y) = F(x)G(y)$ of a function of x and a function of y. Then the integral of f over the rectangle R: $a \leq x \leq b$, $c \leq y \leq d$ can be evaluated as a product as well, by the formula

$$\iint_R f(x, y)\,dA = \left(\int_a^b F(x)\,dx\right)\left(\int_c^d G(y)\,dy\right). \tag{1}$$

The argument is that

$$\iint_R f(x, y)\,dA = \int_c^d \left(\int_a^b F(x)G(y)\,dx\right)dy \tag{i}$$

$$= \int_c^d \left(G(y)\int_a^b F(x)\,dx\right)dy \tag{ii}$$

$$= \int_c^d \left(\int_a^b F(x)\,dx\right)G(y)\,dy \tag{iii}$$

$$= \left(\int_a^b F(x)\,dx\right)\int_c^d G(y)\,dy. \tag{iv}$$

a. Give reasons for steps (i) through (v).

When it applies, Equation (1) can be a time saver. Use it to evaluate the following integrals.

b. $\int_0^{\ln 2}\int_0^{\pi/2} e^x \cos y \, dy\, dx$ c. $\int_1^2\int_{-1}^1 \frac{x}{y^2}\, dx\, dy$

22. Let $D_{\mathbf{u}}f$ denote the derivative of $f(x, y) = (x^2 + y^2)/2$ in the direction of the unit vector $\mathbf{u} = u_1\mathbf{i} + u_2\mathbf{j}$.

a. **Finding average value** Find the average value of $D_{\mathbf{u}}f$ over the triangular region cut from the first quadrant by the line $x + y = 1$.

b. **Average value and centroid** Show in general that the average value of $D_{\mathbf{u}}f$ over a region in the xy-plane is the value of $D_{\mathbf{u}}f$ at the centroid of the region.

23. **The value of $\Gamma(1/2)$** The gamma function,

$$\Gamma(x) = \int_0^\infty t^{x-1}e^{-t}\, dt,$$

extends the factorial function from the nonnegative integers to other real values. Of particular interest in the theory of differential equations is the number

$$\Gamma\left(\frac{1}{2}\right) = \int_0^\infty t^{(1/2)-1}e^{-t}\, dt = \int_0^\infty \frac{e^{-t}}{\sqrt{t}}\, dt. \qquad (2)$$

a. If you have not yet done Exercise 37 in Section 15.3, do it now to show that

$$I = \int_0^\infty e^{-y^2}\, dy = \frac{\sqrt{\pi}}{2}.$$

b. Substitute $y = \sqrt{t}$ in Equation (2) to show that $\Gamma(1/2) = 2I = \sqrt{\pi}$.

24. **Total electrical charge over circular plate** The electrical charge distribution on a circular plate of radius R meters is $\sigma(r, \theta) = kr(1 - \sin\theta)$ coulomb/m^2 (k a constant). Integrate σ over the plate to find the total charge Q.

25. **A parabolic rain gauge** A bowl is in the shape of the graph of $z = x^2 + y^2$ from $z = 0$ to $z = 10$ in. You plan to calibrate the bowl to make it into a rain gauge. What height in the bowl would correspond to 1 in. of rain? 3 in. of rain?

26. **Water in a satellite dish** A parabolic satellite dish is 2 m wide and 1/2 m deep. Its axis of symmetry is tilted 30 degrees from the vertical.

a. Set up, but do not evaluate, a triple integral in rectangular coordinates that gives the amount of water the satellite dish will hold. (*Hint:* Put your coordinate system so that the satellite dish is in "standard position" and the plane of the water level is slanted.) (*Caution:* The limits of integration are not "nice.")

b. What would be the smallest tilt of the satellite dish so that it holds no water?

27. **An infinite half-cylinder** Let D be the interior of the infinite right circular half-cylinder of radius 1 with its single-end face suspended 1 unit above the origin and its axis the ray from (0, 0, 1) to ∞. Use cylindrical coordinates to evaluate

$$\iiint_D z(r^2 + z^2)^{-5/2}\, dV.$$

28. **Hypervolume** We have learned that $\int_a^b 1\, dx$ is the length of the interval $[a, b]$ on the number line (one-dimensional space), $\iint_R 1\, dA$ is the area of region R in the xy-plane (two-dimensional space), and $\iiint_D 1\, dV$ is the volume of the region D in three-dimensional space (xyz-space). We could continue: If Q is a region in 4-space ($xyzw$-space), then $\iiiint_Q 1\, dV$ is the "hypervolume" of Q. Use your generalizing abilities and a Cartesian coordinate system of 4-space to find the hypervolume inside the unit 3-dimensional sphere $x^2 + y^2 + z^2 + w^2 = 1$.

Chapter 15 Technology Application Projects

Mathematica/Maple Module

Take Your Chances: Try the Monte Carlo Technique for Numerical Integration in Three Dimensions

Use the Monte Carlo technique to integrate numerically in three dimensions.

Mathematica/Maple Module

Means and Moments and Exploring New Plotting Techniques, Part II.

Use the method of moments in a form that makes use of geometric symmetry as well as multiple integration.

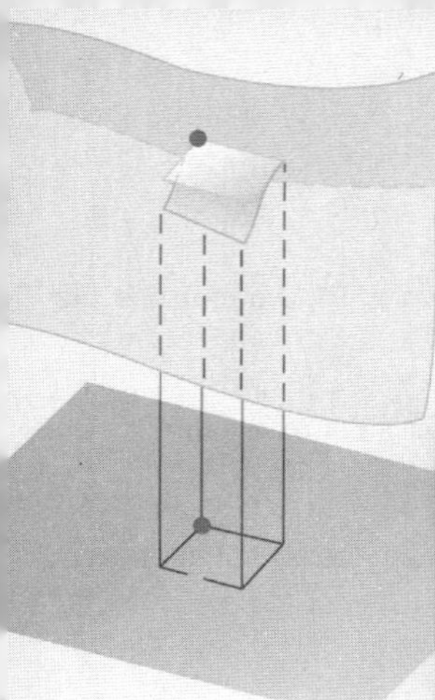

Chapter 16 INTEGRATION IN VECTOR FIELDS

OVERVIEW This chapter treats integration in vector fields. It is the mathematics that engineers and physicists use to describe fluid flow, design underwater transmission cables, explain the flow of heat in stars, and put satellites in orbit. In particular, we define line integrals, which are used to find the work done by a force field in moving an object along a path through the field. We also define surface integrals so we can find the rate that a fluid flows across a surface. Along the way we develop key concepts and results, such as *conservative* force fields and Green's Theorem, to simplify our calculations of these new integrals by connecting them to the single, double, and triple integrals we have already studied.

16.1 Line Integrals

In Chapter 5 we defined the definite integral of a function over a finite closed interval $[a, b]$ on the x-axis. We used definite integrals to find the mass of a thin straight rod, or the work done by a variable force directed along the x-axis. Now we would like to calculate the masses of thin rods or wires lying along a *curve* in the plane or space, or to find the work done by a variable force acting along such a curve. For these calculations we need a more general notion of a "line" integral than integrating over a line segment on the x-axis. Instead we need to integrate over a curve C in the plane or in space. These more general integrals are called *line integrals*, although "curve" integrals might be more descriptive. We make our definitions for space curves, remembering that curves in the xy-plane are just a special case with z-coordinate identically zero.

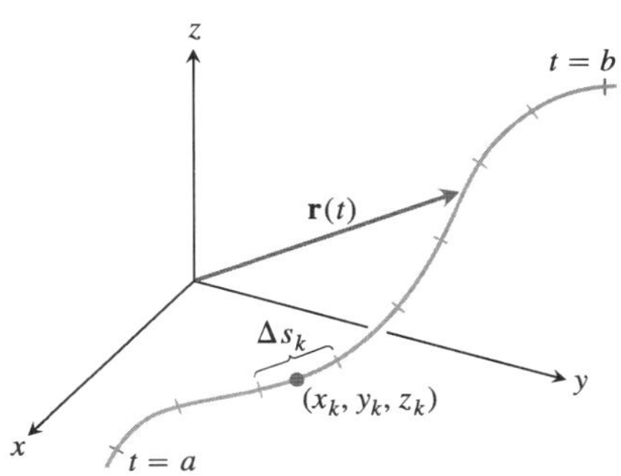

FIGURE 16.1 The curve $\mathbf{r}(t)$ partitioned into small arcs from $t = a$ to $t = b$. The length of a typical subarc is Δs_k.

Suppose that $f(x, y, z)$ is a real-valued function we wish to integrate over the curve $\mathbf{r}(t) = g(t)\mathbf{i} + h(t)\mathbf{j} + k(t)\mathbf{k}$, $a \le t \le b$, lying within the domain of f. The values of f along the curve are given by the composite function $f(g(t), h(t), k(t))$. We are going to integrate this composite with respect to arc length from $t = a$ to $t = b$. To begin, we first partition the curve into a finite number n of subarcs (Figure 16.1). The typical subarc has length Δs_k. In each subarc we choose a point (x_k, y_k, z_k) and form the sum

$$S_n = \sum_{k=1}^{n} f(x_k, y_k, z_k)\, \Delta s_k.$$

If f is continuous and the functions g, h, and k have continuous first derivatives, then these sums approach a limit as n increases and the lengths Δs_k approach zero. We call this limit the **line integral of f over the curve from a to b**. If the curve is denoted by a single letter, C for example, the notation for the integral is

$$\int_C f(x, y, z)\, ds \qquad \text{"The integral of } f \text{ over } C\text{"} \tag{1}$$

If $\mathbf{r}(t)$ is smooth for $a \le t \le b$ ($\mathbf{v} = d\mathbf{r}/dt$ is continuous and never $\mathbf{0}$), we can use the equation

$$s(t) = \int_a^t |\mathbf{v}(\tau)|\, d\tau \qquad \text{Equation (3) of Section 13.3 with } t_0 = a$$

to express ds in Equation (1) as $ds = |\mathbf{v}(t)|\, dt$. A theorem from advanced calculus says that we can then evaluate the integral of f over C as

$$\int_C f(x, y, z)\, ds = \int_a^b f(g(t), h(t), k(t))|\mathbf{v}(t)|\, dt.$$

Notice that the integral on the right side of this last equation is just an ordinary (single) definite integral, as defined in Chapter 5, where we are integrating with respect to the parameter t. The formula evaluates the line integral on the left side correctly no matter what parametrization is used, as long as the parametrization is smooth.

How to Evaluate a Line Integral

To integrate a continuous function $f(x, y, z)$ over a curve C:

1. Find a smooth parametrization of C,

$$\mathbf{r}(t) = g(t)\mathbf{i} + h(t)\mathbf{j} + k(t)\mathbf{k}, \qquad a \le t \le b$$

2. Evaluate the integral as

$$\int_C f(x, y, z)\, ds = \int_a^b f(g(t), h(t), k(t))|\mathbf{v}(t)|\, dt. \tag{2}$$

If f has the constant value 1, then the integral of f over C gives the length of C.

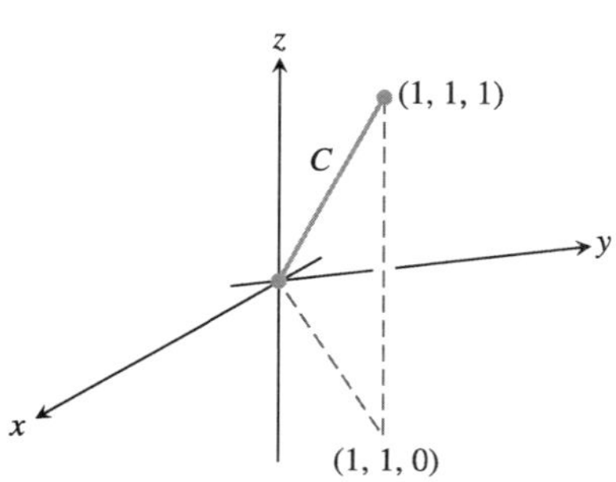

FIGURE 16.2 The integration path in Example 1.

EXAMPLE 1 Evaluating a Line Integral

Integrate $f(x, y, z) = x - 3y^2 + z$ over the line segment C joining the origin to the point $(1, 1, 1)$ (Figure 16.2).

Solution We choose the simplest parametrization we can think of:

$$\mathbf{r}(t) = t\mathbf{i} + t\mathbf{j} + t\mathbf{k}, \qquad 0 \le t \le 1.$$

The components have continuous first derivatives and $|\mathbf{v}(t)| = |\mathbf{i} + \mathbf{j} + \mathbf{k}| = \sqrt{1^2 + 1^2 + 1^2} = \sqrt{3}$ is never 0, so the parametrization is smooth. The integral of f over C is

$$\begin{aligned}\int_C f(x, y, z)\, ds &= \int_0^1 f(t, t, t)\left(\sqrt{3}\right) dt \qquad \text{Equation (2)}\\ &= \int_0^1 (t - 3t^2 + t)\sqrt{3}\, dt\\ &= \sqrt{3}\int_0^1 (2t - 3t^2)\, dt = \sqrt{3}\left[t^2 - t^3\right]_0^1 = 0.\end{aligned}$$

■

Additivity

Line integrals have the useful property that if a curve C is made by joining a finite number of curves $C_1, C_2, \dots, C_n$ end to end, then the integral of a function over C is the sum of the integrals over the curves that make it up:

$$\int_C f\,ds = \int_{C_1} f\,ds + \int_{C_2} f\,ds + \cdots + \int_{C_n} f\,ds. \tag{3}$$

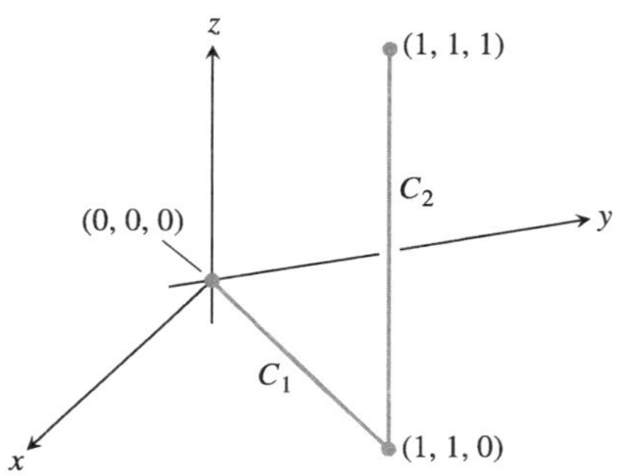

FIGURE 16.3 The path of integration in Example 2.

EXAMPLE 2 Line Integral for Two Joined Paths

Figure 16.3 shows another path from the origin to (1, 1, 1), the union of line segments C_1 and C_2. Integrate $f(x, y, z) = x - 3y^2 + z$ over $C_1 \cup C_2$.

Solution We choose the simplest parametrizations for C_1 and C_2 we can think of, checking the lengths of the velocity vectors as we go along:

$$C_1:\quad \mathbf{r}(t) = t\mathbf{i} + t\mathbf{j},\quad 0 \le t \le 1;\quad |\mathbf{v}| = \sqrt{1^2 + 1^2} = \sqrt{2}$$

$$C_2:\quad \mathbf{r}(t) = \mathbf{i} + \mathbf{j} + t\mathbf{k},\quad 0 \le t \le 1;\quad |\mathbf{v}| = \sqrt{0^2 + 0^2 + 1^2} = 1.$$

With these parametrizations we find that

$$\begin{aligned}
\int_{C_1 \cup C_2} f(x, y, z)\,ds &= \int_{C_1} f(x, y, z)\,ds + \int_{C_2} f(x, y, z)\,ds && \text{Equation (3)}\\
&= \int_0^1 f(t, t, 0)\sqrt{2}\,dt + \int_0^1 f(1, 1, t)(1)\,dt && \text{Equation (2)}\\
&= \int_0^1 (t - 3t^2 + 0)\sqrt{2}\,dt + \int_0^1 (1 - 3 + t)(1)\,dt\\
&= \sqrt{2}\left[\frac{t^2}{2} - t^3\right]_0^1 + \left[\frac{t^2}{2} - 2t\right]_0^1 = -\frac{\sqrt{2}}{2} - \frac{3}{2}.
\end{aligned}$$

■

Notice three things about the integrations in Examples 1 and 2. First, as soon as the components of the appropriate curve were substituted into the formula for f, the integration became a standard integration with respect to t. Second, the integral of f over $C_1 \cup C_2$ was obtained by integrating f over each section of the path and adding the results. Third, the integrals of f over C and $C_1 \cup C_2$ had different values. For most functions, the value of the integral along a path joining two points changes if you change the path between them. For some functions, however, the value remains the same.

Mass and Moment Calculations

We treat coil springs and wires like masses distributed along smooth curves in space. The distribution is described by a continuous density function $\delta(x, y, z)$ (mass per unit length). The spring's or wire's mass, center of mass, and moments are then calculated with the formulas in Table 16.1. The formulas also apply to thin rods.

TABLE 16.1 Mass and moment formulas for coil springs, thin rods, and wires lying along a smooth curve C in space

Mass: $M = \int_C \delta(x, y, z)\, ds \qquad (\delta = \delta(x, y, z) = \text{density})$

First moments about the coordinate planes:

$$M_{yz} = \int_C x\,\delta\, ds, \qquad M_{xz} = \int_C y\,\delta\, ds, \qquad M_{xy} = \int_C z\,\delta\, ds$$

Coordinates of the center of mass:

$$\bar{x} = M_{yz}/M, \qquad \bar{y} = M_{xz}/M, \qquad \bar{z} = M_{xy}/M$$

Moments of inertia about axes and other lines:

$$I_x = \int_C (y^2 + z^2)\,\delta\, ds, \qquad I_y = \int_C (x^2 + z^2)\,\delta\, ds$$

$$I_z = \int_C (x^2 + y^2)\,\delta\, ds, \qquad I_L = \int_C r^2\,\delta\, ds$$

$$r(x, y, z) = \text{distance from the point } (x, y, z) \text{ to line } L$$

Radius of gyration about a line L: $R_L = \sqrt{I_L/M}$

EXAMPLE 3 Finding Mass, Center of Mass, Moment of Inertia, Radius of Gyration

A coil spring lies along the helix

$$\mathbf{r}(t) = (\cos 4t)\mathbf{i} + (\sin 4t)\mathbf{j} + t\mathbf{k}, \qquad 0 \le t \le 2\pi.$$

The spring's density is a constant, $\delta = 1$. Find the spring's mass and center of mass, and its moment of inertia and radius of gyration about the z-axis.

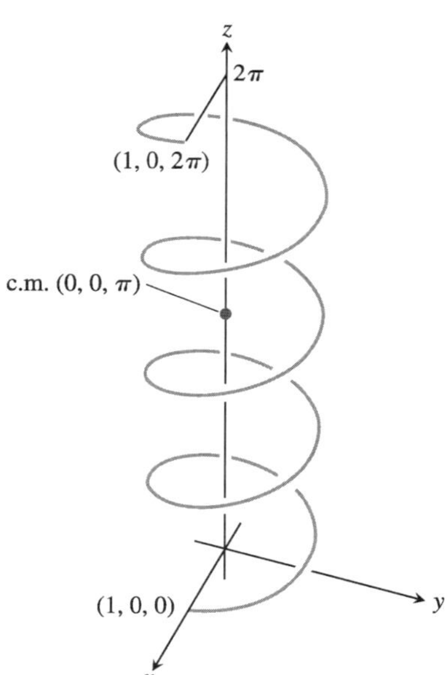

FIGURE 16.4 The helical spring in Example 3.

Solution We sketch the spring (Figure 16.4). Because of the symmetries involved, the center of mass lies at the point $(0, 0, \pi)$ on the z-axis.

For the remaining calculations, we first find $|\mathbf{v}(t)|$:

$$|\mathbf{v}(t)| = \sqrt{\left(\frac{dx}{dt}\right)^2 + \left(\frac{dy}{dt}\right)^2 + \left(\frac{dz}{dt}\right)^2}$$

$$= \sqrt{(-4\sin 4t)^2 + (4\cos 4t)^2 + 1} = \sqrt{17}.$$

We then evaluate the formulas from Table 16.1 using Equation (2):

$$M = \int_{\text{Helix}} \delta\, ds = \int_0^{2\pi} (1)\sqrt{17}\, dt = 2\pi\sqrt{17}$$

$$I_z = \int_{\text{Helix}} (x^2 + y^2)\delta\, ds = \int_0^{2\pi} (\cos^2 4t + \sin^2 4t)(1)\sqrt{17}\, dt$$

$$= \int_0^{2\pi} \sqrt{17}\, dt = 2\pi\sqrt{17}$$

$$R_z = \sqrt{I_z/M} = \sqrt{2\pi\sqrt{17}/(2\pi\sqrt{17})} = 1.$$

Notice that the radius of gyration about the z-axis is the radius of the cylinder around which the helix winds. ■

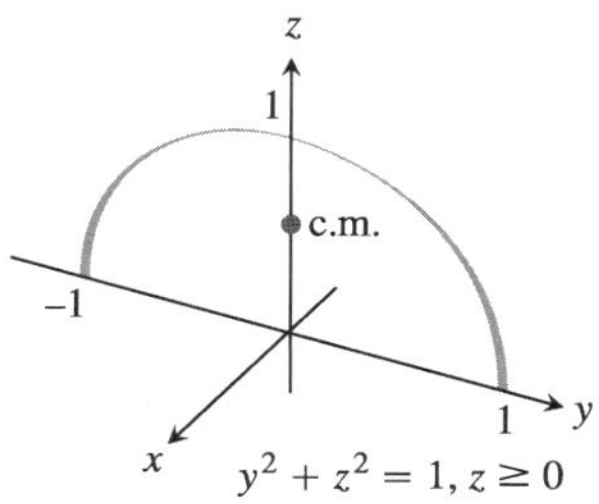

FIGURE 16.5 Example 4 shows how to find the center of mass of a circular arch of variable density.

EXAMPLE 4 Finding an Arch's Center of Mass

A slender metal arch, denser at the bottom than top, lies along the semicircle $y^2 + z^2 = 1, z \geq 0$, in the yz-plane (Figure 16.5). Find the center of the arch's mass if the density at the point (x, y, z) on the arch is $\delta(x, y, z) = 2 - z$.

Solution We know that $\bar{x} = 0$ and $\bar{y} = 0$ because the arch lies in the yz-plane with its mass distributed symmetrically about the z-axis. To find $\bar{z}$, we parametrize the circle as

$$\mathbf{r}(t) = (\cos t)\mathbf{j} + (\sin t)\mathbf{k}, \qquad 0 \leq t \leq \pi.$$

For this parametrization,

$$|\mathbf{v}(t)| = \sqrt{\left(\frac{dx}{dt}\right)^2 + \left(\frac{dy}{dt}\right)^2 + \left(\frac{dz}{dt}\right)^2} = \sqrt{(0)^2 + (-\sin t)^2 + (\cos t)^2} = 1.$$

The formulas in Table 16.1 then give

$$M = \int_C \delta\, ds = \int_C (2 - z)\, ds = \int_0^{\pi} (2 - \sin t)(1)\, dt = 2\pi - 2$$

$$M_{xy} = \int_C z\delta\, ds = \int_C z(2 - z)\, ds = \int_0^{\pi} (\sin t)(2 - \sin t)\, dt$$

$$= \int_0^{\pi} (2 \sin t - \sin^2 t)\, dt = \frac{8 - \pi}{2}$$

$$\bar{z} = \frac{M_{xy}}{M} = \frac{8 - \pi}{2} \cdot \frac{1}{2\pi - 2} = \frac{8 - \pi}{4\pi - 4} \approx 0.57.$$

With $\bar{z}$ to the nearest hundredth, the center of mass is $(0, 0, 0.57)$. ■

EXERCISES 16.1

Graphs of Vector Equations

Match the vector equations in Exercises 1–8 with the graphs (a)–(h) given here.

a.

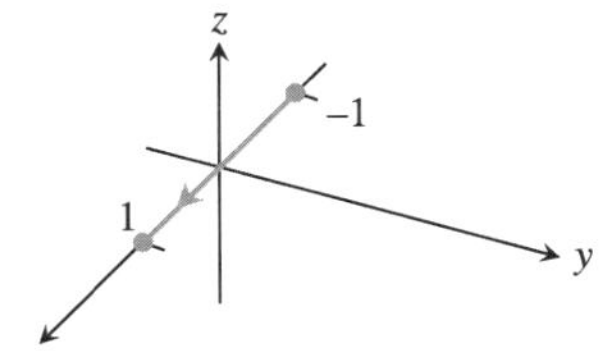

b.

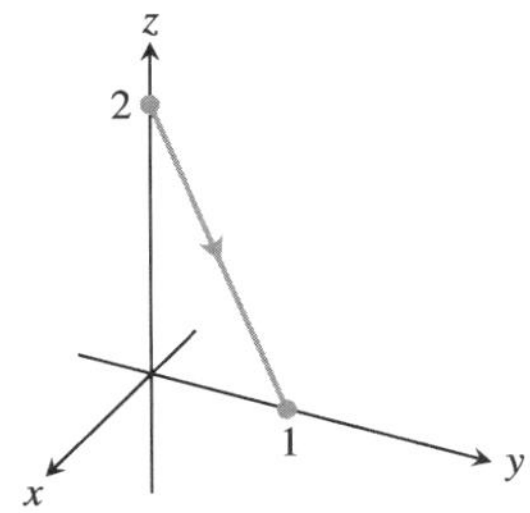

c.

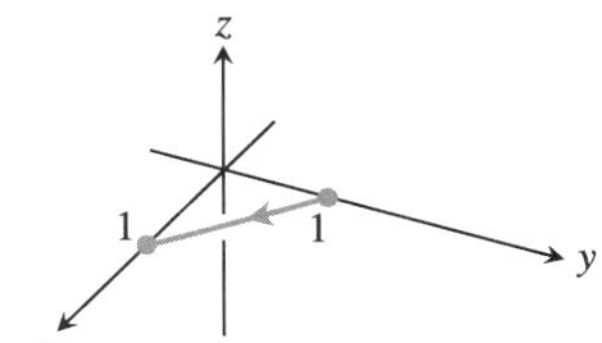

d.

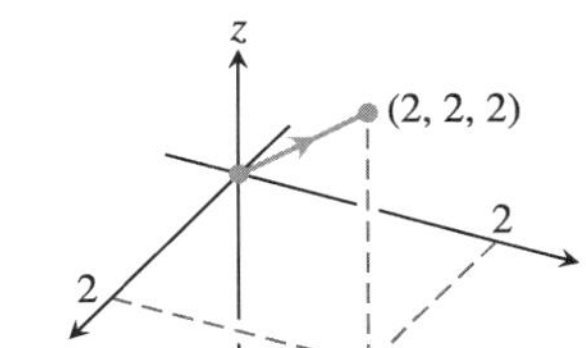

e.

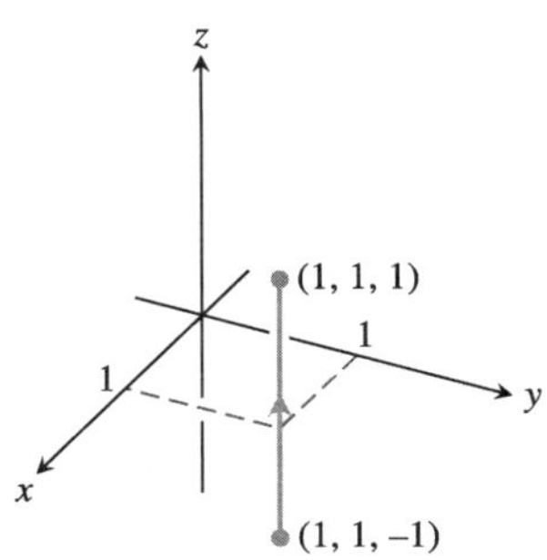

f.

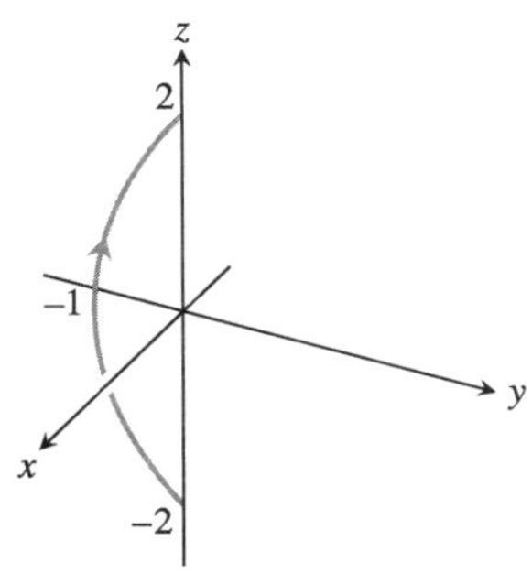

g.

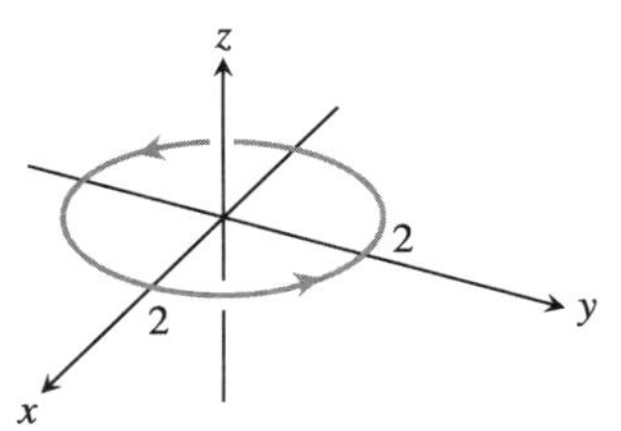

h.

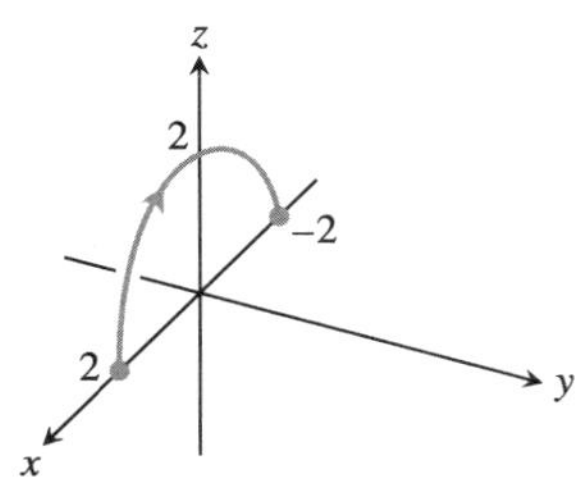

1. $\mathbf{r}(t) = t\mathbf{i} + (1 - t)\mathbf{j}, \quad 0 \le t \le 1$
2. $\mathbf{r}(t) = \mathbf{i} + \mathbf{j} + t\mathbf{k}, \quad -1 \le t \le 1$
3. $\mathbf{r}(t) = (2\cos t)\mathbf{i} + (2\sin t)\mathbf{j}, \quad 0 \le t \le 2\pi$
4. $\mathbf{r}(t) = t\mathbf{i}, \quad -1 \le t \le 1$
5. $\mathbf{r}(t) = t\mathbf{i} + t\mathbf{j} + t\mathbf{k}, \quad 0 \le t \le 2$
6. $\mathbf{r}(t) = t\mathbf{j} + (2 - 2t)\mathbf{k}, \quad 0 \le t \le 1$
7. $\mathbf{r}(t) = (t^2 - 1)\mathbf{j} + 2t\mathbf{k}, \quad -1 \le t \le 1$
8. $\mathbf{r}(t) = (2\cos t)\mathbf{i} + (2\sin t)\mathbf{k}, \quad 0 \le t \le \pi$

Evaluating Line Integrals over Space Curves

9. Evaluate $\int_C (x + y)\,ds$ where C is the straight-line segment $x = t, y = (1 - t), z = 0$, from $(0, 1, 0)$ to $(1, 0, 0)$.
10. Evaluate $\int_C (x - y + z - 2)\,ds$ where C is the straight-line segment $x = t, y = (1 - t), z = 1$, from $(0, 1, 1)$ to $(1, 0, 1)$.
11. Evaluate $\int_C (xy + y + z)\,ds$ along the curve $\mathbf{r}(t) = 2t\mathbf{i} + t\mathbf{j} + (2 - 2t)\mathbf{k}, 0 \le t \le 1$.
12. Evaluate $\int_C \sqrt{x^2 + y^2}\,ds$ along the curve $\mathbf{r}(t) = (4\cos t)\mathbf{i} + (4\sin t)\mathbf{j} + 3t\mathbf{k}, -2\pi \le t \le 2\pi$.
13. Find the line integral of $f(x, y, z) = x + y + z$ over the straight-line segment from $(1, 2, 3)$ to $(0, -1, 1)$.
14. Find the line integral of $f(x, y, z) = \sqrt{3}/(x^2 + y^2 + z^2)$ over the curve $\mathbf{r}(t) = t\mathbf{i} + t\mathbf{j} + t\mathbf{k}, 1 \le t \le \infty$.
15. Integrate $f(x, y, z) = x + \sqrt{y} - z^2$ over the path from $(0, 0, 0)$ to $(1, 1, 1)$ (Figure 16.6a) given by

$$C_1: \quad \mathbf{r}(t) = t\mathbf{i} + t^2\mathbf{j}, \quad 0 \le t \le 1$$
$$C_2: \quad \mathbf{r}(t) = \mathbf{i} + \mathbf{j} + t\mathbf{k}, \quad 0 \le t \le 1$$

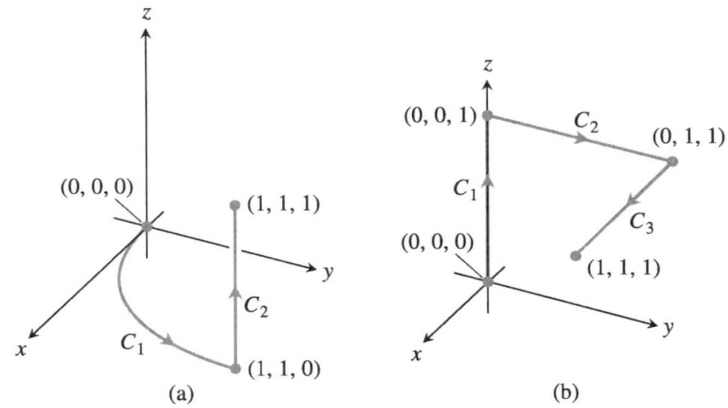

FIGURE 16.6 The paths of integration for Exercises 15 and 16.

16. Integrate $f(x, y, z) = x + \sqrt{y} - z^2$ over the path from $(0, 0, 0)$ to $(1, 1, 1)$ (Figure 16.6b) given by

$$C_1: \quad \mathbf{r}(t) = t\mathbf{k}, \quad 0 \le t \le 1$$
$$C_2: \quad \mathbf{r}(t) = t\mathbf{j} + \mathbf{k}, \quad 0 \le t \le 1$$
$$C_3: \quad \mathbf{r}(t) = t\mathbf{i} + \mathbf{j} + \mathbf{k}, \quad 0 \le t \le 1$$

17. Integrate $f(x, y, z) = (x + y + z)/(x^2 + y^2 + z^2)$ over the path $\mathbf{r}(t) = t\mathbf{i} + t\mathbf{j} + t\mathbf{k}, 0 < a \le t \le b$.
18. Integrate $f(x, y, z) = -\sqrt{x^2 + z^2}$ over the circle

$$\mathbf{r}(t) = (a\cos t)\mathbf{j} + (a\sin t)\mathbf{k}, \quad 0 \le t \le 2\pi.$$

Line Integrals over Plane Curves

In Exercises 19–22, integrate f over the given curve.

19. $f(x, y) = x^3/y, \quad C: \quad y = x^2/2, \quad 0 \le x \le 2$
20. $f(x, y) = (x + y^2)/\sqrt{1 + x^2}, \quad C: \quad y = x^2/2$ from $(1, 1/2)$ to $(0, 0)$
21. $f(x, y) = x + y, \quad C: \quad x^2 + y^2 = 4$ in the first quadrant from $(2, 0)$ to $(0, 2)$
22. $f(x, y) = x^2 - y, \quad C: \quad x^2 + y^2 = 4$ in the first quadrant from $(0, 2)$ to $(\sqrt{2}, \sqrt{2})$

Mass and Moments

23. **Mass of a wire** Find the mass of a wire that lies along the curve $\mathbf{r}(t) = (t^2 - 1)\mathbf{j} + 2t\mathbf{k}, 0 \le t \le 1$, if the density is $\delta = (3/2)t$.
24. **Center of mass of a curved wire** A wire of density $\delta(x, y, z) = 15\sqrt{y + 2}$ lies along the curve $\mathbf{r}(t) = (t^2 - 1)\mathbf{j} + 2t\mathbf{k}, -1 \le t \le 1$. Find its center of mass. Then sketch the curve and center of mass together.
25. **Mass of wire with variable density** Find the mass of a thin wire lying along the curve $\mathbf{r}(t) = \sqrt{2}t\mathbf{i} + \sqrt{2}t\mathbf{j} + (4 - t^2)\mathbf{k}, 0 \le t \le 1$, if the density is **(a)** $\delta = 3t$ and **(b)** $\delta = 1$.

26. Center of mass of wire with variable density Find the center of mass of a thin wire lying along the curve $\mathbf{r}(t) = t\mathbf{i} + 2t\mathbf{j} + (2/3)t^{3/2}\mathbf{k}$, $0 \le t \le 2$, if the density is $\delta = 3\sqrt{5 + t}$.

27. Moment of inertia and radius of gyration of wire hoop A circular wire hoop of constant density δ lies along the circle $x^2 + y^2 = a^2$ in the xy-plane. Find the hoop's moment of inertia and radius of gyration about the z-axis.

28. Inertia and radii of gyration of slender rod A slender rod of constant density lies along the line segment $\mathbf{r}(t) = t\mathbf{j} + (2 - 2t)\mathbf{k}$, $0 \le t \le 1$, in the yz-plane. Find the moments of inertia and radii of gyration of the rod about the three coordinate axes.

29. Two springs of constant density A spring of constant density δ lies along the helix

$$\mathbf{r}(t) = (\cos t)\mathbf{i} + (\sin t)\mathbf{j} + t\mathbf{k}, \qquad 0 \le t \le 2\pi.$$

a. Find I_z and R_z.

b. Suppose that you have another spring of constant density δ that is twice as long as the spring in part (a) and lies along the helix for $0 \le t \le 4\pi$. Do you expect I_z and R_z for the longer spring to be the same as those for the shorter one, or should they be different? Check your predictions by calculating I_z and R_z for the longer spring.

30. Wire of constant density A wire of constant density $\delta = 1$ lies along the curve

$$\mathbf{r}(t) = (t\cos t)\mathbf{i} + (t\sin t)\mathbf{j} + \left(2\sqrt{2}/3\right)t^{3/2}\mathbf{k}, \qquad 0 \le t \le 1.$$

Find $\bar{z}$, I_z, and R_z.

31. The arch in Example 4 Find I_x and R_x for the arch in Example 4.

32. Center of mass, moments of inertia, and radii of gyration for wire with variable density Find the center of mass, and the moments of inertia and radii of gyration about the coordinate axes of a thin wire lying along the curve

$$\mathbf{r}(t) = t\mathbf{i} + \frac{2\sqrt{2}}{3}t^{3/2}\mathbf{j} + \frac{t^2}{2}\mathbf{k}, \qquad 0 \le t \le 2,$$

if the density is $\delta = 1/(t + 1)$

COMPUTER EXPLORATIONS

Evaluating Line Integrals Numerically

In Exercises 33–36, use a CAS to perform the following steps to evaluate the line integrals.

a. Find $ds = |\mathbf{v}(t)|\,dt$ for the path $\mathbf{r}(t) = g(t)\mathbf{i} + h(t)\mathbf{j} + k(t)\mathbf{k}$.

b. Express the integrand $f(g(t), h(t), k(t))|\mathbf{v}(t)|$ as a function of the parameter t.

c. Evaluate $\int_C f\,ds$ using Equation (2) in the text.

33. $f(x, y, z) = \sqrt{1 + 30x^2 + 10y}$; $\mathbf{r}(t) = t\mathbf{i} + t^2\mathbf{j} + 3t^2\mathbf{k}$, $0 \le t \le 2$

34. $f(x, y, z) = \sqrt{1 + x^3 + 5y^3}$; $\mathbf{r}(t) = t\mathbf{i} + \frac{1}{3}t^2\mathbf{j} + \sqrt{t}\mathbf{k}$, $0 \le t \le 2$

35. $f(x, y, z) = x\sqrt{y} - 3z^2$; $\mathbf{r}(t) = (\cos 2t)\mathbf{i} + (\sin 2t)\mathbf{j} + 5t\mathbf{k}$, $0 \le t \le 2\pi$

36. $f(x, y, z) = \left(1 + \frac{9}{4}z^{1/3}\right)^{1/4}$; $\mathbf{r}(t) = (\cos 2t)\mathbf{i} + (\sin 2t)\mathbf{j} + t^{5/2}\mathbf{k}$, $0 \le t \le 2\pi$

16.2 Vector Fields, Work, Circulation, and Flux

When we study physical phenomena that are represented by vectors, we replace integrals over closed intervals by integrals over paths through vector fields. We use such integrals to find the work done in moving an object along a path against a variable force (such as a vehicle sent into space against Earth's gravitational field) or to find the work done by a vector field in moving an object along a path through the field (such as the work done by an accelerator in raising the energy of a particle). We also use line integrals to find the rates at which fluids flow along and across curves.

Vector Fields

Suppose a region in the plane or in space is occupied by a moving fluid such as air or water. Imagine that the fluid is made up of a very large number of particles, and that at any instant of time a particle has a velocity $\mathbf{v}$. If we take a picture of the velocities of some particles at

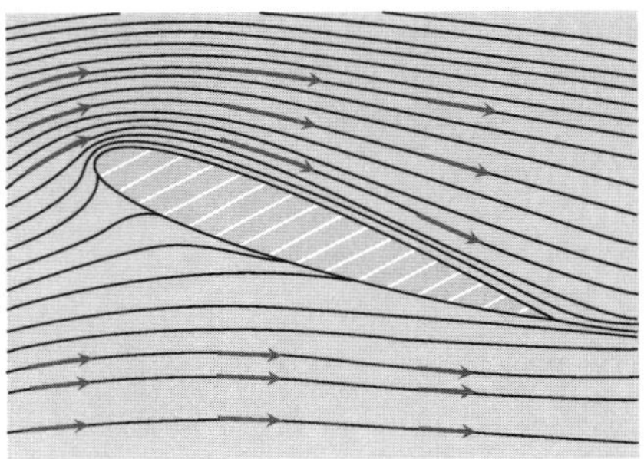

FIGURE 16.7 Velocity vectors of a flow around an airfoil in a wind tunnel. The streamlines were made visible by kerosene smoke.

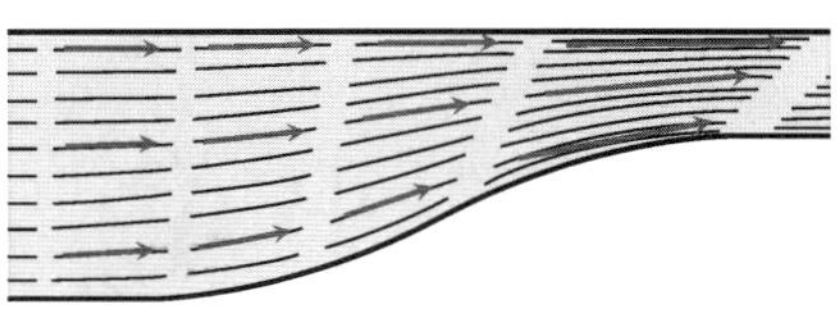

FIGURE 16.8 Streamlines in a contracting channel. The water speeds up as the channel narrows and the velocity vectors increase in length.

different position points at the same instant, we would expect to find that these velocities vary from position to position. We can think of a velocity vector as being attached to each point of the fluid. Such a fluid flow exemplifies a *vector field*. For example, Figure 16.7 shows a velocity vector field obtained by attaching a velocity vector to each point of air flowing around an airfoil in a wind tunnel. Figure 16.8 shows another vector field of velocity vectors along the streamlines of water moving through a contracting channel. In addition to vector fields associated with fluid flows, there are vector force fields that are associated with gravitational attraction (Figure 16.9), magnetic force fields, electric fields, and even purely mathematical fields.

Generally, a **vector field** on a domain in the plane or in space is a function that assigns a vector to each point in the domain. A field of three-dimensional vectors might have a formula like

$$\mathbf{F}(x, y, z)=M(x, y, z)\mathbf{i}+N(x, y, z)\mathbf{j}+P(x, y, z)\mathbf{k}.$$

The field is **continuous** if the **component functions** M, N, and P are continuous, **differentiable** if M, N, and P are differentiable, and so on. A field of two-dimensional vectors might have a formula like

$$\mathbf{F}(x, y)=M(x, y)\mathbf{i}+N(x, y)\mathbf{j}.$$

If we attach a projectile's velocity vector to each point of the projectile's trajectory in the plane of motion, we have a two-dimensional field defined along the trajectory. If we attach the gradient vector of a scalar function to each point of a level surface of the function, we have a three-dimensional field on the surface. If we attach the velocity vector to each point of a flowing fluid, we have a three-dimensional field defined on a region in space. These and other fields are illustrated in Figures 16.10–16.15. Some of the illustrations give formulas for the fields as well.

To sketch the fields that had formulas, we picked a representative selection of domain points and sketched the vectors attached to them. The arrows representing the vectors are drawn with their tails, not their heads, at the points where the vector functions are

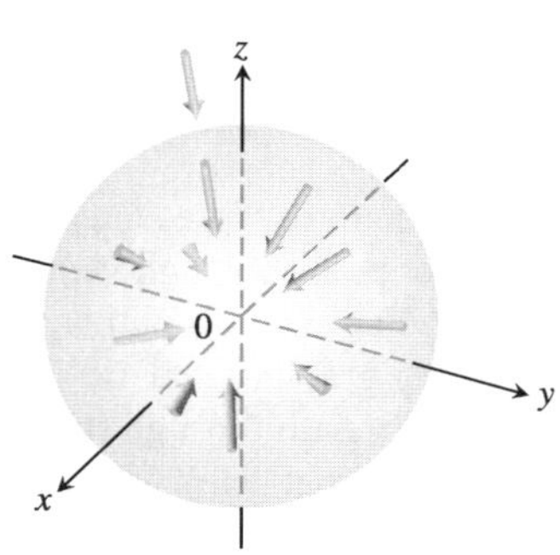

FIGURE 16.9 Vectors in a gravitational field point toward the center of mass that gives the source of the field.

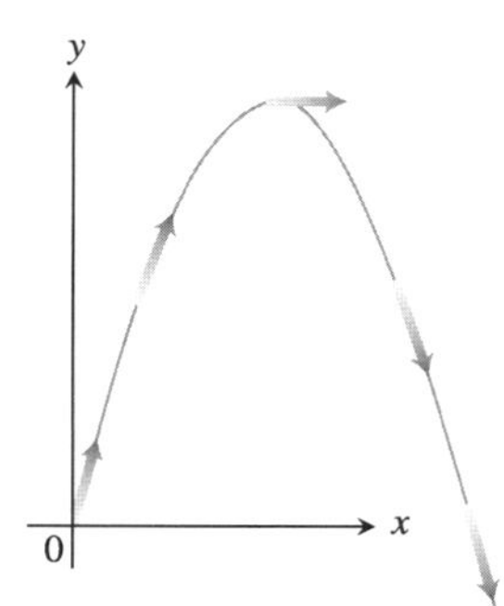

FIGURE 16.10 The velocity vectors $\mathbf{v}(t)$ of a projectile's motion make a vector field along the trajectory.

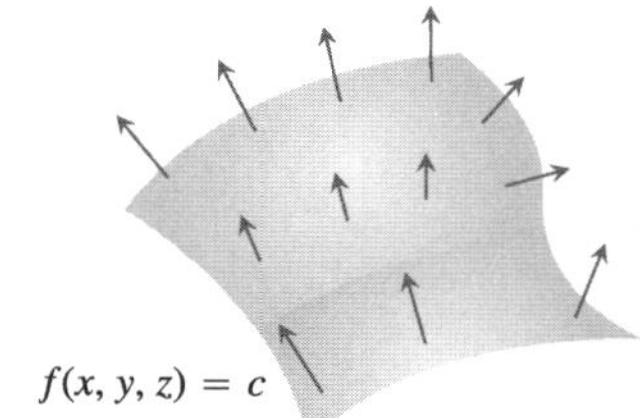

FIGURE 16.11 The field of gradient vectors ∇f on a surface $f(x, y, z)=c$.

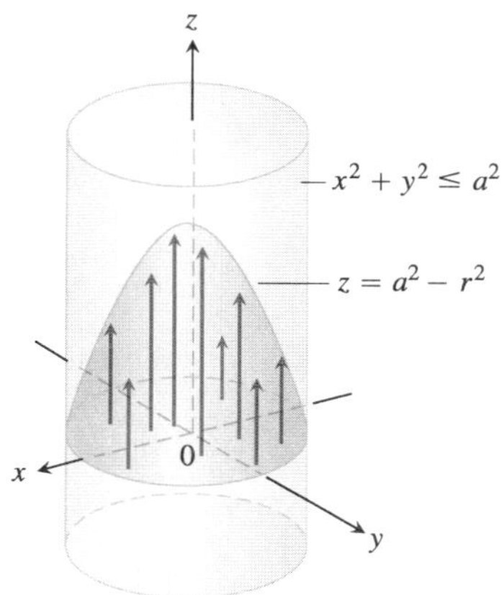

FIGURE 16.12 The flow of fluid in a long cylindrical pipe. The vectors $\mathbf{v} = (a^2 - r^2)\mathbf{k}$ inside the cylinder that have their bases in the xy-plane have their tips on the paraboloid $z = a^2 - r^2$.

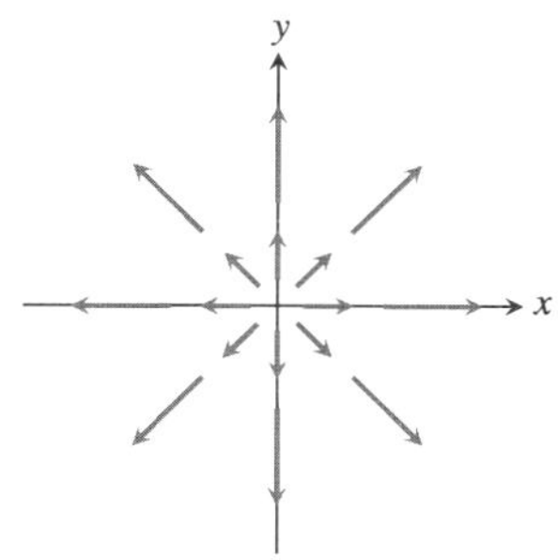

FIGURE 16.13 The radial field $\mathbf{F} = x\mathbf{i} + y\mathbf{j}$ of position vectors of points in the plane. Notice the convention that an arrow is drawn with its tail, not its head, at the point where $\mathbf{F}$ is evaluated.

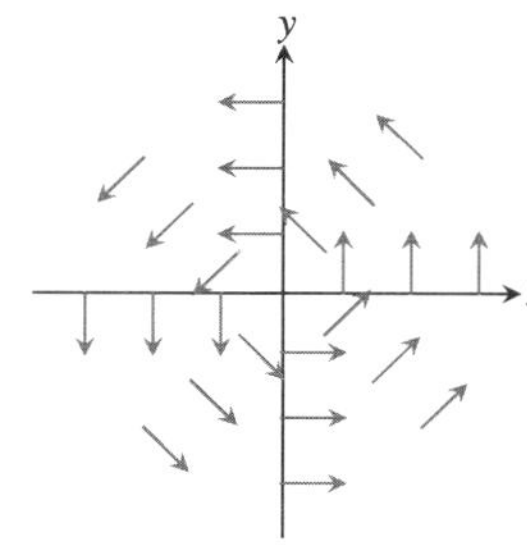

FIGURE 16.14 The circumferential or "spin" field of unit vectors

$$\mathbf{F} = (-y\mathbf{i} + x\mathbf{j})/(x^2 + y^2)^{1/2}$$

in the plane. The field is not defined at the origin.

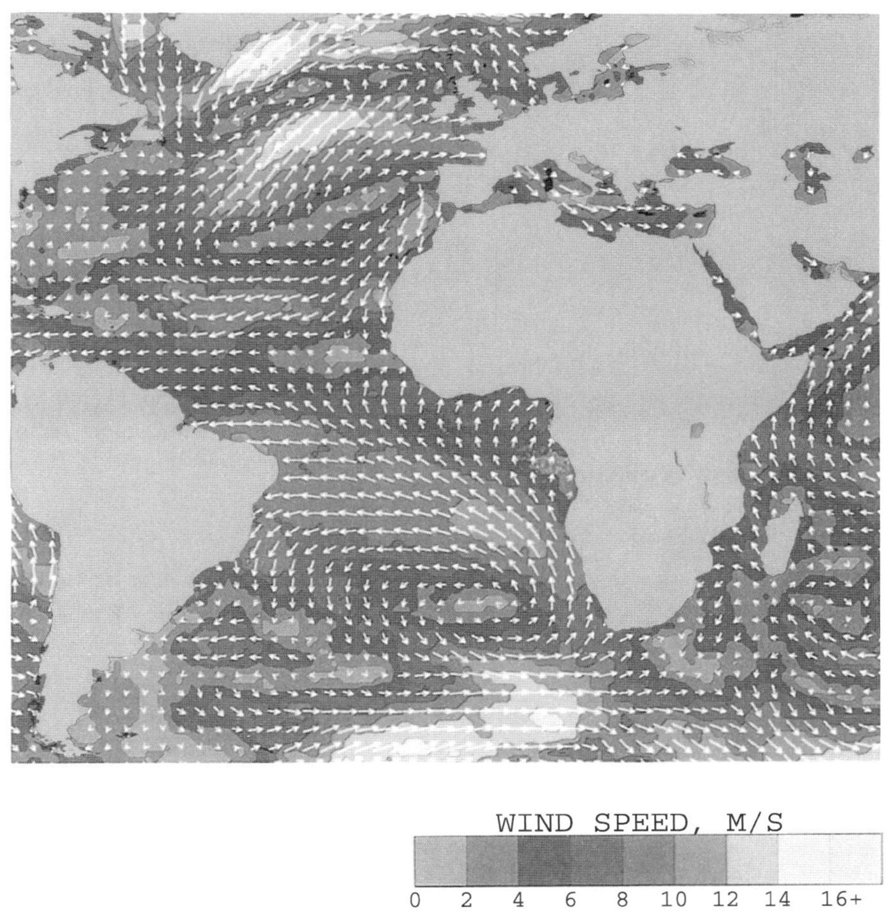

FIGURE 16.15 NASA's *Seasat* used radar to take 350,000 wind measurements over the world's oceans. The arrows show wind direction; their length and the color contouring indicate speed. Notice the heavy storm south of Greenland.

evaluated. This is different from the way we draw position vectors of planets and projectiles, with their tails at the origin and their heads at the planet's and projectile's locations.

Gradient Fields

> **DEFINITION Gradient Field**
> The **gradient field** of a differentiable function $f(x, y, z)$ is the field of gradient vectors
> $$\nabla f = \frac{\partial f}{\partial x}\mathbf{i} + \frac{\partial f}{\partial y}\mathbf{j} + \frac{\partial f}{\partial z}\mathbf{k}.$$

EXAMPLE 1 Finding a Gradient Field

Find the gradient field of $f(x, y, z) = xyz$.

Solution The gradient field of f is the field $\mathbf{F} = \nabla f = yz\mathbf{i} + xz\mathbf{j} + xy\mathbf{k}$. ■

As we will see in Section 16.3, gradient fields are of special importance in engineering, mathematics, and physics.

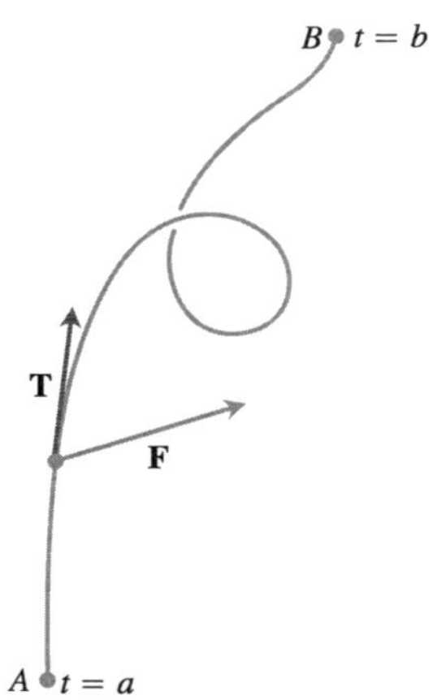

FIGURE 16.16 The work done by a force **F** is the line integral of the scalar component **F** · **T** over the smooth curve from A to B.

Work Done by a Force over a Curve in Space

Suppose that the vector field $\mathbf{F} = M(x, y, z)\mathbf{i} + N(x, y, z)\mathbf{j} + P(x, y, z)\mathbf{k}$ represents a force throughout a region in space (it might be the force of gravity or an electromagnetic force of some kind) and that

$$\mathbf{r}(t) = g(t)\mathbf{i} + h(t)\mathbf{j} + k(t)\mathbf{k}, \qquad a \le t \le b,$$

is a smooth curve in the region. Then the integral of $\mathbf{F} \cdot \mathbf{T}$, the scalar component of **F** in the direction of the curve's unit tangent vector, over the curve is called the work done by **F** over the curve from a to b (Figure 16.16).

> **DEFINITION Work over a Smooth Curve**
> The **work** done by a force $\mathbf{F} = M\mathbf{i} + N\mathbf{j} + P\mathbf{k}$ over a smooth curve $\mathbf{r}(t)$ from $t = a$ to $t = b$ is
> $$W = \int_{t=a}^{t=b} \mathbf{F} \cdot \mathbf{T}\, ds. \qquad (1)$$

We motivate Equation (1) with the same kind of reasoning we used in Chapter 6 to derive the formula $W = \int_a^b F(x)\,dx$ for the work done by a continuous force of magnitude $F(x)$ directed along an interval of the x-axis. We divide the curve into short segments, apply the (constant-force) × (distance) formula for work to approximate the work over each curved segment, add the results to approximate the work over the entire curve, and calculate the work as the limit of the approximating sums as the segments become shorter and more numerous. To find exactly what the limiting integral should be, we partition the parameter interval $[a, b]$ in the usual way and choose a point c_k in each subinterval $[t_k, t_{k+1}]$. The partition of $[a, b]$ determines ("induces," we say) a partition of the curve, with the point P_k being the tip of the position vector $\mathbf{r}(t_k)$ and Δs_k being the length of the curve segment P_kP_{k+1} (Figure 16.17).

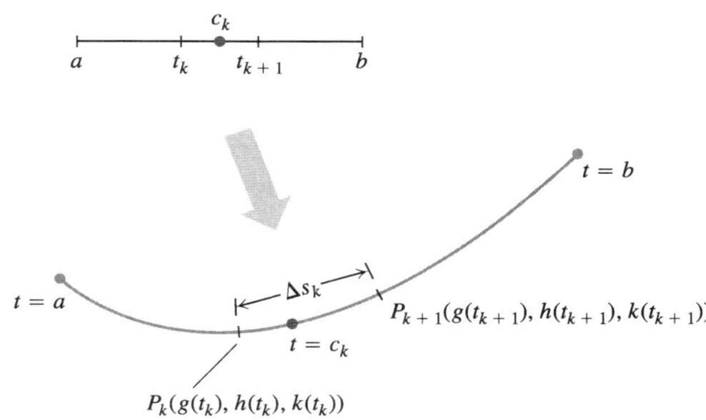

FIGURE 16.17 Each partition of $[a, b]$ induces a partition of the curve $\mathbf{r}(t) = g(t)\mathbf{i} + h(t)\mathbf{j} + k(t)\mathbf{k}$.

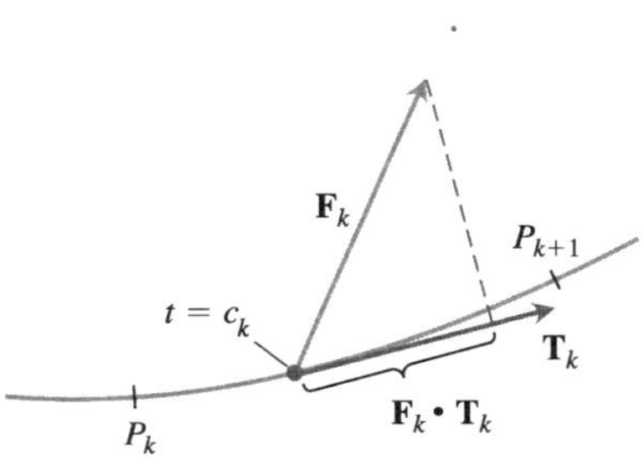

FIGURE 16.18 An enlarged view of the curve segment P_kP_{k+1} in Figure 16.17, showing the force and unit tangent vectors at the point on the curve where $t = c_k$.

If $\mathbf{F}_k$ denotes the value of $\mathbf{F}$ at the point on the curve corresponding to $t = c_k$ and $\mathbf{T}_k$ denotes the curve's unit tangent vector at this point, then $\mathbf{F}_k \cdot \mathbf{T}_k$ is the scalar component of $\mathbf{F}$ in the direction of $\mathbf{T}$ at $t = c_k$ (Figure 16.18). The work done by $\mathbf{F}$ along the curve segment P_kP_{k+1} is approximately

$$\begin{pmatrix}\text{Force component in}\\ \text{direction of motion}\end{pmatrix} \times \begin{pmatrix}\text{distance}\\ \text{applied}\end{pmatrix} = \mathbf{F}_k \cdot \mathbf{T}_k\, \Delta s_k.$$

The work done by $\mathbf{F}$ along the curve from $t = a$ to $t = b$ is approximately

$$\sum_{k=1}^{n} \mathbf{F}_k \cdot \mathbf{T}_k\, \Delta s_k.$$

As the norm of the partition of $[a, b]$ approaches zero, the norm of the induced partition of the curve approaches zero and these sums approach the line integral

$$\int_{t=a}^{t=b} \mathbf{F} \cdot \mathbf{T}\, ds.$$

The sign of the number we calculate with this integral depends on the direction in which the curve is traversed as t increases. If we reverse the direction of motion, we reverse the direction of $\mathbf{T}$ and change the sign of $\mathbf{F} \cdot \mathbf{T}$ and its integral.

Table 16.2 shows six ways to write the work integral in Equation (1). Despite their variety, the formulas in Table 16.2 are all evaluated the same way. In the table, $\mathbf{r}(t) = g(t)\mathbf{i} + h(t)\mathbf{j} + k(t)\mathbf{k} = x\mathbf{i} + y\mathbf{j} + z\mathbf{k}$ is a smooth curve, and

$$d\mathbf{r} = \frac{d\mathbf{r}}{dt}\, dt = dg\mathbf{i} + dh\mathbf{j} + dk\mathbf{k}$$

is its differential.

TABLE 16.2 Six different ways to write the work integral

$\mathbf{W} = \displaystyle\int_{t=a}^{t=b} \mathbf{F} \cdot \mathbf{T}\, ds$	The definition
$= \displaystyle\int_{t=a}^{t=b} \mathbf{F} \cdot d\mathbf{r}$	Compact differential form
$= \displaystyle\int_{a}^{b} \mathbf{F} \cdot \frac{d\mathbf{r}}{dt}\, dt$	Expanded to include dt; emphasizes the parameter t and velocity vector $d\mathbf{r}/dt$
$= \displaystyle\int_{a}^{b} \left(M\frac{dg}{dt} + N\frac{dh}{dt} + P\frac{dk}{dt} \right) dt$	Emphasizes the component functions
$= \displaystyle\int_{a}^{b} \left(M\frac{dx}{dt} + N\frac{dy}{dt} + P\frac{dz}{dt} \right) dt$	Abbreviates the components of $\mathbf{r}$
$= \displaystyle\int_{a}^{b} M\, dx + N\, dy + P\, dz$	dt's canceled; the most common form

Evaluating a Work Integral

To evaluate the work integral along a smooth curve $\mathbf{r}(t)$, take these steps:

1. Evaluate $\mathbf{F}$ on the curve as a function of the parameter t.
2. Find $d\mathbf{r}/dt$
3. Integrate $\mathbf{F} \cdot d\mathbf{r}/dt$ from $t = a$ to $t = b$.

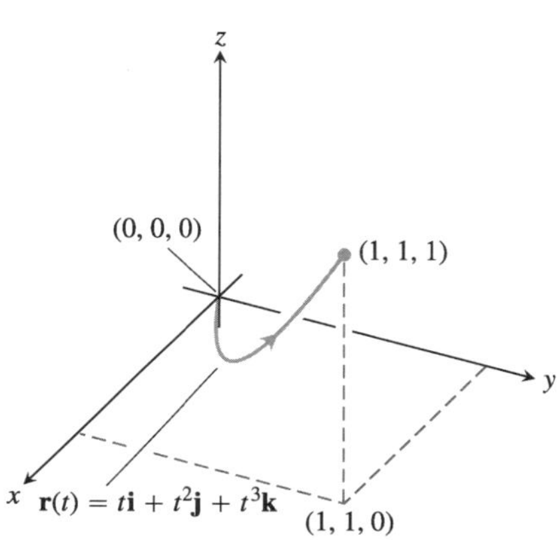

FIGURE 16.19 The curve in Example 2.

EXAMPLE 2 Finding Work Done by a Variable Force over a Space Curve

Find the work done by $\mathbf{F} = (y - x^2)\mathbf{i} + (z - y^2)\mathbf{j} + (x - z^2)\mathbf{k}$ over the curve $\mathbf{r}(t) = t\mathbf{i} + t^2\mathbf{j} + t^3\mathbf{k}$, $0 \le t \le 1$, from (0, 0, 0) to (1, 1, 1) (Figure 16.19).

Solution First we evaluate $\mathbf{F}$ on the curve:

$$\begin{aligned}\mathbf{F} &= (y - x^2)\mathbf{i} + (z - y^2)\mathbf{j} + (x - z^2)\mathbf{k} \\ &= \underbrace{(t^2 - t^2)}_{0}\mathbf{i} + (t^3 - t^4)\mathbf{j} + (t - t^6)\mathbf{k}\end{aligned}$$

Then we find $d\mathbf{r}/dt$,

$$\frac{d\mathbf{r}}{dt} = \frac{d}{dt}(t\mathbf{i} + t^2\mathbf{j} + t^3\mathbf{k}) = \mathbf{i} + 2t\mathbf{j} + 3t^2\mathbf{k}$$

Finally, we find $\mathbf{F} \cdot d\mathbf{r}/dt$ and integrate from $t = 0$ to $t = 1$:

$$\begin{aligned}\mathbf{F} \cdot \frac{d\mathbf{r}}{dt} &= [(t^3 - t^4)\mathbf{j} + (t - t^6)\mathbf{k}] \cdot (\mathbf{i} + 2t\mathbf{j} + 3t^2\mathbf{k}) \\ &= (t^3 - t^4)(2t) + (t - t^6)(3t^2) = 2t^4 - 2t^5 + 3t^3 - 3t^8,\end{aligned}$$

so

$$\text{Work} = \int_0^1 (2t^4 - 2t^5 + 3t^3 - 3t^8)\,dt$$

$$= \left[\frac{2}{5}t^5 - \frac{2}{6}t^6 + \frac{3}{4}t^4 - \frac{3}{9}t^9\right]_0^1 = \frac{29}{60}.$$ ■

Flow Integrals and Circulation for Velocity Fields

Instead of being a force field, suppose that **F** represents the velocity field of a fluid flowing through a region in space (a tidal basin or the turbine chamber of a hydroelectric generator, for example). Under these circumstances, the integral of $\mathbf{F}\cdot\mathbf{T}$ along a curve in the region gives the fluid's flow along the curve.

DEFINITIONS Flow Integral, Circulation

If $\mathbf{r}(t)$ is a smooth curve in the domain of a continuous velocity field **F**, the **flow** along the curve from $t = a$ to $t = b$ is

$$\text{Flow} = \int_a^b \mathbf{F}\cdot\mathbf{T}\,ds. \tag{2}$$

The integral in this case is called a **flow integral**. If the curve is a closed loop, the flow is called the **circulation** around the curve.

We evaluate flow integrals the same way we evaluate work integrals.

EXAMPLE 3 Finding Flow Along a Helix

A fluid's velocity field is $\mathbf{F} = x\mathbf{i} + z\mathbf{j} + y\mathbf{k}$. Find the flow along the helix $\mathbf{r}(t) = (\cos t)\mathbf{i} + (\sin t)\mathbf{j} + t\mathbf{k}$, $0 \le t \le \pi/2$.

Solution We evaluate **F** on the curve,

$$\mathbf{F} = x\mathbf{i} + z\mathbf{j} + y\mathbf{k} = (\cos t)\mathbf{i} + t\mathbf{j} + (\sin t)\mathbf{k}$$

and then find $d\mathbf{r}/dt$:

$$\frac{d\mathbf{r}}{dt} = (-\sin t)\mathbf{i} + (\cos t)\mathbf{j} + \mathbf{k}.$$

Then we integrate $\mathbf{F}\cdot(d\mathbf{r}/dt)$ from $t = 0$ to $t = \frac{\pi}{2}$:

$$\mathbf{F}\cdot\frac{d\mathbf{r}}{dt} = (\cos t)(-\sin t) + (t)(\cos t) + (\sin t)(1)$$

$$= -\sin t\cos t + t\cos t + \sin t$$

so,

$$\text{Flow} = \int_{t=a}^{t=b} \mathbf{F} \cdot \frac{d\mathbf{r}}{dt}\, dt = \int_0^{\pi/2} (-\sin t \cos t + t \cos t + \sin t)\, dt$$

$$= \left[\frac{\cos^2 t}{2} + t \sin t\right]_0^{\pi/2} = \left(0 + \frac{\pi}{2}\right) - \left(\frac{1}{2} + 0\right) = \frac{\pi}{2} - \frac{1}{2}.$$

EXAMPLE 4 Finding Circulation Around a Circle

Find the circulation of the field $\mathbf{F} = (x - y)\mathbf{i} + x\mathbf{j}$ around the circle $\mathbf{r}(t) = (\cos t)\mathbf{i} + (\sin t)\mathbf{j}$, $0 \le t \le 2\pi$.

Solution On the circle, $\mathbf{F} = (x - y)\mathbf{i} + x\mathbf{j} = (\cos t - \sin t)\mathbf{i} + (\cos t)\mathbf{j}$, and

$$\frac{d\mathbf{r}}{dt} = (-\sin t)\mathbf{i} + (\cos t)\mathbf{j}.$$

Then

$$\mathbf{F} \cdot \frac{d\mathbf{r}}{dt} = -\sin t \cos t + \underbrace{\sin^2 t + \cos^2 t}_{1}$$

gives

$$\text{Circulation} = \int_0^{2\pi} \mathbf{F} \cdot \frac{d\mathbf{r}}{dt}\, dt = \int_0^{2\pi} (1 - \sin t \cos t)\, dt$$

$$= \left[t - \frac{\sin^2 t}{2}\right]_0^{2\pi} = 2\pi.$$

Flux Across a Plane Curve

To find the rate at which a fluid is entering or leaving a region enclosed by a smooth curve C in the xy-plane, we calculate the line integral over C of $\mathbf{F} \cdot \mathbf{n}$, the scalar component of the fluid's velocity field in the direction of the curve's outward-pointing normal vector. The value of this integral is the *flux* of $\mathbf{F}$ across C. *Flux* is Latin for *flow*, but many flux calculations involve no motion at all. If $\mathbf{F}$ were an electric field or a magnetic field, for instance, the integral of $\mathbf{F} \cdot \mathbf{n}$ would still be called the flux of the field across C.

DEFINITION **Flux Across a Closed Curve in the Plane**

If C is a smooth closed curve in the domain of a continuous vector field $\mathbf{F} = M(x, y)\mathbf{i} + N(x, y)\mathbf{j}$ in the plane and if $\mathbf{n}$ is the outward-pointing unit normal vector on C, the **flux** of $\mathbf{F}$ across C is

$$\text{Flux of } \mathbf{F} \text{ across } C = \int_C \mathbf{F} \cdot \mathbf{n}\, ds. \quad (3)$$

Notice the difference between flux and circulation. The flux of $\mathbf{F}$ across C is the line integral with respect to arc length of $\mathbf{F} \cdot \mathbf{n}$, the scalar component of $\mathbf{F}$ in the direction of the

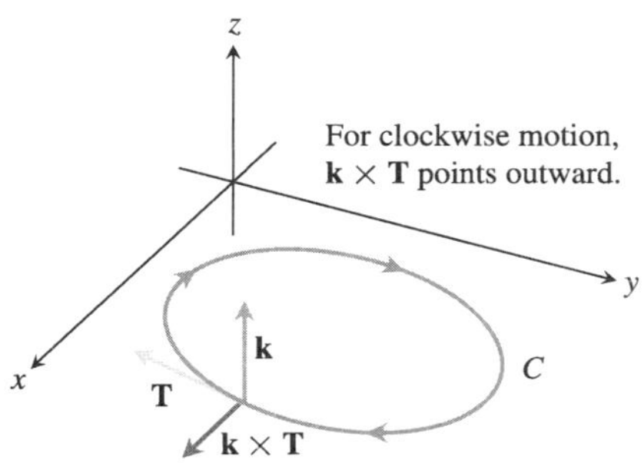

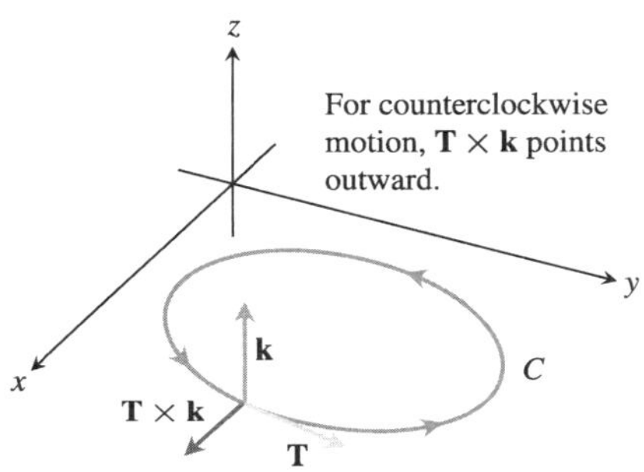

FIGURE 16.20 To find an outward unit normal vector for a smooth curve C in the xy-plane that is traversed counterclockwise as t increases, we take $\mathbf{n} = \mathbf{T} \times \mathbf{k}$. For clockwise motion, we take $\mathbf{n} = \mathbf{k} \times \mathbf{T}$.

outward normal. The circulation of $\mathbf{F}$ around C is the line integral with respect to arc length of $\mathbf{F} \cdot \mathbf{T}$, the scalar component of $\mathbf{F}$ in the direction of the unit tangent vector. Flux is the integral of the normal component of $\mathbf{F}$; circulation is the integral of the tangential component of $\mathbf{F}$.

To evaluate the integral in Equation (3), we begin with a smooth parametrization

$$x = g(t), \qquad y = h(t), \qquad a \le t \le b,$$

that traces the curve C exactly once as t increases from a to b. We can find the outward unit normal vector $\mathbf{n}$ by crossing the curve's unit tangent vector $\mathbf{T}$ with the vector $\mathbf{k}$. But which order do we choose, $\mathbf{T} \times \mathbf{k}$ or $\mathbf{k} \times \mathbf{T}$? Which one points outward? It depends on which way C is traversed as t increases. If the motion is clockwise, $\mathbf{k} \times \mathbf{T}$ points outward; if the motion is counterclockwise, $\mathbf{T} \times \mathbf{k}$ points outward (Figure 16.20). The usual choice is $\mathbf{n} = \mathbf{T} \times \mathbf{k}$, the choice that assumes counterclockwise motion. Thus, although the value of the arc length integral in the definition of flux in Equation (3) does not depend on which way C is traversed, the formulas we are about to derive for evaluating the integral in Equation (3) will assume counterclockwise motion.

In terms of components,

$$\mathbf{n} = \mathbf{T} \times \mathbf{k} = \left(\frac{dx}{ds}\mathbf{i} + \frac{dy}{ds}\mathbf{j}\right) \times \mathbf{k} = \frac{dy}{ds}\mathbf{i} - \frac{dx}{ds}\mathbf{j}.$$

If $\mathbf{F} = M(x, y)\mathbf{i} + N(x, y)\mathbf{j}$, then

$$\mathbf{F} \cdot \mathbf{n} = M(x, y)\frac{dy}{ds} - N(x, y)\frac{dx}{ds}.$$

Hence,

$$\int_C \mathbf{F} \cdot \mathbf{n}\, ds = \int_C \left(M\frac{dy}{ds} - N\frac{dx}{ds}\right) ds = \oint_C M\, dy - N\, dx.$$

We put a directed circle $\circlearrowleft$ on the last integral as a reminder that the integration around the closed curve C is to be in the counterclockwise direction. To evaluate this integral, we express M, dy, N, and dx in terms of t and integrate from $t = a$ to $t = b$. We do not need to know either $\mathbf{n}$ or ds to find the flux.

Calculating Flux Across a Smooth Closed Plane Curve

$$(\text{Flux of } \mathbf{F} = M\mathbf{i} + N\mathbf{j} \text{ across } C) = \oint_C M\, dy - N\, dx \tag{4}$$

The integral can be evaluated from any smooth parametrization $x = g(t), y = h(t)$, $a \le t \le b$, that traces C counterclockwise exactly once.

EXAMPLE 5 Finding Flux Across a Circle

Find the flux of $\mathbf{F} = (x - y)\mathbf{i} + x\mathbf{j}$ across the circle $x^2 + y^2 = 1$ in the xy-plane.

Solution The parametrization $\mathbf{r}(t) = (\cos t)\mathbf{i} + (\sin t)\mathbf{j}$, $0 \le t \le 2\pi$, traces the circle counterclockwise exactly once. We can therefore use this parametrization in Equation (4). With

$$M = x - y = \cos t - \sin t, \qquad dy = d(\sin t) = \cos t\, dt$$
$$N = x = \cos t, \qquad dx = d(\cos t) = -\sin t\, dt,$$

We find

$$\text{Flux} = \int_C M\, dy - N\, dx = \int_0^{2\pi} (\cos^2 t - \sin t \cos t + \cos t \sin t)\, dt \qquad \text{Equation (4)}$$
$$= \int_0^{2\pi} \cos^2 t\, dt = \int_0^{2\pi} \frac{1 + \cos 2t}{2}\, dt = \left[\frac{t}{2} + \frac{\sin 2t}{4}\right]_0^{2\pi} = \pi.$$

The flux of $\mathbf{F}$ across the circle is π. Since the answer is positive, the net flow across the curve is outward. A net inward flow would have given a negative flux. ■

EXERCISES 16.2

Vector and Gradient Fields

Find the gradient fields of the functions in Exercises 1–4.

1. $f(x, y, z) = (x^2 + y^2 + z^2)^{-1/2}$
2. $f(x, y, z) = \ln \sqrt{x^2 + y^2 + z^2}$
3. $g(x, y, z) = e^z - \ln (x^2 + y^2)$
4. $g(x, y, z) = xy + yz + xz$
5. Give a formula $\mathbf{F} = M(x, y)\mathbf{i} + N(x, y)\mathbf{j}$ for the vector field in the plane that has the property that $\mathbf{F}$ points toward the origin with magnitude inversely proportional to the square of the distance from (x, y) to the origin. (The field is not defined at $(0, 0)$.)
6. Give a formula $\mathbf{F} = M(x, y)\mathbf{i} + N(x, y)\mathbf{j}$ for the vector field in the plane that has the properties that $\mathbf{F} = \mathbf{0}$ at $(0, 0)$ and that at any other point (a, b), $\mathbf{F}$ is tangent to the circle $x^2 + y^2 = a^2 + b^2$ and points in the clockwise direction with magnitude $|\mathbf{F}| = \sqrt{a^2 + b^2}$.

Work

In Exercises 7–12, find the work done by force $\mathbf{F}$ from $(0, 0, 0)$ to $(1, 1, 1)$ over each of the following paths (Figure 16.21):

a. The straight-line path C_1: $\mathbf{r}(t) = t\mathbf{i} + t\mathbf{j} + t\mathbf{k}$, $0 \le t \le 1$
b. The curved path C_2: $\mathbf{r}(t) = t\mathbf{i} + t^2\mathbf{j} + t^4\mathbf{k}$, $0 \le t \le 1$
c. The path $C_3 \cup C_4$ consisting of the line segment from $(0, 0, 0)$ to $(1, 1, 0)$ followed by the segment from $(1, 1, 0)$ to $(1, 1, 1)$

7. $\mathbf{F} = 3y\mathbf{i} + 2x\mathbf{j} + 4z\mathbf{k}$
8. $\mathbf{F} = [1/(x^2 + 1)]\mathbf{j}$
9. $\mathbf{F} = \sqrt{z}\mathbf{i} - 2x\mathbf{j} + \sqrt{y}\mathbf{k}$
10. $\mathbf{F} = xy\mathbf{i} + yz\mathbf{j} + xz\mathbf{k}$
11. $\mathbf{F} = (3x^2 - 3x)\mathbf{i} + 3z\mathbf{j} + \mathbf{k}$
12. $\mathbf{F} = (y + z)\mathbf{i} + (z + x)\mathbf{j} + (x + y)\mathbf{k}$

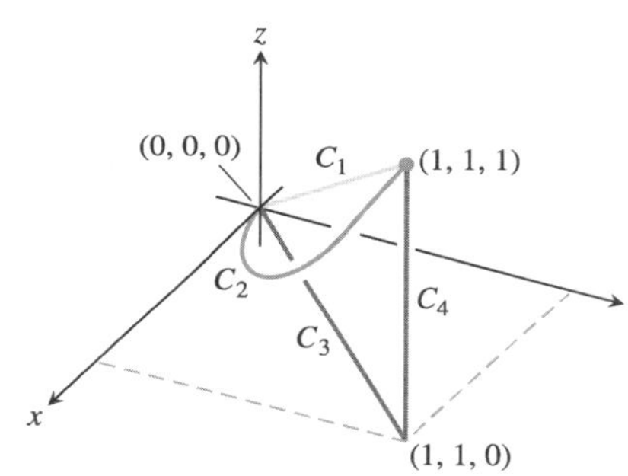

FIGURE 16.21 The paths from $(0, 0, 0)$ to $(1, 1, 1)$.

In Exercises 13–16, find the work done by $\mathbf{F}$ over the curve in the direction of increasing t.

13. $\mathbf{F} = xy\mathbf{i} + y\mathbf{j} - yz\mathbf{k}$
 $\mathbf{r}(t) = t\mathbf{i} + t^2\mathbf{j} + t\mathbf{k}$, $0 \le t \le 1$
14. $\mathbf{F} = 2y\mathbf{i} + 3x\mathbf{j} + (x + y)\mathbf{k}$
 $\mathbf{r}(t) = (\cos t)\mathbf{i} + (\sin t)\mathbf{j} + (t/6)\mathbf{k}$, $0 \le t \le 2\pi$
15. $\mathbf{F} = z\mathbf{i} + x\mathbf{j} + y\mathbf{k}$
 $\mathbf{r}(t) = (\sin t)\mathbf{i} + (\cos t)\mathbf{j} + t\mathbf{k}$, $0 \le t \le 2\pi$
16. $\mathbf{F} = 6z\mathbf{i} + y^2\mathbf{j} + 12x\mathbf{k}$
 $\mathbf{r}(t) = (\sin t)\mathbf{i} + (\cos t)\mathbf{j} + (t/6)\mathbf{k}$, $0 \le t \le 2\pi$

Line Integrals and Vector Fields in the Plane

17. Evaluate $\int_C xy\, dx + (x + y)\, dy$ along the curve $y = x^2$ from $(-1, 1)$ to $(2, 4)$.
18. Evaluate $\int_C (x - y)\, dx + (x + y)\, dy$ counterclockwise around the triangle with vertices $(0, 0)$, $(1, 0)$, and $(0, 1)$.

19. Evaluate $\int_C \mathbf{F}\cdot\mathbf{T}\,ds$ for the vector field $\mathbf{F} = x^2\mathbf{i} - y\mathbf{j}$ along the curve $x = y^2$ from $(4, 2)$ to $(1, -1)$.

20. Evaluate $\int_C \mathbf{F}\cdot d\mathbf{r}$ for the vector field $\mathbf{F} = y\mathbf{i} - x\mathbf{j}$ counterclockwise along the unit circle $x^2 + y^2 = 1$ from $(1, 0)$ to $(0, 1)$.

21. **Work** Find the work done by the force $\mathbf{F} = xy\mathbf{i} + (y - x)\mathbf{j}$ over the straight line from $(1, 1)$ to $(2, 3)$.

22. **Work** Find the work done by the gradient of $f(x, y) = (x + y)^2$ counterclockwise around the circle $x^2 + y^2 = 4$ from $(2, 0)$ to itself.

23. **Circulation and flux** Find the circulation and flux of the fields

$$\mathbf{F}_1 = x\mathbf{i} + y\mathbf{j} \quad \text{and} \quad \mathbf{F}_2 = -y\mathbf{i} + x\mathbf{j}$$

around and across each of the following curves.

a. The circle $\mathbf{r}(t) = (\cos t)\mathbf{i} + (\sin t)\mathbf{j}, \quad 0 \le t \le 2\pi$

b. The ellipse $\mathbf{r}(t) = (\cos t)\mathbf{i} + (4\sin t)\mathbf{j}, \quad 0 \le t \le 2\pi$

24. **Flux across a circle** Find the flux of the fields

$$\mathbf{F}_1 = 2x\mathbf{i} - 3y\mathbf{j} \quad \text{and} \quad \mathbf{F}_2 = 2x\mathbf{i} + (x - y)\mathbf{j}$$

across the circle

$$\mathbf{r}(t) = (a\cos t)\mathbf{i} + (a\sin t)\mathbf{j}, \qquad 0 \le t \le 2\pi.$$

Circulation and Flux

In Exercises 25–28, find the circulation and flux of the field $\mathbf{F}$ around and across the closed semicircular path that consists of the semicircular arch $\mathbf{r}_1(t) = (a\cos t)\mathbf{i} + (a\sin t)\mathbf{j}$, $0 \le t \le \pi$, followed by the line segment $\mathbf{r}_2(t) = t\mathbf{i}$, $-a \le t \le a$.

25. $\mathbf{F} = x\mathbf{i} + y\mathbf{j}$

26. $\mathbf{F} = x^2\mathbf{i} + y^2\mathbf{j}$

27. $\mathbf{F} = -y\mathbf{i} + x\mathbf{j}$

28. $\mathbf{F} = -y^2\mathbf{i} + x^2\mathbf{j}$

29. **Flow integrals** Find the flow of the velocity field $\mathbf{F} = (x + y)\mathbf{i} - (x^2 + y^2)\mathbf{j}$ along each of the following paths from $(1, 0)$ to $(-1, 0)$ in the xy-plane.

a. The upper half of the circle $x^2 + y^2 = 1$

b. The line segment from $(1, 0)$ to $(-1, 0)$

c. The line segment from $(1, 0)$ to $(0, -1)$ followed by the line segment from $(0, -1)$ to $(-1, 0)$.

30. **Flux across a triangle** Find the flux of the field $\mathbf{F}$ in Exercise 29 outward across the triangle with vertices $(1, 0)$, $(0, 1)$, $(-1, 0)$.

Sketching and Finding Fields in the Plane

31. **Spin field** Draw the spin field

$$\mathbf{F} = -\frac{y}{\sqrt{x^2 + y^2}}\mathbf{i} + \frac{x}{\sqrt{x^2 + y^2}}\mathbf{j}$$

(see Figure 16.14) along with its horizontal and vertical components at a representative assortment of points on the circle $x^2 + y^2 = 4$.

32. **Radial field** Draw the radial field

$$\mathbf{F} = x\mathbf{i} + y\mathbf{j}$$

(see Figure 16.13) along with its horizontal and vertical components at a representative assortment of points on the circle $x^2 + y^2 = 1$.

33. **A field of tangent vectors**

a. Find a field $\mathbf{G} = P(x, y)\mathbf{i} + Q(x, y)\mathbf{j}$ in the xy-plane with the property that at any point $(a, b) \ne (0, 0)$, $\mathbf{G}$ is a vector of magnitude $\sqrt{a^2 + b^2}$ tangent to the circle $x^2 + y^2 = a^2 + b^2$ and pointing in the counterclockwise direction. (The field is undefined at $(0, 0)$.)

b. How is $\mathbf{G}$ related to the spin field $\mathbf{F}$ in Figure 16.14?

34. **A field of tangent vectors**

a. Find a field $\mathbf{G} = P(x, y)\mathbf{i} + Q(x, y)\mathbf{j}$ in the xy-plane with the property that at any point $(a, b) \ne (0, 0)$, $\mathbf{G}$ is a unit vector tangent to the circle $x^2 + y^2 = a^2 + b^2$ and pointing in the clockwise direction.

b. How is $\mathbf{G}$ related to the spin field $\mathbf{F}$ in Figure 16.14?

35. **Unit vectors pointing toward the origin** Find a field $\mathbf{F} = M(x, y)\mathbf{i} + N(x, y)\mathbf{j}$ in the xy-plane with the property that at each point $(x, y) \ne (0, 0)$, $\mathbf{F}$ is a unit vector pointing toward the origin. (The field is undefined at $(0, 0)$.)

36. **Two "central" fields** Find a field $\mathbf{F} = M(x, y)\mathbf{i} + N(x, y)\mathbf{j}$ in the xy-plane with the property that at each point $(x, y) \ne (0, 0)$, $\mathbf{F}$ points toward the origin and $|\mathbf{F}|$ is **(a)** the distance from (x, y) to the origin, **(b)** inversely proportional to the distance from (x, y) to the origin. (The field is undefined at $(0, 0)$.)

Flow Integrals in Space

In Exercises 37–40, $\mathbf{F}$ is the velocity field of a fluid flowing through a region in space. Find the flow along the given curve in the direction of increasing t.

37. $\mathbf{F} = -4xy\mathbf{i} + 8y\mathbf{j} + 2\mathbf{k}$

$\mathbf{r}(t) = t\mathbf{i} + t^2\mathbf{j} + \mathbf{k}, \quad 0 \le t \le 2$

38. $\mathbf{F} = x^2\mathbf{i} + yz\mathbf{j} + y^2\mathbf{k}$

$r(t) = 3t\mathbf{j} + 4t\mathbf{k}, \quad 0 \le t \le 1$

39. $\mathbf{F} = (x - z)\mathbf{i} + x\mathbf{k}$

$\mathbf{r}(t) = (\cos t)\mathbf{i} + (\sin t)\mathbf{k}, \quad 0 \le t \le \pi$

40. $\mathbf{F} = -y\mathbf{i} + x\mathbf{j} + 2\mathbf{k}$

$\mathbf{r}(t) = (-2\cos t)\mathbf{i} + (2\sin t)\mathbf{j} + 2t\mathbf{k}, \qquad 0 \le t \le 2\pi$

41. **Circulation** Find the circulation of $\mathbf{F} = 2x\mathbf{i} + 2z\mathbf{j} + 2y\mathbf{k}$ around the closed path consisting of the following three curves traversed in the direction of increasing t:

C_1: $\mathbf{r}(t) = (\cos t)\mathbf{i} + (\sin t)\mathbf{j} + t\mathbf{k}, \quad 0 \le t \le \pi/2$

C_2: $\mathbf{r}(t) = \mathbf{j} + (\pi/2)(1 - t)\mathbf{k}, \quad 0 \le t \le 1$

C_3: $\mathbf{r}(t) = t\mathbf{i} + (1 - t)\mathbf{j}, \quad 0 \le t \le 1$

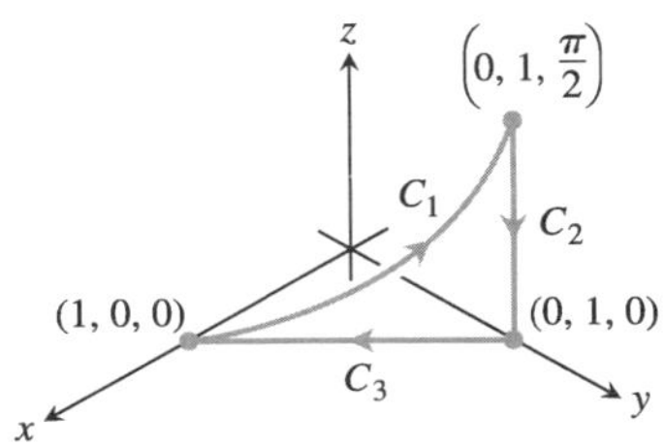

42. **Zero circulation** Let C be the ellipse in which the plane $2x + 3y - z = 0$ meets the cylinder $x^2 + y^2 = 12$. Show, without evaluating either line integral directly, that the circulation of the field $\mathbf{F} = x\mathbf{i} + y\mathbf{j} + z\mathbf{k}$ around C in either direction is zero.

43. **Flow along a curve** The field $\mathbf{F} = xy\mathbf{i} + y\mathbf{j} - yz\mathbf{k}$ is the velocity field of a flow in space. Find the flow from (0, 0, 0) to (1, 1, 1) along the curve of intersection of the cylinder $y = x^2$ and the plane $z = x$. (*Hint:* Use $t = x$ as the parameter.)

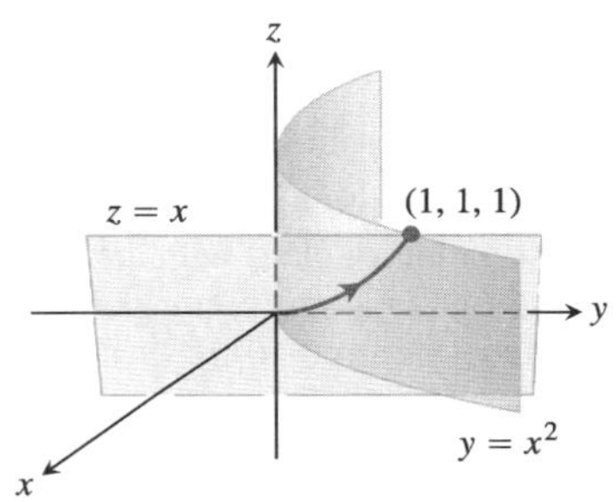

44. **Flow of a gradient field** Find the flow of the field $\mathbf{F} = \nabla(xy^2z^3)$:
   a. Once around the curve C in Exercise 42, clockwise as viewed from above
   b. Along the line segment from (1, 1, 1) to (2, 1, −1),

Theory and Examples

45. **Work and area** Suppose that $f(t)$ is differentiable and positive for $a \le t \le b$. Let C be the path $\mathbf{r}(t) = t\mathbf{i} + f(t)\mathbf{j}$, $a \le t \le b$, and $\mathbf{F} = y\mathbf{i}$. Is there any relation between the value of the work integral

$$\int_C \mathbf{F} \cdot d\mathbf{r}$$

and the area of the region bounded by the t-axis, the graph of f, and the lines $t = a$ and $t = b$? Give reasons for your answer.

46. **Work done by a radial force with constant magnitude** A particle moves along the smooth curve $y = f(x)$ from $(a, f(a))$ to $(b, f(b))$. The force moving the particle has constant magnitude k and always points away from the origin. Show that the work done by the force is

$$\int_C \mathbf{F} \cdot \mathbf{T}\, ds = k\left[(b^2 + (f(b))^2)^{1/2} - (a^2 + (f(a))^2)^{1/2}\right].$$

COMPUTER EXPLORATIONS

Finding Work Numerically

In Exercises 47–52, use a CAS to perform the following steps for finding the work done by force $\mathbf{F}$ over the given path:

a. Find $d\mathbf{r}$ for the path $\mathbf{r}(t) = g(t)\mathbf{i} + h(t)\mathbf{j} + k(t)\mathbf{k}$.

b. Evaluate the force $\mathbf{F}$ along the path.

c. Evaluate $\int_C \mathbf{F} \cdot d\mathbf{r}$.

47. $\mathbf{F} = xy^6\mathbf{i} + 3x(xy^5 + 2)\mathbf{j}$; $\mathbf{r}(t) = (2\cos t)\mathbf{i} + (\sin t)\mathbf{j}$, $0 \le t \le 2\pi$

48. $\mathbf{F} = \dfrac{3}{1 + x^2}\mathbf{i} + \dfrac{2}{1 + y^2}\mathbf{j}$; $\mathbf{r}(t) = (\cos t)\mathbf{i} + (\sin t)\mathbf{j}$, $0 \le t \le \pi$

49. $\mathbf{F} = (y + yz\cos xyz)\mathbf{i} + (x^2 + xz\cos xyz)\mathbf{j} + (z + xy\cos xyz)\mathbf{k}$; $\mathbf{r}(t) = (2\cos t)\mathbf{i} + (3\sin t)\mathbf{j} + \mathbf{k}$, $0 \le t \le 2\pi$

50. $\mathbf{F} = 2xy\mathbf{i} - y^2\mathbf{j} + ze^x\mathbf{k}$; $\mathbf{r}(t) = -t\mathbf{i} + \sqrt{t}\mathbf{j} + 3t\mathbf{k}$, $1 \le t \le 4$

51. $\mathbf{F} = (2y + \sin x)\mathbf{i} + (z^2 + (1/3)\cos y)\mathbf{j} + x^4\mathbf{k}$; $\mathbf{r}(t) = (\sin t)\mathbf{i} + (\cos t)\mathbf{j} + (\sin 2t)\mathbf{k}$, $-\pi/2 \le t \le \pi/2$

52. $\mathbf{F} = (x^2y)\mathbf{i} + \frac{1}{3}x^3\mathbf{j} + xy\mathbf{k}$; $\mathbf{r}(t) = (\cos t)\mathbf{i} + (\sin t)\mathbf{j} + (2\sin^2 t - 1)\mathbf{k}$, $0 \le t \le 2\pi$

16.3 Path Independence, Potential Functions, and Conservative Fields

In gravitational and electric fields, the amount of work it takes to move a mass or a charge from one point to another depends only on the object's initial and final positions and not on the path taken in between. This section discusses the notion of path independence of work integrals and describes the properties of fields in which work integrals are path independent. Work integrals are often easier to evaluate if they are path independent.

Path Independence

If A and B are two points in an open region D in space, the work $\int \mathbf{F} \cdot d\mathbf{r}$ done in moving a particle from A to B by a field $\mathbf{F}$ defined on D usually depends on the path taken. For some special fields, however, the integral's value is the same for all paths from A to B.

> **DEFINITIONS Path Independence, Conservative Field**
> Let $\mathbf{F}$ be a field defined on an open region D in space, and suppose that for any two points A and B in D the work $\int_A^B \mathbf{F} \cdot d\mathbf{r}$ done in moving from A to B is the same over all paths from A to B. Then the integral $\int \mathbf{F} \cdot d\mathbf{r}$ is **path independent in D** and the field $\mathbf{F}$ is **conservative on D**.

The word *conservative* comes from physics, where it refers to fields in which the principle of conservation of energy holds (it does, in conservative fields).

Under differentiability conditions normally met in practice, a field $\mathbf{F}$ is conservative if and only if it is the gradient field of a scalar function f; that is, if and only if $\mathbf{F} = \nabla f$ for some f. The function f then has a special name.

> **DEFINITION Potential Function**
> If $\mathbf{F}$ is a field defined on D and $\mathbf{F} = \nabla f$ for some scalar function f on D, then f is called a **potential function for F**.

An electric potential is a scalar function whose gradient field is an electric field. A gravitational potential is a scalar function whose gradient field is a gravitational field, and so on. As we will see, once we have found a potential function f for a field $\mathbf{F}$, we can evaluate all the work integrals in the domain of $\mathbf{F}$ over any path between A and B by

$$\int_A^B \mathbf{F} \cdot d\mathbf{r} = \int_A^B \nabla f \cdot d\mathbf{r} = f(B) - f(A). \tag{1}$$

If you think of ∇f for functions of several variables as being something like the derivative f' for functions of a single variable, then you see that Equation (1) is the vector calculus analogue of the Fundamental Theorem of Calculus formula

$$\int_a^b f'(x)\, dx = f(b) - f(a).$$

Conservative fields have other remarkable properties we will study as we go along. For example, saying that $\mathbf{F}$ is conservative on D is equivalent to saying that the integral of $\mathbf{F}$ around every closed path in D is zero. Naturally, certain conditions on the curves, fields, and domains must be satisfied for Equation (1) to be valid. We discuss these conditions below.

Assumptions in Effect from Now On: Connectivity and Simple Connectivity

We assume that all curves are **piecewise smooth**, that is, made up of finitely many smooth pieces connected end to end, as discussed in Section 13.1. We also assume that the components of $\mathbf{F}$ have continuous first partial derivatives. When $\mathbf{F} = \nabla f$, this continuity requirement guarantees that the mixed second derivatives of the potential function f are equal, a result we will find revealing in studying conservative fields $\mathbf{F}$.

We assume D to be an *open* region in space. This means that every point in D is the center of an open ball that lies entirely in D. We assume D to be **connected**, which in an open region means that every point can be connected to every other point by a smooth curve that lies in the region. Finally, we assume D is **simply connected**, which means every loop in D can be contracted to a point in D without ever leaving D. (If D consisted of space with a line removed, for example, D would not be simply connected. There would be no way to contract a loop around the line to a point without leaving D.)

Connectivity and simple connectivity are not the same, and neither implies the other. Think of connected regions as being in "one piece" and simply connected regions as not having any "holes that catch loops." All of space itself is both connected and simply connected. Some of the results in this chapter can fail to hold if applied to domains where these conditions do not hold. For example, the component test for conservative fields, given later in this section, is not valid on domains that are not simply connected.

Line Integrals in Conservative Fields

The following result provides a convenient way to evaluate a line integral in a conservative field. The result establishes that the value of the integral depends only on the endpoints and not on the specific path joining them.

THEOREM 1 The Fundamental Theorem of Line Integrals

1. Let $\mathbf{F} = M\mathbf{i} + N\mathbf{j} + P\mathbf{k}$ be a vector field whose components are continuous throughout an open connected region D in space. Then there exists a differentiable function f such that

$$\mathbf{F} = \nabla f = \frac{\partial f}{\partial x}\mathbf{i} + \frac{\partial f}{\partial y}\mathbf{j} + \frac{\partial f}{\partial z}\mathbf{k}$$

if and only if for all points A and B in D the value of $\int_A^B \mathbf{F}\cdot d\mathbf{r}$ is independent of the path joining A to B in D.

2. If the integral is independent of the path from A to B, its value is

$$\int_A^B \mathbf{F}\cdot d\mathbf{r} = f(B) - f(A).$$

Proof that $\mathbf{F} = \nabla f$ Implies Path Independence of the Integral Suppose that A and B are two points in D and that C: $\mathbf{r}(t) = g(t)\mathbf{i} + h(t)\mathbf{j} + k(t)\mathbf{k}$, $a \le t \le b$, is a smooth curve in D joining A and B. Along the curve, f is a differentiable function of t and

$$\frac{df}{dt} = \frac{\partial f}{\partial x}\frac{dx}{dt} + \frac{\partial f}{\partial y}\frac{dy}{dt} + \frac{\partial f}{\partial z}\frac{dz}{dt} \qquad \text{Chain Rule with } x = g(t),\ y = h(t),\ z = k(t)$$

$$= \nabla f\cdot\left(\frac{dx}{dt}\mathbf{i} + \frac{dy}{dt}\mathbf{j} + \frac{dz}{dt}\mathbf{k}\right) = \nabla f\cdot\frac{d\mathbf{r}}{dt} = \mathbf{F}\cdot\frac{d\mathbf{r}}{dt}. \qquad \text{Because } \mathbf{F} = \nabla f$$

Therefore,

$$\int_C \mathbf{F}\cdot d\mathbf{r} = \int_{t=a}^{t=b} \mathbf{F}\cdot\frac{d\mathbf{r}}{dt}\,dt = \int_a^b \frac{df}{dt}\,dt$$

$$= f(g(t), h(t), k(t))\Big]_a^b = f(B) - f(A).$$

Thus, the value of the work integral depends only on the values of f at A and B and not on the path in between. This proves Part 2 as well as the forward implication in Part 1. We omit the more technical proof of the reverse implication. ■

EXAMPLE 1 Finding Work Done by a Conservative Field

Find the work done by the conservative field

$$\mathbf{F} = yz\mathbf{i} + xz\mathbf{j} + xy\mathbf{k} = \nabla(xyz)$$

along any smooth curve C joining the point $A(-1, 3, 9)$ to $B(1, 6, -4)$.

Solution With $f(x, y, z) = xyz$, we have

$$\int_A^B \mathbf{F}\cdot d\mathbf{r} = \int_A^B \nabla f\cdot d\mathbf{r} \qquad \mathbf{F} = \nabla f$$

$$= f(B) - f(A) \qquad \text{Fundamental Theorem, Part 2}$$

$$= xyz|_{(1,6,-4)} - xyz|_{(-1,3,9)}$$

$$= (1)(6)(-4) - (-1)(3)(9)$$

$$= -24 + 27 = 3.$$ ■

THEOREM 2 **Closed-Loop Property of Conservative Fields**

The following statements are equivalent.

1. $\oint \mathbf{F}\cdot d\mathbf{r} = 0$ around every closed loop in D.
2. The field $\mathbf{F}$ is conservative on D.

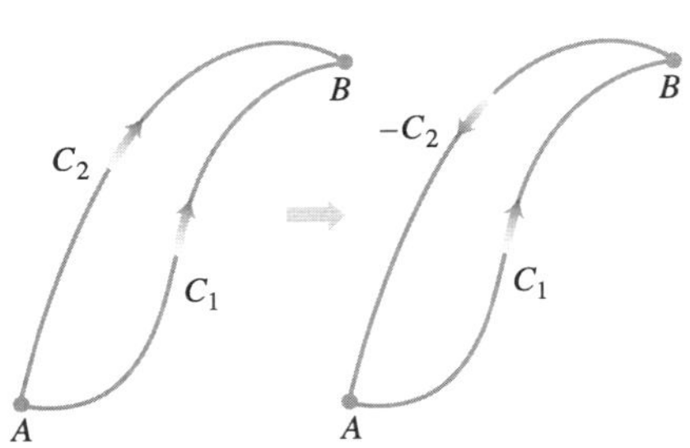

FIGURE 16.22 If we have two paths from A to B, one of them can be reversed to make a loop.

Proof that Part 1 ⇒ Part 2 We want to show that for any two points A and B in D, the integral of $\mathbf{F}\cdot d\mathbf{r}$ has the same value over any two paths C_1 and C_2 from A to B. We reverse the direction on C_2 to make a path $-C_2$ from B to A (Figure 16.22). Together, C_1 and $-C_2$ make a closed loop C, and

$$\int_{C_1} \mathbf{F}\cdot d\mathbf{r} - \int_{C_2} \mathbf{F}\cdot d\mathbf{r} = \int_{C_1} \mathbf{F}\cdot d\mathbf{r} + \int_{-C_2} \mathbf{F}\cdot d\mathbf{r} = \int_C \mathbf{F}\cdot d\mathbf{r} = 0.$$

Thus, the integrals over C_1 and C_2 give the same value. Note that the definition of line integral shows that changing the direction along a curve reverses the sign of the line integral.

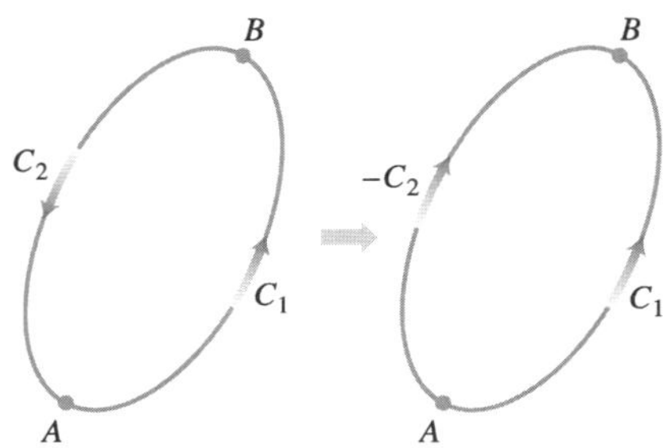

FIGURE 16.23 If A and B lie on a loop, we can reverse part of the loop to make two paths from A to B.

Proof that Part 2 $\Rightarrow$ Part 1 We want to show that the integral of $\mathbf{F}\cdot d\mathbf{r}$ is zero over any closed loop C. We pick two points A and B on C and use them to break C into two pieces: C_1 from A to B followed by C_2 from B back to A (Figure 16.23). Then

$$\oint_C \mathbf{F}\cdot d\mathbf{r} = \int_{C_1} \mathbf{F}\cdot d\mathbf{r} + \int_{C_2} \mathbf{F}\cdot d\mathbf{r} = \int_A^B \mathbf{F}\cdot d\mathbf{r} - \int_A^B \mathbf{F}\cdot d\mathbf{r} = 0. \qquad \blacksquare$$

The following diagram summarizes the results of Theorems 1 and 2.

	Theorem 1		Theorem 2	
$\mathbf{F} = \nabla f$ on D	$\Leftrightarrow$	$\mathbf{F}$ conservative on D	$\Leftrightarrow$	$\oint_C \mathbf{F}\cdot d\mathbf{r} = 0$ over any closed path in D

Now that we see how convenient it is to evaluate line integrals in conservative fields, two questions remain.

1. How do we know when a given field $\mathbf{F}$ is conservative?
2. If $\mathbf{F}$ is in fact conservative, how do we find a potential function f (so that $\mathbf{F} = \nabla f$)?

Finding Potentials for Conservative Fields

The test for being conservative is the following. Keep in mind our assumption that the domain of $\mathbf{F}$ is connected and simply connected.

> **Component Test for Conservative Fields**
> Let $\mathbf{F} = M(x, y, z)\mathbf{i} + N(x, y, z)\mathbf{j} + P(x, y, z)\mathbf{k}$ be a field whose component functions have continuous first partial derivatives. Then, $\mathbf{F}$ is conservative if and only if
>
> $$\frac{\partial P}{\partial y} = \frac{\partial N}{\partial z}, \quad \frac{\partial M}{\partial z} = \frac{\partial P}{\partial x}, \quad \text{and} \quad \frac{\partial N}{\partial x} = \frac{\partial M}{\partial y}. \tag{2}$$

Proof that Equations (2) hold if F is conservative There is a potential function f such that

$$\mathbf{F} = M\mathbf{i} + N\mathbf{j} + P\mathbf{k} = \frac{\partial f}{\partial x}\mathbf{i} + \frac{\partial f}{\partial y}\mathbf{j} + \frac{\partial f}{\partial z}\mathbf{k}.$$

Hence,

$$\begin{aligned} \frac{\partial P}{\partial y} &= \frac{\partial}{\partial y}\left(\frac{\partial f}{\partial z}\right) = \frac{\partial^2 f}{\partial y\, \partial z} \\ &= \frac{\partial^2 f}{\partial z\, \partial y} \qquad \text{Continuity implies that the mixed partial derivatives are equal.} \\ &= \frac{\partial}{\partial z}\left(\frac{\partial f}{\partial y}\right) = \frac{\partial N}{\partial z}. \end{aligned}$$

The others in Equations (2) are proved similarly. $\blacksquare$

The second half of the proof, that Equations (2) imply that $\mathbf{F}$ is conservative, is a consequence of Stokes' Theorem, taken up in Section 16.7, and requires our assumption that the domain of $\mathbf{F}$ be simply connected.

Once we know that **F** is conservative, we usually want to find a potential function for **F**. This requires solving the equation $\nabla f = \mathbf{F}$ or

$$\frac{\partial f}{\partial x}\mathbf{i} + \frac{\partial f}{\partial y}\mathbf{j} + \frac{\partial f}{\partial z}\mathbf{k} = M\mathbf{i} + N\mathbf{j} + P\mathbf{k}$$

for f. We accomplish this by integrating the three equations

$$\frac{\partial f}{\partial x} = M, \qquad \frac{\partial f}{\partial y} = N, \qquad \frac{\partial f}{\partial z} = P,$$

as illustrated in the next example.

EXAMPLE 2 Finding a Potential Function

Show that $\mathbf{F} = (e^x \cos y + yz)\mathbf{i} + (xz - e^x \sin y)\mathbf{j} + (xy + z)\mathbf{k}$ is conservative and find a potential function for it.

Solution We apply the test in Equations (2) to

$$M = e^x \cos y + yz, \qquad N = xz - e^x \sin y, \qquad P = xy + z$$

and calculate

$$\frac{\partial P}{\partial y} = x = \frac{\partial N}{\partial z}, \qquad \frac{\partial M}{\partial z} = y = \frac{\partial P}{\partial x}, \qquad \frac{\partial N}{\partial x} = -e^x \sin y + z = \frac{\partial M}{\partial y}.$$

Together, these equalities tell us that there is a function f with $\nabla f = \mathbf{F}$.

We find f by integrating the equations

$$\frac{\partial f}{\partial x} = e^x \cos y + yz, \qquad \frac{\partial f}{\partial y} = xz - e^x \sin y, \qquad \frac{\partial f}{\partial z} = xy + z. \tag{3}$$

We integrate the first equation with respect to x, holding y and z fixed, to get

$$f(x, y, z) = e^x \cos y + xyz + g(y, z).$$

We write the constant of integration as a function of y and z because its value may change if y and z change. We then calculate $\partial f/\partial y$ from this equation and match it with the expression for $\partial f/\partial y$ in Equations (3). This gives

$$-e^x \sin y + xz + \frac{\partial g}{\partial y} = xz - e^x \sin y,$$

so $\partial g/\partial y = 0$. Therefore, g is a function of z alone, and

$$f(x, y, z) = e^x \cos y + xyz + h(z).$$

We now calculate $\partial f/\partial z$ from this equation and match it to the formula for $\partial f/\partial z$ in Equations (3). This gives

$$xy + \frac{dh}{dz} = xy + z, \qquad \text{or} \qquad \frac{dh}{dz} = z,$$

so

$$h(z) = \frac{z^2}{2} + C.$$

Hence,

$$f(x, y, z) = e^x \cos y + xyz + \frac{z^2}{2} + C.$$

We have infinitely many potential functions of **F**, one for each value of C. ■

EXAMPLE 3 Showing That a Field Is Not Conservative

Show that $\mathbf{F} = (2x - 3)\mathbf{i} - z\mathbf{j} + (\cos z)\mathbf{k}$ is not conservative.

Solution We apply the component test in Equations (2) and find immediately that

$$\frac{\partial P}{\partial y} = \frac{\partial}{\partial y}(\cos z) = 0, \qquad \frac{\partial N}{\partial z} = \frac{\partial}{\partial z}(-z) = -1.$$

The two are unequal, so **F** is not conservative. No further testing is required. ■

Exact Differential Forms

As we see in the next section and again later on, it is often convenient to express work and circulation integrals in the "differential" form

$$\int_A^B M\,dx + N\,dy + P\,dz$$

mentioned in Section 16.2. Such integrals are relatively easy to evaluate if $M\,dx + N\,dy + P\,dz$ is the total differential of a function f. For then

$$\begin{aligned}\int_A^B M\,dx + N\,dy + P\,dz &= \int_A^B \frac{\partial f}{\partial x}dx + \frac{\partial f}{\partial y}dy + \frac{\partial f}{\partial z}dz \\ &= \int_A^B \nabla f \cdot d\mathbf{r} \\ &= f(B) - f(A). \qquad \text{Theorem 1}\end{aligned}$$

Thus,

$$\int_A^B df = f(B) - f(A),$$

just as with differentiable functions of a single variable.

> **DEFINITIONS** **Exact Differential Form**
>
> Any expression $M(x, y, z)\,dx + N(x, y, z)\,dy + P(x, y, z)\,dz$ is a **differential form**. A differential form is **exact** on a domain D in space if
>
> $$M\,dx + N\,dy + P\,dz = \frac{\partial f}{\partial x}dx + \frac{\partial f}{\partial y}dy + \frac{\partial f}{\partial z}dz = df$$
>
> for some scalar function f throughout D.

Notice that if $M\,dx + N\,dy + P\,dz = df$ on D, then $\mathbf{F} = M\mathbf{i} + N\mathbf{j} + P\mathbf{k}$ is the gradient field of f on D. Conversely, if $\mathbf{F} = \nabla f$, then the form $M\,dx + N\,dy + P\,dz$ is exact. The test for the form's being exact is therefore the same as the test for **F**'s being conservative.

Component Test for Exactness of $M\,dx + N\,dy + P\,dz$
The differential form $M\,dx + N\,dy + P\,dz$ is exact if and only if

$$\frac{\partial P}{\partial y} = \frac{\partial N}{\partial z}, \quad \frac{\partial M}{\partial z} = \frac{\partial P}{\partial x}, \quad \text{and} \quad \frac{\partial N}{\partial x} = \frac{\partial M}{\partial y}.$$

This is equivalent to saying that the field $\mathbf{F} = M\mathbf{i} + N\mathbf{j} + P\mathbf{k}$ is conservative.

EXAMPLE 4 Showing That a Differential Form Is Exact

Show that $y\,dx + x\,dy + 4\,dz$ is exact and evaluate the integral

$$\int_{(1,1,1)}^{(2,3,-1)} y\,dx + x\,dy + 4\,dz$$

over the line segment from $(1, 1, 1)$ to $(2, 3, -1)$.

Solution We let $M = y, N = x, P = 4$ and apply the Test for Exactness:

$$\frac{\partial P}{\partial y} = 0 = \frac{\partial N}{\partial z}, \quad \frac{\partial M}{\partial z} = 0 = \frac{\partial P}{\partial x}, \quad \frac{\partial N}{\partial x} = 1 = \frac{\partial M}{\partial y}.$$

These equalities tell us that $y\,dx + x\,dy + 4\,dz$ is exact, so

$$y\,dx + x\,dy + 4\,dz = df$$

for some function f, and the integral's value is $f(2, 3, -1) - f(1, 1, 1)$.

We find f up to a constant by integrating the equations

$$\frac{\partial f}{\partial x} = y, \quad \frac{\partial f}{\partial y} = x, \quad \frac{\partial f}{\partial z} = 4. \tag{4}$$

From the first equation we get

$$f(x, y, z) = xy + g(y, z).$$

The second equation tells us that

$$\frac{\partial f}{\partial y} = x + \frac{\partial g}{\partial y} = x, \quad \text{or} \quad \frac{\partial g}{\partial y} = 0.$$

Hence, g is a function of z alone, and

$$f(x, y, z) = xy + h(z).$$

The third of Equations (4) tells us that

$$\frac{\partial f}{\partial z} = 0 + \frac{dh}{dz} = 4, \quad \text{or} \quad h(z) = 4z + C.$$

Therefore,

$$f(x, y, z) = xy + 4z + C.$$

The value of the integral is

$$f(2, 3, -1) - f(1, 1, 1) = 2 + C - (5 + C) = -3.$$

■

EXERCISES 16.3

Testing for Conservative Fields

Which fields in Exercises 1–6 are conservative, and which are not?

1. $\mathbf{F} = yz\mathbf{i} + xz\mathbf{j} + xy\mathbf{k}$
2. $\mathbf{F} = (y \sin z)\mathbf{i} + (x \sin z)\mathbf{j} + (xy \cos z)\mathbf{k}$
3. $\mathbf{F} = y\mathbf{i} + (x + z)\mathbf{j} - y\mathbf{k}$
4. $\mathbf{F} = -y\mathbf{i} + x\mathbf{j}$
5. $\mathbf{F} = (z + y)\mathbf{i} + z\mathbf{j} + (y + x)\mathbf{k}$
6. $\mathbf{F} = (e^x \cos y)\mathbf{i} - (e^x \sin y)\mathbf{j} + z\mathbf{k}$

Finding Potential Functions

In Exercises 7–12, find a potential function f for the field $\mathbf{F}$.

7. $\mathbf{F} = 2x\mathbf{i} + 3y\mathbf{j} + 4z\mathbf{k}$
8. $\mathbf{F} = (y + z)\mathbf{i} + (x + z)\mathbf{j} + (x + y)\mathbf{k}$
9. $\mathbf{F} = e^{y+2z}(\mathbf{i} + x\mathbf{j} + 2x\mathbf{k})$
10. $\mathbf{F} = (y \sin z)\mathbf{i} + (x \sin z)\mathbf{j} + (xy \cos z)\mathbf{k}$
11. $\mathbf{F} = (\ln x + \sec^2(x + y))\mathbf{i} + \left(\sec^2(x + y) + \dfrac{y}{y^2 + z^2}\right)\mathbf{j} + \dfrac{z}{y^2 + z^2}\mathbf{k}$
12. $\mathbf{F} = \dfrac{y}{1 + x^2y^2}\mathbf{i} + \left(\dfrac{x}{1 + x^2y^2} + \dfrac{z}{\sqrt{1 - y^2z^2}}\right)\mathbf{j} + \left(\dfrac{y}{\sqrt{1 - y^2z^2}} + \dfrac{1}{z}\right)\mathbf{k}$

Evaluating Line Integrals

In Exercises 13–17, show that the differential forms in the integrals are exact. Then evaluate the integrals.

13. $\displaystyle\int_{(0,0,0)}^{(2,3,-6)} 2x\,dx + 2y\,dy + 2z\,dz$
14. $\displaystyle\int_{(1,1,2)}^{(3,5,0)} yz\,dx + xz\,dy + xy\,dz$
15. $\displaystyle\int_{(0,0,0)}^{(1,2,3)} 2xy\,dx + (x^2 - z^2)\,dy - 2yz\,dz$
16. $\displaystyle\int_{(0,0,0)}^{(3,3,1)} 2x\,dx - y^2\,dy - \frac{4}{1 + z^2}\,dz$
17. $\displaystyle\int_{(1,0,0)}^{(0,1,1)} \sin y \cos x\,dx + \cos y \sin x\,dy + dz$

Although they are not defined on all of space R^3, the fields associated with Exercises 18–22 have simply connected domains and the Component Test can be used to show they are conservative. Find a potential function for each field and evaluate the integrals as in Example 4.

18. $\displaystyle\int_{(0,2,1)}^{(1,\pi/2,2)} 2 \cos y\,dx + \left(\frac{1}{y} - 2x \sin y\right) dy + \frac{1}{z}\,dz,\ y > 0$
19. $\displaystyle\int_{(1,1,1)}^{(1,2,3)} 3x^2\,dx + \frac{z^2}{y}\,dy + 2z \ln y\,dz,\ y > 0$
20. $\displaystyle\int_{(1,2,1)}^{(2,1,1)} (2x \ln y - yz)\,dx + \left(\frac{x^2}{y} - xz\right) dy - xy\,dz,\ y > 0$
21. $\displaystyle\int_{(1,1,1)}^{(2,2,2)} \frac{1}{y}\,dx + \left(\frac{1}{z} - \frac{x}{y^2}\right) dy - \frac{y}{z^2}\,dz,\ y > 0, z > 0$
22. $\displaystyle\int_{(-1,-1,-1)}^{(2,2,2)} \frac{2x\,dx + 2y\,dy + 2z\,dz}{x^2 + y^2 + z^2}$
23. **Revisiting Example 4** Evaluate the integral
$$\int_{(1,1,1)}^{(2,3,-1)} y\,dx + x\,dy + 4\,dz$$
from Example 4 by finding parametric equations for the line segment from (1, 1, 1) to (2, 3, −1) and evaluating the line integral of $\mathbf{F} = y\mathbf{i} + x\mathbf{j} + 4\mathbf{k}$ along the segment. Since $\mathbf{F}$ is conservative, the integral is independent of the path.
24. Evaluate
$$\int_C x^2\,dx + yz\,dy + (y^2/2)\,dz$$
along the line segment C joining (0, 0, 0) to (0, 3, 4).

Theory, Applications, and Examples

Independence of path Show that the values of the integrals in Exercises 25 and 26 do not depend on the path taken from A to B.

25. $\displaystyle\int_A^B z^2\,dx + 2y\,dy + 2xz\,dz$
26. $\displaystyle\int_A^B \frac{x\,dx + y\,dy + z\,dz}{\sqrt{x^2 + y^2 + z^2}}$

In Exercises 27 and 28, find a potential function for $\mathbf{F}$.

27. $\mathbf{F} = \dfrac{2x}{y}\mathbf{i} + \left(\dfrac{1 - x^2}{y^2}\right)\mathbf{j},\ y > 0$
28. $\mathbf{F} = (e^x \ln y)\mathbf{i} + \left(\dfrac{e^x}{y} + \sin z\right)\mathbf{j} + (y \cos z)\mathbf{k},\ y > 0$
29. **Work along different paths** Find the work done by $\mathbf{F} = (x^2 + y)\mathbf{i} + (y^2 + x)\mathbf{j} + ze^z\mathbf{k}$ over the following paths from (1, 0, 0) to (1, 0, 1).
    a. The line segment $x = 1, y = 0, 0 \le z \le 1$
    b. The helix $\mathbf{r}(t) = (\cos t)\mathbf{i} + (\sin t)\mathbf{j} + (t/2\pi)\mathbf{k},\ 0 \le t \le 2\pi$
    c. The x-axis from (1, 0, 0) to (0, 0, 0) followed by the parabola $z = x^2, y = 0$ from (0, 0, 0) to (1, 0, 1)
30. **Work along different paths** Find the work done by $\mathbf{F} = e^{yz}\mathbf{i} + (xze^{yz} + z \cos y)\mathbf{j} + (xye^{yz} + \sin y)\mathbf{k}$ over the following paths from (1, 0, 1) to $(1, \pi/2, 0)$.

a. The line segment $x = 1, y = \pi t/2, z = 1 - t, 0 \le t \le 1$

b. The line segment from $(1, 0, 1)$ to the origin followed by the line segment from the origin to $(1, \pi/2, 0)$

c. The line segment from $(1, 0, 1)$ to $(1, 0, 0)$, followed by the x-axis from $(1, 0, 0)$ to the origin, followed by the parabola $y = \pi x^2/2, z = 0$ from there to $(1, \pi/2, 0)$

31. **Evaluating a work integral two ways** Let $\mathbf{F} = \nabla(x^3y^2)$ and let C be the path in the xy-plane from $(-1, 1)$ to $(1, 1)$ that consists of the line segment from $(-1, 1)$ to $(0, 0)$ followed by the line segment from $(0, 0)$ to $(1, 1)$. Evaluate $\int_C \mathbf{F} \cdot d\mathbf{r}$ in two ways.

a. Find parametrizations for the segments that make up C and evaluate the integral.

b. Using $f(x, y) = x^3y^2$ as a potential function for $\mathbf{F}$.

32. **Integral along different paths** Evaluate $\int_C 2x \cos y\, dx - x^2 \sin y\, dy$ along the following paths C in the xy-plane.

a. The parabola $y = (x - 1)^2$ from $(1, 0)$ to $(0, 1)$

b. The line segment from $(-1, \pi)$ to $(1, 0)$

c. The x-axis from $(-1, 0)$ to $(1, 0)$

d. The astroid $\mathbf{r}(t) = (\cos^3 t)\mathbf{i} + (\sin^3 t)\mathbf{j}, 0 \le t \le 2\pi$, counterclockwise from $(1, 0)$ back to $(1, 0)$

33. a. **Exact differential form** How are the constants a, b, and c related if the following differential form is exact?

$$(ay^2 + 2czx)\, dx + y(bx + cz)\, dy + (ay^2 + cx^2)\, dz$$

b. **Gradient field** For what values of b and c will

$$\mathbf{F} = (y^2 + 2czx)\mathbf{i} + y(bx + cz)\mathbf{j} + (y^2 + cx^2)\mathbf{k}$$

be a gradient field?

34. **Gradient of a line integral** Suppose that $\mathbf{F} = \nabla f$ is a conservative vector field and

$$g(x, y, z) = \int_{(0,0,0)}^{(x,y,z)} \mathbf{F} \cdot d\mathbf{r}.$$

Show that $\nabla g = \mathbf{F}$.

35. **Path of least work** You have been asked to find the path along which a force field $\mathbf{F}$ will perform the least work in moving a particle between two locations. A quick calculation on your part shows $\mathbf{F}$ to be conservative. How should you respond? Give reasons for your answer.

36. **A revealing experiment** By experiment, you find that a force field $\mathbf{F}$ performs only half as much work in moving an object along path C_1 from A to B as it does in moving the object along path C_2 from A to B. What can you conclude about $\mathbf{F}$? Give reasons for your answer.

37. **Work by a constant force** Show that the work done by a constant force field $\mathbf{F} = a\mathbf{i} + b\mathbf{j} + c\mathbf{k}$ in moving a particle along any path from A to B is $W = \mathbf{F} \cdot \overrightarrow{AB}$.

38. **Gravitational field**

a. Find a potential function for the gravitational field

$$\mathbf{F} = -GmM \frac{x\mathbf{i} + y\mathbf{j} + z\mathbf{k}}{(x^2 + y^2 + z^2)^{3/2}} \qquad (G, m, \text{ and } M \text{ are constants}).$$

b. Let P_1 and P_2 be points at distance s_1 and s_2 from the origin. Show that the work done by the gravitational field in part (a) in moving a particle from P_1 to P_2 is

$$GmM\left(\frac{1}{s_2} - \frac{1}{s_1}\right).$$

16.4 Green's Theorem in the Plane

From Table 16.2 in Section 16.2, we know that every line integral $\int_C M\, dx + N\, dy$ can be written as a flow integral $\int_a^b \mathbf{F} \cdot \mathbf{T}\, ds$. If the integral is independent of path, so the field $\mathbf{F}$ is conservative (over a domain satisfying the basic assumptions), we can evaluate the integral easily from a potential function for the field. In this section we consider how to evaluate the integral if it is *not* associated with a conservative vector field, but is a flow or flux integral across a closed curve in the xy-plane. The means for doing so is a result known as Green's Theorem, which converts the line integral into a double integral over the region enclosed by the path.

We frame our discussion in terms of velocity fields of fluid flows because they are easy to picture. However, Green's Theorem applies to any vector field satisfying certain mathematical conditions. It does not depend for its validity on the field's having a particular physical interpretation.

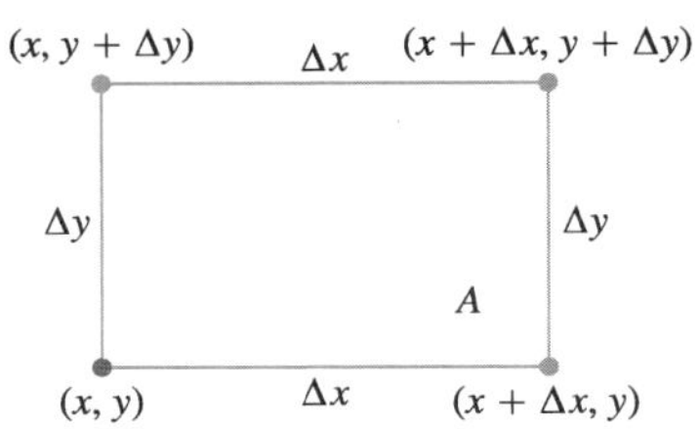

FIGURE 16.24 The rectangle for defining the divergence (flux density) of a vector field at a point (x, y).

Divergence

We need two new ideas for Green's Theorem. The first is the idea of the *divergence* of a vector field at a point, sometimes called the *flux density* of the vector field by physicists and engineers. We obtain it in the following way.

Suppose that $\mathbf{F}(x, y) = M(x, y)\mathbf{i} + N(x, y)\mathbf{j}$ is the velocity field of a fluid flow in the plane and that the first partial derivatives of M and N are continuous at each point of a region R. Let (x, y) be a point in R and let A be a small rectangle with one corner at (x, y) that, along with its interior, lies entirely in R (Figure 16.24). The sides of the rectangle, parallel to the coordinate axes, have lengths of Δx and Δy. The rate at which fluid leaves the rectangle across the bottom edge is approximately

$$\mathbf{F}(x, y) \cdot (-\mathbf{j})\,\Delta x = -N(x, y)\Delta x.$$

This is the scalar component of the velocity at (x, y) in the direction of the outward normal times the length of the segment. If the velocity is in meters per second, for example, the exit rate will be in meters per second times meters or square meters per second. The rates at which the fluid crosses the other three sides in the directions of their outward normals can be estimated in a similar way. All told, we have

$$\begin{array}{lll} \textbf{Exit Rates:} & \text{Top:} & \mathbf{F}(x, y + \Delta y) \cdot \mathbf{j}\,\Delta x = N(x, y + \Delta y)\Delta x \\ & \text{Bottom:} & \mathbf{F}(x, y) \cdot (-\mathbf{j})\,\Delta x = -N(x, y)\Delta x \\ & \text{Right:} & \mathbf{F}(x + \Delta x, y) \cdot \mathbf{i}\,\Delta y = M(x + \Delta x, y)\Delta y \\ & \text{Left:} & \mathbf{F}(x, y) \cdot (-\mathbf{i})\,\Delta y = -M(x, y)\Delta y. \end{array}$$

Combining opposite pairs gives

$$\text{Top and bottom:} \quad (N(x, y + \Delta y) - N(x, y))\Delta x \approx \left(\frac{\partial N}{\partial y}\Delta y\right)\Delta x$$

$$\text{Right and left:} \quad (M(x + \Delta x, y) - M(x, y))\Delta y \approx \left(\frac{\partial M}{\partial x}\Delta x\right)\Delta y.$$

Adding these last two equations gives

$$\text{Flux across rectangle boundary} \approx \left(\frac{\partial M}{\partial x} + \frac{\partial N}{\partial y}\right)\Delta x \Delta y.$$

We now divide by $\Delta x \Delta y$ to estimate the total flux per unit area or flux density for the rectangle:

$$\frac{\text{Flux across rectangle boundary}}{\text{rectangle area}} \approx \left(\frac{\partial M}{\partial x} + \frac{\partial N}{\partial y}\right).$$

Finally, we let Δx and Δy approach zero to define what we call the *flux density* of $\mathbf{F}$ at the point (x, y). In mathematics, we call the flux density the *divergence* of $\mathbf{F}$. The symbol for it is div $\mathbf{F}$, pronounced "divergence of $\mathbf{F}$" or "div $\mathbf{F}$."

DEFINITION **Divergence (Flux Density)**
The **divergence (flux density)** of a vector field $\mathbf{F} = M\mathbf{i} + N\mathbf{j}$ at the point (x, y) is

$$\text{div}\,\mathbf{F} = \frac{\partial M}{\partial x} + \frac{\partial N}{\partial y}. \tag{1}$$

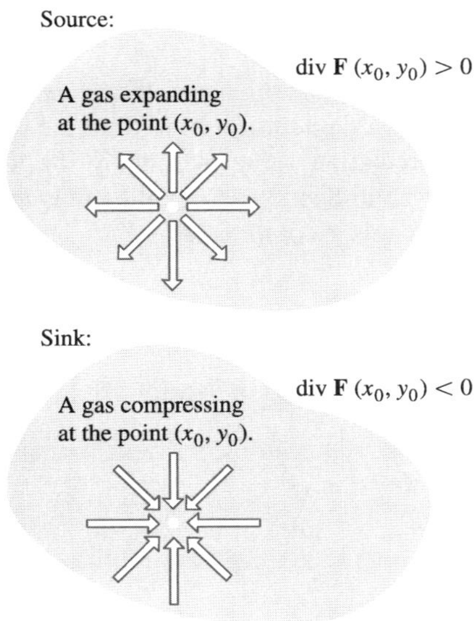

FIGURE 16.25 If a gas is expanding at a point (x_0, y_0), the lines of flow have positive divergence; if the gas is compressing, the divergence is negative.

Intuitively, if a gas is expanding at the point (x_0, y_0), the lines of flow would diverge there (hence the name) and, since the gas would be flowing out of a small rectangle about (x_0, y_0) the divergence of $\mathbf{F}$ at (x_0, y_0) would be positive. If the gas were compressing instead of expanding, the divergence would be negative (see Figure 16.25).

EXAMPLE 1 Finding Divergence

Find the divergence of $\mathbf{F}(x, y) = (x^2 - y)\mathbf{i} + (xy - y^2)\mathbf{j}$.

Solution We use the formula in Equation (1):

$$\begin{aligned}\text{div }\mathbf{F} &= \frac{\partial M}{\partial x} + \frac{\partial N}{\partial y} = \frac{\partial}{\partial x}(x^2 - y) + \frac{\partial}{\partial y}(xy - y^2)\\ &= 2x + x - 2y = 3x - 2y.\end{aligned}$$

■

Spin Around an Axis: The k-Component of Curl

The second idea we need for Green's Theorem has to do with measuring how a paddle wheel spins at a point in a fluid flowing in a plane region. This idea gives some sense of how the fluid is circulating around axes located at different points and perpendicular to the region. Physicists sometimes refer to this as the *circulation density* of a vector field $\mathbf{F}$ at a point. To obtain it, we return to the velocity field

$$\mathbf{F}(x, y) = M(x, y)\mathbf{i} + N(x, y)\mathbf{j}$$

and the rectangle A. The rectangle is redrawn here as Figure 16.26.

The counterclockwise circulation of $\mathbf{F}$ around the boundary of A is the sum of flow rates along the sides. For the bottom edge, the flow rate is approximately

$$\mathbf{F}(x, y)\cdot\mathbf{i}\,\Delta x = M(x, y)\Delta x.$$

This is the scalar component of the velocity $\mathbf{F}(x, y)$ in the direction of the tangent vector $\mathbf{i}$ times the length of the segment. The rates of flow along the other sides in the counterclockwise direction are expressed in a similar way. In all, we have

$$\begin{aligned}&\text{Top:} && \mathbf{F}(x, y + \Delta y)\cdot(-\mathbf{i})\,\Delta x = -M(x, y + \Delta y)\Delta x\\ &\text{Bottom:} && \mathbf{F}(x, y)\cdot\mathbf{i}\,\Delta x = M(x, y)\Delta x\\ &\text{Right:} && \mathbf{F}(x + \Delta x, y)\cdot\mathbf{j}\,\Delta y = N(x + \Delta x, y)\Delta y\\ &\text{Left:} && \mathbf{F}(x, y)\cdot(-\mathbf{j})\,\Delta y = -N(x, y)\Delta y.\end{aligned}$$

We add opposite pairs to get

Top and bottom:

$$-(M(x, y + \Delta y) - M(x, y))\Delta x \approx -\left(\frac{\partial M}{\partial y}\Delta y\right)\Delta x$$

Right and left:

$$(N(x + \Delta x, y) - N(x, y))\Delta y \approx \left(\frac{\partial N}{\partial x}\Delta x\right)\Delta y.$$

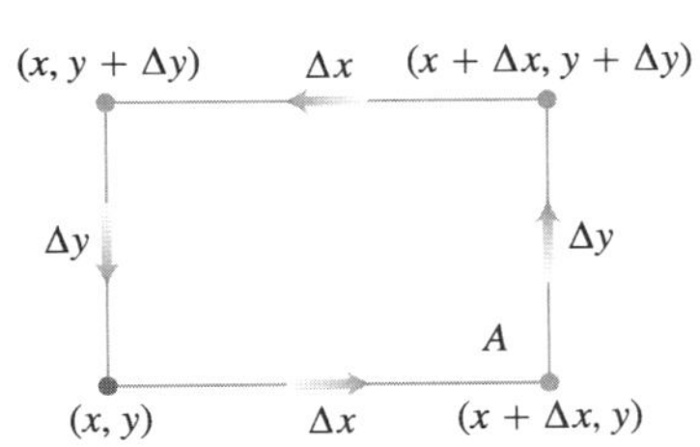

FIGURE 16.26 The rectangle for defining the curl (circulation density) of a vector field at a point (x, y).

Adding these last two equations and dividing by $\Delta x \Delta y$ gives an estimate of the circulation density for the rectangle:

$$\frac{\text{Circulation around rectangle}}{\text{rectangle area}} \approx \frac{\partial N}{\partial x} - \frac{\partial M}{\partial y}.$$

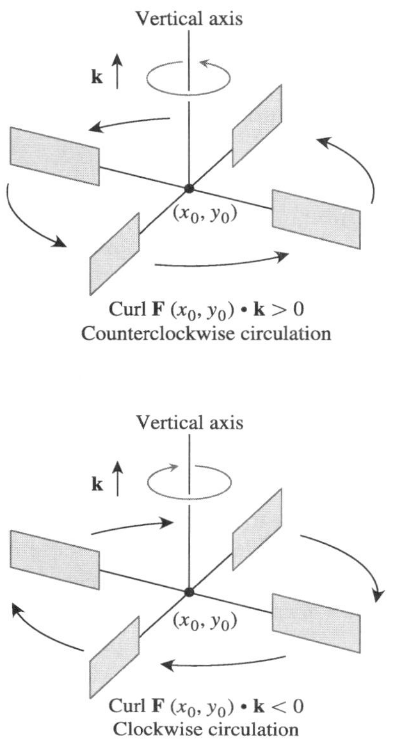

FIGURE 16.27 In the flow of an incompressible fluid over a plane region, the **k**-component of the curl measures the rate of the fluid's rotation at a point. The **k**-component of the curl is positive at points where the rotation is counterclockwise and negative where the rotation is clockwise.

We let Δx and Δy approach zero to define what we call the *circulation density* of $\mathbf{F}$ at the point (x, y).

The positive orientation of the circulation density for the plane is the *counterclockwise* rotation around the vertical axis, looking downward on the xy-plane from the tip of the (vertical) unit vector $\mathbf{k}$ (Figure 16.27). The circulation value is actually the $\mathbf{k}$-component of a more general circulation vector we define in Section 16.7, called the *curl* of the vector field $\mathbf{F}$. For Green's Theorem, we need only this $\mathbf{k}$-component.

> **DEFINITION k-Component of Curl (Circulation Density)**
>
> **The k-component of the curl (circulation density)** of a vector field $\mathbf{F} = M\mathbf{i} + N\mathbf{j}$ at the point (x, y) is the scalar
>
> $$(\text{curl } \mathbf{F}) \cdot \mathbf{k} = \frac{\partial N}{\partial x} - \frac{\partial M}{\partial y}. \tag{2}$$

If water is moving about a region in the xy-plane in a thin layer, then the $\mathbf{k}$-component of the circulation, or curl, at a point (x_0, y_0) gives a way to measure how fast and in what direction a small paddle wheel will spin if it is put into the water at (x_0, y_0) with its axis perpendicular to the plane, parallel to $\mathbf{k}$ (Figure 16.27).

EXAMPLE 2 Finding the k-Component of the Curl

Find the $\mathbf{k}$-component of the curl for the vector field

$$\mathbf{F}(x, y) = (x^2 - y)\mathbf{i} + (xy - y^2)\mathbf{j}.$$

Solution We use the formula in Equation (2):

$$(\text{curl } \mathbf{F}) \cdot \mathbf{k} = \frac{\partial N}{\partial x} - \frac{\partial M}{\partial y} = \frac{\partial}{\partial x}(xy - y^2) - \frac{\partial}{\partial y}(x^2 - y) = y + 1. \qquad \blacksquare$$

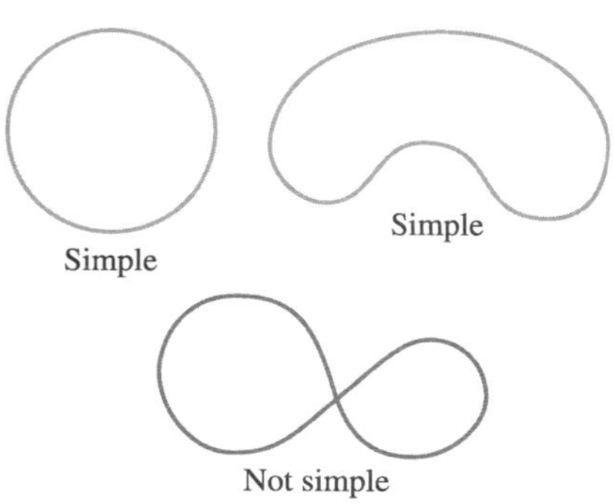

FIGURE 16.28 In proving Green's Theorem, we distinguish between two kinds of closed curves, simple and not simple. Simple curves do not cross themselves. A circle is simple but a figure 8 is not.

Two Forms for Green's Theorem

In one form, Green's Theorem says that under suitable conditions the outward flux of a vector field across a simple closed curve in the plane (Figure 16.28) equals the double integral of the divergence of the field over the region enclosed by the curve. Recall the formulas for flux in Equations (3) and (4) in Section 16.2.

> **THEOREM 3 Green's Theorem (Flux-Divergence or Normal Form)**
>
> The outward flux of a field $\mathbf{F} = M\mathbf{i} + N\mathbf{j}$ across a simple closed curve C equals the double integral of div $\mathbf{F}$ over the region R enclosed by C.
>
> $$\underbrace{\oint_C \mathbf{F} \cdot \mathbf{n}\, ds}_{\text{Outward flux}} = \oint_C M\, dy - N\, dx = \underbrace{\iint_R \left(\frac{\partial M}{\partial x} + \frac{\partial N}{\partial y} \right) dx\, dy}_{\text{Divergence integral}} \tag{3}$$

In another form, Green's Theorem says that the counterclockwise circulation of a vector field around a simple closed curve is the double integral of the **k**-component of the curl of the field over the region enclosed by the curve. Recall the defining Equation (2) for circulation in Section 16.2.

THEOREM 4 Green's Theorem (Circulation-Curl or Tangential Form)
The counterclockwise circulation of a field $\mathbf{F} = M\mathbf{i} + N\mathbf{j}$ around a simple closed curve C in the plane equals the double integral of $(\text{curl } \mathbf{F}) \cdot \mathbf{k}$ over the region R enclosed by C.

$$\underbrace{\oint_C \mathbf{F} \cdot \mathbf{T}\, ds = \oint_C M\,dx + N\,dy}_{\text{Counterclockwise circulation}} = \underbrace{\iint_R \left(\frac{\partial N}{\partial x} - \frac{\partial M}{\partial y}\right) dx\,dy}_{\text{Curl integral}} \tag{4}$$

The two forms of Green's Theorem are equivalent. Applying Equation (3) to the field $\mathbf{G}_1 = N\mathbf{i} - M\mathbf{j}$ gives Equation (4), and applying Equation (4) to $\mathbf{G}_2 = -N\mathbf{i} + M\mathbf{j}$ gives Equation (3).

Mathematical Assumptions

We need two kinds of assumptions for Green's Theorem to hold. First, we need conditions on M and N to ensure the existence of the integrals. The usual assumptions are that M, N, and their first partial derivatives are continuous at every point of some open region containing C and R. Second, we need geometric conditions on the curve C. It must be simple, closed, and made up of pieces along which we can integrate M and N. The usual assumptions are that C is piecewise smooth. The proof we give for Green's Theorem, however, assumes things about the shape of R as well. You can find proofs that are less restrictive in more advanced texts. First let's look at examples.

EXAMPLE 3 Supporting Green's Theorem

Verify both forms of Green's Theorem for the field

$$\mathbf{F}(x, y) = (x - y)\mathbf{i} + x\mathbf{j}$$

and the region R bounded by the unit circle

$$C: \quad \mathbf{r}(t) = (\cos t)\mathbf{i} + (\sin t)\mathbf{j}, \qquad 0 \le t \le 2\pi.$$

Solution We have

$$M = \cos t - \sin t, \qquad dx = d(\cos t) = -\sin t\,dt,$$

$$N = \cos t, \qquad dy = d(\sin t) = \cos t\,dt,$$

$$\frac{\partial M}{\partial x} = 1, \qquad \frac{\partial M}{\partial y} = -1, \qquad \frac{\partial N}{\partial x} = 1, \qquad \frac{\partial N}{\partial y} = 0.$$

The two sides of Equation (3) are

$$\oint_C M\,dy - N\,dx = \int_{t=0}^{t=2\pi} (\cos t - \sin t)(\cos t\,dt) - (\cos t)(-\sin t\,dt)$$

$$= \int_0^{2\pi} \cos^2 t\,dt = \pi$$

$$\iint_R \left(\frac{\partial M}{\partial x} + \frac{\partial N}{\partial y}\right) dx\,dy = \iint_R (1 + 0)\,dx\,dy$$

$$= \iint_R dx\,dy = \text{area inside the unit circle} = \pi.$$

The two sides of Equation (4) are

$$\oint_C M\,dx + N\,dy = \int_{t=0}^{t=2\pi} (\cos t - \sin t)(-\sin t\,dt) + (\cos t)(\cos t\,dt)$$

$$= \int_0^{2\pi} (-\sin t \cos t + 1)\,dt = 2\pi$$

$$\iint_R \left(\frac{\partial N}{\partial x} - \frac{\partial M}{\partial y}\right) dx\,dy = \iint_R (1 - (-1))\,dx\,dy = 2\iint_R dx\,dy = 2\pi.$$ ■

Using Green's Theorem to Evaluate Line Integrals

If we construct a closed curve C by piecing a number of different curves end to end, the process of evaluating a line integral over C can be lengthy because there are so many different integrals to evaluate. If C bounds a region R to which Green's Theorem applies, however, we can use Green's Theorem to change the line integral around C into one double integral over R.

EXAMPLE 4 Evaluating a Line Integral Using Green's Theorem

Evaluate the integral

$$\oint_C xy\,dy - y^2\,dx,$$

where C is the square cut from the first quadrant by the lines $x = 1$ and $y = 1$.

Solution We can use either form of Green's Theorem to change the line integral into a double integral over the square.

1. *With the Normal Form Equation* (3): Taking $M = xy$, $N = y^2$, and C and R as the square's boundary and interior gives

$$\oint_C xy\,dy - y^2\,dx = \iint_R (y + 2y)\,dx\,dy = \int_0^1\int_0^1 3y\,dx\,dy$$

$$= \int_0^1 \left[3xy\right]_{x=0}^{x=1} dy = \int_0^1 3y\,dy = \frac{3}{2}y^2\Big]_0^1 = \frac{3}{2}.$$

2. *With the Tangential Form Equation* (4): Taking $M = -y^2$ and $N = xy$ gives the same result:

$$\oint_C -y^2\,dx + xy\,dy = \iint_R (y - (-2y))\,dx\,dy = \frac{3}{2}.$$ ■

EXAMPLE 5 Finding Outward Flux

Calculate the outward flux of the field $\mathbf{F}(x, y) = x\mathbf{i} + y^2\mathbf{j}$ across the square bounded by the lines $x = \pm 1$ and $y = \pm 1$.

Solution Calculating the flux with a line integral would take four integrations, one for each side of the square. With Green's Theorem, we can change the line integral to one double integral. With $M = x$, $N = y^2$, C the square, and R the square's interior, we have

$$\begin{aligned}\text{Flux} &= \oint_C \mathbf{F}\cdot\mathbf{n}\,ds = \oint_C M\,dy - N\,dx \\ &= \iint_R \left(\frac{\partial M}{\partial x} + \frac{\partial N}{\partial y}\right) dx\,dy \qquad \text{Green's Theorem} \\ &= \int_{-1}^{1}\int_{-1}^{1} (1 + 2y)\,dx\,dy = \int_{-1}^{1}\Big[x + 2xy\Big]_{x=-1}^{x=1} dy \\ &= \int_{-1}^{1} (2 + 4y)\,dy = \Big[2y + 2y^2\Big]_{-1}^{1} = 4.\end{aligned}$$ ■

Proof of Green's Theorem for Special Regions

Let C be a smooth simple closed curve in the xy-plane with the property that lines parallel to the axes cut it in no more than two points. Let R be the region enclosed by C and suppose that M, N, and their first partial derivatives are continuous at every point of some open region containing C and R. We want to prove the circulation-curl form of Green's Theorem,

$$\oint_C M\,dx + N\,dy = \iint_R \left(\frac{\partial N}{\partial x} - \frac{\partial M}{\partial y}\right) dx\,dy. \tag{5}$$

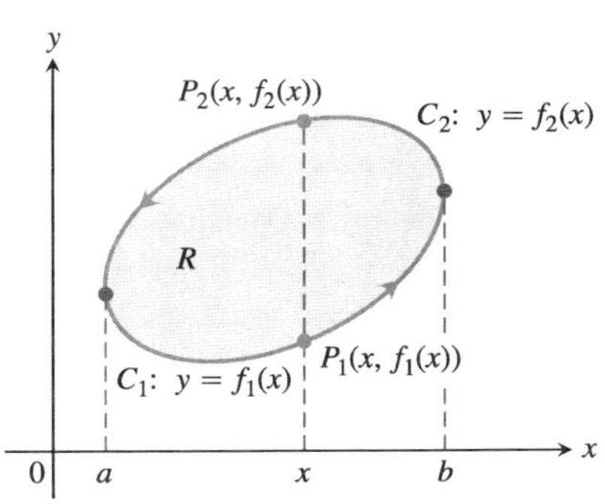

FIGURE 16.29 The boundary curve C is made up of C_1, the graph of $y = f_1(x)$, and C_2, the graph of $y = f_2(x)$.

Figure 16.29 shows C made up of two directed parts:

$$C_1:\quad y = f_1(x),\quad a \le x \le b, \qquad C_2:\quad y = f_2(x),\quad b \ge x \ge a.$$

For any x between a and b, we can integrate $\partial M/\partial y$ with respect to y from $y = f_1(x)$ to $y = f_2(x)$ and obtain

$$\int_{f_1(x)}^{f_2(x)} \frac{\partial M}{\partial y}\,dy = M(x, y)\Big]_{y=f_1(x)}^{y=f_2(x)} = M(x, f_2(x)) - M(x, f_1(x)).$$

We can then integrate this with respect to x from a to b:

$$\begin{aligned}\int_a^b \int_{f_1(x)}^{f_2(x)} \frac{\partial M}{\partial y}\, dy\, dx &= \int_a^b [M(x, f_2(x)) - M(x, f_1(x))]\, dx \\ &= -\int_b^a M(x, f_2(x))\, dx - \int_a^b M(x, f_1(x))\, dx \\ &= -\int_{C_2} M\, dx - \int_{C_1} M\, dx \\ &= -\oint_C M\, dx.\end{aligned}$$

Therefore

$$\oint_C M\, dx = \iint_R \left(-\frac{\partial M}{\partial y}\right) dx\, dy. \qquad (6)$$

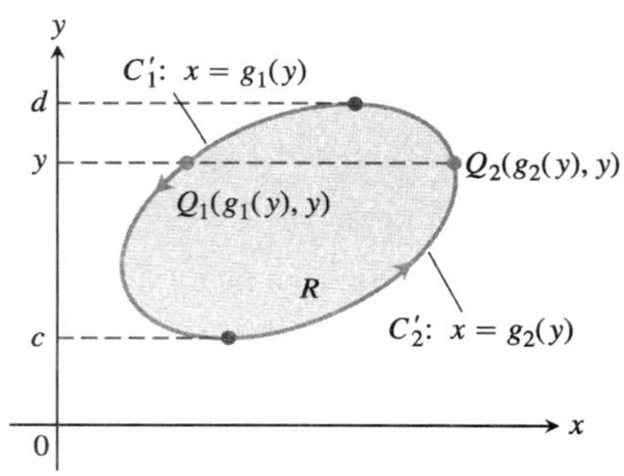

FIGURE 16.30 The boundary curve C is made up of C_1', the graph of $x = g_1(y)$, and C_2', the graph of $x = g_2(y)$.

Equation (6) is half the result we need for Equation (5). We derive the other half by integrating $\partial N/\partial x$ first with respect to x and then with respect to y, as suggested by Figure 16.30. This shows the curve C of Figure 16.29 decomposed into the two directed parts C_1': $x = g_1(y)$, $d \ge y \ge c$ and C_2': $x = g_2(y)$, $c \le y \le d$. The result of this double integration is

$$\oint_C N\, dy = \iint_R \frac{\partial N}{\partial x}\, dx\, dy. \qquad (7)$$

Summing Equations (6) and (7) gives Equation (5). This concludes the proof. ■

Extending the Proof to Other Regions

The argument we just gave does not apply directly to the rectangular region in Figure 16.31 because the lines $x = a$, $x = b$, $y = c$, and $y = d$ meet the region's boundary in more than two points. If we divide the boundary C into four directed line segments, however,

$$C_1:\ y = c,\quad a \le x \le b, \qquad C_2:\ x = b,\quad c \le y \le d$$

$$C_3:\ y = d,\quad b \ge x \ge a, \qquad C_4:\ x = a,\quad d \ge y \ge c,$$

we can modify the argument in the following way.

Proceeding as in the proof of Equation (7), we have

$$\begin{aligned}\int_c^d \int_a^b \frac{\partial N}{\partial x}\, dx\, dy &= \int_c^d (N(b, y) - N(a, y))\, dy \\ &= \int_c^d N(b, y)\, dy + \int_d^c N(a, y)\, dy \\ &= \int_{C_2} N\, dy + \int_{C_4} N\, dy. \qquad (8)\end{aligned}$$

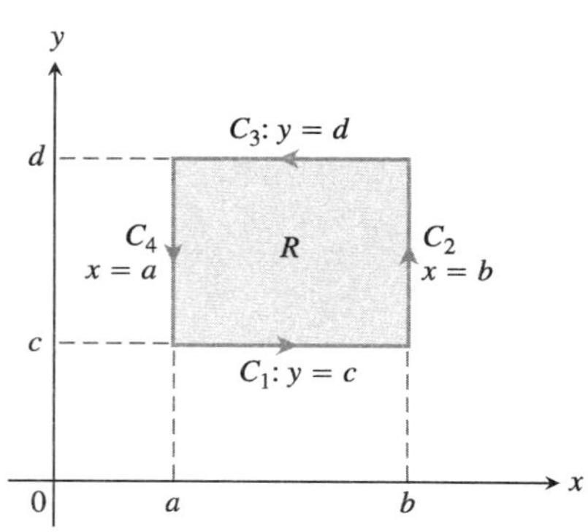

FIGURE 16.31 To prove Green's Theorem for a rectangle, we divide the boundary into four directed line segments.

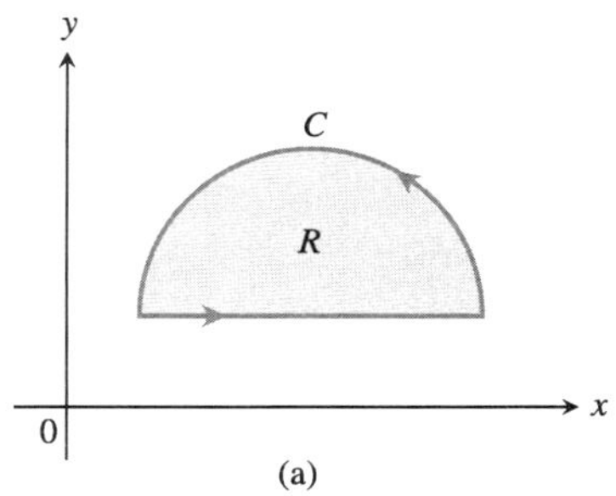

FIGURE 16.32 Other regions to which Green's Theorem applies.

Because y is constant along C_1 and C_3, $\int_{C_1} N\,dy = \int_{C_3} N\,dy = 0$, so we can add $\int_{C_1} N\,dy = \int_{C_3} N\,dy$ to the right-hand side of Equation (8) without changing the equality. Doing so, we have

$$\int_c^d \int_a^b \frac{\partial N}{\partial x}\,dx\,dy = \oint_C N\,dy. \tag{9}$$

Similarly, we can show that

$$\int_a^b \int_c^d \frac{\partial M}{\partial y}\,dy\,dx = -\oint_C M\,dx. \tag{10}$$

Subtracting Equation (10) from Equation (9), we again arrive at

$$\oint_C M\,dx + N\,dy = \iint_R \left(\frac{\partial N}{\partial x} - \frac{\partial M}{\partial y}\right) dx\,dy.$$

Regions like those in Figure 16.32 can be handled with no greater difficulty. Equation (5) still applies. It also applies to the horseshoe-shaped region R shown in Figure 16.33, as we see by putting together the regions R_1 and R_2 and their boundaries. Green's Theorem applies to C_1, R_1 and to C_2, R_2, yielding

$$\int_{C_1} M\,dx + N\,dy = \iint_{R_1} \left(\frac{\partial N}{\partial x} - \frac{\partial M}{\partial y}\right) dx\,dy$$

$$\int_{C_2} M\,dx + N\,dy = \iint_{R_2} \left(\frac{\partial N}{\partial x} - \frac{\partial M}{\partial y}\right) dx\,dy.$$

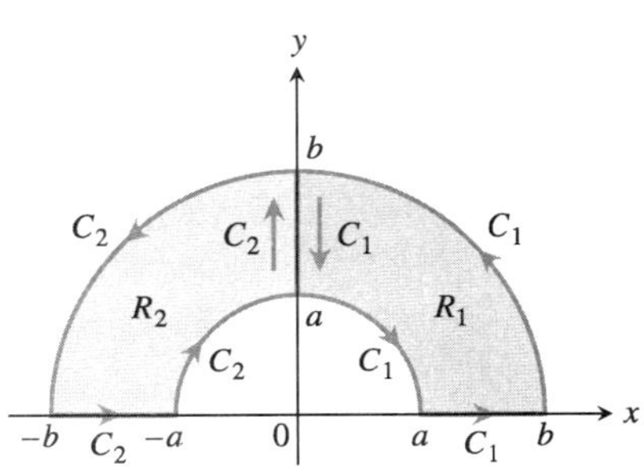

FIGURE 16.33 A region R that combines regions R_1 and R_2.

When we add these two equations, the line integral along the y-axis from b to a for C_1 cancels the integral over the same segment but in the opposite direction for C_2. Hence,

$$\oint_C M\,dx + N\,dy = \iint_R \left(\frac{\partial N}{\partial x} - \frac{\partial M}{\partial y}\right) dx\,dy,$$

where C consists of the two segments of the x-axis from $-b$ to $-a$ and from a to b and of the two semicircles, and where R is the region inside C.

The device of adding line integrals over separate boundaries to build up an integral over a single boundary can be extended to any finite number of subregions. In Figure 16.34a let C_1 be the boundary, oriented counterclockwise, of the region R_1 in the first quadrant. Similarly, for the other three quadrants, C_i is the boundary of the region R_i, $i = 2, 3, 4$. By Green's Theorem,

$$\oint_{C_i} M\,dx + N\,dy = \iint_{R_i} \left(\frac{\partial N}{\partial x} - \frac{\partial M}{\partial y}\right) dx\,dy. \tag{11}$$

We sum Equation (11) over $i = 1, 2, 3, 4$, and get (Figure 16.34b):

$$\oint_{r=b} (M\,dx + N\,dy) + \oint_{r=a} (M\,dx + N\,dy) = \iint_{\cup R_i} \left(\frac{\partial N}{\partial x} - \frac{\partial M}{\partial y}\right) dx\,dy. \tag{12}$$

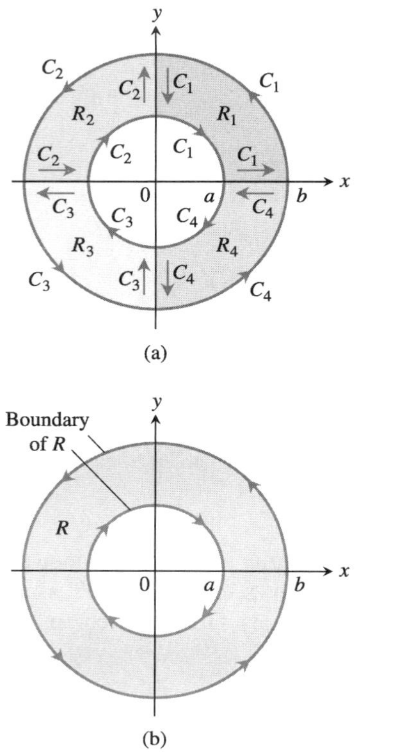

FIGURE 16.34 The annular region R combines four smaller regions. In polar coordinates, $r = a$ for the inner circle, $r = b$ for the outer circle, and $a \leq r \leq b$ for the region itself.

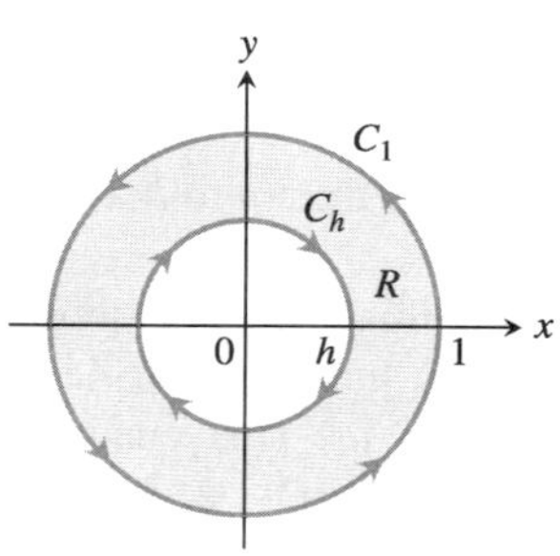

FIGURE 16.35 Green's Theorem may be applied to the annular region R by integrating along the boundaries as shown (Example 6).

Equation (12) says that the double integral of $(\partial N/\partial x) - (\partial M/\partial y)$ over the annular ring R equals the line integral of $M\,dx + N\,dy$ over the complete boundary of R in the direction that keeps R on our left as we progress (Figure 16.34b).

EXAMPLE 6 Verifying Green's Theorem for an Annular Ring

Verify the circulation form of Green's Theorem (Equation 4) on the annular ring R: $h^2 \leq x^2 + y^2 \leq 1$, $0 < h < 1$ (Figure 16.35), if

$$M = \frac{-y}{x^2 + y^2}, \qquad N = \frac{x}{x^2 + y^2}.$$

Here R is not simply connected.

Solution The boundary of R consists of the circle

$$C_1: \quad x = \cos t, \qquad y = \sin t, \qquad 0 \leq t \leq 2\pi,$$

traversed counterclockwise as t increases, and the circle

$$C_h: \quad x = h\cos\theta, \qquad y = -h\sin\theta, \qquad 0 \leq \theta \leq 2\pi,$$

traversed clockwise as θ increases. The functions M and N and their partial derivatives are continuous throughout R. Moreover,

$$\frac{\partial M}{\partial y} = \frac{(x^2 + y^2)(-1) + y(2y)}{(x^2 + y^2)^2} = \frac{y^2 - x^2}{(x^2 + y^2)^2} = \frac{\partial N}{\partial x},$$

so

$$\iint_R \left(\frac{\partial N}{\partial x} - \frac{\partial M}{\partial y}\right) dx\,dy = \iint_R 0\,dx\,dy = 0.$$

The integral of $M\,dx + N\,dy$ over the boundary of R is

$$\begin{aligned}\int_C M\,dx + N\,dy &= \oint_{C_1} \frac{x\,dy - y\,dx}{x^2 + y^2} + \oint_{C_h} \frac{x\,dy - y\,dx}{x^2 + y^2}\\ &= \int_0^{2\pi} (\cos^2 t + \sin^2 t)\,dt - \int_0^{2\pi} \frac{h^2(\cos^2\theta + \sin^2\theta)}{h^2}\,d\theta\\ &= 2\pi - 2\pi = 0.\end{aligned}$$

■

The functions M and N in Example 6 are discontinuous at $(0, 0)$, so we cannot apply Green's Theorem to the circle C_1 and the region inside it. We must exclude the origin. We do so by excluding the points interior to C_h.

We could replace the circle C_1 in Example 6 by an ellipse or any other simple closed curve K surrounding C_h (Figure 16.36). The result would still be

$$\oint_K (M\,dx + N\,dy) + \oint_{C_h} (M\,dx + N\,dy) = \iint_R \left(\frac{\partial N}{\partial x} - \frac{\partial M}{\partial y}\right) dy\,dx = 0,$$

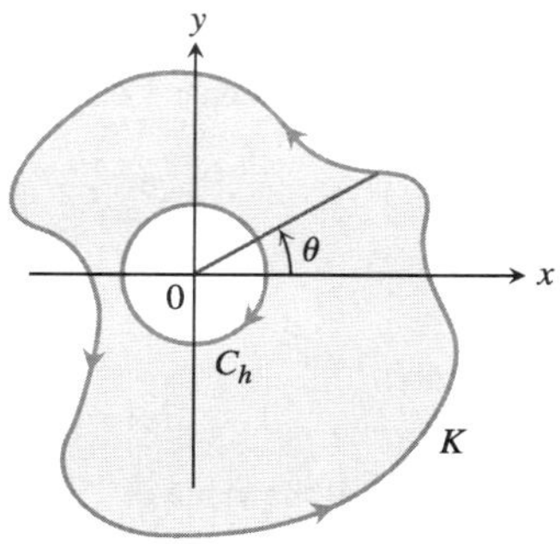

FIGURE 16.36 The region bounded by the circle C_h and the curve K.

which leads to the conclusion that

$$\oint_K (M\,dx + N\,dy) = 2\pi$$

for any such curve K. We can explain this result by changing to polar coordinates. With

$$x = r\cos\theta, \qquad y = r\sin\theta,$$
$$dx = -r\sin\theta\,d\theta + \cos\theta\,dr, \qquad dy = r\cos\theta\,d\theta + \sin\theta\,dr,$$

we have

$$\frac{x\,dy - y\,dx}{x^2 + y^2} = \frac{r^2(\cos^2\theta + \sin^2\theta)\,d\theta}{r^2} = d\theta,$$

and θ increases by 2π as we traverse K once counterclockwise.

EXERCISES 16.4

Verifying Green's Theorem

In Exercises 1–4, verify the conclusion of Green's Theorem by evaluating both sides of Equations (3) and (4) for the field $\mathbf{F} = M\mathbf{i} + N\mathbf{j}$. Take the domains of integration in each case to be the disk R: $x^2 + y^2 \le a^2$ and its bounding circle C: $\mathbf{r} = (a\cos t)\mathbf{i} + (a\sin t)\mathbf{j}$, $0 \le t \le 2\pi$.

1. $\mathbf{F} = -y\mathbf{i} + x\mathbf{j}$
2. $\mathbf{F} = y\mathbf{i}$
3. $\mathbf{F} = 2x\mathbf{i} - 3y\mathbf{j}$
4. $\mathbf{F} = -x^2y\mathbf{i} + xy^2\mathbf{j}$

Counterclockwise Circulation and Outward Flux

In Exercises 5–10, use Green's Theorem to find the counterclockwise circulation and outward flux for the field $\mathbf{F}$ and curve C.

5. $\mathbf{F} = (x - y)\mathbf{i} + (y - x)\mathbf{j}$
   C: The square bounded by $x = 0, x = 1, y = 0, y = 1$
6. $\mathbf{F} = (x^2 + 4y)\mathbf{i} + (x + y^2)\mathbf{j}$
   C: The square bounded by $x = 0, x = 1, y = 0, y = 1$
7. $\mathbf{F} = (y^2 - x^2)\mathbf{i} + (x^2 + y^2)\mathbf{j}$
   C: The triangle bounded by $y = 0, x = 3$, and $y = x$
8. $\mathbf{F} = (x + y)\mathbf{i} - (x^2 + y^2)\mathbf{j}$
   C: The triangle bounded by $y = 0, x = 1$, and $y = x$
9. $\mathbf{F} = (x + e^x \sin y)\mathbf{i} + (x + e^x \cos y)\mathbf{j}$
   C: The right-hand loop of the lemniscate $r^2 = \cos 2\theta$
10. $\mathbf{F} = \left(\tan^{-1}\frac{y}{x}\right)\mathbf{i} + \ln(x^2 + y^2)\mathbf{j}$
   C: The boundary of the region defined by the polar coordinate inequalities $1 \le r \le 2, 0 \le \theta \le \pi$
11. Find the counterclockwise circulation and outward flux of the field $\mathbf{F} = xy\mathbf{i} + y^2\mathbf{j}$ around and over the boundary of the region enclosed by the curves $y = x^2$ and $y = x$ in the first quadrant.
12. Find the counterclockwise circulation and the outward flux of the field $\mathbf{F} = (-\sin y)\mathbf{i} + (x\cos y)\mathbf{j}$ around and over the square cut from the first quadrant by the lines $x = \pi/2$ and $y = \pi/2$.
13. Find the outward flux of the field

$$\mathbf{F} = \left(3xy - \frac{x}{1 + y^2}\right)\mathbf{i} + (e^x + \tan^{-1} y)\mathbf{j}$$

   across the cardioid $r = a(1 + \cos\theta)$, $a > 0$.
14. Find the counterclockwise circulation of $\mathbf{F} = (y + e^x \ln y)\mathbf{i} + (e^x/y)\mathbf{j}$ around the boundary of the region that is bounded above by the curve $y = 3 - x^2$ and below by the curve $y = x^4 + 1$.

Work

In Exercises 15 and 16, find the work done by $\mathbf{F}$ in moving a particle once counterclockwise around the given curve.

15. $\mathbf{F} = 2xy^3\mathbf{i} + 4x^2y^2\mathbf{j}$
   C: The boundary of the "triangular" region in the first quadrant enclosed by the x-axis, the line $x = 1$, and the curve $y = x^3$
16. $\mathbf{F} = (4x - 2y)\mathbf{i} + (2x - 4y)\mathbf{j}$
   C: The circle $(x - 2)^2 + (y - 2)^2 = 4$

Evaluating Line Integrals in the Plane

Apply Green's Theorem to evaluate the integrals in Exercises 17–20.

17. $\oint_C (y^2\,dx + x^2\,dy)$
   C: The triangle bounded by $x = 0, x + y = 1, y = 0$
18. $\oint_C (3y\,dx + 2x\,dy)$
   C: The boundary of $0 \le x \le \pi, 0 \le y \le \sin x$

19. $\oint_C (6y + x)\,dx + (y + 2x)\,dy$

C: The circle $(x - 2)^2 + (y - 3)^2 = 4$

20. $\oint_C (2x + y^2)\,dx + (2xy + 3y)\,dy$

C: Any simple closed curve in the plane for which Green's Theorem holds

Calculating Area with Green's Theorem

If a simple closed curve C in the plane and the region R it encloses satisfy the hypotheses of Green's Theorem, the area of R is given by

Green's Theorem Area Formula

$$\text{Area of } R = \frac{1}{2}\oint_C x\,dy - y\,dx \qquad (13)$$

The reason is that by Equation (3), run backward,

$$\text{Area of } R = \iint_R dy\,dx = \iint_R \left(\frac{1}{2} + \frac{1}{2}\right) dy\,dx$$

$$= \oint_C \frac{1}{2}x\,dy - \frac{1}{2}y\,dx.$$

Use the Green's Theorem area formula (Equation 13) to find the areas of the regions enclosed by the curves in Exercises 21–24.

21. The circle $\mathbf{r}(t) = (a\cos t)\mathbf{i} + (a\sin t)\mathbf{j}, \quad 0 \le t \le 2\pi$
22. The ellipse $\mathbf{r}(t) = (a\cos t)\mathbf{i} + (b\sin t)\mathbf{j}, \quad 0 \le t \le 2\pi$
23. The astroid $\mathbf{r}(t) = (\cos^3 t)\mathbf{i} + (\sin^3 t)\mathbf{j}, \quad 0 \le t \le 2\pi$
24. The curve $\mathbf{r}(t) = t^2\mathbf{i} + ((t^3/3) - t)\mathbf{j}, \quad -\sqrt{3} \le t \le \sqrt{3}$ (see accompanying figure).

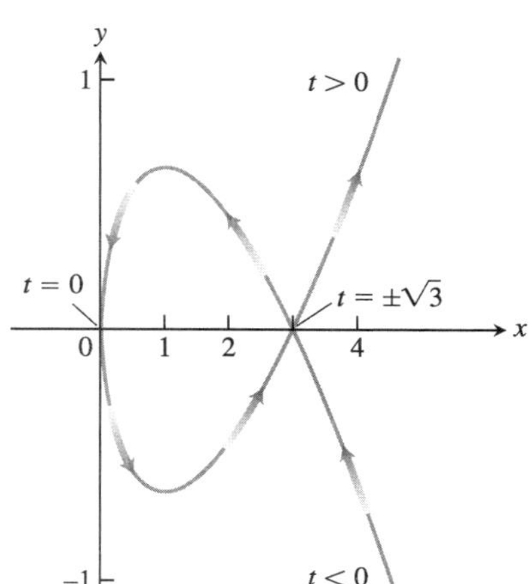

Theory and Examples

25. Let C be the boundary of a region on which Green's Theorem holds. Use Green's Theorem to calculate

a. $\oint_C f(x)\,dx + g(y)\,dy$

b. $\oint_C ky\,dx + hx\,dy$ (k and h constants).

26. **Integral dependent only on area** Show that the value of

$$\oint_C xy^2\,dx + (x^2y + 2x)\,dy$$

around any square depends only on the area of the square and not on its location in the plane.

27. What is special about the integral

$$\oint_C 4x^3y\,dx + x^4\,dy?$$

Give reasons for your answer.

28. What is special about the integral

$$\oint_C -y^3\,dy + x^3\,dx?$$

Give reasons for your answer.

29. **Area as a line integral** Show that if R is a region in the plane bounded by a piecewise-smooth simple closed curve C, then

$$\text{Area of } R = \oint_C x\,dy = -\oint_C y\,dx.$$

30. **Definite integral as a line integral** Suppose that a nonnegative function $y = f(x)$ has a continuous first derivative on $[a, b]$. Let C be the boundary of the region in the xy-plane that is bounded below by the x-axis, above by the graph of f, and on the sides by the lines $x = a$ and $x = b$. Show that

$$\int_a^b f(x)\,dx = -\oint_C y\,dx.$$

31. **Area and the centroid** Let A be the area and $\bar{x}$ the x-coordinate of the centroid of a region R that is bounded by a piecewise-smooth simple closed curve C in the xy-plane. Show that

$$\frac{1}{2}\oint_C x^2\,dy = -\oint_C xy\,dx = \frac{1}{3}\oint_C x^2\,dy - xy\,dx = A\bar{x}.$$

32. **Moment of inertia** Let I_y be the moment of inertia about the y-axis of the region in Exercise 31. Show that

$$\frac{1}{3}\oint_C x^3\,dy = -\oint_C x^2y\,dx = \frac{1}{4}\oint_C x^3\,dy - x^2y\,dx = I_y.$$

33. **Green's Theorem and Laplace's equation** Assuming that all the necessary derivatives exist and are continuous, show that if $f(x, y)$ satisfies the Laplace equation

$$\frac{\partial^2 f}{\partial x^2} + \frac{\partial^2 f}{\partial y^2} = 0,$$

then

$$\oint_C \frac{\partial f}{\partial y}\,dx - \frac{\partial f}{\partial x}\,dy = 0$$

for all closed curves C to which Green's Theorem applies. (The converse is also true: If the line integral is always zero, then f satisfies the Laplace equation.)

34. **Maximizing work** Among all smooth simple closed curves in the plane, oriented counterclockwise, find the one along which the work done by

$$\mathbf{F} = \left(\frac{1}{4}x^2y + \frac{1}{3}y^3\right)\mathbf{i} + x\mathbf{j}$$

is greatest. (*Hint:* Where is (curl $\mathbf{F}$) $\cdot$ $\mathbf{k}$ positive?)

35. **Regions with many holes** Green's Theorem holds for a region R with any finite number of holes as long as the bounding curves are smooth, simple, and closed and we integrate over each component of the boundary in the direction that keeps R on our immediate left as we go along (Figure 16.37).

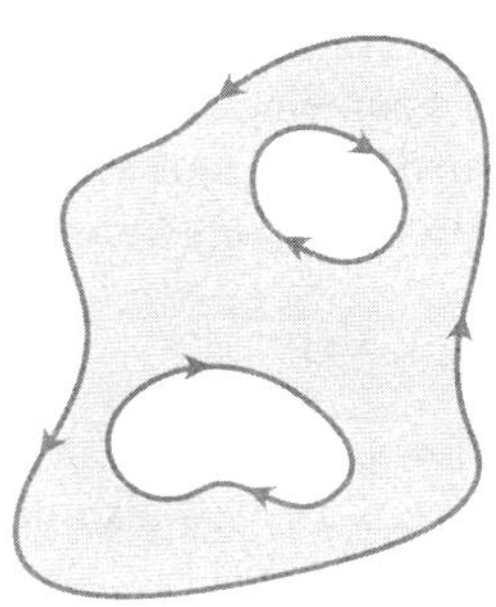

FIGURE 16.37 Green's Theorem holds for regions with more than one hole (Exercise 35).

a. Let $f(x, y) = \ln(x^2 + y^2)$ and let C be the circle $x^2 + y^2 = a^2$. Evaluate the flux integral

$$\oint_C \nabla f \cdot \mathbf{n}\,ds.$$

b. Let K be an arbitrary smooth simple closed curve in the plane that does not pass through (0, 0). Use Green's Theorem to show that

$$\oint_K \nabla f \cdot \mathbf{n}\,ds$$

has two possible values, depending on whether (0, 0) lies inside K or outside K.

36. **Bendixson's criterion** The *streamlines* of a planar fluid flow are the smooth curves traced by the fluid's individual particles. The vectors $\mathbf{F} = M(x, y)\mathbf{i} + N(x, y)\mathbf{j}$ of the flow's velocity field are the tangent vectors of the streamlines. Show that if the flow takes place over a simply connected region R (no holes or missing points) and that if $M_x + N_y \neq 0$ throughout R, then none of the streamlines in R is closed. In other words, no particle of fluid ever has a closed trajectory in R. The criterion $M_x + N_y \neq 0$ is called **Bendixson's criterion** for the nonexistence of closed trajectories.

37. Establish Equation (7) to finish the proof of the special case of Green's Theorem.

38. Establish Equation (10) to complete the argument for the extension of Green's Theorem.

39. **Curl component of conservative fields** Can anything be said about the curl component of a conservative two-dimensional vector field? Give reasons for your answer.

40. **Circulation of conservative fields** Does Green's Theorem give any information about the circulation of a conservative field? Does this agree with anything else you know? Give reasons for your answer.

COMPUTER EXPLORATIONS

Finding Circulation

In Exercises 41–44, use a CAS and Green's Theorem to find the counterclockwise circulation of the field $\mathbf{F}$ around the simple closed curve C. Perform the following CAS steps.

a. Plot C in the xy-plane.

b. Determine the integrand $(\partial N/\partial x) - (\partial M/\partial y)$ for the curl form of Green's Theorem.

c. Determine the (double integral) limits of integration from your plot in part (a) and evaluate the curl integral for the circulation.

41. $\mathbf{F} = (2x - y)\mathbf{i} + (x + 3y)\mathbf{j}$, C: The ellipse $x^2 + 4y^2 = 4$

42. $\mathbf{F} = (2x^3 - y^3)\mathbf{i} + (x^3 + y^3)\mathbf{j}$, C: The ellipse $\frac{x^2}{4} + \frac{y^2}{9} = 1$

43. $\mathbf{F} = x^{-1}e^y\mathbf{i} + (e^y \ln x + 2x)\mathbf{j}$,
C: The boundary of the region defined by $y = 1 + x^4$ (below) and $y = 2$ (above)

44. $\mathbf{F} = xe^y\mathbf{i} + 4x^2 \ln y\,\mathbf{j}$,
C: The triangle with vertices (0, 0), (2, 0), and (0, 4)

16.5 Surface Area and Surface Integrals

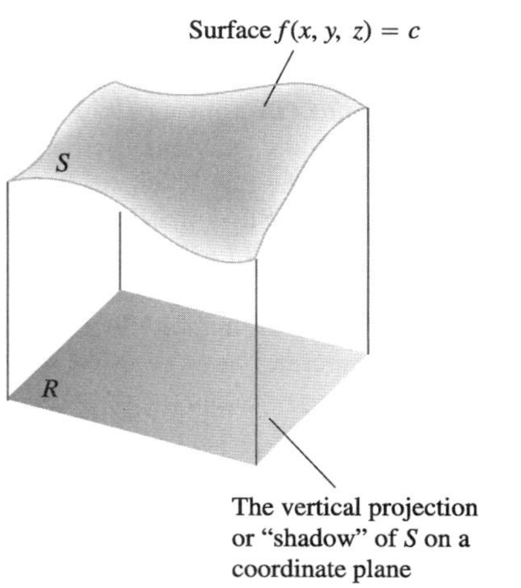

FIGURE 16.38 As we soon see, the integral of a function $g(x, y, z)$ over a surface S in space can be calculated by evaluating a related double integral over the vertical projection or "shadow" of S on a coordinate plane.

We know how to integrate a function over a flat region in a plane, but what if the function is defined over a curved surface? To evaluate one of these so-called surface integrals, we rewrite it as a double integral over a region in a coordinate plane beneath the surface (Figure 16.38). Surface integrals are used to compute quantities such as the flow of liquid across a membrane or the upward force on a falling parachute.

Surface Area

Figure 16.39 shows a surface S lying above its "shadow" region R in a plane beneath it. The surface is defined by the equation $f(x, y, z) = c$. If the surface is **smooth** (∇f is continuous and never vanishes on S), we can define and calculate its area as a double integral over R. We assume that this projection of the surface onto its shadow R is one-to-one. That is, each point in R corresponds to exactly one point (x, y, z) satisfying $f(x, y, z) = c$.

The first step in defining the area of S is to partition the region R into small rectangles ΔA_k of the kind we would use if we were defining an integral over R. Directly above each ΔA_k lies a patch of surface $\Delta\sigma_k$ that we may approximate by a parallelogram ΔP_k in the tangent plane to S at a point $T_k(x_k, y_k, z_k)$ in $\Delta\sigma_k$. This parallelogram in the tangent plane projects directly onto ΔA_k. To be specific, we choose the point $T_k(x_k, y_k, z_k)$ lying directly above the back corner C_k of ΔA_k, as shown in Figure 16.39. If the tangent plane is parallel to R, then ΔP_k will be congruent to ΔA_k. Otherwise, it will be a parallelogram whose area is somewhat larger than the area of ΔA_k.

Figure 16.40 gives a magnified view of $\Delta\sigma_k$ and ΔP_k, showing the gradient vector $\nabla f(x_k, y_k, z_k)$ at T_k and a unit vector $\mathbf{p}$ that is normal to R. The figure also shows the angle γ_k between ∇f and $\mathbf{p}$. The other vectors in the picture, $\mathbf{u}_k$ and $\mathbf{v}_k$, lie along the edges of the patch ΔP_k in the tangent plane. Thus, both $\mathbf{u}_k \times \mathbf{v}_k$ and ∇f are normal to the tangent plane.

We now need to know from advanced vector geometry that $|(\mathbf{u}_k \times \mathbf{v}_k)\cdot\mathbf{p}|$ is the area of the projection of the parallelogram determined by $\mathbf{u}_k$ and $\mathbf{v}_k$ onto any plane whose normal is $\mathbf{p}$. (A proof is given in Appendix 8.) In our case, this translates into the statement

$$|(\mathbf{u}_k \times \mathbf{v}_k)\cdot\mathbf{p}| = \Delta A_k.$$

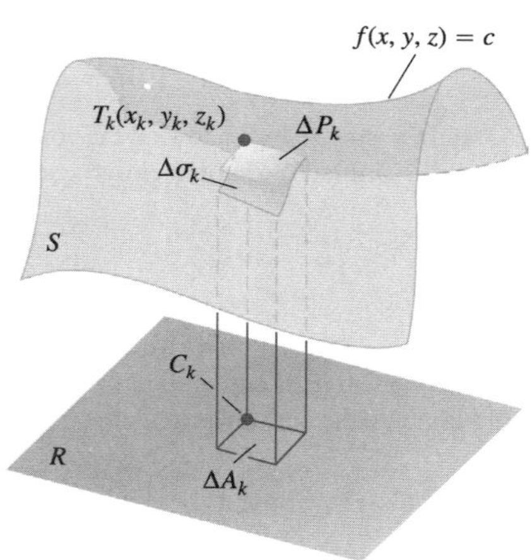

FIGURE 16.39 A surface S and its vertical projection onto a plane beneath it. You can think of R as the shadow of S on the plane. The tangent plane ΔP_k approximates the surface patch $\Delta\sigma_k$ above ΔA_k.

To simplify the notation in the derivation that follows, we are now denoting the *area* of the small rectangular region by ΔA_k as well. Likewise, ΔP_k will also denote the area of the portion of the tangent plane directly above this small region.

Now, $|\mathbf{u}_k \times \mathbf{v}_k|$ itself is the area ΔP_k (standard fact about cross products) so this last equation becomes

$$\underbrace{|\mathbf{u}_k \times \mathbf{v}_k|}_{\Delta P_k}\ \underbrace{|\mathbf{p}|}_{1}\ \underbrace{|\cos(\text{angle between } \mathbf{u}_k \times \mathbf{v}_k \text{ and } \mathbf{p})|}_{\substack{\text{Same as } |\cos\gamma_k| \text{ because } \nabla f \text{ and } \mathbf{u}_k \times \mathbf{v}_k \\ \text{are both normal to the tangent plane}}} = \Delta A_k$$

or

$$\Delta P_k |\cos\gamma_k| = \Delta A_k$$

or

$$\Delta P_k = \frac{\Delta A_k}{|\cos\gamma_k|},$$

provided $\cos \gamma_k \neq 0$. We will have $\cos \gamma_k \neq 0$ as long as ∇f is not parallel to the ground plane and $\nabla f \cdot \mathbf{p} \neq 0$.

Since the patches ΔP_k approximate the surface patches $\Delta \sigma_k$ that fit together to make S, the sum

$$\sum \Delta P_k = \sum \frac{\Delta A_k}{|\cos \gamma_k|} \tag{1}$$

looks like an approximation of what we might like to call the surface area of S. It also looks as if the approximation would improve if we refined the partition of R. In fact, the sums on the right-hand side of Equation (1) are approximating sums for the double integral

$$\iint_R \frac{1}{|\cos \gamma|}\, dA. \tag{2}$$

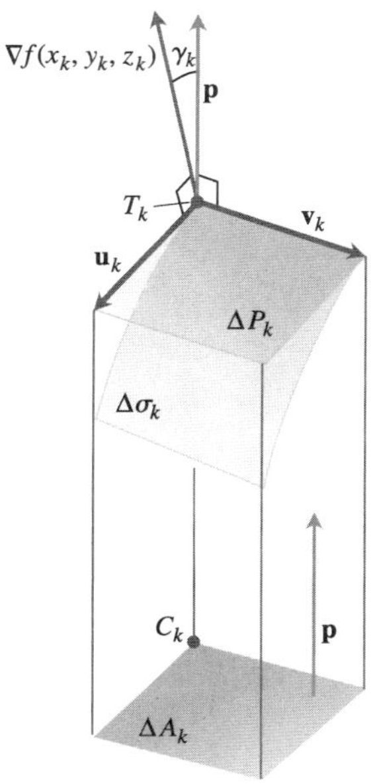

FIGURE 16.40 Magnified view from the preceding figure. The vector $\mathbf{u}_k \times \mathbf{v}_k$ (not shown) is parallel to the vector ∇f because both vectors are normal to the plane of ΔP_k.

We therefore define the **area** of S to be the value of this integral whenever it exists. For any surface $f(x, y, z) = c$, we have $|\nabla f \cdot \mathbf{p}| = |\nabla f||\mathbf{p}||\cos \gamma|$, so

$$\frac{1}{|\cos \gamma|} = \frac{|\nabla f|}{|\nabla f \cdot \mathbf{p}|}.$$

This combines with Equation (2) to give a practical formula for surface area.

Formula for Surface Area

The area of the surface $f(x, y, z) = c$ over a closed and bounded plane region R is

$$\text{Surface area} = \iint_R \frac{|\nabla f|}{|\nabla f \cdot \mathbf{p}|}\, dA, \tag{3}$$

where $\mathbf{p}$ is a unit vector normal to R and $\nabla f \cdot \mathbf{p} \neq 0$.

Thus, the area is the double integral over R of the magnitude of ∇f divided by the magnitude of the scalar component of ∇f normal to R.

We reached Equation (3) under the assumption that $\nabla f \cdot \mathbf{p} \neq 0$ throughout R and that ∇f is continuous. Whenever the integral exists, however, we define its value to be the area of the portion of the surface $f(x, y, z) = c$ that lies over R. (Recall that the projection is assumed to be one-to-one.)

In the exercises (see Equation 11), we show how Equation (3) simplifies if the surface is defined by $z = f(x, y)$.

EXAMPLE 1 Finding Surface Area

Find the area of the surface cut from the bottom of the paraboloid $x^2 + y^2 - z = 0$ by the plane $z = 4$.

Solution We sketch the surface S and the region R below it in the xy-plane (Figure 16.41). The surface S is part of the level surface $f(x, y, z) = x^2 + y^2 - z = 0$, and R is the disk $x^2 + y^2 \leq 4$ in the xy-plane. To get a unit vector normal to the plane of R, we can take $\mathbf{p} = \mathbf{k}$.

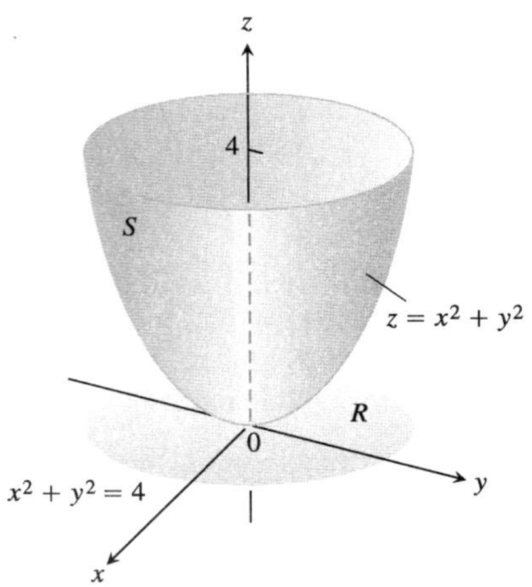

FIGURE 16.41 The area of this parabolic surface is calculated in Example 1.

At any point (x, y, z) on the surface, we have

$$\begin{aligned} f(x, y, z) &= x^2 + y^2 - z \\ \nabla f &= 2x\mathbf{i} + 2y\mathbf{j} - \mathbf{k} \\ |\nabla f| &= \sqrt{(2x)^2 + (2y)^2 + (-1)^2} \\ &= \sqrt{4x^2 + 4y^2 + 1} \\ |\nabla f \cdot \mathbf{p}| &= |\nabla f \cdot \mathbf{k}| = |-1| = 1. \end{aligned}$$

In the region R, $dA = dx\,dy$. Therefore,

$$\begin{aligned} \text{Surface area} &= \iint_R \frac{|\nabla f|}{|\nabla f \cdot \mathbf{p}|}\,dA && \text{Equation (3)} \\ &= \iint_{x^2+y^2\le 4} \sqrt{4x^2 + 4y^2 + 1}\,dx\,dy \\ &= \int_0^{2\pi}\int_0^2 \sqrt{4r^2 + 1}\,r\,dr\,d\theta && \text{Polar coordinates} \\ &= \int_0^{2\pi} \left[\frac{1}{12}(4r^2 + 1)^{3/2}\right]_0^2 d\theta \\ &= \int_0^{2\pi} \frac{1}{12}(17^{3/2} - 1)\,d\theta = \frac{\pi}{6}\left(17\sqrt{17} - 1\right). \end{aligned}$$

■

EXAMPLE 2 Finding Surface Area

Find the area of the cap cut from the hemisphere $x^2 + y^2 + z^2 = 2$, $z \ge 0$, by the cylinder $x^2 + y^2 = 1$ (Figure 16.42).

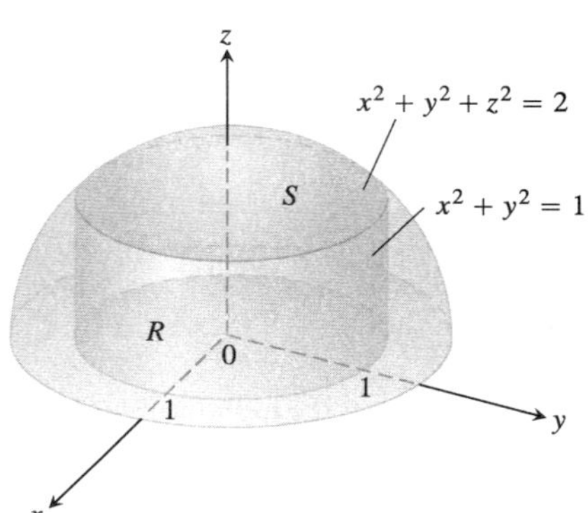

FIGURE 16.42 The cap cut from the hemisphere by the cylinder projects vertically onto the disk R: $x^2 + y^2 \le 1$ in the xy-plane (Example 2).

Solution The cap S is part of the level surface $f(x, y, z) = x^2 + y^2 + z^2 = 2$. It projects one-to-one onto the disk R: $x^2 + y^2 \le 1$ in the xy-plane. The unit vector $\mathbf{p} = \mathbf{k}$ is normal to the plane of R.

At any point on the surface,

$$\begin{aligned} f(x, y, z) &= x^2 + y^2 + z^2 \\ \nabla f &= 2x\mathbf{i} + 2y\mathbf{j} + 2z\mathbf{k} \\ |\nabla f| &= 2\sqrt{x^2 + y^2 + z^2} = 2\sqrt{2} && \text{Because } x^2 + y^2 + z^2 = 2 \text{ at points of } S \\ |\nabla f \cdot \mathbf{p}| &= |\nabla f \cdot \mathbf{k}| = |2z| = 2z. \end{aligned}$$

Therefore,

$$\text{Surface area} = \iint_R \frac{|\nabla f|}{|\nabla f \cdot \mathbf{p}|}\,dA = \iint_R \frac{2\sqrt{2}}{2z}\,dA = \sqrt{2}\iint_R \frac{dA}{z}. \tag{4}$$

What do we do about the z?

Since z is the z-coordinate of a point on the sphere, we can express it in terms of x and y as

$$z = \sqrt{2 - x^2 - y^2}.$$

We continue the work of Equation (4) with this substitution:

$$\begin{aligned}\text{Surface area} &= \sqrt{2}\iint_R \frac{dA}{z} = \sqrt{2}\iint_{x^2+y^2\le 1}\frac{dA}{\sqrt{2-x^2-y^2}}\\ &= \sqrt{2}\int_0^{2\pi}\int_0^1 \frac{r\,dr\,d\theta}{\sqrt{2-r^2}} \qquad \text{Polar coordinates}\\ &= \sqrt{2}\int_0^{2\pi}\left[-(2-r^2)^{1/2}\right]_{r=0}^{r=1} d\theta\\ &= \sqrt{2}\int_0^{2\pi}\left(\sqrt{2}-1\right)d\theta = 2\pi\left(2-\sqrt{2}\right).\end{aligned}$$

■

Surface Integrals

We now show how to integrate a function over a surface, using the ideas just developed for calculating surface area.

Suppose, for example, that we have an electrical charge distributed over a surface $f(x, y, z) = c$ like the one shown in Figure 16.43 and that the function $g(x, y, z)$ gives the charge per unit area (charge density) at each point on S. Then we may calculate the total charge on S as an integral in the following way.

We partition the shadow region R on the ground plane beneath the surface into small rectangles of the kind we would use if we were defining the surface area of S. Then directly above each ΔA_k lies a patch of surface $\Delta\sigma_k$ that we approximate with a parallelogram-shaped portion of tangent plane, ΔP_k. (See Figure 16.43.)

Up to this point the construction proceeds as in the definition of surface area, but now we take an additional step: We evaluate g at (x_k, y_k, z_k) and approximate the total charge on the surface path $\Delta\sigma_k$ by the product $g(x_k, y_k, z_k)\,\Delta P_k$. The rationale is that when the partition of R is sufficiently fine, the value of g throughout $\Delta\sigma_k$ is nearly constant and ΔP_k is nearly the same as $\Delta\sigma_k$. The total charge over S is then approximated by the sum

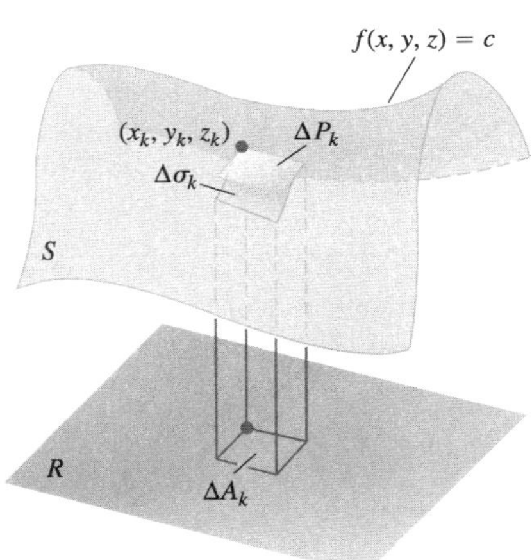

FIGURE 16.43 If we know how an electrical charge $g(x, y, z)$ is distributed over a surface, we can find the total charge with a suitably modified surface integral.

$$\text{Total charge} \approx \sum g(x_k, y_k, z_k)\,\Delta P_k = \sum g(x_k, y_k, z_k)\frac{\Delta A_k}{|\cos\gamma_k|}.$$

If f, the function defining the surface S, and its first partial derivatives are continuous, and if g is continuous over S, then the sums on the right-hand side of the last equation approach the limit

$$\iint_R g(x, y, z)\frac{dA}{|\cos\gamma|} = \iint_R g(x, y, z)\frac{|\nabla f|}{|\nabla f\cdot\mathbf{p}|}\,dA \qquad (5)$$

as the partition of R is refined in the usual way. This limit is called the integral of g over the surface S and is calculated as a double integral over R. The value of the integral is the total charge on the surface S.

As you might expect, the formula in Equation (5) defines the integral of *any* function g over the surface S as long as the integral exists.

DEFINITION Surface Integral

If R is the shadow region of a surface S defined by the equation $f(x, y, z) = c$, and g is a continuous function defined at the points of S, then the **integral of g over S** is the integral

$$\iint_R g(x, y, z) \frac{|\nabla f|}{|\nabla f \cdot \mathbf{p}|} dA, \tag{6}$$

where $\mathbf{p}$ is a unit vector normal to R and $\nabla f \cdot \mathbf{p} \neq 0$. The integral itself is called a **surface integral**.

The integral in Equation (6) takes on different meanings in different applications. If g has the constant value 1, the integral gives the area of S. If g gives the mass density of a thin shell of material modeled by S, the integral gives the mass of the shell.

We can abbreviate the integral in Equation (6) by writing $d\sigma$ for $(|\nabla f| / |\nabla f \cdot \mathbf{p}|)\, dA$.

The Surface Area Differential and the Differential Form for Surface Integrals

$$d\sigma = \frac{|\nabla f|}{|\nabla f \cdot \mathbf{p}|} dA \qquad \iint_S g\, d\sigma \tag{7}$$

Surface area differential — Differential formula for surface integrals

Surface integrals behave like other double integrals, the integral of the sum of two functions being the sum of their integrals and so on. The domain Additivity Property takes the form

$$\iint_S g\, d\sigma = \iint_{S_1} g\, d\sigma + \iint_{S_2} g\, d\sigma + \cdots + \iint_{S_n} g\, d\sigma.$$

The idea is that if S is partitioned by smooth curves into a finite number of nonoverlapping smooth patches (i.e., if S is **piecewise smooth**), then the integral over S is the sum of the integrals over the patches. Thus, the integral of a function over the surface of a cube is the sum of the integrals over the faces of the cube. We integrate over a turtle shell of welded plates by integrating one plate at a time and adding the results.

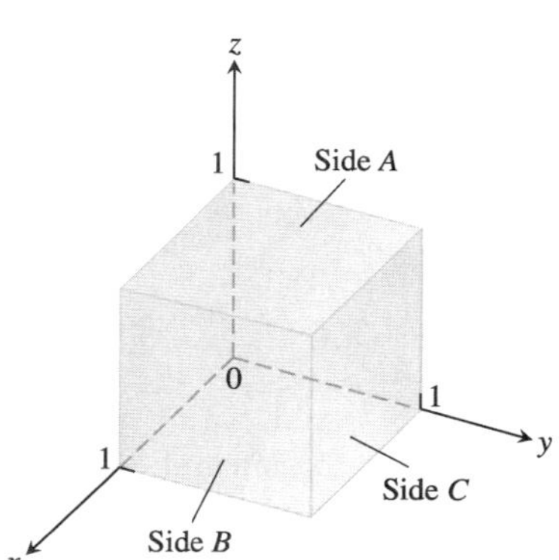

FIGURE 16.44 The cube in Example 3.

EXAMPLE 3 Integrating Over a Surface

Integrate $g(x, y, z) = xyz$ over the surface of the cube cut from the first octant by the planes $x = 1$, $y = 1$, and $z = 1$ (Figure 16.44).

Solution We integrate xyz over each of the six sides and add the results. Since $xyz = 0$ on the sides that lie in the coordinate planes, the integral over the surface of the cube reduces to

$$\iint_{\text{Cube surface}} xyz\, d\sigma = \iint_{\text{Side } A} xyz\, d\sigma + \iint_{\text{Side } B} xyz\, d\sigma + \iint_{\text{Side } C} xyz\, d\sigma.$$

Side A is the surface $f(x, y, z) = z = 1$ over the square region R_{xy}: $0 \le x \le 1$, $0 \le y \le 1$, in the xy-plane. For this surface and region,

$$\mathbf{p} = \mathbf{k}, \qquad \nabla f = \mathbf{k}, \qquad |\nabla f| = 1, \qquad |\nabla f \cdot \mathbf{p}| = |\mathbf{k} \cdot \mathbf{k}| = 1$$

$$d\sigma = \frac{|\nabla f|}{|\nabla f \cdot \mathbf{p}|}\, dA = \frac{1}{1}\, dx\, dy = dx\, dy$$

$$xyz = xy(1) = xy$$

and

$$\iint\limits_{\text{Side } A} xyz\, d\sigma = \iint\limits_{R_{xy}} xy\, dx\, dy = \int_0^1 \int_0^1 xy\, dx\, dy = \int_0^1 \frac{y}{2}\, dy = \frac{1}{4}.$$

Symmetry tells us that the integrals of xyz over sides B and C are also $1/4$. Hence,

$$\iint\limits_{\substack{\text{Cube}\\ \text{surface}}} xyz\, d\sigma = \frac{1}{4} + \frac{1}{4} + \frac{1}{4} = \frac{3}{4}.$$

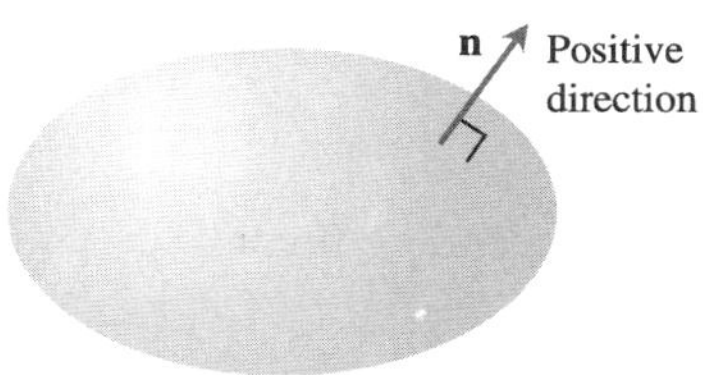

FIGURE 16.45 Smooth closed surfaces in space are orientable. The outward unit normal vector defines the positive direction at each point.

Orientation

We call a smooth surface S **orientable** or **two-sided** if it is possible to define a field $\mathbf{n}$ of unit normal vectors on S that varies continuously with position. Any patch or subportion of an orientable surface is orientable. Spheres and other smooth closed surfaces in space (smooth surfaces that enclose solids) are orientable. By convention, we choose $\mathbf{n}$ on a closed surface to point outward.

Once $\mathbf{n}$ has been chosen, we say that we have **oriented** the surface, and we call the surface together with its normal field an **oriented surface**. The vector $\mathbf{n}$ at any point is called the **positive direction** at that point (Figure 16.45).

The Möbius band in Figure 16.46 is not orientable. No matter where you start to construct a continuous-unit normal field (shown as the shaft of a thumbtack in the figure), moving the vector continuously around the surface in the manner shown will return it to the starting point with a direction opposite to the one it had when it started out. The vector at that point cannot point both ways and yet it must if the field is to be continuous. We conclude that no such field exists.

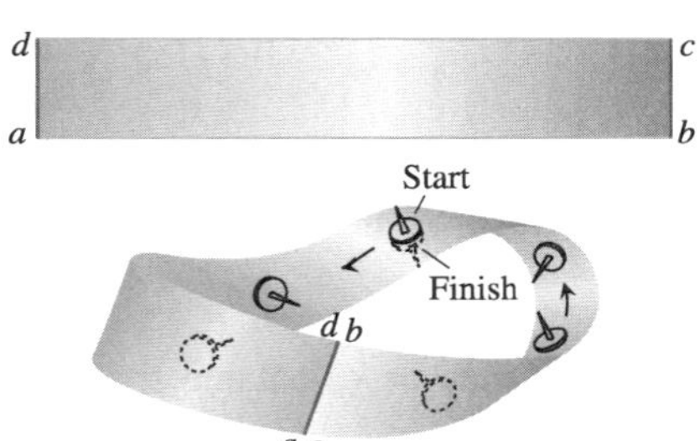

FIGURE 16.46 To make a Möbius band, take a rectangular strip of paper *abcd*, give the end *bc* a single twist, and paste the ends of the strip together to match *a* with *c* and *b* with *d*. The Möbius band is a nonorientable or one-sided surface.

Surface Integral for Flux

Suppose that $\mathbf{F}$ is a continuous vector field defined over an oriented surface S and that $\mathbf{n}$ is the chosen unit normal field on the surface. We call the integral of $\mathbf{F} \cdot \mathbf{n}$ over S the flux of $\mathbf{F}$ across S in the positive direction. Thus, the flux is the integral over S of the scalar component of $\mathbf{F}$ in the direction of $\mathbf{n}$.

DEFINITION Flux

The **flux** of a three-dimensional vector field $\mathbf{F}$ across an oriented surface S in the direction of $\mathbf{n}$ is

$$\text{Flux} = \iint\limits_S \mathbf{F} \cdot \mathbf{n}\, d\sigma. \tag{8}$$

The definition is analogous to the flux of a two-dimensional field $\mathbf{F}$ across a plane curve C. In the plane (Section 16.2), the flux is

$$\int_C \mathbf{F}\cdot\mathbf{n}\, ds,$$

the integral of the scalar component of $\mathbf{F}$ normal to the curve.

If $\mathbf{F}$ is the velocity field of a three-dimensional fluid flow, the flux of $\mathbf{F}$ across S is the net rate at which fluid is crossing S in the chosen positive direction. We discuss such flows in more detail in Section 16.7.

If $\mathbf{S}$ is part of a level surface $g(x, y, z) = c$, then $\mathbf{n}$ may be taken to be one of the two fields

$$\mathbf{n} = \pm\frac{\nabla g}{|\nabla g|}, \tag{9}$$

depending on which one gives the preferred direction. The corresponding flux is

$$\begin{aligned}\text{Flux} &= \iint_S \mathbf{F}\cdot\mathbf{n}\, d\sigma \\ &= \iint_R \left(\mathbf{F}\cdot\frac{\pm\nabla g}{|\nabla g|}\right)\frac{|\nabla g|}{|\nabla g\cdot\mathbf{p}|}\, dA \qquad \text{Equations (9) and (7)} \qquad (8) \\ &= \iint_R \mathbf{F}\cdot\frac{\pm\nabla g}{|\nabla g\cdot\mathbf{p}|}\, dA. \qquad (10)\end{aligned}$$

EXAMPLE 4 Finding Flux

Find the flux of $\mathbf{F} = yz\mathbf{j} + z^2\mathbf{k}$ outward through the surface S cut from the cylinder $y^2 + z^2 = 1$, $z \geq 0$, by the planes $x = 0$ and $x = 1$.

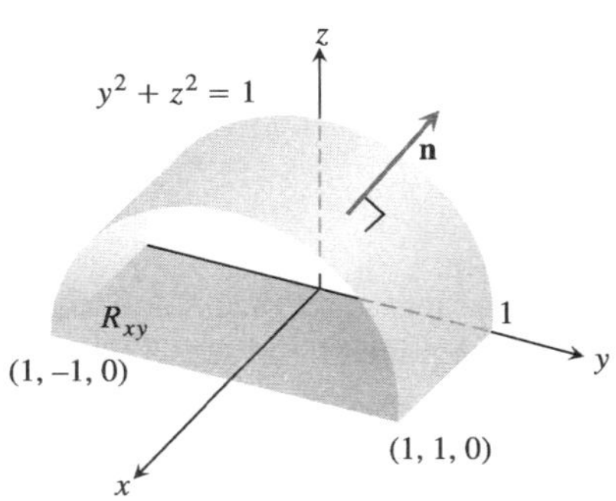

FIGURE 16.47 Calculating the flux of a vector field outward through this surface. The area of the shadow region R_{xy} is 2 (Example 4).

Solution The outward normal field on S (Figure 16.47) may be calculated from the gradient of $g(x, y, z) = y^2 + z^2$ to be

$$\mathbf{n} = +\frac{\nabla g}{|\nabla g|} = \frac{2y\mathbf{j} + 2z\mathbf{k}}{\sqrt{4y^2 + 4z^2}} = \frac{2y\mathbf{j} + 2z\mathbf{k}}{2\sqrt{1}} = y\mathbf{j} + z\mathbf{k}.$$

With $\mathbf{p} = \mathbf{k}$, we also have

$$d\sigma = \frac{|\nabla g|}{|\nabla g\cdot\mathbf{k}|}\, dA = \frac{2}{|2z|}\, dA = \frac{1}{z}\, dA.$$

We can drop the absolute value bars because $z \geq 0$ on S.

The value of $\mathbf{F}\cdot\mathbf{n}$ on the surface is

$$\begin{aligned}\mathbf{F}\cdot\mathbf{n} &= (yz\mathbf{j} + z^2\mathbf{k})\cdot(y\mathbf{j} + z\mathbf{k}) \\ &= y^2z + z^3 = z(y^2 + z^2) \\ &= z. \qquad y^2 + z^2 = 1 \text{ on } S\end{aligned}$$

Therefore, the flux of $\mathbf{F}$ outward through S is

$$\iint_S \mathbf{F}\cdot\mathbf{n}\, d\sigma = \iint_S (z)\left(\frac{1}{z}\, dA\right) = \iint_{R_{xy}} dA = \text{area}(R_{xy}) = 2. \qquad \blacksquare$$

Moments and Masses of Thin Shells

Thin shells of material like bowls, metal drums, and domes are modeled with surfaces. Their moments and masses are calculated with the formulas in Table 16.3.

TABLE 16.3 Mass and moment formulas for very thin shells

Mass: $M = \iint_S \delta(x, y, z)\, d\sigma \qquad (\delta(x, y, z) = \text{density at } (x, y, z), \text{ mass per unit area})$

First moments about the coordinate planes:

$$M_{yz} = \iint_S x\,\delta\, d\sigma, \qquad M_{xz} = \iint_S y\,\delta\, d\sigma, \qquad M_{xy} = \iint_S z\,\delta\, d\sigma$$

Coordinates of center of mass:

$$\bar{x} = M_{yz}/M, \qquad \bar{y} = M_{xz}/M, \qquad \bar{z} = M_{xy}/M$$

Moments of inertia about coordinate axes:

$$I_x = \iint_S (y^2 + z^2)\,\delta\, d\sigma, \qquad I_y = \iint_S (x^2 + z^2)\,\delta\, d\sigma,$$

$$I_z = \iint_S (x^2 + y^2)\,\delta\, d\sigma, \qquad I_L = \iint_S r^2\delta\, d\sigma,$$

$$r(x, y, z) = \text{distance from point } (x, y, z) \text{ to line } L$$

Radius of gyration about a line L: $R_L = \sqrt{I_L/M}$

EXAMPLE 5 Finding Center of Mass

Find the center of mass of a thin hemispherical shell of radius a and constant density δ.

Solution We model the shell with the hemisphere

$$f(x, y, z) = x^2 + y^2 + z^2 = a^2, \qquad z \geq 0$$

(Figure 16.48). The symmetry of the surface about the z-axis tells us that $\bar{x} = \bar{y} = 0$. It remains only to find $\bar{z}$ from the formula $\bar{z} = M_{xy}/M$.

The mass of the shell is

$$M = \iint_S \delta\, d\sigma = \delta \iint_S d\sigma = (\delta)(\text{area of } S) = 2\pi a^2 \delta.$$

To evaluate the integral for M_{xy}, we take $\mathbf{p} = \mathbf{k}$ and calculate

$$|\nabla f| = |2x\mathbf{i} + 2y\mathbf{j} + 2z\mathbf{k}| = 2\sqrt{x^2 + y^2 + z^2} = 2a$$

$$|\nabla f \cdot \mathbf{p}| = |\nabla f \cdot \mathbf{k}| = |2z| = 2z$$

$$d\sigma = \frac{|\nabla f|}{|\nabla f \cdot \mathbf{p}|}\, dA = \frac{a}{z}\, dA.$$

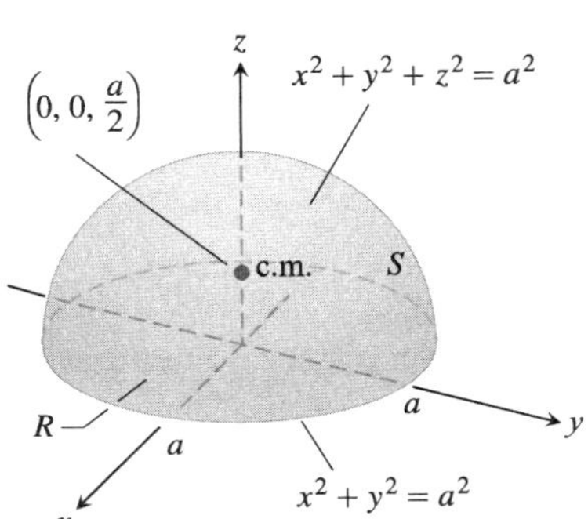

FIGURE 16.48 The center of mass of a thin hemispherical shell of constant density lies on the axis of symmetry halfway from the base to the top (Example 5).

Then

$$M_{xy} = \iint_S z\delta \, d\sigma = \delta \iint_R z \frac{a}{z} \, dA = \delta a \iint_R dA = \delta a(\pi a^2) = \delta \pi a^3$$

$$\bar{z} = \frac{M_{xy}}{M} = \frac{\pi a^3 \delta}{2\pi a^2 \delta} = \frac{a}{2}.$$

The shell's center of mass is the point $(0, 0, a/2)$. ■

EXERCISES 16.5

Surface Area

1. Find the area of the surface cut from the paraboloid $x^2 + y^2 - z = 0$ by the plane $z = 2$.
2. Find the area of the band cut from the paraboloid $x^2 + y^2 - z = 0$ by the planes $z = 2$ and $z = 6$.
3. Find the area of the region cut from the plane $x + 2y + 2z = 5$ by the cylinder whose walls are $x = y^2$ and $x = 2 - y^2$.
4. Find the area of the portion of the surface $x^2 - 2z = 0$ that lies above the triangle bounded by the lines $x = \sqrt{3}, y = 0$, and $y = x$ in the xy-plane.
5. Find the area of the surface $x^2 - 2y - 2z = 0$ that lies above the triangle bounded by the lines $x = 2, y = 0$, and $y = 3x$ in the xy-plane.
6. Find the area of the cap cut from the sphere $x^2 + y^2 + z^2 = 2$ by the cone $z = \sqrt{x^2 + y^2}$.
7. Find the area of the ellipse cut from the plane $z = cx$ (c a constant) by the cylinder $x^2 + y^2 = 1$.
8. Find the area of the upper portion of the cylinder $x^2 + z^2 = 1$ that lies between the planes $x = \pm 1/2$ and $y = \pm 1/2$.
9. Find the area of the portion of the paraboloid $x = 4 - y^2 - z^2$ that lies above the ring $1 \le y^2 + z^2 \le 4$ in the yz-plane.
10. Find the area of the surface cut from the paraboloid $x^2 + y + z^2 = 2$ by the plane $y = 0$.
11. Find the area of the surface $x^2 - 2 \ln x + \sqrt{15}y - z = 0$ above the square R: $1 \le x \le 2, 0 \le y \le 1$, in the xy-plane.
12. Find the area of the surface $2x^{3/2} + 2y^{3/2} - 3z = 0$ above the square R: $0 \le x \le 1, 0 \le y \le 1$, in the xy-plane.

Surface Integrals

13. Integrate $g(x, y, z) = x + y + z$ over the surface of the cube cut from the first octant by the planes $x = a, y = a, z = a$.
14. Integrate $g(x, y, z) = y + z$ over the surface of the wedge in the first octant bounded by the coordinate planes and the planes $x = 2$ and $y + z = 1$.
15. Integrate $g(x, y, z) = xyz$ over the surface of the rectangular solid cut from the first octant by the planes $x = a, y = b$, and $z = c$.
16. Integrate $g(x, y, z) = xyz$ over the surface of the rectangular solid bounded by the planes $x = \pm a, y = \pm b$, and $z = \pm c$.
17. Integrate $g(x, y, z) = x + y + z$ over the portion of the plane $2x + 2y + z = 2$ that lies in the first octant.
18. Integrate $g(x, y, z) = x\sqrt{y^2 + 4}$ over the surface cut from the parabolic cylinder $y^2 + 4z = 16$ by the planes $x = 0, x = 1$, and $z = 0$.

Flux Across a Surface

In Exercises 19 and 20, find the flux of the field $\mathbf{F}$ across the portion of the given surface in the specified direction.

19. $\mathbf{F}(x, y, z) = -\mathbf{i} + 2\mathbf{j} + 3\mathbf{k}$

    S: rectangular surface $z = 0, \quad 0 \le x \le 2, \quad 0 \le y \le 3$, direction $\mathbf{k}$

20. $\mathbf{F}(x, y, z) = yx^2\mathbf{i} - 2\mathbf{j} + xz\mathbf{k}$

    S: rectangular surface $y = 0, \quad -1 \le x \le 2, \quad 2 \le z \le 7$, direction $-\mathbf{j}$

In Exercises 21–26, find the flux of the field $\mathbf{F}$ across the portion of the sphere $x^2 + y^2 + z^2 = a^2$ in the first octant in the direction away from the origin.

21. $\mathbf{F}(x, y, z) = z\mathbf{k}$
22. $\mathbf{F}(x, y, z) = -y\mathbf{i} + x\mathbf{j}$
23. $\mathbf{F}(x, y, z) = y\mathbf{i} - x\mathbf{j} + \mathbf{k}$
24. $\mathbf{F}(x, y, z) = zx\mathbf{i} + zy\mathbf{j} + z^2\mathbf{k}$
25. $\mathbf{F}(x, y, z) = x\mathbf{i} + y\mathbf{j} + z\mathbf{k}$
26. $\mathbf{F}(x, y, z) = \dfrac{x\mathbf{i} + y\mathbf{j} + z\mathbf{k}}{\sqrt{x^2 + y^2 + z^2}}$

27. Find the flux of the field $\mathbf{F}(x, y, z) = z^2\mathbf{i} + x\mathbf{j} - 3z\mathbf{k}$ outward through the surface cut from the parabolic cylinder $z = 4 - y^2$ by the planes $x = 0, x = 1$, and $z = 0$.

28. Find the flux of the field $\mathbf{F}(x, y, z) = 4x\mathbf{i} + 4y\mathbf{j} + 2\mathbf{k}$ outward (away from the z-axis) through the surface cut from the bottom of the paraboloid $z = x^2 + y^2$ by the plane $z = 1$.

29. Let S be the portion of the cylinder $y = e^x$ in the first octant that projects parallel to the x-axis onto the rectangle R_{yz}: $1 \le y \le 2$, $0 \le z \le 1$ in the yz-plane (see the accompanying figure). Let $\mathbf{n}$ be the unit vector normal to S that points away from the yz-plane. Find the flux of the field $\mathbf{F}(x, y, z) = -2\mathbf{i} + 2y\mathbf{j} + z\mathbf{k}$ across S in the direction of $\mathbf{n}$.

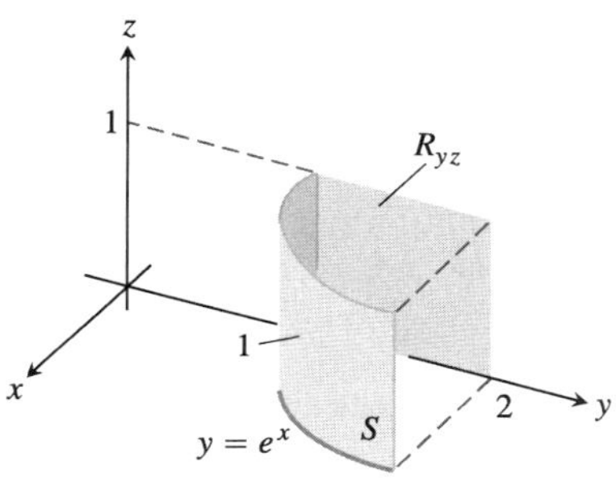

30. Let S be the portion of the cylinder $y = \ln x$ in the first octant whose projection parallel to the y-axis onto the xz-plane is the rectangle R_{xz}: $1 \le x \le e, 0 \le z \le 1$. Let $\mathbf{n}$ be the unit vector normal to S that points away from the xz-plane. Find the flux of $\mathbf{F} = 2y\mathbf{j} + z\mathbf{k}$ through S in the direction of $\mathbf{n}$.

31. Find the outward flux of the field $\mathbf{F} = 2xy\mathbf{i} + 2yz\mathbf{j} + 2xz\mathbf{k}$ across the surface of the cube cut from the first octant by the planes $x = a, y = a, z = a$.

32. Find the outward flux of the field $\mathbf{F} = xz\mathbf{i} + yz\mathbf{j} + \mathbf{k}$ across the surface of the upper cap cut from the solid sphere $x^2 + y^2 + z^2 \le 25$ by the plane $z = 3$.

Moments and Masses

33. Centroid Find the centroid of the portion of the sphere $x^2 + y^2 + z^2 = a^2$ that lies in the first octant.

34. Centroid Find the centroid of the surface cut from the cylinder $y^2 + z^2 = 9, z \ge 0$, by the planes $x = 0$ and $x = 3$ (resembles the surface in Example 4).

35. Thin shell of constant density Find the center of mass and the moment of inertia and radius of gyration about the z-axis of a thin shell of constant density δ cut from the cone $x^2 + y^2 - z^2 = 0$ by the planes $z = 1$ and $z = 2$,

36. Conical surface of constant density Find the moment of inertia about the z-axis of a thin shell of constant density δ cut from the cone $4x^2 + 4y^2 - z^2 = 0, z \ge 0$, by the circular cylinder $x^2 + y^2 = 2x$ (see the accompanying figure).

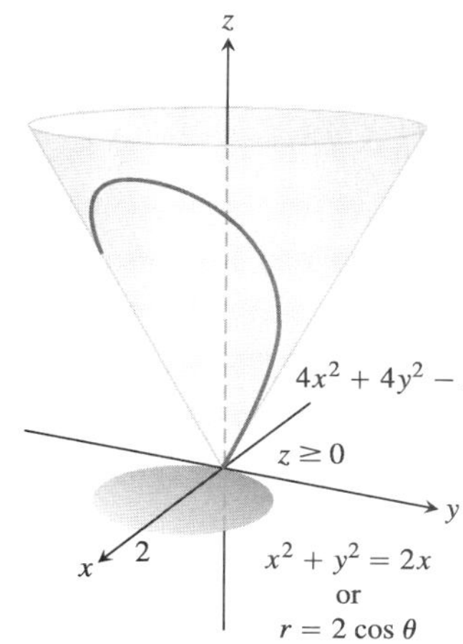

37. Spherical shells

a. Find the moment of inertia about a diameter of a thin spherical shell of radius a and constant density δ. (Work with a hemispherical shell and double the result.)

b. Use the Parallel Axis Theorem (Exercises 15.5) and the result in part (a) to find the moment of inertia about a line tangent to the shell.

38. a. Cones with and without ice cream Find the centroid of the lateral surface of a solid cone of base radius a and height h (cone surface minus the base).

b. Use Pappus's formula (Exercises 15.5) and the result in part (a) to find the centroid of the complete surface of a solid cone (side plus base).

c. A cone of radius a and height h is joined to a hemisphere of radius a to make a surface S that resembles an ice cream cone. Use Pappus's formula and the results in part (a) and Example 5 to find the centroid of S. How high does the cone have to be to place the centroid in the plane shared by the bases of the hemisphere and cone?

Special Formulas for Surface Area

If S is the surface defined by a function $z = f(x, y)$ that has continuous first partial derivatives throughout a region R_{xy} in the xy-plane (Figure 16.49), then S is also the level surface $F(x, y, z) = 0$ of the function $F(x, y, z) = f(x, y) - z$. Taking the unit normal to R_{xy} to be $\mathbf{p} = \mathbf{k}$ then gives

$$|\nabla F| = |f_x\mathbf{i} + f_y\mathbf{j} - \mathbf{k}| = \sqrt{f_x^2 + f_y^2 + 1}$$

$$|\nabla F \cdot \mathbf{p}| = |(f_x\mathbf{i} + f_y\mathbf{j} - \mathbf{k}) \cdot \mathbf{k}| = |-1| = 1$$

and

$$\iint_{R_{xy}} \frac{|\nabla F|}{|\nabla F \cdot \mathbf{p}|} dA = \iint_{R_{xy}} \sqrt{f_x^2 + f_y^2 + 1}\, dx\, dy, \qquad (11)$$

Similarly, the area of a smooth surface $x = f(y, z)$ over a region R_{yz} in the yz-plane is

$$A = \iint_{R_{yz}} \sqrt{f_y^2 + f_z^2 + 1}\, dy\, dz, \tag{12}$$

and the area of a smooth $y = f(x, z)$ over a region R_{xz} in the xz-plane is

$$A = \iint_{R_{xz}} \sqrt{f_x^2 + f_z^2 + 1}\, dx\, dz. \tag{13}$$

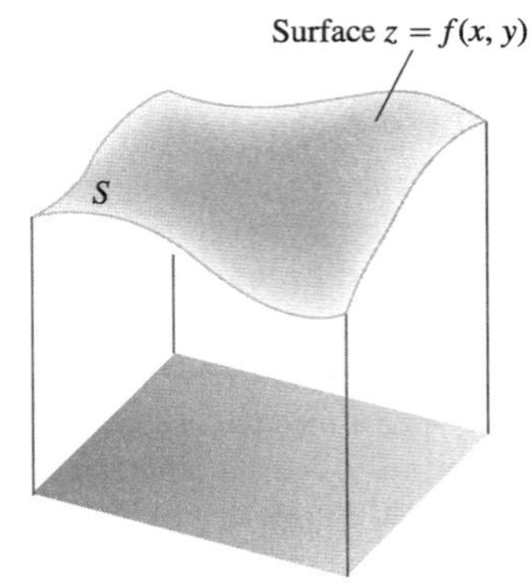

FIGURE 16.49 For a surface $z = f(x, y)$, the surface area formula in Equation (3) takes the form

$$A = \iint_{R_{xy}} \sqrt{f_x^2 + f_y^2 + 1}\, dx\, dy.$$

Use Equations (11)–(13) to find the area of the surfaces in Exercises 39–44.

39. The surface cut from the bottom of the paraboloid $z = x^2 + y^2$ by the plane $z = 3$

40. The surface cut from the "nose" of the paraboloid $x = 1 - y^2 - z^2$ by the yz-plane

41. The portion of the cone $z = \sqrt{x^2 + y^2}$ that lies over the region between the circle $x^2 + y^2 = 1$ and the ellipse $9x^2 + 4y^2 = 36$ in the xy-plane. (*Hint:* Use formulas from geometry to find the area of the region.)

42. The triangle cut from the plane $2x + 6y + 3z = 6$ by the bounding planes of the first octant. Calculate the area three ways, once with each area formula

43. The surface in the first octant cut from the cylinder $y = (2/3)z^{3/2}$ by the planes $x = 1$ and $y = 16/3$

44. The portion of the plane $y + z = 4$ that lies above the region cut from the first quadrant of the xz-plane by the parabola $x = 4 - z^2$

16.6 Parametrized Surfaces

We have defined curves in the plane in three different ways:

Explicit form:	$y = f(x)$
Implicit form:	$F(x, y) = 0$
Parametric vector form:	$\mathbf{r}(t) = f(t)\mathbf{i} + g(t)\mathbf{j}, \quad a \le t \le b.$

We have analogous definitions of surfaces in space:

Explicit form:	$z = f(x, y)$
Implicit form:	$F(x, y, z) = 0.$

There is also a parametric form that gives the position of a point on the surface as a vector function of two variables. The present section extends the investigation of surface area and surface integrals to surfaces described parametrically.

Parametrizations of Surfaces

Let

$$\mathbf{r}(u, v) = f(u, v)\mathbf{i} + g(u, v)\mathbf{j} + h(u, v)\mathbf{k} \tag{1}$$

be a continuous vector function that is defined on a region R in the uv-plane and one-to-one on the interior of R (Figure 16.50). We call the range of $\mathbf{r}$ the **surface** S defined or traced by $\mathbf{r}$. Equation (1) together with the domain R constitute a **parametrization** of the surface. The variables u and v are the **parameters**, and R is the **parameter domain**.

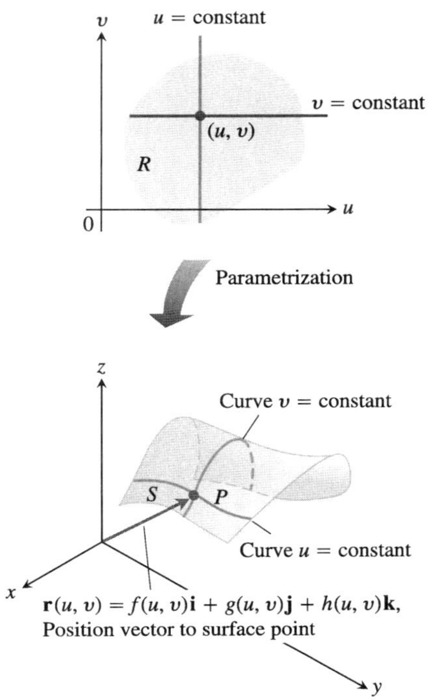

FIGURE 16.50 A parametrized surface S expressed as a vector function of two variables defined on a region R.

To simplify our discussion, we take R to be a rectangle defined by inequalities of the form $a \leq u \leq b, c \leq v \leq d$. The requirement that $\mathbf{r}$ be one-to-one on the interior of R ensures that S does not cross itself. Notice that Equation (1) is the vector equivalent of *three* parametric equations:

$$x = f(u, v), \qquad y = g(u, v), \qquad z = h(u, v).$$

EXAMPLE 1 Parametrizing a Cone

Find a parametrization of the cone

$$z = \sqrt{x^2 + y^2}, \qquad 0 \leq z \leq 1.$$

Solution Here, cylindrical coordinates provide everything we need. A typical point (x, y, z) on the cone (Figure 16.51) has $x = r\cos\theta$, $y = r\sin\theta$, and $z = \sqrt{x^2 + y^2} = r$, with $0 \leq r \leq 1$ and $0 \leq \theta \leq 2\pi$. Taking $u = r$ and $v = \theta$ in Equation (1) gives the parametrization

$$\mathbf{r}(r, \theta) = (r\cos\theta)\mathbf{i} + (r\sin\theta)\mathbf{j} + r\mathbf{k}, \qquad 0 \leq r \leq 1, \quad 0 \leq \theta \leq 2\pi.$$ ■

EXAMPLE 2 Parametrizing a Sphere

Find a parametrization of the sphere $x^2 + y^2 + z^2 = a^2$.

Solution Spherical coordinates provide what we need. A typical point (x, y, z) on the sphere (Figure 16.52) has $x = a\sin\phi\cos\theta$, $y = a\sin\phi\sin\theta$, and $z = a\cos\phi$, $0 \leq \phi \leq \pi$, $0 \leq \theta \leq 2\pi$. Taking $u = \phi$ and $v = \theta$ in Equation (1) gives the parametrization

$$\mathbf{r}(\phi, \theta) = (a\sin\phi\cos\theta)\mathbf{i} + (a\sin\phi\sin\theta)\mathbf{j} + (a\cos\phi)\mathbf{k},$$
$$0 \leq \phi \leq \pi, \quad 0 \leq \theta \leq 2\pi.$$ ■

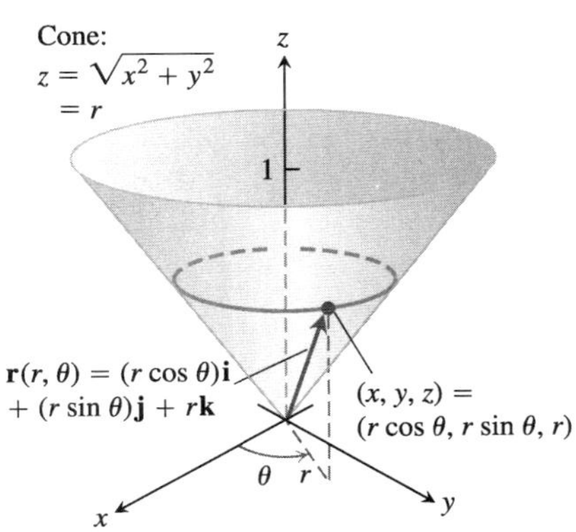

FIGURE 16.51 The cone in Example 1 can be parametrized using cylindrical coordinates.

EXAMPLE 3 Parametrizing a Cylinder

Find a parametrization of the cylinder

$$x^2 + (y - 3)^2 = 9, \qquad 0 \leq z \leq 5.$$

Solution In cylindrical coordinates, a point (x, y, z) has $x = r\cos\theta$, $y = r\sin\theta$, and $z = z$. For points on the cylinder $x^2 + (y - 3)^2 = 9$ (Figure 16.53), the equation is the same as the polar equation for the cylinder's base in the xy-plane:

$$x^2 + (y^2 - 6y + 9) = 9$$
$$r^2 - 6r\sin\theta = 0$$

or

$$r = 6\sin\theta, \qquad 0 \leq \theta \leq \pi.$$

A typical point on the cylinder therefore has

$$x = r\cos\theta = 6\sin\theta\cos\theta = 3\sin 2\theta$$
$$y = r\sin\theta = 6\sin^2\theta$$
$$z = z.$$

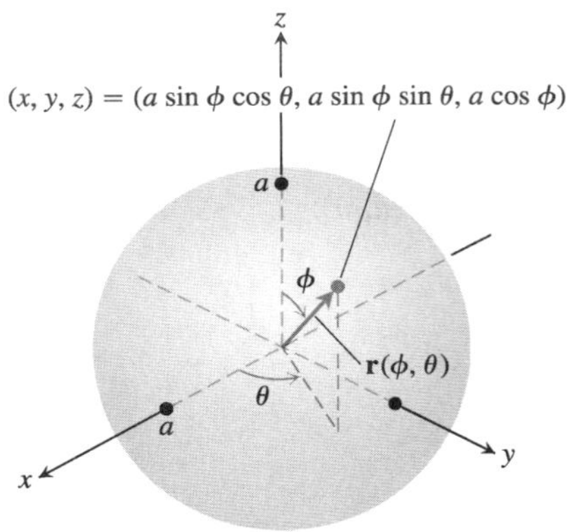

FIGURE 16.52 The sphere in Example 2 can be parametrized using spherical coordinates.

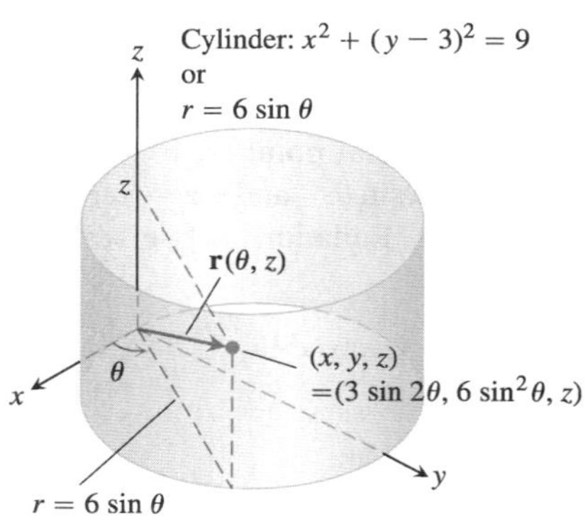

FIGURE 16.53 The cylinder in Example 3 can be parametrized using cylindrical coordinates.

Taking $u = \theta$ and $v = z$ in Equation (1) gives the parametrization

$$\mathbf{r}(\theta, z) = (3\sin 2\theta)\mathbf{i} + (6\sin^2\theta)\mathbf{j} + z\mathbf{k}, \quad 0 \le \theta \le \pi, \quad 0 \le z \le 5. \quad \blacksquare$$

Surface Area

Our goal is to find a double integral for calculating the area of a curved surface S based on the parametrization

$$\mathbf{r}(u, v) = f(u, v)\mathbf{i} + g(u, v)\mathbf{j} + h(u, v)\mathbf{k}, \qquad a \le u \le b, \quad c \le v \le d.$$

We need S to be smooth for the construction we are about to carry out. The definition of smoothness involves the partial derivatives of $\mathbf{r}$ with respect to u and v:

$$\mathbf{r}_u = \frac{\partial \mathbf{r}}{\partial u} = \frac{\partial f}{\partial u}\mathbf{i} + \frac{\partial g}{\partial u}\mathbf{j} + \frac{\partial h}{\partial u}\mathbf{k}$$

$$\mathbf{r}_v = \frac{\partial \mathbf{r}}{\partial v} = \frac{\partial f}{\partial v}\mathbf{i} + \frac{\partial g}{\partial v}\mathbf{j} + \frac{\partial h}{\partial v}\mathbf{k}.$$

DEFINITION Smooth Parametrized Surface

A parametrized surface $\mathbf{r}(u, v) = f(u, v)\mathbf{i} + g(u, v)\mathbf{j} + h(u, v)\mathbf{k}$ is **smooth** if $\mathbf{r}_u$ and $\mathbf{r}_v$ are continuous and $\mathbf{r}_u \times \mathbf{r}_v$ is never zero on the parameter domain.

The condition that $\mathbf{r}_u \times \mathbf{r}_v$ is never the zero vector in the definition of smoothness means that the two vectors $\mathbf{r}_u$ and $\mathbf{r}_v$ are nonzero and never lie along the same line, so they always determine a plane tangent to the surface.

Now consider a small rectangle ΔA_{uv} in R with sides on the lines $u = u_0$, $u = u_0 + \Delta u$, $v = v_0$ and $v = v_0 + \Delta v$ (Figure 16.54). Each side of ΔA_{uv} maps to a curve on the surface S, and together these four curves bound a "curved area element" $\Delta\sigma_{uv}$. In the notation of the figure, the side $v = v_0$ maps to curve C_1, the side $u = u_0$ maps to C_2, and their common vertex (u_0, v_0) maps to P_0.

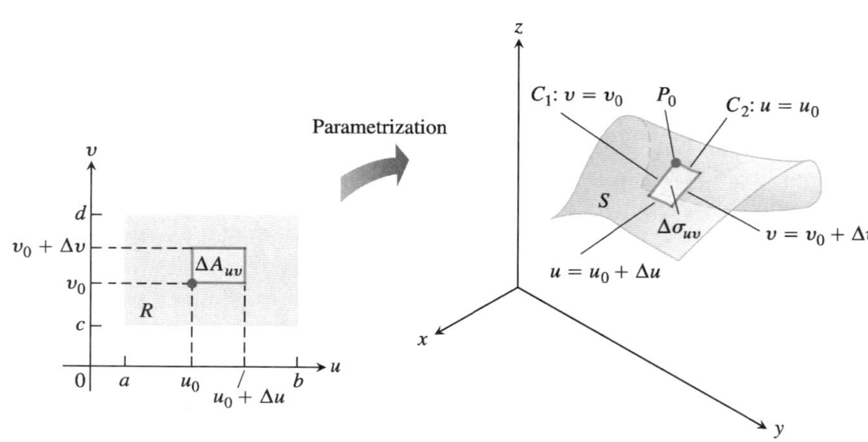

FIGURE 16.54 A rectangular area element ΔA_{uv} in the uv-plane maps onto a curved area element $\Delta\sigma_{uv}$ on S.

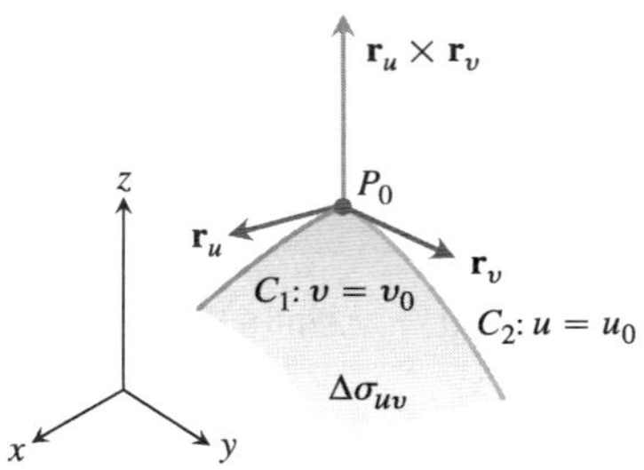

FIGURE 16.55 A magnified view of a surface area element $\Delta\sigma_{uv}$.

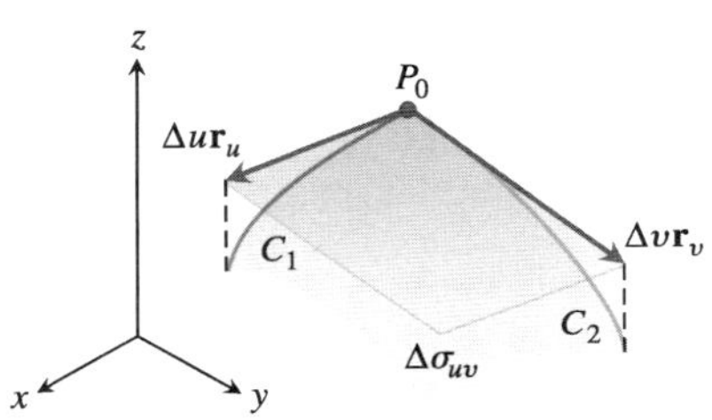

FIGURE 16.56 The parallelogram determined by the vectors $\Delta u\mathbf{r}_u$ and $\Delta v\mathbf{r}_v$ approximates the surface area element $\Delta\sigma_{uv}$.

Figure 16.55 shows an enlarged view of $\Delta\sigma_{uv}$. The vector $\mathbf{r}_u(u_0, v_0)$ is tangent to C_1 at P_0. Likewise, $\mathbf{r}_v(u_0, v_0)$ is tangent to C_2 at P_0. The cross product $\mathbf{r}_u \times \mathbf{r}_v$ is normal to the surface at P_0. (Here is where we begin to use the assumption that S is smooth. We want to be sure that $\mathbf{r}_u \times \mathbf{r}_v \neq \mathbf{0}$.)

We next approximate the surface element $\Delta\sigma_{uv}$ by the parallelogram on the tangent plane whose sides are determined by the vectors $\Delta u\mathbf{r}_u$ and $\Delta v\mathbf{r}_v$ (Figure 16.56). The area of this parallelogram is

$$|\Delta u\mathbf{r}_u \times \Delta v\mathbf{r}_v| = |\mathbf{r}_u \times \mathbf{r}_v|\,\Delta u\,\Delta v. \tag{2}$$

A partition of the region R in the uv-plane by rectangular regions ΔA_{uv} generates a partition of the surface S into surface area elements $\Delta\sigma_{uv}$. We approximate the area of each surface element $\Delta\sigma_{uv}$ by the parallelogram area in Equation (2) and sum these areas together to obtain an approximation of the area of S:

$$\sum_u \sum_v |\mathbf{r}_u \times \mathbf{r}_v|\,\Delta u\,\Delta v. \tag{3}$$

As Δu and Δv approach zero independently, the continuity of $\mathbf{r}_u$ and $\mathbf{r}_v$ guarantees that the sum in Equation (3) approaches the double integral $\int_c^d \int_a^b |\mathbf{r}_u \times \mathbf{r}_v|\,du\,dv$. This double integral defines the area of the surface S and agrees with previous definitions of area, though it is more general.

DEFINITION Area of a Smooth Surface

The **area** of the smooth surface

$$\mathbf{r}(u, v) = f(u, v)\mathbf{i} + g(u, v)\mathbf{j} + h(u, v)\mathbf{k}, \qquad a \le u \le b, \quad c \le v \le d$$

is

$$A = \int_c^d \int_a^b |\mathbf{r}_u \times \mathbf{r}_v|\,du\,dv. \tag{4}$$

As in Section 16.5, we can abbreviate the integral in Equation (4) by writing $d\sigma$ for $|\mathbf{r}_u \times \mathbf{r}_v|\,du\,dv$.

Surface Area Differential and Differential Formula for Surface Area

$$d\sigma = |\mathbf{r}_u \times \mathbf{r}_v|\,du\,dv \qquad \iint_S d\sigma \tag{5}$$

Surface area differential — Differential formula for surface area

EXAMPLE 4 Finding Surface Area (Cone)

Find the surface area of the cone in Example 1 (Figure 16.51).

Solution In Example 1, we found the parametrization

$$\mathbf{r}(r, \theta) = (r\cos\theta)\mathbf{i} + (r\sin\theta)\mathbf{j} + r\mathbf{k}, \qquad 0 \le r \le 1, \quad 0 \le \theta \le 2\pi.$$

To apply Equation (4), we first find $\mathbf{r}_r \times \mathbf{r}_\theta$:

$$\mathbf{r}_r \times \mathbf{r}_\theta = \begin{vmatrix} \mathbf{i} & \mathbf{j} & \mathbf{k} \\ \cos\theta & \sin\theta & 1 \\ -r\sin\theta & r\cos\theta & 0 \end{vmatrix}$$

$$= -(r\cos\theta)\mathbf{i} - (r\sin\theta)\mathbf{j} + \underbrace{(r\cos^2\theta + r\sin^2\theta)}_{r}\mathbf{k}.$$

Thus, $|\mathbf{r}_r \times \mathbf{r}_\theta| = \sqrt{r^2\cos^2\theta + r^2\sin^2\theta + r^2} = \sqrt{2r^2} = \sqrt{2}r$. The area of the cone is

$$A = \int_0^{2\pi}\int_0^1 |\mathbf{r}_r \times \mathbf{r}_\theta|\, dr\, d\theta \qquad \text{Equation (4) with } u = r, v = \theta$$

$$= \int_0^{2\pi}\int_0^1 \sqrt{2}\, r\, dr\, d\theta = \int_0^{2\pi} \frac{\sqrt{2}}{2}\, d\theta = \frac{\sqrt{2}}{2}(2\pi) = \pi\sqrt{2} \text{ units squared.}$$ ■

EXAMPLE 5 Finding Surface Area (Sphere)

Find the surface area of a sphere of radius a.

Solution We use the parametrization from Example 2:

$$\mathbf{r}(\phi, \theta) = (a\sin\phi\cos\theta)\mathbf{i} + (a\sin\phi\sin\theta)\mathbf{j} + (a\cos\phi)\mathbf{k},$$
$$0 \le \phi \le \pi, \quad 0 \le \theta \le 2\pi.$$

For $\mathbf{r}_\phi \times \mathbf{r}_\theta$, we get

$$\mathbf{r}_\phi \times \mathbf{r}_\theta = \begin{vmatrix} \mathbf{i} & \mathbf{j} & \mathbf{k} \\ a\cos\phi\cos\theta & a\cos\phi\sin\theta & -a\sin\phi \\ -a\sin\phi\sin\theta & a\sin\phi\cos\theta & 0 \end{vmatrix}$$

$$= (a^2\sin^2\phi\cos\theta)\mathbf{i} + (a^2\sin^2\phi\sin\theta)\mathbf{j} + (a^2\sin\phi\cos\phi)\mathbf{k}.$$

Thus,

$$|\mathbf{r}_\phi \times \mathbf{r}_\theta| = \sqrt{a^4\sin^4\phi\cos^2\theta + a^4\sin^4\phi\sin^2\theta + a^4\sin^2\phi\cos^2\phi}$$
$$= \sqrt{a^4\sin^4\phi + a^4\sin^2\phi\cos^2\phi} = \sqrt{a^4\sin^2\phi(\sin^2\phi + \cos^2\phi)}$$
$$= a^2\sqrt{\sin^2\phi} = a^2\sin\phi,$$

since $\sin\phi \ge 0$ for $0 \le \phi \le \pi$. Therefore, the area of the sphere is

$$A = \int_0^{2\pi}\int_0^{\pi} a^2\sin\phi\, d\phi\, d\theta$$

$$= \int_0^{2\pi}\Big[-a^2\cos\phi\Big]_0^{\pi} d\theta = \int_0^{2\pi} 2a^2\, d\theta = 4\pi a^2 \text{ units squared.}$$

This agrees with the well-known formula for the surface area of a sphere. ■

Surface Integrals

Having found a formula for calculating the area of a parametrized surface, we can now integrate a function over the surface using the parametrized form.

> **DEFINITION Parametric Surface Integral**
> If S is a smooth surface defined parametrically as $\mathbf{r}(u, v) = f(u, v)\mathbf{i} + g(u, v)\mathbf{j} + h(u, v)\mathbf{k}$, $a \le u \le b$, $c \le v \le d$, and $G(x, y, z)$ is a continuous function defined on S, then the **integral of G over S** is
> $$\iint_S G(x, y, z)\, d\sigma = \int_c^d \int_a^b G(f(u, v), g(u, v), h(u, v))\,|\mathbf{r}_u \times \mathbf{r}_v|\, du\, dv.$$

EXAMPLE 6 Integrating Over a Surface Defined Parametrically

Integrate $G(x, y, z) = x^2$ over the cone $z = \sqrt{x^2 + y^2}$, $0 \le z \le 1$.

Solution Continuing the work in Examples 1 and 4, we have $|\mathbf{r}_r \times \mathbf{r}_\theta| = \sqrt{2}r$ and

$$\iint_S x^2\, d\sigma = \int_0^{2\pi}\int_0^1 \left(r^2\cos^2\theta\right)\left(\sqrt{2}r\right) dr\, d\theta \qquad x = r\cos\theta$$

$$= \sqrt{2}\int_0^{2\pi}\int_0^1 r^3\cos^2\theta\, dr\, d\theta$$

$$= \frac{\sqrt{2}}{4}\int_0^{2\pi}\cos^2\theta\, d\theta = \frac{\sqrt{2}}{4}\left[\frac{\theta}{2} + \frac{1}{4}\sin 2\theta\right]_0^{2\pi} = \frac{\pi\sqrt{2}}{4}.$$ ■

EXAMPLE 7 Finding Flux

Find the flux of $\mathbf{F} = yz\mathbf{i} + x\mathbf{j} - z^2\mathbf{k}$ outward through the parabolic cylinder $y = x^2$, $0 \le x \le 1$, $0 \le z \le 4$ (Figure 16.57).

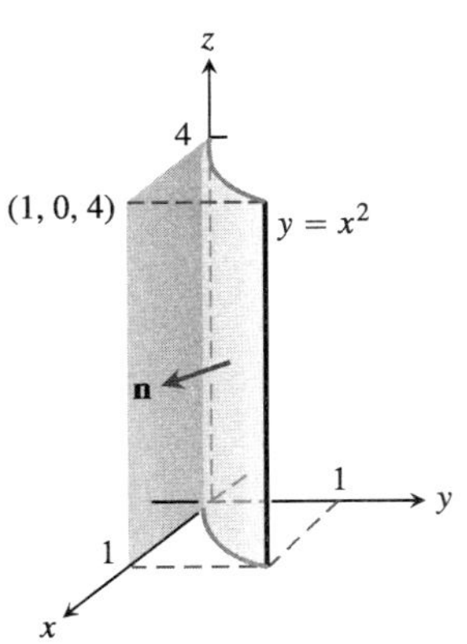

FIGURE 16.57 Finding the flux through the surface of a parabolic cylinder (Example 7).

Solution On the surface we have $x = x$, $y = x^2$, and $z = z$, so we automatically have the parametrization $\mathbf{r}(x, z) = x\mathbf{i} + x^2\mathbf{j} + z\mathbf{k}$, $0 \le x \le 1$, $0 \le z \le 4$. The cross product of tangent vectors is

$$\mathbf{r}_x \times \mathbf{r}_z = \begin{vmatrix} \mathbf{i} & \mathbf{j} & \mathbf{k} \\ 1 & 2x & 0 \\ 0 & 0 & 1 \end{vmatrix} = 2x\mathbf{i} - \mathbf{j}.$$

The unit normal pointing outward from the surface is

$$\mathbf{n} = \frac{\mathbf{r}_x \times \mathbf{r}_z}{|\mathbf{r}_x \times \mathbf{r}_z|} = \frac{2x\mathbf{i} - \mathbf{j}}{\sqrt{4x^2 + 1}}.$$

On the surface, $y = x^2$, so the vector field there is

$$\mathbf{F} = yz\mathbf{i} + x\mathbf{j} - z^2\mathbf{k} = x^2z\mathbf{i} + x\mathbf{j} - z^2\mathbf{k}.$$

Thus,

$$\mathbf{F}\cdot\mathbf{n} = \frac{1}{\sqrt{4x^2 + 1}}\left((x^2z)(2x) + (x)(-1) + (-z^2)(0)\right)$$

$$= \frac{2x^3z - x}{\sqrt{4x^2 + 1}}.$$

The flux of $\mathbf{F}$ outward through the surface is

$$\begin{aligned}\iint_S \mathbf{F}\cdot\mathbf{n}\,d\sigma &= \int_0^4\int_0^1 \frac{2x^3z - x}{\sqrt{4x^2+1}}\,|\mathbf{r}_x\times\mathbf{r}_z|\,dx\,dz\\ &= \int_0^4\int_0^1 \frac{2x^3z - x}{\sqrt{4x^2+1}}\sqrt{4x^2+1}\,dx\,dz\\ &= \int_0^4\int_0^1 (2x^3z - x)\,dx\,dz = \int_0^4\left[\frac{1}{2}x^4z - \frac{1}{2}x^2\right]_{x=0}^{x=1} dz\\ &= \int_0^4 \frac{1}{2}(z-1)\,dz = \frac{1}{4}(z-1)^2\Big]_0^4\\ &= \frac{1}{4}(9) - \frac{1}{4}(1) = 2.\end{aligned}$$

■

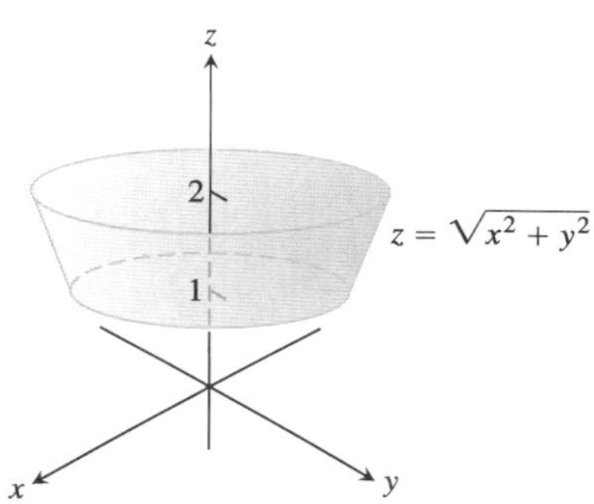

FIGURE 16.58 The cone frustum formed when the cone $z = \sqrt{x^2+y^2}$ is cut by the planes $z = 1$ and $z = 2$ (Example 8).

EXAMPLE 8 Finding a Center of Mass

Find the center of mass of a thin shell of constant density δ cut from the cone $z = \sqrt{x^2+y^2}$ by the planes $z = 1$ and $z = 2$ (Figure 16.58).

Solution The symmetry of the surface about the z-axis tells us that $\bar{x} = \bar{y} = 0$. We find $\bar{z} = M_{xy}/M$. Working as in Examples 1 and 4, we have

$$\mathbf{r}(r,\theta) = r\cos\theta\mathbf{i} + r\sin\theta\mathbf{j} + r\mathbf{k},\qquad 1\le r\le 2,\quad 0\le\theta\le 2\pi,$$

and

$$|\mathbf{r}_r\times\mathbf{r}_\theta| = \sqrt{2}r.$$

Therefore,

$$\begin{aligned}M &= \iint_S \delta\,d\sigma = \int_0^{2\pi}\int_1^2 \delta\sqrt{2}r\,dr\,d\theta\\ &= \delta\sqrt{2}\int_0^{2\pi}\left[\frac{r^2}{2}\right]_1^2 d\theta = \delta\sqrt{2}\int_0^{2\pi}\left(2-\frac{1}{2}\right)d\theta\\ &= \delta\sqrt{2}\left[\frac{3\theta}{2}\right]_0^{2\pi} = 3\pi\delta\sqrt{2}\\ M_{xy} &= \iint_S \delta z\,d\sigma = \int_0^{2\pi}\int_1^2 \delta r\sqrt{2}r\,dr\,d\theta\\ &= \delta\sqrt{2}\int_0^{2\pi}\int_1^2 r^2\,dr\,d\theta = \delta\sqrt{2}\int_0^{2\pi}\left[\frac{r^3}{3}\right]_1^2 d\theta\\ &= \delta\sqrt{2}\int_0^{2\pi}\frac{7}{3}\,d\theta = \frac{14}{3}\pi\delta\sqrt{2}\\ \bar{z} &= \frac{M_{xy}}{M} = \frac{14\pi\delta\sqrt{2}}{3\left(3\pi\delta\sqrt{2}\right)} = \frac{14}{9}.\end{aligned}$$

The shell's center of mass is the point $(0, 0, 14/9)$.

■

EXERCISES 16.6

Finding Parametrizations for Surfaces

In Exercises 1–16, find a parametrization of the surface. (There are many correct ways to do these, so your answers may not be the same as those in the back of the book.)

1. The paraboloid $z = x^2 + y^2, z \leq 4$
2. The paraboloid $z = 9 - x^2 - y^2, z \geq 0$
3. **Cone frustum** The first-octant portion of the cone $z = \sqrt{x^2 + y^2}/2$ between the planes $z = 0$ and $z = 3$
4. **Cone frustum** The portion of the cone $z = 2\sqrt{x^2 + y^2}$ between the planes $z = 2$ and $z = 4$
5. **Spherical cap** The cap cut from the sphere $x^2 + y^2 + z^2 = 9$ by the cone $z = \sqrt{x^2 + y^2}$
6. **Spherical cap** The portion of the sphere $x^2 + y^2 + z^2 = 4$ in the first octant between the xy-plane and the cone $z = \sqrt{x^2 + y^2}$
7. **Spherical band** The portion of the sphere $x^2 + y^2 + z^2 = 3$ between the planes $z = \sqrt{3}/2$ and $z = -\sqrt{3}/2$
8. **Spherical cap** The upper portion cut from the sphere $x^2 + y^2 + z^2 = 8$ by the plane $z = -2$
9. **Parabolic cylinder between planes** The surface cut from the parabolic cylinder $z = 4 - y^2$ by the planes $x = 0, x = 2$, and $z = 0$
10. **Parabolic cylinder between planes** The surface cut from the parabolic cylinder $y = x^2$ by the planes $z = 0, z = 3$ and $y = 2$
11. **Circular cylinder band** The portion of the cylinder $y^2 + z^2 = 9$ between the planes $x = 0$ and $x = 3$
12. **Circular cylinder band** The portion of the cylinder $x^2 + z^2 = 4$ above the xy-plane between the planes $y = -2$ and $y = 2$
13. **Tilted plane inside cylinder** The portion of the plane $x + y + z = 1$
    a. Inside the cylinder $x^2 + y^2 = 9$
    b. Inside the cylinder $y^2 + z^2 = 9$
14. **Tilted plane inside cylinder** The portion of the plane $x - y + 2z = 2$
    a. Inside the cylinder $x^2 + z^2 = 3$
    b. Inside the cylinder $y^2 + z^2 = 2$
15. **Circular cylinder band** The portion of the cylinder $(x - 2)^2 + z^2 = 4$ between the planes $y = 0$ and $y = 3$
16. **Circular cylinder band** The portion of the cylinder $y^2 + (z - 5)^2 = 25$ between the planes $x = 0$ and $x = 10$

Areas of Parametrized Surfaces

In Exercises 17–26, use a parametrization to express the area of the surface as a double integral. Then evaluate the integral. (There are many correct ways to set up the integrals, so your integrals may not be the same as those in the back of the book. They should have the same values, however.)

17. **Titled plane inside cylinder** The portion of the plane $y + 2z = 2$ inside the cylinder $x^2 + y^2 = 1$
18. **Plane inside cylinder** The portion of the plane $z = -x$ inside the cylinder $x^2 + y^2 = 4$
19. **Cone frustum** The portion of the cone $z = 2\sqrt{x^2 + y^2}$ between the planes $z = 2$ and $z = 6$
20. **Cone frustum** The portion of the cone $z = \sqrt{x^2 + y^2}/3$ between the planes $z = 1$ and $z = 4/3$
21. **Circular cylinder band** The portion of the cylinder $x^2 + y^2 = 1$ between the planes $z = 1$ and $z = 4$
22. **Circular cylinder band** The portion of the cylinder $x^2 + z^2 = 10$ between the planes $y = -1$ and $y = 1$
23. **Parabolic cap** The cap cut from the paraboloid $z = 2 - x^2 - y^2$ by the cone $z = \sqrt{x^2 + y^2}$
24. **Parabolic band** The portion of the paraboloid $z = x^2 + y^2$ between the planes $z = 1$ and $z = 4$
25. **Sawed-off sphere** The lower portion cut from the sphere $x^2 + y^2 + z^2 = 2$ by the cone $z = \sqrt{x^2 + y^2}$
26. **Spherical band** The portion of the sphere $x^2 + y^2 + z^2 = 4$ between the planes $z = -1$ and $z = \sqrt{3}$

Integrals Over Parametrized Surfaces

In Exercises 27–34, integrate the given function over the given surface.

27. **Parabolic cylinder** $G(x, y, z) = x$, over the parabolic cylinder $y = x^2, 0 \leq x \leq 2, 0 \leq z \leq 3$
28. **Circular cylinder** $G(x, y, z) = z$, over the cylindrical surface $y^2 + z^2 = 4, z \geq 0, 1 \leq x \leq 4$
29. **Sphere** $G(x, y, z) = x^2$, over the unit sphere $x^2 + y^2 + z^2 = 1$
30. **Hemisphere** $G(x, y, z) = z^2$, over the hemisphere $x^2 + y^2 + z^2 = a^2, z \geq 0$
31. **Portion of plane** $F(x, y, z) = z$, over the portion of the plane $x + y + z = 4$ that lies above the square $0 \leq x \leq 1$, $0 \leq y \leq 1$, in the xy-plane
32. **Cone** $F(x, y, z) = z - x$, over the cone $z = \sqrt{x^2 + y^2}$, $0 \leq z \leq 1$
33. **Parabolic dome** $H(x, y, z) = x^2\sqrt{5 - 4z}$, over the parabolic dome $z = 1 - x^2 - y^2, z \geq 0$
34. **Spherical cap** $H(x, y, z) = yz$, over the part of the sphere $x^2 + y^2 + z^2 = 4$ that lies above the cone $z = \sqrt{x^2 + y^2}$

Flux Across Parametrized Surfaces

In Exercises 35–44, use a parametrization to find the flux $\iint_S \mathbf{F} \cdot \mathbf{n}\, d\sigma$ across the surface in the given direction.

35. **Parabolic cylinder** $\mathbf{F} = z^2\mathbf{i} + x\mathbf{j} - 3z\mathbf{k}$ outward (normal away from the x-axis) through the surface cut from the parabolic cylinder $z = 4 - y^2$ by the planes $x = 0, x = 1$, and $z = 0$

36. **Parabolic cylinder** $\mathbf{F} = x^2\mathbf{j} - xz\mathbf{k}$ outward (normal away from the yz-plane) through the surface cut from the parabolic cylinder $y = x^2, -1 \le x \le 1$, by the planes $z = 0$ and $z = 2$

37. **Sphere** $\mathbf{F} = z\mathbf{k}$ across the portion of the sphere $x^2 + y^2 + z^2 = a^2$ in the first octant in the direction away from the origin

38. **Sphere** $\mathbf{F} = x\mathbf{i} + y\mathbf{j} + z\mathbf{k}$ across the sphere $x^2 + y^2 + z^2 = a^2$ in the direction away from the origin

39. **Plane** $\mathbf{F} = 2xy\mathbf{i} + 2yz\mathbf{j} + 2xz\mathbf{k}$ upward across the portion of the plane $x + y + z = 2a$ that lies above the square $0 \le x \le a, 0 \le y \le a$, in the xy-plane

40. **Cylinder** $\mathbf{F} = x\mathbf{i} + y\mathbf{j} + z\mathbf{k}$ outward through the portion of the cylinder $x^2 + y^2 = 1$ cut by the planes $z = 0$ and $z = a$

41. **Cone** $\mathbf{F} = xy\mathbf{i} - z\mathbf{k}$ outward (normal away from the z-axis) through the cone $z = \sqrt{x^2 + y^2}, 0 \le z \le 1$

42. **Cone** $\mathbf{F} = y^2\mathbf{i} + xz\mathbf{j} - \mathbf{k}$ outward (normal away from the z-axis) through the cone $z = 2\sqrt{x^2 + y^2}, 0 \le z \le 2$

43. **Cone frustum** $\mathbf{F} = -x\mathbf{i} - y\mathbf{j} + z^2\mathbf{k}$ outward (normal away from the z-axis) through the portion of the cone $z = \sqrt{x^2 + y^2}$ between the planes $z = 1$ and $z = 2$

44. **Paraboloid** $\mathbf{F} = 4x\mathbf{i} + 4y\mathbf{j} + 2\mathbf{k}$ outward (normal way from the z-axis) through the surface cut from the bottom of the paraboloid $z = x^2 + y^2$ by the plane $z = 1$

Moments and Masses

45. Find the centroid of the portion of the sphere $x^2 + y^2 + z^2 = a^2$ that lies in the first octant.

46. Find the center of mass and the moment of inertia and radius of gyration about the z-axis of a thin shell of constant density δ cut from the cone $x^2 + y^2 - z^2 = 0$ by the planes $z = 1$ and $z = 2$.

47. Find the moment of inertia about the z-axis of a thin spherical shell $x^2 + y^2 + z^2 = a^2$ of constant density δ.

48. Find the moment of inertia about the z-axis of a thin conical shell $z = \sqrt{x^2 + y^2}, 0 \le z \le 1$, of constant density δ.

Planes Tangent to Parametrized Surfaces

The tangent plane at a point $P_0(f(u_0, v_0), g(u_0, v_0), h(u_0, v_0))$ on a parametrized surface $\mathbf{r}(u, v) = f(u, v)\mathbf{i} + g(u, v)\mathbf{j} + h(u, v)\mathbf{k}$ is the plane through P_0 normal to the vector $\mathbf{r}_u(u_0, v_0) \times \mathbf{r}_v(u_0, v_0)$, the cross product of the tangent vectors $\mathbf{r}_u(u_0, v_0)$ and $\mathbf{r}_v(u_0, v_0)$ at P_0. In Exercises 49–52, find an equation for the plane tangent to the surface at P_0. Then find a Cartesian equation for the surface and sketch the surface and tangent plane together.

49. **Cone** The cone $\mathbf{r}(r, \theta) = (r\cos\theta)\mathbf{i} + (r\sin\theta)\mathbf{j} + r\mathbf{k}, r \ge 0, 0 \le \theta \le 2\pi$ at the point $P_0(\sqrt{2}, \sqrt{2}, 2)$ corresponding to $(r, \theta) = (2, \pi/4)$

50. **Hemisphere** The hemisphere surface $\mathbf{r}(\phi, \theta) = (4\sin\phi\cos\theta)\mathbf{i} + (4\sin\phi\sin\theta)\mathbf{j} + (4\cos\phi)\mathbf{k}, 0 \le \phi \le \pi/2, 0 \le \theta \le 2\pi$, at the point $P_0(\sqrt{2}, \sqrt{2}, 2\sqrt{3})$ corresponding to $(\phi, \theta) = (\pi/6, \pi/4)$

51. **Circular cylinder** The circular cylinder $\mathbf{r}(\theta, z) = (3\sin 2\theta)\mathbf{i} + (6\sin^2\theta)\mathbf{j} + z\mathbf{k}, 0 \le \theta \le \pi$, at the point $P_0(3\sqrt{3}/2, 9/2, 0)$ corresponding to $(\theta, z) = (\pi/3, 0)$ (See Example 3.)

52. **Parabolic cylinder** The parabolic cylinder surface $\mathbf{r}(x, y) = x\mathbf{i} + y\mathbf{j} - x^2\mathbf{k}, -\infty < x < \infty, -\infty < y < \infty$, at the point $P_0(1, 2, -1)$ corresponding to $(x, y) = (1, 2)$

Further Examples of Parametrizations

53. a. A *torus of revolution* (doughnut) is obtained by rotating a circle C in the xz-plane about the z-axis in space. (See the accompanying figure.) If C has radius $r > 0$ and center $(R, 0, 0)$, show that a parametrization of the torus is

$$\mathbf{r}(u, v) = ((R + r\cos u)\cos v)\mathbf{i} + ((R + r\cos u)\sin v)\mathbf{j} + (r\sin u)\mathbf{k},$$

where $0 \le u \le 2\pi$ and $0 \le v \le 2\pi$ are the angles in the figure.

b. Show that the surface area of the torus is $A = 4\pi^2 Rr$.

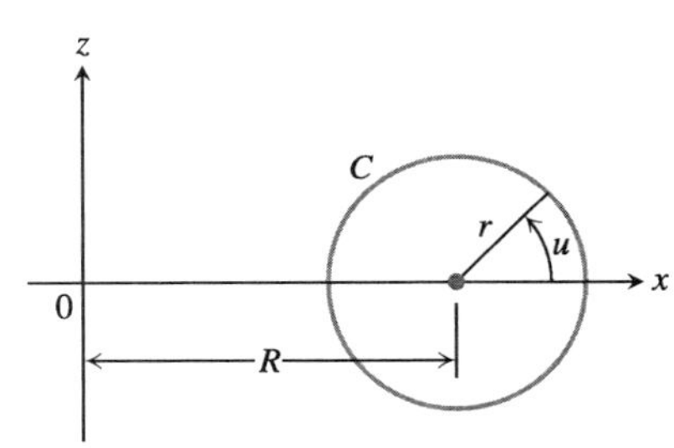

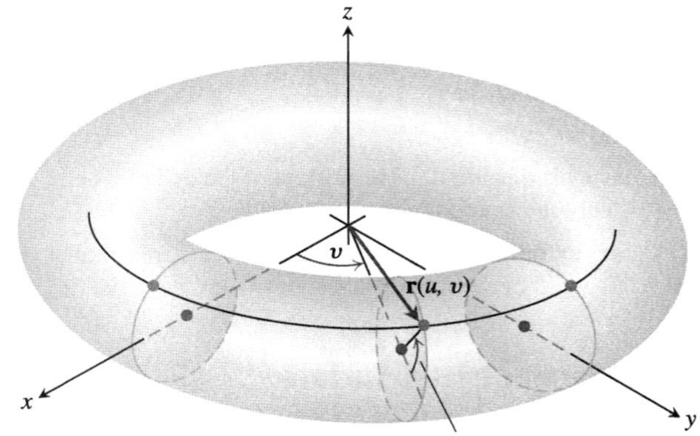

54. Parametrization of a surface of revolution Suppose that the parametrized curve C: $(f(u), g(u))$ is revolved about the x-axis, where $g(u) > 0$ for $a \le u \le b$.

a. Show that

$$\mathbf{r}(u, v) = f(u)\mathbf{i} + (g(u)\cos v)\mathbf{j} + (g(u)\sin v)\mathbf{k}$$

is a parametrization of the resulting surface of revolution, where $0 \le v \le 2\pi$ is the angle from the xy-plane to the point $\mathbf{r}(u, v)$ on the surface. (See the accompanying figure.) Notice that $f(u)$ measures distance *along* the axis of revolution and $g(u)$ measures distance *from* the axis of revolution.

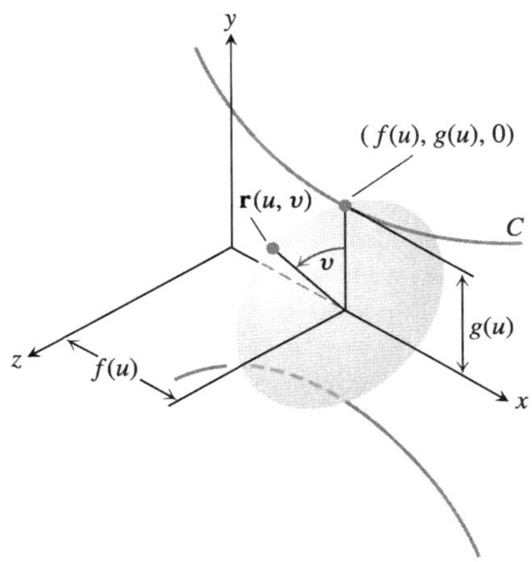

b. Find a parametrization for the surface obtained by revolving the curve $x = y^2, y \ge 0$, about the x-axis.

55. a. Parametrization of an ellipsoid Recall the parametrization $x = a\cos\theta, y = b\sin\theta, 0 \le \theta \le 2\pi$ for the ellipse $(x^2/a^2) + (y^2/b^2) = 1$ (Section 3.5, Example 13). Using the angles θ and ϕ in spherical coordinates, show that

$$\mathbf{r}(\theta, \phi) = (a\cos\theta\cos\phi)\mathbf{i} + (b\sin\theta\cos\phi)\mathbf{j} + (c\sin\phi)\mathbf{k}$$

is a parametrization of the ellipsoid $(x^2/a^2) + (y^2/b^2) + (z^2/c^2) = 1$.

b. Write an integral for the surface area of the ellipsoid, but do not evaluate the integral.

56. Hyperboloid of one sheet

a. Find a parametrization for the hyperboloid of one sheet $x^2 + y^2 - z^2 = 1$ in terms of the angle θ associated with the circle $x^2 + y^2 = r^2$ and the hyperbolic parameter u associated with the hyperbolic function $r^2 - z^2 = 1$. (See Section 7.8, Exercise 84.)

b. Generalize the result in part (a) to the hyperboloid $(x^2/a^2) + (y^2/b^2) - (z^2/c^2) = 1$.

57. (*Continuation of Exercise 56.*) Find a Cartesian equation for the plane tangent to the hyperboloid $x^2 + y^2 - z^2 = 25$ at the point $(x_0, y_0, 0)$, where $x_0^2 + y_0^2 = 25$.

58. Hyperboloid of two sheets Find a parametrization of the hyperboloid of two sheets $(z^2/c^2) - (x^2/a^2) - (y^2/b^2) = 1$.

16.7 Stokes' Theorem

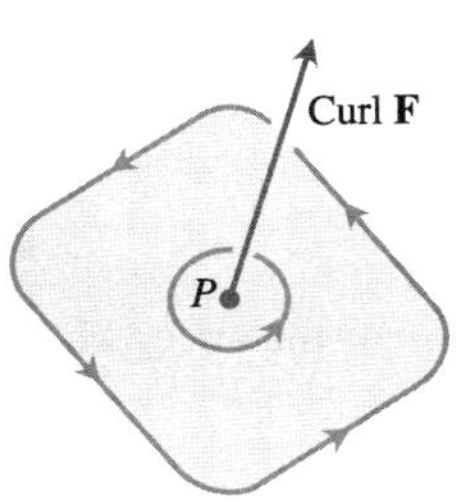

FIGURE 16.59 The circulation vector at a point P in a plane in a three-dimensional fluid flow. Notice its right-hand relation to the circulation line.

As we saw in Section 16.4, the circulation density or curl component of a two-dimensional field $\mathbf{F} = M\mathbf{i} + N\mathbf{j}$ at a point (x, y) is described by the scalar quantity $(\partial N/\partial x - \partial M/\partial y)$. In three dimensions, the circulation around a point P in a plane is described with a vector. This vector is normal to the plane of the circulation (Figure 16.59) and points in the direction that gives it a right-hand relation to the circulation line. The length of the vector gives the rate of the fluid's rotation, which usually varies as the circulation plane is tilted about P. It turns out that the vector of greatest circulation in a flow with velocity field $\mathbf{F} = M\mathbf{i} + N\mathbf{j} + P\mathbf{k}$ is the **curl vector**

$$\text{curl}\,\mathbf{F} = \left(\frac{\partial P}{\partial y} - \frac{\partial N}{\partial z}\right)\mathbf{i} + \left(\frac{\partial M}{\partial z} - \frac{\partial P}{\partial x}\right)\mathbf{j} + \left(\frac{\partial N}{\partial x} - \frac{\partial M}{\partial y}\right)\mathbf{k}. \quad (1)$$

We get this information from Stokes' Theorem, the generalization of the circulation-curl form of Green's Theorem to space.

Notice that $(\text{curl}\,\mathbf{F}) \cdot \mathbf{k} = (\partial N/\partial x - \partial M/\partial y)$ is consistent with our definition in Section 16.4 when $\mathbf{F} = M(x, y)\mathbf{i} + N(x, y)\mathbf{j}$. The formula for curl $\mathbf{F}$ in Equation (1) is often written using the symbolic operator

$$\nabla = \mathbf{i}\frac{\partial}{\partial x} + \mathbf{j}\frac{\partial}{\partial y} + \mathbf{k}\frac{\partial}{\partial z}. \quad (2)$$

(The symbol ∇ is pronounced "del.") The curl of $\mathbf{F}$ is $\nabla \times \mathbf{F}$:

$$\begin{aligned}\nabla \times \mathbf{F} &= \begin{vmatrix} \mathbf{i} & \mathbf{j} & \mathbf{k} \\ \dfrac{\partial}{\partial x} & \dfrac{\partial}{\partial y} & \dfrac{\partial}{\partial z} \\ M & N & P \end{vmatrix} \\ &= \left(\frac{\partial P}{\partial y} - \frac{\partial N}{\partial z}\right)\mathbf{i} + \left(\frac{\partial M}{\partial z} - \frac{\partial P}{\partial x}\right)\mathbf{j} + \left(\frac{\partial N}{\partial x} - \frac{\partial M}{\partial y}\right)\mathbf{k} \\ &= \text{curl } \mathbf{F}.\end{aligned}$$

$$\text{curl } \mathbf{F} = \nabla \times \mathbf{F} \tag{3}$$

EXAMPLE 1 Finding Curl F

Find the curl of $\mathbf{F} = (x^2 - y)\mathbf{i} + 4z\mathbf{j} + x^2\mathbf{k}$.

Solution

$$\begin{aligned}\text{curl } \mathbf{F} &= \nabla \times \mathbf{F} \qquad \text{Equation (3)} \\ &= \begin{vmatrix} \mathbf{i} & \mathbf{j} & \mathbf{k} \\ \dfrac{\partial}{\partial x} & \dfrac{\partial}{\partial y} & \dfrac{\partial}{\partial z} \\ x^2 - y & 4z & x^2 \end{vmatrix} \\ &= \left(\frac{\partial}{\partial y}(x^2) - \frac{\partial}{\partial z}(4z)\right)\mathbf{i} - \left(\frac{\partial}{\partial x}(x^2) - \frac{\partial}{\partial z}(x^2 - y)\right)\mathbf{j} \\ &\quad + \left(\frac{\partial}{\partial x}(4z) - \frac{\partial}{\partial y}(x^2 - y)\right)\mathbf{k} \\ &= (0 - 4)\mathbf{i} - (2x - 0)\mathbf{j} + (0 + 1)\mathbf{k} \\ &= -4\mathbf{i} - 2x\mathbf{j} + \mathbf{k}\end{aligned}$$

■

As we will see, the operator ∇ has a number of other applications. For instance, when applied to a scalar function $f(x, y, z)$, it gives the gradient of f:

$$\nabla f = \frac{\partial f}{\partial x}\mathbf{i} + \frac{\partial f}{\partial y}\mathbf{j} + \frac{\partial f}{\partial z}\mathbf{k}.$$

This may now be read as "del f" as well as "grad f."

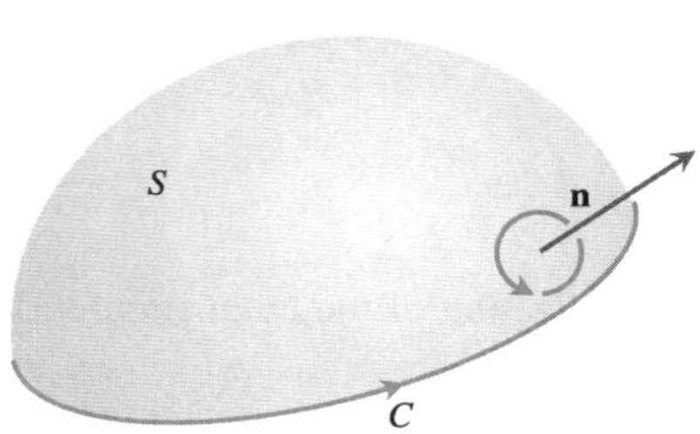

FIGURE 16.60 The orientation of the bounding curve C gives it a right-handed relation to the normal field $\mathbf{n}$.

Stokes' Theorem

Stokes' Theorem says that, under conditions normally met in practice, the circulation of a vector field around the boundary of an oriented surface in space in the direction counterclockwise with respect to the surface's unit normal vector field $\mathbf{n}$ (Figure 16.60) equals the integral of the normal component of the curl of the field over the surface.

THEOREM 5 Stokes' Theorem
The circulation of a vector field $\mathbf{F} = M\mathbf{i} + N\mathbf{j} + P\mathbf{k}$ around the boundary C of an oriented surface S in the direction counterclockwise with respect to the surface's unit normal vector $\mathbf{n}$ equals the integral of $\nabla \times \mathbf{F} \cdot \mathbf{n}$ over S.

$$\underbrace{\oint_C \mathbf{F} \cdot d\mathbf{r}}_{\text{Counterclockwise circulation}} = \underbrace{\iint_S \nabla \times \mathbf{F} \cdot \mathbf{n}\, d\sigma}_{\text{Curl integral}} \tag{4}$$

Notice from Equation (4) that if two different oriented surfaces S_1 and S_2 have the same boundary C, their curl integrals are equal:

$$\iint_{S_1} \nabla \times \mathbf{F} \cdot \mathbf{n}_1\, d\sigma = \iint_{S_2} \nabla \times \mathbf{F} \cdot \mathbf{n}_2\, d\sigma.$$

Both curl integrals equal the counterclockwise circulation integral on the left side of Equation (4) as long as the unit normal vectors $\mathbf{n}_1$ and $\mathbf{n}_2$ correctly orient the surfaces.

Naturally, we need some mathematical restrictions on $\mathbf{F}$, C, and S to ensure the existence of the integrals in Stokes' equation. The usual restrictions are that all functions, vector fields, and their derivatives be continuous.

If C is a curve in the xy-plane, oriented counterclockwise, and R is the region in the xy-plane bounded by C, then $d\sigma = dx\,dy$ and

$$(\nabla \times \mathbf{F}) \cdot \mathbf{n} = (\nabla \times \mathbf{F}) \cdot \mathbf{k} = \left(\frac{\partial N}{\partial x} - \frac{\partial M}{\partial y}\right).$$

Under these conditions, Stokes' equation becomes

$$\oint_C \mathbf{F} \cdot d\mathbf{r} = \iint_R \left(\frac{\partial N}{\partial x} - \frac{\partial M}{\partial y}\right) dx\,dy,$$

which is the circulation-curl form of the equation in Green's Theorem. Conversely, by reversing these steps we can rewrite the circulation-curl form of Green's Theorem for two-dimensional fields in del notation as

$$\oint_C \mathbf{F} \cdot d\mathbf{r} = \iint_R \nabla \times \mathbf{F} \cdot \mathbf{k}\, dA. \tag{5}$$

See Figure 16.61.

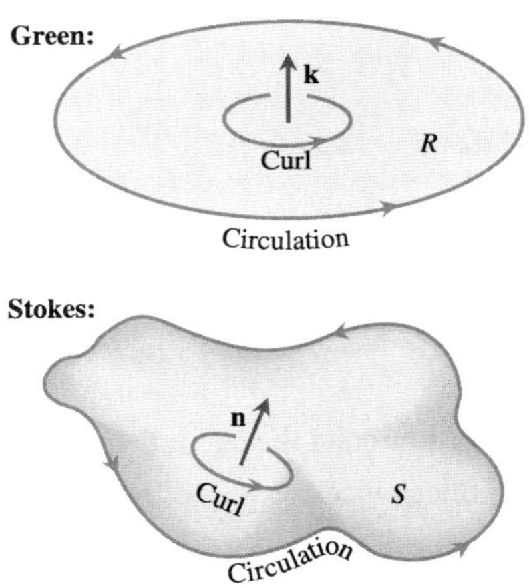

FIGURE 16.61 Comparison of Green's Theorem and Stokes' Theorem.

EXAMPLE 2 Verifying Stokes' Equation for a Hemisphere

Evaluate Equation (4) for the hemisphere $S: x^2 + y^2 + z^2 = 9,\ z \geq 0$, its bounding circle $C: x^2 + y^2 = 9,\ z = 0$, and the field $\mathbf{F} = y\mathbf{i} - x\mathbf{j}$.

Solution We calculate the counterclockwise circulation around C (as viewed from above) using the parametrization $\mathbf{r}(\theta) = (3\cos\theta)\mathbf{i} + (3\sin\theta)\mathbf{j}$, $0 \le \theta \le 2\pi$:

$$d\mathbf{r} = (-3\sin\theta\, d\theta)\mathbf{i} + (3\cos\theta\, d\theta)\mathbf{j}$$

$$\mathbf{F} = y\mathbf{i} - x\mathbf{j} = (3\sin\theta)\mathbf{i} - (3\cos\theta)\mathbf{j}$$

$$\mathbf{F}\cdot d\mathbf{r} = -9\sin^2\theta\, d\theta - 9\cos^2\theta\, d\theta = -9\, d\theta$$

$$\oint_C \mathbf{F}\cdot d\mathbf{r} = \int_0^{2\pi} -9\, d\theta = -18\pi.$$

For the curl integral of $\mathbf{F}$, we have

$$\begin{aligned}\nabla\times\mathbf{F} &= \left(\frac{\partial P}{\partial y} - \frac{\partial N}{\partial z}\right)\mathbf{i} + \left(\frac{\partial M}{\partial z} - \frac{\partial P}{\partial x}\right)\mathbf{j} + \left(\frac{\partial N}{\partial x} - \frac{\partial M}{\partial y}\right)\mathbf{k}\\ &= (0-0)\mathbf{i} + (0-0)\mathbf{j} + (-1-1)\mathbf{k} = -2\mathbf{k}\\ \mathbf{n} &= \frac{x\mathbf{i} + y\mathbf{j} + z\mathbf{k}}{\sqrt{x^2+y^2+z^2}} = \frac{x\mathbf{i} + y\mathbf{j} + z\mathbf{k}}{3} \qquad \text{Outer unit normal}\\ d\sigma &= \frac{3}{z}\, dA \qquad \text{Section 16.5, Example 5, with } a = 3\\ \nabla\times\mathbf{F}\cdot\mathbf{n}\, d\sigma &= -\frac{2z}{3}\frac{3}{z}\, dA = -2\, dA\end{aligned}$$

and

$$\iint_S \nabla\times\mathbf{F}\cdot\mathbf{n}\, d\sigma = \iint_{x^2+y^2\le 9} -2\, dA = -18\pi.$$

The circulation around the circle equals the integral of the curl over the hemisphere, as it should. ■

EXAMPLE 3 Finding Circulation

Find the circulation of the field $\mathbf{F} = (x^2 - y)\mathbf{i} + 4z\mathbf{j} + x^2\mathbf{k}$ around the curve C in which the plane $z = 2$ meets the cone $z = \sqrt{x^2+y^2}$, counterclockwise as viewed from above (Figure 16.62).

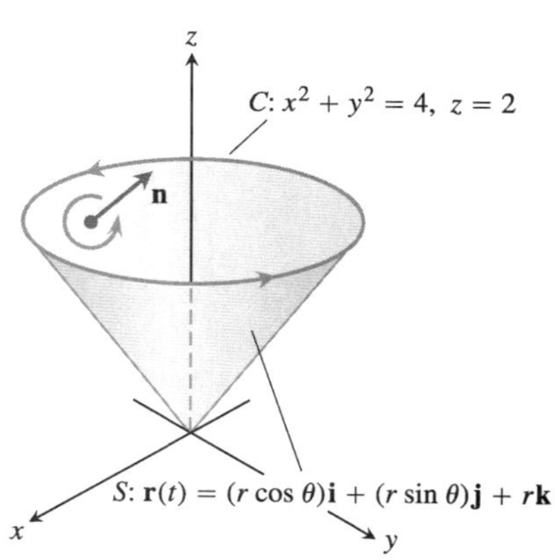

FIGURE 16.62 The curve C and cone S in Example 3.

Solution Stokes' Theorem enables us to find the circulation by integrating over the surface of the cone. Traversing C in the counterclockwise direction viewed from above corresponds to taking the *inner* normal $\mathbf{n}$ to the cone, the normal with a positive z-component.

We parametrize the cone as

$$\mathbf{r}(r,\theta) = (r\cos\theta)\mathbf{i} + (r\sin\theta)\mathbf{j} + r\mathbf{k}, \qquad 0 \le r \le 2, \quad 0 \le \theta \le 2\pi.$$

We then have

$$\begin{aligned}\mathbf{n} &= \frac{\mathbf{r}_r \times \mathbf{r}_\theta}{|\mathbf{r}_r \times \mathbf{r}_\theta|} = \frac{-(r\cos\theta)\mathbf{i} - (r\sin\theta)\mathbf{j} + r\mathbf{k}}{r\sqrt{2}} \qquad \text{Section 16.6, Example 4}\\ &= \frac{1}{\sqrt{2}}\left(-(\cos\theta)\mathbf{i} - (\sin\theta)\mathbf{j} + \mathbf{k}\right)\end{aligned}$$

$$\begin{aligned} d\sigma &= r\sqrt{2}\,dr\,d\theta && \text{Section 16.6, Example 4} \\ \nabla \times \mathbf{F} &= -4\mathbf{i} - 2x\mathbf{j} + \mathbf{k} && \text{Example 1} \\ &= -4\mathbf{i} - 2r\cos\theta\mathbf{j} + \mathbf{k}. && x = r\cos\theta \end{aligned}$$

Accordingly,

$$\begin{aligned} \nabla \times \mathbf{F}\cdot\mathbf{n} &= \frac{1}{\sqrt{2}}\left(4\cos\theta + 2r\cos\theta\sin\theta + 1\right) \\ &= \frac{1}{\sqrt{2}}\left(4\cos\theta + r\sin 2\theta + 1\right) \end{aligned}$$

and the circulation is

$$\begin{aligned} \oint_C \mathbf{F}\cdot d\mathbf{r} &= \iint_S \nabla \times \mathbf{F}\cdot\mathbf{n}\,d\sigma && \text{Stokes' Theorem, Equation (4)} \\ &= \int_0^{2\pi}\int_0^2 \frac{1}{\sqrt{2}}\left(4\cos\theta + r\sin 2\theta + 1\right)\left(r\sqrt{2}\,dr\,d\theta\right) = 4\pi. \end{aligned}$$

■

Paddle Wheel Interpretation of $\nabla \times \mathbf{F}$

Suppose that $\mathbf{v}(x, y, z)$ is the velocity of a moving fluid whose density at (x, y, z) is $\delta(x, y, z)$ and let $\mathbf{F} = \delta\mathbf{v}$. Then

$$\oint_C \mathbf{F}\cdot d\mathbf{r}$$

is the circulation of the fluid around the closed curve C. By Stokes' Theorem, the circulation is equal to the flux of $\nabla \times \mathbf{F}$ through a surface S spanning C:

$$\oint_C \mathbf{F}\cdot d\mathbf{r} = \iint_S \nabla \times \mathbf{F}\cdot\mathbf{n}\,d\sigma.$$

Suppose we fix a point Q in the domain of $\mathbf{F}$ and a direction $\mathbf{u}$ at Q. Let C be a circle of radius ρ, with center at Q, whose plane is normal to $\mathbf{u}$. If $\nabla \times \mathbf{F}$ is continuous at Q, the average value of the $\mathbf{u}$-component of $\nabla \times \mathbf{F}$ over the circular disk S bounded by C approaches the $\mathbf{u}$-component of $\nabla \times \mathbf{F}$ at Q as $\rho \to 0$:

$$(\nabla \times \mathbf{F}\cdot\mathbf{u})_Q = \lim_{\rho\to 0}\frac{1}{\pi\rho^2}\iint_S \nabla \times \mathbf{F}\cdot\mathbf{u}\,d\sigma.$$

If we replace the surface integral in this last equation by the circulation, we get

$$(\nabla \times \mathbf{F}\cdot\mathbf{u})_Q = \lim_{\rho\to 0}\frac{1}{\pi\rho^2}\oint_C \mathbf{F}\cdot d\mathbf{r}. \tag{6}$$

The left-hand side of Equation (6) has its maximum value when $\mathbf{u}$ is the direction of $\nabla \times \mathbf{F}$. When ρ is small, the limit on the right-hand side of Equation (6) is approximately

$$\frac{1}{\pi\rho^2}\oint_C \mathbf{F}\cdot d\mathbf{r},$$

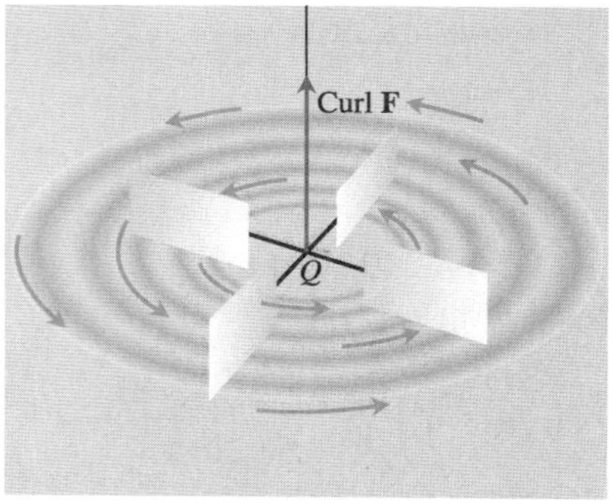

FIGURE 16.63 The paddle wheel interpretation of curl **F**.

which is the circulation around C divided by the area of the disk (circulation density). Suppose that a small paddle wheel of radius ρ is introduced into the fluid at Q, with its axle directed along $\mathbf{u}$. The circulation of the fluid around C will affect the rate of spin of the paddle wheel. The wheel will spin fastest when the circulation integral is maximized; therefore it will spin fastest when the axle of the paddle wheel points in the direction of $\nabla \times \mathbf{F}$ (Figure 16.63).

EXAMPLE 4 Relating $\nabla \times \mathbf{F}$ to Circulation Density

A fluid of constant density rotates around the z-axis with velocity $\mathbf{v} = \omega(-y\mathbf{i} + x\mathbf{j})$, where ω is a positive constant called the *angular velocity* of the rotation (Figure 16.64). If $\mathbf{F} = \mathbf{v}$, find $\nabla \times \mathbf{F}$ and relate it to the circulation density.

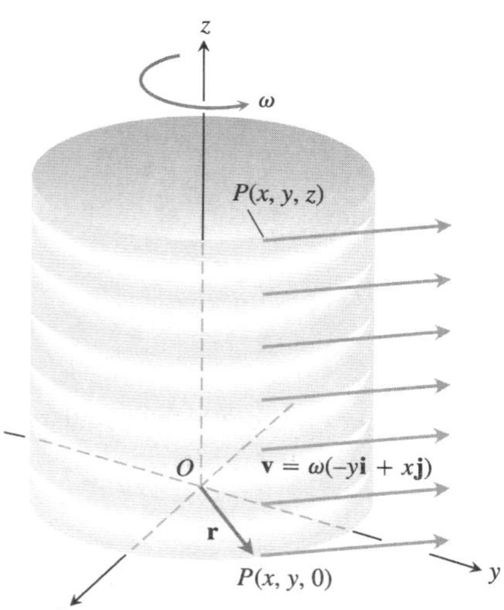

FIGURE 16.64 A steady rotational flow parallel to the xy-plane, with constant angular velocity ω in the positive (counterclockwise) direction (Example 4).

Solution With $\mathbf{F} = \mathbf{v} = -\omega y\mathbf{i} + \omega x\mathbf{j}$,

$$\nabla \times \mathbf{F} = \left(\frac{\partial P}{\partial y} - \frac{\partial N}{\partial z}\right)\mathbf{i} + \left(\frac{\partial M}{\partial z} - \frac{\partial P}{\partial x}\right)\mathbf{j} + \left(\frac{\partial N}{\partial x} - \frac{\partial M}{\partial y}\right)\mathbf{k}$$

$$= (0 - 0)\mathbf{i} + (0 - 0)\mathbf{j} + (\omega - (-\omega))\mathbf{k} = 2\omega\mathbf{k}.$$

By Stokes' Theorem, the circulation of $\mathbf{F}$ around a circle C of radius ρ bounding a disk S in a plane normal to $\nabla \times \mathbf{F}$, say the xy-plane, is

$$\oint_C \mathbf{F} \cdot d\mathbf{r} = \iint_S \nabla \times \mathbf{F} \cdot \mathbf{n}\, d\sigma = \iint_S 2\omega\mathbf{k} \cdot \mathbf{k}\, dx\, dy = (2\omega)(\pi\rho^2).$$

Thus,

$$(\nabla \times \mathbf{F}) \cdot \mathbf{k} = 2\omega = \frac{1}{\pi\rho^2} \oint_C \mathbf{F} \cdot d\mathbf{r},$$

consistent with Equation (6) when $\mathbf{u} = \mathbf{k}$. ■

EXAMPLE 5 Applying Stokes' Theorem

Use Stokes' Theorem to evaluate $\int_C \mathbf{F} \cdot d\mathbf{r}$, if $\mathbf{F} = xz\mathbf{i} + xy\mathbf{j} + 3xz\mathbf{k}$ and C is the boundary of the portion of the plane $2x + y + z = 2$ in the first octant, traversed counterclockwise as viewed from above (Figure 16.65).

Solution The plane is the level surface $f(x, y, z) = 2$ of the function $f(x, y, z) = 2x + y + z$. The unit normal vector

$$\mathbf{n} = \frac{\nabla f}{|\nabla f|} = \frac{(2\mathbf{i} + \mathbf{j} + \mathbf{k})}{|2\mathbf{i} + \mathbf{j} + \mathbf{k}|} = \frac{1}{\sqrt{6}}\left(2\mathbf{i} + \mathbf{j} + \mathbf{k}\right)$$

is consistent with the counterclockwise motion around C. To apply Stokes' Theorem, we find

$$\text{curl } \mathbf{F} = \nabla \times \mathbf{F} = \begin{vmatrix} \mathbf{i} & \mathbf{j} & \mathbf{k} \\ \dfrac{\partial}{\partial x} & \dfrac{\partial}{\partial y} & \dfrac{\partial}{\partial z} \\ xz & xy & 3xz \end{vmatrix} = (x - 3z)\mathbf{j} + y\mathbf{k}.$$

On the plane, z equals $2 - 2x - y$, so

$$\nabla \times \mathbf{F} = (x - 3(2 - 2x - y))\mathbf{j} + y\mathbf{k} = (7x + 3y - 6)\mathbf{j} + y\mathbf{k}$$

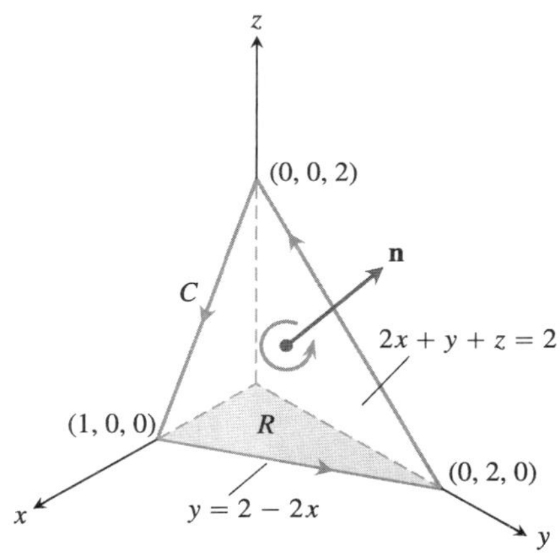

FIGURE 16.65 The planar surface in Example 5.

and

$$\nabla \times \mathbf{F} \cdot \mathbf{n} = \frac{1}{\sqrt{6}}\left(7x + 3y - 6 + y\right) = \frac{1}{\sqrt{6}}\left(7x + 4y - 6\right).$$

The surface area element is

$$d\sigma = \frac{|\nabla f|}{|\nabla f \cdot \mathbf{k}|}\,dA = \frac{\sqrt{6}}{1}\,dx\,dy.$$

The circulation is

$$\oint_C \mathbf{F} \cdot d\mathbf{r} = \iint_S \nabla \times \mathbf{F} \cdot \mathbf{n}\,d\sigma \qquad \text{Stokes' Theorem, Equation (4)}$$

$$= \int_0^1 \int_0^{2-2x} \frac{1}{\sqrt{6}}\left(7x + 4y - 6\right)\sqrt{6}\,dy\,dx$$

$$= \int_0^1 \int_0^{2-2x} (7x + 4y - 6)\,dy\,dx = -1.$$

Proof of Stokes' Theorem for Polyhedral Surfaces

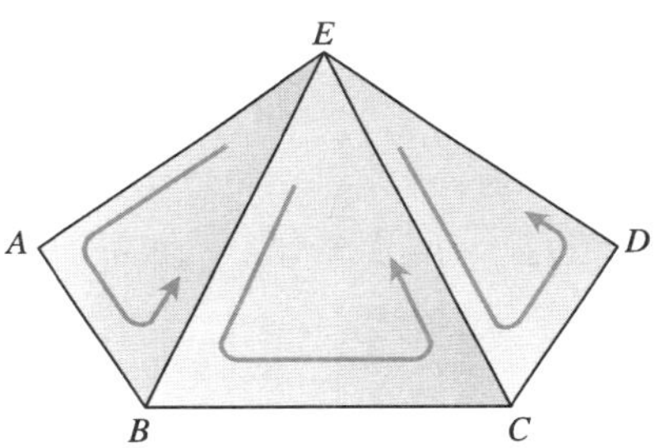

FIGURE 16.66 Part of a polyhedral surface.

Let S be a polyhedral surface consisting of a finite number of plane regions. (See Figure 16.66 for an example.) We apply Green's Theorem to each separate panel of S. There are two types of panels:

1. Those that are surrounded on all sides by other panels
2. Those that have one or more edges that are not adjacent to other panels.

The boundary Δ of S consists of those edges of the type 2 panels that are not adjacent to other panels. In Figure 16.66, the triangles EAB, BCE, and CDE represent a part of S, with $ABCD$ part of the boundary Δ. Applying Green's Theorem to the three triangles in turn and adding the results, we get

$$\left(\oint_{EAB} + \oint_{BCE} + \oint_{CDE}\right)\mathbf{F} \cdot d\mathbf{r} = \left(\iint_{EAB} + \iint_{BCE} + \iint_{CDE}\right)\nabla \times \mathbf{F} \cdot \mathbf{n}\,d\sigma. \qquad (7)$$

The three line integrals on the left-hand side of Equation (7) combine into a single line integral taken around the periphery $ABCDE$ because the integrals along interior segments cancel in pairs. For example, the integral along segment BE in triangle ABE is opposite in sign to the integral along the same segment in triangle EBC. The same holds for segment CE. Hence, Equation (7) reduces to

$$\oint_{ABCDE} \mathbf{F} \cdot d\mathbf{r} = \iint_{ABCDE} \nabla \times \mathbf{F} \cdot \mathbf{n}\,d\sigma.$$

When we apply Green's Theorem to all the panels and add the results, we get

$$\oint_{\Delta} \mathbf{F} \cdot d\mathbf{r} = \iint_S \nabla \times \mathbf{F} \cdot \mathbf{n}\,d\sigma.$$

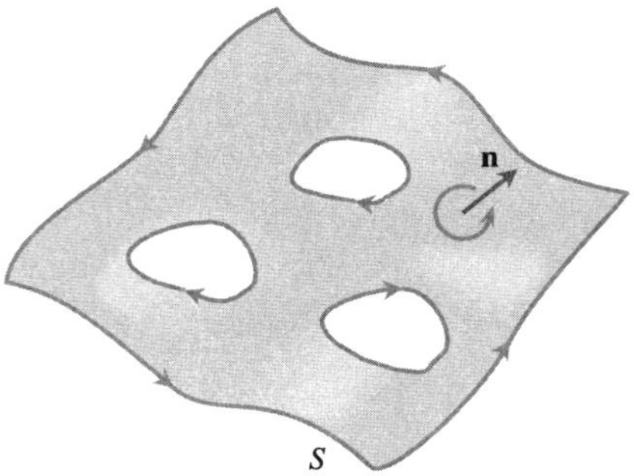

FIGURE 16.67 Stokes' Theorem also holds for oriented surfaces with holes.

This is Stokes' Theorem for a polyhedral surface S. You can find proofs for more general surfaces in advanced calculus texts.

Stokes' Theorem for Surfaces with Holes

Stokes' Theorem can be extended to an oriented surface S that has one or more holes (Figure 16.67), in a way analogous to the extension of Green's Theorem: The surface integral over S of the normal component of $\nabla \times \mathbf{F}$ equals the sum of the line integrals around all the boundary curves of the tangential component of $\mathbf{F}$, where the curves are to be traced in the direction induced by the orientation of S.

An Important Identity

The following identity arises frequently in mathematics and the physical sciences.

$$\text{curl grad } f = \mathbf{0} \qquad \text{or} \qquad \nabla \times \nabla f = \mathbf{0} \tag{8}$$

This identity holds for any function $f(x, y, z)$ whose second partial derivatives are continuous. The proof goes like this:

$$\nabla \times \nabla f = \begin{vmatrix} \mathbf{i} & \mathbf{j} & \mathbf{k} \\ \dfrac{\partial}{\partial x} & \dfrac{\partial}{\partial y} & \dfrac{\partial}{\partial z} \\ \dfrac{\partial f}{\partial x} & \dfrac{\partial f}{\partial y} & \dfrac{\partial f}{\partial z} \end{vmatrix} = (f_{zy} - f_{yz})\mathbf{i} - (f_{zx} - f_{xz})\mathbf{j} + (f_{yx} - f_{xy})\mathbf{k}.$$

If the second partial derivatives are continuous, the mixed second derivatives in parentheses are equal (Theorem 2, Section 14.3) and the vector is zero.

Conservative Fields and Stokes' Theorem

In Section 16.3, we found that a field $\mathbf{F}$ is conservative in an open region D in space is equivalent to the integral of $\mathbf{F}$ around every closed loop in D being zero. This, in turn, is equivalent in *simply connected* open regions to saying that $\nabla \times \mathbf{F} = \mathbf{0}$.

THEOREM 6 Curl F = 0 Related to the Closed-Loop Property
If $\nabla \times \mathbf{F} = \mathbf{0}$ at every point of a simply connected open region D in space, then on any piecewise-smooth closed path C in D,

$$\oint_C \mathbf{F} \cdot d\mathbf{r} = 0.$$

Sketch of a Proof Theorem 6 is usually proved in two steps. The first step is for simple closed curves. A theorem from topology, a branch of advanced mathematics, states that every differentiable simple closed curve C in a simply connected open region D is the boundary of a smooth two-sided surface S that also lies in D. Hence, by Stokes' Theorem,

$$\oint_C \mathbf{F} \cdot d\mathbf{r} = \iint_S \nabla \times \mathbf{F} \cdot \mathbf{n}\, d\sigma = 0.$$

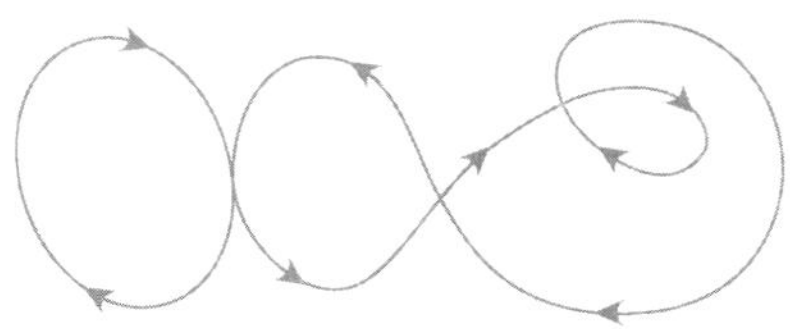

FIGURE 16.68 In a simply connected open region in space, differentiable curves that cross themselves can be divided into loops to which Stokes' Theorem applies.

The second step is for curves that cross themselves, like the one in Figure 16.68. The idea is to break these into simple loops spanned by orientable surfaces, apply Stokes' Theorem one loop at a time, and add the results. ■

The following diagram summarizes the results for conservative fields defined on connected, simply connected open regions.

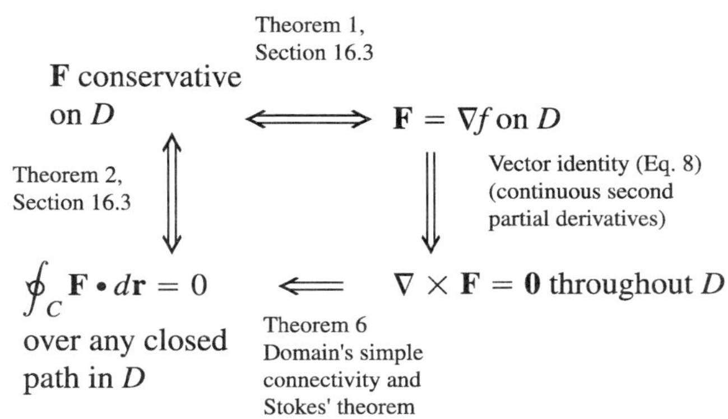

EXERCISES 16.7

Using Stokes' Theorem to Calculate Circulation

In Exercises 1–6, use the surface integral in Stokes' Theorem to calculate the circulation of the field **F** around the curve C in the indicated direction.

1. $\mathbf{F} = x^2\mathbf{i} + 2x\mathbf{j} + z^2\mathbf{k}$

   C: The ellipse $4x^2 + y^2 = 4$ in the xy-plane, counterclockwise when viewed from above

2. $\mathbf{F} = 2y\mathbf{i} + 3x\mathbf{j} - z^2\mathbf{k}$

   C: The circle $x^2 + y^2 = 9$ in the xy-plane, counterclockwise when viewed from above

3. $\mathbf{F} = y\mathbf{i} + xz\mathbf{j} + x^2\mathbf{k}$

   C: The boundary of the triangle cut from the plane $x + y + z = 1$ by the first octant, counterclockwise when viewed from above

4. $\mathbf{F} = (y^2 + z^2)\mathbf{i} + (x^2 + z^2)\mathbf{j} + (x^2 + y^2)\mathbf{k}$

   C: The boundary of the triangle cut from the plane $x + y + z = 1$ by the first octant, counterclockwise when viewed from above

5. $\mathbf{F} = (y^2 + z^2)\mathbf{i} + (x^2 + y^2)\mathbf{j} + (x^2 + y^2)\mathbf{k}$

   C: The square bounded by the lines $x = \pm 1$ and $y = \pm 1$ in the xy-plane, counterclockwise when viewed from above

6. $\mathbf{F} = x^2y^3\mathbf{i} + \mathbf{j} + z\mathbf{k}$

   C: The intersection of the cylinder $x^2 + y^2 = 4$ and the hemisphere $x^2 + y^2 + z^2 = 16, z \geq 0$, counterclockwise when viewed from above.

Flux of the Curl

7. Let **n** be the outer unit normal of the elliptical shell

   $$S:\quad 4x^2 + 9y^2 + 36z^2 = 36, \qquad z \geq 0,$$

   and let

   $$\mathbf{F} = y\mathbf{i} + x^2\mathbf{j} + (x^2 + y^4)^{3/2} \sin e^{\sqrt{xyz}}\, \mathbf{k}.$$

   Find the value of

   $$\iint_S \nabla \times \mathbf{F} \cdot \mathbf{n}\, d\sigma.$$

   (*Hint:* One parametrization of the ellipse at the base of the shell is $x = 3\cos t, y = 2\sin t, 0 \leq t \leq 2\pi$.)

8. Let **n** be the outer unit normal (normal away from the origin) of the parabolic shell

   $$S:\quad 4x^2 + y + z^2 = 4, \qquad y \geq 0,$$

and let

$$\mathbf{F} = \left(-z + \frac{1}{2+x}\right)\mathbf{i} + (\tan^{-1} y)\mathbf{j} + \left(x + \frac{1}{4+z}\right)\mathbf{k}.$$

Find the value of

$$\iint_S \nabla \times \mathbf{F} \cdot \mathbf{n}\, d\sigma.$$

9. Let S be the cylinder $x^2 + y^2 = a^2, 0 \le z \le h$, together with its top, $x^2 + y^2 \le a^2, z = h$. Let $\mathbf{F} = -y\mathbf{i} + x\mathbf{j} + x^2\mathbf{k}$. Use Stokes' Theorem to find the flux of $\nabla \times \mathbf{F}$ outward through S.

10. Evaluate

$$\iint_S \nabla \times (y\mathbf{i}) \cdot \mathbf{n}\, d\sigma,$$

where S is the hemisphere $x^2 + y^2 + z^2 = 1, z \ge 0$.

11. **Flux of curl F** Show that

$$\iint_S \nabla \times \mathbf{F} \cdot \mathbf{n}\, d\sigma$$

has the same value for all oriented surfaces S that span C and that induce the same positive direction on C.

12. Let $\mathbf{F}$ be a differentiable vector field defined on a region containing a smooth closed oriented surface S and its interior. Let $\mathbf{n}$ be the unit normal vector field on S. Suppose that S is the union of two surfaces S_1 and S_2 joined along a smooth simple closed curve C. Can anything be said about

$$\iint_S \nabla \times \mathbf{F} \cdot \mathbf{n}\, d\sigma?$$

Give reasons for your answer.

Stokes' Theorem for Parametrized Surfaces

In Exercises 13–18, use the surface integral in Stokes' Theorem to calculate the flux of the curl of the field $\mathbf{F}$ across the surface S in the direction of the outward unit normal $\mathbf{n}$.

13. $\mathbf{F} = 2z\mathbf{i} + 3x\mathbf{j} + 5y\mathbf{k}$

S: $\mathbf{r}(r, \theta) = (r\cos\theta)\mathbf{i} + (r\sin\theta)\mathbf{j} + (4 - r^2)\mathbf{k}$, $0 \le r \le 2, \quad 0 \le \theta \le 2\pi$

14. $\mathbf{F} = (y - z)\mathbf{i} + (z - x)\mathbf{j} + (x + z)\mathbf{k}$

S: $\mathbf{r}(r, \theta) = (r\cos\theta)\mathbf{i} + (r\sin\theta)\mathbf{j} + (9 - r^2)\mathbf{k}$, $0 \le r \le 3, \quad 0 \le \theta \le 2\pi$

15. $\mathbf{F} = x^2y\mathbf{i} + 2y^3z\mathbf{j} + 3z\mathbf{k}$

S: $\mathbf{r}(r, \theta) = (r\cos\theta)\mathbf{i} + (r\sin\theta)\mathbf{j} + r\mathbf{k}$, $0 \le r \le 1, \quad 0 \le \theta \le 2\pi$

16. $\mathbf{F} = (x - y)\mathbf{i} + (y - z)\mathbf{j} + (z - x)\mathbf{k}$

S: $\mathbf{r}(r, \theta) = (r\cos\theta)\mathbf{i} + (r\sin\theta)\mathbf{j} + (5 - r)\mathbf{k}$, $0 \le r \le 5, \quad 0 \le \theta \le 2\pi$

17. $\mathbf{F} = 3y\mathbf{i} + (5 - 2x)\mathbf{j} + (z^2 - 2)\mathbf{k}$

S: $\mathbf{r}(\phi, \theta) = \left(\sqrt{3}\sin\phi\cos\theta\right)\mathbf{i} + \left(\sqrt{3}\sin\phi\sin\theta\right)\mathbf{j} + \left(\sqrt{3}\cos\phi\right)\mathbf{k}, \quad 0 \le \phi \le \pi/2, \quad 0 \le \theta \le 2\pi$

18. $\mathbf{F} = y^2\mathbf{i} + z^2\mathbf{j} + x\mathbf{k}$

S: $\mathbf{r}(\phi, \theta) = (2\sin\phi\cos\theta)\mathbf{i} + (2\sin\phi\sin\theta)\mathbf{j} + (2\cos\phi)\mathbf{k}$, $0 \le \phi \le \pi/2, \quad 0 \le \theta \le 2\pi$

Theory and Examples

19. **Zero circulation** Use the identity $\nabla \times \nabla f = \mathbf{0}$ (Equation (8) in the text) and Stokes' Theorem to show that the circulations of the following fields around the boundary of any smooth orientable surface in space are zero.

a. $\mathbf{F} = 2x\mathbf{i} + 2y\mathbf{j} + 2z\mathbf{k}$

b. $\mathbf{F} = \nabla(xy^2z^3)$

c. $\mathbf{F} = \nabla \times (x\mathbf{i} + y\mathbf{j} + z\mathbf{k})$

d. $\mathbf{F} = \nabla f$

20. **Zero circulation** Let $f(x, y, z) = (x^2 + y^2 + z^2)^{-1/2}$. Show that the clockwise circulation of the field $\mathbf{F} = \nabla f$ around the circle $x^2 + y^2 = a^2$ in the xy-plane is zero

a. by taking $\mathbf{r} = (a\cos t)\mathbf{i} + (a\sin t)\mathbf{j}, 0 \le t \le 2\pi$, and integrating $\mathbf{F} \cdot d\mathbf{r}$ over the circle.

b. by applying Stokes' Theorem.

21. Let C be a simple closed smooth curve in the plane $2x + 2y + z = 2$, oriented as shown here. Show that

$$\oint_C 2y\,dx + 3z\,dy - x\,dz$$

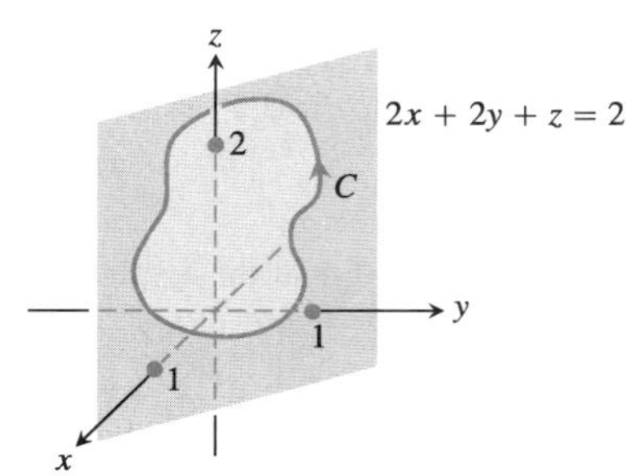

depends only on the area of the region enclosed by C and not on the position or shape of C.

22. Show that if $\mathbf{F} = x\mathbf{i} + y\mathbf{j} + z\mathbf{k}$, then $\nabla \times \mathbf{F} = \mathbf{0}$.

23. Find a vector field with twice-differentiable components whose curl is $x\mathbf{i} + y\mathbf{j} + z\mathbf{k}$ or prove that no such field exists.

24. Does Stokes' Theorem say anything special about circulation in a field whose curl is zero? Give reasons for your answer.

25. Let R be a region in the xy-plane that is bounded by a piecewise-smooth simple closed curve C and suppose that the moments of

inertia of R about the x- and y-axes are known to be I_x and I_y. Evaluate the integral

$$\oint_C \nabla(r^4)\cdot \mathbf{n}\, ds,$$

where $r = \sqrt{x^2 + y^2}$, in terms of I_x and I_y.

26. **Zero curl, yet field not conservative** Show that the curl of

$$\mathbf{F} = \frac{-y}{x^2+y^2}\mathbf{i} + \frac{x}{x^2+y^2}\mathbf{j} + z\mathbf{k}$$

is zero but that

$$\oint_C \mathbf{F}\cdot d\mathbf{r}$$

is not zero if C is the circle $x^2 + y^2 = 1$ in the xy-plane. (Theorem 6 does not apply here because the domain of $\mathbf{F}$ is not simply connected. The field $\mathbf{F}$ is not defined along the z-axis so there is no way to contract C to a point without leaving the domain of $\mathbf{F}$.)

16.8 The Divergence Theorem and a Unified Theory

The divergence form of Green's Theorem in the plane states that the net outward flux of a vector field across a simple closed curve can be calculated by integrating the divergence of the field over the region enclosed by the curve. The corresponding theorem in three dimensions, called the Divergence Theorem, states that the net outward flux of a vector field across a closed surface in space can be calculated by integrating the divergence of the field over the region enclosed by the surface. In this section, we prove the Divergence Theorem and show how it simplifies the calculation of flux. We also derive Gauss's law for flux in an electric field and the continuity equation of hydrodynamics. Finally, we unify the chapter's vector integral theorems into a single fundamental theorem.

Divergence in Three Dimensions

The **divergence** of a vector field $\mathbf{F} = M(x, y, z)\mathbf{i} + N(x, y, z)\mathbf{j} + P(x, y, z)\mathbf{k}$ is the scalar function

$$\text{div}\,\mathbf{F} = \nabla\cdot\mathbf{F} = \frac{\partial M}{\partial x} + \frac{\partial N}{\partial y} + \frac{\partial P}{\partial z}. \tag{1}$$

The symbol "div **F**" is read as "divergence of **F**" or "div **F**." The notation $\nabla\cdot\mathbf{F}$ is read "del dot **F**."

Div **F** has the same physical interpretation in three dimensions that it does in two. If **F** is the velocity field of a fluid flow, the value of div **F** at a point (x, y, z) is the rate at which fluid is being piped in or drained away at (x, y, z). The divergence is the flux per unit volume or flux density at the point.

EXAMPLE 1 Finding Divergence

Find the divergence of $\mathbf{F} = 2xz\mathbf{i} - xy\mathbf{j} - z\mathbf{k}$.

Solution The divergence of **F** is

$$\nabla\cdot\mathbf{F} = \frac{\partial}{\partial x}(2xz) + \frac{\partial}{\partial y}(-xy) + \frac{\partial}{\partial z}(-z) = 2z - x - 1.$$

■

Divergence Theorem

The Divergence Theorem says that under suitable conditions, the outward flux of a vector field across a closed surface (oriented outward) equals the triple integral of the divergence of the field over the region enclosed by the surface.

THEOREM 7 Divergence Theorem

The flux of a vector field $\mathbf{F}$ across a closed oriented surface S in the direction of the surface's outward unit normal field $\mathbf{n}$ equals the integral of $\nabla \cdot \mathbf{F}$ over the region D enclosed by the surface:

$$\underbrace{\iint_S \mathbf{F} \cdot \mathbf{n}\, d\sigma}_{\text{Outward flux}} = \underbrace{\iiint_D \nabla \cdot \mathbf{F}\, dV}_{\text{Divergence integral}}. \tag{2}$$

EXAMPLE 2 Supporting the Divergence Theorem

Evaluate both sides of Equation (2) for the field $\mathbf{F} = x\mathbf{i} + y\mathbf{j} + z\mathbf{k}$ over the sphere $x^2 + y^2 + z^2 = a^2$.

Solution The outer unit normal to S, calculated from the gradient of $f(x, y, z) = x^2 + y^2 + z^2 - a^2$, is

$$\mathbf{n} = \frac{2(x\mathbf{i} + y\mathbf{j} + z\mathbf{k})}{\sqrt{4(x^2 + y^2 + z^2)}} = \frac{x\mathbf{i} + y\mathbf{j} + z\mathbf{k}}{a}.$$

Hence,

$$\mathbf{F} \cdot \mathbf{n}\, d\sigma = \frac{x^2 + y^2 + z^2}{a}\, d\sigma = \frac{a^2}{a}\, d\sigma = a\, d\sigma$$

because $x^2 + y^2 + z^2 = a^2$ on the surface. Therefore,

$$\iint_S \mathbf{F} \cdot \mathbf{n}\, d\sigma = \iint_S a\, d\sigma = a \iint_S d\sigma = a(4\pi a^2) = 4\pi a^3.$$

The divergence of $\mathbf{F}$ is

$$\nabla \cdot \mathbf{F} = \frac{\partial}{\partial x}(x) + \frac{\partial}{\partial y}(y) + \frac{\partial}{\partial z}(z) = 3,$$

so

$$\iiint_D \nabla \cdot \mathbf{F}\, dV = \iiint_D 3\, dV = 3\left(\frac{4}{3}\pi a^3\right) = 4\pi a^3. \qquad \blacksquare$$

EXAMPLE 3 Finding Flux

Find the flux of $\mathbf{F} = xy\mathbf{i} + yz\mathbf{j} + xz\mathbf{k}$ outward through the surface of the cube cut from the first octant by the planes $x = 1$, $y = 1$, and $z = 1$.

Solution Instead of calculating the flux as a sum of six separate integrals, one for each face of the cube, we can calculate the flux by integrating the divergence

$$\nabla \cdot \mathbf{F} = \frac{\partial}{\partial x}(xy) + \frac{\partial}{\partial y}(yz) + \frac{\partial}{\partial z}(xz) = y + z + x$$

over the cube's interior:

$$\text{Flux} = \iint_{\substack{\text{Cube}\\\text{surface}}} \mathbf{F} \cdot \mathbf{n}\, d\sigma = \iiint_{\substack{\text{Cube}\\\text{interior}}} \nabla \cdot \mathbf{F}\, dV \qquad \text{The Divergence Theorem}$$

$$= \int_0^1 \int_0^1 \int_0^1 (x + y + z)\, dx\, dy\, dz = \frac{3}{2}. \qquad \text{Routine integration}$$

■

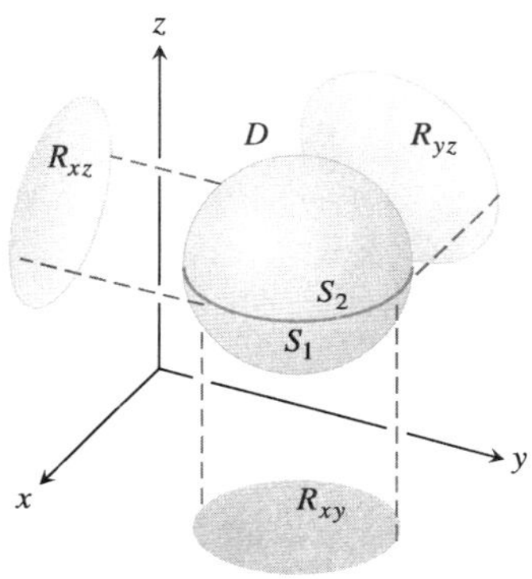

FIGURE 16.69 We first prove the Divergence Theorem for the kind of three-dimensional region shown here. We then extend the theorem to other regions.

Proof of the Divergence Theorem for Special Regions

To prove the Divergence Theorem, we assume that the components of **F** have continuous first partial derivatives. We also assume that D is a convex region with no holes or bubbles, such as a solid sphere, cube, or ellipsoid, and that S is a piecewise smooth surface. In addition, we assume that any line perpendicular to the xy-plane at an interior point of the region R_{xy} that is the projection of D on the xy-plane intersects the surface S in exactly two points, producing surfaces

$$S_1:\quad z = f_1(x, y), \qquad (x, y) \text{ in } R_{xy}$$

$$S_2:\quad z = f_2(x, y), \qquad (x, y) \text{ in } R_{xy},$$

with $f_1 \le f_2$. We make similar assumptions about the projection of D onto the other coordinate planes. See Figure 16.69.

The components of the unit normal vector $\mathbf{n} = n_1\mathbf{i} + n_2\mathbf{j} + n_3\mathbf{k}$ are the cosines of the angles α, β, and γ that **n** makes with **i**, **j**, and **k** (Figure 16.70). This is true because all the vectors involved are unit vectors. We have

$$n_1 = \mathbf{n} \cdot \mathbf{i} = |\mathbf{n}||\mathbf{i}| \cos \alpha = \cos \alpha$$

$$n_2 = \mathbf{n} \cdot \mathbf{j} = |\mathbf{n}||\mathbf{j}| \cos \beta = \cos \beta$$

$$n_3 = \mathbf{n} \cdot \mathbf{k} = |\mathbf{n}||\mathbf{k}| \cos \gamma = \cos \gamma$$

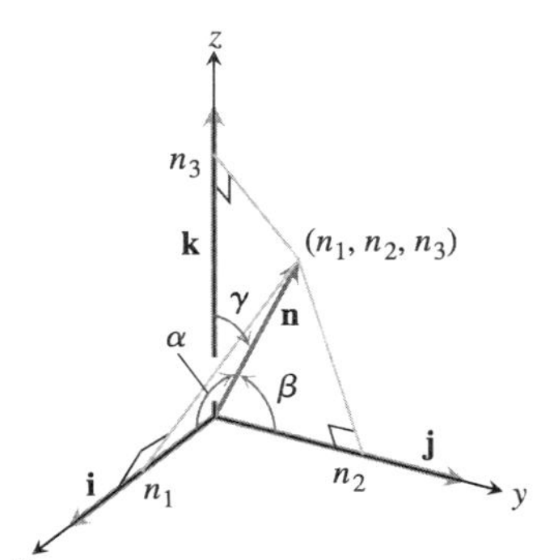

FIGURE 16.70 The scalar components of the unit normal vector **n** are the cosines of the angles α, β, and γ that it makes with **i**, **j**, and **k**.

Thus,

$$\mathbf{n} = (\cos \alpha)\mathbf{i} + (\cos \beta)\mathbf{j} + (\cos \gamma)\mathbf{k}$$

and

$$\mathbf{F} \cdot \mathbf{n} = M \cos \alpha + N \cos \beta + P \cos \gamma.$$

In component form, the Divergence Theorem states that

$$\iint_S (M \cos \alpha + N \cos \beta + P \cos \gamma)\, d\sigma = \iiint_D \left(\frac{\partial M}{\partial x} + \frac{\partial N}{\partial y} + \frac{\partial P}{\partial z}\right) dx\, dy\, dz.$$

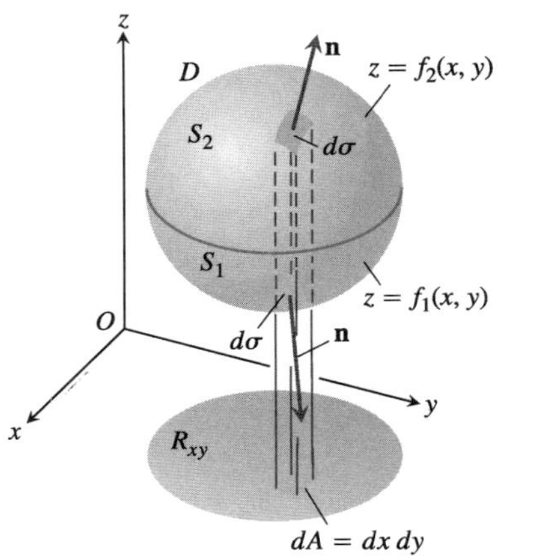

FIGURE 16.71 The three-dimensional region D enclosed by the surfaces S_1 and S_2 shown here projects vertically onto a two-dimensional region R_{xy} in the xy-plane.

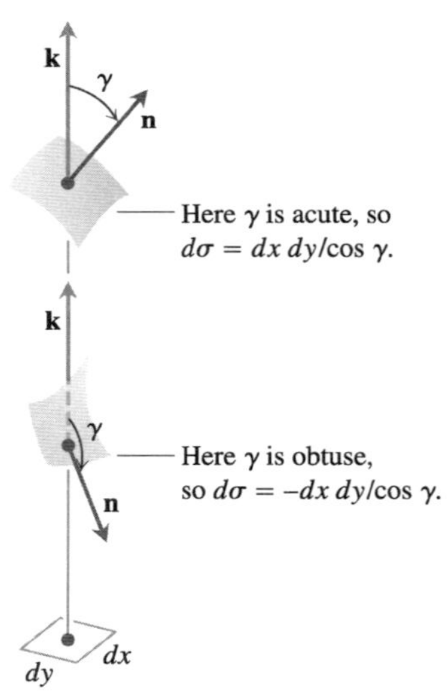

FIGURE 16.72 An enlarged view of the area patches in Figure 16.71. The relations $d\sigma = \pm dx\,dy/\cos\gamma$ are derived in Section 16.5.

We prove the theorem by proving the three following equalities:

$$\iint_S M\cos\alpha\,d\sigma = \iiint_D \frac{\partial M}{\partial x}\,dx\,dy\,dz \tag{3}$$

$$\iint_S N\cos\beta\,d\sigma = \iiint_D \frac{\partial N}{\partial y}\,dx\,dy\,dz \tag{4}$$

$$\iint_S P\cos\gamma\,d\sigma = \iiint_D \frac{\partial P}{\partial z}\,dx\,dy\,dz \tag{5}$$

Proof of Equation (5) We prove Equation (5) by converting the surface integral on the left to a double integral over the projection R_{xy} of D on the xy-plane (Figure 16.71). The surface S consists of an upper part S_2 whose equation is $z = f_2(x, y)$ and a lower part S_1 whose equation is $z = f_1(x, y)$. On S_2, the outer normal $\mathbf{n}$ has a positive $\mathbf{k}$-component and

$$\cos\gamma\,d\sigma = dx\,dy \qquad \text{because} \qquad d\sigma = \frac{dA}{|\cos\gamma|} = \frac{dx\,dy}{\cos\gamma}.$$

See Figure 16.72. On S_1, the outer normal $\mathbf{n}$ has a negative $\mathbf{k}$-component and

$$\cos\gamma\,d\sigma = -dx\,dy.$$

Therefore,

$$\begin{aligned}\iint_S P\cos\gamma\,d\sigma &= \iint_{S_2} P\cos\gamma\,d\sigma + \iint_{S_1} P\cos\gamma\,d\sigma\\ &= \iint_{R_{xy}} P(x, y, f_2(x, y))\,dx\,dy - \iint_{R_{xy}} P(x, y, f_1(x, y))\,dx\,dy\\ &= \iint_{R_{xy}} [P(x, y, f_2(x, y)) - P(x, y, f_1(x, y))]\,dx\,dy\\ &= \iint_{R_{xy}} \left[\int_{f_1(x,y)}^{f_2(x,y)} \frac{\partial P}{\partial z}\,dz\right] dx\,dy = \iiint_D \frac{\partial P}{\partial z}\,dz\,dx\,dy.\end{aligned}$$

This proves Equation (5). ■

The proofs for Equations (3) and (4) follow the same pattern; or just permute x, y, z; M, N, P; α, β, γ, in order, and get those results from Equation (5).

Divergence Theorem for Other Regions

The Divergence Theorem can be extended to regions that can be partitioned into a finite number of simple regions of the type just discussed and to regions that can be defined as limits of simpler regions in certain ways. For example, suppose that D is the region between two concentric spheres and that $\mathbf{F}$ has continuously differentiable components throughout D and on the bounding surfaces. Split D by an equatorial plane and apply the

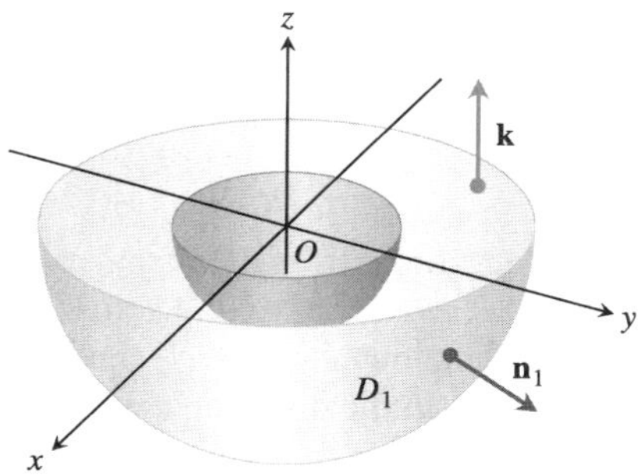

FIGURE 16.73 The lower half of the solid region between two concentric spheres.

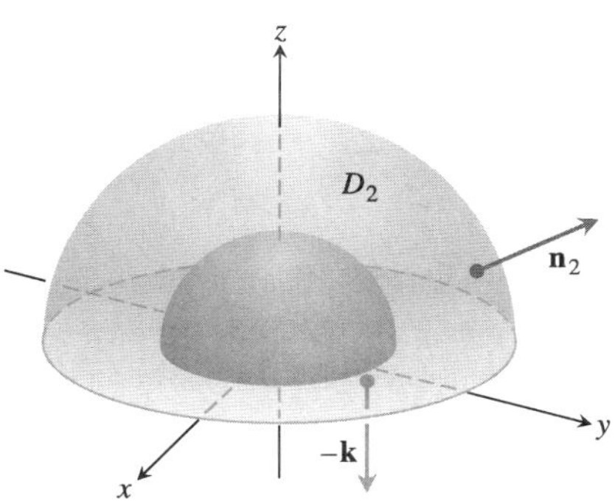

FIGURE 16.74 The upper half of the solid region between two concentric spheres.

Divergence Theorem to each half separately. The bottom half, D_1, is shown in Figure 16.73. The surface S_1 that bounds D_1 consists of an outer hemisphere, a plane washer-shaped base, and an inner hemisphere. The Divergence Theorem says that

$$\iint_{S_1} \mathbf{F}\cdot\mathbf{n}_1\, d\sigma_1 = \iiint_{D_1} \nabla\cdot\mathbf{F}\, dV_1. \tag{6}$$

The unit normal $\mathbf{n}_1$ that points outward from D_1 points away from the origin along the outer surface, equals $\mathbf{k}$ along the flat base, and points toward the origin along the inner surface. Next apply the Divergence Theorem to D_2, and its surface S_2 (Figure 16.74):

$$\iint_{S_2} \mathbf{F}\cdot\mathbf{n}_2\, d\sigma_2 = \iiint_{D_2} \nabla\cdot\mathbf{F}\, dV_2. \tag{7}$$

As we follow $\mathbf{n}_2$ over S_2, pointing outward from D_2, we see that $\mathbf{n}_2$ equals $-\mathbf{k}$ along the washer-shaped base in the xy-plane, points away from the origin on the outer sphere, and points toward the origin on the inner sphere. When we add Equations (6) and (7), the integrals over the flat base cancel because of the opposite signs of $\mathbf{n}_1$ and $\mathbf{n}_2$. We thus arrive at the result

$$\iint_{S} \mathbf{F}\cdot\mathbf{n}\, d\sigma = \iiint_{D} \nabla\cdot\mathbf{F}\, dV,$$

with D the region between the spheres, S the boundary of D consisting of two spheres, and $\mathbf{n}$ the unit normal to S directed outward from D.

EXAMPLE 4 Finding Outward Flux

Find the net outward flux of the field

$$\mathbf{F} = \frac{x\mathbf{i} + y\mathbf{j} + z\mathbf{k}}{\rho^3}, \qquad \rho = \sqrt{x^2 + y^2 + z^2}$$

across the boundary of the region D: $0 < a^2 \le x^2 + y^2 + z^2 \le b^2$.

Solution The flux can be calculated by integrating $\nabla\cdot\mathbf{F}$ over D. We have

$$\frac{\partial\rho}{\partial x} = \frac{1}{2}(x^2 + y^2 + z^2)^{-1/2}(2x) = \frac{x}{\rho}$$

and

$$\frac{\partial M}{\partial x} = \frac{\partial}{\partial x}(x\rho^{-3}) = \rho^{-3} - 3x\rho^{-4}\frac{\partial\rho}{\partial x} = \frac{1}{\rho^3} - \frac{3x^2}{\rho^5}.$$

Similarly,

$$\frac{\partial N}{\partial y} = \frac{1}{\rho^3} - \frac{3y^2}{\rho^5} \quad \text{and} \quad \frac{\partial P}{\partial z} = \frac{1}{\rho^3} - \frac{3z^2}{\rho^5}.$$

Hence,

$$\text{div}\,\mathbf{F} = \frac{3}{\rho^3} - \frac{3}{\rho^5}(x^2 + y^2 + z^2) = \frac{3}{\rho^3} - \frac{3\rho^2}{\rho^5} = 0$$

and

$$\iiint_D \nabla \cdot \mathbf{F}\, dV = 0.$$

So the integral of $\nabla \cdot \mathbf{F}$ over D is zero and the net outward flux across the boundary of D is zero. There is more to learn from this example, though. The flux leaving D across the inner sphere S_a is the negative of the flux leaving D across the outer sphere S_b (because the sum of these fluxes is zero). Hence, the flux of $\mathbf{F}$ across S_a in the direction away from the origin equals the flux of $\mathbf{F}$ across S_b in the direction away from the origin. Thus, the flux of $\mathbf{F}$ across a sphere centered at the origin is independent of the radius of the sphere. What is this flux?

To find it, we evaluate the flux integral directly. The outward unit normal on the sphere of radius a is

$$\mathbf{n} = \frac{x\mathbf{i} + y\mathbf{j} + z\mathbf{k}}{\sqrt{x^2 + y^2 + z^2}} = \frac{x\mathbf{i} + y\mathbf{j} + z\mathbf{k}}{a}.$$

Hence, on the sphere,

$$\mathbf{F} \cdot \mathbf{n} = \frac{x\mathbf{i} + y\mathbf{j} + z\mathbf{k}}{a^3} \cdot \frac{x\mathbf{i} + y\mathbf{j} + z\mathbf{k}}{a} = \frac{x^2 + y^2 + z^2}{a^4} = \frac{a^2}{a^4} = \frac{1}{a^2}$$

and

$$\iint_{S_a} \mathbf{F} \cdot \mathbf{n}\, d\sigma = \frac{1}{a^2} \iint_{S_a} d\sigma = \frac{1}{a^2}(4\pi a^2) = 4\pi.$$

The outward flux of $\mathbf{F}$ across any sphere centered at the origin is 4π. ■

Gauss's Law: One of the Four Great Laws of Electromagnetic Theory

There is still more to be learned from Example 4. In electromagnetic theory, the electric field created by a point charge q located at the origin is

$$\mathbf{E}(x, y, z) = \frac{1}{4\pi\epsilon_0} \frac{q}{|\mathbf{r}|^2} \left(\frac{\mathbf{r}}{|\mathbf{r}|} \right) = \frac{q}{4\pi\epsilon_0} \frac{\mathbf{r}}{|\mathbf{r}|^3} = \frac{q}{4\pi\epsilon_0} \frac{x\mathbf{i} + y\mathbf{j} + z\mathbf{k}}{\rho^3},$$

where ϵ_0 is a physical constant, $\mathbf{r}$ is the position vector of the point (x, y, z), and $\rho = |\mathbf{r}| = \sqrt{x^2 + y^2 + z^2}$. In the notation of Example 4,

$$\mathbf{E} = \frac{q}{4\pi\epsilon_0}\mathbf{F}.$$

The calculations in Example 4 show that the outward flux of $\mathbf{E}$ across any sphere centered at the origin is q/ϵ_0, but this result is not confined to spheres. The outward flux of $\mathbf{E}$ across any closed surface S that encloses the origin (and to which the Divergence Theorem applies) is also q/ϵ_0. To see why, we have only to imagine a large sphere S_a centered at the origin and enclosing the surface S. Since

$$\nabla \cdot \mathbf{E} = \nabla \cdot \frac{q}{4\pi\epsilon_0}\mathbf{F} = \frac{q}{4\pi\epsilon_0}\nabla \cdot \mathbf{F} = 0$$

when $\rho > 0$, the integral of $\nabla \cdot \mathbf{E}$ over the region D between S and S_a is zero. Hence, by the Divergence Theorem,

$$\iint_{\substack{\text{Boundary}\\ \text{of } D}} \mathbf{E} \cdot \mathbf{n}\, d\sigma = 0,$$

and the flux of $\mathbf{E}$ across S in the direction away from the origin must be the same as the flux of $\mathbf{E}$ across S_a in the direction away from the origin, which is q/ϵ_0. This statement, called *Gauss's Law*, also applies to charge distributions that are more general than the one assumed here, as you will see in nearly any physics text.

$$\text{Gauss's law:} \quad \iint_S \mathbf{E} \cdot \mathbf{n}\, d\sigma = \frac{q}{\epsilon_0}$$

Continuity Equation of Hydrodynamics

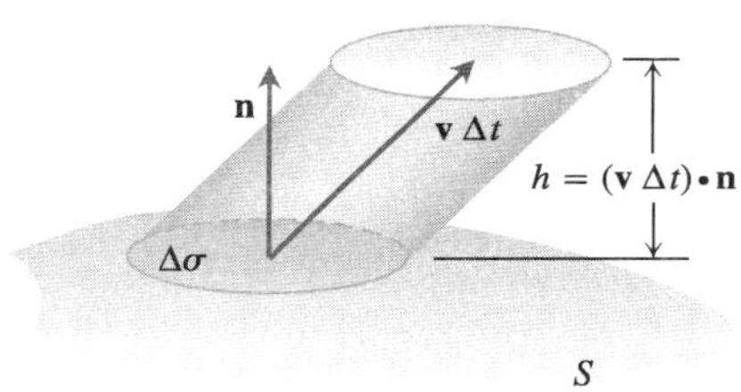

FIGURE 16.75 The fluid that flows upward through the patch $\Delta\sigma$ in a short time Δt fills a "cylinder" whose volume is approximately base $\times$ height $=$ $\mathbf{v} \cdot \mathbf{n}\, \Delta\sigma\, \Delta t$.

Let D be a region in space bounded by a closed oriented surface S. If $\mathbf{v}(x, y, z)$ is the velocity field of a fluid flowing smoothly through D, $\delta = \delta(t, x, y, z)$ is the fluid's density at (x, y, z) at time t, and $\mathbf{F} = \delta\mathbf{v}$, then the **continuity equation** of hydrodynamics states that

$$\nabla \cdot \mathbf{F} + \frac{\partial \delta}{\partial t} = 0.$$

If the functions involved have continuous first partial derivatives, the equation evolves naturally from the Divergence Theorem, as we now see.

First, the integral

$$\iint_S \mathbf{F} \cdot \mathbf{n}\, d\sigma$$

is the rate at which mass leaves D across S (leaves because $\mathbf{n}$ is the outer normal). To see why, consider a patch of area $\Delta\sigma$ on the surface (Figure 16.75). In a short time interval Δt, the volume ΔV of fluid that flows across the patch is approximately equal to the volume of a cylinder with base area $\Delta\sigma$ and height $(\mathbf{v}\Delta t) \cdot \mathbf{n}$, where $\mathbf{v}$ is a velocity vector rooted at a point of the patch:

$$\Delta V \approx \mathbf{v} \cdot \mathbf{n}\, \Delta\sigma\, \Delta t.$$

The mass of this volume of fluid is about

$$\Delta m \approx \delta\mathbf{v} \cdot \mathbf{n}\, \Delta\sigma\, \Delta t,$$

so the rate at which mass is flowing out of D across the patch is about

$$\frac{\Delta m}{\Delta t} \approx \delta\mathbf{v} \cdot \mathbf{n}\, \Delta\sigma.$$

This leads to the approximation

$$\frac{\sum \Delta m}{\Delta t} \approx \sum \delta\mathbf{v} \cdot \mathbf{n}\, \Delta\sigma$$

as an estimate of the average rate at which mass flows across S. Finally, letting $\Delta\sigma \to 0$ and $\Delta t \to 0$ gives the instantaneous rate at which mass leaves D across S as

$$\frac{dm}{dt} = \iint_S \delta \mathbf{v} \cdot \mathbf{n}\, d\sigma,$$

which for our particular flow is

$$\frac{dm}{dt} = \iint_S \mathbf{F} \cdot \mathbf{n}\, d\sigma.$$

Now let B be a solid sphere centered at a point Q in the flow. The average value of $\nabla \cdot \mathbf{F}$ over B is

$$\frac{1}{\text{volume of } B} \iiint_B \nabla \cdot \mathbf{F}\, dV.$$

It is a consequence of the continuity of the divergence that $\nabla \cdot \mathbf{F}$ actually takes on this value at some point P in B. Thus,

$$\begin{aligned}(\nabla \cdot \mathbf{F})_P &= \frac{1}{\text{volume of } B} \iiint_B \nabla \cdot \mathbf{F}\, dV = \frac{\iint_S \mathbf{F} \cdot \mathbf{n}\, d\sigma}{\text{volume of } B} \\ &= \frac{\text{rate at which mass leaves } B \text{ across its surface } S}{\text{volume of } B}\end{aligned} \tag{8}$$

The fraction on the right describes decrease in mass per unit volume.

Now let the radius of B approach zero while the center Q stays fixed. The left side of Equation (8) converges to $(\nabla \cdot \mathbf{F})_Q$, the right side to $(-\partial\delta/\partial t)_Q$. The equality of these two limits is the continuity equation

$$\nabla \cdot \mathbf{F} = -\frac{\partial \delta}{\partial t}.$$

The continuity equation "explains" $\nabla \cdot \mathbf{F}$: The divergence of $\mathbf{F}$ at a point is the rate at which the density of the fluid is decreasing there.

The Divergence Theorem

$$\iint_S \mathbf{F} \cdot \mathbf{n}\, d\sigma = \iiint_D \nabla \cdot \mathbf{F}\, dV$$

now says that the net decrease in density of the fluid in region D is accounted for by the mass transported across the surface S. So, the theorem is a statement about conservation of mass (Exercise 31).

Unifying the Integral Theorems

If we think of a two-dimensional field $\mathbf{F} = M(x, y)\mathbf{i} + N(x, y)\mathbf{j}$ as a three-dimensional field whose $\mathbf{k}$-component is zero, then $\nabla \cdot \mathbf{F} = (\partial M/\partial x) + (\partial N/\partial y)$ and the normal form of Green's Theorem can be written as

$$\oint_C \mathbf{F} \cdot \mathbf{n}\, ds = \iint_R \left(\frac{\partial M}{\partial x} + \frac{\partial N}{\partial y}\right) dx\, dy = \iint_R \nabla \cdot \mathbf{F}\, dA.$$

Similarly, $\nabla \times \mathbf{F} \cdot \mathbf{k} = (\partial N/\partial x) - (\partial M/\partial y)$, so the tangential form of Green's Theorem can be written as

$$\oint_C \mathbf{F} \cdot d\mathbf{r} = \iint_R \left(\frac{\partial N}{\partial x} - \frac{\partial M}{\partial y} \right) dx\, dy = \iint_R \nabla \times \mathbf{F} \cdot \mathbf{k}\, dA.$$

With the equations of Green's Theorem now in del notation, we can see their relationships to the equations in Stokes' Theorem and the Divergence Theorem.

Green's Theorem and Its Generalization to Three Dimensions

Normal form of Green's Theorem: $\oint_C \mathbf{F} \cdot \mathbf{n}\, ds = \iint_R \nabla \cdot \mathbf{F}\, dA$

Divergence Theorem: $\iint_S \mathbf{F} \cdot \mathbf{n}\, d\sigma = \iiint_D \nabla \cdot \mathbf{F}\, dV$

Tangential form of Green's Theorem: $\oint_C \mathbf{F} \cdot d\mathbf{r} = \iint_R \nabla \times \mathbf{F} \cdot \mathbf{k}\, dA$

Stokes' Theorem: $\oint_C \mathbf{F} \cdot d\mathbf{r} = \iint_S \nabla \times \mathbf{F} \cdot \mathbf{n}\, d\sigma$

Notice how Stokes' Theorem generalizes the tangential (curl) form of Green's Theorem from a flat surface in the plane to a surface in three-dimensional space. In each case, the integral of the normal component of curl **F** over the interior of the surface equals the circulation of **F** around the boundary.

Likewise, the Divergence Theorem generalizes the normal (flux) form of Green's Theorem from a two-dimensional region in the plane to a three-dimensional region in space. In each case, the integral of $\nabla \cdot \mathbf{F}$ over the interior of the region equals the total flux of the field across the boundary.

There is still more to be learned here. All these results can be thought of as forms of a *single fundamental theorem*. Think back to the Fundamental Theorem of Calculus in Section 5.4. It says that if $f(x)$ is differentiable on (a, b) and continuous on $[a, b]$, then

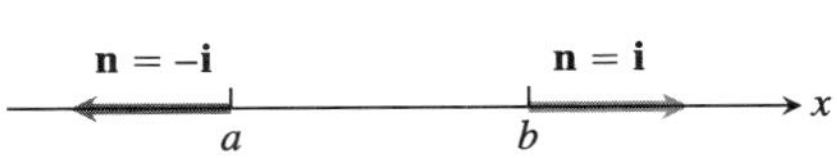

FIGURE 16.76 The outward unit normals at the boundary of $[a, b]$ in one-dimensional space.

$$\int_a^b \frac{df}{dx}\, dx = f(b) - f(a).$$

If we let $\mathbf{F} = f(x)\mathbf{i}$ throughout $[a, b]$, then $(df/dx) = \nabla \cdot \mathbf{F}$. If we define the unit vector field $\mathbf{n}$ normal to the boundary of $[a, b]$ to be $\mathbf{i}$ at b and $-\mathbf{i}$ at a (Figure 16.76), then

$$\begin{aligned} f(b) - f(a) &= f(b)\mathbf{i} \cdot (\mathbf{i}) + f(a)\mathbf{i} \cdot (-\mathbf{i}) \\ &= \mathbf{F}(b) \cdot \mathbf{n} + \mathbf{F}(a) \cdot \mathbf{n} \\ &= \text{total outward flux of } \mathbf{F} \text{ across the boundary of } [a, b]. \end{aligned}$$

The Fundamental Theorem now says that

$$\mathbf{F}(b) \cdot \mathbf{n} + \mathbf{F}(a) \cdot \mathbf{n} = \int_{[a,b]} \nabla \cdot \mathbf{F}\, dx.$$

The Fundamental Theorem of Calculus, the normal form of Green's Theorem, and the Divergence Theorem all say that the integral of the differential operator $\nabla \cdot$ operating on a field **F** over a region equals the sum of the normal field components over the boundary of the region. (Here we are interpreting the line integral in Green's Theorem and the surface integral in the Divergence Theorem as "sums" over the boundary.)

Stokes' Theorem and the tangential form of Green's Theorem say that, when things are properly oriented, the integral of the normal component of the curl operating on a field equals the sum of the tangential field components on the boundary of the surface.

The beauty of these interpretations is the observance of a single unifying principle, which we might state as follows.

> The integral of a differential operator acting on a field over a region equals the sum of the field components appropriate to the operator over the boundary of the region.

EXERCISES 16.8

Calculating Divergence

In Exercises 1–4, find the divergence of the field.

1. The spin field in Figure 16.14.
2. The radial field in Figure 16.13.
3. The gravitational field in Figure 16.9.
4. The velocity field in Figure 16.12.

Using the Divergence Theorem to Calculate Outward Flux

In Exercises 5–16, use the Divergence Theorem to find the outward flux of **F** across the boundary of the region D.

5. **Cube** $\mathbf{F} = (y - x)\mathbf{i} + (z - y)\mathbf{j} + (y - x)\mathbf{k}$
   D: The cube bounded by the planes $x = \pm 1, y = \pm 1$, and $z = \pm 1$
6. $\mathbf{F} = x^2\mathbf{i} + y^2\mathbf{j} + z^2\mathbf{k}$
   a. **Cube** D: The cube cut from the first octant by the planes $x = 1, y = 1$, and $z = 1$
   b. **Cube** D: The cube bounded by the planes $x = \pm 1$, $y = \pm 1$, and $z = \pm 1$
   c. **Cylindrical can** D: The region cut from the solid cylinder $x^2 + y^2 \leq 4$ by the planes $z = 0$ and $z = 1$
7. **Cylinder and paraboloid** $\mathbf{F} = y\mathbf{i} + xy\mathbf{j} - z\mathbf{k}$
   D: The region inside the solid cylinder $x^2 + y^2 \leq 4$ between the plane $z = 0$ and the paraboloid $z = x^2 + y^2$
8. **Sphere** $\mathbf{F} = x^2\mathbf{i} + xz\mathbf{j} + 3z\mathbf{k}$
   D: The solid sphere $x^2 + y^2 + z^2 \leq 4$
9. **Portion of sphere** $\mathbf{F} = x^2\mathbf{i} - 2xy\mathbf{j} + 3xz\mathbf{k}$
   D: The region cut from the first octant by the sphere $x^2 + y^2 + z^2 = 4$
10. **Cylindrical can** $\mathbf{F} = (6x^2 + 2xy)\mathbf{i} + (2y + x^2z)\mathbf{j} + 4x^2y^3\mathbf{k}$
    D: The region cut from the first octant by the cylinder $x^2 + y^2 = 4$ and the plane $z = 3$
11. **Wedge** $\mathbf{F} = 2xz\mathbf{i} - xy\mathbf{j} - z^2\mathbf{k}$
    D: The wedge cut from the first octant by the plane $y + z = 4$ and the elliptical cylinder $4x^2 + y^2 = 16$
12. **Sphere** $\mathbf{F} = x^3\mathbf{i} + y^3\mathbf{j} + z^3\mathbf{k}$
    D: The solid sphere $x^2 + y^2 + z^2 \leq a^2$
13. **Thick sphere** $\mathbf{F} = \sqrt{x^2 + y^2 + z^2}\,(x\mathbf{i} + y\mathbf{j} + z\mathbf{k})$
    D: The region $1 \leq x^2 + y^2 + z^2 \leq 2$
14. **Thick sphere** $\mathbf{F} = (x\mathbf{i} + y\mathbf{j} + z\mathbf{k})/\sqrt{x^2 + y^2 + z^2}$
    D: The region $1 \leq x^2 + y^2 + z^2 \leq 4$
15. **Thick sphere** $\mathbf{F} = (5x^3 + 12xy^2)\mathbf{i} + (y^3 + e^y \sin z)\mathbf{j} + (5z^3 + e^y \cos z)\mathbf{k}$
    D: The solid region between the spheres $x^2 + y^2 + z^2 = 1$ and $x^2 + y^2 + z^2 = 2$
16. **Thick cylinder** $\mathbf{F} = \ln(x^2 + y^2)\mathbf{i} - \left(\frac{2z}{x}\tan^{-1}\frac{y}{x}\right)\mathbf{j} + z\sqrt{x^2 + y^2}\,\mathbf{k}$
    D: The thick-walled cylinder $1 \leq x^2 + y^2 \leq 2, \quad -1 \leq z \leq 2$

Properties of Curl and Divergence

17. div (curl G) is zero

a. Show that if the necessary partial derivatives of the components of the field $\mathbf{G} = M\mathbf{i} + N\mathbf{j} + P\mathbf{k}$ are continuous, then $\nabla \cdot \nabla \times \mathbf{G} = 0$.

b. What, if anything, can you conclude about the flux of the field $\nabla \times \mathbf{G}$ across a closed surface? Give reasons for your answer.

18. Let $\mathbf{F}_1$ and $\mathbf{F}_2$ be differentiable vector fields and let a and b be arbitrary real constants. Verify the following identities.

a. $\nabla \cdot (a\mathbf{F}_1 + b\mathbf{F}_2) = a\nabla \cdot \mathbf{F}_1 + b\nabla \cdot \mathbf{F}_2$

b. $\nabla \times (a\mathbf{F}_1 + b\mathbf{F}_2) = a\nabla \times \mathbf{F}_1 + b\nabla \times \mathbf{F}_2$

c. $\nabla \cdot (\mathbf{F}_1 \times \mathbf{F}_2) = \mathbf{F}_2 \cdot \nabla \times \mathbf{F}_1 - \mathbf{F}_1 \cdot \nabla \times \mathbf{F}_2$

19. Let $\mathbf{F}$ be a differentiable vector field and let $g(x, y, z)$ be a differentiable scalar function. Verify the following identities.

a. $\nabla \cdot (g\mathbf{F}) = g\nabla \cdot \mathbf{F} + \nabla g \cdot \mathbf{F}$

b. $\nabla \times (g\mathbf{F}) = g\nabla \times \mathbf{F} + \nabla g \times \mathbf{F}$

20. If $\mathbf{F} = M\mathbf{i} + N\mathbf{j} + P\mathbf{k}$ is a differentiable vector field, we define the notation $\mathbf{F} \cdot \nabla$ to mean

$$M\frac{\partial}{\partial x} + N\frac{\partial}{\partial y} + P\frac{\partial}{\partial z}.$$

For differentiable vector fields $\mathbf{F}_1$ and $\mathbf{F}_2$, verify the following identities.

a. $\nabla \times (\mathbf{F}_1 \times \mathbf{F}_2) = (\mathbf{F}_2 \cdot \nabla)\mathbf{F}_1 - (\mathbf{F}_1 \cdot \nabla)\mathbf{F}_2 + (\nabla \cdot \mathbf{F}_2)\mathbf{F}_1 - (\nabla \cdot \mathbf{F}_1)\mathbf{F}_2$

b. $\nabla(\mathbf{F}_1 \cdot \mathbf{F}_2) = (\mathbf{F}_1 \cdot \nabla)\mathbf{F}_2 + (\mathbf{F}_2 \cdot \nabla)\mathbf{F}_1 + \mathbf{F}_1 \times (\nabla \times \mathbf{F}_2) + \mathbf{F}_2 \times (\nabla \times \mathbf{F}_1)$

Theory and Examples

21. Let $\mathbf{F}$ be a field whose components have continuous first partial derivatives throughout a portion of space containing a region D bounded by a smooth closed surface S. If $|\mathbf{F}| \le 1$, can any bound be placed on the size of

$$\iiint_D \nabla \cdot \mathbf{F}\, dV?$$

Give reasons for your answer.

22. The base of the closed cubelike surface shown here is the unit square in the xy-plane. The four sides lie in the planes $x = 0, x = 1, y = 0$, and $y = 1$. The top is an arbitrary smooth surface whose identity is unknown. Let $\mathbf{F} = x\mathbf{i} - 2y\mathbf{j} + (z + 3)\mathbf{k}$ and suppose the outward flux of $\mathbf{F}$ through side A is 1 and through side B is -3. Can you conclude anything about the outward flux through the top? Give reasons for your answer.

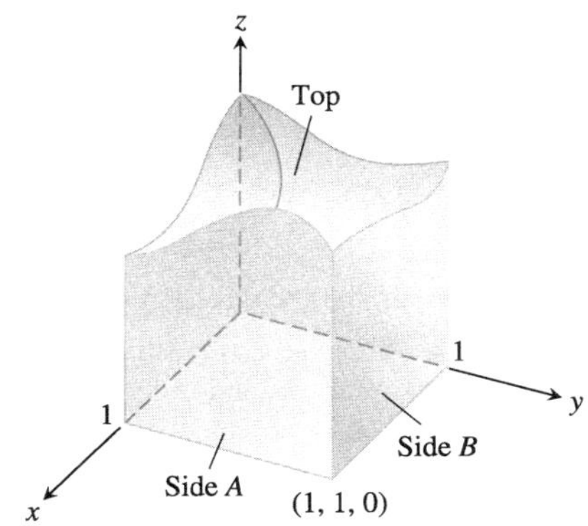

23. a. Show that the flux of the position vector field $\mathbf{F} = x\mathbf{i} + y\mathbf{j} + z\mathbf{k}$ outward through a smooth closed surface S is three times the volume of the region enclosed by the surface.

b. Let $\mathbf{n}$ be the outward unit normal vector field on S. Show that it is not possible for $\mathbf{F}$ to be orthogonal to $\mathbf{n}$ at every point of S.

24. Maximum flux Among all rectangular solids defined by the inequalities $0 \le x \le a, 0 \le y \le b, 0 \le z \le 1$, find the one for which the total flux of $\mathbf{F} = (-x^2 - 4xy)\mathbf{i} - 6yz\mathbf{j} + 12z\mathbf{k}$ outward through the six sides is greatest. What *is* the greatest flux?

25. Volume of a solid region Let $\mathbf{F} = x\mathbf{i} + y\mathbf{j} + z\mathbf{k}$ and suppose that the surface S and region D satisfy the hypotheses of the Divergence Theorem. Show that the volume of D is given by the formula

$$\text{Volume of } D = \frac{1}{3}\iint_S \mathbf{F} \cdot \mathbf{n}\, d\sigma.$$

26. Flux of a constant field Show that the outward flux of a constant vector field $\mathbf{F} = \mathbf{C}$ across any closed surface to which the Divergence Theorem applies is zero.

27. Harmonic functions A function $f(x, y, z)$ is said to be *harmonic* in a region D in space if it satisfies the Laplace equation

$$\nabla^2 f = \nabla \cdot \nabla f = \frac{\partial^2 f}{\partial x^2} + \frac{\partial^2 f}{\partial y^2} + \frac{\partial^2 f}{\partial z^2} = 0$$

throughout D.

a. Suppose that f is harmonic throughout a bounded region D enclosed by a smooth surface S and that $\mathbf{n}$ is the chosen unit normal vector on S. Show that the integral over S of $\nabla f \cdot \mathbf{n}$, the derivative of f in the direction of $\mathbf{n}$, is zero.

b. Show that if f is harmonic on D, then

$$\iint_S f\, \nabla f \cdot \mathbf{n}\, d\sigma = \iiint_D |\nabla f|^2\, dV.$$

28. Flux of a gradient field Let S be the surface of the portion of the solid sphere $x^2 + y^2 + z^2 \le a^2$ that lies in the first octant and let $f(x, y, z) = \ln\sqrt{x^2 + y^2 + z^2}$. Calculate

$$\iint_S \nabla f \cdot \mathbf{n}\, d\sigma.$$

($\nabla f \cdot \mathbf{n}$ is the derivative of f in the direction of $\mathbf{n}$.)

29. Green's first formula Suppose that f and g are scalar functions with continuous first- and second-order partial derivatives throughout a region D that is bounded by a closed piecewise-smooth surface S. Show that

$$\iint_S f\,\nabla g \cdot \mathbf{n}\, d\sigma = \iiint_D (f\,\nabla^2 g + \nabla f \cdot \nabla g)\, dV. \qquad (9)$$

Equation (9) is **Green's first formula.** (*Hint:* Apply the Divergence Theorem to the field $\mathbf{F} = f\,\nabla g$.)

30. Green's second formula (*Continuation of Exercise 29.*) Interchange f and g in Equation (9) to obtain a similar formula. Then subtract this formula from Equation (9) to show that

$$\iint_S (f\,\nabla g - g\nabla f) \cdot \mathbf{n}\, d\sigma = \iiint_D (f\,\nabla^2 g - g\nabla^2 f)\, dV. \qquad (10)$$

This equation is **Green's second formula.**

31. Conservation of mass Let $\mathbf{v}(t, x, y, z)$ be a continuously differentiable vector field over the region D in space and let $p(t, x, y, z)$ be a continuously differentiable scalar function. The variable t represents the time domain. The Law of Conservation of Mass asserts that

$$\frac{d}{dt}\iiint_D p(t, x, y, z)\, dV = -\iint_S p\mathbf{v} \cdot \mathbf{n}\, d\sigma,$$

where S is the surface enclosing D.

a. Give a physical interpretation of the conservation of mass law if $\mathbf{v}$ is a velocity flow field and p represents the density of the fluid at point (x, y, z) at time t.

b. Use the Divergence Theorem and Leibniz's Rule,

$$\frac{d}{dt}\iiint_D p(t, x, y, z)\, dV = \iiint_D \frac{\partial p}{\partial t}\, dV,$$

to show that the Law of Conservation of Mass is equivalent to the continuity equation,

$$\nabla \cdot p\mathbf{v} + \frac{\partial p}{\partial t} = 0.$$

(In the first term $\nabla \cdot p\mathbf{v}$, the variable t is held fixed, and in the second term $\partial p/\partial t$, it is assumed that the point (x, y, z) in D is held fixed.)

32. The heat diffusion equation Let $T(t, x, y, z)$ be a function with continuous second derivatives giving the temperature at time t at the point (x, y, z) of a solid occupying a region D in space. If the solid's heat capacity and mass density are denoted by the constants c and ρ, respectively, the quantity $c\rho T$ is called the solid's **heat energy per unit volume.**

a. Explain why $-\nabla T$ points in the direction of heat flow.

b. Let $-k\nabla T$ denote the **energy flux vector.** (Here the constant k is called the **conductivity**.) Assuming the Law of Conservation of Mass with $-k\nabla T = \mathbf{v}$ and $c\rho T = p$ in Exercise 31, derive the diffusion (heat) equation

$$\frac{\partial T}{\partial t} = K\nabla^2 T,$$

where $K = k/(c\rho) > 0$ is the *diffusivity* constant. (Notice that if $T(t, x)$ represents the temperature at time t at position x in a uniform conducting rod with perfectly insulated sides, then $\nabla^2 T = \partial^2 T/\partial x^2$ and the diffusion equation reduces to the one-dimensional heat equation in Chapter 14's Additional Exercises.)

Chapter 16 Questions to Guide Your Review

1. What are line integrals? How are they evaluated? Give examples.
2. How can you use line integrals to find the centers of mass of springs? Explain.
3. What is a vector field? A gradient field? Give examples.
4. How do you calculate the work done by a force in moving a particle along a curve? Give an example.
5. What are flow, circulation, and flux?
6. What is special about path independent fields?
7. How can you tell when a field is conservative?
8. What is a potential function? Show by example how to find a potential function for a conservative field.
9. What is a differential form? What does it mean for such a form to be exact? How do you test for exactness? Give examples.
10. What is the divergence of a vector field? How can you interpret it?
11. What is the curl of a vector field? How can you interpret it?
12. What is Green's theorem? How can you interpret it?
13. How do you calculate the area of a curved surface in space? Give an example.

14. What is an oriented surface? How do you calculate the flux of a three-dimensional vector field across an oriented surface? Give an example.
15. What are surface integrals? What can you calculate with them? Give an example.
16. What is a parametrized surface? How do you find the area of such a surface? Give examples.
17. How do you integrate a function over a parametrized surface? Give an example.
18. What is Stokes' Theorem? How can you interpret it?
19. Summarize the chapter's results on conservative fields.
20. What is the Divergence Theorem? How can you interpret it?
21. How does the Divergence Theorem generalize Green's Theorem?
22. How does Stokes' Theorem generalize Green's Theorem?
23. How can Green's Theorem, Stokes' Theorem, and the Divergence Theorem be thought of as forms of a single fundamental theorem?

Chapter 16 Practice Exercises

Evaluating Line Integrals

1. The accompanying figure shows two polygonal paths in space joining the origin to the point (1, 1, 1). Integrate $f(x, y, z) = 2x - 3y^2 - 2z + 3$ over each path.

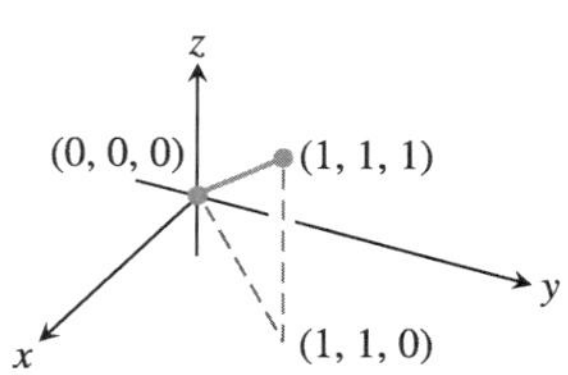

Path 1

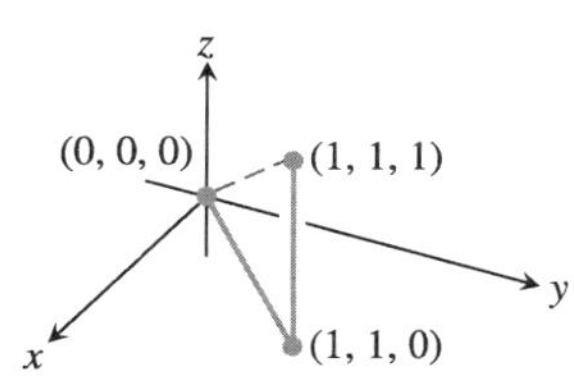

Path 2

2. The accompanying figure shows three polygonal paths joining the origin to the point (1, 1, 1). Integrate $f(x, y, z) = x^2 + y - z$ over each path.

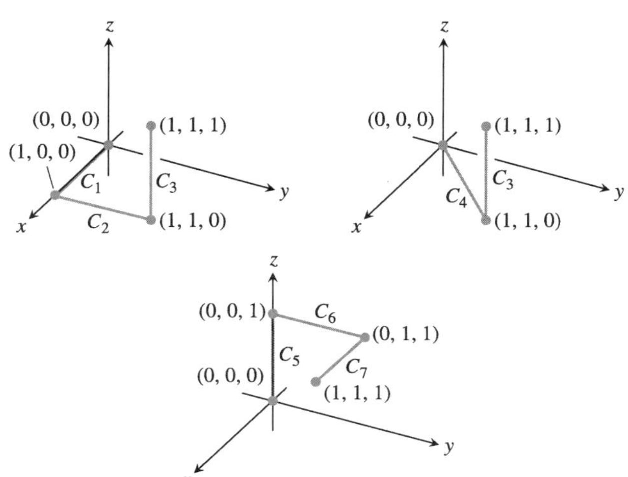

3. Integrate $f(x, y, z) = \sqrt{x^2 + z^2}$ over the circle

$$\mathbf{r}(t) = (a \cos t)\mathbf{j} + (a \sin t)\mathbf{k}, \qquad 0 \le t \le 2\pi.$$

4. Integrate $f(x, y, z) = \sqrt{x^2 + y^2}$ over the involute curve

$$\mathbf{r}(t) = (\cos t + t \sin t)\mathbf{i} + (\sin t - t \cos t)\mathbf{j}, \qquad 0 \le t \le \sqrt{3}.$$

Evaluate the integrals in Exercises 5 and 6.

5. $\displaystyle\int_{(-1,1,1)}^{(4,-3,0)} \frac{dx + dy + dz}{\sqrt{x + y + z}}$

6. $\displaystyle\int_{(1,1,1)}^{(10,3,3)} dx - \sqrt{\frac{z}{y}}\, dy - \sqrt{\frac{y}{z}}\, dz$

7. Integrate $\mathbf{F} = -(y \sin z)\mathbf{i} + (x \sin z)\mathbf{j} + (xy \cos z)\mathbf{k}$ around the circle cut from the sphere $x^2 + y^2 + z^2 = 5$ by the plane $z = -1$, clockwise as viewed from above.

8. Integrate $\mathbf{F} = 3x^2y\mathbf{i} + (x^3 + 1)\mathbf{j} + 9z^2\mathbf{k}$ around the circle cut from the sphere $x^2 + y^2 + z^2 = 9$ by the plane $x = 2$.

Evaluate the integrals in Exercises 9 and 10.

9. $\displaystyle\int_C 8x \sin y\, dx - 8y \cos x\, dy$

   C is the square cut from the first quadrant by the lines $x = \pi/2$ and $y = \pi/2$.

10. $\displaystyle\int_C y^2\, dx + x^2\, dy$

    C is the circle $x^2 + y^2 = 4$.

Evaluating Surface Integrals

11. **Area of an elliptical region** Find the area of the elliptical region cut from the plane $x + y + z = 1$ by the cylinder $x^2 + y^2 = 1$.

12. **Area of a parabolic cap** Find the area of the cap cut from the paraboloid $y^2 + z^2 = 3x$ by the plane $x = 1$.

13. **Area of a spherical cap** Find the area of the cap cut from the top of the sphere $x^2 + y^2 + z^2 = 1$ by the plane $z = \sqrt{2}/2$.

14. a. **Hemisphere cut by cylinder** Find the area of the surface cut from the hemisphere $x^2 + y^2 + z^2 = 4$, $z \geq 0$, by the cylinder $x^2 + y^2 = 2x$.

b. Find the area of the portion of the cylinder that lies inside the hemisphere. (*Hint:* Project onto the xz-plane. Or evaluate the integral $\int h\, ds$, where h is the altitude of the cylinder and ds is the element of arc length on the circle $x^2 + y^2 = 2x$ in the xy-plane.)

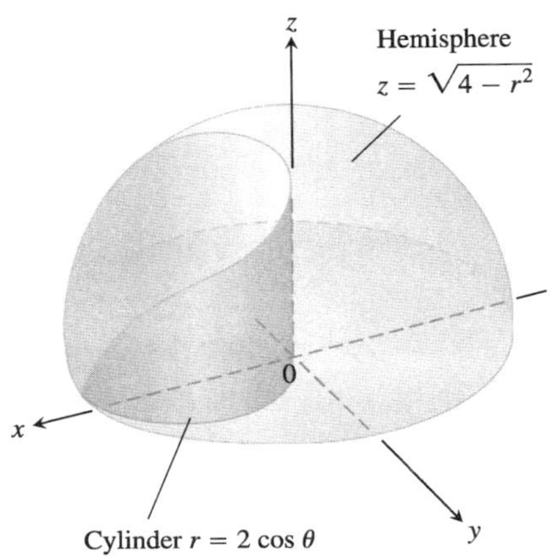

15. **Area of a triangle** Find the area of the triangle in which the plane $(x/a) + (y/b) + (z/c) = 1$ $(a, b, c > 0)$ intersects the first octant. Check your answer with an appropriate vector calculation.

16. **Parabolic cylinder cut by planes** Integrate

a. $g(x, y, z) = \dfrac{yz}{\sqrt{4y^2 + 1}}$ b. $g(x, y, z) = \dfrac{z}{\sqrt{4y^2 + 1}}$

over the surface cut from the parabolic cylinder $y^2 - z = 1$ by the planes $x = 0$, $x = 3$, and $z = 0$.

17. **Circular cylinder cut by planes** Integrate $g(x, y, z) = x^4 y(y^2 + z^2)$ over the portion of the cylinder $y^2 + z^2 = 25$ that lies in the first octant between the planes $x = 0$ and $x = 1$ and above the plane $z = 3$.

18. **Area of Wyoming** The state of Wyoming is bounded by the meridians 111°3′ and 104°3′ west longitude and by the circles 41° and 45° north latitude. Assuming that Earth is a sphere of radius $R = 3959$ mi, find the area of Wyoming.

Parametrized Surfaces

Find the parametrizations for the surfaces in Exercises 19–24. (There are many ways to do these, so your answers may not be the same as those in the back of the book.)

19. **Spherical band** The portion of the sphere $x^2 + y^2 + z^2 = 36$ between the planes $z = -3$ and $z = 3\sqrt{3}$

20. **Parabolic cap** The portion of the paraboloid $z = -(x^2 + y^2)/2$ above the plane $z = -2$

21. **Cone** The cone $z = 1 + \sqrt{x^2 + y^2}$, $z \leq 3$

22. **Plane above square** The portion of the plane $4x + 2y + 4z = 12$ that lies above the square $0 \leq x \leq 2$, $0 \leq y \leq 2$ in the first quadrant

23. **Portion of paraboloid** The portion of the paraboloid $y = 2(x^2 + z^2)$, $y \leq 2$, that lies above the xy-plane

24. **Portion of hemisphere** The portion of the hemisphere $x^2 + y^2 + z^2 = 10$, $y \geq 0$, in the first octant

25. **Surface area** Find the area of the surface

$$\mathbf{r}(u, v) = (u + v)\mathbf{i} + (u - v)\mathbf{j} + v\mathbf{k},\quad 0 \leq u \leq 1,\quad 0 \leq v \leq 1.$$

26. **Surface integral** Integrate $f(x, y, z) = xy - z^2$ over the surface in Exercise 25.

27. **Area of a helicoid** Find the surface area of the helicoid

$$\mathbf{r}(r, \theta) = (r\cos\theta)\mathbf{i} + (r\sin\theta)\mathbf{j} + \theta\mathbf{k},\quad 0 \leq \theta \leq 2\pi,\quad 0 \leq r \leq 1,$$

in the accompanying figure.

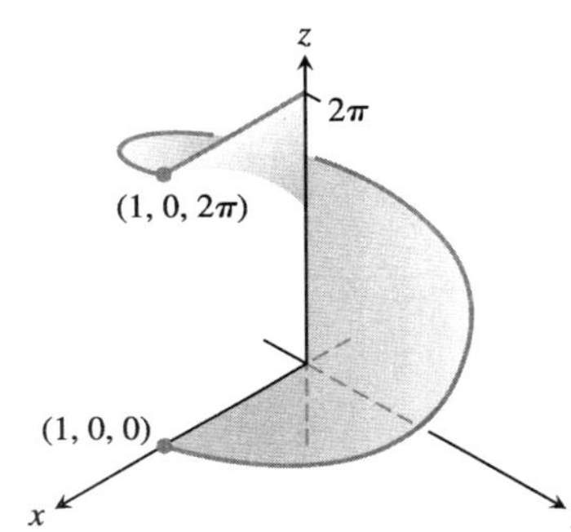

28. **Surface integral** Evaluate the integral $\iint_S \sqrt{x^2 + y^2 + 1}\, d\sigma$, where S is the helicoid in Exercise 27.

Conservative Fields

Which of the fields in Exercises 29–32 are conservative, and which are not?

29. $\mathbf{F} = x\mathbf{i} + y\mathbf{j} + z\mathbf{k}$

30. $\mathbf{F} = (x\mathbf{i} + y\mathbf{j} + z\mathbf{k})/(x^2 + y^2 + z^2)^{3/2}$

31. $\mathbf{F} = xe^y\mathbf{i} + ye^z\mathbf{j} + ze^x\mathbf{k}$

32. $\mathbf{F} = (\mathbf{i} + z\mathbf{j} + y\mathbf{k})/(x + yz)$

Find potential functions for the fields in Exercises 33 and 34.

33. $\mathbf{F} = 2\mathbf{i} + (2y + z)\mathbf{j} + (y + 1)\mathbf{k}$

34. $\mathbf{F} = (z\cos xz)\mathbf{i} + e^y\mathbf{j} + (x\cos xz)\mathbf{k}$

Work and Circulation

In Exercises 35 and 36, find the work done by each field along the paths from (0, 0, 0) to (1, 1, 1) in Exercise 1.

35. $\mathbf{F} = 2xy\mathbf{i} + \mathbf{j} + x^2\mathbf{k}$ **36.** $\mathbf{F} = 2xy\mathbf{i} + x^2\mathbf{j} + \mathbf{k}$

37. Finding work in two ways Find the work done by

$$\mathbf{F} = \frac{x\mathbf{i} + y\mathbf{j}}{(x^2 + y^2)^{3/2}}$$

over the plane curve $\mathbf{r}(t) = (e^t \cos t)\mathbf{i} + (e^t \sin t)\mathbf{j}$ from the point $(1, 0)$ to the point $(e^{2\pi}, 0)$ in two ways:

a. By using the parametrization of the curve to evaluate the work integral

b. By evaluating a potential function for $\mathbf{F}$.

38. Flow along different paths Find the flow of the field $\mathbf{F} = \nabla(x^2ze^y)$

a. Once around the ellipse C in which the plane $x + y + z = 1$ intersects the cylinder $x^2 + z^2 = 25$, clockwise as viewed from the positive y-axis

b. Along the curved boundary of the helicoid in Exercise 27 from $(1, 0, 0)$ to $(1, 0, 2\pi)$.

In Exercises 39 and 40, use the surface integral in Stokes' Theorem to find the circulation of the field $\mathbf{F}$ around the curve C in the indicated direction.

39. Circulation around an ellipse $\mathbf{F} = y^2\mathbf{i} - y\mathbf{j} + 3z^2\mathbf{k}$

C: The ellipse in which the plane $2x + 6y - 3z = 6$ meets the cylinder $x^2 + y^2 = 1$, counterclockwise as viewed from above

40. Circulation around a circle $\mathbf{F} = (x^2 + y)\mathbf{i} + (x + y)\mathbf{j} + (4y^2 - z)\mathbf{k}$

C: The circle in which the plane $z = -y$ meets the sphere $x^2 + y^2 + z^2 = 4$, counterclockwise as viewed from above

Mass and Moments

41. Wire with different densities Find the mass of a thin wire lying along the curve $\mathbf{r}(t) = \sqrt{2}t\mathbf{i} + \sqrt{2}t\mathbf{j} + (4 - t^2)\mathbf{k}$, $0 \le t \le 1$, if the density at t is **(a)** $\delta = 3t$ and **(b)** $\delta = 1$.

42. Wire with variable density Find the center of mass of a thin wire lying along the curve $\mathbf{r}(t) = t\mathbf{i} + 2t\mathbf{j} + (2/3)t^{3/2}\mathbf{k}$, $0 \le t \le 2$, if the density at t is $\delta = 3\sqrt{5 + t}$.

43. Wire with variable density Find the center of mass and the moments of inertia and radii of gyration about the coordinate axes of a thin wire lying along the curve

$$\mathbf{r}(t) = t\mathbf{i} + \frac{2\sqrt{2}}{3}t^{3/2}\mathbf{j} + \frac{t^2}{2}\mathbf{k}, \qquad 0 \le t \le 2,$$

if the density at t is $\delta = 1/(t + 1)$.

44. Center of mass of an arch A slender metal arch lies along the semicircle $y = \sqrt{a^2 - x^2}$ in the xy-plane. The density at the point (x, y) on the arch is $\delta(x, y) = 2a - y$. Find the center of mass.

45. Wire with constant density A wire of constant density $\delta = 1$ lies along the curve $\mathbf{r}(t) = (e^t \cos t)\mathbf{i} + (e^t \sin t)\mathbf{j} + e^t\mathbf{k}$, $0 \le t \le \ln 2$. Find $\bar{z}$, I_z, and R_z.

46. Helical wire with constant density Find the mass and center of mass of a wire of constant density δ that lies along the helix $\mathbf{r}(t) = (2 \sin t)\mathbf{i} + (2 \cos t)\mathbf{j} + 3t\mathbf{k}$, $0 \le t \le 2\pi$.

47. Inertia, radius of gyration, center of mass of a shell Find I_z, R_z, and the center of mass of a thin shell of density $\delta(x, y, z) = z$ cut from the upper portion of the sphere $x^2 + y^2 + z^2 = 25$ by the plane $z = 3$.

48. Moment of inertia of a cube Find the moment of inertia about the z-axis of the surface of the cube cut from the first octant by the planes $x = 1, y = 1$, and $z = 1$ if the density is $\delta = 1$.

Flux Across a Plane Curve or Surface

Use Green's Theorem to find the counterclockwise circulation and outward flux for the fields and curves in Exercises 49 and 50.

49. Square $\mathbf{F} = (2xy + x)\mathbf{i} + (xy - y)\mathbf{j}$

C: The square bounded by $x = 0, x = 1, y = 0, y = 1$

50. Triangle $\mathbf{F} = (y - 6x^2)\mathbf{i} + (x + y^2)\mathbf{j}$

C: The triangle made by the lines $y = 0, y = x$, and $x = 1$

51. Zero line integral Show that

$$\oint_C \ln x \sin y \, dy - \frac{\cos y}{x} dx = 0$$

for any closed curve C to which Green's Theorem applies.

52. a. Outward flux and area Show that the outward flux of the position vector field $\mathbf{F} = x\mathbf{i} + y\mathbf{j}$ across any closed curve to which Green's Theorem applies is twice the area of the region enclosed by the curve.

b. Let $\mathbf{n}$ be the outward unit normal vector to a closed curve to which Green's Theorem applies. Show that it is not possible for $\mathbf{F} = x\mathbf{i} + y\mathbf{j}$ to be orthogonal to $\mathbf{n}$ at every point of C.

In Exercises 53–56, find the outward flux of $\mathbf{F}$ across the boundary of D.

53. Cube $\mathbf{F} = 2xy\mathbf{i} + 2yz\mathbf{j} + 2xz\mathbf{k}$

D: The cube cut from the first octant by the planes $x = 1, y = 1, z = 1$

54. Spherical cap $\mathbf{F} = xz\mathbf{i} + yz\mathbf{j} + \mathbf{k}$

D: The entire surface of the upper cap cut from the solid sphere $x^2 + y^2 + z^2 \le 25$ by the plane $z = 3$

55. Spherical cap $\mathbf{F} = -2x\mathbf{i} - 3y\mathbf{j} + z\mathbf{k}$

D: The upper region cut from the solid sphere $x^2 + y^2 + z^2 \le 2$ by the paraboloid $z = x^2 + y^2$

56. Cone and cylinder $\mathbf{F} = (6x + y)\mathbf{i} - (x + z)\mathbf{j} + 4yz\mathbf{k}$

D: The region in the first octant bounded by the cone $z = \sqrt{x^2 + y^2}$, the cylinder $x^2 + y^2 = 1$, and the coordinate planes

57. **Hemisphere, cylinder, and plane** Let S be the surface that is bounded on the left by the hemisphere $x^2 + y^2 + z^2 = a^2, y \leq 0$, in the middle by the cylinder $x^2 + z^2 = a^2, 0 \leq y \leq a$, and on the right by the plane $y = a$. Find the flux of $\mathbf{F} = y\mathbf{i} + z\mathbf{j} + x\mathbf{k}$ outward across S.

58. **Cylinder and planes** Find the outward flux of the field $\mathbf{F} = 3xz^2\mathbf{i} + y\mathbf{j} - z^3\mathbf{k}$ across the surface of the solid in the first octant that is bounded by the cylinder $x^2 + 4y^2 = 16$ and the planes $y = 2z, x = 0$, and $z = 0$.

59. **Cylindrical can** Use the Divergence Theorem to find the flux of $\mathbf{F} = xy^2\mathbf{i} + x^2y\mathbf{j} + y\mathbf{k}$ outward through the surface of the region enclosed by the cylinder $x^2 + y^2 = 1$ and the planes $z = 1$ and $z = -1$.

60. **Hemisphere** Find the flux of $\mathbf{F} = (3z + 1)\mathbf{k}$ upward across the hemisphere $x^2 + y^2 + z^2 = a^2, z \geq 0$ **(a)** with the Divergence Theorem and **(b)** by evaluating the flux integral directly.

Chapter 16 Additional and Advanced Exercises

Finding Areas with Green's Theorem

Use the Green's Theorem area formula, Equation (13) in Exercises 16.4, to find the areas of the regions enclosed by the curves in Exercises 1–4.

1. The limaçon $x = 2\cos t - \cos 2t$, $y = 2\sin t - \sin 2t$, $0 \leq t \leq 2\pi$

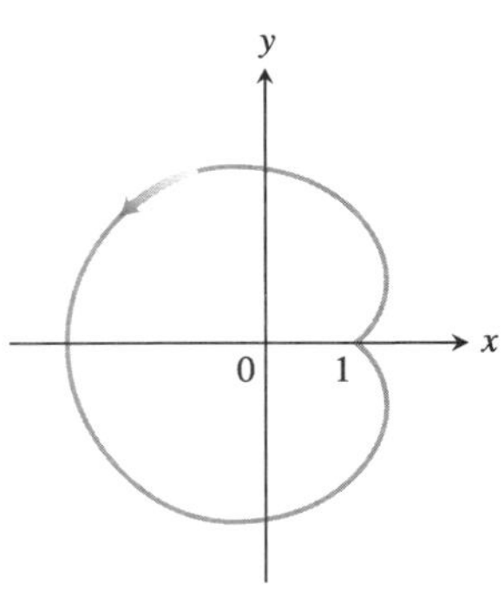

2. The deltoid $x = 2\cos t + \cos 2t$, $y = 2\sin t - \sin 2t$, $0 \leq t \leq 2\pi$

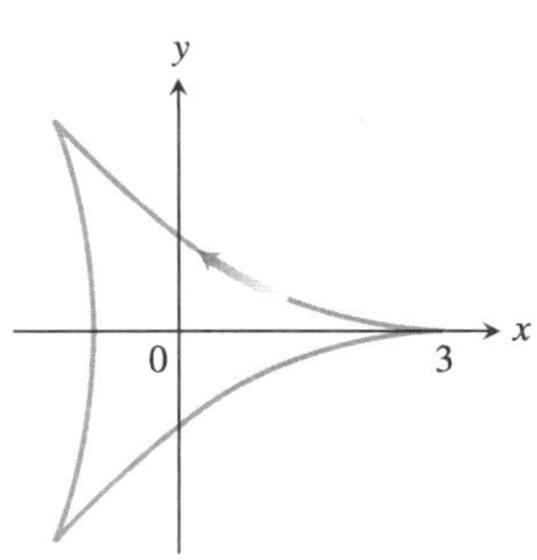

3. The eight curve $x = (1/2)\sin 2t, y = \sin t, 0 \leq t \leq \pi$ (one loop)

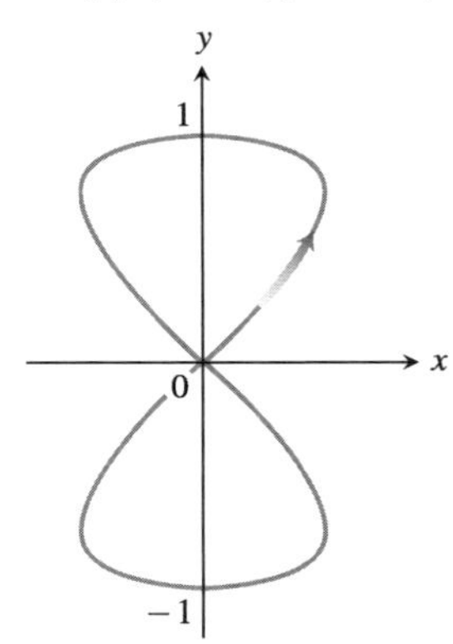

4. The teardrop $x = 2a\cos t - a\sin 2t, y = b\sin t, 0 \leq t \leq 2\pi$

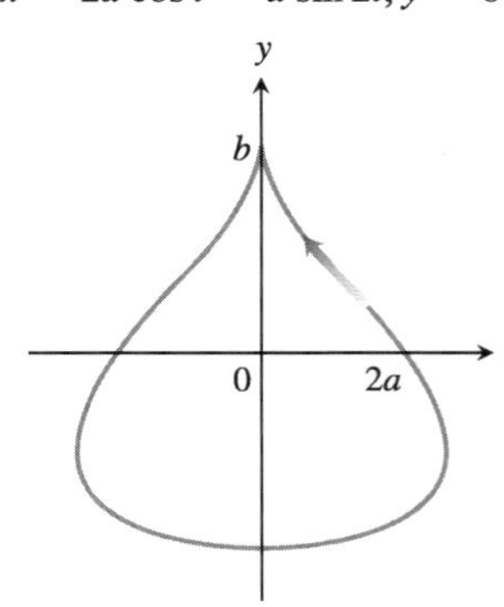

Theory and Applications

5. **a.** Give an example of a vector field $\mathbf{F}(x, y, z)$ that has value $\mathbf{0}$ at only one point and such that curl $\mathbf{F}$ is nonzero everywhere. Be sure to identify the point and compute the curl.

b. Give an example of a vector field $\mathbf{F}(x, y, z)$ that has value $\mathbf{0}$ on precisely one line and such that curl $\mathbf{F}$ is nonzero everywhere. Be sure to identify the line and compute the curl.

c. Give an example of a vector field $\mathbf{F}(x, y, z)$ that has value $\mathbf{0}$ on a surface and such that curl $\mathbf{F}$ is nonzero everywhere. Be sure to identify the surface and compute the curl.

6. Find all points (a, b, c) on the sphere $x^2 + y^2 + z^2 = R^2$ where the vector field $\mathbf{F} = yz^2\mathbf{i} + xz^2\mathbf{j} + 2xyz\mathbf{k}$ is normal to the surface and $\mathbf{F}(a, b, c) \neq \mathbf{0}$.

7. Find the mass of a spherical shell of radius R such that at each point (x, y, z) on the surface the mass density $\delta(x, y, z)$ is its distance to some fixed point (a, b, c) of the surface.

8. Find the mass of a helicoid

$$\mathbf{r}(r, \theta) = (r\cos\theta)\mathbf{i} + (r\sin\theta)\mathbf{j} + \theta\mathbf{k},$$

$0 \le r \le 1, 0 \le \theta \le 2\pi$, if the density function is $\delta(x, y, z) = 2\sqrt{x^2 + y^2}$. See Practice Exercise 27 for a figure.

9. Among all rectangular regions $0 \le x \le a, 0 \le y \le b$, find the one for which the total outward flux of $\mathbf{F} = (x^2 + 4xy)\mathbf{i} - 6y\mathbf{j}$ across the four sides is least. What *is* the least flux?

10. Find an equation for the plane through the origin such that the circulation of the flow field $\mathbf{F} = z\mathbf{i} + x\mathbf{j} + y\mathbf{k}$ around the circle of intersection of the plane with the sphere $x^2 + y^2 + z^2 = 4$ is a maximum.

11. A string lies along the circle $x^2 + y^2 = 4$ from (2, 0) to (0, 2) in the first quadrant. The density of the string is $\rho(x, y) = xy$

a. Partition the string into a finite number of subarcs to show that the work done by gravity to move the string straight down to the x-axis is given by

$$\text{Work} = \lim_{n\to\infty} \sum_{k=1}^{n} g\, x_k y_k^2 \Delta s_k = \int_C g\, xy^2\, ds,$$

where g is the gravitational constant.

b. Find the total work done by evaluating the line integral in part (a).

c. Show that the total work done equals the work required to move the string's center of mass $(\bar{x}, \bar{y})$ straight down to the x-axis.

12. A thin sheet lies along the portion of the plane $x + y + z = 1$ in the first octant. The density of the sheet is $\delta(x, y, z) = xy$.

a. Partition the sheet into a finite number of subpieces to show that the work done by gravity to move the sheet straight down to the xy-plane is given by

$$\text{Work} = \lim_{n\to\infty} \sum_{k=1}^{n} g\, x_k y_k z_k\, \Delta\sigma_k = \iint_S g\, xyz\, d\sigma,$$

where g is the gravitational constant.

b. Find the total work done by evaluating the surface integral in part (a).

c. Show that the total work done equals the work required to move the sheet's center of mass $(\bar{x}, \bar{y}, \bar{z})$ straight down to the xy-plane.

13. Archimedes' principle If an object such as a ball is placed in a liquid, it will either sink to the bottom, float, or sink a certain distance and remain suspended in the liquid. Suppose a fluid has constant weight density w and that the fluid's surface coincides with the plane $z = 4$. A spherical ball remains suspended in the fluid and occupies the region $x^2 + y^2 + (z - 2)^2 \le 1$.

a. Show that the surface integral giving the magnitude of the total force on the ball due to the fluid's pressure is

$$\text{Force} = \lim_{n\to\infty} \sum_{k=1}^{n} w(4 - z_k)\, \Delta\sigma_k = \iint_S w(4 - z)\, d\sigma.$$

b. Since the ball is not moving, it is being held up by the buoyant force of the liquid. Show that the magnitude of the buoyant force on the sphere is

$$\text{Buoyant force} = \iint_S w(z - 4)\mathbf{k}\cdot\mathbf{n}\, d\sigma,$$

where $\mathbf{n}$ is the outer unit normal at (x, y, z). This illustrates Archimedes' principle that the magnitude of the buoyant force on a submerged solid equals the weight of the displaced fluid.

c. Use the Divergence Theorem to find the magnitude of the buoyant force in part (b).

14. Fluid force on a curved surface A cone in the shape of the surface $z = \sqrt{x^2 + y^2}, 0 \le z \le 2$ is filled with a liquid of constant weight density w. Assuming the xy-plane is "ground level," show that the total force on the portion of the cone from $z = 1$ to $z = 2$ due to liquid pressure is the surface integral

$$F = \iint_S w(2 - z)\, d\sigma.$$

Evaluate the integral.

15. Faraday's Law If $\mathbf{E}(t, x, y, z)$ and $\mathbf{B}(t, x, y, z)$ represent the electric and magnetic fields at point (x, y, z) at time t, a basic principle of electromagnetic theory says that $\nabla \times \mathbf{E} = -\partial\mathbf{B}/\partial t$. In this expression $\nabla \times \mathbf{E}$ is computed with t held fixed and $\partial\mathbf{B}/\partial t$ is calculated with (x, y, z) fixed. Use Stokes' Theorem to derive Faraday's Law

$$\oint_C \mathbf{E}\cdot d\mathbf{r} = -\frac{\partial}{\partial t}\iint_S \mathbf{B}\cdot\mathbf{n}\, d\sigma,$$

where C represents a wire loop through which current flows counterclockwise with respect to the surface's unit normal $\mathbf{n}$, giving rise to the voltage

$$\oint_C \mathbf{E}\cdot d\mathbf{r}$$

around C. The surface integral on the right side of the equation is called the *magnetic flux*, and S is any oriented surface with boundary C.

16. Let

$$\mathbf{F} = -\frac{GmM}{|\mathbf{r}|^3}\mathbf{r}$$

be the gravitational force field defined for $\mathbf{r} \neq \mathbf{0}$. Use Gauss's Law in Section 16.8 to show that there is no continuously differentiable vector field $\mathbf{H}$ satisfying $\mathbf{F} = \nabla \times \mathbf{H}$.

17. If $f(x, y, z)$ and $g(x, y, z)$ are continuously differentiable scalar functions defined over the oriented surface S with boundary curve C, prove that

$$\iint_S (\nabla f \times \nabla g) \cdot \mathbf{n}\, d\sigma = \oint_C f\, \nabla g \cdot d\mathbf{r}.$$

18. Suppose that $\nabla \cdot \mathbf{F}_1 = \nabla \cdot \mathbf{F}_2$ and $\nabla \times \mathbf{F}_1 = \nabla \times \mathbf{F}_2$ over a region D enclosed by the oriented surface S with outward unit normal $\mathbf{n}$ and that $\mathbf{F}_1 \cdot \mathbf{n} = \mathbf{F}_2 \cdot \mathbf{n}$ on S. Prove that $\mathbf{F}_1 = \mathbf{F}_2$ throughout D.

19. Prove or disprove that if $\nabla \cdot \mathbf{F} = 0$ and $\nabla \times \mathbf{F} = \mathbf{0}$, then $\mathbf{F} = \mathbf{0}$.

20. Let S be an oriented surface parametrized by $\mathbf{r}(u, v)$. Define the notation $d\boldsymbol{\sigma} = \mathbf{r}_u\, du \times \mathbf{r}_v\, dv$ so that $d\boldsymbol{\sigma}$ is a vector normal to the surface. Also, the magnitude $d\sigma = |d\boldsymbol{\sigma}|$ is the element of surface area (by Equation 5 in Section 16.6). Derive the identity

$$d\sigma = (EG - F^2)^{1/2}\, du\, dv$$

where

$$E = |\mathbf{r}_u|^2, \quad F = \mathbf{r}_u \cdot \mathbf{r}_v, \quad \text{and} \quad G = |\mathbf{r}_v|^2.$$

21. Show that the volume V of a region D in space enclosed by the oriented surface S with outward normal $\mathbf{n}$ satisfies the identity

$$V = \frac{1}{3}\iint_S \mathbf{r} \cdot \mathbf{n}\, d\sigma,$$

where $\mathbf{r}$ is the position vector of the point (x, y, z) in D.

Chapter 16 Technology Application Projects

Mathematica/Maple Module

Work in Conservative and Nonconservative Force Fields

Explore integration over vector fields and experiment with conservative and nonconservative force functions along different paths in the field.

Mathematica/Maple Module

How Can You Visualize Green's Theorem?

Explore integration over vector fields and use parametrizations to compute line integrals. Both forms of Green's Theorem are explored.

Mathematica/Maple Module

Visualizing and Interpreting the Divergence Theorem

Verify the Divergence Theorem by formulating and evaluating certain divergence and surface integrals.

APPENDICES

A.1 Mathematical Induction

Many formulas, like

$$1 + 2 + \cdots + n = \frac{n(n+1)}{2},$$

can be shown to hold for every positive integer n by applying an axiom called the *mathematical induction principle*. A proof that uses this axiom is called a *proof by mathematical induction* or a *proof by induction*.

The steps in proving a formula by induction are the following:

1. Check that the formula holds for $n = 1$.
2. Prove that if the formula holds for any positive integer $n = k$, then it also holds for the next integer, $n = k + 1$.

The induction axiom says that once these steps are completed, the formula holds for all positive integers n. By Step 1 it holds for $n = 1$. By Step 2 it holds for $n = 2$, and therefore by Step 2 also for $n = 3$, and by Step 2 again for $n = 4$, and so on. If the first domino falls, and the kth domino always knocks over the $(k + 1)$st when it falls, all the dominoes fall.

From another point of view, suppose we have a sequence of statements $S_1, S_2, \ldots, S_n, \ldots$, one for each positive integer. Suppose we can show that assuming any one of the statements to be true implies that the next statement in line is true. Suppose that we can also show that S_1 is true. Then we may conclude that the statements are true from S_1 on.

EXAMPLE 1 Use mathematical induction to prove that for every positive integer n,

$$1 + 2 + \cdots + n = \frac{n(n+1)}{2}.$$

Solution We accomplish the proof by carrying out the two steps above.

1. The formula holds for $n = 1$ because

$$1 = \frac{1(1+1)}{2}.$$

2. If the formula holds for $n = k$, does it also hold for $n = k + 1$? The answer is yes, as we now show. If

$$1 + 2 + \cdots + k = \frac{k(k+1)}{2},$$

then

$$\begin{aligned} 1 + 2 + \cdots + k + (k+1) &= \frac{k(k+1)}{2} + (k+1) = \frac{k^2 + k + 2k + 2}{2} \\ &= \frac{(k+1)(k+2)}{2} = \frac{(k+1)((k+1)+1)}{2}. \end{aligned}$$

The last expression in this string of equalities is the expression $n(n+1)/2$ for $n = (k+1)$.

The mathematical induction principle now guarantees the original formula for all positive integers n. ■

In Example 4 of Section 5.2 we gave another proof for the formula giving the sum of the first n integers. However, proof by mathematical induction is more general. It can be used to find the sums of the squares and cubes of the first n integers (Exercises 9 and 10). Here is another example.

EXAMPLE 2 Show by mathematical induction that for all positive integers n,

$$\frac{1}{2^1} + \frac{1}{2^2} + \cdots + \frac{1}{2^n} = 1 - \frac{1}{2^n}.$$

Solution We accomplish the proof by carrying out the two steps of mathematical induction.

1. The formula holds for $n = 1$ because

$$\frac{1}{2^1} = 1 - \frac{1}{2^1}.$$

2. If

$$\frac{1}{2^1} + \frac{1}{2^2} + \cdots + \frac{1}{2^k} = 1 - \frac{1}{2^k},$$

then

$$\begin{aligned} \frac{1}{2^1} + \frac{1}{2^2} + \cdots + \frac{1}{2^k} + \frac{1}{2^{k+1}} &= 1 - \frac{1}{2^k} + \frac{1}{2^{k+1}} = 1 - \frac{1 \cdot 2}{2^k \cdot 2} + \frac{1}{2^{k+1}} \\ &= 1 - \frac{2}{2^{k+1}} + \frac{1}{2^{k+1}} = 1 - \frac{1}{2^{k+1}}. \end{aligned}$$

Thus, the original formula holds for $n = (k+1)$ whenever it holds for $n = k$.

With these steps verified, the mathematical induction principle now guarantees the formula for every positive integer n. ■

Other Starting Integers

Instead of starting at $n = 1$ some induction arguments start at another integer. The steps for such an argument are as follows.

1. Check that the formula holds for $n = n_1$ (the first appropriate integer).
2. Prove that if the formula holds for any integer $n = k \geq n_1$, then it also holds for $n = (k + 1)$.

Once these steps are completed, the mathematical induction principle guarantees the formula for all $n \geq n_1$.

EXAMPLE 3 Show that $n! > 3^n$ if n is large enough.

Solution How large is large enough? We experiment:

n	1	2	3	4	5	6	7
$n!$	1	2	6	24	120	720	5040
3^n	3	9	27	81	243	729	2187

It looks as if $n! > 3^n$ for $n \geq 7$. To be sure, we apply mathematical induction. We take $n_1 = 7$ in Step 1 and complete Step 2.

Suppose $k! > 3^k$ for some $k \geq 7$. Then

$$(k + 1)! = (k + 1)(k!) > (k + 1)3^k > 7 \cdot 3^k > 3^{k+1}.$$

Thus, for $k \geq 7$,

$$k! > 3^k \quad \text{implies} \quad (k + 1)! > 3^{k+1}.$$

The mathematical induction principle now guarantees $n! \geq 3^n$ for all $n \geq 7$. ■

EXERCISES A.1

1. Assuming that the triangle inequality $|a + b| \leq |a| + |b|$ holds for any two numbers a and b, show that

$$|x_1 + x_2 + \cdots + x_n| \leq |x_1| + |x_2| + \cdots + |x_n|$$

for any n numbers.

2. Show that if $r \neq 1$, then

$$1 + r + r^2 + \cdots + r^n = \frac{1 - r^{n+1}}{1 - r}$$

for every positive integer n.

3. Use the Product Rule, $\frac{d}{dx}(uv) = u\frac{dv}{dx} + v\frac{du}{dx}$, and the fact that $\frac{d}{dx}(x) = 1$ to show that $\frac{d}{dx}(x^n) = nx^{n-1}$ for every positive integer n.

4. Suppose that a function $f(x)$ has the property that $f(x_1x_2) = f(x_1) + f(x_2)$ for any two positive numbers x_1 and x_2. Show that

$$f(x_1x_2\cdots x_n) = f(x_1) + f(x_2) + \cdots + f(x_n)$$

for the product of any n positive numbers $x_1, x_2 \ldots, x_n$.

5. Show that

$$\frac{2}{3^1} + \frac{2}{3^2} + \cdots + \frac{2}{3^n} = 1 - \frac{1}{3^n}$$

for all positive integers n.

6. Show that $n! > n^3$ if n is large enough.
7. Show that $2^n > n^2$ if n is large enough.
8. Show that $2^n \geq 1/8$ for $n \geq -3$.
9. **Sums of squares** Show that the sum of the squares of the first n positive integers is

$$\frac{n\left(n + \frac{1}{2}\right)(n + 1)}{3}.$$

10. **Sums of cubes** Show that the sum of the cubes of the first n positive integers is $(n(n + 1)/2)^2$.
11. **Rules for finite sums** Show that the following finite sum rules hold for every positive integer n.

 a. $\sum_{k=1}^{n}(a_k + b_k) = \sum_{k=1}^{n} a_k + \sum_{k=1}^{n} b_k$

b. $\sum_{k=1}^{n}(a_k - b_k) = \sum_{k=1}^{n} a_k - \sum_{k=1}^{n} b_k$

c. $\sum_{k=1}^{n} ca_k = c \cdot \sum_{k=1}^{n} a_k$ (Any number c)

d. $\sum_{k=1}^{n} a_k = n \cdot c$ (if a_k has the constant value c)

12. Show that $|x^n| = |x|^n$ for every positive integer n and every real number x.

A.2 Proofs of Limit Theorems

This appendix proves Theorem 1, Parts 2–5, and Theorem 4 from Section 2.2.

THEOREM 1 Limit Laws

If L, M, c, and k are real numbers and

$$\lim_{x \to c} f(x) = L \quad \text{and} \quad \lim_{x \to c} g(x) = M, \quad \text{then}$$

1. *Sum Rule:* $\lim_{x \to c} (f(x) + g(x)) = L + M$
2. *Difference Rule:* $\lim_{x \to c} (f(x) - g(x)) = L - M$
3. *Product Rule:* $\lim_{x \to c} (f(x) \cdot g(x)) = L \cdot M$
4. *Constant Multiple Rule:* $\lim_{x \to c} (kf(x)) = kL$ (any number k)
5. *Quotient Rule:* $\lim_{x \to c} \frac{f(x)}{g(x)} = \frac{L}{M}$, if $M \neq 0$
6. *Power Rule:* If r and s are integers with no common factor and $s \neq 0$, then

$$\lim_{x \to c} (f(x))^{r/s} = L^{r/s}$$

provided that $L^{r/s}$ is a real number. (If s is even, we assume that $L > 0$.)

We proved the Sum Rule in Section 2.3 and the Power Rule is proved in more advanced texts. We obtain the Difference Rule by replacing $g(x)$ by $-g(x)$ and M by $-M$ in the Sum Rule. The Constant Multiple Rule is the special case $g(x) = k$ of the Product Rule. This leaves only the Product and Quotient Rules.

Proof of the Limit Product Rule We show that for any $\epsilon > 0$ there exists a $\delta > 0$ such that for all x in the intersection D of the domains of f and g,

$$0 < |x - c| < \delta \quad \Rightarrow \quad |f(x)g(x) - LM| < \epsilon.$$

Suppose then that ϵ is a positive number, and write $f(x)$ and $g(x)$ as

$$f(x) = L + (f(x) - L), \qquad g(x) = M + (g(x) - M).$$

Multiply these expressions together and subtract LM:

$$\begin{aligned} f(x)\cdot g(x) - LM &= (L + (f(x) - L))(M + (g(x) - M)) - LM \\ &= LM + L(g(x) - M) + M(f(x) - L) \\ &\quad + (f(x) - L)(g(x) - M) - LM \\ &= L(g(x) - M) + M(f(x) - L) + (f(x) - L)(g(x) - M). \end{aligned} \tag{1}$$

Since f and g have limits L and M as $x \to c$, there exist positive numbers δ_1, δ_2, δ_3, and δ_4 such that for all x in D

$$\begin{aligned} 0 < |x - c| < \delta_1 \quad &\Rightarrow \quad |f(x) - L| < \sqrt{\epsilon/3} \\ 0 < |x - c| < \delta_2 \quad &\Rightarrow \quad |g(x) - M| < \sqrt{\epsilon/3} \\ 0 < |x - c| < \delta_3 \quad &\Rightarrow \quad |f(x) - L| < \epsilon/(3(1 + |M|)) \\ 0 < |x - c| < \delta_4 \quad &\Rightarrow \quad |g(x) - M| < \epsilon/(3(1 + |L|)) \end{aligned} \tag{2}$$

If we take δ to be the smallest numbers δ_1 through δ_4, the inequalities on the right-hand side of the Implications (2) will hold simultaneously for $0 < |x - c| < \delta$. Therefore, for all x in D, $0 < |x - c| < \delta$ implies

$$|f(x)\cdot g(x) - LM|$$

Triangle inequality applied to Equation (1)

$$\begin{aligned} &\le |L||g(x) - M| + |M||f(x) - L| + |f(x) - L||g(x) - M| \\ &\le (1 + |L|)|g(x) - M| + (1 + |M|)|f(x) - L| + |f(x) - L||g(x) - M| \\ &< \frac{\epsilon}{3} + \frac{\epsilon}{3} + \sqrt{\frac{\epsilon}{3}}\sqrt{\frac{\epsilon}{3}} = \epsilon. \end{aligned}$$

Values from (2)

This completes the proof of the Limit Product Rule. ■

Proof of the Limit Quotient Rule We show that $\lim_{x\to c}(1/g(x)) = 1/M$. We can then conclude that

$$\lim_{x\to c}\frac{f(x)}{g(x)} = \lim_{x\to c}\left(f(x)\cdot\frac{1}{g(x)}\right) = \lim_{x\to c} f(x)\cdot \lim_{x\to c}\frac{1}{g(x)} = L\cdot\frac{1}{M} = \frac{L}{M}$$

by the Limit Product Rule.

Let $\epsilon > 0$ be given. To show that $\lim_{x\to c}(1/g(x)) = 1/M$, we need to show that there exists a $\delta > 0$ such that for all x.

$$0 < |x - c| < \delta \quad \Rightarrow \quad \left|\frac{1}{g(x)} - \frac{1}{M}\right| < \epsilon.$$

Since $|M| > 0$, there exists a positive number δ_1 such that for all x

$$0 < |x - c| < \delta_1 \quad \Rightarrow \quad |g(x) - M| < \frac{M}{2}. \tag{3}$$

For any numbers A and B it can be shown that $|A| - |B| \le |A - B|$ and $|B| - |A| \le |A - B|$, from which it follows that $||A| - |B|| \le |A - B|$. With $A = g(x)$ and $B = M$, this becomes

$$||g(x)| - |M|| \le |g(x) - M|,$$

which can be combined with the inequality on the right in Implication (3) to get, in turn,

$$||g(x)| - |M|| < \frac{|M|}{2}$$

$$-\frac{|M|}{2} < |g(x)| - |M| < \frac{|M|}{2}$$

$$\frac{|M|}{2} < |g(x)| < \frac{3|M|}{2}$$

$$|M| < 2|g(x)| < 3|M|$$

$$\frac{1}{|g(x)|} < \frac{2}{|M|} < \frac{3}{|g(x)|} \tag{4}$$

Therefore, $0 < |x - c| < \delta_1$ implies that

$$\left|\frac{1}{g(x)} - \frac{1}{M}\right| = \left|\frac{M - g(x)}{Mg(x)}\right| \leq \frac{1}{|M|} \cdot \frac{1}{|g(x)|} \cdot |M - g(x)|$$

$$< \frac{1}{|M|} \cdot \frac{2}{|M|} \cdot |M - g(x)|. \quad \text{Inequality (4)} \tag{5}$$

Since $(1/2)|M|^2\epsilon > 0$, there exists a number $\delta_2 > 0$ such that for all x

$$0 < |x - c| < \delta_2 \quad \Rightarrow \quad |M - g(x)| < \frac{\epsilon}{2}|M|^2. \tag{6}$$

If we take δ to be the smaller of δ_1 and δ_2, the conclusions in (5) and (6) both hold for all x such that $0 < |x - c| < \delta$. Combining these conclusions gives

$$0 < |x - c| < \delta \quad \Rightarrow \quad \left|\frac{1}{g(x)} - \frac{1}{M}\right| < \epsilon.$$

This concludes the proof of the Limit Quotient Rule. ■

THEOREM 4 The Sandwich Theorem
Suppose that $g(x) \leq f(x) \leq h(x)$ for all x in some open interval I containing c, except possibly at $x = c$ itself. Suppose also that $\lim_{x\to c} g(x) = \lim_{x\to c} h(x) = L$. Then $\lim_{x\to c} f(x) = L$.

Proof for Right-Hand Limits Suppose $\lim_{x\to c^+} g(x) = \lim_{x\to c^+} h(x) = L$. Then for any $\epsilon > 0$ there exists a $\delta > 0$ such that for all x the interval $c < x < c + \delta$ is contained in I and the inequality implies

$$L - \epsilon < g(x) < L + \epsilon \qquad \text{and} \qquad L - \epsilon < h(x) < L + \epsilon.$$

These inequalities combine with the inequality $g(x) \leq f(x) \leq h(x)$ to give

$$L - \epsilon < g(x) \leq f(x) \leq h(x) < L + \epsilon,$$

$$L - \epsilon < f(x) < L + \epsilon,$$

$$-\epsilon < f(x) - L < \epsilon.$$

Therefore, for all x, the inequality $c < x < c + \delta$ implies $|f(x) - L| < \epsilon$. ■

Proof for Left-Hand Limits Suppose $\lim_{x\to c^-} g(x) = \lim_{x\to c^-} h(x) = L$. Then for any $\epsilon > 0$ there exists a $\delta > 0$ such that for all x the interval $c - \delta < x < c$ is contained in I and the inequality implies

$$L - \epsilon < g(x) < L + \epsilon \quad \text{and} \quad L - \epsilon < h(x) < L + \epsilon.$$

We conclude as before that for all x, $c - \delta < x < c$ implies $|f(x) - L| < \epsilon$. ∎

Proof for Two-Sided Limits If $\lim_{x\to c} g(x) = \lim_{x\to c} h(x) = L$, then $g(x)$ and $h(x)$ both approach L as $x \to c^+$ and as $x \to c^-$; so $\lim_{x\to c^+} f(x) = L$ and $\lim_{x\to c^-} f(x) = L$. Hence $\lim_{x\to c} f(x)$ exists and equals L. ∎

EXERCISES A.2

1. Suppose that functions $f_1(x)$, $f_2(x)$, and $f_3(x)$ have limits L_1, L_2, and L_3, respectively, as $x \to c$. Show that their sum has limit $L_1 + L_2 + L_3$. Use mathematical induction (Appendix 1) to generalize this result to the sum of any finite number of functions.
2. Use mathematical induction and the Limit Product Rule in Theorem 1 to show that if functions $f_1(x), f_2(x), \ldots, f_n(x)$ have limits $L_1, L_2, \ldots, L_n$ as $x \to c$, then
$$\lim_{x\to c} f_1(x)f_2(x)\cdot \cdots \cdot f_n(x) = L_1 \cdot L_2 \cdot \cdots \cdot L_n.$$
3. Use the fact that $\lim_{x\to c} x = c$ and the result of Exercise 2 to show that $\lim_{x\to c} x^n = c^n$ for any integer $n > 1$.
4. **Limits of polynomials** Use the fact that $\lim_{x\to c}(k) = k$ for any number k together with the results of Exercises 1 and 3 to show that $\lim_{x\to c} f(x) = f(c)$ for any polynomial function
$$f(x) = a_n x^n + a_{n-1}x^{n-1} + \cdots + a_1 x + a_0.$$
5. **Limits of rational functions** Use Theorem 1 and the result of Exercise 4 to show that if $f(x)$ and $g(x)$ are polynomial functions and $g(c) \neq 0$, then
$$\lim_{x\to c} \frac{f(x)}{g(x)} = \frac{f(c)}{g(c)}.$$
6. **Composites of continuous functions** Figure A.1 gives the diagram for a proof that the composite of two continuous functions is continuous. Reconstruct the proof from the diagram. The statement to be proved is this: If f is continuous at $x = c$ and g is continuous at $f(c)$, then $g \circ f$ is continuous at c.

   Assume that c is an interior point of the domain of f and that $f(c)$ is an interior point of the domain of g. This will make the limits involved two-sided. (The arguments for the cases that involve one-sided limits are similar.)

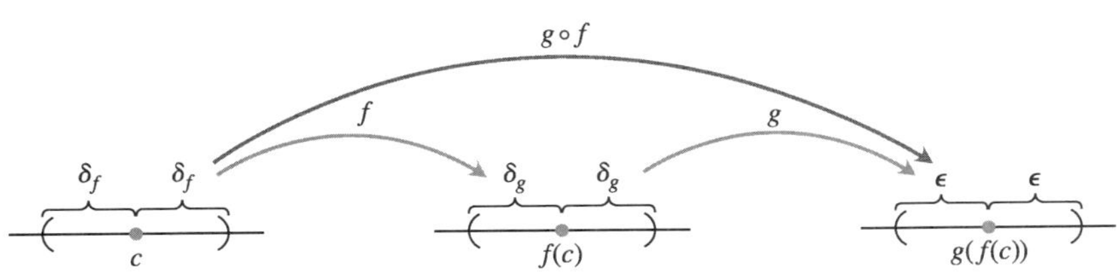

FIGURE A.1 The diagram for a proof that the composite of two continuous functions is continuous.

A.3 Commonly Occurring Limits

This appendix verifies limits (4)–(6) in Theorem 5 of Section 11.1.

Limit 4: If $|x| < 1$, $\lim_{n\to\infty} x^n = 0$ We need to show that to each $\epsilon > 0$ there corresponds an integer N so large that $|x^n| < \epsilon$ for all n greater than N. Since $\epsilon^{1/n} \to 1$, while

$|x| < 1$, there exists an integer N for which $\epsilon^{1/N} > |x|$. In other words,

$$|x^N| = |x|^N < \epsilon. \tag{1}$$

This is the integer we seek because, if $|x| < 1$, then

$$|x^n| < |x^N| \quad \text{for all } n > N. \tag{2}$$

Combining (1) and (2) produces $|x^n| < \epsilon$ for all $n > N$, concluding the proof. ■

Limit 5: For any number x, $\lim_{n\to\infty}\left(1 + \frac{x}{n}\right)^n = e^x$ Let

$$a_n = \left(1 + \frac{x}{n}\right)^n.$$

Then

$$\ln a_n = \ln\left(1 + \frac{x}{n}\right)^n = n\ln\left(1 + \frac{x}{n}\right) \to x,$$

as we can see by the following application of l'Hôpital's Rule, in which we differentiate with respect to n:

$$\lim_{n\to\infty} n\ln\left(1 + \frac{x}{n}\right) = \lim_{n\to\infty}\frac{\ln(1 + x/n)}{1/n}$$

$$= \lim_{n\to\infty}\frac{\left(\dfrac{1}{1 + x/n}\right)\cdot\left(-\dfrac{x}{n^2}\right)}{-1/n^2} = \lim_{n\to\infty}\frac{x}{1 + x/n} = x.$$

Apply Theorem 4, Section 11.1, with $f(x) = e^x$ to conclude that

$$\left(1 + \frac{x}{n}\right)^n = a_n = e^{\ln a_n} \to e^x.$$ ■

Limit 6: For any number x, $\lim_{n\to\infty}\frac{x^n}{n!} = 0$ Since

$$-\frac{|x|^n}{n!} \le \frac{x^n}{n!} \le \frac{|x|^n}{n!},$$

all we need to show is that $|x|^n/n! \to 0$. We can then apply the Sandwich Theorem for Sequences (Section 11.1, Theorem 2) to conclude that $x^n/n! \to 0$.

The first step in showing that $|x|^n/n! \to 0$ is to choose an integer $M > |x|$, so that $(|x|/M) < 1$. By Limit 4, just proved, we then have $(|x|/M)^n \to 0$. We then restrict our attention to values of $n > M$. For these values of n, we can write

$$\frac{|x|^n}{n!} = \frac{|x|^n}{1\cdot 2\cdot\cdots\cdot M\cdot\underbrace{(M+1)(M+2)\cdot\cdots\cdot n}_{(n-M)\text{ factors}}}$$

$$\le \frac{|x|^n}{M!M^{n-M}} = \frac{|x|^n M^M}{M!M^n} = \frac{M^M}{M!}\left(\frac{|x|}{M}\right)^n.$$

Thus,

$$0 \le \frac{|x|^n}{n!} \le \frac{M^M}{M!}\left(\frac{|x|}{M}\right)^n.$$

Now, the constant $M^M/M!$ does not change as n increases. Thus the Sandwich Theorem tells us that $|x|^n/n! \to 0$ because $(|x|/M)^n \to 0$. ■

A.4 Theory of the Real Numbers

A rigorous development of calculus is based on properties of the real numbers. Many results about functions, derivatives, and integrals would be false if stated for functions defined only on the rational numbers. In this appendix we briefly examine some basic concepts of the theory of the reals that hint at what might be learned in a deeper, more theoretical study of calculus.

Three types of properties make the real numbers what they are. These are the **algebraic**, **order**, and **completeness** properties. The algebraic properties involve addition and multiplication, subtraction and division. They apply to rational or complex numbers as well as to the reals.

The structure of numbers is built around a set with addition and multiplication operations. The following properties are required of addition and multiplication.

A1 $a + (b + c) = (a + b) + c$ for all a, b, c.

A2 $a + b = b + a$ for all a, b, c.

A3 There is a number called "0" such that $a + 0 = a$ for all a.

A4 For each number a, there is a b such that $a + b = 0$.

M1 $a(bc) = (ab)c$ for all a, b, c.

M2 $ab = ba$ for all a, b.

M3 There is a number called "1" such that $a \cdot 1 = a$ for all a.

M4 For each nonzero a, there is a b such that $ab = 1$.

D $a(b + c) = ab + bc$ for all a, b, c.

A1 and M1 are *associative laws*, A2 and M2 are *commutativity laws*, A3 and M3 are *identity laws*, and D is the *distributive law*. Sets that have these algebraic properties are examples of **fields**, and are studied in depth in the area of theoretical mathematics called abstract algebra.

The **order** properties allow us to compare the size of any two numbers. The order properties are

O1 For any a and b, either $a \le b$ or $b \le a$ or both.

O2 If $a \le b$ and $b \le a$ then $a = b$.

O3 If $a \le b$ and $b \le c$ then $a \le c$.

O4 If $a \le b$ then $a + c \le b + c$.

O5 If $a \le b$ and $0 \le c$ then $ac \le bc$.

O3 is the *transitivity law*, and O4 and O5 relate ordering to addition and multiplication.

We can order the reals, the integers, and the rational numbers, but we cannot order the complex numbers (see Appendix A.5). There is no reasonable way to decide whether a number like $i = \sqrt{-1}$ is bigger or smaller than zero. A field in which the size of any two elements can be compared as above is called an **ordered field**. Both the rational numbers and the real numbers are ordered fields, and there are many others.

We can think of real numbers geometrically, lining them up as points on a line. The **completeness property** says that the real numbers correspond to all points on the line, with no "holes" or "gaps." The rationals, in contrast, omit points such as $\sqrt{2}$ and π, and the integers even leave out fractions like $1/2$. The reals, having the completeness property, omit no points.

What exactly do we mean by this vague idea of missing holes? To answer this we must give a more precise description of completeness. A number M is an **upper bound** for a set of numbers if all numbers in the set are smaller than or equal to M. M is a **least upper bound** if it is the smallest upper bound. For example, $M = 2$ is an upper bound for the negative numbers. So is $M = 1$, showing that 2 is not a least upper bound. The least upper bound for the set of negative numbers is $M = 0$. We define a **complete** ordered field to be one in which every nonempty set bounded above has a least upper bound.

If we work with just the rational numbers, the set of numbers less than $\sqrt{2}$ is bounded, but it does not have a rational least upper bound, since any rational upper bound M can be replaced by a slightly smaller rational number that is still larger than $\sqrt{2}$. So the rationals are not complete. In the real numbers, a set that is bounded above always has a least upper bound. The reals are a complete ordered field.

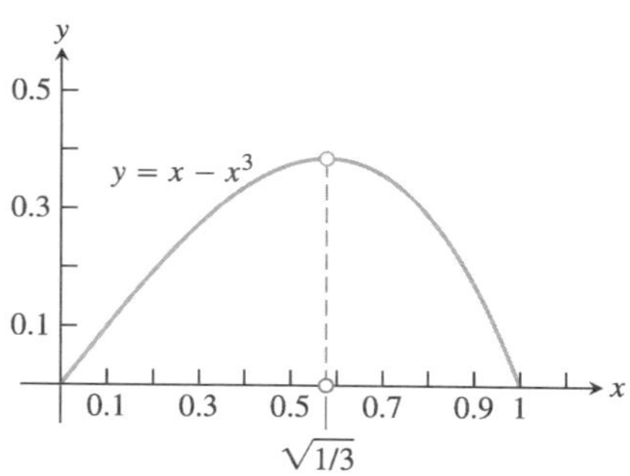

FIGURE A.2 The maximum value of $y = x - x^3$ on $[0, 1]$ occurs at the irrational number $x = \sqrt{1/3}$.

The completeness property is at the heart of many results in calculus. One example occurs when searching for a maximum value for a function on a closed interval $[a, b]$, as in Section 4.1. The function $y = x - x^3$ has a maximum value on $[0, 1]$ at the point x satisfying $1 - 3x^2 = 0$, or $x = \sqrt{1/3}$. If we limited our consideration to functions defined only on rational numbers, we would have to conclude that the function has no maximum, since $\sqrt{1/3}$ is irrational (Figure A.2). The Extreme Value Theorem (Section 4.1), which implies that continuous functions on closed intervals $[a, b]$ have a maximum value, is not true for functions defined only on the rationals.

The Intermediate Value Theorem implies that a continuous function f on an interval $[a, b]$ with $f(a) < 0$ and $f(b) > 0$ must be zero somewhere in $[a, b]$. The function values cannot jump from negative to positive without there being some point x in $[a, b]$ where $f(x) = 0$. The Intermediate Value Theorem also relies on the completeness of the real numbers and is false for continuous functions defined only on the rationals. The function $f(x) = 3x^2 - 1$ has $f(0) = -1$ and $f(1) = 2$, but if we consider f only on the rational numbers, it never equals zero. The only value of x for which $f(x) = 0$ is $x = \sqrt{1/3}$, an irrational number.

We have captured the desired properties of the reals by saying that the real numbers are a complete ordered field. But we're not quite finished. Greek mathematicians in the school of Pythagoras tried to impose another property on the numbers of the real line, the condition that all numbers are ratios of integers. They learned that their effort was doomed when they discovered irrational numbers such as $\sqrt{2}$. How do we know that our efforts to specify the real numbers are not also flawed, for some unseen reason? The artist Escher drew optical illusions of spiral staircases that went up and up until they rejoined themselves at the bottom. An engineer trying to build such a staircase would find that no structure realized the plans the architect had drawn. Could it be that our design for the reals contains some subtle contradiction, and that no construction of such a number system can be made?

We resolve this issue by giving a specific description of the real numbers and verifying that the algebraic, order, and completeness properties are satisfied in this model. This is called a **construction** of the reals, and just as stairs can be built with wood, stone, or steel, there are several approaches to constructing the reals. One construction treats the reals as all the infinite decimals,

$$a.d_1d_2d_3d_4\ldots$$

In this approach a real number is an integer a followed by a sequence of decimal digits $d_1, d_2, d_3, \ldots$, each between 0 and 9. This sequence may stop, or repeat in a periodic pattern, or keep going forever with no pattern. In this form, $2.00, 0.3333333\ldots$ and $3.1415926535898\ldots$ represent three familiar real numbers. The real meaning of the dots "$\ldots$" following these digits requires development of the theory of sequences and series, as in Chapter 11. Each real number is constructed as the limit of a sequence of rational numbers given by its finite decimal approximations. An infinite decimal is then the same as a series

$$a + \frac{d_1}{10} + \frac{d_2}{100} + \cdots.$$

This decimal construction of the real numbers is not entirely straightforward. It's easy enough to check that it gives numbers that satisfy the completeness and order properties, but verifying the algebraic properties is rather involved. Even adding or multiplying two numbers requires an infinite number of operations. Making sense of division requires a careful argument involving limits of rational approximations to infinite decimals.

A different approach was taken by Richard Dedekind (1831–1916), a German mathematician, who gave the first rigorous construction of the real numbers in 1872. Given any real number x, we can divide the rational numbers into two sets: those less than or equal to x and those greater. Dedekind cleverly reversed this reasoning and defined a real number to be a division of the rational numbers into two such sets. This seems like a strange approach, but such indirect methods of constructing new structures from old are common in theoretical mathematics.

These and other approaches (see Appendix A.5) can be used to construct a system of numbers having the desired algebraic, order, and completeness properties. A final issue that arises is whether all the constructions give the same thing. Is it possible that different constructions result in different number systems satisfying all the required properties? If yes, which of these is the real numbers? Fortunately, the answer turns out to be no. The reals are the only number system satisfying the algebraic, order, and completeness properties.

Confusion about the nature of real numbers and about limits caused considerable controversy in the early development of calculus. Calculus pioneers such as Newton, Leibniz, and their successors, when looking at what happens to the difference quotient

$$\frac{\Delta y}{\Delta x} = \frac{f(x + \Delta x) - f(x)}{\Delta x}$$

as each of Δy and Δx approach zero, talked about the resulting derivative being a quotient of two infinitely small quantities. These "infinitesimals," written dx and dy, were thought to be some new kind of number, smaller than any fixed number but not zero. Similarly, a definite integral was thought of as a sum of an infinite number of infinitesimals

$$f(x) \cdot dx$$

as x varied over a closed interval. While the approximating difference quotients $\Delta y/\Delta x$ were understood much as today, it was the quotient of infinitesimal quantities, rather than a limit, that was thought to encapsulate the meaning of the derivative. This way of thinking led to logical difficulties, as attempted definitions and manipulations of infinitesimals ran into contradictions and inconsistencies. The more concrete and computable difference quotients did not cause such trouble, but they were thought of merely as useful calculation tools. Difference quotients were used to work out the numerical value of the derivative and to derive general formulas for calculation, but were not considered to be at the heart of the question of what the derivative actually was. Today we realize that the logical problems associated with infinitesimals can be avoided by *defining* the derivative to be the limit of its approximating difference quotients. The ambiguities of the old approach are no longer present, and in the standard theory of calculus, infinitesimals are neither needed nor used.

A.5 Complex Numbers

Complex numbers are expressions of the form $a + ib$, where a and b are real numbers and i is a symbol for $\sqrt{-1}$. Unfortunately, the words "real" and "imaginary" have connotations that somehow place $\sqrt{-1}$ in a less favorable position in our minds than $\sqrt{2}$. As a matter of fact, a good deal of imagination, in the sense of *inventiveness*, has been required to construct the *real* number system, which forms the basis of the calculus (see Appendix A.4). In this appendix we review the various stages of this invention. The further invention of a complex number system is then presented.

The Development of the Real Numbers

The earliest stage of number development was the recognition of the **counting numbers** $1, 2, 3, \ldots$, which we now call the **natural numbers** or the **positive integers**. Certain simple arithmetical operations can be performed with these numbers without getting outside the system. That is, the system of positive integers is **closed** under the operations of addition and multiplication. By this we mean that if m and n are any positive integers, then

$$m + n = p \qquad \text{and} \qquad mn = q \tag{1}$$

are also positive integers. Given the two positive integers on the left side of either equation in (1), we can find the corresponding positive integer on the right side. More than this, we can sometimes specify the positive integers m and p and find a positive integer n such that $m + n = p$. For instance, $3 + n = 7$ can be solved when the only numbers we know are the positive integers. But the equation $7 + n = 3$ cannot be solved unless the number system is enlarged.

The number zero and the negative integers were invented to solve equations like $7 + n = 3$. In a civilization that recognizes all the **integers**

$$\ldots, -3, -2, -1, 0, 1, 2, 3, \ldots, \tag{2}$$

an educated person can always find the missing integer that solves the equation $m + n = p$ when given the other two integers in the equation.

Suppose our educated people also know how to multiply any two of the integers in the list (2). If, in Equations (1), they are given m and q, they discover that sometimes they can find n and sometimes they cannot. Using their imagination, they may be

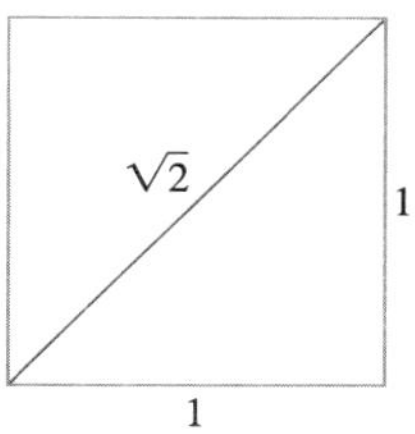

FIGURE A.3 With a straightedge and compass, it is possible to construct a segment of irrational length.

inspired to invent still more numbers and introduce fractions, which are just ordered pairs m/n of integers m and n. The number zero has special properties that may bother them for a while, but they ultimately discover that it is handy to have all ratios of integers m/n, excluding only those having zero in the denominator. This system, called the set of **rational numbers**, is now rich enough for them to perform the **rational operations** of arithmetic:

1. **(a)** addition
(b) subtraction

2. **(a)** multiplication
(b) division

on any two numbers in the system, *except that they cannot divide by zero* because it is meaningless.

The geometry of the unit square (Figure A.3) and the Pythagorean theorem showed that they could construct a geometric line segment that, in terms of some basic unit of length, has length equal to $\sqrt{2}$. Thus they could solve the equation

$$x^2 = 2$$

by a geometric construction. But then they discovered that the line segment representing $\sqrt{2}$ is an incommensurable quantity. This means that $\sqrt{2}$ cannot be expressed as the ratio of two *integer* multiples of some unit of length. That is, our educated people could not find a rational number solution of the equation $x^2 = 2$.

There *is* no rational number whose square is 2. To see why, suppose that there were such a rational number. Then we could find integers p and q with no common factor other than 1, and such that

$$p^2 = 2q^2. \qquad (3)$$

Since p and q are integers, p must be even; otherwise its product with itself would be odd. In symbols, $p = 2p_1$, where p_1 is an integer. This leads to $2p_1^2 = q^2$ which says q must be even, say $q = 2q_1$, where q_1 is an integer. This makes 2 a factor of both p and q, contrary to our choice of p and q as integers with no common factor other than 1. Hence there is no rational number whose square is 2.

Although our educated people could not find a rational solution of the equation $x^2 = 2$, they could get a sequence of rational numbers

$$\frac{1}{1}, \quad \frac{7}{5}, \quad \frac{41}{29}, \quad \frac{239}{169}, \quad \ldots, \qquad (4)$$

whose squares form a sequence

$$\frac{1}{1}, \quad \frac{49}{25}, \quad \frac{1681}{841}, \quad \frac{57{,}121}{28{,}561}, \quad \ldots, \qquad (5)$$

that converges to 2 as its limit. This time their imagination suggested that they needed the concept of a limit of a sequence of rational numbers. If we accept the fact that an increasing sequence that is bounded from above always approaches a limit (Theorem 6, Section 11.1) and observe that the sequence in (4) has these properties, then we want it to have a limit L. This would also mean, from (5), that $L^2 = 2$, and hence L is *not* one of our rational numbers. If to the rational numbers we further add the limits of all bounded increasing sequences of rational numbers, we arrive at the system of all "real" numbers. The word *real* is placed in quotes because there is nothing that is either "more real" or "less real" about this system than there is about any other mathematical system.

The Complex Numbers

Imagination was called upon at many stages during the development of the real number system. In fact, the art of invention was needed at least three times in constructing the systems we have discussed so far:

1. The *first invented* system: the set of *all integers* as constructed from the counting numbers.
2. The *second invented* system: the set of *rational numbers* m/n as constructed from the integers.
3. The *third invented* system: the set of all *real numbers* x as constructed from the rational numbers.

These invented systems form a hierarchy in which each system contains the previous system. Each system is also richer than its predecessor in that it permits additional operations to be performed without going outside the system:

1. In the system of all integers, we can solve all equations of the form
$$x + a = 0, \tag{6}$$
where a can be any integer.
2. In the system of all rational numbers, we can solve all equations of the form
$$ax + b = 0, \tag{7}$$
provided a and b are rational numbers and $a \neq 0$.
3. In the system of all real numbers, we can solve all of Equations (6) and (7) and, in addition, all quadratic equations
$$ax^2 + bx + c = 0 \quad \text{having} \quad a \neq 0 \quad \text{and} \quad b^2 - 4ac \geq 0. \tag{8}$$

You are probably familiar with the formula that gives the solutions of Equation (8), namely,

$$x = \frac{-b \pm \sqrt{b^2 - 4ac}}{2a}, \tag{9}$$

and are familiar with the further fact that when the discriminant, $b^2 - 4ac$, is negative, the solutions in Equation (9) do *not* belong to any of the systems discussed above. In fact, the very simple quadratic equation

$$x^2 + 1 = 0$$

is impossible to solve if the only number systems that can be used are the three invented systems mentioned so far.

Thus we come to the *fourth invented* system, the set of *all complex numbers* $a + ib$. We could dispense entirely with the symbol i and use the ordered pair notation (a, b). Since, under algebraic operations, the numbers a and b are treated somewhat differently, it is essential to keep the *order* straight. We therefore might say that the **complex number system** consists of the set of all ordered pairs of real numbers (a, b), together with the rules by which they are to be equated, added, multiplied, and so on, listed below. We will use both the (a, b) notation and the notation $a + ib$ in the discussion that follows. We call a the **real part** and b the **imaginary part** of the complex number (a, b).

We make the following definitions.

Equality	
$a + ib = c + id$ if and only if $a = c$ and $b = d$.	Two complex numbers (a, b) and (c, d) are *equal* if and only if $a = c$ and $b = d$.
Addition	
$(a + ib) + (c + id) = (a + c) + i(b + d)$	The *sum* of the two complex numbers (a, b) and (c, d) is the complex number $(a + c, b + d)$.
Multiplication	
$(a + ib)(c + id) = (ac - bd) + i(ad + bc)$	The *product* of two complex numbers (a, b) and (c, d) is the complex number $(ac - bd, ad + bc)$.
$c(a + ib) = ac + i(bc)$	The product of a real number c and the complex number (a, b) is the complex number (ac, bc).

The set of all complex numbers (a, b) in which the second number b is zero has all the properties of the set of real numbers a. For example, addition and multiplication of $(a, 0)$ and $(c, 0)$ give

$$(a, 0) + (c, 0) = (a + c, 0),$$
$$(a, 0) \cdot (c, 0) = (ac, 0),$$

which are numbers of the same type with imaginary part equal to zero. Also, if we multiply a "real number" $(a, 0)$ and the complex number (c, d), we get

$$(a, 0) \cdot (c, d) = (ac, ad) = a(c, d).$$

In particular, the complex number $(0, 0)$ plays the role of *zero* in the complex number system, and the complex number $(1, 0)$ plays the role of *unity* or *one*.

The number pair $(0, 1)$, which has real part equal to zero and imaginary part equal to one, has the property that its square,

$$(0, 1)(0, 1) = (-1, 0),$$

has real part equal to minus one and imaginary part equal to zero. Therefore, in the system of complex numbers (a, b) there is a number $x = (0, 1)$ whose square can be added to unity $= (1, 0)$ to produce zero $= (0, 0)$, that is,

$$(0, 1)^2 + (1, 0) = (0, 0).$$

The equation

$$x^2 + 1 = 0$$

therefore has a solution $x = (0, 1)$ in this new number system.

You are probably more familiar with the $a + ib$ notation than you are with the notation (a, b). And since the laws of algebra for the ordered pairs enable us to write

$$(a, b) = (a, 0) + (0, b) = a(1, 0) + b(0, 1),$$

while $(1, 0)$ behaves like unity and $(0, 1)$ behaves like a square root of minus one, we need not hesitate to write $a + ib$ in place of (a, b). The i associated with b is like a tracer element that tags the imaginary part of $a + ib$. We can pass at will from the realm of ordered pairs (a, b) to the realm of expressions $a + ib$, and conversely. But there is nothing less "real" about the symbol $(0, 1) = i$ than there is about the symbol $(1, 0) = 1$, once we have learned the laws of algebra in the complex number system of ordered pairs (a, b).

To reduce any rational combination of complex numbers to a single complex number, we apply the laws of elementary algebra, replacing i^2 wherever it appears by -1. Of course, we cannot divide by the complex number $(0, 0) = 0 + i0$. But if $a + ib \neq 0$, then we may carry out a division as follows:

$$\frac{c + id}{a + ib} = \frac{(c + id)(a - ib)}{(a + ib)(a - ib)} = \frac{(ac + bd) + i(ad - bc)}{a^2 + b^2}.$$

The result is a complex number $x + iy$ with

$$x = \frac{ac + bd}{a^2 + b^2}, \qquad y = \frac{ad - bc}{a^2 + b^2},$$

and $a^2 + b^2 \neq 0$, since $a + ib = (a, b) \neq (0, 0)$.

The number $a - ib$ that is used as multiplier to clear the i from the denominator is called the **complex conjugate** of $a + ib$. It is customary to use $\bar{z}$ (read "z bar") to denote the complex conjugate of z; thus

$$z = a + ib, \qquad \bar{z} = a - ib.$$

Multiplying the numerator and denominator of the fraction $(c + id)/(a + ib)$ by the complex conjugate of the denominator will always replace the denominator by a real number.

EXAMPLE 1 Arithmetic Operations with Complex Numbers

(a) $(2 + 3i) + (6 - 2i) = (2 + 6) + (3 - 2)i = 8 + i$

(b) $(2 + 3i) - (6 - 2i) = (2 - 6) + (3 - (-2))i = -4 + 5i$

(c) $(2 + 3i)(6 - 2i) = (2)(6) + (2)(-2i) + (3i)(6) + (3i)(-2i)$

$$= 12 - 4i + 18i - 6i^2 = 12 + 14i + 6 = 18 + 14i$$

(d)
$$\frac{2 + 3i}{6 - 2i} = \frac{2 + 3i}{6 - 2i}\frac{6 + 2i}{6 + 2i} = \frac{12 + 4i + 18i + 6i^2}{36 + 12i - 12i - 4i^2} = \frac{6 + 22i}{40} = \frac{3}{20} + \frac{11}{20}i$$

■

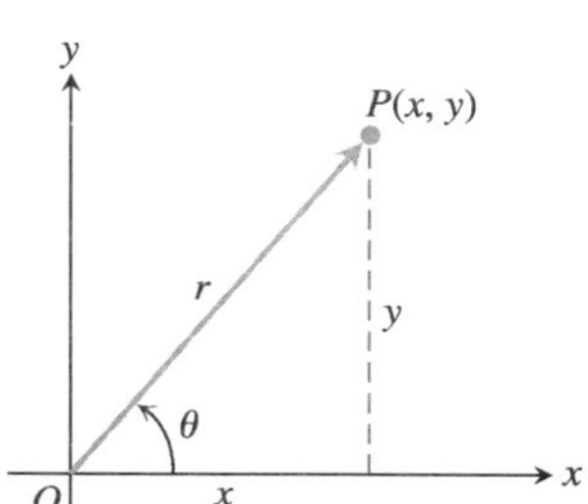

FIGURE A.4 This Argand diagram represents $z = x + iy$ both as a point $P(x, y)$ and as a vector $\overrightarrow{OP}$.

Argand Diagrams

There are two geometric representations of the complex number $z = x + iy$:

1. as the point $P(x, y)$ in the xy-plane
2. as the vector $\overrightarrow{OP}$ from the origin to P.

In each representation, the x-axis is called the **real axis** and the y-axis is the **imaginary axis**. Both representations are **Argand diagrams** for $x + iy$ (Figure A.4).

In terms of the polar coordinates of x and y, we have

$$x = r\cos\theta, \qquad y = r\sin\theta,$$

and

$$z = x + iy = r(\cos\theta + i\sin\theta). \tag{10}$$

We define the **absolute value** of a complex number $x + iy$ to be the length r of a vector $\overrightarrow{OP}$ from the origin to $P(x, y)$. We denote the absolute value by vertical bars; thus,

$$|x + iy| = \sqrt{x^2 + y^2}.$$

If we always choose the polar coordinates r and θ so that r is nonnegative, then

$$r = |x + iy|.$$

The polar angle θ is called the **argument** of z and is written $\theta = \arg z$. Of course, any integer multiple of 2π may be added to θ to produce another appropriate angle.

The following equation gives a useful formula connecting a complex number z, its conjugate $\bar{z}$, and its absolute value $|z|$, namely,

$$z \cdot \bar{z} = |z|^2.$$

Euler's Formula

The identity

$$e^{i\theta} = \cos\theta + i\sin\theta,$$

called **Euler's formula**, enables us to rewrite Equation (10) as

$$z = re^{i\theta}.$$

This formula, in turn, leads to the following rules for calculating products, quotients, powers, and roots of complex numbers. It also leads to Argand diagrams for $e^{i\theta}$. Since $\cos\theta + i\sin\theta$ is what we get from Equation (10) by taking $r = 1$, we can say that $e^{i\theta}$ is represented by a unit vector that makes an angle θ with the positive x-axis, as shown in Figure A.5.

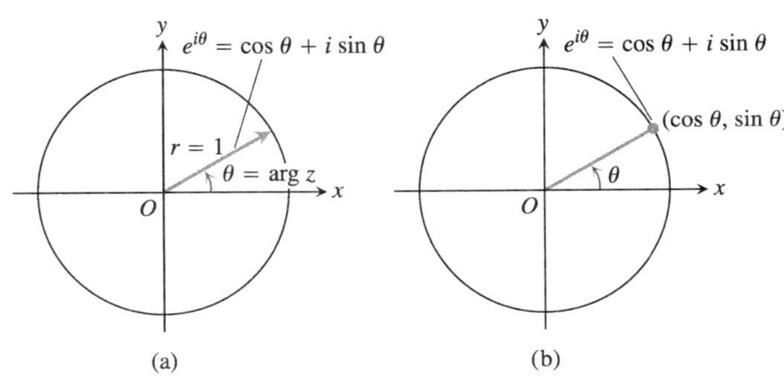

FIGURE A.5 Argand diagrams for $e^{i\theta} = \cos\theta + i\sin\theta$ (a) as a vector and (b) as a point.

Products

To multiply two complex numbers, we multiply their absolute values and add their angles. Let

$$z_1 = r_1 e^{i\theta_1}, \qquad z_2 = r_2 e^{i\theta_2}, \tag{11}$$

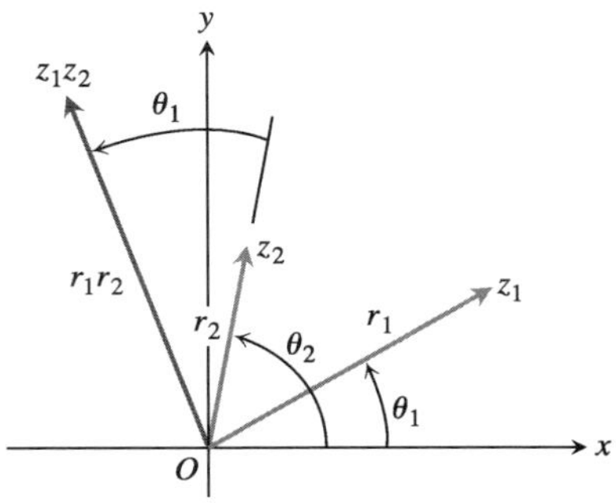

FIGURE A.6 When z_1 and z_2 are multiplied, $|z_1z_2| = r_1 \cdot r_2$ and $\arg(z_1z_2) = \theta_1 + \theta_2$.

so that

$$|z_1| = r_1, \qquad \arg z_1 = \theta_1; \qquad |z_2| = r_2, \qquad \arg z_2 = \theta_2.$$

Then

$$z_1z_2 = r_1e^{i\theta_1} \cdot r_2e^{i\theta_2} = r_1r_2e^{i(\theta_1+\theta_2)}$$

and hence

$$\begin{aligned} |z_1z_2| &= r_1r_2 = |z_1| \cdot |z_2| \\ \arg(z_1z_2) &= \theta_1 + \theta_2 = \arg z_1 + \arg z_2. \end{aligned} \tag{12}$$

Thus, the product of two complex numbers is represented by a vector whose length is the product of the lengths of the two factors and whose argument is the sum of their arguments (Figure A.6). In particular, from Equation (12) a vector may be rotated counterclockwise through an angle θ by multiplying it by $e^{i\theta}$. Multiplication by i rotates 90°, by -1 rotates 180°, by $-i$ rotates 270°, and so on.

EXAMPLE 2 Finding a Product of Complex Numbers

Let $z_1 = 1 + i$, $z_2 = \sqrt{3} - i$. We plot these complex numbers in an Argand diagram (Figure A.7) from which we read off the polar representations

$$z_1 = \sqrt{2}e^{i\pi/4}, \qquad z_2 = 2e^{-i\pi/6}.$$

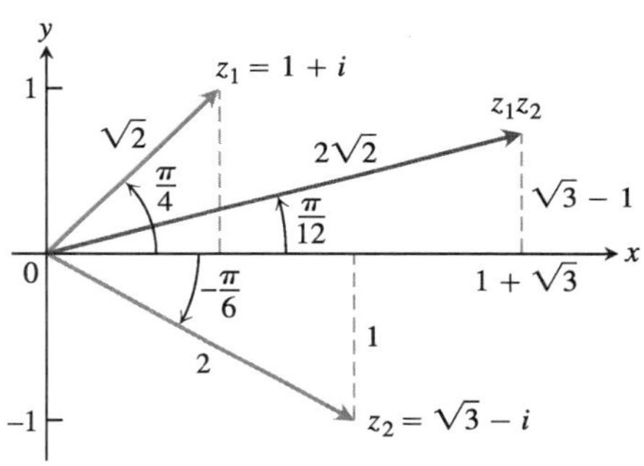

FIGURE A.7 To multiply two complex numbers, multiply their absolute values and add their arguments.

Then

$$\begin{aligned} z_1z_2 &= 2\sqrt{2}\exp\left(\frac{i\pi}{4} - \frac{i\pi}{6}\right) = 2\sqrt{2}\exp\left(\frac{i\pi}{12}\right) \\ &= 2\sqrt{2}\left(\cos\frac{\pi}{12} + i\sin\frac{\pi}{12}\right) \approx 2.73 + 0.73i. \end{aligned}$$

The notation $\exp(A)$ stands for e^A. ■

Quotients

Suppose $r_2 \neq 0$ in Equation (11). Then

$$\frac{z_1}{z_2} = \frac{r_1e^{i\theta_1}}{r_2e^{i\theta_2}} = \frac{r_1}{r_2}e^{i(\theta_1-\theta_2)}.$$

Hence

$$\left|\frac{z_1}{z_2}\right| = \frac{r_1}{r_2} = \frac{|z_1|}{|z_2|} \quad \text{and} \quad \arg\left(\frac{z_1}{z_2}\right) = \theta_1 - \theta_2 = \arg z_1 - \arg z_2.$$

That is, we divide lengths and subtract angles for the quotient of complex numbers.

EXAMPLE 3 Let $z_1 = 1 + i$ and $z_2 = \sqrt{3} - i$, as in Example 2. Then

$$\begin{aligned} \frac{1 + i}{\sqrt{3} - i} &= \frac{\sqrt{2}e^{i\pi/4}}{2e^{-i\pi/6}} = \frac{\sqrt{2}}{2}e^{5\pi i/12} \approx 0.707\left(\cos\frac{5\pi}{12} + i\sin\frac{5\pi}{12}\right) \\ &\approx 0.183 + 0.683i. \end{aligned}$$

■

Powers

If n is a positive integer, we may apply the product formulas in Equation (12) to find

$$z^n = z \cdot z \cdot \cdots \cdot z. \qquad n \text{ factors}$$

With $z = re^{i\theta}$, we obtain

$$\begin{aligned} z^n = (re^{i\theta})^n &= r^n e^{i(\theta+\theta+\cdots+\theta)} \qquad n \text{ summands} \\ &= r^n e^{in\theta}. \end{aligned} \tag{13}$$

The length $r = |z|$ is raised to the nth power and the angle $\theta = \arg z$ is multiplied by n.

If we take $r = 1$ in Equation (13), we obtain De Moivre's Theorem.

De Moivre's Theorem

$$(\cos\theta + i\sin\theta)^n = \cos n\theta + i\sin n\theta. \tag{14}$$

If we expand the left side of De Moivre's equation above by the Binomial Theorem and reduce it to the form $a + ib$, we obtain formulas for $\cos n\theta$ and $\sin n\theta$ as polynomials of degree n in $\cos\theta$ and $\sin\theta$.

EXAMPLE 4 If $n = 3$ in Equation (14), we have

$$(\cos\theta + i\sin\theta)^3 = \cos 3\theta + i\sin 3\theta.$$

The left side of this equation expands to

$$\cos^3\theta + 3i\cos^2\theta\sin\theta - 3\cos\theta\sin^2\theta - i\sin^3\theta.$$

The real part of this must equal $\cos 3\theta$ and the imaginary part must equal $\sin 3\theta$. Therefore,

$$\begin{aligned} \cos 3\theta &= \cos^3\theta - 3\cos\theta\sin^2\theta, \\ \sin 3\theta &= 3\cos^2\theta\sin\theta - \sin^3\theta. \end{aligned}$$

■

Roots

If $z = re^{i\theta}$ is a complex number different from zero and n is a positive integer, then there are precisely n different complex numbers $w_0, w_1, \ldots, w_{n-1}$, that are nth roots of z. To see why, let $w = \rho e^{i\alpha}$ be an nth root of $z = re^{i\theta}$, so that

$$w^n = z$$

or

$$\rho^n e^{in\alpha} = re^{i\theta}.$$

Then

$$\rho = \sqrt[n]{r}$$

is the real, positive nth root of r. For the argument, although we cannot say that $n\alpha$ and θ must be equal, we can say that they may differ only by an integer multiple of 2π. That is,

$$n\alpha = \theta + 2k\pi, \qquad k = 0, \pm 1, \pm 2, \ldots.$$

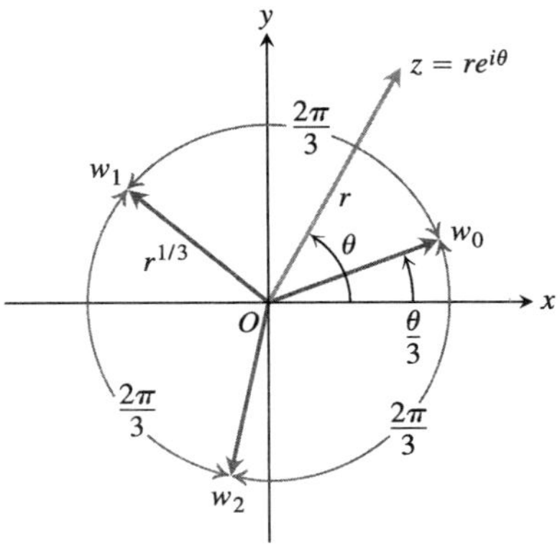

FIGURE A.8 The three cube roots of $z = re^{i\theta}$.

Therefore,

$$\alpha = \frac{\theta}{n} + k\frac{2\pi}{n}.$$

Hence, all the nth roots of $z = re^{i\theta}$ are given by

$$\sqrt[n]{re^{i\theta}} = \sqrt[n]{r}\exp i\left(\frac{\theta}{n} + k\frac{2\pi}{n}\right), \qquad k = 0, \pm1, \pm2, \ldots. \tag{15}$$

There might appear to be infinitely many different answers corresponding to the infinitely many possible values of k, but $k = n + m$ gives the same answer as $k = m$ in Equation (15). Thus, we need only take n consecutive values for k to obtain all the different nth roots of z. For convenience, we take

$$k = 0, 1, 2, \ldots, n - 1.$$

All the nth roots of $re^{i\theta}$ lie on a circle centered at the origin and having radius equal to the real, positive nth root of r. One of them has argument $\alpha = \theta/n$. The others are uniformly spaced around the circle, each being separated from its neighbors by an angle equal to $2\pi/n$. Figure A.8 illustrates the placement of the three cube roots, w_0, w_1, w_2, of the complex number $z = re^{i\theta}$.

EXAMPLE 5 Finding Fourth Roots

Find the four fourth roots of -16.

Solution As our first step, we plot the number -16 in an Argand diagram (Figure A.9) and determine its polar representation $re^{i\theta}$. Here, $z = -16$, $r = +16$, and $\theta = \pi$. One of the fourth roots of $16e^{i\pi}$ is $2e^{i\pi/4}$. We obtain others by successive additions of $2\pi/4 = \pi/2$ to the argument of this first one. Hence,

$$\sqrt[4]{16\exp i\pi} = 2\exp i\left(\frac{\pi}{4}, \frac{3\pi}{4}, \frac{5\pi}{4}, \frac{7\pi}{4}\right),$$

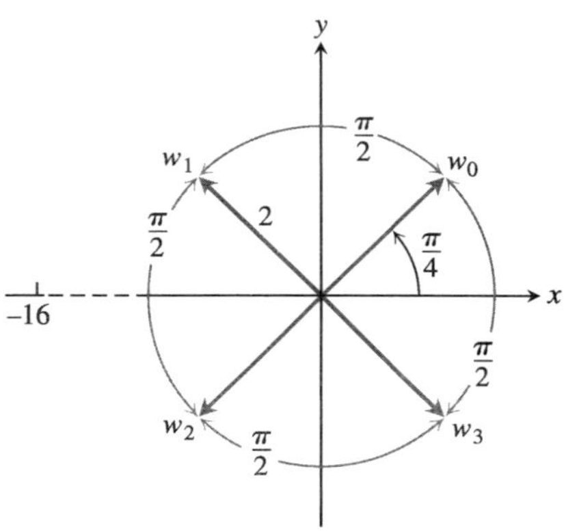

FIGURE A.9 The four fourth roots of -16.

and the four roots are

$$w_0 = 2\left[\cos\frac{\pi}{4} + i\sin\frac{\pi}{4}\right] = \sqrt{2}(1 + i)$$

$$w_1 = 2\left[\cos\frac{3\pi}{4} + i\sin\frac{3\pi}{4}\right] = \sqrt{2}(-1 + i)$$

$$w_2 = 2\left[\cos\frac{5\pi}{4} + i\sin\frac{5\pi}{4}\right] = \sqrt{2}(-1 - i)$$

$$w_3 = 2\left[\cos\frac{7\pi}{4} + i\sin\frac{7\pi}{4}\right] = \sqrt{2}(1 - i).$$

■

The Fundamental Theorem of Algebra

One might say that the invention of $\sqrt{-1}$ is all well and good and leads to a number system that is richer than the real number system alone; but where will this process end? Are we also going to invent still more systems so as to obtain $\sqrt[4]{-1}$, $\sqrt[6]{-1}$, and so on? But it turns out this is not necessary. These numbers are already expressible in terms of the complex number system $a + ib$. In fact, the Fundamental Theorem of Algebra says that with the introduction of the complex numbers we now have enough numbers to factor every polynomial into a product of linear factors and so enough numbers to solve every possible polynomial equation.

The Fundamental Theorem of Algebra

Every polynomial equation of the form

$$a_n z^n + a_{n-1} z^{n-1} + \cdots + a_1 z + a_0 = 0,$$

in which the coefficients $a_0, a_1, \ldots, a_n$ are any complex numbers, whose degree n is greater than or equal to one, and whose leading coefficient a_n is not zero, has exactly n roots in the complex number system, provided each multiple root of multiplicity m is counted as m roots.

A proof of this theorem can be found in almost any text on the theory of functions of a complex variable.

EXERCISES A.5

Operations with Complex Numbers

1. **How computers multiply complex numbers** Find $(a, b) \cdot (c, d) = (ac - bd, ad + bc)$.

   a. $(2, 3) \cdot (4, -2)$ b. $(2, -1) \cdot (-2, 3)$

   c. $(-1, -2) \cdot (2, 1)$

   (This is how complex numbers are multiplied by computers.)

2. Solve the following equations for the real numbers, x and y.

   a. $(3 + 4i)^2 - 2(x - iy) = x + iy$

   b. $\left(\dfrac{1 + i}{1 - i}\right)^2 + \dfrac{1}{x + iy} = 1 + i$

   c. $(3 - 2i)(x + iy) = 2(x - 2iy) + 2i - 1$

Graphing and Geometry

3. How may the following complex numbers be obtained from $z = x + iy$ geometrically? Sketch.

   a. $\bar{z}$ b. $\overline{(-z)}$

   c. $-z$ d. $1/z$

4. Show that the distance between the two points z_1 and z_2 in an Argand diagram is $|z_1 - z_2|$.

In Exercises 5–10, graph the points $z = x + iy$ that satisfy the given conditions.

5. a. $|z| = 2$ b. $|z| < 2$ c. $|z| > 2$

6. $|z - 1| = 2$

7. $|z + 1| = 1$

8. $|z + 1| = |z - 1|$

9. $|z + i| = |z - 1|$

10. $|z + 1| \geq |z|$

Express the complex numbers in Exercises 11–14 in the form $re^{i\theta}$, with $r \geq 0$ and $-\pi < \theta \leq \pi$. Draw an Argand diagram for each calculation.

11. $\left(1 + \sqrt{-3}\right)^2$

12. $\dfrac{1 + i}{1 - i}$

13. $\dfrac{1 + i\sqrt{3}}{1 - i\sqrt{3}}$

14. $(2 + 3i)(1 - 2i)$

Powers and Roots

Use De Moivre's Theorem to express the trigonometric functions in Exercises 15 and 16 in terms of $\cos\theta$ and $\sin\theta$.

15. $\cos 4\theta$

16. $\sin 4\theta$

17. Find the three cube roots of 1.

18. Find the two square roots of i.
19. Find the three cube roots of $-8i$.
20. Find the six sixth roots of 64.
21. Find the four solutions of the equation $z^4 - 2z^2 + 4 = 0$.
22. Find the six solutions of the equation $z^6 + 2z^3 + 2 = 0$.
23. Find all solutions of the equation $x^4 + 4x^2 + 16 = 0$.
24. Solve the equation $x^4 + 1 = 0$.

Theory and Examples

25. **Complex numbers and vectors in the plane** Show with an Argand diagram that the law for adding complex numbers is the same as the parallelogram law for adding vectors.
26. **Complex arithmetic with conjugates** Show that the conjugate of the sum (product, or quotient) of two complex numbers, z_1 and z_2, is the same as the sum (product, or quotient) of their conjugates.
27. **Complex roots of polynomials with real coefficients come in complex-conjugate pairs**
    a. Extend the results of Exercise 26 to show that $f(\bar{z}) = \overline{f(z)}$ if
    $$f(z) = a_n z^n + a_{n-1}z^{n-1} + \cdots + a_1 z + a_0$$
    is a polynomial with real coefficients $a_0, \ldots, a_n$.
    b. If z is a root of the equation $f(z) = 0$, where $f(z)$ is a polynomial with real coefficients as in part (a), show that the conjugate $\bar{z}$ is also a root of the equation. (*Hint:* Let $f(z) = u + iv = 0$; then both u and v are zero. Use the fact that $f(\bar{z}) = \overline{f(z)} = u - iv$.)
28. **Absolute value of a conjugate** Show that $|\bar{z}| = |z|$.
29. **When $\mathbf{z} = \bar{\mathbf{z}}$** If z and $\bar{z}$ are equal, what can you say about the location of the point z in the complex plane?
30. **Real and imaginary parts** Let Re(z) denote the real part of z and Im(z) the imaginary part. Show that the following relations hold for any complex numbers z, z_1, and z_2.
    a. $z + \bar{z} = 2\mathrm{Re}(z)$ b. $z - \bar{z} = 2i\mathrm{Im}(z)$
    c. $|\mathrm{Re}(z)| \le |z|$
    d. $|z_1 + z_2|^2 = |z_1|^2 + |z_2|^2 + 2\mathrm{Re}(z_1\bar{z}_2)$
    e. $|z_1 + z_2| \le |z_1| + |z_2|$

A.6 The Distributive Law for Vector Cross Products

In this appendix, we prove the Distributive Law

$$\mathbf{u} \times (\mathbf{v} + \mathbf{w}) = \mathbf{u} \times \mathbf{v} + \mathbf{u} \times \mathbf{w}$$

which is Property 2 in Section 12.4.

Proof To derive the Distributive Law, we construct $\mathbf{u} \times \mathbf{v}$ a new way. We draw $\mathbf{u}$ and $\mathbf{v}$ from the common point O and construct a plane M perpendicular to $\mathbf{u}$ at O (Figure A.10). We then project $\mathbf{v}$ orthogonally onto M, yielding a vector $\mathbf{v}'$ with length $|\mathbf{v}|\sin\theta$. We rotate $\mathbf{v}'$ 90° about $\mathbf{u}$ in the positive sense to produce a vector $\mathbf{v}''$. Finally, we multiply $\mathbf{v}''$ by the

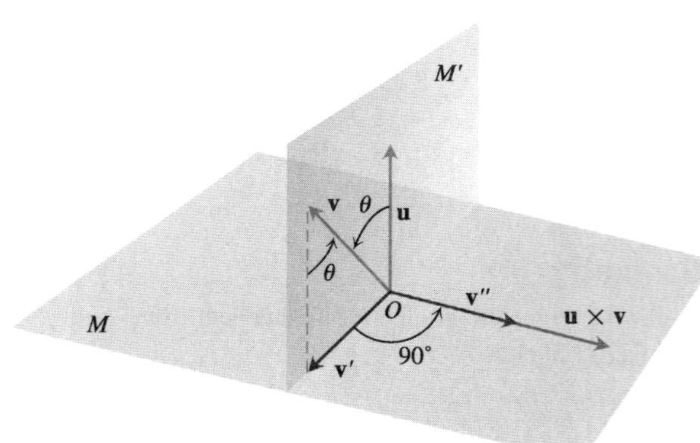

FIGURE A.10 As explained in the text, $\mathbf{u} \times \mathbf{v} = |\mathbf{u}|\mathbf{v}''$.

length of $\mathbf{u}$. The resulting vector $|\mathbf{u}|\mathbf{v}''$ is equal to $\mathbf{u} \times \mathbf{v}$ since $\mathbf{v}''$ has the same direction as $\mathbf{u} \times \mathbf{v}$ by its construction (Figure A.10) and

$$|\mathbf{u}||\mathbf{v}''| = |\mathbf{u}||\mathbf{v}'| = |\mathbf{u}||\mathbf{v}|\sin\theta = |\mathbf{u} \times \mathbf{v}|.$$

Now each of these three operations, namely,

1. projection onto M
2. rotation about $\mathbf{u}$ through 90°
3. multiplication by the scalar $|\mathbf{u}|$

when applied to a triangle whose plane is not parallel to $\mathbf{u}$, will produce another triangle. If we start with the triangle whose sides are $\mathbf{v}$, $\mathbf{w}$, and $\mathbf{v} + \mathbf{w}$ (Figure A.11) and apply these three steps, we successively obtain the following:

1. A triangle whose sides are $\mathbf{v}'$, $\mathbf{w}'$, and $(\mathbf{v} + \mathbf{w})'$ satisfying the vector equation
$$\mathbf{v}' + \mathbf{w}' = (\mathbf{v} + \mathbf{w})'$$
2. A triangle whose sides are $\mathbf{v}''$, $\mathbf{w}''$, and $(\mathbf{v} + \mathbf{w})''$ satisfying the vector equation
$$\mathbf{v}'' + \mathbf{w}'' = (\mathbf{v} + \mathbf{w})''$$
(the double prime on each vector has the same meaning as in Figure A.10)

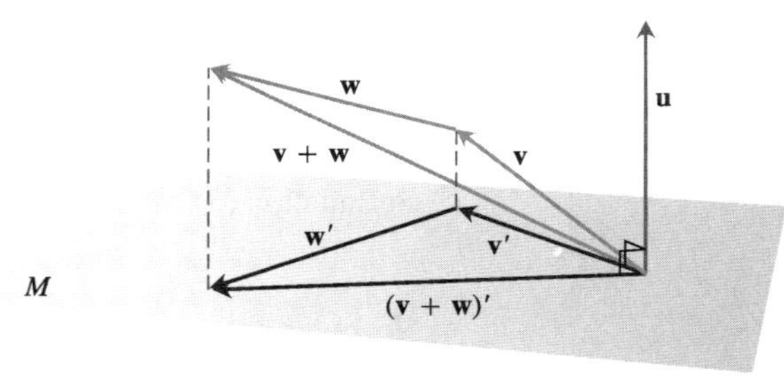

FIGURE A.11 The vectors, $\mathbf{v}$, $\mathbf{w}$, $\mathbf{v} + \mathbf{w}$, and their projections onto a plane perpendicular to $\mathbf{u}$.

3. A triangle whose sides are $|\mathbf{u}|\mathbf{v}''$, $|\mathbf{u}|\mathbf{w}''$, and $|\mathbf{u}|(\mathbf{v} + \mathbf{w})''$ satisfying the vector equation
$$|\mathbf{u}|\mathbf{v}'' + |\mathbf{u}|\mathbf{w}'' = |\mathbf{u}|(\mathbf{v} + \mathbf{w})''.$$

Substituting $|\mathbf{u}|\mathbf{v}'' = \mathbf{u} \times \mathbf{v}$, $|\mathbf{u}|\mathbf{w}'' = \mathbf{u} \times \mathbf{w}$, and $|\mathbf{u}|(\mathbf{v} + \mathbf{w})'' = \mathbf{u} \times (\mathbf{v} + \mathbf{w})$ from our discussion above into this last equation gives

$$\mathbf{u} \times \mathbf{v} + \mathbf{u} \times \mathbf{w} = \mathbf{u} \times (\mathbf{v} + \mathbf{w}),$$

which is the law we wanted to establish. ■

A.7 The Mixed Derivative Theorem and the Increment Theorem

This appendix derives the Mixed Derivative Theorem (Theorem 2, Section 14.3) and the Increment Theorem for Functions of Two Variables (Theorem 3, Section 14.3). Euler first published the Mixed Derivative Theorem in 1734, in a series of papers he wrote on hydrodynamics.

THEOREM 2 The Mixed Derivative Theorem
If $f(x, y)$ and its partial derivatives f_x, f_y, f_{xy}, and f_{yx} are defined throughout an open region containing a point (a, b) and are all continuous at (a, b), then $f_{xy}(a, b) = f_{yx}(a, b)$.

Proof The equality of $f_{xy}(a, b)$ and $f_{yx}(a, b)$ can be established by four applications of the Mean Value Theorem (Theorem 4, Section 4.2). By hypothesis, the point (a, b) lies in the interior of a rectangle R in the xy-plane on which f, f_x, f_y, f_{xy}, and f_{yx} are all defined. We let h and k be the numbers such that the point $(a + h, b + k)$ also lies in R, and we consider the difference

$$\Delta = F(a + h) - F(a), \tag{1}$$

where

$$F(x) = f(x, b + k) - f(x, b). \tag{2}$$

We apply the Mean Value Theorem to F, which is continuous because it is differentiable. Then Equation (1) becomes

$$\Delta = hF'(c_1), \tag{3}$$

where c_1 lies between a and $a + h$. From Equation (2).

$$F'(x) = f_x(x, b + k) - f_x(x, b),$$

so Equation (3) becomes

$$\Delta = h[f_x(c_1, b + k) - f_x(c_1, b)]. \tag{4}$$

Now we apply the Mean Value Theorem to the function $g(y) = f_x(c_1, y)$ and have

$$g(b + k) - g(b) = kg'(d_1),$$

or

$$f_x(c_1, b + k) - f_x(c_1, b) = kf_{xy}(c_1, d_1)$$

for some d_1 between b and $b + k$. By substituting this into Equation (4), we get

$$\Delta = hkf_{xy}(c_1, d_1) \tag{5}$$

for some point (c_1, d_1) in the rectangle R' whose vertices are the four points (a, b), $(a + h, b)$, $(a + h, b + k)$, and $(a, b + k)$. (See Figure A.12.)

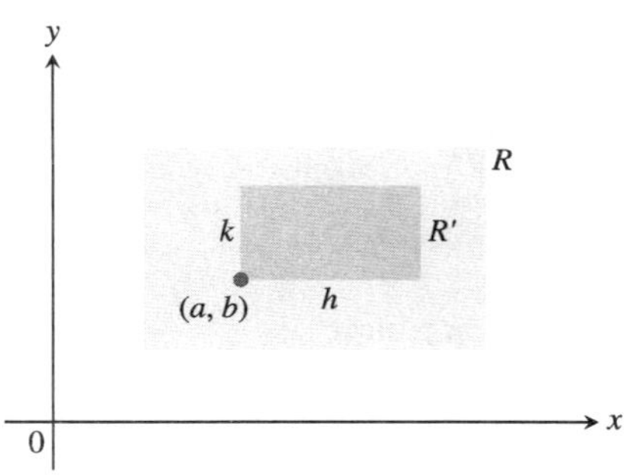

FIGURE A.12 The key to proving $f_{xy}(a, b) = f_{yx}(a, b)$ is that no matter how small R' is, f_{xy} and f_{yx} take on equal values somewhere inside R' (although not necessarily at the same point).

By substituting from Equation (2) into Equation (1), we may also write

$$\begin{aligned} \Delta &= f(a + h, b + k) - f(a + h, b) - f(a, b + k) + f(a, b) \\ &= [f(a + h, b + k) - f(a, b + k)] - [f(a + h, b) - f(a, b)] \\ &= \phi(b + k) - \phi(b), \end{aligned} \tag{6}$$

where

$$\phi(y) = f(a + h, y) - f(a, y). \tag{7}$$

The Mean Value Theorem applied to Equation (6) now gives

$$\Delta = k\phi'(d_2) \tag{8}$$

for some d_2 between b and $b + k$. By Equation (7),

$$\phi'(y) = f_y(a + h, y) - f_y(a, y). \tag{9}$$

Substituting from Equation (9) into Equation (8) gives

$$\Delta = k[f_y(a + h, d_2) - f_y(a, d_2)].$$

Finally, we apply the Mean Value Theorem to the expression in brackets and get

$$\Delta = khf_{yx}(c_2, d_2) \tag{10}$$

for some c_2 between a and $a + h$.

Together, Equations (5) and (10) show that

$$f_{xy}(c_1, d_1) = f_{yx}(c_2, d_2), \tag{11}$$

where (c_1, d_1) and (c_2, d_2) both lie in the rectangle R' (Figure A.12). Equation (11) is not quite the result we want, since it says only that f_{xy} has the same value at (c_1, d_1) that f_{yx} has at (c_2, d_2). The numbers h and k in our discussion, however, may be made as small as we wish. The hypothesis that f_{xy} and f_{yx} are both continuous at (a, b) means that $f_{xy}(c_1, d_1) = f_{xy}(a, b) + \epsilon_1$ and $f_{yx}(c_2, d_2) = f_{yx}(a, b) + \epsilon_2$, where each of $\epsilon_1, \epsilon_2 \to 0$ as both $h, k \to 0$. Hence, if we let h and $k \to 0$, we have $f_{xy}(a, b) = f_{yx}(a, b)$. ■

The equality of $f_{xy}(a, b)$ and $f_{yx}(a, b)$ can be proved with hypotheses weaker than the ones we assumed. For example, it is enough for f, f_x, and f_y to exist in R and for f_{xy} to be continuous at (a, b). Then f_{yx} will exist at (a, b) and equal f_{xy} at that point.

> **THEOREM 3 The Increment Theorem for Functions of Two Variables**
> Suppose that the first partial derivatives of $z = f(x, y)$ are defined throughout an open region R containing the point (x_0, y_0) and that f_x and f_y are continuous at (x_0, y_0). Then the change $\Delta z = f(x_0 + \Delta x, y_0 + \Delta y) - f(x_0, y_0)$ in the value of f that results from moving from (x_0, y_0) to another point $(x_0 + \Delta x, y_0 + \Delta y)$ in R satisfies an equation of the form
>
> $$\Delta z = f_x(x_0, y_0)\Delta x + f_y(x_0, y_0)\Delta y + \epsilon_1\Delta x + \epsilon_2\Delta y,$$
>
> in which each of $\epsilon_1, \epsilon_2 \to 0$ as both $\Delta x, \Delta y \to 0$.

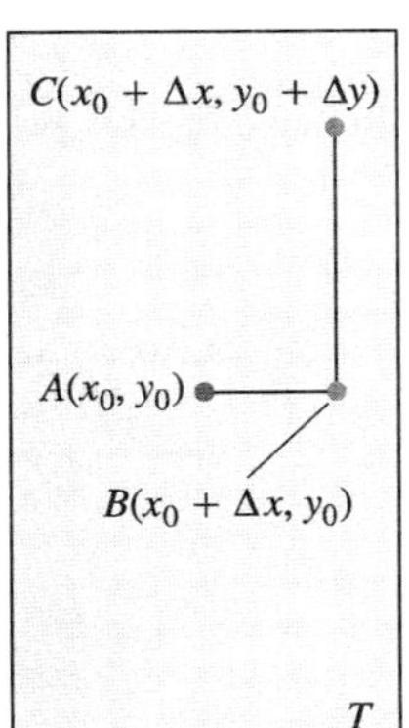

FIGURE A.13 The rectangular region T in the proof of the Increment Theorem. The figure is drawn for Δx and Δy positive, but either increment might be zero or negative.

Proof We work within a rectangle T centered at $A(x_0, y_0)$ and lying within R, and we assume that Δx and Δy are already so small that the line segment joining A to $B(x_0 + \Delta x, y_0)$ and the line segment joining B to $C(x_0 + \Delta x, y_0 + \Delta y)$ lie in the interior of T (Figure A.13).

We may think of Δz as the sum $\Delta z = \Delta z_1 + \Delta z_2$ of two increments, where

$$\Delta z_1 = f(x_0 + \Delta x, y_0) - f(x_0, y_0)$$

is the change in the value of f from A to B and

$$\Delta z_2 = f(x_0 + \Delta x, y_0 + \Delta y) - f(x_0 + \Delta x, y_0)$$

is the change in the value of f from B to C (Figure A.14).

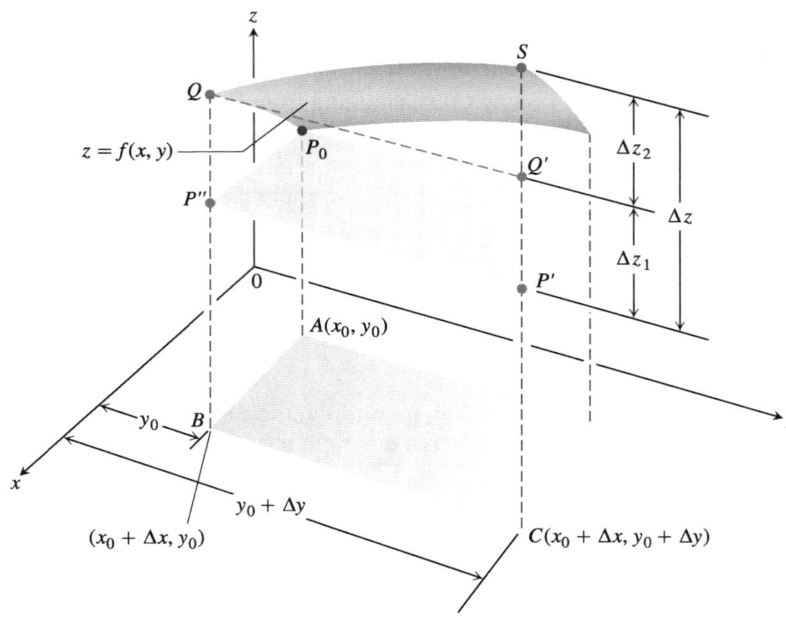

FIGURE A.14 Part of the surface $z = f(x, y)$ near $P_0(x_0, y_0, f(x_0, y_0))$. The points P_0, P', and P'' have the same height $z_0 = f(x_0, y_0)$ above the xy-plane. The change in z is $\Delta z = P'S$. The change

$$\Delta z_1 = f(x_0 + \Delta x, y_0) - f(x_0, y_0),$$

shown as $P''Q = P'Q'$, is caused by changing x from x_0 to $x_0 + \Delta x$ while holding y equal to y_0. Then, with x held equal to $x_0 + \Delta x$,

$$\Delta z_2 = f(x_0 + \Delta x, y_0 + \Delta y) - f(x_0 + \Delta x, y_0)$$

is the change in z caused by changing y_0 from $y_0 + \Delta y$, which is represented by $Q'S$? The total change in z is the sum of Δz_1 and Δz_2.

On the closed interval of x-values joining x_0 to $x_0 + \Delta x$, the function $F(x) = f(x, y_0)$ is a differentiable (and hence continuous) function of x, with derivative

$$F'(x) = f_x(x, y_0).$$

By the Mean Value Theorem (Theorem 4, Section 4.2), there is an x-value c between x_0 and $x_0 + \Delta x$ at which

$$F(x_0 + \Delta x) - F(x_0) = F'(c)\Delta x$$

or

$$f(x_0 + \Delta x, y_0) - f(x_0, y_0) = f_x(c, y_0)\Delta x$$

or

$$\Delta z_1 = f_x(c, y_0)\Delta x. \tag{12}$$

Similarly, $G(y) = f(x_0 + \Delta x, y)$ is a differentiable (and hence continuous) function of y on the closed y-interval joining y_0 and $y_0 + \Delta y$, with derivative

$$G'(y) = f_y(x_0 + \Delta x, y).$$

Hence, there is a y-value d between y_0 and $y_0 + \Delta y$ at which

$$G(y_0 + \Delta y) - G(y_0) = G'(d)\Delta y$$

or

$$f(x_0 + \Delta x, y_0 + \Delta y) - f(x_0 + \Delta x, y) = f_y(x_0 + \Delta x, d)\Delta y$$

or

$$\Delta z_2 = f_y(x_0 + \Delta x, d)\Delta y. \tag{13}$$

Now, as both Δx and $\Delta y \to 0$, we know that $c \to x_0$ and $d \to y_0$. Therefore, since f_x and f_y are continuous at (x_0, y_0), the quantities

$$\begin{aligned} \epsilon_1 &= f_x(c, y_0) - f_x(x_0, y_0), \\ \epsilon_2 &= f_y(x_0 + \Delta x, d) - f_y(x_0, y_0) \end{aligned} \tag{14}$$

both approach zero as both Δx and $\Delta y \to 0$.

Finally,

$$\begin{aligned} \Delta z &= \Delta z_1 + \Delta z_2 \\ &= f_x(c, y_0)\Delta x + f_y(x_0 + \Delta x, d)\Delta y && \text{From Equations (12) and (13)} \\ &= [f_x(x_0, y_0) + \epsilon_1]\Delta x + [f_y(x_0, y_0) + \epsilon_2]\Delta y && \text{From Equation (14)} \\ &= f_x(x_0, y_0)\Delta x + f_y(x_0, y_0)\Delta y + \epsilon_1\Delta x + \epsilon_2\Delta y, \end{aligned}$$

where both ϵ_1 and $\epsilon_2 \to 0$ as both Δx and $\Delta y \to 0$, which is what we set out to prove. ■

Analogous results hold for functions of any finite number of independent variables. Suppose that the first partial derivatives of $w = f(x, y, z)$ are defined throughout an open region containing the point (x_0, y_0, z_0) and that f_x, f_y, and f_z are continuous at (x_0, y_0, z_0). Then

$$\begin{aligned} \Delta w &= f(x_0 + \Delta x, y_0 + \Delta y, z_0 + \Delta z) - f(x_0, y_0, z_0) \\ &= f_x\Delta x + f_y\Delta y + f_z\Delta z + \epsilon_1\Delta x + \epsilon_2\Delta y + \epsilon_3\Delta z, \end{aligned} \tag{15}$$

where $\epsilon_1, \epsilon_2, \epsilon_3 \to 0$ as Δx, Δy, and $\Delta z \to 0$.

The partial derivatives f_x, f_y, f_z in Equation (15) are to be evaluated at the point (x_0, y_0, z_0).

Equation (15) can be proved by treating Δw as the sum of three increments,

$$\Delta w_1 = f(x_0 + \Delta x, y_0, z_0) - f(x_0, y_0, z_0) \tag{16}$$

$$\Delta w_2 = f(x_0 + \Delta x, y_0 + \Delta y, z_0) - f(x_0 + \Delta x, y_0, z_0) \tag{17}$$

$$\Delta w_3 = f(x_0 + \Delta x, y_0 + \Delta y, z_0 + \Delta z) - f(x_0 + \Delta x, y_0 + \Delta y, z_0), \tag{18}$$

and applying the Mean Value Theorem to each of these separately. Two coordinates remain constant and only one varies in each of these partial increments $\Delta w_1, \Delta w_2, \Delta w_3$. In Equation (17), for example, only y varies, since x is held equal to $x_0 + \Delta x$ and z is held equal to z_0. Since $f(x_0 + \Delta x, y, z_0)$ is a continuous function of y with a derivative f_y, it is subject to the Mean Value Theorem, and we have

$$\Delta w_2 = f_y(x_0 + \Delta x, y_1, z_0)\Delta y$$

for some y_1 between y_0 and $y_0 + \Delta y$.

A.8 The Area of a Parallelogram's Projection on a Plane

This appendix proves the result needed in Section 16.5 that $|(\mathbf{u} \times \mathbf{v}) \cdot \mathbf{p}|$ is the area of the projection of the parallelogram with sides determined by $\mathbf{u}$ and $\mathbf{v}$ onto any plane whose normal is $\mathbf{p}$. (See Figure A.15.)

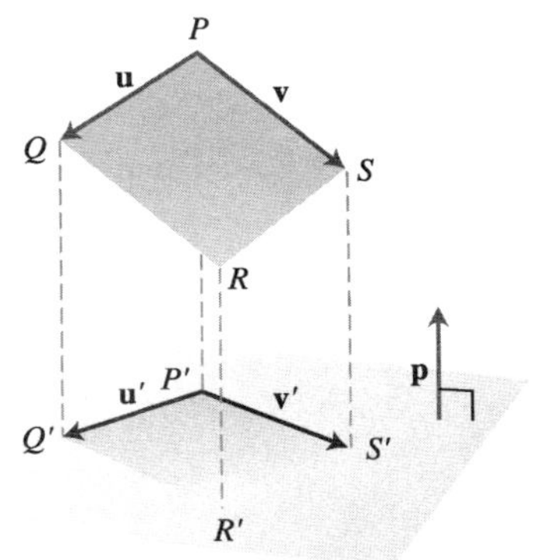

FIGURE A.15 The parallelogram determined by two vectors $\mathbf{u}$ and $\mathbf{v}$ in space and the orthogonal projection of the parallelogram onto a plane. The projection lines, orthogonal to the plane, lie parallel to the unit normal vector $\mathbf{p}$.

THEOREM

The area of the orthogonal projection of the parallelogram determined by two vectors $\mathbf{u}$ and $\mathbf{v}$ in space onto a plane with unit normal vector $\mathbf{p}$ is

$$\text{Area} = |(\mathbf{u} \times \mathbf{v}) \cdot \mathbf{p}|.$$

Proof In the notation of Figure A.15, which shows a typical parallelogram determined by vectors $\mathbf{u}$ and $\mathbf{v}$ and its orthogonal projection onto a plane with unit normal vector $\mathbf{p}$,

$$\begin{aligned}\mathbf{u} &= \overrightarrow{PP'} + \mathbf{u}' + \overrightarrow{Q'Q} \\ &= \mathbf{u}' + \overrightarrow{PP'} - \overrightarrow{QQ'} && (\overrightarrow{Q'Q} = -\overrightarrow{QQ'}) \\ &= \mathbf{u}' + s\mathbf{p}. && \text{(For some scalar } s \text{ because } (\overrightarrow{PP'} - \overrightarrow{QQ'}) \text{ is parallel to } \mathbf{p})\end{aligned}$$

Similarly,

$$\mathbf{v} = \mathbf{v}' + t\mathbf{p}$$

for some scalar t. Hence,

$$\begin{aligned}\mathbf{u} \times \mathbf{v} &= (\mathbf{u}' + s\mathbf{p}) \times (\mathbf{v}' + t\mathbf{p}) \\ &= (\mathbf{u}' \times \mathbf{v}') + s(\mathbf{p} \times \mathbf{v}') + t(\mathbf{u}' \times \mathbf{p}) + st\underbrace{(\mathbf{p} \times \mathbf{p})}_{0}. \end{aligned} \tag{1}$$

The vectors $\mathbf{p} \times \mathbf{v}'$ and $\mathbf{u}' \times \mathbf{p}$ are both orthogonal to $\mathbf{p}$. Hence, when we dot both sides of Equation (1) with $\mathbf{p}$, the only nonzero term on the right is $(\mathbf{u}' \times \mathbf{v}') \cdot \mathbf{p}$. That is,

$$(\mathbf{u} \times \mathbf{v}) \cdot \mathbf{p} = (\mathbf{u}' \times \mathbf{v}') \cdot \mathbf{p}.$$

In particular,

$$|(\mathbf{u} \times \mathbf{v}) \cdot \mathbf{p}| = |(\mathbf{u}' \times \mathbf{v}') \cdot \mathbf{p}|. \tag{2}$$

The absolute value on the right is the volume of the box determined by $\mathbf{u}'$, $\mathbf{v}'$, and $\mathbf{p}$. The height of this particular box is $|\mathbf{p}| = 1$, so the box's volume is numerically the same as its base area, the area of parallelogram $P'Q'R'S'$. Combining this observation with Equation (2) gives

$$\text{Area of } P'Q'R'S' = |(\mathbf{u}' \times \mathbf{v}') \cdot \mathbf{p}| = |(\mathbf{u} \times \mathbf{v}) \cdot \mathbf{p}|,$$

which says that the area of the orthogonal projection of the parallelogram determined by $\mathbf{u}$ and $\mathbf{v}$ onto a plane with unit normal vector $\mathbf{p}$ is $|(\mathbf{u} \times \mathbf{v}) \cdot \mathbf{p}|$. This is what we set out to prove. ■

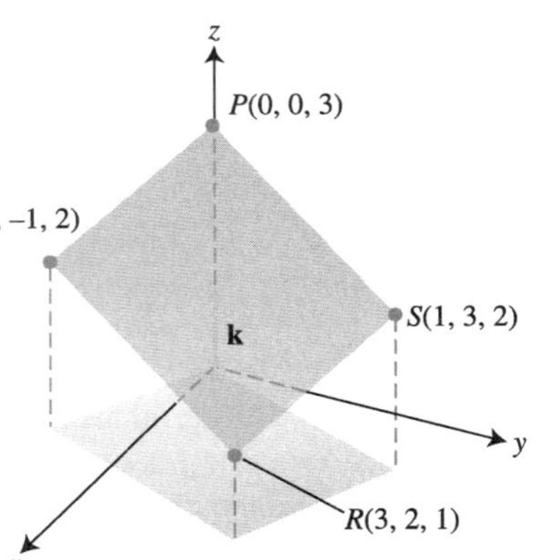

FIGURE A.16 Example 1 calculates the area of the orthogonal projection of parallelogram $PQRS$ on the xy-plane.

EXAMPLE 1 Finding the Area of a Projection

Find the area of the orthogonal projection onto the xy-plane of the parallelogram determined by the points $P(0, 0, 3)$, $Q(2, -1, 2)$, $R(3, 2, 1)$, and $S(1, 3, 2)$ (Figure A.16).

Solution With

$$\mathbf{u} = \overrightarrow{PQ} = 2\mathbf{i} - \mathbf{j} - \mathbf{k}, \qquad \mathbf{v} = \overrightarrow{PS} = \mathbf{i} + 3\mathbf{j} - \mathbf{k}, \qquad \text{and} \qquad \mathbf{p} = \mathbf{k},$$

we have

$$(\mathbf{u} \times \mathbf{v}) \cdot \mathbf{p} = \begin{vmatrix} 2 & -1 & -1 \\ 1 & 3 & -1 \\ 0 & 0 & 1 \end{vmatrix} = \begin{vmatrix} 2 & -1 \\ 1 & 3 \end{vmatrix} = 7,$$

so the area is $|(\mathbf{u} \times \mathbf{v}) \cdot \mathbf{p}| = |7| = 7$. ■

A.9 Basic Algebra, Geometry, and Trigonometry Formulas

Algebra

Arithmetic Operations

$$a(b + c) = ab + ac, \qquad \frac{a}{b} \cdot \frac{c}{d} = \frac{ac}{bd}$$

$$\frac{a}{b} + \frac{c}{d} = \frac{ad + bc}{bd}, \qquad \frac{a/b}{c/d} = \frac{a}{b} \cdot \frac{d}{c}$$

Laws of Signs

$$-(-a) = a, \qquad \frac{-a}{b} = -\frac{a}{b} = \frac{a}{-b}$$

Zero Division by zero is not defined.

$$\text{If } a \neq 0\text{:}\ \frac{0}{a} = 0, \quad a^0 = 1, \quad 0^a = 0$$

$$\text{For any number } a\text{:}\ a \cdot 0 = 0 \cdot a = 0$$

Laws of Exponents

$$a^m a^n = a^{m+n}, \qquad (ab)^m = a^m b^m, \qquad (a^m)^n = a^{mn}, \qquad a^{m/n} = \sqrt[n]{a^m} = \left(\sqrt[n]{a}\right)^m$$

If $a \neq 0$,

$$\frac{a^m}{a^n} = a^{m-n}, \quad a^0 = 1, \quad a^{-m} = \frac{1}{a^m}.$$

The Binomial Theorem For any positive integer n,

$$(a + b)^n = a^n + na^{n-1}b + \frac{n(n-1)}{1 \cdot 2} a^{n-2}b^2 + \frac{n(n-1)(n-2)}{1 \cdot 2 \cdot 3} a^{n-3}b^3 + \cdots + nab^{n-1} + b^n.$$

For instance,

$$(a+b)^2 = a^2 + 2ab + b^2, \qquad (a-b)^2 = a^2 - 2ab + b^2$$

$$(a+b)^3 = a^3 + 3a^2b + 3ab^2 + b^3, \qquad (a-b)^3 = a^2 - 3a^2b + 3ab^2 - b^3.$$

Factoring the Difference of Like Integer Powers, $n > 1$

$$a^n - b^n = (a-b)(a^{n-1} + a^{n-2}b + a^{n-3}b^2 + \cdots + ab^{n-2} + b^{n-1})$$

For instance,

$$a^2 - b^2 = (a-b)(a+b),$$
$$a^3 - b^3 = (a-b)(a^2 + ab + b^2),$$
$$a^4 - b^4 = (a-b)(a^3 + a^2b + ab^2 + b^3).$$

Completing the Square If $a \neq 0$,

$$ax^2 + bx + c = a\left(x^2 + \frac{b}{a}x\right) + c$$

$$= a\left(x^2 + \frac{b}{a}x + \frac{b^2}{4a^2} - \frac{b^2}{4a^2}\right) + c$$

$$= a\left(x^2 + \frac{b}{a}x + \frac{b^2}{4a^2}\right) + a\left(-\frac{b^2}{4a^2}\right) + c$$

$$= \underbrace{a\left(x^2 + \frac{b}{a}x + \frac{b^2}{4a^2}\right)}_{\text{This is } \left(x + \frac{b}{2a}\right)^2.} + \underbrace{c - \frac{b^2}{4a}}_{\text{Call this part } C.}$$

$$= au^2 + C \qquad (u = x + (b/2a))$$

The Quadratic Formula If $a \neq 0$ and $ax^2 + bx + c = 0$, then

$$x = \frac{-b \pm \sqrt{b^2 - 4ac}}{2a}.$$

Geometry

Formulas for area, circumference, and volume: (A = area, B = area of base, C = circumference, S = lateral area or surface area, V = volume)

Triangle

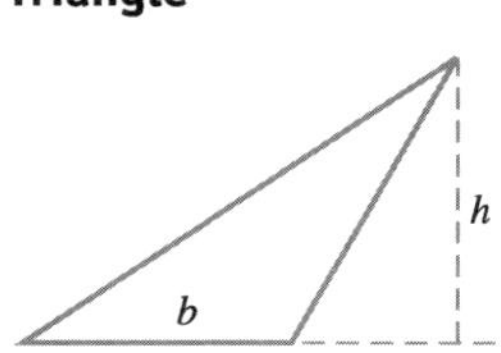

$$A = \frac{1}{2}bh$$

Similar Triangles

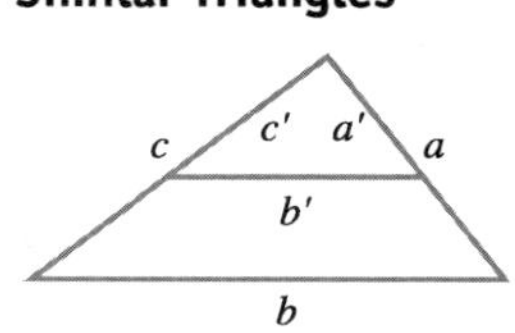

$$\frac{a'}{a} = \frac{b'}{b} = \frac{c'}{c}$$

Pythagorean Theorem

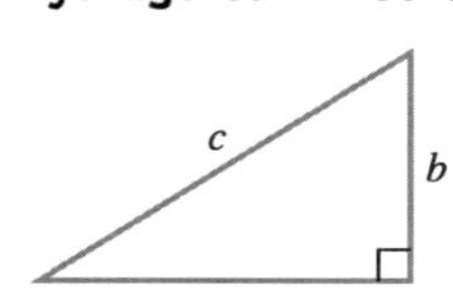

$$a^2 + b^2 = c^2$$

Parallelogram

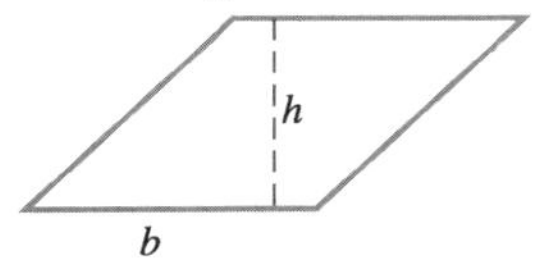

$A = bh$

Trapezoid

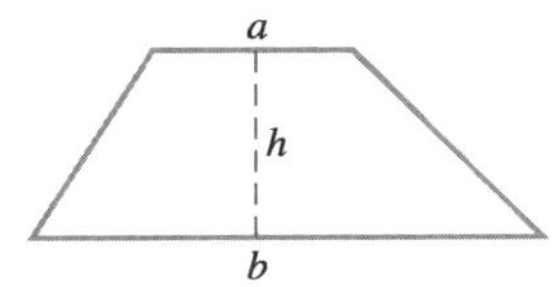

$A = \frac{1}{2}(a + b)h$

Circle

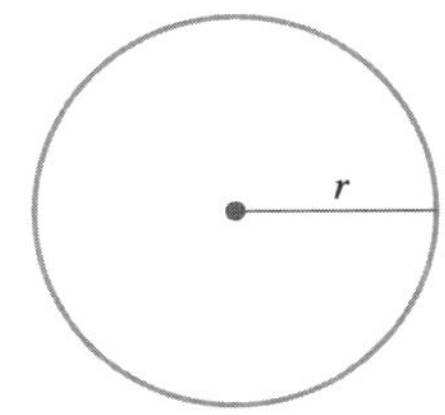

$A = \pi r^2,$
$C = 2\pi r$

Any Cylinder or Prism with Parallel Bases

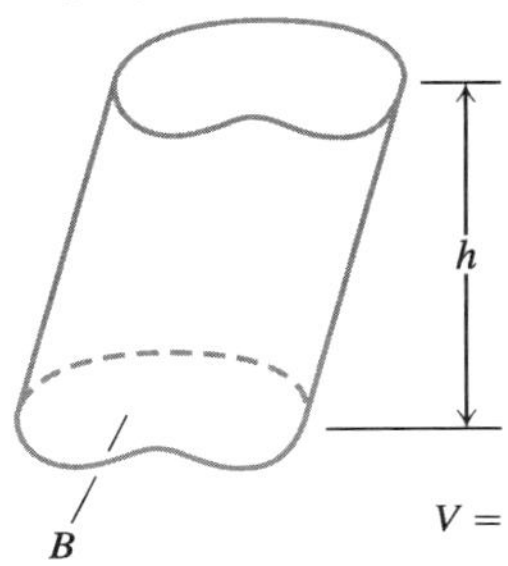

$V = Bh$

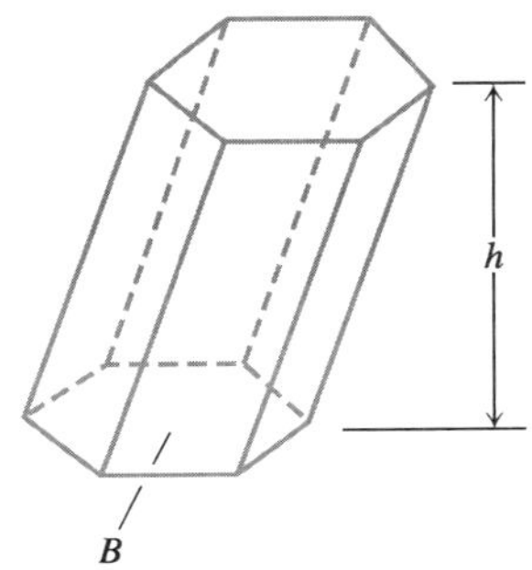

Right Circular Cylinder

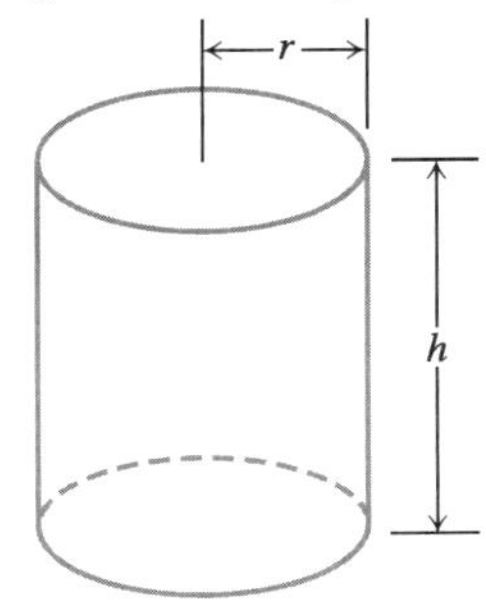

$V = \pi r^2 h$
$S = 2\pi rh =$ Area of side

Any Cone or Pyramid

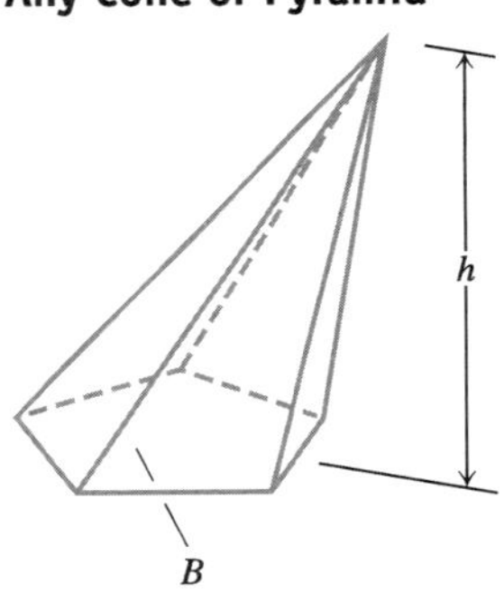

$V = \frac{1}{3}Bh$

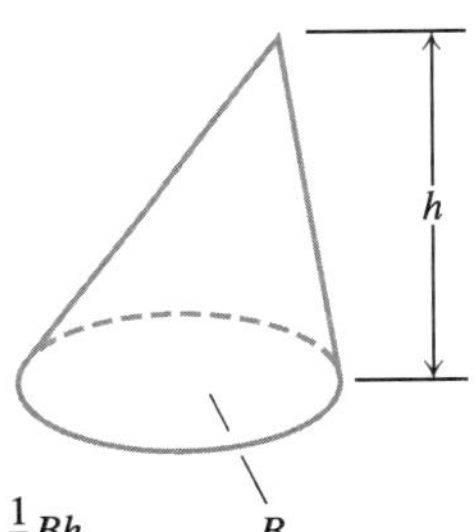

Right Circular Cone

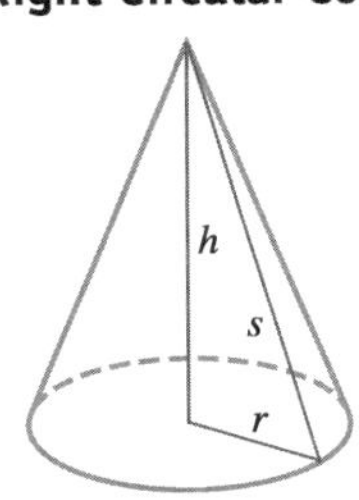

$V = \frac{1}{3}\pi r^2 h$
$S = \pi rs =$ Area of side

Sphere

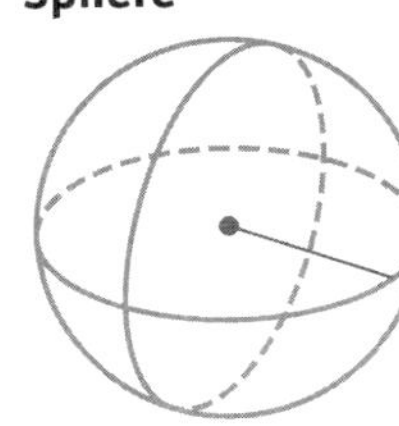

$V = \frac{4}{3}\pi r^3, S = 4\pi r^2$

Trigonometry Formulas

Definitions and Fundamental Identities

Sine: $\sin\theta = \frac{y}{r} = \frac{1}{\csc\theta}$

Cosine: $\cos\theta = \frac{x}{r} = \frac{1}{\sec\theta}$

Tangent: $\tan\theta = \frac{y}{x} = \frac{1}{\cot\theta}$

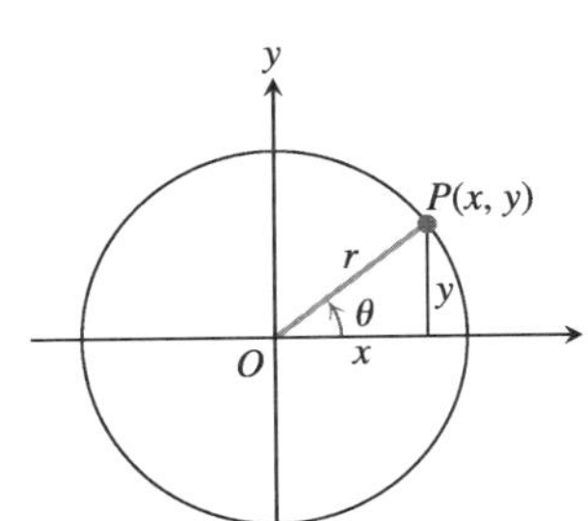

Identities

$\sin(-\theta) = -\sin\theta, \quad \cos(-\theta) = \cos\theta$

$\sin^2\theta + \cos^2\theta = 1, \quad \sec^2\theta = 1 + \tan^2\theta, \quad \csc^2\theta = 1 + \cot^2\theta$

$\sin 2\theta = 2\sin\theta\cos\theta, \quad \cos 2\theta = \cos^2\theta - \sin^2\theta$

$\cos^2\theta = \dfrac{1 + \cos 2\theta}{2}, \quad \sin^2\theta = \dfrac{1 - \cos 2\theta}{2}$

$\sin(A + B) = \sin A\cos B + \cos A\sin B$

$\sin(A - B) = \sin A\cos B - \cos A\sin B$

$\cos(A + B) = \cos A\cos B - \sin A\sin B$

$\cos(A - B) = \cos A\cos B + \sin A\sin B$

$\tan(A + B) = \dfrac{\tan A + \tan B}{1 - \tan A\tan B}, \qquad \tan(A - B) = \dfrac{\tan A - \tan B}{1 + \tan A\tan B}$

$\sin\left(A - \dfrac{\pi}{2}\right) = -\cos A, \qquad \cos\left(A - \dfrac{\pi}{2}\right) = \sin A$

$\sin\left(A + \dfrac{\pi}{2}\right) = \cos A, \qquad \cos\left(A + \dfrac{\pi}{2}\right) = -\sin A$

$\sin A\sin B = \dfrac{1}{2}\cos(A - B) - \dfrac{1}{2}\cos(A + B)$

$\cos A\cos B = \dfrac{1}{2}\cos(A - B) + \dfrac{1}{2}\cos(A + B)$

$\sin A\cos B = \dfrac{1}{2}\sin(A - B) + \dfrac{1}{2}\sin(A + B)$

$\sin A + \sin B = 2\sin\dfrac{1}{2}(A + B)\cos\dfrac{1}{2}(A - B)$

$\sin A - \sin B = 2\cos\dfrac{1}{2}(A + B)\sin\dfrac{1}{2}(A - B)$

$\cos A + \cos B = 2\cos\dfrac{1}{2}(A + B)\cos\dfrac{1}{2}(A - B)$

$\cos A - \cos B = -2\sin\dfrac{1}{2}(A + B)\sin\dfrac{1}{2}(A - B)$

Trigonometric Functions

Radian Measure

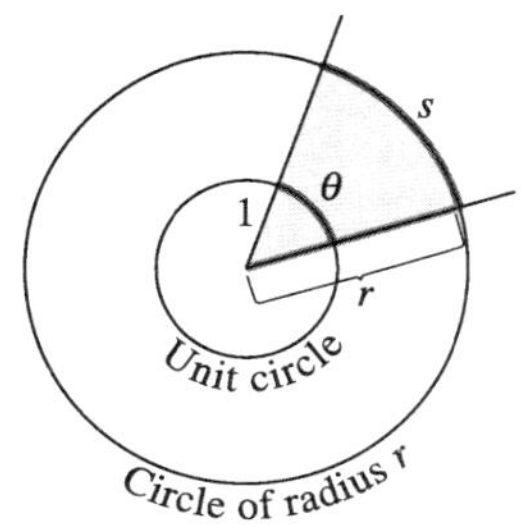

$$\frac{s}{r} = \frac{\theta}{1} = \theta \quad \text{or} \quad \theta = \frac{s}{r},$$

$180° = \pi$ radians.

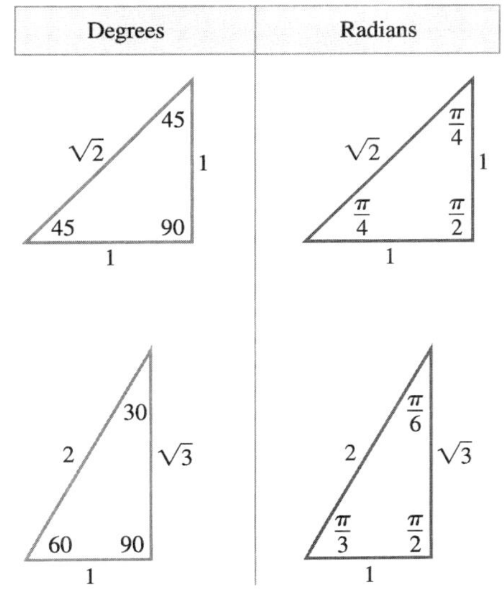

The angles of two common triangles, in degrees and radians.

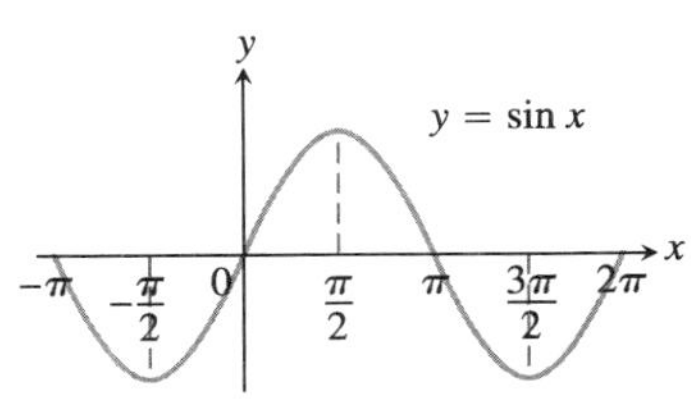

Domain: $(-\infty, \infty)$
Range: $[-1, 1]$

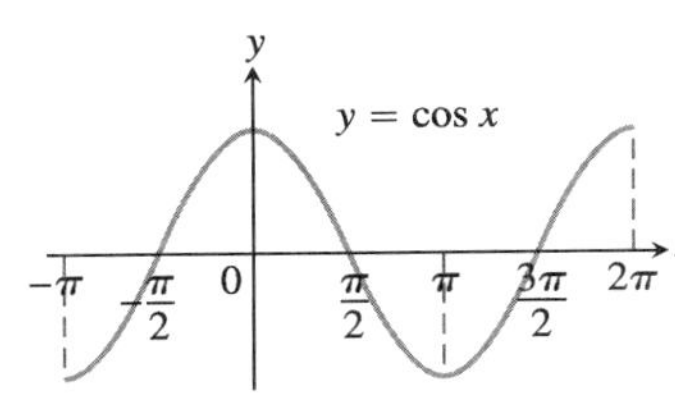

Domain: $(-\infty, \infty)$
Range: $[-1, 1]$

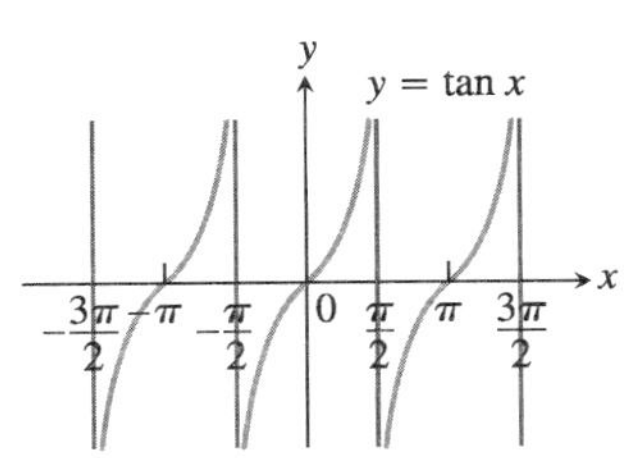

Domain: All real numbers except odd integer multiples of $\pi/2$
Range: $(-\infty, \infty)$

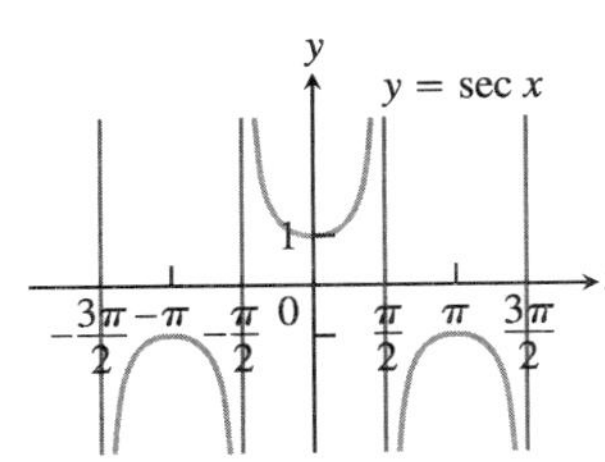

Domain: $x \neq \pm\frac{\pi}{2}, \pm\frac{3\pi}{2}, \ldots$
Range: $(-\infty, -1] \cup [1, \infty)$

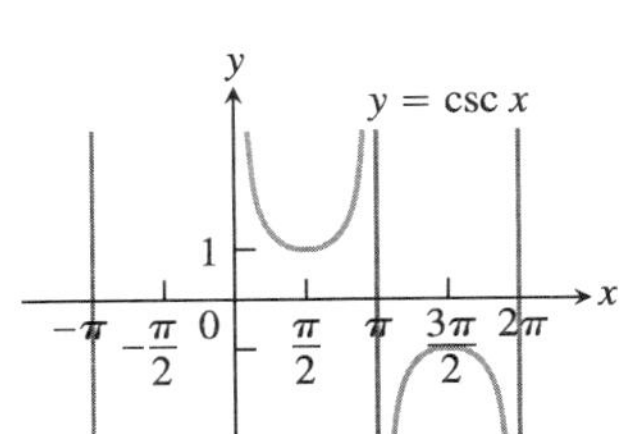

Domain: $x \neq 0, \pm\pi, \pm 2\pi, \ldots$
Range: $(-\infty, -1] \cup [1, \infty)$

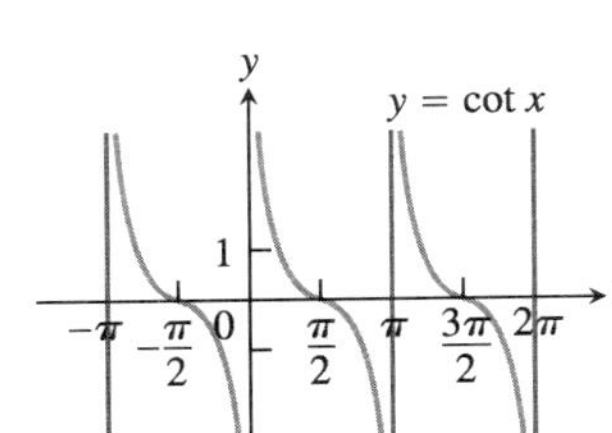

Domain: $x \neq 0, \pm\pi, \pm 2\pi, \ldots$
Range: $(-\infty, \infty)$

ANSWERS

CHAPTER 1

Section 1.1, pp. 7–8

1. $0.\bar{1}, 0.\bar{2}, 0.\bar{3}, 0.\bar{8}, 0.\bar{9}$ or 1

3. **(a)** Not necessarily true **(b)** True **(c)** True **(d)** True **(e)** True **(f)** True **(g)** True **(h)** True

5. $x < -2$

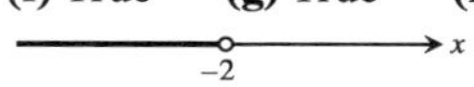

7. $x \le \frac{5}{4}$

9. $x \le -\frac{1}{3}$

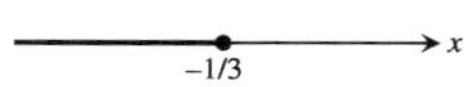

11. $x < -\frac{6}{7}$

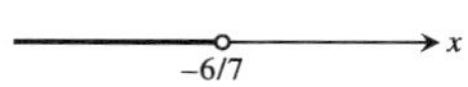

13. ± 3 **15.** $-\frac{1}{2}, -\frac{9}{2}$ **17.** $\frac{7}{6}, \frac{25}{6}$

19. $-2 < x < 2$

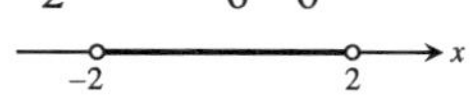

21. $-2 \le t \le 4$

23. $1 < y < \frac{11}{3}$

25. $0 \le z \le 10$

27. $\frac{2}{7} < x < \frac{2}{5}$ or $\frac{10}{35} < x < \frac{14}{35}$

29. $(-\infty, -2] \cup [2, \infty)$

31. $(-\infty, 0) \cup (2, \infty)$

33. $(-\infty, -3] \cup [1, \infty)$

35. $(-\sqrt{2}, \sqrt{2})$ **37.** $(-3, -2) \cup (2, 3)$ **39.** $(-1, 3)$

41. $(0, 1)$ **43.** $a \ge 0$; any negative real number

47. $-\frac{1}{2} < x \le 3$

Section 1.2, pp. 16–19

1. $2, -4; 2\sqrt{5}$ **3.** $-4.9, 0; 4.9$ **5.** Unit circle

7. The circle centered at the origin with points less than a radius of $\sqrt{3}$ and its interior

9. $m_{\perp} = -\frac{1}{3}$

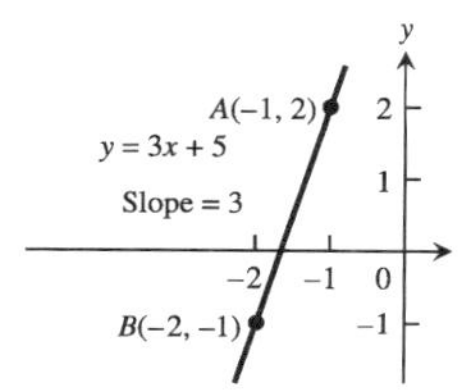

11. $m_{\perp}$ is undefined.

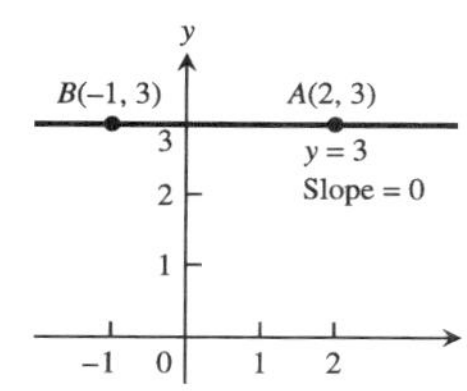

13. **(a)** $x = -1$ **(b)** $y = 4/3$

15. **(a)** $x = 0$ **(b)** $y = -\sqrt{2}$

17. $y = -x$ **19.** $y = -\frac{x}{5} + \frac{23}{5}$ **21.** $y = -\frac{5}{4}x + 6$

23. $y = -9$ **25.** $y = 4x + 4$ **27.** $y = -\frac{2}{5}x + 1$

29. $y = -\frac{x}{2} + 12$

31. x-intercept $= 4$, y-intercept $= 3$

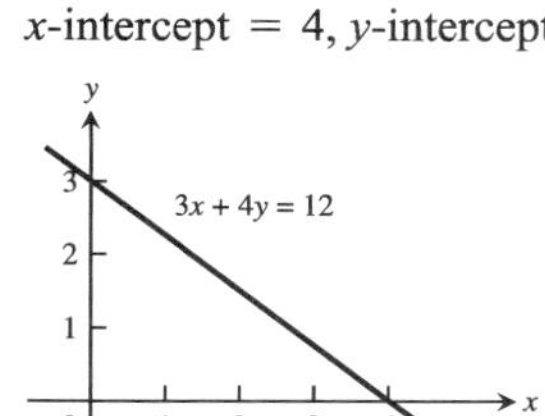

33. x-intercept $= \sqrt{3}$, y-intercept $= -\sqrt{2}$

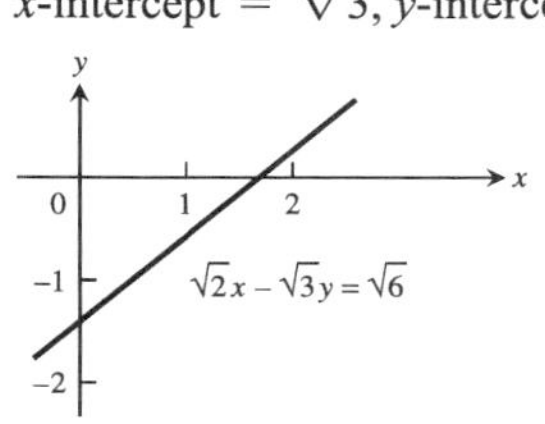

35. Yes. The lines are perpendicular because their slopes, $-A/B$ and B/A, are negative reciprocals of one another.

37. $(3, -3)$ **39.** $(-2, -9)$

41. $x^2 + (y - 2)^2 = 4$

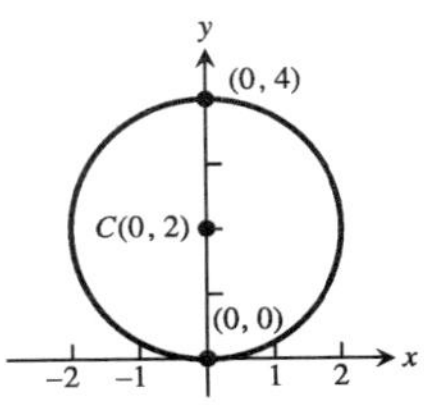

43. $(x + 1)^2 + (y - 5)^2 = 10$

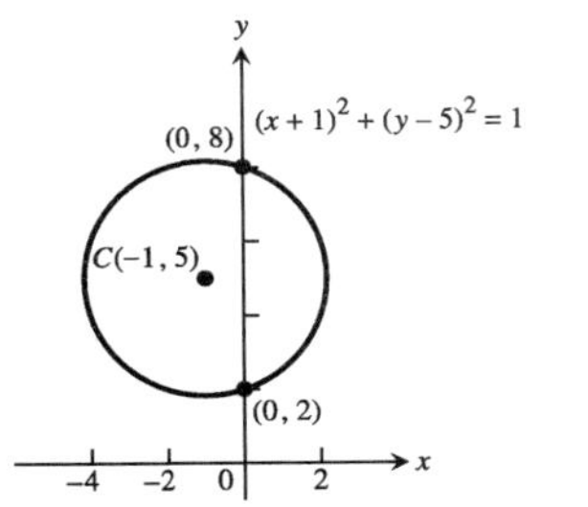

45. $(x + \sqrt{3})^2 + (y + 2)^2 = 4$

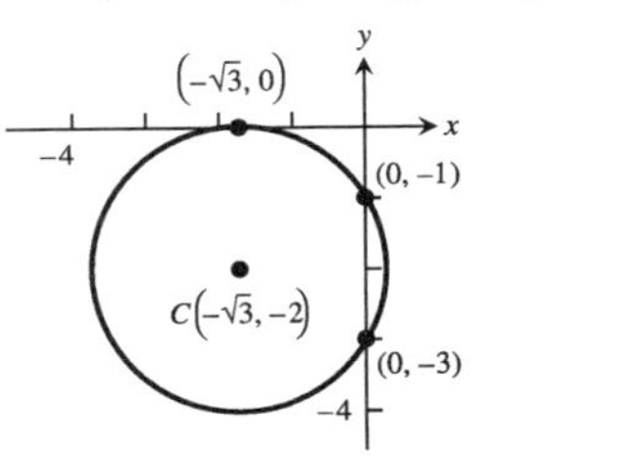

47. $(x + 2)^2 + (y - 2)^2 = 4$

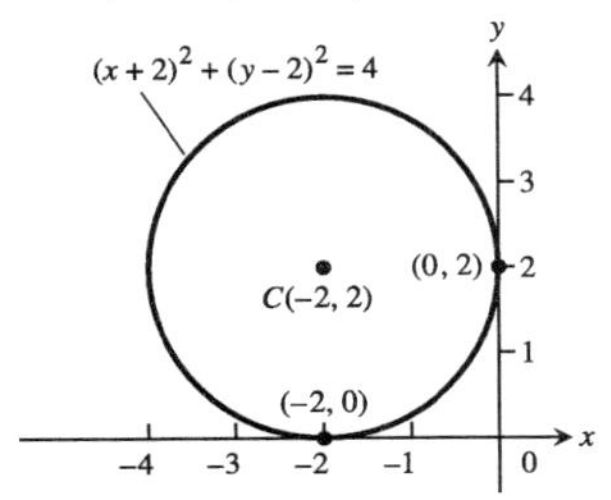

49. $x^2 + (y - 3/2)^2 = 25/4$

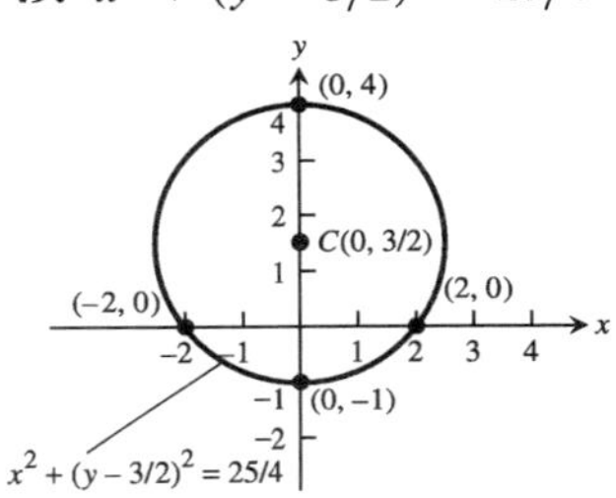

51. $(x - 2)^2 + (y + 2)^2 = 8$

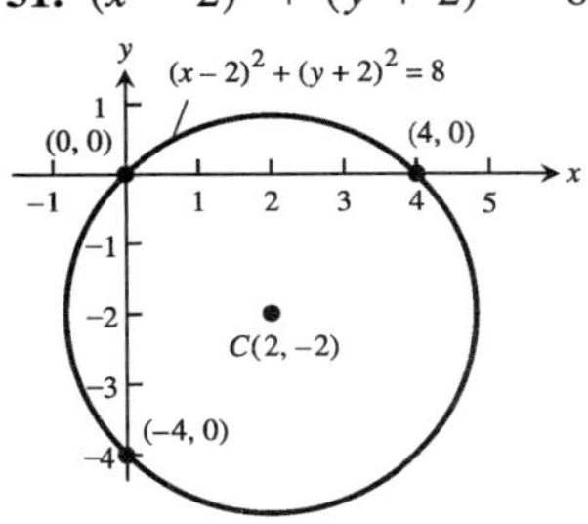

53.

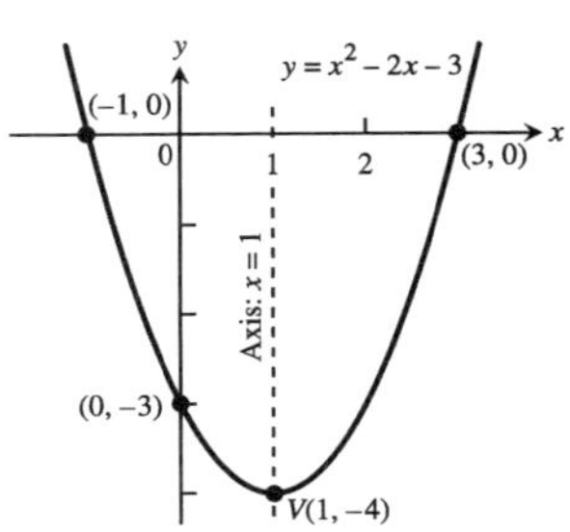

55.

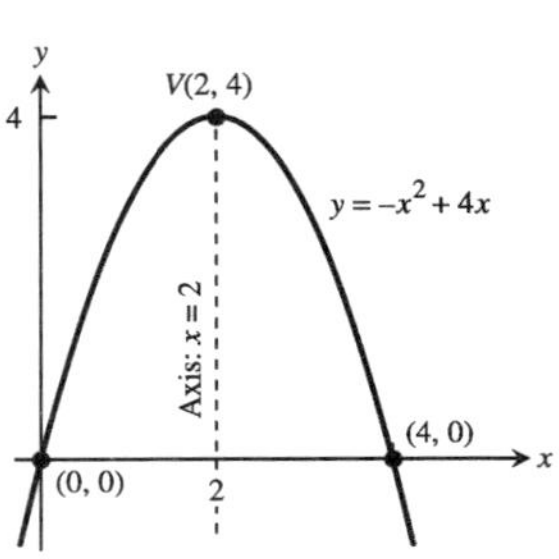

57.

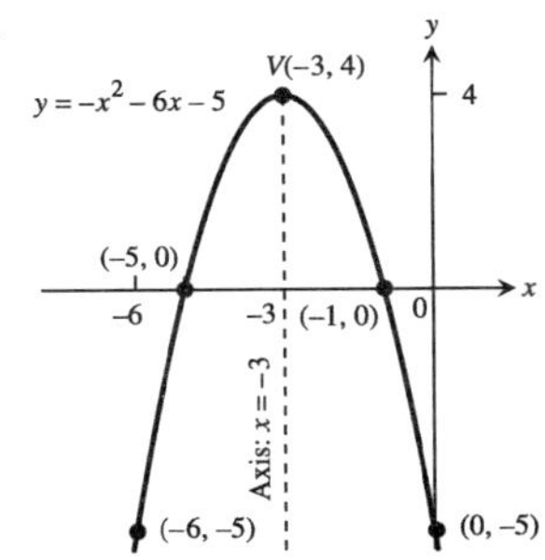

59.

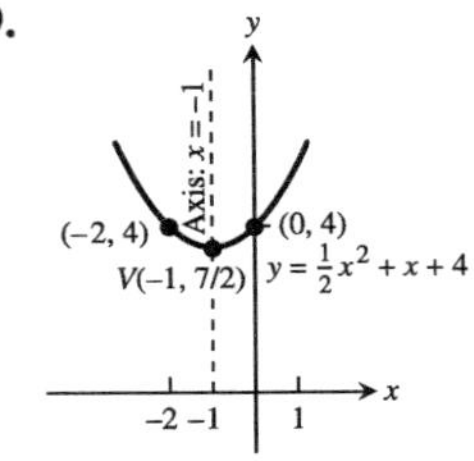

61. Exterior points of a circle of radius $\sqrt{7}$, centered at the origin

63. A circle of radius 2, centered at (1, 0), together with its interior

65. The washer between the circles $x^2 + y^2 = 1$ and $x^2 + y^2 = 4$ (points with distance from the origin between 1 and 2)

67. The interior points of a circle centered at $(0, -3)$ with a radius of 3 that lie above the line $y = -3$

69. $(x + 2)^2 + (y - 1)^2 < 6$ **71.** $x^2 + y^2 \le 2, \quad x \ge 1$

73. $\left(\frac{1}{\sqrt{5}}, \frac{2}{\sqrt{5}}\right), \quad \left(-\frac{1}{\sqrt{5}}, -\frac{2}{\sqrt{5}}\right)$

75. $\left(\frac{1 - \sqrt{5}}{2}, \frac{3 - \sqrt{5}}{2}\right), \quad \left(\frac{1 + \sqrt{5}}{2}, \frac{3 + \sqrt{5}}{2}\right)$

77. $\left(-\frac{1}{\sqrt{3}}, -\frac{1}{3}\right), \quad \left(\frac{1}{\sqrt{3}}, -\frac{1}{3}\right)$

79. $\left(\frac{1}{2}, -\frac{\sqrt{3}}{2}\right), \quad \left(\frac{1}{2}, \frac{\sqrt{3}}{2}\right)$

81. **(a)** ≈ -2.5 degrees/inch **(b)** ≈ -16.1 degrees/inch **(c)** ≈ -8.3 degrees/inch **83.** 5.97 atm

85. Yes: $C = F = -40°$

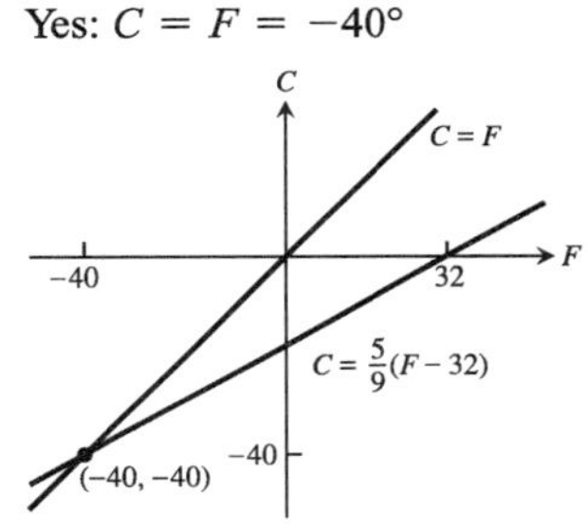

91.

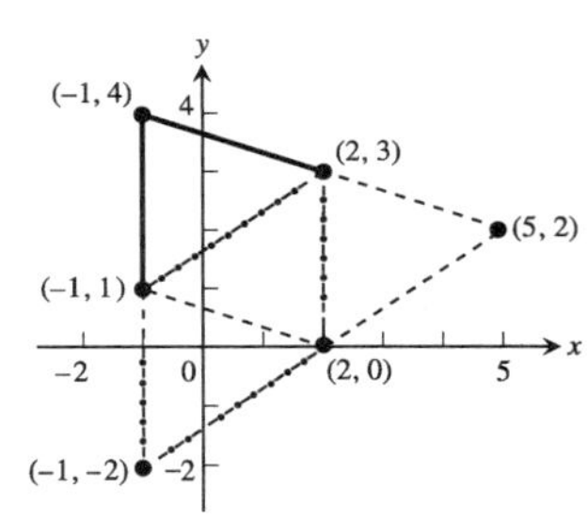

93. $k = -8, \quad k = 1/2$

Section 1.3, pp. 26–28

1. $D: (-\infty, \infty), \quad R: [1, \infty)$ **3.** $D: (0, \infty), \quad R: (0, \infty)$

5. $D: [-2, 2], \quad R: [0, 2]$

7. **(a)** Not a function of *x* because some values of *x* have two values of *y* **(b)** A function of *x* because for every *x* there is only one possible *y*

9. **(a)** No **(b)** No **(c)** No **(d)** $(0, 1]$

11. $A = \dfrac{\sqrt{3}}{4}x^2, \quad p = 3x$

13. $x = \dfrac{d}{\sqrt{3}}, \quad A = 2d^2, \quad V = \dfrac{d^3}{3\sqrt{3}}$

15. $(-\infty, \infty)$

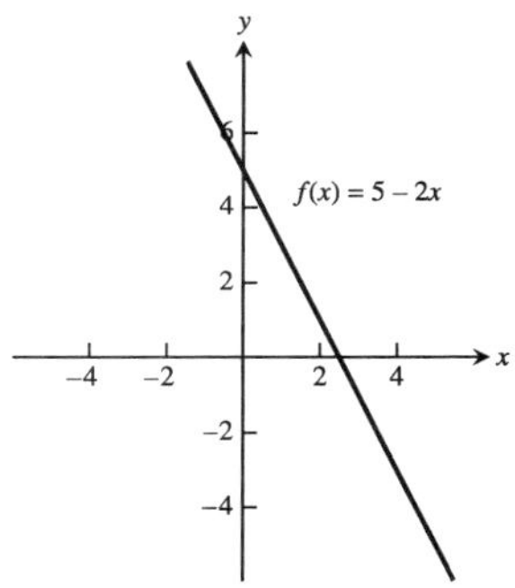

17. $(-\infty, \infty)$

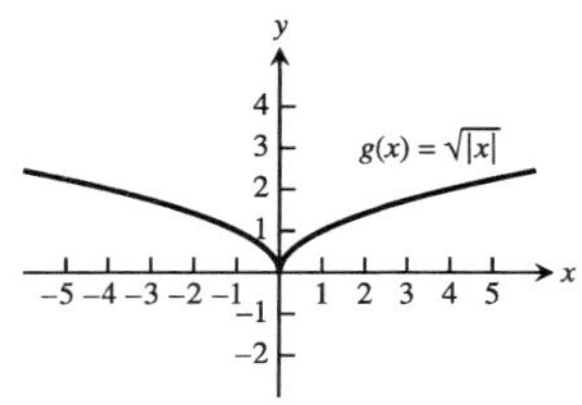

19. $(-\infty, 0) \cup (0, \infty)$

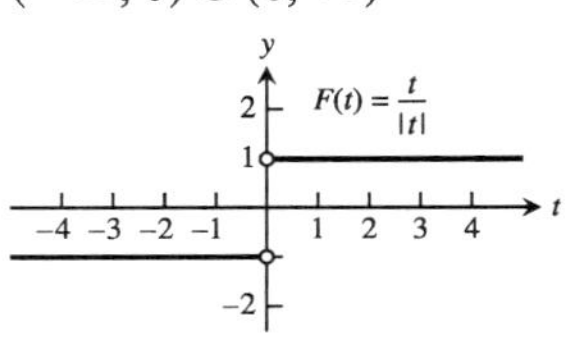

21. **(a)** For each positive value of *x*, there are two values of *y*.

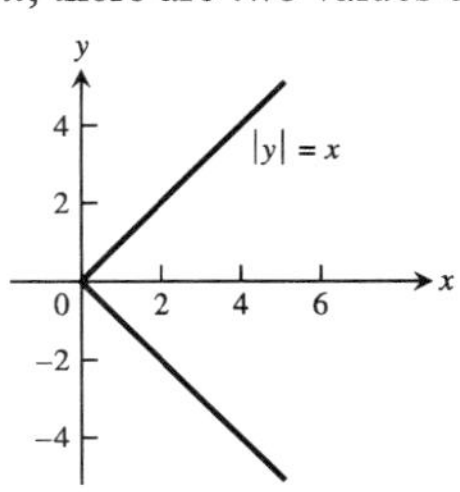

(b) For each value of $x \neq 0$, there are two values of *y*.

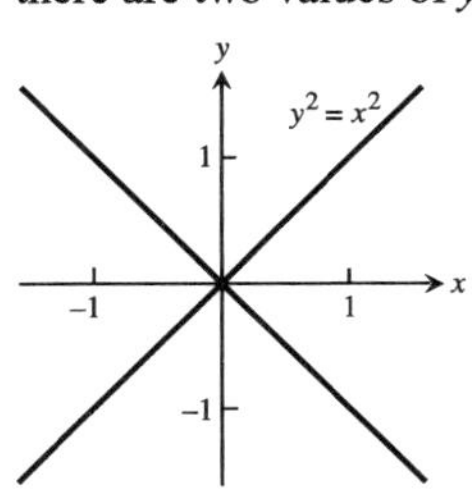

23.

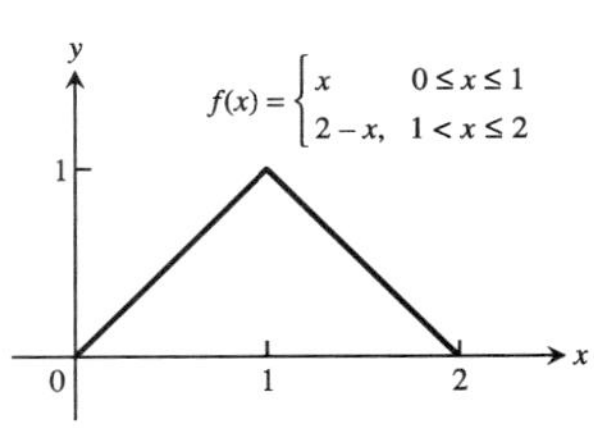

25.

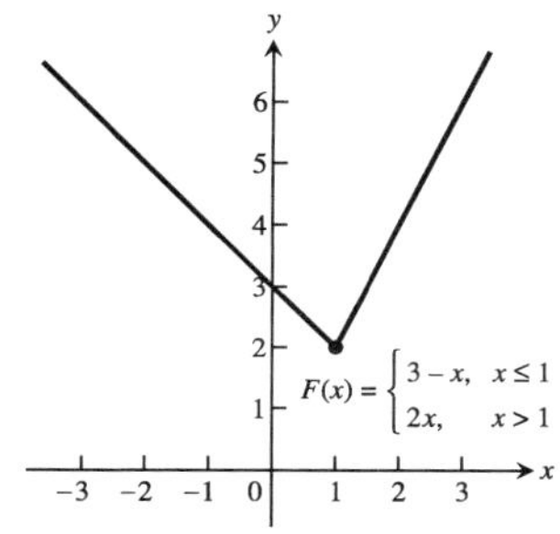

27. **(a)** $f(x) = \begin{cases} x, & 0 \le x \le 1 \\ -x + 2, & 1 < x \le 2 \end{cases}$

(b) $f(x) = \begin{cases} 2, & 0 \le x < 1 \\ 0, & 1 \le x < 2 \\ 2, & 2 \le x < 3 \\ 0, & 3 \le x \le 4 \end{cases}$

29. **(a)** $f(x) = \begin{cases} -x, & -1 \le x < 0 \\ 1, & 0 < x \le 1 \\ -\frac{1}{2}x + \frac{3}{2}, & 1 < x < 3 \end{cases}$

(b) $f(x) = \begin{cases} \frac{1}{2}x, & -2 \le x \le 0 \\ -2x + 2, & 0 < x \le 1 \\ -1, & 1 < x \le 3 \end{cases}$

31. **(a)** $(-2, 0) \cup (4, \infty)$

33. **(a)** $0 \le x < 1$ **(b)** $-1 < x \le 0$

35. Yes **37.** $V = x(14 - 2x)(22 - 2x)$

39. **(a)** Because the circumference of the original circle was 8π and a piece of length *x* was removed

(b) $r = \dfrac{8\pi - x}{2\pi} = 4 - \dfrac{x}{2\pi}$

(c) $h = \sqrt{16 - r^2} = \dfrac{\sqrt{16\pi x - x^2}}{2\pi}$

(d) $V = \dfrac{1}{3}\pi r^2 h = \dfrac{(8\pi - x)^2\sqrt{16\pi x - x^2}}{24\pi^2}$

Section 1.4, pp. 37–38

1. **(a)** linear, algebraic, polynomial of degree 1 **(b)** power, algebraic **(c)** rational, algebraic **(d)** exponential

3. **(a)** rational, algebraic **(b)** algebraic **(c)** trigonometric **(d)** logarithmic

5. **(a)** *h* **(b)** *f* **(c)** *g*

7. Symmetric about the origin

Dec. $-\infty < x < \infty$

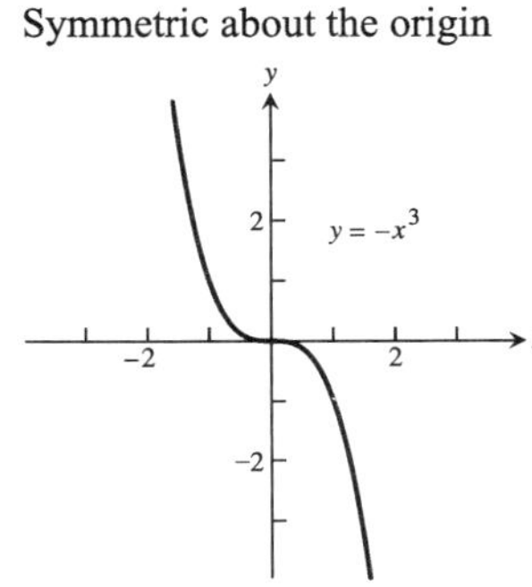

9. Symmetric about the origin

Inc. $-\infty < x < 0$ and $0 < x < \infty$

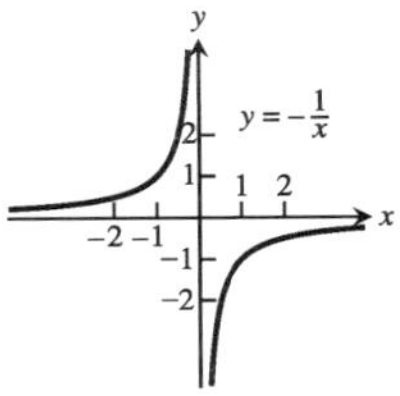

11. Symmetric about the y-axis

Dec. $-\infty < x \leq 0$;
inc. $0 \leq x < \infty$

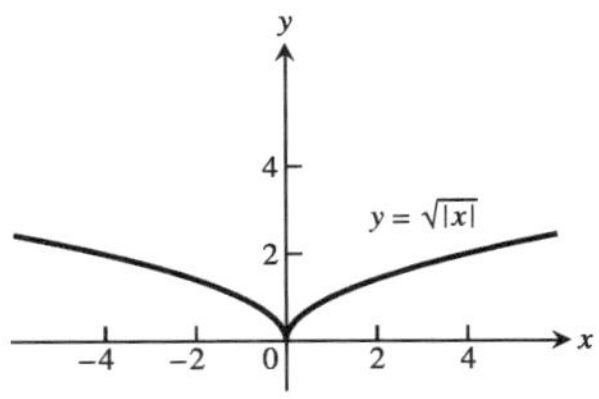

13. Symmetric about the origin

Inc. $-\infty < x < \infty$

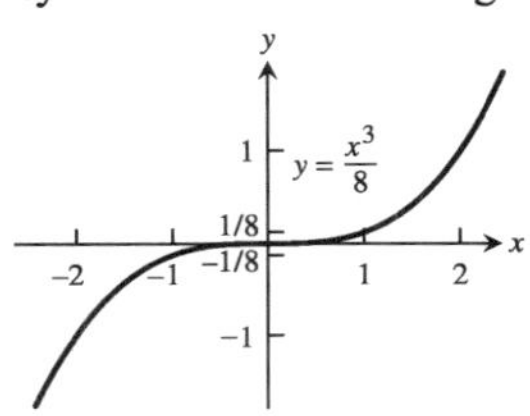

15. No symmetry

Dec. $0 \leq x < \infty$

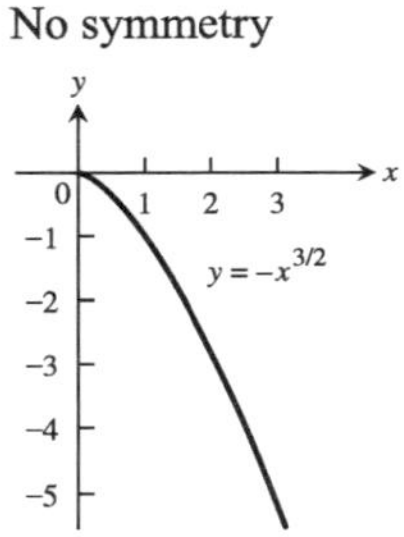

17. Symmetric about the y-axis

Dec. $-\infty < x \leq 0$;
inc. $0 \leq x < \infty$

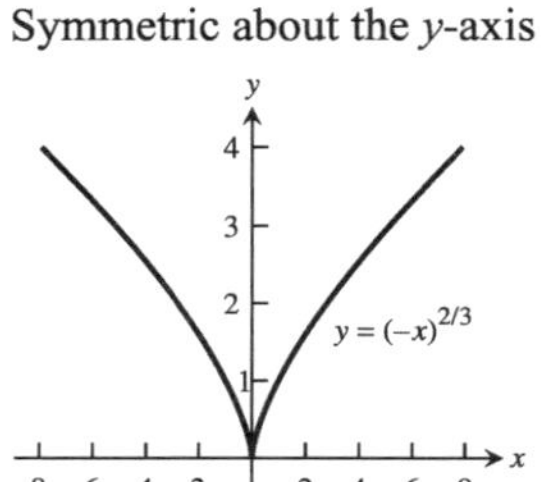

19. Even **21.** Even **23.** Odd **25.** Even **27.** Neither
29. Neither

31. (a) The graph supports the assumption that y is proportional to x. The constant of proportionality is estimated from the slope of the line, which is 0.166.

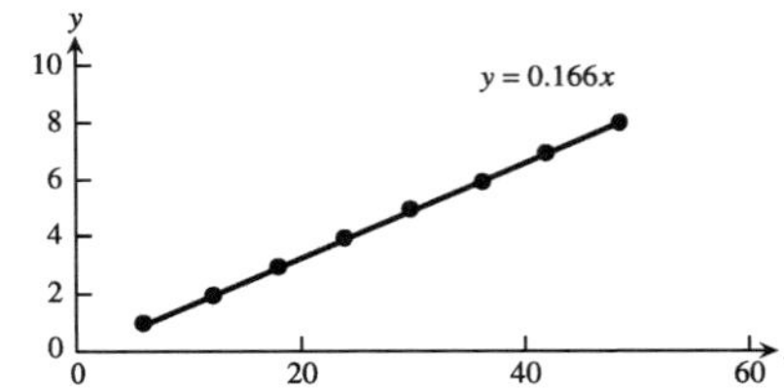

(b) The graph supports the assumption that y is proportional to $x^{1/2}$. The constant of proportionality is estimated from the slope of the line, which is 2.03.

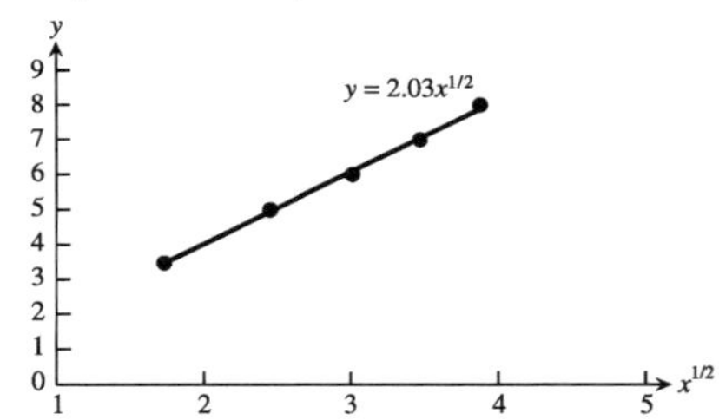

33. (a) $k \approx 1.1$ **(b)** $k \approx 0.059$

35. (a)

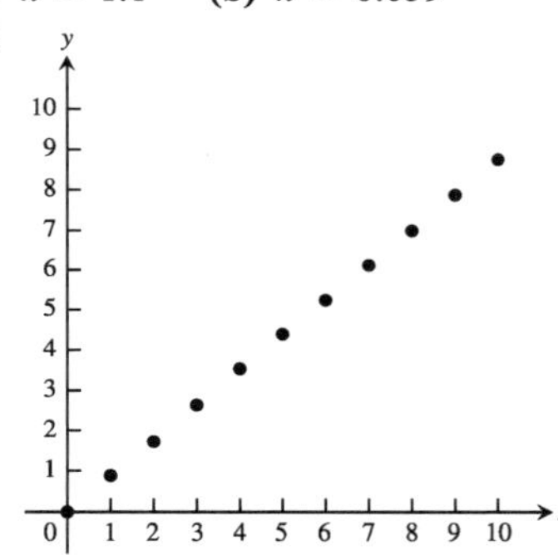

(b) $k \approx 0.87$
(c) Using $y = 0.87x$ with $x = 13$, we get $y = 11.31$.

Section 1.5, pp. 45–48

1. $D_f: -\infty < x < \infty$, $D_g: x \geq 1$, $R_f: -\infty < y < \infty$, $R_g: y \geq 0$, $D_{f+g} = D_{f\cdot g} = D_g$, $R_{f+g}: y \geq 1$, $R_{f\cdot g}: y \geq 0$

3. $D_f: -\infty < x < \infty$, $D_g: -\infty < x < \infty$, $R_f: y = 2$, $R_g: y \geq 1$, $D_{f/g}: -\infty < x < \infty$, $R_{f/g}: 0 < y \leq 2$, $D_{g/f}: -\infty < x < \infty$, $R_{g/f}: y \geq 1/2$

5. (a) 2 **(b)** 22 **(c)** $x^2 + 2$ **(d)** $x^2 + 10x + 22$ **(e)** 5 **(f)** -2 **(g)** $x + 10$ **(h)** $x^4 - 6x^2 + 6$

7. (a) $\dfrac{4}{x^2} - 5$ **(b)** $\dfrac{4}{x^2} - 5$ **(c)** $\left(\dfrac{4}{x} - 5\right)^2$ **(d)** $\left(\dfrac{1}{4x - 5}\right)^2$

(e) $\dfrac{1}{4x^2 - 5}$ **(f)** $\dfrac{1}{(4x - 5)^2}$

9. **(a)** $f(g(x))$ **(b)** $j(g(x))$ **(c)** $g(g(x))$ **(d)** $j(j(x))$
(e) $g(h(f(x)))$ **(f)** $h(j(f(x)))$

11.

	$g(x)$	$f(x)$	$f \circ g(x)$
(a)	$x - 7$	$\sqrt{x}$	$\sqrt{x - 7}$
(b)	$x + 2$	$3x$	$3x + 6$
(c)	x^2	$\sqrt{x - 5}$	$\sqrt{x^2 - 5}$
(d)	$\dfrac{x}{x - 1}$	$\dfrac{x}{x - 1}$	x
(e)	$\dfrac{1}{x - 1}$	$1 + \dfrac{1}{x}$	x
(f)	$\dfrac{1}{x}$	$\dfrac{1}{x}$	x

13. **(a)** $f(g(x)) = \sqrt{\dfrac{1}{x} + 1}, g(f(x)) = \dfrac{1}{\sqrt{x + 1}}$

(b) $D_{f \circ g} = (0, \infty), D_{g \circ f} = (-1, \infty)$

(c) $R_{f \circ g} = (1, \infty), R_{g \circ f} = (0, \infty)$

15. **(a)** $y = -(x + 7)^2$ **(b)** $y = -(x - 4)^2$

17. **(a)** Position 4 **(b)** Position 1 **(c)** Position 2 **(d)** Position 3

19. $(x + 2)^2 + (y + 3)^2 = 49$

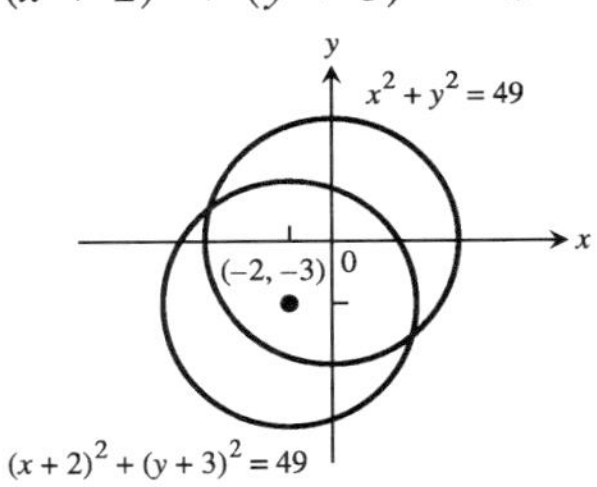

21. $y + 1 = (x + 1)^3$

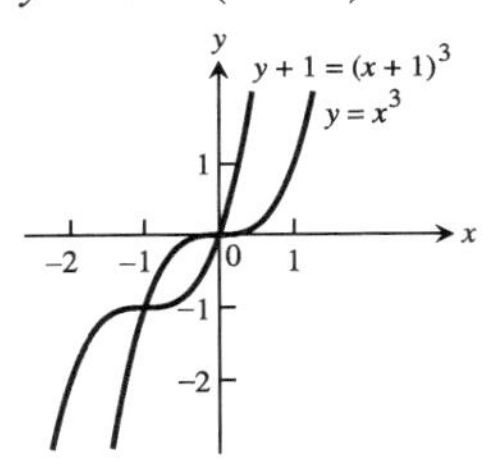

23. $y = \sqrt{x + 0.81}$

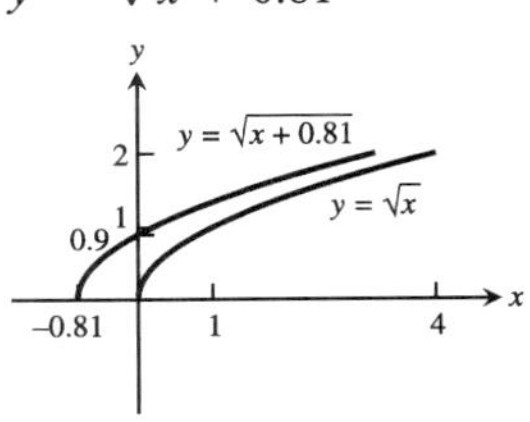

25. $y = 2x$

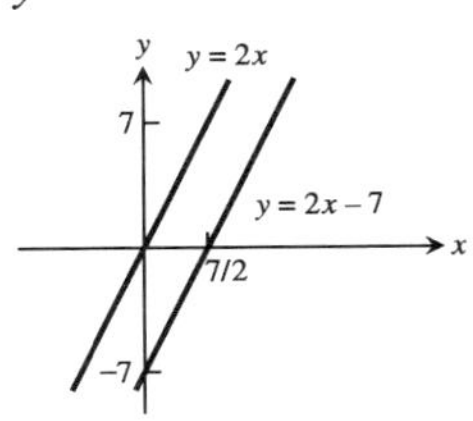

27. $y - 1 = \dfrac{1}{x - 1}$

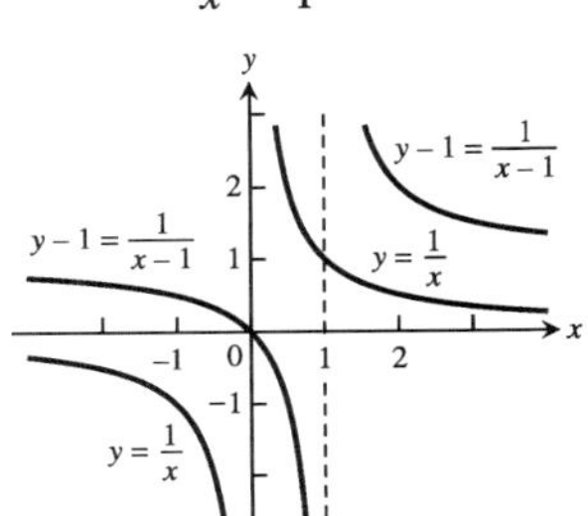

29.

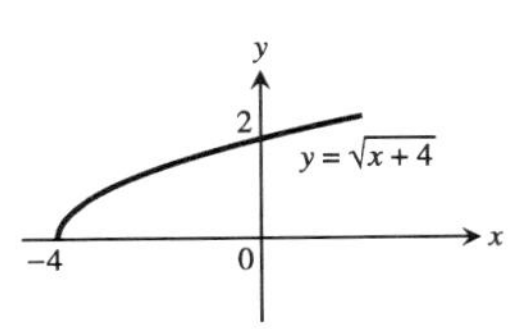

31.

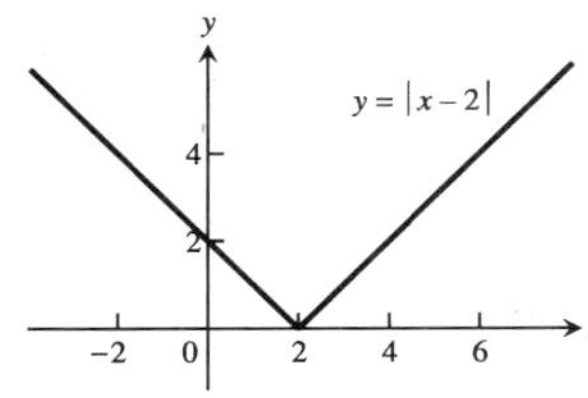

33.

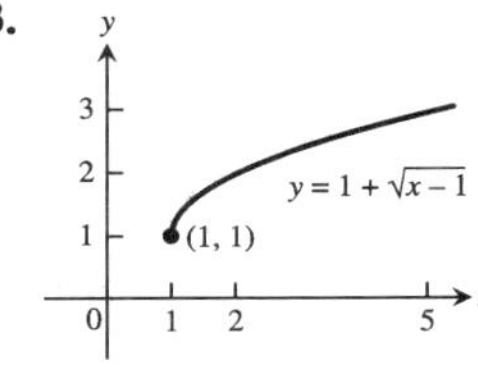

35.

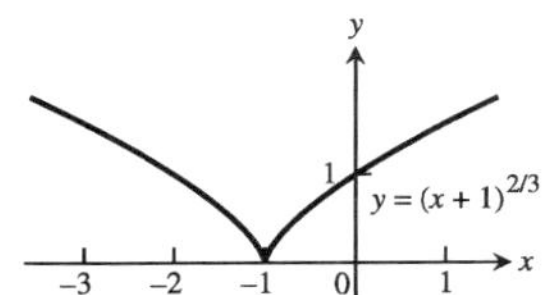

37.

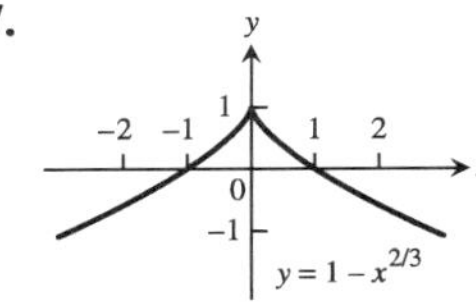

39.

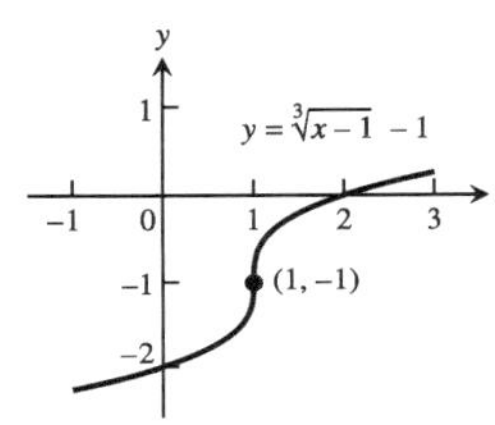

41.

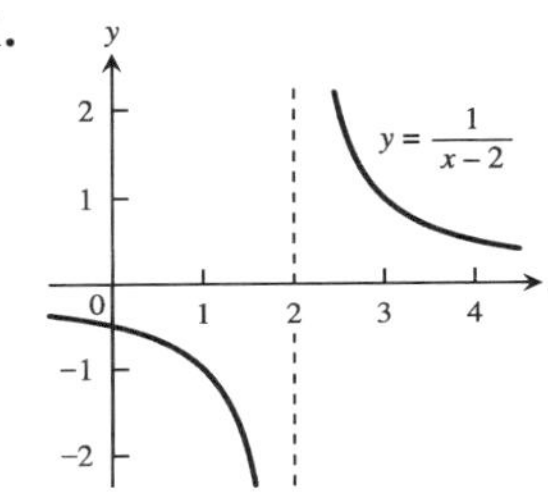

43.

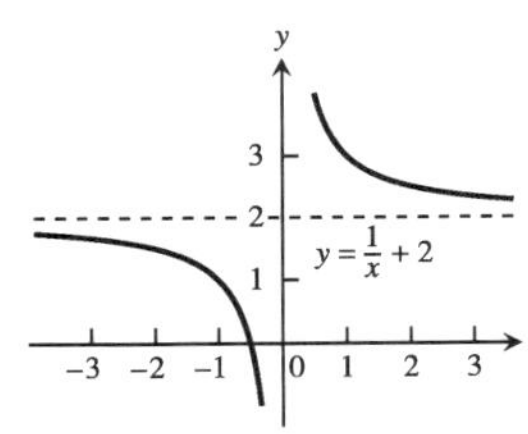

45.

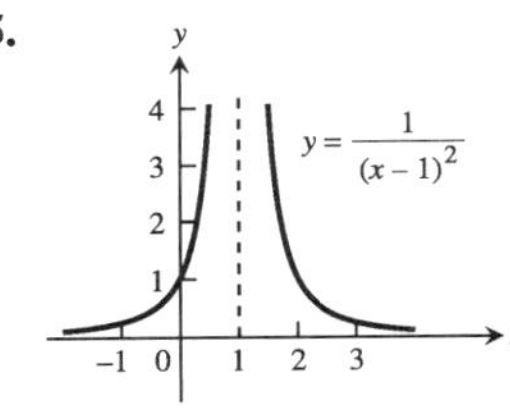

47.

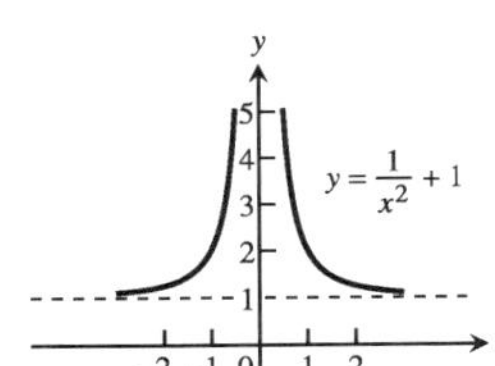

49. **(a)** $D : [0, 2], \quad R : [2, 3]$

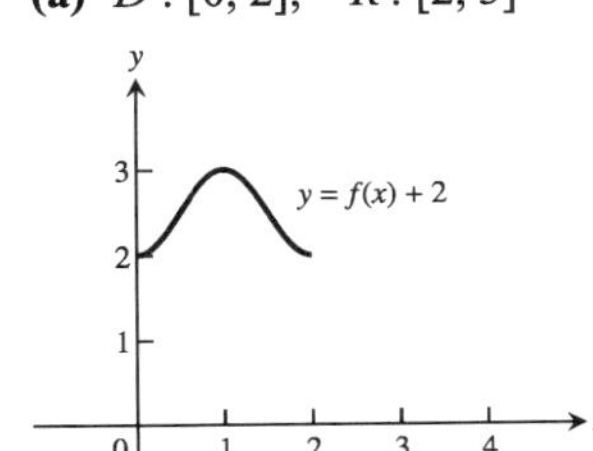

(b) $D : [0, 2], \quad R : [-1, 0]$

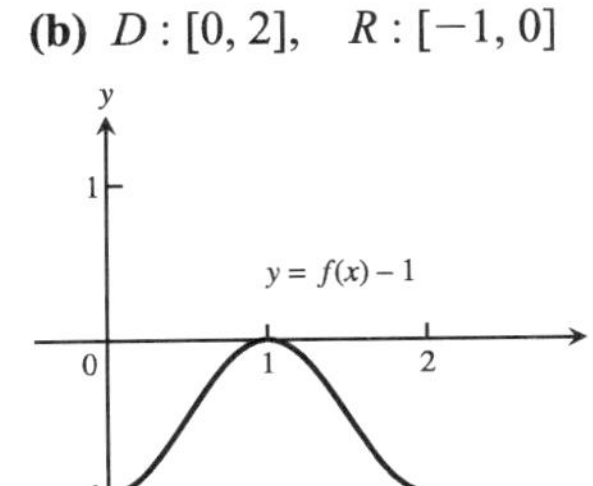

(c) $D: [0, 2], \quad R: [0, 2]$

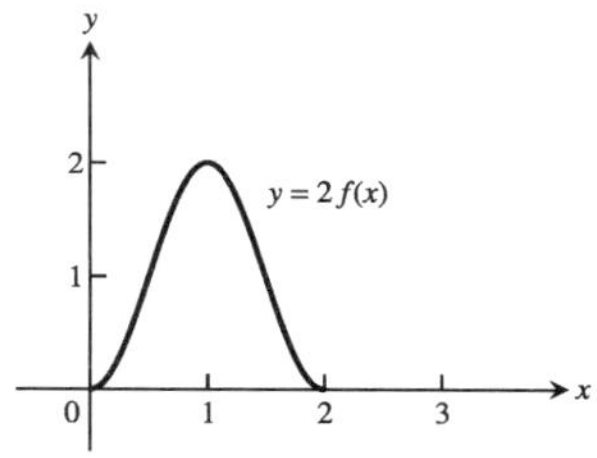

(d) $D: [0, 2], \quad R: [-1, 0]$

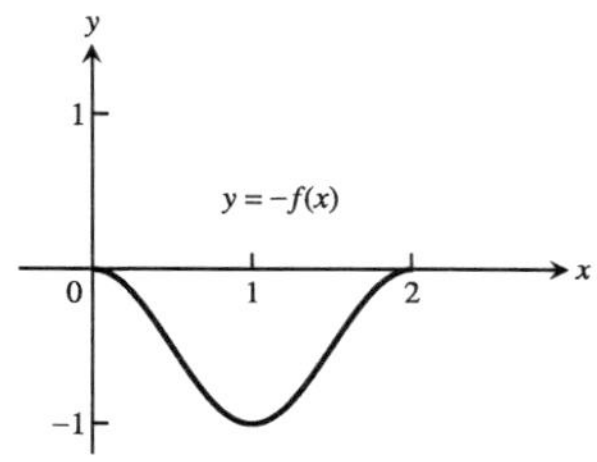

(e) $D: [-2, 0], \quad R: [0, 1]$

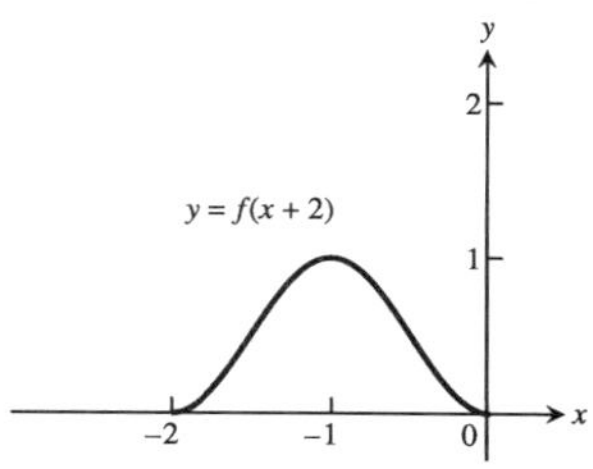

(f) $D: [1, 3], R: [0, 1]$

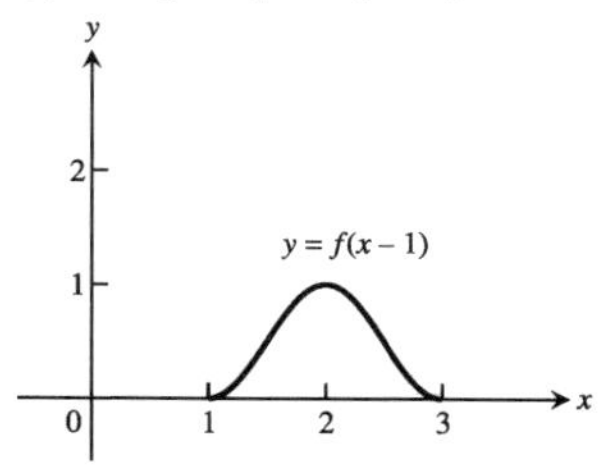

(g) $D: [-2, 0], \quad R: [0, 1]$

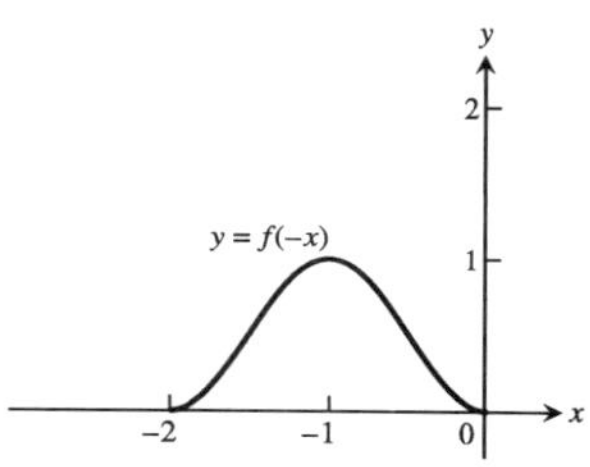

(h) $D: [-1, 1], \quad R: [0, 1]$

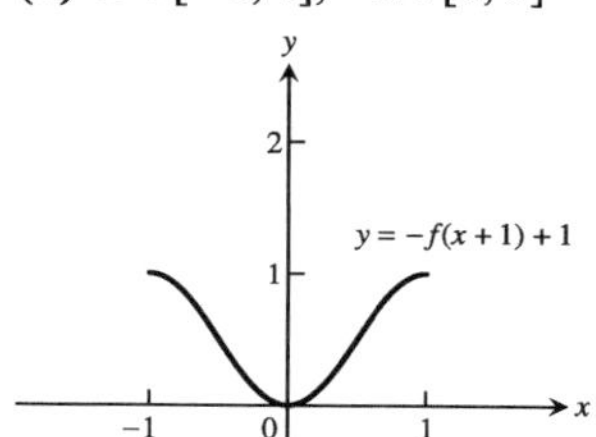

51. $y = 3x^2 - 3$ **53.** $y = \frac{1}{2} + \frac{1}{2x^2}$ **55.** $y = \sqrt{4x + 1}$

57. $y = \sqrt{4 - \frac{x^2}{4}}$ **59.** $y = 1 - 27x^3$

61.

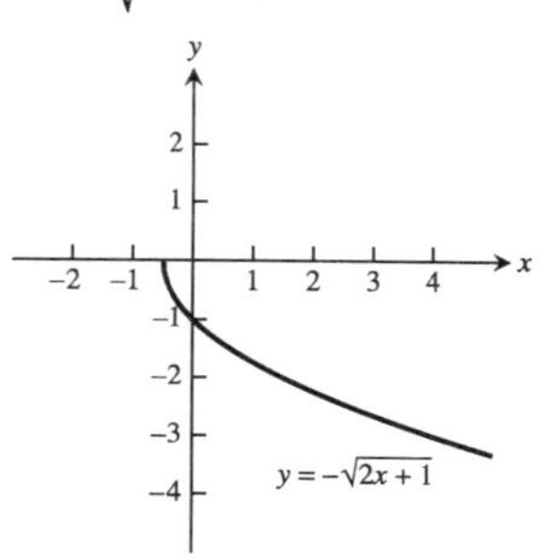

63.

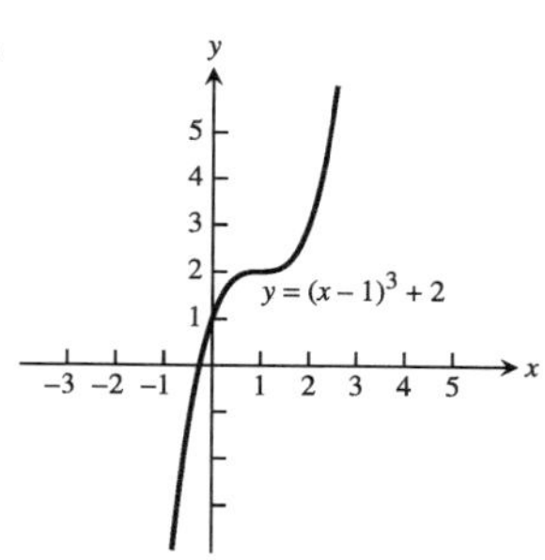

65.

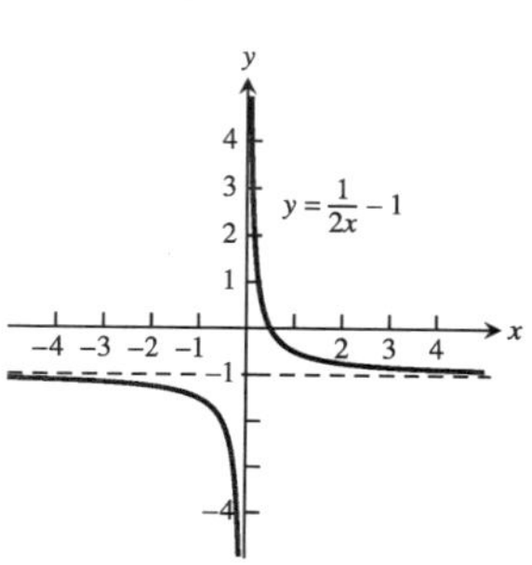

67.

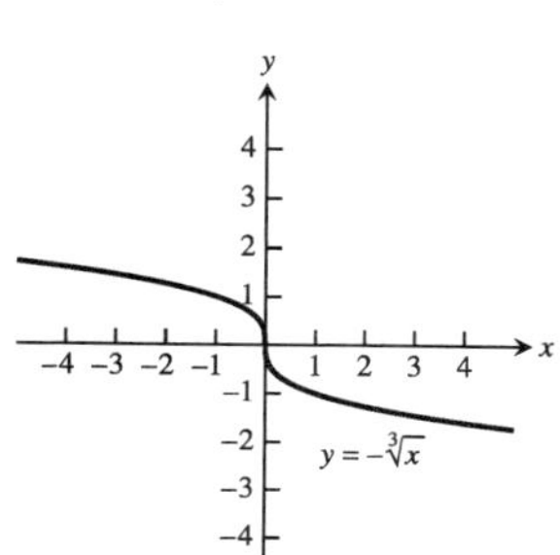

69.

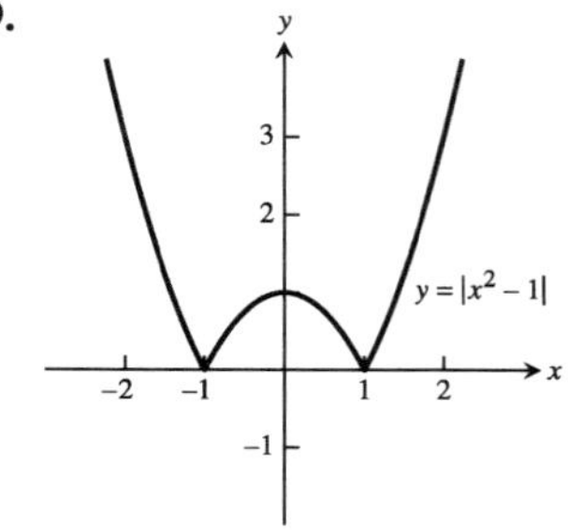

71.

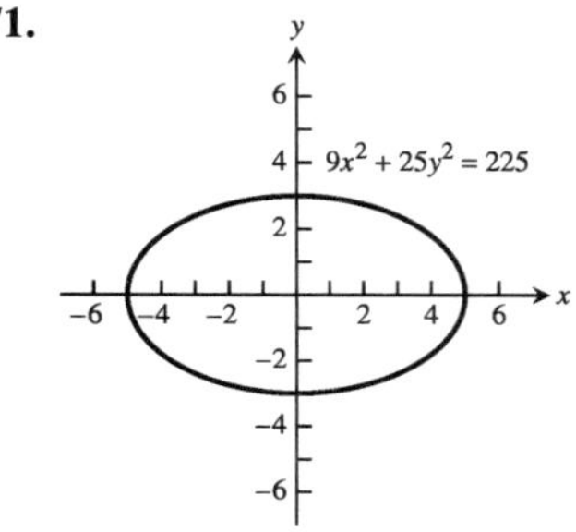

73.

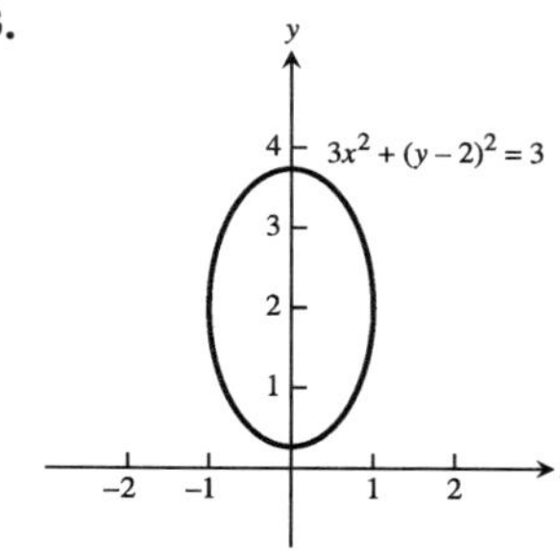

75.

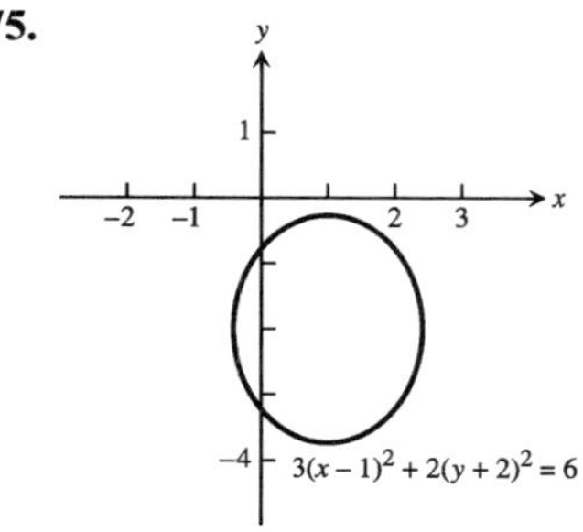

77. $\frac{(x + 4)^2}{16} + \frac{(y - 3)^2}{9} = 1$ Center: $(-4, 3)$

The major axis is the line segment between $(-8, 3)$ and $(0, 3)$.

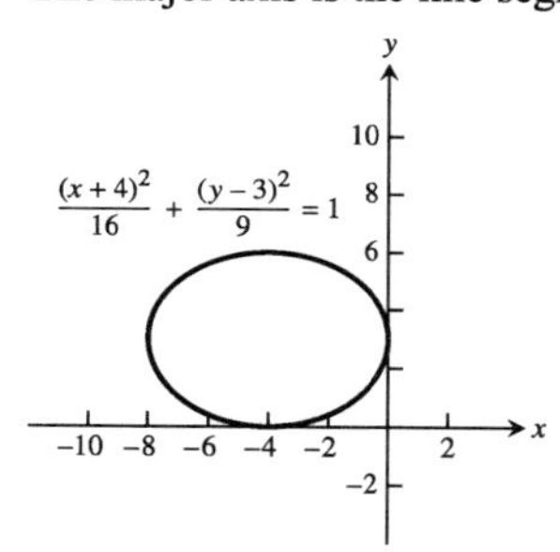

79. **(a)** Odd **(b)** Odd **(c)** Odd **(d)** Even **(e)** Even **(f)** Even **(g)** Even **(h)** Even **(i)** Odd

Section 1.6, pp. 56–58

1. **(a)** 8π m **(b)** $\frac{55\pi}{9}$ m **3.** 8.4 in.

5.

θ	$-\pi$	$-2\pi/3$	0	$\pi/2$	$3\pi/4$
$\sin\theta$	0	$-\frac{\sqrt{3}}{2}$	0	1	$\frac{1}{\sqrt{2}}$
$\cos\theta$	-1	$-\frac{1}{2}$	1	0	$-\frac{1}{\sqrt{2}}$
$\tan\theta$	0	$\sqrt{3}$	0	UND	-1
$\cot\theta$	UND	$\frac{1}{\sqrt{3}}$	UND	0	-1
$\sec\theta$	-1	-2	1	UND	$-\sqrt{2}$
$\csc\theta$	UND	$-\frac{2}{\sqrt{3}}$	UND	1	$\sqrt{2}$

7. $\cos x = -4/5, \tan x = -3/4$

9. $\sin x = -\frac{\sqrt{8}}{3}, \tan x = -\sqrt{8}$

11. $\sin x = -\frac{1}{\sqrt{5}}, \cos x = -\frac{2}{\sqrt{5}}$

13. Period π

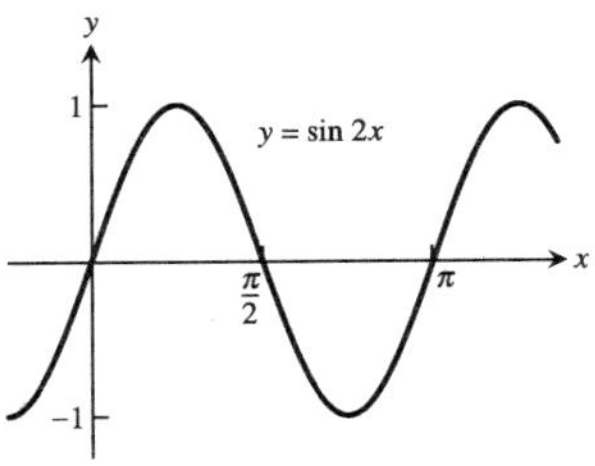

15. Period 2

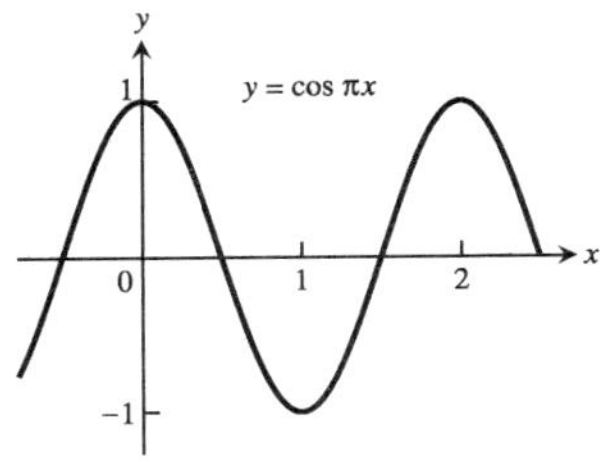

17. Period 6

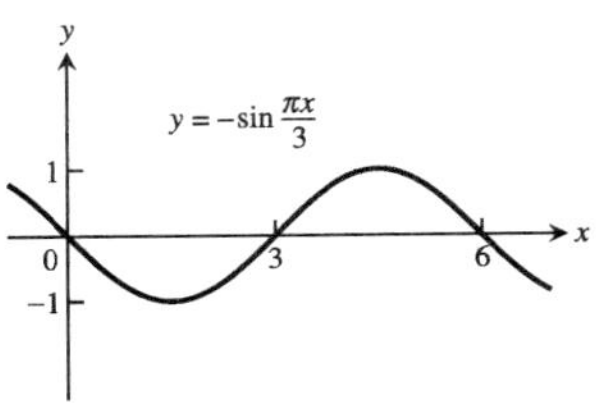

19. Period 2π

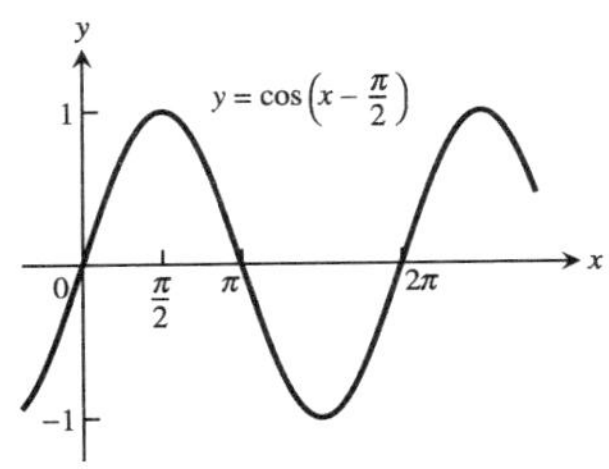

21. Period 2π

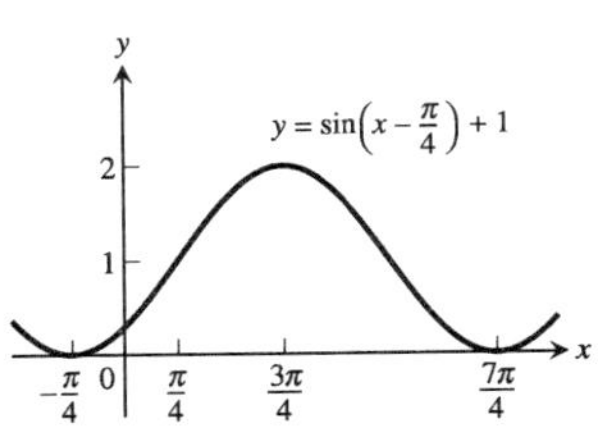

23. Period $\pi/2$, symmetric about the origin

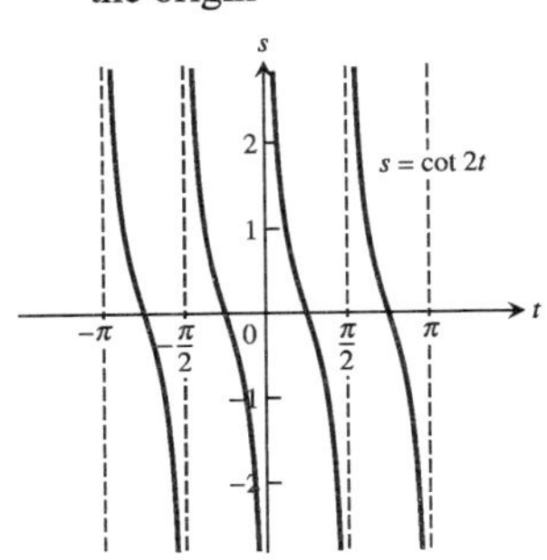

25. Period 4, symmetric about the y-axis

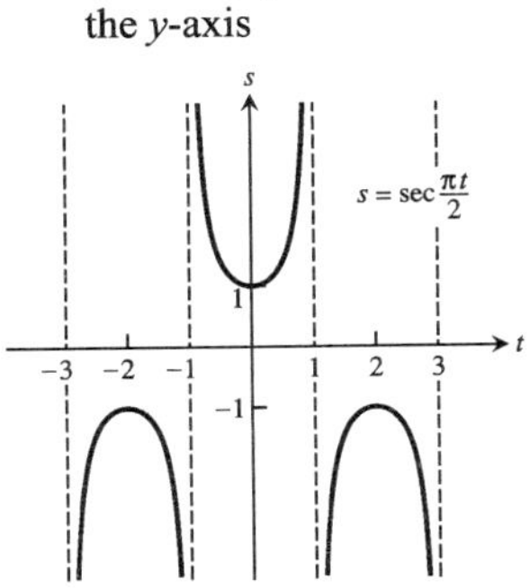

29. $D: (-\infty, \infty)$,
$R: y = -1, 0, 1$

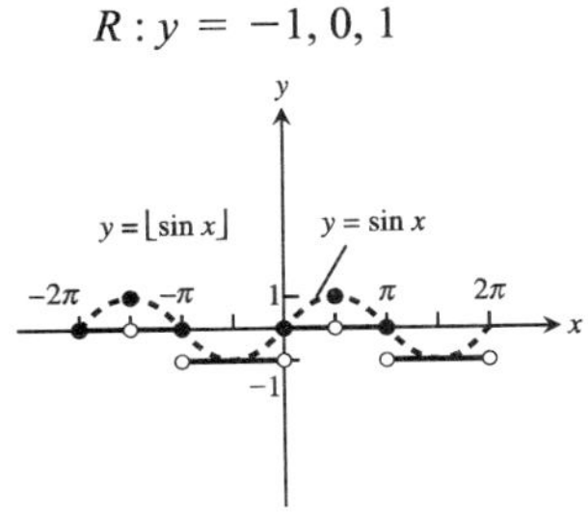

39. $-\cos x$ **41.** $-\cos x$ **43.** $\frac{\sqrt{6}+\sqrt{2}}{4}$ **45.** $\frac{1+\sqrt{3}}{2\sqrt{2}}$

47. $\frac{2+\sqrt{2}}{4}$ **49.** $\frac{2-\sqrt{3}}{4}$ **55.** $c = \sqrt{7} \approx 2.646$

59. $a = 1.464$

61. $A = 2, B = 2\pi, C = -\pi, D = -1$

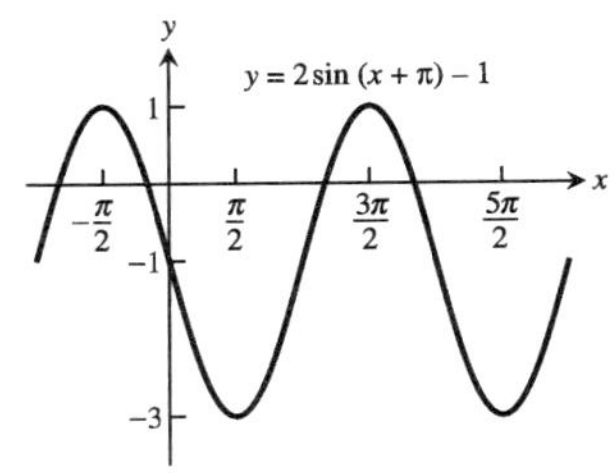

63. $A = -\frac{2}{\pi}, B = 4, C = 0, D = \frac{1}{\pi}$

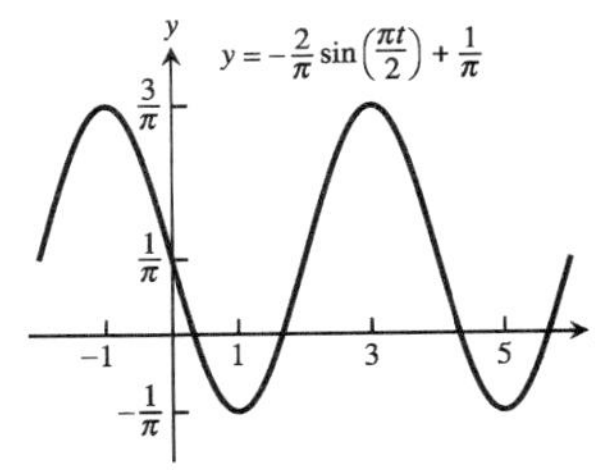

65. **(a)** 37 **(b)** 365 **(c)** Right 101 **(d)** Up 25

Section 1.7, pp. 66–68

1. d) **3. d)**

5. $[-3, 5]$ by $[-15, 40]$

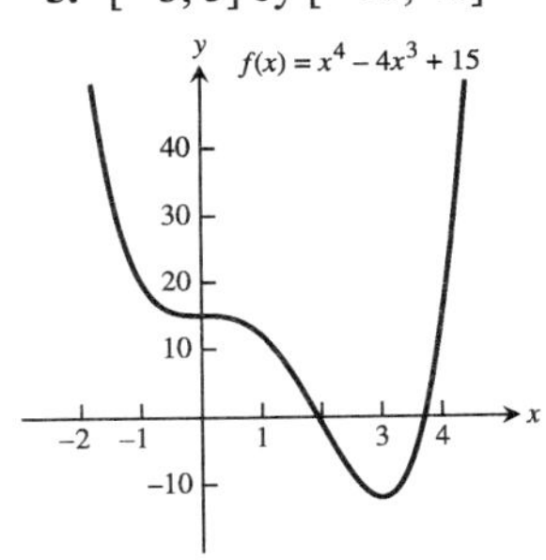

7. $[-3, 6]$ by $[-250, 50]$

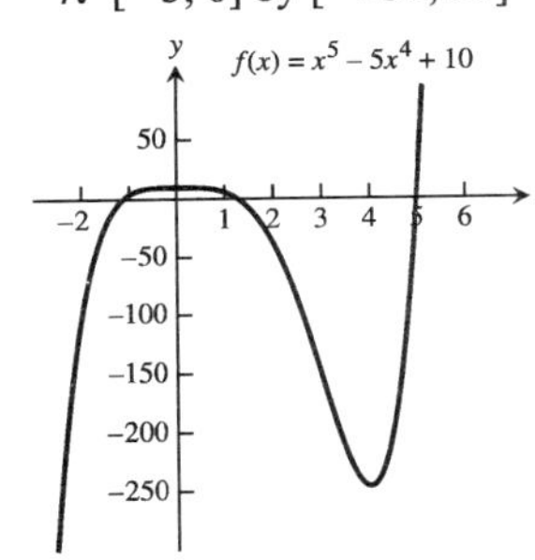

9. $[-3, 3]$ by $[-6, 6]$

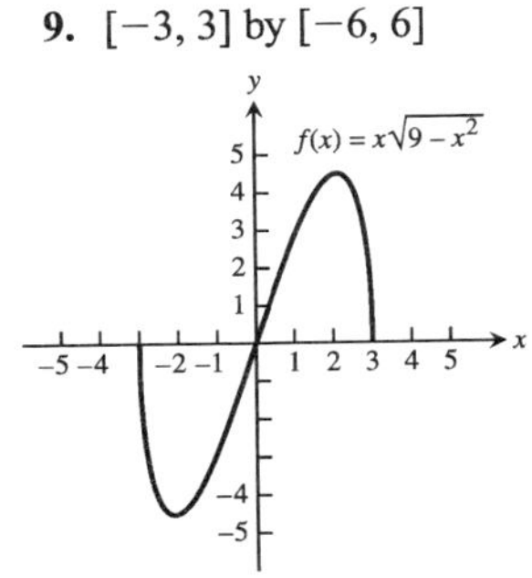

11. $[-2, 6]$ by $[-5, 4]$

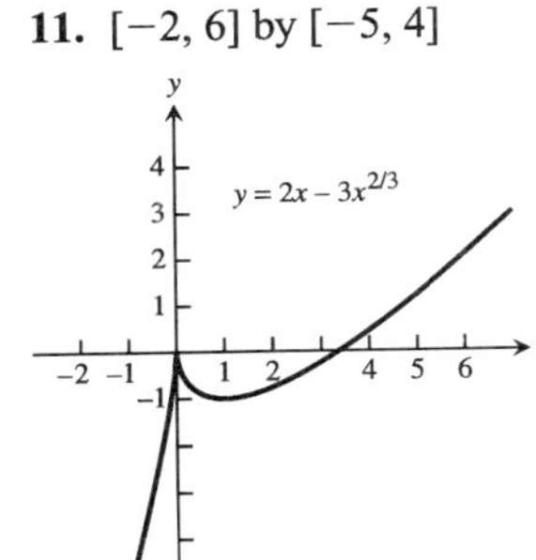

13. $[-2, 8]$ by $[-5, 10]$

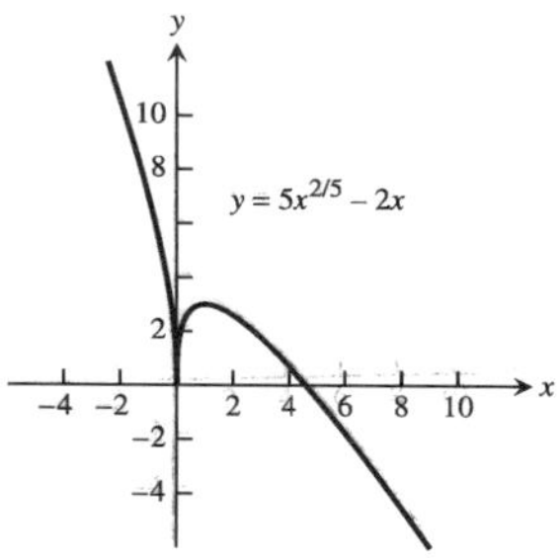

15. $[-3, 3]$ by $[0, 10]$

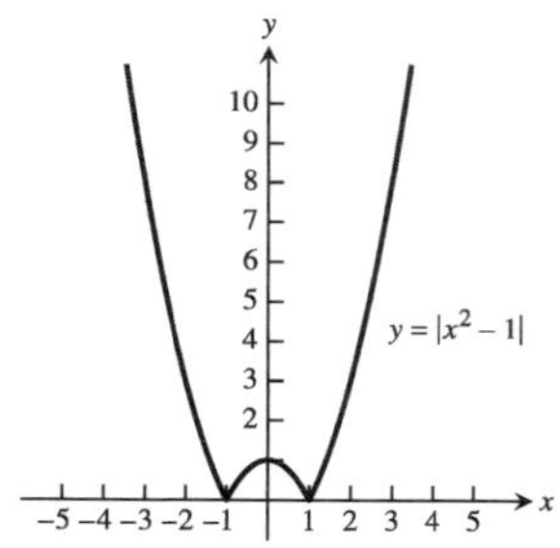

17. $[-15, 5]$ by $[-10, 10]$

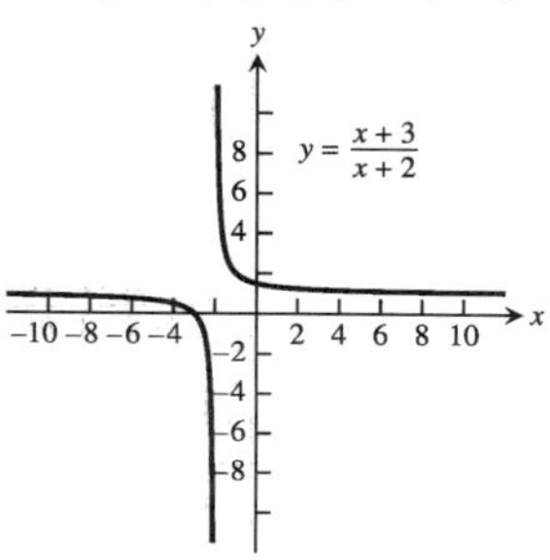

19. $[-4, 4]$ by $[0, 3]$

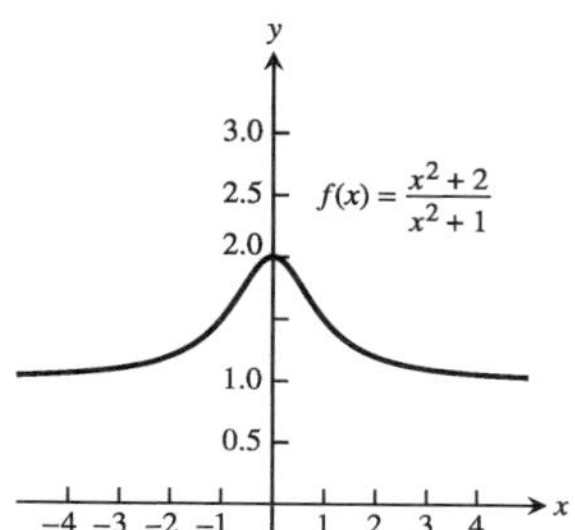

21. $[-10, 10]$ by $[-6, 6]$

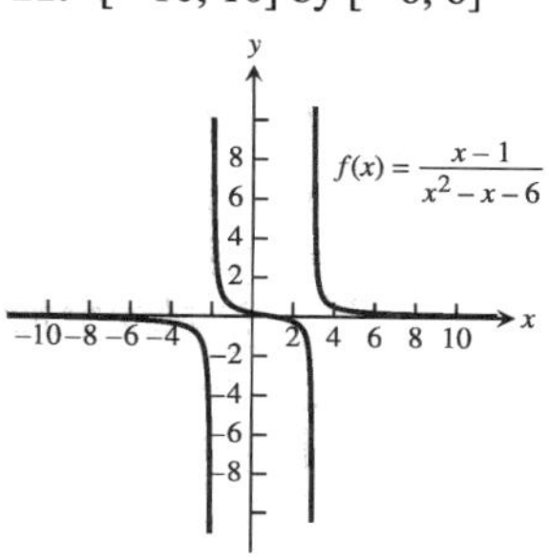

23. $[-6, 10]$ by $[-6, 6]$

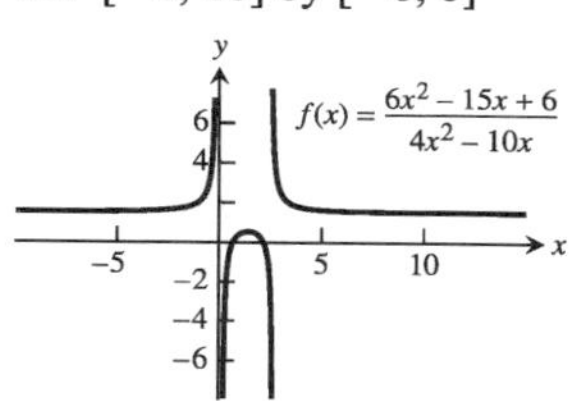

25. $\left[-\frac{\pi}{125}, \frac{\pi}{125}\right]$ by $[-1.25, 1.25]$

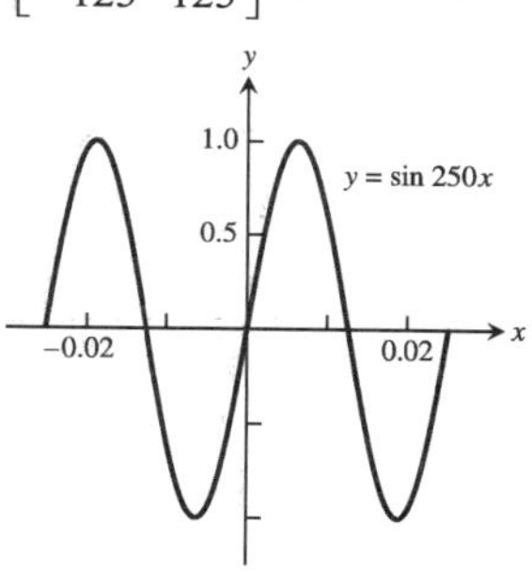

27. $[-100\pi, 100\pi]$ by $[-1.25, 1.25]$

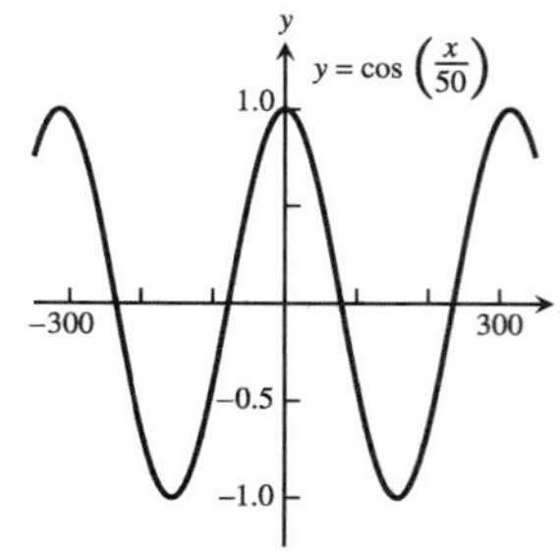

29. $\left[-\frac{\pi}{15}, \frac{\pi}{15}\right]$ by $[-0.25, 0.25]$

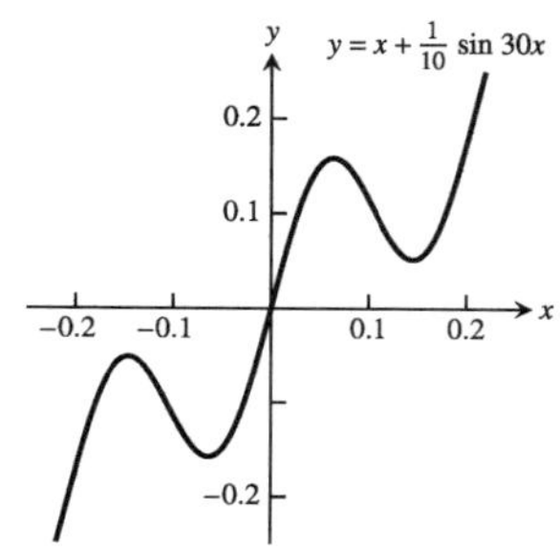

31.

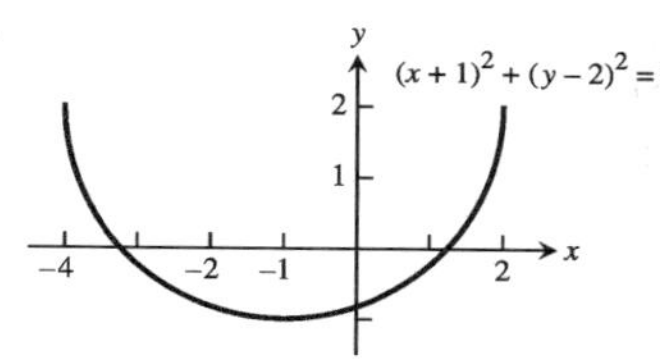

33.

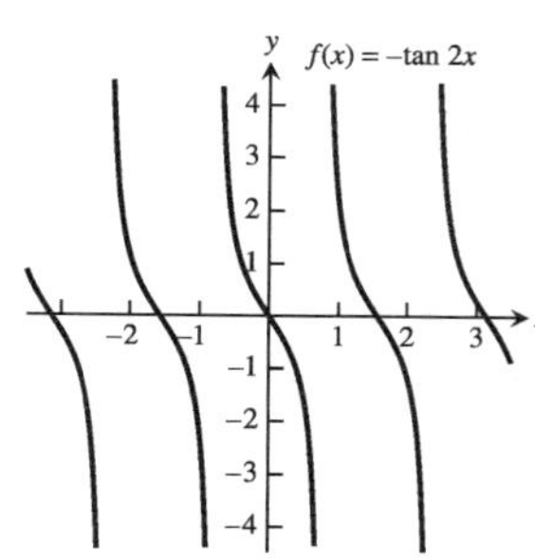

35.

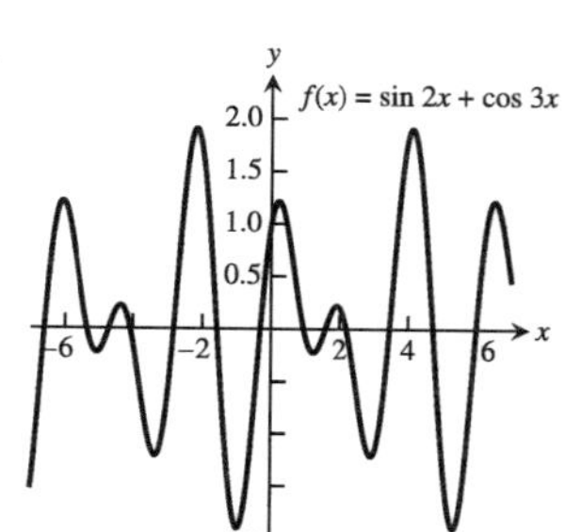

37.

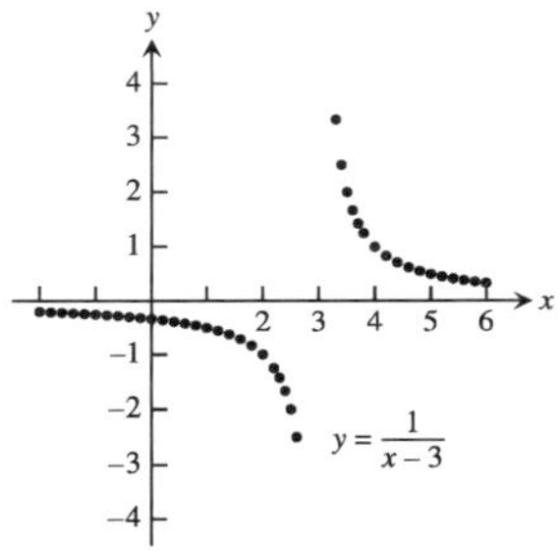

39.

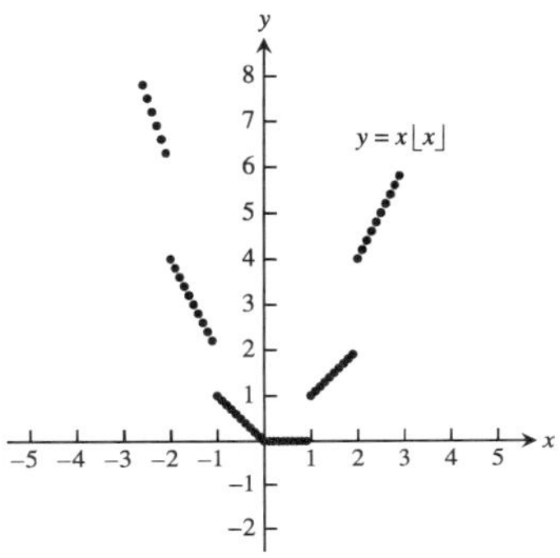

41. **(a)** $y = 1059.14x - 2074972.23$
(b) $m = 1059.14$; this is the amount the compensation will increase by each year.
(c)

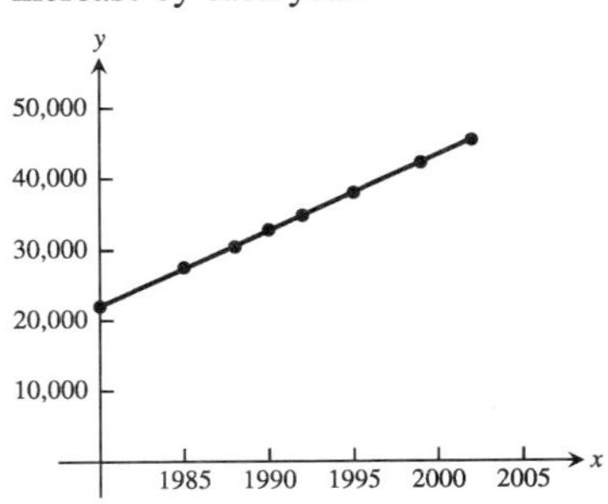

(d) \$53,899.17

43. **(a)** $y = 0.0866x^2 - 1.9701x + 50.0594$
(b)

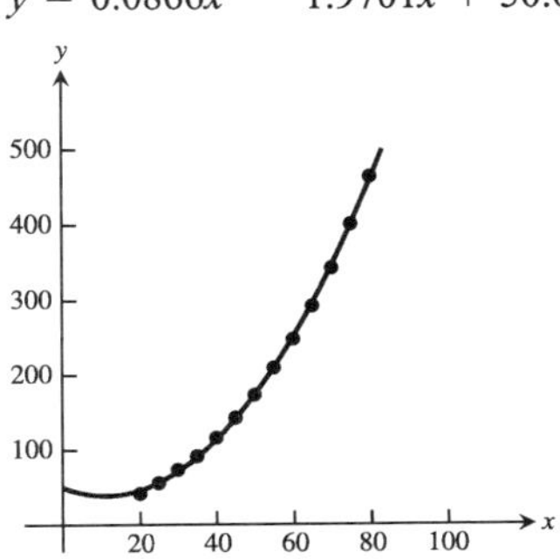

(c) If the speed is 72 mph, the approximate stopping distance is 367.50 ft. If the speed is 85 mph, the approximate stopping distance is 522.67 ft.

(d) $y = -140.4121 + 6.889x$

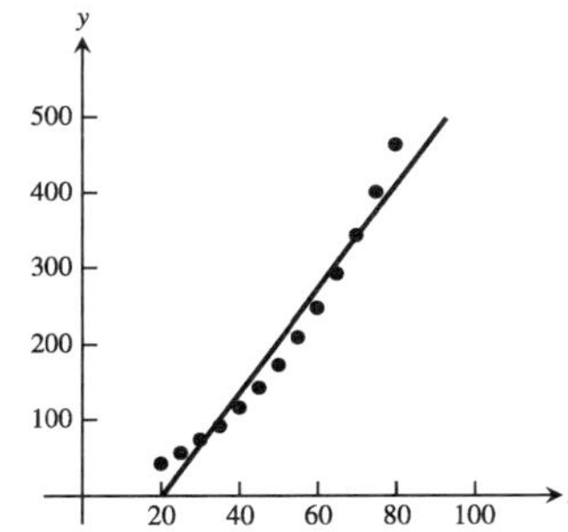

If the speed is 72 mph, the approximate stopping distance is 355.60 ft. If the speed is 85 mph, the approximate stopping distance is 445.15 ft
The quadratic regression equation is a better fit.

Practice Exercises, pp. 69–70

1. $x \geq -2$ 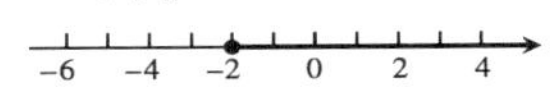

3. $x > 6$ 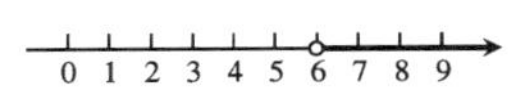

5. $-8, 6$ **7.** $x < -1$ or $x > 5$ **9.** $(0, 11)$
11. No, no two sides have the same length; no, no two sides are perpendicular
13. $y = 3x - 9$ **15.** $x = 0$ **17.** $y = 2$ **19.** $y = -3x + 3$
21. $y = -\frac{4}{3}x - \frac{20}{3}$ **23.** $y = \frac{2}{3}x + \frac{8}{3}$
25. $A = \pi r^2, C = 2\pi r, A = \frac{C^2}{4\pi}$ **27.** $x = \tan\theta, y = \tan^2\theta$
29. Origin **31.** Neither **33.** Even **35.** Even **37.** Odd
39. Neither **41.** **(a)** Domain: all reals **(b)** Range: $[-2, \infty)$
43. **(a)** Domain: $[-4, 4]$ **(b)** Range: $[0, 4]$
45. **(a)** Domain: all reals **(b)** Range: $(-3, \infty)$
47. **(a)** Domain: all reals **(b)** Range: $[-3, 1]$
49. **(a)** Domain: $(3, \infty)$ **(b)** Range: all reals
51. **(a)** Domain: $[-4, 4]$ **(b)** Range: $[0, 2]$
53. $f(x) = \begin{cases} 1 - x, & 0 \leq x < 1 \\ 2 - x, & 1 \leq x \leq 2 \end{cases}$
55. **(a)** 1 **(b)** $\frac{1}{\sqrt{2.5}} = \sqrt{\frac{2}{5}}$ **(c)** $x, x \neq 0$
(d) $\frac{1}{\sqrt{1/\sqrt{x+2}+2}}$
57. **(a)** $(f \circ g)(x) = -x, x \geq -2, (g \circ f)(x) = \sqrt{4 - x^2}$
(b) Domain $(f \circ g)$: $[-2, \infty)$, domain $(g \circ f)$: $[-2, 2]$
(c) Range $(f \circ g)$: $(-\infty, 2]$, range $(g \circ f)$: $[0, 2]$

59. Replace the portion for $x < 0$ with mirror image of the portion for $x > 0$ to make the new graph symmetric with respect to the y-axis.

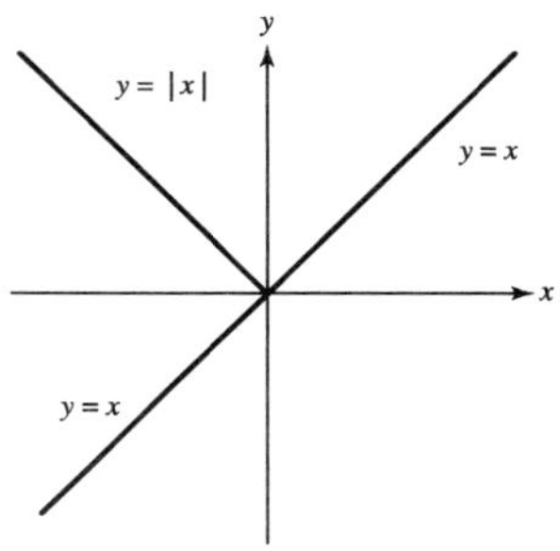

61. It does not change it.
63. Adds the mirror image of the portion for $x > 0$ to make the new graph symmetric with respect to the y-axis
65. Reflects the portion for $y < 0$ across the x-axis
67. Reflects the portion for $y < 0$ across the x-axis
69. Period π

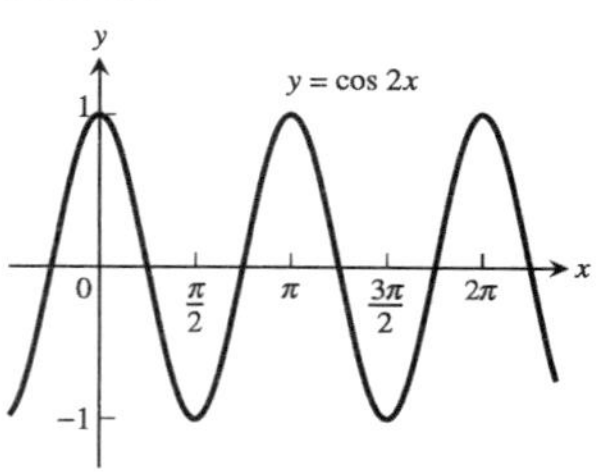

71. Period 2

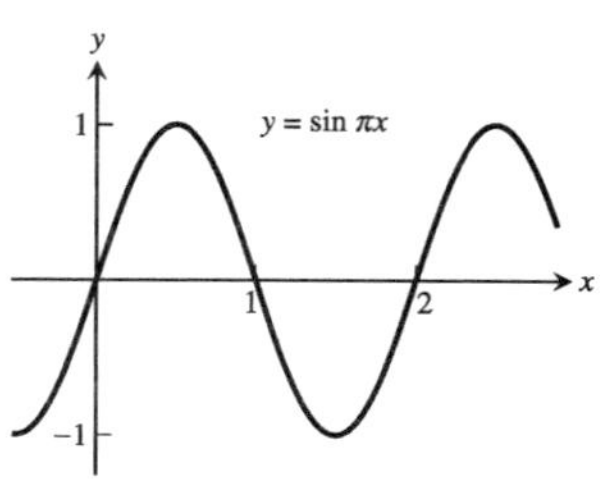

73.

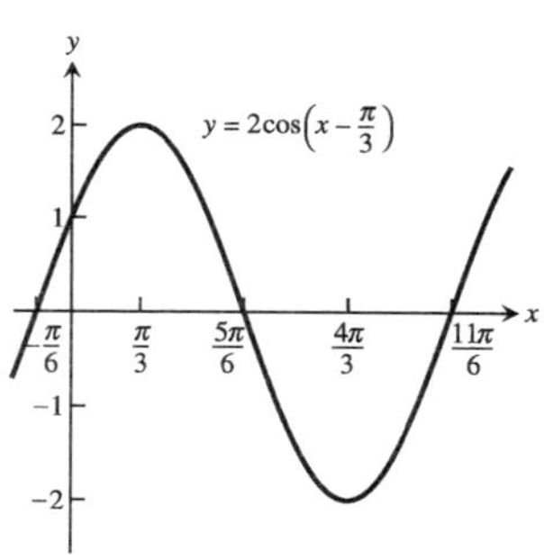

75. **(a)** $a = 1 \quad b = \sqrt{3}$ **(b)** $a = 2\sqrt{3}/3 \quad c = 4\sqrt{3}/3$

77. **(a)** $a = \dfrac{b}{\tan B}$ **(b)** $c = \dfrac{a}{\sin A}$

79. ≈ 16.98 m **81.** **(b)** 4π

Additional and Advanced Exercises, pp. 71–72

1. **(a)**

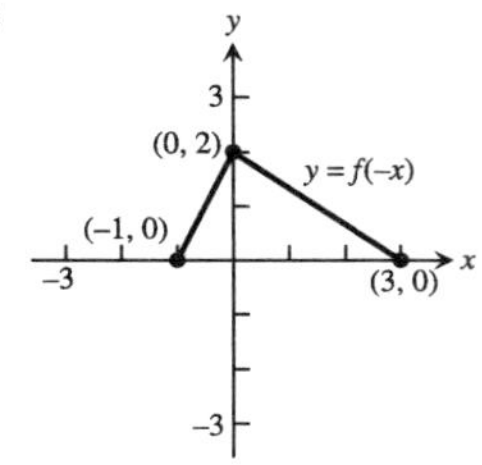

(b)

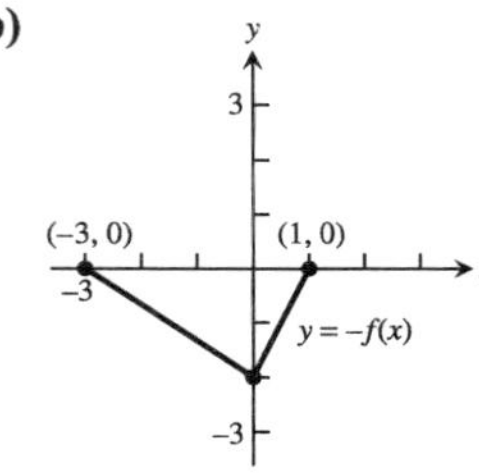

(c)

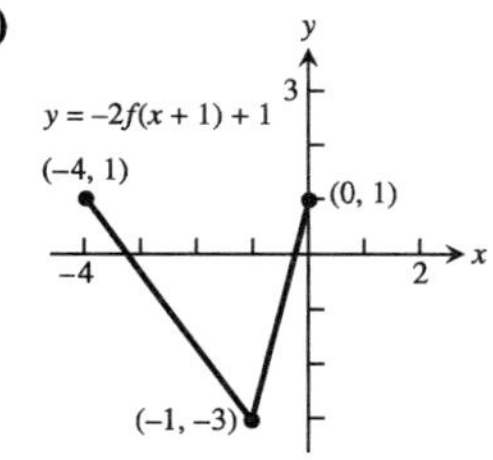

(d)

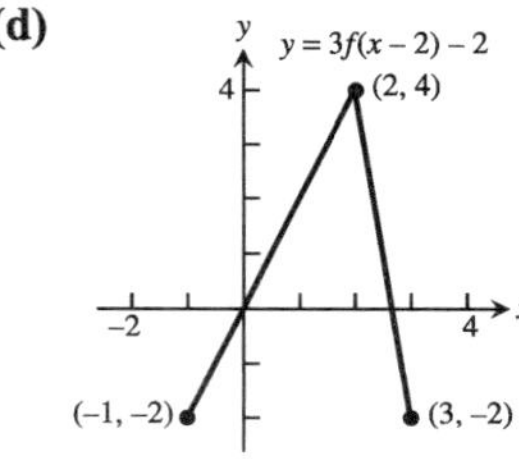

3. Yes. For instance: $f(x) = 1/x$ and $g(x) = 1/x$, or $f(x) = 2x$ and $g(x) = x/2$, or $f(x) = e^x$ and $g(x) = \ln x$.
5. If $f(x)$ is odd, then $g(x) = f(x) - 2$ is not odd. Nor is $g(x)$ even, unless $f(x) = 0$ for all x. If f is even, then $g(x) = f(x) - 2$ is also even.
7.

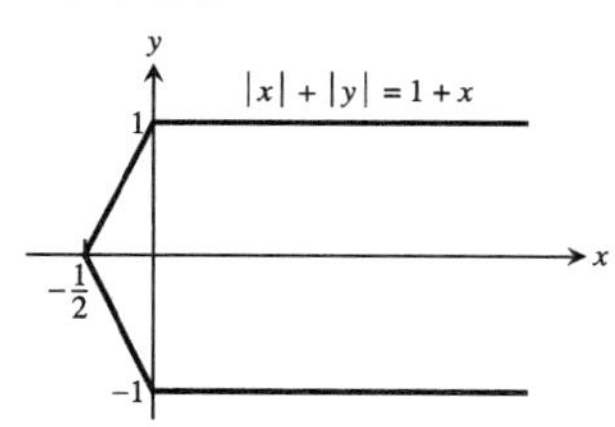

9. $\sqrt{2}$ **11.** 3/4 **13.** $3\sqrt{15}/16$ **27.** $-4 < m < 0$

CHAPTER 2

Section 2.1, pp. 81–84

1. **(a)** Does not exist. As x approaches 1 from the right, $g(x)$ approaches 0. As x approaches 1 from the left, $g(x)$ approaches 1. There is no single number L that all the values $g(x)$ get arbitrarily close to as $x \to 1$. **(b)** 1 **(c)** 0
3. **(a)** True **(b)** True **(c)** False
(d) False **(e)** False **(f)** True
5. As x approaches 0 from the left, $x/|x|$ approaches -1. As x approaches 0 from the right, $x/|x|$ approaches 1. There is no single number L that the function values all get arbitrarily close to as $x \to 0$.
7. Nothing can be said. **9.** No; no; no

11. **(a)** $f(x) = (x^2 - 9)/(x + 3)$

x	-3.1	-3.01	-3.001	-3.0001	-3.00001	-3.000001
$f(x)$	-6.1	-6.01	-6.001	-6.0001	-6.00001	-6.000001

x	-2.9	-2.99	-2.999	-2.9999	-2.99999	-2.999999
$f(x)$	-5.9	-5.99	-5.999	-5.9999	-5.99999	-5.999999

(c) $\lim_{x \to -3} f(x) = -6$

13. **(a)** $G(x) = (x + 6)/(x^2 + 4x - 12)$

x	-5.9	-5.99	-5.999	-5.9999	-5.99999	-5.999999
$G(x)$	$-.126582$	$-.1251564$	$-.1250156$	$-.1250015$	$-.1250001$	$-.1250000$

x	-6.1	-6.01	-6.001	-6.0001	-6.00001	-6.000001
$G(x)$	$-.123456$	$-.124843$	$-.124984$	$-.124998$	$-.124999$	$-.124999$

(c) $\lim_{x \to -6} G(x) = -1/8 = -0.125$

15. **(a)** $f(x) = (x^2 - 1)/(|x| - 1)$

x	-1.1	-1.01	-1.001	-1.0001	-1.00001	-1.000001
$f(x)$	2.1	2.01	2.001	2.0001	2.00001	2.000001

x	$-.9$	$-.99$	$-.999$	$-.9999$	$-.99999$	$-.999999$
$f(x)$	1.9	1.99	1.999	1.9999	1.99999	1.999999

(c) $\lim_{x \to -1} f(x) = 2$

17. **(a)** $g(\theta) = (\sin \theta)/\theta$

θ	.1	.01	.001	.0001	.00001	.000001
$g(\theta)$	.998334	.999983	.999999	.999999	.999999	.999999

θ	$-.1$	$-.01$	$-.001$	$-.0001$	$-.00001$	$-.000001$
$g(\theta)$	.998334	.999983	.999999	.999999	.999999	.999999

$\lim_{\theta \to 0} g(\theta) = 1$

19. **(a)** $f(x) = x^{1/(1-x)}$

x	.9	.99	.999	.9999	.99999	.999999
$f(x)$	.348678	.366032	.367695	.367861	.367877	.367879

x	1.1	1.01	1.001	1.0001	1.00001	1.000001
$f(x)$	.385543	.369711	.368063	.367897	.367881	.367878

$\lim_{x \to 1} f(x) \approx 0.36788$

21. 4 **23.** 0 **25.** 9 **27.** $\pi/2$ **29.** **(a)** 19 **(b)** 1

31. **(a)** $-\frac{4}{\pi}$ **(b)** $-\frac{3\sqrt{3}}{\pi}$ **33.** 1

35. Graphs can shift during a press run, so your estimates may not completely agree with these.

(a)

PQ_1	PQ_2	PQ_3	PQ_4
43	46	49	50

The appropriate units are m/sec.

(b) $\approx$ 50 m/sec or 180 km/h

37. **(a)**

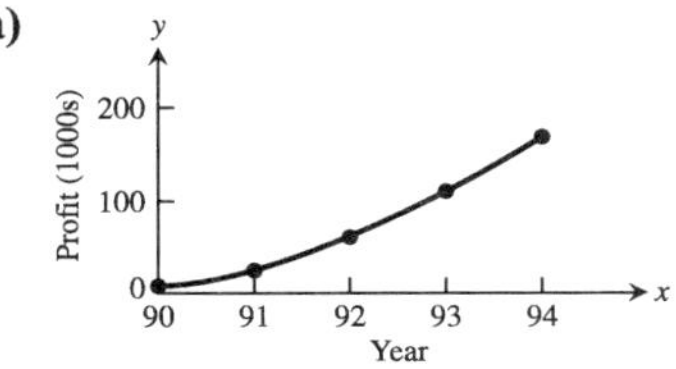

(b) $\approx$ \$56,000/year
(c) $\approx$ \$42,000/year

39. **(a)** 0.414213, 0.449489, $(\sqrt{1 + h} - 1)/h$ **(b)** $g(x) = \sqrt{x}$

$1 + h$	1.1	1.01	1.001	1.0001	1.00001	1.000001
$\sqrt{1 + h}$	1.04880	1.004987	1.0004998	1.0000499	1.000005	1.0000005
$(\sqrt{1 + h} - 1)/h$	0.4880	0.4987	0.4998	0.499	0.5	0.5

(c) 0.5 **(d)** 0.5

Section 2.2, pp. 89–91

1. -9 **3.** 4 **5.** -8 **7.** 5/8 **9.** 5/2 **11.** 27 **13.** 16
15. 3/2 **17.** 3/2 **19.** 1/10 **21.** -7 **23.** 3/2 **25.** $-1/2$
27. 4/3 **29.** 1/6 **31.** 4 **33.** 1/2 **35.** 3/2
37. **(a)** Quotient Rule **(b)** Difference and Power Rules
(c) Sum and Constant Multiple Rules
39. **(a)** -10 **(b)** -20 **(c)** -1 **(d)** 5/7
41. **(a)** 4 **(b)** -21 **(c)** -12 **(d)** $-7/3$
43. 2 **45.** 3 **47.** $1/(2\sqrt{7})$ **49.** $\sqrt{5}$
51. **(a)** The limit is 1. **53.** $c = 0, 1, -1$; The limit is 0 at $c = 0$, and 1 at $c = 1, -1$ **55.** 7 **57.** **(a)** 5 **(b)** 5

Section 2.3, pp. 98–101

1. $\delta = 2$

3. $\delta = 1/2$

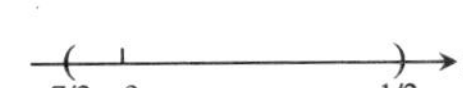

5. $\delta = 1/18$

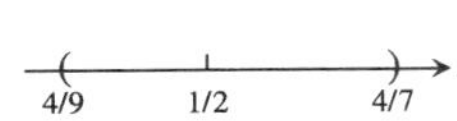

7. $\delta = 0.1$ **9.** $\delta = 7/16$ **11.** $\delta = \sqrt{5} - 2$ **13.** $\delta = 0.36$
15. $(3.99, 4.01)$, $\delta = 0.01$ **17.** $(-0.19, 0.21)$, $\delta = 0.19$
19. $(3, 15)$, $\delta = 5$ **21.** $(10/3, 5)$, $\delta = 2/3$
23. $(-\sqrt{4.5}, -\sqrt{3.5})$, $\delta = \sqrt{4.5} - 2 \approx 0.12$
25. $(\sqrt{15}, \sqrt{17})$, $\delta = \sqrt{17} - 4 \approx 0.12$

27. $\left(2 - \frac{0.03}{m}, 2 + \frac{0.03}{m}\right), \quad \delta = \frac{0.03}{m}$

29. $\left(\frac{1}{2} - \frac{c}{m}, \frac{c}{m} + \frac{1}{2}\right), \quad \delta = \frac{c}{m}$

31. $L = -3, \quad \delta = 0.01$ **33.** $L = 4, \quad \delta = 0.05$

35. $L = 4, \quad \delta = 0.75$

55. [3.384, 3.387]. To be safe, the left endpoint was rounded up and the right endpoint rounded down.

59. The limit does not exist as x approaches 3.

Section 2.4, pp. 111–114

1. **(a)** True **(b)** True **(c)** False **(d)** True **(e)** True **(f)** True **(g)** False **(h)** False **(i)** False **(j)** False **(k)** True **(l)** False

3. **(a)** 2, 1 **(b)** No, $\lim_{x\to 2^+} f(x) \neq \lim_{x\to 2^-} f(x)$ **(c)** 3, 3 **(d)** Yes, 3

5. **(a)** No **(b)** Yes, 0 **(c)** No

7. **(a)**

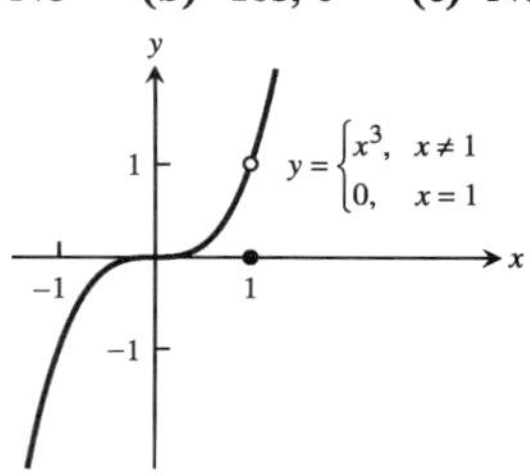

(b) 1, 1 **(c)** Yes, 1

9. **(a)** $D: 0 \le x \le 2, R: 0 < y \le 1$ and $y = 2$.
(b) $(0, 1) \cup (1, 2)$ **(c)** $x = 2$ **(d)** $x = 0$

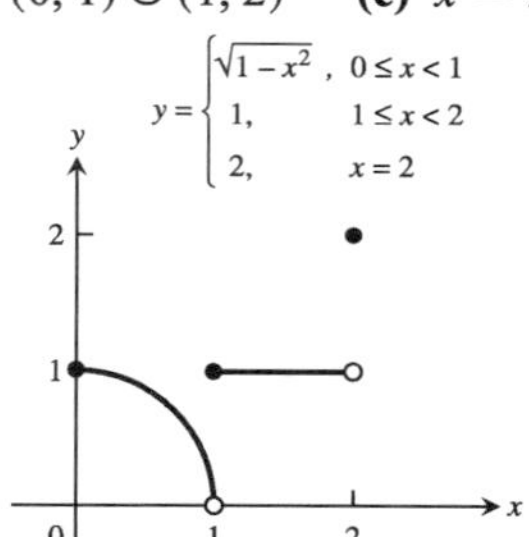

11. $\sqrt{3}$ **13.** 1 **15.** $2/\sqrt{5}$ **17.** **(a)** 1 **(b)** −1
19. **(a)** 1 **(b)** 2/3 **21.** 1 **23.** 3/4 **25.** 2 **27.** 1/2
29. 2 **31.** 1 **33.** 1/2 **35.** 3/8 **37.** **(a)** −3 **(b)** −3
39. **(a)** 1/2 **(b)** 1/2 **41.** **(a)** −5/3 **(b)** −5/3 **43.** 0
45. −1 **47.** **(a)** 2/5 **(b)** 2/5 **49.** **(a)** 0 **(b)** 0
51. **(a)** 7 **(b)** 7 **53.** **(a)** 0 **(b)** 0 **55.** **(a)** −2/3 **(b)** −2/3 **57.** 0 **59.** 1 **61.** ∞ **69.** 1
73. $\delta = \epsilon^2, \lim_{x\to 5^+} \sqrt{x-5} = 0$
77. **(a)** 400 **(b)** 399 **(c)** The limit does not exist.
79. 1 **81.** 3/2 **83.** 3

Section 2.5, pp. 122–123

1. ∞ **3.** $-\infty$ **5.** $-\infty$ **7.** ∞ **9.** **(a)** ∞ **(b)** $-\infty$
11. ∞ **13.** ∞ **15.** $-\infty$ **17.** **(a)** ∞ **(b)** $-\infty$ **(c)** $-\infty$ **(d)** ∞ **19.** **(a)** $-\infty$ **(b)** ∞ **(c)** 0 **(d)** 3/2 **21.** **(a)** $-\infty$ **(b)** 1/4 **(c)** 1/4 **(d)** 1/4 **(e)** It will be $-\infty$. **23.** **(a)** $-\infty$ **(b)** ∞ **25.** **(a)** ∞ **(b)** ∞ **(c)** ∞ **(d)** ∞

27.

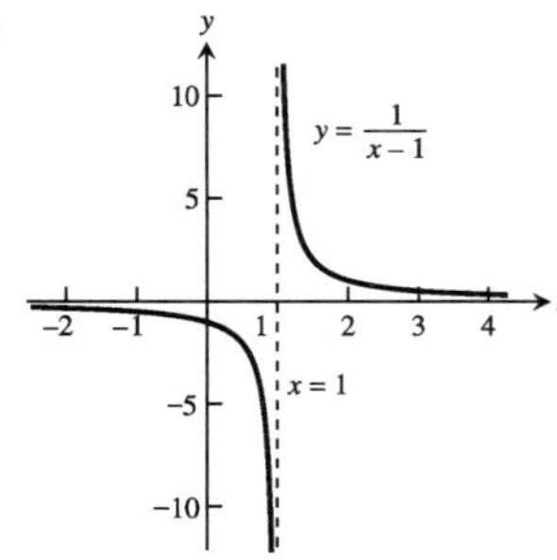

29.

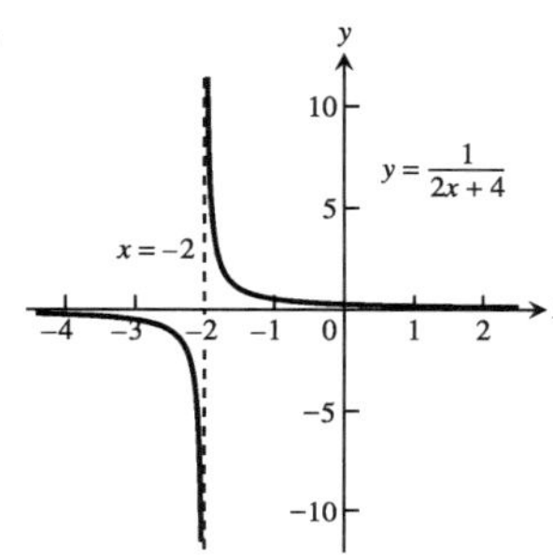

31.

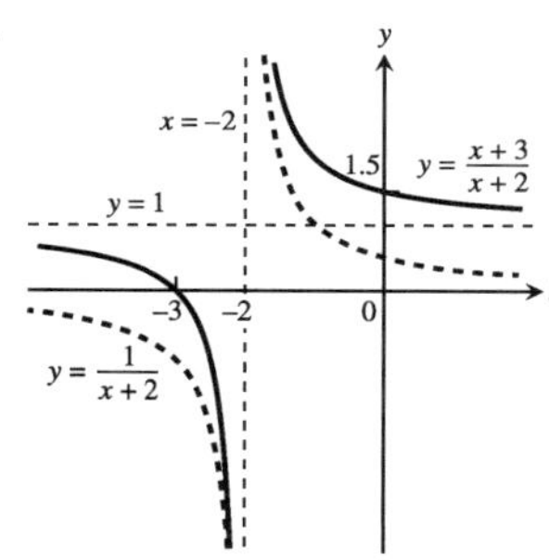

33.

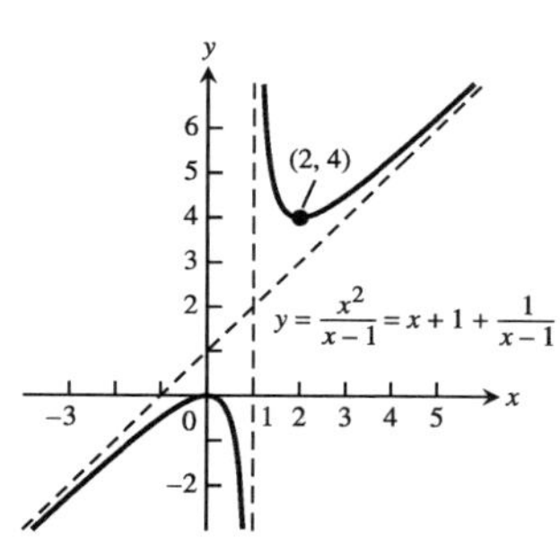

35.

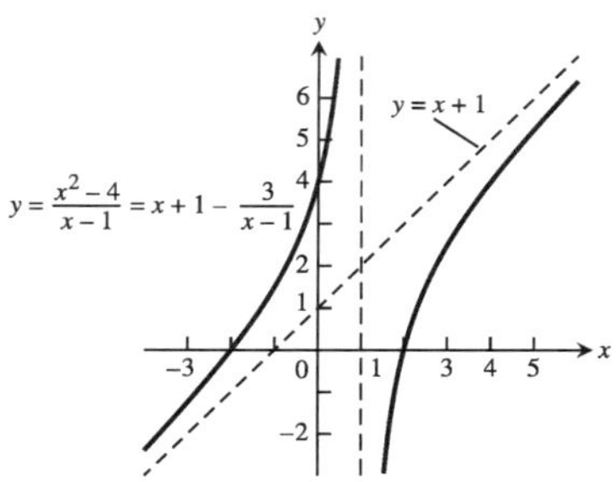

37.

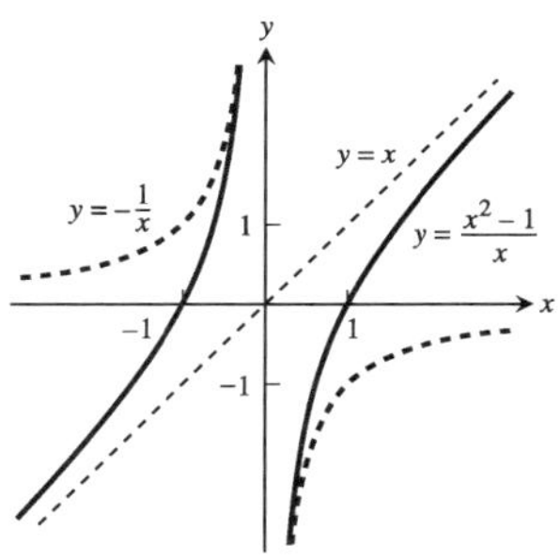

39. Here is one possibility.

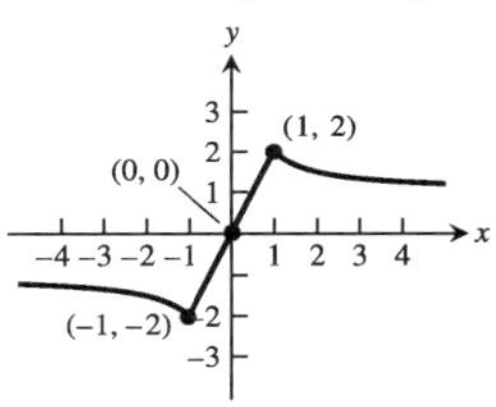

41. Here is one possibility.

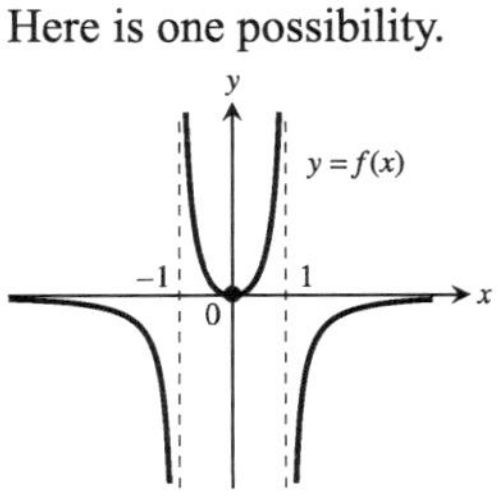

43. Here is one possibility.

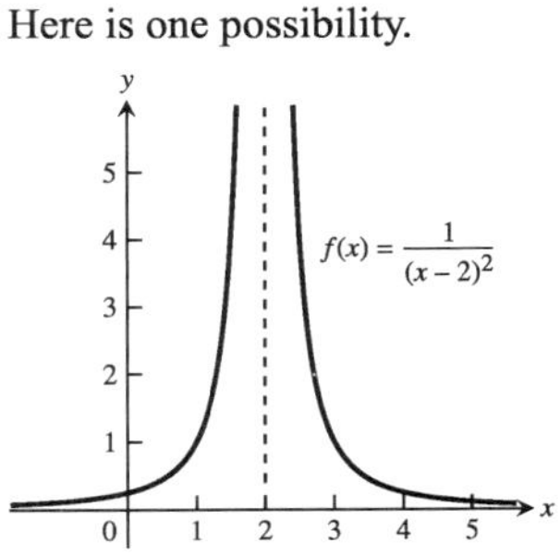

45. Here is one possibility.

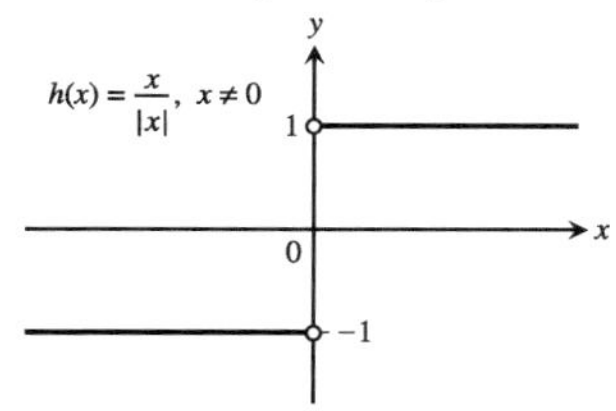

51. **(a)** For every positive real number B there exists a corresponding number $\delta > 0$ such that for all x

$$x_0 - \delta < x < x_0 \Rightarrow f(x) > B.$$

(b) For every negative real number $-B$ there exists a corresponding number $\delta > 0$ such that for all x

$$x_0 < x < x_0 + \delta \Rightarrow f(x) < -B.$$

(c) For every negative real number $-B$ there exists a corresponding number $\delta > 0$ such that for all x

$$x_0 - \delta < x < x_0 \Rightarrow f(x) < -B.$$

57.

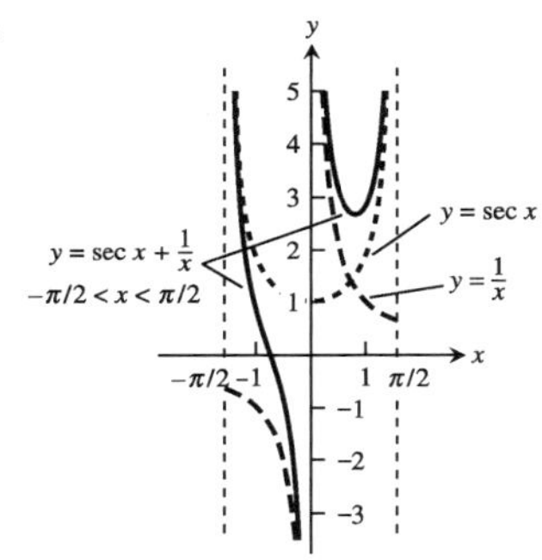

59.

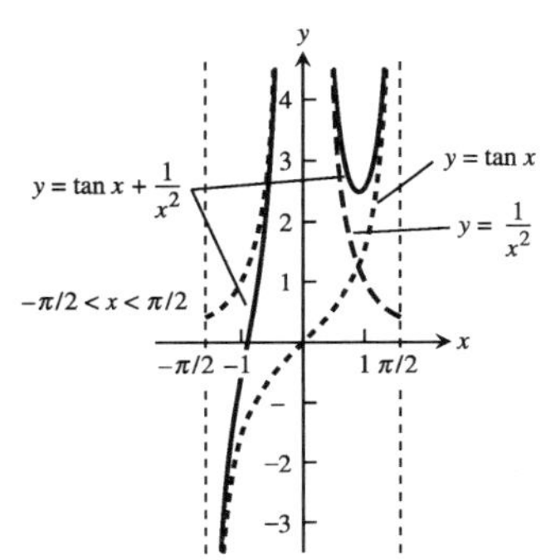

61.

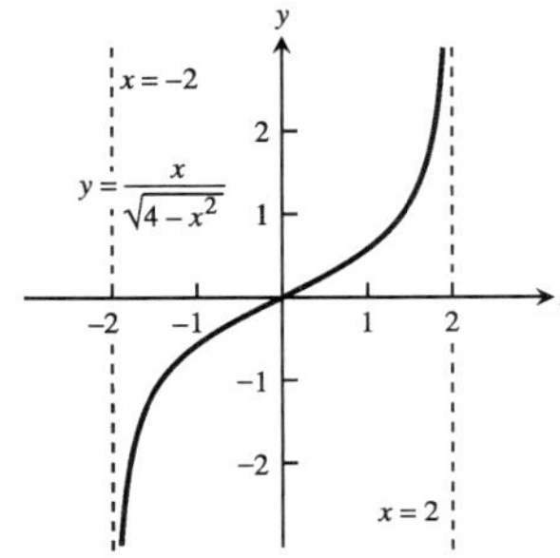

63.

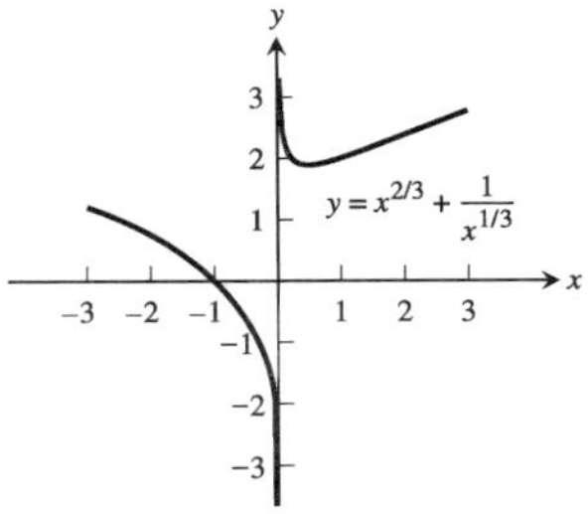

Section 2.6, pp. 132–134

1. No; discontinuous at $x = 2$; not defined at $x = 2$
3. Continuous **5. (a)** Yes **(b)** Yes **(c)** Yes **(d)** Yes
7. (a) No **(b)** No **9.** 0 **11.** 1, nonremovable; 0, removable **13.** All x except $x = 2$ **15.** All x except $x = 3, x = 1$ **17.** All x **19.** All x except $x = 0$
21. All x except $x = n\pi/2$, n any integer **23.** All x except $n\pi/2$, n an odd integer **25.** All $x \geq -3/2$ **27.** All x
29. 0; continuous at $x = \pi$ **31.** 1; continuous at $y = 1$
33. $\sqrt{2}/2$; continuous at $t = 0$ **35.** $g(3) = 6$
37. $f(1) = 3/2$ **39.** $a = 4/3$
63. $x \approx 1.8794, -1.5321, -0.3473$
65. $x \approx 1.7549$ **67.** $x \approx 3.5156$ **69.** $x \approx 0.7391$

Section 2.7, pp. 140–141

1. P_1: $m_1 = 1$, P_2: $m_2 = 5$ **3.** P_1: $m_1 = 5/2$, P_2: $m_2 = -1/2$
5. $y = 2x + 5$

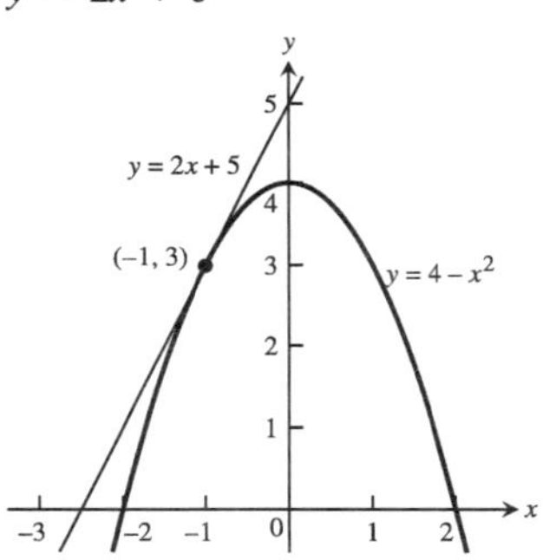

7. $y = x + 1$

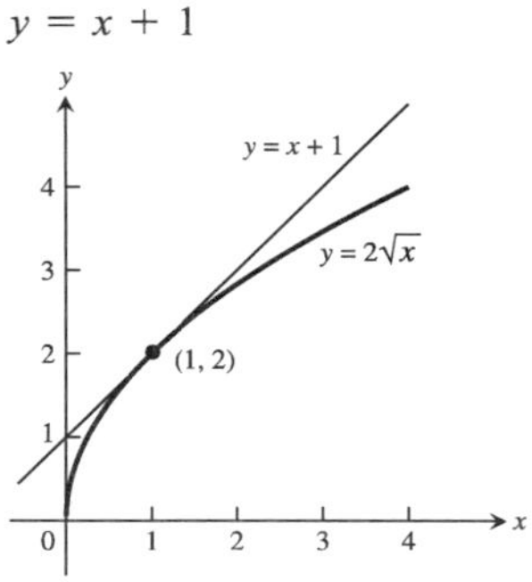

9. $y = 12x + 16$

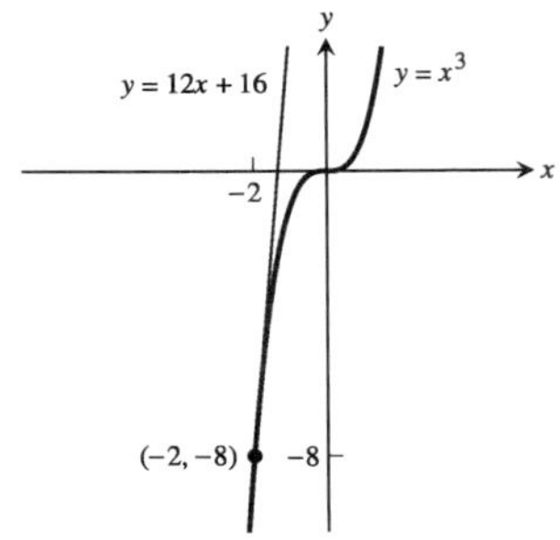

11. $m = 4, y - 5 = 4(x - 2)$
13. $m = -2, y - 3 = -2(x - 3)$
15. $m = 12, y - 8 = 12(t - 2)$
17. $m = \frac{1}{4}, y - 2 = \frac{1}{4}(x - 4)$
19. $m = -10$ **21.** $m = -1/4$ **23.** $(-2, -5)$
25. $y = -(x + 1), y = -(x - 3)$ **27.** 19.6 m/sec
29. 6π **31.** Yes **33.** Yes **35. (a)** Nowhere
37. (a) At $x = 0$ **39. (a)** Nowhere **41. (a)** At $x = 1$
43. (a) At $x = 0$

Practice Exercises, pp. 142–143

1. At $x = -1$: $\lim_{x \to -1^-} f(x) = \lim_{x \to -1^+} f(x) = 1$, so $\lim_{x \to -1} f(x) = 1 = f(-1)$; continuous at $x = -1$

At $x = 0$: $\lim_{x \to 0^-} f(x) = \lim_{x \to 0^+} f(x) = 0$, so $\lim_{x \to 0} f(x) = 0$. However, $f(0) \neq 0$, so f is discontinuous at $x = 0$. The discontinuity can be removed by redefining $f(0)$ to be 0.

At $x = 1$: $\lim_{x \to 1^-} f(x) = -1$ and $\lim_{x \to 1^+} f(x) = 1$, so $\lim_{x \to 1} f(x)$ does not exist. The function is discontinuous at $x = 1$, and the discontinuity is not removable.

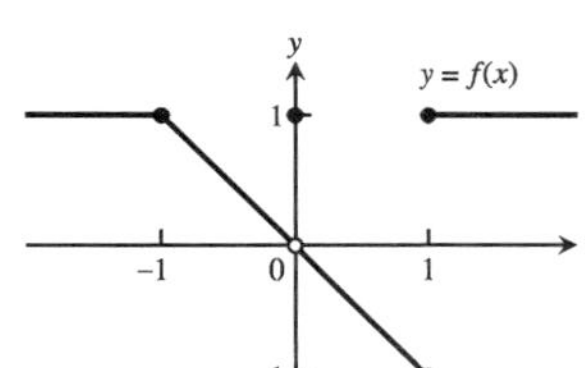

3. (a) -21 **(b)** 49 **(c)** 0 **(d)** 1 **(e)** 1 **(f)** 7 **(g)** -7 **(h)** $-\frac{1}{7}$ **5.** 4
7. (a) $(-\infty, +\infty)$ **(b)** $[0, \infty)$ **(c)** $(-\infty, 0)$ and $(0, \infty)$ **(d)** $(0, \infty)$
9. (a) Does not exist **(b)** 0
11. $\frac{1}{2}$ **13.** $2x$ **15.** $-\frac{1}{4}$ **17.** 2 **19.** 0 **21.** $\frac{2}{5}$ **23.** 0
25. $-\infty$ **27.** 0 **29.** 1 **31.** No in both cases, because $\lim_{x \to 1} f(x)$ does not exist, and $\lim_{x \to -1} f(x)$ does not exist.
37. (b) 1.324717957

Additional and Advanced Exercises, pp. 144–146

3. 0; the left-hand limit was needed because the function is undefined for $v > c$. **5.** $65 < t < 75$; within 5°F
13. (a) B (b) A (c) A (d) A
21. (a) $\lim_{a\to 0} r_+(a) = 0.5$, $\lim_{a\to -1^+} r_+(a) = 1$
(b) $\lim_{a\to 0} r_-(a)$ does not exist, $\lim_{a\to -1^+} r_-(a) = 1$
25. 0 **27.** 1 **29.** 4

CHAPTER 3

Section 3.1, pp. 155–159

1. $-2x, 6, 0, -2$ **3.** $-\frac{2}{t^3}, 2, -\frac{1}{4}, -\frac{2}{3\sqrt{3}}$
5. $\frac{3}{2\sqrt{3\theta}}, \frac{3}{2\sqrt{3}}, \frac{1}{2}, \frac{3}{2\sqrt{2}}$ **7.** $6x^2$ **9.** $\frac{1}{(2t+1)^2}$
11. $\frac{-1}{2(q+1)\sqrt{q+1}}$ **13.** $1 - \frac{9}{x^2}, 0$ **15.** $3t^2 - 2t, 5$
17. $\frac{-4}{(x-2)\sqrt{x-2}}$, $y - 4 = -\frac{1}{2}(x-6)$ **19.** 6
21. 1/8 **23.** $\frac{-1}{(x+2)^2}$ **25.** $\frac{-1}{(x-1)^2}$ **27.** b **29.** d
31. (a) $x = 0, 1, 4$ (b)

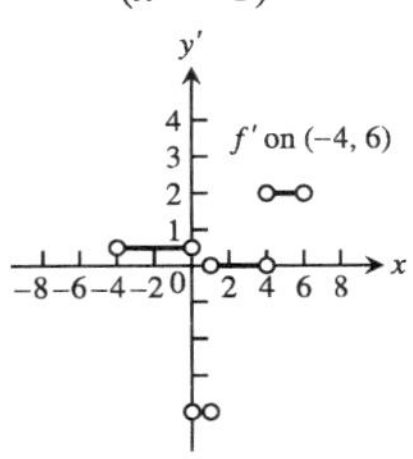

33.

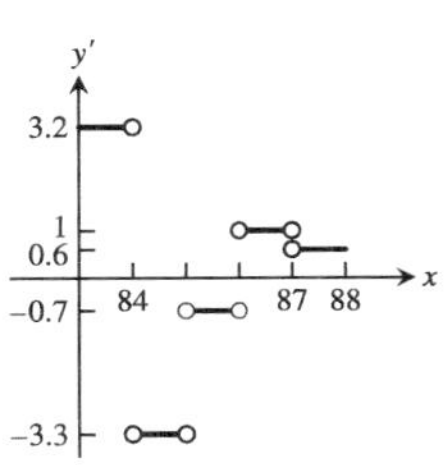

35. Since $\lim_{x\to 0^+} f'(x) = 1$ while $\lim_{x\to 0^-} f'(x) = 0$, $f(x)$ is not differentiable at $x = 0$.
37. Since $\lim_{x\to 1^+} f'(x) = 2$ while $\lim_{x\to 1^-} f'(x) = 1/2$, $f(x)$ is not differentiable at $x = 1$.
39. (a) $-3 \le x \le 2$ (b) None (c) None
41. (a) $-3 \le x < 0, 0 < x \le 3$ (b) None (c) $x = 0$
43. (a) $-1 \le x < 0, 0 < x \le 2$ (b) $x = 0$ (c) None
45. (a) $y' = -2x$ (c) $x < 0, x = 0, x > 0$
(d) $-\infty < x < 0, 0 < x < \infty$
47. (a) $y' = x^2$
(b)

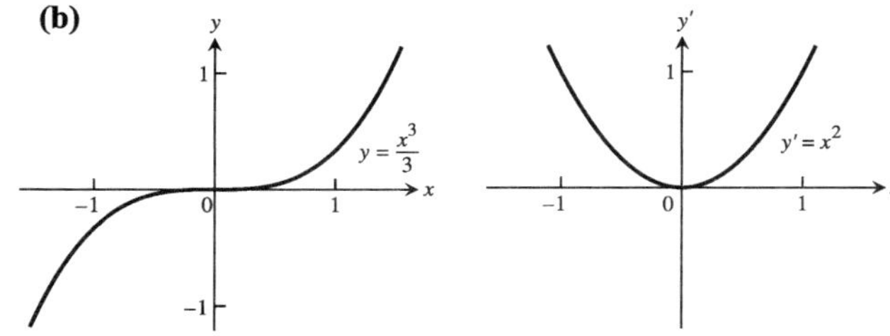

(c) $x \ne 0, x = 0$, none (d) $-\infty < x < \infty$, none
49. $y' = 3x^2$ is never negative
51. Yes, $y + 16 = -(x-3)$ is tangent at $(3, -16)$
53. No, the function $y = \lfloor x \rfloor$ does not satisfy the intermediate value property of derivatives.
55. Yes, $(-f)'(x) = -(f'(x))$
57. For $g(t) = mt$ and $h(t) = t$, $\lim_{t\to 0} \frac{g(t)}{h(t)} = m$, which need not be zero.

Section 3.2, pp. 169–171

1. $\frac{dy}{dx} = -2x, \frac{d^2y}{dx^2} = -2$
3. $\frac{ds}{dt} = 15t^2 - 15t^4, \frac{d^2s}{dt^2} = 30t - 60t^3$
5. $\frac{dy}{dx} = 4x^2 - 1, \frac{d^2y}{dx^2} = 8x$
7. $\frac{dw}{dz} = -\frac{6}{z^3} + \frac{1}{z^2}, \frac{d^2w}{dz^2} = \frac{18}{z^4} - \frac{2}{z^3}$
9. $\frac{dy}{dx} = 12x - 10 + 10x^{-3}, \frac{d^2y}{dx^2} = 12 - 30x^{-4}$
11. $\frac{dr}{ds} = \frac{-2}{3s^3} + \frac{5}{2s^2}, \frac{d^2r}{ds^2} = \frac{2}{s^4} - \frac{5}{s^3}$
13. $y' = -5x^4 + 12x^2 - 2x - 3$
15. $y' = 3x^2 + 10x + 2 - \frac{1}{x^2}$ **17.** $y' = \frac{-19}{(3x-2)^2}$
19. $g'(x) = \frac{x^2 + x + 4}{(x+0.5)^2}$ **21.** $\frac{dv}{dt} = \frac{t^2 - 2t - 1}{(1+t^2)^2}$
23. $f'(s) = \frac{1}{\sqrt{s}(\sqrt{s}+1)^2}$ **25.** $v' = -\frac{1}{x^2} + 2x^{-3/2}$
27. $y' = \frac{-4x^3 - 3x^2 + 1}{(x^2-1)^2(x^2+x+1)^2}$
29. $y' = 2x^3 - 3x - 1, y'' = 6x^2 - 3, y''' = 12x, y^{(4)} = 12, y^{(n)} = 0$ for $n \ge 5$
31. $y' = 2x - 7x^{-2}, y'' = 2 + 14x^{-3}$
33. $\frac{dr}{d\theta} = 3\theta^{-4}, \frac{d^2r}{d\theta^2} = -12\theta^{-5}$
35. $\frac{dw}{dz} = -z^{-2} - 1, \frac{d^2w}{dz^2} = 2z^{-3}$
37. $\frac{dp}{dq} = \frac{1}{6}q + \frac{1}{6}q^{-3} + q^{-5}, \frac{d^2p}{dq^2} = \frac{1}{6} - \frac{1}{2}q^{-4} - 5q^{-6}$

39. **(a)** 13 **(b)** −7 **(c)** 7/25 **(d)** 20

41. **(a)** $y = -\frac{x}{8} + \frac{5}{4}$ **(b)** $m = -4$ at $(0, 1)$

(c) $y = 8x - 15, y = 8x + 17$

43. $y = 4x, y = 2$ **45.** $a = 1, b = 1, c = 0$

47. **(a)** $y = 2x + 2,$ **(c)** $(2, 6)$

49. $P'(x) = na_n x^{n-1} + (n-1)a_{n-1}x^{n-2} + \cdots + 2a_2 x + a_1$

51. The Product Rule is then the Constant Multiple Rule, so the latter is a special case of the Product Rule.

53. **(a)** $\frac{d}{dx}(uvw) = uvw' + uv'w + u'vw$

(b) $\frac{d}{dx}(u_1 u_2 u_3 u_4) = u_1 u_2 u_3 u_4' + u_1 u_2 u_3' u_4 + u_1 u_2' u_3 u_4 + u_1' u_2 u_3 u_4$

(c) $\frac{d}{dx}(u_1 \cdots u_n) = u_1 u_2 \cdots u_{n-1} u_n' + u_1 u_2 \cdots u_{n-2} u_{n-1}' u_n + \cdots + u_1' u_2 \cdots u_n$

55. $\frac{dP}{dV} = -\frac{nRT}{(V - nb)^2} + \frac{2an^2}{V^3}$

Section 3.3, pp. 179–183

1. **(a)** −2 m, −1 m/sec **(b)** 3 m/sec, 1 m/sec; 2 m/sec^2, 2 m/sec^2 **(c)** changes direction at $t = 3/2$ sec

3. **(a)** −9 m, −3 m/sec **(b)** 3 m/sec, 12 m/sec; 6 m/sec^2, −12 m/sec^2 **(c)** no change in direction

5. **(a)** −20 m, −5 m/sec **(b)** 45 m/sec, (1/5) m/sec; 140 m/sec^2, (4/25) m/sec^2 **(c)** no change in direction

7. **(a)** $a(1) = -6$ m/sec^2, $a(3) = 6$ m/sec^2

(b) $v(2) = 3$ m/sec **(c)** 6 m

9. Mars: ≈ 7.5 sec, Jupiter: ≈ 1.2 sec **11.** $g_s = 0.75$ m/sec^2

13. **(a)** $v = -32t, |v| = 32t$ ft/sec, $a = -32$ ft/sec^2

(b) $t \approx 3.3$ sec **(c)** $v \approx -107.0$ ft/sec

15. **(a)** $t = 2, t = 7$ **(b)** $3 \le t \le 6$

(c)

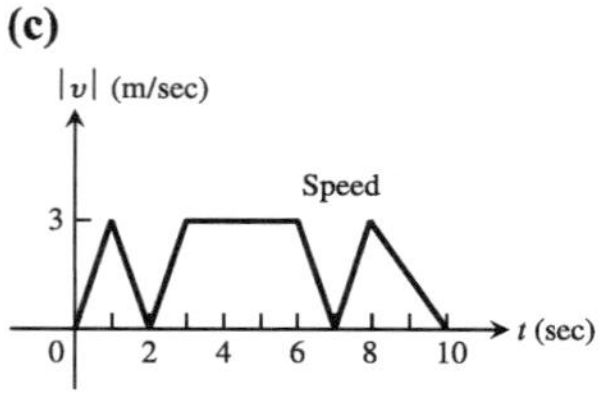

(d)

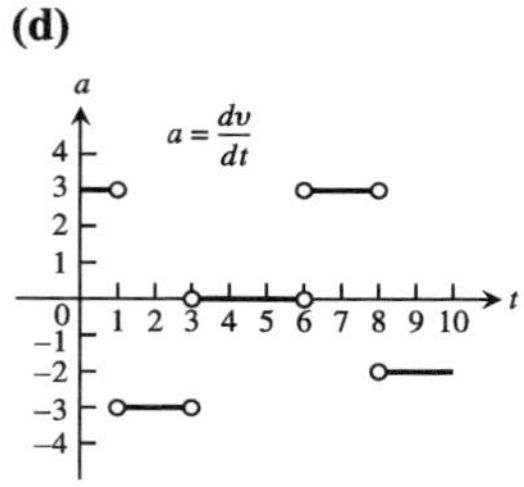

17. **(a)** 190 ft/sec **(b)** 2 sec **(c)** 8 sec, 0 ft/sec,

(d) 10.8 sec, 90 ft/sec **(e)** 2.8 sec

(f) greatest acceleration happens 2 sec after launch

(g) constant acceleration between 2 and 10.8 sec, −32 ft/sec^2

19. **(a)** $\frac{4}{7}$ sec, 280 cm/sec **(b)** 560 cm/sec, 980 cm/sec^2

(c) 29.75 flashes/sec

21. C = position, A = velocity, B = acceleration

23. **(a)** \$110/machine **(b)** \$80 **(c)** \$79.90

25. **(a)** $b'(0) = 10^4$ bacteria/h **(b)** $b'(5) = 0$ bacteria/h

(c) $b'(10) = -10^4$ bacteria/h

27. **(a)** $\frac{dy}{dt} = \frac{t}{12} - 1$ **(b)** The largest value of $\frac{dy}{dt}$ is 0 m/h when $t = 12$ and the smallest value of $\frac{dy}{dt}$ is −1 m/h, when $t = 0$.

(c)

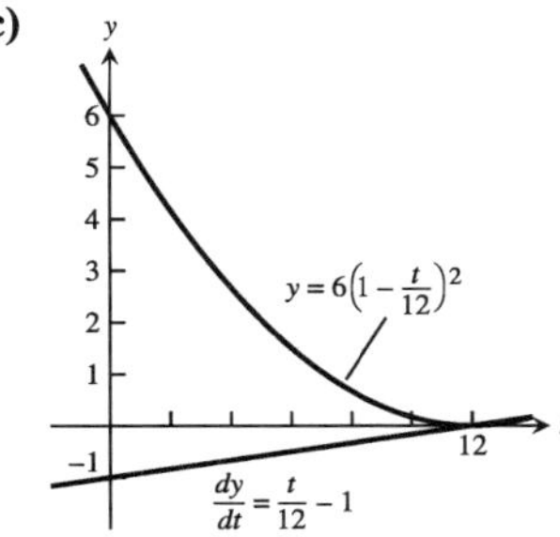

29. $t = 25$ sec $D = \frac{6250}{9}$ m

31.

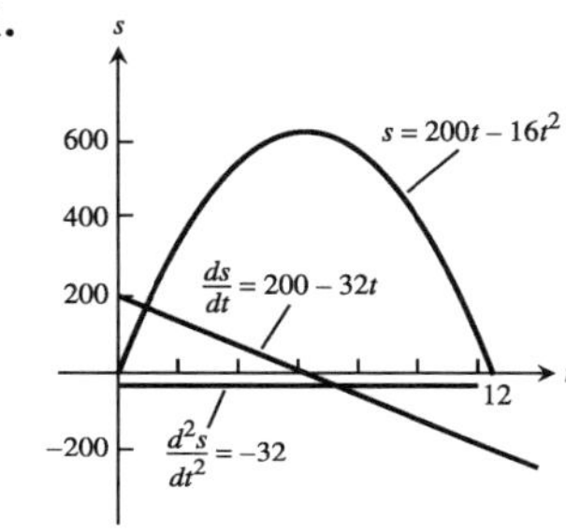

(a) $v = 0$ when $t = 6.25$ sec. **(b)** $v > 0$ when $0 \le t < 6.25 \Rightarrow$ body moves up; $v < 0$ when $6.25 < t \le 12.5 \Rightarrow$ body moves down. **(c)** Body changes direction at $t = 6.25$ sec. **(d)** Body speeds up on (6.25, 12.5] and slows down on [0, 6.25). **(e)** The body is moving fastest at the endpoints $t = 0$ and $t = 12.5$ when it is traveling 200 ft/sec. It's moving slowest at $t = 6.25$ when the speed is 0. **(f)** When $t = 6.25$ the body is $s = 625$ m from the origin and farthest away.

33.

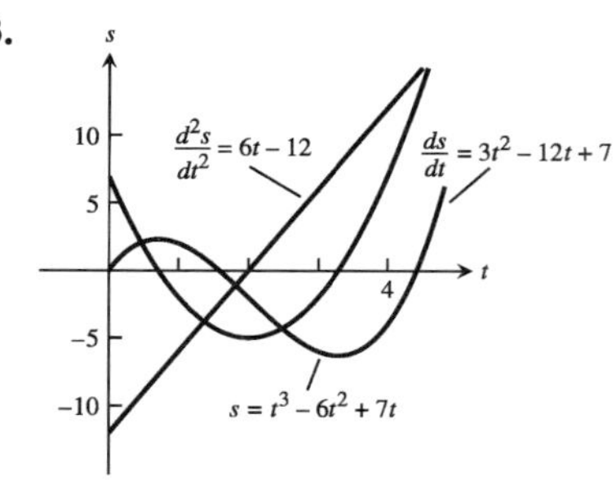

(a) $v = 0$ when $t = \frac{6 \pm \sqrt{15}}{3}$ sec.

(b) $v < 0$ when $\frac{6 - \sqrt{15}}{3} < t < \frac{6 + \sqrt{15}}{3} \Rightarrow$ body moves left; $v > 0$ when $0 \le t < \frac{6 - \sqrt{15}}{3}$ or $\frac{6 + \sqrt{15}}{3} < t \le 4 \Rightarrow$ body moves right.

(c) Body changes direction at $t = \dfrac{6 \pm \sqrt{15}}{3}$ sec.

(d) Body speeds up on $\left(\dfrac{6 - \sqrt{15}}{3}, 2\right) \cup \left(\dfrac{6 + \sqrt{15}}{3}, 4\right]$ and slows down on $\left[0, \dfrac{6 - \sqrt{15}}{3}\right) \cup \left(2, \dfrac{6 + \sqrt{15}}{3}\right)$.

(e) The body is moving fastest at $t = 0$ and $t = 4$ when it is moving 7 units/sec and slowest at $t = \dfrac{6 \pm \sqrt{15}}{3}$ sec.

(f) When $t = \dfrac{6 + \sqrt{15}}{3}$ the body is at position $s \approx -6.303$ units and farthest from the origin.

35. (a) It takes 135 sec. (b) Average speed $= \dfrac{\Delta F}{\Delta t} = \dfrac{5 - 0}{73 - 0} = \dfrac{5}{73} \approx 0.068$ furlongs/sec. (c) Using a centered difference quotient, the horse's speed is approximately (Section 3.4, Exercise 53) $\dfrac{\Delta F}{\Delta t} = \dfrac{4 - 2}{59 - 33} = \dfrac{2}{26} = \dfrac{1}{13} \approx 0.077$ furlongs/sec.
(d) The horse is running the fastest during the last furlong (between 9th and 10th furlong markers). This furlong takes only 11 sec to run, which is the least amount of time for a furlong.
(e) The horse accelerates the fastest during the first furlong (between markers 0 and 1).

Section 3.4, pp. 188–190

1. $-10 - 3\sin x$ **3.** $-\csc x \cot x - \dfrac{2}{\sqrt{x}}$ **5.** 0

7. $\dfrac{-\csc^2 x}{(1 + \cot x)^2}$ **9.** $4\tan x \sec x - \csc^2 x$ **11.** $x^2 \cos x$

13. $\sec^2 t - 1$ **15.** $\dfrac{-2\csc t \cot t}{(1 - \csc t)^2}$ **17.** $-\theta(\theta\cos\theta + 2\sin\theta)$

19. $\sec\theta\csc\theta(\tan\theta - \cot\theta) = \sec^2\theta - \csc^2\theta$

21. $\sec^2 q$ **23.** $\sec^2 q$ **25.** (a) $2\csc^3 x - \csc x$
(b) $2\sec^3 x - \sec x$

27.

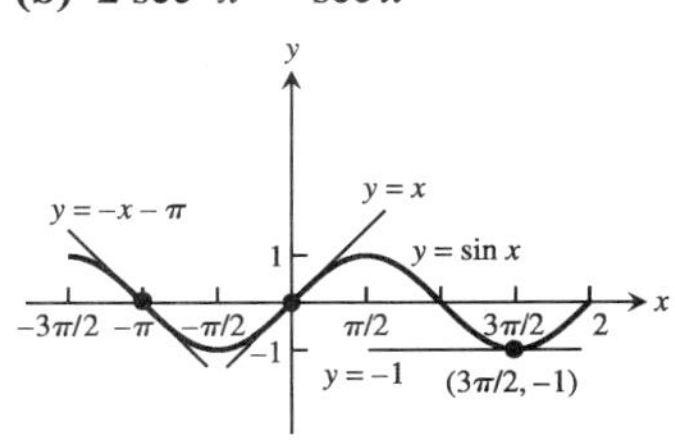

29.

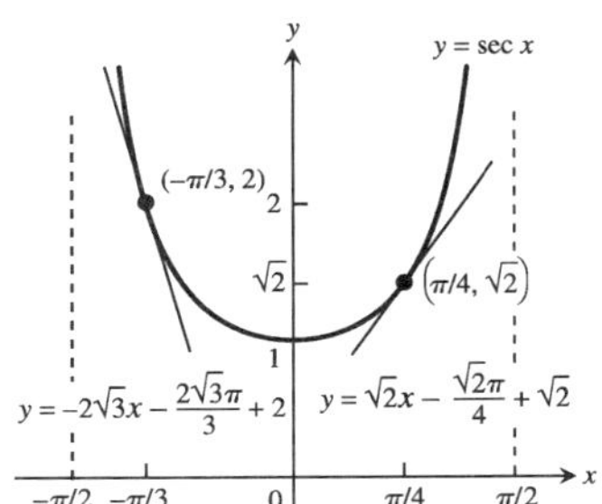

31. Yes, at $x = \pi$ **33.** No

35. $\left(-\dfrac{\pi}{4}, -1\right); \left(\dfrac{\pi}{4}, 1\right)$

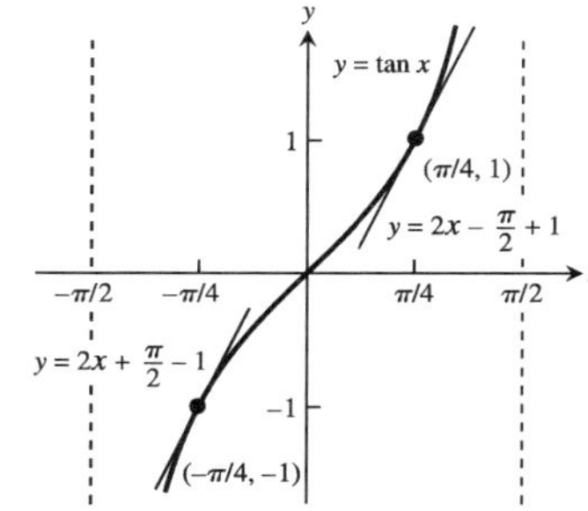

37. (a) $y = -x + \pi/2 + 2$ (b) $y = 4 - \sqrt{3}$

39. 0 **41.** -1 **43.** 0

45. $-\sqrt{2}$ m/sec, $\sqrt{2}$ m/sec, $\sqrt{2}$ m/sec^2, $\sqrt{2}$ m/sec^3

47. $c = 9$ **49.** $\sin x$

Section 3.5, pp. 201–205

1. $12x^3$ **3.** $3\cos(3x + 1)$ **5.** $-\sin(\sin x)\cos x$

7. $10\sec^2(10x - 5)$

9. With $u = (2x + 1), y = u^5: \dfrac{dy}{dx} = \dfrac{dy}{du}\dfrac{du}{dx} = 5u^4 \cdot 2 = 10(2x + 1)^4$

11. With $u = (1 - (x/7)), y = u^{-7}: \dfrac{dy}{dx} = \dfrac{dy}{du}\dfrac{du}{dx} = -7u^{-8} \cdot \left(-\dfrac{1}{7}\right) = \left(1 - \dfrac{x}{7}\right)^{-8}$

13. With $u = ((x^2/8) + x - (1/x)), y = u^4: \dfrac{dy}{dx} = \dfrac{dy}{du}\dfrac{du}{dx} = 4u^3 \cdot \left(\dfrac{x}{4} + 1 + \dfrac{1}{x^2}\right) = 4\left(\dfrac{x^2}{8} + x - \dfrac{1}{x}\right)^3\left(\dfrac{x}{4} + 1 + \dfrac{1}{x^2}\right)$

15. With $u = \tan x, y = \sec u: \dfrac{dy}{dx} = \dfrac{dy}{du}\dfrac{du}{dx} = (\sec u \tan u)(\sec^2 x) = \sec(\tan x)\tan(\tan x)\sec^2 x$

17. With $u = \sin x, y = u^3: \dfrac{dy}{dx} = \dfrac{dy}{du}\dfrac{du}{dx} = 3u^2 \cos x = 3\sin^2 x(\cos x)$

19. $-\dfrac{1}{2\sqrt{3 - t}}$ **21.** $\dfrac{4}{\pi}(\cos 3t - \sin 5t)$ **23.** $\dfrac{\csc\theta}{\cot\theta + \csc\theta}$

25. $2x\sin^4 x + 4x^2\sin^3 x\cos x + \cos^{-2} x + 2x\cos^{-3} x \sin x$

27. $(3x - 2)^6 - \dfrac{1}{x^3\left(4 - \dfrac{1}{2x^2}\right)^2}$ **29.** $\dfrac{(4x + 3)^3(4x + 7)}{(x + 1)^4}$

31. $\sqrt{x}\sec^2(2\sqrt{x}) + \tan(2\sqrt{x})$ **33.** $\dfrac{2\sin\theta}{(1 + \cos\theta)^2}$

35. $\dfrac{dr}{d\theta} = -2\sin(\theta^2)\sin 2\theta + 2\theta\cos(2\theta)\cos(\theta^2)$

37. $\frac{dq}{dt} = \left(\frac{t+2}{2(t+1)^{3/2}}\right)\cos\left(\frac{t}{\sqrt{t+1}}\right)$

39. $2\pi \sin(\pi t - 2)\cos(\pi t - 2)$ **41.** $\frac{8\sin(2t)}{(1+\cos 2t)^5}$

43. $-2\cos(\cos(2t-5))(\sin(2t-5))$

45. $\left(1+\tan^4\left(\frac{t}{12}\right)\right)^2\left(\tan^3\left(\frac{t}{12}\right)\sec^2\left(\frac{t}{12}\right)\right)$

47. $-\frac{t\sin(t^2)}{\sqrt{1+\cos(t^2)}}$ **49.** $\frac{6}{x^3}\left(1+\frac{1}{x}\right)\left(1+\frac{2}{x}\right)$

51. $2\csc^2(3x-1)\cot(3x-1)$ **53.** $5/2$ **55.** $-\pi/4$ **57.** 0

59. **(a)** $2/3$ **(b)** $2\pi+5$ **(c)** $15-8\pi$ **(d)** $37/6$ **(e)** -1 **(f)** $\sqrt{2}/24$ **(g)** $5/32$ **(h)** $-5/(3\sqrt{17})$ **61.** 5

63. **(a)** 1 **(b)** 1 **65. (a)** $y = \pi x + 2 - \pi$ **(b)** $\pi/2$

67.

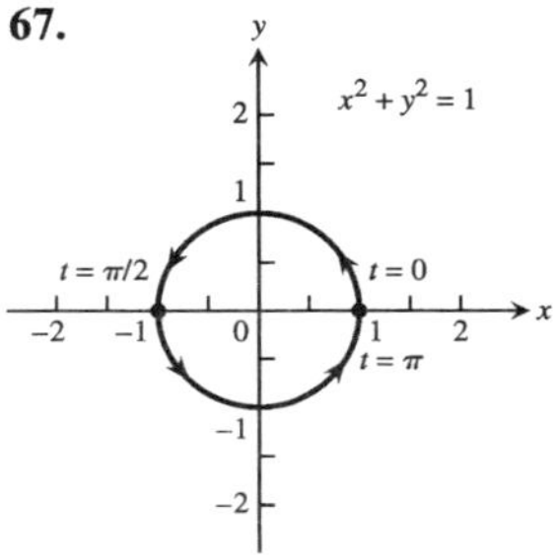

69.

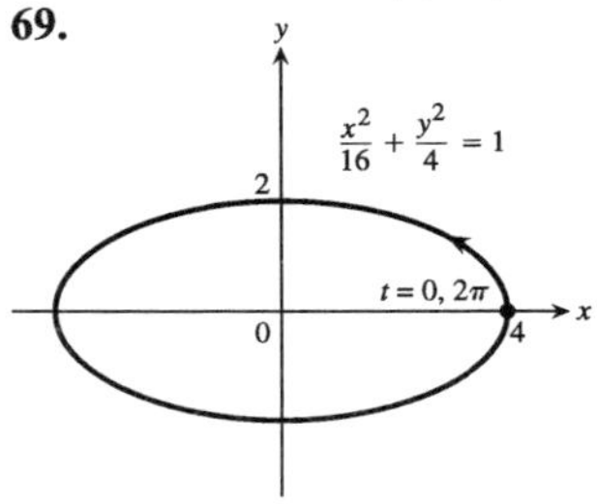

71.

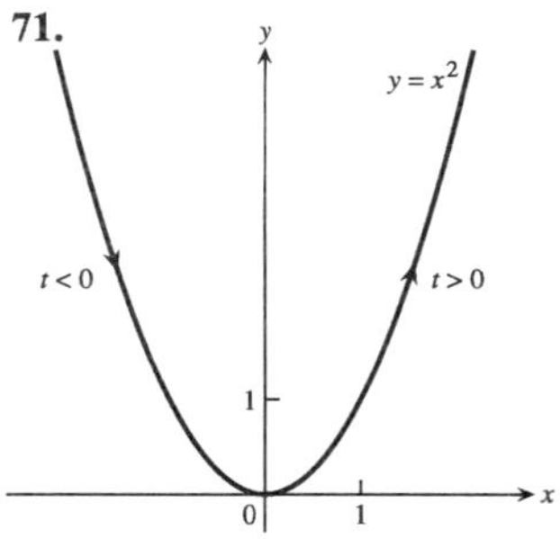

73.

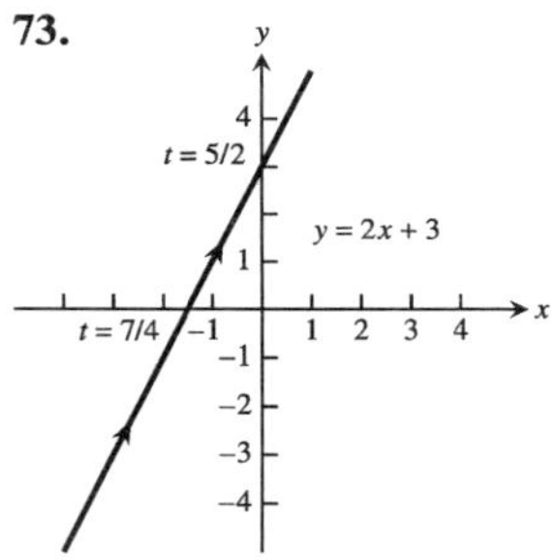

75.

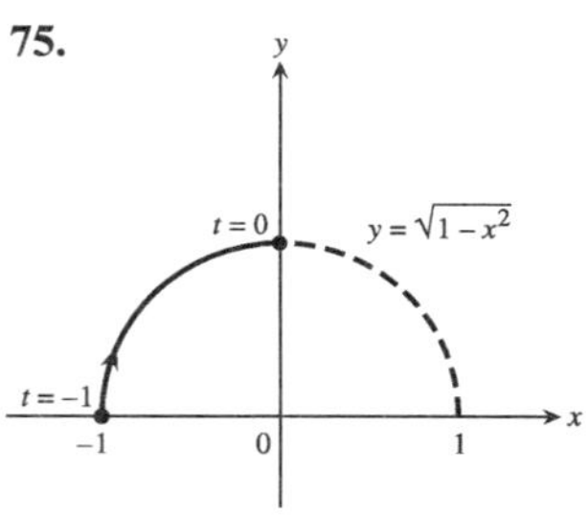

77.

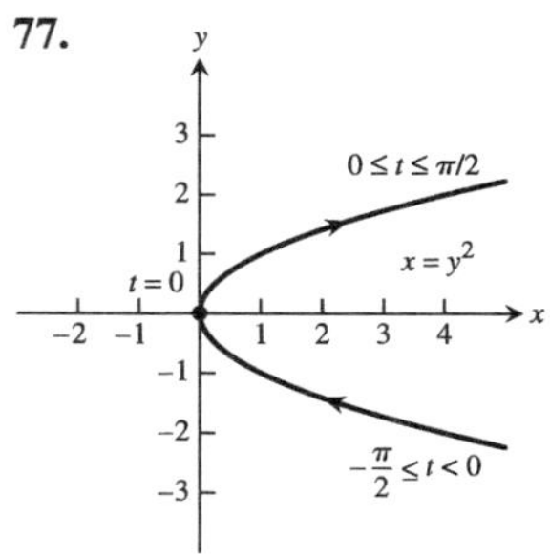

79. **(a)** $x = a\cos t,\ y = -a\sin t,\ 0 \le t \le 2\pi$
(b) $x = a\cos t,\ y = a\sin t,\ 0 \le t \le 2\pi$
(c) $x = a\cos t,\ y = -a\sin t,\ 0 \le t \le 4\pi$
(d) $x = a\cos t,\ y = a\sin t,\ 0 \le t \le 4\pi$

81. Possible answer: $x = -1 + 5t,\ y = -3 + 4t,\ 0 \le t \le 1$

83. Possible answer: $x = t^2 + 1,\ y = t,\ t \le 0$

85. Possible answer: $x = 2 - 3t,\ y = 3 - 4t,\ t \ge 0$

87. $y = -x + 2,\ \left.\frac{d^2y}{dx^2}\right|_{t=\pi/4} = -\sqrt{2}$

89. $y = x + \frac{1}{4},\ \left.\frac{d^2y}{dx^2}\right|_{t=1/4} = -2$

91. $y = x - 4,\ \left.\frac{d^2y}{dx^2}\right|_{t=-1} = \frac{1}{2}$

93. $y = 2,\ \left.\frac{d^2y}{dx^2}\right|_{t=\pi/2} = -1$

95. It multiplies the velocity, acceleration, and jerk by 2, 4, and 8, respectively.

97. $v(6) = \frac{2}{5}$ m/sec, $a(6) = -\frac{4}{125}$ m/sec^2

107. $\left(\frac{\sqrt{2}}{2}, 1\right)$, $y = 2x$ at $t = 0$, $y = -2x$ at $t = \pi$

Section 3.6, pp. 211–213

1. $\frac{9}{4}x^{5/4}$ **3.** $\frac{2^{1/3}}{3x^{2/3}}$ **5.** $\frac{7}{2(x+6)^{1/2}}$ **7.** $-(2x+5)^{-3/2}$

9. $\frac{2x^2+1}{(x^2+1)^{1/2}}$ **11.** $\frac{ds}{dt} = \frac{2}{7}t^{-5/7}$

13. $\frac{dy}{dt} = -\frac{4}{3}(2t+5)^{-5/3}\cos\left[(2t+5)^{-2/3}\right]$

15. $f'(x) = \frac{-1}{4\sqrt{x(1-\sqrt{x})}}$

17. $h'(\theta) = -\frac{2}{3}(\sin 2\theta)(1+\cos 2\theta)^{-2/3}$ **19.** $\frac{-2xy-y^2}{x^2+2xy}$

21. $\frac{1-2y}{2x+2y-1}$ **23.** $\frac{-2x^3+3x^2y-xy^2+x}{x^2y-x^3+y}$

25. $\frac{1}{y(x+1)^2}$ **27.** $\cos^2 y$ **29.** $\frac{-\cos^2(xy)-y}{x}$

31. $\frac{-y^2}{y\sin\left(\frac{1}{y}\right)-\cos\left(\frac{1}{y}\right)+xy}$ **33.** $-\frac{\sqrt{r}}{\sqrt{\theta}}$ **35.** $\frac{-r}{\theta}$

37. $y' = -\frac{x}{y},\ y'' = \frac{-y^2-x^2}{y^3}$

39. $y' = \frac{x+1}{y},\ y'' = \frac{y^2-(x+1)^2}{y^3}$

41. $y' = \frac{\sqrt{y}}{\sqrt{y}+1},\ y'' = \frac{1}{2(\sqrt{y}+1)^3}$

43. -2 **45.** $(-2, 1): m = -1,\ (-2, -1): m = 1$

47. **(a)** $y = \frac{7}{4}x - \frac{1}{2}$, **(b)** $y = -\frac{4}{7}x + \frac{29}{7}$

49. **(a)** $y = 3x + 6$, **(b)** $y = -\frac{1}{3}x + \frac{8}{3}$

51. **(a)** $y = \frac{6}{7}x + \frac{6}{7}$, **(b)** $y = -\frac{7}{6}x - \frac{7}{6}$

53. **(a)** $y = -\frac{\pi}{2}x + \pi$, **(b)** $y = \frac{2}{\pi}x - \frac{2}{\pi} + \frac{\pi}{2}$

55. **(a)** $y = 2\pi x - 2\pi$, **(b)** $y = -\frac{x}{2\pi} + \frac{1}{2\pi}$

57. Points: $(-\sqrt{7}, 0)$ and $(\sqrt{7}, 0)$, Slope: -2

59. $m = -1$ at $\left(\frac{\sqrt{3}}{4}, \frac{\sqrt{3}}{2}\right)$, $m = \sqrt{3}$ at $\left(\frac{\sqrt{3}}{4}, \frac{1}{2}\right)$

61. $(-3, 2): m = -\frac{27}{8}$; $(-3, -2): m = \frac{27}{8}$; $(3, 2): m = \frac{27}{8}$; $(3, -2): m = -\frac{27}{8}$

63. 0 **65.** -6 **67.** **(a)** False **(b)** True **(c)** True **(d)** True **69.** $(3, -1)$

73. $\frac{dy}{dx} = \frac{y^3 + 2xy}{x^2 + 3xy^2}$, $\frac{dx}{dy} = -\frac{x^2 + 3xy^2}{y^3 + 2xy}$, $\frac{dx}{dy} = \frac{1}{dy/dx}$

Section 3.7, pp. 218–221

1. $\frac{dA}{dt} = 2\pi r \frac{dr}{dt}$ **3.** **(a)** $\frac{dV}{dt} = \pi r^2 \frac{dh}{dt}$ **(b)** $\frac{dV}{dt} = 2\pi hr \frac{dr}{dt}$
(c) $\frac{dV}{dt} = \pi r^2 \frac{dh}{dt} + 2\pi hr \frac{dr}{dt}$ **5.** **(a)** 1 volt/sec
(b) $-\frac{1}{3}$ amp/sec **(c)** $\frac{dR}{dt} = \frac{1}{I}\left(\frac{dV}{dt} - \frac{V}{I}\frac{dI}{dt}\right)$
(d) 3/2 ohms/sec, R is increasing.

7. **(a)** $\frac{ds}{dt} = \frac{x}{\sqrt{x^2 + y^2}}\frac{dx}{dt}$
(b) $\frac{ds}{dt} = \frac{x}{\sqrt{x^2 + y^2}}\frac{dx}{dt} + \frac{y}{\sqrt{x^2 + y^2}}\frac{dy}{dt}$
(c) $\frac{dx}{dt} = -\frac{y}{x}\frac{dy}{dt}$

9. **(a)** $\frac{dA}{dt} = \frac{1}{2}ab\cos\theta \frac{d\theta}{dt}$
(b) $\frac{dA}{dt} = \frac{1}{2}ab\cos\theta \frac{d\theta}{dt} + \frac{1}{2}b\sin\theta \frac{da}{dt}$
(c) $\frac{dA}{dt} = \frac{1}{2}ab\cos\theta \frac{d\theta}{dt} + \frac{1}{2}b\sin\theta \frac{da}{dt} + \frac{1}{2}a\sin\theta \frac{db}{dt}$

11. **(a)** 14 cm^2/sec, increasing **(b)** 0 cm/sec, constant **(c)** $-14/13$ cm/sec, decreasing

13. **(a)** -12 ft/sec **(b)** -59.5 ft^2/sec **(c)** -1 rad/sec

15. 20 ft/sec

17. **(a)** $\frac{dh}{dt} = 11.19$ cm/min **(b)** $\frac{dr}{dt} = 14.92$ cm/min

19. **(a)** $\frac{-1}{24\pi}$ m/min **(b)** $r = \sqrt{26y - y^2}$ m,
(c) $\frac{dr}{dt} = -\frac{5}{288\pi}$ m/min

21. 1 ft/min, 40π ft^2/min **23.** 11 ft/sec **25.** Increasing at 466/1681 L/min **27.** 1 rad/sec **29.** -5 m/sec

31. -1500 ft/sec **33.** $\frac{5}{72\pi}$ in./min, $\frac{10}{3}$ in.^2/min

35. 7.1 in./min **37.** **(a)** $-32/\sqrt{13} \approx -8.875$ ft/sec,
(b) $d\theta_1/dt = 8/65$ rad/sec, $d\theta_2/dt = -8/65$ rad/sec
(c) $d\theta_1/dt = 1/6$ rad/sec, $d\theta_2/dt = -1/6$ rad/sec

Section 3.8, pp. 231–234

1. $L(x) = 10x - 13$ **3.** $L(x) = 2$ **5.** $2x$ **7.** -5

9. $\frac{1}{12}x + \frac{4}{3}$ **11.** **(a)** $L(x) = x$ **(b)** $L(x) = \pi - x$

13. **(a)** $L(x) = 1$ **(b)** $L(x) = 2 - 2\sqrt{3}\left(x + \frac{\pi}{3}\right)$

15. $f(0) = 1$. Also, $f'(x) = k(1 + x)^{k-1}$, so $f'(0) = k$. This means the linearization at $x = 0$ is $L(x) = 1 + kx$.

17. **(a)** 1.01 **(b)** 1.003

19. $\left(3x^2 - \frac{3}{2\sqrt{x}}\right)dx$ **21.** $\frac{2 - 2x^2}{(1 + x^2)^2}dx$

23. $\frac{1 - y}{3\sqrt{y} + x}dx$ **25.** $\frac{5}{2\sqrt{x}}\cos(5\sqrt{x})\,dx$

27. $(4x^2)\sec^2\left(\frac{x^3}{3}\right)dx$

29. $\frac{3}{\sqrt{x}}(\csc(1 - 2\sqrt{x})\cot(1 - 2\sqrt{x}))\,dx$

31. **(a)** .41 **(b)** .4 **(c)** .01
33. **(a)** .231 **(b)** .2 **(c)** .031
35. **(a)** $-1/3$ **(b)** $-2/5$ **(c)** $1/15$
37. $dV = 4\pi r_0^2\,dr$ **39.** $dS = 12x_0\,dx$ **41.** $dV = 2\pi r_0 h\,dr$
43. **(a)** 0.08π m^2 **(b)** 2% **45.** $dV \approx 565.5$ in.^3

47. $\frac{1}{3}\%$ **49.** 0.05%

51. The ratio equals 37.87, so a change in the acceleration of gravity on the moon has about 38 times the effect that a change of the same magnitude has on Earth.

53. 3% **55.** 3%

59. $\lim_{x\to 0}\frac{\sqrt{1 + x}}{1 + \left(\frac{x}{2}\right)} = \frac{\sqrt{1 + 0}}{1 + \left(\frac{0}{2}\right)} = \frac{1}{1} = 1$ **65.** $0.07c$

Practice Exercises, pp. 235–240

1. $5x^4 - 0.25x + 0.25$ **3.** $3x(x - 2)$
5. $2(x + 1)(2x^2 + 4x + 1)$
7. $3(\theta^2 + \sec\theta + 1)^2(2\theta + \sec\theta\tan\theta)$

9. $\frac{1}{2\sqrt{t}(1 + \sqrt{t})^2}$ **11.** $2\sec^2 x\tan x$

13. $8\cos^3(1 - 2t)\sin(1 - 2t)$ **15.** $5(\sec t)(\sec t + \tan t)^5$

17. $\frac{\theta\cos\theta + \sin\theta}{\sqrt{2\theta\sin\theta}}$ **19.** $\frac{\cos\sqrt{2\theta}}{\sqrt{2\theta}}$

21. $x\csc\left(\frac{2}{x}\right) + \csc\left(\frac{2}{x}\right)\cot\left(\frac{2}{x}\right)$

23. $\frac{1}{2}x^{1/2}\sec(2x)^2\left[16\tan(2x)^2 - x^{-2}\right]$

25. $-10x\csc^2(x^2)$ **27.** $8x^3\sin(2x^2)\cos(2x^2) + 2x\sin^2(2x^2)$

29. $\frac{-(t + 1)}{8t^3}$ **31.** $\frac{1 - x}{(x + 1)^3}$ **33.** $\frac{-1}{2x^2\left(1 + \frac{1}{x}\right)^{1/2}}$

35. $\dfrac{-2\sin\theta}{(\cos\theta - 1)^2}$ **37.** $3\sqrt{2x+1}$ **39.** $-9\left[\dfrac{5x+\cos 2x}{(5x^2+\sin 2x)^{5/2}}\right]$

41. $-\dfrac{y+2}{x+3}$ **43.** $\dfrac{-3x^2-4y+2}{4x-4y^{1/3}}$ **45.** $-\dfrac{y}{x}$

47. $\dfrac{1}{2y(x+1)^2}$ **49.** $\dfrac{dp}{dq} = \dfrac{6q-4p}{3p^2+4q}$

51. $\dfrac{dr}{ds} = (2r-1)(\tan 2s)$

53. **(a)** $\dfrac{d^2y}{dx^2} = \dfrac{-2xy^3-2x^4}{y^5}$ **(b)** $\dfrac{d^2y}{dx^2} = \dfrac{-2xy^2-1}{x^4y^3}$

55. **(a)** 7 **(b)** −2 **(c)** 5/12 **(d)** 1/4 **(e)** 12 **(f)** 9/2 **(g)** 3/4

57. 0 **59.** $\sqrt{3}$ **61.** $-\dfrac{1}{2}$ **63.** $\dfrac{-2}{(2t+1)^2}$

65. **(a)**

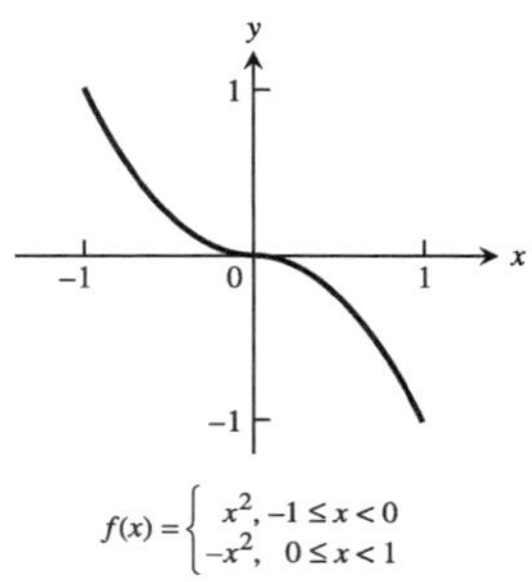

(b) Yes **(c)** Yes

67. **(a)**

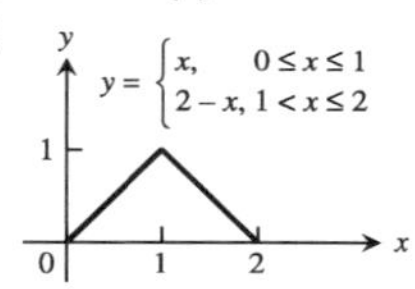

(b) Yes **(c)** No

69. $\left(\dfrac{5}{2}, \dfrac{9}{4}\right)$ and $\left(\dfrac{3}{2}, -\dfrac{1}{4}\right)$ **71.** $(-1, 27)$ and $(2, 0)$

73. **(a)** $(-2, 16)$, $(3, 11)$ **(b)** $(0, 20)$, $(1, 7)$

75.

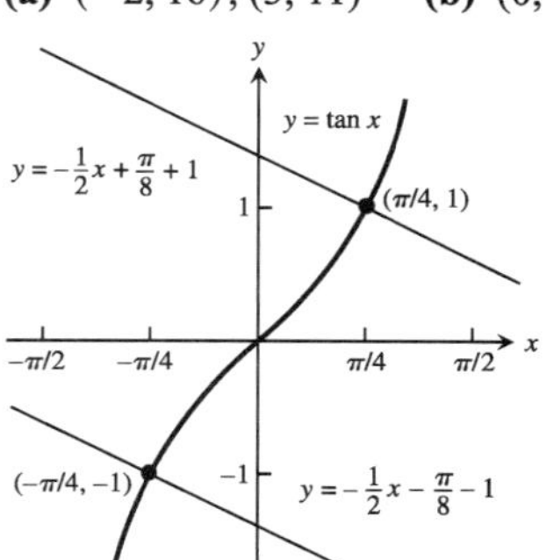

77. $\dfrac{1}{4}$ **79.** 4 **81.** Tangent: $y = -\dfrac{1}{4}x + \dfrac{9}{4}$, normal: $y = 4x - 2$

83. Tangent: $y = 2x - 4$, normal: $y = -\dfrac{1}{2}x + \dfrac{7}{2}$

85. Tangent: $y = -\dfrac{5}{4}x + 6$, normal: $y = \dfrac{4}{5}x - \dfrac{11}{5}$

87. $(1, 1)$: $m = -\dfrac{1}{2}$; $(1, -1)$: m not defined

89. $y = \left(\dfrac{\sqrt{3}}{2}\right)x + \dfrac{1}{4}, \dfrac{1}{4}$ **91.** B = graph of f, A = graph of f'

93.

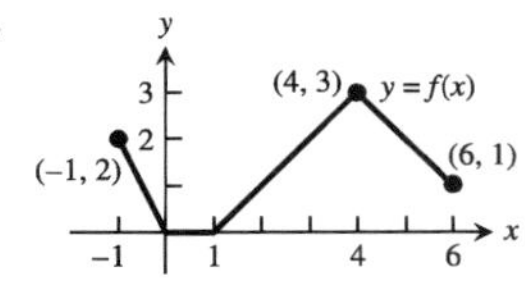

95. **(a)** 0, 0 **(b)** 1700 rabbits, ≈1400 rabbits

97. −1 **99.** 1/2 **101.** 4 **103.** 1

107. **(a)** $\dfrac{dS}{dt} = (4\pi r + 2\pi h)\dfrac{dr}{dt}$ **(b)** $\dfrac{dS}{dt} = 2\pi r\dfrac{dh}{dt}$

(c) $\dfrac{dS}{dt} = (4\pi r + 2\pi h)\dfrac{dr}{dt} + 2\pi r\dfrac{dh}{dt}$

(d) $\dfrac{dr}{dt} = -\dfrac{r}{2r+h}\dfrac{dh}{dt}$

109. $-40\ \text{m}^2/\text{sec}$ **111.** 0.02 ohm/sec **113.** 22 m/sec

115. **(a)** $r = \dfrac{2}{5}h$ **(b)** $-\dfrac{125}{144\pi}$ ft/min

117. **(a)** $\dfrac{3}{5}$ km/sec or 600 m/sec **(b)** $\dfrac{18}{\pi}$ rpm

119. **(a)** $L(x) = 2x + \dfrac{\pi - 2}{2}$

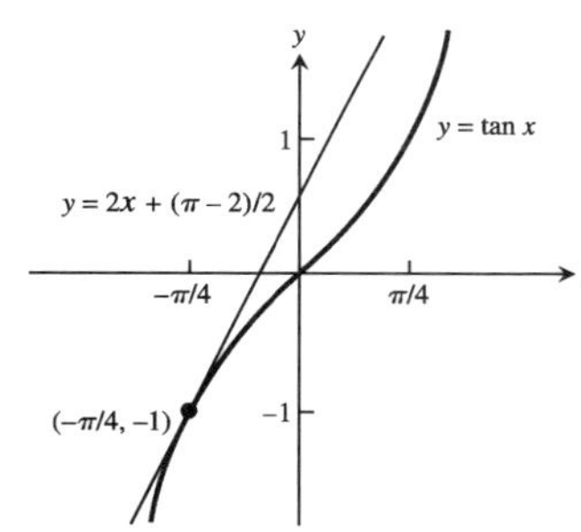

(b) $L(x) = -\sqrt{2}x + \dfrac{\sqrt{2}(4-\pi)}{4}$

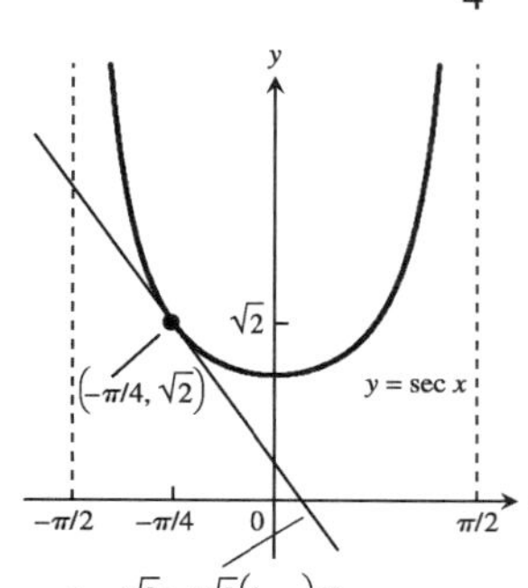

121. $L(x) = 1.5x + 0.5$ **123.** $dS = \dfrac{\pi r h_0}{\sqrt{r^2 + h_0^2}}\, dh$

125. **(a)** 4% **(b)** 8% **(c)** 12%

Additional and Advanced Exercises, pp. 240–243

1. **(a)** $\sin 2\theta = 2 \sin\theta \cos\theta$; $2\cos 2\theta = 2\sin\theta(-\sin\theta) + \cos\theta(2\cos\theta)$; $2\cos 2\theta = -2\sin^2\theta + 2\cos^2\theta$; $\cos 2\theta = \cos^2\theta - \sin^2\theta$
(b) $\cos 2\theta = \cos^2\theta - \sin^2\theta$; $-2\sin 2\theta = 2\cos\theta(-\sin\theta) - 2\sin\theta(\cos\theta)$; $\sin 2\theta = \cos\theta\sin\theta + \sin\theta\cos\theta$; $\sin 2\theta = 2\sin\theta\cos\theta$

3. **(a)** $a = 1, b = 0, c = -\dfrac{1}{2}$ **(b)** $b = \cos a, c = \sin a$

5. $h = -4, k = \dfrac{9}{2}, a = \dfrac{5\sqrt{5}}{2}$

7. **(a)** $0.09y$ **(b)** Increasing at 1% per year

9. Answers will vary. Here is one possibility.

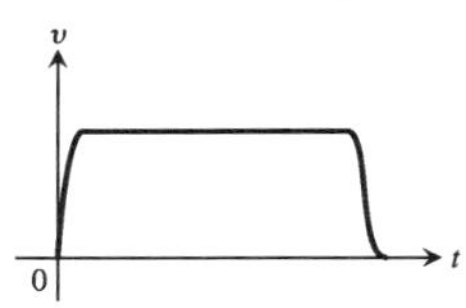

11. **(a)** 2 sec, 64 ft/sec **(b)** 12.31 sec, 393.85 ft

15. **(a)** $m = -\dfrac{b}{\pi}$ **(b)** $m = -1, b = \pi$

17. **(a)** $a = \dfrac{3}{4}, b = \dfrac{9}{4}$ **19.** f odd $\Rightarrow f'$ is even

23. h' is defined but not continuous at $x = 0$; k' is defined *and* continuous at $x = 0$.

27. **(a)** 0.8156 ft **(b)** 0.00613 sec **(c)** It will lose about 8.83 min/day.

CHAPTER 4

Section 4.1, pp. 252–255

1. Absolute minimum at $x = c_2$; absolute maximum at $x = b$

3. Absolute maximum at $x = c$; no absolute minimum

5. Absolute minimum at $x = a$; absolute maximum at $x = c$

7. Local minimum at $(-1, 0)$; local maximum at $(1, 0)$

9. Maximum at $(0, 5)$ **11.** (c) **13.** (d)

15. Absolute maximum: -3; absolute minimum: $-19/3$

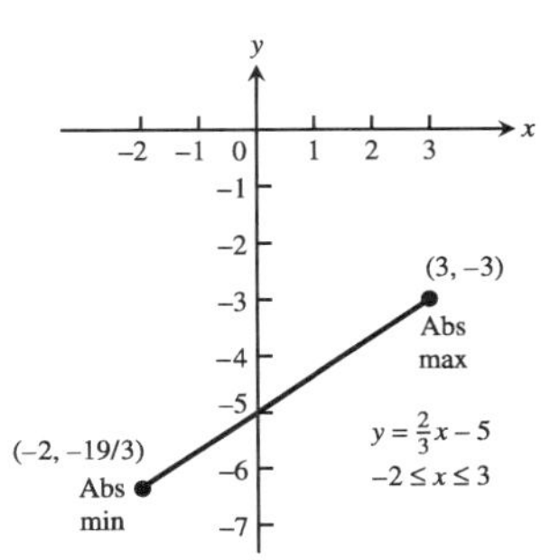

17. Absolute maximum: 3; absolute minimum: -1

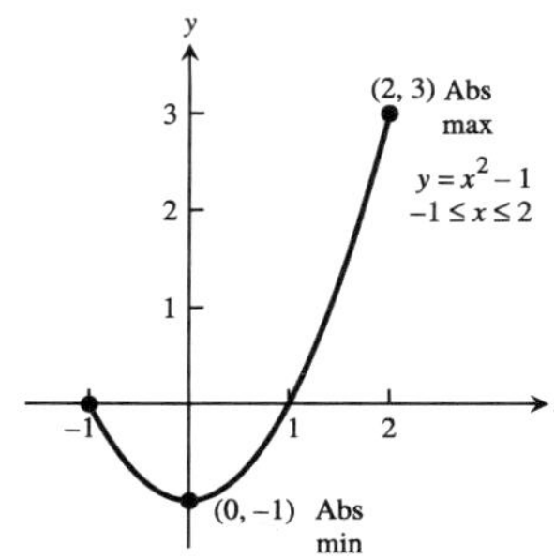

19. Absolute maximum: -0.25; absolute minimum: -4

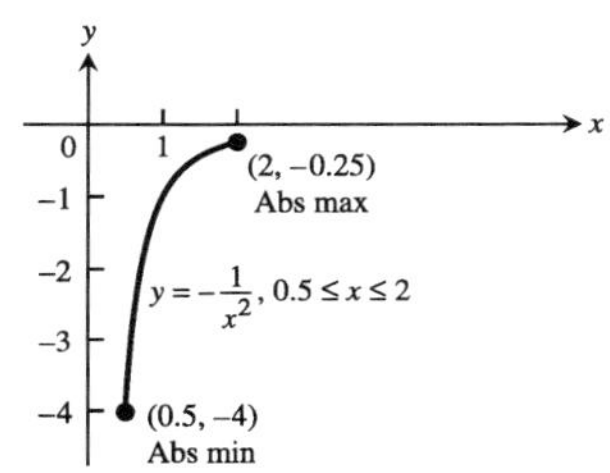

21. Absolute maximum: 2; absolute minimum: -1

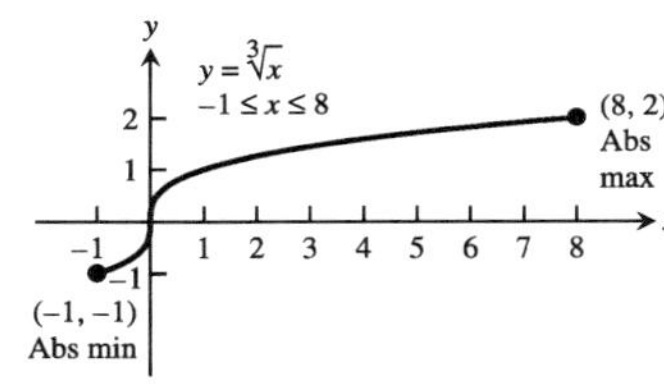

23. Absolute maximum: 2; absolute minimum: 0

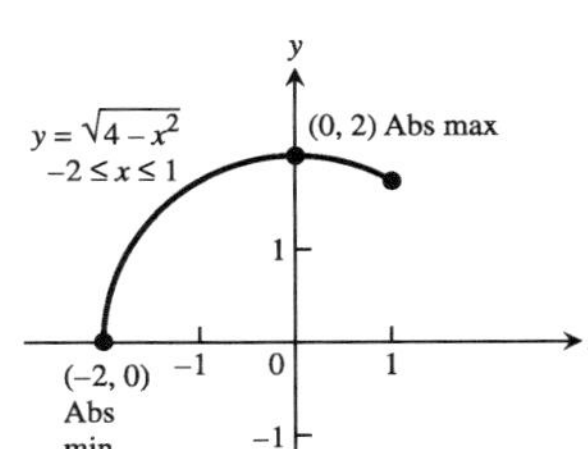

25. Absolute maximum: 1; absolute minimum: -1

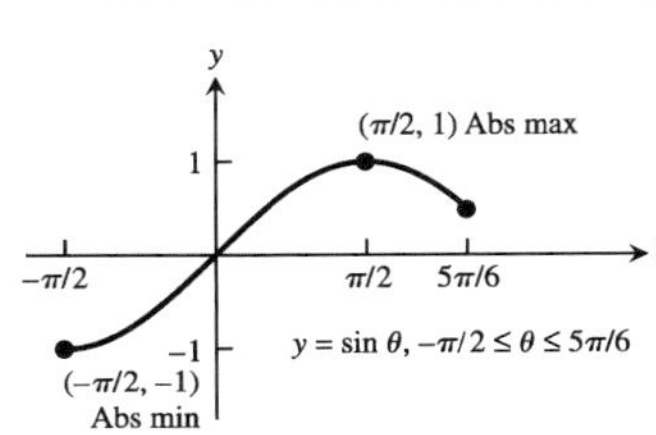

27. Absolute maximum: $2/\sqrt{3}$; absolute minimum: 1

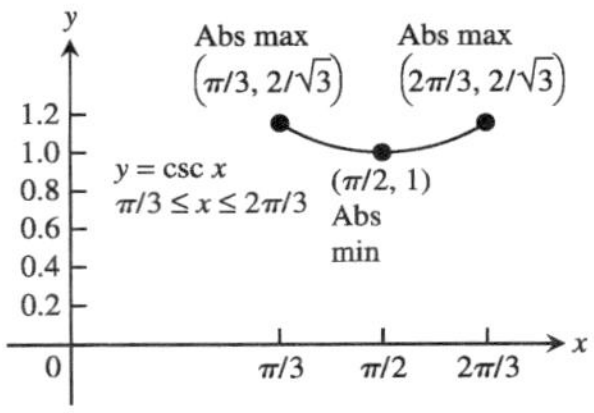

29. Absolute maximum: 2; absolute minimum: -1

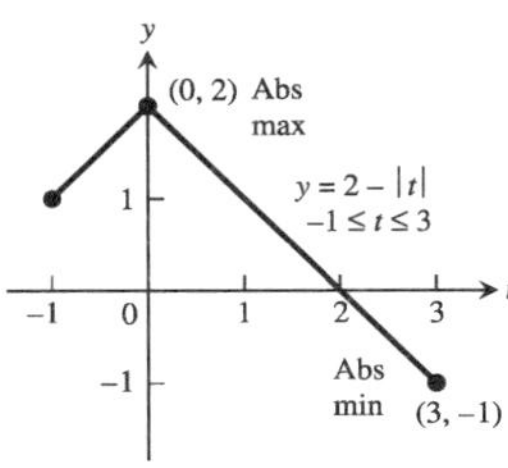

31. Increasing on $(0, 8)$, decreasing on $(-1, 0)$; absolute maximum: 16 at $x = 8$; absolute minimum: 0 at $x = 0$

33. Increasing on $(-32, 1)$; absolute maximum: 1 at $\theta = 1$; absolute minimum: -8 at $\theta = -32$

35. Minimum value is 1 at $x = 2$.

37. Local maximum at $(-2, 17)$; local minimum at $\left(\frac{4}{3}, -\frac{41}{27}\right)$

39. Minimum value is 0 at $x = -1$ and $x = 1$.

41. There is a local minimum at $(0, 1)$.

43. Maximum value is $\frac{1}{2}$ at $x = 1$; minimum value is $-\frac{1}{2}$ at $x = -1$.

45.

Critical point	Derivative	Extremum	Value
$x = -\frac{4}{5}$	0	Local max	$\frac{12}{25}10^{1/3} = 1.034$
$x = 0$	Undefined	Local min	0

47.

Critical point	Derivative	Extremum	Value
$x = -2$	Undefined	Local max	0
$x = -\sqrt{2}$	0	Minimum	-2
$x = \sqrt{2}$	0	Maximum	2
$x = 2$	Undefined	Local min	0

49.

Critical point	Derivative	Extremum	Value
$x = 1$	Undefined	Minimum	2

51.

Critical point	Derivative	Extremum	Value
$x = -1$	0	Maximum	5
$x = 1$	Undefined	Local min	1
$x = 3$	0	Maximum	5

53. **(a)** No
(b) The derivative is defined and nonzero for $x \ne 2$. Also, $f(2) = 0$ and $f(x) > 0$ for all $x \ne 2$.
(c) No, because $(-\infty, \infty)$ is not a closed interval.
(d) The answers are the same as parts (a) and (b) with 2 replaced by a.

55. **(a)** $C(x) = 0.3\sqrt{16 + x^2} + 0.2(9 - x)$ million dollars, where $0 \le x \le 9$ mi. To minimize the cost of construction, the pipeline should be placed from the docking facility to point B, 3.58 mi along the shore from point A, and then along the shore from point B to the refinery.
(b) In theory, the underwater pipe cost per mile p would have to be infinite to justify running the pipe directly from the docking facility to point A (i.e., for x_c to be zero). For all values of $p > 0.218864$, there is always an x_c in $(0, 9)$ that will give a minimum value for C. This is proved by looking at $C''(x_c) = \frac{16p}{(16 + x_c^2)^{3/2}}$, which is always positive for $p > 0$.

57. The length of pipeline is $L(x) = \sqrt{4 + x^2} + \sqrt{25 + (10 - x)^2}$ for $0 \le x \le 10$. $x = \frac{20}{7} \approx 2.857$ mi along the coast from Town A to Town B.

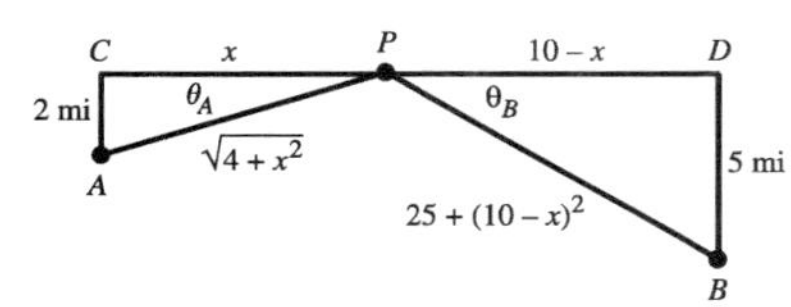

59. **(a)** Maximum value is 144 at $x = 2$.
(b) The largest volume of the box is 144 cubic units, and it occurs when $x = 2$.

61. The largest possible area is $A\left(\frac{5}{\sqrt{2}}\right) = \frac{25}{4}$ cm^2.

63. $\frac{v_0^2}{2g} + s_0$ **65.** Yes **67.** g assumes a local maximum at $-c$.

69. **(a)** $f'(x) = 3ax^2 + 2bx + c$ is a quadratic, so it can have 0, 1, or 2 zeros, which would be the critical points of f. Examples: The function $f(x) = x^3 - 3x$ has two critical points at $x = -1$ and $x = 1$.

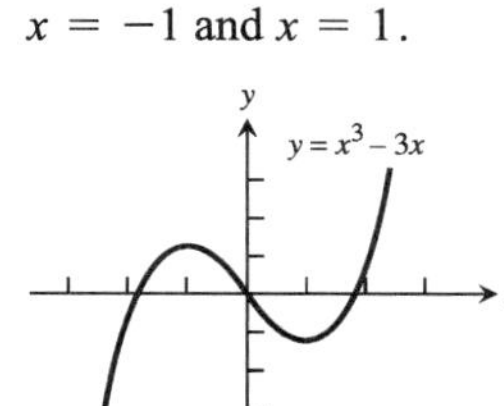

The function $f(x) = x^3 - 1$ has one critical point at $x = 0$.

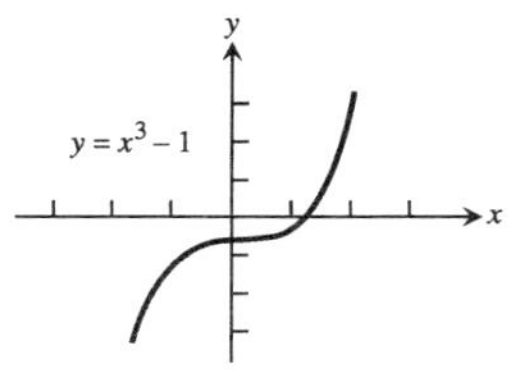

The function $f(x) = x^3 + x$ has no critical points.

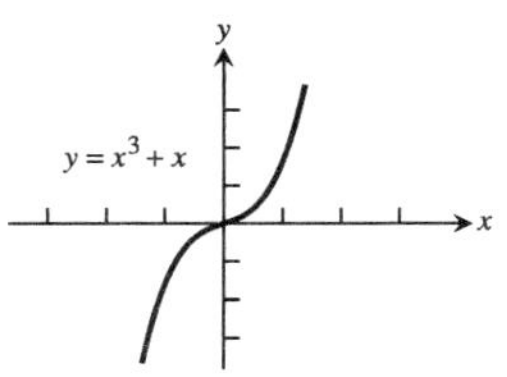

(b) Two or none

71. Maximum value is 11 at $x = 5$; minimum value is 5 on the interval $[-3, 2]$; local maximum at $(-5, 9)$.

73. Maximum value is 5 on the interval $[3, \infty)$; minimum value is -5 on the interval $(-\infty, -2]$.

Section 4.2, pp. 260–262

1. 1/2 **3.** 1 **5.** Does not; f is not differentiable at the interior domain point $x = 0$. **7.** Does

11. (a)

i) 

ii) 

iii) 

iv) 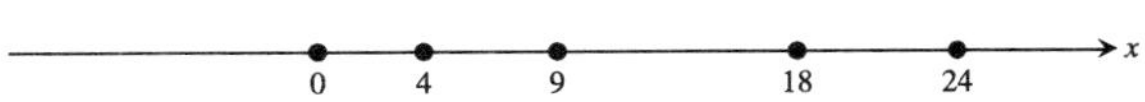

23. Yes **25. (a)** 4 **(b)** 3 **(c)** 3

27. (a) $\frac{x^2}{2} + C$ **(b)** $\frac{x^3}{3} + C$ **(c)** $\frac{x^4}{4} + C$

29. (a) $\frac{1}{x} + C$ **(b)** $x + \frac{1}{x} + C$ **(c)** $5x - \frac{1}{x} + C$

31. (a) $-\frac{1}{2}\cos 2t + C$ **(b)** $2\sin\frac{t}{2} + C$

(c) $-\frac{1}{2}\cos 2t + 2\sin\frac{t}{2} + C$

33. $f(x) = x^2 - x$ **35.** $r(\theta) = 8\theta + \cot\theta - 2\pi - 1$

37. $s = 4.9t^2 + 5t + 10$ **39.** $s = \frac{1 - \cos(\pi t)}{\pi}$

41. $s = 16t^2 + 20t + 5$ **43.** $s = \sin(2t) - 3$

45. If $T(t)$ is the temperature of the thermometer at time t, then $T(0) = -19$ °C and $T(14) = 100$ °C. From the Mean Value Theorem, there exists a $0 < t_0 < 14$ such that $\frac{T(14) - T(0)}{14 - 0} = 8.5$ °C/sec $= T'(t_0)$, the rate at which the temperature was changing at $t = t_0$ as measured by the rising mercury on the thermometer.

47. Because its average speed was approximately 7.667 knots, and by the Mean Value Theorem, it must have been going that speed at least once during the trip.

51. The conclusion of the Mean Value Theorem yields

$$\frac{\frac{1}{b} - \frac{1}{a}}{b - a} = -\frac{1}{c^2} \Rightarrow c^2\left(\frac{a - b}{ab}\right) = a - b \Rightarrow c = \sqrt{ab}.$$

55. $f(x)$ must be zero at least once between a and b by the Intermediate Value Theorem. Now suppose that $f(x)$ is zero twice between a and b. Then, by the Mean Value Theorem, $f'(x)$ would have to be zero at least once between the two zeros of $f(x)$, but this can't be true since we are given that $f'(x) \neq 0$ on this interval. Therefore, $f(x)$ is zero once and only once between a and b.

61. $1.09999 \le f(0.1) \le 1.1$

Section 4.3, pp. 266–267

1. (a) 0, 1 **(b)** increasing on $(-\infty, 0)$ and $(1, \infty)$, decreasing on $(0, 1)$ **(c)** local maximum at $x = 0$, local minimum at $x = 1$

3. (a) $-2, 1$ **(b)** increasing on $(-2, 1)$ and $(1, \infty)$, decreasing on $(-\infty, -2)$ **(c)** no local maximum, local minimum at $x = -2$

5. (a) $-2, 1, 3$ **(b)** increasing on $(-2, 1)$ and $(3, \infty)$, decreasing on $(-\infty, -2)$ and $(1, 3)$ **(c)** local maximum at $x = 1$, local minima at $x = -2, 3$

7. (a) $-2, 0$ **(b)** increasing on $(-\infty, -2)$ and $(0, \infty)$, decreasing on $(-2, 0)$ **(c)** local maximum at $x = -2$, local minimum at $x = 0$

9. (a) Increasing on $(-\infty, -1.5)$, decreasing on $(-1.5, \infty)$ **(b)** local maximum: 5.25 at $t = -1.5$ **(c)** absolute maximum: 5.25 at $t = -1.5$

11. (a) Decreasing on $(-\infty, 0)$, increasing on $(0, 4/3)$, decreasing on $(4/3, \infty)$ **(b)** local minimum at $x = 0$ $(0, 0)$, local maximum at $x = 4/3$ $(4/3, 32/27)$ **(c)** no absolute extrema

13. (a) Decreasing on $(-\infty, 0)$, increasing on $(0, 1/2)$, decreasing on $(1/2, \infty)$ **(b)** local minimum at $\theta = 0$ $(0, 0)$, local maximum at $\theta = 1/2$ $(1/2, 1/4)$ **(c)** no absolute extrema

15. (a) Increasing on $(-\infty, \infty)$, never decreasing **(b)** no local extrema **(c)** no absolute extrema

17. (a) Increasing on $(-2, 0)$ and $(2, \infty)$, decreasing on $(-\infty, -2)$ and $(0, 2)$ **(b)** local maximum: 16 at $x = 0$, local minimum: 0 at $x = \pm 2$ **(c)** no absolute maximum; absolute minimum: 0 at $x = \pm 2$

19. (a) Increasing on $(-\infty, -1)$, decreasing on $(-1, 0)$, increasing on $(0, 1)$, decreasing on $(1, \infty)$ **(b)** local maximum at $x = \pm 1$ $(1, 0.5)$, $(-1, 0.5)$, local minimum at $x = 0$ $(0, 0)$ **(c)** absolute maximum: 1/2 at $x = \pm 1$; no absolute minimum

21. **(a)** Decreasing on $(-2\sqrt{2}, -2)$, increasing on $(-2, 2)$, decreasing on $(2, 2\sqrt{2})$ **(b)** local minima: $g(-2) = -4$, $g(2\sqrt{2}) = 0$; local maxima: $g(-2\sqrt{2}) = 0$, $g(2) = 4$ **(c)** absolute maximum: 4 at $x = 2$; absolute minimum: -4 at $x = -2$

23. **(a)** Increasing on $(-\infty, 1)$, decreasing when $1 < x < 2$, decreasing when $2 < x < 3$, discontinuous at $x = 2$, increasing on $(3, \infty)$ **(b)** local minimum at $x = 3$ $(3, 6)$, local maximum at $x = 1$ $(1, 2)$ **(c)** no absolute extrema

25. **(a)** Increasing on $(-2, 0)$ and $(0, \infty)$, decreasing on $(-\infty, -2)$ **(b)** local minimum: $-6\sqrt[3]{2}$ at $x = -2$ **(c)** no absolute maximum; absolute minimum: $-6\sqrt[3]{2}$ at $x = -2$

27. **(a)** Increasing on $\left(-\infty, -2/\sqrt{7}\right)$ and $\left(2/\sqrt{7}, \infty\right)$, decreasing on $\left(-2/\sqrt{7}, 0\right)$ and $\left(0, 2/\sqrt{7}\right)$ **(b)** local maximum: $24\sqrt[3]{2}/7^{7/6} \approx 3.12$ at $x = -2/\sqrt{7}$; local minimum: $-24\sqrt[3]{2}/7^{7/6} \approx -3.12$ at $x = 2/\sqrt{7}$ **(c)** no absolute extrema

29. **(a)** Local maximum: 1 at $x = 1$; local minimum: 0 at $x = 2$ **(b)** absolute maximum: 1 at $x = 1$; no absolute minimum

31. **(a)** Local maximum: 1 at $x = 1$; local minimum: 0 at $x = 2$ **(b)** no absolute maximum; absolute minimum: 0 at $x = 2$

33. **(a)** Local maxima: -9 at $t = -3$ and 16 at $t = 2$; local minimum: -16 at $t = -2$ **(b)** absolute maximum: 16 at $t = 2$; no absolute minimum

35. **(a)** Local minimum: 0 at $x = 0$ **(b)** no absolute maximum; absolute minimum: 0 at $x = 0$

37. **(a)** Local minimum: $(\pi/3) - \sqrt{3}$ at $x = 2\pi/3$; local maximum: 0 at $x = 0$; local maximum: π at $x = 2\pi$

39. **(a)** Local minimum: 0 at $x = \pi/4$

41. Local maximum: 3 at $\theta = 0$; local minimum: -3 at $\theta = 2\pi$

43.

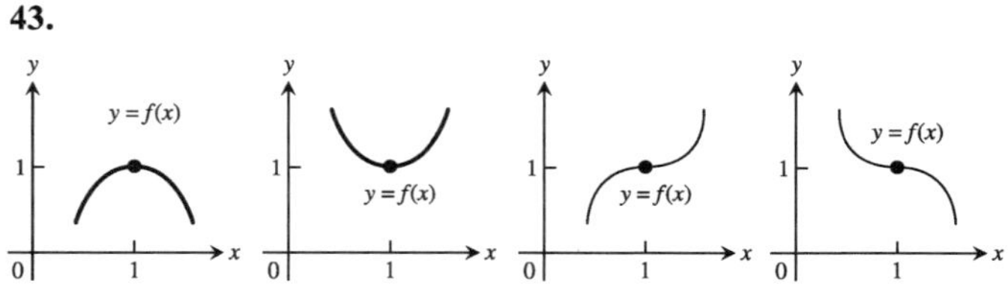

(a) (b) (c) (d)

45. **(a)**

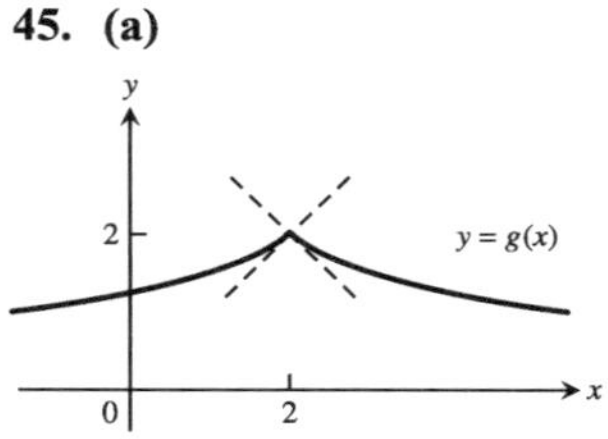

(b)

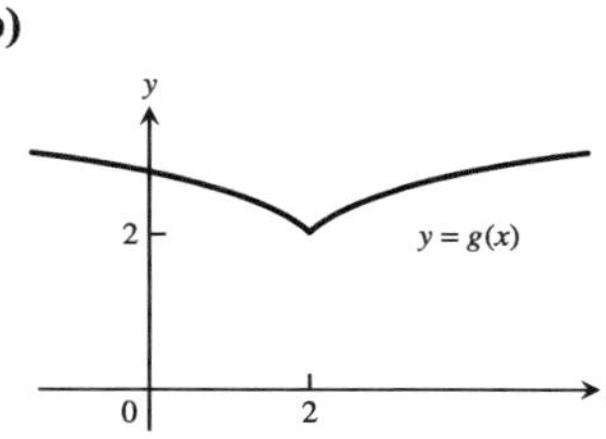

47. Rising

Section 4.4, pp. 274–277

1. Local maximum: 3/2 at $x = -1$, local minimum: -3 at $x = 2$, point of inflection at $(1/2, -3/4)$, rising on $(-\infty, -1)$ and $(2, \infty)$, falling on $(-1, 2)$, concave up on $(1/2, \infty)$, concave down on $(-\infty, 1/2)$

3. Local maximum: 3/4 at $x = 0$, local minimum: 0 at $x = \pm 1$, points of inflection at $\left(-\sqrt{3}, \frac{3\sqrt[3]{4}}{4}\right)$ and $\left(\sqrt{3}, \frac{3\sqrt[3]{4}}{4}\right)$, rising on $(-1, 0)$ and $(1, \infty)$, falling on $(-\infty, -1)$ and $(0, 1)$, concave up on $(-\infty, -\sqrt{3})$ and $(\sqrt{3}, \infty)$, concave down on $(-\sqrt{3}, \sqrt{3})$

5. Local maxima: $-2\pi/3 + \sqrt{3}/2$ at $x = -2\pi/3$; $\frac{\pi}{3} + \frac{\sqrt{3}}{2}$ at $x = \frac{\pi}{3}$, local minima: $-\frac{\pi}{3} - \frac{\sqrt{3}}{2}$ at $x = -\frac{\pi}{3}$; $2\pi/3 - \sqrt{3}/2$ at $x = \frac{2\pi}{3}$, points of inflection at $(-\pi/2, -\pi/2)$, $(0, 0)$, and $(\pi/2, \pi/2)$, rising on $(-\pi/3, \pi/3)$, falling on $(-2\pi/3, -\pi/3)$ and $(\pi/3, 2\pi/3)$, concave up on $(-\pi/2, 0)$ and $(\pi/2, 2\pi/3)$, concave down on $(-2\pi/3, -\pi/2)$ and $(0, \pi/2)$

7. Local maxima: 1 at $x = -\frac{\pi}{2}$ and $x = \frac{\pi}{2}$; 0 at $x = -2\pi$ and $x = 2\pi$; local minima: -1 at $x = -\frac{3\pi}{2}$ and $x = \frac{3\pi}{2}$, 0 at $x = 0$, points of inflection at $(-\pi, 0)$ and $(\pi, 0)$, rising on $(-3\pi/2, -\pi/2)$, $(0, \pi/2)$ and $(3\pi/2, 2\pi)$, falling on $(-2\pi, -3\pi/2)$, $(-\pi/2, 0)$ and $(\pi/2, 3\pi/2)$, concave up on $(-2\pi, -\pi)$ and $(\pi, 2\pi)$, concave down on $(-\pi, \pi)$

9.

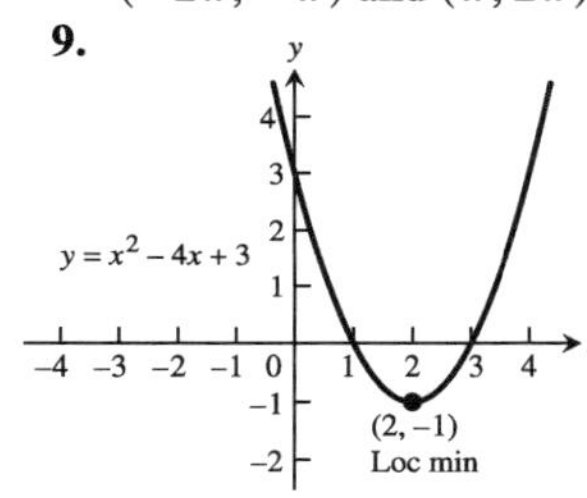

11.

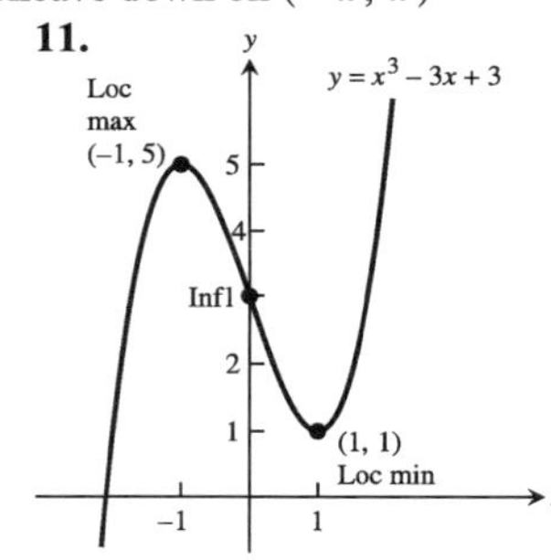

13.

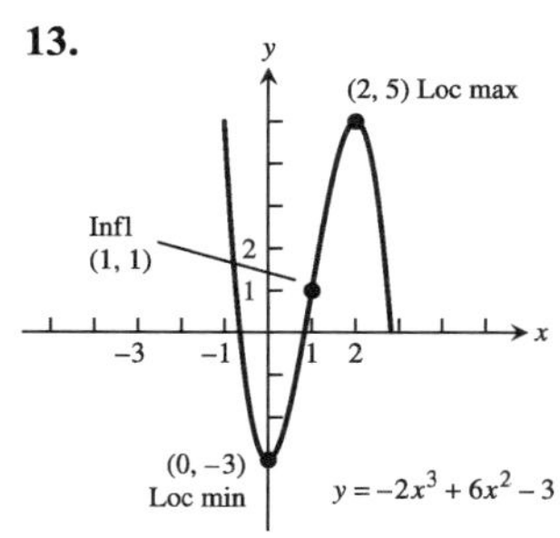

15.

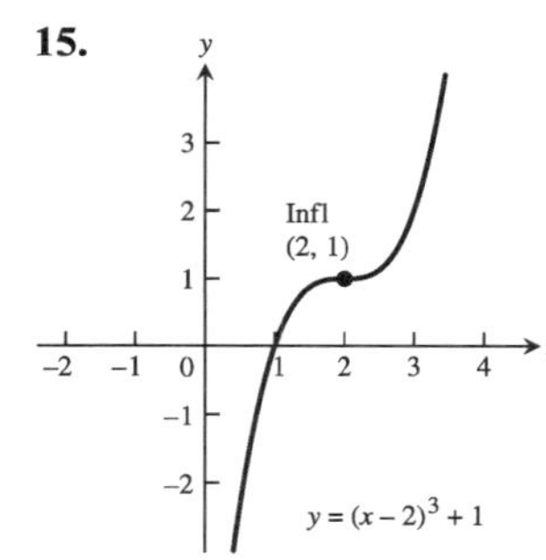

17.

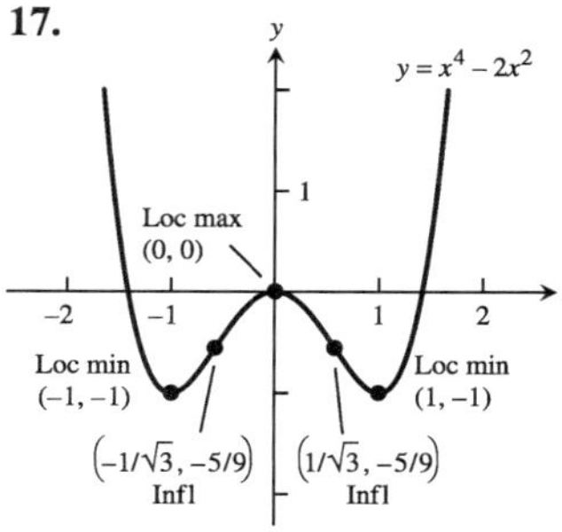

19.

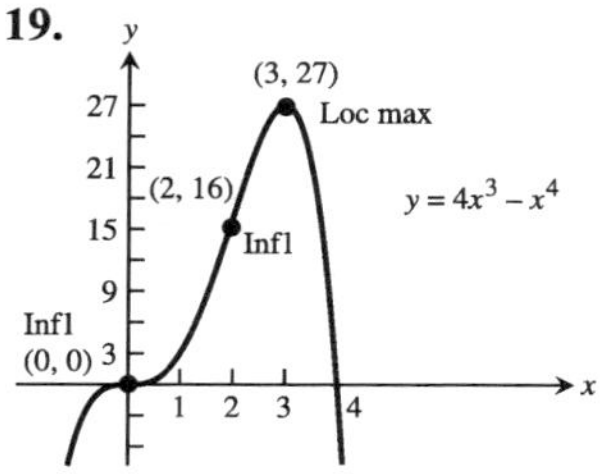

21.

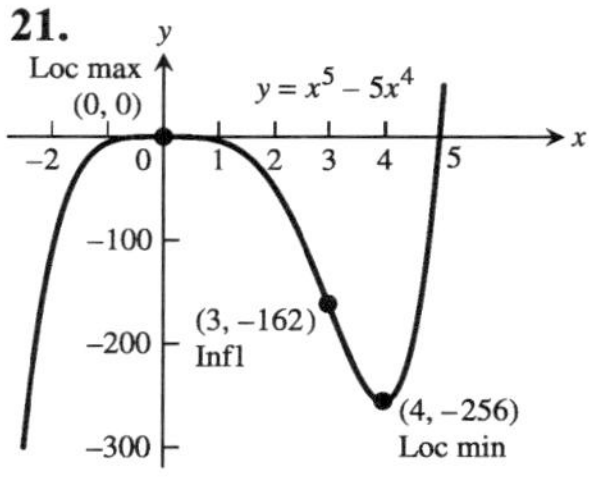

23.

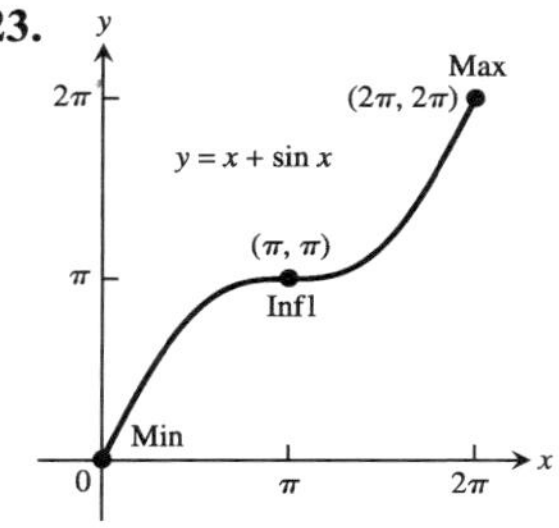

25.

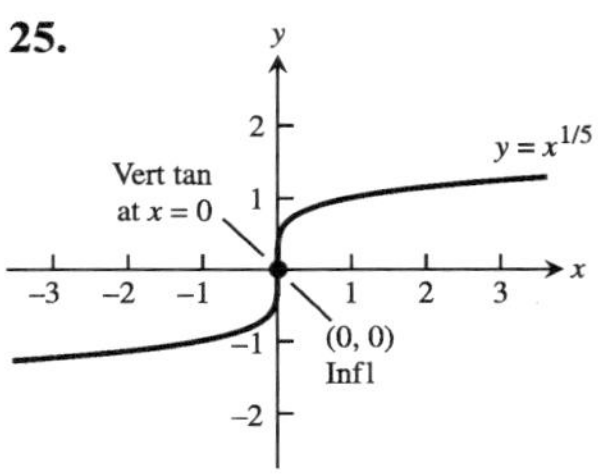

27.

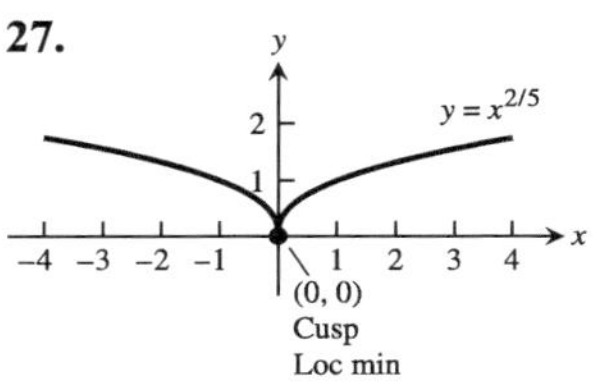

29.

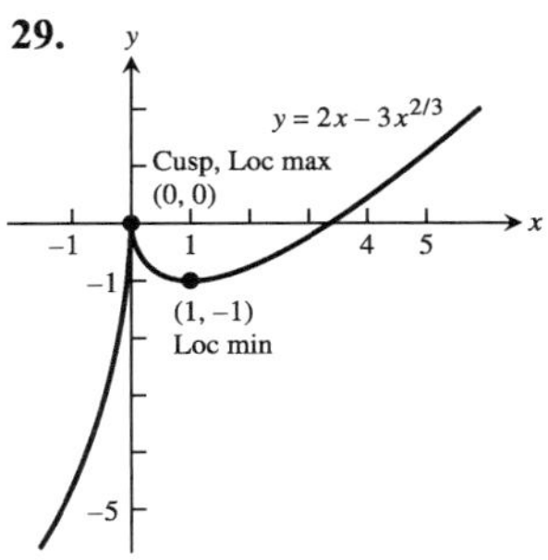

31.

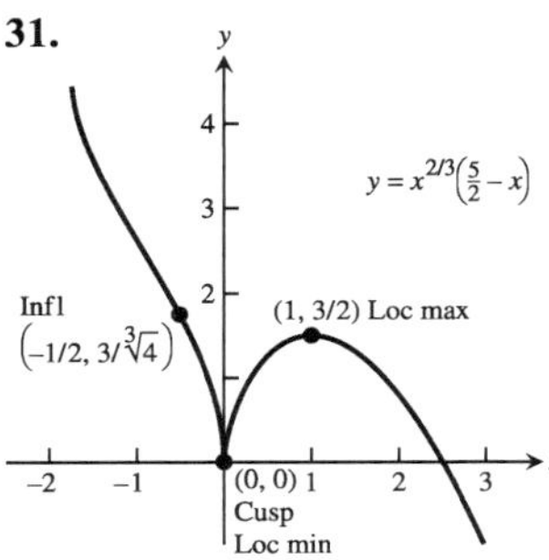

33.

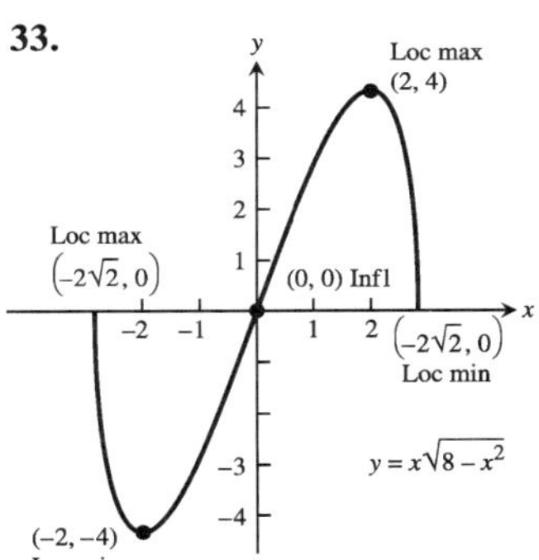

35.

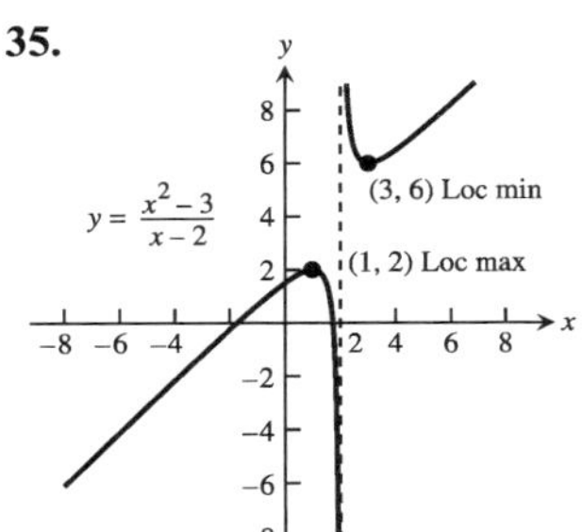

37.

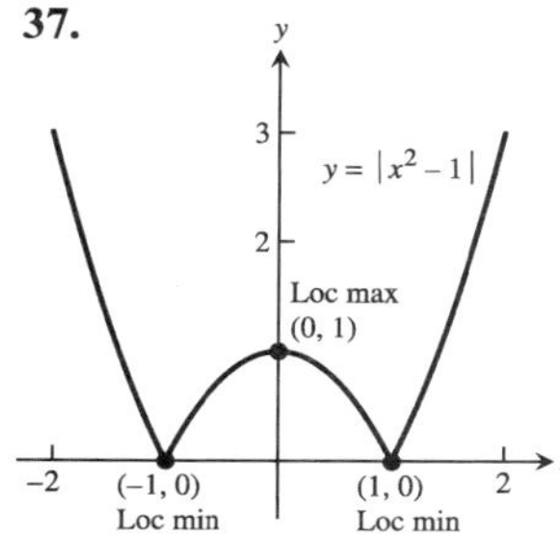

39.

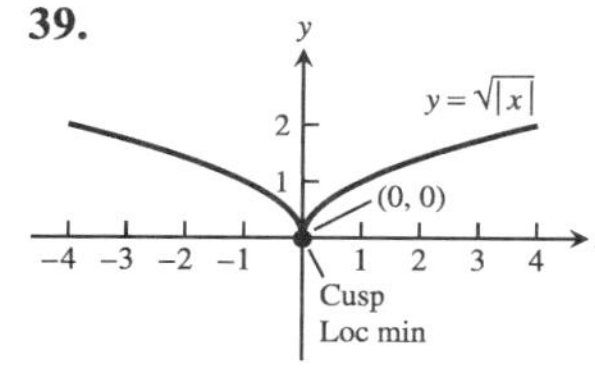

41. $y'' = 1 - 2x$

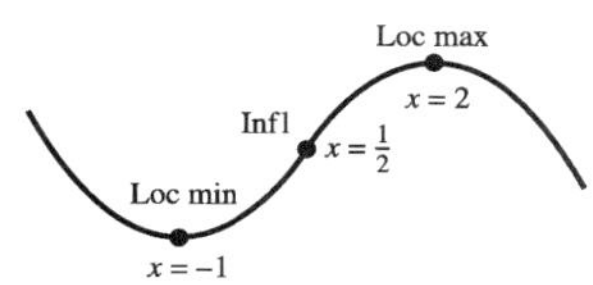

43. $y'' = 3(x - 3)(x - 1)$

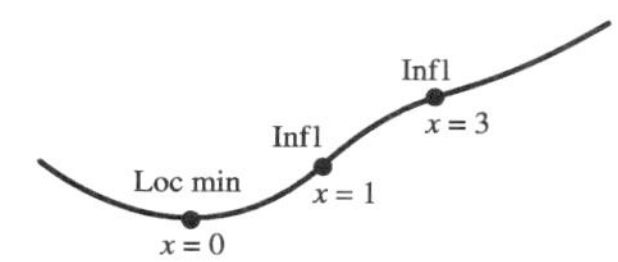

45. $y'' = 3(x - 2)(x + 2)$

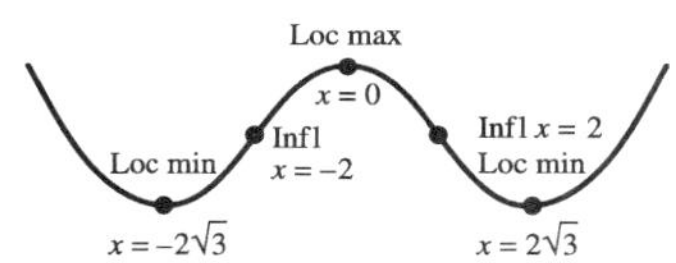

47. $y'' = 4(4 - x)(5x^2 - 16x + 8)$

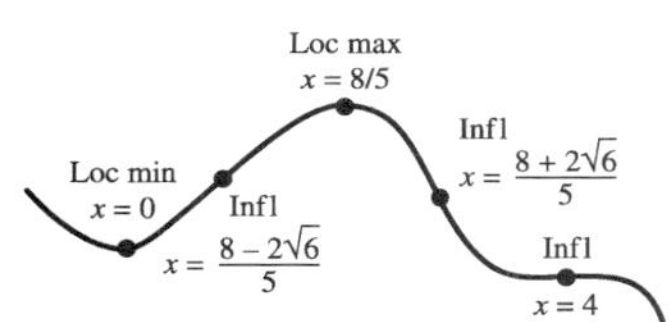

49. $y'' = 2\sec^2 x \tan x$

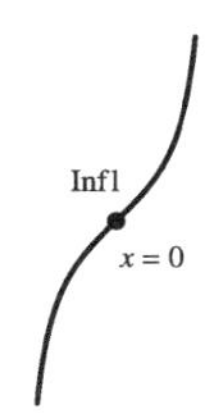

51. $y'' = -\frac{1}{2}\csc^2\frac{\theta}{2}, 0 < \theta < 2\pi$

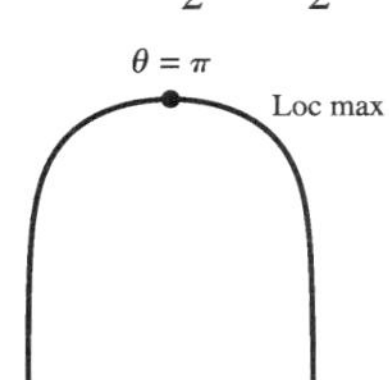

53. $y'' = 2\tan\theta\sec^2\theta,\ -\dfrac{\pi}{2} < \theta < \dfrac{\pi}{2}$

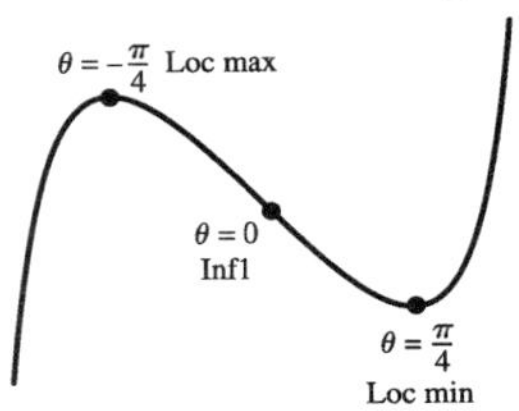

55. $y'' = -\sin t,\ 0 \le t \le 2\pi$

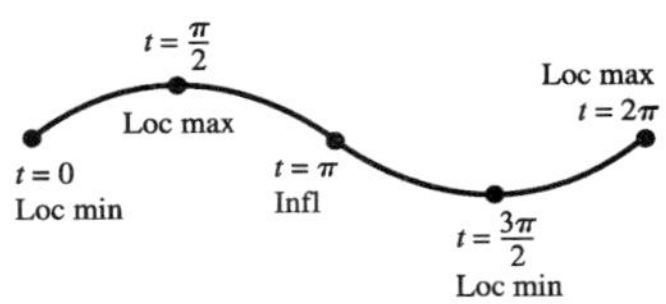

57. $y'' = -\dfrac{2}{3}(x+1)^{-5/3}$

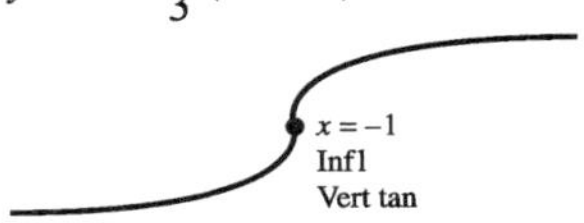

59. $y'' = \dfrac{1}{3}x^{-2/3} + \dfrac{2}{3}x^{-5/3}$

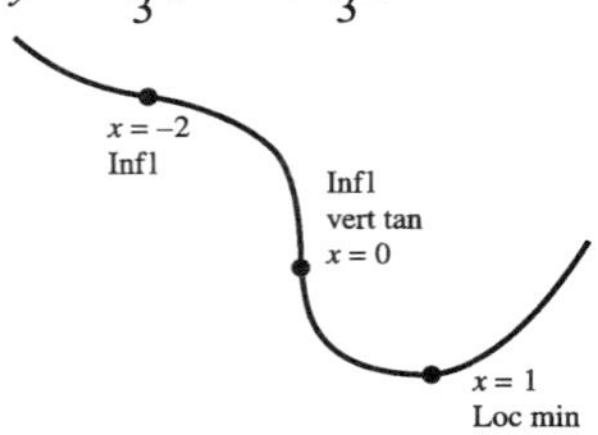

61. $y'' = \begin{cases} -2, & x < 0 \\ 2, & x > 0 \end{cases}$

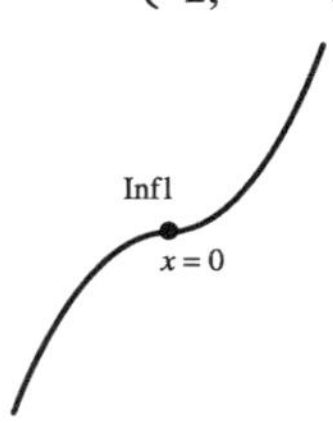

63.

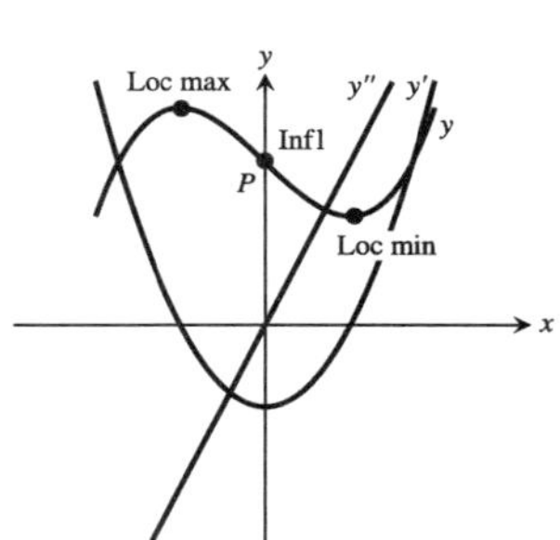

65.

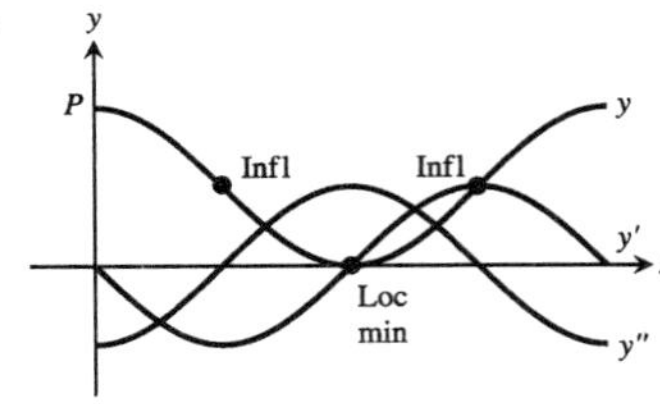

67.

Point	y'	y''
P	$-$	$+$
Q	$+$	0
R	$+$	$-$
S	0	$-$
T	$-$	$-$

69.

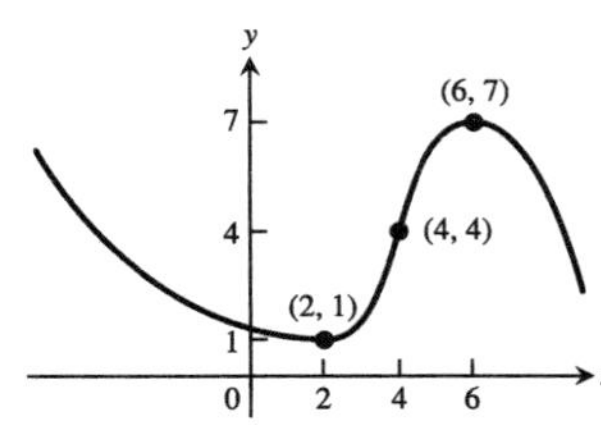

73. ≈ 60 thousand units **75.** Local minimum at $x = 2$, inflection points at $x = 1$ and $x = 5/3$ **79.** $b = -3$

81. **(a)** $\left(-\dfrac{b}{2a}, \dfrac{4ac - b^2}{4a}\right)$ **(b)** concave up if $a > 0$, concave down if $a < 0$

85. The zeros of $y' = 0$ and $y'' = 0$ are extrema and points of inflection, respectively. Inflection at $x = 3$, local maximum at $x = 0$, local minimum at $x = 4$.

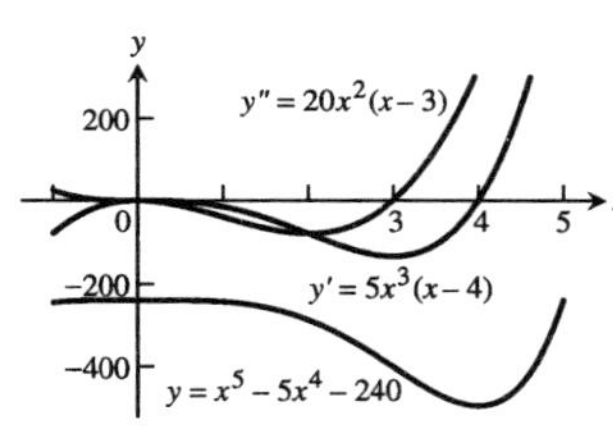

87. The zeros of $y' = 0$ and $y'' = 0$ are extrema and points of inflection, respectively. Inflection at $x = -\sqrt[3]{2}$, local maximum at $x = -2$, local minimum at $x = 0$.

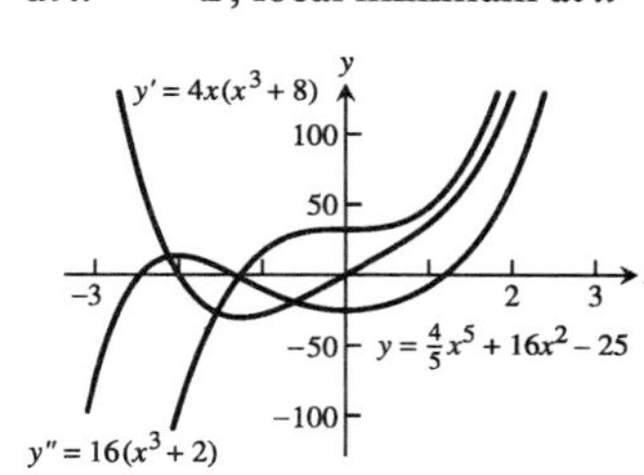

91. **(b)** $f'(x) = 3x^2 + k$; $-12k$; positive if $k < 0$, negative if $k > 0$, 0 if $k = 0$; f' has two zeros if $k < 0$, one zero if $k = 0$, no zeros if $k > 0$; that is, the sign of k controls the number of local extrema.

93. **(b)** A cusp since $\lim_{x\to 0^-} y' = \infty$ and $\lim_{x\to 0^+} y' = -\infty$

95. Yes, the graph of y' crosses through zero near -3, so y has a horizontal tangent near -3.

Section 4.5, pp. 285–292

1. 16 in., 4 in. by 4 in. **3.** **(a)** $(x, 1 - x)$ **(b)** $A(x) = 2x(1 - x)$ **(c)** $\frac{1}{2}$ square units, 1 by $\frac{1}{2}$

5. $\frac{14}{3} \times \frac{35}{3} \times \frac{5}{3}$ in., $\frac{2450}{27}$ in.^{3} **7.** 80,000 m^2; 400 m by 200 m

9. **(a)** The optimum dimensions of the tank are 10 ft on the base edges and 5 ft deep.
(b) Minimizing the surface area of the tank minimizes its weight for a given wall thickness. The thickness of the steel walls would likely be determined by other considerations such as structural requirements.

11. 9×18 in. **13.** $\frac{\pi}{2}$ **15.** $h : r = 8 : \pi$

17. **(a)** $V(x) = 2x(24 - 2x)(18 - 2x)$ **(b)** Domain: (0, 9)

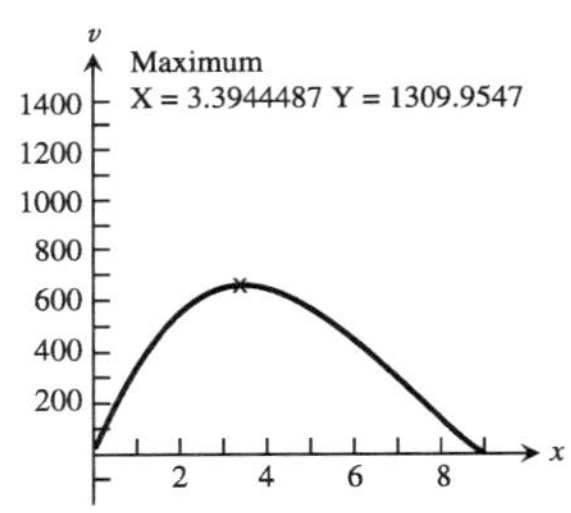

(c) Maximum volume ≈ 1309.95 in.^{3} when $x \approx 3.39$ in.
(d) $V'(x) = 24x^2 - 336x + 864$, so the critical point is at $x = 7 - \sqrt{13}$, which confirms the result in part (c).
(e) $x = 2$ in. or $x = 5$ in.

19. ≈ 2418.40 cm^3

21. **(a)** $h = 24$, $w = 18$
(b)

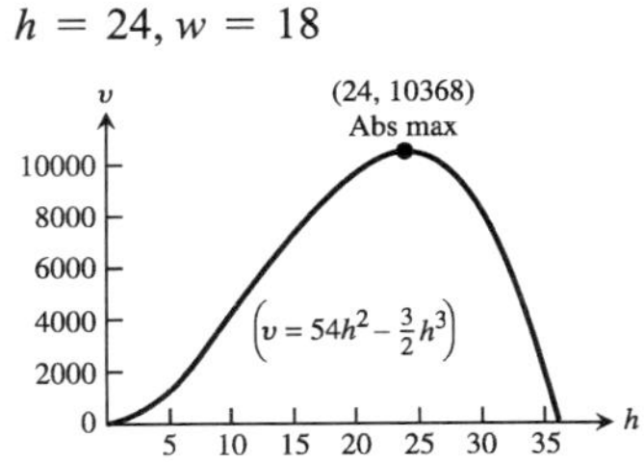

23. If r is the radius of the hemisphere, h the height of the cylinder, and V the volume, then $r = \left(\frac{3V}{8\pi}\right)^{1/3}$ and $h = \left(\frac{3V}{\pi}\right)^{1/3}$.

25. **(b)** $x = \frac{51}{8}$ **(c)** $L \approx 11$ in.

27. Radius $= \sqrt{2}$ m, height $= 1$ m, volume $\frac{2\pi}{3}$ m^3

31. **(a)** $v(0) = 96$ ft/sec **(b)** 256 ft at $t = 3$ sec
(c) Velocity when $s = 0$ is $v(7) = -128$ ft/sec

33. ≈ 46.87 ft **35.** **(a)** $6 \times 6\sqrt{3}$ in.

37. **(a)** $10\pi \approx 31.42$ cm/sec; when $t = 0.5$ sec, 1.5 sec, 2.5 sec, 3.5 sec; $s = 0$, acceleration is 0 **(b)** 10 cm from rest position; speed is 0

39. **(a)** $s = ((12 - 12t)^2 + 64t^2)^{1/2}$ **(b)** -12 knots, 8 knots
(c) No **(e)** $4\sqrt{13}$. This limit is the square root of the sums of the squares of the individual speeds.

41. $x = \frac{a}{2}$, $v = \frac{ka^2}{4}$ **43.** $\frac{c}{2} + 50$

45. **(a)** $\sqrt{\frac{2km}{h}}$ **(b)** $\sqrt{\frac{2km}{h}}$

49. **(a)** The cabinetmaker should order px units of material to have enough until the next delivery.
(c) Average cost per day $= \dfrac{\left(d + \frac{ps}{2}x^2\right)}{x} = \frac{d}{x} + \frac{ps}{2}x$;
$x^* = \sqrt{\frac{2d}{ps}}$; $px^* = \sqrt{\frac{2pd}{s}}$ gives a minimum.
(d) The line and hyperbola intersect when $\frac{d}{x} = \frac{ps}{2}x$. For $x > 0$, $x_{\text{intersection}} = \sqrt{\frac{2d}{ps}} = x^*$. The average cost per day is minimized when the average daily cost of delivery is equal to the average daily cost of storage.

51. $M = \frac{C}{2}$ **57.** **(a)** $y = -1$

59. **(a)** The minimum distance is $\frac{\sqrt{5}}{2}$.
(b) The minimum distance is from the point (3/2, 0) to the point (1, 1) on the graph of $y = \sqrt{x}$, and this occurs at the value $x = 1$, where $D(x)$, the distance squared, has its minimum value.

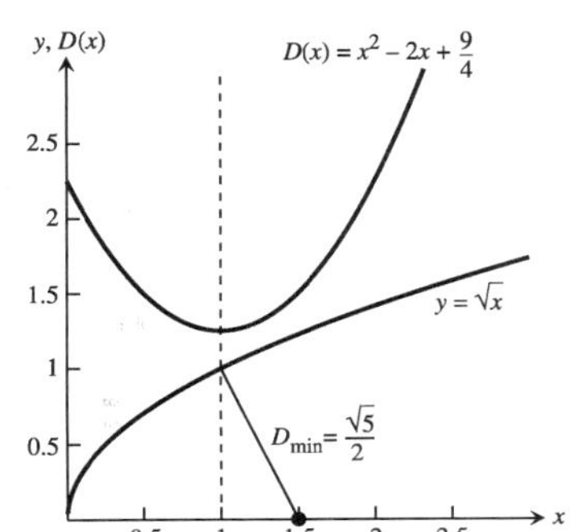

61. **(a)** $V(x) = \frac{\pi}{3}\left(\frac{2\pi a - x}{2\pi}\right)^2 \sqrt{a^2 - \left(\frac{2\pi a - x}{2\pi}\right)^2}$

(b) When $a = 4$: $r = \dfrac{4\sqrt{6}}{3}$, $h = \dfrac{4\sqrt{3}}{3}$; when $a = 5$: $r = \dfrac{5\sqrt{6}}{3}$, $h = \dfrac{5\sqrt{3}}{3}$; when $a = 6$: $r = 2\sqrt{6}$, $h = 2\sqrt{3}$; when $a = 8$: $r = \dfrac{8\sqrt{6}}{3}$, $h = \dfrac{8\sqrt{3}}{3}$

(c) Since $r = \dfrac{a\sqrt{6}}{3}$ and $h = \dfrac{a\sqrt{3}}{3}$, the relationship is $\dfrac{r}{h} = \sqrt{2}$.

Section 4.6, pp. 298–299

1. $\frac{1}{4}$ **3.** $\frac{5}{7}$ **5.** $\frac{1}{2}$ **7.** 0 **9.** 1 **11.** $\sqrt{2}$ **13.** +1

15. −1 **17.** $\frac{1}{2}$ **19.** 3 **21.** na **23.** $-\frac{1}{2}$ **25.** 0 **27.** 3

29. 1 **31.** (b) is correct, but (a) is not.

33. $c = \frac{27}{10}$ **35.** −1

Section 4.7, pp. 305–306

1. $x_2 = -\frac{5}{3}, \frac{13}{21}$ **3.** $x_2 = -\frac{51}{31}, \frac{5763}{4945}$ **5.** $x_2 = \frac{2387}{2000}$

7. x, and all later approximations will equal x_0.

9.

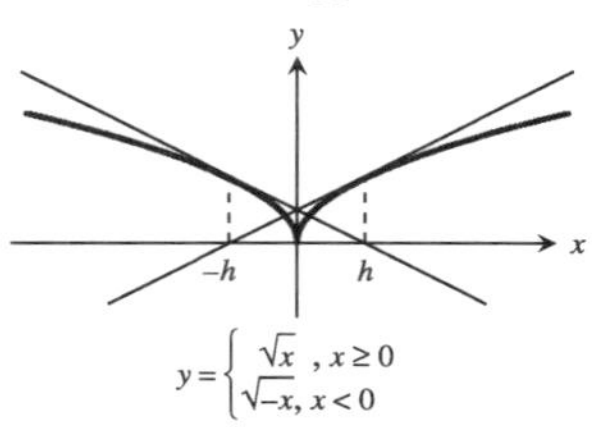

11. The points of intersection of $y = x^3$ and $y = 3x + 1$ or $y = x^3 - 3x$ and $y = 1$ have the same x-values as the roots of part (i) or the solutions of part (iv). **15.** 1.165561185

17. **(a)** Two **(b)** 0.35003501505249 and −1.0261731615301

19. ±1.3065629648764, ±0.5411961001462 **21.** $x \approx 0.45$

23. The root is 1.17951.

25. **(a)** For $x_0 = -2$ or $x_0 = -0.8$, $x_i \to -1$ as i gets large.
(b) For $x_0 = -0.5$ or $x_0 = 0.25$, $x_i \to 0$ as i gets large.
(c) For $x_0 = 0.8$ or $x_0 = 2$, $x_i \to 1$ as i gets large.
(d) For $x_0 = -\sqrt{21}/7$ or $x_0 = \sqrt{21}/7$, Newton's method does not converge. The values of x_i alternate between $-\sqrt{21}/7$ and $\sqrt{21}/7$ as i increases.

27. Answers will vary with machine speed. **29.** 2.45, 0.000245

Section 4.8, pp. 314–318

1. **(a)** x^2 **(b)** $\frac{x^3}{3}$ **(c)** $\frac{x^3}{3} - x^2 + x$

3. **(a)** x^{-3} **(b)** $-\frac{1}{3}x^{-3}$ **(c)** $-\frac{1}{3}x^{-3} + x^2 + 3x$

5. **(a)** $-\frac{1}{x}$ **(b)** $-\frac{5}{x}$ **(c)** $2x + \frac{5}{x}$

7. **(a)** $\sqrt{x^3}$ **(b)** $\sqrt{x}$ **(c)** $\frac{2\sqrt{x^3}}{3} + 2\sqrt{x}$

9. **(a)** $x^{2/3}$ **(b)** $x^{1/3}$ **(c)** $x^{-1/3}$

11. **(a)** $\cos(\pi x)$ **(b)** $-3\cos x$ **(c)** $-\frac{1}{\pi}\cos(\pi x) + \cos(3x)$

13. **(a)** $\tan x$ **(b)** $2\tan\left(\frac{x}{3}\right)$ **(c)** $-\frac{2}{3}\tan\left(\frac{3x}{2}\right)$

15. **(a)** $-\csc x$ **(b)** $\frac{1}{5}\csc(5x)$ **(c)** $2\csc\left(\frac{\pi x}{2}\right)$

17. $\frac{x^2}{2} + x + C$ **19.** $t^3 + \frac{t^2}{4} + C$ **21.** $\frac{x^4}{2} - \frac{5x^2}{2} + 7x + C$

23. $-\frac{1}{x} - \frac{x^3}{3} - \frac{x}{3} + C$ **25.** $\frac{3}{2}x^{2/3} + C$

27. $\frac{2}{3}x^{3/2} + \frac{3}{4}x^{4/3} + C$ **29.** $4y^2 - \frac{8}{3}y^{3/4} + C$

31. $x^2 + \frac{2}{x} + C$ **33.** $2\sqrt{t} - \frac{2}{\sqrt{t}} + C$ **35.** $-2\sin t + C$

37. $-21\cos\frac{\theta}{3} + C$ **39.** $3\cot x + C$ **41.** $-\frac{1}{2}\csc\theta + C$

43. $4\sec x - 2\tan x + C$ **45.** $-\frac{1}{2}\cos 2x + \cot x + C$

47. $\frac{t}{2} + \frac{\sin 4t}{8} + C$ **49.** $\tan\theta + C$

51. $-\cot x - x + C$ **53.** $-\cos\theta - \theta + C$

61. **(a)** Wrong: $\frac{d}{dx}\left(\frac{x^2}{2}\sin x + C\right) = \frac{2x}{2}\sin x + \frac{x^2}{2}\cos x = x\sin x + \frac{x^2}{2}\cos x$

(b) Wrong: $\frac{d}{dx}(-x\cos x + C) = -\cos x + x\sin x$

(c) Right: $\frac{d}{dx}(-x\cos x + \sin x + C) = -\cos x + x\sin x + \cos x = x\sin x$

63. **(a)** Wrong: $\frac{d}{dx}\left(\frac{(2x+1)^3}{3} + C\right) = \frac{3(2x+1)^2(2)}{3} = 2(2x+1)^2$

(b) Wrong: $\frac{d}{dx}((2x+1)^3 + C) = 3(2x+1)^2(2) = 6(2x+1)^2$

(c) Right: $\frac{d}{dx}((2x+1)^3 + C) = 6(2x+1)^2$

65. (b) **67.** $y = x^2 - 7x + 10$ **69.** $y = -\frac{1}{x} + \frac{x^2}{2} - \frac{1}{2}$

71. $y = 9x^{1/3} + 4$ **73.** $s = t + \sin t + 4$

75. $r = \cos(\pi\theta) - 1$ **77.** $v = \frac{1}{2}\sec t + \frac{1}{2}$

79. $y = x^2 - x^3 + 4x + 1$ **81.** $r = \frac{1}{t} + 2t - 2$

83. $y = x^3 - 4x^2 + 5$ **85.** $y = -\sin t + \cos t + t^3 - 1$

87. $y = 2x^{3/2} - 50$ **89.** $y = x - x^{4/3} + \dfrac{1}{2}$

91. $y = -\sin x - \cos x - 2$
93. **(a)** **(i)** 33.2 units, **(ii)** 33.2 units, **(iii)** 33.2 units **(b)** True
95. $t = 88/k, k = 16$
97. **(a)** $v = 10t^{3/2} - 6t^{1/2}$ **(b)** $s = 4t^{5/2} - 4t^{3/2}$
101. **(a)** $-\sqrt{x} + C$ **(b)** $x + C$ **(c)** $\sqrt{x} + C$
(d) $-x + C$ **(e)** $x - \sqrt{x} + C$ **(f)** $-x - \sqrt{x} + C$

Practice Exercises, pp. 318–321

1. No **3.** No minimum; absolute maximum: $f(1) = 16$; critical points: $x = 1$ and $11/3$ **5.** Yes, except at $x = 0$ **7.** No
11. **(b)** one
13. **(b)** 0.8555 99677 2 **19.** Global minimum value of $\dfrac{1}{2}$ at $x = 2$
21. **(a)** $t = 0, 6, 12$ **(b)** $t = 3, 9$ **(c)** $6 < t < 12$
(d) $0 < t < 6, 12 < t < 14$

23.

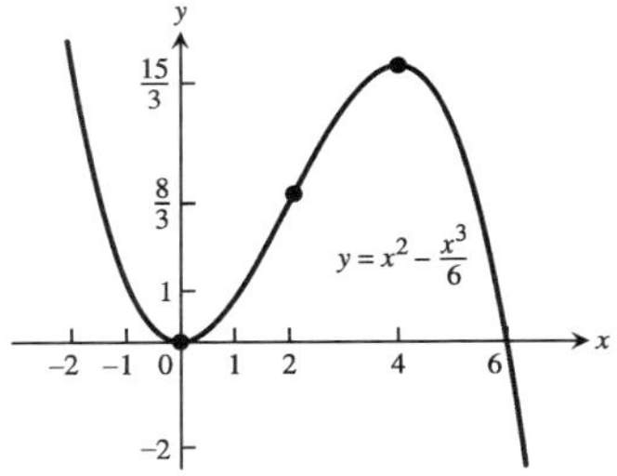

25.

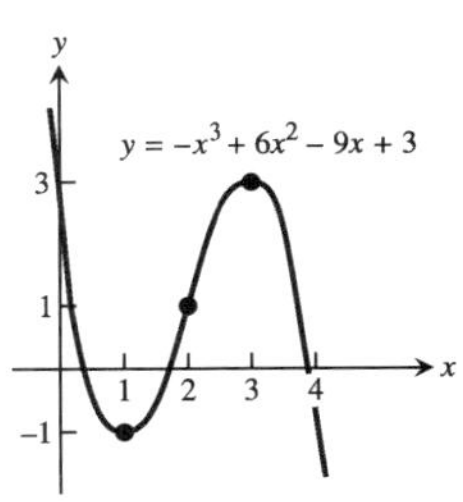

27.

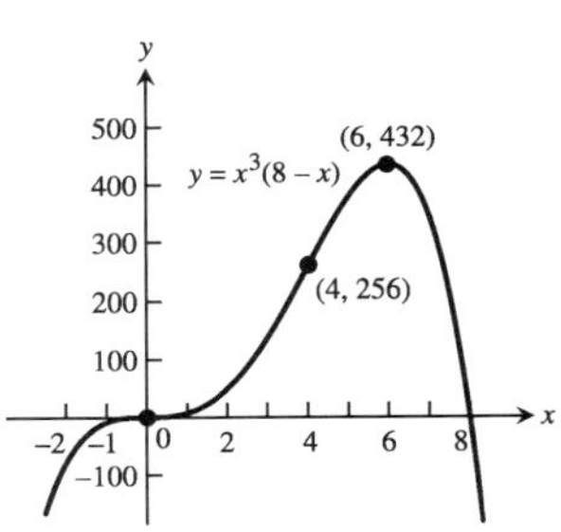

29.

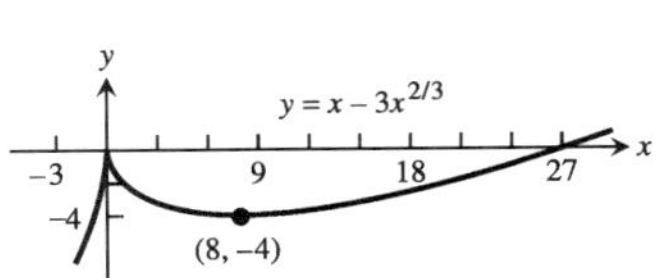

31.

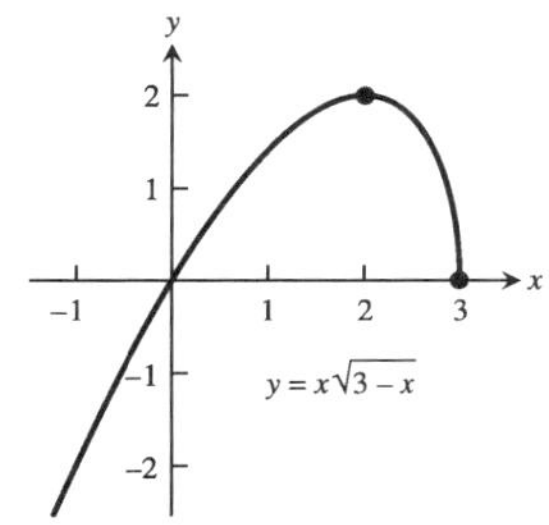

33. **(a)** Local maximum at $x = 4$, local minimum at $x = -4$, inflection point at $x = 0$

(b)

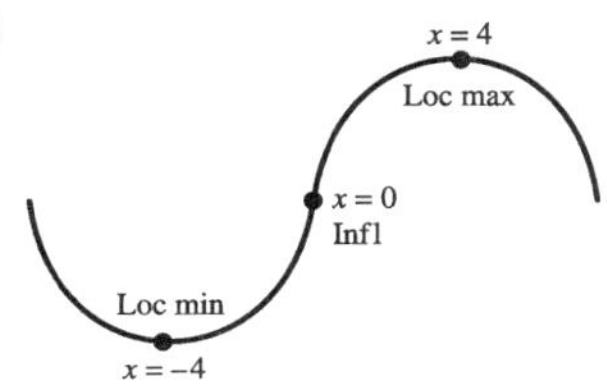

35. **(a)** Local maximum at $x = 0$, local minima at $x = -1$ and $x = 2$, inflection points at $x = \left(1 \pm \sqrt{7}\right)/3$

(b)

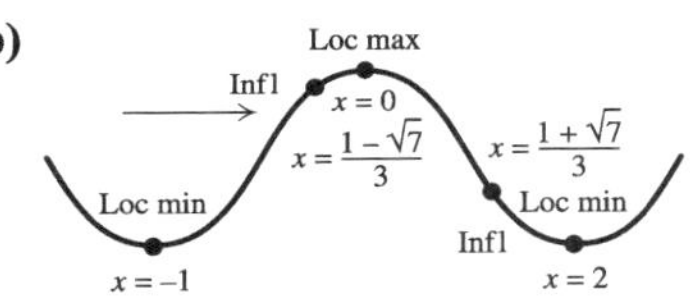

37. **(a)** Local maximum at $x = -\sqrt{2}$, local minimum at $x = \sqrt{2}$, inflection points at $x = \pm 1$ and 0

(b)

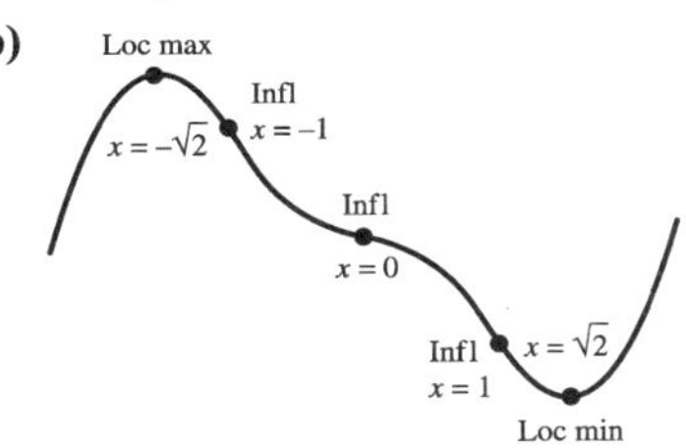

43.

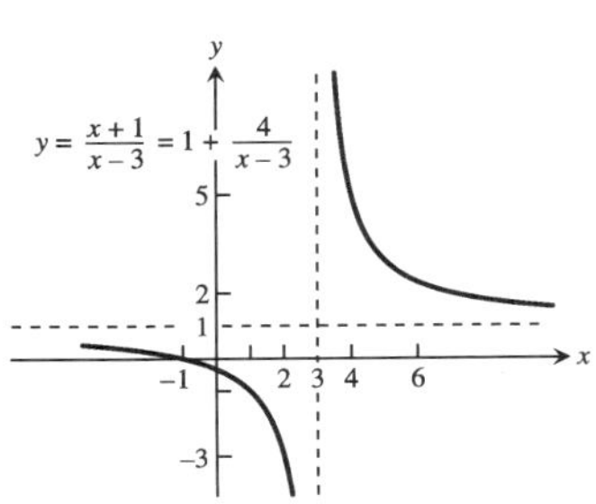

45.

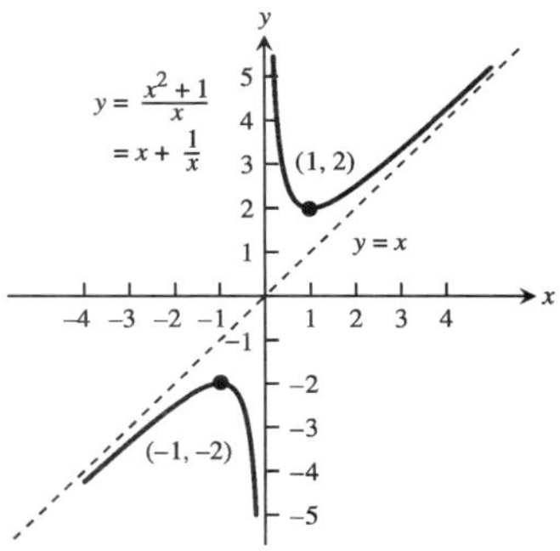

47.

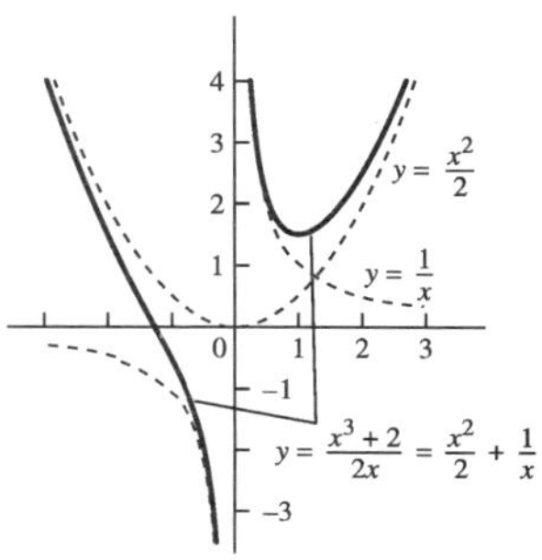

49.

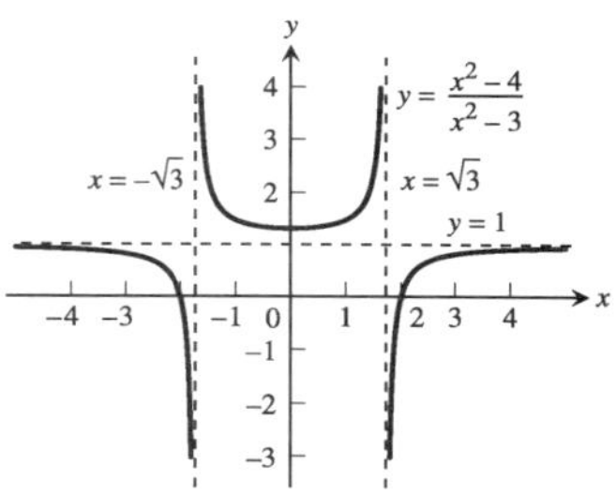

51. 5 **53.** 0 **55.** 1 **57.** 3/7 **59.** 0 **61.** 1
63. **(a)** 0, 36 **(b)** 18, 18 **65.** 54 square units
67. height = 2, radius = $\sqrt{2}$
69. $x = 5 - \sqrt{5}$ hundred ≈ 276 tires, $y = 2(5 - \sqrt{5})$ hundred ≈ 553 tires
71. Dimensions: base is 6 in. by 12 in., height = 2 in.; maximum volume = 144 in.^{3}
73. $x_5 = 2.1958\,23345$ **75.** $\frac{x^4}{4} + \frac{5}{2}x^2 - 7x + C$
77. $2t^{3/2} - \frac{4}{t} + C$ **79.** $-\frac{1}{r+5} + C$
81. $(\theta^2 + 1)^{3/2} + C$ **83.** $\frac{1}{3}(1 + x^4)^{3/4} + C$
85. $10 \tan \frac{s}{10} + C$ **87.** $-\frac{1}{\sqrt{2}} \csc \sqrt{2}\,\theta + C$
89. $\frac{1}{2}x - \sin \frac{x}{2} + C$ **91.** $y = x - \frac{1}{x} - 1$
93. $r = 4t^{5/2} + 4t^{3/2} - 8t$

Additional and Advanced Exercises, pp. 322–324

1. The function is constant on the interval.
3. The extreme points will not be at the end of an open interval.
5. **(a)** A local minimum at $x = -1$, points of inflection at $x = 0$ and $x = 2$ **(b)** A local maximum at $x = 0$ and local minima at $x = -1$ and $x = 2$, points of inflection at $x = \frac{1 \pm \sqrt{7}}{3}$
9. No **11.** $a = 1, b = 0, c = 1$ **13.** Yes **15.** Drill the hole at $y = h/2$.
17. $r = \frac{RH}{2(H - R)}$ for $H > 2R$, $r = R$ if $H \le 2R$
19. **(a)** $\frac{10}{3}$ **(b)** $\frac{5}{3}$ **(c)** $\frac{1}{2}$ **(d)** 0 **(e)** $-\frac{1}{2}$ **(f)** 1 **(g)** $\frac{1}{2}$ **(h)** 3
21. **(a)** $\frac{c - b}{2e}$ **(b)** $\frac{c + b}{2}$ **(c)** $\frac{b^2 - 2bc + c^2 + 4ae}{4e}$ **(d)** $\frac{c + b + t}{2}$
23. $m_0 = 1 - \frac{1}{q}$, $m_1 = \frac{1}{q}$
25. **(a)** $k = -38.72$ **(b)** 25 ft
27. Yes, $y = x + C$ **29.** $v_0 = \frac{2\sqrt{2}}{3} b^{3/4}$

CHAPTER 5

Section 5.1, pp. 333–335

1. **(a)** 0.125 **(b)** 0.21875 **(c)** 0.625 **(d)** 0.46875
3. **(a)** 1.066667 **(b)** 1.283333 **(c)** 2.666667 **(d)** 2.083333
5. 0.3125, 0.328125 **7.** 1.5, 1.574603
9. **(a)** 87 in. **(b)** 87 in.
11. **(a)** 3490 ft **(b)** 3840 ft
13. **(a)** 74.65 ft/sec **(b)** 45.28 ft/sec **(c)** 146.59 ft
15. $\frac{31}{16}$ **17.** 1
19. **(a)** Upper = 758 gal, lower = 543 gal
(b) Upper = 2363 gal, lower = 1693 gal
(c) ≈ 31.4 h, ≈ 32.4 h
21. **(a)** 2 **(b)** $2\sqrt{2} \approx 2.828$
(c) $8 \sin\left(\frac{\pi}{8}\right) \approx 3.061$
(d) Each area is less than the area of the circle, π. As n increases, the polygon area approaches π.

Section 5.2, pp. 342–343

1. $\frac{6(1)}{1+1} + \frac{6(2)}{2+1} = 7$
3. $\cos(1)\pi + \cos(2)\pi + \cos(3)\pi + \cos(4)\pi = 0$
5. $\sin \pi - \sin \frac{\pi}{2} + \sin \frac{\pi}{3} = \frac{\sqrt{3} - 2}{2}$

7. All of them **9.** b **11.** $\sum_{k=1}^{6} k$ **13.** $\sum_{k=1}^{4} \frac{1}{2^k}$

15. $\sum_{k=1}^{5} (-1)^{k+1} \frac{1}{k}$

17. **(a)** -15 **(b)** 1 **(c)** 1 **(d)** -11 **(e)** 16

19. **(a)** 55 **(b)** 385 **(c)** 3025

21. -56 **23.** -73 **25.** 240 **27.** 3376

29. **(a)**

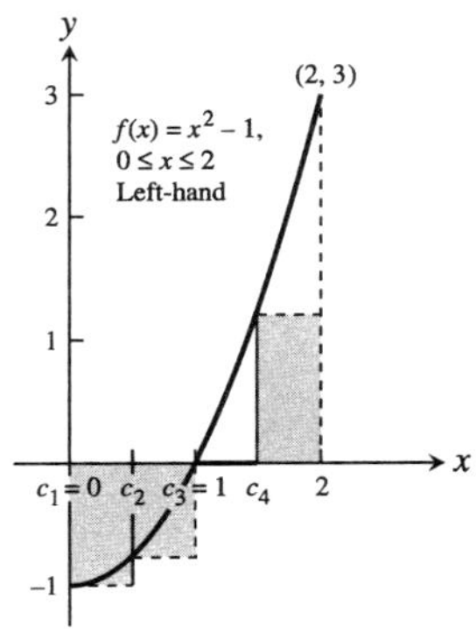

(b)

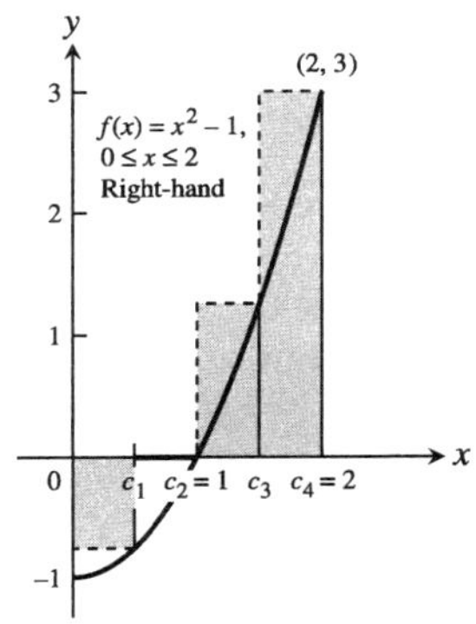

(c)

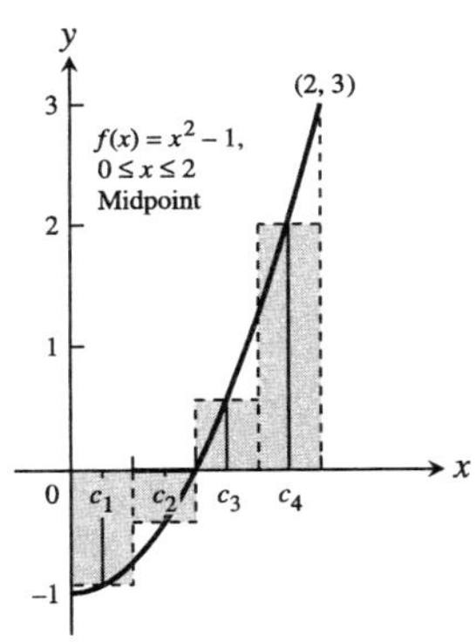

31. **(a)**

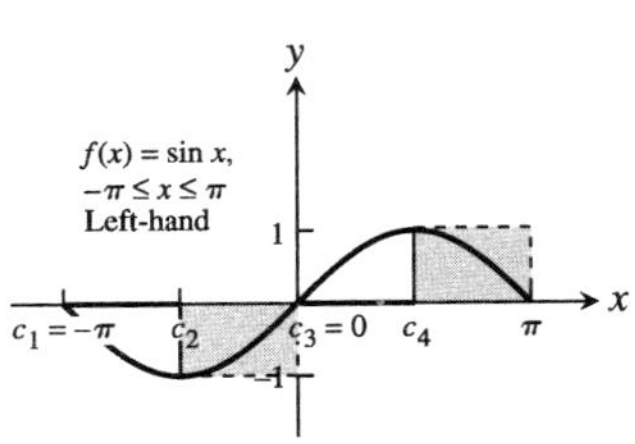

(b)

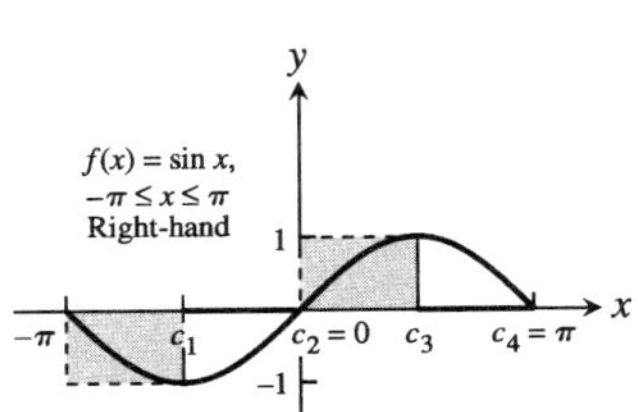

(c)

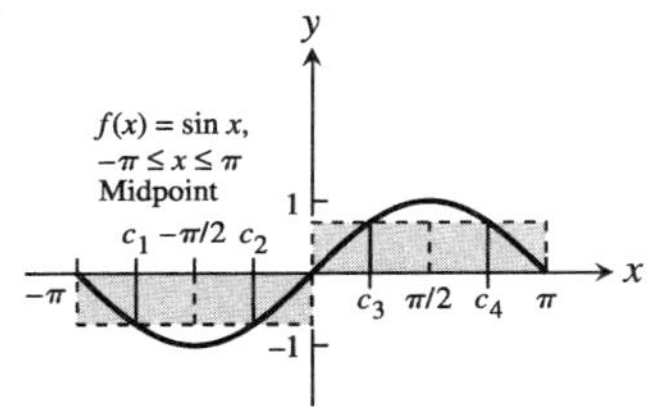

33. 1.2

35. $\frac{2}{3} + \frac{3n-1}{6n^2}, \frac{2}{3}$

37. $12 + \frac{27n+9}{2n^2}, 12$

39. $\frac{5}{6} + \frac{6n+1}{6n^2}, \frac{5}{6}$

Section 5.3, pp. 352–356

1. $\int_0^2 x^2\,dx$ **3.** $\int_{-7}^{5} (x^2 - 3x)\,dx$ **5.** $\int_2^3 \frac{1}{1-x}\,dx$

7. $\int_{-\pi/4}^{0} \sec x\,dx$

9. **(a)** 0 **(b)** -8 **(c)** -12 **(d)** 10 **(e)** -2 **(f)** 16

11. **(a)** 5 **(b)** $5\sqrt{3}$ **(c)** -5 **(d)** -5

13. **(a)** 4 **(b)** -4 **15.** Area $= 21$ square units

17. Area $= 9\pi/2$ square units **19.** Area $= 2.5$ square units

21. Area $= 3$ square units **23.** $b^2/4$ **25.** $b^2 - a^2$ **27.** $1/2$

29. $3\pi^2/2$ **31.** $7/3$ **33.** $1/24$ **35.** $3a^2/2$ **37.** $b/3$

39. -14 **41.** 10 **43.** -2 **45.** $-7/4$ **47.** 7 **49.** 0

51. Using n subintervals of length $\Delta x = b/n$ and right-endpoint values:

$$\text{Area} = \int_0^b 3x^2\,dx = b^3$$

53. Using n subintervals of length $\Delta x = b/n$ and right-endpoint values:

$$\text{Area} = \int_0^b 2x\,dx = b^2$$

55. $\text{av}(f) = 0$ **57.** $\text{av}(f) = -2$ **59.** $\text{av}(f) = 1$

61. **(a)** $\text{av}(g) = -1/2$ **(b)** $\text{av}(g) = 1$ **(c)** $\text{av}(g) = 1/4$

63. $a = 0$ and $b = 1$ maximize the integral.

65. Upper bound $= 1$, lower bound $= 1/2$

67. For example, $\int_0^1 \sin(x^2)\,dx \le \int_0^1 dx = 1$

69. $\int_a^b f(x)\,dx \ge \int_a^b 0\,dx = 0$ **71.** Upper bound $= 1/2$

Section 5.4, pp. 365–368

1. 6 **3.** 8 **5.** 1 **7.** $5/2$ **9.** 2 **11.** $2\sqrt{3}$ **13.** 0

15. $-\pi/4$ **17.** $\frac{2\pi^3}{3}$ **19.** $-8/3$ **21.** $-3/4$

23. $\sqrt{2} - \sqrt[4]{8} + 1$ **25.** 16 **27.** $(\cos\sqrt{x})\left(\frac{1}{2\sqrt{x}}\right)$

29. $4t^5$ **31.** $\sqrt{1+x^2}$ **33.** $-\frac{1}{2}x^{-1/2}\sin x$ **35.** 1

37. 28/3 **39.** 1/2 **41.** 51/4 **43.** π **45.** $\frac{\sqrt{2}\pi}{2}$

47. d, since $y' = \frac{1}{x}$ and $y(\pi) = \int_{\pi}^{\pi} \frac{1}{t}\,dt - 3 = -3$

49. b, since $y' = \sec x$ and $y(0) = \int_0^0 \sec t\,dt + 4 = 4$

51. $y = \int_2^x \sec t\,dt + 3$ **53.** $s = \int_{t_0}^t f(x)\,dx + s_0$

55. $\frac{2}{3}bh$ **57.** \$9.00

59. **(a)** $v = \frac{ds}{dt} = \frac{d}{dt}\int_0^t f(x)\,dx = f(t) \Rightarrow v(5) = f(5) = 2$ m/sec

(b) $a = df/dt$ is negative since the slope of the tangent line at $t = 5$ is negative.

(c) $s = \int_0^3 f(x)\,dx = \frac{1}{2}(3)(3) = \frac{9}{2}$ m since the integral is the area of the triangle formed by $y = f(x)$, the x-axis, and $x = 3$.

(d) $t = 6$ since after $t = 6$ to $t = 9$, the region lies below the x-axis.

(e) At $t = 4$ and $t = 7$, since there are horizontal tangents there.

(f) Toward the origin between $t = 6$ and $t = 9$ since the velocity is negative on this interval. Away from the origin between $t = 0$ and $t = 6$ since the velocity is positive there.

(g) Right or positive side, because the integral of f from 0 to 9 is positive, there being more area above the x-axis than below.

63. $2x - 2$ **65.** $-3x + 5$

67. **(a)** True. Since f is continuous, g is differentiable by Part 1 of the Fundamental Theorem of Calculus.

(b) True: g is continuous because it is differentiable.

(c) True, since $g'(1) = f(1) = 0$.

(d) False, since $g''(1) = f'(1) > 0$.

(e) True, since $g'(1) = 0$ and $g''(1) = f'(1) > 0$.

(f) False: $g''(x) = f'(x) > 0$, so g'' never changes sign.

(g) True, since $g'(1) = f(1) = 0$ and $g'(x) = f(x)$ is an increasing function of x (because $f'(x) > 0$).

Section 5.5, pp. 374–376

1. $-\frac{1}{3}\cos 3x + C$ **3.** $\frac{1}{2}\sec 2t + C$ **5.** $-(7x-2)^{-4} + C$

7. $-6(1 - r^3)^{1/2} + C$

9. $\frac{1}{3}(x^{3/2} - 1) - \frac{1}{6}\sin(2x^{3/2} - 2) + C$

11. **(a)** $-\frac{1}{4}(\cot^2 2\theta) + C$ **(b)** $-\frac{1}{4}(\csc^2 2\theta) + C$

13. $-\frac{1}{3}(3 - 2s)^{3/2} + C$ **15.** $\frac{2}{5}(5s + 4)^{1/2} + C$

17. $-\frac{2}{5}(1 - \theta^2)^{5/4} + C$ **19.** $-\frac{1}{3}(7 - 3y^2)^{3/2} + C$

21. $(-2/(1 + \sqrt{x})) + C$ **23.** $\frac{1}{3}\sin(3z + 4) + C$

25. $\frac{1}{3}\tan(3x + 2) + C$ **27.** $\frac{1}{2}\sin^6\left(\frac{x}{3}\right) + C$

29. $\left(\frac{r^3}{18} - 1\right)^6 + C$ **31.** $-\frac{2}{3}\cos(x^{3/2} + 1) + C$

33. $\sec\left(v + \frac{\pi}{2}\right) + C$ **35.** $\frac{1}{2\cos(2t + 1)} + C$

37. $-\frac{2}{3}(\cot^3 y)^{1/2} + C$ **39.** $-\sin\left(\frac{1}{t} - 1\right) + C$

41. $-\frac{\sin^2(1/\theta)}{2} + C$ **43.** $\frac{(s^3 + 2s^2 - 5s + 5)^2}{2} + C$

45. $\frac{1}{16}(1 + t^4)^4 + C$

47. $\frac{1}{5}(x^2 + 1)^{5/2} - \frac{1}{3}(x^2 + 1)^{3/2} + C$

49. **(a)** $-\frac{6}{2 + \tan^3 x} + C$ **(b)** $-\frac{6}{2 + \tan^3 x} + C$

(c) $-\frac{6}{2 + \tan^3 x} + C$

51. $\frac{1}{6}\sin\sqrt{3(2r - 1)^2 + 6} + C$

53. $s = \frac{1}{2}(3t^2 - 1)^4 - 5$

55. $s = 4t - 2\sin\left(2t + \frac{\pi}{6}\right) + 9$

57. $s = \sin\left(2t - \frac{\pi}{2}\right) + 100t + 1$

59. 6 m **63.** b) 399 Volts

Section 5.6, pp. 383–387

1. **(a)** 14/3 **(b)** 2/3

3. **(a)** 1/2 **(b)** −1/2

5. **(a)** 15/16 **(b)** 0

7. **(a)** 0 **(b)** 1/8

9. **(a)** 4 **(b)** 0

11. **(a)** 1/6 **(b)** 1/2

13. **(a)** 0 **(b)** 0

15. $2\sqrt{3}$ **17.** 3/4 **19.** $3^{5/2} - 1$ **21.** 3 **23.** $\pi/3$

25. 16/3 **27.** $2^{5/2}$ **29.** $\pi/2$ **31.** 128/15 **33.** 4/3

35. 5/6 **37.** 38/3 **39.** 49/6 **41.** 32/3 **43.** 48/5

45. 8/3 **47.** 8 **49.** 5/3 (There are three intersection points.)

51. 18 **53.** 243/8 **55.** 8/3 **57.** 2 **59.** 104/15

61. 56/15 **63.** 4 **65.** $\frac{4}{3} - \frac{4}{\pi}$ **67.** $\pi/2$ **69.** 2 **71.** 1/2

73. 1

75. **(a)** $(\pm\sqrt{c}, c)$ **(b)** $c = 4^{2/3}$ **(c)** $c = 4^{2/3}$

77. 11/3 **79.** 3/4 **81.** Neither **83.** $F(6) - F(2)$

85. **(a)** −3 **(b)** 3

87. $I = a/2$

Practice Exercises, pp. 388–391

1. (a) about 680 ft **(b)**

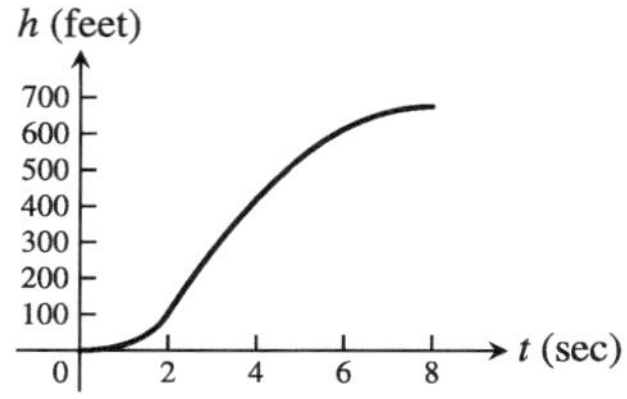

3. (a) $-1/2$ **(b)** 31 **(c)** 13 **(d)** 0

5. $\int_1^5 (2x-1)^{-1/2}\,dx = 2$ **7.** $\int_{-\pi}^{0} \cos\frac{x}{2}\,dx = 2$

9. (a) 4 **(b)** 2 **(c)** -2 **(d)** -2π **(e)** 8/5

11. 8/3 **13.** 62 **15.** 1 **17.** 1/6 **19.** 18 **21.** 9/8

23. $\frac{\pi^2}{32} + \frac{\sqrt{2}}{2} - 1$ **25.** 4 **27.** $\frac{8\sqrt{2}-7}{6}$

29. Min: -4, max: 0, area: 27/4 **31.** 6/5

35. $y = \int_5^x \left(\frac{\sin t}{t}\right) dt - 3$ **37.** $-4(\cos x)^{1/2} + C$

39. $\theta^2 + \theta + \sin(2\theta + 1) + C$ **41.** $\frac{t^3}{3} + \frac{4}{t} + C$

43. $-\frac{1}{3}\cos(2t^{3/2}) + C$ **45.** 16 **47.** 2 **49.** 1 **51.** 8

53. $27\sqrt{3}/160$ **55.** $\pi/2$ **57.** $\sqrt{3}$ **59.** $6\sqrt{3} - 2\pi$

61. -1 **63.** 2 **65.** -2 **67.** 1 **69.** $\sqrt{2} - 1$

71. (a) b **(b)** b

75. 25°F **77.** $\sqrt{2 + \cos^3 x}$ **79.** $\frac{-6}{3 + x^4}$ **81.** Yes

83. $-\sqrt{1 + x^2}$

85. cost $\approx$ \$10,899 using a lower sum estimate

87. 600, \$18.00 **89.** 300, \$6.00

Additional and Advanced Exercises, pp. 391–394

1. (a) Yes **(b)** No

5. (a) 1/4 **(b)** $\sqrt[3]{12}$

7. $f(x) = \frac{x}{\sqrt{x^2 + 1}}$ **9.** $y = x^3 + 2x - 4$

11. 36/5

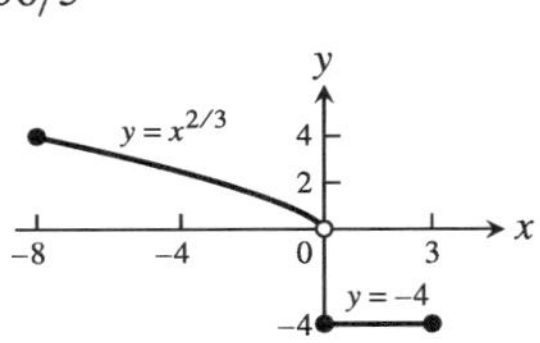

13. $\frac{1}{2} - \frac{2}{\pi}$

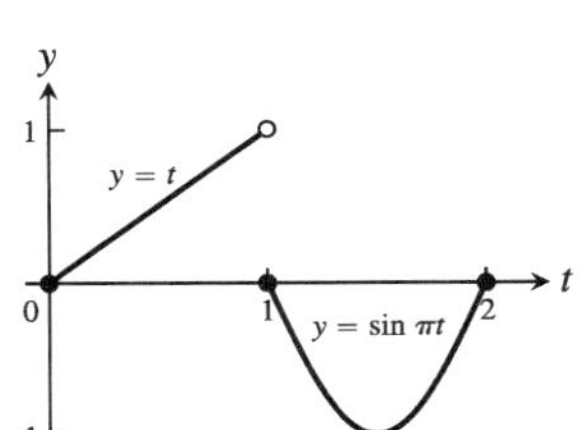

15. 13/3

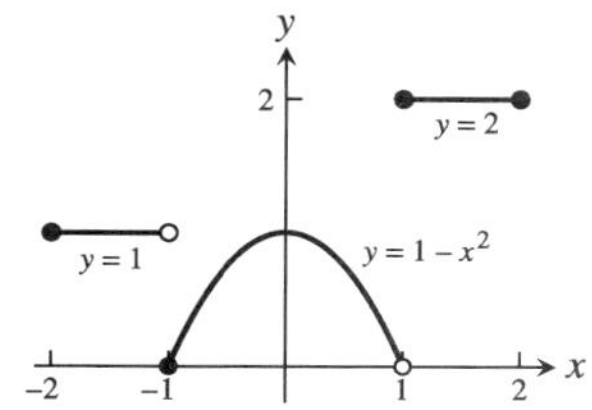

17. 1/2 **19.** $2/x$

21. $\frac{\sin 4y}{\sqrt{y}} - \frac{\sin y}{2\sqrt{y}}$ **23.** 1/6 **25.** $\int_0^1 f(x)\,dx$

29. (a) 0 **(b)** -1 **(c)** $-\pi$ **(d)** $x = 1$
(e) $y = 2x + 2 - \pi$ **(f)** $x = -1, x = 2$ **(g)** $[-2\pi, 0]$

CHAPTER 6

Section 6.1, pp. 405–409

1. (a) $A(x) = \pi(1 - x^2)$ **(b)** $A(x) = 4(1 - x^2)$
(c) $A(x) = 2(1 - x^2)$ **(d)** $A(x) = \sqrt{3}(1 - x^2)$

3. 16 **5.** $\frac{16}{3}$ **7. (a)** $2\sqrt{3}$ **(b)** 8 **9.** 8π

11. (a) s^2h **(b)** s^2h **13.** $\frac{2\pi}{3}$ **15.** $4 - \pi$ **17.** $\frac{32\pi}{5}$

19. 36π **21.** π **23.** $\pi\left(\frac{\pi}{2} + 2\sqrt{2} - \frac{11}{3}\right)$ **25.** 2π

27. 2π **29.** 3π **31.** $\pi^2 - 2\pi$ **33.** $\frac{2\pi}{3}$ **35.** $\frac{117\pi}{5}$

37. $\pi(\pi - 2)$ **39.** $\frac{4\pi}{3}$ **41.** 8π **43.** $\frac{7\pi}{6}$

45. (a) 8π **(b)** $\frac{32\pi}{5}$ **(c)** $\frac{8\pi}{3}$ **(d)** $\frac{224\pi}{15}$

47. (a) $\frac{16\pi}{15}$ **(b)** $\frac{56\pi}{15}$ **(c)** $\frac{64\pi}{15}$

49. $V = 2a^2b\pi^2$ **51. (a)** $V = \frac{\pi h^2(3a - h)}{3}$ **(b)** $\frac{1}{120\pi}$ m/sec

55. $V = 3308\ \text{cm}^3$

57. (a) $c = \frac{2}{\pi}$ **(b)** $c = 0$
(c)

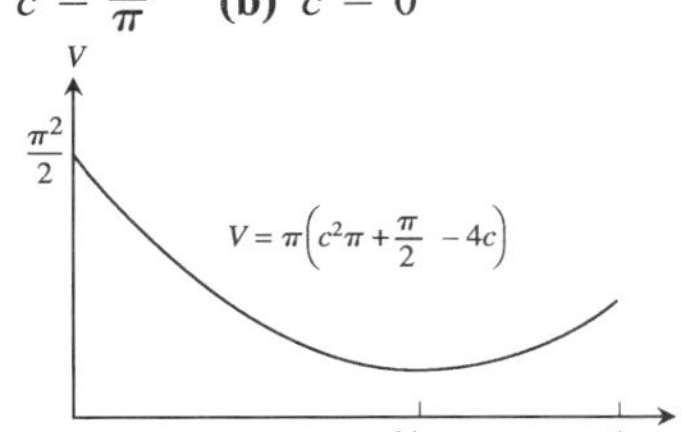

Section 6.2, pp. 414–416

1. 6π **3.** 2π **5.** $\frac{14\pi}{3}$ **7.** 8π **9.** $\frac{5\pi}{6}$ **11.** $\frac{7\pi}{15}$

13. (b) 4π **15.** $\frac{16\pi}{15}(3\sqrt{2} + 5)$ **17.** $\frac{8\pi}{3}$ **19.** $\frac{4\pi}{3}$

21. $\frac{16\pi}{3}$ **23. (a)** $\frac{6\pi}{5}$ **(b)** $\frac{4\pi}{5}$ **(c)** 2π **(d)** 2π

25. **(a)** About the x-axis: $V = \frac{2\pi}{15}$; about the y-axis: $V = \frac{\pi}{6}$
(b) About the x-axis: $V = \frac{2\pi}{15}$; about the y-axis: $V = \frac{\pi}{6}$

27. **(a)** $\frac{5\pi}{3}$ **(b)** $\frac{4\pi}{3}$ **(c)** 2π **(d)** $\frac{2\pi}{3}$

29. **(a)** $\frac{4\pi}{15}$ **(b)** $\frac{7\pi}{30}$ **31.** **(a)** $\frac{24\pi}{5}$ **(b)** $\frac{48\pi}{5}$

33. **(a)** $\frac{9\pi}{16}$ **(b)** $\frac{9\pi}{16}$

35. Disk: 2 integrals; washer: 2 integrals; shell: 1 integral

Section 6.3, pp. 423–424

1. $\frac{5\sqrt{10}}{3}$ **3.** 7 **5.** $\frac{21}{2}$ **7.** 12 **9.** $\frac{53}{6}$ **11.** $\frac{123}{32}$

13. $\frac{99}{8}$ **15.** 2 **17.** **(a)** $\int_{-1}^{2} \sqrt{1 + 4x^2}\, dx$ **(c)** ≈ 6.13

19. **(a)** $\int_{0}^{\pi} \sqrt{1 + \cos^2 y}\, dy$ **(c)** ≈ 3.82

21. **(a)** $\int_{-1}^{3} \sqrt{1 + (y + 1)^2}\, dy$ **(c)** ≈ 9.29

23. **(a)** $\int_{0}^{\pi/6} \sec x\, dx$ **(c)** ≈ 0.55

25. Yes, $f(x) = \pm x + C$ where C is any real number.

27. **(a)** $y = \sqrt{x}$ from (1, 1) to (4, 2)
(b) Only one. We know the derivative of the function and the value of the function at one value of x.

29. **(a)** π **(b)** π

Section 6.4, pp. 434–435

1. 4 ft **3.** $(L/4, L/4)$ **5.** $M_0 = 8, M = 8, \bar{x} = 1$
7. $M_0 = 15/2, M = 9/2, \bar{x} = 5/3$
9. $M_0 = 73/6, M = 5, \bar{x} = 73/30$ **11.** $M_0 = 3, M = 3, \bar{x} = 1$
13. $\bar{x} = 0, \bar{y} = 12/5$ **15.** $\bar{x} = 1, \bar{y} = -3/5$
17. $\bar{x} = 16/105, \bar{y} = 8/15$ **19.** $\bar{x} = 0, \bar{y} = \pi/8$
21. $\bar{x} = 1, \bar{y} = -2/5$ **23.** $\bar{x} = \bar{y} = \frac{2}{4 - \pi}$
25. $\bar{x} = 3/2, \bar{y} = 1/2$
27. **(a)** $\frac{224\pi}{3}$ **(b)** $\bar{x} = 2, \bar{y} = 0$
(c)

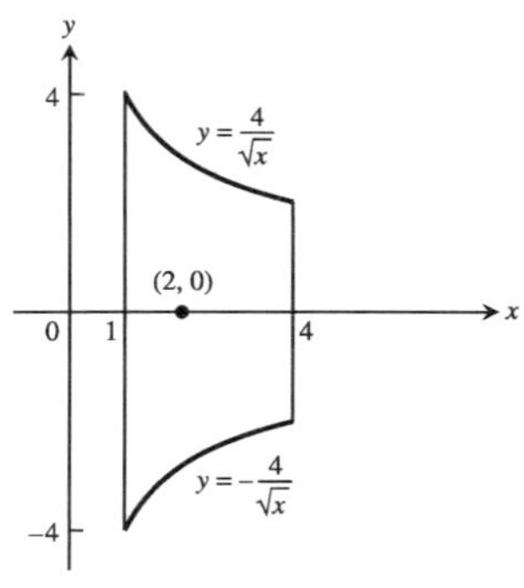

31. $\bar{x} = \bar{y} = 1/3$ **33.** $\bar{x} = a/3, \bar{y} = b/3$ **35.** $13\delta/6$
37. $\bar{x} = 0, \bar{y} = \frac{a\pi}{4}$

Section 6.5, pp. 444–447

1. **(a)** $2\pi \int_{0}^{\pi/4} \tan x \sqrt{1 + \sec^4 x}\, dx$ **(c)** ≈ 3.84

3. **(a)** $2\pi \int_{1}^{2} \frac{1}{y} \sqrt{1 + y^{-4}}\, dy$ **(c)** ≈ 5.02

5. **(a)** $2\pi \int_{1}^{4} (3 - \sqrt{x})^2 \sqrt{1 + (1 - 3x^{-1/2})^2}\, dx$ **(c)** ≈ 63.37

7. **(a)** $2\pi \int_{0}^{\pi/3} \left(\int_{0}^{y} \tan t\, dt \right) \sec y\, dy$ **(c)** ≈ 2.08

9. $4\pi\sqrt{5}$ **11.** $3\pi\sqrt{5}$ **13.** $98\pi/81$ **15.** 2π
17. $\pi(\sqrt{8} - 1)/9$ **19.** $35\pi\sqrt{5}/3$ **21.** $253\pi/20$

25. $2\pi \int_{-\pi/2}^{\pi/2} (\cos x) \sqrt{1 + \sin^2 x}\, dx$

27. Order 226.2 liters of each color. **31.** $5\sqrt{2}\pi$ **33.** $8\pi^2$
35. $52\pi/3$ **37.** $3\pi\sqrt{5}$ **41.** $V = 32\pi, S = 32\sqrt{2}\pi$
43. $4\pi^2$ **45.** $\bar{x} = 0, \bar{y} = \frac{2a}{\pi}$ **47.** $\bar{x} = 0, \bar{y} = \frac{4b}{3\pi}$
49. $\sqrt{2}\pi a^3(4 + 3\pi)/6$ **51.** $\frac{2a^3}{3}$

Section 6.6, pp. 452–455

1. 400 N·m **3.** 4 cm, 0.08 J
5. **(a)** 7238 lb/in. **(b)** 905 in.-lb, 2714 in.-lb **7.** 780 J
9. 72,900 ft-lb **13.** 160 ft-lb
15. **(a)** 1,497,600 ft-lb **(b)** 1 hr, 40 min **(d)** At 62.26 lb/ft^3: a) 1,494,240 ft-lb b) 1 hr, 40.1 min At 62.59 lb/ft^3: a) 1,502,160 ft-lb b) 1 hr, 40.1 min
17. 37,306 ft-lb **19.** 7,238,229.47 ft-lb
21. **(a)** 34,583 ft-lb **(b)** 53,483 ft-lb **23.** 15,073,100.75 J
27. 85.1 ft-lb **29.** 64.6 ft-lb **31.** 110.6 ft-lb
33. **(a)** $r(y) = 60 - \sqrt{50^2 - (y - 325)^2}$ for $325 \le y \le 375$ ft
(b) $\Delta V \approx \pi[60 - \sqrt{2500 - (y - 325)^2}]^2\, \Delta y$
(c) $W = 6.3358 \cdot 10^7$ ft-lb
35. 91.32 in.-oz **37.** 5.144×10^{10} J

Section 6.7, pp. 459–461

1. 1684.8 lb **3.** 2808 lb **5.** **(a)** 1164.8 lb **(b)** 1194.7 lb
7. 1309 lb **9.** 41.6 lb **11.** **(a)** 93.33 lb **(b)** 3 ft
13. 1035 ft^3 **15.** $wb/2$
17. No. The tank will overflow because the movable end will have moved only $3\frac{1}{3}$ ft by the time the tank is full.
19. 4.2 lb **21.** **(a)** 374.4 lb **(b)** 7.5 in. **(c)** No

Practice Exercises, pp. 461–464

1. $\frac{9\pi}{280}$ **3.** π^2 **5.** $\frac{72\pi}{35}$

7. **(a)** 2π **(b)** π **(c)** $12\pi/5$ **(d)** $26\pi/5$
9. **(a)** 8π **(b)** $1088\pi/15$ **(c)** $512\pi/15$
11. $\pi(3\sqrt{3} - \pi)/3$
13. **(a)** $16\pi/15$ **(b)** $8\pi/5$ **(c)** $8\pi/3$ **(d)** $32\pi/5$
15. $\frac{28\pi}{3}$ ft^3 **17.** $\frac{10}{3}$ **19.** $\frac{285}{8}$ **21.** 10 **23.** $\frac{9\pi}{2}$
25. $\bar{x} = 0, \bar{y} = 8/5$ **27.** $\bar{x} = 3/2, \bar{y} = 12/5$
29. $\bar{x} = 9/5, \bar{y} = 11/10$ **31.** $28\pi\sqrt{2}/3$ **33.** 4π
35. $76\pi/3$ **37.** 4640 J **39.** 10 ft-lb, 30 ft-lb
41. 418,208.81 ft-lb **43.** $22{,}500\pi$ ft-lb, 257 sec
45. 332.8 lb **47.** 2196.48 lb **49.** $216w_1 + 360w_2$

Additional and Advanced Exercises, pp. 464–465

1. $f(x) = \sqrt{\frac{2x - a}{\pi}}$ **3.** $f(x) = \sqrt{C^2 - 1}\, x + a$, where $C \geq 1$
5. $\bar{x} = 0, \bar{y} = \frac{n}{2n + 1}$, $(0, 1/2)$
9. **(a)** $\bar{x} = \bar{y} = 4(a^2 + ab + b^2)/(3\pi(a + b))$
(b) $(2a/\pi, 2a/\pi)$
11. $28/3$ **13.** $\frac{4h\sqrt{3mh}}{3}$ **15.** ≈ 2329.6 lb
17. **(a)** $2h/3$ **(b)** $(6a^2 + 8ah + 3h^2)/(6a + 4h)$

CHAPTER 7

Section 7.1, 473–475

1. One-to-one **3.** Not one-to-one **5.** One-to-one
7. D: $(0, 1]$ R: $[0, \infty)$

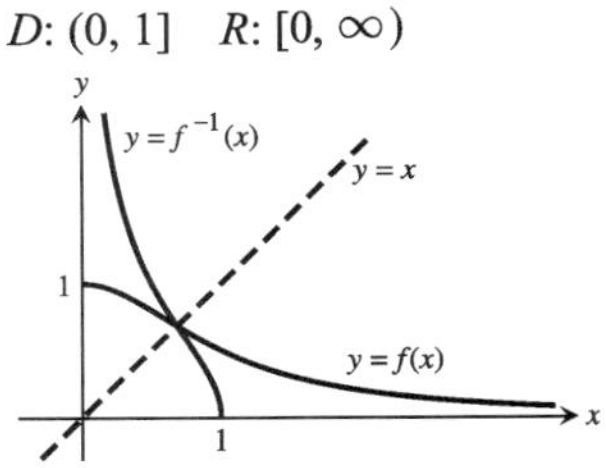

9. D: $[-1, 1]$ R: $[-\pi/2, \pi/2]$

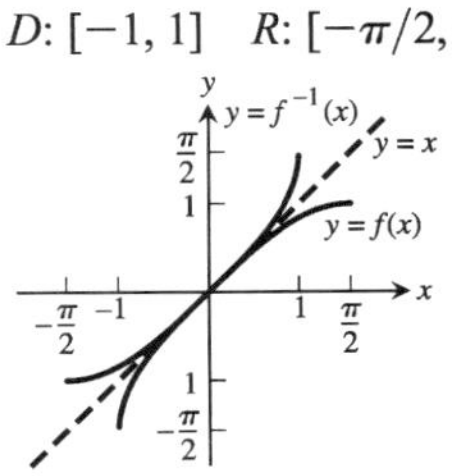

11. **(a)** Symmetric about the line $y = x$

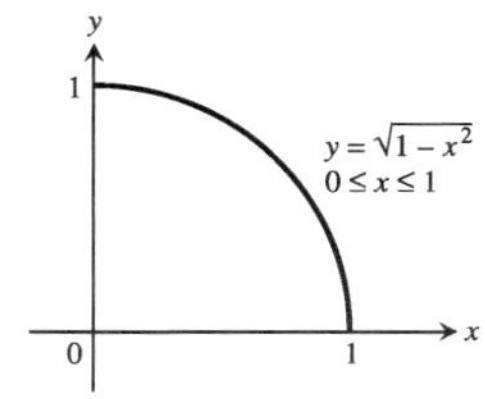

13. $f^{-1}(x) = \sqrt{x - 1}$ **15.** $f^{-1}(x) = \sqrt[3]{x + 1}$
17. $f^{-1}(x) = \sqrt{x} - 1$
19. $f^{-1}(x) = \sqrt[5]{x}$;domain: $-\infty < x < \infty$; range: $-\infty < y < \infty$
21. $f^{-1}(x) = 5\sqrt{x - 1}$; domain: $-\infty < x < \infty$;
range: $-\infty < y < \infty$
23. $f^{-1}(x) = \frac{1}{\sqrt{x}}$; domain: $x > 0$; range: $y > 0$
25. **(a)** $f^{-1}(x) = \frac{x}{2} - \frac{3}{2}$
(b)

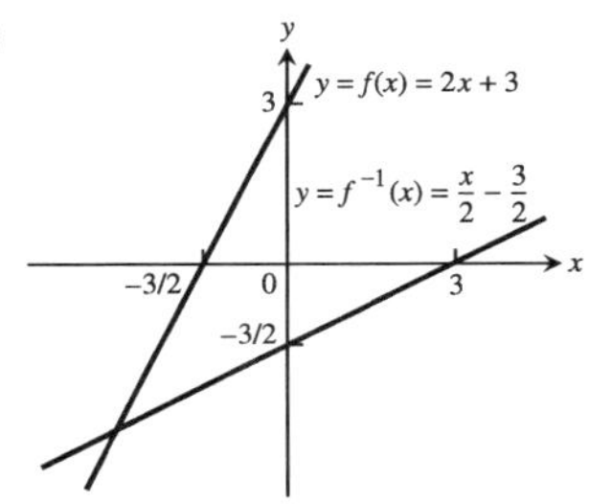

(c) 2, 1/2
27. **(a)** $f^{-1}(x) = -\frac{x}{4} + \frac{5}{4}$
(b)

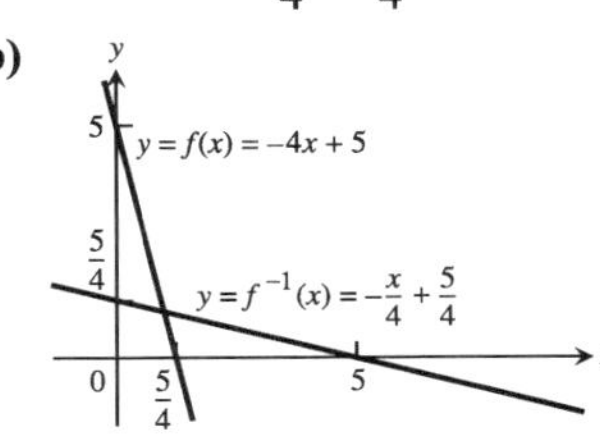

(c) $-4, -1/4$
29. **(b)**

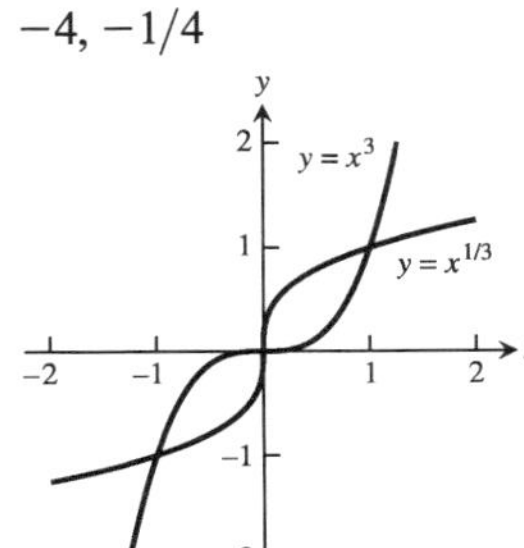

(c) Slope of f at $(1, 1)$: 3; slope of g at $(1, 1)$: 1/3; slope of f at $(-1, -1)$: 3; slope of g at $(-1, -1)$: 1/3
(d) $y = 0$ is tangent to $y = x^3$ at $x = 0$; $x = 0$ is tangent to $y = \sqrt[3]{x}$ at $x = 0$

31. 1/9 **33.** 3

35. **(a)** $f^{-1}(x) = \frac{1}{m}x$

(b) The graph of f^{-1} is the line through the origin with slope $1/m$.

37. **(a)** $f^{-1}(x) = x - 1$

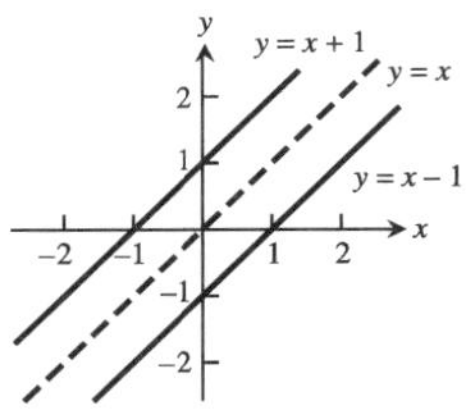

(b) $f^{-1}(x) = x - b$. The graph of f^{-1} is a line parallel to the graph of f. The graphs of f and f^{-1} lie on opposite sides of the line $y = x$ and are equidistant from that line.

(c) Their graphs will be parallel to one another and lie on opposite sides of the line $y = x$ equidistant from that line.

41. Increasing, therefore one-to-one; $df^{-1}/dx = \frac{1}{9}x^{-2/3}$

43. Decreasing, therefore one-to-one; $df^{-1}/dx = -\frac{1}{3}x^{-2/3}$

Section 7.2, pp. 484–485

1. **(a)** $\ln 3 - 2\ln 2$ **(b)** $2(\ln 2 - \ln 3)$ **(c)** $-\ln 2$, **(d)** $\frac{2}{3}\ln 3$ **(e)** $\ln 3 + \frac{1}{2}\ln 2$ **(f)** $\frac{1}{2}(3\ln 3 - \ln 2)$

3. **(a)** $\ln 5$ **(b)** $\ln(x - 3)$ **(c)** $\ln(t^2)$

5. $1/x$ **7.** $2/t$ **9.** $-1/x$ **11.** $\frac{1}{\theta + 1}$ **13.** $3/x$

15. $2(\ln t) + (\ln t)^2$ **17.** $x^3 \ln x$ **19.** $\frac{1 - \ln t}{t^2}$

21. $\frac{1}{x(1 + \ln x)^2}$ **23.** $\frac{1}{x\ln x}$ **25.** $2\cos(\ln\theta)$

27. $-\frac{3x + 2}{2x(x + 1)}$ **29.** $\frac{2}{t(1 - \ln t)^2}$ **31.** $\frac{\tan(\ln\theta)}{\theta}$

33. $\frac{10x}{x^2 + 1} + \frac{1}{2(1 - x)}$ **35.** $2x\ln|x| - x\ln\frac{|x|}{\sqrt{2}}$ **37.** $\ln\left(\frac{2}{3}\right)$

39. $\ln|y^2 - 25| + C$ **41.** $\ln 3$ **43.** $(\ln 2)^2$ **45.** $\frac{1}{\ln 4}$

47. $\ln|6 + 3\tan t| + C$ **49.** $\ln 2$ **51.** $\ln 27$

53. $\ln(1 + \sqrt{x}) + C$

55. $\left(\frac{1}{2}\right)\sqrt{x(x + 1)}\left(\frac{1}{x} + \frac{1}{x + 1}\right) = \frac{2x + 1}{2\sqrt{x(x + 1)}}$

57. $\left(\frac{1}{2}\right)\sqrt{\frac{t}{t + 1}}\left(\frac{1}{t} - \frac{1}{t + 1}\right) = \frac{1}{2\sqrt{t}(t + 1)^{3/2}}$

59. $\sqrt{\theta + 3}(\sin\theta)\left(\frac{1}{2(\theta + 3)} + \cot\theta\right)$

61. $t(t + 1)(t + 2)\left[\frac{1}{t} + \frac{1}{t + 1} + \frac{1}{t + 2}\right] = 3t^2 + 6t + 2$

63. $\frac{\theta + 5}{\theta\cos\theta}\left[\frac{1}{\theta + 5} - \frac{1}{\theta} + \tan\theta\right]$

65. $\frac{x\sqrt{x^2 + 1}}{(x + 1)^{2/3}}\left[\frac{1}{x} + \frac{x}{x^2 + 1} - \frac{2}{3(x + 1)}\right]$

67. $\frac{1}{3}\sqrt[3]{\frac{x(x - 2)}{x^2 + 1}}\left(\frac{1}{x} + \frac{1}{x - 2} - \frac{2x}{x^2 + 1}\right)$

69. **(a)** Max $= 0$ at $x = 0$, min $= -\ln 2$ at $x = \pi/3$

(b) Max $= 1$ at $x = 1$, min $= \cos(\ln 2)$ at $x = 1/2$ and $x = 2$

71. $\ln 16$ **73.** $4\pi\ln 4$ **75.** $\pi\ln 16$

77. **(a)** $6 + \ln 2$ **(b)** $8 + \ln 9$

79. **(a)** $\bar{x} \approx 1.44, \bar{y} \approx 0.36$

(b)

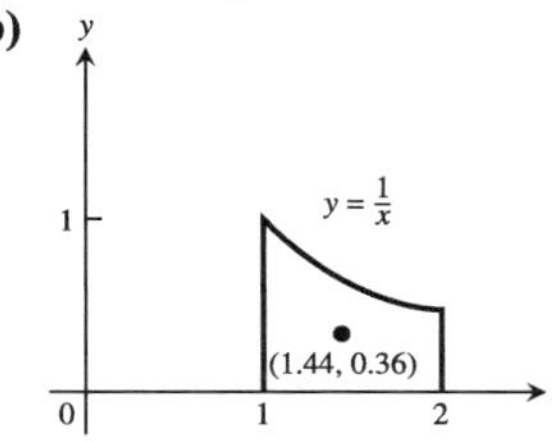

81. $y = x + \ln|x| + 2$ **83.** **(b)** 0.00469

Section 7.3, pp. 493–495

1. **(a)** 7.2 **(b)** $\frac{1}{x^2}$ **(c)** $\frac{x}{y}$

3. **(a)** 1 **(b)** 1 **(c)** $-x^2 - y^2$

5. e^{2t+4} **7.** $e^{5t} + 40$ **9.** $y = 2xe^x + 1$

11. **(a)** $k = \ln 2$ **(b)** $k = (1/10)\ln 2$ **(c)** $k = 1000\ln a$

13. **(a)** $t = -10\ln 3$ **(b)** $t = -\frac{\ln 2}{k}$ **(c)** $t = \frac{\ln .4}{\ln .2}$

15. $4(\ln x)^2$ **17.** $-5e^{-5x}$ **19.** $-7e^{(5-7x)}$ **21.** xe^x

23. x^2e^x **25.** $2e^\theta\cos\theta$ **27.** $2\theta e^{-\theta^2}\sin(e^{-\theta^2})$

29. $\frac{1 - t}{t}$ **31.** $1/(1 + e^\theta)$ **33.** $e^{\cos t}(1 - t\sin t)$

35. $(\sin x)/x$ **37.** $\frac{ye^y\cos x}{1 - ye^y\sin x}$ **39.** $\frac{2e^{2x} - \cos(x + 3y)}{3\cos(x + 3y)}$

41. $\frac{1}{3}e^{3x} - 5e^{-x} + C$ **43.** 1 **45.** $8e^{(x+1)} + C$ **47.** 2

49. $2e^{\sqrt{r}} + C$ **51.** $-e^{-t^2} + C$ **53.** $-e^{1/x} + C$ **55.** e

57. $\frac{1}{\pi}e^{\sec\pi t} + C$ **59.** 1 **61.** $\ln(1 + e^r) + C$

63. $y = 1 - \cos(e^t - 2)$ **65.** $y = 2(e^{-x} + x) - 1$

67. Maximum: 1 at $x = 0$, minimum: $2 - 2\ln 2$ at $x = \ln 2$

69. Abs max of $1/(2e)$ assumed at $x = 1/\sqrt{e}$

71. 2 **73.** $y = e^{x/2} - 1$

75. **(a)** $\frac{d}{dx}(x\ln x - x + C) = x\cdot\frac{1}{x} + \ln x - 1 + 0 = \ln x$

(b) $\frac{1}{e - 1}$

77. **(b)** $|\text{error}| \approx 0.02140$ **79.** 2.71828183

Section 7.4, pp. 500–502

1. **(a)** 7 **(b)** $\sqrt{2}$ **(c)** 75 **(d)** 2 **(e)** 0.5 **(f)** -1

3. **(a)** $\sqrt{x}$ **(b)** x^2 **(c)** $\sin x$ **5.** **(a)** $\frac{\ln 3}{\ln 2}$ **(b)** 3 **(c)** 2

7. $x = 12$ **9.** $x = 3$ or $x = 2$ **11.** $2^x\ln x$

13. $\left(\frac{\ln 5}{2\sqrt{s}}\right)5^{\sqrt{s}}$ **15.** $\pi x^{(\pi-1)}$ **17.** $-\sqrt{2}\cos\theta^{(\sqrt{2}-1)}\sin\theta$

19. $7^{\sec\theta}(\ln 7)^2(\sec\theta\tan\theta)$ **21.** $(3\cos 3t)(2^{\sin 3t})\ln 2$

23. $\frac{1}{\theta\ln 2}$ **25.** $\frac{3}{x\ln 4}$ **27.** $\frac{2(\ln r)}{r(\ln 2)(\ln 4)}$

29. $\frac{-2}{(x+1)(x-1)}$ **31.** $\sin(\log_7\theta) + \frac{1}{\ln 7}\cos(\log_7\theta)$

33. $\frac{1}{\ln 5}$ **35.** $\frac{1}{t}(\log_2 3)3^{\log_2 t}$ **37.** $\frac{1}{t}$

39. $(x+1)^x\left(\frac{x}{x+1} + \ln(x+1)\right)$ **41.** $(\sqrt{t})^t\left(\frac{\ln t}{2} + \frac{1}{2}\right)$

43. $(\sin x)^x(\ln\sin x + x\cot x)$ **45.** $(x^{\ln x})\left(\frac{\ln x^2}{x}\right)$

47. $\frac{5^x}{\ln 5} + C$ **49.** $\frac{1}{2\ln 2}$ **51.** $\frac{1}{\ln 2}$ **53.** $\frac{6}{\ln 7}$ **55.** 32760

57. $\frac{3x^{(\sqrt{3}+1)}}{\sqrt{3}+1} + C$ **59.** $3^{\sqrt{2}+1}$ **61.** $\frac{1}{\ln 10}\left(\frac{(\ln x)^2}{2}\right) + C$

63. $2(\ln 2)^2$ **65.** $\frac{3\ln 2}{2}$ **67.** $\ln 10$ **69.** $(\ln 10)\ln|\ln x| + C$

71. $\ln(\ln x), x > 1$ **73.** $-\ln x$ **75.** $2\ln 5$
77. $[10^{-7.44}, 10^{-7.37}]$ **79.** $k = 10$
81. **(a)** 10^{-7} **(b)** 7 **(c)** 1 : 1 **83.** $x \approx -0.76666$
85. **(a)** $L(x) = 1 + (\ln 2)x \approx 0.69x + 1$
87. **(a)** 1.89279 **(b)** −0.35621 **(c)** 0.94575 **(d)** −2.80735
(e) 5.29595 **(f)** 0.97041 **(g)** −1.03972 **(h)** −1.61181
91. $1/e$ **93.** 1 **95.** $1/e$ **97.** $e^{1/2}$ **99.** 1

Section 7.5, pp. 508–511

1. **(a)** −0.00001 **(b)** 10,536 years **(c)** 82%
3. 54.88 g **5.** 59.8 ft **7.** 2.8147498×10^{14}
9. **(a)** 8 years **(b)** 32.02 years **11.** 15.28 years
13. **(a)** $A_0e^{0.2}$ **(b)** 17.33 years; 27.47 years
15. 4.50% **17.** 0.585 days
21. **(a)** 17.5 min. **(b)** 13.26 min.
23. −3°C **25.** About 6659 years **27.** 41 years old

Section 7.6, pp. 515–517

1. **(a)** slower **(b)** slower **(c)** slower **(d)** faster
(e) slower **(f)** slower **(g)** same **(h)** slower
3. **(a)** same **(b)** faster **(c)** same **(d)** same **(e)** slower
(f) faster **(g)** slower **(h)** same
5. **(a)** same **(b)** same **(c)** same **(d)** faster **(e)** faster
(f) same **(g)** slower **(h)** faster
7. d, a, c, b
9. **(a)** false **(b)** false **(c)** true **(d)** true **(e)** true
(f) true **(g)** false **(h)** true
13. When the degree of f is less than or equal to the degree of g.
15. 1, 1
21. **(b)** $\ln(e^{17000000}) = 17{,}000{,}000 < (e^{17\times10^6})^{1/10^6} = e^{17} \approx 24{,}154{,}952.75$
(c) $x \approx 3.4306311 \times 10^{15}$
(d) They cross at $x \approx 3.4306311 \times 10^{15}$

23. **(a)** The algorithm that takes $O(n\log_2 n)$ steps
25. It could take one million for a sequential search; at most 20 steps for a binary search.

Section 7.7, pp. 530–534

1. **(a)** $\pi/4$ **(b)** $-\pi/3$ **(c)** $\pi/6$
3. **(a)** $-\pi/6$ **(b)** $\pi/4$ **(c)** $-\pi/3$
5. **(a)** $\pi/3$ **(b)** $3\pi/4$ **(c)** $\pi/6$
7. **(a)** $3\pi/4$ **(b)** $\pi/6$ **(c)** $2\pi/3$
9. **(a)** $\pi/4$ **(b)** $-\pi/3$ **(c)** $\pi/6$
11. **(a)** $3\pi/4$ **(b)** $\pi/6$ **(c)** $2\pi/3$

13. $\cos\alpha = \frac{12}{13}, \tan\alpha = \frac{5}{12}, \sec\alpha = \frac{13}{12}, \csc\alpha = \frac{13}{5}, \cot\alpha = \frac{12}{5}$

15. $\sin\alpha = \frac{2}{\sqrt{5}}, \cos\alpha = -\frac{1}{\sqrt{5}}, \tan\alpha = -2, \csc\alpha = \frac{\sqrt{5}}{2},$ $\cot\alpha = -\frac{1}{2}$

17. $1/\sqrt{2}$ **19.** $-1/\sqrt{3}$ **21.** $\frac{4+\sqrt{3}}{2\sqrt{3}}$ **23.** 1

25. $-\sqrt{2}$ **27.** $\pi/6$ **29.** $\frac{\sqrt{x^2+4}}{2}$ **31.** $\sqrt{9y^2-1}$

33. $\sqrt{1-x^2}$ **35.** $\frac{\sqrt{x^2-2x}}{x-1}$ **37.** $\frac{\sqrt{9-4y^2}}{3}$

39. $\frac{\sqrt{x^2-16}}{x}$ **41.** $\pi/2$ **43.** $\pi/2$ **45.** $\pi/2$

47. 0 **49.** $\frac{-2x}{\sqrt{1-x^4}}$ **51.** $\frac{\sqrt{2}}{\sqrt{1-2t^2}}$

53. $\frac{1}{|2s+1|\sqrt{s^2+s}}$ **55.** $\frac{-2x}{(x^2+1)\sqrt{x^4+2x^2}}$

57. $\frac{-1}{\sqrt{1-t^2}}$ **59.** $\frac{-1}{2\sqrt{t}(1+t)}$ **61.** $\frac{1}{(\tan^{-1}x)(1+x^2)}$

63. $\frac{-e^t}{|e^t|\sqrt{(e^t)^2-1}} = \frac{-1}{\sqrt{e^{2t}-1}}$ **65.** $\frac{-2s^n}{\sqrt{1-s^2}}$ **67.** 0

69. $\sin^{-1}x$ **71.** $\sin^{-1}\frac{x}{7} + C$ **73.** $\frac{1}{\sqrt{17}}\tan^{-1}\frac{x}{\sqrt{17}} + C$

75. $\frac{1}{\sqrt{2}}\sec^{-1}\left|\frac{5x}{\sqrt{2}}\right| + C$ **77.** $2\pi/3$ **79.** $\pi/16$

81. $-\pi/12$ **83.** $\frac{3}{2}\sin^{-1}2(r-1) + C$

85. $\frac{\sqrt{2}}{2}\tan^{-1}\left(\frac{x-1}{\sqrt{2}}\right) + C$ **87.** $\frac{1}{4}\sec^{-1}\left|\frac{2x-1}{2}\right| + C$

89. π **91.** $\pi/12$ **93.** $\frac{1}{2}\sin^{-1}y^2 + C$ **95.** $\sin^{-1}(x-2) + C$

97. π **99.** $\frac{1}{2}\tan^{-1}\left(\frac{y-1}{2}\right) + C$ **101.** 2π

103. $\sec^{-1}|x+1| + C$ **105.** $e^{\sin^{-1}x} + C$ **107.** $\frac{1}{3}(\sin^{-1}(x))^3 + C$

109. $\ln|\tan^{-1}y| + C$ **111.** $\sqrt{3}-1$ **113.** 5 **115.** 2

121. $y = \sin^{-1}x$ **123.** $y = \sec^{-1}x + \frac{2\pi}{3}, x > 1$

127. $\theta = \cos^{-1}\left(\frac{1}{\sqrt{3}}\right) \approx 54.7°$

133. (a) Defined; there is an angle whose tangent is 2.
(b) Not defined; there is no angle whose cosine is 2.

135. (a) Not defined; no angle has secant 0.
(b) Not defined; no angle has sine $\sqrt{2}$.

137. $3\sqrt{5}$ ft.

139. Yes, $\sin^{-1}(x)$ and $-\cos^{-1}(x)$ differ by the constant $\pi/2$.

147. $\pi^2/2$ **149. (a)** $\pi^2/2$ **(b)** 2π

151. (a) 0.84107 **(b)** -0.72973 **(c)** 0.46365

153. (a) Domain: all real numbers except those having the form $\frac{\pi}{2} + k\pi$ where k is an integer; range: $-\pi/2 < y < \pi/2$.
(b) Domain: $-\infty < x < \infty$; range: $-\infty < y < \infty$

155. (a) Domain: $-\infty < x < \infty$; range: $0 \le y \le \pi$
(b) Domain: $-1 \le x \le 1$; range: $-1 \le y \le 1$

157. The graphs are identical.

Section 7.8, pp. 542–546

1. $\cosh x = 5/4$, $\tanh x = -3/5$, $\coth x = -5/3$, $\operatorname{sech} x = 4/5$, $\operatorname{csch} x = -4/3$

3. $\sinh x = 8/15$, $\tanh x = 8/17$, $\coth x = 17/8$, $\operatorname{sech} x = 15/17$, $\operatorname{csch} x = 15/8$

5. $x + \frac{1}{x}$ **7.** e^{5x} **9.** e^{4x} **13.** $2\cosh\frac{x}{3}$

15. $\operatorname{sech}^2\sqrt{t} + \frac{\tanh\sqrt{t}}{\sqrt{t}}$ **17.** $\coth z$

19. $(\ln \operatorname{sech}\theta)(\operatorname{sech}\theta\tanh\theta)$ **21.** $\tanh^3 v$ **23.** 2

25. $\frac{1}{2\sqrt{x(1+x)}}$ **27.** $\frac{1}{1+\theta} - \tanh^{-1}\theta$

29. $\frac{1}{2\sqrt{t}} - \coth^{-1}\sqrt{t}$ **31.** $-\operatorname{sech}^{-1}x$ **33.** $\frac{\ln 2}{\sqrt{1 + \left(\frac{1}{2}\right)^{2\theta}}}$

35. $|\sec x|$ **41.** $\frac{\cosh 2x}{2} + C$

43. $12\sinh\left(\frac{x}{2} - \ln 3\right) + C$ **45.** $7\ln|e^{x/7} + e^{-x/7}| + C$

47. $\tanh\left(x - \frac{1}{2}\right) + C$ **49.** $-2\operatorname{sech}\sqrt{t} + C$ **51.** $\ln\frac{5}{2}$

53. $\frac{3}{32} + \ln 2$ **55.** $e - e^{-1}$ **57.** 3/4 **59.** $\frac{3}{8} + \ln\sqrt{2}$

61. $\ln(2/3)$ **63.** $\frac{-\ln 3}{2}$ **65.** $\ln 3$

67. (a) $\sinh^{-1}(\sqrt{3})$ **(b)** $\ln(\sqrt{3} + 2)$

69. (a) $\coth^{-1}(2) - \coth^{-1}(5/4)$ **(b)** $\left(\frac{1}{2}\right)\ln\left(\frac{1}{3}\right)$

71. (a) $-\operatorname{sech}^{-1}\left(\frac{12}{13}\right) + \operatorname{sech}^{-1}\left(\frac{4}{5}\right)$

(b) $-\ln\left(\frac{1 + \sqrt{1 - (12/13)^2}}{(12/13)}\right) + \ln\left(\frac{1 + \sqrt{1 - (4/5)^2}}{(4/5)}\right) = -\ln\left(\frac{3}{2}\right) + \ln(2) = \ln(4/3)$

73. (a) 0 **(b)** 0

75. (b) i) $f(x) = \frac{2f(x)}{2} + 0 = f(x)$, ii) $f(x) = 0 + \frac{2f(x)}{2} = f(x)$

77. (b) $\sqrt{\frac{mg}{k}}$ **(c)** $80\sqrt{5} \approx 178.89$ ft/sec

79. $y = \operatorname{sech}^{-1}(x) - \sqrt{1 - x^2}$ **81.** 2π **83.** $\frac{6}{5}$

85. $16\pi\ln 6 + \frac{455\pi}{9}$

89. (c) $a \approx 0.0417525$ **(d)** ≈ 47.90 lb

Practice Exercises, pp. 547–550

1. $-2e^{-x/5}$ **3.** xe^{4x} **5.** $\frac{2\sin\theta\cos\theta}{\sin^2\theta} = 2\cot\theta$ **7.** $\frac{2}{(\ln 2)x}$

9. $-8^{-t}(\ln 8)$ **11.** $18x^{2.6}$

13. $(x + 2)^{x+2}(\ln(x + 2) + 1)$ **15.** $-\frac{1}{\sqrt{1 - u^2}}$

17. $\frac{-1}{\sqrt{1 - x^2}\cos^{-1}x}$ **19.** $\tan^{-1}(t) + \frac{t}{1 + t^2} - \frac{1}{2t}$

21. $\frac{1 - z}{\sqrt{z^2 - 1}} + \sec^{-1}z$ **23.** -1

25. $\frac{2(x^2 + 1)}{\sqrt{\cos 2x}}\left[\frac{2x}{x^2 + 1} + \tan 2x\right]$

27. $5\left[\frac{(t + 1)(t - 1)}{(t - 2)(t + 3)}\right]^5\left[\frac{1}{t + 1} + \frac{1}{t - 1} - \frac{1}{t - 2} - \frac{1}{t + 3}\right]$

29. $\frac{1}{\sqrt{\theta}}(\sin\theta)^{\sqrt{\theta}}\left(\frac{\ln\sqrt{\sin\theta}}{2} + \theta\cot\theta\right)$ **31.** $-\cos e^x + C$

33. $\tan(e^x - 7) + C$ **35.** $e^{\tan x} + C$ **37.** $\frac{-\ln 7}{3}$

39. $\ln 8$ **41.** $\ln(9/25)$ **43.** $-[\ln|\cos(\ln v)|] + C$

45. $-\frac{1}{2}(\ln x)^{-2} + C$ **47.** $-\cot(1 + \ln r) + C$

49. $\frac{1}{2\ln 3}(3^{x^2}) + C$ **51.** $3\ln 7$ **53.** $15/16 + \ln 2$

55. $e - 1$ **57.** 1/6 **59.** 9/14

61. $\frac{1}{3}\left[(\ln 4)^3 - (\ln 2)^3\right]$ or $\frac{7}{3}(\ln 2)^3$ **63.** $\frac{9\ln 2}{4}$ **65.** π

67. $\pi/\sqrt{3}$ **69.** $\sec^{-1}|2y| + C$ **71.** $\pi/12$

73. $\sin^{-1}(x + 1) + C$ **75.** $\pi/2$ **77.** $\frac{1}{3}\sec^{-1}\left(\frac{t + 1}{3}\right) + C$

79. $y = \frac{\ln 2}{\ln(3/2)}$ **81.** $y = \ln x - \ln 3$ **83.** $y = \frac{1}{1 - e^x}$

85. $\ln 10$ **87.** $\ln 2$ **89.** 5 **91.** $-\infty$ **93.** 1 **95.** e^3

97. (a) same rate **(b)** same rate **(c)** faster **(d)** faster **(e)** same rate **(f)** same rate

99. (a) true **(b)** false **(c)** false **(d)** true **(e)** true **(f)** true

101. 1/3

103. Absolute maximum $= 0$ at $x = e/2$, absolute minimum $= -0.5$ at $x = 0.5$

105. 1 **107.** $1/e$ m/sec

109. $1/\sqrt{2}$ units long by $1/\sqrt{e}$ units high, $A = 1/\sqrt{2e} \approx 0.43$ units^2

111. $\ln 5x - \ln 3x = \ln(5/3)$ **113.** 1/2

115. (a) Absolute maximum of $2/e$ at $x = e^2$, inflection point $(e^{8/3}, (8/3)e^{-4/3})$, concave up on $(e^{8/3}, \infty)$, concave down on $(0, e^{8/3})$
(b) Absolute maximum of 1 at $x = 0$, inflection points $(\pm 1/\sqrt{2}, 1/\sqrt{e})$, concave up on $(-\infty, -1/\sqrt{2}) \cup (1/\sqrt{2}, \infty)$, concave down on $(-1/\sqrt{2}, 1/\sqrt{2})$
(c) Absolute maximum of 1 at $x = 0$, inflection point $(1, 2/e)$, concave up on $(1, \infty)$, concave down on $(-\infty, 1)$

117. 18,935 years **119.** $20(5 - \sqrt{17})$ m

Additional and Advanced Exercises, pp. 550–552

1. $\pi/2$ **3.** $1/\sqrt{e}$ **5.** $\ln 2$ **7. (a)** 1 **(b)** $\pi/2$ **(c)** π
9. $\frac{1}{\ln 2}, \frac{1}{2\ln 2}, 2:1$ **11.** $x = 2$ **13.** $2/17$
21. $\bar{x} = \frac{\ln 4}{\pi}, \bar{y} = 0$ **25. (b)** 61°

CHAPTER 8

Section 8.1, pp. 558–560

1. $2\sqrt{8x^2 + 1} + C$ **3.** $2(\sin v)^{3/2} + C$ **5.** $\ln 5$
7. $2\ln\left(\sqrt{x} + 1\right) + C$ **9.** $-\frac{1}{7}\ln|\sin(3 - 7x)| + C$
11. $-\ln|\csc(e^\theta + 1) + \cot(e^\theta + 1)| + C$
13. $3\ln\left|\sec\frac{t}{3} + \tan\frac{t}{3}\right| + C$
15. $-\ln|\csc(s - \pi) + \cot(s - \pi)| + C$ **17.** 1
19. $e^{\tan v} + C$ **21.** $\frac{3^{(x+1)}}{\ln 3} + C$ **23.** $\frac{2^{\sqrt{w}}}{\ln 2} + C$
25. $3\tan^{-1} 3u + C$ **27.** $\pi/18$ **29.** $\sin^{-1} s^2 + C$
31. $6\sec^{-1}|5x| + C$ **33.** $\tan^{-1} e^x + C$ **35.** $\ln\left(2 + \sqrt{3}\right)$
37. 2π **39.** $\sin^{-1}(t - 2) + C$
41. $\sec^{-1}|x + 1| + C$, when $|x + 1| > 1$
43. $\tan x - 2\ln|\csc x + \cot x| - \cot x - x + C$
45. $x + \sin 2x + C$ **47.** $x - \ln|x + 1| + C$ **49.** $7 + \ln 8$
51. $2t^2 - t + 2\tan^{-1}\left(\frac{t}{2}\right) + C$ **53.** $\sin^{-1} x + \sqrt{1 - x^2} + C$
55. $\sqrt{2}$ **57.** $\tan x - \sec x + C$ **59.** $\ln|1 + \sin\theta| + C$
61. $\cot x + x + \csc x + C$ **63.** 4 **65.** $\sqrt{2}$ **67.** 2
69. $\ln\left|\sqrt{2} + 1\right| - \ln\left|\sqrt{2} - 1\right|$ **71.** $4 - \frac{\pi}{2}$
73. $-\ln|\csc(\sin\theta) + \cot(\sin\theta)| + C$
75. $\ln|\sin x| + \ln|\cos x| + C$ **77.** $12\tan^{-1}\left(\sqrt{y}\right) + C$
79. $\sec^{-1}\left|\frac{x - 1}{7}\right| + C$ **81.** $\ln|\sec(\tan t)| + C$

83. (a) $\sin\theta - \frac{1}{3}\sin^3\theta + C$
(b) $\sin\theta - \frac{2}{3}\sin^3\theta + \frac{1}{5}\sin^5\theta + C$
(c) $\int \cos^9\theta\, d\theta = \int \cos^8\theta(\cos\theta)\, d\theta = \int (1 - \sin^2\theta)^4(\cos\theta)\, d\theta$

85. (a) $\int \tan^3\theta\, d\theta = \frac{1}{2}\tan^2\theta - \int \tan\theta\, d\theta = \frac{1}{2}\tan^2\theta + \ln|\cos\theta| + C$
(b) $\int \tan^5\theta\, d\theta = \frac{1}{4}\tan^4\theta - \int \tan^3\theta\, d\theta$
(c) $\int \tan^7\theta\, d\theta = \frac{1}{6}\tan^6\theta - \int \tan^5\theta\, d\theta$
(d) $\int \tan^{2k+1}\theta\, d\theta = \frac{1}{2k}\tan^{2k}\theta - \int \tan^{2k-1}\theta\, d\theta$

87. $2\sqrt{2} - \ln\left(3 + 2\sqrt{2}\right)$ **89.** π^2
91. $\ln\left(2 + \sqrt{3}\right)$ **93.** $\bar{x} = 0, \bar{y} = \frac{1}{\ln\left(2\sqrt{2} + 3\right)}$

Section 8.2, pp. 568–570

1. $-2x\cos(x/2) + 4\sin(x/2) + C$
3. $t^2\sin t + 2t\cos t - 2\sin t + C$ **5.** $\ln 4 - \frac{3}{4}$
7. $y\tan^{-1}(y) - \ln\sqrt{1 + y^2} + C$
9. $x\tan x + \ln|\cos x| + C$
11. $(x^3 - 3x^2 + 6x - 6)e^x + C$
13. $(x^2 - 7x + 7)e^x + C$
15. $(x^5 - 5x^4 + 20x^3 - 60x^2 + 120x - 120)e^x + C$
17. $\frac{\pi^2 - 4}{8}$ **19.** $\frac{5\pi - 3\sqrt{3}}{9}$
21. $\frac{1}{2}(-e^\theta\cos\theta + e^\theta\sin\theta) + C$
23. $\frac{e^{2x}}{13}(3\sin 3x + 2\cos 3x) + C$
25. $\frac{2}{3}\left(\sqrt{3s + 9}\, e^{\sqrt{3s+9}} - e^{\sqrt{3s+9}}\right) + C$
27. $\frac{\pi\sqrt{3}}{3} - \ln(2) - \frac{\pi^2}{18}$
29. $\frac{1}{2}[-x\cos(\ln x) + x\sin(\ln x)] + C$
31. (a) π **(b)** 3π **(c)** 5π **(d)** $(2n + 1)\pi$
33. $2\pi(1 - \ln 2)$ **35. (a)** $\pi(\pi - 2)$ **(b)** 2π
37. $\frac{1}{2\pi}(1 - e^{-2\pi})$ **39.** $u = x^n, dv = \cos x\, dx$
41. $u = x^n, dv = e^{ax}\, dx$ **43.** $x\sin^{-1} x + \cos(\sin^{-1} x) + C$

45. $x \sec^{-1} x - \ln\left|x + \sqrt{x^2 - 1}\right| + C$ **47.** Yes

49. (a) $x \sinh^{-1} x - \cosh(\sinh^{-1} x) + C$

(b) $x \sinh^{-1} x - (1 + x^2)^{1/2} + C$

Section 8.3, pp. 579–581

1. $\frac{2}{x-3} + \frac{3}{x-2}$ **3.** $\frac{1}{x+1} + \frac{3}{(x+1)^2}$

5. $\frac{-2}{z} + \frac{-1}{z^2} + \frac{2}{z-1}$ **7.** $1 + \frac{17}{t-3} + \frac{-12}{t-2}$

9. $\frac{1}{2}[\ln|1 + x| - \ln|1 - x|] + C$

11. $\frac{1}{7}\ln|(x+6)^2(x-1)^5| + C$ **13.** $(\ln 15)/2$

15. $-\frac{1}{2}\ln|t| + \frac{1}{6}\ln|t+2| + \frac{1}{3}\ln|t-1| + C$ **17.** $3\ln 2 - 2$

19. $\frac{1}{4}\ln\left|\frac{x+1}{x-1}\right| - \frac{x}{2(x^2-1)} + C$ **21.** $(\pi + 2\ln 2)/8$

23. $\tan^{-1} y - \frac{1}{y^2+1} + C$

25. $-(s-1)^{-2} + (s-1)^{-1} + \tan^{-1} s + C$

27. $\frac{-1}{\theta^2 + 2\theta + 2} + \ln(\theta^2 + 2\theta + 2) - \tan^{-1}(\theta + 1) + C$

29. $x^2 + \ln\left|\frac{x-1}{x}\right| + C$

31. $9x + 2\ln|x| + \frac{1}{x} + 7\ln|x-1| + C$

33. $\frac{y^2}{2} - \ln|y| + \frac{1}{2}\ln(1 + y^2) + C$ **35.** $\ln\left(\frac{e^t+1}{e^t+2}\right) + C$

37. $\frac{1}{5}\ln\left|\frac{\sin y - 2}{\sin y + 3}\right| + C$

39. $\frac{(\tan^{-1} 2x)^2}{4} - 3\ln|x-2| + \frac{6}{x-2} + C$

41. $x = \ln|t-2| - \ln|t-1| + \ln 2$ **43.** $x = \frac{6t}{t+2} - 1$

45. $3\pi\ln 25$ **47.** 1.10

49. (a) $x = \frac{1000e^{4t}}{499 + e^{4t}}$ **(b)** 1.55 days

51. (a) $\frac{22}{7} - \pi$ **(b)** 0.04% **(c)** The area is less than 0.003.

Section 8.4, pp. 585–586

1. 8/15 **3.** 4/3 **5.** 16/35 **7.** 3π **9.** π **11.** 2

13. 1 **15.** 4 **17.** 2 **19.** $2\ln\left(1 + \sqrt{2}\right)$ **21.** $\sqrt{2}$

23. $2\sqrt{3} + \ln\left(2 + \sqrt{3}\right)$ **25.** 4/3 **27.** 4/3

29. $2(1 - \ln 2)$ **31.** $\frac{4}{3} - \ln\sqrt{3}$ **33.** $-6/5$ **35.** π

37. 0 **39.** $\frac{2\pi\left(\left(9\sqrt[3]{4} + 1\right)^{3/2} - 1\right)}{27}$ **41.** $\ln\left(1 + \sqrt{2}\right)$

43. $\pi^2/2$

Section 8.5, pp. 591–592

1. $\ln\left|\sqrt{9 + y^2} + y\right| + C$ **3.** $\pi/4$ **5.** $\pi/6$

7. $\frac{25}{2}\sin^{-1}\left(\frac{t}{5}\right) + \frac{t\sqrt{25 - t^2}}{2} + C$

9. $\frac{1}{2}\ln\left|\frac{2x}{7} + \frac{\sqrt{4x^2 - 49}}{7}\right| + C$

11. $7\left[\frac{\sqrt{y^2 - 49}}{7} - \sec^{-1}\left(\frac{y}{7}\right)\right] + C$ **13.** $\frac{\sqrt{x^2 - 1}}{x} + C$

15. $\frac{1}{3}(x^2 + 4)^{3/2} - 4\sqrt{x^2 + 4} + C$ **17.** $\frac{-2\sqrt{4 - w^2}}{w} + C$

19. $4\sqrt{3} - 4\pi/3$ **21.** $-\frac{x}{\sqrt{x^2 - 1}} + C$

23. $-\frac{1}{5}\left(\frac{\sqrt{1 - x^2}}{x}\right)^5 + C$ **25.** $2\tan^{-1} 2x + \frac{4x}{(4x^2 + 1)} + C$

27. $\frac{1}{3}\left(\frac{v}{\sqrt{1 - v^2}}\right)^3 + C$ **29.** $\ln 9 - \ln\left(1 + \sqrt{10}\right)$

31. $\pi/6$ **33.** $\sec^{-1}|x| + C$ **35.** $\sqrt{x^2 - 1} + C$

37. $y = 2\left[\frac{\sqrt{x^2 - 4}}{2} - \sec^{-1}\left(\frac{x}{2}\right)\right]$

39. $y = \frac{3}{2}\tan^{-1}\left(\frac{x}{2}\right) - \frac{3\pi}{8}$ **41.** $3\pi/4$

43. $\frac{2}{1 - \tan(x/2)} + C$ **45.** 1 **47.** $\frac{\sqrt{3}\pi}{9}$

49. $\frac{1}{\sqrt{2}}\ln\left|\frac{\tan(t/2) + 1 - \sqrt{2}}{\tan(t/2) + 1 + \sqrt{2}}\right| + C$

51. $\ln\left|\frac{1 + \tan(\theta/2)}{1 - \tan(\theta/2)}\right| + C$

Section 8.6, pp. 600–603

1. $\frac{2}{\sqrt{3}}\left(\tan^{-1}\sqrt{\frac{x-3}{3}}\right) + C$

3. $\sqrt{x-2}\left(\frac{2(x-2)}{3} + 4\right) + C$

5. $\frac{(2x-3)^{3/2}(x+1)}{5} + C$

7. $\frac{-\sqrt{9 - 4x}}{x} - \frac{2}{3}\ln\left|\frac{\sqrt{9 - 4x} - 3}{\sqrt{9 - 4x} + 3}\right| + C$

9. $\frac{(x+2)(2x-6)\sqrt{4x - x^2}}{6} + 4\sin^{-1}\left(\frac{x-2}{2}\right) + C$

11. $-\frac{1}{\sqrt{7}}\ln\left|\frac{\sqrt{7} + \sqrt{7 + x^2}}{x}\right| + C$

13. $\sqrt{4 - x^2} - 2\ln\left|\frac{2 + \sqrt{4 - x^2}}{x}\right| + C$

15. $\frac{p}{2}\sqrt{25 - p^2} + \frac{25}{2}\sin^{-1}\frac{p}{5} + C$

17. $2\sin^{-1}\frac{r}{2}-\frac{1}{2}r\sqrt{4-r^2}+C$

19. $-\frac{1}{3}\tan^{-1}\left[\frac{1}{3}\tan\left(\frac{\pi}{4}-\theta\right)\right]+C$

21. $\frac{e^{2t}}{13}(2\cos 3t+3\sin 3t)+C$

23. $\frac{x^2}{2}\cos^{-1}(x)+\frac{1}{4}\sin^{-1}(x)-\frac{1}{4}x\sqrt{1-x^2}+C$

25. $\frac{s}{18(9-s^2)}+\frac{1}{108}\ln\left|\frac{s+3}{s-3}\right|+C$

27. $-\frac{\sqrt{4x+9}}{x}+\frac{2}{3}\ln\left|\frac{\sqrt{4x+9}-3}{\sqrt{4x+9}+3}\right|+C$

29. $2\sqrt{3t-4}-4\tan^{-1}\sqrt{\frac{3t-4}{4}}+C$

31. $\frac{x^3}{3}\tan^{-1}x-\frac{x^2}{6}+\frac{1}{6}\ln(1+x^2)+C$

33. $-\frac{\cos 5x}{10}-\frac{\cos x}{2}+C$ **35.** $8\left[\frac{\sin(7t/2)}{7}-\frac{\sin(9t/2)}{9}\right]+C$

37. $6\sin(\theta/12)+\frac{6}{7}\sin(7\theta/12)+C$

39. $\frac{1}{2}\ln(x^2+1)+\frac{x}{2(1+x^2)}+\frac{1}{2}\tan^{-1}x+C$

41. $\left(x-\frac{1}{2}\right)\sin^{-1}\sqrt{x}+\frac{1}{2}\sqrt{x-x^2}+C$

43. $\sin^{-1}\sqrt{x}-\sqrt{x-x^2}+C$

45. $\sqrt{1-\sin^2 t}-\ln\left|\frac{1+\sqrt{1-\sin^2 t}}{\sin t}\right|+C$

47. $\ln\left|\ln y+\sqrt{3+(\ln y)^2}\right|+C$

49. $\ln\left|3r+\sqrt{9r^2-1}\right|+C$

51. $x\cos^{-1}\sqrt{x}+\frac{1}{2}\sin^{-1}\sqrt{x}-\frac{1}{2}\sqrt{x-x^2}+C$

53. $-\frac{\sin^4 2x\cos 2x}{10}-\frac{2\sin^2 2x\cos 2x}{15}-\frac{4\cos 2x}{15}+C$

55. $\frac{\cos^3 2\pi t\sin 2\pi t}{\pi}+\frac{3}{2}\frac{\cos 2\pi t\sin 2\pi t}{\pi}+3t+C$

57. $\frac{\sin^3 2\theta\cos^2 2\theta}{10}+\frac{\sin^3 2\theta}{15}+C$ **59.** $\frac{2}{3}\tan^3 t+C$

61. $\tan^2 2x-2\ln|\sec 2x|+C$

63. $8\left[-\frac{1}{3}\cot^3 t+\cot t+t\right]+C$

65. $\frac{(\sec\pi x)(\tan\pi x)}{\pi}+\frac{1}{\pi}\ln|\sec\pi x+\tan\pi x|+C$

67. $\frac{\sec^2 3x\tan 3x}{3}+\frac{2}{3}\tan 3x+C$

69. $\frac{-\csc^3 x\cot x}{4}-\frac{3\csc x\cot x}{8}-\frac{3}{8}\ln|\csc x+\cot x|+C$

71. $4x^4(\ln x)^2-2x^4(\ln x)+\frac{x^2}{2}+C$ **73.** $\frac{e^{3x}}{9}(3x-1)+C$

75. $2x^3e^{x/2}-12x^2e^{x/2}+96e^{x/2}\left(\frac{x}{2}-1\right)+C$

77. $\frac{x^2 2^x}{\ln 2}-\frac{2}{\ln 2}\left[\frac{x2^x}{\ln 2}-\frac{2^x}{(\ln 2)^2}\right]+C$ **79.** $\frac{x\pi^x}{\ln\pi}-\frac{\pi^x}{(\ln\pi)^2}+C$

81. $\frac{1}{2}[\sec(e^t-1)\tan(e^t-1)+\ln|\sec(e^t-1)+\tan(e^t-1)|]+C$

83. $\sqrt{2}+\ln\left(\sqrt{2}+1\right)$ **85.** $\pi/3$

87. $\frac{1}{120}\sinh^4 3x\cosh 3x-\frac{1}{90}\sinh^2 3x\cosh 3x+\frac{1}{45}\cosh 3x+C$

89. $\frac{x^2}{3}\sinh 3x-\frac{2x}{9}\cosh 3x+\frac{2}{27}\sinh 3x+C$

91. $-\frac{\operatorname{sech}^7 x}{7}+C$ **101.** $2\pi\sqrt{3}+\pi\sqrt{2}\ln(\sqrt{2}+\sqrt{3})$

103. $\bar{x}=4/3, \bar{y}=\ln\sqrt{2}$ **105.** 7.62 **107.** $\pi/8$ **111.** $\pi/4$

Section 8.7, pp. 613–619

1. **I:** **(a)** 1.5, 0 **(b)** 1.5, 0 **(c)** 0%
II: **(a)** 1.5, 0 **(b)** 1.5, 0 **(c)** 0%

3. **I:** **(a)** 2.75, 0.08 **(b)** 2.67, 0.08 **(c)** $0.0312 \approx 3\%$
II: **(a)** 2.67, 0 **(b)** 2.67, 0 **(c)** 0%

5. **I:** **(a)** 6.25, 0.5 **(b)** 6, 0.25 **(c)** $0.0417 \approx 4\%$
II: **(a)** 6, 0 **(b)** 6, 0 **(c)** 0%

7. **I:** **(a)** 0.509, 0.03125 **(b)** 0.5, 0.009 **(c)** $0.018 \approx 2\%$
II: **(a)** 0.5, 0.002604 **(b)** 0.5, 0.0004 **(c)** 0%

9. **I:** **(a)** 1.8961, 0.161 **(b)** 2, 0.1039 **(c)** $0.052 \approx 5\%$
II: **(a)** 2.0045, 0.0066 **(b)** 2, 0.00454 **(c)** 0%

11. **(a)** 0.31929 **(b)** 0.32812 **(c)** 1/3, 0.01404, 0.00521

13. **(a)** 1.95643 **(b)** 2.00421 **(c)** 2, 0.04357, −0.00421

15. **(a)** 1 **(b)** 2

17. **(a)** 116 **(b)** 2

19. **(a)** 283 **(b)** 2

21. **(a)** 71 **(b)** 10

23. **(a)** 76 **(b)** 12

25. **(a)** 82 **(b)** 8

27. 15,990 ft³ **29.** 5166.346 ft ≈ 0.9785 mi **31.** ≈10.63 ft

33. **(a)** ≈0.00021 **(b)** ≈1.37079 **(c)** ≈0.015%

35. **(a)** 3.11571 **(b)** 0.02588
(c) With $M = 3.11$, we get $|E_T| \le (\pi^3/1200)(3.11) < 0.081$

39. 1.08943 **41.** 0.82812

43. **(a)** $T_{10} \approx 1.983523538$, $T_{100} \approx 1.999835504$, $T_{1000} \approx 1.999998355$

(b)

n	$\lvert E_T\rvert = 2 - T_n$
10	$0.016476462 = 1.6476462 \times 10^{-2}$
100	1.64496×10^{-4}
1000	1.645×10^{-6}

(c) $|E_{10n}| \approx 10^{-2}|E_n|$

(d) $b-a=\pi,\ h^2=\frac{\pi^2}{n^2},\ M=1$

$$|E_n| \le \frac{\pi}{12}\left(\frac{\pi^2}{n^2}\right)=\frac{\pi^3}{12n^2}$$

$$|E_{10n}| \le \frac{\pi^3}{12(10n)^2}=10^{-2}|E_n|$$

45. (a) $f''(x) = 2\cos(x^2) - 4x^2\sin(x^2)$
(b)

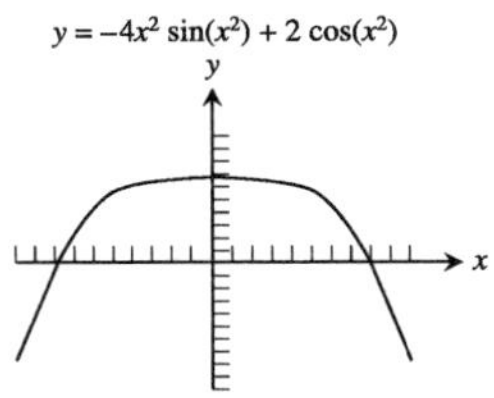

(c) The graph shows that $-3 \le f''(x) \le 2$ for $-1 \le x \le 1$.
(d) $|E_T| \le \frac{1-(-1)}{12}(\Delta x^2)(3) = \frac{\Delta x^2}{2}$
(e) $|E_T| \le \frac{\Delta x^2}{2} \le \frac{0.1^2}{2} < 0.01$ (f) $n \ge 20$

47. (a) 2.3, 1.6, 1.5, 2.1, 3.2, 4.8, 7.0, 9.3, 10.7, 10.7, 9.3, 6.4, 3.2
(b) $\frac{1}{4\pi}\int_0^6 (C(y))^2\,dy$ (c) ≈ 34.7 in.^{3}
(d) $V \approx 34.79$ in.^{3} by Simpson's Rule. Simpson's Rule estimate should be more accurate than the trapezoid estimate. The error in Simpson's Rule estimate is proportional to $\Delta x^4 = 0.0625$, whereas the error in the trapezoid estimate is proportional to $\Delta x^2 = 0.25$, a larger number when $\Delta x = 0.5$ in.

49. (a) ≈ 5.870 (b) $|E_T| \le 0.0032$

51. 21.07 in. 53. 14.4 55. 54.9

Section 8.8, pp. 631–633

1. $\pi/2$ 3. 2 5. 6 7. $\pi/2$ 9. ln 3 11. ln 4 13. 0
15. $\sqrt{3}$ 17. π 19. $\ln\left(1 + \frac{\pi}{2}\right)$ 21. -1 23. 1
25. $-1/4$ 27. $\pi/2$ 29. $\pi/3$ 31. 6 33. ln 2
35. Diverges 37. Converges 39. Converges 41. Converges
43. Diverges 45. Converges 47. Converges 49. Diverges
51. Converges 53. Converges 55. Diverges 57. Converges
59. Diverges 61. Converges 63. Converges
65. (a) Converges when $p < 1$ (b) Converges when $p > 1$
67. 1 69. 2π 71. ln 2 73. (b) ≈ 0.88621
75. (a)

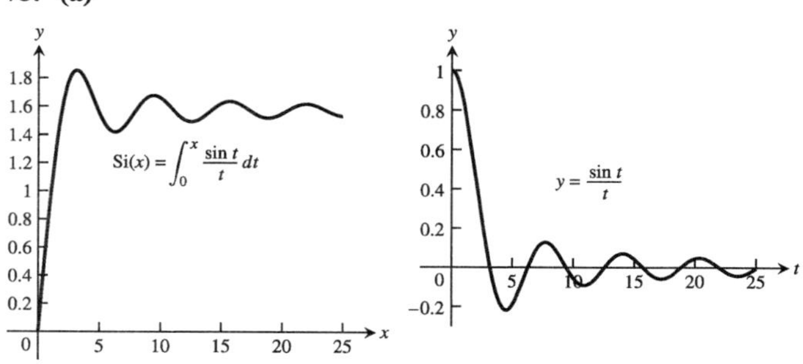

(b) $\pi/2$

77. (a)

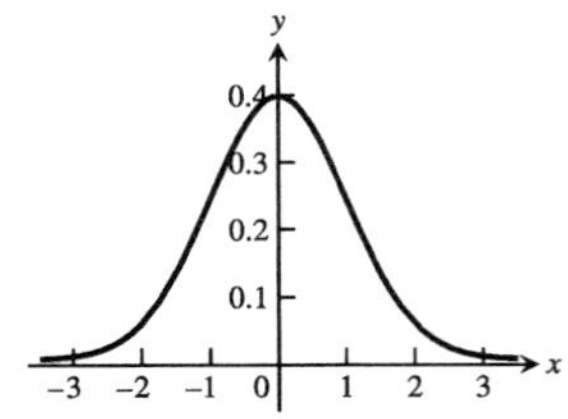

(b) ≈ 0.683, ≈ 0.954, ≈ 0.997

81. Diverges 83. Converges 85. Converges 87. Diverges

Practice Exercises, pp. 634–638

1. $\frac{1}{12}(4x^2-9)^{3/2} + C$ 3. $\frac{(2x+1)^{5/2}}{10} - \frac{(2x+1)^{3/2}}{6} + C$
5. $\frac{\sqrt{8x^2+1}}{8} + C$ 7. $\frac{1}{2}\ln(25+y^2) + C$
9. $\frac{-\sqrt{9-4t^4}}{8} + C$ 11. $\frac{9}{25}(z^{5/3}+1)^{5/3} + C$
13. $-\frac{1}{2(1-\cos 2\theta)} + C$ 15. $-\frac{1}{4}\ln|3 + 4\cos t| + C$
17. $-\frac{1}{2}e^{\cos 2x} + C$ 19. $-\frac{1}{3}\cos^3(e^\theta) + C$ 21. $\frac{2^{x-1}}{\ln 2} + C$
23. $\ln|\ln v| + C$ 25. $\ln|2 + \tan^{-1}x| + C$
27. $\sin^{-1}(2x) + C$ 29. $\frac{1}{3}\sin^{-1}\left(\frac{3t}{4}\right) + C$
31. $\frac{1}{3}\tan^{-1}\left(\frac{t}{3}\right) + C$ 33. $\frac{1}{5}\sec^{-1}\left|\frac{5x}{4}\right| + C$
35. $\sin^{-1}\left(\frac{x-2}{2}\right) + C$ 37. $\frac{1}{2}\tan^{-1}\left(\frac{y-2}{2}\right) + C$
39. $\sec^{-1}|x-1| + C$ 41. $\frac{x}{2} - \frac{\sin 2x}{4} + C$
43. $\frac{2}{3}\cos^3\left(\frac{\theta}{2}\right) - 2\cos\left(\frac{\theta}{2}\right) + C$
45. $\frac{\tan^2(2t)}{4} - \frac{1}{2}\ln|\sec 2t| + C$
47. $-\frac{1}{2}\ln|\csc(2x) + \cot(2x)| + C$ 49. $\ln\sqrt{2}$ 51. 2
53. $2\sqrt{2}$ 55. $x - 2\tan^{-1}\left(\frac{x}{2}\right) + C$
57. $x + x^2 + 2\ln|2x-1| + C$
59. $\ln(y^2+4) - \frac{1}{2}\tan^{-1}\left(\frac{y}{2}\right) + C$
61. $-\sqrt{4-t^2} + 2\sin^{-1}\left(\frac{t}{2}\right) + C$ 63. $x - \tan x + \sec x + C$
65. $-\frac{1}{3}\ln|\sec(5-3x) + \tan(5-3x)| + C$
67. $4\ln\left|\sin\left(\frac{x}{4}\right)\right| + C$
69. $-2\left(\frac{(\sqrt{1-x})^3}{3} - \frac{(\sqrt{1-x})^5}{5}\right) + C$

71. $\frac{1}{2}\left(z\sqrt{z^2+1}+\ln|z+\sqrt{z^2+1}|\right)+C$

73. $\ln|y+\sqrt{25+y^2}|+C$ **75.** $\frac{-\sqrt{1-x^2}}{x}+C$

77. $\frac{\sin^{-1}x}{2}-\frac{x\sqrt{1-x^2}}{2}+C$ **79.** $\ln\left|\frac{x}{3}+\frac{\sqrt{x^2-9}}{3}\right|+C$

81. $\sqrt{w^2-1}-\sec^{-1}(w)+C$

83. $(x+1)(\ln(x+1))-(x+1)+C$

85. $x\tan^{-1}(3x)-\frac{1}{6}\ln(1+9x^2)+C$

87. $(x+1)^2e^x-2(x+1)e^x+2e^x+C$

89. $\frac{2e^x\sin 2x}{5}+\frac{e^x\cos 2x}{5}+C$

91. $2\ln|x-2|-\ln|x-1|+C$

93. $\ln|x|-\ln|x+1|+\frac{1}{x+1}+C$

95. $-\frac{1}{3}\ln\left|\frac{\cos\theta-1}{\cos\theta+2}\right|+C$

97. $4\ln|x|-\frac{1}{2}\ln(x^2+1)+4\tan^{-1}x+C$

99. $\frac{1}{16}\ln\left|\frac{(v-2)^5(v+2)}{v^6}\right|+C$

101. $\frac{1}{2}\tan^{-1}t-\frac{\sqrt{3}}{6}\tan^{-1}\frac{t}{\sqrt{3}}+C$

103. $\frac{x^2}{2}+\frac{4}{3}\ln|x+2|+\frac{2}{3}\ln|x-1|+C$

105. $\frac{x^2}{2}-\frac{9}{2}\ln|x+3|+\frac{3}{2}\ln|x+1|+C$

107. $\frac{1}{3}\ln\left|\frac{\sqrt{x+1}-1}{\sqrt{x+1}+1}\right|+C$ **109.** $\ln|1-e^{-s}|+C$

111. $-\sqrt{16-y^2}+C$ **113.** $-\frac{1}{2}\ln|4-x^2|+C$

115. $\ln\frac{1}{\sqrt{9-x^2}}+C$ **117.** $\frac{1}{6}\ln\left|\frac{x+3}{x-3}\right|+C$

119. $-\frac{\cos^5 x}{5}+\frac{\cos^7 x}{7}+C$ **121.** $\frac{\tan^5 x}{5}+C$

123. $\frac{\cos\theta}{2}-\frac{\cos 11\theta}{22}+C$ **125.** $4\sqrt{1-\cos(t/2)}+C$

127. At least 16 **129.** $T=\pi, S=\pi$ **131.** 25°F
133. **(a)** ≈2.42 gal **(b)** ≈24.83 mi/gal
135. $\pi/2$ **137.** 6 **139.** ln 3 **141.** 2 **143.** $\pi/6$
145. Diverges **147.** Diverges **149.** Converges

151. $\frac{2x^{3/2}}{3}-x+2\sqrt{x}-2\ln(\sqrt{x}+1)+C$

153. $\ln\left|\frac{\sqrt{x}}{\sqrt{x^2+1}}\right|-\frac{1}{2}\left(\frac{x}{\sqrt{x^2+1}}\right)^2+C$

155. $\sin^{-1}(x+1)+C$ **157.** $\ln|u+\sqrt{1+u^2}|+C$

159. $-2\cot x-\ln|\csc x+\cot x|+\csc x+C$

161. $\frac{1}{12}\ln\left|\frac{3+v}{3-v}\right|+\frac{1}{6}\tan^{-1}\frac{v}{3}+C$

163. $\frac{\theta\sin(2\theta+1)}{2}+\frac{\cos(2\theta+1)}{4}+C$

165. $\frac{x^2}{2}+2x+3\ln|x-1|-\frac{1}{x-1}+C$

167. $-\cos(2\sqrt{x})+C$ **169.** $-\ln|\csc(2y)+\cot(2y)|+C$

171. $\frac{1}{2}\tan^2 x+C$ **173.** $-\sqrt{4-(r+2)^2}+C$

175. $\frac{1}{4}\sec^2\theta+C$ **177.** $\frac{\sqrt{2}}{2}$

179. $2\left(\frac{(\sqrt{2-x})^3}{3}-2\sqrt{2-x}\right)+C$ **181.** $\tan^{-1}(y-1)+C$

183. $\frac{1}{3}\ln|\sec\theta^3|+C$

185. $\frac{1}{4}\ln|z|-\frac{1}{4z}-\frac{1}{4}\left[\frac{1}{2}\ln(z^2+4)+\frac{1}{2}\tan^{-1}\left(\frac{z}{2}\right)\right]+C$

187. $-\frac{1}{4}\sqrt{9-4t^2}+C$ **189.** $\ln|\sin\theta|-\frac{1}{2}\ln(1+\sin^2\theta)+C$

191. $\ln|\sec\sqrt{y}|+C$ **193.** $-\theta\ln\left|\frac{\theta+2}{\theta-2}\right|+C$ **195.** $x+C$

197. $-\frac{\cos x}{2}+C$ **199.** $\ln(1+e^t)+C$ **201.** 1/4

203. $\ln|\ln\sin v|+C$ **205.** $\frac{2}{3}x^{3/2}+C$

207. $-\frac{1}{5}\tan^{-1}\cos(5t)+C$ **209.** $\frac{1}{3}\left(\frac{27^{3\theta+1}}{\ln 27}\right)+C$

211. $2\sqrt{r}-2\ln(1+\sqrt{r})+C$

213. $\ln\left|\frac{y}{y+2}\right|+\frac{2}{y}-\frac{2}{y^2}+C$ **215.** $4\sec^{-1}\left(\frac{7m}{2}\right)+C$

217. $\frac{\sqrt{8}-1}{6}$ **219.** $\frac{\pi}{2}(3b-a)+2$

Additional and Advanced Exercises, pp. 638–641

1. $x(\sin^{-1}x)^2+2(\sin^{-1}x)\sqrt{1-x^2}-2x+C$

3. $\frac{x^2\sin^{-1}x}{2}+\frac{x\sqrt{1-x^2}-\sin^{-1}x}{4}+C$

5. $\frac{\ln|\sec 2\theta+\tan 2\theta|+2\theta}{4}+C$

7. $\frac{1}{2}\left(\ln\left(t-\sqrt{1-t^2}\right)-\sin^{-1}t\right)+C$

9. $\frac{1}{16}\ln\left|\frac{x^2+2x+2}{x^2-2x+2}\right|+\frac{1}{8}(\tan^{-1}(x+1)+\tan^{-1}(x-1))+C$

11. 0 **13.** $\ln(4)-1$ **15.** 1 **17.** $32\pi/35$ **19.** 2π

21. **(a)** π **(b)** $\pi(2e-5)$

23. **(b)** $\pi\left(\frac{8(\ln 2)^2}{3}-\frac{16(\ln 2)}{9}+\frac{16}{27}\right)$ **25.** $\left(\frac{e^2+1}{4},\frac{e-2}{2}\right)$

27. $\sqrt{1+e^2}-\ln\left(\frac{\sqrt{1+e^2}}{e}+\frac{1}{e}\right)-\sqrt{2}+\ln\left(1+\sqrt{2}\right)$

29. 6 **31.** $y=\sqrt{x},\ 0\le x\le 4$ **33.** **(b)** 1

37. $a=\frac{1}{2},-\frac{\ln 2}{4}$ **39.** $\frac{1}{2}<p\le 1$

41. $\frac{e^{2x}}{13}(3\sin 3x + 2\cos 3x) + C$

43. $\frac{\cos x \sin 3x - 3\sin x \cos 3x}{8} + C$

45. $\frac{e^{ax}}{a^2 + b^2}(a \sin bx - b\cos bx) + C$ **47.** $x\ln(ax) - x + C$

CHAPTER 9

Section 9.1, pp. 648–650

9. $\frac{2}{3}y^{3/2} - x^{1/2} = C$ **11.** $e^y - e^x = C$

13. $-x + 2\tan\sqrt{y} = C$ **15.** $e^{-y} + 2e^{\sqrt{x}} = C$

17. $y = \sin(x^2 + C)$ **19.** (d) **21.** (a)

23.

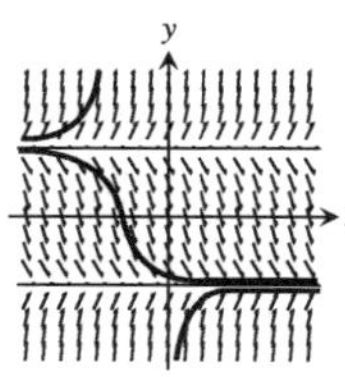

25.

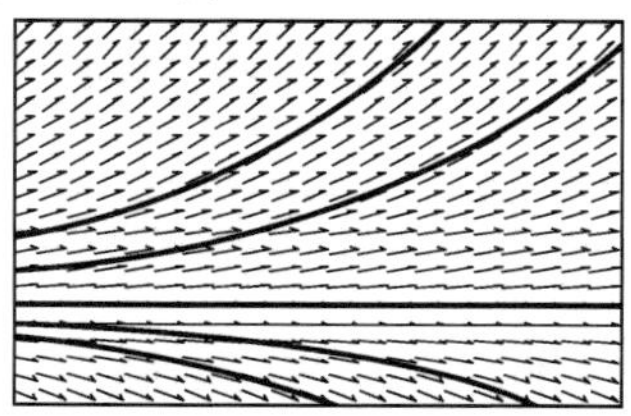

27.

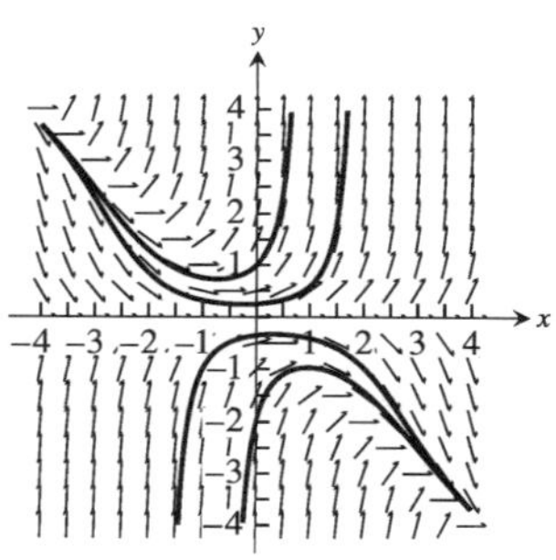

29.

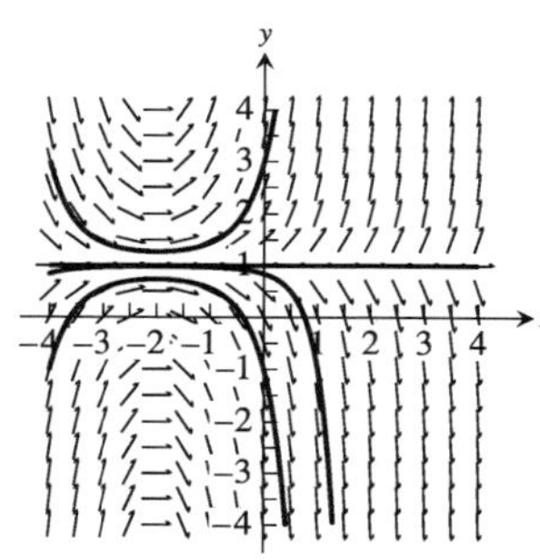

Section 9.2, pp. 657–659

1. $y = \frac{e^x + C}{x}, \quad x > 0$ **3.** $y = \frac{C - \cos x}{x^3}, \quad x > 0$

5. $y = \frac{1}{2} - \frac{1}{x} + \frac{C}{x^2}, \quad x > 0$ **7.** $y = \frac{1}{2}xe^{x/2} + Ce^{x/2}$

9. $y = x(\ln x)^2 + Cx$

11. $s = \frac{t^3}{3(t-1)^4} - \frac{t}{(t-1)^4} + \frac{C}{(t-1)^4}$

13. $r = (\csc\theta)(\ln|\sec\theta| + C), \quad 0 < \theta < \pi/2$

15. $y = \frac{3}{2} - \frac{1}{2}e^{-2t}$ **17.** $y = -\frac{1}{\theta}\cos\theta + \frac{\pi}{2\theta}$

19. $y = 6e^{x^2} - \frac{e^{x^2}}{x+1}$ **21.** $y = y_0e^{kt}$

23. **(b)** is correct, but **(a)** is not.

25. **(a)** 10 lb/min **(b)** $(100 + t)$ gal

(c) $4\left(\frac{y}{100 + t}\right)$ lb/min

(d) $\frac{dy}{dt} = 10 - \frac{4y}{100 + t}, \quad y(0) = 50,$

$y = 2(100 + t) - \frac{150}{\left(1 + \frac{t}{100}\right)^4}$

(e) Concentration $= \frac{y(25)}{\text{amt. brine in tank}} = \frac{188.6}{125} \approx 1.5$ lb/gal

27. $y(27.8) \approx 14.8$ lb, $t \approx 27.8$ min **29.** $t = \frac{L}{R}\ln 2$ sec

31. **(a)** $i = \frac{V}{R} - \frac{V}{R}e^{-3} = \frac{V}{R}(1 - e^{-3}) \approx 0.95\frac{V}{R}$ amp **(b)** 86%

33. $y = \frac{1}{1 + Ce^{-x}}$ **35.** $y^3 = 1 + Cx^{-3}$

Section 9.3, pp. 664–665

1. $y\text{ (exact)} = \frac{x}{2} - \frac{4}{x}, \; y_1 = -0.25, \; y_2 = 0.3, \; y_3 = 0.75$

3. $y\text{ (exact)} = 3e^{x(x+2)}, \; y_1 = 4.2, \; y_2 = 6.216, \; y_3 = 9.697$

5. $y\text{ (exact)} = e^{x^2} + 1, \; y_1 = 2.0, \; y_2 = 2.0202, \; y_3 = 2.0618$

7. $y \approx 2.48832$, exact value is e

9. $y \approx -0.2272$, exact value is $1/\left(1 - 2\sqrt{5}\right) \approx -0.2880$

11.

x	z	y-approx.	y-exact	Error
0	1	3	3	0
0.2	4.2	4.608	4.658122	0.050122
0.4	6.81984	7.623475	7.835089	0.211614
0.6	11.89262	13.56369	14.27646	0.712777

13. Euler's method gives $y \approx 3.45835$; the exact solution is $y = 1 + e \approx 3.71828$

15. $y \approx 1.5000$; exact value is 1.5275.

17. **(a)** $y = \frac{1}{x^2 - 2x + 2}, \quad y(3) = -0.2$

(b) -0.1851, error ≈ 0.0149 **(c)** -0.1929, error ≈ 0.0071

(d) -0.1965, error ≈ 0.0035

19. The exact solution in $y = \frac{1}{x^2 - 2x + 2}$, so $y(3) = -0.2$. To find the approximation, let $z_n = y_{n-1} + 2y_{n-1}(x_{n-1} - 1)\,dx$ and $y_n = y_{n-1} + \left(y_{n-1}^2 (x_{n-1} - 1) + z_n^2 (x_n^2 - 1)\right)dx$ with initial values $x_0 = 2$ and $y_0 = -\frac{1}{2}$. Use a spreadsheet, calculator, or CAS as indicated in parts (a) through (d).

(a) -0.2024, error ≈ 0.0024

(b) -0.2005, error ≈ 0.0005

(c) -0.2001, error ≈ 0.0001

(d) Each time the step size is cut in half, the error is reduced to approximately one-fourth of what it was for the larger step size.

Section 9.4, pp. 671–672

1. $y' = (y + 2)(y - 3)$

(a) $y = -2$ is a stable equilibrium value and $y = 3$ is an unstable equilibrium.

(b) $y'' = 2(y+2)\left(y-\frac{1}{2}\right)(y-3)$

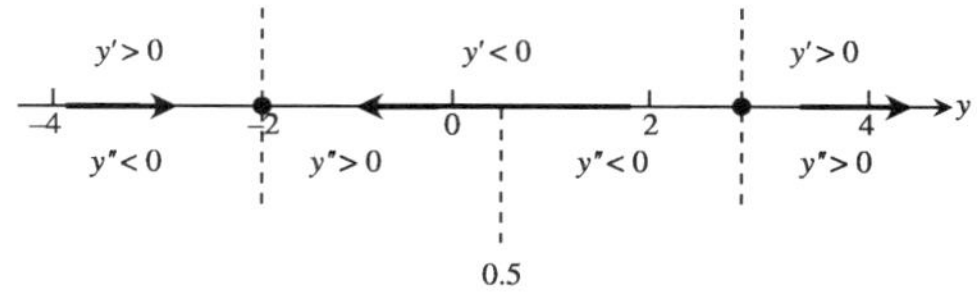

(c)

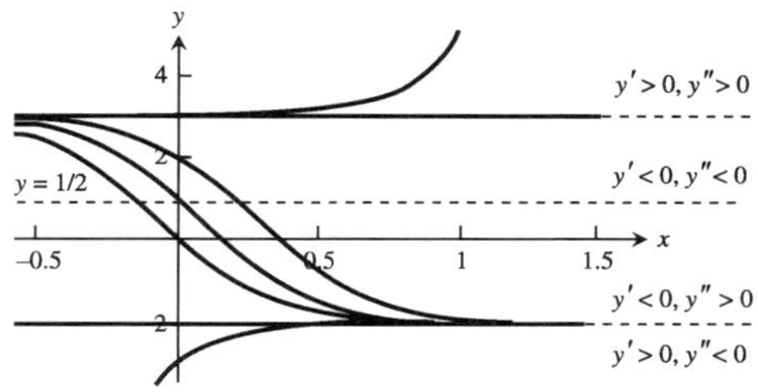

3. $y' = y^3 - y = (y+1)y(y-1)$

(a) $y = -1$ and $y = 1$ are unstable equilibria and $y = 0$ is a stable equilibrium.

(b) $y'' = (3y^2 - 1)y' = 3(y+1)\left(y + 1/\sqrt{3}\right)y\left(y - 1/\sqrt{3}\right)(y-1)$

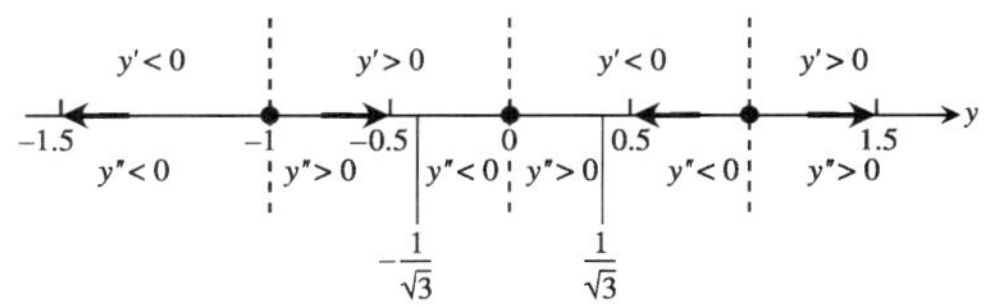

(c)

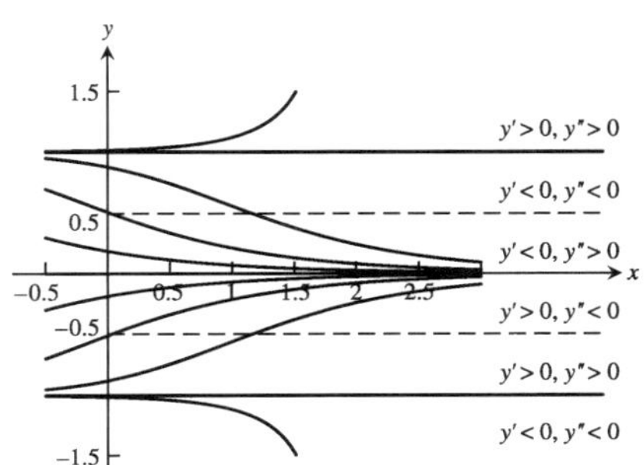

5. $y' = \sqrt{y}, y > 0$

(a) There are no equilibrium values.

(b) $y'' = \frac{1}{2}$

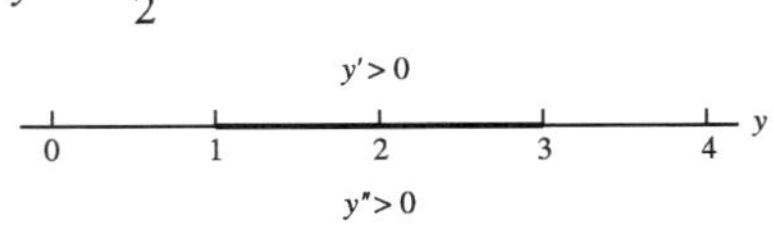

(c)

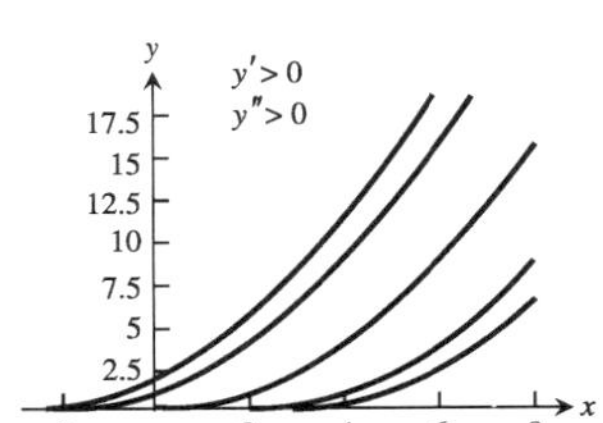

7. $y' = (y-1)(y-2)(y-3)$

(a) $y = 1$ and $y = 3$ are unstable equilibria and $y = 2$ is a stable equilibrium.

(b) $y'' = (3y^2 - 12y + 11)(y-1)(y-2)(y-3) = (y-1)\left(y - \frac{6-\sqrt{3}}{3}\right)(y-2)\left(y - \frac{6+\sqrt{3}}{3}\right)(y-3)$

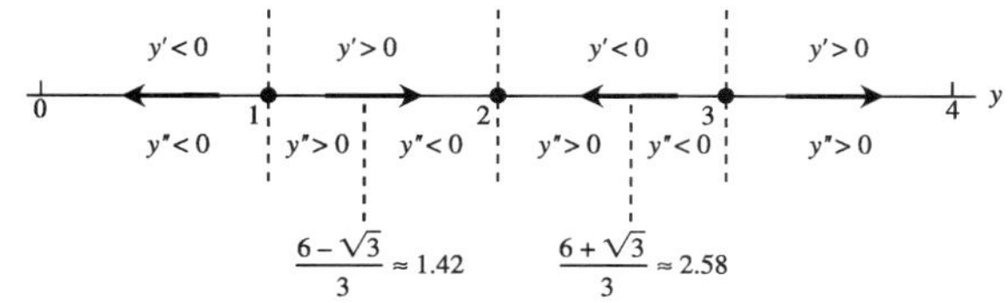

(c)

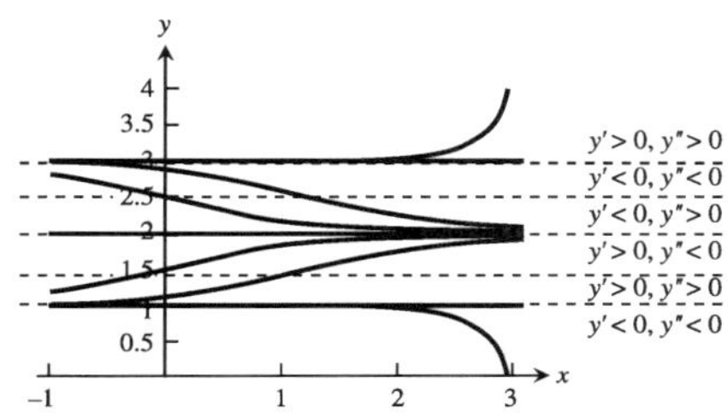

9. $\frac{dP}{dt} = 1 - 2P$ has a stable equilibrium at $P = \frac{1}{2}$; $\frac{d^2P}{dt^2} = -2\frac{dP}{dt} = -2(1-2P)$.

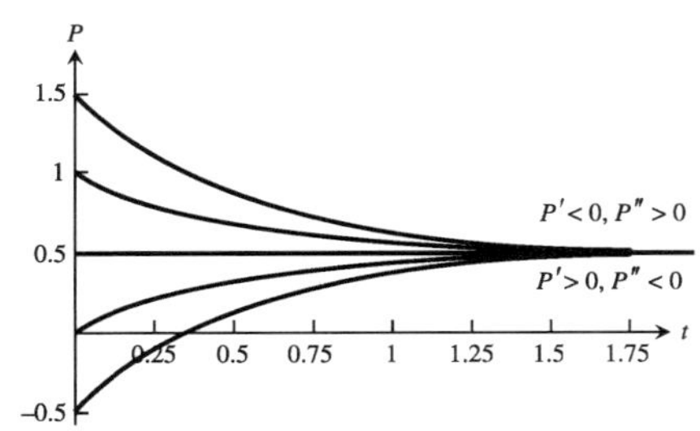

11. $\frac{dP}{dt} = 2P(P-3)$ has a stable equilibrium at $P = 0$ and an unstable equilibrium at $P = 3$; $\frac{d^2P}{dt^2} = 2(2P-3)\frac{dP}{dt} = 4P(2P-3)(P-3)$

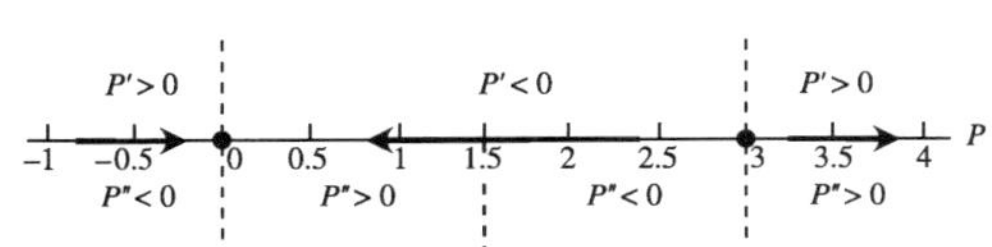

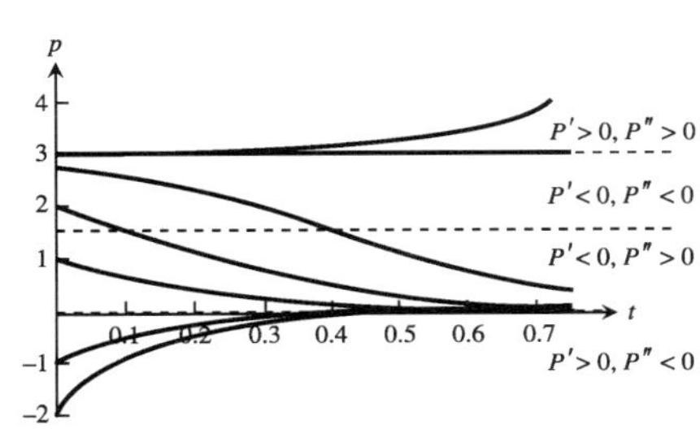

13. Before the catastrophe, the population exhibits logistic growth and $P(t)$ increases toward M_0, the stable equilibrium. After the catastrophe, the population declines logistically and $P(t)$ decreases toward M_1, the new stable equilibrium.

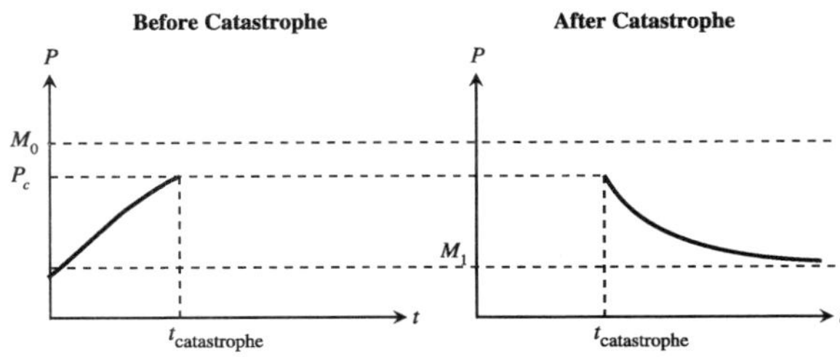

15. $\frac{dv}{dt} = g - \frac{k}{m}v^2, \quad g, k, m > 0$ and $v(t) \geq 0$

Equilibrium: $\frac{dv}{dt} = g - \frac{k}{m}v^2 = 0 \Rightarrow v = \sqrt{\frac{mg}{k}}$

Concavity: $\frac{d^2v}{dt^2} = -2\left(\frac{k}{m}v\right)\frac{dv}{dt} = -2\left(\frac{k}{m}v\right)\left(g - \frac{k}{m}v^2\right)$

(a)

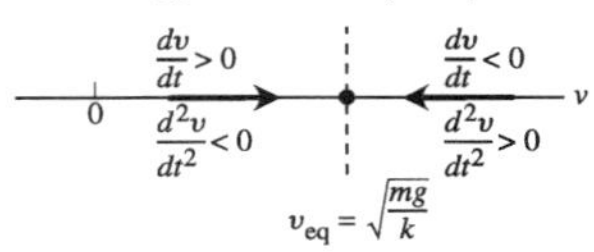

(b)

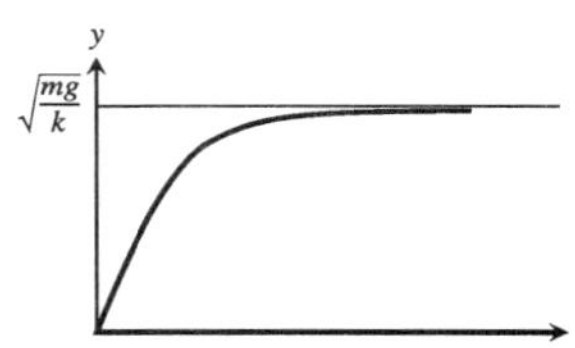

(c) $v_{\text{terminal}} = \sqrt{\frac{160}{0.005}} = 178.9$ ft/sec $= 122$ mph

17. $F = F_p - F_r$; $ma = 50 - 5|v|$; $\frac{dv}{dt} = \frac{1}{m}(50 - 5|v|)$. The maximum velocity occurs when $\frac{dv}{dt} = 0$ or $v = 10$ ft/sec.

19. Phase line:

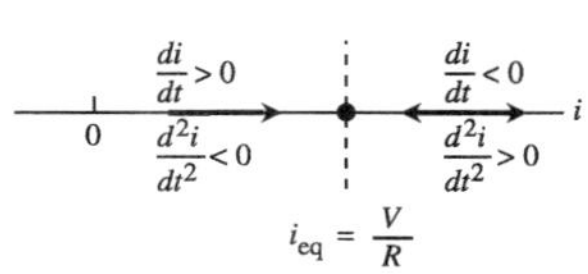

If the switch is closed at $t = 0$, then $i(0) = 0$, and the graph of the solution looks like this:

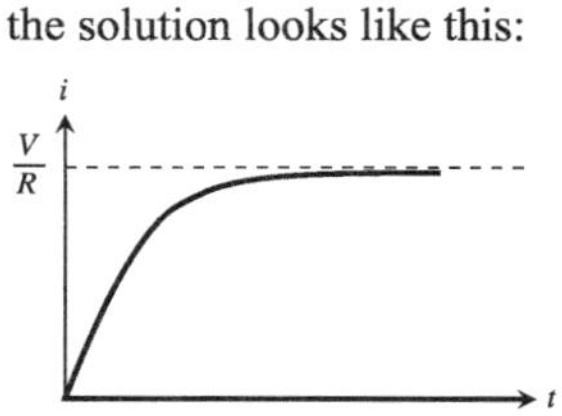

As $t \to \infty$, $i(t) \to i_{\text{steady state}} = \frac{V}{R}$.

Section 9.5, pp. 680–681

1. **(a)** 168.5 m **(b)** 41.13 sec

3. $s(t) = 4.91(1 - e^{-(22.36/39.92)t})$

5. **(a)** $P(t) = \frac{150}{1 + 24e^{-0.225t}}$

(b) About 17.21 weeks; 21.28 weeks

7. **(a)** $y(t) = \frac{8 \times 10^7}{1 + 4e^{-0.71t}} \Rightarrow y(1) \approx 2.69671 \times 10^7$ kg

(b) $t \approx 1.95253$ years

9. **(a)** $y = 2e^t - 1$ **(b)** $y(t) = \frac{400}{1 + 199e^{-200t}}$

11. **(a)** $P(t) = \frac{P_0}{1 - kP_0 t}$ **(b)** Vertical asymptote at $t = \frac{1}{kP_0}$

13. $x^2 + y^2 = C$

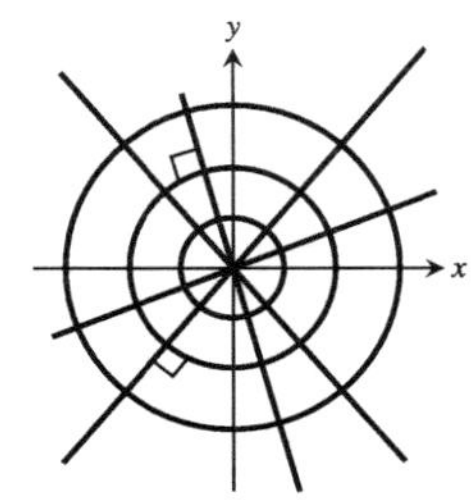

15. $\ln|y| - \frac{1}{2}y^2 = \frac{1}{2}x^2 + C$

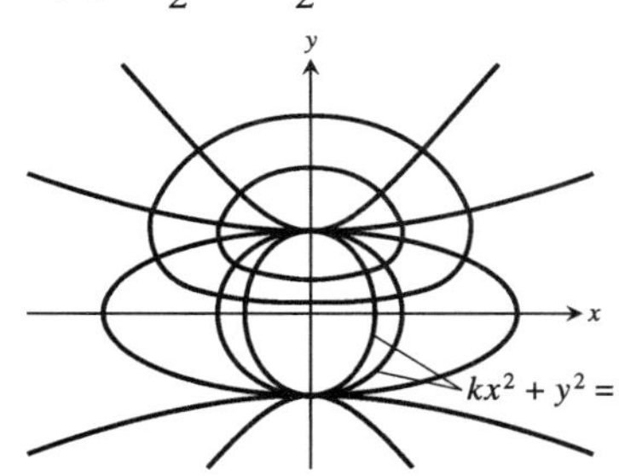

17. $y = \pm\sqrt{2x + C}$

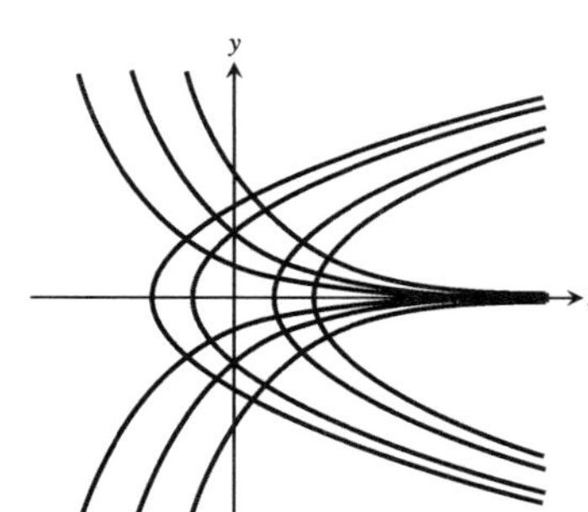

Practice Exercises, pp. 682–683

1. $y = \left(\tan^{-1}\left(\frac{x + C}{2}\right)\right)^2$ **3.** $y^2 = \sin^{-1}(2\tan x + C)$

5. $y = -\ln\left(C - \frac{2}{5}(x - 2)^{5/2} - \frac{4}{3}(x - 2)^{3/2}\right)$

7. $\tan y = -x\sin x - \cos x + C$ **9.** $(y + 1)e^{-y} = -\ln|x| + C$

11. $y = C\frac{x - 1}{x}$ **13.** $y = \frac{x^4}{4}e^{x/2} + Ce^{x/2}$

15. $y = \frac{x^2 - 2x + C}{2x^2}$ **17.** $y = \frac{e^{-x} + C}{1 + e^x}$ **19.** $xy + y^3 = C$

21. $y = -2 + \ln(2 - e^{-x})$ **23.** $y = \frac{2x^3 + 3x^2 + 6}{6(x + 1)^2}$

25. $y = \frac{1}{3}(1 - 4e^{-x^3})$ **27.** $y = 4x - 4\sqrt{x} + 1$

29. $y = e^{-x}(3x^3 - 3x^2)$

31.

x	y
0	0
0.1	0.1000
0.2	0.2095
0.3	0.3285
0.4	0.4568
0.5	0.5946
0.6	0.7418
0.7	0.8986
0.8	1.0649
0.9	1.2411
1.0	1.4273

x	y
1.1	1.6241
1.2	1.8319
1.3	2.0513
1.4	2.2832
1.5	2.5285
1.6	2.7884
1.7	3.0643
1.8	3.3579
1.9	3.6709
2.0	4.0057

33. $y(3) \approx 0.9063$

35.

(a)

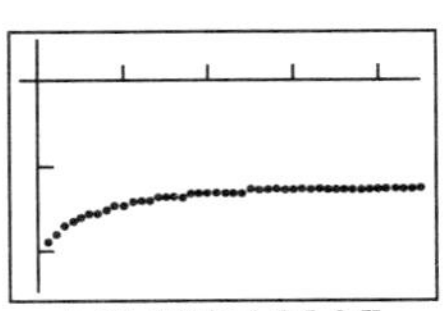

[−0.2, 4.5] by [−2.5, 0.5]

(b) Note that we choose a small interval of x-values because the y-values decrease very rapidly and our calculator cannot handle the calculations for $x \le -1$. (This occurs because the analytic solution is $y = -2 + \ln(2 - e^{-x})$, which has an asymptote at $x = -\ln 2 \approx -0.69$. Obviously, the Euler approximations are misleading for $x \le -0.7$.)

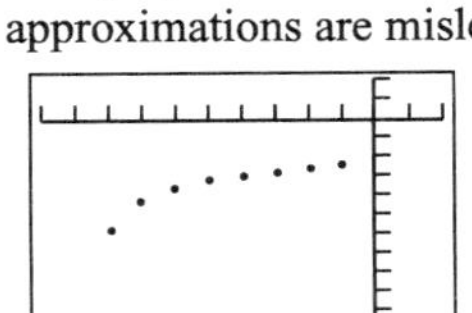

[−1, 0.2] by [−10, 2]

37. $y(\text{exact}) = \frac{1}{2}x^2 - \frac{3}{2}$; $y(2) \approx 0.4$; exact value is $\frac{1}{2}$

39. $y(\text{exact}) = -e^{(x^2-1)/2}$; $y(2) \approx -3.4192$; exact value is $-e^{3/2} \approx -4.4817$.

41. (a) $y = -1$ is stable and $y = 1$ is unstable.

(b) $\frac{d^2y}{dx^2} = 2y\frac{dy}{dx} = 2y(y^2 - 1)$

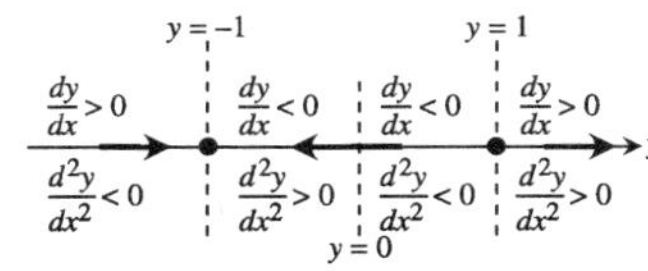

(c)

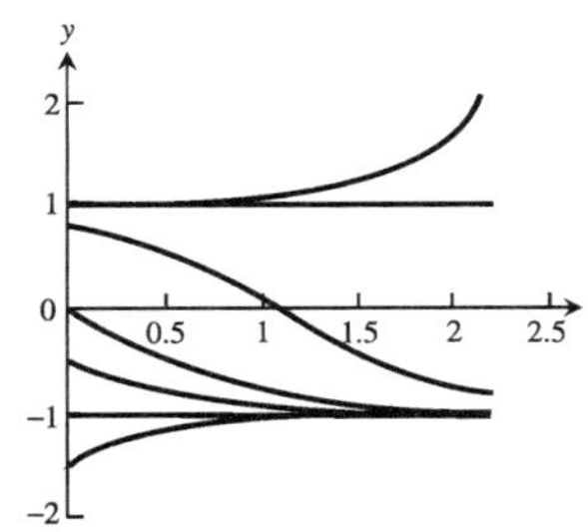

Additional and Advanced Exercises, pp. 683–684

1. (a) $y = c + (y_0 - c)e^{-k(A/V)t}$

(b) Steady-state solution: $y_\infty = c$

3. 0.179%

CHAPTER 10

Section 10.1, pp. 693–697

1. $y^2 = 8x$, $F(2, 0)$, directrix: $x = -2$

3. $x^2 = -6y$, $F(0, -3/2)$, directrix: $y = 3/2$

5. $\frac{x^2}{4} - \frac{y^2}{9} = 1$, $F(\pm\sqrt{13}, 0)$, $V(\pm 2, 0)$, asymptotes: $y = \pm\frac{3}{2}x$

7. $\frac{x^2}{2} + y^2 = 1$, $F(\pm 1, 0)$, $V(\pm\sqrt{2}, 0)$

9.

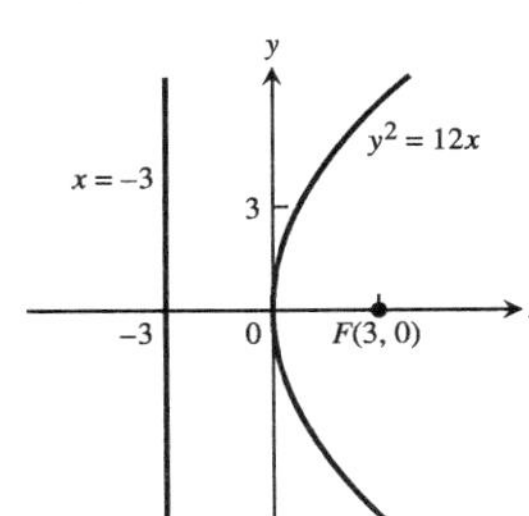

11.

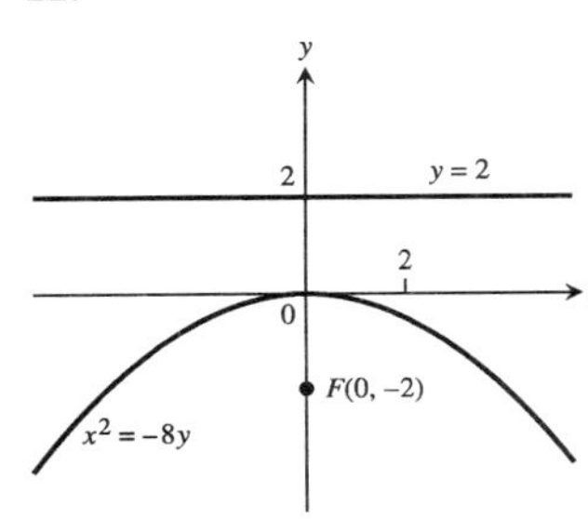

13.

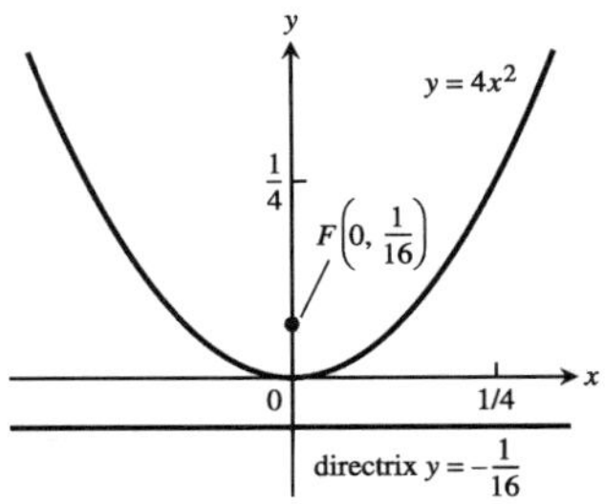

15.

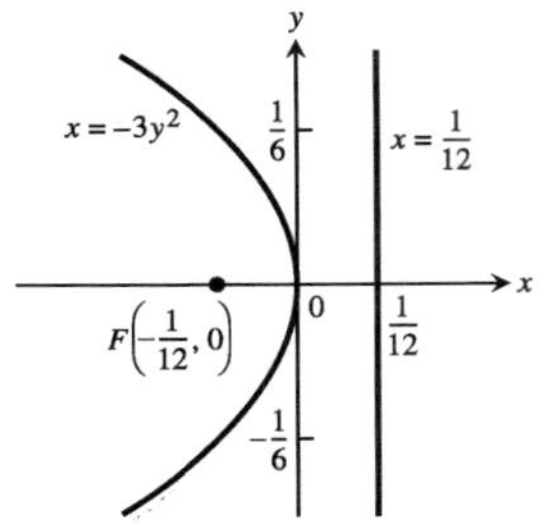

17.

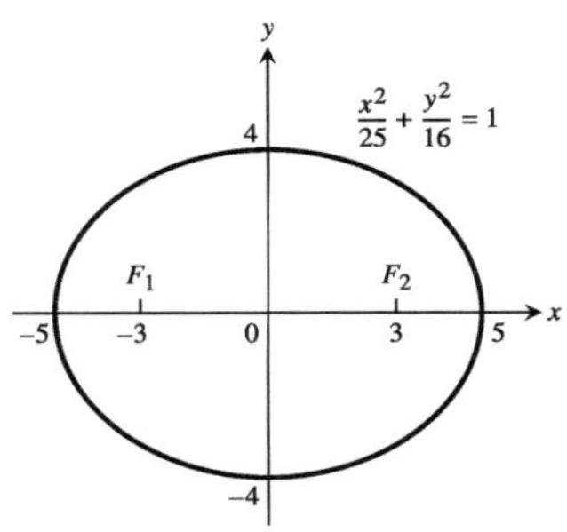

19.

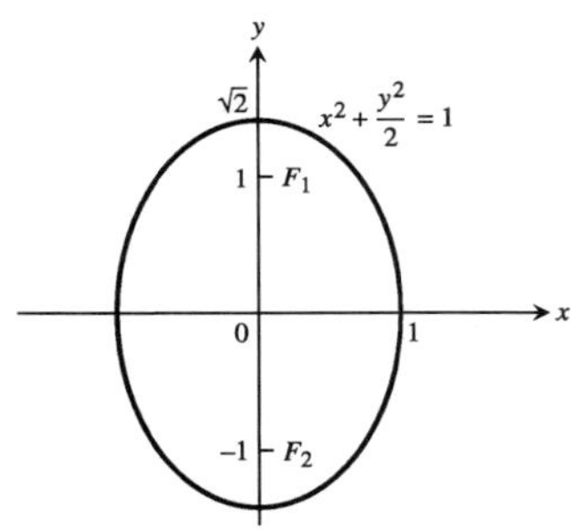

21.

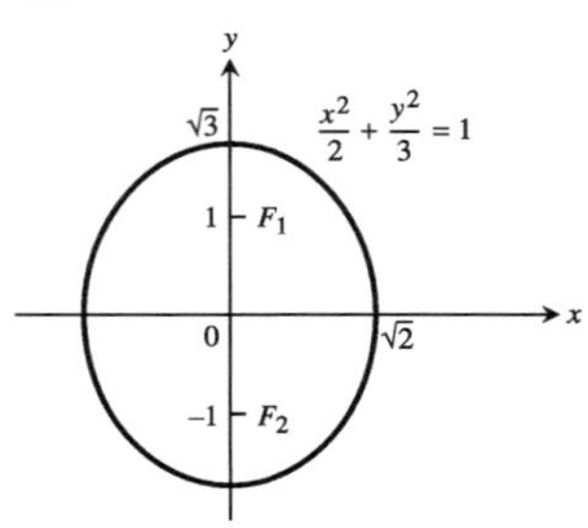

23.

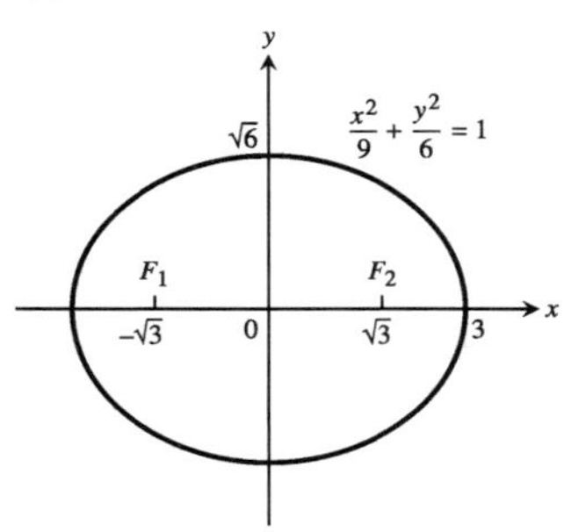

25. $\dfrac{x^2}{4} + \dfrac{y^2}{2} = 1$

27. Asymptotes: $y = \pm x$

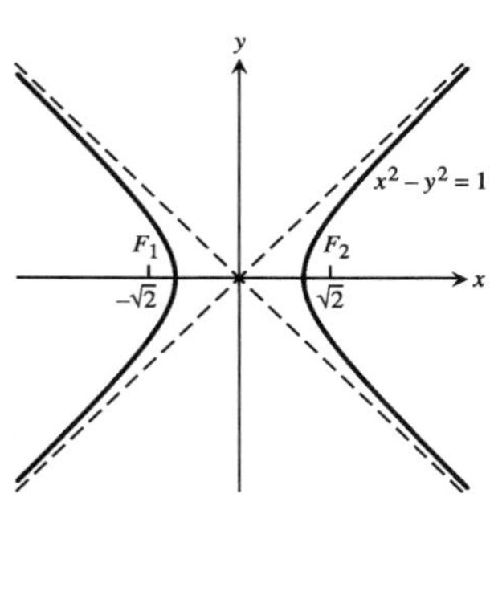

29. Asymptotes: $y = \pm x$

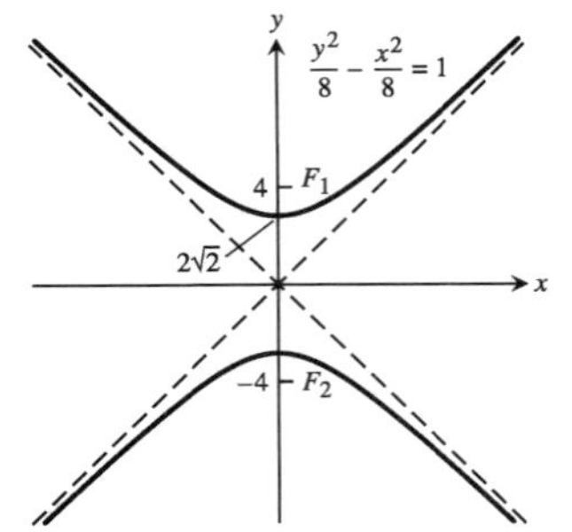

31. Asymptotes: $y = \pm 2x$

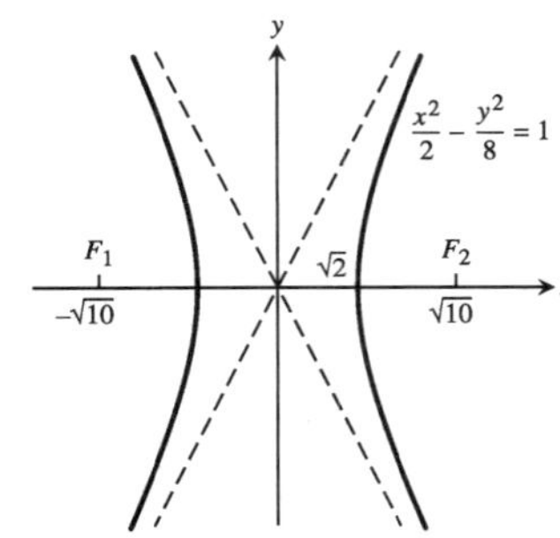

33. Asymptotes: $y = \pm \dfrac{x}{2}$

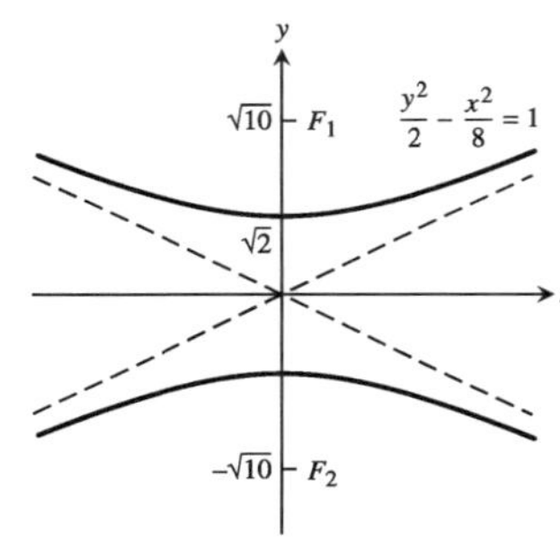

35. $y^2 - x^2 = 1$ **37.** $\dfrac{x^2}{9} - \dfrac{y^2}{16} = 1$

39. **(a)** Vertex: $(1, -2)$; focus: $(3, -2)$; directrix: $x = -1$

(b)

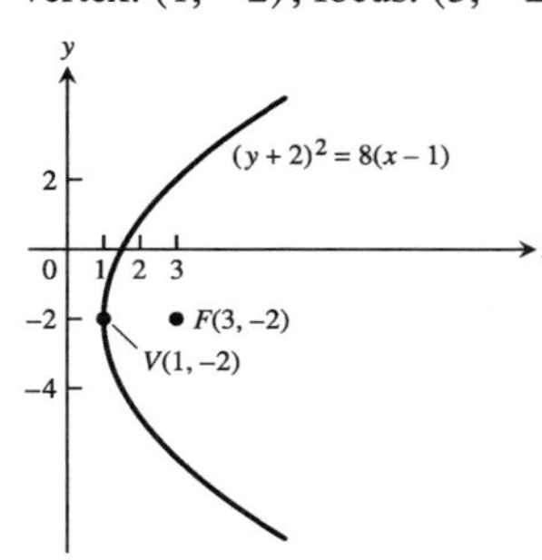

41. **(a)** Foci: $\left(4 \pm \sqrt{7}, 3\right)$; vertices: $(8, 3)$ and $(0, 3)$; center: $(4, 3)$
(b)

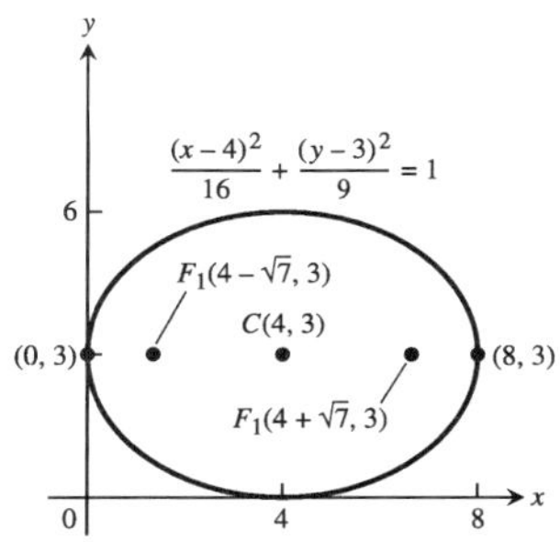

43. **(a)** Center: $(2, 0)$; foci: $(7, 0)$ and $(-3, 0)$; vertices: $(6, 0)$ and $(-2, 0)$; asymptotes: $y = \pm\frac{3}{4}(x - 2)$
(b)

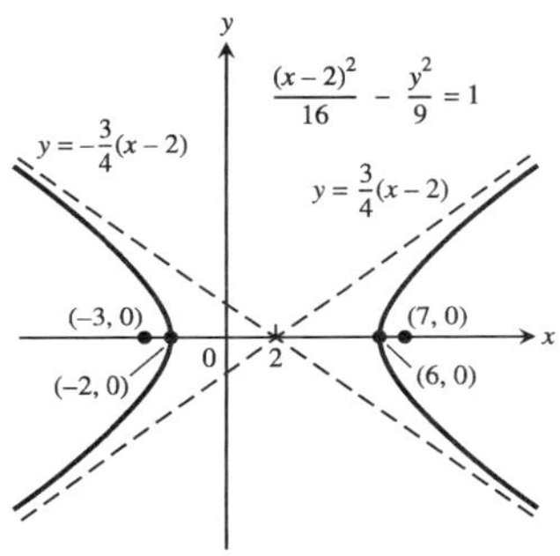

45. $(y + 3)^2 = 4(x + 2)$, $V(-2, -3)$, $F(-1, -3)$, directrix: $x = -3$

47. $(x - 1)^2 = 8(y + 7)$, $V(1, -7)$, $F(1, -5)$, directrix: $y = -9$

49. $\frac{(x + 2)^2}{6} + \frac{(y + 1)^2}{9} = 1$, $F\left(-2, \pm\sqrt{3} - 1\right)$, $V(-2, \pm 3 - 1)$, $C(-2, -1)$

51. $\frac{(x - 2)^2}{3} + \frac{(y - 3)^2}{2} = 1$, $F(3, 3)$ and $F(1, 3)$, $V\left(\pm\sqrt{3} + 2, 3\right)$, $C(2, 3)$

53. $\frac{(x - 2)^2}{4} - \frac{(y - 2)^2}{5} = 1$, $C(2, 2)$, $F(5, 2)$ and $F(-1, 2)$, $V(4, 2)$ and $V(0, 2)$; asymptotes: $(y - 2) = \pm\frac{\sqrt{5}}{2}(x - 2)$

55. $(y + 1)^2 - (x + 1)^2 = 1$, $C(-1, -1)$, $F\left(-1, \sqrt{2} - 1\right)$ and $F\left(-1, -\sqrt{2} - 1\right)$, $V(-1, 0)$ and $V(-1, -2)$; asymptotes $(y + 1) = \pm(x + 1)$

57. $C(-2, 0)$, $a = 4$ **59.** $V(-1, 1)$, $F(-1, 0)$

61. Ellipse: $\frac{(x + 2)^2}{5} + y^2 = 1$, $C(-2, 0)$, $F(0, 0)$ and $F(-4, 0)$, $V\left(\sqrt{5} - 2, 0\right)$ and $V\left(-\sqrt{5} - 2, 0\right)$

63. Ellipse: $\frac{(x - 1)^2}{2} + (y - 1)^2 = 1$, $C(1, 1)$, $F(2, 1)$ and $F(0, 1)$, $V\left(\sqrt{2} + 1, 1\right)$ and $V\left(-\sqrt{2} + 1, 1\right)$

65. Hyperbola: $(x - 1)^2 - (y - 2)^2 = 1$, $C(1, 2)$, $F\left(1 + \sqrt{2}, 2\right)$ and $F\left(1 - \sqrt{2}, 2\right)$, $V(2, 2)$ and $V(0, 2)$; asymptotes: $(y - 2) = \pm(x - 1)$

67. Hyperbola: $\frac{(y - 3)^2}{6} - \frac{x^2}{3} = 1$, $C(0, 3)$, $F(0, 6)$ and $F(0, 0)$, $V\left(0, \sqrt{6} + 3\right)$ and $V\left(0, -\sqrt{6} + 3\right)$; asymptotes: $y = \sqrt{2}x + 3$ or $y = -\sqrt{2}x + 3$

69.

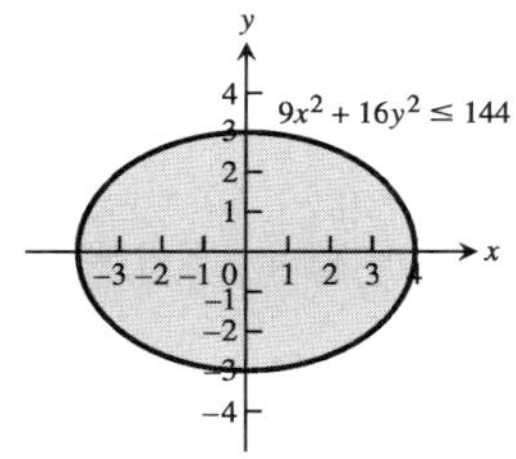

71.

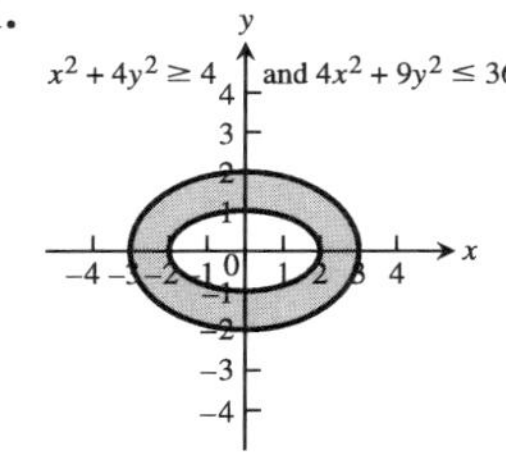

73.

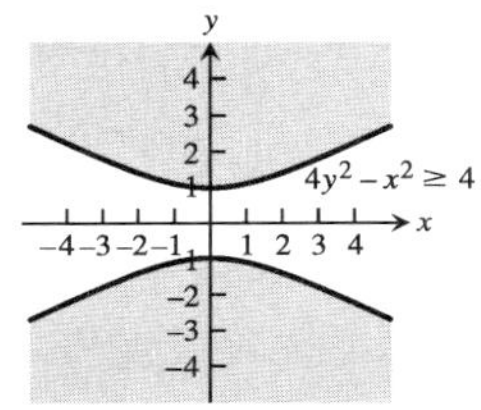

77. $3x^2 + 3y^2 - 7x - 7y + 4 = 0$

79. $(x + 2)^2 + (y - 1)^2 = 13$. The point is inside the circle.

81. **(b)** $1 : 1$ **83.** Length $= 2\sqrt{2}$, width $= \sqrt{2}$, area $= 4$

85. 24π **87.** $(0, 16/(3\pi))$

Section 10.2, pp. 701–702

1. $e = 3/5$, $F(\pm 3, 0)$, $x = \pm 25/3$

3. $e = 1/\sqrt{2}$, $F(0, \pm 1)$, $y = \pm 2$

5. $e = 1/\sqrt{3}$, $F(0, \pm 1)$, $y = \pm 3$

7. $e = \sqrt{3}/3$, $F\left(\pm\sqrt{3}, 0\right)$, $x = \pm 3\sqrt{3}$ **9.** $\frac{x^2}{27} + \frac{y^2}{36} = 1$

11. $\frac{x^2}{4851} + \frac{y^2}{4900} = 1$ **13.** $e = \frac{\sqrt{5}}{3}$, $\frac{x^2}{9} + \frac{y^2}{4} = 1$

15. $e = 1/2$, $\frac{x^2}{64} + \frac{y^2}{48} = 1$

19. $\frac{(x - 1)^2}{4} + \frac{(y - 4)^2}{9} = 1$, $F\left(1, 4 \pm \sqrt{5}\right)$, $e = \sqrt{5}/3$, $y = 4 \pm \left(9\sqrt{5}/5\right)$

21. $a = 0$, $b = -4$, $c = 0$, $e = \sqrt{3}/2$

23. $e = \sqrt{2}$, $F\left(\pm\sqrt{2}, 0\right)$, $x = \pm 1/\sqrt{2}$

25. $e = \sqrt{2}$, $F(0, \pm 4)$, $y = \pm 2$

27. $e = \sqrt{5}$, $F\left(\pm\sqrt{10}, 0\right)$, $x = \pm 2/\sqrt{10}$

29. $e = \sqrt{5}$, $F\left(0, \pm\sqrt{10}\right)$, $y = \pm 2/\sqrt{10}$

31. $y^2 - \frac{x^2}{8} = 1$ **33.** $x^2 - \frac{y^2}{8} = 1$

35. $e = \sqrt{2}$, $\frac{x^2}{8} - \frac{y^2}{8} = 1$ **37.** $e = 2$, $x^2 - \frac{y^2}{3} = 1$

39. $\dfrac{(y-6)^2}{36} - \dfrac{(x-1)^2}{45} = 1$

Section 10.3, pp. 707–709

1. Hyperbola 3. Ellipse 5. Parabola 7. Parabola
9. Hyperbola 11. Hyperbola 13. Ellipse 15. Ellipse
17. $x'^2 - y'^2 = 4$, hyperbola 19. $4x'^2 + 16y' = 0$, parabola
21. $y'^2 = 1$, parallel lines 23. $2\sqrt{2}x'^2 + 8\sqrt{2}y' = 0$, parabola
25. $4x'^2 + 2y'^2 = 19$, ellipse
27. $\sin\alpha = 1/\sqrt{5}$, $\cos\alpha = 2/\sqrt{5}$
29. $A' = 0.88$, $B' = 0.00$, $C' = 3.10$, $D' = 0.74$, $E' = -1.20$, $F' = -3$, $0.88x'^2 + 3.10y'^2 + 0.74x' - 1.20y' - 3 = 0$, ellipse
31. $A' = 0.00$, $B' = 0.00$, $C' = 5.00$, $D' = 0$, $E' = 0$, $F' = -5$, $5.00y'^2 - 5 = 0$ or $y' = \pm 1.00$, parallel lines
33. $A' = 5.05$, $B' = 0.00$, $C' = -0.05$, $D' = -5.07$, $E' = -6.18$, $F' = -1$, $5.05x'^2 - 0.05y'^2 - 5.07x' - 6.18y' - 1 = 0$, hyperbola
35. **(a)** $\dfrac{x'^2}{b^2} + \dfrac{y'^2}{a^2} = 1$ **(b)** $\dfrac{y'^2}{a^2} - \dfrac{x'^2}{b^2} = 1$
(c) $x'^2 + y'^2 = a^2$ **(d)** $y' = -\dfrac{1}{m}x'$
(e) $y' = -\dfrac{1}{m}x' + \dfrac{b}{m}$
37. **(a)** $x'^2 - y'^2 = 2$ **(b)** $x'^2 - y'^2 = 2a$ 43. **(a)** Parabola
45. **(a)** Hyperbola
(b)

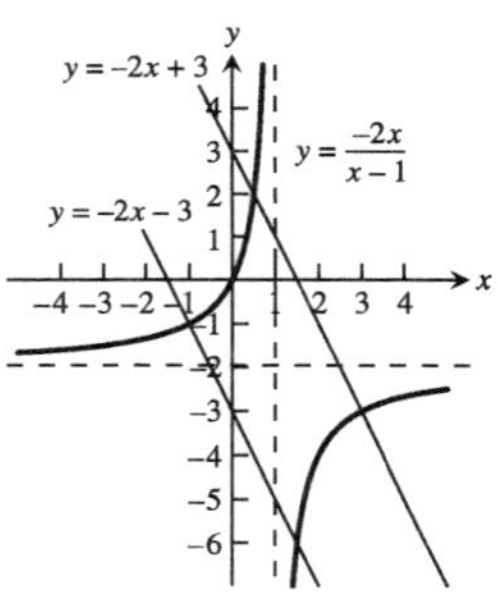

(c) $y = -2x - 3$, $y = -2x + 3$

Section 10.4, pp. 712–713

1.

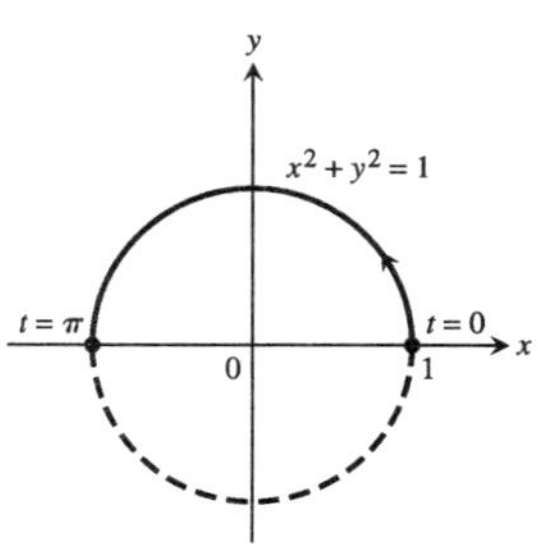

3.

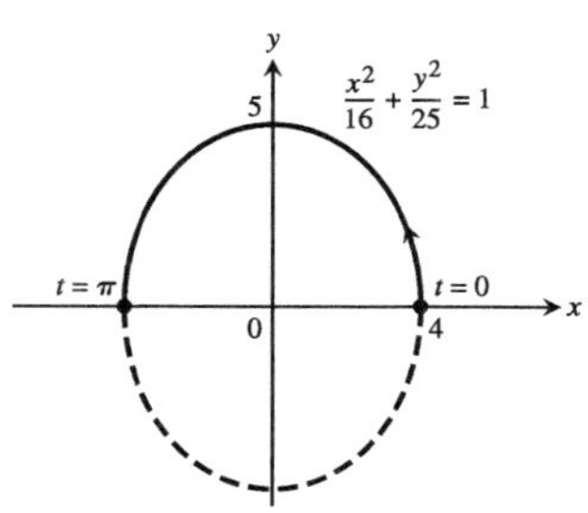

5.

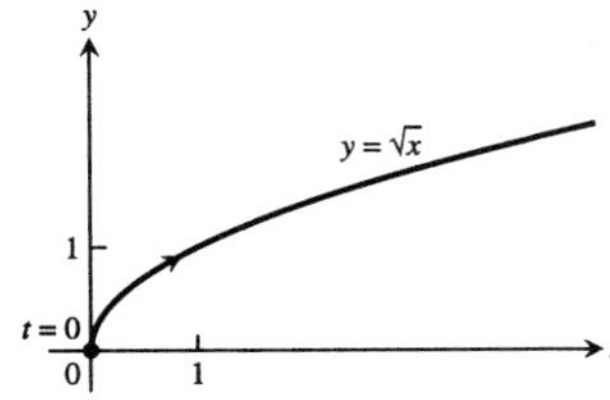

7.

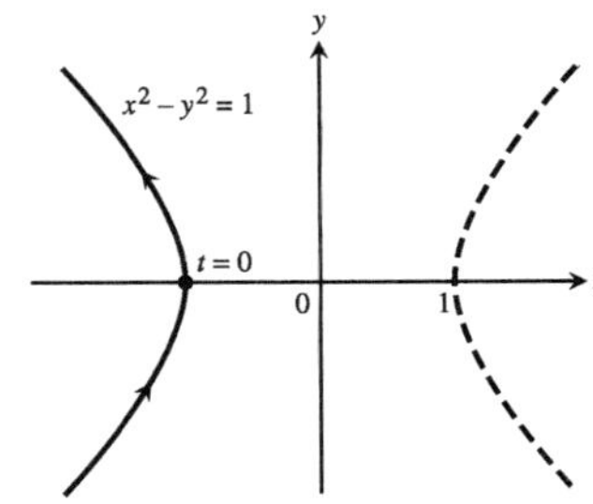

9.

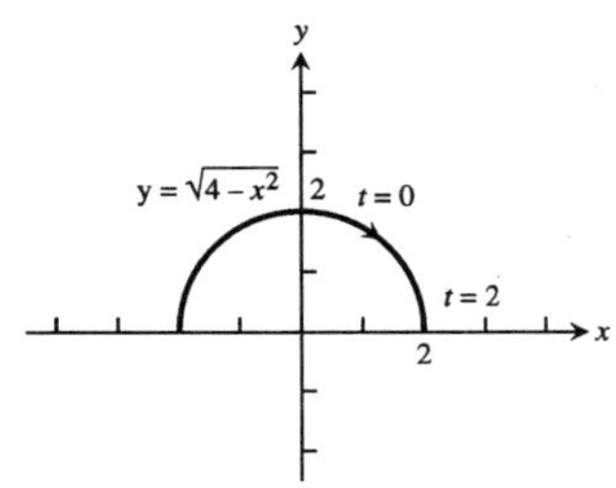

11.

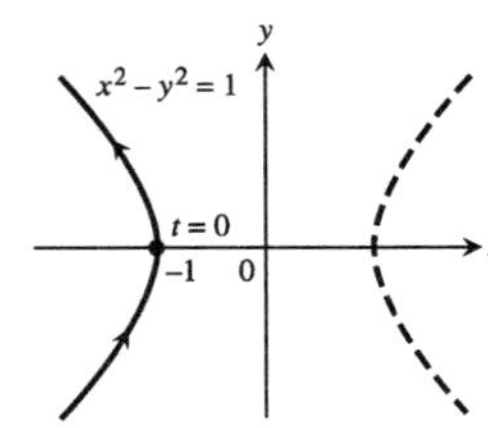

13. $x = (a-b)\cos\theta + b\cos\left(\dfrac{a-b}{b}\theta\right)$,
$y = (a-b)\sin\theta - b\sin\left(\dfrac{a-b}{b}\theta\right)$

15. $x = a\sin^2 t\tan t$, $y = a\sin^2 t$ 17. $(1, 1)$

Section 10.5, pp. 718–719

1. a, e; b, g; c, h; d, f

3.

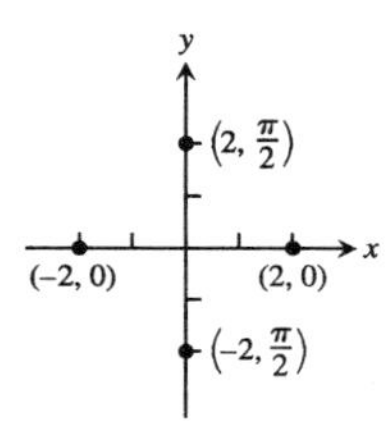

(a) $\left(2, \dfrac{\pi}{2} + 2n\pi\right)$ and $\left(-2, \dfrac{\pi}{2} + (2n+1)\pi\right)$, n an integer
(b) $(2, 2n\pi)$ and $(-2, (2n+1)\pi)$, n an integer
(c) $\left(2, \dfrac{3\pi}{2} + 2n\pi\right)$ and $\left(-2, \dfrac{3\pi}{2} + (2n+1)\pi\right)$, n an integer
(d) $(2, (2n+1)\pi)$ and $(-2, 2n\pi)$, n an integer

5. **(a)** $(3, 0)$ **(b)** $(-3, 0)$ **(c)** $(-1, \sqrt{3})$ **(d)** $(1, \sqrt{3})$
(e) $(3, 0)$ **(f)** $(1, \sqrt{3})$ **(g)** $(-3, 0)$ **(h)** $(-1, \sqrt{3})$

7.

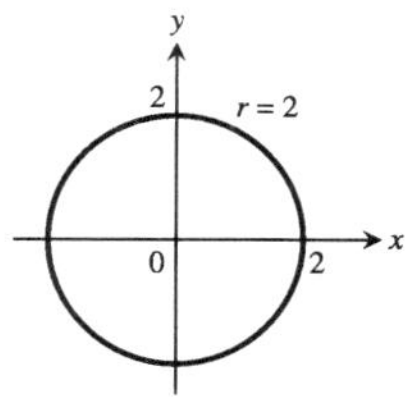

9.

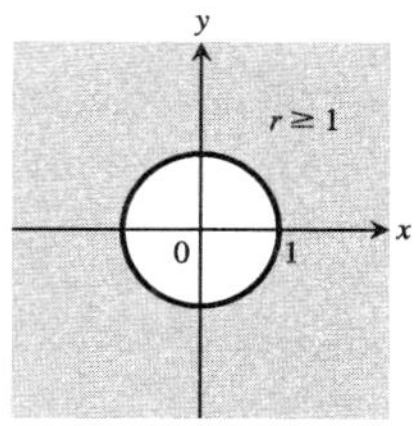

11.

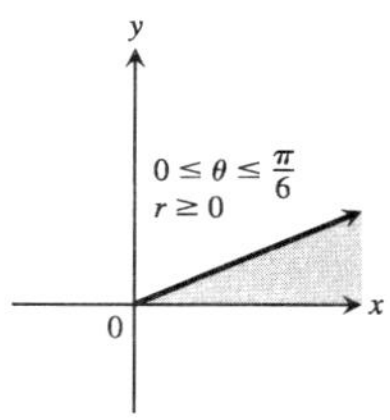

13.

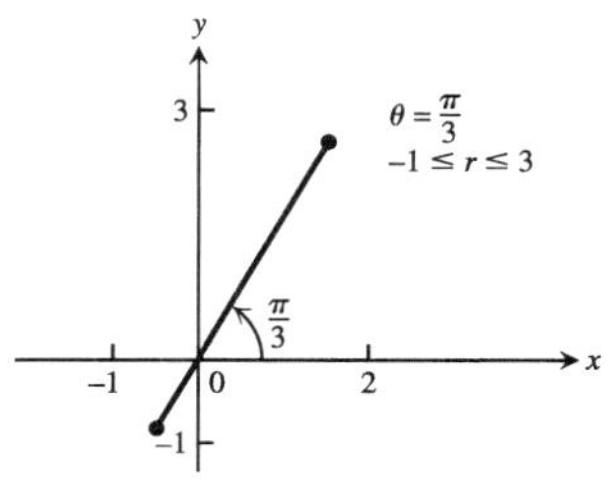

15.

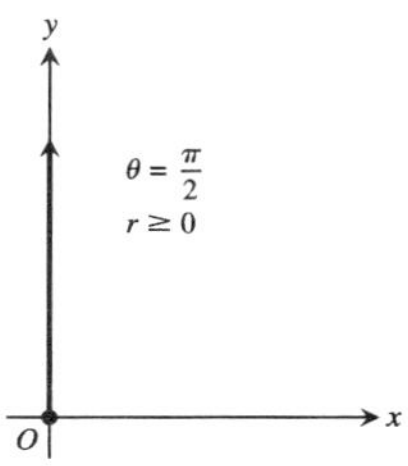

17.

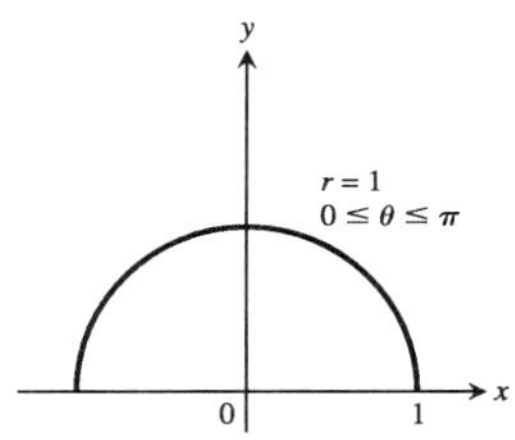

19.

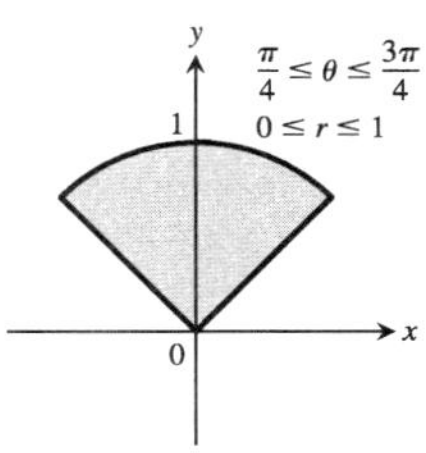

21.

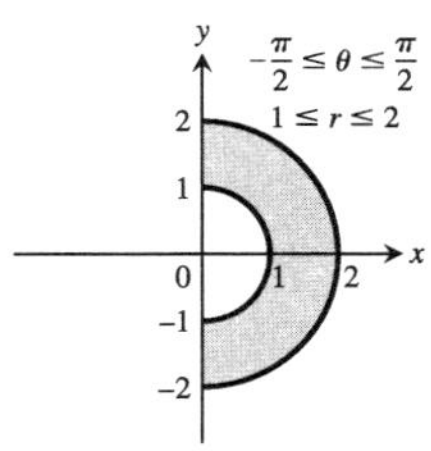

23. $x = 2$, vertical line through (2, 0)
25. $y = 0$, the x-axis
27. $y = 4$, horizontal line through (0, 4)
29. $x + y = 1$, line, $m = -1, b = 1$
31. $x^2 + y^2 = 1$, circle, $C(0, 0)$, radius 1
33. $y - 2x = 5$, line; $m = 2, b = 5$
35. $y^2 = x$, parabola, vertex (0, 0), opens right
37. $y = e^x$, graph of natural exponential function
39. $x + y = \pm 1$, two straight lines of slope -1, y-intercepts $b = \pm 1$
41. $(x + 2)^2 + y^2 = 4$, circle, $C(-2, 0)$, radius 2
43. $x^2 + (y - 4)^2 = 16$, circle, $C(0, 4)$, radius 4
45. $(x - 1)^2 + (y - 1)^2 = 2$, circle, $C(1, 1)$, radius $\sqrt{2}$
47. $\sqrt{3}y + x = 4$ **49.** $r\cos\theta = 7$ **51.** $\theta = \pi/4$
53. $r = 2$ or $r = -2$ **55.** $4r^2\cos^2\theta + 9r^2\sin^2\theta = 36$
57. $r\sin^2\theta = 4\cos\theta$ **59.** $r = 4\sin\theta$
61. $r^2 = 6r\cos\theta - 2r\sin\theta - 6$
63. $(0, \theta)$, where θ is any angle

Section 10.6, pp. 725–726

1. x-axis

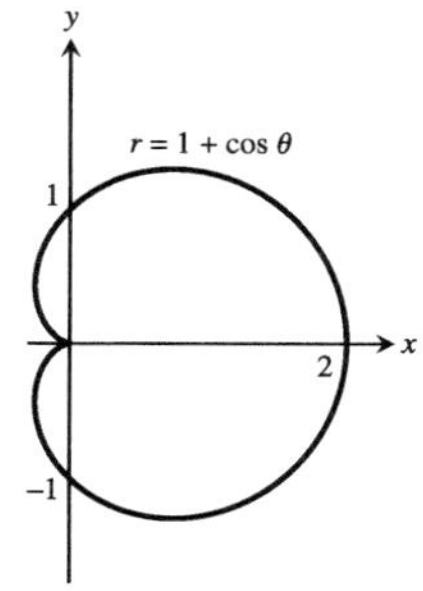

3. y-axis

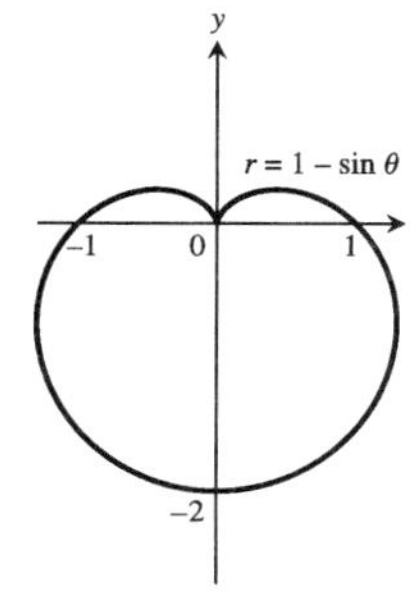

5. y-axis

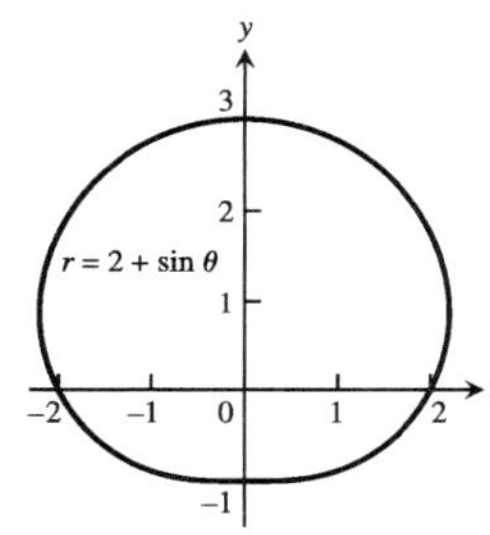

7. x-axis

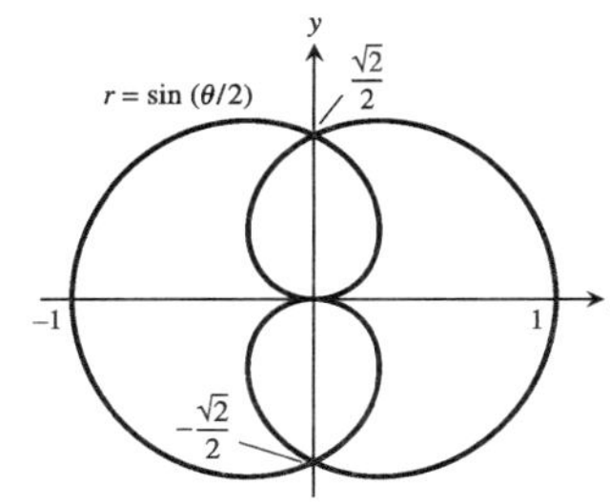

9. x-axis, y-axis, origin

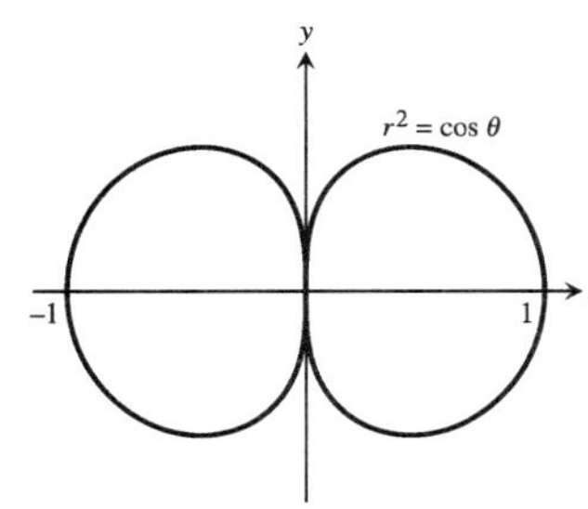

11. y-axis, x-axis, origin

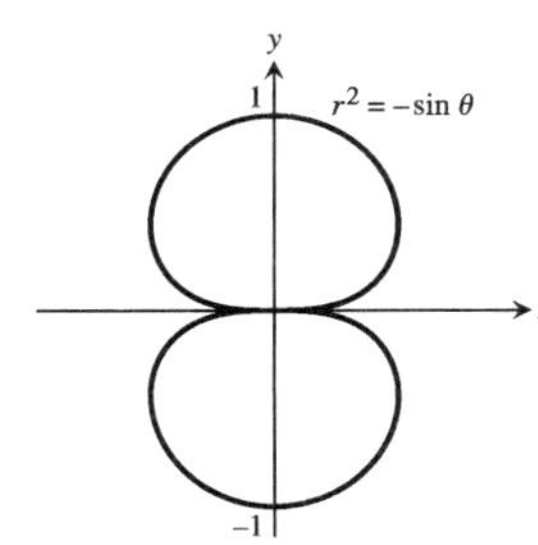

13. x-axis, y-axis, origin **15.** Origin

17. The slope at $(-1, \pi/2)$ is -1, at $(-1, -\pi/2)$ is 1.

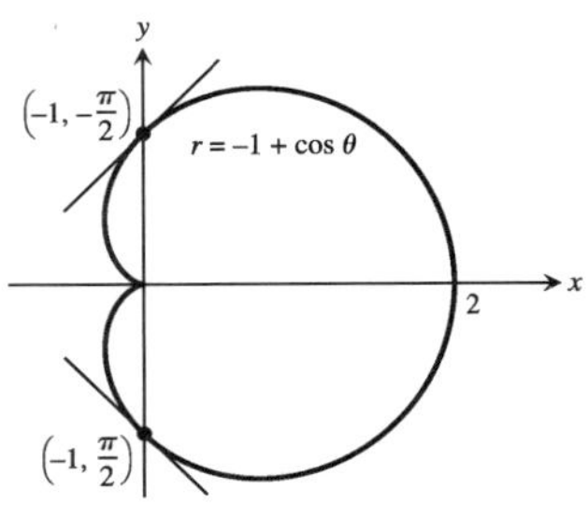

19. The slope at $(1, \pi/4)$ is -1, at $(-1, -\pi/4)$ is 1, at $(-1, 3\pi/4)$ is 1, at $(1, -3\pi/4)$ is -1.

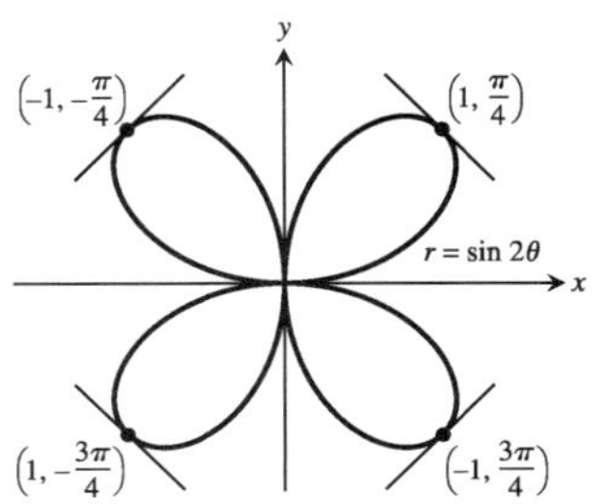

21. **(a)**

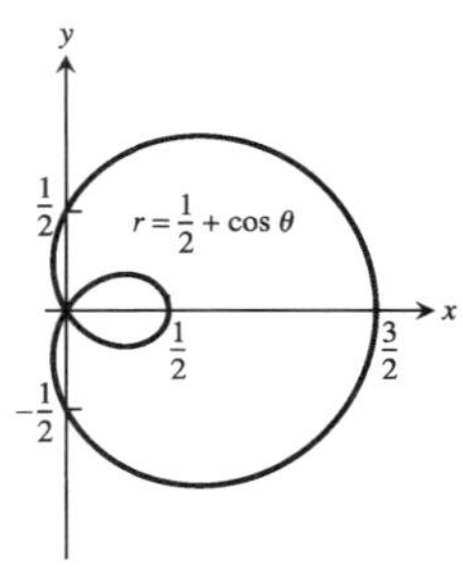

(b)

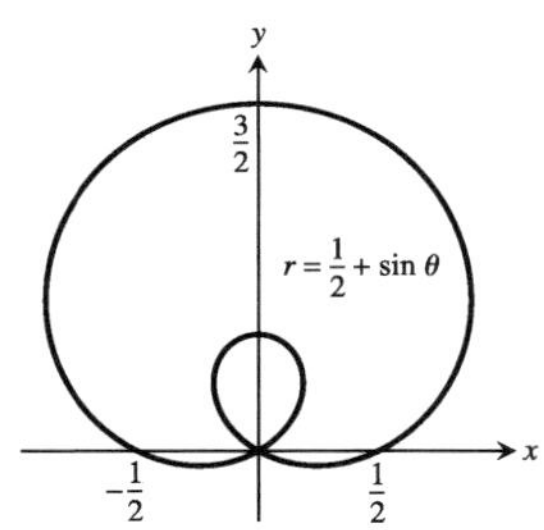

23. **(a)**

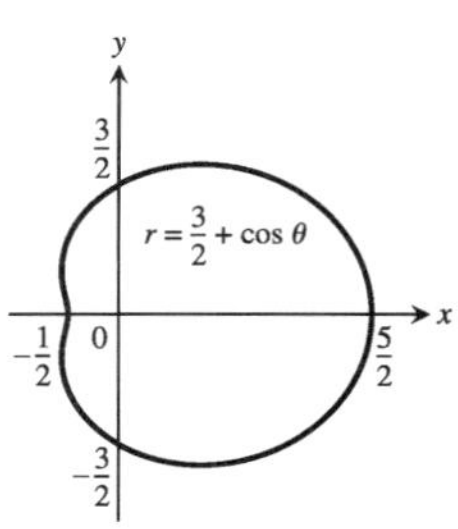

(b)

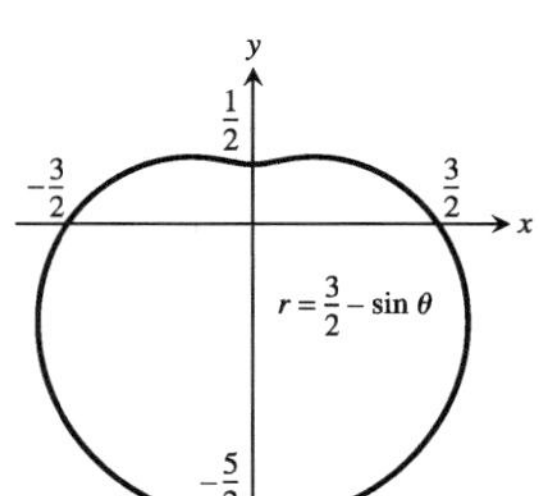

25.

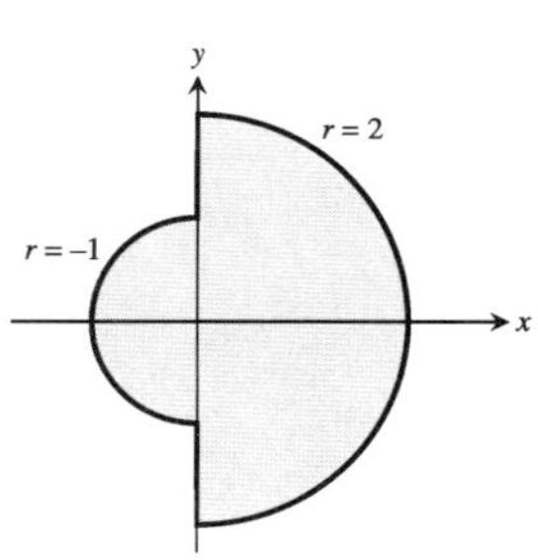

27.

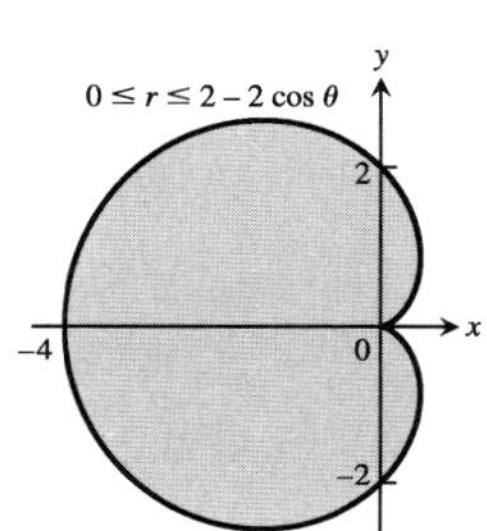

31. $(0, 0), (1, \pi/2), (1, 3\pi/2)$

33. $(0, 0), \left(\sqrt{3}, \pi/3\right), \left(-\sqrt{3}, -\pi/3\right)$

35. $\left(\sqrt{2}, \pm\pi/6\right), \left(\sqrt{2}, \pm 5\pi/6\right)$

37. $(1, \pi/12), (1, 5\pi/12), (1, 13\pi/12), (1, 17\pi/12)$

43. (a) **51.** $2y = \dfrac{2\sqrt{6}}{9}$

Section 10.7, pp. 730–731

1. 18π **3.** $\pi/8$ **5.** 2 **7.** $\dfrac{\pi}{2} - 1$ **9.** $5\pi - 8$

11. $3\sqrt{3} - \pi$ **13.** $\dfrac{\pi}{3} + \dfrac{\sqrt{3}}{2}$ **15.** $12\pi - 9\sqrt{3}$

17. **(a)** $\dfrac{3}{2} - \dfrac{\pi}{4}$ **19.** 19/3 **21.** 8

23. $3\left(\sqrt{2} + \ln\left(1 + \sqrt{2}\right)\right)$ **25.** $\dfrac{\pi}{8} + \dfrac{3}{8}$ **27.** 2π

29. $\pi\sqrt{2}$ **31.** $2\pi\left(2 - \sqrt{2}\right)$ **37.** $\left(\dfrac{5}{6}a, 0\right)$

Section 10.8, pp. 737–739

1. $r\cos(\theta - \pi/6) = 5, y = -\sqrt{3}x + 10$

3. $r\cos(\theta - 4\pi/3) = 3, y = -\left(\sqrt{3}/3\right)x - 2\sqrt{3}$

5. $y = 2 - x$ **7.** $y = \left(\sqrt{3}/3\right)x + 2\sqrt{3}$

9. $r\cos\left(\theta - \dfrac{\pi}{4}\right) = 3$ **11.** $r\cos\left(\theta + \dfrac{\pi}{2}\right) = 5$

13. $r = 8\cos\theta$ **15.** $r = 2\sqrt{2}\sin\theta$ **17.** $C(2, 0)$, radius $= 2$

19. $C(1, \pi)$, radius $= 1$ **21.** $(x - 6)^2 + y^2 = 36, r = 12\cos\theta$

23. $x^2 + (y - 5)^2 = 25, r = 10\sin\theta$

25. $(x + 1)^2 + y^2 = 1, r = -2\cos\theta$

27. $x^2 + (y + 1/2)^2 = 1/4, r = -\sin\theta$ **29.** $r = 2/(1 + \cos\theta)$

31. $r = 30/(1 - 5\sin\theta)$ **33.** $r = 1/(2 + \cos\theta)$

35. $r = 10/(5 - \sin\theta)$

37.

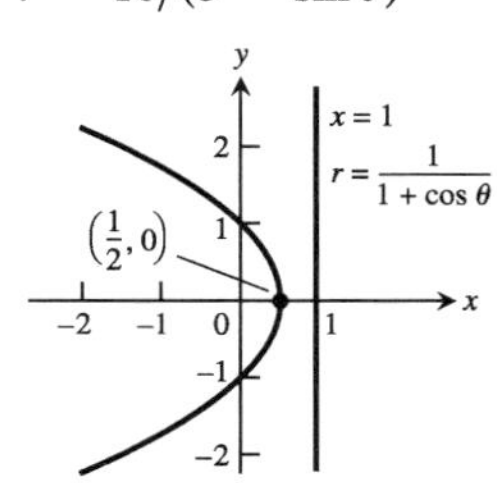

39.

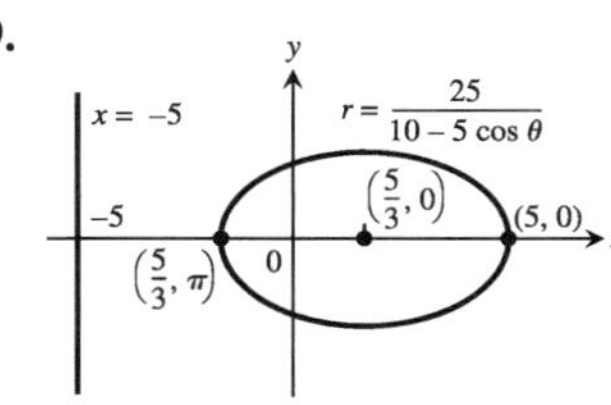

41.

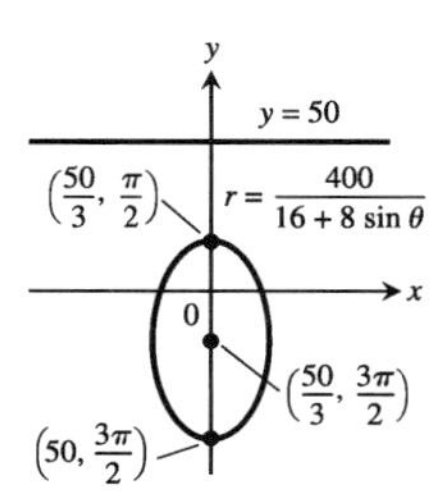

43.

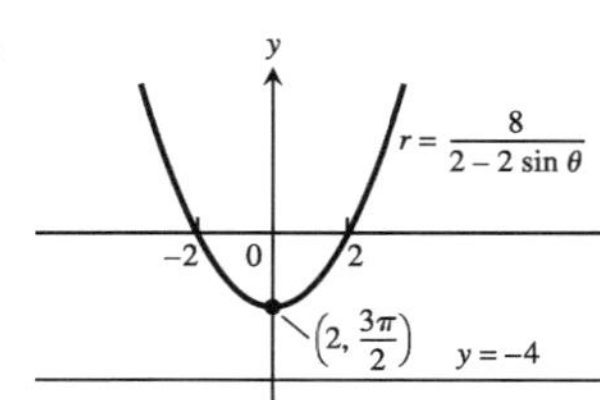

45.

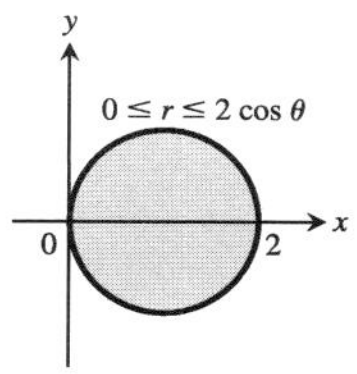

57. (b)

Planet	Perihelion	Aphelion
Mercury	0.3075 AU	0.4667 AU
Venus	0.7184 AU	0.7282 AU
Earth	0.9833 AU	1.0167 AU
Mars	1.3817 AU	1.6663 AU
Jupiter	4.9512 AU	5.4548 AU
Saturn	9.0210 AU	10.0570 AU
Uranus	18.2977 AU	20.0623 AU
Neptune	29.8135 AU	30.3065 AU
Pluto	29.6549 AU	49.2251 AU

59. (a) $x^2 + (y - 2)^2 = 4, x = \sqrt{3}$

(b)

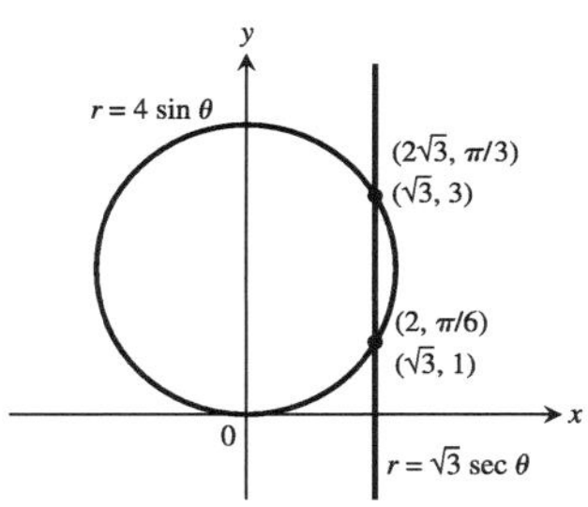

61. $r = 4/(1 + \cos\theta)$ **63. (b)** The pins should be 2 in. apart.
65. $r = 2a\sin\theta$ (a circle) **67.** $r\cos(\theta - \alpha) = p$ (a line)

Practice Exercises, pp. 740–743

1.

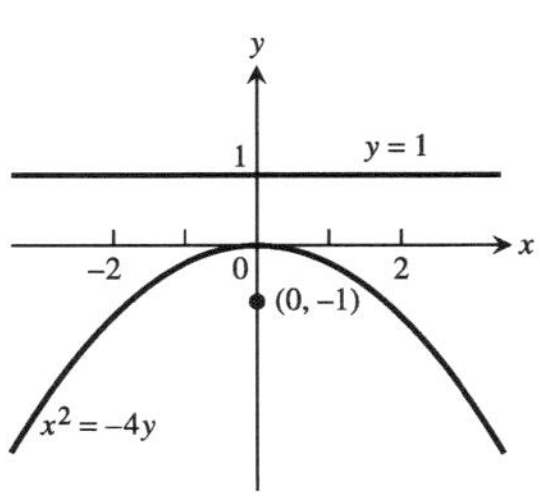

3.

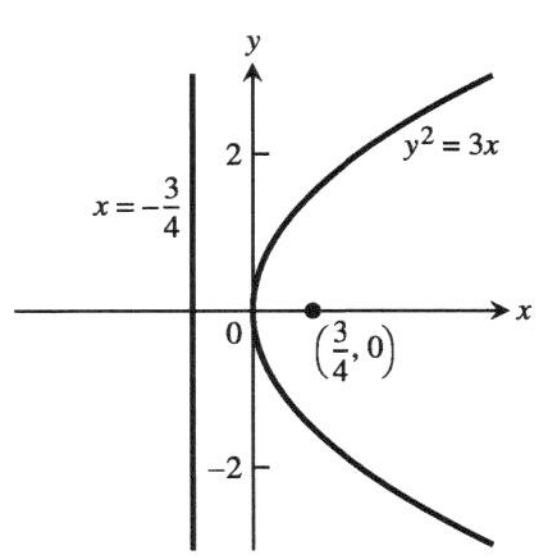

5. $e = 3/4$

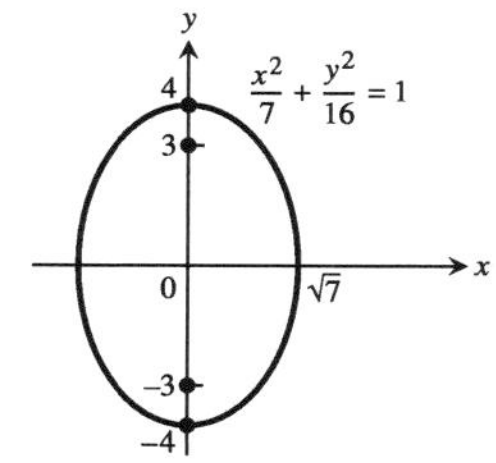

7. $e = 2$

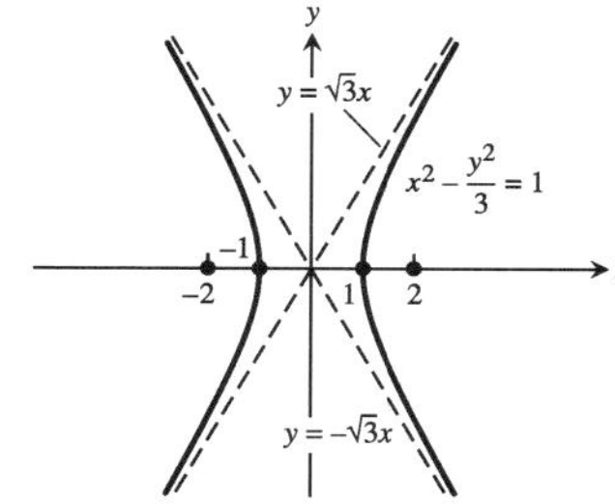

9. $(x - 2)^2 = -12(y - 3)$, $V(2, 3)$, $F(2, 0)$; directrix: $y = 6$

11. $\dfrac{(x + 3)^2}{9} + \dfrac{(y + 5)^2}{25} = 1$, $C(-3, -5)$, $V(-3, 0)$ and $V(-3, -10)$, $F(-3, -1)$ and $F(-3, -9)$

13. $\dfrac{\left(y - 2\sqrt{2}\right)^2}{8} - \dfrac{(x - 2)^2}{2} = 1$, $C\left(2, 2\sqrt{2}\right)$, $V\left(2, 4\sqrt{2}\right)$ and $V(2, 0)$, $F\left(2, \sqrt{10} + 2\sqrt{2}\right)$ and $F\left(2, -\sqrt{10} + 2\sqrt{2}\right)$; asymptotes: $y = 2x - 4 + 2\sqrt{2}$ and $y = -2x + 4 + 2\sqrt{2}$

15. Hyperbola: $\dfrac{(x - 2)^2}{4} - y^2 = 1$, $F\left(2 \pm \sqrt{5}, 0\right)$, $V(2 \pm 2, 0)$, $C(2, 0)$; asymptotes: $y = \pm\dfrac{1}{2}(x - 2)$

17. Parabola: $(y - 1)^2 = -16(x + 3)$, $V(-3, 1)$, $F(-7, 1)$; directrix: $x = 1$

19. Ellipse: $\dfrac{(x + 3)^2}{16} + \dfrac{(y - 2)^2}{9} = 1$, $F\left(\pm\sqrt{7} - 3, 2\right)$, $V(\pm 4 - 3, 2)$, $C(-3, 2)$

21. Circle: $(x - 1)^2 + (y - 1)^2 = 2$, $C(1, 1)$, radius $= \sqrt{2}$
23. Ellipse **25.** Hyperbola **27.** Line
29. Ellipse, $5x'^2 + 3y'^2 = 30$ **31.** Hyperbola, $y'^2 - x'^2 = 2$

33.

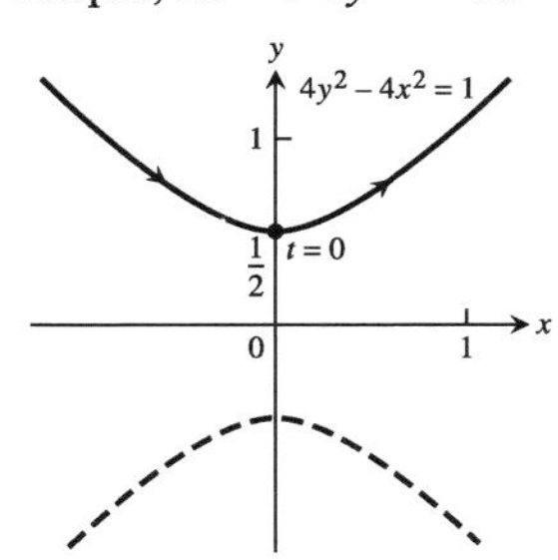

35.

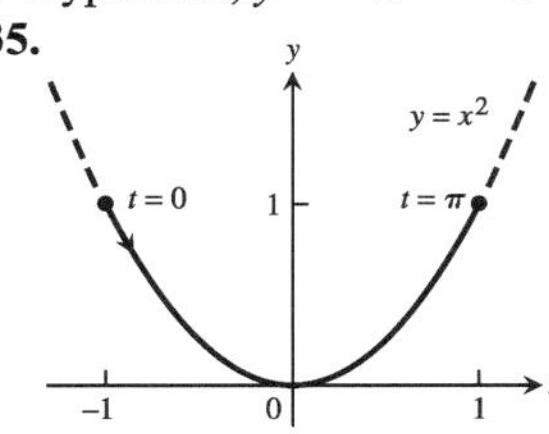

37.

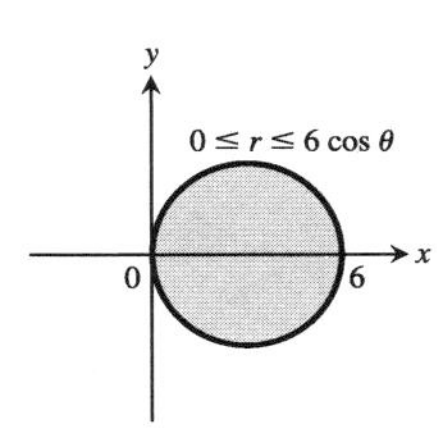

39. (d) **41.** (l) **43.** (k)

45. (i) **47.** (0, 0) **49.** (0, 0), $(1, \pm\pi/2)$
51. The graphs coincide. **53.** $\left(\sqrt{2}, \pi/4\right)$

55. $y = (\sqrt{3}/3)x - 4$ **57.** $x = 2$ **59.** $y = -3/2$
61. $x^2 + (y + 2)^2 = 4$ **63.** $(x - \sqrt{2})^2 + y^2 = 2$
65. $r = -5 \sin \theta$ **67.** $r = 3 \cos \theta$

69.

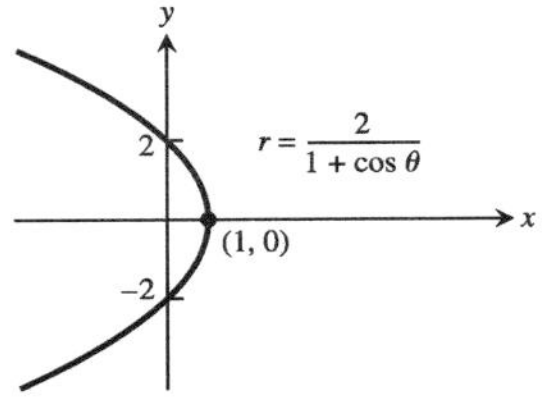

71.

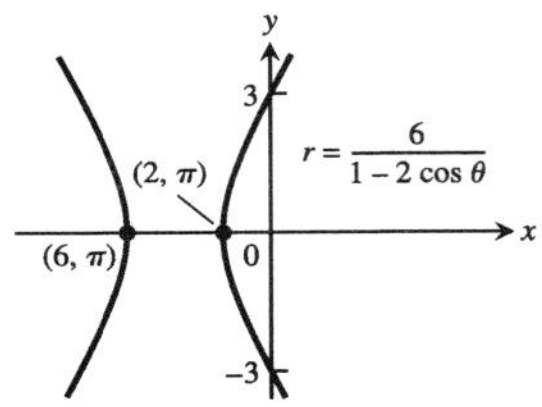

73. $r = \dfrac{4}{1 + 2\cos\theta}$ **75.** $r = \dfrac{2}{2 + \sin\theta}$ **77.** $9\pi/2$
79. $2 + \pi/4$ **81.** 8 **83.** $\pi - 3$ **85.** $(2 - \sqrt{2})\pi$
87. **(a)** 24π **(b)** 16π

Additional and Advanced Exercises, pp. 743–745

1.

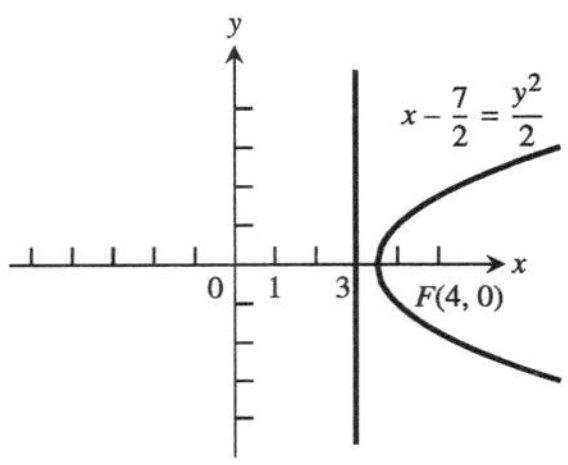

3. $3x^2 + 3y^2 - 8y + 4 = 0$

5. $(0, \pm 1)$

7. **(a)** $\dfrac{(y - 1)^2}{16} - \dfrac{x^2}{48} = 1$ **(b)** $\dfrac{16\left(y + \frac{3}{4}\right)^2}{25} - \dfrac{2x^2}{75} = 1$

11.

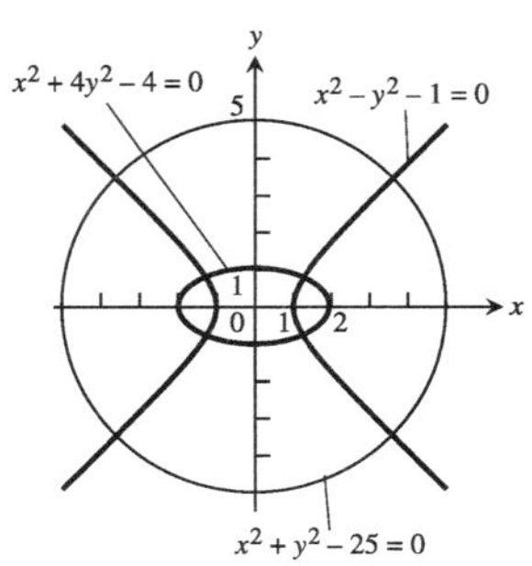

13.

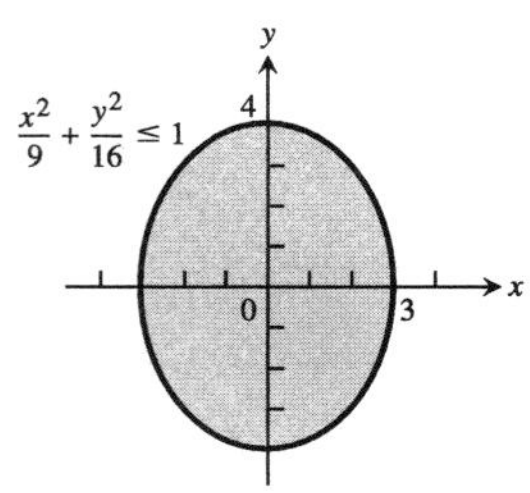

15.

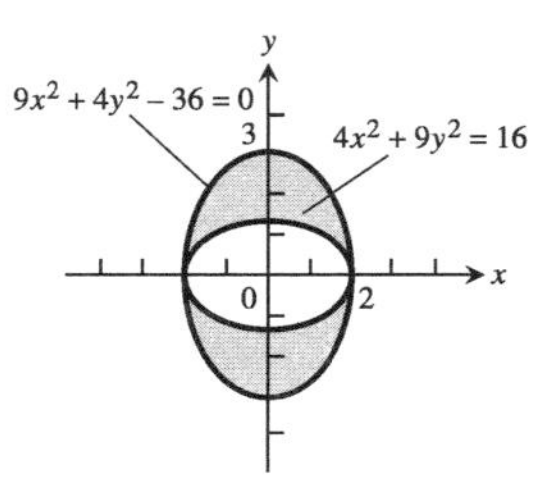

17.

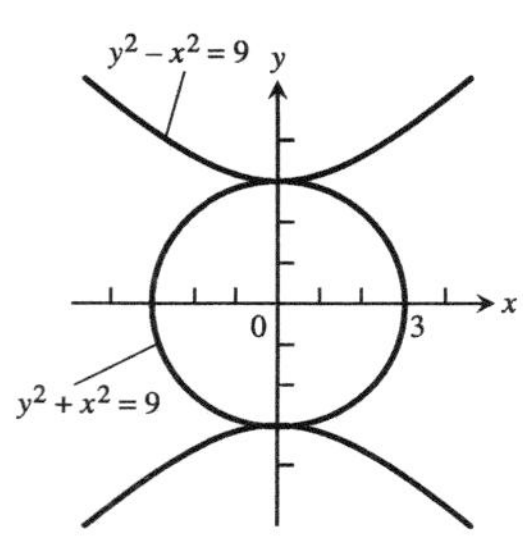

19. $x = (a + b)\cos\theta - b\cos\left(\dfrac{a + b}{b}\theta\right)$,
$y = (a + b)\sin\theta - b\sin\left(\dfrac{a + b}{b}\theta\right)$

21. **(a)** $r = e^{2\theta}$ **(b)** $\dfrac{\sqrt{5}}{2}(e^{4\pi} - 1)$ **23.** $\dfrac{32\pi - 4\pi\sqrt{2}}{5}$

25. $r = \dfrac{4}{1 + 2\cos\theta}$ **27.** $r = \dfrac{2}{2 + \sin\theta}$ **29.** **(a)** 120°

31. 1×10^7 miles **33.** $e = \sqrt{2/3}$ **35.** Yes, a parabola

37. **(a)** $r = \dfrac{2a}{1 + \cos\left(\theta - \dfrac{\pi}{4}\right)}$ **(b)** $r = \dfrac{8}{3 - \cos\theta}$

(c) $r = \dfrac{3}{1 + 2\sin\theta}$

43. $\pi/2$ **47.** $\left(2, \pm\dfrac{\pi}{3}\right), \dfrac{\pi}{2}$ **51.** $\pi/2$ **53.** $\pi/4$

CHAPTER 11

Section 11.1, pp. 757–761

1. $a_1 = 0, a_2 = -1/4, a_3 = -2/9, a_4 = -3/16$
3. $a_1 = 1, a_2 = -1/3, a_3 = 1/5, a_4 = -1/7$
5. $a_1 = 1/2, a_2 = 1/2, a_3 = 1/2, a_4 = 1/2$
7. $1, \frac{3}{2}, \frac{7}{4}, \frac{15}{8}, \frac{31}{16}, \frac{63}{32}, \frac{127}{64}, \frac{255}{128}, \frac{511}{256}, \frac{1023}{512}$
9. $2, 1, -\frac{1}{2}, -\frac{1}{4}, \frac{1}{8}, \frac{1}{16}, -\frac{1}{32}, -\frac{1}{64}, \frac{1}{128}, \frac{1}{256}$
11. 1, 1, 2, 3, 5, 8, 13, 21, 34, 55 **13.** $a_n = (-1)^{n+1}, n \ge 1$
15. $a_n = (-1)^{n+1}(n)^2, n \ge 1$ **17.** $a_n = n^2 - 1, n \ge 1$
19. $a_n = 4n - 3, n \ge 1$ **21.** $a_n = \dfrac{1 + (-1)^{n+1}}{2}, n \ge 1$
23. Converges, 2 **25.** Converges, −1 **27.** Converges, −5
29. Diverges **31.** Diverges **33.** Converges, 1/2
35. Converges, 0 **37.** Converges, $\sqrt{2}$ **39.** Converges, 1
41. Converges, 0 **43.** Converges, 0 **45.** Converges, 0
47. Converges, 1 **49.** Converges, e^7 **51.** Converges, 1
53. Converges, 1 **55.** Diverges **57.** Converges, 4
59. Converges, 0 **61.** Diverges **63.** Converges, e^{-1}
65. Converges, $e^{2/3}$ **67.** Converges, x ($x > 0$)
69. Converges, 0 **71.** Converges, 1 **73.** Converges, 1/2
75. Converges, $\pi/2$ **77.** Converges, 0 **79.** Converges, 0
81. Converges, 1/2 **83.** Converges, 0 **85.** $x_n = 2^{n-2}$
87. **(a)** $f(x) = x^2 - 2$, $1.414213562 \approx \sqrt{2}$
(b) $f(x) = \tan(x) - 1$, $0.7853981635 \approx \pi/4$
(c) $f(x) = e^x$, diverges
89. **(b)** 1 **97.** Nondecreasing, bounded
99. Not nondecreasing, bounded
101. Converges, nondecreasing sequence theorem
103. Converges, nondecreasing sequence theorem
105. Diverges, definition of divergence **109.** Converges
111. Converges **121.** $N = 692, a_n = \sqrt[n]{0.5}, L = 1$
123. $N = 65, a_n = (0.9)^n, L = 0$ **125.** **(b)** $\sqrt{3}$

Section 11.2, pp. 769–771

1. $s_n = \dfrac{2(1 - (1/3)^n)}{1 - (1/3)}, 3$ **3.** $s_n = \dfrac{1 - (-1/2)^n}{1 - (-1/2)}, 2/3$

5. $s_n = \dfrac{1}{2} - \dfrac{1}{n+2}, \dfrac{1}{2}$ **7.** $1 - \dfrac{1}{4} + \dfrac{1}{16} - \dfrac{1}{64} + \cdots, \dfrac{4}{5}$

9. $\dfrac{7}{4} + \dfrac{7}{16} + \dfrac{7}{64} + \cdots, \dfrac{7}{3}$

11. $(5 + 1) + \left(\dfrac{5}{2} + \dfrac{1}{3}\right) + \left(\dfrac{5}{4} + \dfrac{1}{9}\right) + \left(\dfrac{5}{8} + \dfrac{1}{27}\right) + \cdots, \dfrac{23}{2}$

13. $(1 + 1) + \left(\dfrac{1}{2} - \dfrac{1}{5}\right) + \left(\dfrac{1}{4} + \dfrac{1}{25}\right) + \left(\dfrac{1}{8} - \dfrac{1}{125}\right) + \cdots, \dfrac{17}{6}$

15. 1 **17.** 5 **19.** 1 **21.** $-\dfrac{1}{\ln 2}$ **23.** Converges, $2 + \sqrt{2}$

25. Converges, 1 **27.** Diverges **29.** Converges, $\dfrac{e^2}{e^2 - 1}$

31. Converges, 2/9 **33.** Converges, 3/2 **35.** Diverges

37. Diverges **39.** Converges, $\dfrac{\pi}{\pi - e}$

41. $a = 1, r = -x$; converges to $1/(1 + x)$ for $|x| < 1$

43. $a = 3, r = (x - 1)/2$; converges to $6/(3 - x)$ for x in $(-1, 3)$

45. $|x| < \dfrac{1}{2}, \dfrac{1}{1 - 2x}$ **47.** $-2 < x < 0, \dfrac{1}{2 + x}$

49. $x \neq (2k + 1)\dfrac{\pi}{2}$, k an integer; $\dfrac{1}{1 - \sin x}$

51. 23/99 **53.** 7/9 **55.** 1/15 **57.** 41333/33300

59. **(a)** $\displaystyle\sum_{n=-2}^{\infty} \frac{1}{(n+4)(n+5)}$ **(b)** $\displaystyle\sum_{n=0}^{\infty} \frac{1}{(n+2)(n+3)}$

(c) $\displaystyle\sum_{n=5}^{\infty} \frac{1}{(n-3)(n-2)}$

69. **(a)** $r = 3/5$ **(b)** $r = -3/10$

71. $|r| < 1, \dfrac{1 + 2r}{1 - r^2}$ **73.** 28 m **75.** 8 m^2

77. **(a)** $3\left(\dfrac{4}{3}\right)^{n-1}$

(b) $A_n = A + \dfrac{1}{3}A + \dfrac{1}{3}\left(\dfrac{4}{9}\right)A + \cdots + \dfrac{1}{3}\left(\dfrac{4}{9}\right)^{n-2} A,$

$A = \dfrac{\sqrt{3}}{4}, \lim_{n\to\infty} A_n = 2\sqrt{3}/5$

Section 11.3, pp. 775–777

1. Converges; geometric series, $r = \dfrac{1}{10} < 1$

3. Diverges; $\lim_{n\to\infty} \dfrac{n}{n+1} = 1 \neq 0$ **5.** Diverges; p-series, $p < 1$

7. Converges; geometric series, $r = \dfrac{1}{8} < 1$

9. Diverges; Integral Test

11. Converges; geometric series, $r = 2/3 < 1$

13. Diverges; Integral Test **15.** Diverges; $\lim_{n\to\infty} \dfrac{2^n}{n+1} \neq 0$

17. Diverges; $\lim_{n\to\infty}\left(\sqrt{n}/\ln n\right) \neq 0$

19. Diverges; geometric series, $r = \dfrac{1}{\ln 2} > 1$

21. Converges; Integral Test **23.** Diverges; nth-Term Test

25. Converges; Integral Test **27.** Converges; Integral Test

29. Converges; Integral Test **31.** $a = 1$ **33.** **(b)** About 41.55

35. True

Section 11.4, p. 781

1. Diverges; limit comparison with $\sum\left(1/\sqrt{n}\right)$

3. Converges; compare with $\sum\left(1/2^n\right)$

5. Diverges; nth-Term Test

7. Converges; $\left(\dfrac{n}{3n+1}\right)^n < \left(\dfrac{n}{3n}\right)^n = \left(\dfrac{1}{3}\right)^n$

9. Diverges; direct comparison with $\sum(1/n)$

11. Converges; limit comparison with $\sum(1/n^2)$

13. Diverges; limit comparison with $\sum(1/n)$

15. Diverges; limit comparison with $\sum(1/n)$

17. Diverges; Integral Test

19. Converges; compare with $\sum(1/n^{3/2})$

21. Converges; $\dfrac{1}{n2^n} \leq \dfrac{1}{2^n}$ **23.** Converges; $\dfrac{1}{3^{n-1} + 1} < \dfrac{1}{3^{n-1}}$

25. Diverges; limit comparison with $\sum(1/n)$

27. Converges; compare with $\sum(1/n^2)$

29. Converges; $\dfrac{\tan^{-1} n}{n^{1.1}} < \dfrac{\pi/2}{n^{1.1}}$

31. Converges; compare with $\sum(1/n^2)$

33. Diverges; limit comparison with $\sum(1/n)$

35. Converges; limit comparison with $\sum(1/n^2)$

Section 11.5, p. 786

1. Converges; Ratio Test **3.** Diverges; Ratio Test

5. Converges; Ratio Test

7. Converges; compare with $\sum(3/(1.25)^n)$

9. Diverges; $\lim_{n\to\infty}\left(1 - \dfrac{3}{n}\right)^n = e^{-3} \neq 0$

11. Converges; compare with $\sum(1/n^2)$

13. Diverges; compare with $\sum(1/(2n))$

15. Diverges; compare with $\sum(1/n)$ **17.** Converges; Ratio Test

19. Converges; Ratio Test **21.** Converges; Ratio Test

23. Converges; Root Test

25. Converges; compare with $\sum(1/n^2)$

27. Converges; Ratio Test **29.** Diverges; Ratio Test

31. Converges; Ratio Test **33.** Converges; Ratio Test

35. Diverges; $a_n = \left(\dfrac{1}{3}\right)^{(1/n!)} \to 1$ **37.** Converges; Ratio Test

39. Diverges; Root Test **41.** Converges; Root Test

43. Converges; Ratio Test **47.** Yes

Section 11.6, pp. 792–794

1. Converges by Theorem 16
3. Diverges; $a_n \nrightarrow 0$
5. Converges by Theorem 16
7. Diverges; $a_n \to 1/2$
9. Converges by Theorem 16
11. Converges absolutely. Series of absolute values is a convergent geometric series.
13. Converges conditionally. $1/\sqrt{n} \to 0$ but $\sum_{n=1}^{\infty} \frac{1}{\sqrt{n}}$ diverges.
15. Converges absolutely. Compare with $\sum_{n=1}^{\infty}(1/n^2)$.
17. Converges conditionally. $1/(n+3) \to 0$ but $\sum_{n=1}^{\infty} \frac{1}{n+3}$ diverges (compare with $\sum_{n=1}^{\infty}(1/n)$).
19. Diverges; $\frac{3+n}{5+n} \to 1$
21. Converges conditionally; $\left(\frac{1}{n^2} + \frac{1}{n}\right) \to 0$ but $(1+n)/n^2 > 1/n$
23. Converges absolutely; Ratio Test
25. Converges absolutely by Integral Test
27. Diverges; $a_n \nrightarrow 0$
29. Converges absolutely by the Ratio Test
31. Converges absolutely; $\frac{1}{n^2+2n+1} < \frac{1}{n^2}$
33. Converges absolutely since $\left|\frac{\cos n\pi}{n\sqrt{n}}\right| = \left|\frac{(-1)^{n+1}}{n^{3/2}}\right| = \frac{1}{n^{3/2}}$ (convergent p-series)
35. Converges absolutely by Root Test
37. Diverges; $a_n \to \infty$
39. Converges conditionally; $\sqrt{n+1} - \sqrt{n} = 1/\left(\sqrt{n} + \sqrt{n+1}\right) \to 0$, but series of absolute values diverges (compare with $\sum\left(1/\sqrt{n}\right)$)
41. Diverges, $a_n \to 1/2 \neq 0$
43. Converges absolutely; $\operatorname{sech} n = \frac{2}{e^n + e^{-n}} = \frac{2e^n}{e^{2n}+1} < \frac{2e^n}{e^{2n}} = \frac{2}{e^n}$, a term from a convergent geometric series.
45. $|\text{Error}| < 0.2$
47. $|\text{Error}| < 2 \times 10^{-11}$
49. 0.54030
51. **(a)** $a_n \geq a_{n+1}$ **(b)** $-1/2$

Section 11.7, pp. 804–805

1. **(a)** $1, -1 < x < 1$ **(b)** $-1 < x < 1$ **(c)** none
3. **(a)** $1/4, -1/2 < x < 0$ **(b)** $-1/2 < x < 0$ **(c)** none
5. **(a)** $10, -8 < x < 12$ **(b)** $-8 < x < 12$ **(c)** none
7. **(a)** $1, -1 < x < 1$ **(b)** $-1 < x < 1$ **(c)** none
9. **(a)** $3, -3 \leq x \leq 3$ **(b)** $-3 \leq x \leq 3$ **(c)** none
11. **(a)** ∞, for all x **(b)** for all x **(c)** none
13. **(a)** ∞, for all x **(b)** for all x **(c)** none
15. **(a)** $1, -1 \leq x < 1$ **(b)** $-1 < x < 1$ **(c)** $x = -1$
17. **(a)** $5, -8 < x < 2$ **(b)** $-8 < x < 2$ **(c)** none
19. **(a)** $3, -3 < x < 3$ **(b)** $-3 < x < 3$ **(c)** none
21. **(a)** $1, -1 < x < 1$ **(b)** $-1 < x < 1$ **(c)** none
23. **(a)** $0, x = 0$ **(b)** $x = 0$ **(c)** none
25. **(a)** $2, -4 < x \leq 0$ **(b)** $-4 < x < 0$ **(c)** $x = 0$
27. **(a)** $1, -1 \leq x \leq 1$ **(b)** $-1 \leq x \leq 1$ **(c)** none
29. **(a)** $1/4, 1 \leq x \leq 3/2$ **(b)** $1 \leq x \leq 3/2$ **(c)** none
31. **(a)** $1, (-1-\pi) \leq x < (1-\pi)$ **(b)** $(-1-\pi) < x < (1-\pi)$ **(c)** $x = -1-\pi$
33. $-1 < x < 3,\ 4/(3 + 2x - x^2)$
35. $0 < x < 16,\ 2/\left(4 - \sqrt{x}\right)$
37. $-\sqrt{2} < x < \sqrt{2},\ 3/(2 - x^2)$
39. $1 < x < 5,\ 2/(x-1), 1 < x < 5, -2/(x-1)^2$
41. **(a)** $\cos x = 1 - \frac{x^2}{2!} + \frac{x^4}{4!} - \frac{x^6}{6!} + \frac{x^8}{8!} - \frac{x^{10}}{10!} + \cdots$; converges for all x
 (b) and
 (c) $2x - \frac{2^3x^3}{3!} + \frac{2^5x^5}{5!} - \frac{2^7x^7}{7!} + \frac{2^9x^9}{9!} - \frac{2^{11}x^{11}}{11!} + \cdots$
43. **(a)** $\frac{x^2}{2} + \frac{x^4}{12} + \frac{x^6}{45} + \frac{17x^8}{2520} + \frac{31x^{10}}{14175}, -\frac{\pi}{2} < x < \frac{\pi}{2}$
 (b) $1 + x^2 + \frac{2x^4}{3} + \frac{17x^6}{45} + \frac{62x^8}{315} + \cdots, -\frac{\pi}{2} < x < \frac{\pi}{2}$

Section 11.8, pp. 810–811

1. $P_0(x) = 0, P_1(x) = x - 1, P_2(x) = (x-1) - \frac{1}{2}(x-1)^2,$
 $P_3(x) = (x-1) - \frac{1}{2}(x-1)^2 + \frac{1}{3}(x-1)^3$
3. $P_0(x) = \frac{1}{2}, P_1(x) = \frac{1}{2} - \frac{1}{4}(x-2),$
 $P_2(x) = \frac{1}{2} - \frac{1}{4}(x-2) + \frac{1}{8}(x-2)^2,$
 $P_3(x) = \frac{1}{2} - \frac{1}{4}(x-2) + \frac{1}{8}(x-2)^2 - \frac{1}{16}(x-2)^3$
5. $P_0(x) = \frac{\sqrt{2}}{2}, P_1(x) = \frac{\sqrt{2}}{2} + \frac{\sqrt{2}}{2}\left(x - \frac{\pi}{4}\right),$
 $P_2(x) = \frac{\sqrt{2}}{2} + \frac{\sqrt{2}}{2}\left(x - \frac{\pi}{4}\right) - \frac{\sqrt{2}}{4}\left(x - \frac{\pi}{4}\right)^2,$
 $P_3(x) = \frac{\sqrt{2}}{2} + \frac{\sqrt{2}}{2}\left(x - \frac{\pi}{4}\right) - \frac{\sqrt{2}}{4}\left(x - \frac{\pi}{4}\right)^2 - \frac{\sqrt{2}}{12}\left(x - \frac{\pi}{4}\right)^3$
7. $P_0(x) = 2, P_1(x) = 2 + \frac{1}{4}(x-4),$
 $P_2(x) = 2 + \frac{1}{4}(x-4) - \frac{1}{64}(x-4)^2,$
 $P_3(x) = 2 + \frac{1}{4}(x-4) - \frac{1}{64}(x-4)^2 + \frac{1}{512}(x-4)^3$
9. $\sum_{n=0}^{\infty} \frac{(-x)^n}{n!} = 1 - x + \frac{x^2}{2!} - \frac{x^3}{3!} + \frac{x^4}{4!} - \cdots$
11. $\sum_{n=0}^{\infty} (-1)^n x^n = 1 - x + x^2 - x^3 + \cdots$
13. $\sum_{n=0}^{\infty} \frac{(-1)^n 3^{2n+1} x^{2n+1}}{(2n+1)!}$
15. $7\sum_{n=0}^{\infty} \frac{(-1)^n x^{2n}}{(2n)!}$
17. $\sum_{n=0}^{\infty} \frac{x^{2n}}{(2n)!}$
19. $x^4 - 2x^3 - 5x + 4$
21. $8 + 10(x-2) + 6(x-2)^2 + (x-2)^3$
23. $21 - 36(x+2) + 25(x+2)^2 - 8(x+2)^3 + (x+2)^4$

25. $\sum_{n=0}^{\infty}(-1)^n(n+1)(x-1)^n$ **27.** $\sum_{n=0}^{\infty}\frac{e^2}{n!}(x-2)^n$

33. $L(x) = 0, Q(x) = -x^2/2$ **35.** $L(x) = 1, Q(x) = 1 + x^2/2$

37. $L(x) = x, Q(x) = x$

Section 11.9, pp. 819–822

1. $\sum_{n=0}^{\infty}\frac{(-5x)^n}{n!} = 1 - 5x + \frac{5^2x^2}{2!} - \frac{5^3x^3}{3!} + \cdots$

3. $\sum_{n=0}^{\infty}\frac{5(-1)^n(-x)^{2n+1}}{(2n+1)!} = \sum_{n=0}^{\infty}\frac{5(-1)^{n+1}x^{2n+1}}{(2n+1)!}$
$= -5x + \frac{5x^3}{3!} - \frac{5x^5}{5!} + \frac{5x^7}{7!} + \cdots$

5. $\sum_{n=0}^{\infty}\frac{(-1)^n(x+1)^n}{(2n)!}$

7. $\sum_{n=0}^{\infty}\frac{x^{n+1}}{n!} = x + x^2 + \frac{x^3}{2!} + \frac{x^4}{3!} + \frac{x^5}{4!} + \cdots$

9. $\sum_{n=2}^{\infty}\frac{(-1)^nx^{2n}}{(2n)!} = \frac{x^4}{4!} - \frac{x^6}{6!} + \frac{x^8}{8!} - \frac{x^{10}}{10!} + \cdots$

11. $x - \frac{\pi^2x^3}{2!} + \frac{\pi^4x^5}{4!} - \frac{\pi^6x^7}{6!} + \cdots = \sum_{n=0}^{\infty}\frac{(-1)^n\pi^{2n}x^{2n+1}}{(2n)!}$

13. $1 + \sum_{n=1}^{\infty}\frac{(-1)^n(2x)^{2n}}{2\cdot(2n)!} =$
$1 - \frac{(2x)^2}{2\cdot 2!} + \frac{(2x)^4}{2\cdot 4!} - \frac{(2x)^6}{2\cdot 6!} + \frac{(2x)^8}{2\cdot 8!} - \cdots$

15. $x^2\sum_{n=0}^{\infty}(2x)^n = x^2 + 2x^3 + 4x^4 + \cdots$

17. $\sum_{n=1}^{\infty}nx^{n-1} = 1 + 2x + 3x^2 + 4x^3 + \cdots$

19. $|x| < (0.06)^{1/5} < 0.56968$

21. $|\text{Error}| < (10^{-3})^3/6 < 1.67 \times 10^{-10}, \quad -10^{-3} < x < 0$

23. $|\text{Error}| < (3^{0.1})(0.1)^3/6 < 1.87 \times 10^{-4}$ **25.** 0.000293653

27. $|x| < 0.02$ **31.** $\sin x,\ x = 0.1;\ \sin(0.1)$

33. $\tan^{-1}x,\ x = \pi/3$

35. $e^x\sin x = x + x^2 + \frac{x^3}{3} - \frac{x^5}{30} - \frac{x^6}{90}\cdots$

43. **(a)** $Q(x) = 1 + kx + \frac{k(k-1)}{2}x^2$ **(b)** for $0 \le x < 100^{-1/3}$

49. **(a)** -1 **(b)** $(1/\sqrt{2})(1+i)$ **(c)** $-i$

53. $x + x^2 + \frac{1}{3}x^3 - \frac{1}{30}x^5\cdots$; will converge for all x

Section 11.10, pp. 831–833

1. $1 + \frac{x}{2} - \frac{x^2}{8} + \frac{x^3}{16}$ **3.** $1 + \frac{1}{2}x + \frac{3}{8}x^2 + \frac{5}{16}x^3 + \cdots$

5. $1 - x + \frac{3x^2}{4} - \frac{x^3}{2}$ **7.** $1 - \frac{x^3}{2} + \frac{3x^6}{8} - \frac{5x^9}{16}$

9. $1 + \frac{1}{2x} - \frac{1}{8x^2} + \frac{1}{16x^3}$

11. $(1+x)^4 = 1 + 4x + 6x^2 + 4x^3 + x^4$

13. $(1-2x)^3 = 1 - 6x + 12x^2 - 8x^3$

15. $y = \sum_{n=0}^{\infty}\frac{(-1)^n}{n!}x^n = e^{-x}$ **17.** $y = \sum_{n=1}^{\infty}(x^n/n!) = e^x - 1$

19. $y = \sum_{n=2}^{\infty}(x^n/n!) = e^x - x - 1$ **21.** $y = \sum_{n=0}^{\infty}\frac{x^{2n}}{2^nn!} = e^{x^2/2}$

23. $y = \sum_{n=0}^{\infty}2x^n = \frac{2}{1-x}$ **25.** $y = \sum_{n=0}^{\infty}\frac{x^{2n+1}}{(2n+1)!} = \sinh x$

27. $y = 2 + x - 2\sum_{n=1}^{\infty}\frac{(-1)^{n+1}x^{2n}}{(2n)!}$

29. $y = x - 2\sum_{n=0}^{\infty}\frac{x^{2n}}{(2n)!} - 3\sum_{n=0}^{\infty}\frac{x^{2n+1}}{(2n+1)!}$

31. $y = a + bx + \frac{1}{6}x^3 - \frac{ax^4}{3\cdot 4} - \frac{bx^5}{4\cdot 5} - \frac{x^7}{6\cdot 6\cdot 7} +$
$\frac{ax^8}{3\cdot 4\cdot 7\cdot 8} + \frac{bx^9}{4\cdot 5\cdot 8\cdot 9}\cdots.$

33. 0.00267 **35.** 0.1 **37.** 0.0999444611 **39.** 0.100001

41. $1/(13\cdot 6!) \approx 0.00011$ **43.** $\frac{x^3}{3} - \frac{x^7}{7\cdot 3!} + \frac{x^{11}}{11\cdot 5!}$

45. **(a)** $\frac{x^2}{2} - \frac{x^4}{12}$

(b) $\frac{x^2}{2} - \frac{x^4}{3\cdot 4} + \frac{x^6}{5\cdot 6} - \frac{x^8}{7\cdot 8} + \cdots + (-1)^{15}\frac{x^{32}}{31\cdot 32}$

47. 1/2 **49.** −1/24 **51.** 1/3 **53.** −1 **55.** 2

59. 500 terms **61.** 4 terms

63. **(a)** $x + \frac{x^3}{6} + \frac{3x^5}{40} + \frac{5x^7}{112}$, radius of convergence = 1

(b) $\frac{\pi}{2} - x - \frac{x^3}{6} - \frac{3x^5}{40} - \frac{5x^7}{112}$

65. $1 - 2x + 3x^2 - 4x^3 + \cdots$ **71.** **(c)** $3\pi/4$

Section 11.11, pp. 838–839

1. $f(x) = 1$

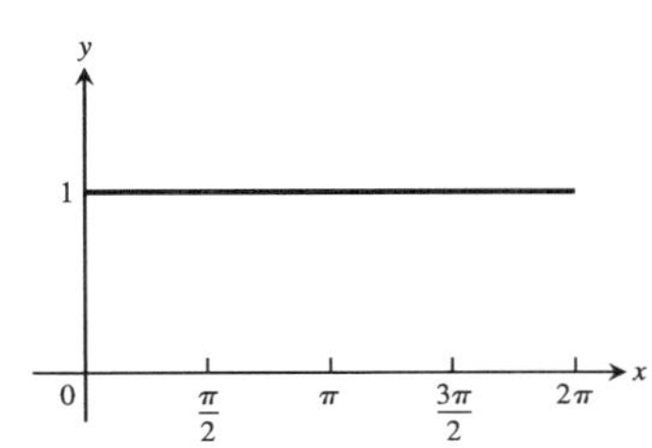

3. $f(x) = \sum_{n=1}^{\infty} \frac{2(-1)^{n+1}\sin(nx)}{n}$

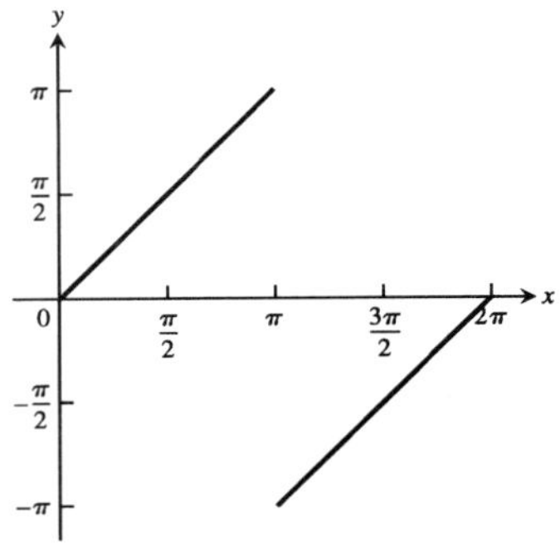

5. $\frac{e^{2\pi}-1}{\pi}\left(\frac{1}{2} + \sum_{n=1}^{\infty}\frac{\cos(nx)}{n^2+1} - \sum_{n=1}^{\infty}\frac{n\sin(nx)}{n^2+1}\right)$

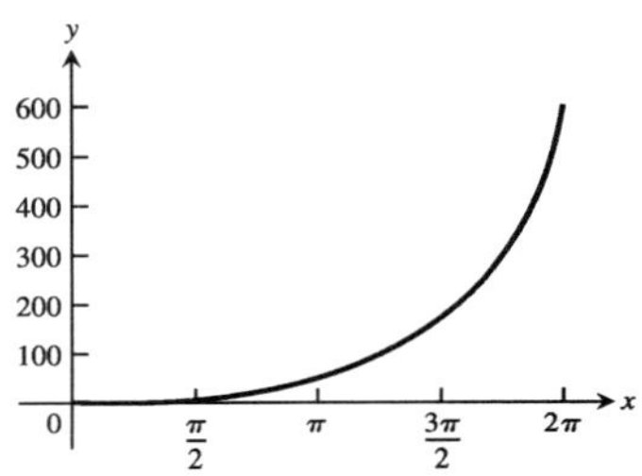

7. $f(x) = \frac{1}{2}\cos x + \frac{1}{\pi}\sum_{n=2}^{\infty}\frac{n(1+(-1)^n)}{n^2-1}\sin nx$

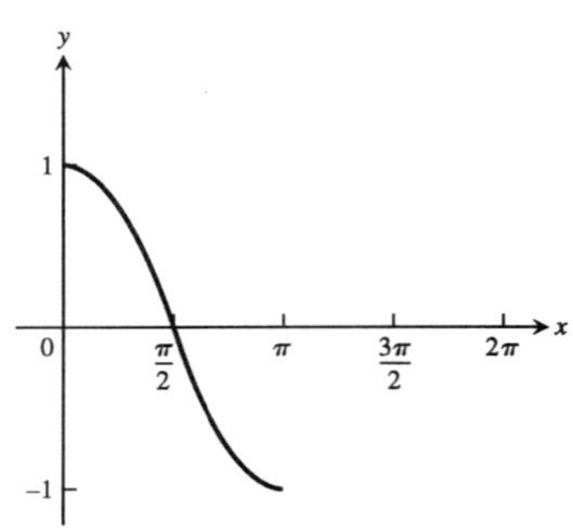

Practice Exercises, pp. 840–842

1. Converges to 1 **3.** Converges to -1 **5.** Diverges
7. Converges to 0 **9.** Converges to 1 **11.** Converges to e^{-5}
13. Converges to 3 **15.** Converges to ln 2 **17.** Diverges
19. $1/6$ **21.** $3/2$ **23.** $e/(e-1)$ **25.** Diverges
27. Converges conditionally **29.** Converges conditionally
31. Converges absolutely **33.** Converges absolutely
35. Converges absolutely **37.** Converges absolutely
39. Converges absolutely
41. (a) $3, -7 \le x < -1$ **(b)** $-7 < x < -1$ **(c)** $x = -7$
43. (a) $1/3, 0 \le x \le 2/3$ **(b)** $0 \le x \le 2/3$ **(c)** none
45. (a) ∞, for all x **(b)** for all x **(c)** none
47. (a) $\sqrt{3}, -\sqrt{3} < x < \sqrt{3}$ **(b)** $-\sqrt{3} < x < \sqrt{3}$ **(c)** none
49. (a) $e, -e < x < e$ **(b)** $-e < x < e$ **(c)** empty set
51. $\frac{1}{1+x}, \frac{1}{4}, \frac{4}{5}$ **53.** $\sin x, \pi, 0$ **55.** $e^x, \ln 2, 2$ **57.** $\sum_{n=0}^{\infty} 2^n x^n$
59. $\sum_{n=0}^{\infty}\frac{(-1)^n\pi^{2n+1}x^{2n+1}}{(2n+1)!}$ **61.** $\sum_{n=0}^{\infty}\frac{(-1)^n x^{5n}}{(2n)!}$
63. $\sum_{n=0}^{\infty}\frac{((\pi x)/2)^n}{n!}$
65. $2 - \frac{(x+1)}{2\cdot 1!} + \frac{3(x+1)^2}{2^3\cdot 2!} + \frac{9(x+1)^3}{2^5\cdot 3!} + \cdots$
67. $\frac{1}{4} - \frac{1}{4^2}(x-3) + \frac{1}{4^3}(x-3)^2 - \frac{1}{4^4}(x-3)^3$
69. $y = \sum_{n=0}^{\infty}\frac{(-1)^{n+1}}{n!}x^n = -e^{-x}$
71. $y = 3\sum_{n=0}^{\infty}\frac{(-1)^n 2^n}{n!}x^n = 3e^{-2x}$
73. $y = -1 - x + 2\sum_{n=2}^{\infty}(x^n/n!) = 2e^x - 3x - 3$
75. $y = 1 + x + 2\sum_{n=0}^{\infty}(x^n/n!) = 2e^x - 1 - x$
77. 0.4849171431 **79.** ≈ 0.4872223583 **81.** $7/2$
83. $1/12$ **85.** -2 **87.** $r = -3, s = 9/2$
89. (b) $|\text{error}| < |\sin(1/42)| < 0.02381$; an underestimate because the remainder is positive
91. $2/3$ **93.** $\ln\left(\frac{n+1}{2n}\right)$; the series converges to $\ln\left(\frac{1}{2}\right)$.
95. (a) ∞ **(b)** $a = 1, \quad b = 0$
97. It converges.
105. $\frac{1}{2} - \sum_{n=1}^{\infty}\frac{2\sin((2n-1)x)}{(2n-1)\pi}$

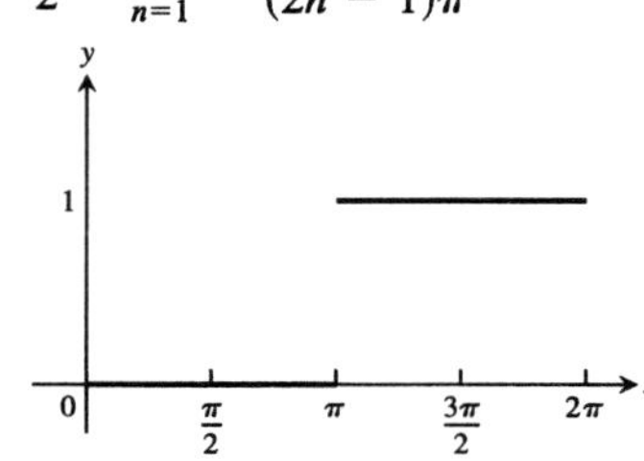

107. $\sum_{n=1}^{\infty} \frac{4\cos((2n-1)x)}{\pi(2n-1)^2} + \sum_{n=1}^{\infty} \frac{2\sin((2n-1)x)}{2n-1}$

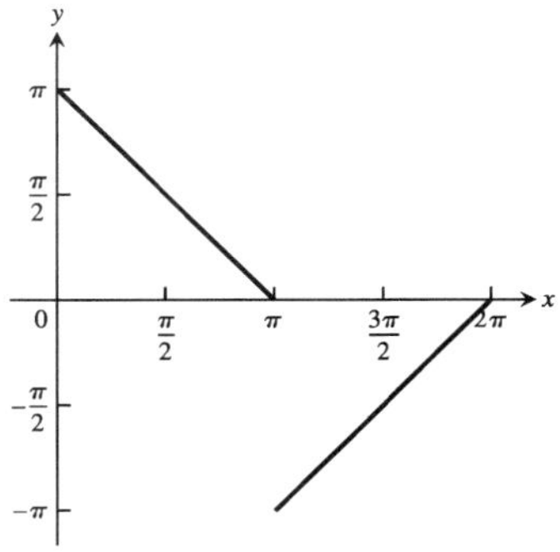

Additional and Advanced Exercises, pp. 843–847

1. Converges; Comparison Test **3.** Diverges; *n*th-Term Test
5. Converges; Comparison Test **7.** Diverges; *n*th-Term Test

9. With $a = \pi/3$, $\cos x = \frac{1}{2} - \frac{\sqrt{3}}{2}(x - \pi/3) - \frac{1}{4}(x - \pi/3)^2 + \frac{\sqrt{3}}{12}(x - \pi/3)^3 + \cdots$

11. With $a = 0$, $e^x = 1 + x + \frac{x^2}{2!} + \frac{x^3}{3!} + \cdots$

13. With $a = 22\pi$, $\cos x = 1 - \frac{1}{2}(x - 22\pi)^2 + \frac{1}{4!}(x - 22\pi)^4 - \frac{1}{6!}(x - 22\pi)^6 + \cdots$

15. Converges, limit $= b$ **17.** $\pi/2$ **23.** $b = \pm\frac{1}{5}$
25. $a = 2, L = -7/6$ **29.** **(b)** Yes

35. **(a)** $\sum_{n=1}^{\infty} nx^{n-1}$ **(b)** 6 **(c)** $1/q$

37. **(a)** $R_n = C_0e^{-kt_0}(1 - e^{-nkt_0})/(1 - e^{-kt_0})$,
$R = C_0(e^{-kt_0})/(1 - e^{-kt_0}) = C_0/(e^{kt_0} - 1)$
(b) $R_1 = 1/e \approx 0.368$,
$R_{10} = R(1 - e^{-10}) \approx R(0.9999546) \approx 0.58195$;
$R \approx 0.58198$; $0 < (R - R_{10})/R < 0.0001$
(c) 7

CHAPTER 12

Section 12.1, pp. 852–853

1. The line through the point (2, 3, 0) parallel to the *z*-axis
3. The *x*-axis **5.** The circle $x^2 + y^2 = 4$ in the *xy*-plane
7. The circle $x^2 + z^2 = 4$ in the *xz*-plane
9. The circle $y^2 + z^2 = 1$ in the *yz*-plane
11. The circle $x^2 + y^2 = 16$ in the *xy*-plane
13. **(a)** The first quadrant of the *xy*-plane
(b) The fourth quadrant of the *xy*-plane
15. **(a)** The ball of radius 1 centered at the origin
(b) All points greater than 1 unit from the origin
17. **(a)** The upper hemisphere of radius 1 centered at the origin
(b) The solid upper hemisphere of radius 1 centered at the origin
19. **(a)** $x = 3$ **(b)** $y = -1$ **(c)** $z = -2$
21. **(a)** $z = 1$ **(b)** $x = 3$ **(c)** $y = -1$
23. **(a)** $x^2 + (y-2)^2 = 4, z = 0$
(b) $(y-2)^2 + z^2 = 4, x = 0$ **(c)** $x^2 + z^2 = 4, y = 2$
25. **(a)** $y = 3, z = -1$ **(b)** $x = 1, z = -1$ **(c)** $x = 1, y = 3$
27. $x^2 + y^2 + z^2 = 25, z = 3$ **29.** $0 \le z \le 1$ **31.** $z \le 0$
33. **(a)** $(x-1)^2 + (y-1)^2 + (z-1)^2 < 1$
(b) $(x-1)^2 + (y-1)^2 + (z-1)^2 > 1$
35. 3 **37.** 7 **39.** $2\sqrt{3}$ **41.** $C(-2, 0, 2), a = 2\sqrt{2}$
43. $C(\sqrt{2}, \sqrt{2}, -\sqrt{2}), a = \sqrt{2}$
45. $(x-1)^2 + (y-2)^2 + (z-3)^2 = 14$
47. $(x+2)^2 + y^2 + z^2 = 3$ **49.** $C(-2, 0, 2), a = \sqrt{8}$
51. $C\left(-\frac{1}{4}, -\frac{1}{4}, -\frac{1}{4}\right), a = \frac{5\sqrt{3}}{4}$
53. **(a)** $\sqrt{y^2 + z^2}$ **(b)** $\sqrt{x^2 + z^2}$ **(c)** $\sqrt{x^2 + y^2}$
55. $\sqrt{17} + \sqrt{33} + 6$

Section 12.2, pp. 860–862

1. **(a)** $\langle 9, -6\rangle$ **(b)** $3\sqrt{13}$ **3.** **(a)** $\langle 1, 3\rangle$ **(b)** $\sqrt{10}$
5. **(a)** $\langle 12, -19\rangle$ **(b)** $\sqrt{505}$ **7.** **(a)** $\left\langle \frac{1}{5}, \frac{14}{5}\right\rangle$ **(b)** $\frac{\sqrt{197}}{5}$
9. $\langle 1, -4\rangle$ **11.** $\langle -2, -3\rangle$ **13.** $\left\langle -\frac{1}{2}, \frac{\sqrt{3}}{2}\right\rangle$
15. $\left\langle -\frac{\sqrt{3}}{2}, -\frac{1}{2}\right\rangle$ **17.** $\langle -3\mathbf{i} + 2\mathbf{j} - \mathbf{k}\rangle$ **19.** $\langle -3\mathbf{i} + 16\mathbf{j}\rangle$
21. $\langle 3\mathbf{i} + 5\mathbf{j} - 8\mathbf{k}\rangle$

23. The vector **v** is horizontal and 1 in. long. The vectors **u** and **w** are $\frac{11}{16}$ in. long. **w** is vertical and **u** makes a 45° angle with the horizontal. All vectors must be drawn to scale.

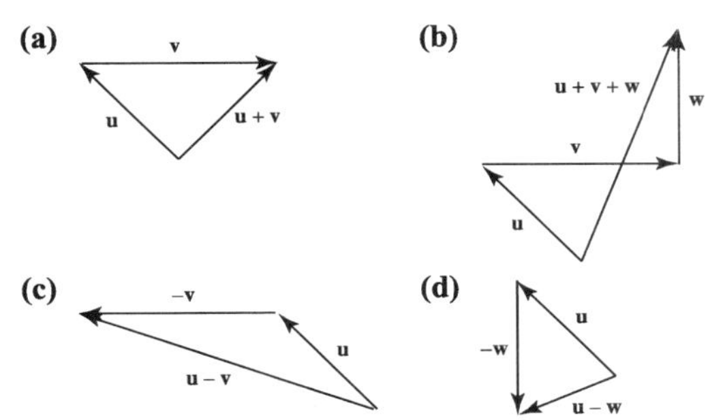

25. $3\left(\frac{2}{3}\mathbf{i} + \frac{1}{3}\mathbf{j} - \frac{2}{3}\mathbf{k}\right)$ **27.** $5(\mathbf{k})$

29. $\sqrt{\frac{1}{2}}\left(\frac{1}{\sqrt{3}}\mathbf{i} - \frac{1}{\sqrt{3}}\mathbf{j} - \frac{1}{\sqrt{3}}\mathbf{k}\right)$

31. **(a)** $2\mathbf{i}$ **(b)** $-\sqrt{3}\mathbf{k}$ **(c)** $\frac{3}{10}\mathbf{j} + \frac{2}{5}\mathbf{k}$ **(d)** $6\mathbf{i} - 2\mathbf{j} + 3\mathbf{k}$

33. $\frac{7}{13}(12\mathbf{i} - 5\mathbf{k})$

35. **(a)** $\frac{3}{5\sqrt{2}}\mathbf{i} + \frac{4}{5\sqrt{2}}\mathbf{j} - \frac{1}{\sqrt{2}}\mathbf{k}$ **(b)** $(1/2, 3, 5/2)$

37. **(a)** $-\frac{1}{\sqrt{3}}\mathbf{i} - \frac{1}{\sqrt{3}}\mathbf{j} - \frac{1}{\sqrt{3}}\mathbf{k}$ **(b)** $\left(\frac{5}{2}, \frac{7}{2}, \frac{9}{2}\right)$

39. $A(4, -3, 5)$ **41.** $a = \frac{3}{2}, b = \frac{1}{2}$ **43.** $5\sqrt{3}\mathbf{i}, 5\mathbf{j}$

45. $\approx\langle -338.095, 725.046\rangle$

47. **(a)** $(5\cos 60°, 5\sin 60°) = \left(\frac{5}{2}, \frac{5\sqrt{3}}{2}\right)$

(b) $(5\cos 60° + 10\cos 315°, 5\sin 60° + 10\sin 315°) = \left(\frac{5 + 10\sqrt{2}}{2}, \frac{5\sqrt{3} - 10\sqrt{2}}{2}\right)$

49. **(a)** $\frac{3}{2}\mathbf{i} + \frac{3}{2}\mathbf{j} - 3\mathbf{k}$ **(b)** $\mathbf{i} + \mathbf{j} - 2\mathbf{k}$ **(c)** $(2, 2, 1)$

Section 12.3, pp. 870–873

1. **(a)** $-25, 5, 5$ **(b)** -1 **(c)** -5 **(d)** $-2\mathbf{i} + 4\mathbf{j} - \sqrt{5}\mathbf{k}$

3. **(a)** $25, 15, 5$ **(b)** $\frac{1}{3}$ **(c)** $\frac{5}{3}$ **(d)** $\frac{1}{9}(10\mathbf{i} + 11\mathbf{j} - 2\mathbf{k})$

5. **(a)** $2, \sqrt{34}, \sqrt{3}$ **(b)** $\frac{2}{\sqrt{3}\sqrt{34}}$ **(c)** $\frac{2}{\sqrt{34}}$

(d) $\frac{1}{17}(5\mathbf{j} - 3\mathbf{k})$

7. **(a)** $10 + \sqrt{17}, \sqrt{26}, \sqrt{21}$ **(b)** $\frac{10 + \sqrt{17}}{\sqrt{546}}$

(c) $\frac{10 + \sqrt{17}}{\sqrt{26}}$ **(d)** $\frac{10 + \sqrt{17}}{26}(5\mathbf{i} + \mathbf{j})$

9. 0.75 rad **11.** 1.77 rad

13. Angle at $A = \cos^{-1}\left(\frac{1}{\sqrt{5}}\right) \approx 63.435$ degrees, angle at $B = \cos^{-1}\left(\frac{3}{5}\right) \approx 53.130$ degrees, angle at $C = \cos^{-1}\left(\frac{1}{\sqrt{5}}\right) \approx 63.435$ degrees.

17. $\left(\frac{3}{2}\mathbf{i} + \frac{3}{2}\mathbf{j}\right) + \left(-\frac{3}{2}\mathbf{i} + \frac{3}{2}\mathbf{j} + 4\mathbf{k}\right)$

19. $\left(\frac{14}{3}\mathbf{i} + \frac{28}{3}\mathbf{j} - \frac{14}{3}\mathbf{k}\right) + \left(\frac{10}{3}\mathbf{i} - \frac{16}{3}\mathbf{j} - \frac{22}{3}\mathbf{k}\right)$

21. The sum of two vectors of equal length is *always* orthogonal to their difference, as we can see from the equation $(\mathbf{v}_1 + \mathbf{v}_2)\cdot(\mathbf{v}_1 - \mathbf{v}_2) = \mathbf{v}_1\cdot\mathbf{v}_1 + \mathbf{v}_2\cdot\mathbf{v}_1 - \mathbf{v}_1\cdot\mathbf{v}_2 - \mathbf{v}_2\cdot\mathbf{v}_2 = |\mathbf{v}_1|^2 - |\mathbf{v}_2|^2 = 0$.

27. Horizontal component: ≈ 1188 ft/sec, vertical component: ≈ 167 ft/sec

29. **(a)** Since $|\cos\theta| \le 1$, we have $|\mathbf{u}\cdot\mathbf{v}| = |\mathbf{u}||\mathbf{v}||\cos\theta| \le |\mathbf{u}||\mathbf{v}|(1) = |\mathbf{u}||\mathbf{v}|$.

(b) We have equality precisely when $|\cos\theta| = 1$ or when one or both of $\mathbf{u}$ and $\mathbf{v}$ are $\mathbf{0}$. In the case of nonzero vectors, we have equality when $\theta = 0$ or π, that is, when the vectors are parallel.

31. *a*

35. $x + 2y = 4$

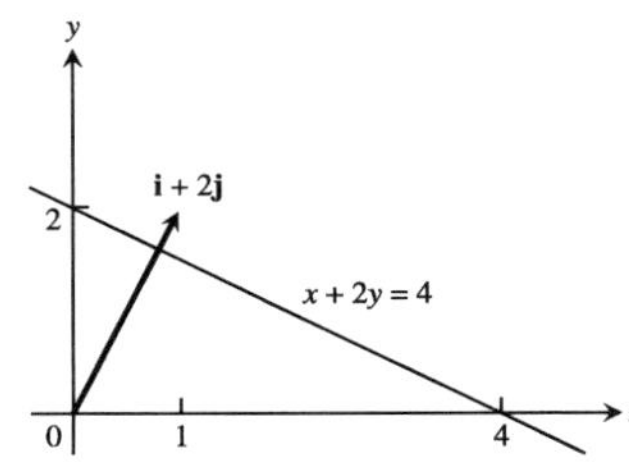

37. $-2x + y = -3$

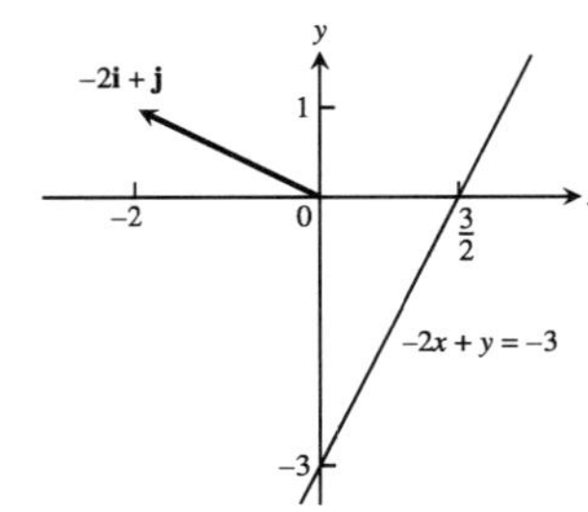

39. $x + y = -1$

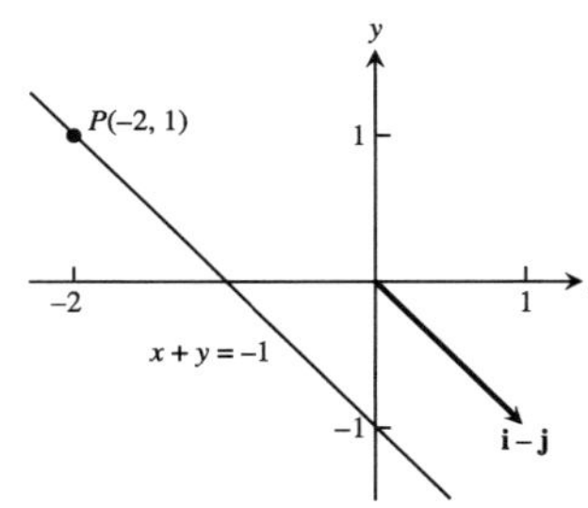

41. $2x - y = 0$

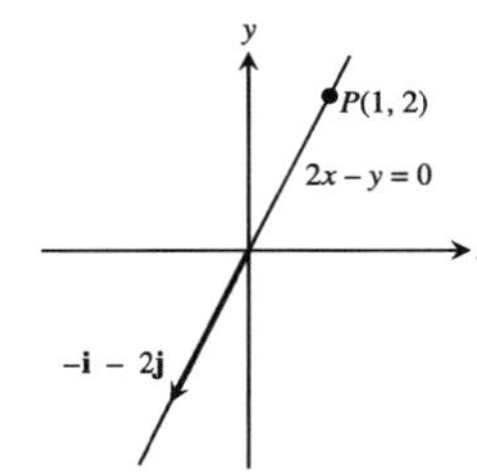

43. 5 J **45.** 3464 J **47.** $\frac{\pi}{4}$ **49.** $\frac{\pi}{6}$ **51.** 0.14

53. $\frac{\pi}{3}$ and $\frac{2\pi}{3}$ at each point **55.** At (0, 0): $\frac{\pi}{2}$; at (1, 1): $\frac{\pi}{4}$ and $\frac{3\pi}{4}$

Section 12.4, pp. 878–879

1. $|\mathbf{u}\times\mathbf{v}| = 3$, direction is $\frac{2}{3}\mathbf{i} + \frac{1}{3}\mathbf{j} + \frac{2}{3}\mathbf{k}$; $|\mathbf{v}\times\mathbf{u}| = 3$, direction is $-\frac{2}{3}\mathbf{i} - \frac{1}{3}\mathbf{j} - \frac{2}{3}\mathbf{k}$

3. $|\mathbf{u}\times\mathbf{v}| = 0$, no direction; $|\mathbf{v}\times\mathbf{u}| = 0$, no direction

5. $|\mathbf{u}\times\mathbf{v}| = 6$, direction is $-\mathbf{k}$; $|\mathbf{v}\times\mathbf{u}| = 6$, direction is $\mathbf{k}$

7. $|\mathbf{u}\times\mathbf{v}| = 6\sqrt{5}$, direction is $\frac{1}{\sqrt{5}}\mathbf{i} - \frac{2}{\sqrt{5}}\mathbf{k}$; $|\mathbf{v}\times\mathbf{u}| = 6\sqrt{5}$, direction is $-\frac{1}{\sqrt{5}}\mathbf{i} + \frac{2}{\sqrt{5}}\mathbf{k}$

9.

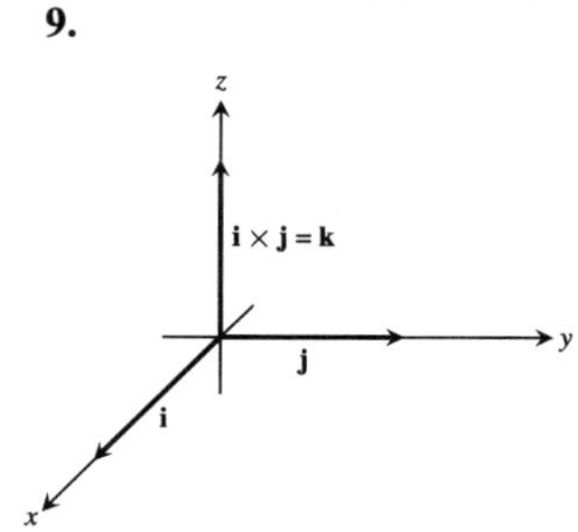

11.

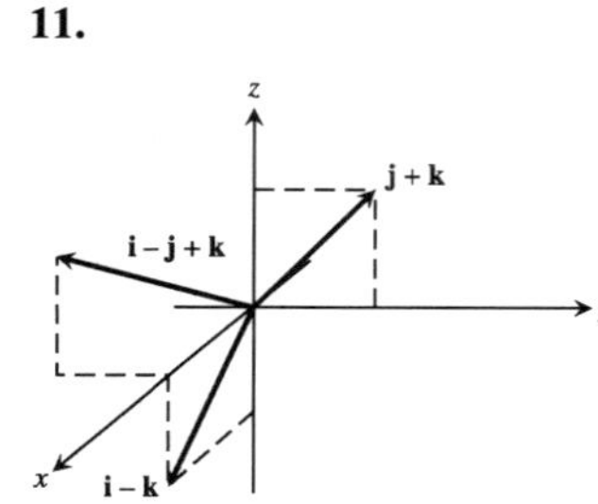

13.

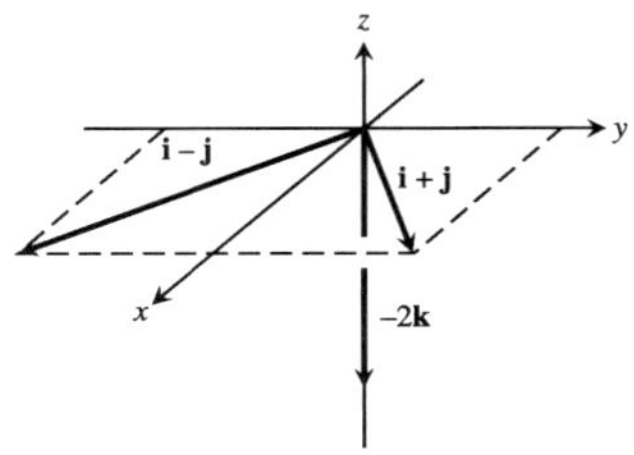

15. **(a)** $2\sqrt{6}$ **(b)** $\pm\frac{1}{\sqrt{6}}(2\mathbf{i}+\mathbf{j}+\mathbf{k})$

17. **(a)** $\frac{\sqrt{2}}{2}$ **(b)** $\pm\frac{1}{\sqrt{2}}(\mathbf{i}-\mathbf{j})$

19. 8 **21.** 7 **23.** **(a)** None **(b)** $\mathbf{u}$ and $\mathbf{w}$ **25.** $10\sqrt{3}$ ft-lb

27. **(a)** True **(b)** Not always true **(c)** True **(d)** True **(e)** Not always true **(f)** True **(g)** True **(h)** True

29. **(a)** $\text{proj}_{\mathbf{v}}\,\mathbf{u}=\frac{\mathbf{u}\cdot\mathbf{v}}{\mathbf{v}\cdot\mathbf{v}}\mathbf{v}$ **(b)** $\pm\,\mathbf{u}\times\mathbf{v}$ **(c)** $\pm\,(\mathbf{u}\times\mathbf{v})\times\mathbf{w}$ **(d)** $|(\mathbf{u}\times\mathbf{v})\cdot\mathbf{w}|$

31. **(a)** Yes **(b)** No **(c)** Yes **(d)** No

33. No, $\mathbf{v}$ need not equal $\mathbf{w}$. For example, $\mathbf{i}+\mathbf{j}\neq-\mathbf{i}+\mathbf{j}$, but $\mathbf{i}\times(\mathbf{i}+\mathbf{j})=\mathbf{i}\times\mathbf{i}+\mathbf{i}\times\mathbf{j}=\mathbf{0}+\mathbf{k}=\mathbf{k}$ and $\mathbf{i}\times(-\mathbf{i}+\mathbf{j})=-\mathbf{i}\times\mathbf{i}+\mathbf{i}\times\mathbf{j}=\mathbf{0}+\mathbf{k}=\mathbf{k}$.

35. 2 **37.** 13 **39.** 11/2 **41.** 25/2

43. If $\mathbf{A}=a_1\mathbf{i}+a_2\mathbf{j}$ and $\mathbf{B}=b_1\mathbf{i}+b_2\mathbf{j}$, then

$$\mathbf{A}\times\mathbf{B}=\begin{vmatrix}\mathbf{i}&\mathbf{j}&\mathbf{k}\\a_1&a_2&0\\b_1&b_2&0\end{vmatrix}=\begin{vmatrix}a_1&a_2\\b_1&b_2\end{vmatrix}\mathbf{k}$$

and the triangle's area is

$$\frac{1}{2}\left|\mathbf{A}\times\mathbf{B}\right|=\pm\frac{1}{2}\begin{vmatrix}a_1&a_2\\b_1&b_2\end{vmatrix}.$$

The applicable sign is (+) if the acute angle from $\mathbf{A}$ to $\mathbf{B}$ runs counterclockwise in the xy-plane, and (−) if it runs clockwise.

Section 12.5, pp. 887–889

1. $x=3+t,\ y=-4+t,\ z=-1+t$

3. $x=-2+5t,\ y=5t,\ z=3-5t$ **5.** $x=0,\ y=2t,\ z=t$

7. $x=1,\ y=1,\ z=1+t$ **9.** $x=t,\ y=-7+2t,\ z=2t$

11. $x=t,\ y=0,\ z=0$

13. $x=t,\ y=t,\ z=\frac{3}{2}t,\ 0\le t\le 1$

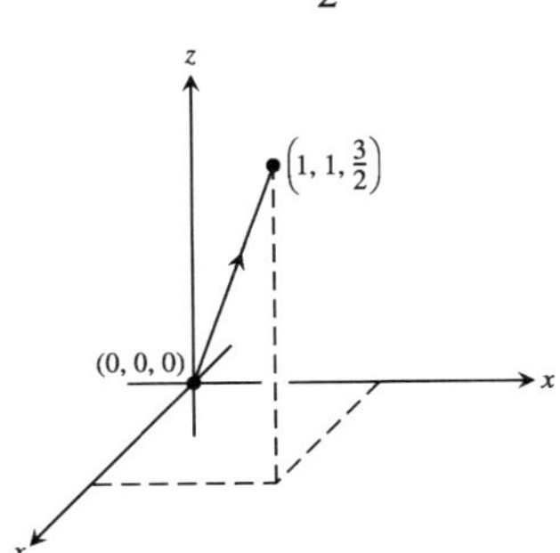

15. $x=1,\ y=1+t,\ z=0,\ -1\le t\le 0$

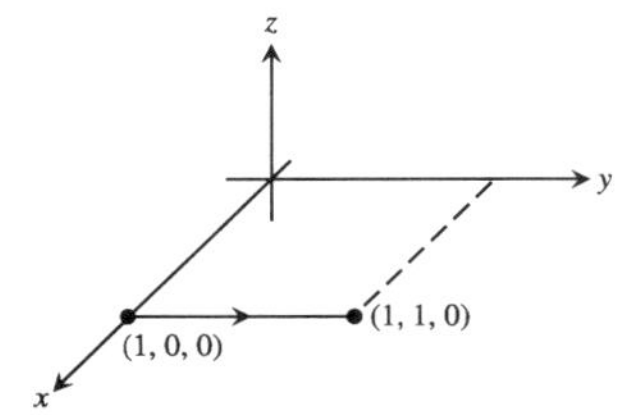

17. $x=0,\ y=1-2t,\ z=1,\ 0\le t\le 1$

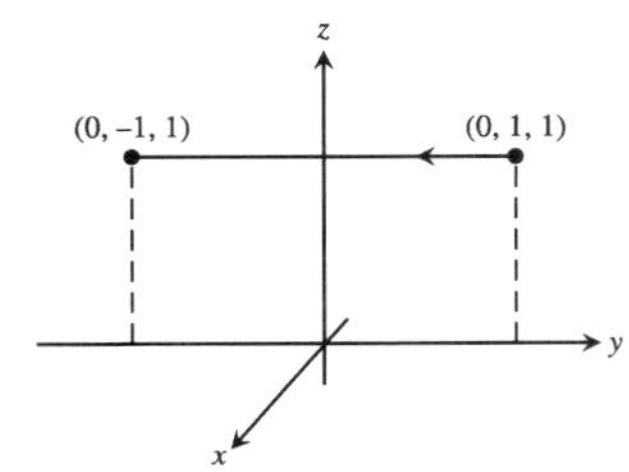

19. $x=2-2t,\ y=2t,\ z=2-2t,\ 0\le t\le 1$

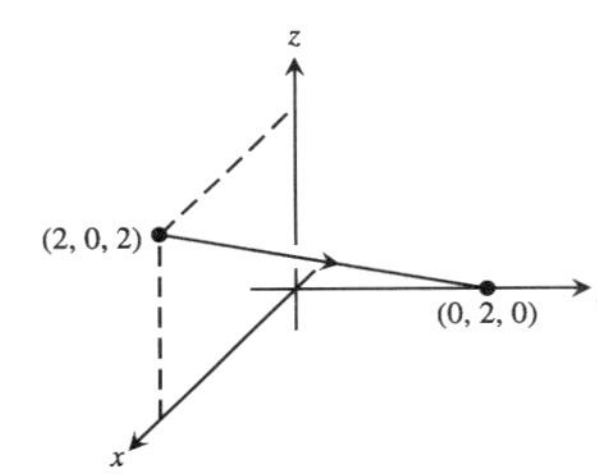

21. $3x-2y-z=-3$ **23.** $7x-5y-4z=6$

25. $x+3y+4z=34$ **27.** $(1,2,3),\ -20x+12y+z=7$

29. $y+z=3$ **31.** $x-y+z=0$ **33.** $2\sqrt{30}$ **35.** 0

37. $\frac{9\sqrt{42}}{7}$ **39.** 3 **41.** 19/5 **43.** 5/3 **45.** $9/\sqrt{41}$

47. $\pi/4$ **49.** 1.76 rad **51.** 0.82 rad **53.** $\left(\frac{3}{2},-\frac{3}{2},\frac{1}{2}\right)$

55. (1, 1, 0) **57.** $x=1-t,\ y=1+t,\ z=-1$

59. $x=4,\ y=3+6t,\ z=1+3t$

61. $L1$ intersects $L2$; $L2$ is parallel to $L3$; $L1$ and $L3$ are skew.

63. $x=2+2t,\ y=-4-t,\ z=7+3t;\ x=-2-t,\ y=-2+(1/2)t,\ z=1-(3/2)t$

65. $\left(0,-\frac{1}{2},-\frac{3}{2}\right),\ (-1,0,-3),\ (1,-1,0)$

69. Many possible answers. One possibility: $x+y=3$ and $2y+z=7$

71. $(x/a)+(y/b)+(z/c)=1$ describes all planes *except* those through the origin or parallel to a coordinate axis.

Section 12.6, pp. 897–899

1. **(d)**, ellipsoid **3.** **(a)**, cylinder **5.** **(l)**, hyperbolic paraboloid
7. **(b)**, cylinder **9.** **(k)**, hyperbolic paraboloid **11.** **(h)**, cone

13.
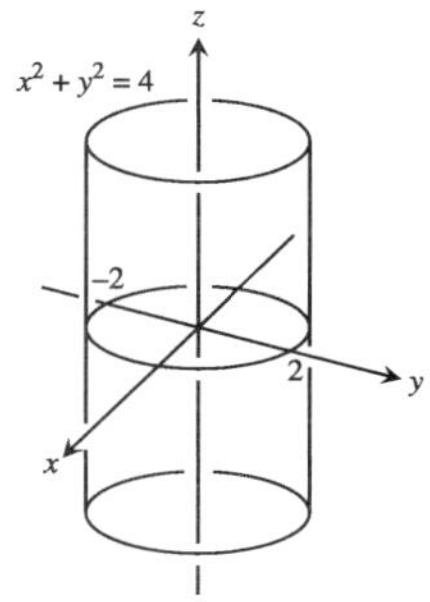

15.
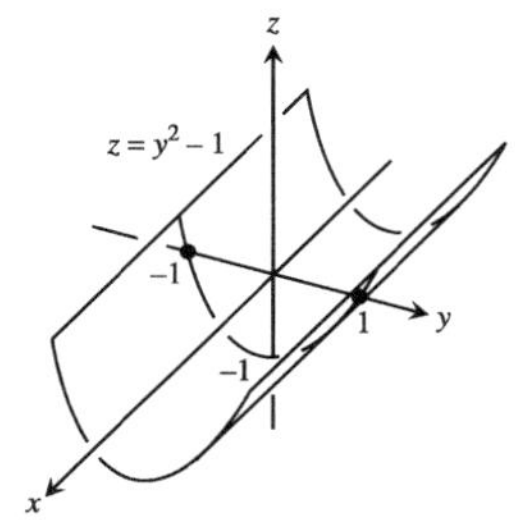

17.
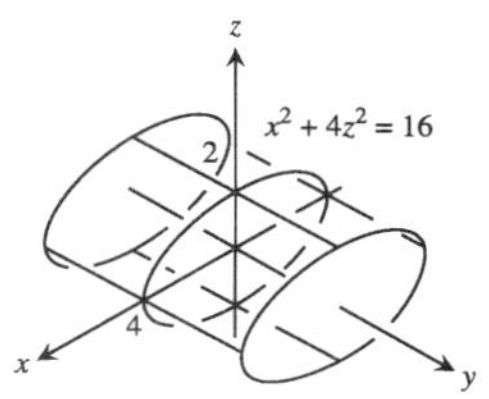

19.
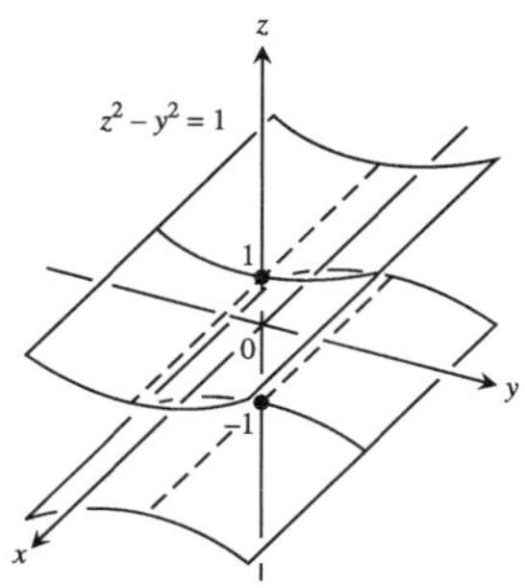

21.
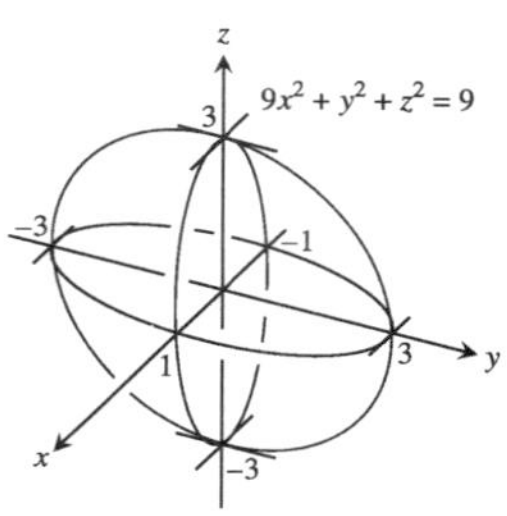

23.
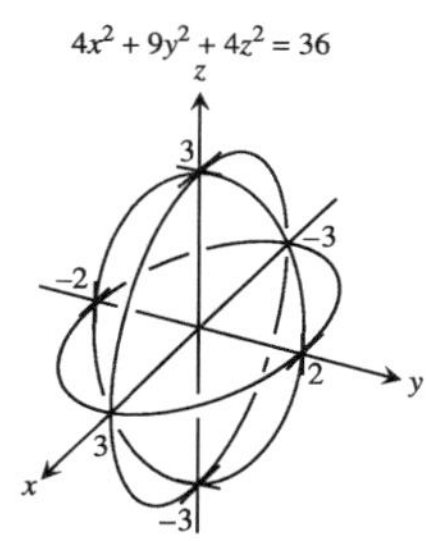

25.
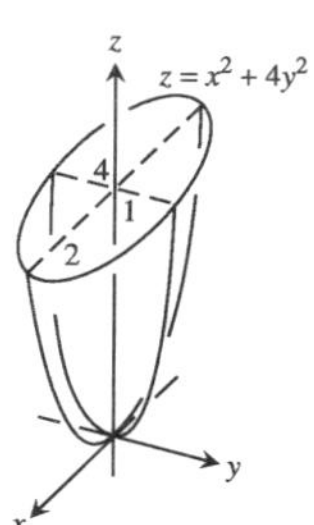

27.
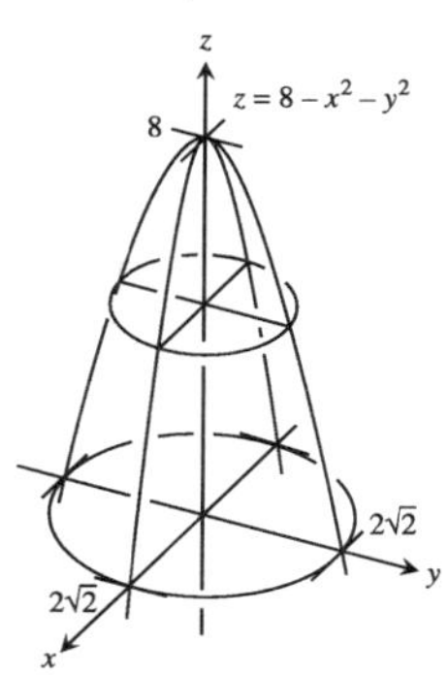

29.
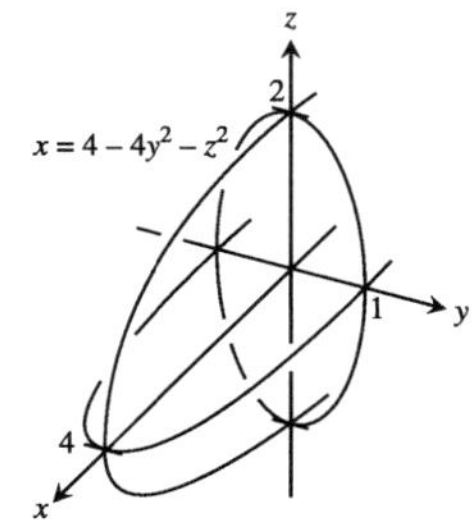

31.
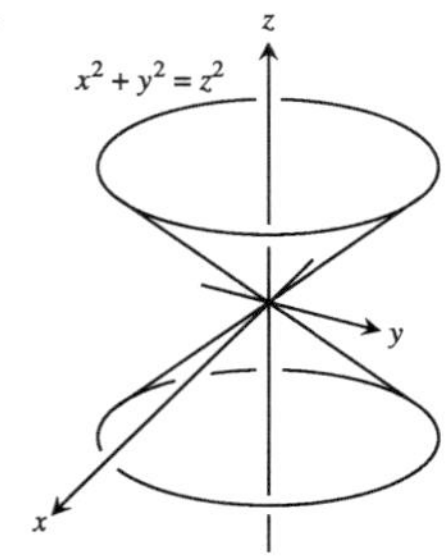

33.
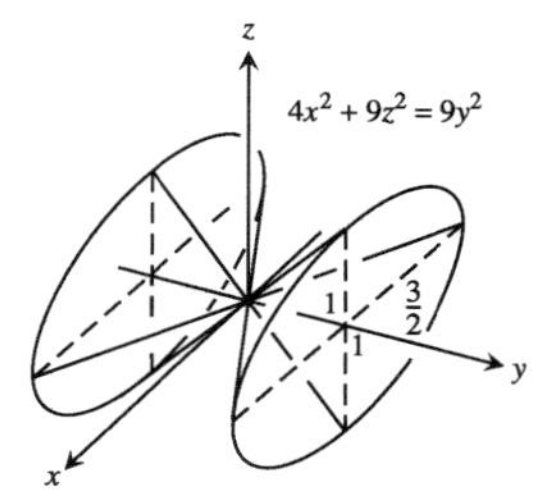

35.
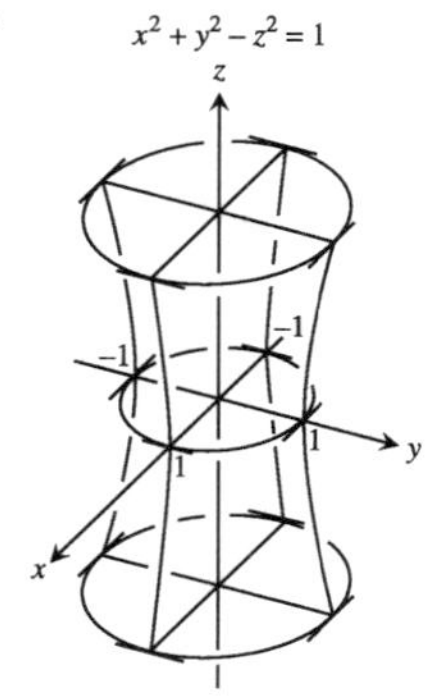

37.
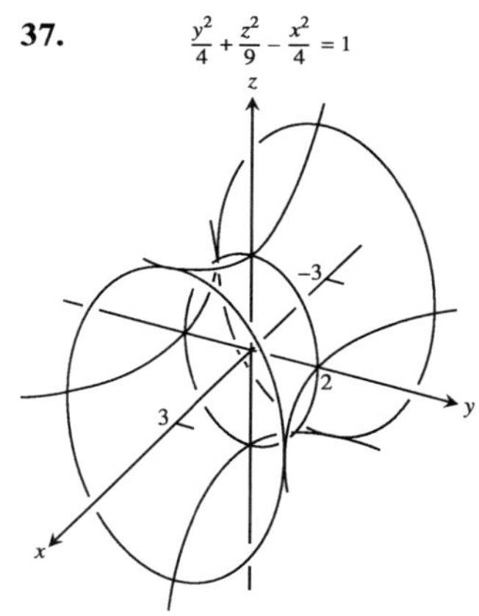

39.
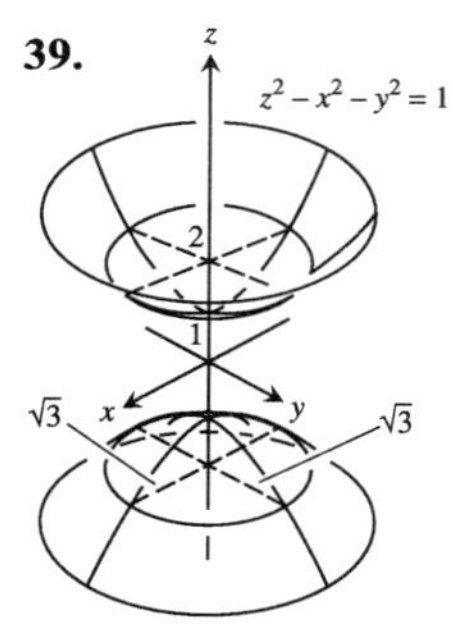

41.
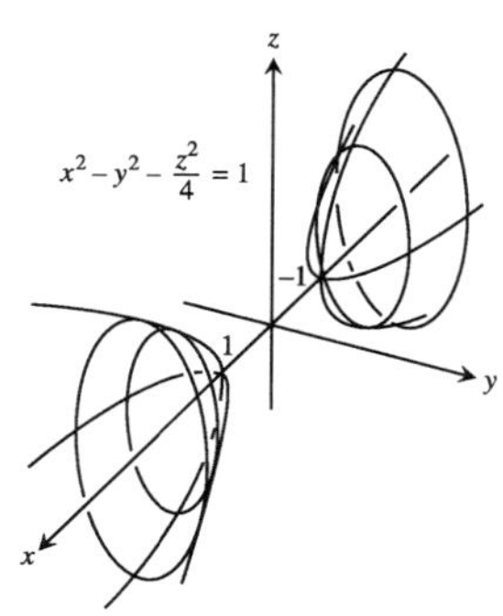

43.
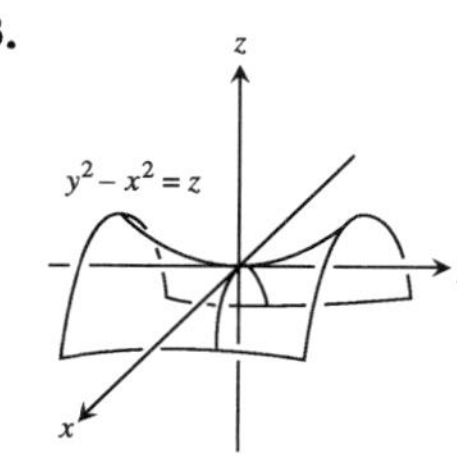

45.

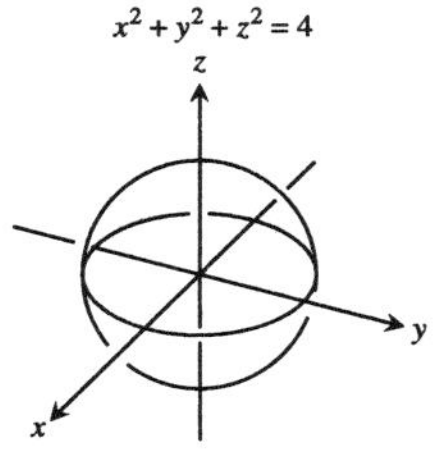

47.

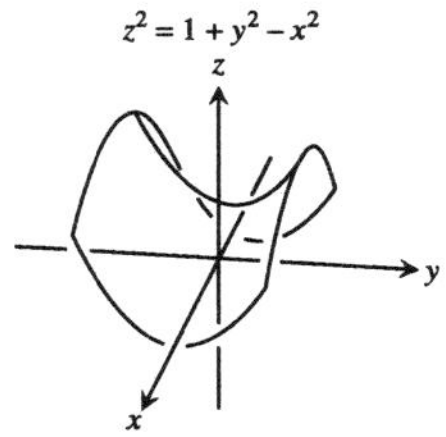

49.

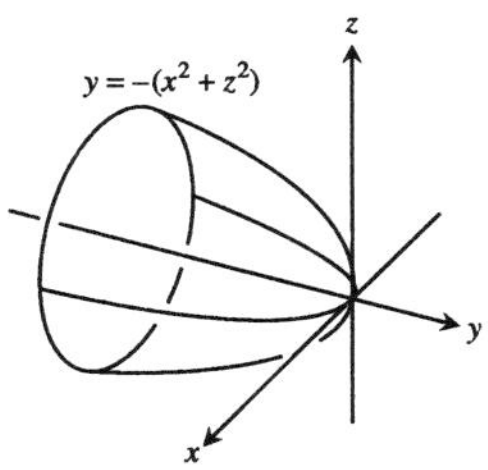

51.

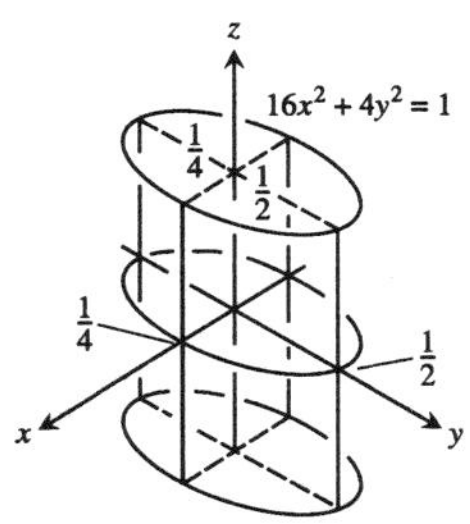

53.

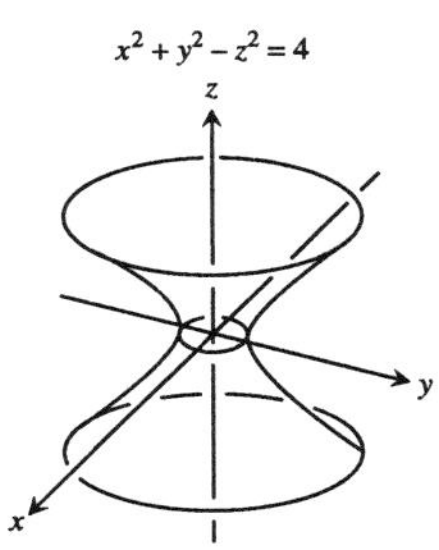

55.

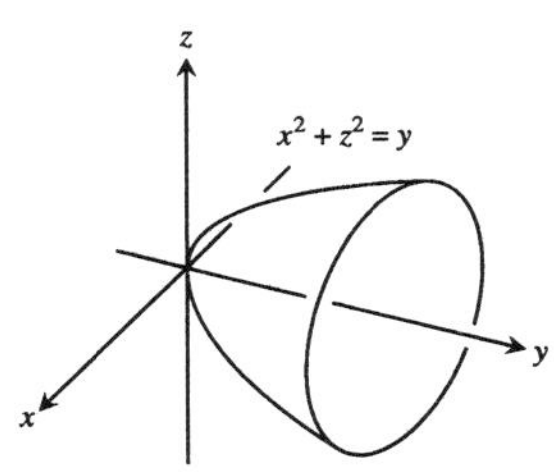

57.

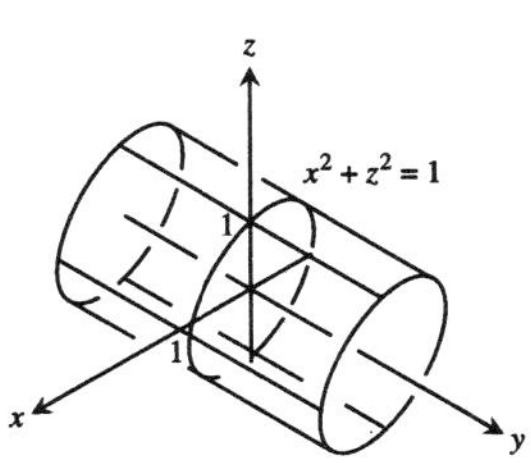

59.

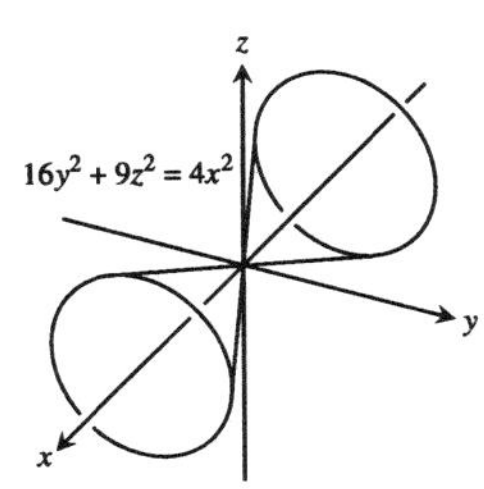

61.

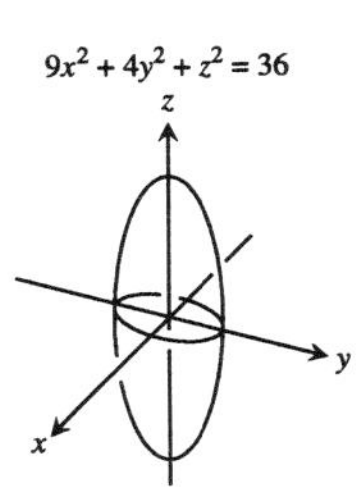

63.

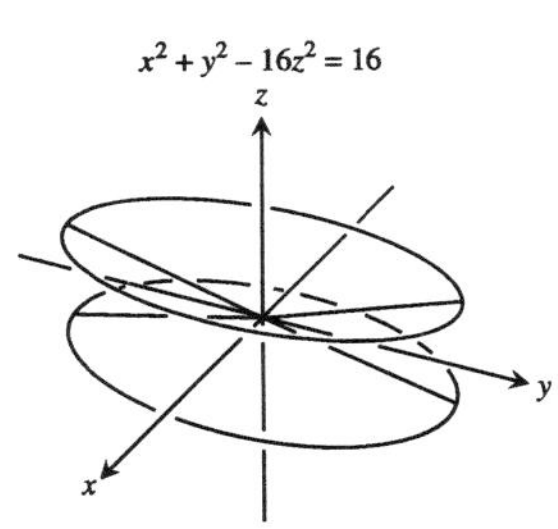

65.

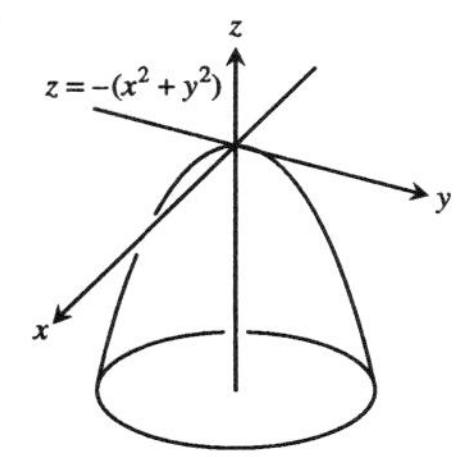

67.

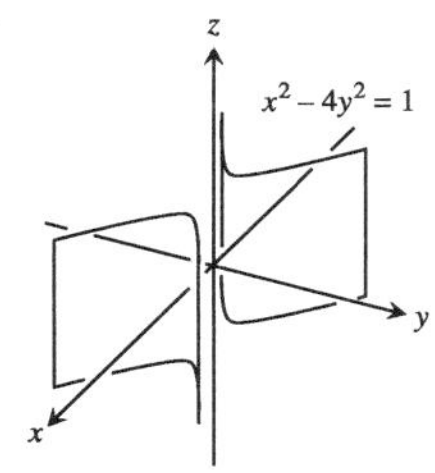

69.

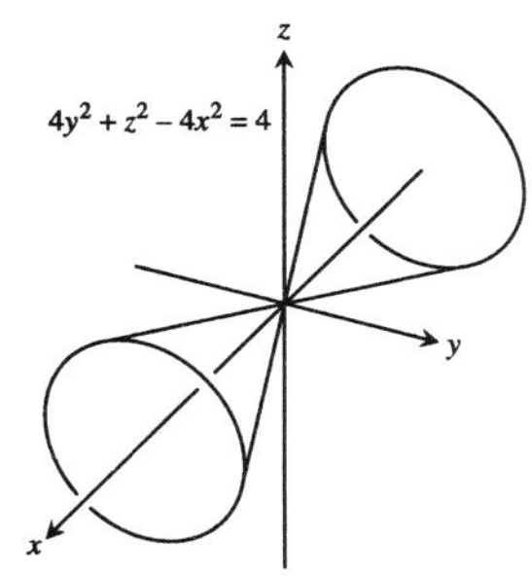

71.

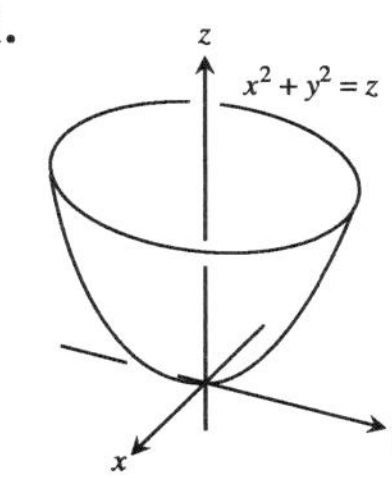

73.

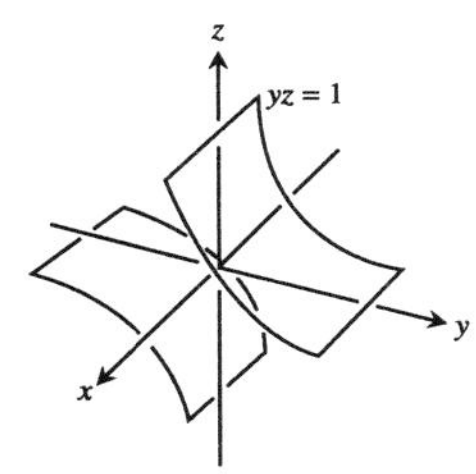

75.

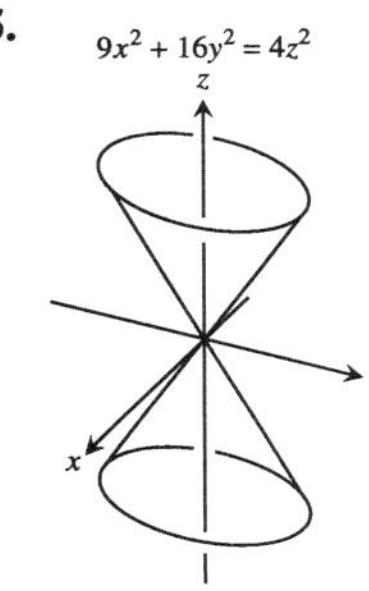

77. **(a)** $\dfrac{2\pi(9 - c^2)}{9}$ **(b)** 8π **(c)** $\dfrac{4\pi abc}{3}$

81. Vertex $(0, y_1, cy_1{}^2/b^2)$, focus $(0, y_1, c(y_1{}^2/b^2) - a^2/(4c))$

Practice Exercises, pp. 900–902

1. **(a)** $\langle -17, 32\rangle$ **(b)** $\sqrt{1313}$ **3.** **(a)** $\langle 6, -8\rangle$ **(b)** 10

5. $\left\langle -\dfrac{\sqrt{3}}{2}, -\dfrac{1}{2}\right\rangle$ [assuming counterclockwise]

7. $\left\langle \dfrac{8}{\sqrt{17}}, -\dfrac{2}{\sqrt{17}}\right\rangle$

9. Length $= 2$, direction is $\dfrac{1}{\sqrt{2}}\mathbf{i} + \dfrac{1}{\sqrt{2}}\mathbf{j}$.

11. $\mathbf{v}(\pi/2) = 2(-\mathbf{i})$

13. Length $= 7$, direction is $\frac{2}{7}\mathbf{i} - \frac{3}{7}\mathbf{j} + \frac{6}{7}\mathbf{k}$.

15. $\dfrac{8}{\sqrt{33}}\mathbf{i} - \dfrac{2}{\sqrt{33}}\mathbf{j} + \dfrac{8}{\sqrt{33}}\mathbf{k}$

17. $|\mathbf{v}| = \sqrt{2}, |\mathbf{u}| = 3, \mathbf{v}\cdot\mathbf{u} = \mathbf{u}\cdot\mathbf{v} = 3, \mathbf{v}\times\mathbf{u} = -2\mathbf{i} + 2\mathbf{j} - \mathbf{k},$
$\mathbf{u}\times\mathbf{v} = 2\mathbf{i} - 2\mathbf{j} + \mathbf{k}, |\mathbf{v}\times\mathbf{u}| = 3, \theta = \cos^{-1}\left(\frac{1}{\sqrt{2}}\right) = \frac{\pi}{4},$
$|\mathbf{u}|\cos\theta = \frac{3}{\sqrt{2}}, \text{proj}_{\mathbf{v}}\,\mathbf{u} = \frac{3}{2}(\mathbf{i} + \mathbf{j})$

19. $\frac{4}{3}(2\mathbf{i} + \mathbf{j} - \mathbf{k}) - \frac{1}{3}(5\mathbf{i} + \mathbf{j} + 11\mathbf{k})$

21. $\mathbf{u}\times\mathbf{v} = \mathbf{k}$

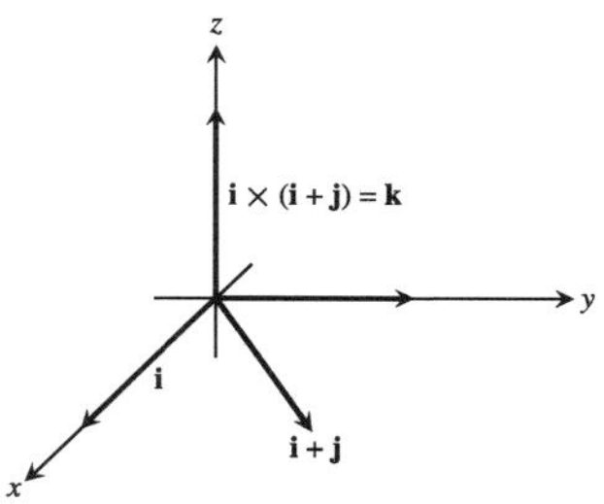

23. $2\sqrt{7}$ **25. (a)** $\sqrt{14}$ **(b)** 1 **29.** $\sqrt{78}/3$
31. $x = 1 - 3t, y = 2, z = 3 + 7t$ **33.** $\sqrt{2}$
35. $2x + y + z = 5$ **37.** $-9x + y + 7z = 4$
39. $\left(0, -\frac{1}{2}, -\frac{3}{2}\right), (-1, 0, -3), (1, -1, 0)$ **41.** $\pi/3$
43. $x = -5 + 5t, y = 3 - t, z = -3t$
45. (b) $x = -12t, y = 19/12 + 15t, z = 1/6 + 6t$
47. Yes; **v** is parallel to the plane. **49.** 3 **51.** $-3\mathbf{j} + 3\mathbf{k}$
53. $\frac{2}{\sqrt{35}}(5\mathbf{i} - \mathbf{j} - 3\mathbf{k})$ **55.** $\left(\frac{11}{9}, \frac{26}{9}, \frac{7}{9}\right)$
57. $(1, -2, -1); x = 1 - 5t, y = -2 + 3t, z = -1 + 4t$
59. $2x + 7y + 2z + 10 = 0$
61. (a) no **(b)** no **(c)** no **(d)** no **(e)** yes
63. $11/\sqrt{107}$

65.

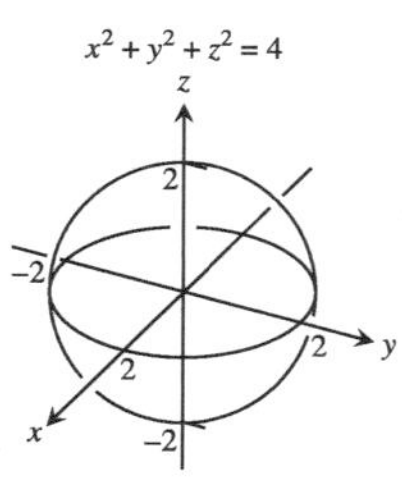

67.

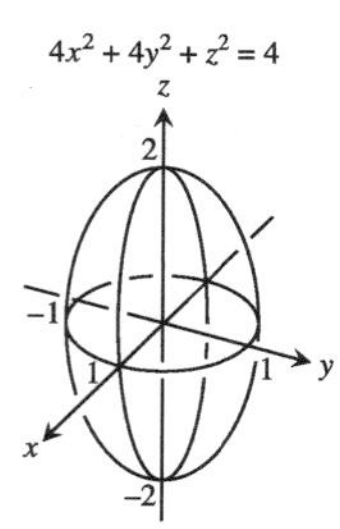

69.

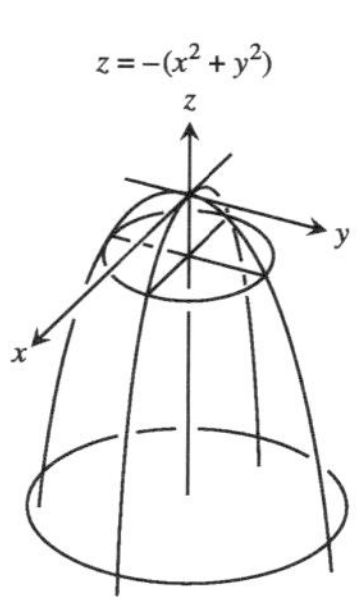

71.

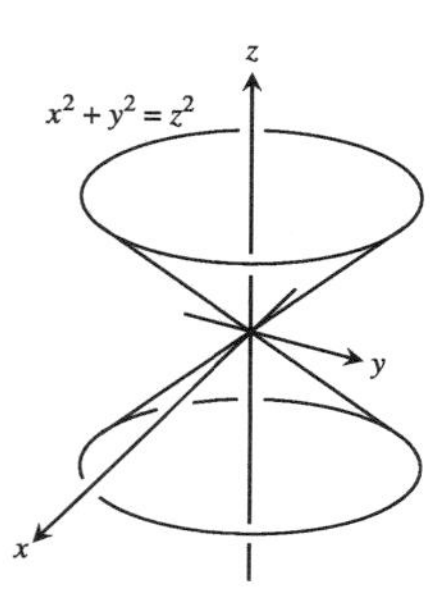

73.

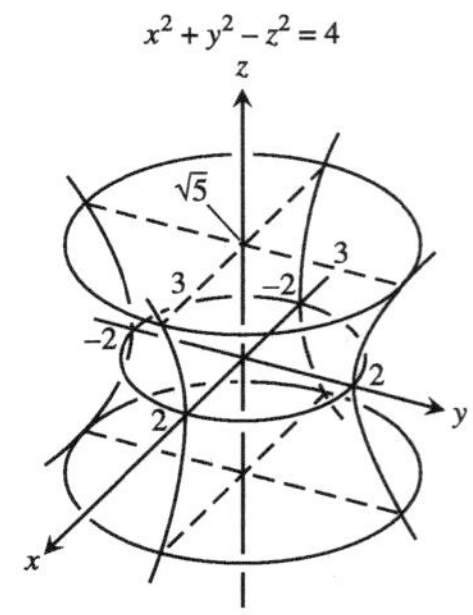

75.

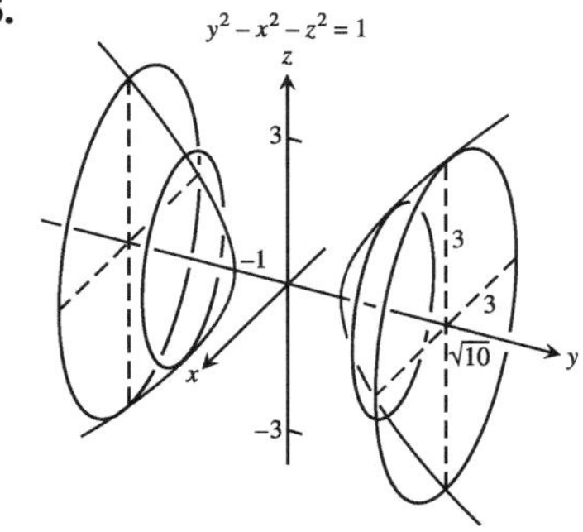

Additional and Advanced Exercises, pp. 902–904

1. $(26, 23, -1/3)$ **3.** $|\mathbf{F}| = 20$ lb

7. (a) $\overrightarrow{BD} = \overrightarrow{AD} - \overrightarrow{AB}$ **(b)** $\overrightarrow{AP} = \frac{1}{2}\overrightarrow{AB} + \frac{1}{2}\overrightarrow{AD}$

13. $\frac{32}{41}\mathbf{i} + \frac{23}{41}\mathbf{j} - \frac{13}{41}\mathbf{k}$

15. (a) 0, 0 **(b)** $-10\mathbf{i} - 2\mathbf{j} + 6\mathbf{k}, -9\mathbf{i} - 2\mathbf{j} + 7\mathbf{k}$
(c) $-4\mathbf{i} - 6\mathbf{j} + 2\mathbf{k}, \mathbf{i} - 2\mathbf{j} - 4\mathbf{k}$
(d) $-10\mathbf{i} - 10\mathbf{k}, -12\mathbf{i} - 4\mathbf{j} - 8\mathbf{k}$

25. (a) $|\mathbf{F}| = \frac{GMm}{d^2}\left(1 + \sum_{i=1}^{n}\frac{2}{(i^2 + 1)^{3/2}}\right)$ **(b)** Yes

CHAPTER 13

Section 13.1, pp. 916–920

1. $y = x^2 - 2x, \mathbf{v} = \mathbf{i} + 2\mathbf{j}, \mathbf{a} = 2\mathbf{j}$

3. $y = \frac{2}{9}x^2, \mathbf{v} = 3\mathbf{i} + 4\mathbf{j}, \mathbf{a} = 3\mathbf{i} + 8\mathbf{j}$

5. $t = \frac{\pi}{4}: \mathbf{v} = \frac{\sqrt{2}}{2}\mathbf{i} - \frac{\sqrt{2}}{2}\mathbf{j}, \mathbf{a} = \frac{-\sqrt{2}}{2}\mathbf{i} - \frac{\sqrt{2}}{2}\mathbf{j};$
$t = \pi/2: \mathbf{v} = -\mathbf{j}, \mathbf{a} = -\mathbf{i}$

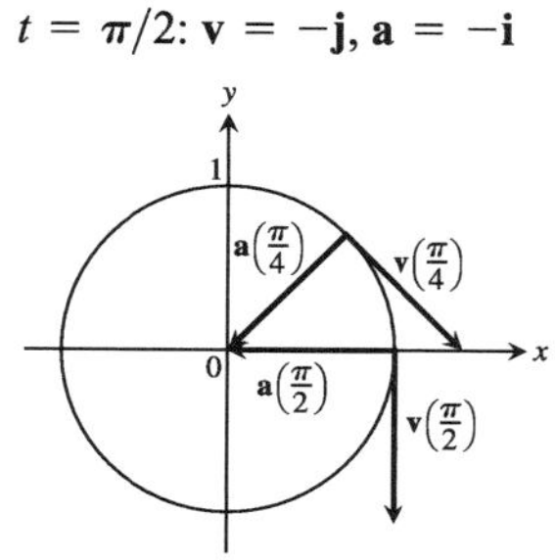

7. $t = \pi: \mathbf{v} = 2\mathbf{i}, \mathbf{a} = -\mathbf{j}; t = \frac{3\pi}{2}: \mathbf{v} = \mathbf{i} - \mathbf{j}, \mathbf{a} = -\mathbf{i}$

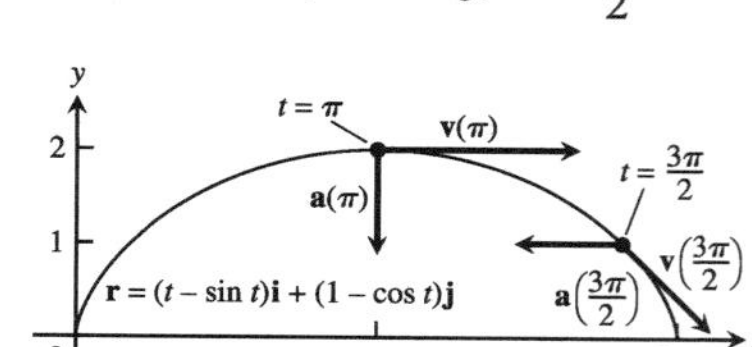

9. $\mathbf{v} = \mathbf{i} + 2t\mathbf{j} + 2\mathbf{k}$; $\mathbf{a} = 2\mathbf{j}$; speed: 3; direction: $\frac{1}{3}\mathbf{i} + \frac{2}{3}\mathbf{j} + \frac{2}{3}\mathbf{k}$; $\mathbf{v}(1) = 3\left(\frac{1}{3}\mathbf{i} + \frac{2}{3}\mathbf{j} + \frac{2}{3}\mathbf{k}\right)$

11. $\mathbf{v} = (-2\sin t)\mathbf{i} + (3\cos t)\mathbf{j} + 4\mathbf{k}$; $\mathbf{a} = (-2\cos t)\mathbf{i} - (3\sin t)\mathbf{j}$; speed: $2\sqrt{5}$; direction: $\left(-1/\sqrt{5}\right)\mathbf{i} + \left(2/\sqrt{5}\right)\mathbf{k}$; $\mathbf{v}(\pi/2) = 2\sqrt{5}\left[\left(-1/\sqrt{5}\right)\mathbf{i} + \left(2/\sqrt{5}\right)\mathbf{k}\right]$

13. $\mathbf{v} = \left(\frac{2}{t+1}\right)\mathbf{i} + 2t\mathbf{j} + t\mathbf{k}$; $\mathbf{a} = \left(\frac{-2}{(t+1)^2}\right)\mathbf{i} + 2\mathbf{j} + \mathbf{k}$; speed: $\sqrt{6}$; direction: $\frac{1}{\sqrt{6}}\mathbf{i} + \frac{2}{\sqrt{6}}\mathbf{j} + \frac{1}{\sqrt{6}}\mathbf{k}$; $\mathbf{v}(1) = \sqrt{6}\left(\frac{1}{\sqrt{6}}\mathbf{i} + \frac{2}{\sqrt{6}}\mathbf{j} + \frac{1}{\sqrt{6}}\mathbf{k}\right)$

15. $\pi/2$ **17.** $\pi/2$ **19.** $t = 0, \pi, 2\pi$

21. $(1/4)\mathbf{i} + 7\mathbf{j} + (3/2)\mathbf{k}$ **23.** $\left(\frac{\pi + 2\sqrt{2}}{2}\right)\mathbf{j} + 2\mathbf{k}$

25. $(\ln 4)\mathbf{i} + (\ln 4)\mathbf{j} + (\ln 2)\mathbf{k}$

27. $\mathbf{r}(t) = \left(\frac{-t^2}{2} + 1\right)\mathbf{i} + \left(\frac{-t^2}{2} + 2\right)\mathbf{j} + \left(\frac{-t^2}{2} + 3\right)\mathbf{k}$

29. $\mathbf{r}(t) = ((t+1)^{3/2} - 1)\mathbf{i} + (-e^{-t} + 1)\mathbf{j} + (\ln(t+1) + 1)\mathbf{k}$

31. $\mathbf{r}(t) = 8t\mathbf{i} + 8t\mathbf{j} + (-16t^2 + 100)\mathbf{k}$

33. $x = t, y = -1, z = 1 + t$ **35.** $x = at, y = a, z = 2\pi b + bt$

37. **(a)** (i): It has constant speed 1 (ii): Yes (iii): Counterclockwise (iv): Yes
(b) (i): It has constant speed 2 (ii): Yes (iii): Counterclockwise (iv): Yes
(c) (i): It has constant speed 1 (ii): Yes (iii): Counterclockwise (iv): It starts at $(0, -1)$ instead of $(1, 0)$
(d) (i): It has constant speed 1 (ii): Yes (iii): Clockwise (iv): Yes
(e) (i): It has variable speed (ii): No (iii): Counterclockwise (iv): Yes

39. $\mathbf{r}(t) = \left(\frac{3}{2}t^2 + \frac{6}{\sqrt{11}}t + 1\right)\mathbf{i} - \left(\frac{1}{2}t^2 + \frac{2}{\sqrt{11}}t - 2\right)\mathbf{j} + \left(\frac{1}{2}t^2 + \frac{2}{\sqrt{11}}t + 3\right)\mathbf{k} = \left(\frac{1}{2}t^2 + \frac{2t}{\sqrt{11}}\right)(3\mathbf{i} - \mathbf{j} + \mathbf{k}) + (\mathbf{i} + 2\mathbf{j} + 3\mathbf{k})$

41. $\mathbf{v} = 2\sqrt{5}\mathbf{i} + \sqrt{5}\mathbf{j}$

43. $\max|\mathbf{v}| = 3, \min|\mathbf{v}| = 2, \max|\mathbf{a}| = 3, \min|\mathbf{a}| = 2$

Section 13.2, pp. 927–930

1. 50 sec

3. **(a)** 72.2 sec; 25,510 m **(b)** 4020 m **(c)** 6378 m

5. $t \approx 2.135$ sec, $x \approx 66.43$ ft

7. **(a)** $v_0 \approx 9.9$ m/sec **(b)** $\alpha \approx 18.4°$ or $71.6°$

9. 190 mph **11.** The golf ball will clip the leaves at the top.

13. **(a)** 149 ft/sec **(b)** 2.25 sec **15.** 39.3° or 50.7°

17. 46.6 ft/sec **21.** 1.92 sec, 73.7 ft (approx.)

23. 4.00 ft, 7.80 ft/sec **25.** **(b)** $\mathbf{v}_0$ would bisect $\angle AOR$

27. **(a)** (Assuming that "x" is zero at the point of impact.) $\mathbf{r}(t) = (x(t))\mathbf{i} + (y(t))\mathbf{j}$, where $x(t) = (35\cos 27°)t$ and $y(t) = 4 + (35\sin 27°)t - 16t^2$.
(b) At $t \approx 0.497$ sec, it reaches its maximum height of about 7.945 ft.
(c) Range ≈ 37.45 ft; flight time ≈ 1.201 sec
(d) At $t \approx 0.254$ and $t \approx 0.740$ sec, when it is ≈ 29.532 and ≈ 14.376 ft from where it will land.
(e) Yes. It changes things because the ball won't clear the net.

31. **(a)** $\mathbf{r}(t) = (x(t))\mathbf{i} + (y(t))\mathbf{j}$, where $x(t) = \left(\frac{1}{0.08}\right)(1 - e^{-0.08t}) \cdot (152\cos 20° - 17.6)$ and $y(t) = 3 + \left(\frac{152}{0.08}\right)(1 - e^{-0.08t}) \cdot (\sin 20°) + \left(\frac{32}{0.08^2}\right)(1 - 0.08t - e^{-0.08t})$
(b) At $t \approx 1.527$ sec, it reaches its maximum height of about 41.893 ft.
(c) Range ≈ 351.734 ft, flight time ≈ 3.181 sec.
(d) At $t \approx 0.877$ and $t \approx 2.190$ sec, when it is about 106.028 and 251.530 ft from home plate.
(e) No. The wind gust would need to be greater than 12.846 ft/sec in the direction of the hit for the ball to clear the fence for a home run.

Section 13.3, pp. 935–936

1. $\mathbf{T} = \left(-\frac{2}{3}\sin t\right)\mathbf{i} + \left(\frac{2}{3}\cos t\right)\mathbf{j} + \frac{\sqrt{5}}{3}\mathbf{k}$, 3π

3. $\mathbf{T} = \frac{1}{\sqrt{1+t}}\mathbf{i} + \frac{\sqrt{t}}{\sqrt{1+t}}\mathbf{k}$, $\frac{52}{3}$

5. $\mathbf{T} = -\cos t\mathbf{j} + \sin t\mathbf{k}$, $\frac{3}{2}$

7. $\mathbf{T} = \left(\frac{\cos t - t\sin t}{t+1}\right)\mathbf{i} + \left(\frac{\sin t + t\cos t}{t+1}\right)\mathbf{j} + \left(\frac{\sqrt{2}t^{1/2}}{t+1}\right)\mathbf{k}$, $\frac{\pi^2}{2} + \pi$

9. $(0, 5, 24\pi)$ **11.** $s(t) = 5t$, $L = \frac{5\pi}{2}$

13. $s(t) = \sqrt{3}e^t - \sqrt{3}$, $L = \frac{3\sqrt{3}}{4}$ **15.** $\sqrt{2} + \ln\left(1 + \sqrt{2}\right)$

17. **(a)** Cylinder is $x^2 + y^2 = 1$, plane is $x + z = 1$.
(b) and **(c)**

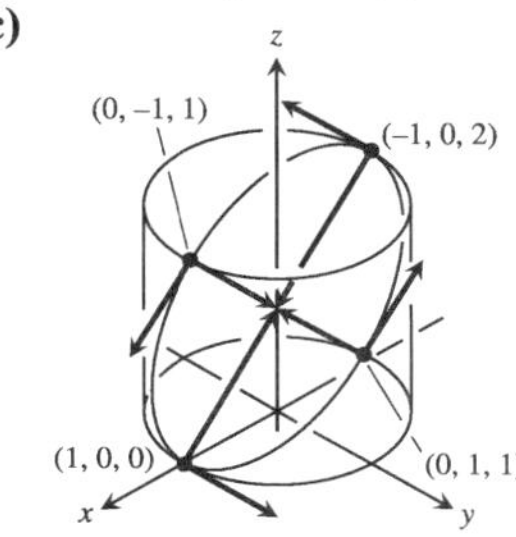

(d) $L = \int_0^{2\pi} \sqrt{1 + \sin^2 t}\, dt$ (e) $L \approx 7.64$

Section 13.4, pp. 942–943

1. $\mathbf{T} = (\cos t)\mathbf{i} - (\sin t)\mathbf{j}$, $\mathbf{N} = (-\sin t)\mathbf{i} - (\cos t)\mathbf{j}$, $\kappa = \cos t$

3. $\mathbf{T} = \dfrac{1}{\sqrt{1 + t^2}}\mathbf{i} - \dfrac{t}{\sqrt{1 + t^2}}\mathbf{j}$, $\mathbf{N} = \dfrac{-t}{\sqrt{1 + t^2}}\mathbf{i} - \dfrac{1}{\sqrt{1 + t^2}}\mathbf{j}$,
$\kappa = \dfrac{1}{2\left(\sqrt{1 + t^2}\right)^3}$

5. (b) $\cos x$

7. (b) $\mathbf{N} = \dfrac{-2e^{2t}}{\sqrt{1 + 4e^{4t}}}\mathbf{i} + \dfrac{1}{\sqrt{1 + 4e^{4t}}}\mathbf{j}$
(c) $\mathbf{N} = -\frac{1}{2}\left(\sqrt{4 - t^2}\,\mathbf{i} + t\mathbf{j}\right)$

9. $\mathbf{T} = \dfrac{3\cos t}{5}\mathbf{i} - \dfrac{3\sin t}{5}\mathbf{j} + \dfrac{4}{5}\mathbf{k}$, $\mathbf{N} = (-\sin t)\mathbf{i} - (\cos t)\mathbf{j}$,
$\kappa = \dfrac{3}{25}$

11. $\mathbf{T} = \left(\dfrac{\cos t - \sin t}{\sqrt{2}}\right)\mathbf{i} + \left(\dfrac{\cos t + \sin t}{\sqrt{2}}\right)\mathbf{j}$,
$\mathbf{N} = \left(\dfrac{-\cos t - \sin t}{\sqrt{2}}\right)\mathbf{i} + \left(\dfrac{-\sin t + \cos t}{\sqrt{2}}\right)\mathbf{j}$,
$\kappa = \dfrac{1}{e^t\sqrt{2}}$

13. $\mathbf{T} = \dfrac{t}{\sqrt{t^2 + 1}}\mathbf{i} + \dfrac{1}{\sqrt{t^2 + 1}}\mathbf{j}$, $\mathbf{N} = \dfrac{\mathbf{i}}{\sqrt{t^2 + 1}} - \dfrac{t\mathbf{j}}{\sqrt{t^2 + 1}}$,
$\kappa = \dfrac{1}{t(t^2 + 1)^{3/2}}$

15. $\mathbf{T} = \left(\operatorname{sech}\dfrac{t}{a}\right)\mathbf{i} + \left(\tanh\dfrac{t}{a}\right)\mathbf{j}$,
$\mathbf{N} = \left(-\tanh\dfrac{t}{a}\right)\mathbf{i} + \left(\operatorname{sech}\dfrac{t}{a}\right)\mathbf{j}$,
$\kappa = \dfrac{1}{a}\operatorname{sech}^2\dfrac{t}{a}$

19. $1/(2b)$ 21. $\left(x - \dfrac{\pi}{2}\right)^2 + y^2 = 1$

23. $\kappa(x) = 2/(1 + 4x^2)^{3/2}$ 25. $\kappa(x) = |\sin x|/(1 + \cos^2 x)^{3/2}$

Section 13.5, pp. 949–950

1. $\mathbf{B} = \left(\dfrac{4}{5}\cos t\right)\mathbf{i} - \left(\dfrac{4}{5}\sin t\right)\mathbf{j} - \dfrac{3}{5}\mathbf{k}$, $\tau = -\dfrac{4}{25}$

3. $\mathbf{B} = \mathbf{k}$, $\tau = 0$ 5. $\mathbf{B} = -\mathbf{k}$, $\tau = 0$ 7. $\mathbf{B} = \mathbf{k}$, $\tau = 0$

9. $\mathbf{a} = |a|\mathbf{N}$ 11. $\mathbf{a}(1) = \dfrac{4}{3}\mathbf{T} + \dfrac{2\sqrt{5}}{3}\mathbf{N}$ 13. $\mathbf{a}(0) = 2\mathbf{N}$

15. $\mathbf{r}\left(\dfrac{\pi}{4}\right) = \dfrac{\sqrt{2}}{2}\mathbf{i} + \dfrac{\sqrt{2}}{2}\mathbf{j} - \mathbf{k}$, $\mathbf{T}\left(\dfrac{\pi}{4}\right) = -\dfrac{\sqrt{2}}{2}\mathbf{i} + \dfrac{\sqrt{2}}{2}\mathbf{j}$,
$\mathbf{N}\left(\dfrac{\pi}{4}\right) = -\dfrac{\sqrt{2}}{2}\mathbf{i} - \dfrac{\sqrt{2}}{2}\mathbf{j}$, $\mathbf{B}\left(\dfrac{\pi}{4}\right) = \mathbf{k}$; osculating plane:
$z = -1$; normal plane: $-x + y = 0$; rectifying plane:
$x + y = \sqrt{2}$

17. Yes. If the car is moving on a curved path ($\kappa \neq 0$), then $a_N = \kappa|\mathbf{v}|^2 \neq 0$ and $\mathbf{a} \neq \mathbf{0}$.

21. $|\mathbf{F}| = \kappa\left(m\left(\dfrac{ds}{dt}\right)^2\right)$ 23. $\kappa = \dfrac{1}{t}$, $\rho = t$

29. Components of **v**: -1.8701, 0.7089, 1.0000
Components of **a**: -1.6960, -2.0307, 0
Speed: 2.2361; Components of **T**: -0.8364, 0.3170, 0.4472
Components of **N**: -0.4143, -0.8998, -0.1369
Components of **B**: 0.3590, -0.2998, 0.8839; Curvature: 0.5060
Torsion: 0.2813; Tangential component of acceleration: 0.7746
Normal component of acceleration: 2.5298

31. Components of **v**: 2.0000, 0, 0.1629
Components of **a**: 0, -1.0000, 0.0086; Speed: 2.0066
Components of **T**: 0.9967, 0, 0.0812
Components of **N**: -0.0007, -1.0000, 0.0086
Components of **B**: 0.0812, -0.0086, -0.9967;
Curvature: 0.2484
Torsion: -0.0411; Tangential component of acceleration: 0.0007
Normal component of acceleration: 1.0000

Section 13.6, pp. 958–959

1. $T = 93.2$ min 3. $a = 6764$ km 5. $D = 6501$ km

7. (a) 42,168 km (b) 35,789 km
(c) *Syncom 3*, *GOES 4*, and *Intelsat 5*

9. $a = 383{,}200$ km from the center of Earth, or about 376,821 km from the surface

11. 2.97×10^{-19} sec^2/m^3, 9.902×10^{-14} sec^2/m^3, 8.045×10^{-12} sec^2/m^3

Practice Exercises, pp. 960–962

1. $\dfrac{x^2}{16} + \dfrac{y^2}{2} = 1$

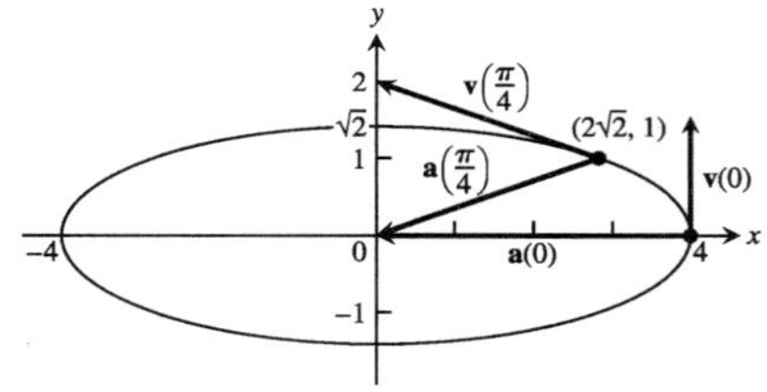

At $t = 0$: $a_T = 0$, $a_N = 4$, $\kappa = 2$;
At $t = \dfrac{\pi}{4}$: $a_T = \dfrac{7}{3}$, $a_N = \dfrac{4\sqrt{2}}{3}$, $\kappa = \dfrac{4\sqrt{2}}{27}$

3. $|\mathbf{v}|_{\max} = 1$ **5.** $\kappa = 1/5$ **7.** $dy/dt = -x$; clockwise
11. Shot put is on the ground, about 66 ft, 3 in. from the stopboard.
15. **(a)** 59.19 ft/sec **(b)** 74.58 ft/sec **19.** $\kappa = \pi s$
21. Length $= \frac{\pi}{4}\sqrt{1+\frac{\pi^2}{16}} + \ln\left(\frac{\pi}{4}+\sqrt{1+\frac{\pi^2}{16}}\right)$
23. $\mathbf{T}(0) = \frac{2}{3}\mathbf{i} - \frac{2}{3}\mathbf{j} + \frac{1}{3}\mathbf{k}$; $\mathbf{N}(0) = \frac{1}{\sqrt{2}}\mathbf{i} + \frac{1}{\sqrt{2}}\mathbf{j}$;

$\mathbf{B}(0) = -\frac{1}{3\sqrt{2}}\mathbf{i} + \frac{1}{3\sqrt{2}}\mathbf{j} + \frac{4}{3\sqrt{2}}\mathbf{k}$; $\kappa = \frac{\sqrt{2}}{3}$; $\tau = \frac{1}{6}$
25. $\mathbf{T}(\ln 2) = \frac{1}{\sqrt{17}}\mathbf{i} + \frac{4}{\sqrt{17}}\mathbf{j}$; $\mathbf{N}(\ln 2) = -\frac{4}{\sqrt{17}}\mathbf{i} + \frac{1}{\sqrt{17}}\mathbf{j}$;

$\mathbf{B}(\ln 2) = \mathbf{k}$; $\kappa = \frac{8}{17\sqrt{17}}$; $\tau = 0$
27. $\mathbf{a}(0) = 10\mathbf{T} + 6\mathbf{N}$
29. $\mathbf{T} = \left(\frac{1}{\sqrt{2}}\cos t\right)\mathbf{i} - (\sin t)\mathbf{j} + \left(\frac{1}{\sqrt{2}}\cos t\right)\mathbf{k}$;

$\mathbf{N} = \left(-\frac{1}{\sqrt{2}}\sin t\right)\mathbf{i} - (\cos t)\mathbf{j} - \left(\frac{1}{\sqrt{2}}\sin t\right)\mathbf{k}$;

$\mathbf{B} = \frac{1}{\sqrt{2}}\mathbf{i} - \frac{1}{\sqrt{2}}\mathbf{k}$; $\kappa = \frac{1}{\sqrt{2}}$; $\tau = 0$
31. $\pi/3$ **33.** $x = 1 + t, y = t, z = -t$
35. 5971 km, 1.639×10^7 km^2, 3.21% visible

Additional and Advanced Exercises, pp. 962–964

1. **(a)** $\mathbf{r}(t) = \left(-\frac{8}{15}t^3 + 4t^2\right)\mathbf{i} + (-20t + 100)\mathbf{j}$; **(b)** $\frac{100}{3}$ m

3. **(a)** $\left.\frac{d\theta}{dt}\right|_{\theta=2\pi} = 2\sqrt{\frac{\pi g b}{a^2+b^2}}$

(b) $\theta = \frac{gbt^2}{2(a^2+b^2)}, z = \frac{gb^2t^2}{2(a^2+b^2)}$

(c) $\mathbf{v}(t) = \frac{gbt}{\sqrt{a^2+b^2}}\mathbf{T}$; $\frac{d^2\mathbf{r}}{dt^2} = \frac{bg}{\sqrt{a^2+b^2}}\mathbf{T} + a\left(\frac{bgt}{a^2+b^2}\right)^2\mathbf{N}$

There is no component in the direction of **B**.

7. **(a)** $\frac{dx}{dt} = \dot{r}\cos\theta - r\dot{\theta}\sin\theta, \frac{dy}{dt} = \dot{r}\sin\theta + r\dot{\theta}\cos\theta$

(b) $\frac{dr}{dt} = \dot{x}\cos\theta + \dot{y}\sin\theta, r\frac{d\theta}{dt} = -\dot{x}\sin\theta + \dot{y}\cos\theta$

9. **(a)** $\mathbf{a}(1) = -9\mathbf{u}_r - 6\mathbf{u}_\theta, \mathbf{v}(1) = -\mathbf{u}_r + 3\mathbf{u}_\theta$ **(b)** 6.5 in.
11. **(c)** $\mathbf{v} = \dot{r}\mathbf{u}_r + r\dot{\theta}\mathbf{u}_\theta + \dot{z}\mathbf{k}, \mathbf{a} = (\ddot{r} - r\dot{\theta}^2)\mathbf{u}_r + (r\ddot{\theta} + 2\dot{r}\dot{\theta})\mathbf{u}_\theta + \ddot{z}\mathbf{k}$

CHAPTER 14

Section 14.1, pp. 973–975

1. **(a)** All points in the xy-plane **(b)** All reals
(c) The lines $y - x = c$ **(d)** No boundary points
(e) Both open and closed **(f)** Unbounded
3. **(a)** All points in the xy-plane **(b)** $z \geq 0$
(c) For $f(x, y) = 0$, the origin; for $f(x, y) \neq 0$, ellipses with the center (0, 0), and major and minor axes, along the x- and y-axes, respectively
(d) No boundary points **(e)** Both open and closed
(f) Unbounded
5. **(a)** All points in the xy-plane **(b)** All reals
(c) For $f(x, y) = 0$, the x- and y-axes; for $f(x, y) \neq 0$, hyperbolas with the x- and y-axes as asymptotes
(d) No boundary points **(e)** Both open and closed
(f) Unbounded
7. **(a)** All (x, y) satisfying $x^2 + y^2 < 16$ **(b)** $z \geq 1/4$
(c) Circles centered at the origin with radii $r < 4$
(d) Boundary is the circle $x^2 + y^2 = 16$
(e) Open **(f)** Bounded
9. **(a)** $(x, y) \neq (0, 0)$ **(b)** All reals
(c) The circles with center (0, 0) and radii $r > 0$
(d) Boundary is the single point (0, 0)
(e) Open **(f)** Unbounded
11. **(a)** All (x, y) satisfying $-1 \leq y - x \leq 1$
(b) $-\pi/2 \leq z \leq \pi/2$
(c) Straight lines of the form $y - x = c$ where $-1 \leq c \leq 1$
(d) Boundary is two straight lines $y = 1 + x$ and $y = -1 + x$
(e) Closed **(f)** Unbounded
13. (f) **15.** (a) **17.** (d)

19. **(a)**

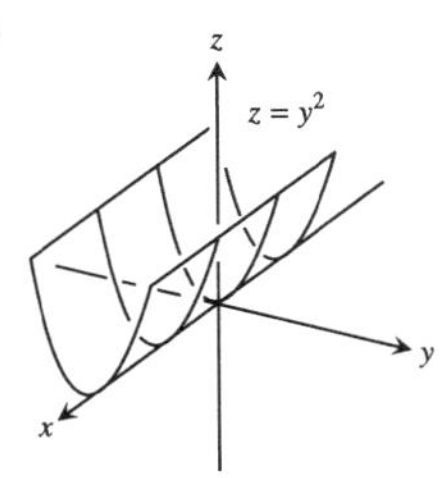

(b)

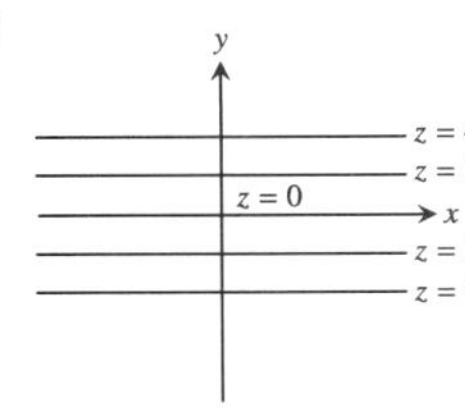

21. **(a)**

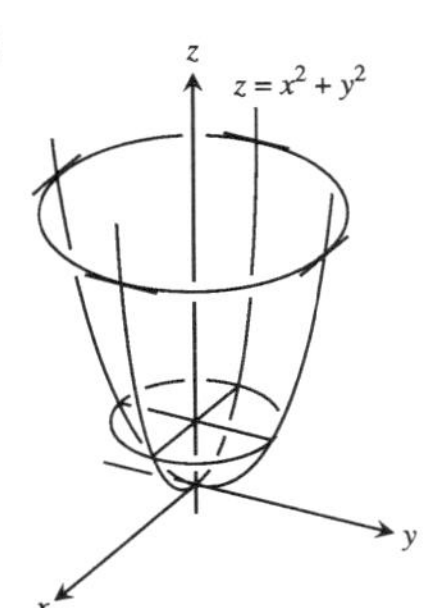

(b)

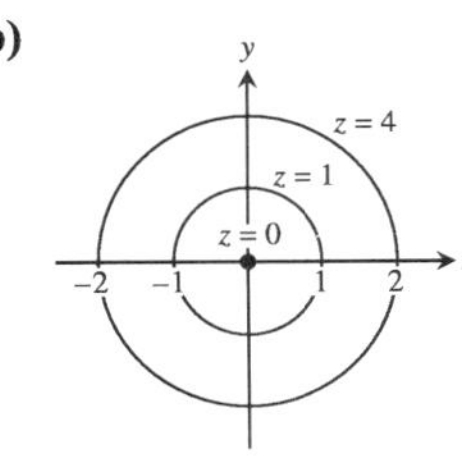

23. (a) 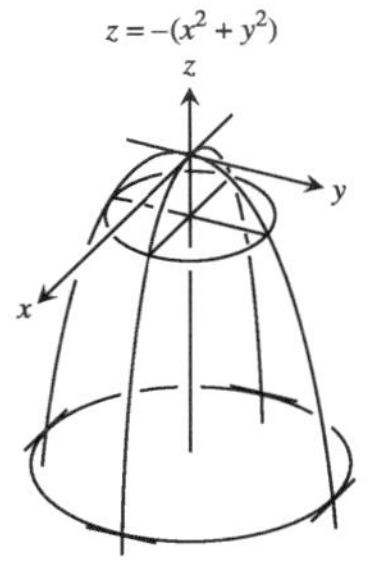

(b) 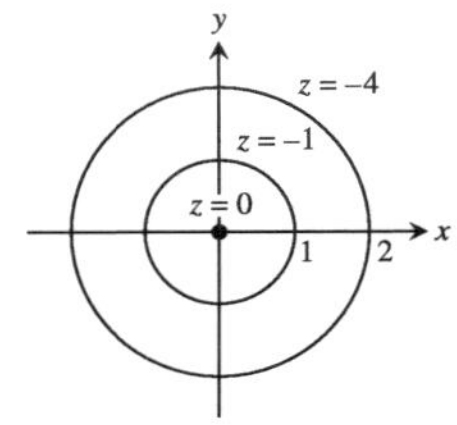

25. (a) 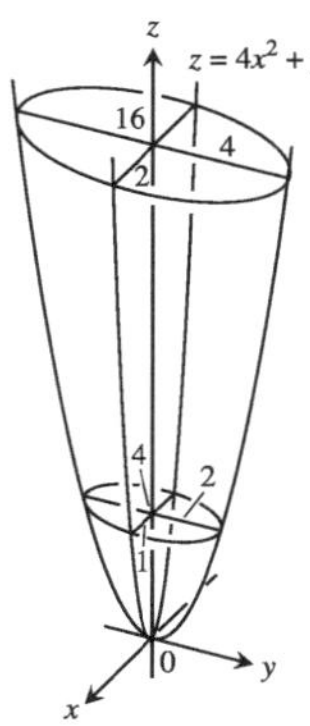

(b) 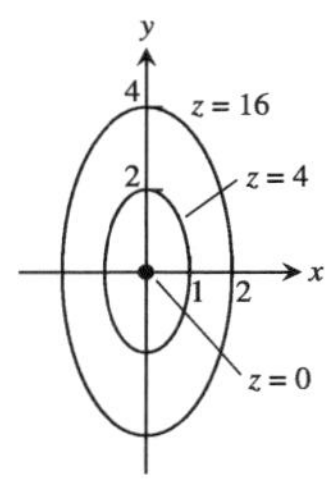

27. (a) 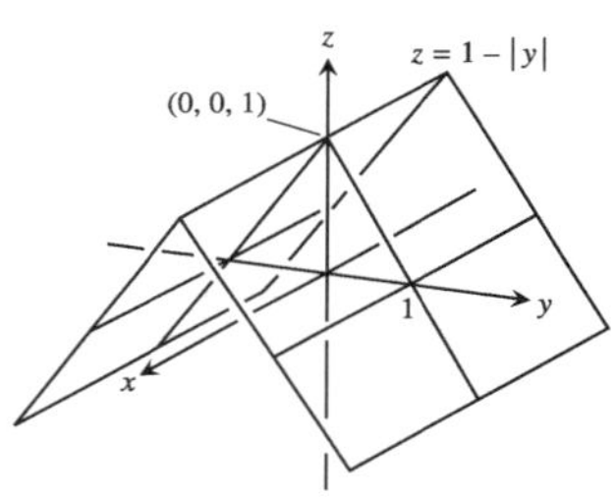

(b) 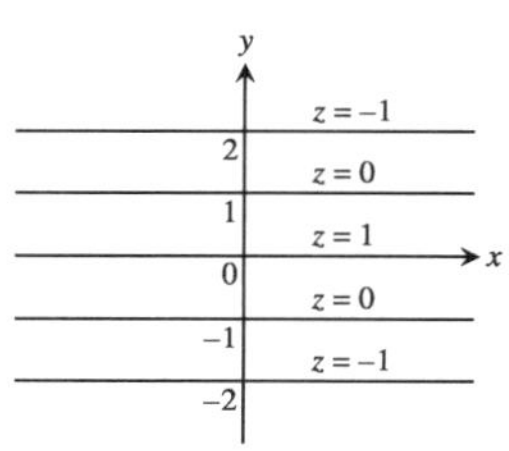

29. $x^2 + y^2 = 10$ **31.** $\tan^{-1} y - \tan^{-1} x = 2 \tan^{-1} \sqrt{2}$

33. 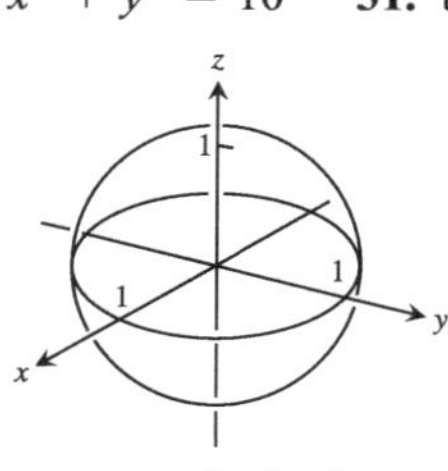

35. 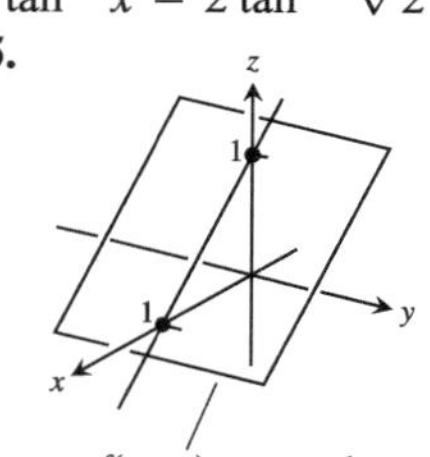

37. 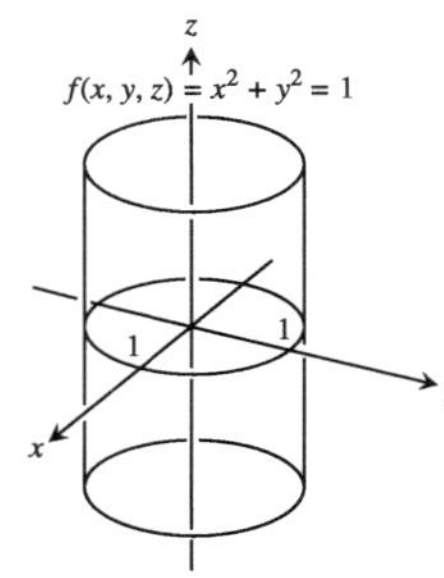

39. 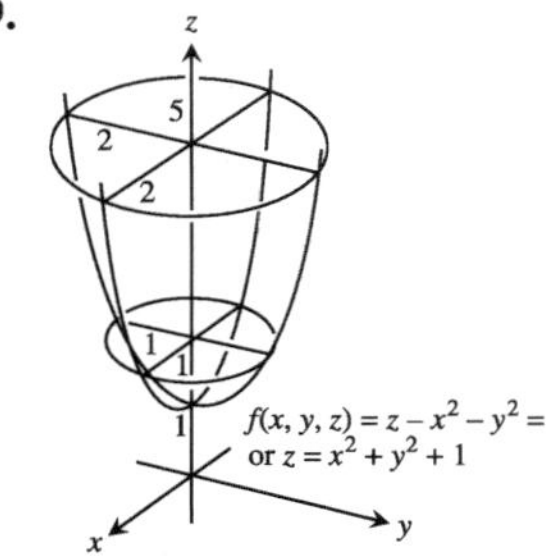

41. $\sqrt{x - y} - \ln z = 2$ **43.** $\dfrac{x + y}{z} = \ln 2$ **45.** Yes, 2000
47. 63 km

Section 14.2, pp. 982–984

1. 5/2 **3.** $2\sqrt{6}$ **5.** 1 **7.** 1/2 **9.** 1 **11.** 0 **13.** 0
15. −1 **17.** 2 **19.** 1/4 **21.** 19/12 **23.** 2 **25.** 3
27. **(a)** All (x, y) **(b)** All (x, y) except $(0, 0)$
29. **(a)** All (x, y) except where $x = 0$ or $y = 0$ **(b)** All (x, y)
31. **(a)** All (x, y, z) **(b)** All (x, y, z) except the interior of the cylinder $x^2 + y^2 = 1$
33. **(a)** All (x, y, z) with $z \neq 0$ **(b)** All (x, y, z) with $x^2 + z^2 \neq 1$
35. Consider paths along $y = x, x > 0$, and along $y = x, x < 0$
37. Consider the paths $y = kx^2$, k a constant
39. Consider the paths $y = mx$, m a constant, $m \neq -1$
41. Consider the paths $y = kx^2$, k a constant, $k \neq 0$
43. No **45.** The limit is 1 **47.** The limit is 0
49. **(a)** $f(x, y)|_{y=mx} = \sin 2\theta$ where $\tan \theta = m$ **51.** 0
53. Does not exist **55.** $\pi/2$ **57.** $f(0, 0) = \ln 3$
59. $\delta = 0.1$ **61.** $\delta = 0.005$ **63.** $\delta = \sqrt{0.015}$
65. $\delta = 0.005$

Section 14.3, pp. 994–996

1. $\dfrac{\partial f}{\partial x} = 4x, \dfrac{\partial f}{\partial y} = -3$ **3.** $\dfrac{\partial f}{\partial x} = 2x(y + 2), \dfrac{\partial f}{\partial y} = x^2 - 1$

5. $\dfrac{\partial f}{\partial x} = 2y(xy - 1), \dfrac{\partial f}{\partial y} = 2x(xy - 1)$

7. $\dfrac{\partial f}{\partial x} = \dfrac{x}{\sqrt{x^2 + y^2}}, \dfrac{\partial f}{\partial y} = \dfrac{y}{\sqrt{x^2 + y^2}}$

9. $\dfrac{\partial f}{\partial x} = \dfrac{-1}{(x + y)^2}, \dfrac{\partial f}{\partial y} = \dfrac{-1}{(x + y)^2}$

11. $\dfrac{\partial f}{\partial x} = \dfrac{-y^2 - 1}{(xy - 1)^2}, \dfrac{\partial f}{\partial y} = \dfrac{-x^2 - 1}{(xy - 1)^2}$

13. $\dfrac{\partial f}{\partial x} = e^{x+y+1}, \dfrac{\partial f}{\partial y} = e^{x+y+1}$ **15.** $\dfrac{\partial f}{\partial x} = \dfrac{1}{x + y}, \dfrac{\partial f}{\partial y} = \dfrac{1}{x + y}$

17. $\dfrac{\partial f}{\partial x} = 2 \sin (x - 3y) \cos (x - 3y),$

$\dfrac{\partial f}{\partial y} = -6 \sin (x - 3y) \cos (x - 3y)$

19. $\frac{\partial f}{\partial x} = yx^{y-1}, \frac{\partial f}{\partial y} = x^y \ln x$ 21. $\frac{\partial f}{\partial x} = -g(x), \frac{\partial f}{\partial y} = g(y)$

23. $f_x = y^2, f_y = 2xy, f_z = -4z$

25. $f_x = 1, f_y = -y(y^2 + z^2)^{-1/2}, f_z = -z(y^2 + z^2)^{-1/2}$

27. $f_x = \frac{yz}{\sqrt{1 - x^2y^2z^2}}, f_y = \frac{xz}{\sqrt{1 - x^2y^2z^2}}, f_z = \frac{xy}{\sqrt{1 - x^2y^2z^2}}$

29. $f_x = \frac{1}{x + 2y + 3z}, f_y = \frac{2}{x + 2y + 3z}, f_z = \frac{3}{x + 2y + 3z}$

31. $f_x = -2xe^{-(x^2+y^2+z^2)}, f_y = -2ye^{-(x^2+y^2+z^2)}, f_z = -2ze^{-(x^2+y^2+z^2)}$

33. $f_x = \operatorname{sech}^2(x + 2y + 3z), f_y = 2\operatorname{sech}^2(x + 2y + 3z),$
$f_z = 3\operatorname{sech}^2(x + 2y + 3z)$

35. $\frac{\partial f}{\partial t} = -2\pi \sin(2\pi t - \alpha), \frac{\partial f}{\partial \alpha} = \sin(2\pi t - \alpha)$

37. $\frac{\partial h}{\partial \rho} = \sin\phi\cos\theta, \frac{\partial h}{\partial \phi} = \rho\cos\phi\cos\theta, \frac{\partial h}{\partial \theta} = -\rho\sin\phi\sin\theta$

39. $W_P(P, V, \delta, v, g) = V, W_V(P, V, \delta, v, g) = P + \frac{\delta v^2}{2g},$
$W_\delta(P, V, \delta, v, g) = \frac{Vv^2}{2g}, W_v(P, V, \delta, v, g) = \frac{V\delta v}{g},$
$W_g(P, V, \delta, v, g) = -\frac{V\delta v^2}{2g^2}$

41. $\frac{\partial f}{\partial x} = 1 + y, \frac{\partial f}{\partial y} = 1 + x, \frac{\partial^2 f}{\partial x^2} = 0, \frac{\partial^2 f}{\partial y^2} = 0,$
$\frac{\partial^2 f}{\partial y\,\partial x} = \frac{\partial^2 f}{\partial x\,\partial y} = 1$

43. $\frac{\partial g}{\partial x} = 2xy + y\cos x, \frac{\partial g}{\partial y} = x^2 - \sin y + \sin x,$
$\frac{\partial^2 g}{\partial x^2} = 2y - y\sin x, \frac{\partial^2 g}{\partial y^2} = -\cos y,$
$\frac{\partial^2 g}{\partial y\,\partial x} = \frac{\partial^2 g}{\partial x\,\partial y} = 2x + \cos x$

45. $\frac{\partial r}{\partial x} = \frac{1}{x + y}, \frac{\partial r}{\partial y} = \frac{1}{x + y}, \frac{\partial^2 r}{\partial x^2} = \frac{-1}{(x + y)^2}, \frac{\partial^2 r}{\partial y^2} = \frac{-1}{(x + y)^2},$
$\frac{\partial^2 r}{\partial y\,\partial x} = \frac{\partial^2 r}{\partial x\,\partial y} = \frac{-1}{(x + y)^2}$

47. $\frac{\partial w}{\partial x} = \frac{2}{2x + 3y}, \frac{\partial w}{\partial y} = \frac{3}{2x + 3y}, \frac{\partial^2 w}{\partial y\,\partial x} = \frac{\partial^2 w}{\partial x\,\partial y} = \frac{-6}{(2x + 3y)^2}$

49. $\frac{\partial w}{\partial x} = y^2 + 2xy^3 + 3x^2y^4, \frac{\partial w}{\partial y} = 2xy + 3x^2y^2 + 4x^3y^3,$
$\frac{\partial^2 w}{\partial y\,\partial x} = \frac{\partial^2 w}{\partial x\,\partial y} = 2y + 6xy^2 + 12x^2y^3$

51. **(a)** x first **(b)** y first **(c)** x first
(d) x first **(e)** y first **(f)** y first

53. $f_x(1, 2) = -13, f_y(1, 2) = -2$ 55. 12 57. -2

59. $\frac{\partial A}{\partial a} = \frac{a}{bc\sin A}, \frac{\partial A}{\partial b} = \frac{c\cos A - b}{bc\sin A}$ 61. $v_x = \frac{\ln v}{(\ln u)(\ln v) - 1}$

77. Yes

Section 14.4, pp. 1003–1005

1. **(a)** $\frac{dw}{dt} = 0,$ **(b)** $\frac{dw}{dt}(\pi) = 0$

3. **(a)** $\frac{dw}{dt} = 1,$ **(b)** $\frac{dw}{dt}(3) = 1$

5. **(a)** $\frac{dw}{dt} = 4t\tan^{-1}t + 1,$ **(b)** $\frac{dw}{dt}(1) = \pi + 1$

7. **(a)** $\frac{\partial z}{\partial u} = 4\cos v\ln(u\sin v) + 4\cos v,$
$\frac{\partial z}{\partial v} = -4u\sin v\ln(u\sin v) + \frac{4u\cos^2 v}{\sin v}$
(b) $\frac{\partial z}{\partial u} = \sqrt{2}(\ln 2 + 2), \frac{\partial z}{\partial v} = -2\sqrt{2}(\ln 2 - 2)$

9. **(a)** $\frac{\partial w}{\partial u} = 2u + 4uv, \frac{\partial w}{\partial v} = -2v + 2u^2$
(b) $\frac{\partial w}{\partial u} = 3, \frac{\partial w}{\partial v} = -\frac{3}{2}$

11. **(a)** $\frac{\partial u}{\partial x} = 0, \frac{\partial u}{\partial y} = \frac{z}{(z - y)^2}, \frac{\partial u}{\partial z} = \frac{-y}{(z - y)^2}$
(b) $\frac{\partial u}{\partial x} = 0, \frac{\partial u}{\partial y} = 1, \frac{\partial u}{\partial z} = -2$

13. $\frac{dz}{dt} = \frac{\partial z}{\partial x}\frac{dx}{dt} + \frac{\partial z}{\partial y}\frac{dy}{dt}$

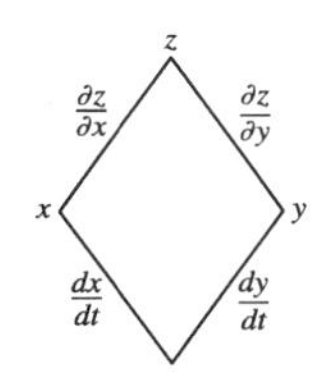

15. $\frac{\partial w}{\partial u} = \frac{\partial w}{\partial x}\frac{\partial x}{\partial u} + \frac{\partial w}{\partial y}\frac{\partial y}{\partial u} + \frac{\partial w}{\partial z}\frac{\partial z}{\partial u},$
$\frac{\partial w}{\partial v} = \frac{\partial w}{\partial x}\frac{\partial x}{\partial v} + \frac{\partial w}{\partial y}\frac{\partial y}{\partial v} + \frac{\partial w}{\partial z}\frac{\partial z}{\partial v}$

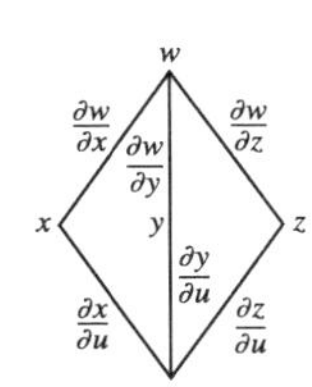

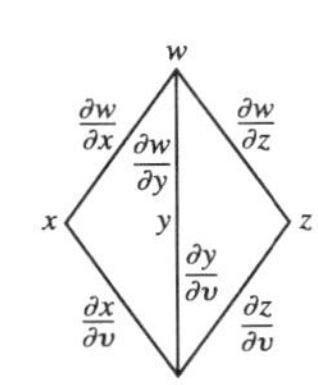

17. $\frac{\partial w}{\partial u} = \frac{\partial w}{\partial x}\frac{\partial x}{\partial u} + \frac{\partial w}{\partial y}\frac{\partial y}{\partial u}, \frac{\partial w}{\partial v} = \frac{\partial w}{\partial x}\frac{\partial x}{\partial v} + \frac{\partial w}{\partial y}\frac{\partial y}{\partial v}$

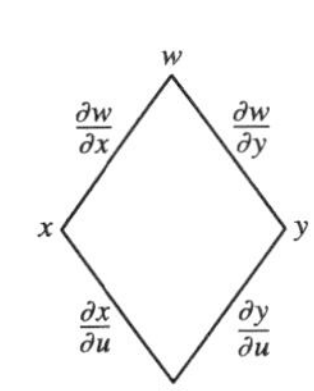

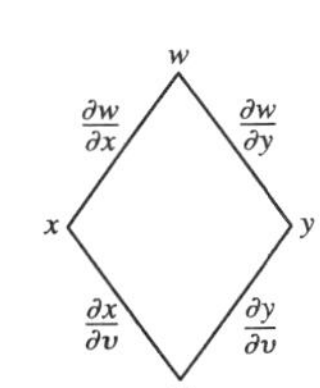

19. $\frac{\partial z}{\partial t} = \frac{\partial z}{\partial x}\frac{\partial x}{\partial t} + \frac{\partial z}{\partial y}\frac{\partial y}{\partial t}, \frac{\partial z}{\partial s} = \frac{\partial z}{\partial x}\frac{\partial x}{\partial s} + \frac{\partial z}{\partial y}\frac{\partial y}{\partial s}$

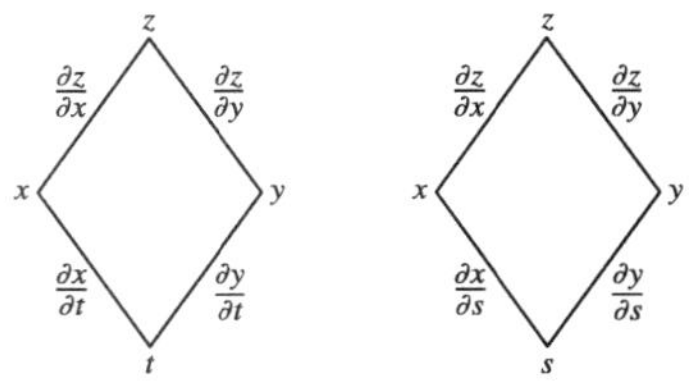

21. $\frac{\partial w}{\partial s} = \frac{dw}{du}\frac{\partial u}{\partial s}, \frac{\partial w}{\partial t} = \frac{dw}{du}\frac{\partial u}{\partial t}$

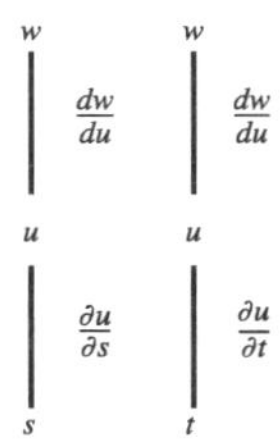

23. $\frac{\partial w}{\partial r} = \frac{\partial w}{\partial x}\frac{dx}{dr} + \frac{\partial w}{\partial y}\frac{dy}{dr} = \frac{\partial w}{\partial x}\frac{dx}{dr}$ since $\frac{dy}{dr} = 0$,

$\frac{\partial w}{\partial s} = \frac{\partial w}{\partial x}\frac{dx}{ds} + \frac{\partial w}{\partial y}\frac{dy}{ds} = \frac{\partial w}{\partial y}\frac{dy}{ds}$ since $\frac{dx}{ds} = 0$

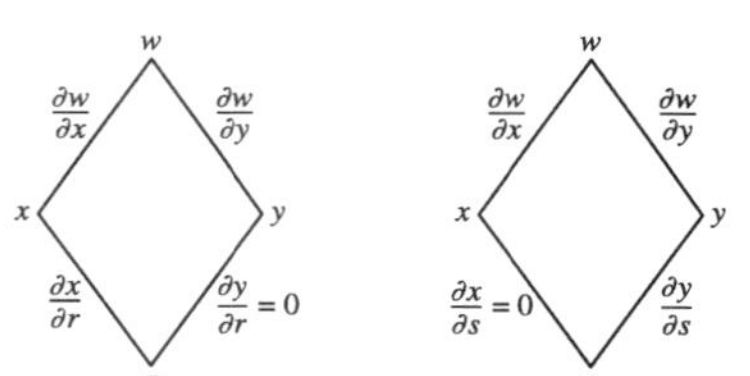

25. $4/3$ 27. $-4/5$ 29. $\frac{\partial z}{\partial x} = \frac{1}{4}, \frac{\partial z}{\partial y} = -\frac{3}{4}$

31. $\frac{\partial z}{\partial x} = -1, \frac{\partial z}{\partial y} = -1$ 33. 12 35. -7

37. $\frac{\partial z}{\partial u} = 2, \frac{\partial z}{\partial v} = 1$ 39. -0.00005 amps/sec

45. $(\cos 1, \sin 1, 1)$ and $(\cos(-2), \sin(-2), -2)$

47. (a) Maximum at $\left(-\frac{\sqrt{2}}{2}, \frac{\sqrt{2}}{2}\right)$ and $\left(\frac{\sqrt{2}}{2}, -\frac{\sqrt{2}}{2}\right)$; minimum at $\left(\frac{\sqrt{2}}{2}, \frac{\sqrt{2}}{2}\right)$ and $\left(-\frac{\sqrt{2}}{2}, -\frac{\sqrt{2}}{2}\right)$

(b) Max $= 6$, min $= 2$

49. $2x\sqrt{x^8 + x^3} + \int_0^{x^2} \frac{3x^2}{2\sqrt{t^4 + x^3}}\,dt$

Section 14.5, pp. 1013–1014

1.

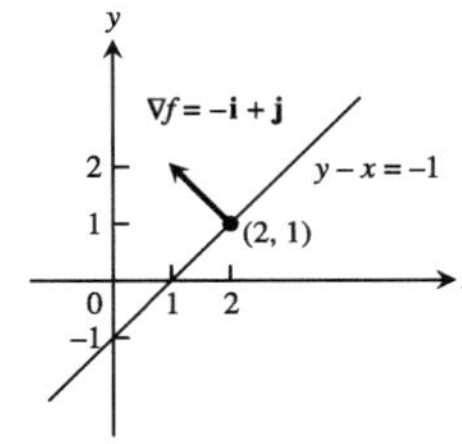

3.

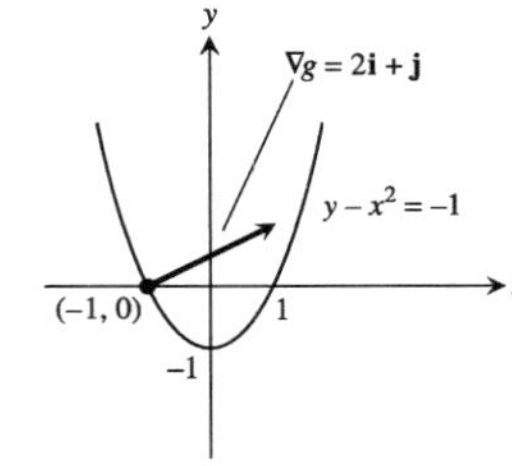

5. $\nabla f = 3\mathbf{i} + 2\mathbf{j} - 4\mathbf{k}$ 7. $\nabla f = -\frac{26}{27}\mathbf{i} + \frac{23}{54}\mathbf{j} - \frac{23}{54}\mathbf{k}$

9. -4 11. $31/13$ 13. 3 15. 2

17. $\mathbf{u} = -\frac{1}{\sqrt{2}}\mathbf{i} + \frac{1}{\sqrt{2}}\mathbf{j}, (D_{\mathbf{u}}f)_{P_0} = \sqrt{2}; -\mathbf{u} = \frac{1}{\sqrt{2}}\mathbf{i} - \frac{1}{\sqrt{2}}\mathbf{j}$,

$(D_{-\mathbf{u}}f)_{P_0} = -\sqrt{2}$

19. $\mathbf{u} = \frac{1}{3\sqrt{3}}\mathbf{i} - \frac{5}{3\sqrt{3}}\mathbf{j} - \frac{1}{3\sqrt{3}}\mathbf{k}, (D_{\mathbf{u}}f)_{P_0} = 3\sqrt{3}$;

$-\mathbf{u} = -\frac{1}{3\sqrt{3}}\mathbf{i} + \frac{5}{3\sqrt{3}}\mathbf{j} + \frac{1}{3\sqrt{3}}\mathbf{k}, (D_{-\mathbf{u}}f)_{P_0} = -3\sqrt{3}$

21. $\mathbf{u} = \frac{1}{\sqrt{3}}(\mathbf{i} + \mathbf{j} + \mathbf{k}), (D_{\mathbf{u}}f)_{P_0} = 2\sqrt{3}$;

$-\mathbf{u} = -\frac{1}{\sqrt{3}}(\mathbf{i} + \mathbf{j} + \mathbf{k}), (D_{-\mathbf{u}}f)_{P_0} = -2\sqrt{3}$

23.

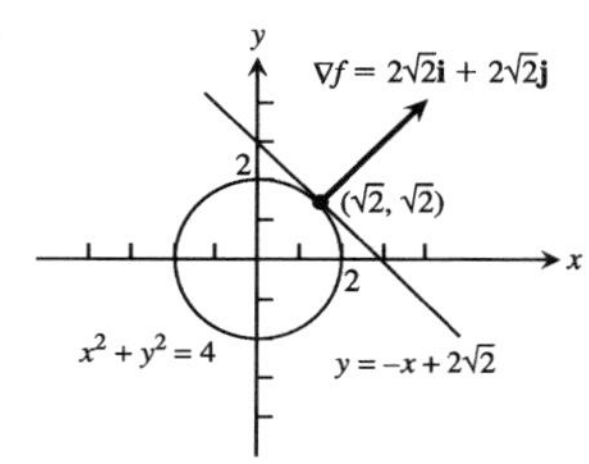

25.

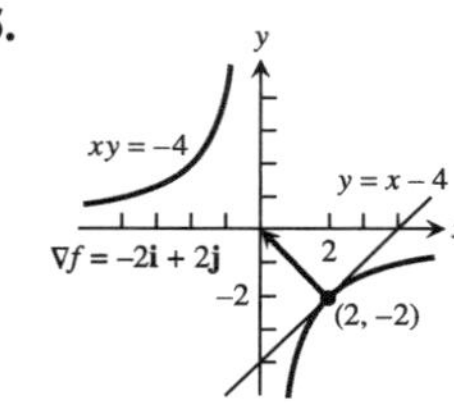

27. $\mathbf{u} = \frac{7}{\sqrt{53}}\mathbf{i} - \frac{2}{\sqrt{53}}\mathbf{j}, -\mathbf{u} = -\frac{7}{\sqrt{53}}\mathbf{i} + \frac{2}{\sqrt{53}}\mathbf{j}$

29. No, the maximum rate of change is $\sqrt{185} < 14$.

31. $-\frac{7}{\sqrt{5}}$

Section 14.6, pp. 1024–1027

1. (a) $x + y + z = 3$
(b) $x = 1 + 2t, y = 1 + 2t, z = 1 + 2t$
3. (a) $2x - z - 2 = 0$ (b) $x = 2 - 4t, y = 0, z = 2 + 2t$
5. (a) $2x + 2y + z - 4 = 0$
(b) $x = 2t, y = 1 + 2t, z = 2 + t$
7. (a) $x + y + z - 1 = 0$ (b) $x = t, y = 1 + t, z = t$
9. $2x - z - 2 = 0$ 11. $x - y + 2z - 1 = 0$
13. $x = 1, y = 1 + 2t, z = 1 - 2t$

15. $x = 1 - 2t, y = 1, z = \frac{1}{2} + 2t$

17. $x = 1 + 90t, y = 1 - 90t, z = 3$

19. $df = \frac{9}{11{,}830} \approx 0.0008$ **21.** $dg = 0$

23. **(a)** $\frac{\sqrt{3}}{2}\sin\sqrt{3} - \frac{1}{2}\cos\sqrt{3} \approx 0.935°\text{C/ft}$

(b) $\sqrt{3}\sin\sqrt{3} - \cos\sqrt{3} \approx 1.87°\text{C/sec}$

25. **(a)** $L(x, y) = 1$ **(b)** $L(x, y) = 2x + 2y - 1$

27. **(a)** $L(x, y) = 3x - 4y + 5$ **(b)** $L(x, y) = 3x - 4y + 5$

29. **(a)** $L(x, y) = 1 + x$ **(b)** $L(x, y) = -y + \frac{\pi}{2}$

31. $L(x, y) = 7 + x - 6y; 0.06$ **33.** $L(x, y) = x + y + 1; 0.08$

35. $L(x, y) = 1 + x; 0.0222$

37. **(a)** $L(x, y, z) = 2x + 2y + 2z - 3$ **(b)** $L(x, y, z) = y + z$

(c) $L(x, y, z) = 0$

39. **(a)** $L(x, y, z) = x$ **(b)** $L(x, y, z) = \frac{1}{\sqrt{2}}x + \frac{1}{\sqrt{2}}y$

(c) $L(x, y, z) = \frac{1}{3}x + \frac{2}{3}y + \frac{2}{3}z$

41. **(a)** $L(x, y, z) = 2 + x$

(b) $L(x, y, z) = x - y - z + \frac{\pi}{2} + 1$

(c) $L(x, y, z) = x - y - z + \frac{\pi}{2} + 1$

43. $L(x, y, z) = 2x - 6y - 2z + 6, 0.0024$

45. $L(x, y, z) = x + y - z - 1, 0.00135$

47. Maximum error (estimate) ≤ 0.31 in magnitude

49. Maximum percentage error $= \pm 4.83\%$

51. Pay more attention to the smaller of the two dimensions. It will generate the larger partial derivative.

53. **(a)** 0.30% **55.** f is most sensitive to a change in d.

57. Q is most sensitive to changes in h.

61. At $-\frac{\pi}{4}, -\frac{\pi}{2\sqrt{2}}$; at 0, 0; at $\frac{\pi}{4}, \frac{\pi}{2\sqrt{2}}$

Section 14.7, pp. 1034–1038

1. $f(-3, 3) = -5$, local minimum

3. $f\left(\frac{2}{3}, \frac{4}{3}\right) = 0$, local maximum **5.** $f(-2, 1)$, saddle point

7. $f\left(\frac{6}{5}, \frac{69}{25}\right)$, saddle point **9.** $f(2, 1)$, saddle point

11. $f(2, -1) = -6$, local minimum **13.** $f(1, 2)$, saddle point

15. $f(0, 0)$, saddle point

17. $f(0, 0)$, saddle point; $f\left(-\frac{2}{3}, \frac{2}{3}\right) = \frac{170}{27}$, local maximum

19. $f(0, 0) = 0$, local minimum; $f(1, -1)$, saddle point

21. $f(0, 0)$, saddle point; $f\left(\frac{4}{9}, \frac{4}{3}\right) = -\frac{64}{81}$, local minimum

23. $f(0, 0)$, saddle point; $f(0, 2) = -12$, local minimum; $f(-2, 0) = -4$, local maximum; $f(-2, 2)$, saddle point

25. $f(0, 0)$, saddle point; $f(1, 1) = 2$, $f(-1, -1) = 2$, local maxima

27. $f(0, 0) = -1$, local maximum

29. $f(n\pi, 0)$, saddle point; $f(n\pi, 0) = 0$ for every n

31. Absolute maximum: 1 at $(0, 0)$; absolute minimum: -5 at $(1, 2)$

33. Absolute maximum: 4 at $(0, 2)$; absolute minimum: 0 at $(0, 0)$

35. Absolute maximum: 11 at $(0, -3)$; absolute minimum: -10 at $(4, -2)$

37. Absolute maximum: 4 at $(2, 0)$; absolute minimum: $\frac{3\sqrt{2}}{2}$ at $\left(3, -\frac{\pi}{4}\right), \left(3, \frac{\pi}{4}\right), \left(1, -\frac{\pi}{4}\right)$, and $\left(1, \frac{\pi}{4}\right)$

39. $a = -3, b = 2$

41. Hottest: $2\frac{1}{4}°$ at $\left(-\frac{1}{2}, \frac{\sqrt{3}}{2}\right)$ and $\left(-\frac{1}{2}, -\frac{\sqrt{3}}{2}\right)$; coldest: $-\frac{1}{4}°$ at $\left(\frac{1}{2}, 0\right)$

43. **(a)** $f(0, 0)$, saddle point **(b)** $f(1, 2)$, local minimum

(c) $f(1, -2)$, local minimum; $f(-1, -2)$, saddle point

49. $\left(\frac{1}{6}, \frac{1}{3}, \frac{355}{36}\right)$

53. **(a)** On the semicircle, max $f = 2\sqrt{2}$ at $t = \pi/4$, min $f = -2$ at $t = \pi$. On the quarter circle, max $f = 2\sqrt{2}$ at $t = \pi/4$, min $f = 2$ at $t = 0, \pi/2$.

(b) On the semicircle, max $g = 2$ at $t = \pi/4$, min $g = -2$ at $t = 3\pi/4$. On the quarter circle, max $g = 2$ at $t = \pi/4$, min $g = 0$ at $t = 0, \pi/2$.

(c) On the semicircle, max $h = 8$ at $t = 0, \pi$; min $h = 4$ at $t = \pi/2$. On the quarter circle, max $h = 8$ at $t = 0$, min $h = 4$ at $t = \pi/2$.

55. i) min $f = -1/2$ at $t = -1/2$; no max ii) max $f = 0$ at $t = -1, 0$; min $f = -1/2$ at $t = -1/2$ iii) max $f = 4$ at $t = 1$; min $f = 0$ at $t = 0$

57. $y = -\frac{20}{13}x + \frac{9}{13}, y|_{x=4} = -\frac{71}{13}$

59. $y = \frac{3}{2}x + \frac{1}{6}, y|_{x=4} = \frac{37}{6}$

61. $y = 0.122x + 3.59$

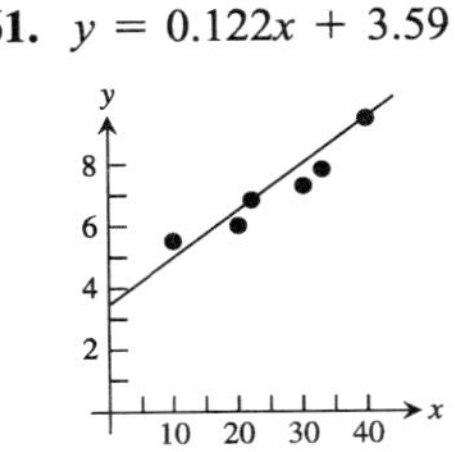

63. (a)

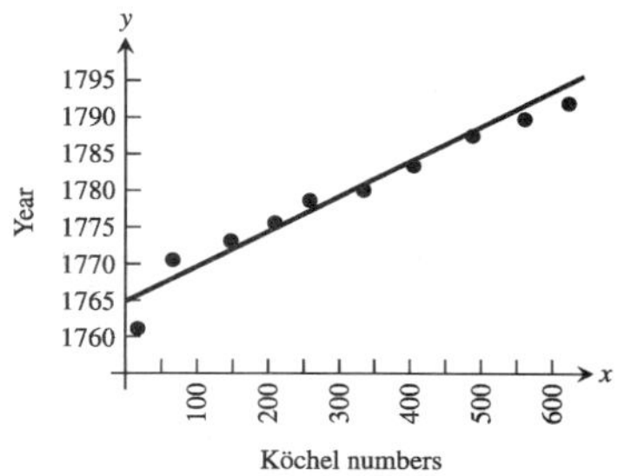

(b) $y = 0.0427\text{K} + 1764.8$ **(c)** 1780

Section 14.8, pp. 1047–1049

1. $\left(\pm\frac{1}{\sqrt{2}}, \frac{1}{2}\right), \left(\pm\frac{1}{\sqrt{2}}, -\frac{1}{2}\right)$ **3.** 39 **5.** $\left(3, \pm 3\sqrt{2}\right)$

7. **(a)** 8 **(b)** 64

9. $r = 2$ cm, $h = 4$ cm **11.** Length $= 4\sqrt{2}$, width $= 3\sqrt{2}$

13. $f(0, 0) = 0$ is minimum, $f(2, 4) = 20$ is maximum.

15. Lowest $= 0°$, highest $= 125°$

17. $\left(\frac{3}{2}, 2, \frac{5}{2}\right)$ **19.** 1 **21.** $(0, 0, 2), (0, 0, -2)$

23. $f(1, -2, 5) = 30$ is maximum, $f(-1, 2, -5) = -30$ is minimum.

25. 3, 3, 3 **27.** $\frac{2}{\sqrt{3}}$ by $\frac{2}{\sqrt{3}}$ by $\frac{2}{\sqrt{3}}$ units

29. $(\pm 4/3, -4/3, -4/3)$ **31.** $U(8, 14) = \$128$

33. $f(2/3, 4/3, -4/3) = \frac{4}{3}$ **35.** $(2, 4, 4)$

37. Maximum is $1 + 6\sqrt{3}$ at $\left(\pm\sqrt{6}, \sqrt{3}, 1\right)$, minimum is $1 - 6\sqrt{3}$ at $\left(\pm\sqrt{6}, -\sqrt{3}, 1\right)$.

39. Maximum is 4 at $(0, 0, \pm 2)$, minimum is 2 at $\left(\pm\sqrt{2}, \pm\sqrt{2}, 0\right)$.

Section 14.9, pp. 1053–1054

1. **(a)** 0 **(b)** $1 + 2z$ **(c)** $1 + 2z$

3. **(a)** $\frac{\partial U}{\partial P} + \frac{\partial U}{\partial T}\left(\frac{V}{nR}\right)$ **(b)** $\frac{\partial U}{\partial P}\left(\frac{nR}{V}\right) + \frac{\partial U}{\partial T}$

5. **(a)** 5 **(b)** 5

7. $\left(\frac{\partial x}{\partial r}\right)_\theta = \cos\theta$

$$\left(\frac{\partial r}{\partial x}\right)_y = \frac{x}{\sqrt{x^2 + y^2}}$$

Section 14.10, pp. 1058–1059

1. Quadratic: $x + xy$; cubic: $x + xy + \frac{1}{2}xy^2$

3. Quadratic: xy; cubic: xy

5. Quadratic: $y + \frac{1}{2}(2xy - y^2)$;

cubic: $y + \frac{1}{2}(2xy - y^2) + \frac{1}{6}(3x^2y - 3xy^2 + 2y^3)$

7. Quadratic: $\frac{1}{2}(2x^2 + 2y^2) = x^2 + y^2$; cubic: $x^2 + y^2$

9. Quadratic: $1 + (x + y) + (x + y)^2$;
cubic: $1 + (x + y) + (x + y)^2 + (x + y)^3$

11. Quadratic: $1 - \frac{1}{2}x^2 - \frac{1}{2}y^2$; $E(x, y) \le 0.00134$

Practice Exercises, pp. 1060–1063

1. Domain: all points in the xy-plane; range: $z \ge 0$. Level curves are ellipses with major axis along the y-axis and minor axis along the x-axis.

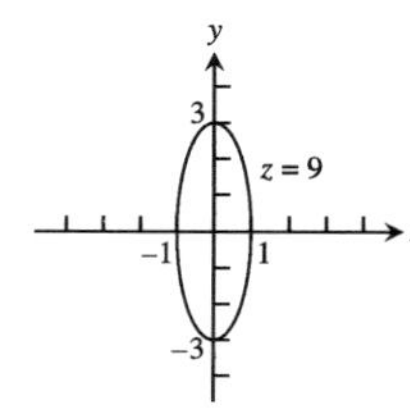

3. Domain: all (x, y) such that $x \ne 0$ and $y \ne 0$; range: $z \ne 0$. Level curves are hyperbolas with the x- and y-axes as asymptotes.

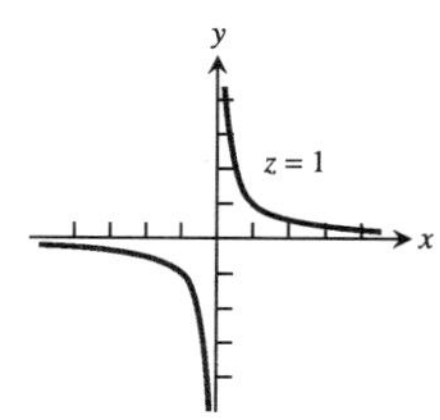

5. Domain: all points in xyz-space; range: all real numbers. Level surfaces are paraboloids of revolution with the z-axis as axis.

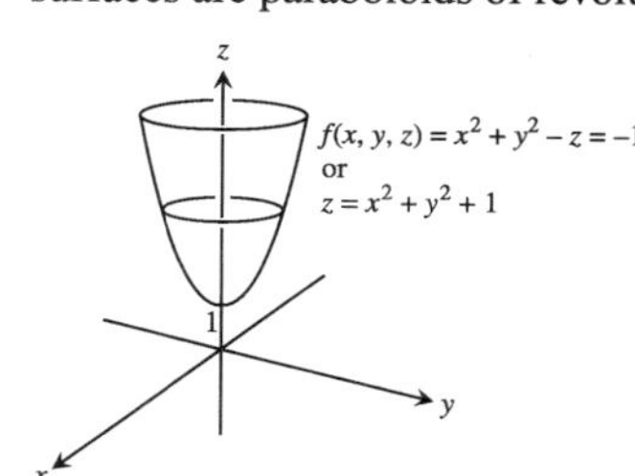

7. Domain: all (x, y, z) such that $(x, y, z) \ne (0, 0, 0)$; range: positive real numbers. Level surfaces are spheres with center $(0, 0, 0)$ and radius $r > 0$.

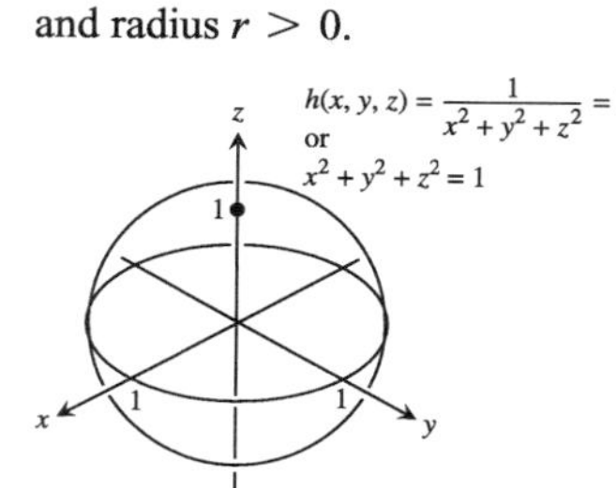

9. -2 **11.** $1/2$ **13.** 1 **15.** Let $y = kx^2, k \neq 1$

17. No; $\lim_{(x,y)\to(0,0)} f(x, y)$ does not exist.

19. $\dfrac{\partial g}{\partial r} = \cos\theta + \sin\theta, \dfrac{\partial g}{\partial \theta} = -r\sin\theta + r\cos\theta$

21. $\dfrac{\partial f}{\partial R_1} = -\dfrac{1}{R_1{}^2}, \dfrac{\partial f}{\partial R_2} = -\dfrac{1}{R_2{}^2}, \dfrac{\partial f}{\partial R_3} = -\dfrac{1}{R_3{}^2}$

23. $\dfrac{\partial P}{\partial n} = \dfrac{RT}{V}, \dfrac{\partial P}{\partial R} = \dfrac{nT}{V}, \dfrac{\partial P}{\partial T} = \dfrac{nR}{V}, \dfrac{\partial P}{\partial V} = -\dfrac{nRT}{V^2}$

25. $\dfrac{\partial^2 g}{\partial x^2} = 0, \dfrac{\partial^2 g}{\partial y^2} = \dfrac{2x}{y^3}, \dfrac{\partial^2 g}{\partial y\,\partial x} = \dfrac{\partial^2 g}{\partial x\,\partial y} = -\dfrac{1}{y^2}$

27. $\dfrac{\partial^2 f}{\partial x^2} = -30x + \dfrac{2 - 2x^2}{(x^2+1)^2}, \dfrac{\partial^2 f}{\partial y^2} = 0, \dfrac{\partial^2 f}{\partial y\,\partial x} = \dfrac{\partial^2 f}{\partial x\,\partial y} = 1$

29. $\left.\dfrac{dw}{dt}\right|_{t=0} = -1$

31. $\left.\dfrac{\partial w}{\partial r}\right|_{(r,s)=(\pi,0)} = 2, \left.\dfrac{\partial w}{\partial s}\right|_{(r,s)=(\pi,0)} = 2 - \pi$

33. $\left.\dfrac{df}{dt}\right|_{t=1} = -(\sin 1 + \cos 2)(\sin 1) + (\cos 1 + \cos 2)(\cos 1)$
$\quad - 2(\sin 1 + \cos 1)(\sin 2)$

35. $\left.\dfrac{dy}{dx}\right|_{(x,y)=(0,1)} = -1$

37. Increases most rapidly in the direction $\mathbf{u} = -\dfrac{\sqrt{2}}{2}\mathbf{i} - \dfrac{\sqrt{2}}{2}\mathbf{j}$; decreases most rapidly in the direction $-\mathbf{u} = \dfrac{\sqrt{2}}{2}\mathbf{i} + \dfrac{\sqrt{2}}{2}\mathbf{j}$; $D_{\mathbf{u}}f = \dfrac{\sqrt{2}}{2}$; $D_{-\mathbf{u}}f = -\dfrac{\sqrt{2}}{2}$; $D_{\mathbf{u}_1}f = -\dfrac{7}{10}$ where $\mathbf{u}_1 = \dfrac{\mathbf{v}}{|\mathbf{v}|}$

39. Increases most rapidly in the direction $\mathbf{u} = \dfrac{2}{7}\mathbf{i} + \dfrac{3}{7}\mathbf{j} + \dfrac{6}{7}\mathbf{k}$; decreases most rapidly in the direction $-\mathbf{u} = -\dfrac{2}{7}\mathbf{i} - \dfrac{3}{7}\mathbf{j} - \dfrac{6}{7}\mathbf{k}$; $D_{\mathbf{u}}f = 7$; $D_{-\mathbf{u}}f = -7$; $D_{\mathbf{u}_1}f = 7$ where $\mathbf{u}_1 = \dfrac{\mathbf{v}}{|\mathbf{v}|}$

41. $\pi/\sqrt{2}$

43. **(a)** $f_x(1, 2) = f_y(1, 2) = 2$ **(b)** $14/5$

45.

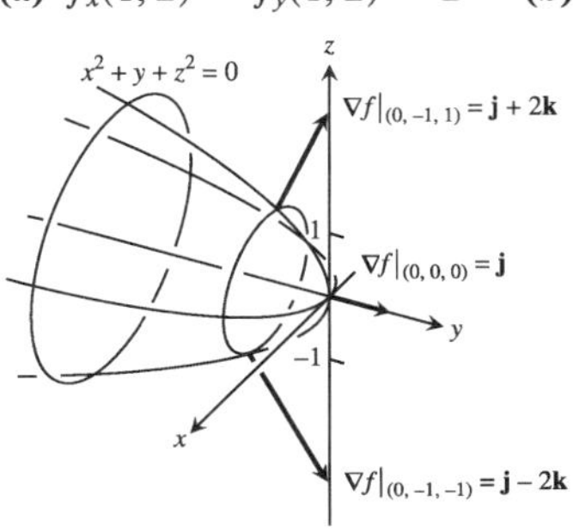

47. Tangent: $4x - y - 5z = 4$; normal line: $x = 2 + 4t, y = -1 - t, z = 1 - 5t$

49. $2y - z - 2 = 0$

51. Tangent: $x + y = \pi + 1$; normal line: $y = x - \pi + 1$

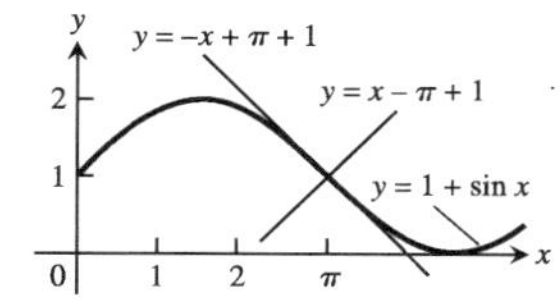

53. $x = 1 - 2t, y = 1, z = 1/2 + 2t$

55. Answers will depend on the upper bound used for $|f_{xx}|, |f_{xy}|, |f_{yy}|$. With $M = \sqrt{2}/2$, $|E| \le 0.0142$. With $M = 1$, $|E| \le 0.02$.

57. $L(x, y, z) = y - 3z$, $L(x, y, z) = x + y - z - 1$

59. Be more careful with the diameter.

61. $dI = 0.038$, % change in $I = 15.83\%$, more sensitive to voltage change

63. **(a)** 5%

65. Local minimum of -8 at $(-2, -2)$

67. Saddle point at $(0, 0)$, $f(0, 0) = 0$; local maximum of $1/4$ at $(-1/2, -1/2)$

69. Saddle point at $(0, 0)$, $f(0, 0) = 0$; local minimum of -4 at $(0, 2)$; local maximum of 4 at $(-2, 0)$; saddle point at $(-2, 2)$, $f(-2, 2) = 0$

71. Absolute maximum: 28 at $(0, 4)$; absolute minimum: $-9/4$ at $(3/2, 0)$

73. Absolute maximum: 18 at $(2, -2)$; absolute minimum: $-17/4$ at $(-2, 1/2)$

75. Absolute maximum: 8 at $(-2, 0)$; absolute minimum: -1 at $(1, 0)$

77. Absolute maximum: 4 at $(1, 0)$; absolute minimum: -4 at $(0, -1)$

79. Absolute maximum: 1 at $(0, \pm 1)$ and $(1, 0)$; absolute minimum: -1 at $(-1, 0)$

81. Maximum: 5 at $(0, 1)$; minimum: $-1/3$ at $(0, -1/3)$

83. Maximum: $\sqrt{3}$ at $\left(\dfrac{1}{\sqrt{3}}, -\dfrac{1}{\sqrt{3}}, \dfrac{1}{\sqrt{3}}\right)$; minimum: $-\sqrt{3}$ at $\left(-\dfrac{1}{\sqrt{3}}, \dfrac{1}{\sqrt{3}}, -\dfrac{1}{\sqrt{3}}\right)$

85. Width $= \left(\dfrac{c^2V}{ab}\right)^{1/3}$, depth $= \left(\dfrac{b^2V}{ac}\right)^{1/3}$, height $= \left(\dfrac{a^2V}{bc}\right)^{1/3}$

87. Maximum: $\dfrac{3}{2}$ at $\left(\dfrac{1}{\sqrt{2}}, \dfrac{1}{\sqrt{2}}, \sqrt{2}\right)$ and $\left(-\dfrac{1}{\sqrt{2}}, -\dfrac{1}{\sqrt{2}}, -\sqrt{2}\right)$; minimum: $\dfrac{1}{2}$ at $\left(-\dfrac{1}{\sqrt{2}}, \dfrac{1}{\sqrt{2}}, -\sqrt{2}\right)$ and $\left(\dfrac{1}{\sqrt{2}}, -\dfrac{1}{\sqrt{2}}, \sqrt{2}\right)$

89. **(a)** $(2y + x^2z)e^{yz}$ **(b)** $x^2e^{yz}\left(y - \dfrac{z}{2y}\right)$ **(c)** $(1 + x^2y)e^{yz}$

91. $\dfrac{\partial w}{\partial x} = \cos\theta\dfrac{\partial w}{\partial r} - \dfrac{\sin\theta}{r}\dfrac{\partial w}{\partial \theta}, \dfrac{\partial w}{\partial y} = \sin\theta\dfrac{\partial w}{\partial r} + \dfrac{\cos\theta}{r}\dfrac{\partial w}{\partial \theta}$

97. $(t, -t \pm 4, t)$, t a real number

Additional and Advanced Exercises, pp. 1063–1066

1. $f_{xy}(0,0) = -1$, $f_{yx}(0,0) = 1$

7. (c) $\dfrac{r^2}{2} = \dfrac{1}{2}(x^2 + y^2 + z^2)$ **13.** $V = \dfrac{\sqrt{3}abc}{2}$

17. $f(x, y) = \dfrac{y}{2} + 4$, $g(x, y) = \dfrac{x}{2} + \dfrac{9}{2}$

19. $y = 2\ln|\sin x| + \ln 2$

21. (a) $\dfrac{1}{\sqrt{53}}(2\mathbf{i} + 7\mathbf{j})$ **(b)** $\dfrac{-1}{\sqrt{29{,}097}}(98\mathbf{i} - 127\mathbf{j} + 58\mathbf{k})$

23. $w = e^{-c^2\pi^2 t}\sin \pi x$

CHAPTER 15

Section 15.1, pp. 1079–1081

1. 16

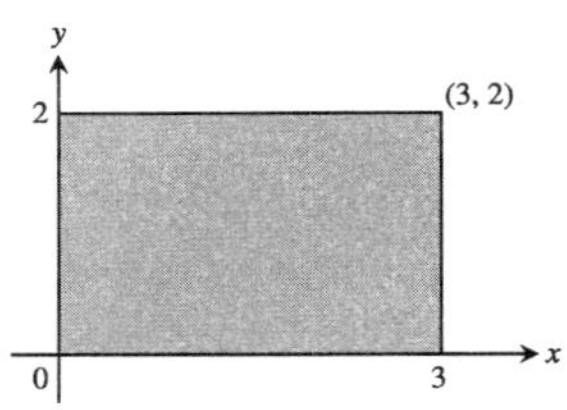

3. 1

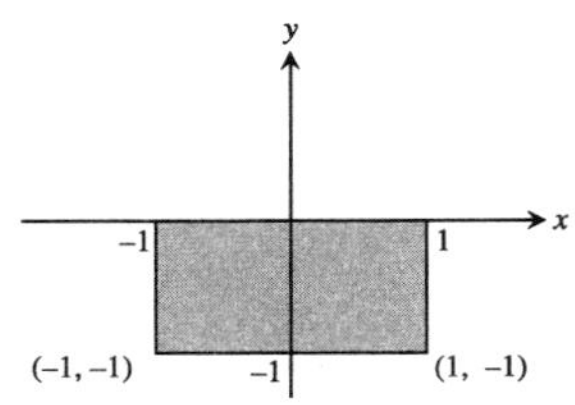

5. $\dfrac{\pi^2}{2} + 2$

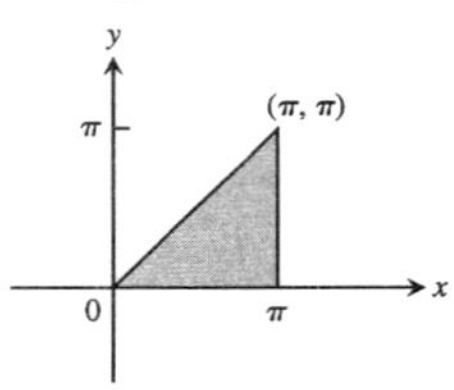

7. $8\ln 8 - 16 + e$

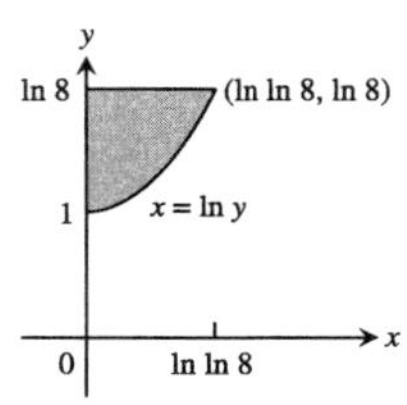

9. $e - 2$

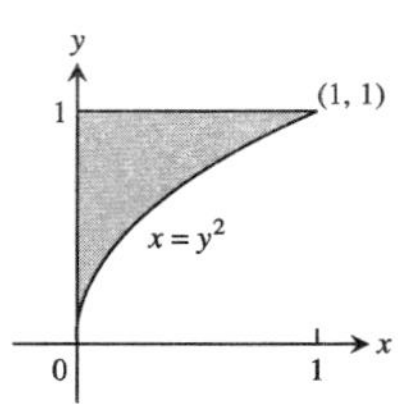

11. $\dfrac{3}{2}\ln 2$ **13.** $1/6$ **15.** $-1/10$

17. 8

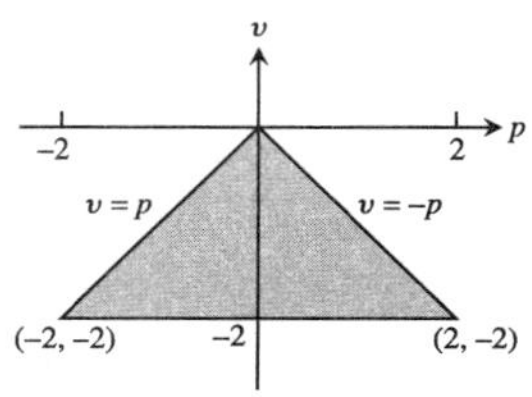

19. 2π

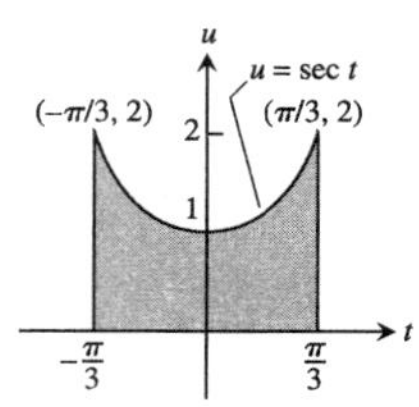

21. $\displaystyle\int_2^4\int_0^{(4-y)/2} dx\, dy$

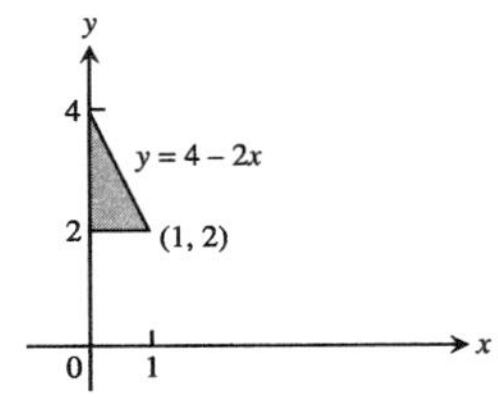

23. $\displaystyle\int_0^1\int_{x^2}^{x} dy\, dx$

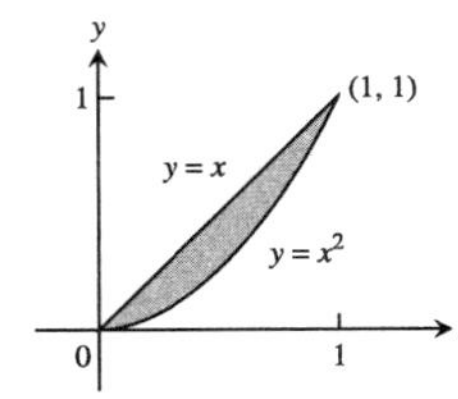

25. $\displaystyle\int_1^e\int_{\ln y}^{1} dx\, dy$

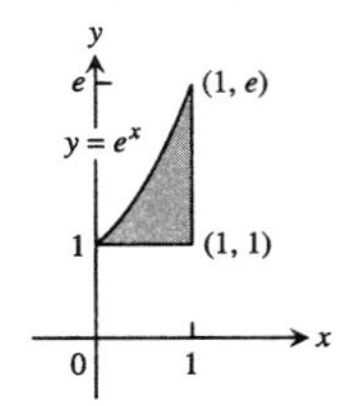

27. $\displaystyle\int_0^9\int_0^{(\sqrt{9-y})/2} 16x\, dx\, dy$

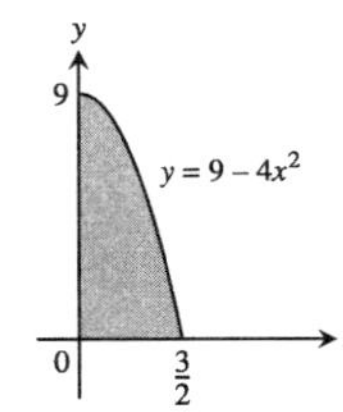

29. $\displaystyle\int_{-1}^1\int_0^{\sqrt{1-x^2}} 3y\, dy\, dx$

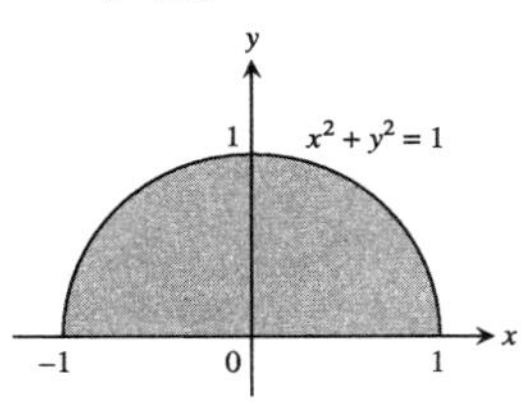

31. 2

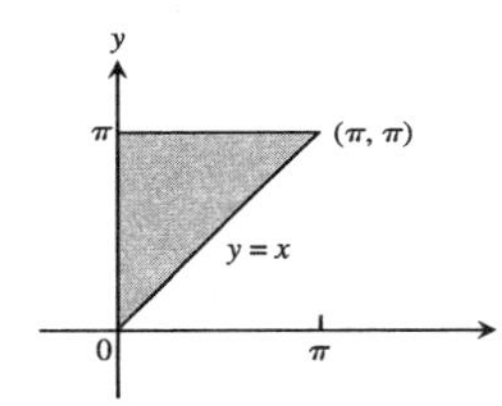

33. $\dfrac{e-2}{2}$

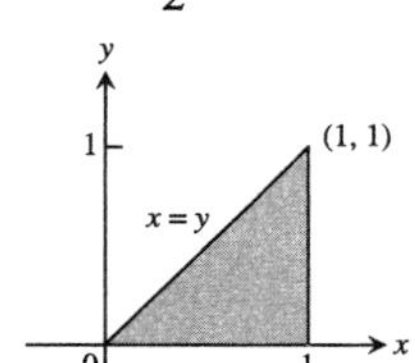

35. 2

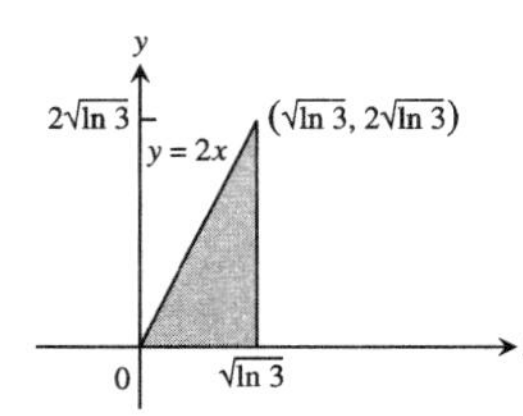

37. $1/(80\pi)$

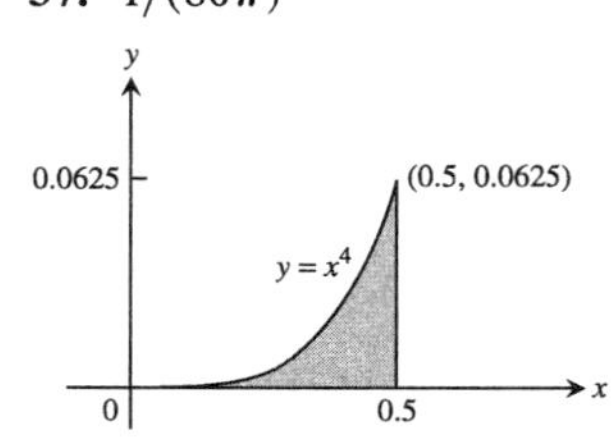

39. $-2/3$

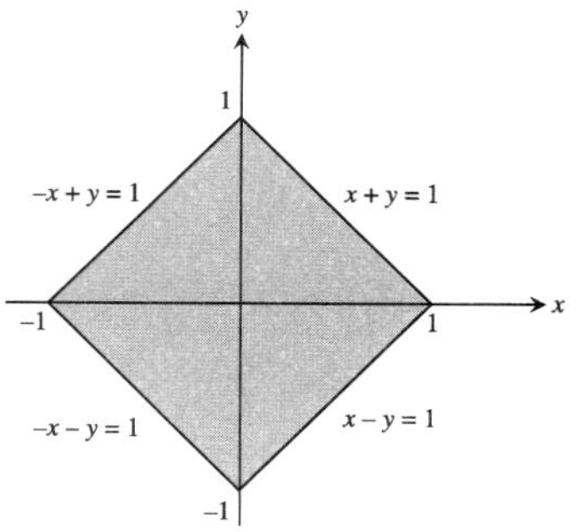

41. $4/3$ **43.** $625/12$ **45.** 16 **47.** 20 **49.** $2(1 + \ln 2)$

51. 1 **53.** π^2 **55.** $-\dfrac{3}{32}$ **57.** $\dfrac{20\sqrt{3}}{9}$

59. $\displaystyle\int_0^1 \int_x^{2-x} (x^2 + y^2)\, dy\, dx = \frac{4}{3}$

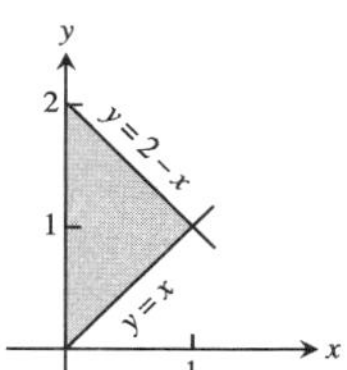

61. R is the set of points (x, y) such that $x^2 + 2y^2 < 4$

63. No, by Fubini's Theorem, the two orders of integration must give the same result.

67. 0.603 **69.** 0.233

Section 15.2, pp. 1089–1091

1. $\displaystyle\int_0^2 \int_0^{2-x} dy\, dx = 2$ or $\displaystyle\int_0^2 \int_0^{2-y} dx\, dy = 2$

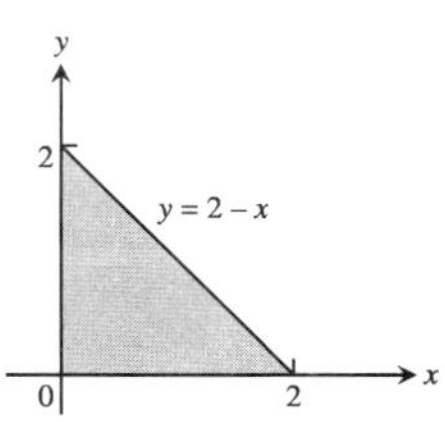

3. $\displaystyle\int_{-2}^1 \int_{y-2}^{-y^2} dx\, dy = \frac{9}{2}$ **5.** $\displaystyle\int_0^{\ln 2} \int_0^{e^x} dy\, dx = 1$

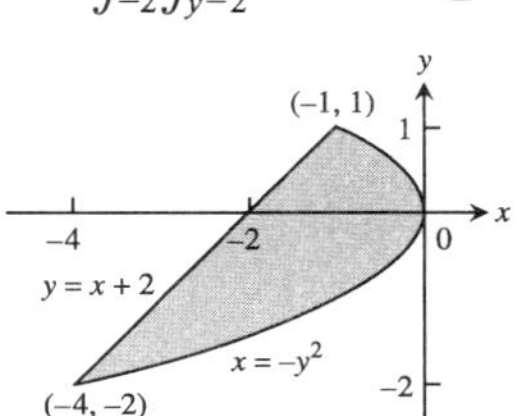

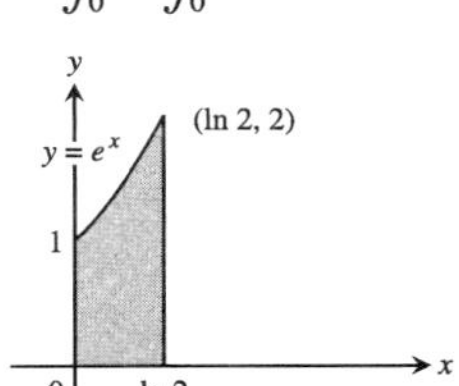

7. $\displaystyle\int_0^1 \int_{y^2}^{2y-y^2} dx\, dy = \frac{1}{3}$ **9.** 12

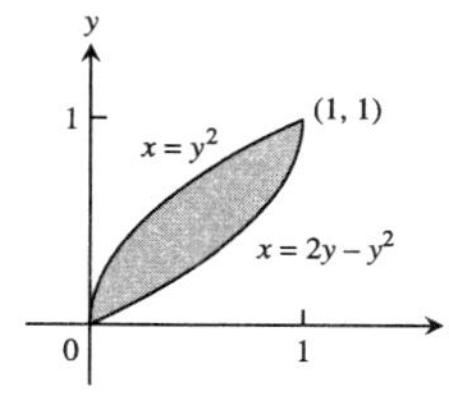

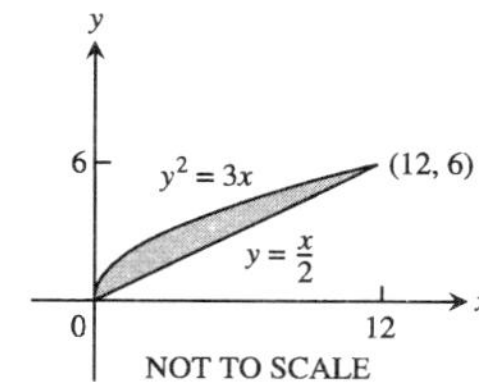

11. $\sqrt{2} - 1$ **13.** $\dfrac{3}{2}$

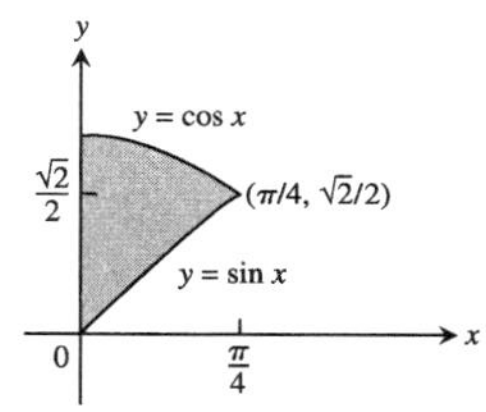

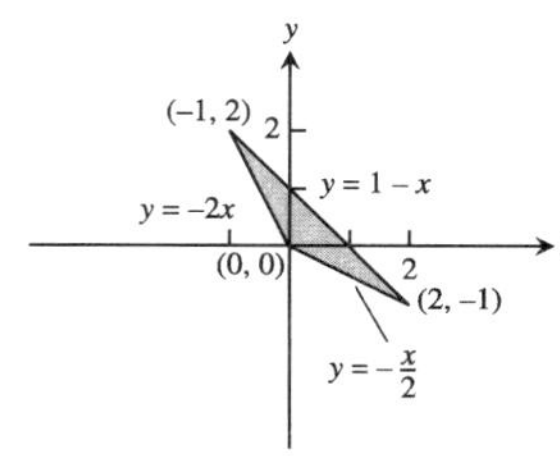

15. **(a)** 0 **(b)** $4/\pi^2$ **17.** $8/3$ **19.** $\bar{x} = 5/14, \bar{y} = 38/35$

21. $\bar{x} = 64/35, \bar{y} = 5/7$ **23.** $\bar{x} = 0, \bar{y} = 4/(3\pi)$

25. $\bar{x} = \bar{y} = 4a/(3\pi)$ **27.** $I_x = I_y = 4\pi, I_0 = 8\pi$

29. $\bar{x} = -1, \bar{y} = 1/4$ **31.** $I_x = 64/105, R_x = 2\sqrt{2/7}$

33. $\bar{x} = 3/8, \bar{y} = 17/16$

35. $\bar{x} = 11/3, \bar{y} = 14/27, I_y = 432, R_y = 4$

37. $\bar{x} = 0, \bar{y} = 13/31, I_y = 7/5, R_y = \sqrt{21/31}$

39. $\bar{x} = 0, \bar{y} = 7/10; I_x = 9/10, I_y = 3/10, I_0 = 6/5;$
$R_x = 3\sqrt{6}/10, R_y = 3\sqrt{2}/10, R_0 = 3\sqrt{2}/5$

41. $40{,}000(1 - e^{-2})\ln(7/2) \approx 43{,}329$

43. If $0 < a \le 5/2$, then the appliance will have to be tipped more than 45° to fall over.

45. $(\bar{x}, \bar{y}) = (2/\pi, 0)$ **47.** **(a)** $3/2$ **(b)** They are the same.

53. **(a)** $(7/5, 31/10)$ **(b)** $(19/7, 18/7)$ **(c)** $(9/2, 19/8)$ **(d)** $(11/4, 43/16)$

55. For the center of mass to be on the common boundary, $h = a\sqrt{2}$. For the center of mass to be inside T, $h > a\sqrt{2}$.

Section 15.3, pp. 1097–1098

1. $\pi/2$ **3.** $\pi/8$ **5.** πa^2 **7.** 36 **9.** $(1 - \ln 2)\pi$

11. $(2\ln 2 - 1)(\pi/2)$ **13.** $(\pi/2) + 1$ **15.** $\pi(\ln 4 - 1)$

17. $2(\pi - 1)$ **19.** 12π **21.** $(3\pi/8) + 1$ **23.** 4

25. $6\sqrt{3} - 2\pi$ **27.** $\bar{x} = 5/6, \bar{y} = 0$ **29.** $\dfrac{2a}{3}$ **31.** $\dfrac{2a}{3}$

33. $2\pi\left(2 - \sqrt{e}\right)$ **35.** $\dfrac{4}{3} + \dfrac{5\pi}{8}$ **37.** **(a)** $\dfrac{\sqrt{\pi}}{2}$ **(b)** 1

39. $\pi \ln 4$, no **41.** $\dfrac{1}{2}(a^2 + 2h^2)$

Section 15.4, pp. 1106–1109

1. $1/6$

3. $\int_0^1\int_0^{2-2x}\int_0^{3-3x-3y/2} dz\,dy\,dx$, $\int_0^2\int_0^{1-y/2}\int_0^{3-3x-3y/2} dz\,dx\,dy$,
$\int_0^1\int_0^{3-3x}\int_0^{2-2x-2z/3} dy\,dz\,dx$, $\int_0^3\int_0^{1-z/3}\int_0^{2-2x-2z/3} dy\,dx\,dz$,
$\int_0^2\int_0^{3-3y/2}\int_0^{1-y/2-z/3} dx\,dz\,dy$,
$\int_0^3\int_0^{2-2z/3}\int_0^{1-y/2-z/3} dx\,dy\,dz$.
The value of all six integrals is 1.

5. $\int_{-2}^2\int_{-\sqrt{4-x^2}}^{\sqrt{4-x^2}}\int_{x^2+y^2}^{8-x^2-y^2} 1\,dz\,dx\,dy$, $\int_{-2}^2\int_{-\sqrt{4-y^2}}^{\sqrt{4-y^2}}\int_{x^2+y^2}^{8-x^2-y^2} 1\,dz\,dx\,dy$,
$\int_{-2}^2\int_4^{8-y^2}\int_{-\sqrt{8-z-y^2}}^{\sqrt{8-z-y^2}} 1\,dx\,dz\,dy + \int_{-2}^2\int_{y^2}^4\int_{-\sqrt{z-y^2}}^{\sqrt{z-y^2}} 1\,dx\,dz\,dy$,
$\int_4^8\int_{-\sqrt{8-z}}^{\sqrt{8-z}}\int_{-\sqrt{8-z-y^2}}^{\sqrt{8-z-y^2}} 1\,dx\,dy\,dz + \int_0^4\int_{-\sqrt{z}}^{\sqrt{z}}\int_{-\sqrt{z-y^2}}^{\sqrt{z-y^2}} 1\,dx\,dy\,dz$,
$\int_{-2}^2\int_4^{8-x^2}\int_{-\sqrt{8-z-x^2}}^{\sqrt{8-z-x^2}} 1\,dy\,dz\,dx + \int_{-2}^2\int_{x^2}^4\int_{-\sqrt{z-x^2}}^{\sqrt{z-x^2}} 1\,dy\,dz\,dx$,
$\int_4^8\int_{-\sqrt{8-z}}^{\sqrt{8-z}}\int_{-\sqrt{8-z-x^2}}^{\sqrt{8-z-x^2}} 1\,dy\,dx\,dz + \int_0^4\int_{-\sqrt{z}}^{\sqrt{z}}\int_{-\sqrt{z-x^2}}^{\sqrt{z-x^2}} 1\,dy\,dx\,dz$.
The value of all six integrals is 16π.

7. 1 **9.** 1 **11.** $\frac{\pi^3}{2}(1-\cos 1)$ **13.** 18 **15.** 7/6

17. 0 **19.** $\frac{1}{2}-\frac{\pi}{8}$

21. **(a)** $\int_{-1}^1\int_0^{1-x^2}\int_{x^2}^{1-z} dy\,dz\,dx$ **(b)** $\int_0^1\int_{-\sqrt{1-z}}^{\sqrt{1-z}}\int_{x^2}^{1-z} dy\,dx\,dz$
(c) $\int_0^1\int_0^{1-z}\int_{-\sqrt{y}}^{\sqrt{y}} dx\,dy\,dz$ **(d)** $\int_0^1\int_0^{1-y}\int_{-\sqrt{y}}^{\sqrt{y}} dx\,dz\,dy$
(e) $\int_0^1\int_{-\sqrt{y}}^{\sqrt{y}}\int_0^{1-y} dz\,dx\,dy$

23. 2/3 **25.** 20/3 **27.** 1 **29.** 16/3 **31.** $8\pi-\frac{32}{3}$
33. 2 **35.** 4π **37.** 31/3 **39.** 1 **41.** 2 sin 4 **43.** 4
45. $a=3$ or $a=13/3$
47. The domain is the set of all point (x, y, z) such that $4x^2+4y^2+z^2\le 4$.

Section 15.5, pp. 1112–1114

1. $R_x=\sqrt{\frac{b^2+c^2}{12}}, R_y=\sqrt{\frac{a^2+c^2}{12}}, R_z=\sqrt{\frac{a^2+b^2}{12}}$

3. $I_x=\frac{M}{3}(b^2+c^2), I_y=\frac{M}{3}(a^2+c^2), I_z=\frac{M}{3}(a^2+b^2)$

5. $\bar{x}=\bar{y}=0, \bar{z}=12/5, I_x=7904/105\approx 75.28$, $I_y=4832/63\approx 76.70, I_z=256/45\approx 5.69$

7. **(a)** $\bar{x}=\bar{y}=0, \bar{z}=8/3$ **(b)** $c=2\sqrt{2}$

9. $I_L=1386, R_L=\sqrt{\frac{77}{2}}$ **11.** $I_L=\frac{40}{3}, R_L=\sqrt{\frac{5}{3}}$

13. **(a)** 4/3 **(b)** $\bar{x}=4/5, \bar{y}=\bar{z}=2/5$

15. **(a)** 5/2 **(b)** $\bar{x}=\bar{y}=\bar{z}=8/15$ **(c)** $I_x=I_y=I_z=11/6$
(d) $R_x=R_y=R_z=\sqrt{\frac{11}{15}}$ **17.** 3 **19.** **(a)** $\frac{4}{3}g$ **(b)** $\frac{4}{3}g$

23. **(a)** $I_{\text{c.m.}}=\frac{abc(a^2+b^2)}{12}, R_{\text{c.m.}}=\sqrt{\frac{a^2+b^2}{12}}$
(b) $I_L=\frac{abc(a^2+7b^2)}{3}, R_L=\sqrt{\frac{a^2+7b^2}{3}}$

27. **(a)** $h=a\sqrt{3}$ **(b)** $h=a\sqrt{2}$

Section 15.6, pp. 1124–1128

1. $\frac{4\pi\left(\sqrt{2}-1\right)}{3}$ **3.** $\frac{17\pi}{5}$ **5.** $\pi\left(6\sqrt{2}-8\right)$ **7.** $\frac{3\pi}{10}$

9. $\pi/3$

11. **(a)** $\int_0^{2\pi}\int_0^1\int_0^{\sqrt{4-r^2}} r\,dz\,dr\,d\theta$
(b) $\int_0^{2\pi}\int_0^{\sqrt{3}}\int_0^1 r\,dr\,dz\,d\theta + \int_0^{2\pi}\int_{\sqrt{3}}^2\int_0^{\sqrt{4-z^2}} r\,dr\,dz\,d\theta$
(c) $\int_0^1\int_0^{\sqrt{4-r^2}}\int_0^{2\pi} r\,d\theta\,dz\,dr$

13. $\int_{-\pi/2}^{\pi/2}\int_0^{\cos\theta}\int_0^{3r^2} f(r,\theta,z)\,dz\,r\,dr\,d\theta$

15. $\int_0^{\pi}\int_0^{2\sin\theta}\int_0^{4-r\sin\theta} f(r,\theta,z)\,dz\,r\,dr\,d\theta$

17. $\int_{-\pi/2}^{\pi/2}\int_1^{1+\cos\theta}\int_0^4 f(r,\theta,z)\,dz\,r\,dr\,d\theta$

19. $\int_0^{\pi/4}\int_0^{\sec\theta}\int_0^{2-r\sin\theta} f(r,\theta,z)\,dz\,r\,dr\,d\theta$ **21.** π^2 **23.** $\pi/3$

25. 5π **27.** 2π **29.** $\left(\frac{8-5\sqrt{2}}{2}\right)\pi$

31. **(a)** $\int_0^{2\pi}\int_0^{\pi/6}\int_0^2 \rho^2\sin\phi\,d\rho\,d\phi\,d\theta +$
$\int_0^{2\pi}\int_{\pi/6}^{\pi/2}\int_0^{\csc\phi} \rho^2\sin\phi\,d\rho\,d\phi\,d\theta$

(b) $\int_0^{2\pi}\int_1^2\int_{\pi/6}^{\sin^{-1}(1/\rho)} \rho^2 \sin\phi \, d\phi \, d\rho \, d\theta + \int_0^{2\pi}\int_0^2\int_0^{\pi/6} \rho^2 \sin\phi \, d\phi \, d\rho \, d\theta$

33. $\int_0^{2\pi}\int_0^{\pi/2}\int_{\cos\phi}^{2} \rho^2 \sin\phi \, d\rho \, d\phi \, d\theta = \frac{31\pi}{6}$

35. $\int_0^{2\pi}\int_0^{\pi}\int_0^{1-\cos\phi} \rho^2 \sin\phi \, d\rho \, d\phi \, d\theta = \frac{8\pi}{3}$

37. $\int_0^{2\pi}\int_{\pi/4}^{\pi/2}\int_0^{2\cos\phi} \rho^2 \sin\phi \, d\rho \, d\phi \, d\theta = \frac{\pi}{3}$

39. **(a)** $8\int_0^{\pi/2}\int_0^{\pi/2}\int_0^2 \rho^2 \sin\phi \, d\rho \, d\phi \, d\theta$

(b) $8\int_0^{\pi/2}\int_0^2\int_0^{\sqrt{4-r^2}} r \, dz \, dr \, d\theta$

(c) $8\int_0^2\int_0^{\sqrt{4-x^2}}\int_0^{\sqrt{4-x^2-y^2}} dz \, dy \, dx$

41. **(a)** $\int_0^{2\pi}\int_0^{\pi/3}\int_{\sec\phi}^{2} \rho^2 \sin\phi \, d\rho \, d\phi \, d\theta$

(b) $\int_0^{2\pi}\int_0^{\sqrt{3}}\int_1^{\sqrt{4-r^2}} r \, dz \, dr \, d\theta$

(c) $\int_{-\sqrt{3}}^{\sqrt{3}}\int_{-\sqrt{3-x^2}}^{\sqrt{3-x^2}}\int_1^{\sqrt{4-x^2-y^2}} dz \, dy \, dx$ **(d)** $5\pi/3$

43. $8\pi/3$ **45.** $9/4$ **47.** $\frac{3\pi - 4}{18}$ **49.** $\frac{2\pi a^3}{3}$ **51.** $5\pi/3$

53. $\pi/2$ **55.** $\frac{4(2\sqrt{2} - 1)\pi}{3}$ **57.** 16π **59.** $5\pi/2$

61. $\frac{4\pi(8 - 3\sqrt{3})}{3}$ **63.** $2/3$ **65.** $3/4$

67. $\bar{x} = \bar{y} = 0, \bar{z} = 3/8$ **69.** $(\bar{x}, \bar{y}, \bar{z}) = (0, 0, 3/8)$

71. $\bar{x} = \bar{y} = 0, \bar{z} = 5/6$ **73.** $I_z = 30\pi, R_z = \sqrt{\frac{5}{2}}$

75. $I_x = \pi/4$ **77.** $\frac{a^4 h\pi}{10}$

79. **(a)** $(\bar{x}, \bar{y}, \bar{z}) = \left(0, 0, \frac{4}{5}\right), I_z = \frac{\pi}{12}, R_z = \sqrt{\frac{1}{3}}$

(b) $(\bar{x}, \bar{y}, \bar{z}) = \left(0, 0, \frac{5}{6}\right), I_z = \frac{\pi}{14}, R_z = \sqrt{\frac{5}{14}}$

83. $(\bar{x}, \bar{y}, \bar{z}) = \left(0, 0, \frac{2h^2 + 3h}{3h + 6}\right), I_z = \frac{\pi a^4(h^2 + 2h)}{4}, R_z = \frac{a}{\sqrt{2}}$

85. $\frac{3M}{\pi R^3}$

89. The surface's equation $r = f(z)$ tells us that the point $(r, \theta, z) = (f(z), \theta, z)$ will lie on the surface for all θ. In particular, $(f(z), \theta + \pi, z)$ lies on the surface whenever $(f(z), \theta, z)$ lies on the surface, so the surface is symmetric with respect to the z-axis.

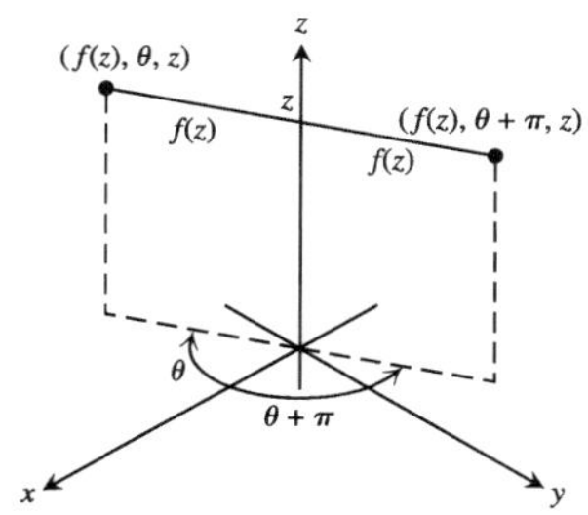

Section 15.7, pp. 1135–1137

1. **(a)** $x = \frac{u + v}{3}, y = \frac{v - 2u}{3}; \frac{1}{3}$
(b) Triangular region with boundaries $u = 0$, $v = 0$, and $u + v = 3$

3. **(a)** $x = \frac{1}{5}(2u - v), y = \frac{1}{10}(3v - u); \frac{1}{10}$
(b) Triangular region with boundaries $3v = u$, $v = 2u$, and $3u + v = 10$

7. $64/5$ **9.** $\int_1^2\int_1^3 (u + v)\frac{2u}{v} \, du \, dv = 8 + \frac{52}{3}\ln 2$

11. $\frac{\pi ab(a^2 + b^2)}{4}$ **13.** $\frac{1}{3}\left(1 + \frac{3}{e^2}\right) \approx 0.4687$

15. **(a)** $\begin{vmatrix} \cos v & -u\sin v \\ \sin v & u\cos v \end{vmatrix} = u\cos^2 v + u\sin^2 v = u$

(b) $\begin{vmatrix} \sin v & u\cos v \\ \cos v & -u\sin v \end{vmatrix} = -u\sin^2 v - u\cos^2 v = -u$

19. 12 **21.** $\frac{a^2b^2c^2}{6}$

Practice Exercises, pp. 1138–1140

1. $9e - 9$

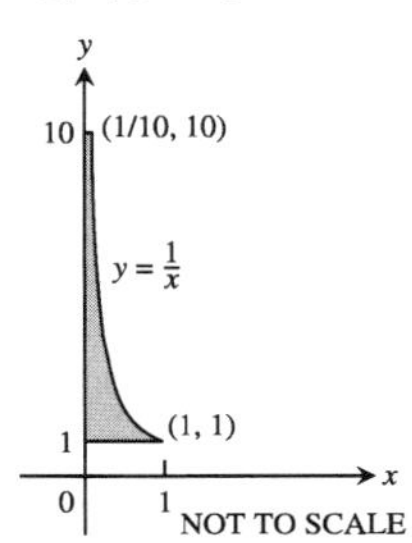

3. $9/2$

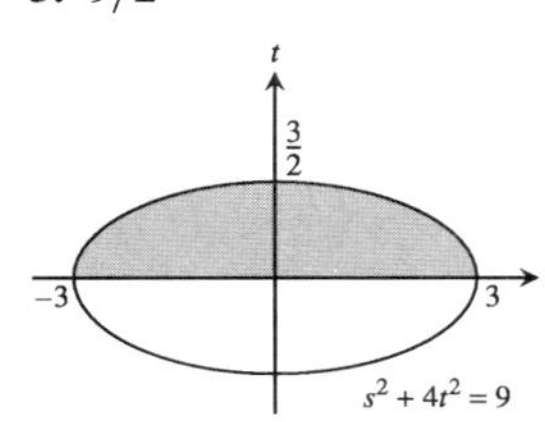

5. $\int_{-2}^{0}\int_{2x+4}^{4-x^2} dy\,dx = \frac{4}{3}$

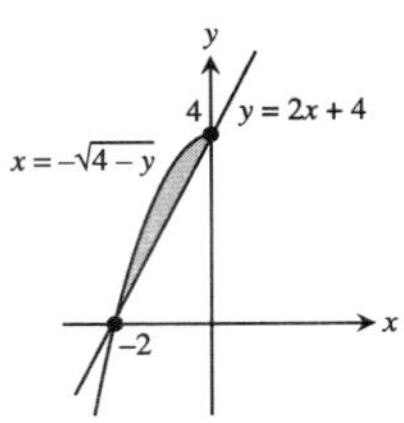

7. $\int_{-3}^{3}\int_{0}^{(1/2)\sqrt{9-x^2}} y\,dy\,dx = \frac{9}{2}$

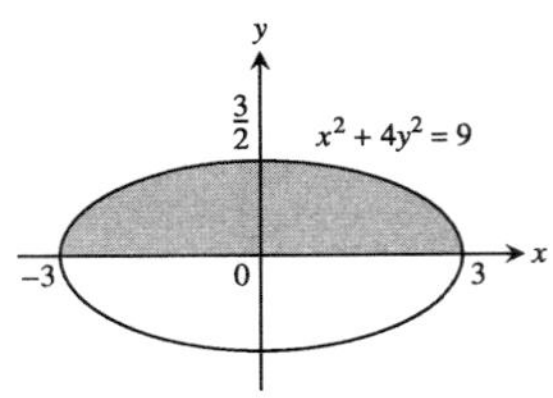

9. $\sin 4$ **11.** $\frac{\ln 17}{4}$ **13.** $4/3$ **15.** $4/3$ **17.** $1/4$

19. $\bar{x} = \bar{y} = \frac{1}{2 - \ln 4}$ **21.** $I_0 = 104$ **23.** $I_x = 2\delta, R_x = \sqrt{\frac{2}{3}}$

25. $M = 4, M_x = 0, M_y = 0$ **27.** π **29.** $\bar{x} = \frac{3\sqrt{3}}{\pi}, \bar{y} = 0$

31. (a) $\bar{x} = \frac{15\pi + 32}{6\pi + 48}, \bar{y} = 0$

(b)

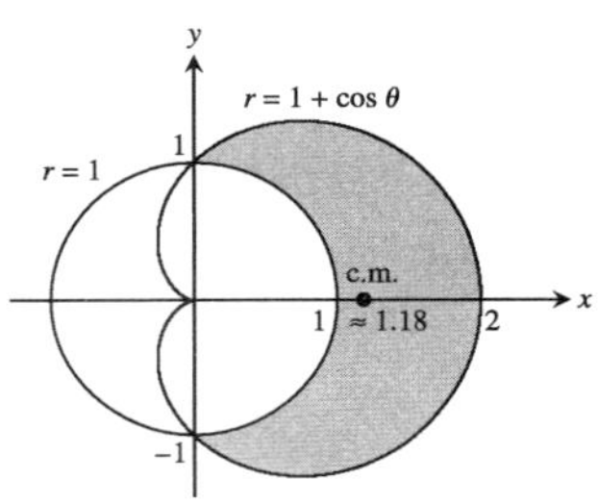

33. $\frac{\pi - 2}{4}$ **35.** 0 **37.** $8/35$ **39.** $\pi/2$ **41.** $\frac{2(31 - 3^{5/2})}{3}$

43. (a) $\int_{-\sqrt{2}}^{\sqrt{2}}\int_{-\sqrt{2-y^2}}^{\sqrt{2-y^2}}\int_{\sqrt{x^2+y^2}}^{\sqrt{4-x^2-y^2}} 3\,dz\,dx\,dy$

(b) $\int_0^{2\pi}\int_0^{\pi/4}\int_0^{2} 3\,\rho^2 \sin\phi\,d\rho\,d\phi\,d\theta$ **(c)** $2\pi\left(8 - 4\sqrt{2}\right)$

45. $\int_0^{2\pi}\int_0^{\pi/4}\int_0^{\sec\phi} \rho^2 \sin\phi\,d\rho\,d\phi\,d\theta = \frac{\pi}{3}$

47. $\int_0^{1}\int_{\sqrt{1-x^2}}^{\sqrt{3-x^2}}\int_1^{\sqrt{4-x^2-y^2}} z^2 xy\,dz\,dy\,dx + \int_1^{\sqrt{3}}\int_0^{\sqrt{3-x^2}}\int_1^{\sqrt{4-x^2-y^2}} z^2 xy\,dz\,dy\,dx$

49. (a) $\frac{8\pi\left(4\sqrt{2} - 5\right)}{3}$ **(b)** $\frac{8\pi\left(4\sqrt{2} - 5\right)}{3}$

51. $I_z = \frac{8\pi\delta(b^5 - a^5)}{15}$

Additional and Advanced Exercises, pp. 1140–1142

1. (a) $\int_{-3}^{2}\int_{x}^{6-x^2} x^2\,dy\,dx$ **(b)** $\int_{-3}^{2}\int_{x}^{6-x^2}\int_0^{x^2} dz\,dy\,dx$

(c) $125/4$

3. 2π **5.** $3\pi/2$ **7. (a)** Hole radius = 1, sphere radius = 2

(b) $4\sqrt{3}\pi$ **9.** $\pi/4$ **11.** $\ln\left(\frac{b}{a}\right)$ **15.** $1/\sqrt[4]{3}$

17. Mass $= a^2\cos^{-1}\left(\frac{b}{a}\right) - b\sqrt{a^2 - b^2}$,

$I_0 = \frac{a^4}{2}\cos^{-1}\left(\frac{b}{a}\right) - \frac{b^3}{2}\sqrt{a^2 - b^2} - \frac{b^3}{6}(a^2 - b^2)^{3/2}$

19. $\frac{1}{ab}(e^{a^2b^2} - 1)$ **21. (b)** 1 **(c)** 0

25. $h = \sqrt{20}$ in., $h = \sqrt{60}$ in. **27.** $2\pi\left[\frac{1}{3} - \left(\frac{1}{3}\right)\frac{\sqrt{2}}{2}\right]$

CHAPTER 16

Section 16.1, pp. 1147–1149

1. Graph (c) **3.** Graph (g) **5.** Graph (d) **7.** Graph (f)

9. $\sqrt{2}$ **11.** $\frac{13}{2}$ **13.** $3\sqrt{14}$ **15.** $\frac{1}{6}\left(5\sqrt{5} + 9\right)$

17. $\sqrt{3}\ln\left(\frac{b}{a}\right)$ **19.** $\frac{10\sqrt{5} - 2}{3}$ **21.** 8 **23.** $2\sqrt{2} - 1$

25. (a) $4\sqrt{2} - 2$ **(b)** $\sqrt{2} + \ln\left(1 + \sqrt{2}\right)$

27. $I_z = 2\pi\delta a^3, R_z = a$

29. (a) $I_z = 2\pi\sqrt{2}\delta, R_z = 1$ **(b)** $I_z = 4\pi\sqrt{2}\delta, R_z = 1$

31. $I_x = 2\pi - 2, R_x = 1$

Section 16.2, pp. 1158–1160

1. $\nabla f = -(x\mathbf{i} + y\mathbf{j} + z\mathbf{k})(x^2 + y^2 + z^2)^{-3/2}$

3. $\nabla g = -\left(\frac{2x}{x^2 + y^2}\right)\mathbf{i} - \left(\frac{2y}{x^2 + y^2}\right)\mathbf{j} + e^z\mathbf{k}$

5. $\mathbf{F} = -\frac{kx}{(x^2 + y^2)^{3/2}}\mathbf{i} - \frac{ky}{(x^2 + y^2)^{3/2}}\mathbf{j}$, any $k > 0$

7. (a) $9/2$ **(b)** $13/3$ **(c)** $9/2$

9. (a) $1/3$ **(b)** $-1/5$ **(c)** 0

11. (a) 2 **(b)** $3/2$ **(c)** $1/2$

13. $1/2$ **15.** $-\pi$ **17.** $69/4$ **19.** $-39/2$ **21.** $25/6$

23. (a) $\text{Circ}_1 = 0$, $\text{circ}_2 = 2\pi$, $\text{flux}_1 = 2\pi$, $\text{flux}_2 = 0$
(b) $\text{Circ}_1 = 0$, $\text{circ}_2 = 8\pi$, $\text{flux}_1 = 8\pi$, $\text{flux}_2 = 0$

25. Circ = 0, flux = $a^2\pi$ **27.** Circ = $a^2\pi$, flux = 0

29. (a) $-\frac{\pi}{2}$ **(b)** 0 **(c)** 1

31.

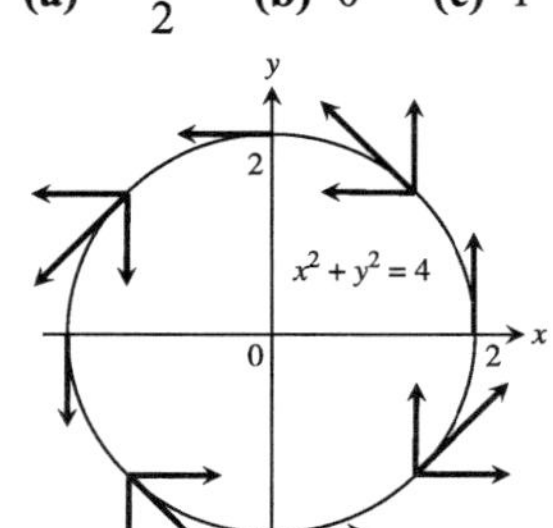

33. **(a)** $\mathbf{G} = -y\mathbf{i} + x\mathbf{j}$ **(b)** $\mathbf{G} = \sqrt{x^2 + y^2}\,\mathbf{F}$

35. $\mathbf{F} = -\dfrac{x\mathbf{i} + y\mathbf{j}}{\sqrt{x^2 + y^2}}$ **37.** 48 **39.** π **41.** 0 **43.** $\frac{1}{2}$

Section 16.3, pp. 1168–1169

1. Conservative **3.** Not conservative **5.** Not conversative

7. $f(x, y, z) = x^2 + \dfrac{3y^2}{2} + 2z^2 + C$

9. $f(x, y, z) = xe^{y+2z} + C$

11. $f(x, y, z) = x \ln x - x + \tan(x + y) + \frac{1}{2}\ln(y^2 + z^2) + C$

13. 49 **15.** -16 **17.** 1 **19.** $9 \ln 2$ **21.** 0 **23.** -3

27. $\mathbf{F} = \nabla\left(\dfrac{x^2 - 1}{y}\right)$ **29.** **(a)** 1 **(b)** 1 **(c)** 1

31. **(a)** 2 **(b)** 2 **33.** **(a)** $c = b = 2a$ **(b)** $c = b = 2$

35. It does not matter what path you use. The work will be the same on any path because the field is conservative.

37. The force $\mathbf{F}$ is conservative because all partial derivatives of M, N, and P are zero. $f(x, y, z) = ax + by + cz + C$; $A = (xa, ya, za)$ *and* $B = (xb, yb, zb)$. Therefore, $\int \mathbf{F} \cdot d\mathbf{r} = f(B) - f(A) = a(xb - xa) + b(yb - ya) + c(zb - za) = \mathbf{F} \cdot \overrightarrow{AB}$.

Section 16.4, pp. 1179–1181

1. Flux $= 0$, circ $= 2\pi a^2$ **3.** Flux $= -\pi a^2$, circ $= 0$
5. Flux $= 2$, circ $= 0$ **7.** Flux $= -9$, circ $= 9$
9. Flux $= 1/2$, circ $= 1/2$ **11.** Flux $= 1/5$, circ $= -1/12$

13. 0 **15.** 2/33 **17.** 0 **19.** -16π **21.** πa^2 **23.** $\frac{3}{8}\pi$

25. **(a)** 4π if C is traversed counterclockwise
(b) $(h - k)$(area of the region) **35.** **(a)** 0

Section 16.5, pp. 1190–1192

1. $\frac{13}{3}\pi$ **3.** 4 **5.** $6\sqrt{6} - 2\sqrt{2}$ **7.** $\pi\sqrt{c^2 + 1}$

9. $\frac{\pi}{6}\left(17\sqrt{17} - 5\sqrt{5}\right)$ **11.** $3 + 2\ln 2$ **13.** $9a^3$

15. $\dfrac{abc}{4}(ab + ac + bc)$ **17.** 2 **19.** 18 **21.** $\dfrac{\pi a^3}{6}$

23. $\dfrac{\pi a^2}{4}$ **25.** $\dfrac{\pi a^3}{2}$ **27.** -32 **29.** -4 **31.** $3a^4$

33. $\left(\dfrac{a}{2}, \dfrac{a}{2}, \dfrac{a}{2}\right)$

35. $(\bar{x}, \bar{y}, \bar{z}) = \left(0, 0, \dfrac{14}{9}\right)$, $I_z = \dfrac{15\pi\sqrt{2}}{2}\delta$, $R_z = \dfrac{\sqrt{10}}{2}$

37. **(a)** $\dfrac{8\pi}{3}a^4\delta$ **(b)** $\dfrac{20\pi}{3}a^4\delta$ **39.** $\frac{\pi}{6}\left(13\sqrt{13} - 1\right)$

41. $5\pi\sqrt{2}$ **43.** $\frac{2}{3}\left(5\sqrt{5} - 1\right)$

Section 16.6, pp. 1199–1201

1. $\mathbf{r}(r, \theta) = (r\cos\theta)\mathbf{i} + (r\sin\theta)\mathbf{j} + r^2\mathbf{k}$, $0 \le r \le 2$, $0 \le \theta \le 2\pi$

3. $\mathbf{r}(r, \theta) = (r\cos\theta)\mathbf{i} + (r\sin\theta)\mathbf{j} + (r/2)\mathbf{k}$, $0 \le r \le 6$, $0 \le \theta \le \pi/2$

5. $\mathbf{r}(r, \theta) = (r\cos\theta)\mathbf{i} + (r\sin\theta)\mathbf{j} + \sqrt{9 - r^2}\,\mathbf{k}$, $0 \le r \le 3\sqrt{2}/2$, $0 \le \theta \le 2\pi$; Also: $\mathbf{r}(\phi, \theta) = (3\sin\phi\cos\theta)\mathbf{i} + (3\sin\phi\sin\theta)\mathbf{j} + (3\cos\phi)\mathbf{k}$, $0 \le \phi \le \pi/4$, $0 \le \theta \le 2\pi$

7. $\mathbf{r}(\phi, \theta) = \left(\sqrt{3}\sin\phi\cos\theta\right)\mathbf{i} + \left(\sqrt{3}\sin\phi\sin\theta\right)\mathbf{j} + \left(\sqrt{3}\cos\phi\right)\mathbf{k}$, $\pi/3 \le \phi \le 2\pi/3$, $0 \le \theta \le 2\pi$

9. $\mathbf{r}(x, y) = x\mathbf{i} + y\mathbf{j} + (4 - y^2)\mathbf{k}$, $0 \le x \le 2$, $-2 \le y \le 2$

11. $\mathbf{r}(u, v) = u\mathbf{i} + (3\cos v)\mathbf{j} + (3\sin v)\mathbf{k}$, $0 \le u \le 3$, $0 \le v \le 2\pi$

13. **(a)** $\mathbf{r}(r, \theta) = (r\cos\theta)\mathbf{i} + (r\sin\theta)\mathbf{j} + (1 - r\cos\theta - r\sin\theta)\mathbf{k}$, $0 \le r \le 3$, $0 \le \theta \le 2\pi$
(b) $\mathbf{r}(u, v) = (1 - u\cos v - u\sin v)\mathbf{i} + (u\cos v)\mathbf{j} + (u\sin v)\mathbf{k}$, $0 \le u \le 3$, $0 \le v \le 2\pi$

15. $\mathbf{r}(u, v) = (4\cos^2 v)\mathbf{i} + u\mathbf{j} + (4\cos v\sin v)\mathbf{k}$, $0 \le u \le 3$, $-(\pi/2) \le v \le (\pi/2)$; Another way: $\mathbf{r}(u, v) = (2 + 2\cos v)\mathbf{i} + u\mathbf{j} + (2\sin v)\mathbf{k}$, $0 \le u \le 3$, $0 \le v \le 2\pi$

17. $\displaystyle\int_0^{2\pi}\int_0^1 \frac{\sqrt{5}}{2}\,r\,dr\,d\theta = \frac{\pi\sqrt{5}}{2}$

19. $\displaystyle\int_0^{2\pi}\int_1^3 r\sqrt{5}\,dr\,d\theta = 8\pi\sqrt{5}$ **21.** $\displaystyle\int_0^{2\pi}\int_1^4 1\,du\,dv = 6\pi$

23. $\displaystyle\int_0^{2\pi}\int_0^1 u\sqrt{4u^2 + 1}\,du\,dv = \frac{\left(5\sqrt{5} - 1\right)}{6}\pi$

25. $\displaystyle\int_0^{2\pi}\int_{\pi/4}^{\pi} 2\sin\phi\,d\phi\,d\theta = \left(4 + 2\sqrt{2}\right)\pi$

27. $\displaystyle\iint_S x\,d\sigma = \int_0^3\int_0^2 u\sqrt{4u^2 + 1}\,du\,dv = \frac{17\sqrt{17} - 1}{4}$

29. $\displaystyle\iint_S x^2\,d\sigma = \int_0^{2\pi}\int_0^{\pi} \sin^3\phi\cos^2\theta\,d\phi\,d\theta = \frac{4\pi}{3}$

31. $\displaystyle\iint_S z\,d\sigma = \int_0^1\int_0^1 (4 - u - v)\sqrt{3}\,dv\,du = 3\sqrt{3}$
(for $x = u$, $y = v$)

33. $\displaystyle\iint_S x^2\sqrt{5 - 4z}\,d\sigma = \int_0^1\int_0^{2\pi} u^2\cos^2 v \cdot \sqrt{4u^2 + 1} \cdot u\sqrt{4u^2 + 1}\,dv\,du = \int_0^1\int_0^{2\pi} u^3(4u^2 + 1)\cos^2 v\,dv\,du = \frac{11\pi}{12}$

35. -32 **37.** $\pi a^3/6$ **39.** $13a^4/6$ **41.** $2\pi/3$ **43.** $-73\pi/6$
45. $(a/2, a/2, a/2)$ **47.** $8\delta\pi a^4/3$

49.

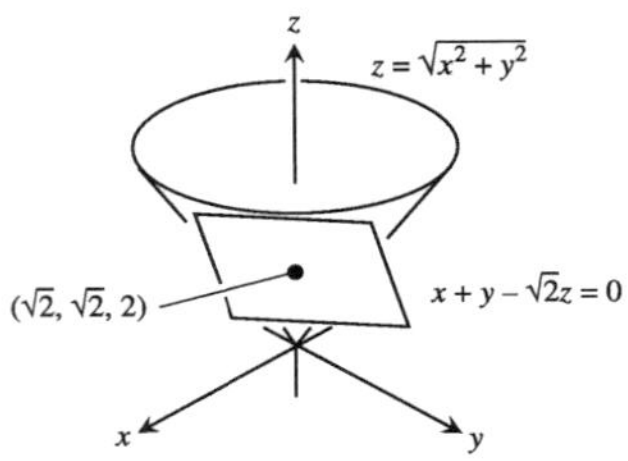

51.

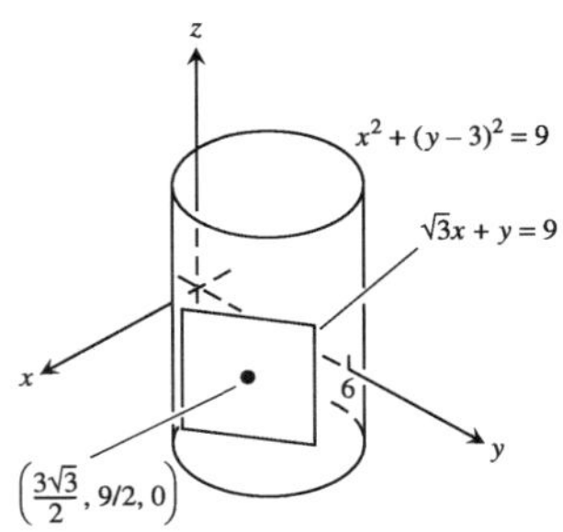

55. **(b)** $A = \int_0^{2\pi}\int_0^{\pi} [a^2b^2 \sin^2\phi \cos^2\phi + b^2c^2\cos^4\phi\cos^2\theta + a^2c^2\cos^4\phi\sin^2\theta]^{1/2}\, d\phi\, d\theta$

57. $x_0x + y_0y = 25$

Section 16.7, pp. 1209–1211

1. 4π **3.** $-5/6$ **5.** 0 **7.** -6π **9.** $2\pi a^2$ **13.** 12π
15. $-\pi/4$ **17.** -15π **25.** $16I_y + 16I_x$

Section 16.8, pp. 1220–1222

1. 0 **3.** 0 **5.** -16 **7.** -8π **9.** 3π **11.** $-40/3$
13. 12π **15.** $12\pi\left(4\sqrt{2} - 1\right)$
21. The integral's value never exceeds the surface area of S.

Practice Exercises, pp. 1223–1226

1. Path 1: $2\sqrt{3}$; path 2: $1 + 3\sqrt{2}$ **3.** $4a^2$ **5.** 0
7. $8\pi\sin(1)$ **9.** 0 **11.** $\pi\sqrt{3}$ **13.** $2\pi\left(1 - \frac{1}{\sqrt{2}}\right)$
15. $\frac{abc}{2}\sqrt{\frac{1}{a^2} + \frac{1}{b^2} + \frac{1}{c^2}}$ **17.** 50
19. $\mathbf{r}(\phi, \theta) = (6\sin\phi\cos\theta)\mathbf{i} + (6\sin\phi\sin\theta)\mathbf{j} + (6\cos\phi)\mathbf{k}$, $\frac{\pi}{6} \le \phi \le \frac{2\pi}{3}, 0 \le \theta \le 2\pi$
21. $\mathbf{r}(r, \theta) = (r\cos\theta)\mathbf{i} + (r\sin\theta)\mathbf{j} + (1 + r)\mathbf{k}, 0 \le r \le 2$, $0 \le \theta \le 2\pi$
23. $\mathbf{r}(u, v) = (u\cos v)\mathbf{i} + 2u^2\mathbf{j} + (u\sin v)\mathbf{k}, 0 \le u \le 1$, $0 \le v \le \pi$
25. $\sqrt{6}$ **27.** $\pi\left[\sqrt{2} + \ln\left(1 + \sqrt{2}\right)\right]$ **29.** Conservative
31. Not conservative **33.** $f(x, y, z) = y^2 + yz + 2x + z$
35. Path 1: 2; path 2: $8/3$ **37.** **(a)** $1 - e^{-2\pi}$ **(b)** $1 - e^{-2\pi}$

39. 0 **41.** **(a)** $4\sqrt{2} - 2$ **(b)** $\sqrt{2} + \ln\left(1 + \sqrt{2}\right)$
43. $(\bar{x}, \bar{y}, \bar{z}) = \left(1, \frac{16}{15}, \frac{2}{3}\right)$; $I_x = \frac{232}{45}, I_y = \frac{64}{15}, I_z = \frac{56}{9}$; $R_x = \frac{2\sqrt{29}}{3\sqrt{5}}, R_y = \frac{4\sqrt{2}}{\sqrt{15}}, R_z = \frac{2\sqrt{7}}{3}$
45. $\bar{z} = \frac{3}{2}, I_z = \frac{7\sqrt{3}}{3}, R_z = \sqrt{\frac{7}{3}}$
47. $(\bar{x}, \bar{y}, \bar{z}) = (0, 0, 49/12), I_z = 640\pi, R_z = 2\sqrt{2}$
49. Flux: $3/2$; circ: $-1/2$ **53.** 3 **55.** $\frac{2\pi}{3}\left(7 - 8\sqrt{2}\right)$
57. 0 **59.** π

Additional and Advanced Exercises, pp. 1226–1228

1. 6π **3.** $2/3$
5. **(a)** $\mathbf{F}(x, y, z) = z\mathbf{i} + x\mathbf{j} + y\mathbf{k}$ **(b)** $\mathbf{F}(x, y, z) = z\mathbf{i} + y\mathbf{k}$
(c) $\mathbf{F}(x, y, z) = z\mathbf{i}$
7. $\frac{16\pi R^3}{3}$ **9.** $a = 2, b = 1$. The minimum flux is -4.
11. **(b)** $\frac{16}{3}g$
(c) Work $= \left(\int_C gxy\, ds\right)\bar{y} = g\int_C xy^2\, ds = \frac{16}{3}g$
13. **(c)** $\frac{4}{3}\pi w$ **19.** False if $\mathbf{F} = y\mathbf{i} + x\mathbf{j}$

APPENDICES

Appendix A.5

1. **(a)** $(14, 8)$ **(b)** $(-1, 8)$ **(c)** $(0, -5)$
3. **(a)** By reflecting z across the real axis
(b) By reflecting z across the imaginary axis
(c) By reflecting z in the real axis and then multiplying the length of the vector by $1/|z|^2$
5. **(a)** Points on the circle $x^2 + y^2 = 4$
(b) Points inside the circle $x^2 + y^2 = 4$
(c) Points outside the circle $x^2 + y^2 = 4$
7. Points on a circle of radius 1, center $(-1, 0)$
9. Points on the line $y = -x$ **11.** $4e^{2\pi i/3}$ **13.** $1e^{2\pi i/3}$
15. $\cos^4\theta - 6\cos^2\theta\sin^2\theta + \sin^4\theta$ **17.** $1, -\frac{1}{2} \pm \frac{\sqrt{3}}{2}i$
19. $2i, -\sqrt{3} - i, \sqrt{3} - i$ **21.** $\frac{\sqrt{6}}{2} \pm \frac{\sqrt{2}}{2}i, -\frac{\sqrt{6}}{2} \pm \frac{\sqrt{2}}{2}i$
23. $1 \pm \sqrt{3}i, -1 \pm \sqrt{3}i$

INDEX

Note: Page numbers in *italics* indicate figures; "t" indicates a table; "e" indicates an exercise.

Abel, Niels, 299
Abscissa, 9
Absolute convergence test, 789–790
Absolute extrema, 244, *244*, *245*, *246*
  on closed interval, 249–250, *251*
  at endpoints, 249, *249*
  finding of, 250, *1031*, 1031–1032, 1034e, 1062e
Absolute maximum, 244, 1031
Absolute minimum, 244, 1031
Absolute value(s), 5, 6, 8e, 69e
Acceleration, 175
  normal component of, 966
  in space, velocity and, 916–917
  tangential and normal components of, 945–947, *946*, *947*, 949e
  velocity and position from, 259–260, 261e
Acceleration vectors, 910
Addition formulas, 53, 57e
Addition vectors, 856, *856*
Additivity Property, 1072, *1072*
Additivity Rule, for integrals, 360, 1145
Albert of Saxony, 551–552e
Algebra, basic, AP-29–AP-30
  Fundamental Theorem of, AP-20–AP-21
Algebra operations, involving vectors, *856*, 856–858, *857*
Algebra rules, 337, 338, 1012, 1014e
Algebra systems, computer (CAS), 593, 598–600, 741e
  visualizing surfaces in space, 897
Algebraic functions, 31
Algebraic properties, 1
Alternating series estimation theorem, 788, 816, 817
Alternating series test, 787
Alternating Series Theorem, 797
Angle(s), of inclination, 10, *11*
  between planes, 887, *887*, 888e
  between vectors, *863*, 863–865, 870–871e, 1063e
Angle convention, 50
Angle of rotation, 704, *704*
Angular momentum, 963e
Antiderivative(s), 307–314
  finding of area using, 363, *363*, *364*, 364
  formulas, 308t, 309
  and motion, 311
Antiderivative linearity rules, 309–310, 309t
Antidifferentiation, 307
Approximation(s), of area, *325*, 325–328, *326*, 328t
  finite, to area, 339–340
  linear. *See* Linear approximation(s)
  trapezoidal, 603–606
  using parabolas, 608–613
Approximation formula, 830
Arbitrary constant, 307
Arc length, 48, 534e, 545e, 602e, 931–933, 935e
  formula for graph, 420
Arccosine, and arcsine, identities involving, 521, *521*
Arccotangent curve, tangent line to, 527
Arch, center of mass of, 1147, *1147*, 1225e
Archer, firing flaming arrow, *924*, 924–926, *925*, 929e
Archimedes, circumference of circle and, 416, *417*
Archimedes' area formula for parabolas, 366e
Archimedes' formula for volume of parabola, 695e
Archimedes' principle, 1227e
Archimedes spirals, 742e
Arcsine, and arccosine, identities involving, 521, *521*
  and arccosine functions, 519–521, *520*
Arctangent(s), 828–829
  and arctangent functions, *522*, 522–524, *523*
Area, approximation of, *325*, 325–328, *326*
  beneath curve, 373, *373*
  of bounded regions in plane, *1081*, 1081–1083, *1082*
  canceling of, *363*, 363–364
  under curve of definite integrals, 349
  between curves, *379*, 379–381, 549e
    substitutions in, 376–387
  of ellipse, *590*, 590–591, 1047e, 1136e
  for evaluation of definite integrals, 353
  finding of, 353e, 565, *727*, 727–728, *728*
    using antiderivatives, 363, *363*, *364*, 364
  finite approximations for, 328t, 328
    limit of, 339–340
  under graph of positive function, 349–351
  between intersecting curves, *380*, 380–381
  and length, in polar coordinates, 726–731
  under line, 350, *350*
  of parallelogram's projection on plane, AP-28–AP-29
  in plane, *725*, 725–727, 741e, 879e
  of smooth surface, 1195
  of surface of revolution, 436–447, 463e, *730*, 730–731
  total, 363, 365e, 388–389e, 384–386e
  of trapezoid, 351, *351*
  of triangle, 876, 879e
Argand diagrams, AP-16–AP-17
Arrow diagram(s), 20, *20*, 1052–1053
Arteries, unclogging of, 230
Astroid, length of, 419, *419*
Astronomical unit, 698
Asymptote(s), *118*, 118–120, *119*, *120*
  horizontal, 109–110, *109*
  of hyperbolas, 691–692, *692*, 697e
  oblique, 111, *111*
  vertical, 622–626
a^u, integral of, 496–497
Average daily cost, 284, *284*
Average rate of change, limits of, 90
  and secant lines, 75
Average speed(s), 73–74, 74t
Average value(s), of integrable function, 1083
  of linear function, 331, *331*
  of nonnegative function, 331, *331*
  of sin x, 331–332, *332*
Average velocity, 172
a^x, 495–497, 500e
Axis, spin around, 1171–1172
Axis of symmetry, 15

Ball, bouncing, *764*, 764–765
Balloon, ascending, dropping package from, 311–312
  inflating, radius of, 219
  rising, rate of change and, *215*, 215–216

Base point, 931
Baseball, hitting of, 926–927, 928e, 930e
Bear population, modeling of, 677–679, *677*
Bernoulli, John, 292
Big-oh notation, 514, 515
Binomial series, 823, 831–832e
  for powers and roots, 822–824
Binomial Theorem, 160, AP-29–AP-30
Biomass, 64, *64*
Blood sugar, concentration of, 150–151, *150*, *151*
Boundary change, changing integrals with, 381, *381*
Boundary points, 3, 967, 1031, 1032
  for space regions, 970, *970*
Bounded region, 967
Bowditch curves, 204e
Box, fabrication of, 278, *278*, 286–287e
Box product, *877*, 877–878, 879e
Brachistochrone(s), 711–712, *712*
Bucket, leaky, 450, *450*

Calculators, graphing with, 59–65, 267e
Calculus, Fundamental Theorem of. *See* Fundamental Theorem of Calculus
Car, jacking up of, 448
Carbon-14 dating, 506–507, 511e
Cardioid(s), 720, *720*, 725e, 744–745e
  length of, 729, *729*
Carrying capacity, 670, 676
Cartesian coordinate system, 848, *848*, 874
Cartesian coordinates, 9, *9*, 848, 1126e, 1139e
  triple integrals in, 1098–1109, 1139e
Cartesian equation(s), and polar equations, *716*, 716–717, 718–719e
  polar equations for lines in, 733, *733*, 741–742e
Cartesian integrals, 1095–1096, *1096*
Cartesian plane, *9*
CAST rule, 50, *51*
Catenary, 33, *33*, 546e
Cauchy condensation test, 776
Cauchy-Schwartz inequality, 872e
Cauchy's Mean Value Theorem, 294, *294*
Cavalieri's principle, 398, *399*, 406e
Center of circle, 14
Center of mass, of arch, 1147, *1147*
  calculation of, *1146*, 1146–1147, 1149e
  of constant-density plate, 431–432, *432*
  of constant-density wire, 433, *433*
  definition of, 426
  finding of, *1189*, 1189–1190, 1198, *1198*
  moments and, 424–435, 464e
  of solid in space, 1110–1111, *1111*
  of thin flat plate, *429*, 429–433, *430*, 1083–1085, *1084*
  of variable-density plate, 432–433, *1084*, 1084–1085
Centroid(s), 433, 462–463e, 602e, 1089e, 1111, 1127e, 1138e, 1141e, 1191e
  finding of, *1118*, 1118–1119
  fluid forces and, 458, *458*
  of geometric figures, *1088*, 1088–1089
  of semicircular region, *443*, 443–444, *444*
Chain Rule, 192–193, 204e, 216, 222, 251, 368, 370, 945, 951, 996–1005, 1003e
  to calculate **N**, 938
  with exponentials, 490
  four-variable form of, 1053
  for functions of three variables, 999, 1000, 1003e
  for functions of two variables, 997, 1000, 1003e
  inverse hyperbolic cosine and, 541
  as "outside-inside" rule, 193
  and power rule, 211
  with powers of function, 194–195
  proof of, 228–229, 913
  tree diagram and, 997–998, *1000*, *1002*
  use of, 193–194, 1063e
Change, directions of, 1013
  estimation of, 1024, 1061–1062e
  exponential, law of, 502–503, 674–675
  rate(s) of, 139, 140e, 1065e
    derivative as, 171–183
    instantaneous, 171
    and limits, 73–81, 90e
  related rates of, 213–217
  sensitivity to, 179, 229–231, 1022, *1022*, 1025–1026e, 1061–1062e
Circle(s), 13, *13*, 17e
  area of, 335e, AP-39
  center of, 14
  circulation around, 1156, 1225e
  circumference(s) of, 416, *417*, 418–419, 732e
  of curvature, 939, 943e
    for plane curves, 939–940
  curvature of, 937
  diameter of, area changes with, 172
  exterior and interior of, 14, *14*
  extreme function values on, 1044–1045, *1045*
  flux across, 1157–1158, 1159e
  osculating, 241e, 939, *939*
    for parabola, 939–940, *940*
  parametric curves and, 196, *196*
  in plane, 13
  polar equations for, *732*, 732–734, *733*, 737e
  radius of, 14
  slope of, *206*, 206–207
  unit, motion on, 935, *935*
Circular arcs, 56
Circulation, around circle, 1156
  finding of, *1204*, 1204–1205
  for velocity fields, 1155–1156
Circulation density, counterclockwise and clockwise, 1172, *1172*, 1179e
  of two-dimensional field, 1201, *1201*
  of vector field, 1171, *1171*
Cissoid of Diocles, 212e
Clairaut's theorem, 991–992
Closed interval, 3
Closed region, 970
Coefficient(s), 30, 571, 578
Common factor, canceling of, 86–87, *87*
  creating of, 87
Comparison test(s), 628, 629, *629*, 777–780
Completeness property, 2, AP-9, AP-10
Completing the square, 529–530, AP-30
Complex conjugate, AP-16
Complex number(s), AP-12–AP-22
Complex number system, AP-14
Component test, for exactness, 1167
Composite(s), of continuous functions, *128*, 128–129, *129*
Composite functions, *40*, 40–41, 45–46e, 133e
  derivative of, *191*, 191–193, *192*
Compounded interest, 504–505
Computer algebra systems (CAS), 593, 598–600, 739e, 1049e
Computers, graphing with, 59–65, 277e
  three dimensional, 970–971, *972*
Concavity, *267*, 267–272
Concavity test, *268*, 268
Cone(s), 893–894, 1097e
  elliptical, *893*, 893–894
  parametrizing of, 1193, *1193*
  surface area of, 240e, 1195–1196
  volume of, 408e, AP-31
Conic section(s), 685, *686*, 740–741e, 743e
  classification by eccentricity, 697–701
  and polar coordinates, 685–745
  in polar coordinates, 732–736, 741e
  polar equations for, 734, *734*, *735*, 737e
Conic section law, 953
Conical bands, surface area and, 442, *442*
Conical tank, filling of, 217, *217*
Conjugate(s), absolute value of, AP-22
  complex arithmetic with, AP-22
Connectivity, 131
  simple, 1161–1162
Conservative field(s), closed-loop property of, *1163*, 1163–1164, *1164*
  component test for, 1164
  path independence and, 1161
  potentials for, 1164–1166
  and Stokes' Theorem, 1208–1209, *1209*
  work done by, 1163
Constant angular velocity, 1206, *1206*
Constant-coordinate equations, 1115, *1115*
Constant density, *427*, 427–428
Constant-depth formula, for fluid forces, 456, *456*
Constant force, work by, 447–448, 868, *868*, 1169e
Constant function(s), 94, *95*
Constant Multiple Rule, 161, *161*, 768
Construction of reals, AP-10–AP-11
Continuity, 124–134
  of composites of continuous functions, *128*, 128–129, *129*, 981

definition of, in terms of limits, 979
and differentiability, 154–155, 157–158e
differentiability implies, 994
limits and, 73–141, 142–143e
partial derivatives and, 990, *990*
at point, 124, *124*
Continuity equation, of hydrodynamics, *1217*, 1217–1218
Continuous, at point, 125
Continuous extension(s), *129*, 129–130, *130*, 133e, 983e, 1060e, 1063e
Continuous function(s), 127–128, *128*, 143e, 345, 909
average value of, *351*, 351–352
on closed bonded sets, 981
composites of, AP-7
continuity of composites of, 981
intermediate value theorem for, 130–131, 357
on interval, 127
at point, 125
throughout domain, 125, *125*
Continuous function theorem, 752
Continuous interest rate, 505
Contour curves, 968, *969*
Convergence, determining of, 622
of Fourier series, 838
power series and, 795–798
testing power series for, 799
testing using ratio test, 796, 847e
tests for, 627–629, 631e
Convergence theorem, power series for, 797–798
Conversion formulas, 48
Cooling soup, 667–671
Coordinate axes, 9
moments of inertia about, 1111, *1111*
rotation of, 703, 707–708e
Coordinate conversion formulas, 1123
Coordinate frame, right-handed, 848, *848*
Coordinate increments, 10, *10*
Coordinate pair, 9
Coordinate plane(s), 848–849, *849*
first moments about, 1110
trigonometric functions in, *52*
Coordinate systems, three-dimensional, 848–851
Coordinates, 69e, 952–953. *See also* Cartesian coordinates; Cylindrical coordinates; Polar coordinates
Cosecant, 50
Cosine(s), 50, 51t
law of, 54
rotations to evaluate, 707, *707*
and sines, products of powers of, 581–583, 585–586e
Cosine function, derivatives of, 184–185, *185*
Cost(s), average daily, 284, *284*
marginal. *See* Marginal cost
minimizing of, 284, *284*
minimum, sensitivity of, 284–285
Cotangent, 50
Counting numbers, AP-12
Cramer's rule, 212e
Critical point(s), 248, 1033, 1035e, *1035e*
definition of, 1029
without extreme values, 250, *250*
Cross product(s), 873–878, *874*
Cross product rule, proof of, 912–913
Cross-section(s), 890
of solid, 396, *397*
Curl. *See also* Circulation density
k-component of, 1171–1172
Curl **F**, finding of, 1202
paddle wheel interpretation of, 1205–1206, *1206*
Curvature, circle of, 939
for plane curves, 939–940
definition of, 936
finding of, *940*, 940–941, 948, 960e
formulas for computing, 947
of helix, *940*, 940–941, 942e
of line as zero, 937, *937*
of plane curve, *936*, 936–939
vector formula for, 947
and vectors, for curves, 940
Curve(s), arccotangent, tangent line to, 527
area beneath, 373, *373*
area between, 379–381, *379*
circulation around, 1155
concavity of, *267*, 267–272
contour, 968, *969*
curvature and normal vectors for, 940
differentiable, angles between, 872–873e
finding of, 310–311, *311*, 316e, 392e
generating, for cylinder, 889, *890*
graph of, 721, *721*
infinite and finite, 619, *619*
with infinitely many asymptotes, 119, *119*
length(s) of, 416–424, 462e, 732e
circumference of circle and, 418–419
defined parametrically, *417*, 417–419
parametric formula for, 419, *419*
level, 968, *969*, 973e, 974e
gradients and tangents to, 1010–1011, *1011*
parametric. *See* Parametric curve(s)
parametrized, 440, *440*
piecewise smooth, 910, *910*, 1161–1162
plane, circle of curvature for, 939–940
flux across, 1156–1158, *1157*, 1225–1226e
polar, length of, 728–729, 731–732e
slope of, 719–721, 725e
quadratic, 277e, 322e, 702, 705t
regression, 63
slope of, 137
smooth, 417
length of, 931
space, arc length along, *931*, 931–932
work done by force over, 1152
in space, 906
continuity of, 909
formulas for, 949
tangent, 135, *135*, 1027e, 1064e
tangent lines to, 1014, 1061e
tangent to, 134–135, *135*, 137, 167, *167*
$y = f(x)$, length of, 419
Cycloid(s), 424e, 709–712, *710*
Cylinder(s), 889–891
definition of, 889
elliptical, 890, *891*
generating curve for, 889, *890*
hyperbolic, 890–891, *891*, *1039*, 1039–1040, *1040*, 1041, *1041*
parabolic, 890, *890*
parametrizing of, 1193–1194, *1194*
volume of, AP-39
estimation of, 1025
Cylindrical bands, versus conical bands, surface area and, 442, *442*
Cylindrical can, designing of, 278–280, *279*
Cylindrical coordinates, 1115, *1116*, 1126e, 1139–1140e
integration in, 1115–1119
limits of, *1116*, 1116–1117
motion in, 951, *951*, 964e
triple integrals in, 1114–1128
Cylindrical shells, volume of, *409*, 409–416, *410*, 1137e
Cylindrical tank, pumping out of, 214–215, *214*

Dam, construction of, 456, *456*
De Moivre's Theorem, AP-19
Decibel scale, 499
Decimals, repeating, 765, 770e
Dedekind, Richard, 381, AP-11
Definite integral(s), applications of, 396–465
area under curve of, 349
definition of, 344, 368
estimating of, 827–828
evaluating by parts, 565
evaluation of, 383–384e, 915
area for, 353
existence of, 345
finding bounds for, 349
Mean Value Theorem for, *356*, 356–357, *357*, 361
notation and existence of, 344–346
properties of, 346–349
rules of, geometric interpretations of, *348*
proof of, 348–349
substitution(s) in, 376–387
of vector functions, 915
Zero Width Interval Rule for, 476
Degree(s), of polynomial, 30
radians versus, 190e, 195
Delta(s), finding of, algebraically, *95*, 95–96, *96*, 99e
applying definition for, 104, *104*
for given epsilons, 94–97
Density, constant, rod of, *427*, 427–428
definition of, 427
Derivations, and proofs, 71–72e

Derivative(s), applications of, 244–324
calculation(s) of, 169e
from definition, *148*, 148–150
of constant function, 159, *159*
of cosine function, 184–185, *185*
directional. *See* Directional derivative(s)
in economics, *177*, 177–178
of exponential functions, 489–491, 495–497
and functions, 147–155, 155–156e, 235–236e, 261e, 273–274
higher order, 168
of higher order, 209
of hyperbolic functions, 537–538, 537t, 543e
intermediate value property, 155, *155*
inverse, value of, 472, *472*
of inverse functions, 474e, 524, *524*, 525, 526, *526*, 527–530
of inverse hyperbolic cosine, 540–541
of inverse hyperbolic functions, 540–542, 540t
of inverses of differentiable functions, 470–472
left-hand, 152
of natural logarithms, 478–479, 487e
Newton's dot notation for, 947
from numerical values, 164–165
one-sided, *152*, 152–153, *153*, 157e
partial. *See* Partial derivative(s)
at point, 139, 153–154
of polynomial, 162–163
as rate of change, 171–183
right-hand, 152
second, 168
second and higher orders, 168
of sine function, 183–184
symbols for, 168
tangents and, 134–139
third, 168
of vector function, and motion, *909*, 909–911
zero, functions with, 258
Derivative formula, application of, 525
Derivative product rule, 163–165
Derivative quotient rule, 165–166
Derivative sum rule, 161–163
Descartes, folium of, 206, 208, *208*, 212e
Determinant(s), cross products and, 875–876
Jacobian, 1129, 1133, 1136–1137e
Determinant formula, 874–876
Devil's curve, 212e
Difference quotient, 139
Difference rule, 162
Differences, 39, 45e, 159–163
Differentiability, 993–994
and continuity, 154–155, 157–158e
implies continuity, 994
Differentiable, 148, *152*, 152–153, *153*
Differentiable function(s), 148, 154–155, 242e, 746, 993
graphing of, 272–273, *273*, 275–276e
inverses of, derivatives of, 470–472
rational powers of, 209–211
Differential(s), 222, 225–227, *226*, 1021–1024
tangent planes and, 1015–1027
total, 1021, 1023
Differential approximation, error in, *227*, 227–229
Differential equation(s), autonomous, definition of, 665
graphing of, 665–671
definition of, 310
first-order, 642–644
applications of, 673–680
solution of, 643
first-order linear, 650–657
and initial value problems, power series solutions of, 824–827
initial value problems and, 310
separable, slope fields and, 642–650
solving of, 825–827
Differential form, 441, *441*
for surface areas, *441*, 441–442
Differential form(s), exact, 1166–1167, 1169e
Differential formula, short, 422, *422*
Differentiation, 147–243, 547e, 578
implicit, *205*, 205–211, *206, 207, 208*, 211e, 236e, 995e, 1001–1002, 1004e, 1060e
logarithmic, 483–484, 485e, 500e, 547e
order of, choosing of, 992
partial, CAS computing, 987
implicit, 988
rules, 159–168
term-by-term, 799–800, 839e
Differentiation operators, 150
Differentiation rules, 911–913
for vector functions, 912
Diocles, cissoid of, 212e
Direction, vectors and, 857–859, *858*
Direction field(s), 644–645, *644*, *645*, 649–650e
Directional derivative(s), 1005–1014, *1008, 1010*
Dirichlet ruler function, 145
Discontinuity(ies), in *dy/dx*, 421, *421*
infinite, 126, *126*
jump, 125, *125*, 126, *126*
oscillating, 126, *126*
point of, 125
removable, 126, 134e
single point of, 979–980
Discriminant of *f*, 1030
Discriminant test, 705–706
Disease, infectious, incidence of, 504, 509e
Disk method, solid of revolution, 399–402, *400, 401, 402*, 406–407e
Displacement, 172, *172*
versus distance traveled, 330
Display windows, 59, *60*
Distance, calculation of, 13
and circles in plane, 13
extremes of, on ellipse, *1046*, 1046–1047
from point to line, 883, 888e
from point to plane, *886*, 886–887
and spheres in space, 850–851
traveled, displacement versus, 330
between two points, 850, *850*, 852e
Distance formula, for points in plane, 13
Distributive Law, for vector cross products, AP-22–AP-23
Divergence, 1211, 1219, 1220
tests for, 627–629
in three dimensions, 1211
of vector field, *1170*, 1170–1171, *1171*
Divergence Theorem, 1219, 1220
and Green's Theorem, 1219, 1220
for special regions, 1213–1214, *1214*
support of, 1212
and unified theory, 1211–1222
for various regions, 1214–1215
Dominant terms, 120–121
Dot product(s), 862–870
definition of, 863
finding of, *863*, 863–864
properties of, 866
triple, *877*, 877–878, 879e
Dot product rule, proof of, 912
Double-angle formulas, 54, 57e
Drift correction, 524, *524*
Dropped cargo, 199–200, *200*

Earthquake, intensity of, 499
Eccentricity(ies), 697–698
of ellipse, 697, *698*
of hyperbola, *699*, 699–700, 702e
of parabola, 700
of planetary orbits, 698, 698t
Economics, derivatives in, *177*, 177–178
Electric current flow, 654–655
Electrical charge, distributed over surface, 1185, *1185*
Electrical resistors, *989*, 989–990
Electricity, household, 374, *374*
Electromagnetic Theory, law of, 1216–1217
Element(s), of set, 3
Ellipse(s), *44*, 44–45, 48e, 688–690, 694e, 701e, 935e
area formula for, 708
area of, *590*, 590–591, 1136e
center of, 44, *45*
center-to-focus distance of, 689
definition of, 688
directrices of, 698, *699*
eccentricity of, 697–698, *698*
equations for, 690
extremes of distance on, *1046*, 1046–1047
focal axis of, 688, *688*
foci of, 688, 698
major axis of, 44, 689, *689*
minor axis of, 44, 689
parametric curves and, 198–199
polar equations for, 734–736, *736*, 737–738e
semimajor axis of, 689
semiminor axis of, 689
tangent line to, 1011, *1011*

vertices of, 688, *688*, 699
Ellipsoid(s), 693, *693*, 891–892, *892*, 1109e
of revolution, 892
Empirical model(ing), 37, 63–65
Empty set, 3
Energy, mass conversion to, 230–231
Engine cylinders, grinding of, 100
Epsilons, finding deltas for, 94–97
Equal area law, *953*, 953–954
Equations, geometric interpretation of, 849, 851, 852e
graphing of, 850, *850*
Equilibrium(a), 667–671
Equilibrium values, 665–666
Error(s), in differential approximation, *227*, 227–229
truncation, 815–817
Error estimation, 793e, 811–819, 820e, 1022, 1025–1026e
Error term, 318
Euler's constant, 776–777
Euler's formula, AP-17
Euler's gamma function, 660e
Euler's identity, 818, 821e
Euler's method, 659–664, *660*, 664e, 677
accuracy of, 661–662, 661t, *662*, 662t
improved, 663, 663t, 664e
use of, 660–661
Exactness, component test for, 1167
Exponential change, law of, 502–503
Exponential function(s), 31, *32*, 486–495
with different bases, 513
even and odd parts of, 535
Exponential growth and decay, 502–511
Exponents, laws of, 488–489, 494e, AP-29
Extension, continuous, 143
Extrema, absolute. *See* Absolute extrema
finding of, 247–252, *248*
local. *See* Local extrema
relative, 247
Extreme function values, on circle, 1044–1045, *1045*
Extreme Value Theorem, 347, AP-10, 247, *247*
Extreme values,
function of two variables and, 1027, *1027*, *1028*
of functions, 244–252
local, 246–247, *247*
derivative tests for, 1027–1031, *1028*
finding of, 1029, *1029*, 1030
first derivative theorem for, 247
maximum, 1028, *1028*, 1033, 1034e
minimum, 1028, 1033, 1034e
searching for, 1031, *1031*
second derivative test for, 1031

Factorial notation $n!$, 754, 759e
Falling body, resistive force and, 669–670, *669*
Faraday's Law, 1227e
Fermat's principle, *281*, 281–282, 289e
Fibonacci numbers, 755
Fick, Adolf, 220e
Field(s), not conservative, 1166
ordered, AP-10
Finite intervals, 3
Finite sum(s), algebra rules for, 337, 338
estimating of, 325–335, 388e
limits of, 339–340
sigma notation and, 335–343
First derivative theorem, 247
First-order differential equations. *See* Differential equation(s), first-order
First-order initial value problem, 643
First-order linear differential equations, 650–657
First-order linear initial value problem, 653–654, 658e
Flow, along helix, 1155–1156
Flow integral(s), 1159e
for velocity fields, 1155–1156
Fluid force(s), 460–461e, 463–464e, 465e
and centroids, 458, *458*
constant-depth formula for, 456, *456*
finding of, 458
integral for, *457*, 457–458
Fluid pressures, 456–461
Flux, across circle, 1157–1158, 1159e
across plane curve, 1156–1158, *1157*, 1225–1226e
circulation and, 1159
definition of, 1187
finding of, *1197*, 1197–1198, 1212–1213
outward. *See* Outward flux
surface integrals for, 1187–1188
of vector field, 1188, *1188*
Flux density, *1170*, 1170–1171, *1171*
Folium of Descartes, 206, 208, *208*, 212e
Force(s), constant, work by, 447–448, 868, *868*, 1169e
effective, 855, *855*
fluid. *See* Fluid force(s)
on spacecraft, 870
variable, work by, 448, 452–453e
Force constant, 449
Force vector, 859, 861–862e
Fourier, Joseph, 833
Fourier approximation functions, 837, *837*
Fourier series, 586e, 833–838, *836*, 842e
Fractal basins, Newton's method and, 303–305, *304*
Fraction(s), integrating of, 573–574
reducing of, 556–557
separating of, 557, 559e
Franklin, Benjamin, will of, 510e
Free fall, 74, 175, *175*
Frenet frame, 943–945, *945*, 950e
Fruit flies (*Drosophila*), average growth rate of, 75–76, *76*, 157e
growth rate on specific day, 76–77, *76*
Fubini, Guido, 1070
Fubini's theorem, *1069*, 1069–1071, *1073*
Function(s), 19, 26e, 69e
absolute value, 128
algebraic, 31
arcsine and arccosine, 519–521, *520*
arctangent and arctangent, 522–524, *522*, *523*
as arrow diagram, 20, *20*
average value of, 331, *331*, 352, *352*, 354e
combining of, 38–45, *40*
component, 906
composite. *See* Composite functions
composition of, 40, 70e
constant, 28, *28*, 79, *79*, 94, *95*
derivative of, 159, *159*
construction of, 360
continuous. *See* Continuous function(s)
continuously differentiable, 417
cube root, 29, *30*
cubic, 30, 254e
decreasing, 262–264
defined by table of values, 23
defined on surfaces, 999–1001
definition of, 79
and derivatives. *See* Derivative(s), and functions
differentiable. *See* Differentiable function(s)
domain(s) of, 19, *19*, 20, 965, 966, 968, 973e
evaluation of, 966
even, integral of, 379
even and odd, 33, 37–38e, 48e
Taylor series for, 821e
exponential. *See* Exponential function(s)
extreme values of, 244–252
graph of, scaling and reflecting of, 42–44
shifting of, 41–42, *42*
and graphs, 19, 21, *21*, 22, *22*, 26e, 69–70e, 71–72e
greatest integer, 24, *25*, 126, *126*
growing at same rate, 513
growth rates of, *511*, 511–513, *512*, 548–549e
hyperbolic. *See* Hyperbolic functions
identification of, 28–38
identity, 79, *79*, 94, *95*
implicitly defined, 205–207
increasing, 262–264
increasing and decreasing, 33, 474e
integer floor, 24, *25*
integrable, 345, 1068
average value of, 1083
integration with respect to y and, 381–382, *382*
inverse. *See* Inverse function(s)
inverse trigonometric. *See* Trigonometric function(s), inverse
left-continuous, 125
limits of, 103, *103*
linear, 28, *28*
average value of, 331, *331*
logarithmic, 31–32, *33*
mean value of, 352, *352*

Function(s) *(continued)*
monotonic, 262–264, *263*
of more than two variables, 981, 989, 1023
linearization of, 1023–1024
near point, behavior of, 77–78, *78*, 78t
nonintegrable, 346
nonnegative, average value of, 331, *331*
numerical representation of, 23
oscillating, 104–105, *105*
periodic, 52
Taylor polynomials for, 821e
piecewise-continuous, 346
piecewise-defined, 24, 25, 26–27e, 70e
polynomial, 30, *30*, 127–128
positive, area under graph of, 349–351
potential, 1165–1166, 1168e
power, 29, *29*, *30*
quadratic, 30
range of, 19, 20, 965, 966, 973e
rapidly oscillating, *61*, 61–62, *62*
rational. *See* Rational function(s)
real-valued, 20, 965
recognizing of, 33, 37e
recovering from derivative, 157
right-continuous, 125
scalar, 907
solution, 643–644
square root, 29, 30e
symmetric, definite integrals of, 378–379, *378*
of three variables, 969–970, 1012–1013, 1025e
Chain Rule for, 995, 1000, 1003e
transcendental, 32–33, *33*, 466–552
trigonometric. *See* Trigonometric function(s)
of two variables, 966–968, 974e
unit step, 125, *125*
limits of, 42–44
of variables, 965–975
vector (vector-valued). *See* Vector functions (vector-valued)
with zero derivatives, 258
zero of (root), 131, *132*
Function in space, average value of, 1105, *1105*
Function values, estimating of, 619
Fundamental Theorem of Algebra, AP-20–AP-21
Fundamental Theorem of Calculus, 312, 356–368, *358*, 367e, 478, 915, 919e, 1219–1220
application of, 359–360

Gabriel's horn, 632e
Galileo's free-fall formula, 180e
Galileo's law, 74
Gateway Arch to the West, 535
Gauss's Law, 1216–1217
General linear equation, 12
General power function, 496
General sine curve, *55*, 58e
General sine function, 55
General solution, 311
Genetic data, sensitivity to change and, 179
Geometry, 72e, AP-30–AP-31
graphing and, AP-21
Glider, distance traveled by, 931–932, *932*
flight of, 915–916
Global extrema, 244
Glory hole, pumping water from, *451*, 451–452, *452*
Gradient(s), algebra rules for, 1012, 1014e
to level curves, 1010–1011, *1011*
Gradient field(s), 1152–1155, 1158e, 1169e
Gradient rules, 1012
Gradient vector, 1008
Graph(s), 9, 69e
arc length formula for, 420
of function, scaling and reflecting of, 42–44
shifting of, 41–42, *42*, 46–47e
of function of two variables, 968
functions and, 26e, 69–70e, 71–72e
identical on large scale, 121, *121*
limits from, 81–82
of rational function, 61, *61*
shifting, 41–42, 46–47e
sketching of, 21–22, *22*
Graphing, with calculators and computers, 59–65
of derivative, 150–151, *151*, 156–157e
of differentiable function, 272–273, *273*, 275–276e
and geometry, AP-21
Graphing windows, 59–63
Gravitational constant, 952
Greatest integer function, *25*, 126, *126*, 158e
Green's formula, 1222e
Green's Theorem, 1169–1181, 1218–1219, 1220, 1225e
to evaluate line integrals, 1174–1175
and Laplace's equation, 1181e
and Stokes' Theorem, 1203, *1203*
Growth, logistic, 670
Growth and decay, exponential, 502–511
Growth model, logistic, 676, *676*
Growth rate(s), comparisons of, 512–513
of functions, *511*, 511–513, *512*, 548–549e
relative, 511–517, 675, 675t

Half-angle formulas, 54
Half-life, of radioactive element, 506
Half-open interval, 3
Halley's comet, 698–699, *699*, 739e
Hang glider, flight of, 911, *911*
Harmonic series, 772–773
Heat transfer, 507–508
Heaviside method, 576–577
integrating with, 577–578
Height,of projectile, 329
Helicopter, flight of, 882
Helix, computer-generated, 908, *908*
curvature of, *940*, 940–941, 942e
flow along, 1155–1156
graphing of, 907, *907*
Hemisphere, Stokes' equation for, 1203–1204
Hessian of *f*, 1030
Hooke's law for springs, 449
Horizontal asymptote(s), *109*, 109–110
Horizontal motion, 174, *174*
Horizontal tangent(s), finding of, 163, *163*
Huygens, Christiaan, pendulum clock of, 710, *710*
Hydrodynamics, continuity equation of, *1217*, 1217–1218
Hydrogen ion concentration, 499
Hyperbola(s), 690–692, 694e, 701–702e, 708e
asymptotes of, 691–692, *692*, 697e
eccentricity of, 699–700, *699*, 702e
equation(s) for, 692, 699–701, *701*, 703–704e, *703*
focal axis of, 691, *691*
foci of, 690, *690*, *699*
parametrization of, 709–710, *710*
polar equations for, 734–736, *736*, 737–738e
vertices of, 691, *691*
Hyperbolic cosine, inverse, derivative of, 540–541
Hyperbolic function(s), 535–536, 535t, 601e
definitions and identities of, 535–537, 535t
derivatives of, 537–538, 537t, 543e
integral formulas for, 537–538, 537t
inverse, 538–539, *539*
derivatives of, 540–542, 540t
evaluation of, 543–544e
identities for, 539t, 539–541
integrals leading to, 541–542, 542t
values and identities of, 542–543e
Hyperboloid(s), 894–896, *895, 896*

Ice skater, coasting, 674
Identity(ies), 53–54, 240–241e, 1208, AP-32
Euler's, 818, 821e
inverse function-inverse cofunction, 527
for inverse hyperbolic functions, 539t, 539–540
involving arcsine and arccosine, 521, *521*
substitutions and, 372
Identity function, 79, *79*, 94, *95*
Image, 1128
Implicit differentiation, *205*, 205–211, *206, 207, 208*, 211e, 236e, 995e, 1001–1002, 1004e, 1060e
Improper integral(s), 553, 619–630
Inclination, angle of, 10, *11*
Increment theorem, for functions of two variables, 993, AP-25–AP-27
Increments, 10–12, 17e
coordinate, 10, *10*
Indefinite integral(s), 312–313, 543e, 553
definition of, 368
finding of, 314–315e, 321e, 914–915
and substitution rule, 368–376

of vector functions, 914–915
Indeterminate form(s), 292, 296–297, 298e, 832e
evaluating of, 829–830, 841e
Index, 747, 764
Index of summation, 336, 337
Inequality(ies), absolute values and, 6–7
Cauchy-Schwartz, 872e
geometric interpretation of, 849, 851, 852e
rules for, 2
solving of, 3–5, *4*
triangle, 6
Infinite half-cylinder, 1142
Infinite intervals, 3
Infinite limits, of integration, *619*, 619–620
Infinite sequence(s), bounded nondecreasing, 755–756, *756*
boundedness of, 756
construction of, recursively, 755
continuous function theorem for, 752
convergence and divergence of, 748–749, 840e, 843e
description of, 747–748
divergent, 750
graphical representation of, 748, *748*
limit(s) of, 749, *749*, 757–758e, 759e
calculation of, 750–752, 760e
nondecreasing sequence theorem of, 756
recursive definitions of, 755, 760e
sandwich theorem for, 751–752
upper bounds of, 756, 759e
Infinite series, 761–769
absolute and conditional convergence of, 789–790
alternating, 787, 793e
harmonic, 787, 788
rearranging of, 791–792
p-series, 790
partial sums of, 788, *788*
conditionally convergent, 789
convergence or divergence of, 770e, 775–776e, 781e, 786e
harmonic, 772–773
infinite sum and, 746
logarithmic *p*-series, 776
rearrangement theorem and, 790, 794e
rearranging of, 790–791
study of, 802
Inflection point(s), 248, 268–269, *269*
Initial value problem(s), 315–316e, 321e, 366e, 375–376e, 389e, 391e, 490–491, 494e, 532e, 580e, 591e, 832e, 841e
definition of, 310
differential equations and, 310
power series solutions of, 824–827
first-order, 643
first-order linear, 653–654, 658e
series solution of, 824–825
Inner product. *See* Dot product(s)
Instantaneous speed, 74–75, 139
Instantaneous velocity, 172
Integers, 2, AP-12
first *n*, sum of, 338
power rule for, 160, 166–168
Integral(s), 325, 481–483, 493–494e, 622
Additivity Rule for, 360, 1145
changing of, to match boundary change, 381, *381*
combining of, with geometry, 383, *383*
definite. *See* Definite integral(s)
divergent improper, 623–624
double, 1067–1081, 1140e
in polar form, 1092–1098
substitutions in, 1128–1132, *1129, 1130*
evaluation of, 353e, 361–363, 365e, 374–375e, 531–532e, 580e
of exponential functions, 489–491, 495–497
flow. *See* Flow integral(s)
for fluid force, 457
improper, 553, 619–630
incorrect calculation of, 626
indefinite. *See* Indefinite integral(s)
iterated, 1070
leading to inverse hyperbolic functions, 541–542, 542t
line. *See* Line integral(s)
matching to basic formulas, 558
multiple, 1067–1142
definition of, 1067
substitutions in, 1128–1137
of natural logarithm, 563
nonelementary, 597–598, 617e, 841e
evaluating of, 827–828
of nonpositive functions, 354
over bounded nonrectangular regions, 1072–1075
path independence of, 1162–1163
in polar coordinates, 1092–1093
of powers of tan x and sec x, 583
repeated, 1070
secant and cosecant, 558
substitutions to evaluate, 371
table of, T-1–T-6
transformation of, 373
trigonometric, 581–586
triple, *1098*, 1098–1099, 1106e, 1140e
in cylindrical and spherical coordinates, 1114–1128
properties of, 1105–1106
in rectangular coordinates, 1098–1109
substitutions in, *1132*, 1132–1135, *1133, 1134*
unknown, solving for, 564–565
of vector functions, 914–916
Integral theorems, 1218–1220
Integral formulas, 528–529
Integral tables, 593–595, 600–601e
Integral test, 772–775, *773, 774*
Integrands, 370, 622–626
Integrate command, 598
Integrating exponentials, 490
Integrating factor, 651
Integration, 325–395, 642–681
with CAS, 598–600
constant of, 313–314
in cylindrical coordinates, 1115–1119
limits of, *1116*, 1116–1117
indefinite, term-by-term, 313–314
infinite limits of, *619*, 619–620
limits of, 1093–1095, *1095*, 1100–1105, *1102, 1103*
finding of, 1076–1077
multiple, 1071
numerical, 603–619, 617e
order(s) of, *1104*, 1104–1105
changing of, 1108–1109e, 1141e
by parts, 561–568, 568e, 569e
with respect to y, functions and, 381–382, *382*
reversing order of, 1077, *1077*, 1079e
tabular, 565–567
techniques of, 553–633
term-by-term, 801–802
variable of, 312, 345
in vector fields, 1143–1228
Integration formulas, 528, 553–558, 554t
Intercepts, 12, 16e
Interest, compounded continuously, 504–505, 510e
Interior point(s), 3, 967, *967*, 1031
for space regions, 970, *970*
vertical asymptotes at, 624, *624*
Intermediate Value Property, 130–131, 155, *155*
Intermediate Value Theorem, 130–131, *131*, AP-10
Intersection of sets, 3
Intersection points, elusive, 722–723, *723*
Interval(s), absolute values and, 6
closed, 249–250, *250*, 253e, 342
of convergence, of power series, 799, 804e
definition of, 3
half-open, extreme values on, 267
open, 5
types of, 4t
Inverse(s), 517–519, 521–524
Inverse equations, 487, 498
Inverse function–inverse cofunction identities, 527
Inverse function(s), 467–472, 538–539, *539*
derivatives of, 474e, 524, *524*, 525, 526, *526*, 527–530
formulas for, 473–474
integration of, 570
one-to-one, 466–467, *467*
Irrational numbers, 3

Jacobi, Carl, 1129
Jacobian determinant(s), 1129, 1130–1131
of transformation, 1133–1134, *1134*
Jerk, 175, 186
Joule, James Prescott, 447
Joules, 447

Kepler equation, 963e
Kepler method for parabolas, 697e
Kepler's first law, 953–956
Kepler's hypothesis, 63
Kepler's second law, *953*, 953–954
Kepler's third law, 35–37, 956, 959e
Kinetic energy, *1085*, 1085–1086
  work and, 457–458e

Lagrange, Joseph-Louis, 257
Lagrange multipliers, 1038–1049, 1062e
Laplace equation(s), 995–996e, 1005e
  Green's Theorem and, 1181e
Law of addition, parallelogram, 856, *856*, *863*, 863–864
Law of cosines, 54
Law of exponential change, 502–503, 674–675
Law of Refraction, *282*, 282–283, *283*
Law of sines, 58e
Laws of exponents, 488–489, 494e, AP-29
Laws of signs, AP-29
Least upper bound, AP-10
Leibniz, Gottfried Wilhelm, 150, 344, 356
Leibniz's formula, 828–829
Leibniz's notation, 222, 225, 418
Leibniz's rule, 243e, 393e, 1064e
Leibniz's theorem, 787
Lemniscate, 722–723, *722*
Length, of arc, 48
  and area, in polar coordinates, 726–731
  of astroid, 419, *419*
  of cardioid, 729, *729*
  constant, vector functions of, *913*, 913–914
  of parametric curves, 418, 423e
  of polar curves, 728–729, 731–732e
  of vector, 855
Lens(es), 207, *208*
Level curves. *See* Curve(s), level
Level surface(s), 969–970
l'Hopital, Guillaume de, 292
l'Hopital's Rule, 292–293, 295, 297, 298e, 320e, 752–753
Limaçon(s), 725e, 727–728, *727*
Limit(s), 77, 531e, 532e, 550e
  calculation of, 79, 84–89, 89–90e, 977–978
    calculators and computers for, 80–81, 81t
  commonly occurring, AP-7–AP-9
  comparison test, 628, 629, *629*
  and continuity, 73–141, 142–143e
  existence of, 82
  finite, as x approaches infinity, *107*, 107–108, 113e
  of finite sums, 339–340
    sigma notation and, 335–343
  of function, 103, *103*
    of two variables, 976–979
  of function values, 77–80
  in higher dimensions, 976–984
  infinite, 115–118, 122e
    of integration, *619*, 619–620
  at infinity, 107–114, 108, *108*
  of integration, 1093–1095, *1095*, 1100–1105, *1102, 1103*
  involving (sin θ)/θ, *105*, 105–107
  left-hand, 102, *102*, 104, *104*
    proof of, AP-7
  nonexistence of, two-path test of, *980*, 980–981
  one-sided, 102–107
  of polynomials, 86, AP-7
  power series using, 829–830
  precise definition of, 91–98, *92, 94*, 145e
  rates of change and, 73–81
  of rational functions, 113–114e, AP-7
  of Riemann sums, 343–356
  right-hand, 102, *102*, 104, *104*
    proof of, AP-6
  two-sided, proof of, AP-7
  upper, of sums, 343
  of vector valued functions, 908
Limit comparison test, 778–780
Limit laws, 84–89, AP-4
Limit product rule, proof of, AP-4–AP-5
Limit quotient rule, proof of, AP-5–AP-6
Limit Theorems, proofs of, AP-4–AP-7
Limiting population, 670
Line(s), area under, 350, *350*
  circles, and parabolas, 9–16
  distance along, 933
  of intersection, 884–886
  long straight, motion on, 918
  motion along, 172, 269–270, 276e, 288e
  normal, parallel to plane, 1063
  parallel, 12–13
  parametric equations for, 881
  parametrizing of, 197, 881
  in plane, intersection of, 885–886
  and planes in space, *880*, 880–887
  polar equations for, 732, *732*, 737e, 741e
  straight, 10–12
    curvature of, 937, *937*
  tangent. *See* Tangent line(s)
  through two points, 11–12, *12*
  vector equation for, 880
Line integral(s), *1143*, 1143–1149
  additivity and, 1145
  in conservative fields, 1162–1164
  evaluation of, 1144, *1144*, 1168e, 1223e
  fundamental theorem of, 1162
  Green's Theorem for, 1174–1175
  for two joined paths, 1145
Line segment, directed, 853, 854
  midpoint of, 18e, 860, *860*, 861e
  parametrizing of, *881*, 881–882
Linear approximation(s), 223, 231e, 232e, 234e, 822e
  in 3-space, 1023–1024
  error formula for, 1056
  finding of, 1058
  standard, 1019, 1020, 1025e
Linear equation(s), 12
  solving of, 651–652
Linear factor(s), distinct, 572–573
  Heaviside "cover-up" method for, 576
  repeated, 573, 579e
Linear function, *91*, 91–92
  average value of, 331, *331*
Linearization(s), 221–225, *222, 223, 224*, 231e, 240e, 494e, 501e
  finding of, 1019–1020, 1025e, 1061e
  functions and, 234e, 1018–1019, *1019*, 1023–1024
  and linear approximations, 223, 231e, 234e
Liquids, pumping of, 450, 453–454e
Lissajous figures, 204e
Little-oh notation, 514
Local extrema, first derivative test for, *264*, 264–266, *266*, 271
  second derivative test for, 270
Local maximum, 247
Local minimum, 247
Logarithmic differentiation, 483–484, 485e, 500e, 547e
Logarithmic function(s), 31–32, *33*
  with different bases, 513
Logarithm(s), base 10, 499–500
  base a, 497, *497*, 498t
    derivatives and integrals involving, 498–499
  natural, 476–485
    derivatives of, 478–479, 484e
    graph and range of, 480–481, *481*
    integrals of, 563
  properties of, 479–480, 484e
Logistic growth, 670
Lorentz contraction, 144e

Maclaurin series, definition of, 806
  finding of, 820
  series representations, 806
  Taylor series and, 805–810
Map, contours on, 1005–1006, *1006*
Marginal cost, 177, 178, 182e, 276e, 282–283, *283*
Marginal profit, 282–283, *283*
Marginal revenue, 178, 182e, 241e, 282–283, *283*
Marginal tax rate, 178
Mass(es), along line, 424–426, *425*
  calculation of, *1146*, 1146–1147
  center of, moments and, 424–435, 464e
  conversion to energy, 230–231
  and moments, calculations of, 1145–1147, *1146*, 1146t
    in three dimensions, 1109–1114
  moments of inertia and, *1109*, 1109–1110
  over plane region, *428*, 428–429
Mathematical induction, AP-1–AP-4

Mathematical models, for functions, 28–38, *35*
Max-min tests, 1033
Maximum(a), absolute, 244
on closed bounded regions, 1031
constrained, 1038–1041
local, 247
Mean Value Theorem, *257*, 257–258, *258*, 260e, 262, 266, 319e, 437, *438*, 812, AP-26–AP-27
corollaries of, 258–259, *259*
for definite integrals, *356*, 356–357, *357*, 361
Taylor's theorem and, 820e
Mendel, Gregor Johann, 179
Mesh size, 603
Midpoint of line segment, 18e, 860, *860*, 861e
Midpoint rule, 327, *327*
Minimum(a), absolute, 244
on closed bounded regions, 1031
constrained, 1038–1041, *1041,* 1047e
local, 247
Mixed derivative theorem, 991–992, AP-23–AP-25
Mixture problems, 655
Möbius band, 1187, *1187*
Moment(s), 1127–1128e, 1138e
and centers of mass, 424–435, 464e
first, 1086
about coordinate planes, 1110
and masses, of thin shells, *1189*, 1189–1190, 1189t
in three dimensions, 1109–1114
polar, 1086–1087, 1138e
second, 1086
of system about origin, 425
Moment(s) of inertia, *1085*, 1085–1088, *1086*, 1089–1090e, 1112e, 1140e, 1180e
about coordinate axes, 1111, *1111*
calculation of, 1146–1147, 1149e
mass and, *1109*, 1109–1110
radius of gyration and, 1087–1088, 1090e, 1112e, 1127e, 1138e
Momentum, angular, 963e
Monotonic functions, 262–264, *263*
Motion, along line, 172, 269–270, 276e, 288e
antiderivatives and, 311
in cylindrical coordinates, 951, *951*, 964e
derivatives of vector function and, *909*, 909–911
direction of, 173, *173*, 910
horizontal, 174, *174*
on long straight line, 918
Newton's law(s) of, 669, 673
planetary, 950–958, *952*, 952–953
in polar coordinates, 951, *951*, 963e
projectile. *See* Projectile motion
simple harmonic, 186, *186*, 189e
in space, 906–964
on spring, 186, *186*
on unit circle, 935, *935*
vertical, *176*, 176–177, 288e
vertical line, 200–201
Moving particle, 525–526
Multiple rule, constant, 161, *161*
Multiples, 159–163
derivative of, 158
Multiplication, scalar, 856
Multiplying by form of 1, 557–558, 559e

Napier, John, 479, 510e
Napier's inequality, 551e
Natural domain, 20
Natural exponential function, 486
Natural logarithm function, 476
Natural logarithms. *See* Logarithm(s), natural
Natural numbers, 2, AP-12
Negative integers, power rule for, 166–168
Nephroid of Freeth, 725e
Newton, Sir Isaac, 150, 356
law of cooling, 507–508, 668, *668*
law(s) of motion, 669, 673, 952, *952*
second, 230
Newton's (Newton–Raphson) method, 299, 321e, 758e, 760e
applications of, 300–302, *301*
convergence of, 302, *302*
failure of, 303, *303*, *304*
fractal basins and, 303–305, *304*
procedure for, 299–300, *300*
Newton's serpentine, 534e
Nonelementary integrals, 597–598, 617e
evaluating of, 827–828
Number *e*, decimal representation of, 494e, 502e
definition of, 477
expressed as limit, 491–492
and inverse of ln *x*, 486, *486*
Numerical integration, 603–619, 617e
Numerical method, 659
Numerical solution, 659
Numerical values, assignment to *x*, 578–579
derivative from, 164–165

Oblique asymptotes, 111, *111*
Octants, 848
Odd fractional power, graphing of, *62*, 62–63
Oh-notation, order and, 514, 516e
Ohm's law, 654
Oil refinery storage tank, 655–657, *656*, 664
One-to-one function(s), 466–467
definition of, 466
domains of, 467
horizontal line test for, 467, *467*
Open interval, 3
Open region, 970
Optimization, 278–285
Orbital data, 957, *957*, 957t
Orbital period(s), 36t, 959e
Orbit(s), 698, *698*
planetary, 957, 957t, 958t
Order, and oh-notation, 514, 516e
Order properties, 2, AP-9
Ordered field, AP-10
Ordinate, 9
Oresme's Theorem, 844e
Origin, of coordinate system, 9
Orthogonal curves, 502e
Orthogonal gradient theorem, 1042
Orthogonal trajectory(ies), *679*, 679–680, *680*
Orthogonal vectors, 865, *869*, 869–870
Orthogonality, 865
Oscillating circles, 939
for parabola, 939–940, *940*
Outward flux, 1179e, 1215–1216
calculation of, 1175

Pappus's formula, 1091e, 1114e
Pappus's theorem(s), 442–444,*443, 444,* 447e
Parabola(s), 14, 17e, 277e, 685–688, 693–694e
approximations using, 608–613
Archimedes' area formula for, 366e
axis, 15, *15*
directrix of, 685, 687, *687*, 687t, 736–737, *736*
eccentricity of, 700
focal length of, 686
focus of, 685, 697e
graphing of, 15–16, *16*
Kepler method of drawing, 697e
oscillating circles for, 939
parametric curves and, 197, *197*
parametrization of, 709, *709*
polar equations for, 734–736, *736*, 737–738e
reflective properties of, 692–693, *693*, 696–697e
tangent line to, 136, *136*, 158e
vertex of, 15, *15*, 686, *686*
Paraboloid(s), 892–893, *893*, 1140e, 1141e
hyperbolic, 896, *896*, 898e
Parallel Axis Theorem, 1091e, 1113–1114e
Parallel lines, 12–13
Parallelepiped, volume of, *877*, 878
Parallelogram(s), 871e, 903e
area of, 874, *874*, AP-31
projection on plane, AP-28–AP-29
law of addition, 856, *856*, *863*, 863–864
Parameter interval, 196
Parametric curve(s), 196, *196*, 205e
length(s) of, 418, 423e
slopes of, 197
Parametric equations, 195–197, *196*, 203e
Cartesian equations from, 202–203e
for conic sections, 712–713e
and cycloids, 743e
in plane, 741e
Parametrized curves, 440, *440*
Parametrized surface(s), 975e, 1192–1201, 1224e
Partial derivative(s), 965–1066, 1000–1001, *1001*
calculations of, 987–989, 1060e
with constrained variables, 1049–1054, 1053–1054e, 1062–1063e, 1064e

Partial derivative(s) (*continued*)
  and continuity, 990, *990*
  first-order, 994e
  fourth-order, 992
  as functions, 984–986, 987–988, 1063–1064e
  of higher order, 992
  second-order, 991–992, 1060e, 994–995e
Partial fraction(s), 570–579
Partition, norm of, 1116
Partition of $[a,b]$, 340
Partition of R, 1068, *1068*
Path, in space, 906, 909
Path independence, 1161, 1162–1163
Peak voltage, 374
Pendulum clock, of Huygens, 710, *710*
Percentage error, 1022–1023, 1025e
Perihelion, 738–739e, *952*, 952–953
Periodic function, 52
Period(s), of trigonometric functions, 53, *52*
Perpendicular Axis Theorem, 1086–1087
Perpendicular lines, 12–13
pH scale, 499, 501e
Phase line(s), 666, 670, *670*, 671e
Pi, estimating of, 305e, 306e, 832e, 833e
Pi/2, fast estimate of, 845e
Piecewise-defined functions, 24, *24*, 25, *25*, 26–27e, 70e
Piecewise smooth, 1186
Piecewise smooth curve(s), 910, *910*, 1162–1163
Piping oil, 250–252, *250*
Plane(s), area in, *725*, 725–727, 741e, 879e
  Green's theorem in, 1169–1181
  intersection of lines and, 885–886
  points in, distance formula for, 13
  in space, *880*, 880–887, 888e
  tangent. *See* Tangent plane(s)
  through three points, 884
  unit vector to, 876
  vectors perpendicular to, *875*, 875–876
Planet(s), distances from Sun, 36t
Planetary motion, 950–958, *952*, 952–953
Planetary orbits, 737, *737*, 739e, 957, 957t, 958t
  eccentricities of, 698, 698t
Plate(s), constant-density, center of mass of, 431–432, *432*
  thin flat, center of mass of, *429*, 429–430, *430*
    mass and first moment formulas for, 1084t
  variable-density, center of mass of, 432–433
  vertical flat, fluid force against, integral for, 457
Pluto, orbit of, 737, *737*
Point-slope equation, 11, 137
Poiseuille, Jean, 230
Polar coordinates, *714*, 714–718, 718e, 1004–1005e, 1138–1139e, 1141e
  area and length in, 725–730, 1095, 1097e
  conic sections and, 685–745, 732–736, 741e
  deceptive, 722
  evaluating integrals using, 1096, *1096*
  graphing of, 719–724
  integrals in, *1092*, 1092–1093, *1093*
  motion in, 951, *951*, 963e
Polar curve(s), 728–729, 731e
Polar equation(s), 715–716, 718e
  and Cartesian equations, *716*, 716–717, 718–719e
  for circles, 732–734, *732*, *733*, 737e
  for conics, 734, *734*, *736*
  for ellipses, parabolas, and hyperbolas, 734–736, *736*, 737–738e
  for lines, 732, *732*, 737e
    in Cartesian form, 732, *732*, 741e
Polar graphs, intersection of, 722–723
  symmetry and, 719, 725e
Polar integrals, 1095–1096, *1096*
Polonium-210, half-life of, 506, 510e
Polyhedral surfaces, Stokes' Theorem for, *1207*, 1207–1208
Polynomial(s), 30, *30*
  complex roots of, AP-22
  cubic, horizontal tangents of, 256
  derivative of, 162–163
  limits of, 86
  Taylor, 807–810, *808*, *809*, *810*, 810e
  trigonometric, 204–205e
Population, limiting, 670
  maximum, 676
  world, 675, 675t, *675*, 676t
Population growth, 670, 671–672e
  modeling of, 674–679
  unlimited, 503–504
Population levels, prediction of, curve for, *64*, 64–65, *65*
Position, from acceleration, 260–261, 262e
Position vector, 1064e
Potential function(s), 1161, 1165–1166, 1168e
Potentials, for conservative fields, 1164–1166
Power(s), 159–163, AP-19
  expanding of, 555–556
  and roots, AP-21–AP-22
    binomial series for, 822–824
  of sines and cosines, products of, 581–583, 585–586e
  of tan x and sec x, 586e
    integrals of, 583
  trigonometric, 560e
Power Chain Rule, 194
Power functions, 29, *29*, *30*, 496
Power Rule, 168, 369
  Chain Rule and, 211
  general form of, 492
  in integral form, 368–370
  with irrational powers, 493
  for positive integers, 160
  for rational powers, 209–211
Power series, 794–803, *796*, 840–841e
  applications of, 822–831
  limits using, 829–830
  multiplication of, 803
  in solutions of problems, 824–827
Preimage, 1128
Pressure-depth equation, 456
Principal unit normal, 940
Principal unit normal vector, 938, *938*
Principal unit normal vector **N**, 940
Prism, AP-31
Product rule, derivative, 163–165
  generalized, 170e, 242e
  in integral form, 561–565
Production, marginal cost of, 177, *177*
Products, 39, 45e
  and quotients, 163–166
  of sines and cosines, 585, 586e
Profit, marginal, 282–283, *283*
Projectile, height of, 329
  ideal, firing of, 921–922, 924–926
  velocity function of, 329
Projectile motion 180e, 871e, 960–961e
  ideal, 923, *923*
    height, flight time, and range of, 922–923, 927e
    vector and parametric equations for, 920–922, *921*
  ideal trajectories of, 923–924, 930e
  modeling of, 920–927
  with wind gusts, 926–928
Proportionality, 35, 38e, 391–392e
p-series, 774–775
Pyramid, volume of, 398
Pythagorean theorem, 53, 251, 850, AP-13, AP-30
Pythagorean triples, 758–759e

Quadrants, 9
Quadratic approximations, 234e, 811e, 822e, 1058–1059e
Quadratic curves, 702, 705t
Quadratic equation(s), graphs of, 705
  and rotations, 702–707
Quadratic factor(s), in denominator, integrating with, 574–575
Quadratic formula, AP-30
Quadratic surface(s), 891–897, 902e
Quotient(s), 39, 45e, AP-18
  products and, 163–166
Quotient rule, 187–188
  derivative, 165–166, 167

Raabe's test, 844e
Radian measure(s), 48–50, *48*, AP-33
  nonzero, 49, *49*
Radians, 190e, 195
Radioactive decay, 505
Radioactive element, half-life of, 506
Radioactivity, 505–507
Radius of circle, 14
Radius of convergence, 798–799
Radius of gyration, calculation of, 1146–1147, 1149e

definition of, 1087
moments of inertia and, 1087–1088, 1090e, 1112e, 1127e
Radon-222, 513e
Rapidly oscillating function, graphs of, *61*, 61–62, *62*
Rate constant, 503
Rates of change, and limits, 73–81
related, 213–217
Ratio Test, 781–784, 796, 799, 844e
Rational function(s), 31, *31*, 61, *61*, 113–114e, 116, 120, 127–128
integration of, by partial fractions, 570–579
limits of, 86
Rational numbers, 2, AP-13
Rational powers, 209–211
Ratios, trigonometric, 50, *50*
Real line, 1
Real numbers, 1–7
development of, AP-12–AP-13
properties of, AP-9
theory of, AP-9–AP-12
Rectangle(s), double integrals over, 1067–1068
inscribed, *280*, 280–281
Rectangular coordinate system, 9
Rectangular coordinates. *See* Cartesian coordinates
Recursion formula, 755
Reduction formula(s), 567–568, 570e, 595–597, 601e
Reflections, and scalings, 43–44, *43*
Reflective properties, of parabolas, 692–693, *693*, 696–697e
Region(s), open and closed, 970, 1099
Regression analysis, 63, 65, 66–67e, 66t, 67t
Regression curve, 63
Regression line(s), 63–64, 63t, *64*
Related rates equations, 214–217
Relative extrema, 247
Relativistic sums, 904e
Remainder Estimation Theorem, 813–814, 815, 816, 817
Remainder of order *n*, 812, 813
Resistance, proportional to velocity, 673–674
Resistive force, 669–670, *669*
Rest points. *See* Equilibrium values
Revenue, marginal, 178, 182e, 241e, 282–283, *283*
Richter scale, 499
Riemann, Bernhard, 340
Riemann sum(s), 340–342, 396, 397, 410, 438, 1067, 1068, 1069, *1069*, 1072, 1078, 1116, 1121
convergence of, 345
limits of, 343–356
rectangles for, 341, 342
Right-hand rule, 873
RL circuit(s), *654*, 654–655, *655*
Rolle's Theorem, *255*, 255–257, *256*, 262e, 819
Root(s), 131, 133e, 143e
complex, 306e, AP-22
fourth, AP-20
powers and, AP-21–AP-22
binomial series for, 822–824
Root finding, 131, *132*, 305e, 306e
Root mean square, 374
Root Test, 784–785
Rotation, angle of, 704, *704*
Rubber band, stretching of, 134, 452e
Rule of 70, 551e
Run and rise, 10

Saddle point, 896–897, 1029, *1029*, 1031, *1031*, 1033
Sandwich theorem, 87–89, *88*, 90e, 110–111, 110e, 983e, AP-6
for infinite sequences, 751–752
Satellite(s), 950–958
orbit of, 742–743e, *957*, 957–958
Savings account, compound interest and, 505
Scalar components, 866–867, *867*, 868
Scalar functions, products of, 919e
Scalar multiplication, 856
Scalar product. *See* Dot product(s)
Scalings, and reflections, *43*, 43–44
vertical and horizontal, 47e
Scatterplot, 63
Search(es), sequential vs. binary, 514–515
Secant, 50, 75
Secant line(s), 75
Second derivative test, 283, 322e, 820e, 1033
derivation of, 1054–1056, *1055*
Semicircle, limits for, 103, *103*
Semicircular region, centroid of, *443*, 443–444, *444*
Sensitivity, to change, 179, 229–231
to medicine, 170e, 290e
of minimum costs, 284–285
Separable equations, 645–647, 648–649e
Sequence(s), 747–756
infinite. *See* Infinite sequence(s)
Series, infinite. *See* Infinite series
Series Multiplication Theorem, 803
Shell formula for revolution, 412
Shift formulas, 41
Shifting graphs, 41–42, 46–47e
Sigma notation, 335–343
Sigmoid shape, 671, *671*
Simple harmonic motion, 186, *186*, 189e
Simpson's rule, *608*, 608–613
Sine(s), 50, 51t, 581–583, 585–586e
rotations to evaluate, 707, *707*
Sine curves, general, 58e, *55*
Sine function, derivatives of, 183–184
Sine-integral function, 616e, 632e
Sinusoid, 55
Skylab 4, 958e, 962e
Slope(s), 16e, 202e, 211–212e, 237e
of circle, *206*, 206–207
of curve, 137
of line, *10*, 10–11
of parametric curves, 197
of polar curve, 719–721, 725e
of surface in y-direction, *988*, 988–989
tangent, 195
and tangent, 138, *138*, 140e, 156e, 169–170e
and y-intercept, 12
Slope field(s), *644*, 644–645, *645*, 649–650e, 675, *676*
and differential equations, 642–650
Slope-intercept equation, 12
Snell's Law, *282*, 282–283, *283*
Snowflake curve, Helga Von Koch's, 771e
Social diffusion, 580e, 672e
Solid(s), cross-sections of, 396,*397*, 405e
infinite, volume of, 626, *626*
moment of inertia of, 1123
in space, center of mass of, 1110–1111, *1111*
twisted, 406
volume(s) of, 396, *397*, 398, 461–462e, 1126–1127e
Solid(s) of revolution, 551e
volume of, 399–404, *400*, *401, 402, 403*, 407e, 589–590, *590*
Solution curves, 666–667, *667*
Sound, 499, 500
Space, geometry of, vectors and, 848–905
Space regions, points for, 970
Spacecraft, force on, 870
Speed, 174, 910
average and instantaneous, 73–75, 139
ground, vectors and, 857–858, *858*, 859
Speeding car, chasing of, *216*, 216–217
Sphere(s), 892
center and radius of, 851, *851*, 852–853e
parametrizing of, 1193, *1194*
in space, distance and, 850–851
surface area of, 1196
volume of, *400*, 400–401, 1140e, AP-31
Spherical coordinates, 1126e, 1139–1140e
definition of, 1119
equations of, 1119–1121, *1120, 1121*
finding volume in, *1122*, 1122–1123
and integration, *1119*, 1119–1122, *1120*
triple integrals in, 1114–1128
Spin, around axis, 1171–1172
Spring(s), compression of, 449, *449*
Hooke's law for, 449
motion on, 186, *186*
stretching of, *449*, 449–450, 452e, 463e
Spring constant, 449, 452e
Square, completing of, 555, 559e, AP-38
Square matrix, AP-24
Square root(s), eliminating of, 556, 559–560e, 583
Square root function, derivative of, 149, *149*
Square windows, 60, *60*
Stable equilibrium(a), 667–671
Standard equation, 13–14, 650–651
Standard position, 48, *49*

Steady-state solution, 655
Steady-state value, 655
Step size, 603
Stirling's formula, 640e
Stokes' equation, for hemisphere, 1203–1204
Stokes' Theorem, 1201–1209, *1207*, 1219
Streamlines, in water in tunnel, 1150, *1150*
Subinterval(s), 340–342, *341*
Substitution(s), 529, 530, 1140e
  and area between curves, 376–387
  in definite integrals, 376–377
  in double integrals, 1128–1132, *1129, 1130*
  to evaluate integral, 371
  finding Taylor series by, 815, 819e
  and identities, 372
  in multiple integrals, 1128–1137
  simplifying, 554–555
  three basic, *587*, 587–591, *588, 589*
  trigonometric, 586–592, 591e
  in triple integrals, *1132*, 1132–1135, *1133, 1134*
  use of, 372–373
Substitution formula, 376–378
Substitution rule, 370, 371, 553
  indefinite integrals and, 368–376
Sum(s), 39, 45e, 159–163
  finite. *See* Finite sum(s)
  infinite, infinite series and, 746
  lower, 326–327, *326*, 345
  relativistic, 904e
  upper, 326, *327*, 345
  upper limits of, 343
Sum rule, 162–163, 168
Summation, index of, 336, 337
Surface(s), defined parametrically, 1197
  functions defined on, 999–1001
  with holes, Stokes' Theorem for, 1208, *1208*
  integrating over, *1186*, 1186–1187, 1197
  orientable, 1187, *1187*
  oriented, 1187
  parametrized, 975e, 1192–1201, 1224e
  smooth, area of, 1195
  in space, visualization of, 897
  two-sided, 1187, *1187*
Surface area(s), *1182*, 1182–1185, *1183*, 1194–1196, *1195*
  applying of, *438*, 438–439
  cylindrical versus conical, 442, *442*
  defining of, *436*, 436–439, *437, 438*
  differential form for, *441*, 441–442
  finding of, 445e, 1183–1185, *1184*, 1195–1196
  formula for, 446–447e, 1183
  Pappus's theorem for, 444, *444*
  special formulas for, 1191–1192, *1192*
  and surface integrals, *1182*, 1182–1192
Surface area differential, 1186
Surface integral(s), 1185–1187, 1190e, 1196–1198
  parametric, 1197
  surface areas and, *1182*, 1182–1192
Surface of revolution, area(s) of, 436–447, 463e, 729–730, *729*
Suspension bridge cables, 695e
Swamp, draining of, 613, *613*
Symmetry(ies), 33–34, *34*, 1128e
  in polar coordinates, 719, *719*
  and polar graphs, 719, 725e

T and **N**, 938–939
Tangent(s), 50, 51t, 202e, 204e, 211–212e, 237
  to curve, 134–135, *135*, 137, 167, *167*
  and derivatives, 134–139
  and gradients, to level curves, 1010–1011, *1011*
  horizontal, of cubic polynomials, 256
    finding of, 163, *163*, 169e
  parallel, 212e, 262e
  to parametric curves, 203e, 237e
  vertical, 140–141e
Tangent line(s), 137, 188–189e, 910
  to arccotangent curve, 527
  to curve(s), 1014, 1061e, 1017, *1017*, 1024e
  to ellipse, 1011, *1011*
  to parabola, 136, *136*, 158e
Tangent plane(s), definition of, 1015, *1015*
  and differentials, 1015–1027
  and normal lines, 1015–1017, *1016*, 1024e, 1063e
Tangent slopes, 195
Tangent vectors, 910, 1159
Tank, conical, pumping oil from, *450*, 450–451
  cylindrical, pumping of, 463e
  draining of, 183e, 239e, 454e, 647, *647*
  filling of, 658e
Tautochrone(s), 711–712, *712*
Tax rate, marginal, 178
Taylor polynomials, 807–810, *808, 809, 810*, 810e
Taylor series, 821e, 830, 841e, 843e
  combining, 817
  convergence of, 811–819
  definition of, 806
  finding of, 807, 810–811e, 815, 819e
  frequently used, 831t
  and Maclaurin series, 805–810
  series representations, 805–806
Taylor's formula, 812, 843e
  for two variables, 1056–1059
Taylor's Theorem, 811–813, 814
  and Mean Value Theorem, 820e
  proof of, 818–819
Telescope, reflecting, 693, *693*
Temperature, in Alaska, *55*, 55–56, *56*, 58e, 203e
  averaging of, 605–606
  beneath Earth's surface, 971, *971*
Term-by-term differentiation, 799–800, 839e
Term-by-term integration, 801–802
Terminal velocity, 670
Thickness variable, 412
Thin shell of constant density, 1191e
Time-distance law, 956, 959e
Tin pest, 289e
TNB frame, 943–945, *945*, 950e
Torque, 425, *876*, 876–877, 902e
Torque system, 425
Torricelli's law, 647–648
Torsion, 943–945, *944*, 950e
  finding of, 948, 949e
  formulas for computing, 947
Torus, volume of, 407–408e, 443, *443*
Tower of Pisa, 241e
Traces, 890
Transcendental functions, 32–33, *33*, 466–552
Transcendental numbers, 487
Transformation(s), integrating and, 1130–1132, 1134–1135
  Jacobian determinant of, 1133–1134, *1134*
  of trigonometric graphs, 55
Transient solution, 655
Trapezoid, area of, 351, *351*, AP-31
Trapezoidal approximation(s), 603–606
Trapezoidal rule, 603–604, *604*, 605,*605*
  approximations of, 611–612, 612t
  error estimates for, 606–607
  steps for accuracy, 608, *608*
Tree diagram, Chain Rule and, 997–998, *1000, 1002*
Triangle(s), AP-30
  area of, 876, 879e, 1224e
Triangle inequality, 72e
Trigonometric function(s), 31, *32*, 48–51, 56–57e, AP-33
  derivatives of, 183–188
  domain restrictions and, 517–519
  inverse, 517–534, 528t
  periodicity and graphs of, 52–53
Trigonometric graphs, 55
Trigonometric identity(ies), 555–556, 559e
Trigonometric integrals, 581–586
Trigonometric polynomials, 204–205e
Trigonometric substitution(s), 586–592, 591e
Trigonometry formulas, AP-31–AP-32
Triple scalar product(s), *877*, 877–878, 879e
Triple vector products, 904e
Trochoid(s), 712–713e
Truncation error, 815–817

Unbounded region, 967
Union of sets, 3
Unit binormal vector **B**, 943, *943*
Unit circle, 13
  motion on, 935, *935*
Unit normal vector **N**, 940
Unit square, geometry of, AP-13
Unit tangent vector **T**, 933–935
Unit vector(s), 858, *858*, 862e, 1159e
  cylindrical coordinates and, 964e
  orthogonal, 872e
  to plane, 876

Unstable equilibrium(a), 667–671
Upper bound, AP-10
U.S. postage stamp, price of, 63, 63t, *64*

Value(s), 19
  average. *See* Average value(s)
  extreme. *See* Extreme values
  table of, function of, 23, *23*
Variable(s), constrained, partial derivatives with, 1049–1054, *1053*, 1062–1063e, 1064e
  dependent, 19
  dummy, 345
  functions of, 965–975
  independent, 19
  input, 965
  more than two, functions of, 981, 989, 1023
  output, 965
  three, functions of, 969–970, 998–999, 1012–1013, 1025e
    Chain Rule for, 999, 1000, 1003e
  two, function(s) of, 966–968, 974e
    Chain Rule for, 997, 1000, 1003e
    continuous, 979, 979
    graphing of, 968, 968
    increment theorem for, 993, AP-25–AP-27
    limits of, 976–977, 978–979
    linearization of, 1018–1019, 1019
    partial derivatives of, 984–986, 985, 986
  Taylor's formula for, 1056–1059
Variable-density rod, 428, *428*
Variable-depth formula, *457*, 457–458
Variable of integration, 312
Vector(s), acceleration, 910
  addition, *856*, 856
  algebra operations, *856*, 856–858, *857*
  angles between, *863*, 863–865, 870–871e, 1063e
  binormal, 949e
  components of, 854–855, 858
  cross product(s) of, *873*, 873–874, 879e
    Distributive Law for, AP-22–AP-23
  and curvature, for curves, 940
  definition of, 853
  as directed line segment, 854, *854*, 862e
  force, 859, 861–862e
  and geometry of space, 848–905
  gradient, 1008
  ground speed and direction and, 857–858, *858*
  magnitude (length) of, 855
  orthogonal (perpendicular), 865
    vector as sum of, *869*, 869–870
  parallel, 873
  perpendicular to plane, *875*, 875–876
  in plane, complex numbers and, AP-22
  position, computer-generated space curves and, 906, *907*
  principal unit normal, 938, *938*
  projections, *866*, 866–868
  resultant, 856
  scalar components of, 866–867, *867*, 868
  in standard position, 854, *854*
  as sum of orthogonal vectors, *869*, 869–870
  tangent, 910
  unit. *See* Unit vector(s)
  unit binormal **B**, 943, *943*
  unit normal **N**, 940
  unit tangent, 934, 935e
  unit tangent **T**, 933–935
  velocity, 853, *853*, 862e, 910
Vector field(s), 1149–1152, *1150, 1152*, 1158e
  circulation density of, 1171, *1171*
  divergence of, *1170*, 1170–1171, *1171*
  flux density of, *1170*, 1170–1171, *1171*
  integration in, 1143–1228
Vector functions (vector-valued), 906–916
  antiderivatives of, 914, 919e
  derivatives of, and motion, *909*, 909–911
  differentiation rules for, 912
  of indefinite integrals, 914–915
  integrals of, 914–916, 917e
  limits of, 908
  and motion in space, limits of, 906–964
Vector operations, 877, *877*
Velocity(ies), from acceleration, 259–260, 261e
  and acceleration in space, 916–917
  average, 172
  instantaneous, 172
  of race car, 172
  resistance proportional to, 673–674
  as speed times direction, 859
  terminal, 670
  of two particles, 242e
Velocity fields, 1155–1156
Velocity function, of projectile, 329
Velocity vector(s), 853, *853*, 862e, 910, *1150*, 1150–1152
Vertex, of parabola, 15, *15*
Vertical line motion, 200–201
Vertical line test, 23, *24*
Vertical motion, *176*, 176–177, 288e
Vertical tangent, 140–141e
Viewing window(s), 59, *60*, 66e
Viking I, orbit of, 958e
Volcanic lava fountains, 183e
Voltage, household, 374, *374*
Volume(s), change in, 1021–1022
  with constraint, 1032–1033
  of cylinder, 218e, 1025
  of cylindrical shells, *409*, 409–416, *410*
  definition of, 1099
  double integrals as, 1068–1069, *1069*
  finding of, 1074, 1101–1102, *1102*
  of infinite solid, 626, *626*
  Pappus's theorem for, 443, *443*
  of prism, 1075, *1075*
  of pyramid, 398
  by slicing and rotation about axis, 396–409
  of solid(s), 396, *397*, 398, 461–462e, 1106e, 1126–1127e
  of solid of revolution, 399–404, *400, 401, 402, 403*, 407e, 589–590, *590*
  of sphere, *400*, 400–401
  of torus, 407–408e, 443, *443*
  of vase, 617
  washer and shell methods for finding, 475
  of wedge, 399, *399*

Washer method, solid of revolution, *403*, 403–404, 407e
Wedge, volume of, 399, *399*
Weierstrass' nowhere differentiable continuous function, 158e
Weight-density, 456
Well, depth of, *227*, 229–230
Whispering galleries, 693
Wilson lot size formula, 290e, 994e, 1026e
Window(s), graphing, 59–63
Wire(s), constant-density, center of mass of, 433, *433*
  and thin rods, 426–428
Work, 447–455, 463e, 465e, 868–869, 872e
  by conservative field, 1163
  by constant force, 447–448, 868, *868*, 1169e
  definition of, 447, 868
  by force over curve in space, *1152*, 1152–1155, *1158*
  by variable force, 448, 452–453e
    over space curve, *1154*, 1154–1155
Work integral, 1155, 1169

x-axis, cylindrical shells revolving about, 413, *413*, 415e
  revolution about, 438

y-axis, cylindrical shells revolving about, *412*, 412–413, 414–415e
  revolution about, 419, *419*

Zero(s), division by, AP-29
Zero denominators, algebraic elimination of, 86–87
Zero (root) of function, 131, *132*
Zero Width Interval Rule, 476
Zipper theorem, 759e

Trigonometry Formulas

1. Definitions and Fundamental Identities

Sine: $\sin\theta = \dfrac{y}{r} = \dfrac{1}{\csc\theta}$

Cosine: $\cos\theta = \dfrac{x}{r} = \dfrac{1}{\sec\theta}$

Tangent: $\tan\theta = \dfrac{y}{x} = \dfrac{1}{\cot\theta}$

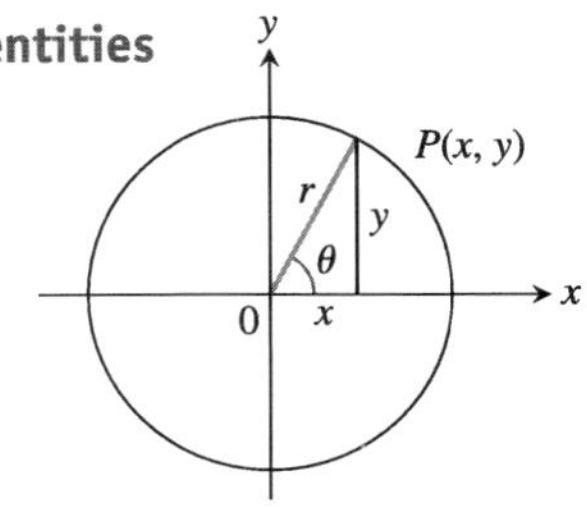

2. Identities

$$\sin(-\theta) = -\sin\theta, \quad \cos(-\theta) = \cos\theta$$

$$\sin^2\theta + \cos^2\theta = 1, \quad \sec^2\theta = 1 + \tan^2\theta, \quad \csc^2\theta = 1 + \cot^2\theta$$

$$\sin 2\theta = 2\sin\theta\cos\theta, \quad \cos 2\theta = \cos^2\theta - \sin^2\theta$$

$$\cos^2\theta = \frac{1+\cos 2\theta}{2}, \quad \sin^2\theta = \frac{1-\cos 2\theta}{2}$$

$$\sin(A+B) = \sin A\cos B + \cos A\sin B$$

$$\sin(A-B) = \sin A\cos B - \cos A\sin B$$

$$\cos(A+B) = \cos A\cos B - \sin A\sin B$$

$$\cos(A-B) = \cos A\cos B + \sin A\sin B$$

$$\tan(A+B) = \frac{\tan A + \tan B}{1 - \tan A\tan B}$$

$$\tan(A-B) = \frac{\tan A - \tan B}{1 + \tan A\tan B}$$

$$\sin\left(A - \frac{\pi}{2}\right) = -\cos A, \qquad \cos\left(A - \frac{\pi}{2}\right) = \sin$$

$$\sin\left(A + \frac{\pi}{2}\right) = \cos A, \qquad \cos\left(A + \frac{\pi}{2}\right) = -\sin$$

$$\sin A\sin B = \frac{1}{2}\cos(A-B) - \frac{1}{2}\cos(A+B)$$

$$\cos A\cos B = \frac{1}{2}\cos(A-B) + \frac{1}{2}\cos(A+B)$$

$$\sin A\cos B = \frac{1}{2}\sin(A-B) + \frac{1}{2}\sin(A+B)$$

$$\sin A + \sin B = 2\sin\frac{1}{2}(A+B)\cos\frac{1}{2}(A-B)$$

$$\sin A - \sin B = 2\cos\frac{1}{2}(A+B)\sin\frac{1}{2}(A-B)$$

$$\cos A + \cos B = 2\cos\frac{1}{2}(A+B)\cos\frac{1}{2}(A-B)$$

$$\cos A - \cos B = -2\sin\frac{1}{2}(A+B)\sin\frac{1}{2}(A-B)$$

Trigonometric Functions

Radian Measure

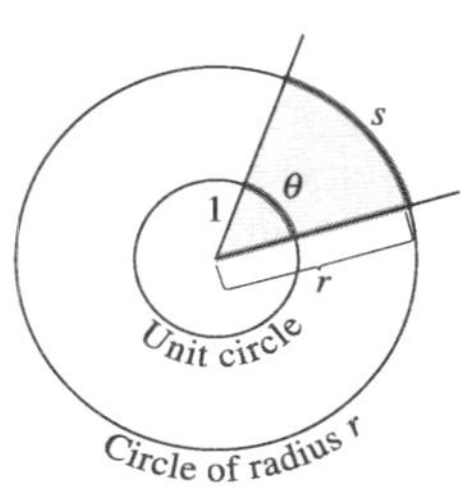

$$\frac{s}{r} = \frac{\theta}{1} = \theta \quad \text{or} \quad \theta = \frac{s}{r},$$

$180° = \pi$ radians.

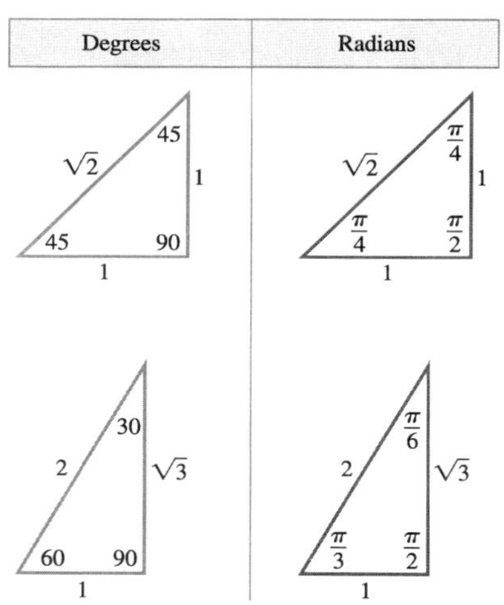

The angles of two common triangles, in degrees and radians.

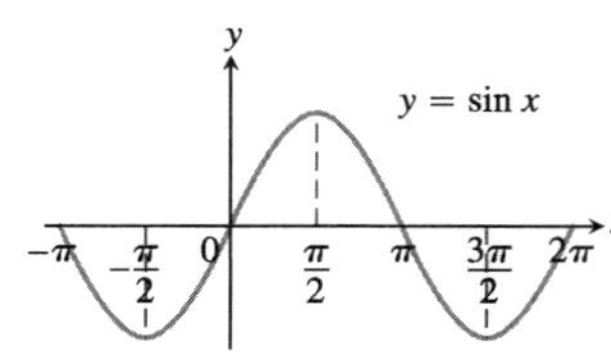

Domain: $(-\infty, \infty)$
Range: $[-1, 1]$

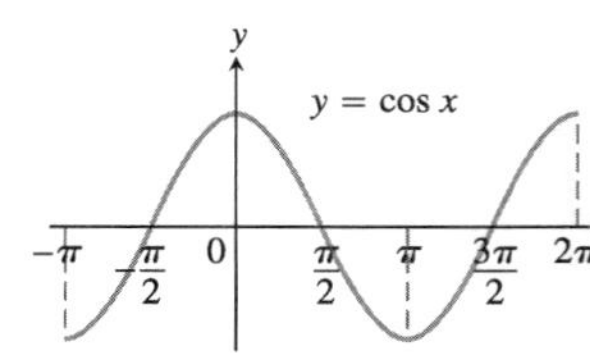

Domain: $(-\infty, \infty)$
Range: $[-1, 1]$

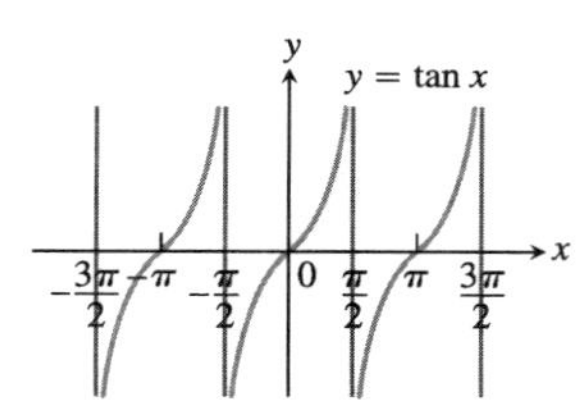

Domain: All real numbers except odd integer multiples of $\pi/2$
Range: $(-\infty, \infty)$

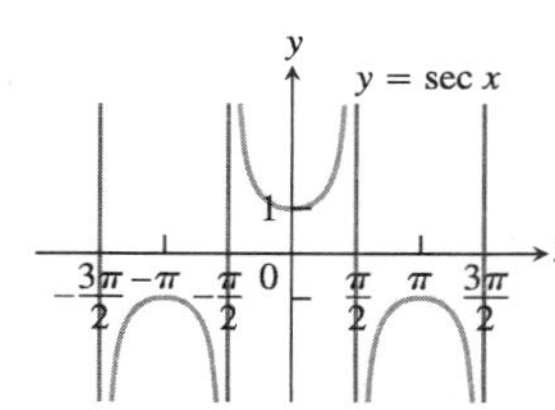

Domain: All real numbers except o[dd] integer multiples of $\pi/2$
Range: $(-\infty, -1] \cup [1, \infty)$

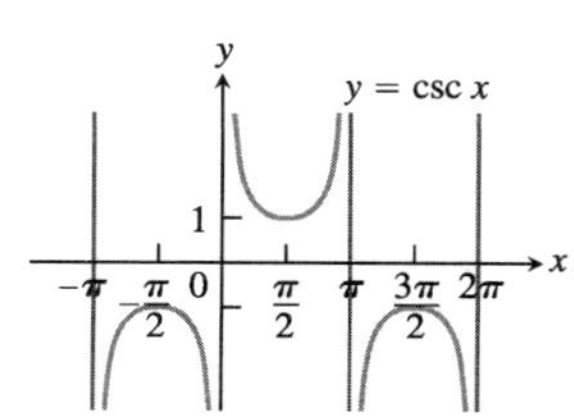

Domain: $x \neq 0, \pm\pi, \pm 2\pi, \ldots$
Range: $(-\infty, -1] \cup [1, \infty)$

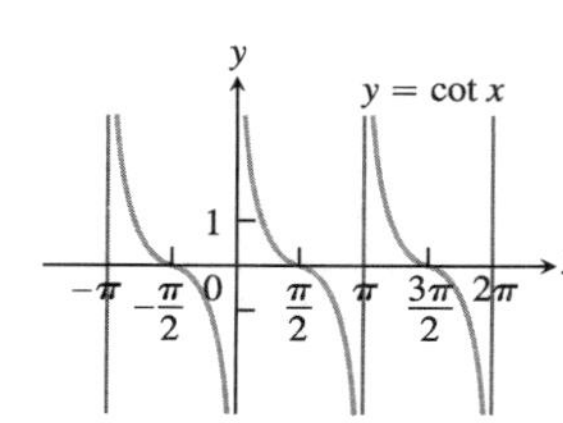

Domain: $x \neq 0, \pm\pi, \pm 2\pi, \ldots$
Range: $(-\infty, \infty)$

A Brief Table of Integrals

1. $\int u\,dv = uv - \int v\,du$

2. $\int a^u\,du = \dfrac{a^u}{\ln a} + C, \quad a \neq 1, \quad a > 0$

3. $\int \cos u\,du = \sin u + C$

4. $\int \sin u\,du = -\cos u + C$

5. $\int (ax+b)^n\,dx = \dfrac{(ax+b)^{n+1}}{a(n+1)} + C, \quad n \neq -1$

6. $\int (ax+b)^{-1}\,dx = \frac{1}{a}\ln|ax+b| + C$

7. $\int x(ax+b)^n\,dx = \dfrac{(ax+b)^{n+1}}{a^2}\left[\dfrac{ax+b}{n+2} - \dfrac{b}{n+1}\right] + C, \quad n \neq -1, -2$

8. $\int x(ax+b)^{-1}\,dx = \frac{x}{a} - \dfrac{b}{a^2}\ln|ax+b| + C$

9. $\int x(ax+b)^{-2}\,dx = \dfrac{1}{a^2}\left[\ln|ax+b| + \dfrac{b}{ax+b}\right] + C$

10. $\int \dfrac{dx}{x(ax+b)} = \dfrac{1}{b}\ln\left|\dfrac{x}{ax+b}\right| + C$

11. $\int \left(\sqrt{ax+b}\right)^n\,dx = \dfrac{2}{a}\dfrac{\left(\sqrt{ax+b}\right)^{n+2}}{n+2} + C, \quad n \neq -2$

12. $\int \dfrac{\sqrt{ax+b}}{x}\,dx = 2\sqrt{ax+b} + b\int \dfrac{dx}{x\sqrt{ax+b}}$

13. (a) $\int \dfrac{dx}{x\sqrt{ax-b}} = \dfrac{2}{\sqrt{b}}\tan^{-1}\sqrt{\dfrac{ax-b}{b}} + C$ (b) $\int \dfrac{dx}{x\sqrt{ax+b}} = \dfrac{1}{\sqrt{b}}\ln\left|\dfrac{\sqrt{ax+b}-\sqrt{b}}{\sqrt{ax+b}+\sqrt{b}}\right| + C$

14. $\int \dfrac{\sqrt{ax+b}}{x^2}\,dx = -\dfrac{\sqrt{ax+b}}{x} + \dfrac{a}{2}\int \dfrac{dx}{x\sqrt{ax+b}} + C$

15. $\int \dfrac{dx}{x^2\sqrt{ax+b}} = -\dfrac{\sqrt{ax+b}}{bx} - \dfrac{a}{2b}\int \dfrac{dx}{x\sqrt{ax+b}} + C$

16. $\int \dfrac{dx}{a^2+x^2} = \frac{1}{a}\tan^{-1}\frac{x}{a} + C$

17. $\int \dfrac{dx}{(a^2+x^2)^2} = \dfrac{x}{2a^2(a^2+x^2)} + \dfrac{1}{2a^3}\tan^{-1}\frac{x}{a} + C$

18. $\int \dfrac{dx}{a^2-x^2} = \dfrac{1}{2a}\ln\left|\dfrac{x+a}{x-a}\right| + C$

19. $\int \dfrac{dx}{(a^2-x^2)^2} = \dfrac{x}{2a^2(a^2-x^2)} + \dfrac{1}{4a^3}\ln\left|\dfrac{x+a}{x-a}\right| + C$

20. $\int \dfrac{dx}{\sqrt{a^2+x^2}} = \sinh^{-1}\frac{x}{a} + C = \ln\left(x + \sqrt{a^2+x^2}\right) + C$

21. $\int \sqrt{a^2+x^2}\,dx = \frac{x}{2}\sqrt{a^2+x^2} + \dfrac{a^2}{2}\ln\left(x+\sqrt{a^2+x^2}\right) + C$

22. $\int x^2\sqrt{a^2+x^2}\,dx = \frac{x}{8}(a^2+2x^2)\sqrt{a^2+x^2} - \dfrac{a^4}{8}\ln\left(x+\sqrt{a^2+x^2}\right) + C$

23. $\int \frac{\sqrt{a^2+x^2}}{x}\,dx = \sqrt{a^2+x^2} - a\ln\left|\frac{a+\sqrt{a^2+x^2}}{x}\right| + C$

24. $\int \frac{\sqrt{a^2+x^2}}{x^2}\,dx = \ln\left(x+\sqrt{a^2+x^2}\right) - \frac{\sqrt{a^2+x^2}}{x} + C$

25. $\int \frac{x^2}{\sqrt{a^2+x^2}}\,dx = -\frac{a^2}{2}\ln\left(x+\sqrt{a^2+x^2}\right) + \frac{x\sqrt{a^2+x^2}}{2} + C$

26. $\int \frac{dx}{x\sqrt{a^2+x^2}} = -\frac{1}{a}\ln\left|\frac{a+\sqrt{a^2+x^2}}{x}\right| + C$

27. $\int \frac{dx}{x^2\sqrt{a^2+x^2}} = -\frac{\sqrt{a^2+x^2}}{a^2x} + C$

28. $\int \frac{dx}{\sqrt{a^2-x^2}} = \sin^{-1}\frac{x}{a} + C$

29. $\int \sqrt{a^2-x^2}\,dx = \frac{x}{2}\sqrt{a^2-x^2} + \frac{a^2}{2}\sin^{-1}\frac{x}{a} + C$

30. $\int x^2\sqrt{a^2-x^2}\,dx = \frac{a^4}{8}\sin^{-1}\frac{x}{a} - \frac{1}{8}x\sqrt{a^2-x^2}\,(a^2-2x^2) + C$

31. $\int \frac{\sqrt{a^2-x^2}}{x}\,dx = \sqrt{a^2-x^2} - a\ln\left|\frac{a+\sqrt{a^2-x^2}}{x}\right| + C$

32. $\int \frac{\sqrt{a^2-x^2}}{x^2}\,dx = -\sin^{-1}\frac{x}{a} - \frac{\sqrt{a^2-x^2}}{x} + C$

33. $\int \frac{x^2}{\sqrt{a^2-x^2}}\,dx = \frac{a^2}{2}\sin^{-1}\frac{x}{a} - \frac{1}{2}x\sqrt{a^2-x^2} + C$

34. $\int \frac{dx}{x\sqrt{a^2-x^2}} = -\frac{1}{a}\ln\left|\frac{a+\sqrt{a^2-x^2}}{x}\right| + C$

35. $\int \frac{dx}{x^2\sqrt{a^2-x^2}} = -\frac{\sqrt{a^2-x^2}}{a^2x} + C$

36. $\int \frac{dx}{\sqrt{x^2-a^2}} = \cosh^{-1}\frac{x}{a} + C = \ln\left|x+\sqrt{x^2-a^2}\right| + C$

37. $\int \sqrt{x^2-a^2}\,dx = \frac{x}{2}\sqrt{x^2-a^2} - \frac{a^2}{2}\ln\left|x+\sqrt{x^2-a^2}\right| + C$

38. $\int \left(\sqrt{x^2-a^2}\right)^n dx = \frac{x\left(\sqrt{x^2-a^2}\right)^n}{n+1} - \frac{na^2}{n+1}\int \left(\sqrt{x^2-a^2}\right)^{n-2} dx, \quad n \neq -1$

39. $\int \frac{dx}{\left(\sqrt{x^2-a^2}\right)^n} = \frac{x\left(\sqrt{x^2-a^2}\right)^{2-n}}{(2-n)a^2} - \frac{n-3}{(n-2)a^2}\int \frac{dx}{\left(\sqrt{x^2-a^2}\right)^{n-2}}, \quad n \neq 2$

40. $\int x\left(\sqrt{x^2-a^2}\right)^n dx = \frac{\left(\sqrt{x^2-a^2}\right)^{n+2}}{n+2} + C, \quad n \neq -2$

41. $\int x^2\sqrt{x^2-a^2}\,dx = \frac{x}{8}(2x^2-a^2)\sqrt{x^2-a^2} - \frac{a^4}{8}\ln\left|x+\sqrt{x^2-a^2}\right| + C$

42. $\int \frac{\sqrt{x^2-a^2}}{x}\,dx = \sqrt{x^2-a^2} - a\sec^{-1}\left|\frac{x}{a}\right| + C$

43. $\int \frac{\sqrt{x^2-a^2}}{x^2}\,dx = \ln\left|x+\sqrt{x^2-a^2}\right| - \frac{\sqrt{x^2-a^2}}{x} + C$

44. $\int \frac{x^2}{\sqrt{x^2-a^2}}\,dx = \frac{a^2}{2}\ln\left|x+\sqrt{x^2-a^2}\right| + \frac{x}{2}\sqrt{x^2-a^2} + C$

45. $\int \frac{dx}{x\sqrt{x^2-a^2}} = \frac{1}{a}\sec^{-1}\left|\frac{x}{a}\right| + C = \frac{1}{a}\cos^{-1}\left|\frac{a}{x}\right| + C$

46. $\int \frac{dx}{x^2\sqrt{x^2-a^2}} = \frac{\sqrt{x^2-a^2}}{a^2x} + C$

47. $\displaystyle\int \frac{dx}{\sqrt{2ax - x^2}} = \sin^{-1}\left(\frac{x - a}{a}\right) + C$

48. $\displaystyle\int \sqrt{2ax - x^2}\, dx = \frac{x - a}{2}\sqrt{2ax - x^2} + \frac{a^2}{2}\sin^{-1}\left(\frac{x - a}{a}\right) + C$

49. $\displaystyle\int \left(\sqrt{2ax - x^2}\right)^n dx = \frac{(x - a)\left(\sqrt{2ax - x^2}\right)^n}{n + 1} + \frac{na^2}{n + 1}\int \left(\sqrt{2ax - x^2}\right)^{n-2} dx$

50. $\displaystyle\int \frac{dx}{\left(\sqrt{2ax - x^2}\right)^n} = \frac{(x - a)\left(\sqrt{2ax - x^2}\right)^{2-n}}{(n - 2)a^2} + \frac{n - 3}{(n - 2)a^2}\int \frac{dx}{\left(\sqrt{2ax - x^2}\right)^{n-2}}$

51. $\displaystyle\int x\sqrt{2ax - x^2}\, dx = \frac{(x + a)(2x - 3a)\sqrt{2ax - x^2}}{6} + \frac{a^3}{2}\sin^{-1}\left(\frac{x - a}{a}\right) + C$

52. $\displaystyle\int \frac{\sqrt{2ax - x^2}}{x}\, dx = \sqrt{2ax - x^2} + a\sin^{-1}\left(\frac{x - a}{a}\right) + C$

53. $\displaystyle\int \frac{\sqrt{2ax - x^2}}{x^2}\, dx = -2\sqrt{\frac{2a - x}{x}} - \sin^{-1}\left(\frac{x - a}{a}\right) + C$

54. $\displaystyle\int \frac{x\, dx}{\sqrt{2ax - x^2}} = a\sin^{-1}\left(\frac{x - a}{a}\right) - \sqrt{2ax - x^2} + C$

55. $\displaystyle\int \frac{dx}{x\sqrt{2ax - x^2}} = -\frac{1}{a}\sqrt{\frac{2a - x}{x}} + C$

56. $\displaystyle\int \sin ax\, dx = -\frac{1}{a}\cos ax + C$

57. $\displaystyle\int \cos ax\, dx = \frac{1}{a}\sin ax + C$

58. $\displaystyle\int \sin^2 ax\, dx = \frac{x}{2} - \frac{\sin 2ax}{4a} + C$

59. $\displaystyle\int \cos^2 ax\, dx = \frac{x}{2} + \frac{\sin 2ax}{4a} + C$

60. $\displaystyle\int \sin^n ax\, dx = -\frac{\sin^{n-1} ax \cos ax}{na} + \frac{n - 1}{n}\int \sin^{n-2} ax\, dx$

61. $\displaystyle\int \cos^n ax\, dx = \frac{\cos^{n-1} ax \sin ax}{na} + \frac{n - 1}{n}\int \cos^{n-2} ax\, dx$

62. (a) $\displaystyle\int \sin ax \cos bx\, dx = -\frac{\cos(a + b)x}{2(a + b)} - \frac{\cos(a - b)x}{2(a - b)} + C, \quad a^2 \neq b^2$

(b) $\displaystyle\int \sin ax \sin bx\, dx = \frac{\sin(a - b)x}{2(a - b)} - \frac{\sin(a + b)x}{2(a + b)} + C, \quad a^2 \neq b^2$

(c) $\displaystyle\int \cos ax \cos bx\, dx = \frac{\sin(a - b)x}{2(a - b)} + \frac{\sin(a + b)x}{2(a + b)} + C, \quad a^2 \neq b^2$

63. $\displaystyle\int \sin ax \cos ax\, dx = -\frac{\cos 2ax}{4a} + C$

64. $\displaystyle\int \sin^n ax \cos ax\, dx = \frac{\sin^{n+1} ax}{(n + 1)a} + C, \quad n \neq -1$

65. $\displaystyle\int \frac{\cos ax}{\sin ax}\, dx = \frac{1}{a}\ln|\sin ax| + C$

66. $\displaystyle\int \cos^n ax \sin ax\, dx = -\frac{\cos^{n+1} ax}{(n + 1)a} + C, \quad n \neq -1$

67. $\displaystyle\int \frac{\sin ax}{\cos ax}\, dx = -\frac{1}{a}\ln|\cos ax| + C$

68. $\int \sin^n ax \cos^m ax\, dx = -\frac{\sin^{n-1} ax \cos^{m+1} ax}{a(m+n)} + \frac{n-1}{m+n}\int \sin^{n-2} ax \cos^m ax\, dx, \quad n \neq -m \quad (\text{reduces } \sin^n ax)$

69. $\int \sin^n ax \cos^m ax\, dx = \frac{\sin^{n+1} ax \cos^{m-1} ax}{a(m+n)} + \frac{m-1}{m+n}\int \sin^n ax \cos^{m-2} ax\, dx, \quad m \neq -n \quad (\text{reduces } \cos^m ax)$

70. $\int \frac{dx}{b + c\sin ax} = \frac{-2}{a\sqrt{b^2 - c^2}} \tan^{-1}\left[\sqrt{\frac{b-c}{b+c}}\tan\left(\frac{\pi}{4} - \frac{ax}{2}\right)\right] + C, \quad b^2 > c^2$

71. $\int \frac{dx}{b + c\sin ax} = \frac{-1}{a\sqrt{c^2 - b^2}} \ln\left|\frac{c + b\sin ax + \sqrt{c^2 - b^2}\cos ax}{b + c\sin ax}\right| + C, \quad b^2 < c^2$

72. $\int \frac{dx}{1 + \sin ax} = -\frac{1}{a}\tan\left(\frac{\pi}{4} - \frac{ax}{2}\right) + C$

73. $\int \frac{dx}{1 - \sin ax} = \frac{1}{a}\tan\left(\frac{\pi}{4} + \frac{ax}{2}\right) + C$

74. $\int \frac{dx}{b + c\cos ax} = \frac{2}{a\sqrt{b^2 - c^2}} \tan^{-1}\left[\sqrt{\frac{b-c}{b+c}}\tan\frac{ax}{2}\right] + C, \quad b^2 > c^2$

75. $\int \frac{dx}{b + c\cos ax} = \frac{1}{a\sqrt{c^2 - b^2}} \ln\left|\frac{c + b\cos ax + \sqrt{c^2 - b^2}\sin ax}{b + c\cos ax}\right| + C, \quad b^2 < c^2$

76. $\int \frac{dx}{1 + \cos ax} = \frac{1}{a}\tan\frac{ax}{2} + C$

77. $\int \frac{dx}{1 - \cos ax} = -\frac{1}{a}\cot\frac{ax}{2} + C$

78. $\int x\sin ax\, dx = \frac{1}{a^2}\sin ax - \frac{x}{a}\cos ax + C$

79. $\int x\cos ax\, dx = \frac{1}{a^2}\cos ax + \frac{x}{a}\sin ax + C$

80. $\int x^n \sin ax\, dx = -\frac{x^n}{a}\cos ax + \frac{n}{a}\int x^{n-1}\cos ax\, dx$

81. $\int x^n \cos ax\, dx = \frac{x^n}{a}\sin ax - \frac{n}{a}\int x^{n-1}\sin ax\, dx$

82. $\int \tan ax\, dx = \frac{1}{a}\ln|\sec ax| + C$

83. $\int \cot ax\, dx = \frac{1}{a}\ln|\sin ax| + C$

84. $\int \tan^2 ax\, dx = \frac{1}{a}\tan ax - x + C$

85. $\int \cot^2 ax\, dx = -\frac{1}{a}\cot ax - x + C$

86. $\int \tan^n ax\, dx = \frac{\tan^{n-1} ax}{a(n-1)} - \int \tan^{n-2} ax\, dx, \quad n \neq 1$

87. $\int \cot^n ax\, dx = -\frac{\cot^{n-1} ax}{a(n-1)} - \int \cot^{n-2} ax\, dx, \quad n \neq 1$

88. $\int \sec ax\, dx = \frac{1}{a}\ln|\sec ax + \tan ax| + C$

89. $\int \csc ax\, dx = -\frac{1}{a}\ln|\csc ax + \cot ax| + C$

90. $\int \sec^2 ax\, dx = \frac{1}{a}\tan ax + C$

91. $\int \csc^2 ax\, dx = -\frac{1}{a}\cot ax + C$

92. $\int \sec^n ax\, dx = \frac{\sec^{n-2} ax \tan ax}{a(n-1)} + \frac{n-2}{n-1}\int \sec^{n-2} ax\, dx, \quad n \neq 1$

93. $\int \csc^n ax\, dx = -\frac{\csc^{n-2} ax \cot ax}{a(n-1)} + \frac{n-2}{n-1}\int \csc^{n-2} ax\, dx, \quad n \neq 1$

94. $\int \sec^n ax \tan ax\, dx = \frac{\sec^n ax}{na} + C, \quad n \neq 0$

95. $\int \csc^n ax \cot ax\, dx = -\frac{\csc^n ax}{na} + C, \quad n \neq 0$

96. $\int \sin^{-1} ax\,dx = x \sin^{-1} ax + \frac{1}{a}\sqrt{1 - a^2x^2} + C$

97. $\int \cos^{-1} ax\,dx = x \cos^{-1} ax - \frac{1}{a}\sqrt{1 - a^2x^2} + C$

98. $\int \tan^{-1} ax\,dx = x \tan^{-1} ax - \frac{1}{2a}\ln(1 + a^2x^2) + C$

99. $\int x^n \sin^{-1} ax\,dx = \frac{x^{n+1}}{n+1}\sin^{-1} ax - \frac{a}{n+1}\int \frac{x^{n+1}\,dx}{\sqrt{1 - a^2x^2}}, \quad n \neq -1$

100. $\int x^n \cos^{-1} ax\,dx = \frac{x^{n+1}}{n+1}\cos^{-1} ax + \frac{a}{n+1}\int \frac{x^{n+1}\,dx}{\sqrt{1 - a^2x^2}}, \quad n \neq -1$

101. $\int x^n \tan^{-1} ax\,dx = \frac{x^{n+1}}{n+1}\tan^{-1} ax - \frac{a}{n+1}\int \frac{x^{n+1}\,dx}{1 + a^2x^2}, \quad n \neq -1$

102. $\int e^{ax}\,dx = \frac{1}{a}e^{ax} + C$

103. $\int b^{ax}\,dx = \frac{1}{a}\frac{b^{ax}}{\ln b} + C, \quad b > 0, b \neq 1$

104. $\int xe^{ax}\,dx = \frac{e^{ax}}{a^2}(ax - 1) + C$

105. $\int x^n e^{ax}\,dx = \frac{1}{a}x^n e^{ax} - \frac{n}{a}\int x^{n-1}e^{ax}\,dx$

106. $\int x^n b^{ax}\,dx = \frac{x^n b^{ax}}{a \ln b} - \frac{n}{a \ln b}\int x^{n-1}b^{ax}\,dx, \quad b > 0, b \neq 1$

107. $\int e^{ax}\sin bx\,dx = \frac{e^{ax}}{a^2 + b^2}(a \sin bx - b \cos bx) + C$

108. $\int e^{ax}\cos bx\,dx = \frac{e^{ax}}{a^2 + b^2}(a \cos bx + b \sin bx) + C$

109. $\int \ln ax\,dx = x \ln ax - x + C$

110. $\int x^n(\ln ax)^m\,dx = \frac{x^{n+1}(\ln ax)^m}{n+1} - \frac{m}{n+1}\int x^n(\ln ax)^{m-1}\,dx, \quad n \neq -1$

111. $\int x^{-1}(\ln ax)^m\,dx = \frac{(\ln ax)^{m+1}}{m+1} + C, \quad m \neq -1$

112. $\int \frac{dx}{x \ln ax} = \ln|\ln ax| + C$

113. $\int \sinh ax\,dx = \frac{1}{a}\cosh ax + C$

114. $\int \cosh ax\,dx = \frac{1}{a}\sinh ax + C$

115. $\int \sinh^2 ax\,dx = \frac{\sinh 2ax}{4a} - \frac{x}{2} + C$

116. $\int \cosh^2 ax\,dx = \frac{\sinh 2ax}{4a} + \frac{x}{2} + C$

117. $\int \sinh^n ax\,dx = \frac{\sinh^{n-1} ax \cosh ax}{na} - \frac{n-1}{n}\int \sinh^{n-2} ax\,dx, \quad n \neq 0$

118. $\int \cosh^n ax\,dx = \frac{\cosh^{n-1} ax \sinh ax}{na} + \frac{n-1}{n}\int \cosh^{n-2} ax\,dx, \quad n \neq 0$

119. $\int x \sinh ax\,dx = \frac{x}{a}\cosh ax - \frac{1}{a^2}\sinh ax + C$

120. $\int x \cosh ax\,dx = \frac{x}{a}\sinh ax - \frac{1}{a^2}\cosh ax + C$

121. $\int x^n \sinh ax\,dx = \frac{x^n}{a}\cosh ax - \frac{n}{a}\int x^{n-1}\cosh ax\,dx$

122. $\int x^n \cosh ax\,dx = \frac{x^n}{a}\sinh ax - \frac{n}{a}\int x^{n-1}\sinh ax\,dx$

123. $\int \tanh ax\,dx = \frac{1}{a}\ln(\cosh ax) + C$

124. $\int \coth ax\,dx = \frac{1}{a}\ln|\sinh ax| + C$

125. $\int \tanh^2 ax\,dx = x - \frac{1}{a}\tanh ax + C$

126. $\int \coth^2 ax\,dx = x - \frac{1}{a}\coth ax + C$

127. $\int \tanh^n ax\,dx = -\frac{\tanh^{n-1} ax}{(n-1)a} + \int \tanh^{n-2} ax\,dx, \quad n \neq 1$

128. $\int \coth^n ax\,dx = -\frac{\coth^{n-1} ax}{(n-1)a} + \int \coth^{n-2} ax\,dx, \quad n \neq 1$

129. $\int \operatorname{sech} ax\,dx = \frac{1}{a}\sin^{-1}(\tanh ax) + C$

130. $\int \operatorname{csch} ax\,dx = \frac{1}{a}\ln\left|\tanh\frac{ax}{2}\right| + C$

131. $\int \operatorname{sech}^2 ax\,dx = \frac{1}{a}\tanh ax + C$

132. $\int \operatorname{csch}^2 ax\,dx = -\frac{1}{a}\coth ax + C$

133. $\int \operatorname{sech}^n ax\,dx = \frac{\operatorname{sech}^{n-2} ax \tanh ax}{(n-1)a} + \frac{n-2}{n-1}\int \operatorname{sech}^{n-2} ax\,dx, \quad n \neq 1$

134. $\int \operatorname{csch}^n ax\,dx = -\frac{\operatorname{csch}^{n-2} ax \coth ax}{(n-1)a} - \frac{n-2}{n-1}\int \operatorname{csch}^{n-2} ax\,dx, \quad n \neq 1$

135. $\int \operatorname{sech}^n ax \tanh ax\,dx = -\frac{\operatorname{sech}^n ax}{na} + C, \quad n \neq 0$

136. $\int \operatorname{csch}^n ax \coth ax\,dx = -\frac{\operatorname{csch}^n ax}{na} + C, \quad n \neq 0$

137. $\int e^{ax}\sinh bx\,dx = \frac{e^{ax}}{2}\left[\frac{e^{bx}}{a+b} - \frac{e^{-bx}}{a-b}\right] + C, \quad a^2 \neq b^2$

138. $\int e^{ax}\cosh bx\,dx = \frac{e^{ax}}{2}\left[\frac{e^{bx}}{a+b} + \frac{e^{-bx}}{a-b}\right] + C, \quad a^2 \neq b^2$

139. $\int_0^\infty x^{n-1}e^{-x}\,dx = \Gamma(n) = (n-1)!, \quad n > 0$

140. $\int_0^\infty e^{-ax^2}\,dx = \frac{1}{2}\sqrt{\frac{\pi}{a}}, \quad a > 0$

141. $$\int_0^{\pi/2} \sin^n x\,dx = \int_0^{\pi/2} \cos^n x\,dx = \begin{cases} \dfrac{1\cdot 3\cdot 5\cdots(n-1)}{2\cdot 4\cdot 6\cdots n}\cdot\dfrac{\pi}{2}, & \text{if } n \text{ is an even integer} \geq 2 \\ \dfrac{2\cdot 4\cdot 6\cdots(n-1)}{3\cdot 5\cdot 7\cdots n}, & \text{if } n \text{ is an odd integer} \geq 3 \end{cases}$$

CREDITS

Page 181, Section 3.3, photo for Exercise 19, *PSSC Physics*, 2nd ed., DC Heath & Co. with Education Development Center, Inc.; **Page 238, Figure 3.53,** NCPMF "Differentiation" by W. U. Walton et al., Project CALC, Education Development Center, Inc.; **Page 241, Chapter 3 Additional and Advanced Exercises, photo for Exercise 9,** AP/Wide World Photos; **Page 304, Figure 4.53,** Scott A. Burns; **Page 425, Figure 6.29a,** *PSSC Physics*, 2nd ed., DC Heath & Co. with Education Development Center, Inc.; **Page 615, Section 8.7, photo for Exercise 30,** Marshall Henrichs; **Page 696, Section 10.1, photo for Exercise 89,** *PSSC Physics*, 2nd ed., DC Heath & Co. with Education Development Center, Inc.; **Page 765, Figure 11.6,** *PSSC Physics*, 2nd ed., DC Heath & Co. with Education Development Center, Inc.; **Page 924, Figure 13.12,** Corbis; **Page 929, Section 13.2, photo for Exercise 23,** *PSSC Physics*, 2nd ed., DC Heath & Co. with Education Development Center, Inc.; **Page 969, Figure 14.6,** Reproduced by permission from Appalachian Mountain Club; **Page 1006, Figure 14.23,** Department of History, U.S. Military Academy, West Point, New York; **Page 1150, Figures 16.7 and 16.8,** *NCFMF Book of Film Notes*, 1974, MIT Press with Education Development Center, Inc.; **Page 1151, Figure 16.15,** Inter-Network Media, Inc., and NASA/JPL.

SERIES

Taylor Series

$$\frac{1}{1-x} = 1 + x + x^2 + \cdots + x^n + \cdots = \sum_{n=0}^{\infty} x^n, \qquad |x| < 1$$

$$\frac{1}{1+x} = 1 - x + x^2 - \cdots + (-x)^n + \cdots = \sum_{n=0}^{\infty} (-1)^n x^n, \qquad |x| < 1$$

$$e^x = 1 + x + \frac{x^2}{2!} + \cdots + \frac{x^n}{n!} + \cdots = \sum_{n=0}^{\infty} \frac{x^n}{n!}, \qquad |x| < \infty$$

$$\sin x = x - \frac{x^3}{3!} + \frac{x^5}{5!} - \cdots + (-1)^n \frac{x^{2n+1}}{(2n+1)!} + \cdots = \sum_{n=0}^{\infty} \frac{(-1)^n x^{2n+1}}{(2n+1)!}, \qquad |x| < \infty$$

$$\cos x = 1 - \frac{x^2}{2!} + \frac{x^4}{4!} - \cdots + (-1)^n \frac{x^{2n}}{(2n)!} + \cdots = \sum_{n=0}^{\infty} \frac{(-1)^n x^{2n}}{(2n)!}, \qquad |x| < \infty$$

$$\ln(1+x) = x - \frac{x^2}{2} + \frac{x^3}{3} - \cdots + (-1)^{n-1} \frac{x^n}{n} + \cdots = \sum_{n=1}^{\infty} \frac{(-1)^{n-1} x^n}{n}, \qquad -1 < x \le 1$$

$$\ln \frac{1+x}{1-x} = 2 \tanh^{-1} x = 2\left(x + \frac{x^3}{3} + \frac{x^5}{5} + \cdots + \frac{x^{2n+1}}{2n+1} + \cdots\right) = 2\sum_{n=0}^{\infty} \frac{x^{2n+1}}{2n+1}, \qquad |x| < 1$$

$$\tan^{-1} x = x - \frac{x^3}{3} + \frac{x^5}{5} - \cdots + (-1)^n \frac{x^{2n+1}}{2n+1} + \cdots = \sum_{n=0}^{\infty} \frac{(-1)^n x^{2n+1}}{2n+1}, \qquad |x| \le 1$$

Binomial Series

$$(1+x)^m = 1 + mx + \frac{m(m-1)x^2}{2!} + \frac{m(m-1)(m-2)x^3}{3!} + \cdots + \frac{m(m-1)(m-2)\cdots(m-k+1)x^k}{k!} + \cdots$$

$$= 1 + \sum_{k=1}^{\infty} \binom{m}{k} x^k, \qquad |x| < 1,$$

where

$$\binom{m}{1} = m, \qquad \binom{m}{2} = \frac{m(m-1)}{2!}, \qquad \binom{m}{k} = \frac{m(m-1)\cdots(m-k+1)}{k!} \qquad \text{for } k \ge 3.$$

VECTOR OPERATOR FORMULAS (CARTESIAN FORM)

Formulas for Grad, Div, Curl, and the Laplacian

	Cartesian (x, y, z) **i, j**, and **k** are unit vectors in the directions of increasing x, y, and z. M, N, and P are the scalar components of $\mathbf{F}(x, y, z)$ in these directions.
Gradient	$\nabla f = \frac{\partial f}{\partial x}\mathbf{i} + \frac{\partial f}{\partial y}\mathbf{j} + \frac{\partial f}{\partial z}\mathbf{k}$
Divergence	$\nabla \cdot \mathbf{F} = \frac{\partial M}{\partial x} + \frac{\partial N}{\partial y} + \frac{\partial P}{\partial z}$
Curl	$\nabla \times \mathbf{F} = \begin{vmatrix} \mathbf{i} & \mathbf{j} & \mathbf{k} \\ \frac{\partial}{\partial x} & \frac{\partial}{\partial y} & \frac{\partial}{\partial z} \\ M & N & P \end{vmatrix}$
Laplacian	$\nabla^2 f = \frac{\partial^2 f}{\partial x^2} + \frac{\partial^2 f}{\partial y^2} + \frac{\partial^2 f}{\partial z^2}$

Vector Triple Products

$(\mathbf{u} \times \mathbf{v}) \cdot \mathbf{w} = (\mathbf{v} \times \mathbf{w}) \cdot \mathbf{u} = (\mathbf{w} \times \mathbf{u}) \cdot \mathbf{v}$

$\mathbf{u} \times (\mathbf{v} \times \mathbf{w}) = (\mathbf{u} \cdot \mathbf{w})\mathbf{v} - (\mathbf{u} \cdot \mathbf{v})\mathbf{w}$

The Fundamental Theorem of Line Integrals

1. Let $\mathbf{F} = M\mathbf{i} + N\mathbf{j} + P\mathbf{k}$ be a vector field whose components are continuous throughout an open connected region D in space. Then there exists a differentiable function f such that

$$\mathbf{F} = \nabla f = \frac{\partial f}{\partial x}\mathbf{i} + \frac{\partial f}{\partial y}\mathbf{j} + \frac{\partial f}{\partial z}\mathbf{k}$$

if and only if for all points A and B in D the value of $\int_A^B \mathbf{F} \cdot d\mathbf{r}$ is independent of the path joining A to B in D.

2. If the integral is independent of the path from A to B, its value is

$$\int_A^B \mathbf{F} \cdot d\mathbf{r} = f(B) - f(A).$$

Green's Theorem and Its Generalization to Three Dimensions

Normal form of Green's Theorem: $\oint_C \mathbf{F} \cdot \mathbf{n}\, ds = \iint_R \nabla \cdot \mathbf{F}\, dA$

Divergence Theorem: $\iint_S \mathbf{F} \cdot \mathbf{n}\, d\sigma = \iiint_D \nabla \cdot \mathbf{F}\, dV$

Tangential form of Green's Theorem: $\oint_C \mathbf{F} \cdot d\mathbf{r} = \iint_R \nabla \times \mathbf{F} \cdot \mathbf{k}\, dA$

Stokes' Theorem: $\oint_C \mathbf{F} \cdot d\mathbf{r} = \iint_S \nabla \times \mathbf{F} \cdot \mathbf{n}\, d\sigma$

Vector Identities

In the identities here, f and g are differentiable scalar functions, $\mathbf{F}$, $\mathbf{F}_1$, and $\mathbf{F}_2$ are differentiable vector fields, and a and b are real constants.

$\nabla \times (\nabla f) = \mathbf{0}$

$\nabla (fg) = f\nabla g + g\nabla f$

$\nabla \cdot (g\mathbf{F}) = g\nabla \cdot \mathbf{F} + \nabla g \cdot \mathbf{F}$

$\nabla \times (g\mathbf{F}) = g\nabla \times \mathbf{F} + \nabla g \times \mathbf{F}$

$\nabla \cdot (a\mathbf{F}_1 + b\mathbf{F}_2) = a\nabla \cdot \mathbf{F}_1 + b\nabla \cdot \mathbf{F}_2$

$\nabla \times (a\mathbf{F}_1 + b\mathbf{F}_2) = a\nabla \times \mathbf{F}_1 + b\nabla \times \mathbf{F}_2$

$\nabla(\mathbf{F}_1 \cdot \mathbf{F}_2) = (\mathbf{F}_1 \cdot \nabla)\mathbf{F}_2 + (\mathbf{F}_2 \cdot \nabla)\mathbf{F}_1 + \mathbf{F}_1 \times (\nabla \times \mathbf{F}_2) + \mathbf{F}_2 \times (\nabla \times \mathbf{F}_1)$

$\nabla \cdot (\mathbf{F}_1 \times \mathbf{F}_2) = \mathbf{F}_2 \cdot \nabla \times \mathbf{F}_1 - \mathbf{F}_1 \cdot \nabla \times \mathbf{F}_2$

$\nabla \times (\mathbf{F}_1 \times \mathbf{F}_2) = (\mathbf{F}_2 \cdot \nabla)\mathbf{F}_1 - (\mathbf{F}_1 \cdot \nabla)\mathbf{F}_2 + (\nabla \cdot \mathbf{F}_2)\mathbf{F}_1 - (\nabla \cdot \mathbf{F}_1)\mathbf{F}_2$

$\nabla \times (\nabla \times \mathbf{F}) = \nabla(\nabla \cdot \mathbf{F}) - (\nabla \cdot \nabla)\mathbf{F} = \nabla(\nabla \cdot \mathbf{F}) - \nabla^2\mathbf{F}$

$(\nabla \times \mathbf{F}) \times \mathbf{F} = (\mathbf{F} \cdot \nabla)\mathbf{F} - \frac{1}{2}\nabla(\mathbf{F} \cdot \mathbf{F})$